"INTENTION"

~ WAR FOR THE HAN FRONTIER ~

BY T. P. M. THORNE

COVER ART BY T. P. M. THORNE

Published by PaMat Publishing

Copyright © 2017 T. P. M. Thorne

Cover art: *artistic depiction of the Han Dynasty China as they were when Cao Cao began his northern campaigns: Han-controlled (or at the least neutral/temporarily ignored) regions are darkest; the northeast region controlled by the Yuans and the Wuhuan is lightest with faint glow; the southeast (governed by the Sun family) and the central region (Jing and Jiaozhi, governed by Liu Biao, Shi Xie and several semi-autonomous prefects) are lighter coloured.*

TABLE OF CONTENTS

FOREWORD

'"Intention" – War for the Han Frontier' is a direct sequel to my earlier works, '"Yellow Sky" – Crisis for the Han Dynasty' and '"Turmoil" – Battle for the Han Empire', and my fifth foray into the era known popularly as 'Three Kingdoms' (approx. 184AD – 280AD when including the Yellow Turban Rebellion and the decline of the Han that precedes). I never planned to write works set in this period beyond '"Yellow Sky"' – which was, by my naïve reckoning, going to serve as the one and only prequel to 'Crouching Dragon' and provide much-needed exploration of the events that led to the fall of the Han – but I had so much material left over at the end of that book – and had failed in my mission to end where 'Crouching Dragon' began (at the Battle of Guandu) – that writing 'East of the River – Home of the Sun Clan' and '"Turmoil"' became an irresistible compulsion for me. When I finally finished that second prequel, I had partially-developed material left over that carried the story as far as the weeks before Red Cliffs (the consequence of planning for the unlikely event of having too little to work with): after a much-needed break, I decided that there was a fairly interesting story to tell by going further, and the project spiralled from there.

The Yuan clan did not simply disappear after Guandu, and their alliance with the Wuhuan tribes of the northeast – whose way of life couldn't have been more different to the lofty Yuans – led to the first major military excursion beyond the Han Empire's famous northern boundary – the Great Wall – since 175AD, when that poorly-equipped Han army was all but destroyed by the Xianbei Confederacy. Cao Cao was making history and 'putting old mistakes to rest' when he embarked on that risky campaign after ending Yuan clan rule in the northeast provinces, and as it is also the strategist Guo Jia's last – and, perhaps, most important – contribution to Cao Cao's career, I felt it deserved proper treatment, and hopefully justice has been served. I do try, as usual, to highlight all sides and be as multilateral as possible: I do, for example, show the effect of Cao Cao's campaign on the Wuhuan race at the same time that I show the impact that the Wuhuan's way of life has had on the Han Chinese that they share the land with (and that the actions of individuals or subgroups should not be taken as the nature of the whole).

The narrative begins after the conclusion of the Battle of Guandu (200AD) and concludes in the weeks prior to the famous Battle of Red Cliffs (the summer of 208AD), which was not at all ideal in many ways but perfect in others: Cao Cao is at the height of his powers prior to Red Cliffs, and the outcome seems to be preordained. The events covered in this work do make some other parts of the whole story make more sense as well, and serve as a prequel and parallel narrative for 'Crouching Dragon – the Journey of Zhuge Liang' and a compliment and partial sequel to 'East of the River – Home of the Sun Clan'; *most* of the famous figures of the era – some well-known, some not so well-known – are featured, along with their subordinates and peers, in order to build as strong, varied narrative as possible (they include Cao Cao and his clan, Yuan Shao and his 3 sons, Liu Bei, Kong Rong, Hua Tuo, Guo Jia, Liu Biao, Sima Yi and Jia Xu to name but a few, but there are only references made to the activities of the Sun clan of Jiangdong, who once again did too much in this time period to include them here and do proper justice).

Cao Cao is a truly complex central character (he cannot be called an 'antagonist', and 'protagonist' would be even more inappropriate), and this work shows many of his contradictions in full: he is often a saviour and murderer, liberator and captor, or protector and destroyer of knowledge at the same time, and his affliction – implied at times to be migraines in this work, but often supposed to be symptoms of a brain tumour – only adds to the mystery surrounding his constant veering between incompetence and brilliance, and between what some might call good and evil. And it must also be noted that Cao Cao's approach to dealing with the Wuhuan provides an interesting contrast to Zhuge Liang's campaign against the Nanman (depicted in 'Crouching Dragon').

A final disclaimer: the work does portray the famous physician Hua Tuo's efforts to cure Cao Cao's headaches, and I have chosen, after much consideration, to follow the portrayals in historical records and portray acupuncture as working effectively. The entirety of what is described – the acupuncture and Hua Tuo's other exploits – is taken from questionable accounts, not a medical dictionary, so please do not take any of it to be sanctioned advice and always consult a qualified doctor!
    It is all part of my usual attempts to write as original and informative a work as possible, partly by looking at people and events that are typically ignored or given reduced roles, by giving focus to social and academic elements instead of keeping the narrative solely targeted on political and military matters, and by relying more on history than the folktales (although, as before, there are some instances of 'artistic license' for the sake of telling a story). And once again, all I can hope is that this book inspires or entertains someone out there as much as I have enjoyed writing it.

T. P. M. Thorne, the author

PROLOGUE: A GRAND ELABORATION

Yet another period of chaos had begun in China: once again, the soldiers donned their armour and fought for to prolong or resist the unrest. The common folk tried to live their lives as they always did while the battles raged around them: one escape was, as it had always been, the storytellers, and the era known as 'Three Kingdoms' – and, unavoidably, the decades-long decline of the Han Dynasty that preceded it – was as popular and timely a source of stories as it had ever been.

"...Right, then, so I last told the story of how Yuan Shao was defeated at Guandu," an old man said to his audience of young and old. "Of course, the next thing that happened was the Battle of Red Cliffs, where-"
"Yay! Red Cliffs! Liu Bei an' Zhuge Liang beat up Cao Cao and summoned the wind and burned up all his boats!" one boy cried.
"You spoiled it!" a girl complained.
"No I never spoiled nothing!" the boy retorted. **"Ever'one knows that Liu Bei and Zhuge Liang-!"**
"No they never!" another boy said. **"It was Zhou Yu and-!"**
"Quiet, both of you!" a woman ordered.
The old storyteller laughed and said, "It's quite alright. Shall I begin, then...?"
"I, uh... I already know about Red Cliffs, and there's one thing that I don't understand, elder," a young farmer said. "Yuan Shao was *defeated* at Guandu: he didn't die at Guandu, then...?"
The storyteller waved his hand dismissively and replied, "I don't really get asked that much, young man, but to elaborate, Yuan died after he lost, and then Cao Cao defeated Yuan Shao's sons, and then Cao went northward and destroyed the Wuhuan tribes, after which he became 'Chancellor of State'; Cao then attacked Liu Biao, who died suddenly, and Biao's son ceded Jing, and-"
"Wait, wait, wait," the farmer pleaded. "We *always* hear about Guandu, and Red Cliffs, and Hefei and Yiling and Wuzhang: can't we hear about what you just described for a change...? It sounds interesting enough."
"That's a good idea!" a young woman said. "Tell us about the things that happened between Guandu and Red Cliffs!"
"I wanted to hear about the boats burning," a boy grumbled.
"...Alright," the storyteller said. "I think I know enough to tell something halfway interesting: I'll begin just after Guandu... now then... let me think..."

The crowd waited patiently while the old man prepared to speak. The story that he would tell would be based upon what he knew: it would be different to the works of 'Luo Guanzhong' that would one day serve as the standard, and it would be different to the records penned by historians: this would be a story told in many ways and for many different audiences in the ages to come.

＊＊＊＊＊＊＊＊＊＊＊＊

ACT I: THE LEGACY OF GUANDU

"...I wonder, sometimes, if my ancestor – if, indeed, all of my ancestors – are ashamed of me."

The short, unassuming Kong Rong – whose 'famous ancestor' was none other than the philosopher Confucius – turned to his long-time acquaintance Wang Lang and awaited a response. Both men were sat on mats in the entertaining quarters of Kong Rong's relatively humble home; while others opted for opulence to impress their guests, Kong had lined the walls with various literary quotes – mostly attributable to his 'famous ancestor' – and simple pieces of art. Kong Rong was only in his forties, but intrigue, personal involvement in the horrors of the day and a growing feeling of responsibility for the current state of things had aged him greatly; he fidgeted with the broad right sleeve of his pale blue silk robes and said, "Well...? Do I speak to myself...?"

Wang Lang smiled, examined the left sleeve of his own patterned silk robes and replied, "How can I answer you? You have given me no way of doing so."

Kong Rong was now adjusting the white silk turban that held his long hair in place; Wang Lang laughed and added, "You plan on letting your hair hang freely, kicking the shoes away from your feet and becoming a hermit...?"

Kong Rong sneered and said, "You are being flippant."

"About *what*...?" Wang Lang chortled. "You invite me here with the pretext that we are to enjoy a hearty drink, perhaps a small meal, and talk about the affairs of the day as we 'men of the pen' like to do... but instead, I get an empty tea dish and a series of vague, self-deprecating statements."

"Oh, right... sorry," Kong Rong said as he leant forward and picked up the small tea kettle that was placed between them on a tray; after pouring some of the hot beverage into Wang's dish, Kong added, "I want someone to tell me that I am so famously unremarkable for some divine purpose, Mister Wang."

Wang Lang hummed ambiguously.

"My ancestor gave us so many of the principles and social rules that we live by," Kong Rong continued as he poured tea into his own dish. "And yet here I am, helplessly watching while Cao Cao does as he-"

"Enough," Wang Lang said coldly. "His Excellency Cao is doing only what is *necessary*."

"Oh, not you as well...!" Kong Rong despaired. "'His Excellency Cao' is guilty of *regicide*!"

"So say some," Wang Lang retorted. "We'll all have things said about us while we live and after we die. What matters to me, Mister Kong, is what is 'fact' and what is-"

"He admitted to the crime!" Kong Rong said. "He is the 'Crafty Villain', the 'Hero of Chaos', just as Xu Shao foretold when he-!"

"The 'Hero of Chaos'...?" Wang Lang scoffed. "So the Han enjoyed stability until he came of age, did it...? Everything was fine until Cao Cao, mm...?"

Kong Rong sighed irritably.

China had long enjoyed the benefits of being an economic power, but that power, built mainly on the value of its exports – most famously silk – was, as with all nations, offset by political and military strife. The previously embattled Roman Empire was enjoying relative stability under the rule of the ambitious unifier, Emperor Septimus Severus – who, while China slowly recovered from 16 years of famines and national rebellion that had weakened its trade links, was looking to regain or strengthen Roman influence in many of the nations that lay along the Silk Road – and the Han Dynasty's perceived strength became an urgent matter as hungry neighbours regained their ability to expand. The problem was that it was becoming all too obvious that the Han was a frail, stricken dynasty, and the proposed and attempted solutions were many and largely controversial.

The Han Dynasty had been an enduring force in China for hundreds of years, but that tenure had not been without problems. Once, an ambitious politician called Wang Mang had managed to depose the Han and found his own dynasty: he had applied the notion of the 'Mandate of Heaven', which asserted that any man – which could, theoretically, mean a peasant as much as a noble – could be deemed a suitable ruler if he had enough support, the 'signs' were right, and the incumbent – in this case, the entire Han Dynasty, rather than the current monarch alone – was said to have 'exhausted their mandate'. Wang fell afoul of a rebellion led by a member of the Liu clan, and their Han Dynasty was restored to power: the whole affair was not without consequences, however, as the weakness of the Chinese rulers had led to rebellions by indigenous tribes around the northwest and the imperial capital, Chang'an – long the centre of trade with the outside world – had to be all but abandoned and the seat of power moved east to Luoyang.

The Han enjoyed relatively stable control of the nation thereafter, but the matter of who would be the next sovereign was a constant internal source of strife. Time and again, different factions would coalesce around a particular candidate and intrigue would take precedence over good government; one particular figure, Liang Ji, used his position as the sister of the Empress Dowager to control the child Emperor Huan and rule through him, although opinions about the nature and success of that rule were infamously mixed. Emperor Huan eventually tired of being a puppet and conspired with his eunuch attendants, whose actions removed Liang Ji and his allies and restored power to the sovereign; their reward – which would have immediate consequences – was power that was normally beyond their caste. The timid attendants – whose emasculation was intended to remove their ambitions, status as real men, and make it possible for them to live and work within the core of the imperial palace, where men were largely forbidden – were suddenly able to have adopted families, possess land and generate wealth; but within a short time, one small faction – which came to be known as the 'Ten Attendants' by their enemies – abused the privilege and started to build an unrivalled power base at court.

"We were all alive when the chaos that you speak of was at its worst, but we were not greying men as we are now," Wang Lang said. "We were children, and the 'Ten' ruled Huandi's court."

"I... I know," Kong Rong conceded. "But-!"
"Cao Cao is exactly what we need right now," Wang Lang insisted. "We must fight the chaos head-on, and he does. He is a hero of an era of chaos, not a hero *to* chaos. He sheltered the partisans during the worst of the eunuchs' rule, did he not...?"
Kong Rong nodded sheepishly.

The 'Ten Attendants' made an already terrible situation far worse: the eunuch clique's corruption added to the existing activities of unscrupulous officials, and it affected everything. The military were underfunded, disaster management was neglected, and only those that fawned on the 'Ten' or paid their sizeable bribes could hold a high post for more than a few months without being slandered and all but destroyed. A public protest by the intelligentsia was met with sustained and disproportionate persecution that came to be known as the 'Partisan Crisis', and when the rot continued into the reign of the child Emperor Ling, many guessed that total disaster was imminent.

A failed military campaign against the 'barbarian' Xianbei Confederacy ended in disaster when the painfully under-resourced and demoralised imperial army – whose leaders were mostly inexperienced, unqualified allies of the 'Ten' – was decimated; subsequent economic and agricultural hardships coincided with the rise of a Taoist cult called the 'Way of Peace', whose leader, Zhang Jue, preached that the calamities were a result of the Han's 'Mandate of Heaven' being exhausted – the same concept cited decades before by Wang Mang – and that a 'Yellow Sky', a sign of change, was coming, and the message reached peasant and disaffected noble alike. Zhang Jue's acolytes in the capital were exposed before they could stage a coup, but by then Zhang had close to two million followers, including disgruntled former soldiers; he called upon them to don yellow turbans – a blatant sign of defiance against imperial rule, for it was decreed that none but the sovereign could 'wear yellow above the head' – and rise up throughout the nation. The army was unable to cope with this 'Yellow Turban Rebellion', so Emperor Ling was forced to ask his nobles to fight the threat as private militias. Zhang Jue was killed and the rebellion crushed, but more rebellions followed, and by the time that Emperor Ling died, the entire country was in turmoil; the trade routes were repeatedly restricted or closed altogether in order to hide the fact that Han Dynasty China was on the verge of total implosion.

"...I still say that Cao has much to answer for," Kong Rong declared. "Yes, he sheltered partisans, but men change! That Cao Cao would not have committed regicide as this one has! And I reiterate that he *confessed to it*!"
"Did he...?" Wang Lang replied. "Or did he 'confess' to eliminating threats to the Empire in the forms of a treacherous vassal, his daughter – a mere concubine – and an unborn child that may or may not have been a future prince, and even more questionable as to whether it would have been a future sovereign...?"
Kong Rong's eyes wandered.
"Dong Cheng was conspiring against His Excellency; we all know that, and that was admitted to by him on many occasions," Wang

Lang noted. "But why, of course, is known only to his wandering spirit: who was he...? Who, truly, was that former vassal of another Dong, Dong *Zhuo* – the most evil man of recent times, without question – that laid waste to Luoyang, raided the imperial tombs, and is known to have actually committed regicide...?"
Kong Rong nodded silently.

Even the most loyal of Han adherents was starting to doubt the chances of avoiding another fall, even if it was as temporary as the last. That fear was made more tangible when the battle to decide who would succeed Emperor Ling ended with a victory for Empress Dowager Hè and her brother, Commander-in-Chief Hè Jin: many feared another Liang Ji, and the 'Ten' feared a reduction in their influence. Further intrigue led to the deaths of Hè Jin, the 'Ten Attendants' and thousands of court eunuchs, and the rise to power of the western general Dong Zhuo, whose rule brought tyranny beyond comprehension.

Dong Zhuo apparently knew no moral low: the nation suffered as he indulged his every vice, and a coalition of nobles quickly formed to oppose him after he deposed the child Emperor Shao and replaced him with his younger half-brother. That latest Emperor, dubbed 'Xian', was forced to watch powerlessly as the increasingly brazen and desperate Dong Zhuo flooded the economy with worthless currency, looted and burned Luoyang, relocated the court back to the original capital Chang'an and ruled as he pleased; when loyal officials and some of Dong Zhuo's disgruntled followers allied to murder Dong and restore control to the court proper, there was a brief glimmer of hope, but it did not glimmer for long. Li Jue and Guo Si, who were two of Dong Zhuo's most powerful vassal-warlords, seized power, fought off all rivals and established an autocratic 'regency' in Chang'an. All the while, the warlords that had once risen up to oppose Dong Zhuo were fighting amongst themselves and carving up the east of the country between them.

It was, ironically, an army of bandits – former Yellow Turbans – that was militarily instrumental to rescuing Emperor Xian when a dispute born out of intrigue divided the regents and led to an embarrassing civil war that tore Chang'an apart and left hundreds dead. The proposed solution was their splitting the country down the middle and running it separately from within Chang'an and Luoyang; the most prominent architects of the 'rescue' that followed were Dong Cheng and Yang Feng, but the latter's use of bandit allies to intercept the emperor's convoy as it travelled to Luoyang's ruins was never popular, and when Yang started to reward himself at Dong Cheng's perceived expense, Dong made a secret alliance with Cao Cao, betrayed Yang Feng and assisted Cao's plan to move Emperor Xian and the weary, famine-stricken court to Cao Cao's base in Yan Province, to the south of Luoyang. That is where the court had been ever since, relying entirely on Cao Cao's magnanimity and ability to project economic and military strength on Emperor Xian's behalf; Cao Cao was now the most influential man in the land, and Dong Cheng quickly shifted his stance yet again and started to become Cao's most dangerous opponent, both publicly and privately.

"You… are right to wonder what Dong Cheng's true motivations were," Kong Rong admitted.
"Who, truly, was Dong Cheng, a man that betrayed his regent masters and 'escorted' His Majesty to the ruins of the capital with the *White Wave Bandits* as his sword and shield…?" Wang Lang asked. "A man who, if I recall, hummed and hawed, wavered and conspired… did he not aid the Bandits' repulsion of His Excellency Cao's armies when he supposed that he would get rank in the Bandit-run court, but betrayed them to the same Cao Cao when the Bandits inevitably reneged…?"
Kong Rong sighed woefully.

Cao Cao had been the friend and later vassal of Yuan Shao, chieftain of the Yuan clan of Ru County and one of the most powerful men in China. When Dong Zhuo took power, Yuan Shao was selected as the leader of the 'Eastern Pass Coalition' that would oppose Dong. Yuan Shao's younger brother Shu resented Shao's place – especially since Shao was born of a maid and not of their father's small harem – and took advantage of growing dissatisfaction at Shao's leadership of the coalition by publicly challenging his legitimacy as clan chieftain in an open letter; Shao responded by shifting his military priorities away from the retreating Dong Zhuo and toward Yuan Shu, and a destructive feud began that lasted for 7 years, ending only when Yuan Shu – who later declared as an emperor and earned universal condemnation for it – died a broken, humiliated fugitive.
        But while that feud was at its peak, Cao Cao took advantage of opportunities and went from the wealthy son of Cao Song – a man that had himself been elevated when he was adopted by a favoured palace eunuch – to Governor of Yan Province, lord to a host of talented future statesmen and leader of a professional army. When the regency collapsed and Emperor Xian was in the care of Dong Cheng, Yang Feng and the White Wave Bandits, Cao Cao answered the sovereign's calls for aid when most – including Yuan Shao – refused to bear the burden.

"Dong Cheng made influential friends and started conspiring against Cao Cao almost as soon as Cao rescued him," Wang Lang scoffed. "Even a high military rank and seeing his beautiful daughter gain favour with His Majesty was not enough… and his wilful, cheerful subservience to Dong Zhuo proved long ago that he had no problem with regicide of a Son of Heaven."
"That is true," Kong Rong admitted.
"Yes, the child might have been a boy, a prince, and if Her Highness the Empress did not have living male issue at the time of His Majesty's passing, then that prince – if, indeed, it existed – might have inherited the throne if that was His Majesty's will," Wang Lang conceded. "But we both know that a living sovereign take precedence over an unborn child or other… 'possibilities'. Were we supposed to repeat one of the 'old mistakes' and let Dong and his daughter do as so many have done before…?"

Yuan Shao and Cao Cao's relationship soured over the years as their power grew and their personal interests became ever more at odds with the other's; by the time that the court was based in the city of Xuchang in Yan Province, Yuan Shao had lost control over Cao and resented the fact that Cao – who was, in his eyes, from an inferior clan – was now going to get the best roles within the recovering government. Petitions went back and forth, but armed conflict was inevitable: once every bandit army, rebel group, tribal alliance and rogue warlord had been pacified or eliminated, Yuan Shao finally released his own open letter denouncing Cao Cao. Dong Cheng had, meanwhile, claimed ownership of a secret imperial edict calling for Cao Cao's destruction; Cao and his allies acted quickly upon learning of it, arresting and executing Dong Cheng and his followers and removing Dong Cheng's daughter, Consort Dong, from Emperor Xian's harem for immediate disposal. It was that last act that had even left some of Cao Cao's followers rattled, since Consort Dong was a known favourite and, most importantly, pregnant with child.

"...There must have been another way," Kong Rong retorted.
"If there had been another way, then one of the many wise men around His Excellency would have found it," Wang Lang insisted. "Our mutual friend Xun Wenruo is as devout a royalist as you will ever find, but even he could see no other way."
"...And I was one of the men that called for the heads of the 'Ten Attendants' at the heights of their villainy," Kong Rong recalled. "This was... ... ...well, it was not 'the same', no, but it had to be... ... ...yes, I suppose that there was no other way."
Wang Lang smiled encouragingly and asked, "So is your conscience eased...?"
"...Perhaps," Kong Rong replied. "Now, perhaps, we should alter the mood."
"Yes!" Wang Lang chuckled. "Why not enlighten me with some of your famous poetry... oh, and some wine would be nice."
Kong Rong summoned a servant and requested wine; the two continued to eat, drink and talk about everything but the state of the nation for the rest of the afternoon.

****

2

"I sense hesitation, Lord Cao."

The prematurely-greyed, hard-faced 'Excellency of Works', Cao Cao, smiled and turned to his frail adviser Guo Jia and replied by saying, "That's to be expected, surely, Guo Fengxiao?"

Cao Cao's court was comprised entirely of clan loyalists that nodded silently. Cao Cao looked down the rows of advisers and officials that sat to his left, and then to the rows of military representatives that sat in rows to his right; there were no signs that anyone intended to address him beyond Guo Jia and two other advisers.

"This is not the moment for hesitation, Lord Cao, not after so much action," Guo Jia countered. "Yuan Shao is down but not decisively defeated; Liu Bei edges closer and closer to Jing Province, where we suspect that he will be received warmly by an increasingly desperate Liu Biao. Sun Quan's loyalty to the Han is questionable, no matter what his man here at court says; the various tribes to the north and northwest are the threat that they have always been, and 'when', rather than 'if', the Qiang tribes in Liang Province put their petty differences aside and unite as they once did against the regents in Chang'an..."

Cao Cao patted the black headpiece that held his long hair in place and said, "This head has many things in it, Guo Fengxiao. Yes, I am hesitant, but not with regard to the matters that you refer to. I am not even hesitant because of the loss of Tian Chou from my service. I am hesitant about addressing the court, nothing more."

A tall, thin, gruff man in his sixties snorted and asked, "Why...?"

"...Because, Elder Cheng, I am not popular, and with good reason," Cao Cao replied wearily. "Even you – on your 'bad days', at least – cannot look me in the eye or confront me confidently, and even now you are uncharacteristically reserved; I am Xu Shao's 'Crafty Villain' come to pass, a murderer of unborn sovereigns and future slayer of the dynasty as a whole!"

"We've discussed that many times, Excellency," Cheng Yu retorted, "and I, for one, am resolved that there was little else that we could do to stop Dong Cheng from being another Liang Ji. My colleague and friend Jia Xu has also been very enlightening with regard to Dong Zhuo's vile circle, and I have no doubt that we are and always have been right in our actions."

"Yes," Cao Cao said as his eyes turned to the unassuming form of the adviser Jia Xu. "You've made quite an impression already, Mister Jia."

Jia Xu bowed humbly and replied, "I merely play the role that I have always wanted to play, Excellency, that which fate has cruelly placed out of reach until now. I now serve in a court dedicated to restoring order as quickly as possible."

"Indeed," Guo Jia chuckled. "The 'quick' part is the most important part. Yuan Shao might be severely weakened, yes, and his options for bringing his demoralised army across the Yellow River reduced to one ford at Cangting, but he still has two-hundred-thousand men at his disposal, the resources of four provinces to draw upon – even though he might not, at the moment, have anywhere to store those resources on this side of the river – and the support of

the Wuhuan tribes that he has forcibly married his vassals'
daughters into. We-"

"Is this not the same discussion that we have every time that we
meet?" Cao Cao interrupted. "Are you all so frightened that I am
going to suffer from the same befuddling disease of the mind
that's afflicted Yuan Shao...? He and I were once friends, but we
shared little more than a love of women and drink. I assure you,
gentlemen, that I am only more determined after having suffered
a forged imperial edict calling for my head and being repeatedly
tricked and betrayed by *Liu Bei*! My hesitation is not in mission but
method... not in advance but in approach. Do I approach the court
as an aggressor, stamping my authority and confronting my
detractors, or do I assume a more humble stance to placate those
– which, of course, currently include His Majesty – that fear that I
have sinister long term intent...?"

"I suggest 'non-aggressive rigidity'," Jia Xu said. "A lot of the men
that made that long, horrible journey from Chang'an to the ruins
of Luoyang are like prey animals at the moment, ears pricked up
and looking for signs of danger; that's why Dong Cheng suspected
that he had an opening to seize power. Instead of meeting their
expectation that you will adopt a particular stance to reflect the
'circumstances' of recent times, be without a stance and address
the court as a man that is, quite rightly, apologetic about nothing
at all."

"Agreed," Cheng Yu said at once.

Cao Cao noted the agreeable murmurs that emanated from both
sides of his court and said, "I shall do as you say, Mister Jia.
Unless there is... another opinion...?"

All eyes turned to Guo Jia, who smiled and said, "I agree with
Mister Jia Xu. After all, the only men that should be feeling guilty
right now are those that took Dong Cheng's forged edict as their
mandate, and only guilty men resort to aggression as a means of
silencing critics. The guilt is a perception in the eyes of a
misguided few that should not dictate your actions, Lord Cao."

"That is very true, Excellency," the adviser Xun Yu – whose
courtesy name was 'Wenruo' – volunteered insistently.

"So, now that the matter of 'how to address the court' is resolved,
might I ask what you intend to address them with, Lord Cao...?"
Guo Jia asked.

"Actions taken thus far, actions for the weeks ahead," Cao Cao
explained. "I admit that I am inclined to launch a full-scale
expedition against Liu Biao and Sun Quan now that Yuan Shao is
humbled and stripped of his best minds and swords, but I am
aware that it is not considered to be 'wise' at present."

"No, it is *most* unwise to disregard Yuan Shao, as we have just
discussed," Xun Wenruo protested. "While he maintains his tight
grip on Cangting, he might just be able to reassemble his forces
and attack us again if we turn our backs for too long, perhaps in
concert with Liu Bei or-"

"Liu Bei cannot do anything of the sort, not while we harass him
as we do," Cheng Yu suggested. "But yes, I agree, we cannot
leave Yuan Shao at Cangting... just as we couldn't afford to let Lü
Bu and Chen Gong have the place seven years ago."

"...So you persist that I am to ignore the threats posed by Liu Biao
and Sun Quan, and continue to peck at a dying animal...?" Cao

Cao asked pointedly.

"*Hardly...!*" Xun Wenruo chortled. "Yuan still has two-hundred-thousand men, as has been said often enough. Yes, he's suffering insurrections across his domains in the wake of Guandu, but he has the men to quell them and the will to return. We cannot leave him with a single scrap of land to the south of the Yellow River that he can use for an easy crossing, no matter how small; and he must intend it, else why hold and reinforce the place...?"

Cao Cao shook his head and said, "But Sun Quan-!"

"Mister Liu Fu is managing well enough," Guo Jia suggested. "He is quite incredible, in fact: we sent him to Hefei to monitor Sun Ce at a moment when we were distracted by Yuan Shao and Liu Bei, little hoping that he might make a little bit of progress with the Qian Hill Bandits while he was there, and yet he has brought stability, pacified rebels, increased security and survived Sun Ce's fearsome rage! I doubt, after all that, that he cannot handle Sun Quan for us for a while... especially when we consider the 'little project' conceived by Mister Liu and Man Chong and what an obstacle that will make when it is finished."

All eyes turned to Assistant Officer Man Chong, who smiled humbly and said, "I did nothing special: I made a small suggestion, that's all."

"A great suggestion that Liu Fu will make real," Guo Jia insisted. "It will ensure that the Sun clan of Jiangdong is as manageable a threat later on as it is now."

"Inspector Liu Fu is certainly more effective than 'Inspector Yan Xiang' was," Cao Cao said. "It's funny: that fool Yan ran back and forth, trying to protect his heretic lord and his own neck, and actually doing everything from feigning his death to trying to recruit mercenaries to finally seeing sense and offering his allegiance to me... and in the end, after achieving a position of relative safety and surviving being the counsel of a traitor, Yan Xiang's as dead as the rest. Ridiculous."

The adviser Yuan Huan – who had once served the renegade warlord Yuan Shu alongside Yan Xiang, but had defected immediately when Shu betrayed the Han Empire – nodded agreeably but offered no words.

"Yan Xiang's not only ridiculous, but irrelevant, so we shall forget him and return to more pressing matters," Guo Jia said. "My lord, I will tell you when it is the right time to fight Liu Biao and Sun Quan, or others will."

"...Fine, we'll content ourselves with ignoring 'Jing Governor Liu Biao' and let Sun Quan keep his undeserved dominions for now," Cao Cao grumbled. "Liu Biao would do well not to shelter Liu Bei, but we all know that he almost certainly will; Bei will doubtlessly urge him to renew his coalition pact with Yuan Shao and gather support for a pincer attack on Xuchang, but while the ambitious Sun Quan continues his harassment of southern Jing and diverts most of Liu Biao's limited resources to that southern front, we can ignore him as well. We now control Yan Province, Central Province, Xu Province, parts of Yang Province, most of Yu Province, and the southwest border regions of Qing Province; and as for Yuan's potential alliance with our other long-standing problem, the Qiang chieftains Ma Teng and Han Sui in Liang Province... Wenruo...?"

"Ma Teng is suffering surprising defeats," Xun Wenruo reported. "His eldest son, Ma Chao, is truly a force to be reckoned with, but Han Sui commands a generally more efficient army that is gaining ground in every place that Ma Chao is not placed to take or defend. That means one of two things in the short term, I suggest: either Ma Teng will capitulate and seek peace in exchange for loss of territory, or he will hand power to Ma Chao and retreat to some far-off place while the tribal war continues."

"...In the short term, we might want the latter, since it keeps them busy, but in the long term, the former is preferable," Jia Xu said. "A Ma Chao that is reined in by Han Sui will not be as much of a threat as a Ma Chao that forces Han Sui to sue for peace and present an opportunity to seize control in the northwest."

"A definitive set of options may exist, but that's entirely up to Heaven," Guo Jia chuckled. "With any luck, it will be one of those options, because either would keep them where we want them."

Jia Xu smiled, rubbed his bearded chin and said, "I do not know the order that your mind chooses for those further options, but I concur that they are most desirable. An alliance against Yuan Shao... or a hostage to control Ma Chao... are both very much desired both now and in the future, but either would do."

"*Ayah*... you advisers are not human, I swear it!" a military official cried; all eyes turned to the one-eyed face of Cao Cao's trusted 'cousin' Xiahou Dun, who added, "All of a sudden, we're looking at the Qiang barbarians giving us hostages or helping us fight Yuan Shao! Why would any of that happen???"

"I admit, Yuanrang, that I consider the possibility myself," Cao Cao replied. "I'm sure that Wenruo, Gongda, Chen Qun and Cheng Yu, at the very least, hope for as much."

"Naturally," Xun Wenruo admitted. "But it is sometimes best to underplay such outcomes to avoid unwanted damage to morale, or at the very least refer to them obliquely. Xuchang is as good a 'far-off place' as any for Ma Teng to flee to, and I made no mention of which side of the Han-Yuan conflict that they might-"

"There is no need to convince us of your insight, Uncle," the adviser Xun Yòu – whose courtesy name was 'Gongda' – interrupted. "Guo Fengxiao is being his usual self, I think."

"If we could have the Qiang tribes with us, that would be perfect," Cao Cao said sadly. "We'd have Yuan cornered then; the Qiang to the west, Zang Ba's agitators in Qing to the east, the fickle Xianbei tribes across the northern border and the Han army to the south. Alas, it cannot be so: the Qiang are as fickle as the other tribes and their 'fee' for assistance will doubtless be too high to pay. In addition, we have yet to see what Liu Biao and Sun Quan's feud will lead to, or what meddlesome role *Liu Bei* will have to play in it. Oh, gentlemen, I cannot say what I would not give to have Liu Bei's severed head in front of me right now! He is the sharpest thorn in my side, just as so many of you predicted!"

"*Pah*... how so?" Xiahou Dun scoffed. "Yeah, I don't like him, or his men... especially that wretched, ungrateful bastard *Guan Yu*... but what can he do? Isn't Yuan Shao, with his two-hundred-thousand men, the only real threat now, like you said before...?"

"Mister Xiahou, you know as well as we do the adage 'it is as when one throws an egg against a rock' when referring to the futility of pitting one force against a vastly superior one, be it due to better trained men, more men or better counsel," Guo Jia chuckled. "You also know, as we all do from the outcome of the encounter at Guandu, that Yuan Shao, 'advised' as he is now by the likes of Guo Tu, Pang Ji and Wenruo's brother Chen, is little more than the owner of the world's largest egg."

Many of the officials laughed at Guo Jia's dismissive response.

"Such a savage analysis, Fengxiao, that makes a toothless dog of my former friend!" Cao Cao chuckled. "But no, Cousin Yuanrang, Fengxiao's statement is nonetheless true beyond the short-term. Yuan Shao needs one last push to finish him off, and then he will bother us no more: it is Bei that is now the long-term worry."

"So intensify the search for Bei and kill him!" Xiahou Dun protested. "He's only got a little army now, and they lack proper supplies! He-!"

"He endured a year-long famine at Haixi, so resource management will be a particular skill of his now," Jia Xu suggested. "Further to that, he-"

"**Don't talk to me!**" Xiahou Dun screamed. "**Don't you *dare* talk to me, Jia Xu! Cousin Mengde might want you in his court because you're a shifty snake, but I'll-!**"

"*Enough*, **Yuanrang!**" Cao Cao scolded.

"**No!**" Xiahou Dun retorted. "**He killed Dian Wei! He killed Anmin! He killed Ang! His advice killed an emperor!**"

A short, uncomfortable silence followed.

"...We... we have been through this several times already, Cousin," Cao Cao replied quietly. "Mister Jia was acting in the best interests of his lord. His advice to Dong Zhuo, his orders to Dong Zhuo's men, his advice to Zhang Xiu-"

"**His 'advice and orders' killed your heir!**" Xiahou Dun bellowed. "**He-!**"

"**He-!** ...*He*, Mister Jia Xu, ordered a decisive repulsion of an enemy force, as ordered to by his lord," Cao Cao insisted as he tried to keep his gaze diverted from Jia Xu, who was visibly uncomfortable. "How many sons, fathers and goodness else knows who have I thoughtlessly given orders to slay...? Did I care what happened to Mengzhuo- I-I mean *Zhang Miao's* family...? No, I did not, because... because it had to be done, it was necessity, just as our first conversation about the fate of Consort Dong and her unborn child had highlighted. Bear him no malice, Yuanrang, for he did what was asked of him, just as you did what was asked of you by me on every campaign that you have fought in... including Xu Province."

Xiahou Dun snorted angrily, turned to Jia Xu and bowed slightly, saying, "I will speak no more of it."

"I understand your anger and grief, Mister Xiahou, and can only hope to atone for my many, many bad choices and poor advice," Jia Xu replied meekly.

"...If we might return to discussing Liu Bei," Cao Cao said as he finally turned to look at Jia Xu. "Mister Jia, you were saying...?"

"Y-yes," Jia Xu replied. "Liu Bei... Liu Bei is a survivor; that much we can all agree on. He'll do whatever it takes to live until he gets to a safe place, at which point he'll start trying to build an army and seize a base of some kind. Preventing him getting to Jing Province might now be impossible, but leaving him to thrive in Jing would be, as many others have suggested, most unwise."

"What, exactly, might he achieve...?" Xiahou Dun asked.

A short, portly man in ostentatious robes laughed haughtily and said, "A lot more than Yuan Shao, I'd imagine, even though he has nothing!"

Many men turned to look at the latest contributor, Xu Yòu, who was an old friend of Cao Cao and Yuan Shao; he had a seat next to Cao Cao's, less because of his lifelong friendship and more because his defection from Yuan Shao to Cao Cao during the Battle of Guandu – and the vital military information that he had brought with him – had handed the Han forces their unexpected early victory.

"So you were impressed with Bei when you met him?" Cheng Yu asked gruffly.

"Not really, but he outwitted Yuan with ease," Xu Yòu replied. "That said, Yuan was mostly drunk, even at meetings, so-"

"We know that Yuan's a drunk," Xiahou Dun said through gritted teeth. "What about *Liu Bei*...?"

"Oh, yes," Xu Yòu chuckled as he turned to face Cao Cao. "Well, he has a few real champions, but it's his way with words, which everyone here knows well enough. I mean, you had Guan Yu for a while, Mengde, and know how good he was; you also know what a way with words Bei has, since he even made a complete fool of *you* when he-"

"**WHAT???**" Xiahou Dun screamed.

"Well he did, didn't he!" Xu Yòu said fearlessly. "Stop being so uppity, Yuanrang."

"Who said you can call me that?" Xiahou Dun complained. "Mengde, he-!"

"Xu Ziyuan is *family*," Cao Cao said pointedly. "For his timely support at Guandu alone, he is family. Do not mind his ways so much, Yuanrang. Bei *did* make a 'complete fool' of me, because I did not heed wise men's advice, so my old friend is quite right."

Xu Yòu sensed the tense atmosphere and laughed awkwardly, saying, "I should not have implied that you were a 'complete fool', Mengde, for you are not. But Bei, yes, I was saying... some of Wen Chou's men joined him, I think, and he has a brigade of cavalrymen from Yòu Province led by... Zhou... Zhao...? ...Something or other, that he begged Yuan to let him have, so they must be good."

"Gongsun Zan must have assigned them to Liu Bei at some point," Guo Jia noted. "Men from that region will be good indeed, in their own right and as mentors to others."

"But Mi Zhu is penniless," the advisor Chen Qun said. "That conniving hankerer exhausted his family fortune on keeping Bei alive at Haixi, and his contacts melted away after that Lü Bu nonsense that he allowed to happen. All that Bei has now is a lot of brawn and one semi-competent ambassador in old Mister Sun. And while he might be very good at crying and fawning and squirming out of the messes that he gets himself into, he couldn't plan a trip to the toilet."

"So his first goal will be to secure good advisers," Guo Jia concluded. "He'll find many a clever mind in Jing. Just look at who that mediocrity Liu Biao has had around him of late: the Pangs, the Kuais and Wang Can, who – when his strange obsession with donkeys does not impede him – is a very sharp sword. I've made my own enquiries in Jing, and Bei could find at least one good man willing to serve him, I fear; it won't make him unbeatable, but it will eliminate any chance of beating him quickly, and time is not on our side."

"It certainly isn't on *yours*," Chen Qun heckled. "You're more often sick than well these days, Guo Jia, and it is, as always, self-inflicted through *vice*! This is your first appearance in days! You-!"

"Not that argument again," Cheng Yu sighed. "For the last time, Mister Chen, don't waste *your* time: Guo Jia is predisposed to reaching Heaven early, and that is that."

Cao Cao shook his head woefully and said, "I only wish you'd listen to reason, Guo Fengxiao. A great genius such as you should not be looking to die early."

"On the contrary, I think that I should be," Guo Jia joked. "After all, my profession is one that is always graded on the list of failures rather than successes. I can win a thousand times, but one careless mistake can cost you an army and undo all of my hard work. And then there is the small matter of being but a mere mortal with only so many ideas in my head. It is far better to live a short but successful life and then die unbeaten, long before a rival 'genius' inevitably appears that outclasses me and consigns my name to a list of forgotten mediocrities."

Cheng Yu grumbled quietly.

"...Except for *you*, of course, Elder Cheng, who still achieves greatness at your advanced age," Guo Jia teased. "'Prodigy of the moment' that I am, I'll have used up all of my best ideas in ten years or less, but *you*, you're-"

"**Liu Bei!**" Xiahou Dun cried. "**What about Liu Bei???**"

"Pray he doesn't find his own genius," Cheng Yu said. "If he does, we'll still be sitting here pondering what to do about him in twenty years' time."

Guo Jia smiled knowingly and lowered his gaze.

"...*Aiee*... well, whatever the future holds, the important thing right now is what I must tell that court of do-nothings," Cao Cao complained. "For now, let us focus on internal matters. What is the state of our supplies?"

Xun Wenruo rummaged through a pile of bamboo books and cloth paper as he tried to find the answer to Cao Cao's question; Jia Xu looked at his latest master and quietly hoped, as he often did, that the 'Crafty Villain' would not be the third infamous tyrant that he had lent his considerable talent to.

✱✱✱✱✱✱✱✱✱✱✱✱

3

A bemused Wang Lang returned to Kong Rong's home on the eve of the next imperial court gathering.

"So are you resolved...?" Wang Lang asked as he took a guest seat in Kong Rong's living quarters once again; he was glad to see that Kong had asked for tea to be brought straight away this time.

"...Resolved...? No, Jingxing, not at all," Kong Rong replied. "As I was saying to Mister Zhi just yesterday, Liu Xuande's fate is-"

Wang Lang harrumphed and said, "*Liu Bei*...? You'd really dare to speak favourably of *Liu Bei*...? You'd guiltlessly refer to that wretched, rotten scion of the royal clan, a man descended from disinherited traitors that carries all of their ailments of the mind, by his courtesy name in front of me...?"

"*Aiee*... You really are persuasive," Kong Rong admitted.

"No, I am not, else Sun Ce would not have bested me and chased me out of Jiangdong," Wang Lang replied. "It is just the case that I speak the obvious truth. I know you well enough, Wenju: you want to believe a distorted account of the last fifteen years, one that makes villains of Cao Cao and Tao Qian and heroes of Liu Bei, Yuan Shao, Sun Ce, Gongsun Zan and-"

"No, no!" Kong Rong insisted. "We were all disappointed by Gongsun Zan, and Sun Ce was a pirate king! But Xuande is a victim of circumstance!"

"Really...?" Wang Lang scoffed. "I saw some of the letters that Gongsun Zan sent out as his little barbarian empire collapsed around him and inevitable defeat and death awaited him at Yuan Shao's hands; one of the arguments for his being spared was that very same protest that he was a 'victim of circumstance'."

Kong Rong started to speak, but he thought better of it and allowed Wang Lang to continue.

"Remember that I served Liu Bei's predecessor in Xu Province," Wang Lang said. "Remember that I served the last rightful governor, Tao Qian, before all of that terrible nonsense that saw first Bei and then Dong Zhuo's treacherous foster son Lü Bu running the province. Bei's a born liar: I'm sure that his flowery speeches, ingratiating letters and empty promises are convincing, but think – truly, seriously ponder it properly – and you'll see someone else."

Kong Rong exhaled loudly.

"Liu Bei is a poor, disinherited member of the Liu clan," Wang Lang continued. "He wove mats and shoes from straw until a wealthy uncle took pity and financed his education: Bei befriended his fellow student Gongsun Zan and the two became as brothers. Yes, he had a moment of 'glory' during the Yellow Turban Crisis, but he was dependent on his growing entourage of pig butchers, fugitives and naïve peasant farmers looking for adventure. Had that two-faced, conniving Mi Zhu not looked to Bei's militia as muscle to facilitate a takeover of Xu Province, Bei would have had to settle for a civil role in a distant rural county."

Kong Rong was forced to nod silently once again.

Liu Bei had been a 'wildcard' during the recent years of the ailing Han Dynasty; schooled with the money of others, Bei had, as so many of his detractors relished pointing out, endured a peasant's life that he had inherited from disinherited ancestors. He lived with his mother and eked out a living weaving mats and shoes from straw that could then be sold for meagre money; his schooling changed that, introducing him to the famous scholar-official Lu Zhi and fellow student Gongsun Zan. Gongsun went on to lead his own impressive militia, which included cavalry at a time when skilled horsemen – and, indeed, horses – were a luxury for a warlord; he was a minor hero during the Yellow Turban Rebellion, as was Liu Bei, although Gongsun enjoyed greater rewards. Gongsun Zan became a county magistrate in northern Yòu Province; Liu Bei was eventually granted the same, but the 'Ten' were keen to maintain their grip on administrative power and Liu Bei was soon forced to abandon the role when confronted with requests for bribes.

Gongsun Zan went from strength to strength while Liu Bei drifted around Yòu, Qing and Xu Provinces, accepting various administrative roles and military assignments; he came to the attention of Xu Governor Tao Qian, who later recalled Bei's valour when faced with an invasion by Cao Cao, who blamed Tao personally for the robbery and murder of his father Cao Song as he passed through Xu. Cao Cao's 'revenge' consisted of a series of 'scorched earth' raids that left thousands dead; one famous attack left the Si River dammed with bodies, and the extent of the genocide made Tao Qian ill. Liu Bei was no match for Cao Cao militarily, leaving victory to come from the most unlikely of sources: Cao's own chief adviser, Chen Gong, and Cao's most trusted friend, Zhang Miao, had asked the late Dong Zhuo's violent, inconstant foster son Lü Bu – who was, at the time, a fugitive from the regency government for betraying and personally murdering Dong Zhuo – to invade Yan Province and help them take it from Cao, an act that forced Cao to withdraw from Xu Province and grant unexpected relief that came too late for Tao Qian's well-being. Opinions and accounts varied greatly, but the outcome – brought about mainly through lobbying by local magnate Mi Zhu – was that Liu Bei inherited the province from Tao Qian and quickly capitulated to Yuan Shao in exchange for Shao demanding that Cao Cao cease his raids; Cao reluctantly obeyed his friend-turned-lord, but the entire affair created enmity between Cao and Liu and irreversibly harmed the friendship of Yuan and Cao.

"His Excellency's actions in Xu Province – which, before you start going on about that again, is a well-worn subject after seven years – gave Liu Bei and Mi Zhu the opportunity to seize power from Tao Qian as he lay dying," Wang Lang said. "Bei mediated with the Yuan brothers, first looking at Tao's genuinely circumstance-driven alliance with the treasonous Yuan Shu and then to Cao's then-master Yuan Shao, who was still, at that point, a loyal Han vassal and not the wretched, covetous seditionist that he has become. But within no time at all, Bei was 'reciprocating goodwill' and giving refuge to Lü Bu, that most wicked of stepsons and vilest of minions, a man that personally slayed his first foster father Ding Yuan, facilitated Dong Zhuo's takeover, and-"
"Didn't *Jia Xu* have more to do with Dong Zhuo's rise to power...?"

Kong Rong asked with sudden confidence. "And isn't that same Jia Xu now a close confidante and adviser to Cao Cao...?"

Wang Lang smiled coldly and replied, "It is indeed true that Mister Jia was one of two advisers that guided Dong Zhuo; which of them guided Dong's worst actions is debatable, methinks, since Mister Jia removed himself from Luoyang before it was sacked and destroyed, and it was his peer Li Ru that was, by all accounts, the focus of His Majesty's wrath. What protest has there been by His Majesty at Jia Xu's return? Isn't it the case that His Majesty was saved on many occasions by Mister Jia, who calmed Dong Zhuo during some of his worst rages, and who kept the self-appointed regents, Li Jue and Guo Si, from committing regicide and seizing power outright...?"

"...As you say, it is debatable," Kong Rong retorted. "But Cao-"

Wang Lang laughed and said, "You truly hate Cao Cao, don't you? But look at the men that you condemn when you berate him – men like Xun Wenruo, Xun Gongda, Zhong Yao, and Chen Qun – and worse still, look at the men that you aggrandise when you speak so ill of Cao and so well of Bei! Were Yuan Shu, Lü Bu, Gongsun Zan, Chen Gong-"

"Alright, *alright*!" Kong Rong pleaded.

"No, it is not alright," Wang Lang insisted. "Someone has to make you see sense, Mister Kong. When Yuan Shao had poor, misguided Chen Lin pen that atrocious condemnation of His Excellency Cao, he committed a multitude of crimes at once. His brother, Yuan Shu, was recently deceased, dead on a roadside like an animal, not a coin to his name nor a building to take shelter within, and why...? ...Because he had dared to declare himself as the first of a new dynasty! Yuan Shu dared to consider the sovereign's mandate exhausted, Mister Kong, and he did so baselessly, purely to further his own career, and only the most wretched of men would do that."

Kong Rong nodded agreeably.

"Heaven punished Yuan Shu; Yuan Shao should then have been affirming his own loyalty to His Majesty by burying his ambitions, but no!" Wang Lang said. "Instead, he pushed for higher rank on the basis that he was descended from great men... which is the same argument used by Liu Bei. You're descended from the great philosopher, and yet you expect nothing that wasn't earned... in fact you constantly berate yourself and bemoan your unworthiness despite being one of the most gifted poets of our day and, when the subject is not too personal, one of our greatest philosophers as well! Why, then, do you then champion men that so openly oppose your ideals...?"

"That... is true," Kong Rong conceded. "But-!"

"*Aiee*... again, you resort to 'But!'" Wang Lang despaired. "Yuan Shao had done nothing to warrant higher rank. He did nothing save for grieving and fawning on Hè Jin during the Yellow Turban Rebellion. He did and does nothing to help the sovereign. He was nominated as the leader of the Eastern Pass Coalition against Dong Zhuo purely because his ancestor was a great man, and he just sat there, watching Dong Zhuo bankrupt the country and loot the capital, and leaving everything to independent actions by Cao Cao and Sun Jian that were militarily and spiritually unsupported... even *condemned*. The only things that Yuan Shao did do were to seize Ji Province from Han Fu – achieved, we now discover, with the aid of Gongsun Zan, whom he later betrayed to cover his tracks – and try to appoint the hapless Yòu Province Governor Liu Yu as an alternative sovereign that he could manipulate! ...And on the latter point, Mister Kong, it may be noted that Yuan's secret ally, Gongsun Zan, killed Liu Yu and seized Yòu Province later on, after Liu Yu publicly rebuked Yuan for embroiling him in selfish politics. Were the two events connected...? Perhaps, but we'll never know. Yuan Shao now rules Yòu Province with the aid of his Wuhuan barbarian allies, having killed Gongsun and taken it from him before his last play for the custody of the sovereign, custody that he had earlier refused because it conflicted economically with his own ambitions.

"It was only when Yuan Shao controlled Ji Province – which he took from Han Fu – Yòu Province – which he took from Gongsun, who had taken it from Liu Yu – Bing Province – which he quietly seized via family connections and exploitation of unrest – and Qing Province – which, most notably, his eldest son Tan took from *you* – that he suddenly decided that his former vassal Cao was unfit to care for His Majesty, after years of doing so very well here in Xuchang and at great personal expense."

"All known to me, and all too painfully!" Kong Rong said. "But-!"

"And yet you stubbornly cling to the myth that Cao Cao is the greatest villain of our age, and all because of one misinterpreted 'prediction' by the appraiser Xu Shao," Wang Lang noted. "That same Xu Shao was less than kind about Yuan Shao, and so it has come to pass. After Dong Zhuo fled west to Chang'an, Yuan Shao perpetuated a feud with his brother for control of his clan instead of pursuing the villain: that alone is wretched. Yuan Shu triggered the seven year feud with a public condemnation that is disturbingly similar to the one that Yuan Shao had Chen Lin write to condemn his former friend Cao Cao: to repeat the crime himself is more wretched still. And when his brother Shu needed aid as his false empire crumbled around him, Shao actually sent men led by his own heir to rescue him, after all that had transpired between them, which proves that to them, that life-consuming feud was just an amusing 'power game' for two bored, spoiled brats! And, dear Wenju, by doing so he aided the survival of a pretender to the throne: isn't that treason in itself, brother or no, and the most wretched thing of all...?"

"Of course it is," Kong Rong protested, "but-!"

"'But', 'but', 'but'," Wang Lang heckled. "Yuan Shao conquered four provinces in his own name and aided his brother as he fled Yang Province – some say in exchange for the stolen Imperial Seal, just so that he could make his own claim to the throne. He then declared war on the appointed Excellency of Works – which, in truth, is declaring war on the court and Majesty – and employed a ragtag army of bandits, barbarians and rebels to serve as his army... which brings us neatly back to Liu Bei. You were here, Kong Rong, as was I: didn't Liu Bei and an army of bandits and *Yellow Turbans* – cultists, plain and simple, whose shared life's mission was to bring an end to Han rule and establish a theocratic dictatorship – repeatedly try to attack the capital while Cao Cao was in Guandu, and at *Yuan Shao's request*...? Liu Bei started his career by fighting them for his sovereign, and ends it by fighting

the sovereign at their side; that is farcical enough, but when Bei is known to want power, it is worse still, since he would, were he to become an emperor, be a *Han* emperor."
Kong Rong nodded silently.
"Liu Bei had an audience with His Majesty after Lü Bu betrayed him, took Xu Province from him and chased him away; he received rank, had his disinheritance placed under review, and enjoyed the friendship of His Excellency Cao, who had every reason to hate him for past actions," Wang Lang continued. "And yet, despite such privilege, Liu Bei took the first opportunity to steal a borrowed army, seize the capital of Xu Province, kill the court-appointed governor of Xu and pledge allegiance to a tiny faction of rebels whose mandate was a blatantly forged Imperial edict crafted by Dong Cheng. Nobody made Liu Bei do that, Wenju. He chose to leave Xuchang, abandon the sovereign, ally with Yuan Shao and a host of criminals and heretics, and try to take Xuchang by military force. In what way, exactly, is Liu Bei a 'victim of circumstance'...?

"Liu Bei now hides in the wastelands along the borders of Yu and Jing Provinces with the remnants of his bandit-and-cultist militia because he made bad choices. Yuan Shao, greedy fool that he is, was humiliated at Guandu despite a massive numerical and tactical advantage because he made bad choices. Neither man deserves your pity or support, Wenju: you are a loyal servant of the Han, while they are fugitive seditionists that will soon face divine retribution. They have far more to answer to their ancestors for than self-perceived mediocrity. They tried to seize the throne, which would have destroyed the Han and made prophets of the Yellow Turbans."
Kong Rong sighed miserably and said, "You put your case well. But I will be watching and listening carefully when we are at court, looking for signs of the truth, whatever that may be. Cao Cao might not be the worst villain of the age, but he is a villain nonetheless, and I fear for the Han while is so powerful and there are no good men with the might to oppose him, only selfish ones."
"We will protect the Han," Wang Lang replied. "So long as men like us continue to support the Han, it will never die."
"...Yes," Kong Rong agreed.
"And now I must go!" Wang Lang chuckled as he got to his feet. "I must prepare for the meeting, as must you."
Kong Rong got to his feet, clasped his hands together and bowed humbly; Wang Lang reciprocated the gesture and departed.

****

4

The Han Imperial court was structured in much the same way as it had been for decades; the great assemblies were, like the infrastructure, largely unchanging. Bearded men filed into the grand hall by the dozens to kneel on the floor in front of the gilded imperial throne; they wore matching brown robes and tough black caps to cover their hair, and their white-socked feet made little noise as they shuffled to places that were predetermined by rank. Shoes were forbidden, as were weapons; only the guards, who were typically eunuchs, could carry arms with the purpose of defending their sovereign.

The Xuchang court was smaller than the 'true' courts of the western capital Chang'an, where the Han Dynasty was born, or the eastern capital Luoyang, where it was reborn following Wang Mang's usurpation of the mandate and founding of his own short-lived dynasty over a hundred years earlier; Cao Cao had made the best palace that his resources could fund, but everyone knew that there would need to be a return to Luoyang – which was still being reconstructed – at some point. Some suggested a return to Chang'an now that the threat of Dong Zhuo's minions, such as Li Jue and Guo Si, had been ended once and for all, but a greater threat existed in the form of the Qiang tribes and disaffected rebel militias, so the idea was quickly dismissed. Xuchang was, as Emperor Xian had once remarked, 'a suitable temporary solution to the crisis', and it would have to remain so at least until one nearby threat to Luoyang's safety – Yuan Shao's vast army in neighbouring Ji Province – was dealt with.

"…Look at us all, sitting here awaiting Heaven-knows-what," Kong Rong whispered to Wang Lang. "What will he say?"
"You ask me, but do I know the answer…?" Wang Lang retorted.
Kong Rong turned to his friend Zhi Xi – who was sat to his right – and said, "It'll be more treasonous bile that I must-"
"Don't risk Cao's wrath!" Zhi Xi hissed.
Xun Wenruo, in his capacity as 'Acting Director of the Imperial Secretariat' and 'Acting Excellency over the Masses', addressed the assembled court by saying, **"Be silent! His Majesty approaches the hall!"**
The audience kowtowed, pressing their foreheads to the floor in a show of united deference as the young Emperor Xian shuffled into the court by way of a side entrance near his throne: he was, as always, accompanied by guards, serving maidens and a small gaggle of meek, fawning eunuch attendants. Emperor Xian paused briefly to inspect the audience that awaited him: his eyes found his father-in-law Fu Wan, his appointed Excellency of Works and 'Acting Commander-in-Chief' Cao Cao, and the humble Jia Xu.
"…Nothing changes, really," Emperor Xian murmured.
The emperor's gold-dragon-emblazoned black and red robes made him the brightest thing in the room; the rows of beads that hung from the front and back of his black mortar-board hat unavoidably made noise as he completed his journey to the gilded throne and took his place upon it. Once Emperor Xian was seated, Xun Wenruo turned to Cao Cao, who got to his feet and moved to

address the court.

"Your Majesty, and gentlemen of the court… I, Cao, am, as always, humbled to be here in your presence, tasked as I am with bringing order to the nation," Cao Cao began. "We are here so that I might, to begin, update the court on matters of state."

"It is our understanding that the 'Alliance of the Girdle Edict', as some have come to know it, is crushed," Emperor Xian said unexpectedly – and cuttingly.

"They are severely harmed, Your Majesty," Cao Cao said with a fearless smile. "Those that chose to follow that seditious and fraudulent document penned by Dong Cheng and his allies have been routed soundly at Guandu and also in Yu Province, after they dared to assault the palace from the west with their unexpected bandit and Yellow Turban allies."

Kong Rong scowled and motioned that he would like to speak; Zhi Xi tried to remonstrate but he was wasting his time.

"Unexpected indeed, Excellency," Kong Rong challenged. "Who would have thought that followers of an edict to smite enemies of the Han and bring peace to the land would then ally themselves with the very people that sought to destroy the Han and plunge the world into darkness…?"

Cao Cao laughed and said, "Well put! Your ancestor smiles."

Kong Rong eyed Cao Cao bitterly.

"For where there was an obvious lack of authenticity with regards to that 'edict', there was no such doubt as to who those chanting lunatics were: they were unmistakably Yellow Turbans," Cao Cao continued. "Yuan Shao has truly lost his way, just as his fool brother did. It is sad. A man that I once called 'Benchu' and sat at tables with as a brother is now the greatest enemy of the Han. But… such is life. Now he hides in Yè City, plotting another attempt to take the capital, and he must be definitively beaten before he can do that. I intend to march northward as soon as weather, supplies and morale permit."

"And… and what of our estranged relative, Liu Bei…?" Emperor Xian asked.

"That traitor…?" Cao Cao scoffed. "O, Majesty, were it only that I could tell you that he was dead, after what he tried to do… marching here at the head of an army of Yellow Turbans to seize the throne for himself while Yuan and I were kept busy with our own battles!"

"So it is confirmed, then… that *he* led the… … … but it is scarcely believable," Emperor Xian admitted.

"But true, nonetheless," Cao Cao sighed. "He made fools of us all, Your Majesty, and me most completely of all, as a good friend so recently – and bluntly – put it."

Xu Yòu smiled at the reference to his recent words.

"Usurpation can be Liu Bei's only intention," Cao Cao continued. "Worse still, Your Majesty, that after being rightly crushed he came back *again* with an army of bandits; what desperate greed."

The court was filled with agreeable murmurs.

"But he will die, I promise that," Cao Cao insisted. "If Yuan should be made to see sense, perhaps he will reassume his place as Commander-in-Chief and help me rout Bei, who is surely the worst villain; stealer of provinces from dead men's hands, friend to rebels and heretics, coveter of thrones… but it will probably be my task alone, for Yuan rebuffs all attempts at parley, and insists upon his rash course."

"Then… he must be destroyed," Emperor Xian said half-heartedly. "Proceed as you have done so far, Mister Cao."

"I shall, Your Majesty," Cao Cao promised. "I shall stop only when every one of Your Majesty's enemies is vanquished."

Emperor Xian nodded uneasily.

"Here in the east, Liu Bei, Liu Biao, Sun Quan, the Wuhuan and the Qiang are the only concerns that remain beside Yuan Shao," Cao Cao continued. "The Wuhuan will fall alongside Yuan, the Qiang are inclined toward self-destruction. Sun Quan shows promising signs of being nowhere near as unmanageable as his brother the 'Little Conqueror' was, and is at worst a long-term nuisance. Liu Biao is old and sick, and unlikely to attack us again, especially when he has a hungry Sun Quan to worry about. The constant concern is Bei: he's a crafty owl that preys on sick, ailing governors for its main source of sustenance, which is ill-gotten land. News from Yu Province indicates that I have failed to keep him away from Jing; one way or another he's going to reach Xiangyang City and trick Liu Biao into giving him first shelter, and then the seal of office. Left unchecked, Liu Bei will be the illegal Governor of Jing within a year."

"That is not at all desirable if he covets the throne at any cost as reports suggest," Emperor Xian said. "Do what must be done, Mister Cao."

"What about enlisting help from Liu Zhang of Yi?" the official Zhong Yao asked.

"…Liu Zhang is a polite gate guard, not a warrior governor," Cao Cao replied diplomatically. "Besides, he has to keep an eye on two of the greatest threats in the west for us, does he not…? The Nan peoples to the west of the empire are hankerers that claim Yi to be ancestral lands, and they can never be ignored. The tribes that live in the lands to the south of Jing are going to be difficult to rein in. The Di and Qiang are a minor threat to the east, but in the northwest they are the main problem before or after Zhang Lu, cultist and tyrant occupier-ruler of the founder's domain and inspiration, the province of Hanzhong."

"If only there were no other problems," Emperor Xian said honestly. "That vile heretic's continued control of Hanzhong – and his chosen name for it – is an ill omen."

"I work tirelessly to restore order," Cao Cao promised. "If I have my way, Hanzhong will be restored to Han control and every other problem dealt with in ten years or less."

"That's an ambitious target," Kong Rong suggested. "Such ambitions will be hard to realise alone, Excellency."

"I will never stop trying to reach out to Liu Biao and Yuan Shao, no matter how futile that may appear to be," Cao Cao retorted. "But then again, I have turned back an army four times the size of mine at Guandu by having good friends at critical moments… so in what sense am I alone…?"

Kong Rong did not answer Cao Cao's question.

"…So that is the military situation," Cao Cao concluded. "I will fight where I must, and negotiate where there is hope of it. I shall turn proceedings over to others now, so that they can report on other matters that are of equal importance to the proper running of a state."

"Indeed, Mister Cao," Emperor Xian said. "Thank... thank you... for your report."

Cao Cao smiled falsely and bowed in respect.

Emperor Xian returned to his private quarters when court proceedings ended; he dismissed all but his trusted confidante Empress Fu so that he could speak openly.

"My lady, I... ... ...*aiee*," Emperor Xian began. "I... I *thanked him*! For *what*???"

"Perhaps... perhaps it was necessary," Empress Fu suggested.

"No, no, there was never a moment where his men dragging Consort Dong out of here and strangling her like a chicken was ever 'necessary'," Emperor Xian said angrily but quietly. "She was carrying my child! I don't care whether it was 'a prince or princess' and whether one was more expendable than another: he insulted me, angered me, disrespected me, and murdered members of my family! He is no better than Dong Zhuo! He might even be *worse*!"

"I... cannot disagree, Majesty," Empress Fu replied. "But when I said what I said, I referred to your thanking him. If you had rebuked him, he might have punished us for it."

"I... yes, well, that's why I thanked him," Emperor Xian sighed. "But when I see him smirking, and then I look at that sea of men, and I see no more than two or three friendly faces... made worse by the return of *Jia Xu*."

Empress Fu shook her head sadly.

"That man is like some sort of family ghoul, the spirit-made-flesh of some vindictive man that one of my ancestors bested," Emperor Xian continued. "Every time I think I've seen the last of him he reappears, retaking his place as chief adviser to the latest monster that has seized power in my court. He guided Dong Zhuo to murder my stepmother and brother, install me as sovereign and leave me with the stain of feeling like a collaborator in my own brother's death; he had Dong murder half of the nobility, loot my ancestors' tombs and burn Luoyang; he ensured that Wang Yun's plot to expunge Dong Zhuo's influence was foiled and installed those two cretins Li Jue and Guo Si as regents to make an even greater fool of me; and now, in the wake of a failed attempt to remove Cao Cao, back he comes again to deliver inexplicable victory at Guandu and ensure that I will never be rid of that hankerer! The followers of that edict were my last chance!"

"...Does... does Cao believe that Your Majesty gave Dong Cheng that edict...?" Empress Fu asked timidly.

"It... it doesn't matter," Emperor Xian replied. "What is done is done, and he will never outright ask or accuse me, and his 'opinion' on the matter will vary according to convenience. What matters, my lady, is that I have very few allies at court now, and... and now I am told that independent sources have confirmed that Liu Bei *was* leading that attack on Xuchang."

Empress Fu was initially taken aback, but once she regained her composure she asked, "Might it have been a necessity...?"

"I tire of people passing off evil acts as 'necessity'," Emperor Xian replied. "Nothing wicked is 'necessary', only easier. If Liu Bei really did march against this city with an army of Yellow Turbans, then... then either he had no choice in his alliance with Yuan Shao,

who would then be the one truly at fault, or he has lost his mind, or he is the worst of them and every bit as wretched as his disinherited ancestors. I... I just wish that I could talk to him, hear his explanation... my heart craves an explanation, something that returns him to the fold, so that I am not isolated and... and..."
"...What about Yuan Shao...?" Empress Fu wondered.
"A lost cause," Emperor Xian said dismissively. "He's no better than his brother; he forges alliance with rebels, bandits and cultists, and he has not once pledged allegiance of late, sent tribute or given written assurance that Bing, Ji, Yòu and Qing were taken in the name of the Han and not his own. Oh, I know that Cao might be withholding correspondence from the court, but there are ways... he got that letter of condemnation distributed easily enough."
"But he fights in the name of the Girdle Edict," Empress Fu noted.
"...So he says," Emperor Xian replied. "But he has long contested my place; I do not know what happened to Governor Liu Yu's son, Liu Hè, but I was told that he travelled northward to aid Yuan's 'reclamation' of Yòu Province from Gongsun Zan. If that's true, and he lives, then Yuan might want to supplant me: remember, my lady, that Yuan's Eastern Pass Coalition fought for the restoration of the glory of the Han, but not for my place on the Han throne. I do not believe that his stance has changed, and cannot until he makes it explicitly clear."
"...So nothing has changed for us, then," Empress Fu sighed.
"No... we are where we have always been," Emperor Xian replied. "That being the case... what use is talking...?"
Empress Fu nodded agreeably, and Emperor Xian called for his servants to return; the young monarchs spent the remainder of the day in near-total silence.

****

5

Yuan Shao's court in his Ji Provincial capital of Yè City was condemned to be a sombre place since his infamous historic defeat at Guandu. Tens of thousands of soldiers had died, been captured or defected to Cao Cao's Han forces in the chaos that followed: in addition to that, Yuan had lost a large number of talented advisers and officers.

At the start of the campaign against Cao Cao's regime in Xuchang City, Yuan Shao had enjoyed more than just a numerical advantage: none but the most shrewd – and aware of Yuan's nature – would have expected the outcome. Firstly, Yuan had prestige and great wealth: his ancestors had been trusted vassals in the Imperial court in Luoyang, and one of his more influential ancestors, Yuan An, had the rare honour of being commemorated with statues; Shao's wealth was such that he could simultaneously fight a 7-year campaign against his brother Yuan Shu and the northern warlord Gongsun Zan and still have the financial security to launch an immediate campaign against Cao Cao in the aftermath. Secondly, Yuan had one of the largest pools of military talent: Generals Yan Liang, Wen Chou and Zhang Hè were only outclassed by the likes of the prodigy Lü Bu; he had a Wuhuan cavalry force that few could match after a serious famine five years earlier; and he had dozens of advisers while others typically had a handful. Thirdly, he had a strong list of third-party supporters: the itinerant warlord Liu Bei, Jing Governor Liu Biao and the north-eastern Wuhuan tribes were publicly united behind him, while the bandit kin Gong Du of Yu, the Yellow Turbans of Runan and a faction of rebellious officials in the capital led by General of Chariots and Cavalry Dong Cheng were silent partners and the southern warlord Sun Ce was said to be considering his own march against Xuchang after deciding that Cao Cao was a threat to his own vision for the south. Fourthly, Yuan Shao enjoyed near-total control of Bing, Ji, Qing and Yòu Provinces and all the resources that those provinces offered.

By contrast, Yuan Shao's opponent Cao Cao was on the defensive. Cao Cao had an army of only a quarter of the size of Yuan's that was tired after simultaneous campaigns against a rebel faction of Southern Xiongnu warriors, the Yellow Turbans of Runan, the warlord Lü Bu, Zang Ba's Mount Tai Bandits and the pretender Yuan Shu. Further to that, the capital Xuchang was surrounded on all sides, the construction of Xuchang's imperial palace and the restoration of Luoyang had drained the already-strained treasury, and the Han enjoyed only limited control over Xu, Yu and Yan Provinces. As a final, apparently deadly blow, Dong Cheng's plotters were found to be in possession of an imperial edict – the so-called 'Girdle Edict' – that condemned Cao Cao as a traitor and called upon the nation to destroy him.

But from the beginning, Yuan Shao was actually doomed: Cao Cao's counsel provided sound advice that led to the exposure of Dong Cheng's conspiracy, enabling Cao to dismiss the edict as a forgery and damage the campaign; Yuan Shao and his allies repeatedly hesitated and failed to coordinate, allowing Cao Cao to make better use of his limited resources and eliminate certain problems one at a time; Sun Ce was assassinated – some said coincidentally, others suspected Cao's involvement – and Ce's successor Sun Quan quickly made it clear that he would not march against the capital; and Yuan's large assembly of advisers quickly proved to be more of a hindrance than a help as they conspired against each other to further their own careers and offered contradictory advice that often led to crippling defeats. Slander caused two of Yuan's capable advisers – Tian Feng and Ju Shou – to be rendered ineffective and a third, Xu Yòu, to defect to Cao Cao, taking precious information with him; Generals Yan Liang and Wen Chou quickly fell in battle, and the slandered Zhang Hè defected after Xu Yòu's revelation of the location of Yuan's supply depot enabled Cao Cao to burn the entire army's food supply and force a retreat. In the wake of that defeat, Ju Shou died in Cao's custody and Tian Feng – who had been in prison since the start of the march – was sentenced to death for allegedly laughing at his master's defeat. Yuan Shao had retreated as a broken man: he still had an army that vastly outnumbered Cao Cao's, but he did not have the capable men to lead it.

"I... I must be resolute!" Yuan Shao said to his assembled court. "This... this cannot be the end of it! I am Yuan Shao, Commander-in-Chief of His Majesty's armed forces and the only man that can stand up to the villain Cao Cao!"
"Time and again you call us here... and time and again you say such things," the scholar and official Cui Yan scolded. "Either act or not."
"Do you accuse your lord of *dithering*, Cui Yan?" an adviser asked.
"*Your* choice of words, Guo Tu, not mine," Cui Yan retorted. "Are you trying to get *me* imprisoned now...?"
"Please... no more," Yuan Shao whimpered. "I regret Tian Feng's death greatly. Yes, he may well have laughed, but he had a right to, for I imprisoned him for trying to tell me the truth."
"B-but that's not right!" Guo Tu said. "He *laughed*! He laughed at your 'foolishness'! Mister Pang, you were the one that reported it, so speak up!"
"He did," the adviser and official Pang Ji insisted. "Is that not so, Gao Fan...?"
The Administrator of Wei Prefecture, Gao Fan, grunted tonelessly.
"I'm a man with an army that is unrivalled anywhere in our Empire, but I cannot beat a tiny mouse like Cao Cao," Yuan Shao complained. "When I next meet him on the battlefield, most of my generals and advisers will be on *his* side!"
"Traitors, one and all," the young officer Ju Hu declared. "My father died serving you loyally, and I shall not disappoint him. Zhang Hè has made a mistake, and he'll pay for it at my hands if I have any say in it."
"You...?" Yuan Shao chortled. "I appreciate your bravery, young man, but you're no match for Zhang Hè. No, I... I must win that valiant hero back to my cause somehow... make him see that-"
"That what?" Guo Tu heckled. "He slandered you, Lord Yuan! He intended defection anyway!"
"That's right!" the adviser Shen Pei cried.
Gao Fan and some of the lesser officials wanted to challenge Guo Tu and Shen Pei, but they knew that the penalty would be career-

destroying slander and said nothing.

"At this moment, Father, it is better to rely on family," Yuan Shao's heir, Yuan Tan, suggested. "I am no Yan Liang or Wen Chou... perhaps I am no Zhang Hè... but I have taken Qing Province for you, Father, and I will toil like a horse or dog to destroy Cao Cao for you. Give me command of a force, and–"

"I always intended it, my son," Yuan Shao said warmly. "I have been harmed by my defeat at Guandu: my innards tremble, my hair greys, my cheeks sink... the sight of anything that reminds me of Cao Cao fills me with rage and horror, so perhaps–"

"I meant to say, 'And I shall fight at your side', Father," Yuan Tan interrupted. "You are the man that led an armed force into the Imperial palace at Luoyang – despite knowing that you risked accusations of high treason – and slayed the eunuch allies of the 'Ten' to rescue the sovereign: I do not believe that you will allow a 'defeat' – a loss caused not by your incompetence but by wanton treachery and the incompetence of others – to harm you for long."

"Your son is right," Yuan Shao's secretary, Chen Lin, said sincerely. "You are a proven hero. You defeated the 'Ten', Gongsun Zan and the Black Mountain Bandits, and those wars were not without setbacks."

Yuan Shao nodded enthusiastically and said, "Yes... yes, yes, you're all quite right! My defeat was because Yan Liang and Wen Chou disappointed me with their poor judgement, and Zhang Hè and Xu Yòu betrayed me, just as so many had predicted that they would! Food and men, they can be replaced! Our cause is not done yet! We shall write to our allies and inspire a second attack!"

"Liu Biao's made it clear that he cannot commit to an attack on what he now calls 'the seat of power', not while the Sun clan harass his southern territory," Cui Yan noted. "And as of the Suns, their ruler Sun Quan is reportedly going further than Liu Biao, ingratiating himself with the imperial court and going through with marriage alliances. The Yellow Turbans of Yu are decimated if not dissolved, Gong Du's gone to ground, and Liu Bei is crawling on his belly to Jing Province with what's left of the army you gave him. Zang Ba's return to Qing Province is losing us vital influence, and the neutrality of the Southern Xiongnu is harming us."

"Do not now try and depress me again after I have finally found hope, Cui Yan!" Yuan Shao said angrily. "I will not simply roll over and die, not when my opponent is Cao Cao, the friendless slayer of princes and seducer of widows!"

"So what do you want to do?" the adviser Xin Pi asked.

"Locate Liu Bei, offer him a militia and propose a pincer," Yuan Shao replied. "No bandits and cultists this time, but a proper army. Despite what I have said in the past, the man didn't really curse me, not when I am being rational... his Guan Yu, alone, is worth trying to maintain relations with him for, and when I ponder it, he actually reached the capital with an army of vagabonds, so he could rescue the Son of Heaven if he had a real force. When Liu Biao sees what Liu Bei and I are achieving he will lend aid, and when Sun Quan sees what is happening he will doubtless show some of his father and brother's spirit and *truly* fight for the Han, not for Cao Cao!"

"...We'll do our best to find Liu Bei," Guo Tu said tonelessly.

"Be sure that you do," Yuan Shao chortled. "It isn't just *my* neck that has one of Cao's blades pressed against it, Guo Tu."

"...It is known to me, Lord Yuan," Guo Tu replied.

Yuan Shao suddenly noticed a familiar face amongst the scholars and said, "Is that... Ying Shao...? Is that Ying Zhongyuan???"

The frail Ying Shao – who was visibly in his early sixties – bowed humbly and replied, "It is, Governor Yuan."

"...Where have you been?" Yuan Shao asked. "I have not seen you in such a time!"

"Your son and heir, who is now Governor of Qing Province, asked that I attend court," Ying Shao replied. "I have been working on additional notes for my piece on folk legends."

"...Gentlemen, here is a man that explains why I must vanquish Cao Cao," Yuan Shao declared. "This fine mind was, like me, a friend of the 'Crafty Villain', and being around fifteen years our senior we looked up to him. Zhongyuan has seen and felt the 'Partisan Crisis', Dong Zhuo's tyranny, and he was Administrator of Mount Tai, where he fought Yellow Turbans and Zang Ba's Bandits: his reward was being forced to flee when Cao Cao began his genocidal war with Tao Qian."

"Mengde often writes and tries to justify his actions," Ying Shao said. "Although I still call him by that familiar name for his kind and selfless efforts to save the so-called 'Partisans', he is sometimes a stranger to me. He invites me to his court in Xuchang, but I always politely refuse. I will stay here and finish my writings, Governor Yuan: I only ask that you make it safe for me to do so."

"...Seeing you... brings back memories," Yuan Shao replied sadly.

Yuan Shao retreated to his private study after the meeting; he was greeted by his principal wife, Lady Liu, and his younger sons, Yuan Xi and Yuan Shang.

"I am weary," Yuan Shao admitted as he took his seat in the entertaining quarters as head of the household. "I did not envisage my grey-haired years as being like this."

"What will you do, Father?" Yuan Shang asked.

"...You're nigh on being a man now, Shang, and *you*, Xi, you *are* a man, though you are yet to experience any burdens," Yuan Shao replied. "I'd not answer your question, normally, but I must. Your father must now risk everything in a last battle with Cao Cao. If I succeed, our place in history as the most loyal and respected of Han servants is assured; if I fail, then it will be up to you and your brothers to continue my efforts to reinvigorate our clan... or there will be no clan."

"Is there no other way?" Lady Liu asked fearfully. "If you cannot win, then-"

"If I could not win, woman, then I would not fight!" Yuan Shao barked. **"If I could not win, then I would get drunk, summon all of you into the bedroom and kill you all before I killed myself, like Gongsun Zan!"**

Lady Liu took a tight hold of her son Yuan Shang's arm and turned to leave the room.

"Release him at once," Yuan Shao ordered. "He isn't your suckling anymore, he's *my son*."

"...As you so wish," Lady Liu muttered as she released Yuan Shang and continued her retreat; the lad turned to face his father and smiled encouragingly.

"You, Shang, only have a little longer to go before you'll be a man!" Yuan Shao chuckled. "But my, what a man you'll make; fine-featured, and showing signs of a statesman's mind already."

"My greatest desire in life is that you are proud of me, Father," Yuan Shang replied.

"...And I, my sons, only want that you are proud of me," Yuan Shao said soberly. "I will not let Cao Cao disgrace me further... I cannot... too much is at stake."

"We... we're proud of you, Father," Yuan Xi said.

"...It is nice of you to say," Yuan Shao replied. "But... but my ancestors... Yuan An, most of all... they will be looking down from the Heavens now, watching me, and... and I wonder... I wonder what... ... ...*aiee*."

Yuan Shao could not fight his angry tears any longer.

"*Damn them all*!" Yuan Shao whined. "Damn Chunyu Qiong, Ju Shou, Wen Chou, Yan Liang, Tian Feng, Zhang Hè, Xu Yòu, Lü Bu, Dong Zhuo, *Cao Cao*, and worst of all, damn that fool brother of mine! Damn him... *damn him*...!"

Neither of Yuan Shao's sons was sure of what to say or do: they retreated, and Shao soon replaced their company with the numbing effects of a jar of strong rice wine. Lady Liu beckoned her biological son Shang to her and fawned on him as she always did; Yuan's elder son by his late first wife, Yuan Xi, and Yuan's consorts kept their distance from the fearsome Lady Liu and wondered what was going through her mind as she glared at her drunken husband.

****

6

The minor warlord Liu Bei's battered forces retreated to an abandoned settlement that was close to the border between Yu and Jing Provinces. Bei looked to his demoralised officers and smiled encouragingly; one of them – a brawny, tanned, wild-eyed man with thick whiskers and tattered robes and armour – was in no mood for false optimism. That man, Zhang Fei, pointed at a cloth letter in Liu Bei's hand and cried, **"Don't do it, Xuande!"**
Liu Bei turned his own gaze to the letter from Yuan Shao's secretary Chen Lin and shook his head with disbelief.
"Don't do it!" Zhang Fei said for a second time. "Don't-!"
"Yide, I'm trying to *think*!" Liu Bei scolded.
"...**Damn that Cao Cao!**" Zhang Fei exclaimed. **"Every time we get just over the border or come near it, he**...!"
A second officer – a tall, imposing man whose weathered green robes were contrasted by his long, shiny, well-kept beard – smiled slightly and said, "Cao *Ren* is our problem right now, Zhang Yide. And he can harry us as much as he wants... we'll be fine."
"Don't humour me, Guan Yunchang," Zhang Fei retorted.
"I wouldn't, Yide," Guan Yu insisted. "Are you still angry...?"
"...No, no, I already said that I wasn't angry at you anymore," Zhang Fei replied. "I didn't just say that so you'd stop boring me senseless with talk after talk about why you joined Cao Cao."
Guan Yu smiled and laughed.
"Is there anything to laugh at...?" Zhang Fei asked.
"...Maybe there is," Liu Bei sighed as he straightened his battle helmet. "Is there anything to laugh at, Xianhe...?"
"Don't ask that clown!" Zhang Fei barked as all eyes turned to Liu Bei's innocuous long-time friend Jian Yong. "He'll just-!"
"*Yide*... stop it," Liu Bei interrupted.
Zhang Fei harrumphed and glared at Jian Yong.
"I'm as sick of all this as you, Zhang Yide," Jian Yong promised. "But then, one can't help wondering how we ended up working side-by-side with *them*."
Jian Yong gestured to one outer part of the hastily-assembled camp: a group of youths were stationed there, and they had one noticeable difference in their attire. Most of Liu Bei's men were outfitted with simple robes, tunics, cuirasses, leather limb guards and simple leather helmets, while the officers were lucky enough to enjoy better protection; the majority of the people within this one outer camp, however, wore yellow turbans on their heads that were an all-too-familiar symbol of dissent against Han rule.
"Didn't we chase them away?" Guan Yu said with surprise.
"No, because Xuande 'doesn't have the heart'!" Zhang Fei heckled.
"Don't say it like that, Yide," Liu Bei retorted. "I didn't mean that I sympathise with their cause, because I'd be a fool to! I want to reach out to them, convince them that their beliefs are the product of a deceitful cultist, and-"
"Sixteen years ago, we were forced to kill hundreds of them because they couldn't be reasoned with," Guan Yu noted. "Fifteen and then fourteen years ago, we fought them again, and the situation was the same every time. Cao Cao was forced to come into Yu Province and quell them three years ago, but yet again

they didn't learn; when we were in Xiaopei, we had no choice but to kill the leaders of the White Wave Bandits that evolved from the Yellow Turbans, for they were still as opposed to order as they had ever been. Anyone that is still wearing that treasonous symbol after all this time is unlikely to be swayed, Xuande. Did you get anywhere with their leader, Liu Pi...?"

"...No, he was obviously lying when he said that he'd changed his mind," Liu Bei admitted. "I suppose that I... ... ...but no, I am being conceited. If I could turn a hardened cultist into a model citizen, I'd not be stuck in the wilds with nothing to my name, would I...?"

"You're being hard on yourself, Lord Liu," the thin, frail official Mi Zhu suggested. "If there was even one of them, as you said, that could be swayed, then-"

"Might we perhaps return to discussing the *letter*...?" the middle-aged official Sun Qian – who most referred to as 'Mister Sun' – asked irritably.

"Ah, yes... the letter," Liu Bei sighed.

"My lord, we should just refuse to answer this," Mi Zhu said.

"How can I?" Liu Bei retorted. "We've given quarters to the messenger! Am I supposed to kill him and throw him in a ditch?"

"By 'refuse to answer', I meant that we should not take up arms against Cao again right now," Mi Zhu explained. "Delay, say that-"

"He promises an army, a proper army, to fight Cao Cao in a pincer!" Liu Bei said excitedly. "If I refuse this, I will be a vagrant, wandering into Jing Province with little more than a band of-!"

"Accept, and you become Yuan's vassal again," Mi Zhu warned. "Taking the army obligates you, and then you will be told to-"

"But if our ultimate objective is to defeat Cao Cao, why refuse a perfectly good army and hide in Jing while Yuan dies alone, only to oppose Cao later with a borrowed army from Liu Biao and die alone as well?" Mister Sun asked. "If he's learned his lessons at Guandu and now proffers a proper army to us, then we-"

"Yuan Shao is a buffoon," Mi Zhu said irritably. "He'll offer us this army now, and then Guo Tu, Pang Ji or one of those other idiots that he has around him will tell him that Lord Liu will steal the borrowed army, 'just as Liu Bei steals everything that he borrows', and then he'll order us to return the men, and we'll be back to where we started."

"*Aiee*... how did I end up with such a reputation?" Liu Bei sighed.

"You were lent the governor's seal of Xu Province and took the place over, stole a borrowed army from Cao Cao and got what's left of this army that you were sneaking into Jing with from Yuan Shao," Jian Yong noted. "To the accuser, just say this: 'Yes, but I only steal from thieves'."

Mi Zhu and Mister Sun covered their faces with their sleeves; Guan Yu, Zhao Yun and Chen Dao lowered their heads to hide their smiles, and Zhang Fei started to laugh uproariously.

"How can you say that, Xianhe???" Liu Bei complained. "I-! ...I am not a thief! Tao Qian bequeathed control of Xu to me! Zhao Yun was returning to my service after a leave of absence! And Yuan Shao gave me two sets of misfits, not a proper army! Yes, okay, the men that Cao assigned to me were his to begin with, but-!"

"You're too touchy," Jian Yong snickered. "I was *joking*, Xuande."

"I'm *not a thief*," Liu Bei insisted. "Cao Cao and Yuan Shao stole everything that they have around them from everyone else and each other! The men that Yuan Shao would be assigning to me now would be 'stolen' from Han Fu, Liu Yu, Gongsun Zan, Qu Yi-"

"Exactly right," Jian Yong interrupted. "So, uh... why do you now want to let him steal *you*?"

Liu Bei's eyes wandered.

"If we accept this army, it'll be as Mi Zhu said," Jian Yong continued. "No offence, Mister Sun, but you're not a strategist. Neither am I, I know, but I have sort of seen what's afoot here, and I really don't trust Yuan Shao's character or his judgement. This isn't about saving the emperor from Cao Cao; this is about *taking* the emperor from Cao Cao. We know that because no good man would ask a wolf to rescue a child, but Yuan Shao enlisted the *Yellow Turbans* to attack Xuchang."

Liu Bei nodded agreeably.

"Jian Xianhe is, thankfully, being serious at what is a very serious moment," Mi Zhu said. "We must be sensible: we don't have-"

Mi Zhu was interrupted by his younger brother, Mi Fang, who approached the gathering and said, **"They're chanting, Lord Liu! We might need to-!"**

"*Chanting...*?" Zhang Fei exclaimed. "Not... not that-!"

"Yes, the mantra, the *Yellow Turban mantra*!" Mi Fang said. "Zhao Yun is trying to calm things down, but the men, they're-!"

"Say no more," Liu Bei interrupted. "Yunchang, Yide..."

Mister Sun coughed deliberately and asked, "And me, Lord Liu...?"

"Stay here with the Mi brothers and continue the debate," Liu Bei ordered. "I will be back soon enough."

Liu Bei's charismatic young officer Zhao Yun was still trying to maintain order as a small group of Yellow Turban acolytes taunted Liu Bei's soldiers with the infamous mantra that had been taught to every follower by the founder of the 'Way of Peace', Zhang Jue:

"Han's mandate has passed!
Yellow Sky, soon here!
In this renewing year,
Prosperous all, at last!"

"Prosperous *what*, you cultist scum???" one soldier screamed as one of Zhao Yun's junior officers reluctantly restrained him.

"Oh, thank the Heavens, Lord Liu is here," Zhao Yun declared as Liu Bei approached the gathering with Guan Yu, Zhang Fei, Jian Yong and his imposing bodyguard force that was led by the silent, towering giant Chen Dao.

"Yellow Sky! Yellow Sky! Prosperous all!" the leader of the Yellow Turbans cackled; his closest followers joined him, but some were visibly wavering.

"You're hated here in Yu, you mad idiots!" one of the bandit Gong Du's former followers shouted angrily. **"All you did was cause more death! Nobody wants you anymore! Take your made-up religion and crawl down a hole!"**

"No, kill them!" one of Liu Bei's soldiers demanded. **"Kill-!"**

"That really shouldn't be necessary!" Liu Bei insisted. **"I don't know what your names are, young people, and perhaps you can tell me later, after this debate is ended."**

"*Debate***'...?"** the Yellow Turban leader scoffed as he gestured for silence. "'**Yellow Sky', Liu Bei! 'Yellow Sky'! I, Bo Ju, say that your emperor is *doomed*! Debate *that*!**"

The acolytes stopped chanting and awaited Liu Bei's response.

"...You're with us because you retreated from the battles with Cao Ren as part of an alliance, an alliance between you, me and Gong Du against the tyrant Cao Cao," Liu Bei suggested. "Cao Cao runs the court: Cao Cao is the one that denies the poor the aid that they need and builds grand homes for himself and his followers while the world outside Xuchang slowly withers. Before him, there were the regents, Li Jue and Guo Si, and before them, there was Dong Zhuo; before him, the 'Ten Attendants'. His Majesty, whom I have met, was but a boy when all of the recent ills occurred, a child that was pushed and pulled this way and that by the ambitious men that surrounded the throne. So it hardly seems fair to condemn him for the actions of the bad men that acted for themselves on his behalf."

"And the one before him...?" one Yellow Turban soldier asked.

"...Lingdi was born surrounded by the 'Ten', and they blinded him to the truth," Liu Bei replied. "Surely you've heard the tales of-?"

"'**Tales'! Yes! 'Tales'! More *lies*!**" Bo Ju taunted. "**The 'Son of Heaven' is the source of our misery! But the Han's time is over! Their mandate *has* passed if eunuchs and fools can control them! Even his relatives, like *you*, and the Yuans of Ru County were attacking the capital to try and seize him! And we got to the capital! We drew blood! It's *over*! Sooner or later, it's *over*! 'Yellow Sky'!**"

The Yellow Turbans began their angry chanting once again.

"**STOP IT!**" Zhang Fei bellowed. "**STOP IT *NOW*, OR...!**"

Many of the Yellow Turbans continued their chanting, but some did obey Zhang Fei, if only because they had been startled by Zhang's cavernous voice; Guan Yu nodded purposefully, and Liu Bei's soldiers raised their weapons.

"**Don't make me order your punishment!**" Liu Bei pleaded. "**Your false prophet is dead, your cause crushed, and despite all of your efforts, the Han persists! There is no 'Yellow Sky', and there never will be!**"

The Yellow Turbans that had not already stopped were never going to: those that had chosen to capitulate backed away from their former peers, and Liu Bei's men quickly encircled the defiant.

"**Prosperous all!**" Bo Ju urged as he realised that death was imminent. "**Yellow Sky, prosperous-!**"

"**SHUT UP!**" Zhang Fei screamed as he thrust his heavy snake-tongued pike toward Bo Ju and ran him through; a short but violent exchange followed, and at the end of it, none of the defiant Yellow Turbans was left alive.

"...*Aiee*... I did not want to do that!" Liu Bei sobbed.

"How could we go into Jing with that lot chanting the whole way?" Jian Yong grumbled. "Liu Biao would have thought we were all-!"

"I...! ...I know that, Xianhe, I know that," Liu Bei said as he turned to face those that had decided to change their stance.

"We're not evil," one young woman pleaded. "W-we just want-!"

"Go home, and be a wife," Zhang Fei jeered.

"**We just want better!**" the woman retorted. "Your emperor-!"

"*Our* Emperor," Liu Bei insisted. "Any men that wish to join our cause and fight to restore the Han's lustre – which, in turn, will

44

bring about the 'prosperous all' you all crave, if only you would be *patient* – may join us. But women must return to their homes. The battlefield is no place for women."

"How patient do you want us to be...?" a young man sobbed. "All I've ever known is having nothing! **All any of my family's ever known is having *nothing*! Nearly *four-hundred years* your Han's been-!**"

"**The great day will come when corruption will be purged and Heaven's will made material!**" Liu Bei declared. "**The Han are part of Heaven's will... all things, good and bad, are Heaven's design. I spent a year starving in Haixi, but I never wavered; even now, out here, with nothing much to smile about, I won't waver. Heaven's design is complex, beyond our meagre understanding, but it is so! I ask of all men and women that they know their place in that design, and do all they can to aid me in the end of that corruption that obstructs the path! Help me defeat Cao Cao, and peace and prosperity *can* belong to us all!**"

The Yellow Turbans exchanged glances and mumbled.

"Nice speech," Jian Yong snickered. "A load of nice-sounding, empty rubbish; have you considered starting your own cult?"

"*Shut up*," Liu Bei muttered.

"Perhaps there are other groups of us left in Yu," one young man sighed as he turned and walked away; a few followed him.

"...I give up," the young woman whimpered as she turned and walked away; a few followed her.

"I'm going home," another man said; a few followed his retreat.

"...I'll stay," one man said as he yanked the yellow turban from his head. "Lord Liu, you are a light in darkness, and I'll follow you if it means bringing peace. Cao Cao is the problem, not the Han."

Most of those that had remained murmured agreeably and removed their yellow turbans; others quietly slipped away.

"**To those of you that have chosen to stay, I give thanks,**" Liu Bei said sombrely. "**To those that left, I wish them well and hope that they find what they are looking for. Now, onward: we must go to Jing's capital and begin our fightback against the 'Crafty Villain' Cao Cao, who slaughtered the people of Xu, seduces widows and aunts, betrays brotherly covenants and murders unborn princes! Glory to the Han! Death to the villain Cao Cao!**"

Zhao Yun and Zhang Fei urged their soldiers to echo their lord's rallying cry; many raised their weapons and chanted repeatedly, "**Glory to the Han! Death to the villain Cao Cao!**"

"...And now, we'd better continue discussing what we're going to do about Chen Lin's letter," Jian Yong suggested as he looked at the self-satisfied Liu Bei. "We might not have long before Cao Ren finds us again; I doubt you'll be able to talk *him* into submission."

Liu Bei's face fell; he nodded seriously and said, "Quite right. **EVERYONE: BACK TO YOUR DUTIES!**"

The small militia quickly obeyed, having been purged of dissenting Yellow Turban elements.

Liu Bei returned to his main camp, where Mi Zhu and Mister Sun were engaged in a heated war of words.

"**Alright, gentlemen, enough!**" Liu Bei ordered.

"You must consider our military strength!" Mister Sun pleaded.

"I do," Liu Bei replied. "I'm not 'responding obediently to this', but I must not abandon the people of Runan."

Jian Yong laughed and said, "Pardon...?"

"Yuan Shao cursed us with heretics for company and damaged our reputation: if I liaise too closely again he'll cause our deaths, I know that," Liu Bei explained. "But when I look at the hated Yellow Turbans that we were just forced to kill, I see that our cause in Yu Province is not lost... we have won hearts and minds in Runan, and we might still do our part in purging the heretics and saving His Majesty if we cultivate support here rather than hiding behind Liu Biao's hall curtains. Yuan Shao's future is his own to preserve or destroy, but we must do what we can for Runan before we simply melt away. We'll resume our march as soon as it is feasible, but it is to about-face and confront Cao Ren, and to hold onto what we have here."

"Finally, a proper fight!" Zhang Fei chuckled.

"...Perhaps," Zhao Yun replied uneasily.

"Cao Cao wants us dead, so why shouldn't we want him dead too?" Zhang Fei asked. "He's taken everything from us, so-!"

"So we should take from him," Jian Yong snickered. "Still trying to justify your scouts capturing Lady Xiahou, then...?"

"*Aiee*... impossible though it might seem, I'd actually forgotten about that," Liu Bei said. "Have you not released her, Yide...?"

"No: I'm marrying her," Zhang Fei retorted.

"She's *Xiahou Yuan's daughter*!" Mister Sun said.

"Yeah... young and pretty, too... lucky me, uh...?" Zhang Fei chuckled. "I hope he gets to know about it, the scruffy bastard."

"You really shouldn't, Yide," Liu Bei said. "I *could* make you give her up, but-"

"But you won't, so leave it," Zhang Fei replied. "My only regret's that she weren't the only one, else I'd have got one for Yunchang too, to make up for Cao Cao stealing Lady Du off him."

Guan Yu shook his head.

"And it's Xiahou's own fault, anyway, sending a pretty girl out alone to chop firewood," Zhang Fei continued. "Doesn't his 'cousin' Cao Cao pay him well enough...? Are his sons all lame...?"

Jian Yong and Mister Sun groaned miserably.

"...If we might get back to our plans...?" Liu Bei asked.

Mi Zhu bowed slightly and said, "A risky decision, Lord Liu: yes, we could do more here than in the untrusting court of Liu Biao, so long as we remember always that we really cannot afford to make any more deadly mistakes or join men that make them for us."

"And we *will* remember," Liu Bei promised. "From now on, we work toward the restoration of the Han in our own way, so that we can be sure that we are truly righteous and certain to win."

Liu Bei's small militia prepared to continue their journey: a few of those that had pledged new allegiance to Liu Bei remained to bury the bodies of their former comrades, after which they kept their promise or went in some new direction.

****

7

Jing Province Governor Liu Biao summoned his officials and allies to a meeting in his northern capital Xiangyang; he viewed the gathering with tired, haggard eyes and asked, "What am I to do about Liu Bei...?"

"Not again," Admiral Cai Mao scoffed. "Lord and Governor... *brother-in-law*... you know that you must not allow this man to take another step in our direction! Why do you keep asking us and then dismissing our opinions?"

"There is no consensus," Liu Biao retorted. "I must be sure, really sure, that he is a hero or a menace; turning him away could be my worst mistake to date."

"But I believe – as do many others – that he is not to be trusted," Cai Mao said. "I know that you and he are related by blood to each other and the royal clan, but he is disinherited, impoverished and a pariah by his own doing! He stole Xu Province from Tao Qian, so why wouldn't he try and steal Jing from you...?"

"*Aiee*... Tao Qian *gave* him the province because he decided that his sons were not best placed to fight a vengeful Cao Cao! I intend no such generosity, for Cao would be fighting for greed, not grief!" Liu Biao insisted. "My eldest son Qi will inherit this province, and if the worst befell Qi, then it would go to my younger son, Cong!"

Some turned to look at the wasted face of Liu Qi and silently guessed that he would not see Liu Biao's age.

"If Cao Cao came here, then I would resist him as a loyal Han governor," Liu Biao declared, "and not crumble as a guilty murderer of innocent fathers!"

The official Huan Jie – whose previous master was Sun Jian, the father of Biao's nemesis Sun Quan – smiled at the statement, since Liu Biao's assassination of Sun Jian had long been the Sun clan's main justification for attacking Jing Province.

"I know that look, and why you wear it," Liu Biao said as he glared at Huan Jie. "I destroyed Sun Jian because he came here to steal my province for his master Yuan Shu, and Heaven let me do it because he was a plunderer. Cao Cao would also be coming here as a thief, and he would meet the same end!"

"I smile because we might be allowing Liu Bei in here to steal the province without a fight," Huan Jie replied. "He is sly, Lord Liu, and possessed of a type of charisma that wins soft hearts and weak minds alike. He'll ingratiate himself with your populace and usurp you with words, the pen and the smiles of naïve peasants, not the sword."

"Too right, Mister Huan," Cai Mao said. "A lot of the young intelligentsia in Xiangyang and Xinye have developed a romantic vision of Bei as some sort of 'underdog hero', the 'only man to face Cao Cao when others flee'."

Liu Biao laughed and said, "Is that so, gentlemen...?"

"It is, Lord Liu," the young scholar-official Wang Can replied. "I make regular trips into town, and-"

"To listen to the donkeys, no doubt!" Liu Biao teased.

"...I make no denial that I find their brays comforting," the frail Wang Can said as he became overwhelmed by a feeling of embarrassment. "But if I may...? Liu Bei is, like Sun Jian, misrepresented by some idealistic types. To the 'thinkers', Bei is an untarnished gem, a man that has not earned a reputation for mass murder, theft, fraud, rape, plunder or deception, but rather for 'heroic action' and 'defiance of evil'; his endurance, tenacity and meek countenance serve as 'evidence' that he is a true hero and a Heaven-sent foil to harry Cao Cao."

"While I, I suppose, am a mediocrity, a toady and a do-nothing, placed into the same category as that spineless fool Liu Zhang," Liu Biao sighed. "I am also, I presume, 'the victim of self-inflicted misery by slaying the hero Sun Jian in so cowardly a fashion'."

Wang Can smiled sheepishly and said, "I cannot deny that they are held opinions. They are wrong, of course, but you know the nature of the naïve tavern scholar. If I had not been blessed with the chance to work for you here, Lord Liu, I would probably be as aloof and romantic as they are."

"...But I am inclined to help Xuande precisely because he has performed so well under duress," Liu Biao admitted. "He was given Xu: that I truly believe, else that brainless thug Lü Bu could not have stolen it so easily."

"It was Chen Gong that connived the province from Liu Bei's hands," the adviser Kuai Yue suggested. "It is simply the case that Chen Gong outplayed Mi Zhu."

"...So it seems that the arguments against inviting Liu Bei here grow by the day," Liu Biao noted. "But I have already offered him refuge! Can I now offend him by turning him away at the border when he arrives?"

"'If' he arrives: he's being harried by Cao Ren, and I suspect that Cao Cao will soon decide to smash him before he gets here," Wang Can explained. "Like many of us, he fears a Liu Bei with Jing Province's defences and options within his grasp. Furthermore, he flounders and procrastinates, perhaps since he was appointed 'Governor of Yu Province' by Tao Qian, and he probably still entertains the idea that the place is rightfully his and worth fighting for. Perhaps he will never reach us here."

"...Yes," Liu Biao murmured.

"You are weary, lord and brother-in-law, and that is muddling your thoughts," Cai Mao suggested. "Sun Quan's continued pressuring of Huang Zu weighs on your mind. We'll deal with Liu Bei *if* he gets here: after all, he'll be tired, broken and lacking in men and food, and in that state he'll be very manageable."

"...Yes," Liu Biao replied. "Yes, Mister Cai, I'll... rest."

Liu Biao coughed uncomfortably as he got to his feet and left the hall by way of a side entrance; he was met almost immediately by his radiant principal wife, Lady Cai.

"I know that expression; I cannot listen to more slandering of Liu Bei!" Liu Biao pleaded. "Your brother and the rest of my court have pecked at me enough!"

"He'll steal everything you've built here," Lady Cai insisted.

"No he won't! He probably won't even get here alive!" Liu Biao retorted as he pushed his way past Lady Cai and retreated to his living quarters.

"...He'll get here," Lady Cai muttered.

A day later, Cao Cao summoned Xun Wenruo, Cheng Yu, Guo Jia and Yuan Huan to his meeting room in the Xuchang chancellery.

"Liu Bei...?" Guo Jia asked mischievously.

"Yes," Cao Cao grumbled. "He is maintaining contact with Yuan Shao... which I cannot risk! And he's so close to Jing now... I cannot let him get to Jing either!"

"Then send a bigger force to Runan," Cheng Yu said impatiently. "Cao Ren's tiny force is merely nibbling at Bei's ankles: devour the wretch in one gulp if you are serious about stopping him."

"But what about Yuan's force at Cangting?" Xun Wenruo fretted.

"I will keep an eye on Yuan Shao," Cheng Yu promised. "Now you must return the favour, my lord."

"What would you have me do...?" Cao Cao asked.

"Take that annoying friend of yours with you to Runan," Cheng Yu replied. "If it is as all possible, *leave him there*."

Cao Cao laughed and said, "You do not like Xu Yòu, then?"

"The man is slimy, dishonest and self-serving, and he manages to be nauseatingly obsequious and shamelessly arrogant at precisely the wrong moments with uncanny timing," Cheng Yu suggested. "He has served his one and only purpose on this world under Heaven, Your Excellency, so be rid of him now."

Cao Cao frowned and said, "You would have me earn a reputation for being the death of *all* of my childhood friends, Cheng Yu...?"

Cheng Yu's expression betrayed nervousness.

"I watched helplessly as Xu Rong's men robbed us of brave, trusting Wei Zi at Xingyang, which was my fault entirely for being reckless," Cao Cao continued. "Confusion led me to harm Lü Boshe and rob the poor man of his family, which was as bad as killing him; I was forced to order the death of Zhang Miao for his betrayal; cruel circumstance led me to the home of Qin Bonan, leading to the poor man giving his life in place of mine; and now I fight Yuan Shao, 'Benchu', who was, perhaps, my dearest friend of all, and the only survivable outcome that I can strive for is his clan's total extermination. I learned a year or so ago – or was it longer? – that Ying Shao, a scholar that I have known since I was a child, hides in Ji Province, and that man who once called me 'friend' now fears me and rejects my calls to come to Xuchang; and Mister Tian Chou, who once came to me and pledged his service, has now retreated to his home region of Wuzhong County and taken a up the position as a Magistrate, which makes him a vassal of Yuan Shao, a man he once accused of colluding with Gongsun Zan to 'remove' poor Liu Yu, and that is doubtless because he felt I went too far in killing Consort Dong. Am I now to kill Xu Yòu for the petty offence of being socially inept...?"

"...I shall make no more such statements, Excellency, for they are, as you say, in poor taste," Cheng Yu promised.

Guo Jia smiled fearlessly and said, "I wouldn't fret, Elder Cheng; Lord Cao failed to realise that it was a joke because he entertains the idea of being rid of him as well: the tone and wording of his retort makes that clear enough."

Cao Cao exhaled fiercely and muttered, "I... I must be aware that he is potentially dangerous, yes, once he no longer needs me to protect him from Yuan Shao. But while that is the case, he will do anything to keep me alive and thwart Yuan Shao, which *could... might...* be useful. After that...? ...That's up to him."

The advisers nodded silently.

"And... and Mister Tian has made it clear that he went back to

Wuzhong to... to be of service to his late lord and governor, Liu Yu, not Yuan Shao, and... and I should trust him," Cao Cao continued.
"He is a good man," Guo Jia said. "You are right to trust him."
"Yes... but enough of that," Cao Cao continued. "*Liu Bei*, who is no friend, must be my focus now. Mister Yuan Huan: as a former adviser to Yuan Shu, you are well acquainted with the various factions in Yu Province, so you will accompany me. Xu Yòu will accompany me to Yu Province, mainly because he will insist upon it. I want to march quickly, and would like to know how quickly."
"Immediately," Guo Jia replied.
"The army is tired," Xun Wenruo protested. "Guandu was costly."
"It will be more costly if we let Liu Bei reach Jing," Guo Jia suggested. "I know that you want their last energies spent on Yuan, but we must destroy Bei first, while Yuan still flounders."
"I'm inclined to agree," Cheng Yu said. "Sorry, Wenruo, but Bei is more dangerous if left alive now: this could be our last chance to destroy him with minimal effort."
"I... I know that," Xun Wenruo admitted. "Yes, Guo Fengxiao is right, we can march immediately."
"Tomorrow evening, then," Cao Cao said.
"Tomorrow morning would be better," Guo Jia declared. "Don't give any of Bei's remaining supporters in the capital a chance to send a warning. And we cannot take Generals Xu Huang or Zhang Liao, because they might hesitate in a confrontation with their friend Guan Yu. Zhang Liao almost certainly would."
"...That reduces our options," Cao Cao complained.
"Those men are better placed on the northern front, facing Cangting and Yuan Shao's army," Xun Wenruo replied. "General Zhang Hè is a better choice, so that he cannot be approached by Yuan Shao's agents and offered a chance to go back to him."
"He wouldn't," Cao Cao said, "but I will take him anyway, since I am unable to take the other two."
"Is taking Xu Yòu *and* Zhang Hè to rout Liu Bei a wise move either...?" Xun Wenruo asked. "One possible scenario is Zhang's deciding to avenge the loss of friends and colleagues at Wuchao depot by taking Xu Yòu's head to Yuan Shao – perhaps alongside your own, Excellency – and pleading forgiveness...?"
"...No," Cao Cao decided. "Zhang Hè is clearly a 'thinking general', and far too shrewd to consider such a silly move. He remembers Qu Yi's fate after the Battle of Jie Bridge: Yuan Shao would believe the slander that endangered Zhang before and kill him anyway."
"Agreed," Guo Jia said. "With Zhang Hè, Cao Ren, Cao Xiu and Xiahou Dun in the vanguard, and if needs be the might of your bodyguard Xu Chu to match blades with Guan Yu or Zhang Fei, you cannot lose. Xu Huang, Zhang Liao, Li Dian and Yue Jin can guard against Yuan's movements and any possible mischief by the Qiang – which, hopefully, Zhang Xiu in Nan County will give us advance warning of – while Yu Jin continues to liaise with Zang Ba and the other former bandit kings in Xu and Qing Provinces."
Cao Cao nodded agreeably and said, "Tomorrow, Liu Bei dies!"

★★★★★★★★★★★★

8

Liu Bei's plan to occupy Runan Prefecture and build a base there instead of retreating to Jing Province was brought to a sudden and humiliating end: Cao Cao's arrival in the region struck fear into many former Yellow Turbans and generated popular support from the people that Cao had defended from those same Yellow Turbans 3 years before. Liu Bei's tiny force reached the prefectural border just as Cao Cao's army was preparing to pursue him; a fight was unavoidable and the outcome was obvious to both sides.

"We're dead," Jian Yong sighed.

"**We should have just gone to Jing!**" Mister Sun whined.

"**Shut up, you old coward!**" Zhang Fei bellowed. "**It's only Cao Cao! We-!**"

"*No*, **Yide!**" Liu Bei said as he watched Cao Cao's forces order themselves with frightening efficiency. "**I've made a mistake: I should have seen that he'd do this! We might have been in Jing, if only I'd...! ...But enough! Yide, you, Mi Fang and Mister Sun shall lead the men back to the west! Zizhong, Yunchang, Zilong, Xianhe and I will-**"

"**That is unwise,**" Liu Bei's bodyguard, Chen Dao, said suddenly.

"**I agree, my lord,**" Zhao Yun said. "**I will hold the rear with my cavalry; everyone else should be advancing westward with all haste!**"

Liu Bei shook his head and cried, "**I cannot be seen to-!**"

"**Now is not the time for such thoughts!**" Mi Zhu scolded. "**You must survive! All is lost if you die! Now please, Lord Liu, go at once, and I shall follow!**"

Cao Cao had deployed a detachment of cavalry to attack Liu Bei's position; there was no time to debate further, and everyone knew it. Chen Dao remained close to his lord while some of his fearsome men – who were all elite Danyang cavalrymen – joined Zhao Yun's efforts to keep Cao Cao's horsemen away.

"**I WANT TO FIGHT!**" Zhang Fei protested. "**LET ME FIGHT!**"

"**So do I, but there will be better times for that!**" Guan Yu said as he led the belligerent Zhang Fei away from the battle.

"**We'll need to split up, Lord Liu, and confuse their efforts!**" Mi Zhu suggested.

"**Whatever it takes!**" Liu Bei said as he kicked his horse to urge it forward.

A scout reported Liu Bei's retreat to Cao Cao.

"**He has to die here!**" Cao Cao shouted over the battle drums and the screams of his soldiers. "**Xiahou Dun!**"

"**Say no more!**" Xiahou Dun replied. "**MEN: WITH ME!**"

Xiahou Dun led a force of infantrymen and cavalrymen after Liu Bei's main force, which was doubly burdened with protecting a convoy of supplies.

"**Their families are not with them,**" Yuan Huan noted. "**They have no base nearby, so... so their families must already be in Jing.**"

"*They* **will not reach Jing!**" Cao Cao barked. "**Zhang Hè, Cao Xiu, Cao Chun!**"

The brawny Zhang Hè nodded obediently and led a third force after Guan Yu, who had separated from the main retreat as a decoy; the less-impressive Cao Xiu shouted, **"For the Han, Cousin Mengde!"** and led his own force after a second decoy force led by Zhang Fei and Mi Fang; Cao Ren's younger brother, Cao Chun, laughed and said, **"I'll fetch Liu Bei's head for you, Mengde!"** before he followed Cao Xiu.

"…We won't get Liu Bei here, will we, Fengxiao…?" Cao Cao asked miserably.

"Probably not," Guo Jia replied, **"but this will ensure that his influence is blunted severely; it would take him years to build enough respect and a following large enough to challenge Liu Biao, and that's if Biao's followers don't remove Bei for us."**

"…We'll need to give them lots of incentives for doing so," Cao Cao said coldly.

"So are we going back to Guandu now, Mengde?" Xu Yòu asked nervously.

Cao Cao smiled and said, **"Yes, Ziyuan, we are."**

"Yuan Shao could be planning anything while we're chasing this nobody Liu Bei!" Xu Yòu fretted. **"You should have left this to someone else!"**

"Calm yourself, Ziyuan," Cao Cao replied. **"It'll all be over soon enough."**

The battle at Runan's western border was the rout that both sides expected; Liu Bei's militia was scattered in all directions, and his closest followers with them, but Cao Cao left the pursuit operations to Cao Ren and returned to Xuchang with his army. Liu Bei, Chen Dao, Jian Yong, Mi Zhu and Mister Sun reached a former encampment on the Yu-Jing border a few days later, and Liu Bei was unable to stifle his tears upon seeing it.

"We were here, so close to Jing…!" Liu Bei lamented. "The sweet, safe air of the place was within a day's march… and I turned us back to be slaughtered at Runan!"

"We showed great courage," Mi Zhu suggested. "That might improve our-"

"Improve *what*, Zizhong?" Liu Bei interrupted. "I had hundreds of men, a small cavalry, and four great generals! Now I have one general, a handful of men, and nothing to show for it!"

"But we resisted the 'Hero of Chaos' and survived," Mi Zhu retorted. "I don't believe that Yunchang, Yide and Zilong are dead, any more than I believe that my brother is dead."

Liu Bei's anger gave way to embarrassment; he smiled awkwardly and said, "Forgive me, Zizhong, for failing to acknowledge your brother's absence."

"There is nothing to forgive," Mi Zhu insisted. "They are all alive. I know it. And now we're going to Jing. They'll cross the border and head for Xinye as planned, and so will we."

"But what about Cao Cao…?" Mister Sun fretted. "What if he pursues us over the border and-?"

"If he intended such a thing, he'd have waited until we crossed in order to give him the excuse to invade Jing," Mi Zhu replied. "He can't invade Jing, not for now at least; he's got to go back to his capital, and then maybe back to the front against Yuan Shao, who still lives, has a base in Cangting and commands close to a quarter of a million men. That battle isn't over."

Liu Bei nodded and said, "You are right as always, Zizhong. If only I'd heeded your advice and crossed into Jing before."

"And if only I'd seen the futility of remaining in Yu Province," Mister Sun sighed. "I should like to go ahead and meet with Liu Biao's court, assess their feelings."

"Do that," Mi Zhu said. "We can't be sure that this attack won't scare Liu Biao into reneging on his previous promise."

"Yes, that's right," Liu Bei gasped. "Go at once, Mister Sun, and ensure that we are still welcome!"

Mister Sun bowed to the ensemble and rode away at speed.

"...Well," Jian Yong sighed, "the-"

"**No jokes!**" Liu Bei barked.

"...'The path is ahead of us', I was about to say, and only fate can know whether we're supposed to get where we want to go," Jian Yong continued. "This proves one thing for certain: one way or another, Xuande, we need our own Guo Jia."

"Quite," Mi Zhu murmured. "To get an army here to smash us with no warning, at such speed... when he faces the threat of a humiliated Yuan Shao bearing down on him from the north... is brave and, for me at least, unexpected. A sharper mind might have foreseen it, planned for it... countered it, perhaps, with the same brilliance that saw Cao Cao defeat Yuan Shao at Guandu."

"We'll make it our priority, as I have said so many times before," Liu Bei promised. "I need a genius if I am to save the Han... and by whatever means, I will gain one."

Jing Governor Liu Biao summoned Kuai Yue, Wang Can and Huan Jie to his private meeting room upon learning of Liu Bei's arrival in Jing Province.

"Any word on your brother's condition...?" Liu Biao asked of Kuai Yue, who smiled sadly and shook his head in response; Liu Biao lowered his gaze and added, "I hope he recovers... selfish though the thought is, I need his brilliant mind."

"Defeating Liu Bei needs no brilliant mind," Wang Can said. "It-"

"I don't intend to 'defeat' him, I intend to welcome him," Liu Biao insisted. "I will be cautious, yes, but I must welcome him. Cao Cao forwarded a particularly nasty letter to me here, hinting that he will one day come for Jing 'in the name of the Han', and reminding me that my halted march on Xuchang – which barely got past my own borders, despite it being greatly exaggerated – was an act of treason against the puppet government that he's built. Normally, I'd write back and publicly remind him which of us has an unborn prince's blood on his hands, but there aren't any heroes left to ally with, are there...? Yuan Shao's a walking corpse, Sun Quan is a hankering pirate, Liu Zhang is a feeble coward and Liu Bei has no army or territory."

"Not *yet*," Kuai Yue said.

"...He intends no usurpation of my governorship... not if he knows what's good for him," Liu Biao retorted. "Now, gentlemen, to business: Liu Bei's envoy, Sun Qian, wants to address the court, and I have allowed it."

"And I presume that I am trusted to go and greet Liu Bei in reciprocation of the protocol...?" Huan Jie prompted.

"Indeed yes, but not at the border," Liu Biao replied. "Liu Bei is headed for Xinye, and I should like you to meet him there and bring him to me here."

"Xinye...?" Kuai Yue noted. "Mm... already, Lord Liu, our guest is presuming too much. He should have stayed at the border."

"No, I invited him to move to Xinye," Liu Biao explained. "Honestly, gentlemen, I am tired of hearing about how untrustworthy Liu Bei is! Who else is there...?"

Wang Can hummed thoughtfully. Liu Biao had pointed out the fact that there were no powerful warlords to turn to as allies in this new phase of conflict, and that the likely victor would be Excellency Cao Cao; Wang's mind quietly turned to the future, and what decisions should be made in order to live to see that future, and his was not the only mind to do so.

Yuan Shao was dismayed to learn that Liu Bei had been driven out of Yu Province, and for a multitude of reasons.

"Cao Cao had his back to us; another missed opportunity!" Yuan Shao complained. "Further to that, I lose my remaining grip in my home region and any chance of a pincer attack on Xuchang!"

"We shouldn't be too upset," the adviser Guo Tu scoffed. "Liu Bei was a poor ally and known for his deceitful-"

"Yet again, *slander*," the official Cui Yan sighed. "No man is without fault, Guo Tu: what matters, in the end, is his main intent. Liu Bei is a scion of the royal clan, and he is determined to see that house restored to glory after years of-"

"We... we know that, Mister Cui," Yuan Shao interrupted. "I apologise for interrupting you, but I must decide what to do now. Without Liu Bei in Yu, my only hopes for pincers reside with the Qiang and Zang Ba; in the case of the latter, some negotiated change of allegiance may be possible, if expensive."

"Zang Ba fears and owes Cao Cao too much," the adviser Xin Pi suggested. "Word coming from Qing indicates that Cao Cao spared Zang and granted him autonomy, even after Zang allied his bandits to Lü Bu. Zang's situation is complicated, and-"

"That's precisely why I pin hopes on reaching out to him, Mister Xin!" Yuan Shao cried. "Zang's past is well known! If I were to convince him that I, not Cao, stand for justice and true restoration of the Han, then he will come over to us and bring the disaffected peoples of Xu and Qing Provinces with him!"

"...It is worth a try, I suppose," Cui Yan sighed.

"Of course it is!" Yuan Shao replied.

"Do we not enjoy the services of Tian Chou, a man that once fled the region citing Lord Yuan as a traitor that colluded with Gongsun Zan to murder his master, Liu Yu...?" the adviser Pang Ji asked.

"Yes!" Yuan Shao said excitedly. "That's right! Does Mister Tian Chou not now live and work in his home region of Wuzhong as a magistrate – *my* magistrate – after abandoning the capital...?"

"*Yes*," Cui Yan sighed, "but-"

"Well then, that settles it!" Yuan Shao chuckled. "Chen Lin!"

Yuan Shao's secretary, Chen Lin, nodded his head obediently.

"Your magnificent skill with the pen is required once more," Yuan Shao continued. "This is what I want to say to Zang Ba..."

****

9

Qing Province was situated to the east of Yuan Shao's base in Ji Province; the region had long been overwhelmed by unrest, and this point in time was no different. Powerful crime families, the Yellow Turbans and the 'Mount Tai Bandits' – so called because the confederacy originated in the hills around the imposing Mount Tai – had been contesting the corrupted and ineffective Han government for more than 10 years, and much of the aforementioned corruption dated back to the activities of the 'Ten Attendants' from a decade before that.

Many innocent people suffered, and one of those people was a prison warder called Zang Jie; his career was brought to a halt when he queried the arrest of innocents while known criminals operated without punishment, and his own imprisonment followed. The false charges that were brought against Zang Jie guaranteed his transportation to Luoyang for quiet disposal; his desperate son, Zang Ba, then turned to the very criminals that his father detested in order to save him. Father and son were then fugitives from the government, and in Zang Ba's case, that meant reassessment of what was right and necessary in a complicated age. Zang Ba joined the ranks of the bandits that operated around Mount Tai Prefecture and quickly ascended to a senior leader; he extended operations into the rest of Qing Province and Xu Province to the south, becoming a feared name and the main founder of the bandit confederacy.

When Cao Cao finally had the resources to move against the rogue warlord Lü Bu – who had just seized Xu Province from Liu Bei and formed an alliance with the pretender Yuan Shu – Zang Ba was forced to decide whether he would fight for Cao Cao – who was hated in Qing and Xu Provinces, and allied to known Legalist Liu Bei, who favoured destroying bandits – or Lü Bu, whose regime had been forced to tolerate and accept nominal allegiance from the Mount Tai Bandits. Zang and his allies chose to support Lü Bu, and that meant that they became a target for Cao Cao's wrath when Bu was finally destroyed at the end of the Battle of Xiapi. Zang and his fellow leaders were persecuted and forced to submit, at which point Cao Cao allowed them to operate as independent forces and aid his campaign against Yuan Shao; Zang was unsurprised by the correspondence from the desperate Yuan Shao, but the response had to be pondered carefully.

"Hey, if it isn't 'prim and proper' Yu Wenze!"
Cao Cao's trusted general Yu Jin – whose courtesy name was 'Wenze' – clasped hands with the former bandit leader Chang Xi as the two met at the gates of Zang Ba's latest military camp; Yu laughed and replied, "Good to see you again, you scruffy rascal!"
"You come to see Zang, Wenze?" Chang Xi asked.
"I have," Yu Jin replied. "But first, how are you?"
"Fine, fine," Chang Xi said. "I took your advice about rations and discipline, and now the men are much happier. S'pose I just have trouble being a regular official. When you wanted discipline in the hills, you just gave a bloke a good smack in the mouth and he learned to be quiet."

Yu Jin smiled and said, "But as I said before, some people only understand that, while other people really don't take to it well. How's the wife and children?"

"...Adjusting to life in a house," Chang Xi admitted. "Missus keeps her belongings all bunched together so we can run at a moment's notice, just as she always has."

Yu Jin laughed at the notion.

"We'll learn," Chang Xi continued. "After all, who'd've thought you and me'd be standing here talking...?"

"And speaking of that, I forgot that I'm supposed to talk to Zang Ba as soon as possible," Yu Jin realised. "We'll have a drink later."

"Right!" Chang Xi said as he stood aside to allow Yu Jin's small entourage to pass him and enter the camp.

"Ah... Yu Jin," the brawny Zang Ba said as Yu Jin entered his command tent. "Let me guess... His Excellency Cao sent you to ask about *this*...?"

Zang Ba waved Chen Lin's letter back and forth; the other bandits smirked and turned to look at Yu Jin.

"Naturally," Yu Jin replied.

"Well, you can tell him not to worry," Zang Ba insisted. "I wasn't born yesterday. Yuan Shao's got next to no authority in Qing anymore, and Yòu and Bing Provinces are reverting to the messes they always were; why would I throw away being a Han officer to join that fool and end up in a coffin?"

Yu Jin turned to a seasoned man that was sat to the right of Zang Ba and asked, "Is that sentiment shared, Sun Guan...?"

"Course it is," Sun Guan replied. "Me and Zang Xuangao are both thinking pretty much the same way. We all are, aren't we, lads...?"

The rest of the bandit leaders mumbled agreeably.

"...Then I have come here needlessly," Yu Jin said.

"Really...?" Sun Guan chuckled. "I thought you were Cao's 'liaison' man, 'Wenze'. Didn't you want to sit with us and 'liaise'...?"

"Yuan Shao isn't 'cold bones' yet, and I have to do my bit to change that," Yu Jin retorted. "Yes, that means liaising with you; no, it doesn't involve looking over your shoulders as you suspect. His Excellency trusts you all, as do I, and so-"

The bandit leader Wu Dun leant forward and said, "Then why'd Cao send you here? If he trusted Xuangao, why'd he send you?"

"...His Excellency trusts you, but he is aware that Yuan Shao is very wealthy and armed with Dong Cheng's fabricated 'Girdle Edict'," Yu Jin explained.

"We know the edict isn't real, and Heaven knows, man, we've said so often enough," Zang Ba replied. "And when we want Yuan's money, we won't wait for him to give it to us, we'll just take it."

Yu Jin smiled dryly and asked, "And that's a consensus...?"

"Stop playing games," the bandit leader Yin Li heckled. "Cao doesn't trust us at all! But he can and should!"

"I'm just being playful," Yu Jin insisted. "You'll all come to understand me as well as Chang Xi does one day, I hope."

"Speaking of him, he should be in this meeting," Zang Ba noted.

"He greeted me at the gates," Yu Jin said. "He may still be there."

"I'll go get him," Wu Dun said as he got to his feet.

"You can escort Yu Wenze to a guest tent on the way there," Zang Ba suggested. "I don't want him thinking we're not hospitable."

"I'll head back to Xiapi, if it's all the same to you," Yu Jin said.

"Mister Wu can escort me back to the gates."

"...Alright," Zang Ba replied; after a thoughtful pause, he clasped his hands together and bowed slightly, adding, "Nice to see you."

Yu Jin reciprocated the gesture and left the tent with Wu Dun.

"...Honestly, I wish we could tell both o' those noblemen warlords where to stick it," Sun Guan complained. "They're the same in the end, aren't they...?"

Zang Ba nodded sombrely and said, "They are, Zhongtai. But Cao's gonna win, and that means we *have* to be nice to him until we know whether we *should* be."

Yin Li shook his head and said, "I don't want to go back to fighting from the hills now. I just hope that Cao's not another Dong Zhuo."

"He isn't," Zang Ba insisted. "It might seem like it, what with the stuff about killing the emperor's consort an' all, but he isn't. Yuan Shao, though... he's not much different to his brother, and there's no way I'm answering his silly letter with anything other than 'Get lost' or 'Drop dead'."

"Agreed," Yin Li said. "Are we all signing the reply?"

"If you want!" Zang Ba chuckled.

Chang Xi patted Yu Jin's arm as the two walked through the camp gates and said, "I was looking forward to that drink, Wenze, but you have orders and I have meetings. Pity..."

"There'll be other times!" Yu Jin replied. "Now go, before Wu Dun burns a hole in the back of your head with that angry gaze of his."

Chang Xi laughed, slapped Yu Jin's arm and returned to the camp.

"You an' him are pretty pally, Chang," Wu Dun noted as he watched Yu Jin's party disappear.

"He's a good sort," Chang Xi replied. "He's a *Juping* man, from Juping in *Mount Tai*! Turns out we knew each other as boys!"

"Yeah, I know," Wu Dun replied. "But Yuan Shao and Cao Cao knew one-another as boys and stayed friends their whole young lives... and now look at 'em. Yu Jin's a Han lackey, mate, and-"

"And we're bandits," Chang Xi interrupted. "I know the way it is. But right now, we're mates, and that's a good thing. Can't hurt to have a man to vouch for us!"

"...In case of *what*...?" Wu Dun asked cautiously.

"Dunno!" Chang Xi said with a grin. "Now are we going to this meeting or what?"

Wu Dun nodded slowly and followed Chang Xi to Zang Ba's command tent.

Cao Cao read Yu Jin's correspondence from Qing Province for a second time and hummed thoughtfully; the majority of his chancellery court waited patiently.

"No Guo Jia *again*," the adviser Chen Qun complained. "Sick *again*, I suppose."

"Please do not start that again," Cao Cao sighed. "We had that unplanned trip to Runan that took a lot out of him."

"Are you going back to Guandu now?" Xun Wenruo asked.

"Mm...? ...Oh, uh... yes," Cao Cao replied as he finished reading Yu Jin's letter for a third time. "We don't need to fear Liu Bei or Zang Ba becoming problematic now, so it is time for me to rout Yuan Shao's force at Cangting."

"What about the Qiang?" Chen Qun asked.

"Ma Teng and Han Sui are still fighting, and Ma is losing badly,"

Xun Gongda reported. "Don't be surprised to see a plea for refuge or negotiated peace."

"I thought that Teng's eldest, Ma Chao, was 'the new Lü Bu'," Chen Qun scoffed. "Still... like Lü Bu, he's but one man."

"Exactly, and like Bu, he's dependant on others for success," Cao Cao said. "So it is your shared belief that Ma Teng will capitulate and Han Sui will not join Yuan Shao?"

"The Qiang respect strength and nothing else," Xun Wenruo noted. "Even if Ma Teng and Han Sui have become schemers with age, the tribes that they command are unchanged. Neither man could convince the rest to follow Yuan now, not after Guandu and especially after what we're about to inflict on Yuan at Cangting."

"Ah, so that's a main reason why you want to strike Cangting with such haste!" Cao Cao realised. "I feel foolish for not seeing it sooner. We guarantee losing Yuan the support of the Qiang, the Southern Xiongnu and, perhaps, the Wuhuan if we humiliate him again so quickly."

"While hesitation prompts suspicion of weakness, that our victory was a fluke," Xun Wenruo replied. "And-"

"And although it wasn't a fluke, it was because I gave you what you needed to know to destroy Wuchao," Xu Yòu suggested.

"For which we are *eternally and repeatedly grateful*," Xun Wenruo said with poorly-hidden irritation; Cao Cao stifled a smile.

"Yes, but what I meant was that Mengde was going to be *smashed* without my help, and the Qiang and the rest might figure that out if we're not careful," Xu Yòu explained; Cao Cao's smile was replaced by a stifled scowl. "If it ever got out..."

"And what bribe do you want to keep your silence?" Xiahou Dun asked snidely.

"Yuanrang!" Cao Cao barked.

"It's my fault," Xu Yòu insisted. "I didn't mean to imply that-"

"It's... fine," Cao Cao said. "It's fine, Ziyuan. And in a way, you have a point; a point that you share with Wenruo. We must 'smash' Yuan at Cangting, and quickly, so that our strength is proven and Yuan's weakness is laid bare. I will not lie, I wanted to wait until Guo Fengxiao had recovered, but that is not an option."

Chen Qun harrumphed audibly.

"...We now have new minds like Liu Yè and Jia Xu to draw upon," Cao Cao said as he turned to look at the men in question; both officials bowed humbly. "Fengxiao wanted it so because... because he is 'fragile', and could 'break' at any time."

A short silence was broken by Xiahou Dun, who said, "Who's going to Cangting?"

"I will go personally, since that will show great strength that will impress the tribes that observe us," Cao Cao replied. "Cheng Yu and Jia Xu will be my main counsel, since Xun Yu and Xun Yòu are best placed here in Xuchang; Yuan Huan will advise Cao Ren on Runan; you, Yuanrang, will join me, of course, as an officer; Cao Hong, Cao Xiu, Zhang Liao, Zhang Hè, Xu Huang and Yue Jin will be my other generals."

The named officials and officers bowed and expressed their gratitude for the trust that Cao Cao was placing in them.

"We are not concerned about the Suns...?" Liu Yè asked suddenly.

"Our new marriage alliances make them unlikely to attack us," Cao Cao replied; the embattled chieftain of the Jiangdong Sun clan, Sun Quan, had agreed to go through with plans to marry Cao's second son, Cao Zhang, to the daughter of Quan's paternal cousin, Sun Ben, and also to marry one of Quan's younger brothers to one of Cao Cao's nieces.

"The Suns are ambitious," Liu Yè suggested. "Xu Gong was not incorrect when he said that."

"But the Suns are also suffering from a lot of internal strife," Cao Cao retorted. "I know that you're monitoring the situation in Lujiang because of 'personal interest', and so I need not tell you that Sun Quan faces a serious rebellion there... half of his standing army has turned on him... Sun Quan's appointment has divided his clan's loyalists, and my son's new father-in-law is, I believe, a future ally that can use his past as acting Sun clan chieftain after Sun Jian's death to help me restore order in the south when I have the resources to deal with it."

"...You have pondered it well," Liu Yè said. "I'll say no more."

"...No more dallying, then," Cao Cao decided. "Benchu's had time enough to lick his wounds and procrastinate; now he will see what fangs this tiger has! We leave in a week or less!"

Yuan Shao was perplexed by the news that Cao Cao had sent a medium-sized force to station and gather supplies around the relatively weak defensive position of Anmin.

"Anmin...?" Yuan Shao prompted. "Not Guandu, or...? ...*Anmin*???"

"Anmin," Guo Tu reiterated.

"...He taunts me, the knave," Yuan Shao muttered. "He is trying to lure me out."

"So do not rise to it," Cui Yan suggested.

"Sitting here will make us look weak to our Wuhuan allies!" Shen Pei cried.

"Rushing to confront Cao Cao and being routed again will make us look even weaker," Cui Yan countered.

"I agree," Xin Pi said. "We should show caution, at least until-"

"Caution isn't an option!" Xun Chen heckled. "I speak as a man that has every reason to demand capitulation or compromise, for my brother and nephew are two of Cao's leading counsel! But I advocate aggression because my duty to the Han comes first! Cao is the greatest villain under Heaven, and-!"

"And therefore we should just madly charge at his conspicuously understaffed camp at Anmin," Cui Yan scoffed. "Oh, I'm certain that will end well...!"

Yuan Shao's gaze darted back and forth as he tried to decide what to do.

"If we do not increase our presence at Cangting, we will look weak!" Guo Tu said. "Do you want us to look *weak*, Cui Yan?"

"*Ayah*... Did I say that we shouldn't reinforce Cangting?" Cui Yan retorted. "I said that we shouldn't blindly *attack*, not that we shouldn't wisely *defend*!"

Xun Chen laughed and said, "But 'defence alone' is a sign of weakness: did Sun Tzu not say that...?"

A heated argument drew in more voices, and the noise became more and more incoherent; Yuan Shao lost his patience – and his temper – and shouted, "**ENOUGH! Enough, enough, ENOUGH! I...!** I... I just want to know what I should *do*, gentlemen! And the only thing that any of you can agree upon is the reinforcement of

Cangting, so **shouldn't we do that and return to the finer points afterward???**"
Guo Tu nodded silently.
"...I shall ready a force and hurry there at once," Ju Hu said.
"Please, yes... *do that*, General Ju," Yuan Shao groaned; once Ju Hu had left the court, Yuan Shao cupped his head in his hands and said, "Heaven spare me this ridiculous *farce* every time I want some answers... I wondered if the absence of Tian Feng and that treacherous *bastard* Xu Yòu might make a difference to the court, but no, it is as loud and confused as it ever was."
"Don't despair, Lord Yuan," Guo Tu pleaded. "Victory is assured in the long term."
"We have innumerable advantages over Cao Cao!" Pang Ji suggested. "Four provinces are yours to control, while Cao relies on bandits to hold Xu and must ingratiate himself with pirates to stop an attack from Yang!"
"...Is there any hope of an alliance with Sun Quan...?" Yuan Shao asked as he raised his head. "Is there any hope of that *at all*...?"
"...Not really, no," Guo Tu admitted. "Sun Quan has closed his ears and eyes to everything but misplaced vengeance; even if you were to condemn Liu Biao and promise to destroy him after Cao is gone – which would be most unwise – I think that Sun Quan is predisposed to hating the Yuans."
"Aye, well, my brother did me another wrong there by forgetting to properly nurture his tigers," Yuan Shao chuckled miserably. "So it's ultimately down to me and Liu Biao, isn't it, since the Qiang are preoccupied and consider me to be 'weak' at the moment. I must show strength to win the tribes around... but does that mean taking unacceptable risks...?"
The advisers looked at one-another but said nothing.
"Ah... so now you are silent!" Yuan Shao sniggered. "But at least I can think for myself when you are silent. I will go to Cangting and reinforce the place personally."
"As... as you wish," Guo Tu said uneasily.
"No," Cui Yan said. "Lord Yuan, you must remain here and personally oversee restoration of order: let Ju Hu, Lü Kuang and Lü Xiang defend Cangting!"
"**How can I not be at Cangting if Cao Cao is there???**" Yuan Shao cried.
"Cao will not fight personally; neither will you," Cui Yan countered. "Two men that never meet on the battlefield are neither of them 'there', regardless of the exact distance from it. Remain where you are needed, Lord Yuan... don't save a remote base and lose your home in the process."
Yuan Shao pondered the words for a moment and said, "I will compromise and camp at Li County. Others will defend Cangting... and we must pray that they are enough."

****

10

Cao Cao's preparations for another encounter with Yuan Shao took him away from his family home for more time than he would have liked; he retired at the end of the third day and had his older sons – Pi, Zhang, Zhi, Xiong and Chong – and two of his adopted sons – Qin Lang and Hè Yan – gather in the living quarters.

"My, my… what a proud father I am!" Cao Cao said as he looked at the 14-year-old Cao Pi, who was now his eldest living son and likely heir. "What fine features and proud countenance! Indeed, you could now join me in battle… were that my wish."

Cao Pi's mother, Lady Bian, stifled a horrified gasp.

"…But it is not," Cao Cao continued. "I have already lost Ang and Shuo. The netherworld has had enough of my sons for now."

"I would gladly fight for you, Father," Cao Pi insisted.

"And so would I," Cao's second son, Cao Zhang, insisted. "I want you to be truly proud of me."

"I am," Cao Cao said. "I am proud of you all… and I include my fine adopted sons when I say that! Yan'er, you are slowly becoming the image of your grandfather, whose heroism saved the nation from the Yellow Turbans and almost rid us of the 'Ten'… and Lang, you do your true father, Qin Yilu, and me proud with your studies and your good nature."

Hè Yan – whose grandfather was Imperial Commander-in-Chief Hè Jin – smiled and bowed silently; Qin Lang bowed and replied, "Thank you, Father."

"All of you are wonderful," Cao Cao said as he turned his gaze to the 8-year-old Cao Zhi. "Now then, Zhi, my boy: have you any poems for me…?"

"Poems…?" Cao Zhang scoffed.

"You're a husband now, Zhang, and soon a father," Cao Cao retorted. "Outside of war, my dear Yellow-beard, where your thoughts reside at all times, there is a beautiful world that is expressed most appropriately through the seamless, structured grace of poetry. Please, Zhi'er, continue."

Cao Zhi laughed haughtily and said, "When blossoms show upon the tree, the spring is truly here; the fruit shows summer's come to be, but autumn's drawing near."

"Mm," Cao Cao mused. "Then winter's grip, so dark and cold, but fleeting as before…"

"And spring returns, a fact foretold, the circle turned once more," Cao Zhi concluded.

"Warmth and happiness, then sadness and cold… so never become too happy in summer, because winter will come soon."

All eyes turned to the 4-year old Cao Chong, who added, "But then more warmth and happiness. So never get sad when it's cold, because summer will come soon."

Cao Cao laughed, applauded his young son and said, "*Four*! He is only *four*, and he already thinks more profoundly than my smartest enemies!"

Cao Pi and Cao Zhi laughed at the suggestion; their mother Lady Bian, Qin Lang's mother Lady Du, Hè Yan's mother Lady Yin and Cao Chong's mother, Lady Huan, giggled and enjoyed the praise that the patriarch was lavishing upon their sons.

"Indeed, we face a harsh winter at present, a long and painful winter that has chilled and harmed us all, but the weather will soon change," Cao Cao said. "Already the worst snows have melted, and spring is within our sights!"
Cao Zhang scoffed quietly and retreated to his quarters.
"...I see that Yellow-beard has left us," Cao Cao sighed. "His disinterest in the arts is unfortunate. States are not governed with swords: they are won with them, yes, and guarded by them, yes, but is that his only ambition...?"
"We're all different," Cao Pi noted. "Zhi is a gifted poet; Chong is a genius; Qin Lang and Hè Yan bring inherited talent from without; Zhang is a future hero that will win battles..."
"...And you, Pi, are as talented as any of your brothers," Cao Cao insisted. "You embrace the importance of all of the disciplines, and it is balance that maintains order."
Cao Cao's cousin Xiu entered the room in full military uniform and said, "Lord and Excellency, I-!"
"No need to be formal at home, Wenlie," Cao Cao insisted. "I did not invite you to this house of mine and have you share quarters with Pi so that you could call me 'Excellency' outside of the court!"
Cao Xiu laughed awkwardly and said, "Of course, Cousin Mengde."
"Now what did you want to tell A'Man that could not wait?" Cao Cao asked as he flicked the 6-year-old Cao Xiong's turban and made the boy laugh.
"Well," Cao Xiu said, "the-"
"Who is A'Man?" Cao Chong asked.
"It is your father's infant name, a name that he does not forget," Cao Cao explained. "I am sometimes... well, I was going to say 'as foolish as a child', but I think that you might be smarter than I am *now*, Chong, never mind when I was your age."
Cao Chong smiled and said, "That would be silly."
"It would, and is, but might be true," Cao Cao replied. "You have a statesman's air about you... a future hero, perhaps."
Cao Pi scowled as he started to suppose that Cao Cao might prefer to appoint one of his brothers as the Cao clan heir; Lady Bian guessed his thoughts and smiled sadly.
"We interrupted Wenlie!" Cao Cao recalled. "Speak, Cousin."
"Yuanrang's just had another 'encounter' with Jia Xu," Cao Xiu said. "He threatened him again... and Xun Yu, he wondered if-"
"*Aiee*... must I warn Yuanrang *again*?" Cao Cao complained.
"But Father," Cao Pi began, "isn't Jia Xu-?"
"He's an adviser of mine that erred in the past, as have I," Cao Cao insisted. "Such men are better used for good than made young bones of. Yuanrang is angry, I know, but... but he would be better placed by being angry at me than at Jia Xu."
Most of the adults within the family assembly lowered their heads.
"I'll talk to him," Cao Cao continued. "Where is he?"
"I told him to come here," Cao Xiu replied. "He really didn't like me ordering him about, though."
"No, he wouldn't," Cao Cao chuckled. "Ah, Yuanrang... even after losing an eye, he can't control his temper. He-"
"**STOP IT!**"
The ensemble turned to face the hall that led to the many sleeping quarters; a portly 10-year-old boy was running toward them.
"Cousin Zhen?" Cao Cao exclaimed. "What's wrong?"

"Why can't he leave me be?" Cao Zhen complained. "I didn't *ask* to be fat! I just *am*!"

"...Cousin Zilian is being cruel again," Cao Pi supposed.

"I didn't do anything!" Cao Hong insisted as he ran after Cao Zhen and stopped dead; he noted the disapproving gazes and added, "Really, honestly, he needs to learn to have a sense of humour."

"And you need to start acting like an adult with more regularity!" Cao Cao scolded. "*Honestly*, Zilian! You and Yuanrang embarrass me with your childish antics! You, a fully grown man with a general's rank, picking fights with a boy, and Yuanrang is no better with all of his secretive attempts to drive Jia Xu from my court while I am elsewhere! Why can you not be more like Cousins Ren and Chun, who impress all with their wits and fists both? How can you stand there with any pride when my four-year-old son Chong has more mature credibility than you?"

Cao Hong eyed Cao Chong irritably.

"So now you want to pick a fight with my son?" Cao Cao asked.

"N-no, Mengde!" Cao Hong replied. "I-I was-!"

"Apologise to Zhen, and then go and make yourself useful, if that is at all possible," Cao Cao ordered. "And I mean it: if I hear that you went and bought a woman to dance on drums for you, I'll-!"

"I won't, I won't," Cao Hong said as he tried to edge past Cao Cao's silent bodyguard, Xu Chu. "Look, Zhen, sorry, okay...? Now can I get past this big- ...I uh, hah-hah, I mean, you know, how Xu Chu is so *tall*..."

The giant Xu Chu – who, unlike his predecessor Dian Wei, was known for his enormous appetite, gentleness in daily life and enormous girth – frowned and said, "Are you calling *me* fat now as well, Mister Hong?"

"Oh, *Heaven forbid that I would*," Cao Hong replied. "Do I want you to snap my neck like a chicken? Mengde, can I go now?"

"*Please, yes*," Cao Cao muttered; Xu Chu moved slightly, and Cao Hong retreated, passing Xiahou Dun as he did so.

"And now here's the other one," Cao Cao sighed.

"What's wrong with Zilian?" Xiahou Dun asked.

"He said I was fat!" Cao Zhen whined.

"You are," Xiahou Dun replied. "But it isn't your fault; I mean, I see how little you eat, and yet you still-"

"Please don't make me hit you, Yuanrang," Cao Cao said irritably.

"I was just going to say that he should tell Zilian that at least he hasn't got a weird fetish for barefoot prostitutes," Xiahou Dun retorted. "That'd-"

Lady Bian and Lady Huan started to usher the younger children from the room; Cao Pi was the only one to remain and observe the exchanges.

"*Aiee*... shut up, and listen to me," Cao Cao ordered. "No more heckling Jia Xu."

"Three guesses who told you I did that," Xiahou Dun said as he turned his eerie monocular gaze toward Cao Xiu. "The only reason that a toady like Xiu'd be dirtying the floor by coming in here in boots would be to tattle on me."

"Don't be like that, Yuanrang," Cao Xiu pleaded. "Part of me wants to gut Jia Xu and hang him from the gates of the city, but what good would that do?"

Cao Cao covered his face with his sleeve.

"It'd avenge Ang, and Anmin, and Dian Wei!" Xiahou Dun suggested. "It would avenge all of the people that were killed by Dong Zhuo!"

"No, Yuanrang, it wouldn't," Cao Cao insisted. "Sometimes one must separate the tools from the craftsmen and the craftsmen from the patron, and in some cases that isn't easy to do but it is always necessary!"

Xiahou Dun turned to look at Cao Cao and asked, "What do you mean, Mengde...?"

Cao Cao lowered his arm from his face and said, "Advisers seem, at first, to be at fault for all things, for they are the craftsmen, and they create the plans that the lords are seen to follow; but it is the lords that are the patrons, those that demand the products of the craftsmen, and they who are to blame. The advisers are the craftsmen, the generals the tools, and the army the materials. But what good are all of those things if there is no patron to desire or request what is made?"

"...I do see what you're saying," Xiahou Dun admitted, "but-!"

"I, too, want to kill Jia Xu every time that I see him," Cao Cao confessed. "I see him and I see the blood of thousands on his hands; I see an architect of the suffering of many, many people, including people dear to me, and I seek his end because of it, even though I know that he was simply doing what Zhang Xiu had asked of him. In Wang Lang I see Tao Qian, who robbed me of my father, and in Jia Xiu I see Dong Zhuo, who did more to us all than can be sanely recounted. But I also see *me*."

Xiahou Dun exhaled loudly.

"...Xu Province was not my finest hour," Cao Cao continued. "There was many a man that probably died needlessly at Guandu, on both sides; such is life. And I lost Chen Gong because he could not make that which I desired at that moment, which was the utter destruction of Xu and all of its peoples. Cheng Yu, Xun Yu, *you*... you all went along with it, but who was to blame? Should you be held responsible for a cruelty of my design alone...?"

Xiahou Dun shook his head and said, "Xu was-!"

"Just as smashing a craftsman's tools does little more than force him to acquire new ones, so killing a craftsman for accepting work and carrying it out effectively is irrational if you then spare the patron," Cao Cao continued. "I must learn to tolerate Jia Xu, we all must, because he is a master craftsman that will help us to build the things that *we* want built now."

"And the 'patron'...?" Cao Xiu asked. "What about Zhang Xiu, his lord, the man that ordered him to plot the deaths of our kin...?"

"He did what he did because I 'defiled' his aunt and plotted his death," Cao Cao replied. "There is no sense in denying that; if I had shown him proper courtesy - deserved or not - then Ang, Anmin and Dian Wei would still be alive and Yuan Shu wouldn't have dared declare himself an emperor when he did."

"But... I cannot hate *you*, Mengde," Xiahou Dun whimpered.

"...You do not need to, for I hate myself enough for our entire clan," Cao Cao replied. "Now, Yuanrang, do I have your word - your solemn word this time - that you will not harm Jia Xu or try to scare him away anymore?"

Xiahou Dun nodded silently.

"Good," Cao Cao said. "Go and rest."

Xiahou Dun nodded, smiled sadly and turned to Cao Xiu, saying, "You were right to tell Mengde about what I did, Wenlie... someone has to control my temper if I can't."

Cao Xiu nodded, and Xiahou Dun left the house.

"...My head is clouding," Cao Cao fretted. "Please, let it not be my affliction... if it can just leave me be for a *few days more*...!"

"Go and rest, Father," Cao Pi suggested.

"...I shall, my son," Cao Cao replied. "I shall..."

Cao Cao retreated to his sleeping quarters; Cao Pi turned to Cao Xiu once his father was gone and said, "You'd better change clothes now, Wenlie."

"Oh, right, yes, I'm still in uniform," Cao Xiu realised. "I'll be back soon, Zihuan."

Cao Pi nodded, and Cao Xiu left the house; Lady Bian entered the room once again and whispered, "Do not be angry at your father for loving us all equally."

"If that is so, Mother, why would I be angry...?" Cao Pi retorted.

Lady Bian sighed and retreated to Cao Cao's sleeping quarters.

"...Who... what... will I be...?" Cao Pi wondered; he could not know at that moment that the answer was quite incredible.

****

11

The chaos in the northwest had barely subsided in 18 years; Liang Province, which made up most of the northwest quarter of the empire, was now all but ruled by the Qiang tribes and not a place that a Han official would gladly administrate.

The current situation had its roots in disaffection amongst the common people; many of the officials were embezzling money and failing to provide famine relief or adequate public order, and the Qiang, amongst other non-Han peoples, were taking advantage of the latter to conduct uncontested raids on towns and villages. The people eventually revolted, and the Han government in far-off Luoyang was forced to intervene: the effectiveness of that government and its armies had been diluted over recent years, however, so the army that did respond, though announcing itself as the Han, was in fact a cobbled-together alliance of private militias, just as the army that had quelled the Yellow Turban Rebellion had been a year earlier. The consequences of the Liang Province Rebellion were many in number: one campaign had elevated the future tyrant Dong Zhuo at the expense of the career of the famous 'Tiger of Jiangdong', Sun Jian, and three former Han officials – Ma Teng, Han Sui and Song Jian – joined the Qiang-rebel alliance that had ironically formed during the uprising and somehow became three of the most powerful Qiang chieftains. The Han almost had a final victory, but protocol halted that last victorious campaign when Emperor Ling died and his funeral forced the senior commander – the famous veteran Huangfu Song – to return to the capital to pay his respects.

Now Ma Teng, Han Sui and Song Jian were the lords of separate independent warrior 'kingdoms' in Liang Province; their initial alliance was short-lived, and any subsequent pooling of resources was tenuous and entirely bound by circumstance or opportunity to expand their influence. Song Jian opted to be satisfied with his lot and guard his borders, but Ma Teng and Han Sui were both hungry for more: they had already made a failed bid to seize the then-capital Chang'an after the death of Dong Zhuo, and each laid claim to what the other had or took as the years went on. Ma Teng and Han Sui's latest feud knew no limits, and that gave Cao Cao's Xuchang government the opportunity to send a new provincial inspector – rather than a fully autonomous governor – to the region and attempt to rebuild order; their choice was a man named Wei Kang. Wei could do little more that prove his administration was an honest one, and he managed to cultivate a good relationship with some of the Han communities, but the warring Qiang chieftains were a different matter altogether; it was difficult to know whether the continuing feud, as violent and costly as it was, was preventing a worse disaster.

"...I tell you, Mister Zhao, that I am at my wit's end already, and I have not been here that long," Wei Kang said to the only guest at a private banquet at his governor's mansion in the provincial capital, Ji City. "What kind of a man could possibly hope to control these maniacal barbarians...?"

"I don't know," Zhao Ang replied. "I... really don't know."

"...I'm being insensitive," Wei Kang realised. "How is your family?"
"It was long enough ago that 'insensitive' is hardly appropriate,"
Zhao Ang said as he adjusted the white scarf that covered his
hair. "I shouldn't be wearing this thing now, not really, but... but
my sons meant a lot to me."
"And I have not given you justice," Wei Kang sighed. "All I can do
now is to improve your standing, since you're too good a man to
be wasted in Qiangdao. I want to give you Liang Shuang's head to
offer to your sons' spirits, but-"
"He didn't just kill my sons," Zhao Ang interrupted. "He killed a lot
of people. But it was necessary that we negotiated with Liang
Shuang from our undeniable position of weakness. That is how
things are in Liang Province, Inspector. My folly was leaving my
family in Xi District in the first place; I was the county magistrate,
and therefore a target for kidnappers and seditionists."
"...I wanted to ask, for I am justifiably cynical," Wei Kang said. "I
wanted to ask... whether it was true, what your wife did...?"
Zhao Ang laughed strangely and replied, "Yes, it is true; my Lady
Wang is quite a formidable woman."
Wei Kang nodded agreeably.

Lady Wang Yi had been left to raise her husband Zhao Ang's three
children – two sons and a daughter – in their family home in Xi
District while Ang travelled to the county capital to take up the
role of Magistrate, the senior administrative figure in the county.
Like every other part of Liang Province, Qiangdao County was
beset by lawlessness, and within weeks of Zhao Ang taking up the
role a local agitator in Xi District, Liang Shuang, led a force of
rebels and seized the area; Zhao Ang's sons fought as part of the
ragtag local defence militia and both of them ultimately died.
Liang Shuang then took up residence close to Zhao Ang's
surviving family, including Lady Wang and her six-year-old
daughter; Lady Wang feared that Shuang would want to molest
her, so after briefly contemplating suicide – which she could not
go through with, since that would involve murdering or
abandoning her daughter – she made herself undesirable by
tearing her clothes, starving herself and rubbing her body with dirt
and excrement. Her bizarre behaviour had the desired effect, and
Liang Shuang kept his distance for the entire year that it took for
a negotiated peace to be reached and a rescue achieved.

"She's quite brave and resourceful, and unwilling to let foolish
pride cost her greater dignity," Wei Kang suggested. "Ruining her
appearance and making herself repugnant to keep Liang Shuang
at bay... very sensible."
"That wasn't how she saw it, Inspector," Zhao Ang sighed. "She
took poison afterwards, saying that she could not bear to live
knowing that other women had borne the hardship or committed
suicide rather than 'disgrace themselves'. She did it to ensure that
our daughter lived, but then... still, she didn't die, so I suppose the
whole thing resolved itself as best it could."
"Liang Shuang will falter, and when he does I swear that I will
punish him for that wrong and all the others," Wei Kang declared.
"...That isn't why I'm here, though," Zhao Ang prompted.
"No, it isn't," Wei Kang replied. "I have been approached by one

of Ma Teng's many relatives with what they called 'an offer'. I'm suspicious of it, and worry that it might mean that my worst fears will come to pass."

"...He wants to broker peace with Han Sui," Zhao Ang guessed.

"Precisely," Wei Kang said. "But we're both early grey heads of hair that know what that might mean..."

"...That two reconciled barbarian kings that vied for Chang'an and eventual control of the entire province on more than one occasion might do so again," Zhao Ang supposed.

"We are of the same mind," Wei Kang said. "But I have no choice but to accept the offer; His Excellency Cao Cao needs them to aid his campaign against Yuan Shao."

"That's more important," Zhao Ang noted. "Peace in the east increases the chance that His Excellency can finally send a proper army to rid us of the 'three Qiang kings' at a later date. But we'd need to have a ready army."

"And that, Mister Zhao, is a role that I would like you to take up," Wei Kang revealed. "As you know, I am looking for the ablest men to assist my administration: I have already recruited Yang Fu, styled 'Yishan', as my senior assistant... I wanted him to meet you here today but he had to manage a judicial case."

"I know of Yang Yishan," Zhao Ang said. "He supposedly predicted the outcome of the Cao-Yuan confrontation at Guandu when all else expected the opposite."

"And did so with such remarkable reason and cogency that he is at the very least a brilliant politician," Wei Kang replied. "Anyhow, Yishan is but one of the many talented men that I must have in my administration and you are another. I want you, your remarkable lady wife and the rest of your family to move here to Ji City, where you will serve as a – the – military consultant to Liang Province's army. I've heard about your work in Qiangdao, and I can see no better candidate."

Zhao Ang bowed slightly and said, "I will serve the Han in any way that I can. I do not believe that I am the best candidate, but if it is your wish then I shall serve as loyally as a dog and as tirelessly as a horse."

"Very good!" Wei Kang exclaimed. "I look forward to our work, rebuilding order in Liang, bearing fruit as it undoubtedly will."

At around the same time, Ma Teng's forces were on the way to securing a rare victory against Han Sui; the reason for the success was the commander in that battle, Ma Teng's heir Ma Chao. The part-Qiang, part-Han Chinese Ma Chao had unique features and a slim, toned physique that he had trained to its limits as an athlete, cavalryman, martial artist and warrior; his armour was a superior combination of Qiang battle dress and Han general's equipment, and his helmet was decorated with feathers, horns or whatever would make him appear to be more fearsome. Many compared Ma Chao to the prodigy Lü Bu, though his character was considered to be less impulsive and self-serving; events during the following years would challenge that last theory, but there was no denying that Ma Chao was a minor 'hero' of the age as he charged about the battlefield on his well-bred Arab steed, tearing into Han Sui's infantry and cavalrymen alike with his decorated spear.

Ma Chao was almost always accompanied by two men

that he trusted completely; the first was his cousin Ma Dai, whose abilities were far less impressive, but whose charisma and loyalty were essential; the second was Pang De, a fearsome warrior that some believed to only be matched or bettered by Ma Chao himself. All three of those men were on the battlefield, and Han Sui's men suspected that their winning streak against Ma Teng was about to be broken.

"**Come, worthless dogs, and lend your corpses to my blade!**" Ma Chao screamed as he ran his spear through the neck of one of Han Sui's cavalrymen. "**And for the blood of my kin, your master's head will be mine!**"

"**He's too fast!**" a cavalryman warned as he saw a colleague try to advance on Ma Chao's unguarded rear; Ma Chao yanked the heavy spear that he had in his left hand from the body of his last victim, wheeled around with unnerving swiftness and cut down the approaching horseman with a sword that he had quickly drawn with his right hand. Many of Han Sui's men were astounded and appalled as Ma Chao – now riding his perfectly-trained horse with the reins wound around the handle of his spear – feigned a rightward dash and then moved left, tearing into two more cavalrymen and unseating them in quick succession.

"**Ma Chao is not the only man you face!**" Pang De cried as he rode toward Ma Chao with six horsemen. "**Here is Pang De!**"

Ma Dai led the main force to attack the enemy infantry, but Han Sui's force was already defeated if it was without a proper cavalry to lead a charge; Han Sui's campaign officer ordered his men to withdraw, and the day belonged to Ma Chao.

"**There's no need for that!**" Ma Dai said as Ma Chao – who was frenzied – pursued and cut down a number or Han Sui's infantry.

"**You're all dead!**" Ma Chao screamed as he killed one retreating man after another. "**Every one of Han Sui's dogs will die by my hand! THEN HIS CHILDREN, AND THEN HIM! I'LL DIG UP HIS ANCESTORS AND GRIND THEIR BONES!**"

Some of Han Sui's non-Qiang followers were weeping as they fled; the full-blooded Qiang men – for whom cowardice in the face of an enemy was a crime – turned and tried to fight, but Ma Chao and his allies had an overwhelming advantage and a ferocity that they could not match.

"**ALL OF YOU WILL DIE!**" Ma Chao cried. "**ALL OF YOU!**"

"**That's enough!**" Ma Dai pleaded as he blocked Ma Chao's path. "**Save your strength! Your father might need us for his battle at-!**"

"**FATHER HAS LOST HIS NERVE!**" Ma Chao replied instinctively. "**FATHER IS A COWARD! HE WANTS TO SURRENDER! He... no! NO! THEY MUST ALL DIE!**"

"**Fine, Cousin, but do they all have to die *right now*...?**" Ma Dai retorted.

Ma Chao glared at Ma Dai, but he could not be angry for long; Ma Dai smiled encouragingly, and Ma Chao started to laugh.

"**They can wait!**" Ma Chao said as he had his horse trample a dying warrior. "**They can have one more day before I kill them to think about their worthlessness!**"

"*Aiee*... what a mess this is," Pang De said as he looked at the sea of bodies. "Why are we killing each other...? Aren't we doing the Han's work for them...?"

"**Send a man to Father at once!**" Ma Chao ordered. "**We cannot be everywhere, but look at what we can do wherever we are! Send a man now and have him renew Father's spirit!**"

"**As you wish, Cousin,**" Ma Dai replied.

Ma Teng received Ma Chao's jubilant communication within a few days, but Teng had suffered two more serious defeats and lost a beloved consort during a raid, and those events had left him further demoralised.

"What will you do now, Father...?" Ma Teng's second son, Ma Tie, asked quietly.

"...Your brother is an incredible man, but he is still just a man," Ma Teng replied. "Were it that I could breed a thousand sons like Chao to lead my men, I would, but I have him and three or four other valiant leaders, and Han Sui has a lot more, and more men than me to go with it now. I will see whether Cao Cao can defeat Yuan Shao for a second time, just in case that first victory was some sort of luck. I will go to whichever of them wins, Yuan or Cao, and ask them to sue for peace. Han Sui and I have been harming each other long enough, and peace is long overdue. I must, therefore, write to Chao in the meantime and ask that he be less violent; if I could win, I probably would slaughter them all, but I can't, so we must show restraint."

"...A lot of the chieftains don't want to show restraint, Father," Ma Tie noted.

"**They are chieftains of a handful of men each, and *I* am *their* chieftain!**" Ma Teng snapped. "**They will obey me, and so will Chao!**"

"I hope so, Father," Ma Tie replied.

✷✷✷✷✷✷✷✷✷✷✷✷

12

There were many factions that were nervously awaiting the outcome of the latest conflict between Yuan Shao and Cao Cao's armies. In the northwest, Wei Kang's government, the Qiang warlords and Zhang Lu, the ruler of the theocratic state of "Han'ning" – or, as it was once known, Hanzhong; to the west, Yi Province Governor Liu Zhang; to the south, the semi-autonomous prefectural administrators to the south of Jing Province and Sun Quan of Jiangdong; to the east, Zang Ba's ex-bandits and the remnants of the Han government that controlled Xu Province and southern Qing Province; to the north, the Han and non-Han peoples in Yuan Shao's increasingly-lawless domains in Ji, Bing, northern Qing and Yòu Provinces; and in the centre, Jing Governor Liu Biao, his invited guest Liu Bei, his uninvited guest Zhang Xiu, and the Han government in Yan Province.

If Cao Cao won, then the apparent fluke at Guandu might be perceived as the 'will of Heaven', and Cao would decide the fate of the nation, whatever his unreadable will might be; if Yuan Shao's army won, then there were two possible outcomes, namely a return to the ways of the past or another attempt to remove Emperor Xian and replace him with kin or Yuan Shao himself, which might then start the cycle of chaos all over again. Eyes, hearts and minds turned to the military installations at Cangting and Anmin, where it could not be denied that something was happening, although few knew exactly what.

"What is he doing...?" Yuan Shao wondered as he studied the reports of Cao Cao's activities in the command centre of his Li County camp, which was to the north the Yellow River. "He's got men stockpiling grain and equipment, but he can't challenge me with such a small force!"

"He must intend a crossing at some other point, and the stockpiling at Anmin is designed to draw you away from the true threat," Guo Tu said.

"Perhaps," Xin Ping said. "But he could also intend to confuse us by giving that impression and then striking here after all."

"How can he do that...?" Guo Tu heckled. "His main army is downriver! How could he march them all the way here without us knowing about it?"

"He got a force of men into Wuchao and reduced it to ash," Xin Ping retorted. "Did you know about *that* at the time...?"

Guo Tu scowled and said, "I was not aware of the exact seriousness of it, perhaps."

"No, you weren't," Xin Ping continued. "Cao Cao's actions are not always so predictable: if nothing else, learn *that*."

"He burned Wuchao because we were betrayed by Xu Yòu!" Guo Tu insisted.

"And our plan to seize Cao's main camp failed because Zhang Hè betrayed us as well!" Shen Pei said. "If he had done as he had been asked, Wuchao would have been an empty victory for Cao!"

Yuan Shao placed his forearm on the easel that held the main battle map and rested his forehead on that arm; he was weary of the constant bickering and sensed that he would soon lose his grip on his temper and his morale.

"Stop going on about who is to blame for yesterday's mistakes!" Xin Ping pleaded. "Isn't the main objective now to *learn* from those mistakes, undo the harm done by those mistakes and restore the order that was lost as a result of those mistakes being made...? We have to guess Cao's next action correctly, gentlemen, or we lose our grip on this side of the Yellow River altogether!"

"My brother is right," Xin Pi said. "My personal concern at one point was that he might cross the river strike at multiple positions, but he hasn't the men for that to result in anything other than a mutually costly maintaining of the current standoff. His main goal, I think, is to drive us out of this area... but how would his counsel interpret this need into action...? Might he attack our outposts on the northern bank to force our withdrawal from Cangting to defend them, or would he just attack us here and push us out without resorting to a scheme...?"

"Cao Cao is a schemer," Yuan Tan scoffed. "He enjoys it: that being the case, Father, I suspect that he'll do something needlessly convoluted."

"...Perhaps," Yuan Shao said as he finally lifted his head away from the easel and turned to face his vassals. "But there was little 'pointless scheming' at Boma or Wuchao. He saw openings and took immediate advantage of them... unlike me."

"Cangting is heavily reinforced now," Xin Ping noted. "Our only weaknesses now would be careless negligence and relaxed vigilance. Surely our past losses have purged the risk of either amongst our forces...?"

"You forget *treachery*, Mister Xin," Shen Pei suggested.

"There's little that we can do about that," Cui Yan said as he glared at Shen Pei. "I would have thought that every man that might have considered defection or desertion has already done so by now."

"I certainly hope so, Mister Cui," Shen Pei said with a cold smile. "Because it would be a shame if-"

"*Weeks... weeks*, that vile, godless knave has been stockpiling and moving men around, and still we are blind!" Yuan Shao cried as his composure finally deserted him. "O, 'Crafty Villain', what mischief are you up to now...? If Heaven truly desires order, then why does it not enlighten me when men have failed to do so...?"

The advisers exchanged glances but said nothing.

Another week passed.

"...I wonder what he's thinking, old 'Benchu'," Cao Cao chuckled as he studied his battle maps with apparent calmness. The Guandu command tent was filled with his officials for the campaign, and the atmosphere was generally tense.

"He's probably wondering what the hell you're doing, like the rest of us," Xiahou Dun complained. "This is another of Guo Jia's strange little plots, isn't it? Marching back and forth from Guandu to Anmin, overseeing tiny movements of supplies for weeks on end! Please tell me we're here to find out what we're doing!"

"If Benchu is even half as angry and confused as you are, Yuanrang, then we have won," Cao Cao replied. "Up and down the riverbank, the men in my camps have been moving suspiciously

and making decoy preparations that will make only half-sense to Yuan Shao and his little band of near-sighted mediocrities. He's floundering and posturing, faltering and procrastinating: now is the moment, gentlemen!"
Xiahou Dun sighed and asked, "For what?"
"No schemes now, Cousin Yuanrang, just action," Cao Cao said with a smile. "I'm going to make another trip to Anmin, one that will be just as banal and bewildering to them as the rest. What happens next will be told to you when the time is right."
"**How is that not a scheme???**" Xiahou Dun complained.
Cao Cao looked at Cheng Yu purposefully and said, "Everyone can go now."
The officials left the tent in a bewildered and irritated state; the only statesmen that remained were Assistant Officer Man Chong, Cheng Yu and Xu Yòu.
"...Are you being so cautious because you fear that I might go back to Yuan Shao and betray you, Mengde...?" Xu Yòu asked worriedly. "Because-"
"If we were concerned about you betraying us, you silly little man, then you'd already be dead," Cheng Yu said cuttingly.
"Then why the secrecy...?" Xu Yòu asked as he stared upward at the tall, scrawny Cheng Yu. "Why the delays? Every day that we do nothing is another day that-!"
"*Patience*, Ziyuan," Cao Cao said calmly. "Yuan Shao must be broken mentally as well as physically; his great power must be confronted as a wolf might size up a bear, and it is with careful planning, numbers and strategy that a wolf bests a bear and forces it to flee needlessly."
"I'm an adviser, Mengde: I know these things," Xu Yòu scoffed. "The problem was that Yuan Shao didn't listen, not that I didn't know what to say, else...!"
Cheng Yu smiled at Xu Yòu's sudden pause and said, "Else 'Mengde' would be long dead, and by *your schemes*...?"
"...I suppose so," Xu Yòu replied meekly.
"Then, as an adviser, you know that Yuan Shao must be treated carefully, but then smashed utterly when a weakness is exposed," Cao Cao said. "I'm going to Anmin, and you're coming with me, Ziyuan. Let's end this charade now, before any more moons come and go."
Xu Yòu nodded sheepishly.

Cao Cao made his one final trip to Anmin with a small supply train; the move was reported to Yuan Shao, who laughed strangely and said, "More small actions! More pointless movements of 'not very much' to 'right in front of my face'!"
"...Maybe we should attack Anmin," Yuan Tan said.
"That might be what he wants, my lord," Xin Ping replied.
"But it's better than sitting here and watching him make fools of us!" Yuan Tan snapped. "Mister Xin, this waiting is unbearable!"
"That's precisely why he does it," Cui Yan said quietly.
"...**You, man!**" Yuan Shao barked at the scout that had brought the news. "I want to know minute-to-minute what he's planning! I want more reports! There must be some hint, some clue as to his plan! *Find it*! **Find it and bring it to me!**"
The scout nodded frantically and fled the command room.

"...*Knave*," Yuan Shao growled. "Cao Cao is a treacherous, conniving knave and churl! I'll have his head put on a spike in the centre of Luoyang when I finally defeat him, and his body carved up and sent to the four corners of the Empire! No mercy for 'Mengde'! He has exhausted my good nature!"
"You'll harm yourself, Father," Yuan Tan pleaded. "Calm down."
Yuan Shao laughed weakly and said, "I am already 'harmed'."

Cao Cao's strange mission ended as it always did, and he started mock preparations for a return to Guandu.
"We're not really just going back, are we...?" Xu Yòu whined.
Cao Cao smiled and said, "No... not this time. This time it will be 'Benchu' that will leave this place."
A soldier approached from the western road; he knelt before Cao Cao's horse and said, "Mister Cheng is ready."
Cao Cao nodded and said, "Very good: tell him to move."
"Move...?" Xu Yòu exclaimed as the soldier retreated westward. "Move what to where? What is the plan, Mengde?"
"Nothing fancy, as I have said often enough," Cao Cao replied. "I'm just going to smash a large egg that rolled too far to the south for its own good."
"Be sure and cross the Yellow River and kill him afterwards, Mengde," Xu Yòu said tonelessly. "Don't keep letting him get away. He wouldn't do the same for you."
Cao Cao's main bodyguard, Xu Chu, was a simple man, but he was still annoyed by what seemed to be a rebuke that was aimed at his lord and master; Cao Cao stifled his own irritation at Xu Yòu's growing arrogance and replied, "If he escapes, Ziyuan, it will not be because I wanted it so."
"I hope not," Xu Yòu scoffed. "It isn't just *my* head that he wants; those childhood days that we shared together are long gone, and all the bonds that went with them."
Cao Cao smiled slightly and said, "I know that. Now, then: let us do our part..."

Yuan Shao's scouts reported Cao Cao's preparations for departure to the command tent of the Cangting camp.
"Not again!" General Jiang Yiqu complained. "If only I had ample grain and men by the tens of thousands in this place! I would have long since torn them to shreds!"
"...What is he doing...?" Ju Hu muttered.
"Nothing yet, by the sounds of it, not if he's going back to Guandu," Lü Xiang said. "I say that if Cao can stockpile at Anmin, then we should do the same here and-"
"**ATTACK...!**"
The officers turned to face a frantic messenger, who scrabbled into the room, fell to the floor in front of them and cried, "**Attacks, on all sides, the-!**"
"No, no not again!" Lü Kuang exclaimed. "He can't have outwitted us again! He *can't have*!"
"We must counterattack at once!" Ju Hu said. "Someone send word to Lord Yuan; General Jiang, let us do our part!"
The formidable Jiang Yiqu nodded and followed Ju Hu's departure.
        Yuan Shao's officers led their men out of the gates of the Cangting camp with newfound resolve, but what met them was a

horrifying sight; Cao Cao had brought some 20,000 men from Guandu to the west and secret eastern positions by water and land, and they now had the camp completely surrounded.

"*How...?*" Ju Hu cried. "**How??? HOW???**"

"**Does it matter???**" Jiang Yiqu retorted. "**We must fight back!**" But it was already too late.

"**The banners of Generals Zhang Liao, Wei Xu and Cao Xing are at the western gates!**" a scout reported. "**The banners of Generals Zhang Hè, Gao Lan and Yue Jin are at the eastern gates; the banners of Generals Xu Huang, Qi Ji and Qin Yi are at the northern gates; the banners of Xiahou Dun, Zhang Xiu and Cao Cao are at the southern gates!**"

What followed was messy and far from the finest hours of those concerned. Jiang Yiqu knew that he was no match for Zhang Liao, who was second only to his former master Lü Bu in terms of prowess on the battlefield, so Jiang resorted to leading his smaller force of men in meandering strikes on Zhang Liao's position; Ju Hu was similarly incapable of defeating Xu Huang, so he resorted to defensive manoeuvres while he looked for a way to pass the enemy; Lü Kuang confronted the hesitant Zhang Hè and Gao Lan, who had both defected from Yuan Shao to Cao Cao at Guandu, and appealed to their honour.

"**Why not do the right thing?**" Lü Kuang bellowed. "**Your true lord is Lord Yuan Shao: come back to him now and we can end Cao's tyranny today!**"

"**And die for 'treason' afterwards...?**" Gao Lan retorted.

"**You will be pardoned!**" Lü Kuang promised.

"**There is no crime to pardon; your words prove that nothing has changed!**" Zhang Hè retorted. "**No mercy for the merciless! FORWARD!**"

Zhang Hè and Gao Lan led their force against Lü Kuang while Yue Jin circled around Kuang's forces to pressure them from the south; Kuang had no choice but to retreat northward, where he met with late reinforcements from Yuan Tan and began an attempt at a counterattack.

Yuan Tan and Cao Cao met at the southern gates.

"*...*For the harm he has inflicted on Father, I will *kill him*," Yuan Tan muttered.

"**Turn back, Yuan Tan!**" Cao Cao heckled. "**I'll take your head another day!**"

"**We should kill him now!**" Xiahou Dun insisted; Zhang Xiu was rattled, as Xiahou Dun's words could just as easily have been aimed at him.

"**Yes!**" Xu Yòu agreed. "**You promised that you wouldn't let them flee!**"

Yuan Tan caught sight of Xu Yòu and pointed angrily, screaming, "**THERE! *There* is the bastard that burned Wuchao! A city and ten-thousand taxable households for the man that brings me the head of Xu Yòu!**"

A few of Yuan Tan's men were tempted by the promise of great wealth and charged at Cao Cao's position; but as they did so, two unannounced generals – Cao Xiu and Cao Hong – appeared to the left and right of Yuan Shao's force with several hundred men and horse. Zhang Xiu's foreign champion Huche'er added his own might to the attack, which tore Tan's front line apart in seconds.

"**More trickery!**" Yuan Tan cried as he faced the realisation that he would have to retreat yet again. "**Curse you and the men that follow you!**"

Cao Cao could not hear Yuan Tan's parting words, but he smiled and asked, "**I wonder what he said, Ziyuan.**"

"**He probably asked why you're letting him get away!**" Xu Yòu replied. "**He wants us both dead, like his father! Chase his ten-thousand from Cangting and laugh if you will, Mengde, but will your fifty-thousand match his quarter-of-a-million when we have to cross to the north?**"

"...**It won't need to,**" Cao Cao said as he watched the first flames of a fire arrow attack start to burn the Cangting camp.

Yuan Tan was coughing and spluttering as he finally escaped the burning camp and started the demoralising journey across the Yellow River; Cao Cao had deliberately given his generals at the northern gates of the camp a smaller force, so Yuan's army had passed them after little more than mild harassment. Yuan Shao brought an army to meet his son's, but it would do little more than serve as an escort as the Yuans retreated to Yè.

"**Cao _mocked_ us!**" Yuan Tan cried angrily. "**Now you're here, Father, we-!**"

"Cangting is lost," Guo Tu said. "Sorry, young lord, but we cannot cross the Yellow River without a viable foothold... that foothold was Cangting, and it is lost."

"_All_ is lost...!" Yuan Shao whimpered. "Now I must face ridicule... my last foothold south of the river, snatched as easily as taking something from a sack!"

"We have to get back to Yè," Guo Tu urged. "I have sent word to Pang Ji, so we should receive reinforcements to prevent Cao Cao from pursuing."

"Beaten by a _mouse_!" Yuan Shao rambled. "I am a _giant_, with four provinces and two-hundred-thousand men, and I have been bested by conniving _mouse_!"

"My lord, calm down," Chen Lin pleaded. "You-"

"Why did I not have my men cross every ford along the Yellow River and overwhelm him?" Yuan Shao lamented. "Why did I guard Cangting as a peasant guards their only valuable possession, when I could have had the entire river blanketed with soldiers and barbarian cavalry?"

"It couldn't be helped," Cui Yan insisted. "Men need food, and-"

"And that's another thing I must face... _Tadun_," Yuan Shao whimpered. "Will that Wuhuan king want such a weakling for an ally, or will he now try and seize all of Yòu Province, or maybe all of my domains...?"

"You let his people do as they please, and married our daughters to his men," Shen Pei said with a tone that betrayed bitterness and contempt. "I'm sure that he will be very amiable."

Yuan Shao laughed and said, "I imagine that you are right, Mister Shen... your words and thoughts both."

"...Cao employed _Zhang Xiu_, Father!" Yuan Tan said. "_Zhang Xiu_!"

"Zhang Xiu???" Yuan Shao exclaimed. "Zhang Xiu, the man that killed his heir??? Is there no low to which the wretch will not stoop, fighting alongside the murderer of his kin???"

"Apparently not," Guo Tu murmured.

"Knave... you are a hankering knave, Cao Cao, a lord of traitors and churls!" Yuan Shao cried angrily. **"He brings here his collection of stolen generals from Dong Zhuo, Lü Bu, my brother and me, and former felons and wastrels!"**

"...And he has won," Cui Yan noted.

"Yes... he has won... *again*," Yuan Shao whimpered. "And I must retreat... *again*."

Cao Cao gathered his officials in the command tent of his Anmin headquarters and said, "A fine victory, gentlemen. Yuan Shao has not one base to the south of the Yellow River now: his grip on the provinces will weaken as his enemies smell blood, and–"

"You let him escape!" Xu Yòu heckled. "I hope that he continues to be as stupid as he has always been when you eventually decide to march on Yè, Mengde, or you might wish that you had not smiled and laughed today!"

"Don't take that from him, Mengde," Cao Hong complained. "He talks to you like he-!"

"Ziyuan is concerned, but he need not be," Cao Cao interrupted. "Yuan Shao will be shuddering, grimacing, heckling, and leaping around on his saddle like a man possessed; he's a man that's making himself sick from the distress of repeated losses against a weaker opponent, and that will end his life soon enough."

"After Yuan's death, chaos will reign," Guo Jia suggested. "Today might seem anticlimactic, especially after the amazing victory at Guandu, but today is special: it marks the beginning of the total decline of Yuan Shao's national influence."

"Today, I drove him from Cangting," Cao Cao chuckled. "One day soon, he will drive himself to the netherworld!" Cao Cao then turned to the isolated Zhang Xiu and said, "General Zhang, thank you for rushing here with your men so quickly. Please return to Nan County and resume your observation of the Qiang and Liu Biao before they notice your absence. Mister Jia Xu, kindly see General Zhang to the gates."

Zhang Xiu bowed to the assembly – which was mostly hostile, since Zhang's ambush at Wan City 3 years before had cost Cao Cao's clan dearly – and replied, "I shall, Excellency, with haste."

Once Zhang Xiu, Jia Xu and Huche'er were gone, Xiahou Dun turned to Cao Cao and said, "You asked *Jia Xu* to walk him out? Aren't you scared that they'll go together, across the river to join Yuan Shao...?"

Cao Cao smiled and replied, "They know my word is honest."

"Here we are, Mister Jia, in one-another's company again so soon, but forced to part again," Zhang Xiu said to his former adviser Jia Xu as soon as they reached the gates of the Anmin camp.

"Indeed," Jia Xu replied. "I imagine that His Excellency wanted us to talk so that we could know we are safe. He is not without fault, but at heart he is truly a statesman."

Zhang Xiu nodded and said, "I am inclined to agree. I can't deny that his actions still leave me feeling tainted, but I took more from him than he from me, and... and..."

"Say no more," Jia Xu said. "Farewell again... for now at least... Lord Zhang."

"*Lord* Zhang...?" Zhang Xiu exclaimed.

"A man can serve many lords, as I have," Jia Xu replied. "It was an honour to serve you, so you retain that title in my heart."
The former lord and vassal exchanged bows and parted ways for the second time in a year; Jia Xu returned to the command tent, and Zhang Xiu returned to Wan City in Nan County, a base that his uncle had stolen and he, he felt, had earned.

The world-weary Yuan Shao was met on the road to Yè City by his nephew – the Governor of Bing Province, Gao Gan – and an army of 20,000 men.
"I am here now, worthy lord and uncle!" Gao Gan declared. "Let us get revenge!"
"What I would have given, Nephew, for these men to have been at Cangting," Yuan Shao bleated as he observed the rows of professional soldiers and horsemen. "What I would give, oh what I would give, to be able to march them back there and wipe that smug smile off of the face of my enemy!"
"Perhaps we should go back, as Cousin Gan suggests, Father," Yuan Tan said.
"No, son," Yuan Shao replied. "We'll need these men for a different task now... restoring the order that will collapse over the coming days as word of my defeat reaches my enemies within."

Yuan Shao was correct: he was not back in Yè City for more than a day before reports of uprisings across Bing, Yòu, Qing and Ji Provinces started to pour in. Cao Cao, by contrast, returned to Xuchang as an unrivalled champion that expected more victories – both military and psychological – over the coming weeks, and he was quickly proved to be correct as well.

****

13

"…Truly unbelievable, gentlemen," Jing Governor Liu Biao said as he placed the reports from the Cangting region to one side and turned his gaze from his assembled courtiers to his guest of honour, Liu Bei.

"Unbelievable and terrible," Liu Bei replied. "If Cao has so easily beaten Yuan Shao again and driven him back, then there are no other heroes left in this world but you."

"And *you*, I think…!" Liu Biao snickered. "You know full well that you are considered to be a hero, so why act as if it isn't so…?"

"Bei is resorting to *flattery*," General Cai Mao scoffed. "It's a poor trait in a 'hero'."

Liu Biao glared at Cai Mao and said, "Brother-in-law, please show more respect to our guest. He has endured much to be here with us now, and he fights for the preservation of the Han Dynasty, the clan to which we both belong and to which you are, by marriage, now a part of yourself. We have common purpose."

Cai Mao harrumphed, bowed slightly and replied, "Your word is final, my lord."

"It is," Liu Biao retorted. "Now then, Xuande… you will be returning to Xinye soon, so that we are ready for any problems that may arise from Cao Cao's latest victory."

"With all haste," Liu Bei said. "He is unlikely to attack, but then again, he is the 'Hero of Chaos', to which no normal rules apply, moral or otherwise."

Liu Biao nodded gratefully, and after a show of respect to the court, Liu Bei and his entourage departed.

"…Cao Cao is now unstoppable," Liu Biao fretted. "I was wrong to challenge him. But what's done is done."

"Indeed," the politician Huan Jie said. "Now thoughts should turn to making peace with the court, whatever that might involve."

The adviser Wang Can laughed and said, "Well put!"

"I will betray no trust," Liu Biao insisted. "But I will try to make my peace with His Majesty, yes… not Cao Cao."

Huan Jie bowed silently and glanced at Wang Can, who nodded purposefully in response.

Ma Teng summoned his sons to a meeting in his current base, which was close to the border with Central Province; Ma Chao ignored the request, but his other sons – Ma Tie and Ma Xiu – arrived promptly.

"…So Chao has decided to forge his own path," Ma Teng realised. "So be it. Tie, Xiu, I must do what I must do; this bloodshed cannot go on."

"Indeed, Father," Ma Tie replied.

"You are both bold warriors, but three sons against the hordes that choose to follow Han Sui are not enough," Ma Teng continued. "Let Chao and his friends fight their own fight: I hope that it does not cost him too dearly. But I must try and restore peace, or we'll lose our lives and our land to the Han, who will simply wait for us to exhaust ourselves and then snatch Liang from our dead hands. I will use the Han to prevent that… I will ask Cao Cao to mediate peace."

"…A lot of blood has been shed," Ma Xiu noted.

"I have killed Han Sui's kin, he has killed mine," Ma Teng replied. "But if we don't want to ruin all that we've achieved, it must stop!"

"…As you wish, Father," Ma Xiu said.

"I don't wish," Ma Teng admitted. "But… but sometimes men must choose between 'bad' and 'worse', between 'wrong' and 'necessary'… that is one lesson that is repeatedly, painfully made clear to me. Today I choose 'bad', I choose 'necessary'… I choose to give us hope."

Ma Tie and Ma Xiu reluctantly agreed to their father's suggestion; Ma Teng hurried a letter to Xuchang and hoped that he would receive a speedy response.

The former bandit Zang Ba was perturbed and irritated when Cao Cao's general Yu Jin returned to his base for another meeting.

"If I wasn't going to defect to Yuan Shao before, I'm certainly not going to now!" Zang Ba complained. "Why are you back here?"

"Go easy," Chang Xi said. "He's alright, Wenze is."

"Marry him, then," Sun Guan heckled.

Chang Xi got to his feet and drew a sword as mocking laughter provoked him to murderous rage, but his friend Wu Dun calmed him, saying, "Find your sense of humour, Chang."

"Ha. Ha. Ha. Bloody *hilarious*," Chang Xi growled as he sheathed his sword and took his seat again; he did not take his eyes off of the fearless, grinning Sun Guan at any point thereafter.

"…What I have to put up with," Zang Ba sighed as he turned to face Yu Jin once again. "So like I asked already, General Yu: why are you here?"

"I am here to ask, on His Excellency's behalf, that you increase your agitation in Qing Province and maybe have some of your people go into eastern Ji," Yu Jin explained. "Nothing more."

"Alright," Zang Ba replied. "We'll do as we're asked. We're not liaising with 'Flying Swallow' Zhang, are we…?"

"No," Yu Jin said. "The Black Mountain Bandits are not allies of ours. Any agitating that they do in Yuan Shao's domains is of their own volition."

"…And that was it…?" Zang Ba asked.

"It is and was," Yu Jin promised.

"…I have to admit, General, that you do seem to be an honest sort," Zang Ba said. "Chang Xi, you're right to trust him. Could you see him out?"

Chang Xi was still transfixed on Sun Guan as he got to his feet to do as he had been asked; Sun Guan got to his feet, walked to Chang Xi and slapped his arm saying, "We're old mates, Chang. Don't let one little joke ruin that. Like Xuangao said, and like you said, Yu Jin's alright. It was just a joke."

Chang Xi relaxed and nodded gratefully, saying, "I knew that. I dunno where me sense o' humour's gone."

"Wherever it went, I reckon you ought to find it," Zang Ba said. "See General Yu to the gates, mate."

Chang Xi guided Yu Jin out of the command tent, and Sun Guan returned to his seat.

"I don't need it," Zang Ba said. "Whatever's wrong with Chang… and I hope it ain't what I think it is… he needs to get a grip."

"…Restlessness…?" Sun Guan supposed.

"Chang's missing the carefree life," Yin Li guessed. "He likes the way we lived before."

"Yeah, well, he can't go back to that now, none of us can," Zang Ba replied. "If he tried, he wouldn't like what'd happen next."

The anxious murmurs that filled the room told Zang Ba that the most difficult days might be seen in the years ahead.

Yuan Shao tried to re-establish normality over the months that followed, although his vassals were disturbed by his apparent focus on life after he was gone; he oversaw the marriage of his second son Xi to the near-peerless beauty Lady Zhen and brought one of his surviving uncles, Yuan Cheng, into the court to assist his preparations for succession.

The wedding was typical for people of Yuan Shao's status; the guests were seated much as they would be in a meeting, with the groom's family sitting on one side and the bride's guests sat on the other. The bride and groom were both wearing red, because it symbolised happiness and prosperity in much the same way as white represented sadness and loss; Yuan Xi wore robes that were decorated with gold dragons and other auspicious imagery, and Lady Zhen wore a trailing dress and a headdress that obscured her face with a row of beads. The two knelt and faced each other, and their matchmakers – Yuan Shao's uncle Cheng for Yuan Xi, and a family friend for Lady Zhen – oversaw a simple exchange of vows and a proclamation by a Taoist priest. At the conclusion of the ceremony – which was a celebrated affair at every level of society, since Lady Zhen was a popular, wealthy philanthropist – there were many that wanted to ask their lord about his plans.

"Forgive me for asking this, esteemed Nephew," the elder Yuan Cheng said, "but aren't you being pessimistic...?"

"Isn't Lady Zhen a sight to behold...?" Yuan Shao asked. "She has the grace and beauty of an Empress, and a heart unblemished by the wicked, unquenchable, self-destructive desire that consumes the rest of us."

Yuan Cheng sighed and said, "You're dodging my questions."

"She will make a good match for Xi, since he lacks ambition... which I do not mean as an insult," Yuan Shao continued as he watched the post-wedding activities from the host seat. "Her generosity towards the common folk with the wealth that her late father left her is, I have to say, highly commendable... I was idealistic like her, once, long ago, before I inherited this burden I now bear..."

"Please answer me," Yuan Cheng prompted.

"She has probably done more to feed the poor during that awful famine than a single one of the men that I assigned, paid and allocated resources to do it," Yuan Shao sighed wistfully. "To see such beauty and such kindness paired... almost makes one believe that there is an inhabited heaven and not just a netherworld full to bursting. Lady Liu, my principal spouse... now there's another story... that woman has a gaze that can cut through-"

"Can you *please answer me*, Nephew???" Yuan Cheng hissed. "My heart is burning with anguish as I watch you plan for your death!"

Yuan Shao laughed and said, "Everyone else plans for my death, Uncle... my wife, my heir, my cronies... so why shouldn't *I*...?"

Yuan Cheng looked at the wedding guests and analysed each group with weary old eyes: Yuan Shao's advisers – Guo Tu, Shen Pei, Pang Ji, Xun Chen and the Xin brothers – were canvassing wealthy invitees and ingratiating themselves with Lady Liu, Yuan Tan or Yuan Shang; Yuan Xi and Lady Zhen were actually enjoying far less attention than the people that were likely to have influence in the years ahead, but it did not seem to be bothering either of them.

"Lady Zhen will have to ask her husband how she should spend her considerable wealth from now on," Yuan Shao continued. "She has been used to an unusually high level of financial autonomy, but reality now bites her and wakes her from a long dream. In a way, it is a shame and I pity her… but it is better than being married to a Wuhuan chieftain."

"Some of your words remind me of the Shao of old," Yuan Cheng noted. "When you were young, carefree, and driven to protect the 'Partisans' from those wicked eunuchs; you were an inspiring lad."

"And now, I am a grey-haired fool with bilious cysts for bodily organs," Yuan Shao chuckled miserably. "I am a master of a quarter of the country, and yet I cannot hold onto that power… hate, humiliation and regret consume me bit by bit, like diseases, and my life shortens with every thought that enters my head."

"But you're better than that!" Yuan Cheng pleaded. "When Dong Zhuo slaughtered our kin, yes you cried and got drunk, but-!"

"I had friends then," Yuan Shao said. "I had respect, I had aspirations and dreams; now, Uncle, I have the land and power that I hungered for, but nothing else. I have sons, yes, but what do they inherit…? This façade, this vision of stability that I have created here today, where people laugh and joke and drink and dance and pretend that there isn't a vicious, hankering tyrant – a man that I once called 'friend' – not more than a month's march away from here that wants me dead, aided by men that I once called 'friends', and… and…!"

Yuan Shao's head fell forward, and he exhaled noisily.

"…*Aiee*… what can I say that could help…?" Yuan Cheng admitted.

"I've fought so hard to retain this power," Yuan Shao whimpered. "Chieftain of the Yuans of Ru County…! Commander of the Eastern Pass Coalition…! Commander-in-Chief of-! …Oh, yes, of course, I forget… Cao Cao demoted me to 'General of Chariots and Cavalry', didn't he, as a warning to me that I have wronged, as a false indication that there is a way to 'return to the light', namely by capitulating to *him*… and, of course, as a *label* and a *curse*, because I inherit the role from *Dong Cheng*…!"

Yuan Shao covered his face with his hands.

"You will attract attention," Yuan Cheng warned.

Yuan Shao lowered his hands and said, "Yes, of course… I must sustain the impression that I am strong, mustn't I…? I must celebrate my son's good fortune… and sustain the illusion…"

Yuan Xi and Lady Zhen had noticed that Yuan Shao was behaving strangely and approached the host seat; Xi bowed slightly and said, "Father, are you alright…?"

"I am overwhelmed by emotion," Yuan Shao replied; he then turned to Lady Zhen and sighed, saying, "My, you are truly a creature doubly blessed by Heaven, dear daughter-in-law! You are an even more magnificent beauty than I realised, now that I see

82

you up close!"
Lady Zhen smiled meekly and said, "I am grateful for your compliments, Father-in-law, but I hope to be remembered for the beauty of my actions."
Yuan Shao laughed strangely and replied, "Well, that's… that's admirable. Yes, very admirable."
"Your actions elevate you to a hero and a magnanimous statesman," Lady Zhen continued. "You protected the intelligentsia and then His Majesty from the evil 'Ten', confronted Dong Zhuo, and even now you strive to restore light to the darkness. I have simply tried to do what I can."
"…You are a good-hearted young woman," Yuan Shao said hoarsely. "I hope that fate doesn't drive it from you as it has me."
Yuan Xi and Lady Zhen exchanged uncomfortable glances, bowed respectfully and retreated.
"Why did you say that?" Yuan Cheng asked.
"I… don't know," Yuan Shao admitted. "I… just want it to be over."
Yuan Cheng sighed woefully, got to his feet and left Yuan Shao to his thoughts; he noticed that Yuan Xi and Lady Zhen had separated and that Yuan Xi had been approached by Lady Liu and two of Yuan Shao's advisers.
"What are you schemers up to…?" Yuan Cheng wondered as he approached the group.
"…To *Yòu Province*…?" Yuan Xi gasped as he absorbed the words of his stepmother Lady Liu. "I must go… to *Yòu Province*…?"
"Your lord and father cannot govern his domains without your help," Lady Liu said. "Isn't that right, Mister Guo Tu…?"
Guo Tu and Shen Pei were standing to Lady Liu's left; Guo Tu nodded and said, "I know that you are only just married, young lord, but you must prepare to travel to the capital Fanyang as soon as your domestic affairs are settled."
"But… I thought that Liu Hè was governor of Yòu Province, a role inherited from his father and restored to him once Gongsun Zan was defeated!" Yuan Xi said.
Shen Pei smiled and said, "That was never the case, young lord. That brash, ill-tempered young man was never the right choice. In any case, he cannot be governor and never will be. He has… retired from public life."
"…But Yòu Province is no place to be starting a family!" Yuan Xi complained. "It will take a long time to stabilise the region!"
"Which is precisely why Lady Zhen shall remain here, in Yè, in your father's household, until you have stabilised the region," Lady Liu replied.
Yuan Xi was exasperated, but he could not argue with his shamelessly contented stepmother: he turned to look at the distant form of his new wife, sighed miserably and said, "If that is Father's wish, then… so be it."
"What is going on…?" Yuan Cheng asked as he reached the gathering. "Why is the groom so folorn…?"
"I… I am to go to Yòu Province while Lady Zhen remains here in Yè, at Father's request," Yuan Xi explained.
"Tan will go back to Qing Province, and Gao Gan will continue to serve as the protector of Bing Province," Lady Liu said cheerfully.
"…So my nephew's older sons will be in far-off places, while your son Shang stays here," Yuan Cheng replied as he glared at Lady

Liu. "And this is my nephew's idea...?"
Lady Liu waved her hand dismissively and giggled, "*Ask him*."
Yuan Cheng turned to look at Yuan Shao and muttered, "No... I won't bother."
"Lord Yuan wants his trusted family members guarding his provincial capitals," Guo Tu said.
Yuan Cheng looked at the smugly-smirking Lady Liu and said, "I can see that... the vision of the future is forming very clearly in my eyes. I only hope that it is the right one." Cheng bowed to each person in turn, said, "Gentlemen... and Lady Liu," and retreated to speak with some of Lady Zhen's relations.
"...It is," Lady Liu said. "It will be."
Guo Tu frowned and looked at Shen Pei; Shen was smiling as well, and Guo Tu – who was quietly currying favour with Yuan Tan – suddenly realised that the future that was being planned might not be one that was entirely to his benefit.

When the festivities were ended, Yuan Shao retired to his private study while servants tidied the living quarters; Lady Liu joined him and said, "Now your eldest boys are grown and gone on to start their own families... Shang will be next."
"I... I say this sincerely, not to appease you," Yuan Shao replied. "I would probably prefer Shang as my heir, as you obviously do."
Lady Liu smiled shamelessly.
"He is not reckless, ill-tempered, hard-faced or lacking in statesman's talents like Tan, nor is he too soft-hearted, like Xi; Shang is handsome, charismatic and confident, as today showed when he handled himself well in conversations with my advisers," Yuan Shao explained. "It goes against the rules that many go by, however, rules that state that the eldest should become the heir."
Lady Liu's smile disappeared.
"Those rules are the only reason that I, not Shu, became clan chieftain, and they must remain," Yuan Shao continued. "But Shang is smarter and more statesmanlike than either of the other two, so I want him to a have a special role, to somehow have chieftain-like influence over Tan when he inherits everything: if I don't ensure that Tan is on a leash, he'll start attacking people and ruin everything."
Lady Liu smiled icily and said, "You know best, my lord. I'm sure that you will resolve things well enough. Perhaps you should consult your advisers."
"...Yes," Yuan Shao replied. "I've had the same thought."
Lady Liu retreated to the bedchambers, and Yuan Shao's five consorts cowered fearfully upon her arrival; Yuan Shao took up a jug of wine and drank joylessly until he passed out. Lady Liu guessed that her husband would not last for much longer, and that she would need more allies to ensure her son Shang's installation as the heir to the Ru County Yuan clan; she wondered who, besides Shen Pei, would aid her quest as she returned to living quarters and watched her husband's frail body writhe and shudder from the nightmares that haunted his sleep.

****

14

Months passed.

Yuan Shao's forces – guided by the forceful hand of Cui Yan – eventually supressed the rebellions in the four provinces and restored a fragile order. But Yuan Shao was a man damaged by the series of ignominious defeats that Cao Cao had inflicted upon him, and his health deteriorated rapidly.

"Poor Benchu...!" Cao Cao chuckled as he sat in his private meeting room and read another report from spies in Ji Province. "Poor, poor old Benchu, fading away like a shadow at the mercy of the morning sun...!"
"So you don't pity him then...?" Guo Jia asked.
"...No," Cao Cao replied.
"Then why did you hesitate...?" Guo Jia asked.
"...Alright, yes, I pity him," Cao Cao admitted as he threw the report to one side. "I laugh because he intended my death, but now, when I think that he might die at any time, I... I wonder what went wrong. I wonder why we have ended up as bitter enemies. And... and I wonder when *I* am destined to die."
"As someone that is indifferent to death's release, I cannot answer the last point," Guo Jia chuckled. "What went wrong between you and Yuan Shao...? Undoubtedly 'ambition', Lord Cao; it consumed the bond between you both long ago."
"...I want to be able to say that I am blameless, but I am not," Cao Cao said. "I took longer... am taking longer... to be fully consumed, but it was always both of us. I just wish that our ambitions had somehow been compatible with friendship."
"Ridiculous," Guo Jia said. "One can have total power or some friends; it is only a madman that tries to have both. You've always known that."
Cao Cao lowered his head, smiled and replied, "Yes, I have."
"...You've been delaying the talks between Ma Teng and Han Sui," Guo Jia noted. "Why...?"
"I'm doubtful that they wouldn't try to kidnap or assassinate me," Cao Cao admitted. "I'm the most powerful statesman in the country, Fengxiao: that makes me a target for such things, and the Qiang are especially untrustworthy."
"Inspector Wei has a competent army, the venue is well-chosen, and their feud is no ruse," Guo Jia replied. "You'll have Xu Chu, Zhang Liao, Xiahou Dun, Cao Xiu and Yue Jin with you, and Jia Xu and Cheng Yu for counsel..."
"Yes!" Cao Cao chuckled. "I'll have Jia Xu at my side, and Zhang Xiu at my rear for a discussion with the Qiang warlords in the middle of Liang Province, surrounded by the remnants of Dong Zhuo's old band... aren't Duan Wei and Wu Xi still around...?"
"That's why you'll have Zhang Liao and quite a few of the other men that followed Lü Bu, all of whom betrayed Dong Zhuo and have no love for the men that were loyal to Dong's memory in the aftermath," Guo Jia explained. "Jia Xu is seen as a man that ultimately betrayed Li Jue and Guo Si, and might I remind you that Duan and Wu were the ones that *killed* Li and Guo...?"

"...It's all so complicated," Cao Cao sighed. "But yes, you're right, Duan and Wu are no threat, and regardless of later divisions, they all dislike the Qiang."

"R-right," Guo Jia said as he winced from a pain in his stomach. "What you... must do, my lord, is... is just go and get them to agree to your terms, as we discussed."

"...I'm losing you for a week again, I see," Cao Cao lamented.

"You don't need me!" Guo Jia said encouragingly. "You have... better men."

"...Go and rest," Cao Cao ordered. "I'll see you when I return."

Guo Jia got to his feet with great difficulty, bowed respectfully and staggered out of the meeting room.

"...*Aiee*... what a waste," Cao Cao murmured as his heir Cao Pi passed Guo Jia and entered the room.

"Guo Jia is sick again," Cao Pi noted.

"Unfortunately, yes," Cao Cao replied.

"You are going to Liang Province to mediate peace between the Qiang, aren't you?" Cao Pi said. "I should like to accompany you."

"I have to pass Wan City," Cao Cao replied. "I don't feel comfortable travelling past that place with my heir, since I came back alone the last time I did that."

"But that's partly why I'd like to go, to pay respects to my cousin and brother, and to Mister Dian," Cao Pi insisted.

"...Not this time," Cao Cao retorted. "There will be safer opportunities for that in the future, son... I doubt that I'll feel safe doing so myself. But it is a nice thought, son. As I said, perhaps we'll go another time."

Cao Pi bowed respectfully and withdrew; Cao Cao turned to the latest correspondence from Ma Teng and frowned sombrely.

"...Do not rile me, Ma Teng," Cao Cao muttered. "And do not challenge me, Han Sui; I feel a migraine poised to strike, and you would do well to be polite."

Cao Cao made the long journey to Liang Province to meet with Ma Teng and Han Sui: he first passed Yingchuan Prefecture in western Yan Province, where his 'cousin' Xiahou Yuan was serving as a prefectural administrator and protector.

"It is good to see you, Miaocai!" Cao Cao said as he ignored protocol and hugged the burly, thick-whiskered Xiahou Yuan at the gates of the prefectural capital.

"You have a migraine," Xiahou Yuan guessed as he patted Cao Cao's back.

"My head is a burden that I would gladly be rid of!" Cao Cao chuckled ironically. "Please, tell one of my many enemies that they are welcome to it!"

Cao Cao backed away and sighed gratefully; it was then that Xiahou Yuan noticed that Xu Yòu was present. Yuan smiled falsely and said, "Mister Xu Yòu, we've not met often but I recognise you immediately nonetheless."

Xu Yòu bowed silently.

"Have you no kind words for me, Miaocai?" Xiahou Dun asked.

"Of course I have, you rascal!" Xiahou Yuan chuckled as he hugged Xiahou Dun.

"We won't be stopping long, sadly," Cao Cao said. "But never fear, Miaocai, for I am hoping that things are about to change for the better: once my worst enemies are eradicated, you can come to Xuchang and we can all be together."

"I'll ensure that your horses are rested and fed and your stocks replenished," Xiahou Yuan promised. "I take it that you're going to Liang Province...?"

"Enough about the Qiang," Cao Cao pleaded. "Day after day, they dominate proceedings as Liu Biao, Yuan Shao and Liu Bei do. Let's have a get-together, just us, where we enjoy wine and only talk about better times!"

"That sounds wonderful," Xu Yòu said. "We're earned it, I think!"

Xiahou Dun fought the urge to attack Xu Yòu, who had effectively invited himself to a private family banquet; Xiahou Yuan grimaced and shook his head discreetly.

"...Of course we've earned it, Ziyuan," Cao Cao replied carefully. "It will be... most pleasant indeed..."

The banquet was, at first, conspicuously devoid of the merriment and reminiscing that Cao Cao had suggested; the five men – Xiahou Yuan, Xiahou Dun, Cao Xiu, Xu Yòu and Cao Cao – did nothing but eat, drink tea or wine and exchange the occasional joke or anecdote. Xu Yòu became very drunk within a short time and excused himself; once he was gone, Xiahou Yuan sighed and said, "What a frustrating, irritating little man he is, Mengde. I know that he is your friend, but..."

Cao Cao clutched his aching head and replied, "He's lucky that I have so much to celebrate at the moment, else I'd have publicly humiliated him at the very least."

Xiahou Dun harrumphed angrily.

"He's drunk so much of my wine!" Xiahou Yuan complained. "Has he forgotten that wine is still a bit of a luxury in famine-hit areas like this one?"

"He's a pain," Cao Xiu admitted. "I really don't like him."

"Look, gentlemen, he is who he is, and that's that!" Cao Cao said desperately. "Can I really worry about 'annoying people' when I have far *worse* to deal with...?"

"...Sorry, Mengde," Xiahou Yuan replied. "It's my fault for moaning about him. It's because we're all tired, I suppose... even though we're not talking about Yellow Turbans, bandits, Yuan Shao and all the rest of it, we're still thinking about it."

"We are," Cao Cao said. "Sad to say... we are."

"...Miaocai, is... is it true that your daughter was taken by *Zhang Fei*...?" Xiahou Dun asked.

Xiahou Yuan nodded silently.

"...I'll kill them *all*, Miaocai," Xiahou Dun promised. "All of them."

"...But how is it not my fault...?" Cao Cao asked. "How is it-?"

"It... it was Zhang's choice, and he alone is to blame," Xiahou Yuan said. "Say no more, Mengde... I beg of you, say no more."

The mood worsened, and the banquet ended sourly with each man retiring to their quarters with a frown on his face, despite the best of intentions.

Cao Cao's next stop was Nan County in northern Jing Province, where Zhang Xiu was a squatter-tenant with the power of a county magistrate. Zhang had erected a memorial site to the fallen at Wan City that recognised both sides of the conflict; Cao

Cao had nonetheless allocated a different, separate place to mourn his fallen son, nephew and bodyguard, and he established his camp at that place.

"I am not going into Wan City, nor am I stopping," Cao Cao said to Jia Xu. "Please compose a letter that conveys my respects to Zhang Xiu for his ensuring our safe passage through this region."

"I shall," Jia Xu replied.

"...If only Tao Qian had been as trustworthy," Cao Cao said suddenly. "And did Tao and I have the difficult past that I share with Zhang Xiu...?"

Jia Xu frowned silently.

"...Things like this are all that's left of my poor Ang," Cao Cao whimpered as he stared at a small pile of rocks, an incense stand and a small, inscribed tablet that had been shielded from the elements by a small wooden shelter. "I want to commission something bigger, but what for...? He's still dead."

The rest of the ensemble – Cao Xiu, Xiahou Dun, Assistant Officer Man Chong, Cheng Yu, Xu Yòu and Cao's bodyguard Xu Chu – were painfully silent.

"I... I'm sorry," Jia Xu pleaded.

"Oh, yes, right... it's I that should apologise to you, Mister Jia, for I did not intend our conversation to imply some attack on you," Cao Cao replied. "I had better leave this place soon. Ma Teng and Han Sui await me... this isn't a pilgrimage."

Cao Cao took one last look at the hastily-assembled shrine to the fallen at Wan and returned to his carriage with Xu Yòu, Man Chong and Xu Chu.

"...You *are* sorry, aren't you, Mister Jia...?" Xiahou Dun prompted.

"My intent was never to harm good men or the Han," Jia Xu replied. "I forgot that I am not an inanimate object to be wielded by others, that I had the option to refuse to serve. I serve a wise lord now, and I won't falter again."

Xiahou Dun nodded thoughtfully and retreated with Cao Xiu.

"...Ours is a strange profession, Mister Jia," Cheng Yu said with a tone that insinuated amusement. "Our lords have us doing all sorts, don't they...? But where does our responsibility end and theirs begin, mm...? I ponder that all the time."

Jia Xu hummed ambiguously, and Cheng Yu retreated; Jia stood and stared at the shrine for a while longer.

"...No one man moves a heavy stone," Jia Xu said at last, and then he joined the procession as it continued the journey to Liang.

The 'mediation camp' in Liang Province was in a designated 'neutral zone' where neither Ma Teng nor Han Sui felt that the other had prevailing influence. Liang's Inspector, Wei Kang, Minister Yang Fu and Army Adviser Zhao Ang were present at the meeting, which was chaired, as promised, by Excellency of Works Cao Cao. Ma Chao was conspicuously absent on the first day, which saddened his father Ma Teng. Both of the warlords were dressed in white garments as a sign of their grief and a sign to the other that compensation was due, which worried the mediators.

The talks went on for three days, and the migraine-stricken Cao Cao was often frustrated to the point of almost walking out as Ma Teng and Han Sui bickered over borders that were not theirs and demands for 'reparation' for personal losses that had been matched by the other; a compromise was eventually found, and both of the Qiang warlords – to the disdain of many of the minor chieftains that they controlled – agreed on a peaceful settlement. It was a relieved government faction that attended the last day of talks; Ma Chao was conspicuously present and defiant in his stance, and that saddened Ma Teng even more.

"My goodness... he *is* like Lü Bu...!" Jia Xu muttered as he stared at Ma Chao.

"Yes, Mister Jia, and we killed Bu easily enough in the end," Cheng Yu replied casually.

"I hope that you have not come to disrupt these talks, Ma Chao," Han Sui said as he glared at the only man to match his ferocity in recent times.

"Not at all," Ma Chao replied tonelessly. "I'm here to support my father and ensure we get a fair deal from these Han lackeys."

Inspector Wei Kang shuddered.

"...I am a man of my word," Cao Cao said. "I've done everything that I ever intended and promised to do."

"Indeed you *have*," Ma Teng chortled.

"I'm prepared to agree to everything that we've discussed," Han Sui declared. "Are *you*, Ma Teng...?"

"No more kin's blood needlessly shed," Ma Teng replied. "I agree to it all."

The two Qiang warlords got up from their seats on opposite sides of the 'command tent' and met at the centre, at which point they clasped hands tightly and nodded tersely to indicate an end to their feud.

"...Now I must go," Han Sui said as he backed away from Ma Teng. "You have your dead to mourn, and I have mine."

"Indeed," Ma Teng replied. "After that... we rebuild what we had."

Ma Chao smiled and stared at Cao Cao, who returned the gesture.

"...*Aiee*... why do they not just announce that they reunite to seize the province???" Wei Kang whispered to Yang Fu, who hummed quietly in response.

"And now," Cao Cao said, "you will honour *your* part of the bargain, Ma Teng."

Ma Chao frowned and asked, "What 'bargain'...?"

"We... have agreed to provide troops to the Han when they are required," Ma Teng revealed. "We-"

"That's ridiculous...!" Ma Chao exclaimed. "**We oppose the rule of the Han in our region! Now you say that we will show weakness and provide our own bodies to protect them??? Does Han Sui lend them men...?**"

"Don't make trouble," Han Sui growled. "A deal's a deal, and yes, I will be lending men when I'm asked to... we all will. The land's divided between us fairly: *evenly*, in fact, which is *very fair*."

"**And I am not 'weak', son!**" Ma Teng barked. "**We aim to benefit from this in the future!**"

"We *won't*," Ma Chao retorted. "**You've handed yourself to them and us as well, given them control of us! When the Yuans are gone, what else will we have to give to Cao and his emperor???**"

Wei Kang and Cao Cao started to argue their point with Ma Chao; Han Sui turned to his adviser Chenggong Ying and whispered, "This could go one of two ways, I think."

Chenggong Ying nodded and said, "Hopefully ours."

Cao Cao left the meeting and returned to his tent as a man torn by success and ill omens; he knew, as many did, that a reconciled Qiang confederacy with ambition was, perhaps, more dangerous than a divided one was harmful in terms of collateral damage from their feuding.

"I came here to begin to avenge Fu Xie and finish what Huangfu Song started," Cao Cao said as he sat at his temporary desk and clutched his aching head. "Instead I am probably going to be remembered as another bumbling Song Nie that tried to smother them with kindness and doomed the region in the process."

The advisers were silent.

"...I need some good news, gentlemen... *proper* good news," Cao Cao muttered.

"Yuan Shao is probably going to be dead within weeks... maybe days," Cheng Yu replied gruffly. "Will that do...?"

Cao Cao looked up, smiled strangely and said, "That... that should be good, shouldn't it..."

"Of *course* it's *good*!" Xu Yòu snapped. "Once he's dead, all our problems are over and done with! Perhaps I might get my poor wife back now, if you'd care to march on Yè as soon as it's confirmed: she's been locked up for 'embezzlement' and a host of other nonsense for too long as it is!"

Cao Cao was not listening to his rambling friend; he was lost in thought. Yuan Shao had been his wealthier, more influential friend since childhood, and now he was dying as a man broken by Cao himself. Cao Cao did not know what to think: like the outcome of the talks between the Qiang, there was no telling what the death of such a powerful figure might lead to in the future.

More months passed: Yuan Shao held on for more than the weeks that Cheng Yu had predicted, but when he reached the first anniversary of his defeat at Cangting, his condition deteriorated rapidly. Shao's eyesight started to fail, and his awareness of his surroundings varied from day to day: his physicians guessed the worst, but Lady Liu had seized control of her husband's affairs and ensured that potential opponents to her plans would not be present at the end.

"Where... where are my sons...?" the bedridden Yuan Shao asked as he had done for days on end: he was only in his mid-forties, but his grey-haired, wrinkled face could have fooled many into thinking that he was much older.

"Your heir is in Qing Province, in his capital, Linzi City," Lady Liu replied icily.

"S'not... his... it's *mine*!" Yuan Shao mumbled. "He... s'in *Qing*...?"

"Yes, and *why*...?" Yuan Shao's uncle Yuan Cheng asked angrily. "Shouldn't he be *here*, now...? Why is he not here???"

"You ask me, as though I am somehow responsible," Lady Liu giggled. "Do I tell Yuan Tan what to do...? He is not my son, and he has always made that clear."

"My s-son...!" Yuan Shao said as he groped at the empty air in front of his mortified third son, Yuan Shang. "S-Shang... T-Tan... Xi... *M-Mai*...!"

Lady Liu shivered at the sound of the fourth name, that of Yuan

Mai, who was not present and never would be.

"I... I am here, Father," Yuan Shang said as he knelt by his father.

"So... so handsome, an' strong, Shang...!" Yuan Shao said. "Every... every b-bit... my *son*."

Yuan Cheng looked at the advisers Pang Ji and Shen Pei and asked, "Usually, it's you two and Guo Tu."

"Mister Guo Tu is in Qing, visiting Yuan Tan and helping him to manage civil affairs at Mister Xin Ping's request, since Tan lacks the ability to do it himself," Lady Liu said before either of Yuan Shao's advisers could reply.

"...I sense some inappropriate motivations," Yuan Cheng replied. "Woman, you are plotting in the presence of your sick husband!"

"What 'plot'?" Lady Liu scoffed. "Look at my lord and husband: see what a fatherly smile he has – has always had – for my Shang...!"

Yuan Cheng looked at his dying nephew, who was fawning on Yuan Shang as Lady Liu suggested; he turned to face Lady Liu again and said, "Favourites are one thing, but this is to decide the heir to the clan! I've lived through the horrors of the fighting between Shao and Shu already, and do not desire to see my nephew's boys torn apart by the same! Tan is the eldest, and the eldest is the heir!"

"It... doesn't necessarily have to be," Pang Ji suggested.

"*Ayah*... here he is, the second-rate Jian Shuo!" Yuan Cheng heckled. "You-!"

"Don't compare me to that wretched eunuch!" Pang Ji retorted. "And this isn't at all like the Han succession issue anyway! Lord Yuan was the *illegitimate* – forgive for saying so, but he *was* – eldest son of a younger brother of the then-chief, and he only ascended to the chieftainship because your eldest brother adopted him, else Yuan Shu – who *was* legitimate, born to a wife and not a maid – might have inherited the mantle, Heaven help us! Lord Yuan wrestled with the enormity of it for his entire life, and it impacts on his-!"

"All of my nephew's children are legitimate," Yuan Cheng noted. "In that case, gentlemen, it is a matter of who is oldest, in order to avoid problems."

"Oldest, *maybe*... or who is most competent," Shen Pei said. "Yuan Tan is, as Lord Yuan has said often enough, aggressive and unstatesmanlike, while Yuan Xi is too meek; Yuan Shang has long been said to have qualities that would be needed to maintain the strength of the Yuan clan, and as Mister Pang has indirectly said, sometimes the first choice is not always the best: what would Yuan Shu have done had he been chieftain, other than drive the entire clan to ruin instead of his own branch alone...?"

Yuan Cheng pondered the point silently as he stared at Yuan Shao and Yuan Shang.

"...See sense, Elder Yuan!" Pang Ji implored. "Tan is too violent, and Xi too quick to yield: we need balance, or the Yuan clan will not survive!"

"...You ask that I risk the destabilisation of the clan domains and the division of the clan itself for a second time in a decade," Yuan Cheng protested. "You think that Tan is going to accept his brother usurping his chieftainship...? You think that-?"

"**Tan!**"

All eyes turned to Yuan Shao, who was grasping at empty air once again while Yuan Shang backed away.

"Tan, where are you???" Yuan Shao cried. "**Tan'er!**"

"...It will not be long now," Yuan Cheng supposed. "What happens then is up to you, it seems, more than me, despite my nephew inviting me here to help him make decisions. Whatever you decide, I'll abide by it, for I feel that I have little choice... but Heaven forgive you all if you are wrong."

Lady Liu scoffed and walked to her husband's side.

"Where... are my other sons...?" Yuan Shao croaked. "Tan... Xi...!"

"I am here, my husband," Lady Liu whispered. "And so is my Shang... the only son you need."

Yuan Shao passed away 'without ever giving any clear indication of who he intended as his heir'. The first actions of Yuan Shao's widow, Lady Liu, were a chilling indication of what might unfold in the years to come: Yuan Shang, Lady Liu's daughter-in-law Lady Zhen and the household staff watched with horror as Lady Liu set about murdering and disfiguring every one of Shao's five beautiful young consorts, saying afterward that "They will not appeal to him in the afterlife now". Lady Liu's son, Yuan Shang, was quickly announced as the heir to the Yuan clan chieftainship, and their new allies – who included and were led by Pang Ji and Shen Pei – began immediate preparations for military reprisals by, at the very least, the eldest of Yuan Shao's sons, Yuan Tan. A new age of Han Dynasty politics was about to begin, one where a new generation of feuding Yuan brothers would play a major role, and the Imperial court – along with the rest of Han Dynasty China - watched with interest and growing discomfort.

****

ACT II: THE SIEGE OF LI COUNTY

15

The death of Yuan Shao – the once-powerful chieftain of the Yuan clan of Ru County – did not come as an enormous surprise, but it was still a sobering announcement. The Yuans had been a near-constant force in Han Dynasty politics over the centuries, with at least one of them occupying a role at the top of the Imperial court; Shao's father and uncles had been no different, with one of them even taking up the role of 'Grand Tutor' and playing a role in the 'moral upbringing' of Emperor Xian's predecessor, Emperor Ling. But Yuan Shao had been tainted: his mother was a maid, and his inheritance of the clan from his adoptive father – who was, in fact, his biological uncle – was always going to come back to haunt him. It led to a seven-year-long feud with his younger, 'legitimate' brother, Yuan Shu, a war that tore the east of the empire apart at a time when the attentions of the warlord nobles should have been focussed on the abduction in all but name of Emperor Xian by Dong Zhuo, a tyrant Chancellor of State that had already added regicide of Xian's brother to his already-startling list of atrocities. Those warlords – including Yuan Shao – built independent 'states' out of the provinces that they acquired during their fighting, and none was more successful than Shao, who governed four provinces – a quarter of the empire – at the end of his many campaigns.

The Yuan feud ended in a changed nation: Emperor Xian had escaped Dong Zhuo's enemies and returned to the ruins of his looted capital Luoyang with the decimated remnants of the court, wherein the governor of nearby Yan Province, Cao Cao, had given the sovereign shelter and a new capital while the extensive damage done by Dong Zhuo was undone. Cao Cao was transformed from a vassal-governor serving Yuan Shao into the highest statesman in the land, and that divided the former friends in Yuan's eyes. Yuan Shu had died a pretender and traitor after trying to seize the throne, so Yuan Shao had much to do to repair his clan's reputation and unseat his friend-turned-rival: he decided to support an edict of dubious origins that called for the death of Cao Cao, and that choice brought the two into conflict at the strategic positions around Guandu, a settlement on the road to the new capital Xuchang. The rout that followed left jaws slackened: Yuan Shao, whose army, officers and counsel outnumbered Cao Cao's considerably, suffered due to the lack of cohesion amongst his high-ranking officials. A succession of in-fighting, high-profile defections and intelligence leaks led to the destruction of his supply depots and a humiliating retreat; Cao Cao followed the victory with a second rout at Cangting, chasing Yuan back to his own domains and leaving him a sick, bitter man. His fortune halved, his lands beset by insurrections and his name tarnished, Yuan Shao was now gone, and his last acts – acts that he could not now offset – would ensure that future historians would look at him with disbelief and disdain. Cao Cao, by contrast, had begun his career with a series of infamous mistakes, but now he was an unrivalled political force that could set his sights on claiming Yuan Shao's vast territory for the Han or for himself.

"Today is a day that divides me," Cao Cao said to his audience of loyal courtiers. "We're gathered here in my meeting hall to discuss the death of an old friend of mine and celebrate it, and yet-"

"There is no 'yet' or 'but', Mengde," Cao's lifelong friend Xu Yòu interrupted. "Yuan Shao is dead, and that's a good thing. He can't try and kill either of us anymore."

"Do you have any idea how rude you are?" the adviser Cheng Yu asked. "You sit there scoffing dumplings, drinking tea and casually interrupting your lord and master when-!"

"It's... alright, Mister Cheng," Cao Cao insisted. "Ziyuan feels at ease, which is a truly gratifying thing for me. It would be nice if others, like Ying Shao, might one day come here from the north and feel as much at ease in my presence as Ziyuan."

"So what now, Cousin Mengde...?" Xiahou Dun asked. "If Yuan's dead, does that mean that we're going to invade Ji Province?"

"Of *course we are*," Xu Yòu said as he took a bite from a steamed dumpling. "The Yuans have to be completely eradicated."

"...I *didn't ask you*," Xiahou Dun growled.

"Nonetheless, Yuanrang, the answer was correct in its purpose if not its phrasing or tone," Cao Cao said. "We must now start to whittle away at the Yuan brothers before they... well, that's something else I don't quite understand. I hear, gentlemen, that they put on a front of being united but that there is deep division born of the distribution of Benchu's estate."

"Quite so," Xun Wenruo replied. "There are a number of 'elements' emerging, and if your head is fine I shall go through them, though they risk giving headaches to the rest of us."

"Go ahead!" Cao Cao chuckled.

"...Yuan Shao's death should have meant that Yuan Tan – his heir – became the new chieftain, but that is not what has happened," Xun Wenruo continued. "Instead, Yuan Shang – his third son – is now the heir, ruling from Yè City in Ji Province, and Yuan Tan is in Qing Province, serving as its Governor. Gao Gan – Yuan Shao's nephew by marriage – is Governor of Bing Province, and Yuan Xi – Yuan Shao's second son – is Governor of Yòu Province."

"Oh...? Yuan Xi, and not Liu Hè...?" Cao Cao exclaimed.

"We can assume that Yuan Shao double-crossed Liu Hè after all," Xun Wenruo said. "There's no word about him, so-"

"Yuan wanted to be emperor," Xu Yòu interrupted. "He never said it outright, but it was obvious... he probably killed Liu Hè quietly."

"...I shall continue," Xun Wenruo said tonelessly. "The provinces divided amongst the sons and nephew, that should have been it, with Yuan Tan as heir, but as I have already said, Shang is nominated as heir... and a strange rumour is emerging that Yuan Tan was posthumously adopted by Yuan Ji, Shao's elder brother."

"...The one that served as Minister Coachman...?" Cao Cao recalled.

"Strange... strange in every sense; Benchu never awarded his late brother a son before, so why would he do so in his will...? Why 'give away' Tan but not Xi if he intended Shang as his heir...? ...I sense intriguing... I sense the meddling efforts of Lady Liu. Tan and Xi are not her children: only Shang is hers."

"I agree," Guo Jia said. "Either Shao wanted to follow natural order and choose Tan, and Lady Liu ruined it with this half-formed scheme, or Shao wanted Xi for his heir – and the adoption *was* his work – but Lady Liu had added to it to favour her own son, or

Shao wanted Shang but died before he could announce a proper method of disinheriting Xi, which I consider unlikely. Regardless of the facts of it, the actual outcome could not have been reached by Lady Liu alone; Yuan Cheng – Shao's uncle – and the advisers have gone along with it."

"I can see why," Cao Cao admitted. "Yuan Tan's administration of Qing Province is embarrassing: Ying Shao's replies to me were deliberately toneless, but they conveyed a concern for Qing nonetheless, him being the former Administrator of Mount Tai. Kong Rong was never going to pacify the place, but he knew who to appoint in key civil roles: Tan's put corrupt, violent men in the jobs that do nothing but bully and steal from the people. He might as well tender the seal to Zang Ba if he's going to carry on like that. Who'd want him governing the entire northeast...?"

"But Yuan Xi is a different kind altogether," Xun Wenruo said. "Yuan Shang is arrogant because he has been so pampered; Xi is a philanthropist and deep thinker, much like Shao used to be as a young man. I wonder if Shao wanted Xi in order to take the region in a new direction..."

"...We'll never know," Cao Cao replied. "The main fact is that Shang is our primary enemy, not Tan: that is good, because Yuan Tan is a competent general, and at present, the Yuans' military ability is our concern, not their adeptness at running a state. The secondary fact is that such a contentious outcome to the succession debate gives us options for sowing discord and dividing the Yuans of they do not willingly divide themselves... that hastens their defeat by years."

"I might even live to see it!" Guo Jia joked.

"Flippancy of the worst kind!" Chen Qun heckled. "Guo Jia, you disgrace your profession with your lack of-!"

"Enough," Cao Cao ordered. "What is our schedule...?"

"We should be looking to march against the Yuans within the next two to three months," Guo Jia suggested. "We'll test their unity and plan from there."

"And how will we attack...?" Cao Cao asked.

"...My first thought is that we need to appoint a talented man as Magistrate of Chang'an," Guo Jia replied.

"What's that got to do with fighting the Yuans...?" Xiahou Dun asked bemusedly.

"...Zhong Yao," Cao Cao said. "He did the job before, after all."

"What's that got to do with fighting the Yuans???" Xiahou Dun asked again.

"Everything," Cao Cao replied. "We cannot fight the quarter-of-a-million without additional muscle that only the Qiang can provide. I control Han Sui and Ma Teng now, but only just: Zhong Yao will aid Wei Kang's efforts to liaise with the Qiang confederacies and secure more military support for us."

"Why not go to Huchuquan of the Southern Xiongnu...?" Xu Yòu asked. "They already have an alliance with the Han: why do business with the Qiang and risk owing them for your success...?"

"Firstly, Huchuquan's heir, Liu Bao... has, in conjunction with Dong Zhuo and Wang Yun, committed a wrong that I intend to put right when I can spare the funds and the time," Cao Cao replied. "I will obviously go to him, but not for all of the help that I need."

"...Dong Zhuo... and *Wang Yun*...?" Xun Wenruo murmured. "But...

but Wang Yun successfully plotted to *murder Dong Zhuo*! When did they ever collaborate? And when did either of them ever collaborate with Liu Bao...?"

"They 'collaborated', as you put it, unintentionally and unconsciously," Cao Cao replied. "It will become clear when the time is right, although I would be more impressed if you figured it out for yourself."

"See it as a fun distraction, Wenruo," Guo Jia chuckled.

"Secondly, the Xiongnu are divided once again, and it is the row over who represents the Han – the Yuans or me – that is to blame," Cao Cao continued. "We have evidence that some tribes favour Gao Gan – who has treated them well – and will follow the Yuans, while others will aid us. With that being the case, we must enlist the aid of the submitted Qiang tribes."

"...Such an age," Chen Qun sighed.

The Imperial court was convened in order for Cao Cao to explain his next actions and issue new appointments; Emperor Xian stifled a scowl as Cao Cao said, "All the enemies of the Han are losing their power and influence; the once-mighty Yuan clan of Ru County, once comprised entirely of noble, loyal followers has recently become tainted, but the death of Yuan Shao has ensured that rebellious branch of the clan will not harm the state for much longer. In addition, the recent agreement with the Qiang tribes of Liang Province gives us access to their finest warriors, meaning that we can now rely upon them as we do the Southern Xiongnu, and with little more than tolerance given in return."

"That is quite an achievement, Mister Cao," Emperor Xian said. "You will be using the Qiang to bring an expedient end to the campaign in the northeast, then...?"

"I will, Your Majesty," Cao Cao replied. "I should like to place a reliable man in Chang'an to liaise with them: I am told that Zhong Yao is that man, and would like to suggest that he be reinstated in his former role."

"...We agree," Emperor Xian said. "It will be so."

Cao Cao turned to the audience and said, "Zhong Yao: you are hereby appointed as Grand Magistrate of Chang'an."

Zhong Yao kowtowed silently.

"We must hurry and bring the threat of the Yuan brothers and their Wuhuan allies to an end," Cao Cao continued. "We will all play our part in this important campaign: when it is over, the northeast will be peaceful at last, and we can turn our attentions to others that defy the will of Heaven."

The ambassador of the Jiangdong region, Zhang Hong, asked, "Who are these 'defiant ones' considered to be, Excellency...?"

Cao Cao smiled and said, "Any who contest the will of Heaven: Zhang Lu, for one, Liu Biao another. Other men are less discernible, but it is their obligation now, not mine, to make their intent clear to the court... your lord Sun Quan included."

Zhang Hong lowered his gaze and hummed thoughtfully.

"Now," Cao Cao said, "we shall move on to other matters..."

****

16

The newly-reappointed Magistrate of Chang'an, Zhong Yao, held a banquet before his departure from Xuchang and invited his fellow officials – including Xun Wenruo, Xun Gongda, Liu Yè, Liu Xun, Kong Rong, Wang Lang and Yang Biao – to attend.

"Are you truly at ease with the appointment, Yuanchang…?" Kong Rong asked of the host, who was visibly haunted.

"…I am quiet for different reasons to those that you assume," Zhong Yao replied. "I am not afraid of the Qiang or the challenges ahead; when I think of Chang'an, I think of Wang Yun executing my tutor and friend Cai Yong for 'mourning Dong Zhuo', of Dong Zhuo torturing and killing my friends until Wang Yun and Lü Bu killed *him*, of the endless raids and sieges, of Li Jue and Guo Si's costly 'civil war' on the streets of that poor city, and, most of all, the long journey to Luoyang that followed that 'war'… I lost family and friends, men that I looked up to such as Shisun Rui, and I saw things that still haunt my rest. But I should not be speaking of these things now, gentlemen: I am about to embark on a mission to bring greater stability to the Empire."

"You cannot be blamed for looking back at that time," Yang Biao said. "I saw what you saw, and I cannot forget either. I am so glad that my son survived by being elsewhere."

Wang Lang looked at Yang Biao's thin and frail son, Yang Xiu, and said, "And now, Dezu, you are a man worthy of serving at the highest level as well! Fortune smiles on you."

"Were I a bird, I'd never see the top of Mount Tai," Yang Xiu replied. "Were I a fish, I'd never know the safest depths of the Great River. As a man, I cannot expect greatness either."

"Your education is second-to-none, and I know you to be a gifted fellow," Zhong Yao said. "You'll impress His Excellency, that I'm certain of. I'd gladly refer you, but my word isn't needed."

"I do not deserve such praise, Mister Zhong," Yang Xiu replied. "What have I endured…?"

"…*Aiee*… Chang'an *does* haunt me, and more than I'd admitted," Yang Biao realised. "Of all the horrors, I still rue the loss of Cai Yong, even more so now that we've lost Zhao Qi."

"I'm glad that I got the chance to see him in his last years," Wang Lang said. "Even at an age over ninety, he was possessed of all of his wits! He leaves a legacy, though – his 'Commentaries on Mencius' – which is more than we can say about poor Cai Yong. Why did Heaven hate him so…?"

"He saved so much with his decision to carve major works into stone," Xun Gongda noted. "What a poor reward he suffered, that great man, for his-"

"That, perhaps, was what Lord Cao meant!" Xun Wenruo gasped. "His riddle… a wrong shared by Dong Zhuo, Wang Yun and Liu Bao! …Or at least, the first two… how did Liu Bao harm Cai Yong?"

"…It is said that Liu Bao of the Southern Xiongnu operated around Chang'an in the time after Yi Governor Liu Yan's treacherous attack on the city alongside the Qiang," Wang Lang prompted.

"We know of it, of course," Yang Biao sighed. "That was another horrible time… surrounded by baying tribesmen that were led by the son of a trusted governor and relative of the Son of Heaven, and our 'saviours' – those that we looked to for our rescue – were Li Jue and Guo Si! And yes, on top of that, the Xiongnu rebels started to cross over from Bing Province to raid villages... and when various good-hearted men went looking for Cai Yong's family in later times, survivors of the attacks said that the Cais were mostly butchered, but that his eldest daughter might have been taken by a chieftain as a consort... that chieftain might well have been Liu Bao."

"...So what does Lord Cao intend...?" Xun Wenruo murmured.

"That's a matter for Lord Cao, Uncle," Xun Gongda replied quietly.

"Chang'an must be restored to its former glory," Zhong Yao declared. "My first objectives must include repairing all of the damage – physical and emotional – that was done by Dong Zhuo, Li Jue, Guo Si, Liu Yan, the Qiang and yes, Wang Yun, as good as his intentions were. I shall look forward to the responsibility."

"I wish that Mengde would allow me to go back to Lujiang and do something about the Sun clan that stole it from me," Liu Xun said. "I'm rotting in a minor role: I was Administrator of Lujiang!"

"At Yuan Shu's command," Zhong Yao retorted.

"And Yuan Shu was a heretic, as much as it pains me to say it," Yang Biao said.

"You *should* be pained," Liu Xun chortled; he then pointed at Yang Xiu and added, "Isn't your son carrying Yuan blood in his veins, Yang Biao...? Isn't it the case that the Yuan brothers are cousins of his, their mother being the sister of Shao and Shu...? You tacitly accuse me of being too closely allied to a heretic when-!"

"**Don't start arguments, Liu Xun!**" Zhong Yao barked.

"You're little better, Mister Zhong," Liu Xun scoffed. "Where's your nephew Guo Yuan now...? Isn't Guo Yuan one of Gao Gan's generals...? Isn't Gao Gan the nephew of Yuan Shao and cousin to the renegade Yuan brothers ...?"

Zhong Yao scowled angrily and said, "Watch your tongue, Liu Xun! In blood matters, one is not able to choose! Yes, I have to stomach Gao Gan being my nephew's lord, but that does not mean I agree with him at all! You're distantly related to Liu Bei, Liu Biao and Liu Yan, but do you agree with their actions...?"

"...No, I don't," Liu Xun conceded. "But I was heckled!"

"No, Mister Liu, you were questioned on questionable thinking," Yang Biao said. "You and Mister Wang Lang have unfinished business with the Sun clan: you were chased out of Lujiang, and Mister Wang out of Kuaiji. I hope that His Excellency gives both of you a chance to return to Yang Province and take those places back for the Han, so that you may both feel at ease. But it must remain to be said that Yuan Shu – who yes, it's true, was my brother-in-law – was a wretch and a heretic that claimed to be an emperor, and he died a deservedly poor death. You and I both benefit from the kind rule of His Majesty and Excellency Cao, Mister Liu Xun, for other, less tolerant rulers might have exterminated those connected to such a man, and we'd neither of us – or Mister Yuan Huan – be alive today."

"...That is true," Liu Xun admitted. "It is also true that I was never made the Administrator by the current government. But I did a good job and could do so again, gentlemen, if only Cao Mengde would give me the chance!"

"Perhaps he will, Mister Liu Xun," Liu Yè said dryly.

"...It was not so long ago that I was your lord," Liu Xun retorted.

"That's true," Liu Yè replied. "This is a time of great upheaval."

Xun Wenruo, Xun Gongda and many others smiled and enjoyed Liu Ye's irreverent conversation with his former master.

"...I hope that I can truly make a difference," Zhong Yao said. "I truly do, gentlemen... I truly hope that His Excellency was right to place such faith in me."

"He was and is," Xun Wenruo insisted. "You'll be fine."

Xun Wenruo reported the events at Zhong Yao's banquet to Cao Cao a day later.

"...He is the right man, Wenruo, partly because he does not believe himself to be," Cao Cao decided. "Arrogance is costly when dealing with the Qiang."

"All of the men that are now in that region are the right men," Xun Wenruo said.

"Yes... so as soon as Zhong Yao has reached Chang'an, all will be ready," Cao Cao replied. "And then I march to Li County: the Yuans have had enough time to mourn their father. And if they do not yield to the Han, Wenruo, they will shortly join him in the netherworld, for I am tired of the circle of chaos. If it takes their shed blood to break the circle, then so be it."

"...And what of Liu Xun's behaviour...?" Xun Wenruo asked.

"That fool can talk all he wants, I'd never send him back to Lujiang," Cao Cao replied. "I'm trying to get the Suns to show greater deference, but the end of the rebellion against Sun Quan by whatever-his-name-was in Lujiang is certainly a setback... we'll see how Sun responds to my request for a hostage. But Liu Xun can wait for another role like that for as long as he likes, for he won't get one... Liu Yè, however, should be close at all times, for he is obviously clever and sensible. Though it might seem to be an ill-fitting clerical role, I will appoint him as my registrar: it won't stop him serving as an adviser, will it, since most posts are flexible when it comes to actual responsibility."

"And the 'conflicting interests' that some officials have...?" Xun Wenruo asked.

"Your brother still serves the Yuans," Cao Cao replied. "Yuan Tan was, at one point, like a son to me. My niece and son are married to members of the Sun clan. The Son of Heaven has relatives that are married to Xiongnu and Wuhuan chiefs. This is a war whose outcome will be decided by loyalties, not relations, and those men know that just as well as we do. This will test us... but for peace, it's worth it."

✳✳✳✳✳✳✳✳✳✳✳✳

17

"...I wonder what he'll do when the Yuans are defeated."

Emperor Xian asked the question with some sense that the answer could not be favourable; the only person present to hear him – Empress Fu – sighed in response.
"They all call barbarians to aid them, and they promise bits of the empire to each other and the savages in exchange for allegiances in a war for control of what is clearly not theirs," Emperor Xian continued. "Everywhere I look, there are...! ...*Aiee*. What's the point of my repetitive lamentations...?"
"They offer you an opportunity to expel pent up rage, Majesty," Empress Fu replied.
"More than that, they... they remind me that I have you," Emperor Xian said. "They have taken so many things from me – dignity, control, land, consorts, unborn children – but I still have you. I will always have *you*."
"I hope so," Empress Fu replied.
"I will," Emperor Xian insisted. "I will always have you, and you are the only person that understands, that I can trust... none of these eunuchs and maids that I am surrounded by, none of the officials... none of them I trust. I only trust you."
Empress Fu smiled meekly.
"But all the same, I... I waste breath talking," Emperor Xian continued. "Yes, I... I 'need' to speak my mind, but it solves nothing. In the end, it is Heaven's will that we are all bound to, and... and that is that."
Empress Fu smiled sadly and replied, "Indeed."
"Yes, it is a simple case of 'that is that'," Emperor Xian continued. "The Yuans, they'll lose, and... and I... *aiee*."

Emperor Xian was at a loss for further words; he lowered his head and sighed while his empress looked on with equal powerlessness.

****

18

The new lord of the northeast, Yuan Shang, was desperate to keep what had been unexpectedly given to him; he summoned officials one by one in an effort to coax declarations of loyalty from them, starting with the scholar Cui Yan. The teenaged chieftain was always accompanied by his uncle Yuan Cheng, his mother, Lady Liu – who was increasingly adopting the mannerisms of an imperial Dowager – and his advisers, Pang Ji and Shen Pei.

"You were my father's conscience at times," Yuan Shang said. "Your great intellect and understanding of the nature of people would be invaluable to me."

"I serve the Yuan clan," Cui Yan retorted. "At present, the-"

"My son is the chieftain of the clan," Lady Liu said menacingly. "By refusing to pledge allegiance to him, you betray your covenant with the Yuan clan!"

"...If I may," Cui Yan continued. "I did not ally with Yuan Shao because I valued his feud with Yuan Shu in any way. If I were now to serve any one of the divided sons of my late lord, I would be advocating an avoidable war between them."

"You dare to compare Lord Yuan Shang's predicament with that old matter...?" Shen Pei heckled. "You're a pedant and a fool!"

"He's neither, which is why I want his service," Yuan Shang said. "I implore you, Mister Cui: it is only by the likes of your good self joining my cause that we can hope to avoid an argument like that between my uncle and my father! My brother Xi has distanced himself, and apart from repeated, ignored requests to send his wife Lady Zhen to Yòu Province, he does not make trouble; my older brother, Tan, is another matter. He's been camped outside this city for weeks now, claiming that the will left by my father is fraudulent, that his adoption to my late elder uncle was contrived by schemers, and that he is the rightful heir to the clan chieftainship and 'General of Chariots and Cavalry', a title awarded by Cao Cao as a slight! He has lost all sense of reality!"

"I am aware of it all," Cui Yan replied.

"...So you sympathise with my brother's view, then?" Yuan Shang asked angrily.

"I want to remain neutral and serve the Yuan clan – in its entirety – when the dispute is resolved," Cui Yan replied. "If I agreed with your elder brother, I would have joined him when I was asked. I did not. I refuse to serve any of you until you-"

"**Lock him up!**" Pang Ji cried.

"The pedant dares to oppose his lord's will!" Shen Pei heckled. "Let him rot in prison like Tian Feng before him!"

"Tian Feng...?" Cui Yan chortled. "You accuse me of making ill-judged comparisons, Shen, and then compare me to Tian Feng...?"

"**Defiance is defiance!**" Lady Liu snapped. "**If you will not serve my son, then you will serve nobody! GUARDS!**"

"You have no authority to call guards!" Cui Yan protested.

"Then I shall do it," Yuan Shang said. "**GUARDS!**"

"**Lord Yuan Shang, see sense!**" Cui Yan pleaded as two soldiers took hold of his arms and started to lead him away. "**I am trying to reunite you and your brothers! This is not what your father wanted!**"

"If you won't serve me, who will you serve?" Yuan Shang retorted. "My younger brother Xi...? *Cao Cao...?*"

"**Ayah! My words fall on deaf ears!**" Cui Yan cried. "**Heaven, open their ears and minds to good sense before the Yuans are destroyed!**"

"**Silence!**" Lady Liu shrieked. "**You deserve death!**"

"He'll stay in prison until he changes his mind," Yuan Shang insisted. "With so many turned from us, we need him."

"...You're right, my son," Lady Liu said.

"We should have arrested the others when we had the chance," Pang Ji grumbled. "Guo Tu and Xin Ping, Xin Pi, Xun Chen... won't the last of those men go and join his brother in Xuchang now...?"

"We... we must win minds and hearts," Yuan Shang replied. "For my leadership to work, we must win minds and hearts. Mister Cui was vital to Father's attempts to quell uprisings and rebellions, so we must show him that we want his help by continuing to follow his advice and regularly allowing him to see that we are doing so. Now who is next...?"

"Secretary Chen Lin 'is ill'," Shen Pei replied. "I suggest that the next man is Yin Kui, who would be an asset if he will join us."

"A pity about Mister Chen Lin; he is a marvel with the pen that could inspire others to join our cause," Yuan Shang said. "I will forget about him for now, though: please fetch Mister Yin."

"Straight away," Shen Pei replied.

"...I wonder how long we have," Yuan Shang said as he watched Shen Pei's retreat.

"Until what...?" Lady Liu asked.

"Until Cao Cao makes his move," Yuan Shang replied. "It will be soon... that I am sure of."

****

19

The Yuan clan's ancestral home, Ru County in Yu Province, was no longer under their control, and had not been since the death of the would-be-emperor Yuan Shu. The vast majority of Yu Province had been under the control of Cao Cao's Han government since Liu Bei's retreat and the defeat of the bandit king Gong Du, but Runan Prefecture was still suffering small, isolated uprisings by the small numbers of Yellow Turban acolytes that had not abandoned their ways. The army of the 'Way of Peace' cult had once been numbered in the hundreds of thousands, but they were no less dangerous for having been reduced to a few thousands; the nation was always one famine or corrupt official away from another insurrection, and Excellency of Works Cao Cao was determined that such an event was not guided by a group that was committed to the downfall of the empire. Cao's cousin Cao Ren was usually tasked with defending Xuchang when the main army was on campaign, but while preparations continued for a war with Yuan Shao's sons, Ren was given instructions to do what he could to purge the remaining Yellow Turbans from Runan.

"Will there ever be a day when these people are not a problem...?" Cao Ren asked of his brother Chun as they rode toward a besieged village at the head of a small army.

"Why do you ask me...?" Cao Chun retorted.

"You're the smart one," Cao Ren replied. "You're always getting praised by the scholars and the officials for your brains."

"'Always'...? ...Hardly," Cao Chun said. "I get the odd compliment, perhaps, but I'm part of the background generally: I'm ordinary."

"You are being dishonestly humble," Cao Ren chuckled. "You know you're clever, Zihe, and you can answer my question."

"...The Yellow Turbans are a product of their time," Cao Chun said. "They arose from the cauldron of the disaffected masses at a time when the nation was ruled by a monarch whose temple name effectively means that he was useless; corruption was the system, the eunuchs were the most powerful 'men', and the people huddled and starved while His Majesty went hunting and collected women. An army that lacked the basic equipment – including, in many cases, clothes or weapons – was destroyed by the Xianbei, and an Empress was branded as a witch instead of the corrupt officials being purged. And that's all after the 'Partisan Crisis', Dou Wu's failed rebellion, and Cai Yong petitioning to have our culture carved in stone to save it from perversion by the 'Ten', who could slander and topple princes despite being less than men... a madman like Zhang Jue could make sense in a world like that."

"...And now...?" Cao Ren asked.

"Now, Zixiao, they are irrelevant," Cao Chun replied. "The people no longer see the 'Way of Peace' as being an answer to an exigent question. 'Prosperous all', when they are now raiding villages to sustain themselves...? The 'Yellow Sky' has been and gone, and the blue sky returned: if the Han survived Dong Zhuo abducting the court and that same court living in the wilderness for a year, what can topple it now...? With Mengde as His Majesty's guardian, stability has returned: the *tuntian* system has generated food and reversed the famine, and even the Qiang are knelt before the court. Good officials have replaced the corrupt ones: only the decadent Yuans remain an obstacle to the much-needed change, and their days are numbered. When people see the Yellow Turbans now, they do not cheer and search for yellow cloth to tie their own hair: they groan and heckle and prepare to defend their village or city from attack. The cultists have been exposed as one of the problems, not a solution, and with the loss of the people's support, we'll see them disappear in three years or less."

"...I'm not as smart as you, Zihe," Cao Ren admitted. "You can talk to clever men as easily as you command soldiers and horses: and on the subject of your military talent, I should say that your cavalry are very impressive."

"Being discerning is the key," Cao Chun replied. "Let's see how the Yellow Turbans like my trained horsemen!"

Cao Ren's militia found the Yellow Turbans as they retreated from their last target with packsaddles and sacks that were filled with stolen food. Cao Chun led his elite riders in an immediate assault on the leaders of the cultists; the Yellow Turbans' horses were laden with goods, so the entire fighting force was on foot and put at an immediate disadvantage.

"PROTECT THE FOOD!" the cultists' leader ordered. **"WE NEED THIS FOOD!"**

The Yellow Turbans were – in addition to being demoralised, surprised and on a forced defensive – poorly armed: their weapons were mostly farm tools and looted army weaponry that was in a very bad condition, and most were wearing little or no armour. Cao Ren's men were, by contrast, nourished, well-equipped and enjoying high morale from previous victories against Liu Bei and Gong Du. Cao Chun's cavalry tore into the enemy 'infantry' with painful ease, and the result was a swift rout; the Yellow Turbans scattered, their leaders were killed and their spoils were collected with minimal loss.

"As easy as taking something from a sack!" Cao Chun said cheerfully. **"I look forward to doing the same to the Yuans!"**

Some of Cao Ren's soldiers were opening the requisitioned packsaddles to steal grain: Cao Chun rode to one group of would-be-thieves and said, **"No! That is all to be returned to the village! There's ample food in our base camp for you! If I am told that you've disobeyed me, I will request permission to execute you!"**

"And my brother will get that permission from me, as well," Cao Ren said as he rode to his brother's side. **"I am _disgusted_!"**

The guilty soldiers fell to their knees and pleaded for forgiveness.

"...Feel lucky that I am in a forgiving mood," Cao Ren continued. **"Let us go and return this stolen food at once!"**

Cao Ren's men finished gathering up corpses, herding surrendered cultists and loading the rescued supplies onto carts while their leaders watched: this was a victory that would increase Cao Cao's popularity, weaken the Yellow Turbans further and make the people forget about the Yuans that once ruled them.

****

20

Yuan Shao's eldest son, Yuan Tan, fumed at the news that his brother Shang had refused a face-to-face meeting.

"He fears that I will kill him, perhaps...?" Yuan Tan chuckled angrily. "Him and his conniving mother, whose honeyed words and sly meddling have led to this...?"

"He's agreed to see *me*, Lord Yuan," the adviser Guo Tu replied. "I think that we can still pluck victory from this dire situation, but we must be patient."

"I am not known for patience," Yuan Tan growled. "I am known as a man that takes what he wants and wins what he seeks. This intrigue will at least end in the deaths of those two bastards Shen and Pang! And Great Uncle Cheng, well... I don't know what madness possesses him, but he endangers his own life by-!"

"He's in a difficult situation," the adviser Xin Ping protested. "He's surrounded by men that have chosen to serve Yuan Shang: scholars, warriors and advisers alike."

"...Yes... 'warriors' flock to him too... I have lost the confidence of Jiang Yiqu, Ju Hu, Lü Kuang and Lü Xiang, Su Yòu... and their subordinates too," Yuan Tan said sadly. "I thought that I commanded the respect of the fighting men..."

"They respect the late lord's will, and unfortunately for us, the truth has been supressed in favour of this farce that sees Shang made the chieftain," Guo Tu replied. "They will fight for Shang because it appears to be the late lord's will, and for no other reason. If the scheme is ever unpicked, they will flock to *you*."

"...So am I to return to Qing Province, then...?" Yuan Tan asked.

"That might be for the best," the adviser Xin Pi replied. "Qing Province is an unstable place: remaining here would-"

"Brother, you're wrong," Xin Ping said. "Lord Yuan must stay and continue to pressure the Yè court with his presence. Wang Xiu and Guan Tong are managing in Qing Province well enough."

Yuan Tan grunted irritably, turned to Guo Tu and said, "Go and speak to my brother. Make him understand that we're under threat of invasion by Cao Cao, that the Black Mountain Bandits are endangering Bing Province again, and that the Wuhuan only respect strength. He'll understand what I'm saying."

Guo Tu bowed humbly and replied, "I'm sure that he will."

Yuan Shang received Guo Tu at the gates of Yè City with as much false warmth as he could muster; Shen Pei and Pang Ji glared at their former colleague with expressions that did nothing to hide their distrust. Yuan Shang and his counsel then invited Guo Tu to Shang's audience hall for a private meeting that, it was hoped, would end with a promise to obtain Yuan Tan's submission.

"I am not the villain that some would portray," Yuan Shang insisted. "I know only this, Mister Guo: when Father neared his end, he would reach out and cry out, and it was my name that passed his lips most often. When the end came, my elder brother was in Qing, where his inability to govern is infamous; the scholar Ying Shao, whose roles included Administrator of Mount Tai, has remarked at least twice that the place has known no order at all in recent times, and he is a man that ruled the place when it was under attack from Zang Ba and the Yellow Turbans."

"I am aware of the troubles in Qing," Guo Tu replied. "I was supposedly sent to him because he lacked the skill to-"

"'Supposedly'...? You are a slanderer, Guo Tu!" Shen Pei heckled. "You resort to slander when you-!"

"**Can we not-!** ...Can we not do that, please...?" Yuan Shang said wearily. "I stood in the shadows and watched enough civil discussions descend into that during my father's time. And yes, Mister Guo Tu, I am aware that you were sent to Qing to aid my brother's administration because of its infamous incompetence. Before I continue, may I ask if you had any success...?"

"...I must confess that there was bullying, incompetence and corruption," Guo Tu replied. "It was rife; I have gone to great lengths to limit the damage."

"If you can admit that the management – or rather, *mis*management – of Qing Province was not understated, Mister Guo, then why can you not see that the living cause – Yuan Tan – is unfit to be clan chieftain, and that Lord Yuan Shao took steps to prevent a disaster...?" Pang Ji asked.

"...I was not consulted," Guo Tu retorted. "I was sent away, supposedly to aid Lord Yuan Tan, but it happened to coincide with Lord Yuan Shao's death and the sudden announcement that – contrary to all that I had been made privy to – Yuan Shang was now the clan chieftain, that my lord Yuan Tan was adopted off to a dead, powerless sibling of Lord Yuan Shao's, and that a 'fair, even distribution of power' had been 'agreed to'. Imagine my surprise."

"I cannot say why you were not confided in," Yuan Shang replied. "I have always thought of you as a most trusted aide of my father, and I would like for you to be a trusted aide of mine."

"Forgive my bluntness, but I cannot serve any but Lord Yuan Shao's chosen heir," Guo Tu said. "My lord Yuan Tan says that he has no knowledge of a plan to adopt him to Yuan Ji nor of the late lord's plan to step over not just him but Xi as well in favour of-"

"Vile wretch!" Shen Pei cried. "**You defy your lord! You-!**"

"**Don't bother, Shen Pei!**" Guo Tu retorted. "**Shouting me down doesn't qualify as a proper counterpoint! If Lord Yuan Tan did not willingly yield his place as chieftain or hear his fate from Lord Yuan Shao – something that, as heir, he was entitled to – then he is the rightful chieftain! That is all! No amount of intrigue or forged documents will-!**"

"Slanderer!" Pang Ji countered. "**You accuse every man in Yè of colluding to defy Lord Yuan Shao's will! It is you that-!**"

"**ENOUGH!**" Yuan Shang screamed. "**ENOUGH, gentlemen!**"

The bickering advisers fell silent.

"...I can see that I will not be able to reason with you, Mister Guo, and... in a way, I understand," Yuan Shang continued. "It must be difficult for my brother to comprehend... that Father, in the end, lacked the faith in him to bequeath the estate to him. But if he cannot run a single province, how can he run four...? I will not yield to him to rectify this, so we must 'agree to disagree'. The question, Mister Guo, is how we move on from this: are we to fight, or are we to return to our corners and establish a fragile peace until tempers ebb and sense prevails...?"

Guo Tu hummed thoughtfully and said, "You are very eloquent and confident, Lord Yuan Shang... I will not change my stance, but

I can see how you might have appeared to be the right choice to some. My lord insists that he is the rightful heir to the chieftainship, and I will follow him until or unless he changes his mind, which is unlikely. I will not oppose his thoughts: I will, however, suggest that he return to Qing Province, although his concerns about Cao Cao are a secondary reason why he is here."
"Ah, so now we finally worry about something valuable!" Shen Pei replied. "The real threat is Cao Cao, and it is to the south that we should aim our swords. We should be fortifying the northern bank of the Yellow River, particularly the fords."
"My lord wants to protect the Yuan legacy as much as anyone else here," Guo Tu said. "I shall return to him and convey your words."
"...I just want us to be resolved," Yuan Shang insisted.

Yuan Tan scoffed when Guo Tu relayed the meeting with Yuan Shang to him two hours later; he shook his head and said, "If he wants us to be resolved, he should give up what is not his and stop playing along with his mother's scheming."
"I stayed a while and spoke to others," Guo Tu revealed. "Xun Chen has put distance between himself and the capital; some say that he has gone to visit family, others that he is on his way to Yòu Province to serve Yuan Xi or on his way here to serve you. Mister Cui Yan is in prison for 'gross insubordination', your father's secretary, Chen Lin, is 'ill', the scholar Ying Shao has retreated to the countryside to 'work on his literary masterpiece on folk matters', and your great uncle Cheng is retiring from the court citing 'weariness'. Oh, and Gao Fan has been put in charge of the naval defences on the Yellow River near Li County."
"...*Gao Fan*...?" Yuan Tan snickered. "Alright, he's competent, but is that it...? Gao Fan is the Administrator of Wei Prefecture, not an admiral! Is there any half-decent land force in Li County?"
"That was Cui Yan's role until this debacle," Guo Tu replied.
"We should go and reinforce Li County, then," Xin Ping suggested.
"It was my own idea," Yuan Tan insisted. "I won't stay here... not if he's being so confrontational about this and the army's mostly with him. Perhaps a victory over Cao at Li County will make them all see that I am the right man to take us forward, and not that pampered, flowery milksop."
"If we don't do something about Shen Pei and Pang Ji, that'll be hard to realise," Xin Ping suggested. "Those two will twist everything we do into something else."
Guo Tu – who was equally guilty of distorting the words and deeds of rivals – grunted irritably and said, "I must concur, Mister Xin Ping. Those two contrived this current mess with Lady Liu, it seems... Gao Gan, Yuan Xi and Yuan Cheng have not really shown much of a 'collective stand', with the last of those putting deliberate distance between himself and his hankering nephew. Shen and Pang are the masterminds, then, and must be divided or eliminated in order to end this."
"And until an opportunity arises to do that, we'll establish a base in Li County," Yuan Tan replied. "We'll depart at once."

❋❋❋❋❋❋❋❋❋❋❋❋

21

One resident family in Li County was less than glad to see the return of large military forces to the region; they were the Simas of Wen County, who had been forced to leave their home and travel to Li County during the 'Dong Zhuo Crisis'. The patriarch of the clan branch was Sima Fang, but his duties as a Han official left his eldest son, Sima Lang, as the acting head of the family; Lang gathered four of his eight brothers in the living quarters of their home and said, "War comes again to Li County… but there are rumours that Gao Gan is massing troops near the Henei border, which puts Wen County at risk. I am at a loss."

"We should really just sell the residence here and go back to Wen County," the third brother, Sima Fu, replied. "Any battle started by Gao Gan will be in Liang and Bing, not Central Province."

"Perhaps," the second brother, Sima Yi, said thoughtfully. "One way or another, we should be joining Kui, Tong and Min in Wen County. Li County will definitely see war in the next year or so – I predict that we'll see war in a matter of months – and that certainty is our first concern. The fact that Cao Cao has brokered peace between the Qiang tribes suggests that he intends to use them against the Yuan brothers, and the Qiang are not known for their ability to remain within borders. We should return to Wen County but remain ready to leave at a moment's notice."

"Agreed," the sixth brother, Sima Jin, said. "Father has made it clear that we are to avoid the conflict at all costs, and we won't do that by repeatedly coming back here to upkeep a family house."

"I'll manage the sale," Sima Lang promised. "But the closeness of the military men raises one other matter: our own futures."

"I've already said that I have no interest in serving the Han," Sima Yi insisted.

"You don't mean that…?" the fifth brother, Sima Xun, asked.

"*Aiee*… if I didn't mean it, I wouldn't say it!" Sima Yi retorted. "None of us should be serving this corrupt, dying beast!"

"That's tantamount to treason, Zhongda," Sima Fu suggested. "You should be careful who you say such things to."

"You're my brothers, the four of you, so I can speak freely," Sima Yi replied. "And I mean what I say: yes, I know that Cao Cao was recommended for his first serious role by Father, but look at what he has become. 'Crafty Villain' he might or might not be, but his actions in Xu Province point to a very violent man, and if you want 'treason', Shuda, look to his killing a pregnant imperial consort."

Sima Fu frowned and exhaled loudly.

"Nothing that I see right now points to the Han enduring more than… more than I shall say 'twenty years'," Sima Yi continued. "The Yellow Turbans and the armies of bandits were the consequences of the corruption sown by the 'Ten' and those that willingly did business with them: some say that Cao Song, Cao Cao's father, was one of the men that benefitted from the 'Ten' and Empress Dowager Dong dismantling the infrastructure and selling it for cheap profit. The damage was already done by the time that Dong Zhuo came along: he sensed that the Han was doomed but chose to rule from the side as Chancellor of State rather than usurp the throne as Wang Mang did. Cao Cao may or may not be trying to save the Han, but the empire is withered from years of mismanagement and nothing can stop it crumbling altogether, not even a loyal hero."

"You are unduly pessimistic!" Sima Fu protested.

"I am not," Sima Yi retorted. "The Han Empire is now divided into a number of regions, and the lords of two of those regions – Cao Cao, who rules Yan, Yu, Xu, Liang and Central Provinces, and Yuan Shang, who rules Qing, Bing, Ji and Yòu Provinces – are about to do battle. The lord of Jing, Liu Biao, sits and watches, as does the lord of Yi, Liu Zhang; to the south, there is the young upstart Sun Quan, who controls an area that we call 'Yang Province' when it is probably bigger than all of the Yuans' domains put together. Liu Biao and Sun Quan are repeatedly butting heads, and one or both of them will one day be forced to fight the 'Imperial army' that Cao Cao commands: the warlords will do as their name implies and be masters of war while the Han government gradually loses more and more credibility as a uniting force, until, eventually, a man – perhaps it will be Cao Cao – steps forth and says 'There must be change'. The Yellow Turbans and Yuan Shu were right about the problem: their only crime was their ineligibility as the solution. The Yuans and Caos are not the answer either: any man that intends to unite the land with violence is only building another future failed state, an empire founded by howling madmen and corrupt financiers that will suck the tree dry of life before it has grown to fullness."

"...Despite what you say, we cannot ignore the calls to join the government," Sima Lang insisted. "Is the patient so sick that medicine is no longer an option...? I will try and save the Han from within and prevent the chaos that would follow its demise."

"So will I," Sima Xun said.

"I will do all that is necessary to preserve order," Sima Fu said.

"Father would scold us for doing anything else," Sima Jin suggested. "Don't you want to make Father proud, Zhongda...?"

"Father is not a fool obsessed with empty pride," Sima Yi retorted. "He would not advocate wasting energy. He dotes on the Han in the way that a loving relative sits at the bedside in the final hours; it isn't every man that has to do that. I will concentrate on the real world that we have right in front of us and build a career around living within it."

"*Aiee*... I will not give up on persuading you to change your mind, Zhongda, nor will I give up on persuading others of your talent," Sima Lang said. "The only thing left is for you to see that the world needs your help to bring order and that you're wasting your life by not serving the government to the fullest."

"Cao Cao has Guo Jia, Cheng Yu, Jia Xu, Xun Yu, Xun Yòu, Chen Qun, Liu Yè, Wang Lang, Zhong Yao, Yuan Huan, Yang Biao, Xu Yòu... to name but a few of the horses in his stables," Sima Yi retorted. "When will he need Sima Yi...?"

"We should just focus on leaving Li County," Sima Fu suggested. "Leave Zhongda be, Elder Brother."

"...I have little choice," Sima Lang sighed.

****

22

Yuan Shang was alarmed when his agents reported that his older brother Tan had moved to Li County instead of returning to Qing Province; he was even more perturbed by the subsequent arrival of a messenger from Tan with a request for reinforcements.

"What should I do, gentlemen...?" Yuan Shang asked of his senior advisers, Shen Pei and Pang Ji. "What can I assume by his making this move...?"

"It's likely that he's getting the same reports as we are about Cao Cao's preparations for war," Pang Ji replied. "It might be that he wants to aid the defence of what he sees as Yuan domain."

"On the other hand, he might want to show his strength and prove that he is the true lord," Shen Pei suggested. "If we refuse the reinforcements, it is an indication of mistrust that could lead to war; if we accept the request, it may then be as when Liu Bei took men from Cao Cao and then used them to seize Xu Province."

"...He is my brother," Yuan Shang said thoughtfully. "We have always been close, so it pains me to think that the succession could divide us as it does. But at the same time, he is now my vassal and must obey me. I did not order him to go to Li County, so this is an affront; I sent Gao Fan to the region to act as the defence commander, and I had plans of my own with regards to the land base. Shouldn't I be ordering him to relocate...?"

"He would certainly see that as an excuse to attack," Shen Pei replied. "I've had time to think about it now, and I suggest that we agree to his request but exploit the wording of his letter in order to spy on him."

"Oh...?" Yuan Shang said. "Please elaborate."

"He cites 'a lack of talents to oversee the army', which obviously hints at his wanting you to send a general – Ju Hu, perhaps, or Jiang Yiqu – that he can try to convince to turn away from you," Shen Pei continued. "But at the same time, a show of humility is protocol, so he acts sensibly... and, at the same time, in the right way for us to respond to our own advantage. We will not give him a large force with any leading generals, opting instead for a small force of average men that will be led by a trusted official, someone that he cannot turn from you but will instead act as our agent and watch him for us."

"I will undertake that mission personally," Pang Ji said. "There can be no mistakes."

"But won't you be very *obvious*, Mister Pang?" Yuan Shang asked.

"In this case, there is more to be gained by letting Yuan Tan know that he is being watched," Pang Ji replied. "I can additionally ensure that he does not court alliances with others – such as Liu Biao, Sun Quan or even Cao Cao – without your knowing about it, and also watch for Cao Cao's advance and ensure that Tan does not deliberately keep such information from you in order to, for example, win surprise victories or 'allow Cao to get past him'."

"But you're very obvious," Yuan Shang insisted.

"...I am also unsure," Shen Pei admitted. "This divides us, Yuantu, at a time when our combined knowledge and talent is essential to preserving order."

"I know, Zhengnan, but Yuan Tan presents the most credible

threat at the moment, and we cannot ignore it," Pang Ji replied. "I hope to find a way to convince him to end his ambitions or coax Guo Tu, Xin Pi and others to our side. Guo, I believe, is simply peeved that he was 'not on the right side' and sees that he supported the wrong man and hence lost influence. He wants to regain his old place in the court's inner circle, and if I can convince him of our desire for him to join us at Lord Yuan Shang's side, then Yuan Tan will be isolated and – with nothing but the Xin brothers and a few other mediocrities like Wang Xiu and Guan Tong left around him – given no choice but to submit."

"...You sound very sure," Yuan Shang conceded. "Very well, Mister Pang: go to him with... with three thousand average troops, two months' grain and some coin for procuring other necessities. That should be enough."

Pang Ji bowed humbly and said, "I will not fail you."

"...And what about our other front...?" Yuan Shang asked.

"Administrator Gao Gan has moved many thousands of his men to Ping County for a sudden offensive," Shen Pei replied. "The Southern Xiongnu Chanyu, Huchuquan, is refusing to get involved, but quite a few of the smaller Southern Xiongnu tribes have joined us for this offensive. If we take Hedong, we can then move west, seize Chang'an, and then – provided that the Qiang warlords, who will turn on Cao Cao when they see how weak his grip is, cause the appropriate havoc – we can seize all or part of Liang Province and start to turn the situation around while support around Cao Cao collapses, especially if we receive the assistance of Liu Biao of Jing Province.

"At the worst, the risk of losing Hedong will harry Cao's attempts to attack us and force him back onto the defensive while he moves his troops westward to rescue the region; in that case, we can cross the Yellow River, re-establish our old bases there and have 'a second Guandu' that ends with the proper result now that we don't have traitors like Xu Yòu and Zhang Hè to worry about. Remember, Lord Yuan, that we outnumber Cao by two-to-one even with the internal problems we face, and that's without factoring the Southern Xiongnu and every single Wuhuan tribe into our number."

"...Your analysis predicts a victory of some kind for us, provided that my brother does not spoil things," Yuan Shang said. "Very well: proceed as you have, gentlemen, and we will soon be able to offer Cao's head to my father's temple. The Yuan clan's lustre will be restored, and after that, the Han's!"

Yuan Tan received word of Pang Ji's imminent arrival and cried out angrily at the thought of it.

"Do not be disheartened," Xin Ping implored.

"Indeed," Guo Tu said. "This is exactly what we want."

"**How so???**" Yuan Tan asked. "**What good are three thousand men and that slimy pedant going to be???**"

"Pang Ji is a shrewd man," Guo Tu replied. "He reported Tian Feng's comments to remove him as a threat; had Tian been forgiven for his earlier remonstrance and allowed to return, things would have transpired very differently. Some say that he slandered Tian wrongly and did it to further his own career, but that is not my view, though I admit that his current position does give strong credibility to that theory."

Yuan Tan glared at Guo Tu silently.

"Pang Ji administrated Yè very competently while we were on campaign," Guo Tu continued. "He is a very capable politician, adviser, officer and ambassador, and I'm sure that he would be of great use to us if he could be persuaded that he has been used by Lady Liu and, perhaps, Shen Pei."

"This is a precursor to another needless game of intrigue," Xin Pi complained. "No more, Guo Tu! We've lost a great many talents and suffered a great many defeats by not keeping things as simple as they can and should be!"

"You're wrong, Xin Pi," Guo Tu insisted. "I propose no new intrigue: I simply propose meeting this obvious attempt at intriguing by Shen and Pang with a simple retort that could bring Pang Ji 'back home' and end this ridiculous plot of Lady Liu's to make her son the chieftain and repeat past mistakes."

"Pang Ji is not going to give up being the adviser to the chieftain and join what Shen Pei will label as a rebellion!" Xin Pi protested.

"Pang Ji brings loyal, inflexible men to us and hopes to twist the minds of our few men to his way of thinking, and I see no way that you can turn that situation into the opposite! Yuan Shang commands tens of thousands – no, hundreds of thousands – while we can barely muster-!"

"Pang Ji wants power," Guo Tu retorted. "Shen Pei will eventually double-cross Pang, and Pang knows it; and Lady Liu – who is truly insane – is like the scheming Empress Dowagers that resort to any tactic to preserve their grip on power, and that can't sustain, for it never has, and Pang knows that too."

Xin Pi harrumphed and said, "Nonsense! This was too well planned to be compared to a dowager's plot! You-!"

"Let Guo Tu speak, Brother," Xin Ping insisted.

"You do not think that Pang Ji looks at Yuan Shang and thinks, 'You cannot last, for you are a suckling with no will of your own, and so it is your mother that truly rules this region now'?" Guo Tu asked. "And you think that Shen Pei won't be thinking, 'Why does Pang Ji leave the safety of Yè to join Yuan Tan?' and perhaps guessing – rightly or wrongly – that Pang intends to defect...? Who picked these men that come here...? Shen or Pang...? Is Pang Ji really so sure that he is supporting the right man...? Let's let them come here, see what happens when they get here, and when the situation is clear we'll plan accordingly."

"...I will do as you say, but I urge you to keep communication between me and Pang Ji to a minimum," Yuan Tan growled. "I can blame the greedy, unstable Lady Liu and that 'suckling' Shang all I want, but the truth is this: Shang would be the subordinate, and *I* would be in Yè City – not a muddy military camp in Li County – if not for Pang Ji and Shen Pei, and I am growing increasingly angry about it."

"I will speak with him, Lord Yuan, so that you do not need to," Guo Tu promised. "I will discover his intentions... and then we can proceed from there."

****

23

The Magistrate of Chang'an, Zhong Yao, arrived at the city gates and stared at the scarred walls of the Han's first capital with sad, distressed eyes as the Inspector of Liang Province, Wei Kang, approached his carriage to greet him.

"...Unwanted memories, I assume...?" Wei Kang prompted.

"Oh, uh... my apologies," Zhong Yao said as he bowed humbly. "I... yes, Inspector, very bad memories, very bad... why are you here, and not in your own capital...?"

"We should continue the discussion privately," Wei Kang replied.

Once Wei Kang had escorted Zhong Yao's carriage to Zhong's mansion residence in Chang'an, the two men sat in the living quarters and continued their conversation over tea.

"Excellency Cao wanted me and my military consultant, Zhao Ang, to oversee the reorganisation of the city guard forces," Wei Kang replied. "There is not as much trust between us and the Qiang as His Excellency would have others believe, admittedly... but they're being quiet enough, them and the Di tribes, to afford us time to ensure that the Yuan brothers cannot encroach on Chang'an without meeting with some resistance."

"*Aiee*... don't get me started on those fools!" Zhong Yao said. "My nephew's a general in Bing, and I'd hoped to reach out to him, but he's devoted to the Yuans now, and vows to 'serve them until his last'! I've remonstrated with my sister and her husband, but they refuse to listen! 'The Yuans are the ones that should prevail', they say: how so? We do what we can to pacify the troublemakers, but the Yuans are making rebellious Wuhuan, Xiongnu and bandits into their vanguard to destroy all of the stability that His Excellency has achieved! What good is there in forcing us to make concessions to the likes of Ma Teng? The Yuans claim that they are restoring the Han's lustre, but all that they are doing now is building a nation that will see nothing but barbarian sectarianism and rampant criminality!"

"I can't disagree," Wei Kang admitted. "So sad, I think, that the once-loyal Yuans that had a place at the side of countless majesties are reduced to wealthy crime lords that wage war on the state for personal gain."

"...So will you be staying here long...?" Zhong Yao asked.

"I wanted to greet you, but I can stay for only a few more days," Wei Kang replied. "I sent Zhao Ang back to Ji City already, as I do not trust Han Sui as much as I probably should."

"How can you trust that man at all?" Zhong Yao chortled. "He was once a Han official: now he rides a saddleless horse, carries a spear and bellows like an animal."

"He's not *that* bad!" Wei Kang chuckled. "The Qiang tribes do have *some* social structure, Zhong Yuanchang, else they'd not have been so successful. Yes, the hierarchy is sadly based entirely around physical strength and bluster, but are we so different most of the time...? What's this current dispute about?"

"...I know, I know," Zhong Yao sighed.

"And by 'trust', I mean 'trust of his sense', not trust of his desire for peace, sad to say," Wei Kang continued. "I know that Han Sui is no friend of ours, but he is not keen to fight while he and Ma

Teng are not properly reconciled; he fears reprisals if he does anything now, but I must still be aware that reconciliation is likely and potentially at any moment, and I should be in Ji City, leading my people, on that day."

"...And I, meanwhile, must liaise with Ma Teng and protect the people of this region from all of its enemies, many and diverse as they are," Zhong Yao said. "Oh, Wei Yuanjiang, this could not be more difficult for me! I lost friends here when Dong Zhuo ruled, I lost family here when Li Jue and Guo Si fought in the streets, and I lost more family and friends when I left here and endured that hellish journey to Luoyang! This city has more familiar ghosts within its walls than living people that I will speak to! I know that I must be strong, but... but I want to weep when I look around this house again after so long. I bring a new family here to live in it... but will they end up like the first?"

"Only Heaven knows," Wei Kang replied. "I imagine that you're more concerned about your nephew at present, though."

"His Excellency's benevolence is beyond question," Zhong Yao said. "Any other lord – Yuan Shao comes to mind, certainly – would have already stripped me of rank when he learned that a senior enemy officer was my nephew. Curse Guo Yuan's idiocy! In a way, he deserves death, but when I see him in my mind's eye as a laughing child in a happy home, I...!"

"...I do not envy your predicament," Wei Kang sighed.

"And worse still, that I might be employing barbarians to fight him!" Zhong Yao continued. "Curse this second generation of bickering, hankering Yuan brothers! They are worse than Shao and Shu were! The sooner they are purged, the better for us all!"

The feud between Yuan Tan and Yuan Shang was not the primary concern of the middle Yuan brother, Yuan Xi, and his wife, Lady Zhen, who had been forcibly parted by Lady Liu before Yuan Shao's death. The decision to keep Lady Zhen in Yè City while Yuan Xi went to his own capital in the remote north was widely seen as a pre-emptive hostage-taking exercise by Lady Liu in order to keep Yuan Xi from acting against her future announcement; Xi reacted by remaining in Yòu Province and refusing all requests for support by his older brother and younger half-brother, while Lady Zhen made repeated pleas to the unsympathetic Lady Liu.

"...My husband means no harm to anyone," Lady Zhen protested as Lady Liu looked at her with condescending eyes. "Please, I... I will make no more hints and be frank, for I am at my wit's end. I just want to visit my husband or have him visit me: is that really so impossible...?"

"Silly girl," Lady Liu giggled. "Do I look like a fool...? Would I really allow you to flee northward and weep before Xi, telling him that you were held against your will by his wicked, conniving stepmother...? Would I be any more foolish and allow him to enter the capital with hidden knives and hidden followers to try and take control and declare himself chieftain?"

"My husband always knew that he was never intended as the heir!" Lady Zhen retorted. "He has no such ambitions! He knew, he *always* knew that his brother- ...that *one of his brothers* would always be the heir, and not him!"

"Knowing that he was never meant to be the chieftain does not stop him wishing it were so... or maybe wanting his brother Tan to rule...?" Lady Liu countered. "Those two have never seen me as their mother: I am not, after all. My son, my only son, Shang, is only their half-brother and does not enjoy their love and loyalty. Those two will connive to take *everything* that my son was **rightly – RIGHTLY – bequeathed by his father, and I will not let them succeed! Go away, girl, and do not have the audacity to confront me again! I am the mother of the clan chieftain, and I will not be so tolerant of any more demands!**"
Lady Zhen fought tears of frustration as she retreated from Lady Liu's quarters; Lady Zhen would not make any more attempts to reason with Yuan Shang's mother, and as the enormity of the blood feud became more apparent to her, she started to give up on the idea of ever seeing her husband again.

Yuan Xi was pining for Lady Zhen with equal frustration, but he was based in the remote north and surrounded by officials that were not necessarily likely to support him for a host of reasons, and that was his immediate concern: he invited many of them to a meeting in his capital Fanyang in order to gauge their loyalty.
"...I see a number of former followers of Liu Yu among you, gentlemen," Yuan Xi said meekly. "Please understand that I am his like-minded successor as Governor of Yòu Province and share his ideals."
"...I must say that I find that difficult to believe," one man said.
"Mister Xianyu Fu, I assure you that I'm sincere," Yuan Xi replied.
"When I see the Yuan 'support base' in this region, I see Wuhuan chieftains such as Tadun, Louban and Supuyan, and crime lords like Huo Nu and Zhao Du," Xianyu Fu retorted. "The Black Mountain Bandits are acting freely again, just as they did when Gongsun Zan was ruling the area: when we gave our support to the Yuans, we did it to end the Wuhuan raids, the bandit raids and the crime lords' hold on the province, not solidify their positions!"
"...And you, Mister Tian...?" Yuan Xi asked as he turned to Tian Chou, who had briefly served Cao Cao in recent times but returned to his native Wuzhong County to serve as its Magistrate.
"I'm here to ensure that the people that I grew up with are treated properly," Tian Chou replied. "I must reluctantly agree with Administrator Xianyu, and not just because he is my superior; the Yuans have courted and acquiesced to most of the enemies of the people in this region and done nothing about the rest. The Xianbei are now harassing the border in addition to the Wuhuan, and that's a bad sign. We cannot go on like this."
"I am at the mercy of politics!" Yuan Xi insisted. "My brother-"
"With all due respect, I know what is going on in Yè, and I don't care, and neither do the people of Wuzhong," Tian Chou said. "I'm here for them: they want something done about the people that make their lives unbearable on a daily basis, but all I can go back and tell them is, 'Our Governor is at the mercy of politics'."
"I, Wang Song, administrate Gongsun Zan's former holding, Zhou Prefecture, as you know, Governor Yuan," another man said. "My loyalty was to Liu Yu in the end, and I am saddened by the 'retirement' of Liu Hè, more so because I believe that he cared for Yòu Province as much as his father did. Gongsun Zan slayed Liu

Yu unjustly, and he turned Zhuo into a famine-ridden wasteland when he consolidated everything he had into Yijing Fortress to defend his ill-gotten gains from your father, who some say helped Gongsun Zan to get Yòu Province in the first place."
"Say no more about that," Yuan Xi pleaded.
"I dare to say more," Wang Song continued. "We reluctantly sided with the Yuans because they were the enemies of Gongsun Zan; if the Yuans would now be as the Gongsuns – and ruin the province whilst fighting the Han that we are all meant to serve – then we must consider our allegiances!"
The gathering murmured agreeably.
"...I will do what I can to curb the Wuhuan, chase the Black Mountain Bandits back into their lairs, punish the criminals and bring stability to the province, even if I am dragged into a war with Cao Cao or my brothers," Yuan Xi promised. "I want what you want, gentlemen... please believe me."
"Is that it...?" Xianyu Fu asked. "I have a troubled region to run."
"Yes, that's it," Yuan Xi replied numbly; the Administrators and Magistrates got to their feet, exchanged half-hearted bows with their Governor and departed from the audience hall.
"...General Jiao, Mister Zhang, I must rely upon your strength," Yuan Xi said as he turned to two of his cynical aides. "You know I am sincere... help me convince others and spare this region further harm!"
General Jiao Chu exchanged weary glances with the official Zhang Nan as he replied, "We will do all things possible, Governor..."

****

24

Cao Cao had started to move soldiers and supplies to the part of the Yellow River's southern bank that faced the road to Li County; the size of the army indicated an invasion force, and that unsettled Yuan Tan.

"Shang's making plans to invade Hedong, but what good will Hedong be if he loses Li County?" Yuan Tan asked of his advisers, Guo Tu and Xin Ping.

"...I will try and talk to Pang Ji again," Guo Tu promised. "I will say again that we need to reinforce the region with more men, and that defence right now is more important than attack... but I fear that the answer will be the same."

"I don't want the men to defend Li County!" Yuan Tan retorted. "I want them to frighten Cao into never coming near Li County, and then I want to seize Cangting, Wuchao, Anmin and Guandu! I want to-!"

"To Pang Ji, the intention is defending Li County," Guo Tu insisted. "I will speak with him again."

Guo Tu met with his old colleague Pang Ji and asked him if they could speak privately in Pang's personal tent.

"...Is this another pathetic attempt to convince me to defect to Yuan Tan?" Pang Ji scoffed as he sat at his host seat in the tent. "Don't bother if it is."

"No, it's another request for more reinforcements," Guo Tu replied. "You've seen the same reports as I have, and you've seen them all before my lord, I'll wager."

"...I am, perhaps, a little obvious," Pang Ji said. "But your lord needs watching, because he will not accept a simple truth and is prepared to shed blood to-"

"If Lord Yuan Tan wanted to shed blood, he'd have done so," Guo Tu replied. "He would do so if left with no alternative. But there *are* alternatives. Lord Yuan Shao could not have intended this cruel end to a loyal, loving relationship between father and sons: to adopt Tan to a dead man at the last without a warning...? Why was I never made aware of it...?"

"I cannot say," Pang Ji said coldly. "Lord Yuan Shao was talking to his uncle at the end... and his lady wife of course... Shen Pei and I were confided in at the last by Lady Liu, who saw you as hostile to Lord Yuan Shao's plan to appoint Lord Yuan Shang as his heir. But as I have said before, 'the door is open': if you would only accept that the will is genuine and that Lord Yuan Shang is the proper heir, then-!"

"I cannot believe that Lord Yuan Tan was intended as the adopted son," Guo Tu insisted. "Yuan Xi, perhaps, for he was never going to be important... but Lord Yuan Tan fought bravely and served loyally! He took Qing Province from Tian Kai and Kong Rong, a feat that made conquering Yòu Province and defeating Gongsun Zan a close reality instead of a distant dream!"

"Yes, and Qing Province was Tan's reward," Pang Ji replied. "And you've admitted that he can barely run *that*. Lord Yuan Shao wasn't blind or deaf or stupid: he could see the unrest, hear the complaints and ponder the response. You talk of alternatives:

what are they...? Lord Yuan Shang agreeing to divide the land down the middle, which would then deny Gao Gan – whose efforts to secure Bing Province are as worthy of reward as Yuan Tan's – and Yuan Xi – who is a much loved son as well – of fiefs...?"

"I see that argument," Guo Tu said, "but-!"

"Each of the three brothers has a province while Gao Gan governs the fourth: if the solution is dividing the chieftainship rather than the land, then we would be creating a precedent for future conflicts," Pang Ji continued. "What good did Li Jue and Guo Si's co-regency do...? Will Han Sui and Ma Teng ever really rule over the Qiang as equals...? Would Yuan Xi, mild-tempered though he is, truly stand by and watch as his older brother and younger half-brother divide the power between them, or would he raise an army of Wuhuan tribes and bandits and march on Yè to 'negotiate his share with swords' as Yuan Tan threatens to do now...?"

"...But surely the matter of reinforcing the Li County region has nothing to do with which of the two brothers should be the clan chieftain...?" Guo Tu asked. "What good is there in putting all of the good men in Bing Province to invade Hedong and leaving Li County exposed?"

"Cao Cao has to pass Gao Fan to reach Li County, which gives Lord Yuan Shang time to place a competent general at the head of a reinforcement army and send them here," Pang Ji retorted. "The worry is that an army without a mission would merely sit here and be lectured to by you and others about the succession issue."

"...So you really see no merit in Lord Yuan Tan at all...?" Guo Tu asked plainly.

"He is a capable officer, but nothing more," Pang Ji replied. "It is right that he was denied the chance to ruin the Yuan legacy as Yuan Shu might have done had Lord Yuan Shao yielded to him any more than he did. And come to think of it, look at what happened when Lord Yuan Shao made concessions and allowed Shu to have unusual autonomy! There, in fact, is the exact example I was looking for, more relevant and obvious than the rest! Lord Yuan Shao allowed his brother to be a co-chieftain in all but name! Look at what that led to! Yuan Shu raised an army and challenged his brother in the end, even after such a show of magnanimity, and drew us all into a seven-year war! Can you see Yuan Tan sharing power forever...?"

"Lord Yuan Tan does not crave the Imperial throne, and he is not mad," Guo Tu retorted. "Can the same be said of Lady Liu...?"

Pang Ji harrumphed angrily.

"She killed and disfigured the lord's consorts before he was even cold!" Guo Tu continued. "She concocted this scheme to keep Lord Yuan Tan and Yuan Xi at bay so she could convince Lord Yuan Shao that her son was the best of the three, and you and Shen went along with it because you knew that it would elevate you! But will it end well...? Will Lady Liu be content with a quarter of the empire, or will that demented creature decide that she would like to be an Empress Dowager...?"

Pang Ji flicked his sleeve.

"...But you do not answer," Guo Tu heckled. "You show the highest contempt, but you do not answer because you cannot tell me that she is not the power behind a paper throne of her own design."

"Say no more!" Pang Ji barked. **"I am not the enemy!** *Cao Cao* is our enemy! I am following the will of Lord Yuan Shao! Lord Yuan Shao favoured Lord Yuan Shang, and that is that! I will forward your request for reinforcements, but that is all that I can do! But do not expect a favourable answer for your lord, because as Sun Tzu said, 'defence alone is a sign of weakness', and Lord Yuan Shang does not want to appear weak!"

"...Sun Tzu also said that causes of division should always be avoided," Guo Tu replied coldly. "He also advocated being aware of enemies within."

"**I will ask for more men!**" Pang Ji snapped. "**That's all! Now I have work to do!**"

Guo Tu bowed, smiled and said, "So do I."

Guo Tu returned to Yuan Tan and asked for a private meeting: the only other attendee was Tan's long-time adviser Xin Ping.

"...The situation is clear now," Guo Tu sighed theatrically.

"No intrigue," Xin Ping pleaded. "I agree with my brother on that: no intrigue!"

"I cannot promise on behalf of others," Guo Tu replied. "I have done nothing: the same cannot be said of Pang Ji and Shen Pei."

"Just say it," Yuan Tan ordered.

"...He has admitted in every sense but an outright admission that he colluded with Shen Pei to bring us to this current situation," Guo Tu said. "Lady Liu could sense that Lord Yuan Shao was wavering as the successive defeats at Cao Cao's hands ate away at his sanity and strength; she started to communicate with Shen and Pang and offered them high rank in exchange for making... 'helpful suggestions'."

"You're sure of this...?" Xin Ping asked.

"As sure as I can be," Guo Tu replied. "Pang Ji and Shen Pei started to cajole Yuan Cheng and others, and tried to have Chen Lin draft various documents, which is why he has drifted away from the government. In the end, a combination of pillow talk, barbed advice, deliberate 'misplacing' of key figures and careful timing ensured that Lord Yuan Shao lay clawing at the air for his eldest son – who was in Qing, with me, for I was also 'misplaced' – and at the last, with Xi also 'misplaced', only Shang was there to show his father pity. A few documents and declarations later... and here we are. But I have no reason to believe that there were any coincidences now. Shen and Pang arranged it all: the posthumous adoption, the 'misplacing', the will, everything. I can see none of Lord Yuan Shao's wishes, only self-serving-"

"*Bastards*," Yuan Tan growled. "Shen and Pang... must **both** *die* for this!*"

"But we must be *careful*," Guo Tu pleaded. "They've been ingratiating themselves with the military and promoting sympathetic officials; we must remember that we have a small army of loyalists and that most others trust Shen and Pang and believe in the validity of the will."

"They have let that vixen coerce them into making that idiot Shang the chieftain, and Heaven only knows what they intend for me!" Yuan Tan said. "Lady Liu disfigured Father's consorts and holds my brother's wife as a hostage; is it too much to ask whether she would have me killed...?"

"For now, she cannot do that, and nor can Shang," Xin Ping insisted. "Cao Cao is too much of a threat, I think. I... I am not saying that I disagree with Mister Guo's analysis, but I suggest being cordial and waiting to see if Shang sends the aid we asked for. If he does, we'll know if he is as bad as his mother."

"...Alright," Yuan Tan replied. "I still care about my brother... just as Father cared about Uncle at the last, even after all that he had done. Pang and Shen are another matter, but alright... we'll see what Shang – or rather, Shen Pei – suggests in response to our request. I just hope that I don't have to get angry."

****

25

Cao Cao periodically left Xuchang and travelled to his base at Guandu to oversee the preparations for his next campaign in the northeast: the time for that campaign was nearing, so he moved east to the site of Yuan Shao's former base at Cangting with two of his advisers, Guo Jia and his long-time friend Xu Yòu.

"Soon we'll be crossing for another encounter with the Yuans," Cao Cao said.

"Let's make this the last time, Mengde," Xu Yòu prompted. "This isn't a game: just cross, kill them all and end it before they regroup or find new allies. Take all of the provinces, not just Ji! Leave them nowhere to run!"

"…Such an outcome is not entirely outside of my expectations, Ziyuan, but I admit that there are many reasons why I probably won't be getting as far as Yòu or Bing Provinces," Cao Cao said tonelessly. "The Wuhuan tribes are extensively employed by the Yuans across Yòu, western Qing and eastern Ji, and they're not going to make things easy, are they…?"

"No, I know that," Xu Yòu replied. "But… but we must try and end it quickly, Mengde!"

Guo Jia laughed and said, "I wonder if the Yuan brothers will show any solidarity. They could be quite formidable if they cooperate."

"Let's hope not, Fengxiao," Cao Cao replied. "I want this over with quickly as well."

Yuan Shang was determined to keep control of his Wuhuan allies, so he invited several chieftains – including the chiefs of them all, Tadun and Louban – to a meeting at a neutral point to the north of Yè City in secret; he took his Registrar of Ji Province, Li Fu, the general Ju Hu and the newly-reacquired Chen Lin as his aides.

"I am glad to have you on my side, great chieftains of the Wuhuan," Yuan Shang said politely.

"Your father was a great man," Tadun replied with sincerity. "He gave us respect, he gave us wives, he let us live as we choose."

Li Fu, Chen Lin and the other officials could barely hide their disgust; the Wuhuan had been given the sisters and daughters of many of Yuan Shao's subordinates as bargaining tools – whether the said subordinates agreed or not – and the phrase 'live as we choose' often included carrying out raids on villages that usually ended in deaths, rapes, kidnappings and the theft of grain, coin and other precious resources.

"As the new Yuan chieftain, I want things to stay the same," Yuan Shang replied carefully. "We must work together to achieve that."

"We are all brothers, all of the tribes and the Yuans," the chieftain Louban said. "My cousin Tadun and I have talked, and we agree that we must remain together as a strong team. This 'Cao Cao' is not like the Yuans. He will try to change us. We will crush him. We have all talked, all the chiefs agree. We all fight as one."

"…What of my brother Tan?" Yuan Shang asked apprehensively.

"I, Tadun, was made chief of chiefs when Qiuliju died," Tadun replied. "I was chief of chiefs because Louban was too young. Now he is older, so I have stood aside, and we rule together, but not quite: I am still strong, but he is chief of chiefs. That is how it is to be. When Yuan Shao died, he made you chief of the Yuan tribe. Your brother came to us, asked us to help him, but Yuan Shao chooses his heir, not his son. If you are the heir, you are the heir. Yuan Tan should stand aside."

"...Thank you, great chieftains," Yuan Shang said.

"We are all great chieftains, you and us," Louban replied. "We will fight together, against Cao Cao!"

"...Then we shall drink to it!" Yuan Shang said with false cheer. "To our brotherhood, and to the destruction of Cao Cao!"

When the brief festivities ended, Yuan Shang hurried back to his capital, where an anxious Shen Pei greeted him at the gates.

"They are with us," Yuan Shang said. "I can't fathom who actually has the authority out of Louban and Tadun... which is an eerily familiar situation, I must say... but whichever one it is, Mister Shen, they are with us."

"We are blessed," Shen Pei replied unhappily.

"I know how it must feel," Yuan Shang insisted. "I truly am sorry that Father deemed it necessary to marry 'daughters and sisters' to them, but their allegiance is essential to our cause. Perhaps, in the future, when the Yuans are restored to their proper place, such things can be put right in some way."

"...Necessity is sometimes a bitter fruit to taste, but I am resigned," Shen Pei replied. "I am just glad that you have returned: Jiang Yiqu was forced to deal with an uprising in Yangping, so I was forced to rely on Su Yòu and Ma Yan."

"Neither man is incompetent, just inexperienced when speaking relatively," Yuan Shang said. "All great men have to start somewhere: Wen Chou and Yan Liang were undecorated captains at some point in the past."

"Now they are undecorated graves," Shen Pei retorted. "Neither Wen nor Yan was inexperienced, but they were stupid, which didn't help them or your father. Su and Ma are no less-!"

"I... understand, Mister Shen," Yuan Shang promised. "Any word from the many, many fronts that we face...? I know of my brother-cousin's request for reinforcements... but now that I know that Tan's been trying to court the Wuhuan and encourage them to rise up against me, I don't know how to respond."

"Don't rush in responding," Shen Pei insisted. "Cao Cao's massing troops along the Yellow River, but we don't know where he intends to strike; Li County is the most favourable place to advance from, but he'll know we'll probably fortify the place and attack somewhere else, like Puyang, Hua, or perhaps go through Henei. Wherever he sends men, then that is where we send ours, not to Li County regardless because Yuan Tan demands it. Our internal problems have drained a lot of our resources and militias from the front line: Zang Ba is still harassing Qing; bandits, former vassals of Gongsun Zan and rebel Wuhuan plague Yòu Province; and even the Black Mountain Bandits are resurfacing now, and there are still tens of thousands of those wretches in northern Bing to deal with. We have over two-hundred-thousand men, but we'll be lucky if we can use a quarter of that, and that spreads us very thin."

"We are certain to see Cao Cao attack us soon, regardless of precisely where and precisely when," Yuan Shang said. "And regardless of the specifics, our counterattack from Bing must ruin his efforts: as soon as we know of one arrow fired, one boat crossing, one man's foot on our soil... *whatever it is*, I want word sent to Gao Gan that Hedong Prefecture is to be taken."

"It shall be done," Shen Pei replied.

Yuan Shang's main entourage passed Shen Pei and entered the city; Shen Pei stopped Chen Lin as he passed and said, "It is good to see you back."

"I was ill," Chen Lin replied. "Now I am recovered."

Shen Pei smiled and said, "Your illness was that great slayer of men... doubt."

"I was ill, but I am recovered," Chen Lin retorted. "I am a vassal of the Yuan clan, Mister Shen, and voluntarily so. I saved the late lord from disaster because I could see he was a hero; I will now do the same for his heir if I can."

"What do you think of Li Fu...?" Shen Pei asked.

"It is a shame that the man has never been made more use of before," Chen Lin replied. "I spoke with him on the way back here... and I think he will be an asset."

"...I wish that Guo Tu could be swayed," Shen Pei admitted. "His being an enemy is-"

"I wonder if 'enemy' is the right word," Chen Lin said. "After all, that makes our late lord's eldest son Yuan Tan an enemy as well, when he is merely confused and disgruntled."

"Yuan Tan is the *nephew* of the late lord," Shen Pei insisted. "And he has no right to be 'disgruntled', no more than Yuan Shu did. And he is courting potential allies to oppose Lord Yuan Shang: you heard it for yourself! How is he not behaving as an enemy...?"

Chen Lin sighed and said, "Perhaps that is true... but I so wish that I was not being asked to turn my sword against a lad that I watched grow up, that I saw as one of his father's most loyal vassals, a man willing to-"

"His motives for loyalty are now called into question," Shen Pei retorted. "Say no more: Lord Yuan Shang is the right choice."

Chen Lin hummed ambiguously in response and continued his journey into the city.

One military front that had never truly quietened was the region around the Qing-Xu provincial border: past combatants included Kong Rong, Ying Shao, Liu Bei, the Mount Tai Bandits, Yellow Turbans and Qing's eventual governor Yuan Tan, but now the main opposing sides were Yuan Tan's Qing defenders – led by Tan's aides, Wang Xiu and Guan Tong – and the Han Imperial forces, who were mostly former Mount Tai Bandits led by the famous agitator Zang Ba. Zang reluctantly convened a meeting of the senior leaders in the area – Sun Guan, Wu Dun, Chang Xi and Yin Li – and announced his immediate plans for advancement of the campaign.

"We're making *another* attempt to take Beihai???" Chang Xi said with surprise. **"It's a bloody waste of time!"**

"It's your mate Yu Jin's request, to be done 'for the Han'," Sun Guan heckled. "If you think it's stupid, go to Cao and tell him!"

"...I lost some good blokes on that last mission, men I've known for years that have watched my back and drank with me," Chang Xi complained. "What are we getting out of this, exactly, other than early coffins?"

"Look, Chang, we're Han agents now," Zang Ba said. "It's that or going back to thieving and risking being hunted down again. I, for one, am glad we're doing good and finally getting something done about the Yuans. If we stabilise Qing, then-"

"That's all it is these days!" Chang Xi barked. **"'Doing good', 'stabilising', 'serving the Han'... that's all just kissing Cao Cao's backside because we're not seen as good enough to kiss the emperor's!"**

"...And all we're getting from you these days is a lot of hints that you're 'tired' of the way things are," Yin Li noted. "Don't do it, Chang. Don't go backwards."

"Where's 'forwards' taking us, mm...?" Chang Xi retorted. "We're 'chaff'! That's all there is to it! Cao Cao can't hold Qing and conquer the rest of the empire with the handful of men he has, so he's getting us to do all the fighting, and-!"

"Shut up," Zang Ba ordered. "What you're saying, it's just your words and I don't want to hear them. The Han had forgiven our crimes because it was seen that we weren't given a choice because the province was corrupt: if we went back to that now after being offered civil posts, military posts and salaries, we'd-"

"How's any of that sound like the king of the Mount Tai Bandits...?" Chang Xi heckled. "How's them the words of the lord of Kaiyang?"

"We're not the Mount Tai Bandits anymore," Zang Ba retorted.

"Aren't we...?" Chang Xi asked. "I thought you said that 'my mate Yu Jin' and the rest of the Han officers don't see us any different!"

"Don't twist the words," Sun Guan said. "You know he meant-"

"What happens when Cao doesn't need us?" Chang Xi asked. "Will we end up like the White Waves...? Will Cao turn on us...?"

"Right now, he's got Zhang Xiu, half of Yuan Shao's generals, Huchuquan's Xiongnu, renegade Wuhuan, half of Lü Bu's generals, a load of Yuan Shu's generals and even the bloody *Qiang* working for him!" Zang Ba replied. "Cao's not like the rest! He won't turn on us! If he *did*, the rest'd feel threatened and turn on *him*!"

"I hope you're right," Chang Xi snickered. "Believe me, though, when I say that I'm watching for signs... I'm always watching..."

"And we're *not*, you idiot?" Yin Li scoffed. "Just shut up and hear Zang out, will you? The sooner we take Beihai and open the road to Linzi, the sooner we get a rest."

"...I don't know about that," Zang Ba chuckled. "Anyhow, here's the plan..."

Yuan Tan's appointed custodians of Qing Province in his absence – Wang Xiu and Guan Tong – had set up a series of checkpoints to monitor Zang Ba; the former bandits were able to surprise the outermost checkpoints, but one man got away and managed to notify Wang Xiu in the provincial capital Linzi.

"Not again," Wang Xiu grumbled. "I seriously think that we should be looking at negotiating with the Han court."

"Are you mad...?" Guan Tong exclaimed. "You want to 'negotiate' with a so-called 'Han court' that sends *Zang Ba and the Mount Tai Bandits* as their vanguard?"

"We're working with the *Wuhuan*," Wang Xiu replied. "The bandits, at least, are not barbarians that abduct people and lay waste to the villages that they raid."

"...I wish I could argue," Guan Tong said. "But what do we do

about the bandits, since they're our enemies anyway...? Doesn't this conflict with our plan to join Lord Yuan at Li County...?"
"Naturally," Guan Tong replied. "I'll report the situation and then we'll advance to meet Zang before he gains too much ground."

The former Mount Tai Bandits were more organised than they had once been, but many of their soldiers were just the same men wearing different clothes and carrying better weapons, and many more were no different at all. No effort had been made to learn military arrays or train for combat with professional soldiers, and the enforcing of discipline varied drastically from leader to leader, with some – like Yin Li and Zang Ba – doing their best to control their followers' rowdy ways while others – like Chang Xi – behaved little better than their men and acted like the bandits that they had always been. Wang Xiu and Guan Tong led their smaller yet more organised army to meet Zang Ba's and observed the hordes that awaited them with interest.
"We'll have less trouble than I expected," Wang Xiu decided. **"They're perhaps less organised than the Black Mountain Bandits: we'll be cautious, in case their disorganised appearance is a ruse, but I think we'll repel them."**
"I agree that this is probably the same old bandits," Guan Tong replied. **"I'll order an attack on their right flank, since there's no apparent organisation there."**
Guan Tong had his drummers signal to his small cavalry force, who immediately charged at Chang Xi's shapeless front lines; Chang's men were sent running in all directions, and Zang Ba was forced to rescue them before they were massacred.
"BLOODY FOOL!" Zang Ba cried. **"WHY NOT SEND THEM YOUR HEAD AND BE DONE WITH IT?!"**
"LIKE ANYONE ELSE IS DOING MUCH BETTER, 'YOUR HIGHNESS'!" Chang Xi retorted; Zang Ba was reluctantly forced to admit that the precision attacks that the defenders were using were picking the larger bandit army apart at the seams and forcing mass retreats.
"RETREAT AND REGROUP!" Zang Ba ordered; the words would take time to reach every part of the army, however, since he had failed to adopt a communication system – such as flags or drums – and relied instead on yelling at the nearest man. The Han militia retreated in an undignified manner while Wang Xiu looked on and laughed; he knew that the enemy might win eventually through sneak attacks and force of numbers, but any victory, no matter how small, was to be savoured.

****

26

Yuan Tan tired of waiting for a response to his request for more reinforcements and summoned Pang Ji to his command tent.

"I don't like you, so I'll keep this brief," Yuan Tan said. "I want an answer, Pang, and I want it soon. I'm not like my brothers: I'm not soft, and I'm not patient. Where are the reinforcements...?"

Pang Ji looked at the small collection of advisers that Yuan Tan had around him and asked, "Will all of you stand by and allow your lord to risk harmony by threatening me thus...?"

"You've had long enough to get a response," Xin Ping replied. "What was it?"

"...There will be no further reinforcements," Pang Ji said at last. "But there are valid reasons for it! We none of us know where Cao Cao intends to strike, and that means that sending troops to one place might endanger another by delaying deployment!"

Pang Ji continued to ramble, but Yuan Tan was not listening: he was lost in a haze of anger and hatred for his brother and the advisers that he believed to be responsible for his demotion from clan chieftain to lesser nephew.

"...Furthermore, Mister Guo Tu, I can see you smirking and do not see why!" Pang Ji heckled. "The matter is closed, and no amount of threats will-!"

Yuan Tan suddenly lunged at Pang Ji with his sword drawn; Pang was barely able to raise his arms and cry out as Yuan Tan – who was practically acting on instinct – cut the adviser down and screamed like a wounded animal.

"**Enough, enough!**" Xin Ping protested. "By the gods, *you've*...!"

No man dared to obstruct Yuan Tan's frenzied attack, which only ended when Tan ran out of breath.

"...That was unwise," Xin Ping said numbly.

"What's the use of saying that now???" Xin Pi asked desperately.

"It... is for the best," Guo Tu suggested.

"How so?" Xin Pi asked. "It's a declaration of war, isn't it...?"

"Cao Cao looms large... so no, it will be seen for what it was... a passionate act by a concerned general-governor who does not wish to lose a battle or a province," Guo Tu replied. "In fact, I imagine that we'll get more reinforcements than we asked for as a result of this..."

"I... I want Shen Pei's head too," Yuan Tan wheezed as he knelt and started to sever Pang Ji's head from his shoulders. "I want them both for what they have taken from me... and then, after that, I-!"

"Do not forget about Cao Cao!" Xin Pi warned. "Lady Liu, Yuan Shang, Shen Pei and the rest must *wait*, Lord Yuan! Let's destroy *Cao Cao* first!"

"...Only because he killed my father," Yuan Tan replied as he got to his feet and turned to face his advisers. "Cao first, and then Shen Pei. But I will have Shen Pei, gentlemen... I will have Shen Pei's head!"

Shen Pei was present when Yuan Tan's messenger brought Pang Ji's head to Yuan Shang's audience hall in Yè City; the officials murmured anxiously and awaited their lord's response as the messenger retreated without incident.

"Should... should that man not have been apprehended?" Yuan Shang asked.

"...Yuan Tan must get the reinforcements now," Shen Pei said.

"Don't be absurd!" Yuan Shang chortled. "How can I acquiesce to my brother's demands after he has shown such contempt by killing my vassal?"

Shen Pei looked at Pang Ji's lifeless head – which was carelessly placed on the ground at Yuan Shang's feet – as he replied, "Send men at once, my lord, and then be ready to march to Li County yourself should Cao Cao appear there, which he most likely will. Yuan Tan will not simply bow to you: we must cooperate or die."

Yuan Shang sighed irritably and said, "Alright... fine, if you say that is the proper course. You are, after all, my adviser."

"...I am," Shen Pei replied; he then looked at Pang Ji's head for a second time and shuddered.

"...Li Fu," Yuan Shang hailed.

"I await your instructions," Li Fu replied.

"...Write... I will write at once to my brother, and have that fellow that delivered Pang's head take the letter, **if someone would please catch up to him and politely detain him...?**" Yuan Shang continued; two guards hurried after the messenger. "...I will give my brother the men he requests... and no more will be said of Pang Ji for now."

"**Nonsense!**" Lady Liu said as she stepped out from behind a screen and knelt beside her son. "**Yuan Tan has insulted you! You have been defied! Show that thug that you are the clan chieftain and-!**"

"**This is not the time for civil war!**" Shen Pei barked. "**Our lord – your son – would be *destroyed*!**"

Lady Liu looked at her son, who smiled and said, "Mister Shen is correct, Mother. I must wait until later to avenge this affront: Cao Cao must die and our family must be restored to greatness first."

"...Of course," Lady Liu murmured.

"My brother and I must cooperate for now," Yuan Shang said. "It's that or... or Cao Cao will be the ruin of us all."

****

27

Cao Cao began his attack on the Yuan brothers by way of a river crossing that would place his army close to Li County; the way was partly barred by Yuan Shang's chosen guardian of the Yellow River, Gao Fan, who allowed Cao's men to cross to the north bank but used his boats to block the movement of the supplies along the water. General Li Dian and the adviser Cheng Yu had been entrusted with transporting the supplies, and it was a miserable, agitated Cheng Yu that was forced to report the situation to Cao Cao in his base on the southern bank.

"His Excellency suggests switching to land-based transport," Cheng Yu sighed as he read Cao Cao's response.

"Don't be hasty!" Li Dian pleaded. "The scouts report that-!"

"Do you think that I want to tell him that we've failed?" Cheng Yu snapped. "I wasted weeks courting bandits and rebels in Li County that are having no effect on Gao Fan's defences whatsoever!"

"Gao Fan's position is partly bluff," Li Dian replied. "Our scouts report that he has far less men on his boats than initially inferred and that they won't survive a direct attack."

"So you advocate destroying them and clearing the waterway, disregarding the topographic advantages that he enjoys...?" Cheng Yu prompted.

"I do, Mister Cheng," Li Dian replied.

"...Agreed, then," Cheng Yu said. "We attack Gao Fan at once!"

Gao Fan was stunned when a soldier ran into his command room on the flagship and shouted, **"REPORT! The enemy is launching a direct attack on this position!"**

"That's ridiculous!" Gao Fan exclaimed. "They don't have the boats to-! ...But...! ...**Why am I just sitting here???**"

Gao Fan got to his feet, pushed the messenger to one side and ran onto the deck of the flagship; he was greeted by the sight of a host of small enemy boats that were overwhelming his with surprising ease, despite the pilots of those boats being far from the best river fighters in the empire.

"Counterattack at once!" Gao Fan ordered. **"We cannot lose control of the river!"**

But the surprise attack had demoralised the defenders, and Li Dian's inspiring charge had galvanised the Han sailors into fighting with every ounce of spirit and strength that they possessed: Gao Fan's boats were sunk or tipped over one by one, and the flagship was quickly surrounded on three sides.

"BACK, BACK!" Gao Fan ordered. **"RETREAT AND REGROUP!"**

Li Dian sailed his boat to the southern bank, where Cheng Yu was waiting with a small band of archers that were now firing on the retreating enemy; Li smiled and asked, **"Can they regroup?"**

"Unlikely," Cheng Yu replied. **"Good call, General: good call!"**

Yuan Shang's messengers reported the arrival of Cao Cao's fleet and the destruction of Gao Fan's inadequate naval defences to Yè City within a day.

"Gao Fan sees no sense in remaining on the river, so he is returning to Yè; Cao Cao's setting up small bases along the riverbank and the roads in the south of Wei Prefecture in preparation for an attack on the capital, but his first target is obviously Li County, more specifically the county capital, as it could serve as a bridgehead for the his campaign," Shen Pei said as he studied the reports. "I expect another request for further reinforcement from Yuan Tan within the next two days."

"Well then we must have all of our forces travel to this region and meet Cao Cao with everything we have!" Yuan Shang declared.

"I say nay," Shen Pei retorted. "We proceed with our original plan: we have Gao Gan stage an immediate attack on Hedong whilst providing extra troops to hold Li County. Cao Cao will have no choice but to divide his armies to save Hedong and undertake a protracted, wasteful siege on Li County City, and in no way will he be able to commit to a two-pronged assault on Li County and Yè."

"...I hope you're right," Yuan Shang said as he turned to Ji Province Registrar Li Fu.

"I am to speed orders to Gao Gan...?" Li Fu supposed.

"You're a smart man," Yuan Shang replied. "Do it at once."

Hedong Prefecture's eastern capital, Anyi, had once been the headquarters of Dong Zhuo's son-in-law, Niu Fu, and his then adviser Jia Xu, during Dong Zhuo's infamous tenure as Chancellor of State; now the city was under the custodianship of Administrator Wang Yi, who sent word of Gao Gan's invasion to the Grand Magistrate of Chang'an City, Zhong Yao.

"...Administrator Wang says that we are facing quite a few thousand men here... mostly Xiongnu infantry and Wuhuan cavalry," Zhong Yao said to his court in Chang'an. "Gao Gan has... has appointed a 'Guo Yuan' as the leading general, sad to say."

The men that knew that Guo Yuan was Zhong Yao's nephew murmured sympathetically.

"...So what do we do...?" an official asked.

"We haven't the troops to hold Chang'an and save Hedong, Mister Jia Kui," Zhong Yao replied. "I will do as His Excellency has already suggested and contact Ma Teng of the Qiang... and may Heaven bless us with a rare show of sincerity."

Gao Gan's assault on Hedong left Bing Province understaffed; that might have been seen as an opportunity by the remnants of the Black Mountain Bandits in times gone by, but their severe defeat at the hands of Yuan Shao during the ill-fated defence of Yijing City – at which time they were allied to the doomed rogue warlord Gongsun Zan, who perished in Yijing – had left their overall leader, 'Flying Swallow' Zhang Yan, a more cautious man.

"So we're not gonna try and take over Bing, then, boss...?" one lesser bandit chieftain asked.

"Nope," Flying Swallow replied. "We'll stick to light raids on villages in western Yòu for now, Circles: Yuan Xi's a bit of a joke, since his whole region's divided up into Liu Yu supporters, Gongsun Zan supporters, Yuan Shao supporters and tribes at the moment, while Gao Gan's prob'ly at his best... there's not a chance that he's left his capital unguarded to attack Hedong, and I don't much fancy getting the Yuans angry while we're still looking to rebuild our numbers."

"Why?" the bandit 'White Circles' asked further. "Yuan Shao's dead, Wen Chou and Yan Liang are dead, Han Juzi's dead, Zhang Hè's gone over to Cao Cao... who are we scared of?"

"Let's just say... let's just say I'm watchin' and waitin'," Flying Swallow replied. "I reckon that things might change quite a bit 'round 'ere in the next couple o' years... Zang Ba's lot joined Cao Cao, and that tells me something... it tells me that we need to be *very* careful, lads, and watch what happens..."

The Bing Province Governor, Gao Gan, moved to the border between Bing and Hedong Prefecture, which was in Central Province; his campaign commander, Guo Yuan, greeted him at the gates of the camp and escorted him to the command tent.

"All is well," Guo Yuan reported. "All of the smaller settlements surrendered without a fight."

"That's good," Gao Gan replied. "And you're not at all distracted by the news that your uncle Zhong Yao now governs Chang'an...?"

Guo Yuan shook his head and said, "I am saddened that my uncle has chosen to serve the wicked villain Cao Cao, but I know what I must do: when we take Hedong, Chang'an will be within our sights, and if I must kill my uncle, then I will. The most important thing is the restoration of order. I will toil like a horse for that great mission, Governor."

"...Very good," Gao Gan replied; he then turned to his cousin Gao Rou and said, "Am I right to say that they've called for aid...?"

"They have," Gao Rou sighed. "But I say again that it will probably not come from Cao Cao but from-"

"Cao Cao must – *must* – send aid from the east, Wenhui, else we are not fulfilling all of our objectives!" Gao Gan insisted. "We want to seize Hedong, harry Chang'an and steal resources and morale from Cao's campaign in Ji Province! No target must go unmet!"

"...We must therefore hope that everything goes according to plan," Gao Rou replied wearily.

The Qiang warlord Ma Teng received Zhong Yao's request for aid and summoned his best officers to his audience hall in Mei City.

"You want to help the Han?" Ma Chao scoffed. "Tell them to-!"

"This is not simple anymore, my son!" Ma Teng barked. "Now then... Pang De, you were one of those that joined me in rebellion against the corrupt officials in Liang Province, young as you were: you've become a fine warrior, one of my finest. You will accompany my son Chao to-"

"I will not!" Ma Chao insisted. "Get some other fool to go!"

"...Son, this is not simple anymore," Ma Teng replied.

"You keep saying that, but it is still *very* simple," Ma Chao retorted. "Nothing has changed: the Han are corrupt, just as they always were. Yuan Shao's sons are like their father, their uncle, their grandfather, uncles, great grandfather and great uncles before them! Cao Cao is a eunuch's adopted grandson: his father bought a good job from the eunuchs! I have heard all about them all! And now they fight each other for who gets to use the boy emperor to do as they please! No more! The tribes should be allied against them, not-!"

"No it *isn't* the same!" Ma Teng insisted. "We've suffered defeats at Han Sui's hands! I'm *tired*! We must stop fighting and work together, as you say, but until then we must work for the Han and make them trust us!"

"...We should not help the Han to fight Xiongnu and Wuhuan men," Ma Chao said. "I will kill as many Han people as you want, but why should we, the people of the land, whose land it is, fight each other for the Han's amusement...?"

"If...! ...If Gao Gan's alliance takes eastern Hedong, they'll advance to Chang'an, and from there, they'll attack Liang Province," Ma Teng explained. "Yes, we might be offered an alliance, but if the Han responds, it will lead to a purge; if we chase them away, we save Liang Province – and Xiliang, our home – from harm. Yuan Shao was no friend of ours... nor is Cao. But we must do this."

"I am happy to go, Great Chief Ma," Pang De said. "If Ma Mengqi would rather not help the Han, then I will-"

"No," Ma Chao interrupted. "You helped Father to destroy the Han before, and you are my friend, so if you are willing to help them now, you've thought it through and I trust your judgement. You and I, Pang Lingming, we'll go and smash the Han men and, if we must, the Xiongnu and Wuhuan that help them."

"...That's good," Ma Teng said wearily. "Go at once, both of you, and relieve Hedong before the fools do too much damage. The rest of you can go as well."

The Qiang warriors indicated their respect for Ma Teng and retreated from the hall; only Ma Teng's second and third sons, Ma Tie and Ma Xiu, remained to await their father's thoughts.

"...Chao is becoming increasingly belligerent and overconfident," Ma Teng said at last. "I love my son and respect him as a warrior, but I am frightened by his fearless challenges to authority. Cao Cao is not like the rest: he is more conciliatory when others might harass us, but if we 'crossed a line', he'd kill us all."

"But Chao is right that we shouldn't be helping the Han, Father," Ma Tie suggested.

"I don't do it out of choice," Ma Teng admitted. "I hate them and do not trust any of them – especially Cao Cao – for a moment, but we have been weakened by fighting each other. Some smaller clans now want to expand their own territories, like Yang Qiu and Li Kan, and that's more fighting that will weaken us further. We must unite... we must forget tribal differences and unite, or the Han will subjugate us as they have done to the Southern Xiongnu, and we will always be their stable and their barracks. If we cooperate now, we can recover, and then, perhaps, at a later time, when we are ready and the Han warlords have weakened each other as they also do, we can act... we must be *patient*."

Cao Cao's forces were barely opposed as they advanced to Li County; the region's self-appointed defender, Yuan Tan, was able to maintain the camps around Li County City with a great display of military skill, but he was seriously outnumbered and had once again called for help from his younger brother Yuan Shang in Yè City. Yuan Tan was doubly surprised when the reinforcements arrived, as there were double the expected number of soldiers and horses, and the army was led by Yuan Shang himself: Cao Cao immediately withdrew his forces to his camp when the new army arrived, and Yuan Shang was able to enter Yuan Tan's camp without a fight.

"You did not expect me to come here," Yuan Shang chuckled.

"...No," Yuan Tan replied. "Who guards Yè?"

"Shen Pei, Su Yòu, Ma Yan, Zhang Yi," Yuan Shang replied. "But what matters, Brother, is who is here in Li County: Jiang Yiqu, Ju Hu, Lü Xiang and Lü Kuang are here, so why won't we send Cao Cao to the netherworld...?"

Yuan Tan smirked and said, "I can see no reason."

"*Aiee*... **they're collaborating!**" Cao Cao cried as he threw his battle helmet to the floor of his command tent. "**They're actually collaborating! That should be *impossible*!**"

"Nothing is impossible in such times," Guo Jia replied as he collected the helmet from the floor and set it upon its stand. "You must watch your temper, Excellency, and let the Yuans be the ones to let passion destroy them."

"Fengxiao is quite right," Cheng Yu said as Cao Cao sat in his host seat and harrumphed. "Yes, they're collaborating: it cannot last."

"Yes, but every moment that it does last is a moment of delay, a moment when others might try and attack me!" Cao Cao replied.

"Who...? Liu Bei and Liu Biao...?" Guo Jia snickered. "One is foolishly brave but toothless, like a new-born puppy; the other is timid, like a sad old dog whose master tortured him, and as toothless as the puppy for different reasons. One might try and cajole the other into attacking you, but you're forgetting Sun Quan! When will it be safe for Liu Biao to attack Xuchang...?"

"Sun Quan also worries me," Cao Cao admitted. "He did not respond as I would have preferred to the request for a hostage, and I wonder if he will 'take the insult stoically' or try to attack Liu Fu now and rob me of yet another Inspector of Yang."

"Sun Quan is as afraid of attacks by the Shanyue tribes and his neighbour Huang Zu as Liu Biao and Huang Zu are afraid of him," Guo Jia insisted. "Those fellows will sit there and keep each other busy for you. Your only concern is the Yuans."

"...I hope that you are as correct," Cao Cao replied.

"*Aiee*... do not miss this opportunity, Cousin!" Liu Bei pleaded, but his host, Jing Province Governor Liu Biao, would not be moved.

"I am not risking an attack on Cao Cao at this point," Liu Biao insisted as his eyes wandered towards the entrance to his study, where his wife Lady Cai was quietly observing the conversation.

"Not even for the cause of saving the Han...?" Liu Bei asked.

"...We would be sticking our heads in the tiger's mouth, and I've done that enough, thank you," Liu Biao replied. "I am watching to see if the Yuans remain united against Cao Cao for more than a few weeks before I do anything: yes, I might pincer Xuchang if the Yuans are there to be 'the other arm', but if I attack now and the Yuans start bickering, I'll be the one caught in a pincer... between Cao Cao and Sun Quan. Is it any wonder that you're here with a handful of men if you make such brash decisions...?"

Liu Bei sighed miserably and said, "Perhaps you are right. I have the nerve to come here and tell you that I know best when-"

"I understand, Xuande," Liu Biao insisted. "You and I, we both want to see Cao Cao destroyed and the Liu clan's fortunes restored, from the lowest prince to the Son of Heaven. But the proper time will come about eventually, and... we must be... patient until then..."

Liu Biao started to cough; Liu Bei bowed humbly and said, "I should leave you now, and let you rest."

"Thank you...!" Liu Biao wheezed; Liu Bei bowed for a second time and retreated, and Lady Cai entered the room once Bei was gone.

"...He tried to goad you into marching on Xuchang... while he would be *where*...?" Lady Cai taunted. "*Here*, perhaps, 'guarding' your province for you...?"

"Hush!" Liu Biao replied breathlessly. "He... he would have been... at my *side*...!"

"I should like to think so," Lady Cai giggled. "After all, he has more to lose, and yet at the same time, more to *gain*. Never let him guard this place for you, Husband, or he will snatch Jing from you as he stole Xu from Tao Qian!"

"...Be gone, woman, and say no more!" Liu Bei protested. "Liu Bei... is distant *family*! Bei... is a close *ally*! Bei... *can* be *trusted*!"

"...You had better hope that you are right and that I, and my brother, and most if not all of your officials and generals are wrong, Husband," Lady Cai retorted as she shuffled away. "Still, he is quite the fighter: your unshared confidence would be well rewarded if he truly *were* a friend..."

"**Be gone!**" Liu Biao cried; he started to cough again, and as he struggled to breathe, he also started to struggle with Liu Bei's well-known reputation.

★★★★★★★★★★★★

28

Ma Chao and Pang De led their Qiang armies to Chang'an and camped outside the city while they awaited further orders from their temporary commander Zhong Yao.

"When we were last here, it was to take the city," Ma Chao said as he stared at the walls of the former capital. "Now we're here to serve as fighting dogs for the Han."

"Don't keep looking at it that way, Mengqi," Pang De replied.

"I see no other way," Ma Chao said. "These lands should be ours, but we are here to help our enemies keep them."

"We're here to prevent the Yuans – who are also Han men – from taking the region with the help of Wuhuan men and Southern Xiongnu men that will not care about us if they get a share," Pang De retorted. "If we help, then Cao Cao must reward us, even if it is only by returning to us what is ours. If they do not reward us properly, then they will deserve what would happen next."

Ma Chao grinned and said, "Put like that, old friend, I can do this!"

Grand Magistrate Zhong Yao arranged for Ma Chao and Pang De to meet him at the gates of Chang'an: Zhong bowed slightly and said, "I welcome you both and thank you in advance for the great service that you do for us."

"We do this for the Qiang, not the Han," Ma Chao retorted. "As long as that is understood, no more needs to be said."

"...Very well," Zhong Yao replied.

Pang De bowed and said, "I, De, am anxious to bring an end to this threat, Grand Magistrate. What are your instructions...?"

Zhong Yao smiled and said, "You are most courteous, Colonel Pang, and I appreciate that, given the difficult relationship that the Han and Qiang have. Sad to say, the defenders of Hedong have been forced to abandon many positions: the city of Anyi is surrounded, but the enemy have advanced past that point and begun a march toward Chang'an without waiting for Anyi to fall."

"They must cross the Yellow River at some point above or at where it meets the Wei River," Ma Chao suggested. "We will march at once and intercept them before they cross."

"My thanks," Zhong Yao replied.

"...It is the Han emperor's thanks, not yours, that I await with interest," Ma Chao retorted. "It doesn't matter how grateful *you* are, 'Grand Magistrate'. A lot of Han cronies have come and gone from Liang and this city, and in the end, swords still-"

"Forgive my interrupting you, General Ma, but we should hurry onward," Pang De said worriedly. "We'll advance at once."

"...Once again, I offer my thanks," Zhong Yao replied.

Yuan Shang and Yuan Tan provided a genuine challenge to Cao Cao's forces when they worked together as a team: both were unafraid of leading men into battle personally, and the defensive positions around Li County City – which included fenced camps, trenches, towers, dirt mounds manned by archers, small walls and wooden palisades – withstood every attack that Cao Cao launched against them.

Over the first few days, Li Dian, Xu Huang, Zhang Liao,

Cao Xiu, Cao Hong, Xiahou Dun, Yu Jin, Yue Jin and Zhang Hè were tasked with breaking through the seas of defences – which were thickest to the south and west, since small rivers and friendly territory lay to the north and the surging Yellow River ran to the east – but every attempt concluded with, at best, a brief removal of some small piece of the vast defensive network that was quickly restored after more fighting, or nothing much achieved at all.

"...This might take a while," Cheng Yu admitted as he sat and watched Cao Cao pace back and forth across the command tent.

"We *can't* be here for too long!" Cao Cao cried angrily. "What games Heaven plays! 'The brothers divided, no longer so tall, once parted by greed, and certain to fail, now are united, as stones in a wall, in an hour of need, and bound to prevail.' Why let me beat their once-invincible father and then do this to me?"

"...You're assuming that this success will last," Guo Jia replied. "Eventually, their tactics of hiding behind defences will start to tax Yuan Tan, and he will suggest an all-out attack, and if not him then one of the generals that fears for their reputation. When they do that, we've won the first battle."

"But how long will that take?" Cao Cao asked desperately. "I'm losing Hedong at the same time: how long can supplies, morale and loyalty sustain us...?"

"At the worst, six months," Guo Jia insisted. "And Hedong will be relieved long before then, Lord Cao."

"*Six months* sieging *defensive works*???" Cao Cao cried. "We need to siege the city afterwards! Sun Tzu would either laugh or cry at such a notion!"

"Sun Tzu said that sieges were undesirable and a last resort, not that they were never to be used," Guo Jia retorted. "And I very much doubt that the Yuan brothers will last long when they are cooped up together in a besieged city, each looking at the other and blaming them for hundreds of years of Yuan clan dominance crumbling before their eyes. They'd yield, betray the other or flee together in that case, and the city will fall within days, Lord Cao, one way or the other."

"I can add little to that, except that the cowardly, wretched citizens of Li County will probably throw the gates of the city open if the Yuans don't do so," Cheng Yu said. "But I do agree that months of fighting in order to clear piles of dirt and fill in trenches is not desirable; that said, Excellency, Yuan Shao faced the same trials around Yijing Fortress when he fought Gongsun Zan, and that ended in the only way that it could."

Cao Cao laughed and said, "A valid point, Mister Cheng! But there is one last opinion that I desire..."

All eyes turned to Jia Xu, who smiled and replied, "Today, Excellency, I am superfluous. Mister Guo Fengxiao and Elder Cheng have said everything that needed to be said. I might, perhaps, add one thing: today, we are the attacker in enemy territory, and rebellions are appearing everywhere, while the commanders are unable to sustain unity forever. Qing Province is divided between friends and enemies and is therefore preoccupied; the men of Yòu Province do nothing to aid either side, for whatever reason; and the men of Bing Province waste time fighting elsewhere as part of some poor stratagem. It might take time, but the outcome is certain."

"...Look how much of one's life is spent *waiting*, gentlemen," Cao Cao sighed. "But wait I must, old as I am and older still that I become... and wait I shall."

In the west of the country, Guo Yuan's invading forces reached the Yellow River and prepared to cross and continue on the road to Chang'an: little stood in their way until a messenger reported the approach of Ma Chao and Pang De's Qiang defence forces.

"**I never thought that I would see this day,**" Guo Yuan chuckled. "**The so-called 'Han Imperial army' resorting to employing Qiang mercenaries!**"

"**Be very careful, my lord,**" Guo Yuan's adviser said. "**The Qiang are dangerous.**"

"**Are they more dangerous than the Wuhuan or Xiongnu that we have among our number?**" Guo Yuan retorted. "**I want a full advance! We cross the river *now*! I will lead the crossing myself!**"

Pang De sped ahead of the unenthusiastic Ma Chao and reached the Yellow River just as General Guo Yuan's men were crossing at a ford.

"**We must strike at once!**" Pang De declared. "**Stay with the supplies, Brother!**"

"**Won't we wait for Mengqi?**" Pang De's older brother, Pang Rou, asked worriedly.

"**They'll have crossed by then!**" Pang De replied as he urged his horse forward.

Guo Yuan was surprised at Pang De's decision to attack his men.

"**This barbarian is outnumbered!**" Guo Yuan said. "**He must want to die!**"

"**No, my lord, we must halt and form a defensive line!**" Guo Yuan's adviser pleaded.

"**What nonsense!**" Guo Yuan retorted. "**He defies Sun Tzu's teachings; he'll achieve nothing but dying!**"

But Pang De's elite cavalrymen were among the finest in the northwest of the land, and Guo Yuan's small Wuhuan and Southern Xiongnu cavalries – who were best placed to counter the attack – were stuck behind the advancing infantry and could not risk crossing at deeper points of the raging river. Pang De's horsemen dashed this way and that, hacking at the Yuan soldiers as they tried to maintain their footing in the shallow waters; Guo Yuan's adviser raised his sword and tried to fight, but he was quickly cut down, which caused Guo to panic and try to turn his horse in order to flee. There was nowhere to run to: the path beneath the shallow, sandy water was rocky and treacherous, and the addition of numerous bodies did nothing to help the situation.

"**Ayah! Heaven hates me!**" Guo Yuan cried. "**I am being punished for defying the Son of Heaven and betraying my good and kindly uncle!**"

Pang De was singling out the few horsemen in the enemy detachment in the hope of killing senior officers, so it was no surprise that he encountered Guo Yuan and challenged him; Guo raised his spear, howled desperately and charged, but his horse stumbled and Pang cut him down with next to no effort. Once the officers had fallen, the Yuan forces scattered; the Southern Xiongnu and Wuhuan men on the eastern bank of the river started a retreat, but Pang De was determined to send a message to his appointed enemies.

"**FIGHT ON!**" Pang De ordered. "**ALL MUST BE CRUSHED!**"

Ma Chao finally arrived and added his men to the rout: Pang De crossed the river and dealt a heavy blow to the retreating Yuan forces, who then staged a general retreat to the region around the city of Anyi.

"**WE SHOULD CONTINUE!**" Pang De cried.

"**No!**" Ma Chao said. "**First we tell the Han what we've done for them! We don't owe them more help just yet!**"

The death of Guo Yuan and the expectation that the Qiang would advance caused mass panic in Gao Gan's ranks; the siege of Anyi was lifted, and Gao Gan retreated to the Bing Province border to prepare for counterattacks. The news delighted the Grand Magistrate of Chang'an, Zhong Yao, who left the city and travelled to the Qiang camp to offer monetary rewards and gratitude for their efforts; a grand banquet was held in the city of Puzhou, where Ma Chao and Pang De were treated as heroes by the grateful populace.

"I am truly amazed at your valour, gentlemen!" Zhong Yao declared. "General Ma, Colonel Pang, you shall be forever regarded as among the greatest men of the era!"

"I only did what was asked of me," Pang De replied humbly.

"It seems that the situation has drastically changed," Jia Kui said. "Anyi was suddenly relieved, and the enemy fled: can it be that Gao Gan or their vanguard general was routed...?"

Zhong Yao hummed ambiguously and replied, "Perhaps, Mister Jia, perhaps: but when did that occur, if that was the case...? Is it that Gao Gan or the aforementioned commanding officer was part of the vanguard that marched toward Chang'an...?"

"I brought with me the heads of the officers for inspection," Pang De declared as he gestured toward a macabre collection of sacks that were positioned behind him.

"...That... that is not unusual," Zhong Yao whimpered as Pang De gestured to his brother, Pang Rou, who then started to look in the sacks as if searching for a particular head.

"Are you squeamish, Mister Zhong?" Ma Chao chuckled.

"N-no, General Ma, I have inspected heads before," Zhong Yao said, "I just-"

"**Aha! That is him!**" Pang De cried. "My apologies, Grand Magistrate, but I have just been handed the head of the leader of those men, whose life was mine to take... here it is."

Pang De placed the head onto the ground in front of him so that Zhong Yao could see the dead man's face; Zhong Yao's sudden, anguished cry took every man present by surprise.

"What kind of reaction is that?" Ma Chao scoffed.

"**Ayah! Ayah!** That...! That is...! ...*Aiee*...!" Zhong Yao lamented as he picked up the familiar head.

"...What is the matter...?" Pang De asked nervously. "He was the enemy, Grand Magistrate! No mistake has been made!"

"...Such... such a good boy, he was once...!" Zhong Yao sobbed as he inspected the lifeless face of Guo Yuan. "I... have no son, and...

and so...! **What will I tell my sister???**"

"*Aiee...* what a shame!" Jia Kui cried.

"...I am confused," Pang De admitted.

"Guo Yuan is – was – the nephew of Grand Magistrate Zhong," Jia Kui explained.

"And he served Gao Gan...?" Ma Chao exclaimed.

"*Aiee...* I have wronged you, Grand Magistrate!" Pang De said miserably. "How can I atone?"

"Even... even I am his uncle, he was a *traitor*, Colonel," Zhong Yao sighed as he lowered Guo Yuan's head to the floor and pushed it away as if rebuking it. "You punished a traitor to the Han: why apologise for that...?"

"...I'm impressed," Ma Chao said. "You adhere to the proper thinking, Mister Zhong: others might have become petty."

"I am Grand Magistrate of the old capital," Zhong Yao replied as he wiped tears from his eyes. "I must think of everything, not live within some small sphere. The rewards will be the same... more, in fact, since we did not expect the campaign to be over so soon. As soon as I have returned to Chang'an, I... I will ensure that more rewards are bestowed: you have my solemn word, gentlemen."

"And your nephew...?" Pang De asked.

"Do with him as you would do with the others," Zhong Yao replied. "He was my nephew once, yes... but not now."

Pang De smiled awkwardly and bowed; Pang Rou removed Guo Yuan's head from its resting place, and the banquet then continued, albeit with a more subdued atmosphere.

The end of the short-lived Hedong campaign put Bing Administrator Gao Gan on the defensive and left the Yuan brothers without a morale-boosting diversion; Cao Cao was able to focus on the siege of Li County, but the defenders did not cede any ground. Yuan Tan and his deputy, Yan Jing, were the ones that surprised and frustrated Cao Cao's forces the most; the two always seemed to be wherever they were needed and pushed their enemies back with relative ease.

"**Curse them all!**" Cao Cao cried as he stood and watched Yan Jing repel Li Dian's infantry for a second time in two days. "**I have thousands more talents than they do! How do they defy me so easily???**"

"**You're the attacker: the attacker always suffers setbacks in situations like these,**" Guo Jia replied calmly. "**What is now their greatest strength will, because of hubris, impatience and ego, soon become their greatest weakness.**"

"**Yes, but when is 'soon'?**" Cao Cao asked. "**How long must I wait for them to undo themselves?**"

"**We have enjoyed a sudden, unexpected victory in Hedong,**" Guo Jia replied. "**I cannot say when we will triumph, but we will.**"

Yan Jing rode to the outer perimeter of the defence works and laughed theatrically before pointing his spear and shouting, "**Here is Yan Jing! Where are the heroes under Cao Cao, or has the villain only got mediocrities?**"

"**Bastard!**" Xiahou Dun cried; he tried to charge at Yan Jing but he was immediately repelled by a hail of arrows that killed several of his infantrymen.

"...**RETREAT!**" Cao Cao ordered. "**BACK TO THE CAMP!**"
The Han forces retreated miserably while Yuan Shang and Yuan Tan looked on.
"Now is the moment for us to strike!" Yuan Tan suggested.
"No it isn't," Yuan Shang retorted. "We must hold our position and wear them down, Brother."
"...Am I not now your *cousin*...?" Yuan Tan scoffed. "And is this 'hide and wait' stratagem the idea of your man Shen Pei...?"
"Partly, but I have other advisers and ideas of my own," Yuan Shang insisted. "We can wear them down easily if we just continue to maintain the defensive works and goad them into walking into traps. They cannot go around us, and they only have limited supplies. The rules of war dictate that a siege should go on no longer than three months if they cannot secure local supplies, which they cannot, not without difficulty; if we are patient, then they will retreat *properly*, and *then* we can attack them and destroy them. Chasing them to their camp will only-"
"We could raid their camp and burn their supplies, if only to get revenge for Wuchao!" Yuan Tan suggested. "This stratagem of waiting costs us supplies as well, and it is weak! The Wuhuan will not support us if we look weak!"
"...I know that," Yuan Shang said, "but we are not being 'weak', we are being 'cautious', and the Wuhuan can be made to understand that."
"For a time," Yuan Tan retorted. "Wait too long though, and-"
"Let us worry about that if and when we are made to remain here 'too long'," Yuan Shang insisted. "For now, we are enjoying victories and riling the old villain: let's make him suffer. For Father, let's make him suffer."
"...Alright," Yuan Tan said. "You win the argument... *for now*."

****

29

For months, Cao Cao's northern campaign and the Yuan brothers' counter-campaigns locked them into a stalemate: the Qiang armies led by Ma Chao and Pang De prevented Gao Gan from returning to Hedong, and Yuan Shang and Yuan Tan kept Cao Cao from reaching Li County City – or any other strategic stronghold – by way of their formidable and enduring defence network. Cao Cao's crippling headaches frequently confined him to his bed, and Guo Jia missed many days through self-inflicted sickness: the morale of the Han forces started to decline, as many saw their inability to pass the outer camps as humiliating and a poor omen when considering the inevitable siege on the city itself.

"…Perhaps we should retreat," Cao Cao said to his assembled officials; it was a rare day when both he and Guo Jia were well enough to be present, and Guo was in surprisingly high spirits.

"We need not consider that just yet," Guo Jia insisted. "Twice now, Yan Jing has almost been provoked into charging beyond the outer perimeter, and Yuan Tan and Yuan Shang have been seen arguing. However ignominious our own situation might seem, Lord Cao, theirs is worse and they know it. To pose one problem of the many that they face: 'Whatever would the Wuhuan say…?'"

"That's right," Cheng Yu said. "The Wuhuan actually owe the Yuans a lot and they fear what will happen if you got the better of the Yuans in the future, Excellency; Yuan Tan, however, is not bright enough to know that."

"…So you think that they will become impatient soon, then…?" Cao Cao asked.

"If I may, Excellency," the brawny, intimidating Zhang Hè said.

"Speak, General Zhang," Cao Cao prompted. "You know them better than us, so your words will be Heaven-sent!"

"Yan Jing isn't as formidable as he seems, although I am not the best man to overcome him," Zhang Hè said. "Yan can be made to disobey orders and charge, but only if he is driven to the heights of anger and knows that he is not the only reckless man in the field; Yuan Tan is a belligerent sort, and he won't like being made to hide behind defences for what is now almost six months, especially when he is being told to do so by his younger brother, whose chieftainship is at his expense. A show of false weakness or a sustained goading campaign might both be considered."

"I suggest the former," Guo Jia said. "Goading risks getting too close to those defences: we want to lure them out of their safety zone and turn their walls, trenches and mounds from a shield to an obstruction."

"…Whatever it takes, gentlemen," Cao Cao replied. "We have been here long enough."

Cao Cao's forces began a series of deliberate failed charges on the outer perimeter of the Yuan brothers' southern defences; Yuan Tan studied the reports and said, "The lack of food, catalogue of failures and pining for home has started to weaken the enemy, just as we said it would!"

"…I'm not sure," Yuan Shang replied. "The incompetence seems a little forced to me, as though-"

"Don't be ridiculous!" Yuan Tan chortled. "What proud man *wants* to lose so gracelessly...?"

"We must be cautious," Xin Pi said. "Cao Cao has already made fools of the Yuans on several occasions, and-"

"Are you defecting, Xin Pi?" Yuan Tan asked angrily. "Do you now want to work for Shang? Is that why you left your family in Yè?"

Xin Pi lowered his head and exhaled woefully.

"...My brother is still your vassal," Xin Ping insisted. "And I have also left my family in Yè: most of us still leave our families in Yè."

"This tactic of waiting has worked for as long as it can!" Yuan Tan insisted. "We must now exploit their weakness and defeat them!"

"I am unsure of their weakness," Yuan Shang replied.

"As much as I regret to say so, Lord Yuan, so do I," Guo Tu said.

"You're all being weak!" Yuan Tan heckled. "You all said, 'Three months is all it will take', but because we have not pressed them when they retreat, they have been able to stay here for *six*! *Six months*! And we know why, as well! They know that we will look weak to our allies! The Wuhuan, the starving peasants, the bandits – including the Black Mountain Bandits – and the rebels that still support former leaders like Han Fu, Liu Yu and Gongsun Zan, they will all start to rise up against us, and-!"

"They already do, but we manage!" Yuan Shang protested. "Your idea is to charge past our own defensive works, putting those works behind us and making them as much *our* enemy as *theirs*!"

"**Cowards and fools!**" Yuan Tan retorted. "**I will not stand by and watch as Cao Cao grinds down our support, starves the populace, takes us down man by man and turns our tribal allies against us! When he next retreats, I will pursue and destroy him!**"

Cao Cao had assigned the task of provoking the enemy to Li Dian and Yue Jin; the two repeatedly charged the southern defences and retreated with false shows of disorganisation and frustration, and General Yan Jing was becoming increasingly irritated with his explicit orders to remain within the perimeter. Yuan Tan located his officer among the defensive positions after one 'successful repulsion' and said, "**No more cowering, Yan Jing! Let's you and I show the world our might!**"

"**I will follow you to victory, Lord Yuan Tan!**" Yan Jing replied.

Li Dian was leading the Han army's retreat, while the short, stocky Yue Jin took the rear; Yan Jing charged at Yue and engaged him in a horseback duel while Yuan Tan raced ahead to challenge Li Dian. The apparent advantage had forced Yuan Shang to let his other officers join the fray: Lü Kuang, Lü Xiang and Jiang Yiqu took their own men beyond the perimeter in order to counterattack on the western front while Yuan Shang, Ju Hu, Guo Tu, Xin Pi and Xin Ping advanced to aid Yuan Tan.

"**Such small, ridiculous-looking men Cao Cao employs!**" Yan Jing heckled. "**No wonder he must content himself with intrigue and cowardly ambushes!**"

Yue Jin smirked silently; Yan Jing was at least a foot taller and obviously quite strong, but he was slower and had not adjusted his swings and lunges to compensate for his opponent's height. Yan Jing repeatedly missed as the agile Yue Jin darted about on his nimble, well-trained horse, and each miss made Yan angrier and less careful. Yue Jin was waiting for Yan Jing to make a mistake that he could not recover from, and several minutes of duelling gave him that opening: Yue lunged as Yan faltered, running him through with his spear and killing him outright.

"Yan Jing is dead!" one Yuan infantryman cried: the effect of the announcement was immediate and devastating. Yuan Tan was forced to break off his attack on Li Dian when he realised that his men were scattering or trying to get back to the city: more of Cao Cao's men were joining the rout, and – just as predicted – the defensive works that had served so well were now an impediment to the defenders' retreat.

"Don't let the Yuan brothers live!" Cao Hong bellowed.

"Don't let _any_ of them live!" Xiahou Dun cackled.

The Yuan soldiers were panicking, abandoning their weapons and fleeing when they could not see a way through their own defences: Yuan Shang waited for his brother before he tried to retreat, and the two fought their way back to the city together.

"Destroy the defences as you pursue!" Li Dian ordered. **"Push them back to the city and trap them there!"**

The Han officers led the majority of their men through the defensive maze while others dedicated their efforts to turning the mounds into landfill to remove the trenches, toppling the flimsy wooden towers and dismantling the palisades; the victory was being partially repeated along the western front as word of the rout reached the defenders there as well. Within hours, the southern defences were almost gone, the accompanying camps were ablaze and the Yuan brothers were trapped within Li County City itself; the western defences were halved and the Yuan men abandoned the positions to take shelter in the city with their lords.

"I told you," Guo Jia said as Cao Cao examined the battle reports and laughed; the command tent was filled with smiling officials and proud officers.

"What can I say?" Cao Cao replied. "They're truly stupid: truly, unbelievably stupid! How can I not win now...?"

"We must seek out supplies," Cheng Yu suggested. "There will be grain in nearby cities and villages, and I advise that we procure some of it."

"...Yes... before you employ your infamous method of obtaining 'meat', Old Cheng," Cao Hong heckled. "I have no desire to eat the enemy corpses – or my own men – if there is grain to be had."

Cheng Yu sneered at Cao Hong but did not respond.

"We will do what must be done!" Cao Cao said cheerfully. "All that matters now is that the Yuans are trapped in Li County City: yes, we'll need to siege the place, but the main obstacle is passed! Only a few of their western defences survive, and they are not worth dismantling: we'll not be letting them out of the city to make use of them! Let us begin the siege at once!"

"...Do not consider blaming me for this!" Yuan Tan said as he stared at the angry, miserable officials – including his own counsel – and his brother, Yuan Shang.

"Who else is to blame?" Li Fu asked. "You–"

"Little worm!" Yuan Tan cried. **"I'll–!"**

"You'll not harm a hair on my registrar's head," Yuan Shang said

insistently. "And in answer to your protest, Brother, I have to say
that the blame is shared between us all: if we had attacked in
concert, or maybe chosen a different time when Cao Cao had not
yet planned to feign weakness... but it has ended thus, and we
must plan for the future."
"...What do you mean...?" Yuan Tan asked.
"We cannot stay here and wait for Cao Cao to start sieging us,"
Guo Tu replied.
"Quite right," Yuan Shang said. "We must flee at once, together,
to Yè, where we can secure more men, regroup, rebuild morale
and work out a way to turn Cao's single victory into a trap, just as
he has just done to us. In fact, let us see if we cannot lure him
into rushing after us... and stretching beyond his reach...!"
"...Alright," Yuan Tan conceded.

Cao Cao was not surprised when a scout brought word of the Yuan
brothers' fighting retreat from Li County City on that same night.
"**We must pursue at once!**" Xu Yòu suggested anxiously.
"...I won't pursue just yet, not in the dark," Cao Cao sighed.
"**Ayah! Sometimes I wonder what...!** ...*Aiee!*" Xu Yòu cried as
he retreated from Cao Cao's command tent.
"You're not alone in your frustration, Ziyuan," Cao Cao murmured.
"I only wish that you would see that, you foolish little man."
"You are disappointed, Lord Cao, but this means that Li County
City – and, in turn, the whole county – is ours," Guo Jia said. "And
we got the city without a fight."
"I wanted the Yuan brothers – dead or alive – to end their careers
here," Cao Cao admitted. "Their retreat to Yè extends their
lifespans and their chances of victory."
"By surrendering Li County, we now have the ability to go in any
direction in Ji Province – or Wei Prefecture, at least – and I
suggest that we begin by advancing to Yè and seizing Yiyang
simultaneously," Guo Jia replied. "If we do that, we'll have
successfully cut off all of the key routes to Qing Province, denying
Yuan Tan's allies an easy way to add their own spears to his."
"...I'll do as you say," Cao Cao decided. "I'll send Xu Huang and Jia
Xu to take Yiyang, and I'll go to Yè in person. You'll come with me,
Fengxiao; Cheng Yu can look after Li County."
"That is the right course, Lord Cao," Guo Jia replied.

****

30

Xu Huang was less than pleased to be travelling to Yiyang with Jia Xu: the adviser guessed as much and said, "You remember our time together under the regents and Dong Zhuo before them, do you not...?"

"I am reminded of our own errors, separate and shared," Xu Huang replied. "I was an affiliate of the White Wave Bandits that abducted His Majesty, and before that a vassal of Dong Zhuo, Li Jue, Guo Si and others that murdered the previous Majesty, who died as the Prince of Hongnong... I was wretched. And you, Mister Jia, have aided a tyrant, empowered regents and harmed our lord greatly. Yet here we are, forgiven and reborn, serving His Excellency Cao and His Majesty. We are fortunate to serve such magnanimous lords."

"...Indeed, yes," Jia Xu said. "Now, uh... I wonder if you had your own thoughts about seizing Yiyang."

"I want to do so bloodlessly, since that will win hearts and minds," Xu Huang replied. "Is that your thought as well...?"

"It is," Jia Xu said. "We shall try diplomacy."

The Magistrate of Yiyang City, Han Fan, stared over the walls of his city and grimaced as he watched 1,000 soldiers approach: he had less than 300, and he knew that a siege or violent battle was very likely. But the Magistrate and his advisers were pleasantly surprised when Xu Huang sent a man to the gates to politely request that the city could yield without a fight and its inhabitants could go about their business as they usually did: Han Fan gathered his officials and asked, "Would I be a traitor if I yielded?"

"Not at all," one adviser said. "The people wouldn't thank you if you subjected them to a siege: if this Xu Huang fellow is honest when he says that the city will be left unharmed, and that this is just a strategic move to block roads and such, then we should agree. If Lord Yuan can relieve us, he will."

"...Fine, fine: I will yield, then!" Han Fan declared.

Cao Cao was pleased to hear that Yiyang had surrendered without a fight, but it was small consolation given that Yuan Shang had managed to rally his men and obstruct Cao Cao's march to Yè City. The Han army's supplies were now starting to run dangerously low, and the distance between the Yellow River, Li County and Yè had thinned the army down to little more than the vanguard by the time that the Yuans' capital was finally within sight after almost a month of fighting and advancing.

We have them!" Yuan Shang said as he watched the depleted enemy forces approach the walls of Yè. **"Cao Cao has finally erred, just as Shen Pei predicted: a newly arrived foe will be an exhausted, demoralised and defeated one! Li Fu: enter the city and have Gao Fan ready the archery divisions to provide cover! Tell Shen Pei that Su Yòu and Ma Yan will lead their men out of the gates! Lü Kuang, Lü Xiang: prepare for a counter-charge! Ju Hu, Jiang Yiqu: we will provide support!"**

Yuan Shang's registrar, Li Fu, turned and moved toward the city gates, which briefly opened to allow him to enter; Lü Kuang and Lü Xiang advanced at speed with their small bands of cavalrymen while their infantry did their best to pursue.

"**And me...?**" Yuan Tan asked of his brother.

"**How do you wish to assist...?**" Yuan Shang said tonelessly.

"**I will join the charge!**" Yuan Tan replied. "**I owe Cao Cao's rat, Yue Jin, for the loss of Yan Jing, and I want to kill Cao Cao personally!**"

"**You need no permission from me to do that, if that is your wish,**" Yuan Shang said. "**By all means, add your formidable spear to the charge!**"

Yuan Tan grinned, leapt onto his horse and shouted, "**Guo Tu, Xin Pi, Xin Ping, Han Xun: you will accompany me! Let us lead our men together and rid the world of Cao Cao for my father and for His Majesty!**"

Yuan Shang waited until his brother's militia had departed before he turned to Ju Hu and said, "**We must be ready in case of treachery. My brother, sad to say, would like to turn this into a play for power if we are successful.**"

"**My father would weep at such a thing,**" Ju Hu replied. "**Never fear, Lord Yuan: I will protect you from Yuan Tan with my very life if that is what I must do.**"

The Yuan forces tore into the reduced ranks of the Han forces and dealt a severe blow; Cao Cao was genuinely taken aback at the ferocity of the attack and its success, but Guo Jia was unfazed.

"They are trying to be cornered tigers," Guo Jia said. "Their ability was within my expectations, but it is nothing to worry about. We won't be able to get near the city, so we should turn about and seek out supplies instead."

"...Just like that...?" Xiahou Dun exclaimed. "Won't they pursue if we do that?"

"A little way, but the wily Shen Pei and Guo Tu will advise their respective lords to remain close to the city and not fall for their own trick," Guo Jia replied. "We'll go to Yin'an, occupy the city, raid the grain stores and rest our men for a month or so. If, once we've done that, it looks like we can come back here and have some success, we'll come back; if we cannot achieve anything, then I have a plan that must not be explained until it is the only option available to us."

"...You advisers," Xiahou Dun muttered.

Cao Cao laughed and said, "Fine! We'll–"

Suddenly, Xu Yòu entered the command tent and said, "Yet again, Mengde, you sent me off on a fool's errand while you plot with that sickly schemer Guo Jia! I'm an adviser as well! Why do you keep leaving me out of discussions? You wanted to leave me in Li County, and before that, you–!"

"You're lucky that I don't break your neck," Xiahou Dun growled.

"*No*, Yuanrang," Cao Cao ordered; he then turned to Xu Yòu and said. "I do not leave you out of discussions because I do not trust you, Ziyuan; I do so because I am trying to reduce your visibility to the enemy. Some of your family are still captive, aren't they...?"

"...Yes," Xu Yòu replied.

"And further to that, this is too personal for you," Cao Cao continued. "You get so passionate, so angry... the reason that we've advanced too far and too fast is because I allowed you to dictate our pace, and look at what a mess it's caused!"

"...You're right," Xu Yòu said. "I... I am just anxious to see the Yuans eradicated."

"But your issues were with Yuan Shao alone, weren't they...?" Guo Jia teased.

"You know quite well that my head will be a fine temple offering for those boys!" Xu Yòu retorted. "They blame me for Wuchao and everything else besides! I do not wish to be assassinated on a road by a fugitive son of the complainant like Sun Ce was: the only way to secure my safety is for that entire clan to be exterminated to the third degree!"

"...I shall be the one to decide the fate of the Yuans, Ziyuan... not you," Cao Cao said coldly.

"Why wouldn't you want them all dead as well, for Heaven's sake??? Why care for their lives? You'd be cold bones in Guandu if I hadn't saved you from Benchu, and they'd have slaughtered your clan to the last child!" Xu Yòu heckled. **"And why shouldn't I-!** ...I... I have... I have said too much. But it is only because I worry about *both of us*, Mengde!"

Cao Cao, Guo Jia, Xiahou Dun and Cao Cao's ever-present bodyguard, Xu Chu, were all glaring at the small, unthreatening Xu Yòu as he continued to ramble; Cao Cao eventually tired of the babbling and said, **"For a man that knows he's said too much, you have certainly insisted on compounding the error!"**

Xu Yòu lowered his head and sighed.

"Go, *please*, and make sure that the 'fool's errands' that I sent you to undertake are properly done," Cao Cao continued. "We are all working as hard as we can to bring an end to the menace of the Yuans, and none works harder – or has more to lose – than I do. Even *you*, lost in blissful conceit, know that to be true."

Xu Yòu bowed silently and retreated.

"...If he had not ensured his certain death for treason at the hands of the Yuans, I might now worry that he might allow our heated exchange to alter his allegiance... but fortunately, he has nowhere to run to," Cao Cao said as he turned to his battle maps. "That... that argument was, perhaps, our shared mistake: he made a valid point about the Yuans and I acknowledge that. I would like to forget it and return to our more pressing concerns. We'll retreat to Yin'an, restock our supplies, rest our men, and plan from there."

"I'll go and prepare my men for departure," Xiahou Dun replied.

Cao Cao nodded tersely, and Xiahou Dun retreated.

"...Are you alright, my lord...?" Guo Jia prompted.

"How I *tire of this*, Fengxiao," Cao Cao sighed.

"And yet you cling to the notion of life being a valuable, exciting treasure trove of experiences," Guo Jia chuckled. "The next ten, twenty, thirty, forty years will be just like this. It will be a relief to me when I am done with it all."

"...Don't go to the netherworld just yet, Guo Fengxiao," Cao Cao said. "I need you to help me finish what I have started."

"I promise nothing," Guo Jia replied, "other than my service while I live."

The news that Cao Cao had suddenly withdrawn from the area around Yè City was greeted with relief by most of the pro-Yuan

settlements in Ji Province, but Yiyang reacted to Cao's next move
– assaulting the city of Yin'an and pillaging the local granaries –
with alarm and suspicion. The surrendered Magistrate of Yiyang,
Han Fan, had been allowed to remain in his post, but he now
considered Xu Huang to be a threat and summoned his officials for
a private discussion.
"I now worry that we have been lied to, gentlemen," Han Fan
said. "Xu Huang and Jia Xu claim that this place is safe, but when
I hear about Yin'an..."
"Firstly, Yin'an resisted, and secondly, Magistrate, we have been
under occupation for a month without incident," an official replied.
"Jia Xu is not here now, only Xu Huang, who–"
"*Who*, I understand, is a former *White Wave Bandit*, taking orders
directly from the main leaders, Han Xian and Yang Feng," Han Fan
declared, "and he, like Yang Feng, was a former vassal of Dong
Zhuo, Li Jue and Guo Si as well."
The officials murmured uneasily.
"We've suffered the raids by the Black Mountain Bandits, who are
bad enough," Han Fan continued. "The White Waves robbed
people at blade-point outside Luoyang – the *capital* – they were so
egregious! And they might well have had a hand in Dong Zhuo's
rise to power if some of their number ended up in his employ!
That's made even more likely by the fact that he knows *Jia Xu*,
Dong Zhuo's counsel during the worst years!"
"So... so we should resist, then...?" a second official asked.
"I'll be honest, gentlemen: I don't trust Cao Cao's word, even if I
was going to trust Xu Huang's," Han Fan replied. "If he's taken to
plundering for food, then he's desperate, and desperate warlords
do horrible things. Remember Xu Province...? That actually *was*
Cao Cao, and has he changed at all, I wonder...?"
The city's chief military officer hummed thoughtfully and said,
"We'll fight. I can close all of the gates before nightfall: Xu
Huang's men remain camped outside at all times. His paltry
thousand cannot siege us, so he will retreat or request
reinforcements, and it is better to fight than be pillaged and
slaughtered like cattle."
"And the rest of you...?" Han Fan asked; the majority voiced their
approval of the idea and the rest remained silent. Han Fan smiled
and said, "Good: those that do not agree can leave the city or
remain at home. Let us teach Cao Cao a lesson!"

Within hours, Xu Huang was staring at the walls of Yiyang City
and sighing miserably.
"...What will you do...?" Xu's deputy, Shi Huan, asked quietly.
"I vowed that I would take the place bloodlessly," Xu Huang
replied. "I will not be forced to go back on my word. Han Fan has
misread our intentions, and I must now convince him of our
sincerity for a second time. There will be one arrow fired from our
side, and that will be fired by my finest archer."
"...Arrow...?" Shi Huan murmured.
Xu Huang took one last look at Yiyang's walls before he returned
to his command tent.

An hour later, Yiyang Magistrate Han Fan was distracted from his
work inside the city by an official that said, "A message from Xu

Huang... tied to an arrow!"

"...I will read it in my study," Han Fan replied.

Han Fan invited three of his officials to his study while his secretary read Xu Huang's correspondence.

"...'Mister Han Fan', he writes, 'you have mistaken our intentions, and see a sword raised in one place as the way that all matters are dealt with in all places'," Han Fan's secretary relayed nervously. "...'The arrow that carried this letter to you is the only one that I want to be fired, and you have my word that no sword, spear or other weapon shall be raised against the city if you submit for a second time. If you do not submit, then'... 'then I will be forced to take action. But I will take a second submission as true, despite military law usually dictating otherwise, because I can see the cause of your mistrust. There will be no harm inflicted on Yiyang while it yields.' ...The rest is affirming the same point in a different way."

Han Fan took the letter from his secretary and read it carefully.

"...So are we submitting again...?" one official asked.

"We... we should," Han Fan replied. "These are the words of a man that is honest: whatever his past faults, these are honest words... yes, honest... and I am resolved that we should trust him after all. Open the gates!"

"...I'm impressed," Cao Cao said as he read Xu Huang's report from Yiyang. "He is a general that understands that every matter must be dealt with uniquely! He has done what many would not, this former friend of bandits, and won Yiyang not once, but twice without bloodshed! Xu Huang is a hero."

"And Yin'an is ours after a short, painful siege," Guo Jia replied. "We will soon have ample stocks for a month or two, but I admit that the signs are not good when I read the scout reports from Yè. The Yuan brothers have fortified the area around the city in much the same way as they did in Li County, and so we're looking at the same nonsense again."

"...You knew that they'd do that," Cao Cao said.

"Of course, but I know other things too!" Guo Jia chuckled.

"So what do we do now...?" Xu Yòu asked.

"...We stay in Yin'an and continue to rest the men and watch Yè closely," Guo Jia replied. "At the first sign of division or some other weakness, we strike: if those signs do not manifest, then we think again."

"...Very well," Cao Cao sighed. "But these many, many months away from Xuchang are starting to make me worry, Fengxiao. I need no more coup attempts and other such nonsense right now."

"But we cannot leave this region until the Yuans are annihilated!" Xu Yòu protested.

"...Wait and see," Guo Jia said calmly. "All will become clear soon enough: we shall wait and see..."

****

31

A month passed: Cao Cao's army collected grain from local supplies and established a second base in Yin'an, but there was no sign of Yè City or the surrounding region having any exploitable weaknesses and the Yuan brothers had remained united against all expectations. Cao Cao invited Guo Jia to his command room in Yin'an City – and, as soon as he learned of it, Xu Yòu invited himself – so that the future of the campaign could be discussed.

"...I think that I know why we are here," Guo Jia said.

"You said that you had a plan if we were unable to take Yè," Cao Cao noted. "Is now not the time to reveal it...?"

Guo Jia smiled and replied, "It is indeed."

Xu Yòu leant forward and waited for what he assumed to be a plan to seize some other place in the Yuan clan's northeast region.

"Yuan Shao loved them both, Tan and Shang – and Xi as well, of course – but died without proclaiming any of them as his heir," Guo Jia said. "In that case, others meddled, and we have the current situation. But the love shown is also love shared: a part of them pines for unity as brothers, and so we will suffer what we have seen: pressure them and they will unite, ignore them and they will divide. We have grain enough to support a retreat to the south bank of the Yellow River; if we-"

"**RETREAT???**" Xu Yòu screeched. "**You-!**"

"**Silence, Ziyuan!**" Cao Cao barked. "**This man Guo Jia has saved me more times than any man, even you, and I will hear his words! Either listen or leave!**"

Xu Yòu harrumphed, sat back and lowered his head.

"...We will retreat to the Yellow River, and see what happens," Guo Jia continued. "If Heaven favours an early victory, they will pursue and be trapped, but I don't imagine that both brothers are that stupid, only Yuan Tan, who enjoys life too much to advance without the troops that his brother will not give him."

"...Go on," Cao Cao prompted as he glared at the sulking Xu Yòu.

"Once we are safely returned to Xuchang, we can turn our attentions to our other long-term problem, Liu Biao of Jing Province and his tenant Liu Bei," Guo Jia continued. "When the Yuans see that we have completely turned away from them, I believe that the divisions that cost Pang Ji his life will return: if the changes are great enough that a sudden, second about-turn to exploit those changes can be justified, then we'll spare the then-bewildered Liu Biao and come back here at speed to destroy the Yuans in a single, decisive blow. I wish that I could advocate our staying and ending it now, but we cannot."

"...If that is what we must do, then fine," Cao Cao replied.

The appointed chieftain of the Yuan clan, Yuan Shang, alternated his time between seeking the counsel of his adviser, Shen Pei, and his mother, Lady Liu, inside Yè City and closely watching his disgruntled older brother Yuan Tan from within the military camps outside of the city walls; the news that Cao Cao was retreating reached both of the Yuan brothers at around the same time, but their reactions could not have differed more.

"**We *must* pursue!**" Yuan Tan barked. "**What else can we do?**"

"We can remain where we are and avoid falling for our own ruse," Yuan Shang retorted. "Have you forgotten why he retreats...? *He* retreats because *we* retreated, and he followed blindly, thinning his forces and leaving them vulnerable and under-resourced! Do you not think that Cao's wily aide Guo Jia hopes to make us do the same...?"

"...So we are to let that man quietly ride back to Xuchang in his golden carriage while we hide behind barricades...?" Yuan Tan asked angrily.

"Do you remember what happened the last time that you and a certain Yan Jing talked everybody into leaving the perimeter of our defences and attacking blindly...?" Yuan Shang retorted. "Only one of you remembers because the other is dead. I will not be tricked or lured again."

Yuan Tan exhaled fiercely and stormed out of Yuan Shang's command tent.

"...He's going to pursue anyway," Jiang Yiqu suggested.

"Let him," Yuan Shang said. "He hasn't the men to do anything."

Yuan Tan took his militia – which now numbered at around 1,200 after a series of terrible losses – and pursued Cao Cao's retreating army to their intended crossing point, which was to the west of Li County. Yuan Tan was forced to camp on the roadside at the end of every night, while Cao Cao actually continued his escape in near-total darkness for some hours to maintain a lead; the need for additional resources was also a pressing problem for Yuan Tan, since the enemy greatly outnumbered him and his militia's equipment was as tired and overused as the men themselves.

"We've heard from Wang Xiu," Guo Tu reported. "He's sending additional men and supplies from Qing Province that will arrive in the next four days."

"That will be too late to capture Cao Cao, who defies all laws of nature and retreats faster than a hare!" Yuan Tan complained. "I must... I must ask Shang for-!"

"He won't help you," Guo Tu said. "He's taking advice from *Shen Pei*, who-"

"*Aiee*... again, you are intriguing, Guo Tu!" Xin Pi cried. "Can you not wait and see whether Shen will refuse before you start antagonising the lord?"

"...I don't like to disagree with you, dear brother, but Shen Pei is the cause of all of our woes," Xin Ping said. "He and Pang were-"

"*Pang Ji is dead, Cao Cao* threatens our lands and *time is running out*!" Xin Pi protested. "I will kill Shen Pei myself if he refuses to aid us, alright...? But can we ask before we point fingers...?"

"...Ask," Guo Tu chuckled. "But he'll refuse."

"Xin Ping: send a man at once," Yuan Tan ordered. "As your brother says, we've not much time."

Yuan Tan's request was hurried back to the military camps around Yè City: Yuan Shang shook his head and said, "I cannot reply favourably right now. Yè must be properly fortified, and we do not know what the Qiang intend to do now that they lurk on Gao Gan's border. This letter suggests that Cao Cao has already made good his escape, so what is my brother pursuing, exactly...?"

The messenger smiled awkwardly.

"...He should put pressure on Li County until I can spare the resources to retake the place myself," Yuan Shang continued. "I'll provide a week's food and some arrows, but that's the best I can manage right now. Go and tell him that, please."
Yuan Tan's messenger retreated.
"...He won't like that," Ju Hu suggested.
Yuan Shang sighed and said, "Probably not."

Cao Cao was forced to send a messenger to Cheng Yu in Li County City, who read the hastily-prepared orders and smiled.
"There's nothing to smile about, is there, Elder Cheng...?" Jia Xu asked. "If His Excellency retreats, then... ... ...or is this the 'ignore and divide' strategy...?"
"I can see that I do not need to elaborate," Cheng Yu replied. "We'll lose Yin'an... but that matters little, the place has been bled dry. We're leaving a downsized garrison in Li County City and returning to Xuchang at once to prepare for a campaign against Liu Biao. I know just the fellow to leave in charge... another 'Jia', in fact. Jia Xin."
"A competent man," Jia Xu said. "But... we'll need to cede Yiyang as well as Yin'an. We had better send urgent word to Xu Huang so we do not lose that fine general. I'll do that at once."
"And I'll ready the retreat of the main army and brief Jia Xin," Cheng Yu replied. "I know this seems ignominious, but... I think we might be rewarded for this ruse sooner that anyone thinks..."

Yuan Tan's returning messenger cowered as his lord loomed over him and screamed, "**He said *what*???**"
Xin Ping shook his head and said, "You heard him well enough, Lord Yuan. Let the poor man go, he's just a messenger!"
Yuan Tan stepped back, half-heartedly smiled at the cowering messenger and said, "You... you have returned quickly after travelling quickly... go, and get some rest and refreshment."
The messenger fled from the command tent.
"...I hate to be correct, but I was," Guo Tu said. "He refused all but the most basic aid to your cause, so we must proceed alone."
"**This is an insult!**" Yuan Tan cried. "**Cao Cao is our clan's worst enemy!**"
"But his answer is his answer," Xin Pi said. "In that case, we-"
"He does not want to help because he plots to be rid of Lord Yuan Tan!" Guo Tu suggested. "This is, as Lord Yuan Tan has said, an insult! The-!"
"We should not be doing what I know you are about to suggest!" Xin Pi protested. "By all means sit here and do nothing, or risk attacking Cao anyway, but do not turn around and attack Yè while Cao is still nearby!"
"**You suggest that I allow him to heckle me, Xin Pi!**" Yuan Tan roared.
"***No, Lord Yuan!***" Xin Pi replied. "**Tell him, Brother!**"
"...My brother is right, for now at least," Xin Ping said. "We should pursue Cao, and if we are unsuccessful we should try to take Li County back to use as a base, for right now we lack even that simple military requirement."
"I didn't mean that we should use it as a base!" Xin Pi retorted. "I meant that-!"

"We must rely on shocks, surprises, and shows of military brilliance if we are to win the minds and hearts of generals!" Guo Tu replied; he then turned to Yuan Tan and added, "Show you are fearless, Lord Yuan. Show you are merciless to your enemies. It can only serve to impress the officers!"

"There is a difference between fearlessness and foolishness!" Xin Pi said. "The-!"

"Wait a moment," Yuan Tan ordered.

"*Aiee*... be careful, Lord Yuan, that's all I ask," Xin Pi replied.

Yuan Tan turned and stared at his battle map; he looked at the marker that represented Cao Cao and said, "If I have the courage to attack Yè with such a small force, then I can attack Cao Cao's cowardly men as they try to get to Guandu. I'll do that first, then I'll harass Li County for a while, and then I'll turn about when Shang assumes me to be 'focussed'. We'll mobilise and get to the riverbank at once."

Guo Tu applauded his lord's decision; Xin Ping hummed ambiguously; Xin Pi shook his head and sighed.

"I'll go and motivate the men personally: follow me please, Xin Pi," Yuan Tan said as he suddenly started toward the entrance to the tent; Xin Pi followed slowly and unenthusiastically, leaving his brother and Guo Tu alone.

"...Don't be so stubborn to the truth," Guo Tu said.

"My brother is right that we shouldn't needlessly intrigue," Xin Ping retorted.

"Ah, but what is the meaning of 'needlessly'...?" Guo Tu asked.

"Shen Pei and Pang Ji have caused all of this with *their* intriguing: you know as well as I do that they manipulated things so that they could be the senior advisers to Yuan Shang. All I ask of you is that you support my efforts to rouse the lord to action."

"Rouse... or *rile*...?" Xin Ping retorted. "And he'll achieve nothing if he attacks blindly and angrily. I have been with Lord Yuan for longer than you, so I know him well enough to tell you that he won't win if he's angry."

"But he won't act if he is not driven to, and if he does not act, then Lady Liu, Shen Pei and Yuan Shang will conspire to be rid of him, and also us," Guo Tu said. "You know that's how it works, Mister Xin: we have to destroy them before they destroy us. There will never be a peace between us now."

"...I must think about it," Xin Ping replied. "I will not keep you waiting long."

"Don't," Guo Tu said. "Every moment is precious."

Cao Cao smiled as he stood on the deck of his small command ship and watched the northern bank of the Yellow River as he slowly moved southward.

"Barely any obstructions," Guo Jia noted.

Cao Cao laughed and said, "I know! This is evidence that you were right once again, Fengxiao. The scouts only report a small militia that may or may not be led by Yuan Tan; if he is poorly supplied, then Yuan Shang has refused to help, and that can only end in a battle between them! But where should we wait for that moment... and for how long...?"

"I was not joking when I said that we should turn westward," Guo Jia replied. "If we turn about too quickly, they'll unite again. We must – as ridiculous as it sounds – make them think that it is safe to be enemies."

"It does sound ridiculous, but I've seen it before," Cao Cao chuckled. "Fine! We'll attack Liu Biao and Liu Bei… and maybe destroy them first!"

Yuan Tan's small army missed Cao Cao's retreat by hours and had to be content with killing some of the men that had bravely volunteered to serve as the rear guard; Tan's army then turned toward the military camps around Li County City, although their failure to capture the Excellency of Works – and Yuan Shang's perceived part in that failure – never left their minds.

****

32

Kong Rong heard that Cao Cao was preparing to return to Xuchang and invited his friends Wang Lang and Zhi Xi to discuss the sudden retreat from Ji Province.

"This is a surprise, is it not?" Kong Rong asked.

"You're hoping that His Excellency was defeated, no doubt," Wang Lang chuckled.

"...No, of course not," Kong Rong replied as he caught sight of Zhi Xi's scolding expression.

"His Excellency Cao Cao is surrounded by brilliant tacticians," Wang Lang continued. "I doubt very much that he was beaten by Yuan Shao's pups... and you, of all men, should not want Yuan Tan to defeat His Excellency, Wenju. I might as well want the Sun clan to triumph if *you* wanted *that*."

"...I have not forgiven Yuan Tan for his cruel mistreatment of my family," Kong Rong replied. "But I have not forgotten Cao Cao's wrongs either, and-!"

Zhi Xi coughed deliberately.

"...But I must think differently," Kong Rong said.

"You certainly should, and not just because your friend does not trust me!" Wang Lang chuckled.

"I do not correct Wenju because I do not trust you," Zhi Xi retorted. "I do so for the same reason as you: Cao Cao is powerful, clever and prone to disproportionate punishments for small offences, but he is ultimately trying to restore the Han, and it is that goal that we must all be reaching for before we look at a man's flaws."

"I do admit that I wonder what could cause a sudden retreat after nine months of fighting with – apparently – nothing much to show for it," Wang Lang said. "Perhaps there is some emergency...? Has Sun Quan been caught scheming, and His Excellency must now turn southward...? Or has Liu Biao done something else foolish, and His Excellency must now turn westward...? I cannot see that there is a reason to retreat: Li County is firmly seized, and the army is intact."

"...And he is coming back *here*, not to Guandu," Kong Rong noted.

"Perhaps he is homesick," Zhi Xi suggested.

"His Excellency would not abandon a campaign for feeling homesick!" Wang Lang chortled. "That is the thinking of a simple soldier or a junior official! No, this is something else..."

Yuan Tan's efforts to act against Cao Cao's stronghold in Li County were proving to be meritless, as he lacked the resources to do any serious damage: Tan sent yet another messenger to Yè City in order to request reinforcements despite his advisers agreeing that it would not be a good idea to do so.

Yuan Shang was inspecting the external camps when the messenger arrived: Shang looked the young man up and down, read his brother's request for a second time and laughed, saying, "He wants – nay, *demands* – men *and* horses *and* weapons *and* food *and* more officers *and* more advisers so that he can 'achieve something where nothing is being achieved'...? Such a tone! Would he also like me to uproot Yè City from its foundations and

transport it to Qing Province stone by stone...?"
The messenger stared at the ground and said nothing.
"...I don't even need to ask Shen Pei about this," Yuan Shang
continued. "You'll go back, little fellow, and tell him that he will
get *nothing*. Nothing... at... all. Now get out of my sight."
The messenger turned and fled.
"...We should prepare for reprisals," Ju Hu suggested.
"I think we were always prepared for a war with my brother,"
Yuan Shang replied. "It is sad to say it, but... that was always how
it was going to end. But can he attack me right now when he lacks
fighting men and had to ask me to supply him with some...? Can
he attack me right now when Cao Cao is still close by...? Yes, I
know the answer is 'he still might', but he could not win. I will, as
you say, prepare... but let us hope that he is not that stupid."

The threat of Gao Gan's army attacking Hedong Prefecture for a
second time had not been dismissed: many local men volunteered
their services, both military and civil, in the hope that any such
attack could be prevented or its impact reduced. One man whose
appearance was a genuine surprise was Wang Ling, who was the
nephew of the late Director of the Imperial Secretariat, Wang Yun:
Yun had successfully rid the country of Dong Zhuo with the aid of
Lü Bu, but the coup was famously short-lived, and his closest
family had been annihilated by Dong Zhuo's loyalists.
"So it's true then! But I thought you had perished with everybody
else!" the official Jia Kui said as he laid eyes on Wang Ling for the
first time.
"Uncle ordered me to flee before the villains breached the city,"
Wang Ling replied. "I could only save a few of my kin, sadly. I had
intended to 'return to the fold' sooner, but when I heard that Cao
Cao had employed Jia Xu and Zhong Yao had been made Grand
Magistrate of Chang'an..."
"...Ah, yes, well, I see the problem," Jia Kui said. "If I read you
correctly, Jia Xu is the cause of your family's destruction, and
Zhong Yao idolised Cai Yong, whose life was cut short by your
uncle for the crime of 'mourning Dong Zhuo', and you wonder how
you will be received."
"I cannot fathom the answer," Wang Ling admitted. "I am nearly
thirty, but I look at the world and feel like a confused child! How is
it that Hedong is protected by the *Qiang*...? How is it that *Jia Xu*
serves the Han's Excellency of Works? What would Zhong Yao do
to me, and would he have a right to harm me if he can work
alongside *Jia Xu*, who caused him more harm than my late uncle
ever did...?"
"I wouldn't worry," Jia Kui insisted. "Zhong Yao is not a petty
man: the Qiang commander Pang De killed his nephew, Guo Yuan,
who was serving as Gao Gan's vanguard general during the
invasion, and he rewarded Pang handsomely whilst condemning
Guo as the traitor that he was."
"Now I am even more confused," Wang Ling admitted. "The *Qiang*
defend Han territory from *Yuan Shao's nephew*, who sent *Zhong
Yao's nephew* to fight *Zhong Yao*, who, in turn, seeks direction
from *Dong Zhuo's chief adviser*. On the other hand, how can I not
have a place in such a world...?"
"Wang Yun executed Cai Yong for publicly mourning a tyrant, and

although it was a loss to the arts, it was a sound decision," Jia Kui said. "Zhong Yao will not rebuke you. You are educated to the appropriate standard for government office, and so I suggest you write to him and ask how you can be of service. He's bound to nominate you and give you a role."

"I shall do as you suggest," Wang Ling replied. "But first, Mister Jia, I want to do something here in Hedong."

"I shall find a suitable role for you," Jia Kui promised. "Administrator Wang Yi will not turn you away: you are, after all, distantly related in some way or another if you bear the same family name, and your late uncle is highly respected anyway."

Wang Ling smiled and said, "If it means that I can serve the Han, I am glad."

Yuan Tan's first instinct upon hearing his brother's relayed message was to strike the messenger down: Xin Ping restrained Tan and shouted, **"That's your own man! Why hurt him after what he's done for you…?"**

Yuan Tan's wild eyes calmed; he smiled at the cowering messenger and said, "I… I apologise. You have returned quickly after travelling quickly… go, and get some rest and refreshment."

The messenger retreated silently and swiftly.

"…That was the wrong reaction," Xin Pi said. "You need your followers to be completely with you, Lord Yuan, to-"

"This is the worst insult yet!" Yuan Tan cried. **"He dares to prevent me from avenging our father??? Shen Pei's advice is *treason*!"**

"The messenger said that your brother 'did not feel the need to consult Shen Pei'," Xin Pi noted. "In that case, the decision was-"

"He didn't consult him because they are now of the same mind: that the destruction of Lord Yuan Tan takes precedence over *all*, even destroying Cao Cao!" Guo Tu said theatrically. "This is, as Lord Yuan Tan has said, the worst insult! The-!"

"Don't do it!" Xin Pi protested. "By all means wait for Wang Xiu's reinforcements and try to take Li County City back from Cao Cao's appointed guardian – I've certainly never heard great things about Jia Xin – but do not turn around and-!"

"This *cannot go unpunished*!" Yuan Tan roared.

"…*Tell him*, Brother!" Xin Pi implored. **"Tell him that such a course is idiocy!"**

"…I can't," Xin Ping replied. "I can't lie. Guo Tu is correct: Shen Pei is our enemy, determined from the start to confound us. In fact, I now know from my own investigations that of them all, Shen Pei was the worst: Yuan Tan is the late lord's nephew because of that man alone, for it was his words alone that-"

"What…?" Yuan Tan exclaimed. "What… did you say…?"

"It was his idea – nobody else's – to have you adopted away," Xin Ping replied. "His plan, approved by Lady Liu… and Pang Ji… and Yuan Cheng, reluctantly…"

Yuan Tan's eyes wandered.

"…This is insanity," Xin Pi said desperately. "Don't do this… don't turn around and pit kin against kin when Cao Cao has barely left! What if he turns about and-?"

"*Let him turn about*," Yuan Tan growled. "I'll fight them both if I have to! But I will not share another month under Heaven with

Shen Pei living and breathing! I will have his head on a spike! We turn around and go to Yè as soon as it is convenient!"
Guo Tu smiled and said, "I'll prepare at once, my lord."
Yuan Tan left the command tent; Xin Pi scowled and turned to Xin Ping and Guo Tu, saying, "I hope you are both pleased with yourselves… look at you, smirking like imbeciles! Yuan Shang enjoys robust fortifications around Yè and the protection of the city itself in addition to a multitude of fine generals and men, an alliance with the Wuhuan, granaries and more besides! Our lord has nothing in comparison! You're goading him into charging at swords! Why would you do that???"
"You underestimate our lord and the men that unwillingly serve the weak, timid Yuan Shang," Guo Tu retorted. "When our lord tells them all of Shen Pei's deception and the true intentions of our late lord Yuan Shao, they'll-!"
"They'll stay at Shang's side!" Xin Pi protested. "Yuan Tan is viewed as reckless, undisciplined, a poor judge of character and a poor administrator of civil affairs! We have to do more to convince the people of his integrity, his benevolence, his wits, his patience; how do we do that by letting him scream 'Betrayal!' and blindly charge at a defence network that recently held Cao Cao's thirty-thousand-strong horde at bay – *thirty-thousand* – when our lord has a thousand men on foot and forty riders?"
"He'll have more when the reinforcements arrive!" Guo Tu said.
"Oh, so Wang Xiu is sending *thirty-thousand men* from Qing Province…?" Xin Pi heckled. "I didn't know we had such an army!"
"Don't be so negative," Xin Ping said. "We'll have the advantage of surprise and the reputation of being the only ones that fought Cao Cao: Yuan Shang is proven to be a coward now, and only a warrior can fight and defeat Cao Cao. Even Ju Hu has been heard commenting that Yuan Shang could not have hoped to win at Li County without Lord Yuan Tan's help."
"*Yes*, but the same men also note that Lord Yuan Tan cannot win any battles without aid from his brother!" Xin Pi retorted. "Didn't this latest row start because he refused men that our lord *needs* in order to chase Cao Cao…?"
Guo Tu harrumphed.
"I'm right," Xin Pi said. "If we go back now and fight Yuan Shang on his own terms, we'll be torn apart."
"…I'm sad that you don't see what we can achieve, Brother," Xin Ping replied. "I truly believe that we can sway them all and bring them to our lord's side."
"So do I, but not like *this*," Xin Pi said powerlessly.

Yuan Shang entered Yè City and visited the main prison, where the scholar-official Cui Yan was still being held for refusing to pledge allegiance.
"You no doubt know from ingratiating yourself with the guards that Cao Cao has been repelled and that my brother and I are working together," Yuan Shang said.
"I am aware of it," Cui Yan replied tonelessly.
"You've been treated relatively well," Yuan Shang continued. "But I should like to treat you better still, Mister Cui. Offer me your support and I can do so!"
"I cannot," Cui Yan replied. "Lord Yuan Shao could be muddle-

headed, but he always understood the need to maintain strong family ties. The Yuan brothers that I see now are divided and bound to fight further. When I see all three of you standing together with the succession matters behind you, then I will reaffirm my pledge of service to the Yuan clan: until then, I shall rot here."

"...If that is what you choose," Yuan Shang sighed as he turned to walk away.

"Are you mad, Mister Cui...?" the warder asked once Yuan Shang's entourage was gone. "You stand not far from where Tian Feng stood three years ago!"

"And if I must suffer the same sorry end, so be it," Cui Yan replied. "But I won't contribute to the in-fighting, which is what I would be doing if I picked a side. I serve the Yuan clan: when it is united, I shall serve it again."

When Yuan Shang returned to his main hall, he was approached by Secretary Chen Lin and the adviser Yin Kui.

"...Is there something that I must know about, gentlemen...?" Yuan Shang asked.

"You already know of it but act incorrectly, Lord Yuan," Chen Lin replied. "You have just been to see Cui Yan in prison. You must not leave him in such a place."

"He intends to continue his stubborn defiance and hence deny my place as his lord!" Yuan Shang retorted. "Until he shows the proper deference, he'll stay where he is!"

"But what will men say...?" Yin Kui asked. "My lord, your father was castigated for his treatment of Qu Yi, Dong Zhao and Tian Feng, to name but three... and their mistreatment became cause for suspicion and disaffection that might have led to other men leaving your father's cause, like Guo Jia, Xun Yu, and-"

"I... see your point, gentlemen," Yuan Shang said. "I will move Mister Cui to his home and place that under guard. But until he truly pledges allegiance, he will not know freedom. I cannot risk his choosing to serve Tan."

"He wouldn't, but... anything is better than a cell," Chen Lin replied. "Your wisdom in this matter is worth more than most men would understand."

"...I know," Yuan Shang said as he turned and retreated toward his private study.

A similar battle of words was being fought by the adviser Xun Chen as he tried to persuade the scholar Ying Shao to leave his rural retreat and return to Yè City.

"Go back there if you want, Mister Xun Chen, but I will remain here and continue my work!" Ying Shao insisted. "I'm too old for all of this nonsense. I retired to this place in the countryside so that I could speak with the people and work undisturbed. I only ask the people to tell me about the old folk tales so that I can record them for posterity, but they often volunteer their opinions about the present time, and they are not flattering. When the Yuans stop fighting, I will pay visits to Yè. Until then, I will stay here. You are an adviser, and hence belong close to the men that do battle."

"I am a scholar as well," Xun Chen insisted. "My clan has always enjoyed closeness to the Son of Heaven, I have long enjoyed the trust of the Yuan chieftain, and I have long admired your work."

"So let me finish it," Ying Shao retorted.

"But if you do not seek protection, I worry that you will become a wandering ghost like Cai Yong!" Xun Chen protested. "You are not safe in the rural outskirts! In the capital, you-!"

"Where did Cai Yong die...?" Ying Shao asked.

"...In Chang'an," Xun Chen conceded. "But this is different! And besides, he eventually returned to Luoyang to escape Dong Zhuo's wrath because he *wasn't* safe in Jiangdong! And Cai Yong only went to Jiangdong because was persecuted by the 'Ten' and fled Luoyang to avoid imprisonment! Lord Yuan Shang would never dream of harming a respected scholar!"

"Where is Cui Yan now...?" Ying Shao asked.

"...I cannot argue," Xun Chen admitted.

"Go back to your lord," Ying Shao said. "I will remain here, among the people, and continue to document what is important to them, since most historians only seem to care for the whims and wills of the shallow few that have and seek power, and our cultural essence is at risk of being lost. If I die, I die: I'll learn nothing about what I want to research by being within the walls of Yè, and my work is my life."

Xun Chen bowed humbly and said, "I shall leave you then, Elder Ying. May Heaven protect your sagely life so that our paths can cross again."

Ying Shao reciprocated the bow, and Xun Chen left the small shack to begin the journey back to Yè City and the unrest that surrounded it.

Cao Cao, meanwhile, prepared to face his critics once again and then begin plans for an entirely different campaign. Jing Province would have to fall eventually, but Cao was left wondering whether he would seize Liu Biao's lands before or after he finally defeated the sons of his late former friend and brought peace to the northeast of the Han Empire: others would wonder the same.

****

ACT III: A CHANGE OF PLAN

33

A chance to establish order in the northeast of the vast Han Empire had apparently been missed: Cao Cao, the Han's Excellency of Works, had aborted an expensive military campaign and returned to the Imperial capital, Xuchang, at short notice, having faced considerable opposition from two sons of the now-deceased super-warlord Yuan Shao. Cao Cao was leaving the Yuan brothers to focus all of his attentions – in some ways truthfully, and in others as a ruse to fool the Yuans – on Jing Province in the centre of the empire, where two old enemies of his – the governor, Liu Biao, and the rogue warlord Liu Bei – stood together in defiance of Cao's regime. That made no sense to many – even Cao's supporters – but this was a complex era.

Cao Cao's famous victory over Yuan Shao at Guandu almost 3 years earlier had broken the spirit of the wealthy magnate and driven him to an early grave, leaving the crucial 'succession question' apparently unanswered; Shao's widow, Lady Liu, had conspired with some of her late husband's advisers and ensured that her biological son, Yuan Shang, would inherit the clan chieftainship and control of the 4 northeast provinces of Ji, Bing, Qing and Yòu, while the eldest son and presumed heir, Yuan Tan, was adopted to a deceased uncle and technically disinherited. The rift that was created by the intrigue had given Cao Cao the greatest of opportunities: he had the support of the Mount Tai Bandits in Qing Province and the Qiang warlords of Liang Province, and his army was stronger after absorbing large numbers of defecting troops in the wake of the Guandu campaign. But what few had accounted for was the strength of the Yuan brothers' 'blood ties' when the situation was dire: Tan and Shang put their differences aside, and they successfully defended their capital, Yè City, despite losing the strategically vital Li County to the enemy.

But Cao Cao had not failed: he had retreated across the Yellow River and returned to Xuchang with his Li County base intact, and he had only done so because his chief adviser, the genius Guo Jia, had suggested that the Yuans would quickly divide when they did not have a common enemy. The Yuans did not disappoint: the bitter, vengeful Yuan Tan was already contemplating attacking Yè City and trying to seize power from Shang before Cao Cao had left the area. And all the while, the second brother, Yuan Xi, watched from his unstable seat in northernmost Yòu Province, and watched for an opportunity to rescue his beautiful young wife, Lady Zhen, who had been taken as a hostage in all but name by his stepmother, Lady Liu, to guarantee his obedience. It was impossible to know what would happen next, and the tension was tangible.

Emperor Xian demanded an explanation for the sudden withdrawal of Cao Cao's army from Ji Province, and an urgent court session was convened as soon as Cao was back in Xuchang.

"We wonder why a nine-month excursion has stalled so obviously," Emperor Xian said as he stared at Cao Cao. "We wonder if we are about to suffer another period of instability akin to that endured after your campaign to reclaim Nan County from

Zhang Xiu, Mister Cao."

"Oh, that nonsense is far behind me now, Your Majesty," Cao Cao replied calmly. "I withdrew from Ji Province, yes, but only after having left a large garrison in Li County City that stands unopposed. I am back because we did, I admit, come across a lot of resistance, and supplies ran out. I want to ensure that we have sufficient supplies and return to battle fresh when the time is right: the Yuans are not united and suffer daily rebellions that drain resources, and their main allies, the Wuhuan, create more enemies for them in the form of their own tortured populace."

"…So this is not a defeat…?" Emperor Xian asked.

Cao Cao smirked and replied, "At the absolute worst, Your Majesty, it might be called 'a setback', but who expected the Yuan brothers – who command three-hundred-thousand men between them and lay a joint treasonous claim to a quarter of the Empire – to be defeated in a few months…? Some said that it would take me a year to establish a stronghold on the northern riverbank: I achieved it in a few months and was able to attack Yè directly. The Yuans will brag, but all that they have managed with their short-lived truce is a reprieve."

"…So we are not to suffer a new spate of insurrections," Emperor Xian prompted.

"The Yuans are the only ones that will suffer such things," Cao Cao promised. "Cao Ren, Yuan Huan and Cao Chun have destroyed the last pockets of Yellow Turbans in Runan; Sun Quan pledges allegiance to the Han, and the Qiang do as they are asked; only the Yuans and Liu Biao pose a threat, and both are at a disadvantage."

"…We are appeased," Emperor Xian said.

Kong Rong motioned that he would like to speak, but Xun Wenruo ignored him.

"Then the court is adjourned," Cao Cao declared. "I shall return to my life's mission now: the obliteration of all who oppose the glory of the Han!"

Emperor Xian returned to his chambers and looked at Empress Fu; the servants expected that they would be dismissed, but no such order was given.

"…There is nothing to discuss…?" Empress Fu prompted.

"We are appeased," Emperor Xian replied tonelessly. "The retreat was merely to regain strength and replenish supplies… the Yuans are bitterly divided and certain to be destroyed, and our sovereignty is not to be harmed further by our outward enemies. We are appeased. Mister Cao pledges that his life's mission is the obliteration of all that oppose our glory… and he is all but indestructible, so… so we are appeased."

Empress Fu smiled sadly and said, "I understand."

Emperor Xian sat facing his empress and exhaled noisily.

Cao Cao convened a meeting of his officials in his chancellery office and said, "I think that His Majesty is suitably calmed."

"I admit that many nervous whispers followed your sudden withdrawal from Ji Province," Xun Wenruo chuckled. "But I think that the grand appearance of the return procession has allayed any fears, Excellency."

"I'm confused, though," Xiahou Dun admitted. "We were doing well! Li County was ours! Li Dian and Yue Jin were taking enemy heads and Xu Huang got Yiyang as easily as taking something from a sack! One little bit of resistance in Yè, though, and-!"

"There is method to what I am doing," Cao Cao promised.

"Yeah, and it's Guo Jia's work, or maybe Old Cheng's or Jia Xu's," Xiahou Dun said. "Explain, Mengde! Why did we retreat?"

"Knowing Fengxiao, he hoped to let the brothers alone and hope that they start bickering," Xun Gongda said. "At that point, the army would return, and-"

"No, no!" Cao Cao chuckled. "We have another problem that we can start to worry about now while we wait and see how well the Yuan brothers get along."

"Liu Bei...?" Xun Wenruo prompted.

"Him and Liu Biao both," Cao Cao replied. "Liu Biao acts as though he thinks that I didn't notice that he was going to sneak up on me while I was in Guandu! But I have simply been biding my time, and he knows that. With 'Benchu' laid to rest, I can finally start to deal with those two errant scions of the royal house, and how nice it is of them to unite so that I can crush them both at once!"

"Give me that role, Mengde!" Xiahou Dun pleaded. "I hate Liu Bei, and I hate Guan Yu even more! I'm aching to get revenge on them all!"

"For what...?" Cao Xiu asked. "They didn't take your eye."

General Zhang Liao sighed miserably and said, "No, that was my old colleague Gao Shun..."

"If Bei's lot'd been any use at all, would I have been out there exposed to get shot in the first place...?" Xiahou Dun said angrily. "Bei showed up after I'd done all the work and paid a price for it! And Guan threatened Mengde and then betrayed him after all those gifts he got! And then there's that bastard Zhang Fei, kidnapping Miaocai's daughter and marrying her! I-!"

"Alright, alright, you can lead the campaign!" Cao Cao sighed.

"*Ayah*... Don't be *ridiculous*!" Cheng Yu heckled. "He's reckless!"

"I did not intend to send him alone, of course," Cao Cao retorted. "He will have help: Yu Jin! Li Dian!"

Yu Jin and Li Dian touched their right fists to their chests.

"You two will aid my cousin and make this campaign our first foray into Jing Province to get it back for our sovereign," Cao Cao ordered. "You're both known for your cool heads, and if two cool heads cannot quench the fire that burns where Yuanrang's brains should be, then I don't know what will."

Some of the officers laughed involuntarily.

"...Okay, I know, I'm reckless," Xiahou Dun conceded. "But I'll bring back the heads of those bastards, Mengde!"

"Please do," Cao Cao said. "As for Yuan Shao's progeny..."

"Let the plotters plot themselves into a corner for us," Guo Jia said. "We'll soon hear of divisions and intrigue, I'll wager."

"Oh, and let division ruin Liu Bei and Liu Biao as well!" Cao Cao declared. "Let them all grant us easy victories!"

"Why can we not attack Liu Biao in greater numbers and destroy him more quickly?" Cao Chun asked. "The three men that you send are great men, don't get me wrong, but only three...? You sent almost everybody against the Yuans!"

"I have my reasons, Yihe," Cao Cao replied. "Oh, yes... I should like to add your impressive cavalry that you've been building to my vanguard armies in the future."

"Add it now, to the front in Jing Province!" Cao Chun said. "I would gladly fight alongside Yuanrang and-!"

"Save your enthusiasm for later campaigns," Cao Cao suggested. "This first attack on Liu Biao is potentially risky, and not necessarily more than a test."

"...I see," Cao Chun replied. "I will not remonstrate further."

Cao Cao smiled and said, "I appreciate your concern, Cousin, and understand it. But it will all become clear."

"Will you be going to Jing yourself...?" Xun Wenruo asked.

"I... I would rather not, since I would be likely based in Wan City to best oversee the campaign, and that place stirs unpleasant memories," Cao Cao replied. "But we'll see: if it looks like my presence is required, then yes, I will go."

"...And you'll be visiting home, I hope," Cao Xiu said.

"Oh, yes!" Cao Cao replied. "In fact, I must confess that I intend to stay here in Xuchang for at least three months before I go anywhere else. I want to stabilise the capital, since I will be spending far less time here in the future."

"...Oh...? What do you mean...?" Xun Wenruo asked.

"Campaigns," Guo Jia said before Cao Cao could answer. "There are a lot of campaigns that will require Lord Cao's presence: he must fight Liu Biao in Jing, the Yuan brothers in Ji, Gao Gan in Bing, the Wuhuan in Yòu, Zhang Lu in Hanzhong and possibly Sun Quan of Jiangdong in the coming years."

"And how long will you be there for, Guo Jia...?" the adviser Chen Qun asked. "Look at you! You're even thinner and paler than you were when you left!"

"Travel fatigue," Guo Jia retorted.

"Nonsense," Chen Qun scoffed. "You're killing yourself, as usual!"

"Leave him be," Cao Cao pleaded. "To answer Wenruo's question more fully, yes, as Fengxiao has said, I will be on campaigns a lot, and in addition to that, I will need a new base to replace Yan Province, which is now a second – or, counting Chang'an, third – Imperial capital and will always be so now, even after the court returns to Luoyang. I intend to make Ji Province my base, and Yè City in Wei Prefecture the capital of that base. I will be closer to the rebellious Wuhuan and the Great Wall, closer to the bandits of Bing and Qing, closer to the Qiang... and such a move will send a message that I am strong, that I am not retreating from problems but advancing to meet them."

"...I see... but are you not worried about sending an incorrect message to your detractors...?" Xun Wenruo asked worriedly. "My lord, our enemies have enough fun at our expense without them accusing you of seizing Yuan Shao's ill-gotten lands for yourself!"

"Let them," Cao Cao replied tonelessly. "Worry more about ensuring that they can do little more than throw words: I want no more Dong Chengs."

Xun Wenruo nodded slowly and uneasily.

****

34

Excellency Cao Cao returned to his mansion, where he was greeted by his ever-growing family; his eldest surviving son, Cao Pi, led the welcome.

"My, how grand a man you are becoming!" Cao Cao said.

"And me as well, I hope, Father...?" Cao Zhang asked.

"Naturally, my dear Yellow-beard," Cao Cao replied as he turned to face his second son by Lady Bian. "You are settling into married life, I hope...?"

"I treat Lady Sun respectfully, if that is what you mean," Cao Zhang said.

"...It wasn't, but that's good to hear," Cao Cao replied.

"Good to see you back, Wenlie!" Cao Pi said as he clasped Cao Xiu's hands.

"It is good to see you again, Zihuan," Cao Xiu replied. "I wonder if we will be serving together when it is time to leave this house once again...?"

"Oh, I hope so," Cao Pi replied. "Zhang and I are hungry for opportunities to show that we are the future heroes!"

Cao Xiu turned to Cao Zhang and said, "You hope to join us...?"

"When have I ever been anything else but a man born for the saddle...?" Cao Zhang replied. "Give me the thrill of battle over a book. Nobody remembers poets and singers, only great generals."

"That's often true, but that's not a good thing," Cao Cao scolded. "Everything from your saddle to your sword and the way your rations are prepared are down to smart men improving the fighting man's lot."

"Good, and let them continue to do so, I won't stop them," Cao Zhang retorted. "But when the history books are written, does anyone know the names of the blacksmiths, the saddle-makers, the farmers and the men that count the arrows...?"

"...For a man that hates scholarly pursuits, you argued that shallow case very well," Cao Cao chuckled. "But glory is fleeting, and history is written with the winner in mind. You might be remembered by one history but forgotten by another. And those history books are written by scholars... scholars that will remember you more fondly if your respect for them is known."

"I don't hate scholars, I just don't want to be one," Cao Zhang insisted. "When will I get to fight for you, Father...?"

Cao Cao shook his head and replied, "Soon, perhaps, if you will not be swayed."

Lady Bian gasped.

"...My lady, our second son seeks war," Cao Cao said. "If I don't provide warfare, he will seek it out. Our third son, Zhi, compensates for that imbalance."

"Will we be composing poetry this evening, Father...?" Cao Zhi asked excitedly.

"I should certainly like to," Cao Cao replied. "Where is Chong...?"

"I am here, Father," Cao Chong said as he moved to the front of the large gathering.

"...In a way, your maturity scares me," Cao Cao admitted. "At seven, your eyes burn with a wisdom and sagacity that I don't often see in grown men of forty."

"I do not know why I am so unusual, Father," Cao Chong replied. "I must confess that I identify more with the scholars that you have in your service than the children of my own age. I find everything fascinating, and I just want to learn more."

"...And that's not normal at all," Cao Zhang muttered. "He's worse than Zhi."

"Cao Cao placed his hand on Cao Chong's head and said, "My library is open, and if you want to learn, learn: it is the intelligentsia that will grow a stable nation, Chong, while we simpler minds are tasked with protecting it with our swords while it grows. What you call 'unusual' can also be called 'extraordinary' and 'wonderful'. Every man with a dose of wits in his head prays for a son like you."

Cao Chong's mother, Lady Huan, smiled happily; Cao Cao's heir, Cao Pi, shuddered at words that could mean yet another obstacle to his retaining his place.

"Will you be staying long, Second Father...?" Cao Cao's adopted son Hè Yan asked politely.

"I will be at home for a while, since I want to leave Xuchang a better place than I find it," Cao Cao replied. "We'll all be able to spend some time together, and I aim to solve some long-term problems as well."

"...Problems...?" Cao Chong prompted.

"Your father suffers greatly with his malady of the head, and he is tiring of the burden," Cao Cao explained. "I want to be rid of the malady, and I think that there is a man that can help: I have been trying to convince him to come here and cure me, but he has been annoyingly evasive."

"...You mean the famous wandering apothecary, acupuncturist, scholar and doctor, Hua Tuo," Cao Chong supposed. "Is he still in Pei County...?"

"*Aiee*... every time that boy speaks, Mengde, it makes me feel like a moron!" Cao Hong complained.

"You *are* a moron," Cao Cao retorted. "And there's no excuse for it! I saw poor Zhen wiping tears from his eyes as he came to greet me! You were chastising him again, mere hours after returning from campaign!"

"...I'm just being playful," Cao Hong insisted.

"Yes, which is an endearing trait in a grown man with his own militia," Cao Cao retorted. "Zhen's proving to be very clever, Hong: be mindful that his intellect will probably carry him over you in years to come."

Cao Zhen smiled, which prompted Cao Hong to involuntarily mutter, "Don't know what *you're* grinning at, Tubby."

"**Did I hear right just then???**" Cao Cao barked.

"...Sorry!" Cao Hong pleaded. "I'm sorry!"

"...And yes, Chong, I did mean the famous Hua Tuo, and yes, he might still be in Pei County," Cao Cao said. "I will have his help... I *need* his help."

"I wish there were something that I could do," Cao Cao's adopted son Qin Lang said with a sigh. "I want to tour the land anyway, Father, and search for knowledge that might include a cure if Hua Tuo cannot help."

"If you want to travel, do so by all means, for it builds character," Cao Cao replied. "I know that you don't want to be an officer, like your birth father, and that you'd avoid any form of military service if you could: I won't force the issue."

The beautiful Lady Du – who was Qin Lang's biological mother – smiled gratefully.

"...I am tired, I realise, and quite hungry," Cao Cao said. "Let us all retire to the living quarters and enjoy a meal together."

Cao Pi was one of the last to follow his father into the house; Lady Bian touched his shoulder and said, "My son, you must not react as you do to your father's praising words for Chong! You are the eldest and therefore his heir, and that is that."

"Wherever I look, I see examples to the contrary, Mother," Cao Pi retorted. "Isn't the lack of adherence to the rules of succession what troubles the Yuans...?"

"...It will not be the same for you," Lady Bian protested. "Your father is not a muddle-headed idiot like Yuan Shao was!"

"No, but he values 'rewriting the rules', and placing academia over the military, and ensuring that it is ability, not social place, that determines what a man can achieve," Cao Pi retorted. "Chong is smarter than me... *Zhi* is smarter than me!"

"Don't speak this way," Lady Bian pleaded. "Your brothers are not your rivals or your enemies! They are your brothers!"

"...I know that," Cao Pi replied. "But I am afraid, Mother... because I want to be a great man, like Father, and there is a risk of me being pushed to the side."

"You won't be," Lady Bian insisted. "You *will* be a great man."

Cao Pi smiled falsely and followed his mother into the house.

****

35

Cao Cao's military preparations for a campaign against Liu Biao were deliberately conspicuous: his efforts to expand the court were no less determined but were easy to miss as the military tensions built. Cao Cao's long-time patron, Sima Fang, had recently returned to the court after a break to manage family affairs: he had brought his eldest son Lang and third son Fu with him from Wen County, and Cao Cao was eager to employ them.

"Ah, how I pine for the day when the 'Eight Da' are all in my employ!" Cao Cao said as he clasped Sima Lang's hand tightly. "For now, I shall enjoy the fact that I have two of you helping me and your father to restore the Han's lustre!"

"I'm nothing special," Sima Lang insisted. "Zhongda has twenty times the wits in his head than I have in mine."

"...Zhongda...?" Cao Cao prompted.

"My second son, Yi," Sima Fang sighed. "He's... not currently able to come to the court. Perhaps later, when his family problems are resolved and his health has improved."

"His health...?" Cao Cao prompted.

"He... he suddenly became unwell, *very* unwell," Sima Fang explained. "It... it is quite unexpected and horrible."

"...I'm sorry to hear that your son is unwell and hope that he recovers quickly," Cao Cao said hesitantly. "It seems that a lot of men are struck down of late: I have had a lot more difficulty convincing men to come to Xuchang and serve the Han because of maladies and family worries."

"I assure you, Mengde, that I only tell you what I know," Sima Fang replied. "My son is, like you once were, a 'free spirit' of sorts, though in different ways. But I would never collude with him to allow him to shirk his responsibilities to the state. He assures me that he will be fine and that he is trying to settle his uneasy relationship with Lady Zhang, his wife, but that illness, it... it is certainly very visible."

"...I owe you for my career, Jiangong, and would never question your integrity," Cao Cao said humbly. "I merely remark that there are a lot of men that are impeded by strife; I have been waylaid by illness and family matters myself."

"One day, Excellency, we will all work for the Han," Sima Lang promised. "And if there is any way that I can be of service to His Majesty now, please tell me, for I am eager to get started."

"As am I, Excellency," Sima Fu said.

"I shall find you both suitable roles," Cao Cao replied.

Yuan Tan had been repeatedly talked out of attacking Yè City by the larger circle of advisers, but he was still subjected to regular prompting by Guo Tu and Xin Ping that went well with his own thoughts. Cao Cao's complete withdrawal to Xuchang was giving Yuan Tan the idea that it would be safe to try to seize power from his brother, using the apparent victory as his reasoning.

"After all," Yuan Tan said to his cynical advisers, "I was the one that chased Cao to the river: where was my brother? The men around him surely saw that I was the one that took decisive action and won a psychological victory, even with an army that was numerically inadequate! Think what I could achieve with the entire two-hundred-and-fifty-thousand under my command!"

"Cao Cao retreated for some other reason," Xin Pi insisted. "He wasn't scared away by us, Lord Yuan. Even with the extra thousands of men that we have now, we are still woefully outnumbered by Yuan Shang's loyalists and Wang Xiu and Guan Tong cannot commit more since Zang Ba's renewed offensive."

"I don't need more!" Yuan Tan insisted. "I can beat my weakling of a brother with what I have! We'll mobilise at once!"

"It is the right course, Lord Yuan!" Guo Tu said.

"No it isn't!" Xin Pi retorted. "My lord, we're acting upon the notion that Cao Cao is planning an attack on Jing Province, as per the rumours that Cao himself is allowing to surface from Yan Province! Until he puts one hoof, sandal or boot in Jing, I refuse to believe that he isn't planning to turn about and attack as soon as he senses division!"

"…That's true," Yuan Tan realised. "But when we're sure that he's going to attack Jing, it will then be safe!"

"*Aiee*… I give up!" Xin Pi cried. "We should all of us be trying to unite right now, not just the Yuans but all the enemies of Cao Cao's villainy: Liu Biao, Gao Gan and any others that might join us, such as Sun Quan of Jiangdong!"

"…That's also true," Yuan Tan said. "Wouldn't we have more to gain from attacking Cao and trapping him in a pincer if he did attack Liu Biao…?"

"Yuan Shang would need to agree to it," Guo Tu suggested dryly. "Of course, he might just see it as an opportunity to attack *you*…"

"…**Damned intrigue! I just want rid of Shen Pei!**" Yuan Tan screamed as he fled from his tent.

"Stop trying to convince him to attack Yè," Xin Pi implored. "It'll end in ruin!"

"If we do not stop Shen Pei's meddling, Lord Yuan Tan will be killed," Guo Tu retorted. "Why can't you understand…?"

"…I understand *completely*," Xin Pi replied.

On one busy morning – and before a court session that had been hastily arranged by Cao Cao – Emperor Xian dismissed his attendants so that he could enjoy one of his liberating private conversations with his confidante Empress Fu.

"One thing is clear now that Yuan Shao is gone: with him went the influence of the Yuans," Emperor Xian mused. "His heirs are boys, and they will be divided, if not by their own choice then by the ambitious courtiers that surround them. Cao moves his troops and makes a show of going west to attack Jing Province, but… would he dare, with the Yuans still at fighting strength…? …That sounds suspicious to me."

"So what does Cao Cao plan now?" Empress Fu asked. "Do we know *anything*…?"

"I was hoping that you might be able to tell me," Emperor Xian admitted. "I had hoped that your father might know something…"

"My father is not that powerful," Empress Fu replied. "He is kept away from great power 'to avoid another Dong Cheng or Liang Ji', and he knows better than to seek it out. He will therefore learn of Cao Cao's plans at the same time as every other official that isn't part of Cao's trusted inner circle."

170

"The man runs my empire like a private business, just like the others!" Emperor Xian complained. "I am his sovereign! I am the Son of Heaven! I should know what he is doing before everyone else, including his vassals!"

"...Do we have any powerful allies now...?" Empress Fu asked.

"Liu Bei might still be someone that we can place our hopes upon, despite his recent 'errors of judgement', which seem to have been the design of Yuan Shao," Emperor Xian replied. "Liu Bei is no longer affiliated to the Yellow Turbans, else Cao Cao would take pleasure in referring to it at every meeting; now Bei is in Jing Province... and allied to Liu Biao. Perhaps... perhaps that really *is* what Cao Cao intends... to announce a full-scale invasion of Jing."

"Can Liu Biao and Liu Bei survive that?" Empress Fu asked.

"If they can avoid division, yes," Emperor Xian replied. "But men are suspicious, and readily lend their ear to slander..."

Cao Cao was visited at his home by Xun Wenruo after the court proceedings ended; Cao frowned and asked, "Is there some business I failed to discuss...?"

"I am here with good news, actually," Xun Wenruo replied. "Do you remember Mister Du Ji, styled 'Bohou', from Duling...?"

"...He's nearly my age, isn't he...?" Cao Cao recalled. "Yes... he was attached to the Director of Retainers, convict labour... Du Bohou was a very honest and competent man, but I'd assumed that he had been killed during Dong Zhuo's purge since I'd heard nothing from him. Is he alive, then...?"

"He is, and he is eager to serve the Han once more!" Xun Wenruo said excitedly. "He contacted me after our recent successes to say that he has been in Jing Province, but that he cannot seek refuge with a traitor any longer and wants to return to the government in any small capacity."

"...So he knows a lot about Jing, then...?" Cao Cao replied thoughtfully. "That would make him a useful man for our imminent campaign... I'll appoint him as 'Rectifier of the Ministry of Works', and take him with me."

"That's... a very high post for a newly returned man, Excellency," Xun Wenruo suggested.

"You're the one that's brought him to my attention, Wenruo!" Cao Cao chuckled. "Why do you now want me to appoint such a decent and honest man in some trifling role and make poor use of him?"

"...I just didn't want to overstate him to you, Excellency," Xun Wenruo replied.

"Bohou is known to me, and I think that such a man is likely to be the same as he was, and such a man is to be properly treated," Cao Cao said. "Have him visit me tomorrow, Wenruo, so that I can finalise his appointment and so on."

"Very good, Your Excellency," Xun Wenruo replied; he then bowed humbly and retreated from the study.

"...Du Bohou, and two of the 'Eight Da of Sima'...!" Cao Cao chuckled. "I wonder, Wenruo, which marvellous talents will ask to serve me next...?"

****

36

A week passed.

Jing Governor Liu Biao summoned Kuai Yue and Wang Can to his private meeting room and said, "I'm hearing word that Cao Cao is plotting an attack on Jing Province. Furthermore, I'm getting word that Liu Bei is becoming very popular in Xinye... some seem to think that his popularity is not a good thing."

"He's recruiting men for his own militia that should be joining *you*, Lord Liu," Wang Can replied. "There are many that fear his reputation for charming provinces away from their governors."

"Especially ailing ones," Liu Biao chortled. "I'm sick from stress: have I a single black hair upon my head now, and do the white not outnumber the grey...? Sun Quan is making a sick man of me, and Liu Bei, who was supposed to help, is making me feel worse with his 'charisma'. My Lady Cai and her brother are driving me out of my mind with their warnings! And if it were only them, but Fu Xun, Han Song, Hè Qia, Huan Jie, the Pang brothers... they all speak ill of Xuande!"

"Solve two problems in one stroke," Wang Can suggested.

"Agreed," Kuai Yue said. "Cao Cao can only enter Jing through Yu Province – which is still riddled with armies of rebels and heretics – or via his strange ally Zhang Xiu's foothold in Nan County. Regardless of his route, have Liu Bei intercept him: if Bei is trustworthy, he'll obey and repel Cao; if he is self-serving then he will make excuses and seek alternative lodgings for his little band of fugitives before he loses any more of them."

"How can Liu Bei repel Cao Cao with a few thousand untested recruits...?" Liu Biao asked desperately. "I'm not sure that Huang Zu or Cai Mao could do it!"

"Cao Cao has, at the most, fifty-thousand men at his disposal," Wang Can replied. "He must keep at least half of them for a possible attack by the Yuan brothers, and he will probably want at least ten-thousand to send to Liang Province if the Qiang warlords decide to start being disobedient again. I estimate that his attack is mainly designed to unnerve you, my lord, and create fear and division, and will involve ten-thousand men and a thousand horses at the most."

"I agree," Kuai Yue said. "And they might well be split to attack us on two fronts."

"...But that suggests that I am being divided from my allies," Liu Biao mused. "Is it not then the case that he tries to divide me from Liu Bei...?"

"Of course, but there are others that he hopes to unnerve," Kuai Yue replied. "He perhaps hopes to weaken your ties to Huang Zu or some of your officials."

"...Men like Huan Jie, men who are quick to turn to new lords when they sense weakness," Liu Biao muttered. "Men like that should be watched closely."

"But what will you do about Liu Bei...?" Kuai Yue asked.

"...I'll do as you've proposed," Liu Biao decided. "Assign him as my buffer: if he is remotely grateful for the shelter that I give him from Cao Cao's wrath, he'll do as I ask. And I might propose a pincer attack to the Yuan brothers, as well... isn't it also in their best interests to be rid of Cao Cao...?"

"It is certainly worth contacting Yuan Shang," Wang Can replied. "But then we must wonder whether we should also contact Yuan Tan and Yuan Xi separately..."

"...Their lack of cooperation is frustrating," Liu Biao said. "I pray that my sons do not behave like that when I die... Jing would be lost in months or less. As for your point, I can only answer that we should just speak to Yuan Shang for now."

"That is the right choice," Wang Can replied.

"To write to each son risks being blamed for divisions that were already there," Kuai Yue said. "Just act as though we believe we are dealing with a united Yuan clan and hope that it shames them into actually uniting."

"...And *hope*, Mister Kuai, that I am not accused of hypocrisy when considering my stance toward Liu Bei," Liu Biao replied.

Liu Bei received Liu Biao's order to oppose Cao Cao's attack within days: he was surprised at the cold language that was being used and summoned his officials to his Xinye residence.

"This is pretty much a request to leave Xinye and relocate to a military camp somewhere, one way or another," Liu Bei's friend Jian Yong exclaimed. "What an ingrate!"

"Liu Biao sees his request to be quite the opposite of ingratitude," the politician Mister Sun Qian said. "To him, we're lucky to have his protection, and we, in turn, should gratefully act as a buffer."

"Xuande's mustered a bigger force here in Xinye than *he* ever could, that old bastard!" Zhang Fei cried. **"This is an insult! This-!"**

"This is a moment for *calm*, Yide," Liu Bei insisted. "Our situation has been steadily improving over the last year, and we should do nothing to compromise that; and by 'we' I mean 'you', because I might have *forgiven* the 'Cao Bao incident' but I haven't forgotten that *or* the Haixi siege and loss of Xu Province that happened as a result... and you haven't either, if you're honest about it and, more importantly, genuinely *repentant*."

Zhang Fei grunted miserably.

"I agree," the long-bearded Guan Yu said. "Keep your temper."

"...But we're being thrown out of Xinye!" Zhang Fei bellowed. **"Liu Biao's a stupid old pile of bones! It's-!"**

"*Yide*... it doesn't matter," Liu Bei interrupted. "We have ample supplies of our own, a good force of men that are adequately trained, and we might soon have our own genius."

"...I get that we've grown our own food, but you don't grow men with brains," Zhang Fei heckled. "And no man with brains in his head is going to join a bunch of evicted fugitives when he can join Liu Biao."

"You're wrong, Yide," the patron-turned-adviser Mi Zhu said. "The intelligentsia around northern Jing are tiring of Liu Biao's floundering. And names are being bandied about... names that we should be putting faces to and then recruiting."

"Like that little man, 'Xu Shu', that you invited to talk to you, I suppose," Zhang Fei scoffed. "He isn't your 'genius', I hope; he had the charisma of a wet rag and stammered even when he wasn't talking."

Guan Yu, Zhao Yun and Mi Zhu's brother Fang stifled smiles.

"Xu Shu has interesting friends," Mi Zhu retorted.

Zhang Fei grinned sarcastically and said, "Yeah, that's nice, really nice, but wouldn't a better idea be to find a man with 'interesting friends' that are more like me, Yunchang or Zilong, and not just another load of scrawny pedants...?"

"*Yide*!" Liu Bei exclaimed.

"Cao Cao isn't sending an army of sleeve-flicking toadies to talk us to death!" Zhang Fei continued. "He'll send that Zhang Liao, or that Xu Huang, or that bastard Xiahou Dun! Or maybe he'll send them men that defected from Yuan Shao!"

"Whoever he sends, it'll be the terrain and a sound plan that will repel them," Mi Zhu insisted. "We must dictate the conditions."

"...Look, I don't know why you ask me to these things," Zhang Fei muttered. "Just tell me who you want me to kill and leave me out of the scheming."

Liu Bei smirked and said, "I have no problem with that. What bothers me is the tone of the letter, but if I do this favour for my host, perhaps he'll start to trust me again."

"And he should stop listening to his wife Lady Cai and his brother-in-law Cai Mao, and the likes of Kuai Yue, Huan Jie and Wang Can as well, because we know that they're the source of this," Jian Yong said. "Honestly, Xuande, I'd expected better than I've found: there are so many able minds in this region, but Liu Biao is a doddering fool, married to a witch and counselled by a band of shifty imps that would make my flesh crawl if I hadn't met Yuan Shao's advisers already. He worries that you'll take the province from him, but I'm not the only one that wouldn't blame you if-"

"That's enough, Xianhe," Liu Bei chortled. "I've done Xu Province twice, and that's enough for me. Liu Biao will see sense after we've repelled Cao Cao's army... he *has to, surely*..."

"And if he doesn't...?" Jian Yong asked plainly. "What then?"

Liu Bei did not answer: he was as aware as everyone else that Liu Biao was not as strong a governor as he had once been, and in yet another reverse of roles, it was Liu Bei who was being tempted to supplant his host, just as Bei had done when Tao Qian invited him to Xu Province and just as Lü Bu had done when he usurped Bei while a guest in that same Xu Province. Ultimately, Liu Bei would leave the arguing to others and the decision to fate: Cao Cao's impending attack was his main concern.

****

37

Cao Chong was a child with intelligence and maturity that far exceeded his 7 years of age: he started to wander the vast mansion that served as his home in order to learn more about the world around him. The servants were bemused by the sight of a young boy pacing the grounds with a serious expression and his arms crossed behind his back, as though he were an official inspector; he looked, at first glance, like a tiny adult, but any fears were quickly allayed when he kept to nodding respectfully and smiling in response to any show of deference or curiosity about his purpose. Chong would often walk around the grounds unaccompanied, which made him seem even more eccentric, but he was in no danger from the hand-picked loyal vassals that staffed the estate.

As the day of the intended attack on Jing Province approached, there was a lot of excitement in the main military barracks and in the stables on the mansion grounds: it was not clear whether Cao Cao would be joining the campaign, and so the stable hands were repeatedly exercising, feeding and saddling the horses as a pre-emptive measure. Such uncertainty was always going to lead to some carelessness, and when one of Cao Cao's favourite saddles – a decorated piece that had been a companion in many battles – was accidentally left hanging over a stable door, the worst occurred: rats chewed the straps and the edge of the seat, causing irreparable damage.

"What do we do…?" one stable hand sobbed as he and his two colleagues stood around the ruined saddle as though it were a human corpse. "We'll be castrated and disembowelled for this if His Excellency has a headache when he finds out!"

"We'll be lashed even if he has no headache!" another man said.

"Do we flee?" the third man asked.

"What's the point?" the first man replied. "He'll hunt us down!"

"…**Is something the matter**…?"

The three men froze; the child's voice was unfamiliar to them, but they knew that it would probably be Cao Chong, and it was.

"…Why are you all standing in a huddle like that?" Cao Chong continued. "I am just interested in knowing what the problem is. Can Father help?"

The three men looked at each other and started to weep.

"…I'm guessing that Father cannot help," Cao Chong said thoughtfully. "You are frightened, gentlemen, but I assure you that I do not want to see you harmed."

One of the men turned to face Cao Chong and fell to his knees, crying, "Have pity, Young Master! Have pity and pray for us when we have told your father-!"

"**Shut up!**" another man barked. "**We must face this like men!**"

"Face what…?" Cao Chong asked. "What it is that you have done?"

"…We left His Excellency's saddle to face the elements by accident, in our haste to clear up yesterday, and it was damaged by rats!" the third stable hand replied. "We were fools, but we know that we must admit our mistake and answer for it!"

The man that had knelt before Cao Chong covered his face with his hands and sobbed, "We… *aiee*… we are *doomed*! Doomed to face horrible ends...!"

"Because of a saddle...?" Cao Chong chuckled. "That doesn't seem to be proportionate to the crime at all. I'm sure that Father will not harm you so gravely for the sake of a few bits of leather."

"It is a military offence!" the second man said. "All such errors are punishable by any means, including death!"

"...Ah, yes, I suppose that it might be classified as a military offence," Cao Chong replied thoughtfully. "Alright, then... I want you all to listen to me."

The three men looked at Cao Chong with horrified expressions.

"I want you to refrain from reporting this for three days, and when you report the loss, explain the cause of the damage – rats – but do not say where the saddle was left unless pressed on the matter," Cao Chong continued. "If you do as I ask, you will not suffer harm."

The three men looked at one-another nervously; the man on his knees shook his head and said, "We would suffer *worse* punishment if it looked like we had delayed reporting it, Young Master! We'd be branded, lashed, our tongues removed, our-!"

"Trust me," Cao Chong interrupted. "Can you do that...? Can you trust me...?"

"...Alright," the second man replied. "So we should wait for three days... and only say how it was destroyed, but not where."

"I promise that you will be fine," Cao Chong insisted.

A day passed; Cao Cao retired from the Imperial court and sat in his study to read a favourite passage of 'The Spring and Autumn Annals' by torchlight.

"...Father...?"

Cao Cao turned from his reading, frowned when he saw the terrified expression on Cao Chong's face and asked, "What is it?"

"...Father, I... I'm frightened," Cao Chong replied.

"*You*...?" Cao Cao said bemusedly. "You're the last of my sons that I expected to hear such things from! What are you afraid of...?"

Cao Chong raised his right arm: he was holding an expensive shirt that his father had procured for him in his right hand.

"...Why are you showing me a shirt...?" Cao Cao asked.

Cao Chong covered his eyes with his left hand and said, "Look, Father, at what has happened to it!"

Cao Cao took the shirt from his son and examined it: it was badly damaged, and the size and pattern of the holes suggested that they were the work of rats.

"...It is a shirt," Cao Cao said. "It is a shame, yes, but if you left it out... but then I know you would not have done so."

"I found it in its proper place, Father, in that condition!" Cao Chong sobbed. "Don't people say that such a thing is bad luck? Won't I come to harm now?"

Cao Cao inspected the shirt and hummed soberly; it was, as Cao Chong suggested, a superstitious belief that rats gnawing at clothes was an ill omen for the owner.

"What do I do, Father?" Cao Chong asked desperately.

"...You will be fine," Cao Cao replied: he then looked up and smiled encouragingly before adding, "You can't believe every tale that's invented by men! Rats nibble things... and it is obviously the case that we have some very tenacious ones on the estate at the moment that can get almost anywhere. But they're rats, not agents of the underworld! Forget about it, my son: I will see if the shirt can be repaired, and if it cannot, I will procure you another."

"...So I won't get sick or die...?" Cao Chong asked.

"You're no more doomed to it than anyone else in this house," Cao Cao replied. "Now go back to your room and forget about it."

"...Thank you, Father," Cao Chong said as he retreated.

Cao Cao turned his gaze to the ruined shirt and muttered, "Blasted rats... for scaring my son, you'll die slow deaths if I catch you personally."

Cao Chong wandered the grounds once again on the following morning: the stable hands watched him cautiously, but he did not approach them or give them any sign of what awaited them. Chong's older half-brother Cao Zhi and his obese cousin Cao Zhen had decided to join him; both were puzzled at the strange, satisfied smile on Chong's face.

"...Has something good happened?" Cao Zhen asked.

"The answer to that is a day away, but the signs are good," Cao Chong replied.

"Father was screaming about rats this morning and ordering the house staff to do something about them," Cao Zhi noted. "I've not seen a rat near the house in a few weeks, though: Father was acting like we were under siege!"

"Yes, I know," Cao Chong replied. "They ruined my shirt."

"Was that what the fuss was about last night...?" Cao Zhen asked.

"It was," Cao Chong replied. "It seems that there is at least one very 'tenacious' – as Father put it – rodent lurking on the grounds. Who knows what else it might damage if it isn't caught soon...?"

"...You seem very happy for someone that lost a shirt and upset Father," Cao Zhi suggested. "I don't understand you, Chong."

"I was frightened, but Father consoled me," Cao Chong replied. "I... am just glad that I will not suffer as superstitions suggested."

"Oh, I see," Cao Zhen said. "You had a 'lucky escape'."

"Hopefully," Cao Chong replied, "I will not be the only one."

The stable hands reported the destruction of the saddle to Cao Cao on the following day, stating only that it had been attacked by rats: Cao Cao surprised the men – just as Cao Chong had promised – by sympathising with them, neglecting to ask where the saddle had been left or found, and reassuring the men that they would face no punishment for what seemed to be an unavoidable loss. It would be years before Cao Chong would confide his actions to one of his brothers: he had used a knife and other implements to cause damage to his shirt that resembled the work of rats in order to falsify a scare and rescue the stable hands from the severe punishment that awaited them. Cao Cao started to suspect that his son might have been acting – just as Cao Cao himself had once done when he feigned a fit in order to ruin his uncle's standing with his father – but he said nothing and continued with his preparations for war with Liu Biao and Liu Bei.

****

38

Yuan Tan was poised to attack his brother's base at Yè City after repeated mobilisations and reconsiderations: the only obstacle had been the belief that Cao Cao might return, but the news that large numbers of Han soldiers – and vast supply convoys – had advanced to Nan County in northern Jing Province dispelled all notions of a sudden attack from the south.

"It's a case of 'now or never'," Yuan Tan said to his assembled officials. "I intend to march on Yè at once and wipe the smug smile from my usurping brother's face! Cao Cao is gone, and we need not fear his immediate return if he is entrenched in Jing: when he does return, it will be to the unopposed rule of Yuan Tan, true lord of the north and the rightful chieftain of the Yuan clan!"

"I beg you to reconsider, Lord Yuan," the adviser Xin Pi said.

"I cannot allow small concerns to rob me of my inheritance and leave my father's hard-fought legacy open to seizure by his worst enemy!" Yuan Tan retorted. **"Yuan Shang is a weakling that takes advice from his mother and that treacherous dog Shen Pei! He willingly conspired with them to rob me of my rightful place, adopt me to a dead uncle and banish Xi to the frontier, where he is surrounded by enemies! Shang is without dignity or decency, and Shen Pei is a creature that I will see dead for what he has done! And it must be done now, before the 'Crafty Villain' can return! We advance now, today, and take Shang by surprise!"**

"It's the only way!" Guo Tu said. "Our might will be undeniable!"

"You have my unyielding support, Lord Yuan!" Xin Ping promised.

"...*Aiee*... a tiger's maw awaits our tiny fist," Xin Pi muttered.

Yuan Shang was alarmed when Ji Province Registrar Li Fu reported Yuan Tan's unprovoked attack on his outer defensive camps.

"His bravery and skill are undeniable," Yuan Shang exclaimed. "He has managed to pass the outermost perimeter once before being repelled...? Granted, he had the element of surprise – or, to be more accurate, 'reaped the benefits of complacency' – but... should I worry...?"

"You should not be concerned," Ju Hu replied. "His army is too small to create a path to the city."

"Can you be certain of that?" Shen Pei asked snidely. "Since he apparently demands my head for 'a catalogue of crimes against him, the people and the clan that can only be atoned for with death', I do not especially want him at the walls!"

"There's no denying that he has got a greater chance of some successful raids on the camps, but I can see no way that he can win now that we are aware of all of his forces," Ju Hu replied.

"But are you certain that he has used every asset?" Shen Pei asked. "Are all of his officers, few though there may be, accounted for? Is every man known? Is every arrow, every horse, every-?"

"He's never had as many followers as Lord Yuan Shang," Ju Hu insisted. "He cannot leave Qing unguarded, so he can use, at best, half of his army, and the numbers reported so far sound correct."

"...Then we meet him on the field and suitably – and deservedly – humiliate him," Yuan Shang decided. "He doubtless intends this to be a show of might to prove his greater worthiness to the title of chieftain, and so I must match – and if possible, outmatch – his valour and might if I do not want to see defections. Shen Pei, Gao Fan, Su Yòu, Chen Lin: you will remain in the city. Mister Shen, please order Ma Yan to oversee the order in the camps and delegate duties to his subordinates where appropriate. Li Fu, Ju Hu, Zhang Yi: you will accompany me. Lü Kuang and Lü Xiang are already engaging my treacherous brother's forces, and with our additional might, victory is assured."

Li Fu bowed silently; Ju Hu and Zhang Yi touched their chests with their fists and said, "**As you command!**"

Yuan Shang led his armies to the eastern perimeter of his defensive network to confront Yuan Tan, who had just been repelled by General Lü Kuang's defenders: Tan spied his brother from a distance and screamed, "**Bring me Shen Pei! Bring me the head of the man that helped you to steal my life!**"

"**…Whatever he's yelling about, it's bound to be nonsense,**" Yuan Shang said. "**Is that really all the men that he has…?**"

"**It seems so, Lord Yuan,**" Lü Kuang replied. "**But it seems to be far less than expected: could he be attempting a ruse?**"

"**…Perhaps,**" Yuan Shang said. "**Guo Tu is not without some talent… and he also has the Xin brothers. Might they try and have a force go around us now that they have lured us here, I wonder…?**"

"**Our supplies are guarded, the road has a network of scout camps along it, and Yè is heavily fortified,**" Ju Hu replied. "**Any such ruse is pointless.**"

"**WHERE IS YUAN SHANG?!**" a voice bellowed: Yuan Tan had sent one of his officers to issue a challenge. "**WILL ANYONE FACE HAN XUN?**"

"**…Who's this?**" Yuan Shang asked.

"**No idea,**" Lü Kuang replied. "**It's some nobody from Qing.**"

"**I'll test his strength!**" Ju Hu declared.

Han Xun and Ju Hu clashed briefly, but they were evenly matched: Guo Tu signalled a retreat order to Han Xun, who reluctantly complied.

"**…I'm… no Lü Bu… and neither is he,**" Ju Hu panted as he returned to Yuan Shang's side. "**Yuan Tan is… severely lacking officers if that's… who he's sending to challenge.**"

"**Then this won't take long,**" Yuan Shang said. "**Full advance!**"

Yuan Tan cursed as his army – which was, as some suspected, not his entire force – buckled under the pressure of Yuan Shang's charge. A scout reported to Guo Tu during the skirmish: Guo silently contemplated the defeat of his ambush pincer forces before they had even settled into place.

"**What should we do???**" Yuan Tan asked.

"**…RETREAT!**" Guo Tu replied.

"**DON'T THINK THAT I AM DONE!**" Yuan Tan screamed as he prepared to flee. "**YOU'LL WISH YOU'D GIVEN ME SHEN PEI!**"

Yuan Shang watched his brother's retreat and smiled.

****

Xiahou Dun, Li Dian and Yu Jin led their armies into Jing Province within the month, whereupon Liu Bei moved to intercept them at the strategically-chosen Bowang Valley. Cao Cao's hope that Xiahou Dun's recklessness could be controlled by two of his more restrained generals was proven to be groundless: Liu Bei employed a fairly straightforward baiting attack, luring Xiahou's force into the wooded valley and then setting fire to it. The outcome was not a rout, because Liu Bei lacked the numbers to oppose Li Dian and Yu Jin's reinforcements, but the loss demoralised Cao Cao's army, and a general retreat was ordered.

Liu Bei had the captured officials brought to his command tent and stood before him with their hands bound behind their backs with rope for final disposal: one such man was Xiahou Lan, a distant relative of the same Xiahou clan that Cao Cao was closely affiliated with. Generals Guan Yu, Zhang Fei and Zhao Yun sat to Bei's right as he deliberated; Bei's recently-adopted son Liu Feng, long-time friend Jian Yong, the politician Mister Sun, sponsor-turned-adviser Mi Zhu and Mi Zhu's brother Fang sat to Bei's left.
"What will we do with you, I wonder...?" Liu Bei asked as he stared at the miserable Xiahou Lan.
"Kill me and be done with it," Xiahou Lan replied.
"Agreed," Zhang Fei chuckled.
"Wait, my lord!" Zhao Yun pleaded. "I know this man!"
"...You vouch for me, Zhao Yun...?" Xiahou Lan murmured.
"We have known each other for a long time," Zhao Yun said. "Lord Liu, we are from the same village; yes, he is a Xiahou, but he is a clever, open-minded man that we can use!"
"How so...?" Guan Yu asked.
"He's a bloody Xiahou!" Zhang Fei heckled. "What can we 'use him' for...? He's Cao Cao's distant cousin!"
"That shouldn't matter, Yide!" Zhao Yun retorted. "Judge his *character*! He is a good man!"
"...Forgive my cynicism, Zilong, but I cannot see what you say," Liu Bei replied. "Yide upsetting the order of things by taking young Lady Xiahou for a bride is one thing and bad enough, but-"
"I treat her well!" Zhang Fei protested. "How she came to be my wife is not to your liking, but too bad! I treat her well, and she is happy to stay now! She's comfortable now, instead of being made to go out and chop wood for that scruffy-!"
"Alright, alright, we get it, Yide," Jian Yong interrupted. "You treat her well... we get it."
"...I will have to settle for that," Liu Bei said with a sigh. "But can I employ a man that could harm my cause and prolong the suffering of the Son of Heaven...? I cannot bring myself to kill him, but it is another thing altogether to give him a job!"
"...You are not at all what I expected," Xiahou Lan admitted.
"We fight for the Han, not some personal ambition," Zhao Yun insisted. "You have known me since we were children, and so you know that I wouldn't serve a wicked, greedy lord. You have tried to be loyal to your clan, I understand that, but Cao Cao is a villain! Yes, I know that our collaborations with Gong Du and Liu Pi

have given us poor reputations, but that was all at Yuan Shao's insistence! Now we're acting as we choose, and we only aspire to be the ones that restore the Han to its former glory! We don't covet lands or the throne! Join us and help us, Mister Xiahou Lan!"

"...I admit that I doubt Cao Mengde's intent, especially after he killed Consort Dong," Xiahou Lan said. "I am a Han loyalist, like you Zilong, and I only want to see the Empire restored and people's lives improved. If... if that is what you want as well, then... then I should like to do all that I can!"

"We're not really going to trust him, are we...?" Zhang Fei asked.

"It is your fine treatment of Lady Xiahou that shows your hearts are not filled with spite and hate, Zhang Yide," Xiahou Lan replied. "Please, Lord Liu: let me serve and repay your kindness!"

Xiahou Lan fell to his knees; Liu Bei hummed thoughtfully and said, "Remove Mister Xiahou's bonds and take him to the barracks to receive a proper meal. I accept your surrender and your service, Mister Xiahou... let us work together for the Han cause!"

"Thank you, Lord Liu!" Xiahou Lan cried.

Zhao Yun had two men free Xiahou Lan and escort him from the command tent; Liu Bei turned to his meek topographer, Xu Shu, and said, "My thanks to you, Yuanzhi. You are, of course, invited to the banquet that we shall have to celebrate our victory."

Xu Shu bowed humbly and said, "Thank you, my lord... might... might I bring my friend Kongming...?" Xu Shu asked.

"...This 'Kongming' is welcome if he is a good friend of yours," Liu Bei replied. "Now please, Mister Xu, go and join the men in the barracks, who would also like to thank you."

Xu Shu bowed and retreated.

"You did well, Feng'er," Liu Bei said as he turned to his adopted son. "A fine effort: I am proud."

"I hope to do more to earn your respect in the future, Father," Liu Feng replied.

"...So *Zhuge Liang* might be at this banquet," Jian Yong said.

"So what...?" Zhang Fei grumbled.

"Stop being petty," Liu Bei sighed. "You know who he is."

"...Well don't expect me to crawl up his arse," Zhang Fei retorted. "We don't need more pedants! Pedants like that Xu Shu didn't beat Cao Cao's generals today!"

"Not directly," Mi Zhu said. "Xu Shu did his part... and now, perhaps, we'll have someone else whose talent will be invaluable. I'll put him to the test, my lord, with your permission."

"You don't have to ask," Liu Bei replied. "I've seen enough men with good reputations that have turned out to be villains or mediocrities... I expect Mister Sun, Xianhe and your brother to test him as well. If he is what he is said to be, we're finally blessed... so let us hope that he is."

Cao Cao received and read the report from Bowang a week later: he summoned Guo Jia and Xun Wenruo and said, "I should have sent one of you to advise them, but I have erred yet again. Now I am seen to be weak, suffering the same fate as Yuan Shao! How is this so? Does Heaven suddenly delight in only awarding victories to the disadvantaged...?"

"There will be no consequences," Guo Jia insisted. "The Qiang will not react, as one defeat cannot be perceived as anything but what it is and even they know that. The Yuans are divided, just as we expected them to be, and are too busy with internecine warfare to be a worry, although they should be our main focus once again, since we cannot attack Jiangdong while Jing stands firm and we cannot annex Jing until the Yuans and their Wuhuan allies are vanquished. Liu Bei can relish this little 'drawing of blood': it is not 'another Wan City', nor is it 'our Guandu or Cangting', and he'll wish he had not laughed when we destroy him later."

Cao Cao looked at Xun Wenruo, who laughed and said, "What can I add to that? Fengxiao is completely right."

"But am I now supposed to go to Jing...?" Cao Cao asked.

Xu Yòu – who had invited himself to the meeting – said, "*No*, Mengde, we should be going to Ji and-!"

"*Enough*, Ziyuan," Cao Cao ordered. "Fengxiao...?"

"In a week or so, yes," Guo Jia replied. "The rumours coming out of Ji Province are very promising... very promising... but not promising enough to risk returning there just yet. We must continue to pressure Liu Biao for now."

"Then I shall do just that," Cao Cao said.

Xu Yòu – whose sole interest was the total destruction of the Yuan clan – huffed irritably but kept his silence.

Jing Governor Liu Biao exhaled angrily when he learned that Cao Cao had advanced to Nan County and set up a base near the border with the rest of Northern Jing; his court was silent as every man present awaited their lord's questions.

"...Liu Bei has embarrassed the 'Crafty Villain', but he advances instead of retreating," Liu Biao said at last. "Cai Mao, Zhang Yun, Wen Ping, Huang Zhong and Wang Wei are all thinly deployed along my many, many borders, and Huang Zu cannot aid me because he rightly fears the return of Sun Quan. Whether they act alone or in concert, Cao and Sun have me trapped in a pincer: how should I proceed, gentlemen...?"

"We must pincer the more dangerous of the two, namely Cao Cao," Kuai Yue replied. "Sun Quan has internal problems that will continually cause him to draw his hand back, whereas Cao Cao can move freely with the help of Zhang Xiu, the Qiang, Zang Ba and the unintended help of the bickering Yuan brothers."

"*Aiee*... do the Yuans still fight?" Liu Biao asked.

"They do," Wang Can replied.

"They must not be allowed to persist while Cao Cao threatens us all," Liu Biao said. "Does anyone have an idea...?"

The politician and junior adviser Han Song gestured meekly.

"...Please speak, Mister Han," Liu Biao prompted.

"I, Song, am a native of Yiyang in Ji Province, and might be best placed to carry messages to the Yuans," Han Song explained. "We should appeal to their sense – which has been seen, and might persist beneath their egos – in order to propose a pincer as Mister Kuai suggests and reverse our situation."

"...We have little choice," Liu Biao replied. "My only friendly neighbour is Liu Zhang, and he's a pathetic sycophant; I *must* seek help from the Yuans."

"Less 'help', more 'cooperation', Governor Liu," the politician Fu Xun suggested. "To suggest that they help us is as wrong as can be: if anything, we help them by giving Cao Cao other targets, and they repay us with idiotic, self-destructive behaviour while his back is turned. We are quite unlucky."

"I agree that we are unlucky to be left with the Yuans as allies," the politician Huan Jie said sadly. "It is a shame that my former lord's son Sun Quan cannot be reasoned with, for he surely will be next if we're defeated, but that family is comprised entirely of stubborn, violent fools, which is why I am here."

"...Sun Quan aids Cao's success, whether he does so deliberately or not," Liu Biao complained. "But... but our relationship is beyond salvage. Who is best placed to pen the letters to the Yuans...?"

"Wang Can," Fu Xun replied immediately.

"Agreed," Huan Jie said. "His is the finest pen of us all."

"If Mister Wang cannot reach their hearts, my lord, then no man can," Han Song suggested.

"You flatter me, gentlemen," Wang Can insisted. "Many others are better than me."

"Not at all," Kuai Yue said. "Your time as a disciple of Cai Yong's teachings has made a grand philosopher of you, Mister Wang, and despite your... unfortunate, shall we say... tendency to be distracted by the sounds of braying beasts of burden – and it is a far better flaw than vice – you are almost without equal. At just twenty-six, you are the envy of the intelligentsia: you shame men twice your age with your mastery of language. If your words fail to appeal, Wang Zhongxuan, it will only be due to the mental inadequacy of the recipients."

Wang Can turned to face Liu Biao and bowed humbly, saying, "If it is truly the belief of the court that I am the best man to write these pleas for good sense to be shown, then I shall retire to your private study and begin immediately."

"Mister Kuai, Mister Han: you will join Mister Wang and me in the study," Liu Biao ordered. "The rest of you should return to your duties. Fu Xun, Huan Jie: if any news from Jiangdong – *any news at all* – is reported, bring it straight to me. Hè Qia, and both Misters Pang: maintain communications with our officers on the borders and report anything immediately. Oh, and make sure that no fool has brought any donkeys to the market today: I can do without my scribe wandering off in mid-sentence."

Wang Can laughed awkwardly as he followed his lord's retreat from the hall; others succumbed to laughter as well, although it did not carry the spiteful intent of past times.

Wang Can's letters reached Yuan Tan and Yuan Shang within a day of each other, but neither of the pleas was responded to with any enthusiasm. The brothers were now irreconcilable, and no amount of praise for their joint defence of Li County or reminders of the other threats that faced them would change that. Liu Biao was distraught, as that left him almost alone in his battle with Cao Cao: Liu did not realise that his plight was just a taste of his future suffering and that Cao was constantly ready to turn around and speed toward Ji Province at the first sign of certain victory over the Yuans.

****

40

Yuan Tan was always at a numerical disadvantage in his struggles with his younger brother Yuan Shang, but he had hoped to sway some of his late father's vassals toward him and away from Shang by attacking the clan's capital, Yè City, and humbling what he declared to be 'a regime built on lies and toothless roaring': the actual outcome was an embarrassing series of routs that weakened Tan further and drove him out of Wei Prefecture altogether. Yuan Shang stopped his pursuit in southern Bohai Prefecture and set up a military camp close to his brother's stronghold at Nanpi City, near the Qing-Ji provincial border, where he then had two options presented to him by his advisers: he could return to Yè – and risk allowing Tan to regroup, seize Bohai Prefecture and regain momentum – or he could force his brother to flee to northern Qing, where the bulk of his support was.

"Don't let him breathe freely, Lord Yuan Shang!" Shen Pei urged. "Yuan Tan is a dim-witted thug that will not just retreat into the hills and accept defeat! Have Louban and Tadun aid us in an invasion of Qing Province! We should capitalise on his loss of support in the south and finish him off!"

"...He is still my brother, Mister Shen," Yuan Shang retorted. "I appreciate that his constant demands for your death must upset you, but please choose your words more carefully. He is not 'dim-witted'... rather he is stubborn, and too quick to favour swift action over cautious planning. He compensates for this, willingly or not, by having Guo Tu, Xin Ping and Xin Pi for counsel."

"And they are useless, thankfully," Shen Pei said. "Whether they're ignored or ignorant, the result is the same: they have achieved nothing. But that's in Ji Province after an impulsive ambush: if they can restore order in Qing and reassemble the army, we might not enjoy such an easy battle when they return! I recommend pursuit and a thorough purge of Tan's supporters."

"Sad to say, Lord Yuan, I agree," Ju Hu admitted. "We mustn't let Tan have a chance to forge alliances, regroup, or anything else."

"...And the rest of you...?" Yuan Shang asked of his other officials: the chorus of murmurings told him that they mostly agreed with Shen Pei.

"We should continue at once," Shen Pei said. "We must not be away from Yè for too long, or Cao Cao might hear of it and attack us again... the distance between Nan County and Wei Prefecture is too small for my liking."

"I'll do as you say," Yuan Shang replied. "We'll destroy my brother's army quickly and then head home."

Yuan Tan stood on the battlements of Nanpi City and stared at Yuan Shang's distant encampment; Xin Ping, Guo Tu and Xin Pi were assembled behind him, awaiting orders that never came.

"...I have written to Wang Xiu," Xin Ping said at last.

"This place was once awarded to my father," Yuan Tan replied. "Before he rightly took Ji Province from Han Fu, this was his seat... Bohai Prefecture. Father moved us all to Wei Prefecture and established Yè as his capital, and good that he did, as our ancestral homelands in Ru County and then Runan Prefecture slipped from his fingers as Uncle became increasingly deranged and started his war to take the chieftainship of the clan... and now I realise something. I was sent to *help him*... a man that would have gladly murdered his own brother – and us, his nephews – to claim something that wasn't his..."

"That's why Yuan Shu ultimately failed and died," Guo Tu said.

"...But he was not the rightful heir, so his claim was false, and he lost as a result!" Yuan Tan retorted. "Why, then, am I the loser in my battle with Shang...? He is the usurper, and I am the rightful heir! How is it that I am losing? I don't even have support here in Bohai, my father's oldest administrative seat!"

"People are confused," Xin Ping insisted. "Yuan Shang's followers have launched an effective slander campaign against you that solely blames you for the unrest."

"But he is ruling at the moment, so how can anything be my fault?" Yuan Tan asked. "Yes, I know I have been blamed for unrest in Qing, and maybe I *am* to blame for that, but what have I done to harm Ji Province?"

"...I do not know how to proceed," Xin Ping admitted. "Have you any ideas, Mister Guo?"

"I have one, but it is reserved for more desperate times than these," Guo Tu replied. "If we can hold Nanpi, then we can wait for Shang to run out of supplies and retreat: if we cannot hold Nanpi, then we must flee southward and-"

"Southward...?" Xin Pi exclaimed. "Do you not mean eastward...?"

"Eastward, as even the most short-sighted man can tell, leads to the banks of the Yellow River as it winds toward the sea," Guo Tu retorted. "After that hazardous crossing – which is, in itself, bound to lose us more men and certain to lose us our supplies – we will then be forced to cross the Ji River in order to reach safety. Hemmed in between two wide rivers, we will not only be caught in a pincer between Yuan Shang and Zang Ba, but between nature's barriers as well. Not only that, but we will lose any hope of retaining a stronghold in Ji Province: has the rightful heir to the Yuan chieftainship got any credibility at all if even the likes of Cao Cao has Li County and he has *nothing*...?"

"...So where would you make this futile stand that you propose...?" Xin Pi asked.

"Pingyuan has long been a good tactical stronghold, regardless of whether it has been part of Qing or Ji Province," Guo Tu replied. "At present, it is part of Ji Province, but we can re-establish the border that we once had if we can hold Pingyuan, get more reinforcements from Qing Province and-"

"But Zang Ba is preventing any such reinforcements, Mister Guo!" Xin Pi protested.

"Zang's support has dwindled after repeated losses and a sense among some bandits that they have betrayed their beliefs by capitulating to Cao Cao," Xin Ping said. "It would serve you well to remember that a lot of newer bandits were from what is now classed as Xu Province, where Cao Cao committed mass murder and made a lot of enemies. And being asked to attack the Yuans means attacking every village, town and city in northern Qing, and that will be affecting the loyalties of the men that hail from northern Qing. In addition, a lot of the crime families that resisted the Yuans initially are now looking, seeing that Lord Yuan Tan fights Cao Cao, recalling Cao's time as Magistrate of Ji'nan and taking up arms against Zang Ba."

"...So reinforcements are not a ludicrous idea...?" Xin Pi asked.

"Not at all," Xin Ping replied. "In fact, I think we might be able to request more men within a few weeks, and we'll be reassembling our existing forces in the meantime. All is far from lost!"

"...Then we shall hold Nanpi for as long as possible, and go to Pingyuan if we cannot hold," Yuan Tan declared. "I will not just roll over and die!"

A week passed in which Yuan Tan's grip on Nanpi weakened: the surrounding settlements surrendered to Yuan Shang's larger army one by one, and with those surrenders came fewer supplies and increased isolation. A small rebellion inside the city by the disaffected local defence forces left Yuan Tan with no option but to throw open the gates and fight his way out of Nanpi.

"Why is he retreating *toward us*?" Yuan Shang asked.

"...He must intend to take some other place and retain a foothold in Bohai!" Li Fu replied.

"We cannot allow that," Yuan Shang said. **"We must force him eastward, toward the Yellow River, and crush him when his back is to it!"**

But Yuan Tan was surprisingly effective as he fought his way to the south: many of Yuan Shang's soldiers and junior officers were hesitant when they were presented with an opportunity to directly attack the older brother of their lord, and when it became clear that Tan was only attacking those that stood in his way, many simply stood aside and let him pass.

"You'll not pass me!" Lü Kuang cried as Yuan Tan reached him; the two clashed briefly before Yuan Tan unseated Kuang and rode on without killing him.

"There is Xin Ping, Yuan Tan's brain trust!" Zhang Yi bellowed. **"After him!"**

Xin Ping was narrowly rescued by his brother Pi, who turned and added his own militia to Ping's: Guo Tu's force passed by without lending aid, but Zhang Yi's efforts were thwarted by Han Xun, who attacked him and allowed the Xin brothers to flee with the remnants of their forces. Fear of traps led Yuan Shang to forbid a pursuit, but the brief battle for control of Nanpi was over, and Shang had won.

"...So they escaped," Yuan Shang sighed.

"But Nanpi is secured," Ju Hu replied.

"But now they head to the south, toward Pingyuan, which we failed to secure effectively," Li Fu said. "In fact, we diverted men and supplies from Pingyuan to aid our advance, so-"

"I... I know that, for it was my order," Yuan Shang interrupted. "But will we now have to siege Pingyuan...? We risk becoming unpopular here."

"Nanpi's people rebuked Yuan Tan; Pingyuan's will doubtless do the same," Ju Hu suggested. "He'll either face opposition and retreat westward – to certain defeat – or somehow take the city, where he can hope to hold out for six months at the most. The roads are ours, so supplies are not a concern."

"Procurement of those supplies for more than a few months will alienate the farmers," Li Fu said. "We cannot afford to undertake a long siege."

"...That's not up to me, sadly," Yuan Shang replied. "Any siege will be entirely my selfish, hankering brother's fault. Ju Hu: once we know where my brother has gone, we will follow. Despatch scouts at once."

Yuan Tan successfully fooled the Pingyuan administration into thinking that his army was his brother's men returned for more supplies: Pingyuan City fell within an hour, and Yuan Tan had an array of camps constructed around its walls.

"...I am the lord of Pingyuan...!" Yuan Tan chuckled sarcastically as he once again observed his brother's distant camps from the walls of a defensive position.

"So what do we do now...?" Xin Pi asked. "We are surrounded by enemies and rivals and cut off from reinforcements from Qing!"

"We're not 'cut off'," Xin Ping retorted. "Have some faith, Brother! We'll soon have a lot of extra men, and Mister Guo Tu has a plan that he is yet to share with us."

"...Yes," Xin Pi said as he glared at Guo Tu. "So please, Mister Guo, share your wisdom."

"...We are further south... and hence closer to Yan Province," Guo Tu replied uneasily. "We now have the option of-"

Xin Pi laughed and asked, "You *dare*, Guo Tu...?"

"...You cannot mean to say what you seem to be about to say," Xin Ping said as he glared at Guo Tu. "Tell me that there is some rebel faction in Yan that has somehow escaped attention that-"

"I... I do not suggest this willingly," Guo Tu insisted. "But the situation is dire! If we now make use of an enemy, we can-"

"I'll hear no more," Yuan Tan ordered. "I know your suggestion without hearing it, Guo Tu, but what you intend is impossible, and actually risks angering me."

"Like it or not, Lord Yuan, you must listen to me!" Guo Tu protested. "Our only hope now is to enlist the aid of Cao Cao-"

"**Silence!**" Yuan Tan barked. "**Silence, man, before I cut out your tongue! Cao humiliated us at Guandu! Cao betrayed and killed my father! Cao holds the Son of Heaven hostage, murders unborn princes, and allies with the Qiang!**"

"...Your father resorted to unpleasant alliances, and so must you," Guo Tu replied. "Without Gongsun Zan, we would not have Ji; without Lü Bu, we would not have Bing; without the Wuhuan, we would not have Yòu. And yes... without Cao, we would not have had Yan until Cao kidnapped the Son of Heaven while our backs were turned. But we destroyed Gongsun once Ji was ours; we hunted down Lü Bu once the Black Mountain Bandits were routed; we will one day destroy the Wuhuan when we no longer need them. Let us use Cao for a second time and then eliminate him once he has served a purpose. While he attacks Yè, we can seize Bohai and-"

"Your idea is *nonsense*," Xin Pi scoffed. "Gongsun Zan and Lü Bu were violent idiots with small armies that destroyed themselves; Cao Cao is the Han's Excellency of Works and master of fifty-thousand men, all of them led by the finest advisers and generals of the day that the man's poached from his defeated foes one by one, including our late lord Yuan Shao!"

"And an alliance with Cao might sway some of the defectors –

Zhang Hè, Gao Lan, Xu Yòu, Dong Zhao, Xun Yu, Xun Yòu, Guo Jia, Zhu Ling – back to us," Guo Tu suggested. "We've seen Tian Chou return to the region, so-!"

"That's *deluded*!" Xin Pi chortled. "Those men left us, each and every one of them, because *you ridiculed, undervalued or slandered them*!"

"…They are all high-minded!" Guo Tu snapped. "When all is said and done, they're Yuan vassals… won't they relish the chance to restore the Yuan clan's glory under its rightful chieftain and turn back to the light…? Will they let my justifiable mistrust prevent them from doing the right thing…?"

"*Aiee*… I want no part of this," Xin Pi replied.

"And neither do I," Yuan Tan said coldly. "Cao Cao is my clan's nemesis, Guo Tu. Cao Cao is the 'Crafty Villain', a Chancellor of State in all but name that will outdo Dong Zhuo as time passes, and be the end of the Han. You'll say no more of alliances!"

"…Very well, my lord," Guo Tu replied.

But as time passed, Yuan Tan's defiance faded: the siege of Pingyuan started to take its toll on morale and leave the defenders with the sense that any plan – even one that involved an alliance with Cao Cao – was better than certain death.

****

41

Cao Cao spent his time in Nan County reading, studying battle maps and trying to forget that he was within a short distance of the place where his eldest son, a beloved nephew and a treasured bodyguard had perished; the squatter-ruler of the region, Zhang Xiu, did his best to remain in Wan City and keep communications with Cao Cao to a minimum, despite their reconciliation. Cao Cao was deliberately limiting the number of actual military exchanges with Jing's defenders, since he hoped for a piece of good news that would take him back to Ji Province; he laughed when a messenger from his appointed guardian of Xuchang, Xun Wenruo, brought news of Yuan Tan's isolation in Pingyuan City.

"Don't consider this to be a reason to return to Xuchang," Guo Jia warned. "We want something more tangible."

"Like what...?" Xu Yòu heckled. "What will it take for us to-?!"

"Ziyuan... *please*," Cao Cao said wearily. "Please go on, Fengxiao."

"We want one of two things," Guo Jia explained. "We want one of the two to be destroyed utterly, or we want something to happen that divides them irrevocably, and that has to be worse than anything we've seen so far. A siege is unpleasant, but we'll still cause them to unite if we go back now."

"That's *nonsense*!" Xu Yòu cried.

"Is it...?" Guo Jia retorted. "So Yuan Shao and Yuan Shu – brothers by birth – never reconciled...? I am imagining that after nearly eight years of conflict that tore the entire east of the empire apart and led to numerous consequential problems, they did not speak amicably at the last...? I am remembering a dream when I recall that even after Yuan Shu had emptied the clan's coffers and dragged their good name into disrepute by claiming to be an emperor in waiting, he reached out a needy hand that Yuan Shao eagerly took...?"

"...I see your point, Fengxiao," Xu Yòu admitted.

"And that happened when Yuan Shao was the mightiest of the warlords, his brother was a humbled, bankrupt pariah, and Lord Cao appeared to be a threat," Guo Jia continued. "The situation now is much the same: one brother is powerful, the other weak, and His Excellency is close by. No, we must wait for something tragic or something quite ludicrous to happen, and knowing Guo Tu as I do... it might well be the latter."

Cao Cao frowned and asked, "You cannot mean...?"

Guo Jia nodded slowly.

"...That's even more ridiculous, but... we live in a world that has descended into madness, so why not...?" Xu Yòu said. "I shall consider you a genius without compare if such a thing happened, Fengxiao... but how would we react...?"

"Let us wait and act at that moment," Guo Jia replied. "For what we do will depend on who is sent, what is asked, where we might go, when we went, and how we might best succeed. That will be up to them."

"...In a way, I almost want such a nonsensical outcome," Cao Cao said. "I could do with something to truly laugh at."

Weeks passed. Cao Cao relocated to Xiping City in Yu Province in order to oversee the eastern wing of his campaign against Liu Biao: that moved him further away from the warring Yuan brothers and Ji Province. Liu Biao's eastern defensive position was guarded by Wen Ping and Admiral Cai Mao's nephew Zhang Yun; they would be facing the generals Lu Zhao and Feng Kai, who would be administratively supported by Man Chong and Du Ji.

"*Aiee*... Cao Cao suddenly places his largest force here, where we are not as strong!" Zhang Yun complained as he studied the battle maps in his command tent. "It's good that you're here now, but further reinforcements cannot get here for three days at least, and we really need Unc- I mean *Admiral Cai* for this-"

"Perhaps not... perhaps Cao Cao is not here to deliver a crushing defeat," Wen Ping said thoughtfully.

"...Why is he here then, in your esteemed opinion...?" Zhang Yun asked gruffly.

"I don't know, but I suspect some ruse that will harm the Yuans more than Governor Liu," Wen Ping replied. "I do not agree with those that say that he intends to attack; I say that he will meander and procrastinate further because he cannot afford to commit to a full-scale war with Governor Liu."

"I disagree," Zhang Yun said. "I know what happened in Bowang, and that was no pretence!"

"We'll see," Wen Ping replied. "I've heard that one or two of Governor Liu's advisers suspect that their heart is not in this campaign, and I suspect the same. At the first sign of an opportunity to destroy the Yuans, Cao will turn about and go northward again... that, General, or he is nobody to be fearful of."

Du Ji took charge of the management of the Han troops and started to drill them in accordance with classic military texts; Man Chong reported the improvements to discipline to an impressed Cao Cao, who said, "Regardless of how long we stay here, P'oning, we'll have gained a better army from it."

"I'm getting intelligence that suggests the famous hermit Lou Gui – styled 'Zibo' – might be giving aid to Liu Biao's forces," Man Chong replied. "That's far from ideal, since he's a man that we want on our side, not theirs."

"...Curious," Cao Cao said. "I thought that hermits typically required a lot of persuasion to abandon their mountain retreats and take to the front line... yet 'Zibo' is here fighting me now, quite possibly. Am I that fearsome...?"

"I cannot say," Man Chong replied. "I hope that it is rumour."

"...I think that I shall see Du Ji's efforts for myself," Cao Cao declared. "I will go at once and watch him at work!"

"I'll remain here," Guo Jia said.

"You most certainly will not," Cao Cao chortled. "You are an expert at managing troops, so won't you be more use there than here...?"

Guo Jia groaned as he got to his feet and said, "Fine."

"And will you be joining me, Ziyuan...?" Cao Cao asked as he turned to Xu Yòu.

"It will be better than remaining here alone," Xu Yòu replied.

Cao Cao and his entourage journeyed to the training grounds and watched as Du Ji raised flags and bellowed single-word commands to the soldiers, who moved as one and reacted as one; Cao turned to General Feng Kai and asked, "**Is this a** considerable improvement...?"

"Mister Du makes me jealous, Excellency," Feng Kai replied. **"He knows how they think, how to manipulate them in order to get the best out of them..."**

"...So it is a great improvement, then...?" Cao Cao prompted.

"Many of them are former Yellow Turbans and recently-surrendered followers of the bandit king Gong Du, Excellency," Feng Kai replied. **"Need I say more...?"**

Cao Cao turned and looked at Guo Jia, who nodded respectfully in lieu of shouting over the military drill and straining his voice; Cao Cao smiled, laughed and said, **"No, General Feng, you do not need to say more! To have instilled such professionalism into such types in such a short time tells me that Du Ji is a man to watch! Perhaps I should strike one or two genuine blows while I am here: we can show Zhang Yun and Wen Ping that we are not to be trifled with!"**

"Yes, Excellency!" General Lu Zhao cried.

"...Alright," Man Chong said. **"When...?"**

"...Now! Let us see *now* whether the enemy can handle a professional army!" Cao Cao decided. **"We will attack the eastern edge of their border camp and see how they react!"**

Cao Cao's advance was reported to Zhang Yun, who glared at Wen Ping and asked, "Will you apologise for your previous predictions being so obviously wrong...?"

"I did not say that they would not advance," Wen Ping retorted. "The reports suggest that Cao's soldiers are chanting like heretics and moving with 'alarming professionalism': this only means that Cao Cao has found himself an unexpectedly fearsome army, that or he has a man that has whipped his wayward recruits into shape, as it were, and he now puts them and us to the test."

"In other words, General Wen, he's posturing," Zhang Yun said.

"I think so," Wen Ping replied. "I think that he will do nothing more than harass our eastern perimeter and wait to see how we react to it."

"...And how *should* we react, in that case...?" Zhang Yun retorted.

"When did you say that Wang Wei's forces were due to arrive...?" Wen Ping asked.

"A matter of hours is doable if we requested that they march double-time for the last part of the journey, otherwise tomorrow," Zhang Yun replied.

"...I suggest that we let Cao exhaust his men for a while," Wen Ping said. "If they don't shout themselves to death between now and morning, then we can chase them away with a pincer."

"Cao has eight to ten thousand, while we have three thousand here and three coming here with Wang Wei," Zhang Yun noted. "If I draw men away from the key defensive points to make the forces equal in size then I'd be leaving those positions vulnerable."

"Nobody said that you needed to," Wen Ping insisted. "War is all about making the best use of the resources that you have... and we can give Cao a small lesson in that philosophy tomorrow."

Cao Cao's forces were startled by sudden attacks from the north and south by men bearing the standards of Wen Ping and Wang Wei; Feng Kai and Lu Zhao met the assaults while Cao Cao, Xu

Yòu, Liu Yè, Du Ji and Man Chong discussed their next move.

"**I regret this now,**" Cao Cao admitted.

"**Then why risk it, Mengde???**" Xu Yòu cried angrily.

"**...I can retreat with minimal risk, so there is little harm done,**" Cao Cao retorted. "**Du Ji's efforts have made good soldiers of most of these men: my Qing Province Corps would have scattered in all directions, but the desertions are very few in number.**"

Du Ji nodded and said, "**I will begin issuing retreat orders at once, Excelle-**"

"**REPORT!**" a messenger cried as he ran toward the commanders. "**General Wen Ping is attacking from the west!**"

"**But Wen Ping is to the *north*!**" Cao Cao exclaimed.

"**So he wanted us to believe!**" Man Chong said as he gestured toward some of Cao Cao's elite guards. "**Go back to the camp, Excellency, and we will cover your escape!**"

"**...Blast it!**" Cao Cao cried as he turned his horse and fled.

Cao Cao's return to his camp was not as sombre as some expected it to be: Zhang Yun had forbidden pursuit, and Wen Ping did little more than harass the line of soldiers that blocked the path to Cao Cao before he retreated.

"...Every attempt to create a breach in the border defences was thwarted," Man Chong said. "Whoever it is – Lou Gui, Kuai Yue, Wang Can – that manages the eastern defences has got a smart head on their shoulders, Excellency. They're making great use of severely limited resources and refusing to panic. If our forces had not been so disciplined, we might have incurred some losses in addition to achieving nothing."

"Yes, well, we're not here to achieve anything really, are we...?" Cao Cao chuckled. "Anything that we do achieve is a bonus, of course, but... ... ...well, anyway, never mind. Mister Du Ji, I am impressed at your work with the men. What is your secret?"

"It is no secret, Excellency," Du Ji replied. "I found the most appropriate way of approaching each 'character', if you will, that I encountered. By being calm, persuasive and certain of intent, I won their respect... or so it seems."

"You've done well, given it wasn't even why I brought you here," Cao Cao said. "A man with the ability to make soldiers out of heretics and brigands might be put to better use: rest assured that I'll be pondering what you should really be doing."

Du Ji bowed silently.

"And what about the enemy here...?" Xu Yòu asked. "We *retreated*: that will *hurt us*."

"We retreated *professionally*: that will *benefit us*," Cao Cao insisted. "They did not pursue, so they saw no advantage in it. Why, then, would they come to Yu Province and risk being routed...? Liu Biao's a defender, not an attacker. All we need to do now is sit and wait for whatever Heaven has in store... and I am sure that it will be very interesting."

✱✱✱✱✱✱✱✱✱✱✱✱

42

Morale within the city of Pingyuan and the defensive ring of camps around it had plummeted as supplies dwindled and the casualties mounted: Yuan Tan finally decided that he was prepared to try anything to have some sort of victory over Yuan Shang.
"Your suggestion, Guo Tu, is not my preferred way of going forward, but I'm facing the people turning on me if I try to hold out any longer," Yuan Tan said.
"No, Lord Yuan!" Xin Pi protested. "You mustn't-!"
"Gentlemen, I've not invited you all here to debate it," Yuan Tan said as he looked at the hungry, frustrated officials that were crammed into the private study of the governor's mansion. "I want to know who to send, what we're asking, and so on."
"...Well Guo Tu can't go," Xin Pi chortled.
"That's quite right," Xin Ping said. "Apart from being one of your senior advisers, Guo Gongze is hated by many in Cao's employ."
"...Alas, yes," Guo Tu sighed.
"I wouldn't send you anyway, since I need you here," Yuan Tan insisted. "No, I need to send a man that had nothing much to do with so many traitors being exposed and the Guandu campaign. I'd send Xun Chen if that wretch hadn't decided to serve somebody else, since his brother and nephew are Cao's close allies; I don't want to send someone of too low a rank, either."
"...Send Xin Pi," Guo Tu suggested.
"Me...?" Xin Pi exclaimed.
"...Perhaps that's best," Xin Ping said. "Brother, you're not as closely linked with the more problematic side of the conflicts, so-"
"You want me to leave here – somehow getting past the siege – and cross the Yellow River, and then the Ji River, and into Yan Province, where I am supposed to go and talk to Cao Cao...?" Xin Pi asked irritably. "Guo Tu suggesting it is not a surprise, but my brother agreeing with it is wholly unexpected. Have I not served loyally enough...? Have I somehow been that poor a sibling...?"
"Stop being melodramatic," Xin Ping chuckled. "You'd rather stay here and die of starvation...? We all trust you to secure a good deal with Cao Cao, one that will save Lord Yuan, deliver Bohai to us while Yuan Shang turns about to rescue Yè, and then enable us to seize the provinces and turn on Cao at our leisure. Your apparent sincerity will fool him, Brother."
"And then we'll achieve through intrigue and the pitting of our enemies against each other a victory that nobody thought possible!" Guo Tu cackled. "Even Sun Tzu would be impressed with such a feat!"
"...And then Guo Tu will be in the history books," Xin Pi chortled. "But where will Xin Pi be, I wonder...?"
"I want you to go, since the others consider you to be the best man for the job," Yuan Tan ordered. "We'll create a distraction: prepare to leave at once."
Xin Pi looked at his lord and his colleagues with tired, angry eyes as he replied, "Yes, Lord Yuan... I shall do as you ask."

Several days passed.

"Where are we going?" Xu Yòu asked as he watched Registrar Liu Yè and Cao Cao's servants frantically packing for a swift retreat from Xiping.
"To Xuchang," Cao Cao replied. "You owe Guo Jia a compliment!"
Xu Yòu looked at Guo Jia and asked, "Has Yuan Tan really…?"
"He has sent Xin Pi to negotiate," Guo Jia replied. "We're going to prepare for a return to Ji Province."
"…But can we trust Yuan Tan…?" Xu Yòu asked.
"It doesn't matter," Guo Jia replied. "What matters, Mister Xu, is whether we can trust Xin Pi. We'll soon know the answer…"

Cao Cao returned to Xuchang within a day and had Xin Pi attend a meeting of his senior advisers in the grand hall of the chancellery.
"I am honoured that you have allowed me to speak with you, Excellency," Xin Pi said as he scanned the room and spotted many familiar faces.
"…It has been a while, Zuozhi," Xun Wenruo said.
"Indeed yes, Wenruo," Xin Pi replied awkwardly. "You look well, as does Gongda."
"And your brother, is he well…?" Xu Yòu asked.
"…He is, Ziyuan," Xin Pi replied. "I should like to say that your family is in Yè and, like mine, is being treated politely by Yuan Shang. And I should also like to say that I regret the way in which you were treated by Lord Yuan."
"Both comments are welcome, and yet they are contradictory," Xu Yòu said before Cao Cao could speak. "If your family is treated well by Yuan Shang, why serve Yuan Tan…? If you regret how men were treated, why do you now work with Guo Tu, who was the source of the poison…?"
"Yuan Shang employs Shen Pei: was he better…?" Xin Pi retorted.
"…No, he was as bad if not worse," Xu Yòu conceded.
"…Perhaps *I* might now be allowed to speak, Ziyuan," Cao Cao said. "Mister Xin, you are invited here to be questioned by my trusted inner circle: I am, as you no doubt understand, dubious about your sudden arrival and this alliance proposal. Is it an act of desperation born of being trapped in Pingyuan…?"
"Undeniably," Xin Pi replied. "Lord Yuan Tan blames you for his father's early death; but sometimes a man must be flexible, mustn't he…?"
Xin Pi turned his gaze toward Jia Xu as he spoke; Cao Cao smirked and said, "You are not only clever but *brave*, Mister Xin. What does your lord propose…?"
"An attack on Yè City to force Yuan Shang to lift the siege on Pingyuan," Xin Pi replied. "He would then pincer Shang's forces, enabling a swift rout."
"…I see," Cao Cao said. "And… what about the time after that, Mister Xin…? If he hates me, as you confess, then we would have a situation where the 'rightful lord of Ji' – and neither His Majesty nor I consider any of the Yuans to be anything of the sort – has routed the 'usurper', Yuan Shang, with my help… what then…?"
Xin Pi was silent.
"I will be honest, Mister Xin: I do not trust Yuan Tan," Cao Cao continued. "The Yuans were once a proud family that I almost felt a part of: Benchu and I saved the 'partisans' together, and we were like brothers. And then the intriguing started. Even before

194

Dong Zhuo, Benchu avoided committing to the suppression of the Yellow Turbans, and after Dong Zhuo, well... you were there, so you know. He started to mistreat me, relegating me from friend to vassal, and he decided that Bohai was too small a fief for a man of his standing: he colluded with others to seize Ji Province from Han Fu, and then he had his nephew, Gao Gan, seize Bing while his son Tan took Qing Province from Kong Rong; and as the Yuan feud raged, the differences between the two lessened in number. By the end, both had seized lands that weren't theirs, slandered trusted brothers and disrespected the Son of Heaven: one refused to rescue His Majesty from the wilderness and proposed alternatives that he could manipulate from the shadows, and the other coveted the throne for himself."

"...More men than the Yuans have been guilty or presumed guilty of such things, Excellency," Xin Pi retorted.

"Yes... myself included, which was, of course, your point," Cao Cao said. "But if I am the villain that I am professed to be, why do so many good men – men that you know to be good – now surround me and assist me...?"

Xin Pi looked at Xun Wenruo and said, "I... I can see that, Excellency. No man is more of a loyalist than Wenruo..."

"...And if His Excellency had truly harmed the throne, I would not be here," Xun Wenruo insisted. "You know that, Xin Zuozhi."

"Every man that left Benchu and came over to me did so because they could not stay," Cao Cao said. "It was not because I was powerful: when Wenruo and Gongda joined me, I was Benchu's vassal. Zhu Ling was loaned to me and chose to remain; Zhang Hè and Gao Lan were forced to flee or face Qu Yi's fate. I've made a lot of mistakes, Mister Xin, and I willingly confess to them; I should not have massacred the people of western Xu, and I only ordered the death of Consort Dong because her unborn child would have been the grandchild of a traitor, and I did what numerous sovereigns and loyal retainers have done in the past... Liu Bei's branch of the royal clan was disinherited, and I think we can all see that it was a sound decision. Yuan Tan is probably right to be angry: Benchu would not have willingly left such an important matter undecided, so I sense intrigue by his widow Lady Liu and a handful of self-serving advisers. But I am being asked to wade into dangerous waters, and I am not keen to do so when Liu Biao is an easier catch for my net."

"You want to go back to Jing...?" Xun Wenruo exclaimed.

"I think that it would be for the best," Cao Cao replied. "I know not whether Xin Zuozhi is being completely honest with me or not, but I have committed to Jing now, and would look quite ridiculous if I changed direction yet again and suffered missed victories and avoidable defeats for it."

"B-but the Yuans are hopelessly divided!" Xun Wenruo protested. "If Xin Zuozhi is here, then they are currently beyond reconciliation! If we continue fighting Liu Biao and Liu Bei, they might suddenly find common ground over some trifling thing and become a united threat again! The-!"

"Wenruo... you're speaking in too unguarded a fashion, methinks," Guo Jia chuckled.

"Oh, Zuozhi is no fool, and knows we'll only say it later!" Xun Wenruo scoffed. "Excellency, the Yuans are divided and Liu Biao is a weak, dithering man that will not advance if you now turn your back again, no matter how much Liu Bei protests: in fact, he'll be grateful for the reprieve and hide in his shell. Don't miss this opportunity to bring peace to the northeast provinces! We can negotiate with Yuan Tan, secure a marriage alliance and give him a fief! But if we don't seize this moment, he'll make peace with his brother and they'll be the cause of a campaign that will tear the region apart and cost thousands of lives! And think of the people! Can the people be left to suffer the Wuhuan doing as they please, raids by the Black Mountain Bandits, and rampant corruption and administrative incompetence...?"

Xin Pi hummed thoughtfully.

"...I do not want to abandon my hopes for the north, but I think that I will return to Jing," Cao Cao said. "That is the safer course."

Xun Wenruo groaned miserably.

"...Your Excellency is doubtful of Yuan Tan's trustworthiness... but you only need to heed his might, which is quite diminished," Xin Pi said suddenly.

"Pardon...?" Xu Yòu exclaimed; Guo Jia hid a smile.

"...Your Excellency, you have stabilised Yan, Xu and Yu Provinces, and partially restored stability to Liang as well: now the Yuans are divided, and one of them comes to you for help, which is indicative, as your best minds have deduced, of the weakness of them both, body and soul," Xin Pi continued. "Yuan Shang is sieging Pingyuan, and yet he cannot pass the camps that surround it, and that is because his army is as wasted as Yuan Tan's. The defences around Yè are reduced as numerous uprisings and raids by bandits divert troops and supplies from the area; if you attacked the city now, Yuan Shang would have no choice other than to abandon his siege and hurry to Yè to rescue it. Yuan Tan will leave Pingyuan and chase his brother's army as it flees: that will weaken Shang further. If you pressed your attack against the rebel at such a time, when he is at breaking point and desperate to hold onto that which he has been improperly bequeathed, then his army will be scattered as leaves in a strong wind. Heaven has given you this opportunity, Excellency: Yuan Shang is yours to crush if you would only act."

Cao Cao hummed ambiguously.

"Fail to act, Excellency, and it will be as others have said," Xin Pi continued. "It will take at least a year to destroy Liu Biao: in that time, another harvest will have yielded grain, and if that harvest is good, the general mood will change, and I agree that the brothers, so like their father, and the men around them, who constantly scheme for entertainment, will change their minds, 'see the error of their ways' and unite once again; they will re-establish government, crush the rebellions and chase the rebels back into the hills, and then they will have their combined two-hundred-thousand to pit against your army, ending any chance of a swift peace for people that have suffered enough. You must act now."

Cao Cao looked to Xun Wenruo, Xun Gongda and Guo Jia, who all nodded solemnly.

"I am not your counsel, but if I were, Excellency, I would say that the right course now is to accept Yuan Tan's offer and send him help," Xin Pi continued. "Of all of your enemies, none is a greater threat than the Yuans and their allies in the northeast: destroy them, Excellency, and the people will flock to you, men of the north will lend their swords to the Han, and the Empire will regain its lustre. Conquer the rebels to the north of the Yellow River, and the Empire will tremble before you: who will oppose you then...?"

"And would you be my counsel, Zuozhi, if you had the chance...?" Cao Cao asked.

"I only wish to serve the Han, Excellency," Xin Pi replied. "I see now that this is the only place where my wish can be granted."

"...You can be trusted," Xun Wenruo said.

"I agree," Xu Yòu said. "Never once did the Xin brothers slander me, and I even recall times when they came to the defence of myself and others. Mengde, I believe that Zuozhi speaks well and that we should heed his advice."

"...Then I shall," Cao Cao decided. "Xin Zuozhi, you came here as an envoy of Yuan Tan, and instead delivered my strategy for restoring order in the north. Return to him with our desire to support him, and we will finally bring an end to an era of chaos that the Yuans have perpetuated for far too long."

Xin Pi sighed and smiled like a man that had just been released from prison: he would now devote his energies to supporting Cao Cao and bringing about the defeat of the Yuan clan that he had, in his mind, wrongly supported for far too long.

Once the meeting had ended, Cao Cao took Xun Wenruo to one side and said, "Du Ji was an immense help in Jing."

"I am glad that my recommending him was beneficial to the Han, Your Excellency," Xun Wenruo replied.

"...Now I must make the best use of him in the wake of the Jing Province campaign," Cao Cao continued. "I want him to go to Xiping, where he will act as Administrator and 'Colonel who protects against the Qiang'."

"...Send him back to Xiping...?" Xun Wenruo exclaimed. "But... but there are no Qiang in Runan, Excellency, not unless we expect them to invade, and with no strong military presence maintained in Xiping, his military appointment makes no-! ...Wait: you don't mean Xiping in Runan, do you?"

Cao Cao shook his head slowly.

"...You mean Xiping in the *northwest*, don't you, Excellency...?" Xun Wenruo asked.

"I do," Cao Cao replied. "I believe that he is the right man to control the Qiang peoples, and we will need such men soon, I fear, since Ma Chao is becoming agitated in his role as a 'Han gate guard' and threatens to withdraw from Hedong, although I actually intend to dismiss the Qiang before he can do that."

"But if you dismiss the Qiang or they leave, doesn't that leave Hedong vulnerable to attack again...?" Xun Wenruo asked.

"It does, but what's the point of 'protecting it' with capricious barbarians...?" Cao Cao retorted. "It would be as when Liu Bei asked Lü Bu to protect Xu Province for him if I left Ma Chao in Hedong now."

"...So Du Ji will go to the northwest frontier... and the Qiang will leave Hedong," Xun Wenruo said soberly. "...All while we intend to fight Yuan Shang..."

"I fear that I am to be remembered as 'The Hero of Chaos' with good reason," Cao Cao replied. "But I am used to it now..."

The lord of Nan County, Zhang Xiu, frowned when his former adviser, Jia Xu, sent word that Cao Cao would be leaving the area and going back to Ji Province to save Yuan Tan.

"I... am truly unable to fathom what is going on anymore," Zhang Xiu said to his trusted general Huche'er. "If Cao Cao leaves now, with Liu Bei emboldened by his victory at Bowang Valley and Liu Biao desperate to regain his reputation for great strength, will I last long...?"

"I wouldn't worry, my lord," Huche'er replied. "Cao Cao has nothing to gain from losing Nan County: he's left Colonel Li Tong here to aid us, and besides, Liu Bei and Liu Biao are reluctant allies and the Sun clan torments southern Jing constantly."

Zhang Xiu nodded and said, "That's all true... but I wonder what will happen next...? The Qiang are his army in Hedong, the Mount Tai Bandits are his army in Qing, I am his gate guard in Nan County, and now he aids Yuan Tan after all that has transpired between those two clans: Cao Mengde is a magnificent statesman indeed... is there any man that could match his brilliance...?"

But Cao Cao's brilliance was being called into question by one of Zang Ba's allies when they received word of the new alliance with Yuan Tan and Cao Cao's desire that they withdraw to southern Qing Province.

"I said, didn't I, that we were just chaff, and that this is all games!" Chang Xi heckled. **"He's had us sacrificing ourselves against Wang Xiu and Guan Tong's defences for months, and now they're all friends! *Bastard*!"**

Many of the former bandit chiefs were at the very least irritated, but some voiced agreement with Chang Xi; Zang Ba could sense that he was going to see some of his followers break away from the confederacy, and he was keen to keep the potential damage to a minimum.

"We shouldn't give these two-faced warlords any more of our blood, Zang Xuangao!" Chang Xi continued. **"We should rebel, and-!"**

"Oh, no-no-no," Zang Ba chuckled. **"You're on your own there, Chang. We rebel, and we'll be next to die. Yeah, I'm annoyed about the truce with Yuan Tan as much as you are, but it's just 'divide and conquer' in action, isn't it? You think they'll be friends in a couple o' years' time...?"**

"I don't care about who's friends with who!" Chang Xi retorted. **"How many good blokes have died??? I've lost good mates, men I've known for-!"**

"You say that every time, and you're not the only one that's lost mates, but we're in this for the long haul, Chang, and that's that!" Zang Ba bellowed.

"...We'll *see*," Chang Xi muttered.

"We're leaving Yuan Tan's men alone now, so that they can go and fight Yuan Shang," Zang Ba continued. **"It's all nonsense, but... we do as we're asked. It'll all make sense in the end... so we do as we're told."**

Zang Ba's words were met with reluctant acceptance; for now, there would be no more war between Cao Cao's allies and Yuan Tan in Qing Province.

And in Hedong, the news that Cao Cao was withdrawing the Qiang armies was met with relief and anger by Hedong Prefecture's Administrator, Wang Yi.

"How will we defend ourselves if Gao Gan invades us again???" Wang Yi asked of his assembled officials. "Yes, I will be glad to see the backs of those western barbarians, but we are not to see much sent here to replace them!"

"His Excellency is knowledgeable, Administrator," the official Jia Kui said. "We are being allocated some troops, and I'm sure that they will be enough."

"They had better be," Wang Yi retorted. "I'm tired of being caught between Cao and Yuan as they fight over the Empire... and there are moments – especially when I am sent *Qiang barbarians* as relief – when I start to wonder which of them is truly fighting for the Empire."

"Gao Gan employed Xiongnu and Wuhuan men!" Jia Kui protested.

"The Southern Xiongnu have long been allies of the Han, and the Wuhuan have never strayed this way," one officer noted.

"Wei Gu is quite right," Wang Yi said. "I hear bad things about the Wuhuan, yes, but the Qiang are surely worse! ...No... I am now unsure of everything..."

"Though I have had personal experiences – bad experiences – with the Qiang, I must insist that His Excellency has not allowed them to do harm, and their intervention saved Hedong from Gao Gan and Guo Yuan," the official Wang Ling said.

"...Nephew of Wang Yun and distant relative, I want to agree with you but cannot," Wang Yi retorted. "The Qiang are wretched, and we are better rid of them, but we are now vulnerable... though to *what* or *who*, exactly, is what we must decide..."

"Administrator, *please*... do not mistake the Yuans and their allies for loyalists," Jia Kui said.

"...Fan Xian, Wei Gu: be prepared to accept and train the new men when they arrive," Wang Yi ordered. "And we'll watch Gao Gan at all times, of course..."

The officers Fan Xian and Wei Gu saluted obediently.

"...And if needs be," Wang Yi added, "we'll... open dialogue."

****

43

Yuan Tan stood on the battlements of Pingyuan City and laughed as he watched his brother Shang begin a hasty retreat to his capital. Cao Cao had arrived in Li County with a large force that immediately gave false indications that it would march toward Yè City, and Cao Cao's eastern agent, Zang Ba, had simultaneously withdrawn his army of former bandits from northern Qing, which allowed Tan's subordinates to commit further reinforcements.

"**Cao Cao's kept his word,**" Guo Tu said.

"**And I shall keep mine!**" Yuan Tan cackled. "**I will work with that treacherous scum until I have reassembled my forces and taken northern Ji: after that, he will die at my hands as I promised long ago!**"

"**...Don't be too obvious,**" Xin Ping warned. "**Shy away from arrogance, my lord, should we need to talk to Cao or any of his advisers.**"

"**I'm not a fool!**" Yuan Tan retorted. "**I will be the model ally, Mister Xin Ping... when do you think your brother will be back here...?**"

"**If he travelled to Li County with Cao Cao, he will arrive within a few days at the most,**" Xin Ping replied.

"**I owe him thanks!**" Yuan Tan said. "**After all, he has fooled our enemy and delivered him to us!**"

"**I hope that you don't intend to pursue Shang's army,**" Guo Tu prompted.

"**...Let him run,**" Yuan Tan replied. "**I know the 'cornered tiger' rule, Mister Guo... and even a cornered tomcat has a nasty scratch. Let him run.**"

Jing Governor Liu Biao was confused by the reports of Cao Cao's retreat; he assembled his officials and asked, "Am I to believe this is true, gentlemen...?"

"Yes, and it is just as well," Kuai Yue replied. "Huang Zhong is saying that he cannot fight any longer, and has to retire; Wen Ping says that he is understaffed, and would not have been able to hold his position; Huang Zu is suffering minor problems in some of his outlying territories and needs more help to rebuild his naval fleet after that last battle at Xiakou; Cai Mao says that-"

"I think I understand, Mister Kuai," Liu Biao chortled.

"...Perhaps we should consider approaching Zhang Xiu with talk of a truce in exchange for recognising his control of Nan County," Huan Jie suggested.

"That would be a waste of time," Fu Xun said. "He'll never risk breaking ties with Cao now that the Qiang are under Han control."

"...Damn those fool Yuan boys!" Liu Biao cried. "I want to aid them if Cao Cao's gone back to Ji, but would they reciprocate when he inevitably turns back to me at the first sign of action...?"

Liu Bei shook his head and said, "Don't miss this opportunity, Jingsheng. Cao Cao is not going to be at full strength after such a sudden turnabout, so he will not be able to react to another distraction with such speed: do not pincer him to save the Yuans, of course, but rather you should advance on Xuchang and rescue the Son of Heaven while he is lightly guarded!"

"A foolish suggestion," Kuai Yue scoffed. "We have to pass though Yu Province, and you are only the governor of that place in dead men's eyes, Liu Bei. Yu is ruled by Cao Cao now, and there are no more bandits and cultists for you to look to for allies."

Liu Bei's adviser Mister Sun pointed at Kuai Yue and cried, "**You–!**"

"He is right, Mister Sun," Liu Bei sighed. "My plan relies on allies in Yu Province – desirable or otherwise – that we do not have."

"...Mister Kuai, you were a little unfair," Liu Biao said. "Xuande has travelled here from Bowang to be congratulated and thanked for his work, not ridiculed."

"...I apologise," Kuai Yue replied.

"But nonetheless, Mister Kuai is right, Xuande, to criticise an unworkable idea," Liu Biao continued. "We must be grateful that Cao has gone back to Ji and use the time to reorganise and build a stronger defensive perimeter; attacking him while his back is turned is guaranteed to cost us if we're barely able to defend."

Liu Bei clasped his hands together and bowed, saying, "I shall return to Xinye and continue my work there."

"Mister Liu: is it true that you have captured and successfully recruited a member of the Xiahou clan...?" Huan Jie asked.

"It is," Liu Bei replied. "He is a Han loyalist that was open-minded enough to realise that Cao Cao is a villain: he saw that Zhang Yide treats Lady Xiahou well and that Cao Cao, by contrast, even disrespects Imperial consorts and puts them to death. He is the first man to defect to us, but he will not be the last."

"...Move as freely as you need to, Xuande," Liu Biao said. "Continue to build your militia and fortify our northern positions... I am fortunate to have a friend and relative such as you."

"And I, Bei, am fortunate to know you, Jingsheng," Liu Bei replied.

Wang Can quietly despaired at the exchange; Liu Bei bowed to the courtiers and left the gathering with his followers.

"...*Undignified sycophant*," Fu Xun muttered.

"Don't put too much faith in Liu Bei, my lord," Wang Can pleaded. "He recruits men for his own purposes, not yours."

"For now, he is my guest-vassal, and his actions benefit me," Liu Biao retorted. "I will damn him when Cao Cao is cold bones, and not before."

Yuan Shang's return to Yè City alarmed Shen Pei, who met the army at the gates and asked, "Is Yuan Tan vanquished, my lord?"

"I am here to fortify Yè against Tan's new ally, *Cao Cao*!" Yuan Shang replied. "My brother's deal with the underworld has bought him a reprieve, but rest assured that I will destroy him for this disgusting act of betrayal!"

"...I am aware that Cao has brought an army to Li County, but I know nothing of an alliance with Yuan Tan," Shen Pei admitted. "Are you *sure*, my lord...?"

"Scouts report Xin Pi being escorted to Pingyuan from Li County by one of Cao's officers as we retreated," Yuan Shang explained. "What else can it be but an alliance, Mister Shen...?"

"...I had not anticipated this," Shen Pei admitted. "I mulled the idea of an alliance if we were ever at a severe loss... how alike we think, Guo Tu and I."

"I would not have agreed to it: that is how *we* differ, my brother and I!" Yuan Shang retorted. "Cao Cao is a wicked villain! He will ultimately betray my brother, and it will be deserved!"

Xin Pi was met at the gates of Pingyuan by a grateful Yuan Tan and his senior advisers; Xin's escort, which was led by Xu Huang, retreated slightly and awaited any correspondence or messengers that might be entrusted to them.
"You are a marvellous envoy!" Yuan Tan said as he clasped Xin Pi's hands tightly. "It can only be that you were sent by Heaven to aid me, Xin Zuozhi!"
"...You flatter me, my lord," Xin Pi replied. "I merely presented our case and spoke as I was directed by Mister Guo and my brother."
"But you were remarkably persuasive," Guo Tu said. "We are rescued from a terrible situation by your efforts. Now we can begin to turn our fortunes around."
"What has Cao Cao proposed...?" Xin Ping asked. "It cannot be that he has settled for invading Ji Province for us and then handing it over to us afterwards."
"It is, of course, expected that Cao does not recognise the legitimacy of the Yuan clan's rule over Ji, Qing, Bing or Yòu," Xin Pi replied. "He has, however, decided that it can be made legitimate by way of marriage alliances and making the proper petitions to the court."
"Marriage alliances...?" Yuan Tan prompted.
"Cao Cao has proposed a marriage between one of his younger sons and your daughter when they are both of the right age," Xin Pi explained. "With such an alliance in place, there would be no problem with His Majesty recognising your place as Governor of Qing at the very least: the rest is negotiable."
"Indeed it is," Yuan Tan chuckled. "I will be Governor of Qing, Governor of Ji, Excellency of Works, Commander-in-Chief, and whatever else my bloodline entitles me to when I've defeated all of my enemies... including Cao Cao... but for now, I'll agree to marry my daughter to his pup..."
"...Should I go back and tell him that you've agreed to his added condition...?" Xin Pi asked.
"Yes," Yuan Tan replied. "Go and tell him..."

Cao Cao smiled when Xin Pi relayed his former lord's reply.
"So what will happen now that you have relieved Pingyuan, Excellency...?" Li County's guardian, Jia Xin, asked cautiously.
"...My work here is done for now," Cao Cao replied. "I am going back to Guandu to make plans for moving a greater amount of supplies here."
"*Again*???" Xu Yòu exclaimed. "Mengde, you-!"
"Please do not question me, Ziyuan," Cao Cao sighed. "I know what I am doing."
"But what about Yuan Shang...?" Xin Pi asked.
"What about him...?" Cao Cao chuckled. "He certainly won't attack here... and he is highly unlikely to go back to Pingyuan and leave Yè undefended either. We're safe to go and make better, more robust plans for a decisive, final campaign."
"I hope that you mean that this time, Mengde," Xu Yòu heckled. "I'm starting to worry that our continual meandering will make it impossible to impress the Wuhuan after the Yuans are dealt with."
"I don't intend to impress them," Cao Cao retorted. "I intend to

break their spirit and either expel or make use of them: they can be the Xianbei or the Xiongnu, it's their choice, but they will not remain in this region and continue to mistreat the Han populace as the Yuans have allowed them to do."

Xin Pi bowed humbly and said, "I have finally found the right lord in you, Excellency: I weep when I think of the daughters and sisters that the Yuans forced us to yield, and I weep still further when I think of the harm that those uncultured monsters inflict on the people, so knowing that they'll be punished and brought to heel at last warms my heart."

"...If I can find and rescue those women, I will," Cao Cao replied. "It... it is a little mission of mine, you might say."

"But our first mission is to destroy the Yuans' grip on these provinces," Guo Jia said. "To properly do that, we will temporarily retreat... and enjoy the easy victories that our 'continual meandering' will deliver."

"...I just hope that you're as clever as you think you are," Xu Yòu said as he glared at Guo Jia. "I saved Mengde from their father; don't waste my efforts."

Cao Cao was forced to stare at his protective bodyguard Xu Chu in order to prevent the giant from attacking the increasingly confident Xu Yòu; Cao did so with increasing reluctance.

Panic had taken hold in the region around Yè City: many were tired of the conflicts between the Yuan clan and Cao Cao and between the Yuan brothers, and some of those saw defection to Cao Cao – and, by the nature of his role, the Han government – as the only way forward.

"I hear that you're wavering," General Su Yòu said as he confronted Lü Kuang in the latter's command tent outside Yè.

"...I don't see why *you're* still here," Lü Kuang retorted. "Like me, you've benefitted from the deaths of other men like Wen Chou and defections by the likes of Zhang Hè, but like me you're up to the job but still underappreciated by that troublemaker Shen Pei and that overpriced mediocrity Gao Fan!"

Su Yòu exhaled wearily and said, "I don't want to report you."

"Then *don't*," Lü Xiang growled as he entered the tent and glared at Su Yòu.

"...So you're both contemplating defection, then," Su Yòu realised.

"Would one of us go without the other...?" Lü Kuang asked. "Come with us. If you disagreed with us, you'd have let us know it."

"...I *can't*," Su Yòu groaned. "I have family in Yè, and besides, I feel that I must stand by my lord... and while I, like you, loathe Shen Pei, that means standing by him as well."

"But you won't obstruct us or warn Shen or Yuan Shang...?" Lü Kuang prompted.

"...No, I won't," Su Yòu replied. "If you feel you must go... go."

Lü Xiang raised his sword and said, "Why should we trust him...?"

"General Su is an honourable man," Lü Xiang replied. "We are free to leave."

"...Then let us go quickly and get to Li County!" Lü Kuang pleaded.

Su Yòu sighed, said, "I saw and heard nothing," and left the tent.

Lü Kuang and Lü Xiang took a large number of their men and fled to Cao Cao on that same night; when the mass defection was discovered on the next morning, Yuan Shang ordered Su Yòu and the other officers to come to his audience hall and asked, "Who knew of this...?"

Jiang Yiqu and Ju Hu exchanged confused glances.

"Are we expected to believe that Lü Kuang and Lü Xiang upped and left here last night with hundreds of men and carts filled with supplies and nobody noticed???" Lady Liu shrieked. **"You must have known, must have seen-!"**

"Mother, please retire and let *me* deal with this," Yuan Shang ordered. "*I* am the clan chieftain... so this is *my* problem to solve."

Lady Liu harrumphed, sneered at the officers and withdrew.

"...This is unfortunate," Shen Pei said. "An atmosphere of mistrust now lingers in the air. But we must overcome this."

"And we will," Yuan Shang replied. "The Lüs defected because my brother now has the aid of 'the Han court' – Cao's puppet court – and that scared them into shifting their support to my brother. He must be our first target if we are to recover ground, for he is the excuse that Cao uses to be here. I will start to make plans... and please, gentlemen, no more defections! Cao Cao is not the Han, he is another Dong Zhuo that must be destroyed, and I must rise to the occasion, just as my father did against that famous tyrant! And I need your help if I am to save the Son of Heaven!"

"...We're yours to command as always," Su Yòu said.

"We can salvage something and strike back," Yuan Shang promised. "You just have to trust in my leadership and never forget what Cao is, no matter what he appears to be. The Lüs will regret their decision one day... just as Zhang Hè, Xu Yòu and all the other defectors will. And the Yuans will once again stand at His Majesty's side, their reputations restored... wait and see."

Cao Cao was delighted when Lü Kuang and Lü Xiang arrived in Li County with their followers and pledged allegiance to his cause; Xin Pi carried word of the defections back to Yuan Tan, who was irritated that his father's generals were submitting to Cao Cao and not to him.

"I know what you intend to ask of me, my lord, but please do not," Xin Pi said. "The Lüs submitted to the *Han*, not Cao Cao, and my asking them to-"

"Am I hearing right...?" Yuan Tan heckled. "You'd refuse to obey my command...?"

"...I am trying to *save you*, my lord," Xin Pi insisted. "If you try to poach the Lüs, Cao Cao will-"

"How can I steal my own property...?" Yuan Tan asked snidely. "The chieftainship of the Yuan clan is mine, is it not...? And those men were my father's men, weren't they...? So they're now mine! They defected from Shang as I knew they eventually would, but they are confused... a few gifts will make them remember their obligations and come here to Pingyuan to aid me."

"...Very well," Xin Pi sighed.

"What else happened...?" Guo Tu asked. "You returned with this useful news and Cao Cao's pledge, but what exactly is it that Cao Cao has 'pledged' to do...? He offers 'support', you say, but what does that mean...?"

"...I cannot say," Xin Pi lied. "His counsel will know such things."

"Xin Pi, you will go back to Li County with gifts for Lü Kuang and

Lü Xiang, and you will buy their souls back from Cao Cao," Yuan Tan ordered. "You will leave as soon as it is possible."
"...As you command," Xin Pi replied.

Cao Cao was surprised and confused when Xin Pi was reported to be returning to Li County yet again: he had Xin visit his command room in the county capital and asked, "Why...?"
Xin Pi smirked and said, "I bring gifts, as you see... none of them for you, Excellency. They are for Lü Kuang and Lü Xiang."
"Wretch!" Xu Yòu cried. "He dares to-!"
"Please be silent, Ziyuan," Cao Cao said. "I must think... since Fengxiao is ill and Mister Jia Xu is busy organising my departure."
"...If I may," Xin Pi prompted.
"You have a solution...?" Cao Cao asked.
"You're angry, and you're right to be," Xin Pi replied. "But we have a dilemma: I should not be here informing you of his plans, and his cooperation is crucial to yours. My suggestion is that you allow me to approach Lü Kuang and Lü Xiang: they will not exchange jade for common stone by going back to the Yuans."
"...Alright," Cao Cao said. "But you're right that I'm annoyed: he has committed his first grave offence, and he is lucky that I am in a forgiving mood."

Xin Pi returned to Pingyuan later that day with a second written pledge of cooperation from Cao Cao, who crossed the Yellow River and travelled to his long-established base at Guandu once he had received a written response from Yuan Tan that was delivered by a junior official.
"...He's gone again...?" Yuan Tan exclaimed when he learned of Cao Cao's departure. "That leaves Pingyuan exposed for a second siege! My brother will come back here!"
"He intends to return with a larger, better-equipped army in due course," Xin Pi explained. "I have seen the preparations first-hand, Lord Yuan, and I am sure that Cao Cao will keep his word."
"...I hope so," Yuan Tan muttered. "Like it or not, I need the villain's help until I have the support of the Wuhuan and a proper base here in Bohai."
"...Such a pity that Lü Kuang and Lü Xiang are not here to aid us," Guo Tu said as he glared at Xin Pi.
"As I said when I returned, they were most unwilling," Xin Pi retorted. "Don't blame me, Mister Guo: they made the choice to break ties with the Yuans."
"But they will be mine again!" Yuan Tan declared. "Them... and everything else that Cao Cao and my brother have taken from me... I *vow it*."

****

ACT IV: THE BATTLE FOR YÈ CITY

44

The Han Empire's Excellency of Works, Cao Cao, had once again defied conventional logic to achieve the near impossible. The powerful Yuan clan ruled a quarter of China with the aid of their Wuhuan tribal allies, but the succession row that followed the death of the clan chieftain Yuan Shao had left Shao's sons divided: Cao Cao tried to exploit that rift to bring the northeast under Han Imperial control but two of Yuan Shao's three sons – the eldest, Tan, and the controversially-chosen clan heir Shang, who was actually the youngest of the three – surprised all by putting aside their newfound hatred for each other and refusing to yield Yè City in Ji Province, which served as the grand capital of the four provinces that the Yuans controlled.

The first campaign against the Yuans neared a year in length with no sign of ending quickly, and many started to expect that Cao Cao had overstretched against a deceptively formidable enemy; Cao's strategist, Guo Jia, prevented disaster by suggesting that the Han army withdraw and focus on Cao's other great enemies, namely Jing Province Governor Liu Biao and Biao's ambitious warlord-tenant Liu Bei. Cao Cao shocked all by complying with Guo Jia and abandoning all but the fully-occupied Li County region; the move risked the reputation of the army and led many to wonder if Cao Cao was incompetent, but it had the desired effect. The Yuan brothers quickly reverted to in-fighting while Cao Cao assaulted Jing Province, and Tan – despite being the fiercer of the two in battle – was forced, due to a lack of followers, to retreat to the city of Pingyuan and forge an alliance with none other than Cao Cao in order to survive the relentless siege that Yuan Shang inflicted upon him.

Cao Cao halted his attack on Jing Province – much to the surprise of all – and returned to Ji Province to defend his unexpected ally Yuan Tan and ensure that a proper contract of cooperation was agreed to. The move led to a number of high-profile defections from Yuan Shang to Cao Cao, and a siege of the well-defended city of Yè was seemingly imminent: Cao then returned to his base in the city of Guandu – surprising everyone again – to prepare for a more prolonged campaign. Cao Cao understood what was at stake: if Yè was taken, Cao would gain control of Ji Province and increase the likelihood that the other provinces under Yuan control – Qing, Bing and Yòu – would also fall in good time, but the plan relied on the trustworthiness of Yuan Tan, who was secretly hoping to betray everyone and seize the region, the Yuan clan chieftainship and anything else that he could obtain. Cao Cao knew, through Tan's adviser Xin Pi, that he could not trust his ally at all, but he had to choose his moment to act before Tan could, and that would, as always, be a matter of luck and judgement.

Two months passed during which Cao Cao remained in Guandu and oversaw the gathering of a vast supply of grain, weapons and other supplies; he then began a gradual return to Li County and commissioned the construction of waterworks along the Yellow River to hasten the transportation of the supplies. Yuan Shang's spies reported it to their lord in Yè City, but his reaction to the news shocked and disappointed his followers.

"Go back to Pingyuan?" Shen Pei exclaimed. "My lord, you cannot go back to Pingyuan when Cao Cao is in Li County with an army of up to forty thousand!"

"I can and I will," Yuan Shang retorted. "I have fortified the region, have I not? Ju Hu holds Handan, which ensures that no northern attack can be carried out without a warning at the very least; Yin Kai has added more layers of defence to the already-impressive Maocheng, so the road to and from Bing Province is secure; Gao Fan and Jiang Yiqu are monitoring and fortifying the roads to the east and south; and you have Su Yòu to rely upon for the defence of the city itself while I take Li Fu, Chen Lin, Xun Chen, Yin Kui, Ma Yan and Zhang Yi with me to finish the siege of Pingyuan City."

"You're mistaken, my lord!" Shen Pei protested. "Xun Chen, agree with me and-!"

"Mister Shen, you act as though I am unaware of the problems we face: what is worse than Cao having justification for this invasion...?" Yuan Shang asked. "Even Father understood the power of working in another's name: he proposed Liu Yu as an alternative sovereign to weaken Dong Zhuo, and then he used Yu's son Liu Hè to destabilise Yòu Province and defeat Gongsun Zan. Cao has learned the same lesson: he uses Tan's selfish claim to the chieftainship as a way to turn support away from me and toward himself whilst simultaneously decrying the Yuans when he addresses his puppet Imperial court. If Tan was routed, Cao Cao would just 'be here', and his plan would be ruined."

"He'd switch to doing what he does to avenge Tan instead of save him," Xun Chen countered. "You are better off trying to appeal to Tan's remaining sanity and make him understand that Cao will betray him later and that blood ties should be restored. If you attack him, you drive him closer to Cao Cao!"

"It would be good if I did!" Yuan Shang said. "It will further prove his lack of eligibility. I will be leaving in the next day or so."

The assembled officials looked at each other and despaired.

Within days, Cao Cao assembled his officials in the audience hall of the governor's mansion in Li County City; they included his eldest son Cao Pi – who was accompanying his father for the first time – and Cao Chun, whose elite 'Tiger and Leopard Cavalry' had gained so much of a reputation during its deployment against the dissenters in Runan that Cao Cao had decided to use them as a vanguard force.

"We're about to siege Yè for what should be – and, with Heaven's blessing, *will be* – the last time," Cao Cao said. "Our latest reports indicate that Yuan Shang has opted for a second offensive against our ally Yuan Tan: I would like to help Tan, and we can best do that by attacking Yè with everything at our disposal."

Li County City's appointed guardian, Jia Xin, raised his hand and asked, "Excellency, what contingency plans have been made in the event of Yuan Shang attacking this city instead of returning to Yè City...?"

"You make a valid point, but never fear, I have accounted for it," Cao Cao replied. "As you can see from looking around you, I have brought most of my most capable officers here: I intend to leave at least one of them here to fortify the city."

"...So can we go and smash some heads now, Mengde...?" Xiahou Dun asked.

Cao Cao laughed and said, "You should try and sound a little less like Zhang Fei or Lü Bu, Cousin Yuanrang. We're going to conduct this siege according to the methods described by the finest strategists of the ages, not as an exercise in random massacre. We will allow the old and very young to leave the city, and we will try to end the matter within the three months that is suggested."

"And if we've not defeated them by then...?" Xu Yòu asked irritably. "We're not going to withdraw *again*, are we Mengde...?"

Cao Cao smiled coldly and said, "I will not leave Yè in another's hands, Ziyuan. If I must extend the campaign, it will be done as it is suggested by the great texts."

"Yeah... now shut up, you annoying little man!" Cao Hong heckled. "You always-!"

"Enough, Cousin Zilian," Cao Cao ordered. "We are to avoid division: we will only succeed by showing the unity that our enemies do not manifest."

"And by being quick, like Guo Jia's always saying," Xiahou Dun suggested. "No more talk, Mengde: let's get going!"

Guo Jia laughed and said, "Indeed I am, and I agree that we should proceed now, Lord Cao, while Yuan Shang is foolishly showing us his back. Let's not give these boys a chance to change their minds."

"Quite so," Cao Cao replied. "Orders will be issued as we march: Gao Lan, Zhu Ling, Qin Yi, Qi Ji and Cao Xing will remain here and double the security around this city and the surrounding area. The rest of you: prepare to depart at once!"

Cao Pi turned to Cao Xiu and whispered, "Are Zilian and Yuanrang always so boisterous at meetings, Cousin...?"

Cao Xiu smiled and replied, "They are."

"...I wonder if I will make my name here," Cao Pi murmured.

"Do not overexert yourself," Cao Xiu said. "The best thing to do is always your regular best: that is how Zihe rose from his brother's assistant to the leader of the Tiger and Leopard Cavalry."

"Zihe is a man to look up to," Cao Pi said as he looked at Cao Chun. "He is a scholar, a warrior and a fine official: I would be the same if my ability permits it."

"You're Mengde's heir," Cao Xiu replied. "You'll be a man worth remembering, Zihuan... that's already foretold."

And so two decisive battles began: in the east of Ji Province, Yuan Shang ignored the warnings that his advisers gave and sieged the city of Pingyuan for a second time while the confused and irritated Yuan Tan looked on from the walls; and in the west, Cao Cao began an attack that placed the city of Yè and its defensive perimeter under insurmountable pressure. The defenders of Yè watched with horror as Cao Cao's massive army amassed near the eastern network of camps, and some saw surrendering as their only chance of survival.

"**You'll do no such thing!**" Shen Pei screamed as he confronted a group of wavering officials in the audience hall of the governor's mansion. "**Any that try to leave this city will be executed!**"

"...That would be bad for morale, Uncle," a young man said.
"And letting these cowards flee would be good for morale, would it, Rong...?" Shen Pei retorted. **"Don't make me regret giving you a commission!"**
Shen Rong sighed and said, "Sorry, Uncle."
"Your nephew is right to say that executing nervous men is far from the right idea," Su Yòu suggested. "Many consider surrender to be a viable solution, and-"
"And are you one of them, Su Yòu?" Shen Pei snapped. **"Are you one of them?"**
"...Mister Shen, I am an appointed defender of Yè," Su Yòu replied. "I don't like the idea of betraying the lord's trust and yielding, but there is a widely held-"
"Maybe I should relieve you of duty!" Shen Pei heckled. **"All of you, you think that he'll spare you! He won't! You think that you can betray your lord and survive, but Cao Cao will kill us all!"**
"...Calm down, Mister Shen," Gao Fan pleaded. "They're just making suggestions!"
"You're the prefectural administrator... *somehow*!" Shen Pei retorted. "Looking at you now, acting as you do, and remembering your failure to stop a few unarmed supply boats from getting here last time, it's easy to see how others suggest that we lack talents these days! Li Cheng's death was your rebirth, Gao Fan, but who else gained...?"
"...You should not be so confrontational," Gao Fan said calmly. "We none of us have anything to gain from panicking or arguing."
"But you all want to surrender, yes, and give Cao Cao my head!" Shen Pei screeched. **"But you'll do no such thing! None of you! Feng Li: arrest these men that say that we should surrender! Treason demands *death*!"**
Su Yòu turned to Feng Li and said, "Stay your hand, Colonel Feng: Mister Shen, you should calm down as others suggest."
Feng Li nodded silently.
"...Gao Fan, go to the walls and monitor Cao's advance," Shen Pei ordered. "Those cowards get a reprieve: Feng Li will escort them out. I don't want to see or hear any more from them."
General Su Yòu nodded to Feng Li, who escorted the group of dissenters from the hall.
"...I will not yield this city!" Shen Pei barked. **"This city is the Yuans' power base! It cannot, must not fall!"**
"That's right!" Yuan Shao's widow, Lady Liu, said as she finally emerged from her hiding place behind a curtain at the back of the hall. **"My son is your lord, and you will give your all or pay for your inaction with your lives!"**
General Su Yòu bowed humbly and followed Feng Li and the rebuked officials.
"There will certainly be more unrest, more treachery, more cowardice," Lady Liu said. "Watch them, Shen Pei: watch them all. Trust nobody."
"I did not survive this long by thinking any other way, my lady," Shen Pei retorted. "I am watching them all, including Su Yòu..."
Shen Rong frowned disapprovingly as he listened to his uncle and Lady Liu.

Cao Cao's forces destroyed the outermost eastern and southern defensive camps around Yè over the next two days, and nerves frayed further: Shen Pei's erratic behaviour worsened and his main ally, General Su Yòu, finally tired of it.

"...Be careful," Feng Li said as he watched Su Yòu pace back and forth along the street outside the gates of the governor's mansion.

"Shen Pei said too much!" Su Yòu replied. "I have done as much as any man to defend this place... how dare he accuse me of underperforming! We fend off a giant with twigs and throw eggs at rocks by trying to hold the city! How can a few thousand repel tens of thousands? And Lord Yuan has abandoned us to chastise his brother... and proved that he is not the right man to lead his clan after all."

"Don't speak that way!" Feng Li pleaded. "Lord Yuan Shang has fallen foul of bad advice! Any man could do the same!"

"...This is an obvious situation," Su Yòu insisted. "And I... I've had enough, Colonel."

"**Wait...!**" Feng Li cried; Su Yòu ignored him and retreated to the eastern wall.

Two days passed: the attack on Yè City and the surrounding region continued relentlessly.

As night approached, Su Yòu gathered a group of like-minded men and advanced to overpower the soldiers that guarded the southern gates: he expected no resistance, but he was confronted on the road to the gates by a small militia led by Gao Fan.

"...Administrator Gao!" Su Yòu hailed. "What brings you here...?"

"I was about to ask the same, General Su," Gao Fan said. "You seem to be on your way to the southern gate with that little band of men... *why*...?"

"I am this city's appointed guardian!" Su Yòu retorted. "I-!"

"Have 'had enough', from what I understand," Gao Fan interrupted. "Of all the men that I might have expected to betray our lord, I least expected it of you. I don't know whether I should have pity or be disgusted."

"What are you talking about?" Su Yòu scoffed.

"There is no point to denying it," Gao Fan said. "You've fired an arrow over the wall, announcing that you intend to open the southern gates to the enemy: they've deployed men that are obviously out at such an hour to exploit your treachery. But the walls are lined with defenders, and the gates will remain closed."

"...I have been betrayed!" Su Yòu exclaimed.

"You betrayed yourself," Gao Fan replied: he then turned to his subordinate captain and said, "**Arrest them all! Mister Shen Pei will decide their fates!**"

"**I'd rather die!**" Su Yòu declared as he raised his sword: his followers knew that they faced death if they surrendered, so they raised their own swords in defiance.

"...**So be it!**" Gao Fan said.

The two militias clashed, and Gao Fan quickly gained the upper hand; the rebels retreated to the eastern gates – where an ally had already overpowered the guards and opened the way – and fled the city. Gao Fan could not pursue, as Cao Cao's men were providing cover fire for the rebels; he settled for having the heads of two of the captured officers collected for presentation to Shen Pei while Su Yòu and his surviving followers fought their way through the remaining defensive camps and officially surrendered to Cao Cao with support from Lü Kuang.

"…We'll display these as a lesson to all of the cowards!" Shen Pei said as he examined the head of one of Su Yòu's accomplices. "It's a pity that Su got away, but… good work, Gao Fan… good work. Reward the man that reported it."
"The informant is one of my junior staff: I will do as you ask and reward him well, Mister Shen," Gao Fan replied.
Colonel Feng Li shuddered as he stared at the severed heads of Su Yòu's allies.
"So who will replace Su Yòu?" Lady Liu asked.
"I won't place that much trust in anyone again," Shen Pei replied. "I'll divide his men between me, Feng Li and Gao Fan, taking the majority for myself. Our main objective now is to keep Cao away from the walls and re-establish the defensive perimeter. We must hold… for the Yuan clan to endure, we must hold."
But Shen Pei's words felt hollow to some: the defences were crumbling, and Yuan Shang was showing no signs of returning to save his capital.

Cao Cao's appointed Han-Qiang liaison in Xiping, Du Ji, arrived in the region with a small retinue and a very small baggage train: the Qiang warlord Han Sui reacted to the new official by demanding that he meet with the local leaders in a neutral place.
"…So Cao feels that we need watching," Han Sui said as he stared at the fearless Du Ji; the tent was filled with Qiang chieftains, local Han officials and junior officers, and the Qiang vastly outnumbered the government representatives.
"I wouldn't be concerned, General Han," Du Ji replied.
"You'd say that," Han Sui scoffed. "I'll decide whether I should be concerned or not after I've decided whether I want you here."
"You could repel me, General Han, but that wouldn't be wise," Du Ji retorted. "I have powerful friends that are not so distracted by worldly matters that they wouldn't send reinforcements here to cause you harm in retaliation."
Han Sui's followers were outraged at the Han official's words and started to heckle him aggressively; Han Sui, by contrast, found Du Ji's courage impressive and started to laugh.
"What's there to laugh about?" one chieftain asked.
"This man is honest!" Han Sui replied. "That's what we want!"
"I was selected for this role because I am not a thief, a deviant or a peddler of false words," Du Ji inisisted. "Believe it or not, but His Excellency Cao Cao wants an eventual peace between us all, and he knows that he won't get it by sending you more corrupt men and agitators. I'm here as a liaison, and that is that."
"…I like you," Han Sui replied. "We'll see how we go, of course, but… I think that you'll be fine, Mister Du Ji."
Du Ji smiled and said, "My thanks, General."

****

45

The last of the defences around Yè City disappeared as mass defections and additional military intelligence from the likes of Su Yòu compromised them; the surrounded and isolated city was further compromised by the building of dirt mounds and the deployment of sappers to tunnel under the walls, but Cao Cao was concerned that something might ruin his relatively easy victory.

"Do not expect too much from our enemies," Guo Jia insisted as he watched Cao Cao pace back and forth across the command tent; Cao Cao's bodyguard Xu Chu watched his master with obvious concern. Cao's long-time friend Xu Yòu was also present, but he was conspicuously silent.

"...I have had a headache," Cao Cao replied. "Now that it is passing, I know that it has been affecting my ability to see things clearly. But I still worry."

"General Su Yòu's defection has proved to be invaluable," Guo Jia said. "The entire defensive network has gone, the walls are exposed, and because there is no moat, we can move back and forth against the city with no impediment."

"So what do we do now...?" Cao Cao asked.

"Yè can be saved by Yuan Shang's return and-or the continued flow of supplies from Bing Province, which is managed at its mid-point by Yin Kai's Maocheng Fortress," Guo Jia explained. "If we block the road into Bing – don't worry about Gao Gan, for he has lost a key general and suffers a resumption of Black Mountain Bandit activity in the north – then we can concentrate on severing supply and reinforcement routes in Ji and Yòu Provinces."

"...I'll do as you suggest," Cao Cao decided. "Zilian can manage the siege for a while, as stupid as he can be: so long as I restrict his budget, he will fight well."

"I agree," Guo Jia said. "Cao Hong can remain, and you can use Cao Chun's magnificent cavalry to attack Maocheng and take it from Yin Kai."

"...And what do I do after that...?" Cao Cao asked. "Should I pincer Yuan Shang, or...?"

"Every military situation should be evaluated at the time in order to make the best decision," Guo Jia replied. "Any plan we made now might – would – need to be revised to take account of the enemy's chosen reaction to our actions."

"I know that, I *know that*...! ...Blasted headache!" Cao Cao groaned. "It makes an imbecile of me! And I should not still be suffering them! Hua Tuo risks making me very angry with his deliberate avoidance, Fengxiao: I have half a mind to-!"

"You must be careful to avoid making Hua Tuo 'the Cai Yong to your Dong Zhuo'," Guo Jia warned. "He is a highly respected physician, scholar, acupuncturist and therapist... to name but four of his many skills. Treat him properly and forgive him for his eccentricities, or you will earn men's scorn."

"...You're right, and I know it," Cao Cao sighed as he finally stopped pacing and covered his face with his hands. "Let us... let us proceed to Maocheng, then. Won't that mean seizing Handan first, though...?"

The impatient Xu Yòu turned his eyes toward Guo Jia, who

smirked and said, "That's the assumption."

Shen Pei was trying to send messengers through the enemy lines to contact Yuan Shang in Pingyuan, but few were getting through: at the same time, the sieges of Yè and Pingyuan were becoming news in Yòu Province, and the lord of the region – the late Yuan Shao's second son, Yuan Xi – despaired.

"My brothers continue to fight over our father's legacy and doom it further with their every move," Yuan Xi said to his adviser, Mister Fan. "Now Cao Cao attacks Yè City, which threatens the future of our clan and, more personally, the safety of my lady wife: I am lacking good generals and have untold amounts of unrest to deal with, else I'd have marched to Yè myself. But... but can I just sit here while my beloved Lady Zhen faces being made another of Cao's consorts or being handed over to one of his wretched subordinates...?"

"I doubt that Cao Cao would risk such as disrespectful move," Mister Fan replied. "You have wisely remained aloof while your brothers argue, and Cao will have seen that. You might even be seen as an alternative to Tan and Shang if Cao wants continuity in order to avoid more chaos."

"I doubt it, all of it," Yuan Xi said. "Father's alliance with the Wuhuan has made us more enemies than friends among the people; and as for Cao's treatment of my lady wife, I recall his treatment of Lady Zou when he conquered Wan City... he is fond of women, particularly young, beautiful women whose relatives and husbands are his enemies. I... I should never have let Lady Liu take her hostage, Mister Fan, and I must apologise for that at least. I... I want to go to her."

"You can't!" Mister Fan protested.

"I... I feel like I *must*, Mister Fan," Yuan Xi replied. "Even if I must go alone, in disguise, and somehow get into Yè to see her... there must be a way... even if I am then trapped in Yè, isn't it better than knowing that she and I have been separately humiliated...?"

"...You do such a thing without my support," Mister Fan said. "It's nonsense, Lord Yuan... nonsense."

"I'll still consider it," Yuan Xi insisted. "I... I *must*."

Yuan Shang, meanwhile, was stubbornly refusing to abandon the siege of Pingyuan and relieve Yè City; he remained in his command tent and ordered an increase in daily attempts to scale Pingyuan's walls instead.

"We've had no communication since the man that told us that the eastern camps had fallen, which is bad news," Registrar Li Fu said. "My lord, we really do have to consider going back!"

"I'm not leaving my brother here in Bohai," Yuan Shang insisted.

"Mister Li Fu is speaking rightly," Yin Kui suggested. "Lord Yuan, we cannot swap a castle for a shack. If we lose Yè, it won't matter whether you defeat Yuan Tan or not: the entire Yuan clan legacy will be lost!"

"We won't lose Yè!" Yuan Shang snapped. **"Shen Pei and ten thousand men guard Yè, with support from Yin Kai at Maocheng and Ju Hu at Handan! If I retreat now, Tan will dog me all the way there, picking off my rear guard and causing even more defections than the retreat inevitably**

will! I *cannot look weak*!"

"...Perhaps we should try and appeal to Yuan Tan's sense again, have Chen Lin write him a letter," Xun Chen suggested.

"No more diplomacy," Yuan Shang insisted. "He invited Cao Cao into my province and asked him to attack Yè: he is no longer my brother! As clan chieftain, I have the right to disinherit him, and when he is captured, I probably will! But I *must* defeat and detain him, else he'll become appealing as my own army falters!"

"...So we are staying then," Li Fu sighed.

"I... I *must*," Yuan Shang replied miserably.

Yuan Tan could not remain on the walls of Pingyuan while Yuan Shang's men attempted to climb them; he withdrew to the governor's mansion with his advisers and vented his frustration at his situation.

"I have been abandoned!" Yuan Tan said. "Cao Cao has allowed Shang to trap me here while he pillages my inheritance!"

"You're mistaken," Xin Pi replied. "Don't lose heart or faith: Shang is being stubborn, that's all. He will withdraw eventually."

"...And when he does, I'll do as my 'ally' does and worry about my own situation," Yuan Tan said. "There will be no cooperation, not after this! I'll harass Shang as he flees, and then I'll seize Bohai, as your brother and Mister Guo proposed before..."

"...I disagree with their analyses," Xin Pi said.

"We'll act as the moment dictates," Guo Tu suggested. "For now, let us try and survive until Yuan Shang finally sees sense."

The Maocheng Fortress was situated at the base of the Taihang Mountains in northwest Ji, and served as a gateway to and from Bing Province to the west: its guardian, Yin Kai, was aware that Yè City was under siege, but he little expected to be at risk at any point in the near future, since any attack on Maocheng would divert personnel away from Yè and require passing Handan, which was guarded by Ju Hu. So when a large army – which was spearheaded by Cao Chun's 'Tiger and Leopard Cavalry' – suddenly appeared and started to attack the outer defensive positions, Yin Kai was left stunned and slightly unnerved.

"**Has Handan fallen???**" Yin Kai cried as he stood on the walls of Maocheng and watched his enemies overwhelm his infantry. "**How is this possible?!**"

Cao Chun's cavalry made quick work of the first line of defence, and the infantry that followed them was inspired by the bloodshed; the two armies clashed while Yin Kai did all he could to prevent Maocheng from being breached. But Maocheng was being used as an inter-provincial transport route, so the gates had been left open for supply trains and even some civilian merchants to pass through: the panic generated by the sudden attack allowed some of Cao Chun's cavalry to outrun the retreating defenders, kill the gate guards and keep the way open for the Han infantry to follow them and enter the fortress. The fighting continued for an hour or more, ending with Yin Kai's humiliating retreat into Bing Province and the seizure of Maocheng Fortress.

"**What next?**" Cao Cao chuckled as he surveyed the scene outside the fortress.

"**We go back the way we came and take Handan City,**" Guo

Jia replied. "**Without Yè or Maocheng to provide support, it will fall more quickly.**"

"**You are without compare, Fengxiao!**" Cao Cao said through grateful laughter. "**To even suggest that I draw resources away from a siege, bypass a major defensive position without compromising it and attack a major supply route with the enemy close behind would unnerve any other man, even Old Cheng, but not you! And look at what we've achieved as a result!**"

"**Only because we were fast,**" Guo Jia insisted. "**Now we must maintain our speed and rid ourselves of Handan's defenders before Yuan Shang reacts.**"

"**It shall be as you say!**" Cao Cao replied; he then turned to Xu Yòu and said, "**Look, Ziyuan! The Yuans will soon trouble us no more!**"

Xu Yòu smiled and replied, "**I am enjoying every minute, Mengde: every single minute!**"

"...Amazin'," 'Flying Swallow' Zhang Yan said when he learned that Cao Cao had captured Maocheng and begun a march on Handan; he knew that his 'Black Mountain Bandit' confederacy now faced an important decision, and so did the assembled lesser chieftains that surrounded him in his hilltop camp near the base of the western Taihang Mountains.

"You must be thinking more than 'Amazing', boss," the bandit 'White Circles' said.

"...O' *course I am*!" Flying Swallow retorted. "I... I jus' can't believe Cao did this so quickly! He's torn Yuan Shang's defences to shreds, an' I don't think he intends to go home with the job half done this time."

"So what do we do...?" White Circles asked.

"...I know a lot o' you ain't gonna like this, but I reckon we should submit to Cao Cao," Flying Swallow declared. "We're a lot of us just here 'cause we don't like the way that the lords o' the manors do things, and now we're lookin' at a lot o' new lords that are really doin' things diff'rently down south. Cao smashed Yufuluo's lot for the raids in Yan, an' he don't like the Wuhuan that harm the locals here much, an' I know that he smashed our lads too, but he works well enough with Zang Ba's blokes in Qing now, don't he...? If this is gonna lead to the Yuans bein' ousted an' us gettin' a better lot in life, then I reckon we should be helpin' the man, not sittin' here watchin'."

The bandit chieftains murmured agreeably.

"...I'm gonna send a man to request a meetin' so's I can submit and offer me help – our help – in gettin' rid o' the Yuans and the Wuhuan an' all," Flying Swallow continued. "If he accepts, then we start *really* makin' life difficult for Yuan Xi and Gao Gan... if he doesn't, we'll think some more."

"Go for it, boss," a second bandit chief said. "We're with you."

General Ju Hu had only become aware that Cao Cao's army had somehow passed his defences at Handan and attacked Maocheng when it was too late to save the vital fortification: Cao Cao had now turned about and started toward Handan with his large army of eager, jubilant troops, and without Yè and Maocheng to defend or act in concert with, Handan had gone from a strong defensive position to an isolated outpost with little chance of holding out. Ju Hu knew that he had to act as quickly as his enemy had if he stood a chance of saving Handan, so he gathered his officials in the governor's mansion's audience hall and stood before them in full armour and wielding his sword of authority.

"Maocheng has obviously fallen, and Handan will be next if we falter... Lord Yuan must be made aware of this!" Ju Hu said. **"I will defend this place until I have either repelled the enemy or died a hero's death! But Handan must hold, with or without me, or we cannot regain Maocheng and relieve Yè! Someone must hurry to Pingyuan at once!"**

"I know the right messenger to send," a major replied.

"Then go and tell him to get moving!" Ju Hu ordered. **"In the meantime, we must all of us double our efforts! There's no time to lose: the wolves are almost at the gates!"**

Ju Hu led his defending army out of the gates of Handan in order to surprise Cao Cao's attacking force with a show of desperate strength: the ploy backfired, as Cao Chun's 'Tiger and Leopard Cavalry' were too disciplined to falter in the face of an unexpected charge. The front line of Ju Hu's infantry and small cavalry force were torn apart in a few minutes by Cao Chun's horsemen, and Ju Hu was forced to retreat into the city before Zhang Liao and Li Dian reached his position with their own men.

"CLOSE THE GATES!" a major ordered as the last of Ju Hu's bodyguards passed the entranceway: the gates were then closed, leaving any men that were still outside to face the might of Cao Cao's army.

"Please, someone, tell... tell me that we... achieved our primary objective!" Ju Hu wheezed as he tugged at his helmet in an effort to remove it.

"Our man escaped to notify Lord Yuan," an official reported.

"...Then we must put every... man we have on the walls," Ju Hu said. "We must hold, damn it! We must *hold*!"

The officials dispersed to fortify Handan; Ju Hu watched them and sighed, saying, "I know... I am too late... may Heaven forgive you... your error... and still give you victory, Lord Yuan... else the world will... belong to the villain."

Events were now moving very quickly: Bing Province Governor Gao Gan had barely learned of the fall of Maocheng when word arrived of the swift fall of Handan and the probable death of Ju Hu. To make matters worse for his administration, the Black Mountain Bandits appeared to be moving to guard the road that led to Maocheng on Cao Cao's behalf: the confused and angry Gao Gan consulted his adviser and relative, Gao Rou, about what he should do next.

"We cannot move, not while we still have to worry about an attack from Hedong, Qiang or no Qiang," Gao Rou said. "We'll need to maintain our defensive stance."

"And let Ji Province fall to Cao Cao???" Gao Gan cried.

"We must have faith that Lord Yuan Shang will somehow turn his fortunes around," Gao Rou replied. "We are in no position to fight now, not if we're at risk of being caught in a pincer."

"Yes, caught in a pincer between the *Qiang* and the *Black*

Mountain Bandits!" Gao Gan despaired. "Is there no wretch that Cao Cao will not befriend...?"

"...Lord Yuan Shao allied with the Wuhuan, the bandit king Gong Du and the Runan Yellow Turbans," Gao Rou noted. "These are difficult times to fathom or apply morals to. In fact, nothing applies... nothing at all."

"...By which you mean *what*...?" Gao Gan asked cautiously.

"I... I merely state that nothing can be classed as 'not for considering'," Gao Rou replied. "Face the facts, Cousin: Lord Yuan Shang may lose, and then we must act as we see fit. If we were faced with Yuan Tan and Cao Cao jointly demanding our surrender, what would we do...?"

"...I realise that I do not know," Gao Gan said. "But... but you're right... we must consider *everything*..."

Cao Cao laughed as an envoy for the Black Mountain Bandits finished his retreat from the Han army's command tent.

"...That ensures that Gao Gan is no threat, for now at least," Xu Yòu said tonelessly.

"It does!" Cao Cao replied. "Oh, yes... it is all proceeding very nicely. Yè has not been relieved, Maocheng and Handan have fallen... we shall now return to Yè, relieve Zilian before his idiocy surfaces and complete the siege of the city!"

"There is only one way in which Yuan Shang can salvage a tiny chance of victory now, but that is up to him, not us," Guo Jia said.

"...What 'chance'...?" Xu Yòu asked. "What can he do to thwart us now, Guo Fengxiao...? What have you seen that I have missed...?"

"His chosen route when he inevitably, eventually returns to Yè," Guo Jia replied. "The path dictates the stance."

"I pondered the same," Cao Cao said.

"...Ah, yes, I see," Xu Yòu said after a moment of thought. "I am clouded by my own desperation to see the Yuans exterminated."

"Which is why you are not my chief strategist on this campaign, Ziyuan!" Cao Cao chuckled. "Fengxiao is indifferent, and so he makes no mistakes! Let us hope that Yuan Shang is even more emotional than you are... for his mistakes will be costly!"

Messengers from Maocheng and Handan had fled the cities as they fell and sped toward Pingyuan, where Yuan Shang was still undertaking a siege that had achieved nothing; Shang absorbed the news and said, "I... I have to stay! I cannot let my brother join Cao Cao! I can still win if I defeat him here!"

"We might have to reconsider our plans now," Xun Chen insisted.

"...We've lost Handan and Maocheng," Li Fu sighed. "My lord, I-!"

"N-no more," Yuan Shang insisted. "We can regain Handan and Maocheng later! Yè will hold! My brother is the excuse for the invasion! We... we *must* stay, gentlemen, or we'll certainly lose!"

Li Fu looked at Yin Kui, who covered his face with his sleeve and muttered quietly; they were not the only ones that despaired that there would be no return to Yè City, which was now completely isolated and certain to fall.

****

46

Shen Pei stood on the eastern battlements of Yè City and looked down at his enemies with contempt as they finished a day of costly effort and completed their retreat; he was certain that he could resist for some time, as the rivers that ran to the north and west were impeding Cao Cao's efforts to properly surround the city and the western mountains were keeping his supply routes restricted to the east and south. General Su Yòu's betrayal had done serious harm, but there were still close to 8,000 men within the city that were willing to fight to the end, and many still clung to the hope that Handan and Maocheng would be regained and that reinforcements from Yuan Shang and Gao Gan were a certainty. But since Cao Cao's return, the ferocity of the attacks had increased, and those hopes were fading.

"...Uncle, we're getting indications that Cao Cao is trying to tunnel under us again," Shen Rong reported.

"Let him try," Shen Pei scoffed. "I'll wait until his men are almost through and bury them alive in their own tunnels! I'll dig more trenches to foil the tunnels!"

"...And what about the mounds...?" Shen Rong asked.

"We'll get out there and topple them at some point," Shen Pei replied. "Look below, Nephew: do you see how many men they lost today...?"

Shen Rong peered over the wall and grimaced.

"At least twenty today at this wall alone," Shen Pei continued. "It doesn't sound like much, I know. But when it is a death toll that is normal for every day, day after day, week after week... even the thousands that Cao has brought here cannot afford to take such losses. Every man is a brother, a father, a son, an uncle, a nephew... every man that dies harms their morale, just as our losses harm us. And as the days and weeks wear on, the losses will be quietly offset against the gains, and the men will start to question why they're here, day after day, hurling themselves at the walls and achieving nothing."

"...Won't Lord Yuan's men in Pingyuan be thinking the same...?" Shen Rong asked pointedly.

Shen Pei huffed irritably and said, "What morale is to be had by such thinking? And I have an answer that may silence your doubts: Lord Yuan is breaking his brother's spirit, punishing him for turning to Cao Cao for help! He's preventing Yuan Tan from joining forces with Cao Cao! And Lord Yuan Shang can sustain his siege because he has local support, while Cao Cao is far from home, reliant on supplies from Yan Province, and he is unpopular. Cao Cao will have to retreat eventually..."

"But Cao has cut our supply route to and from Bing and set up waterworks that ease the transport of supplies from Yan Province this time!" Shen Rong protested. "We're completely isolated!"

"He took Li County, Yiyang and Yin'an last time, and all seemed lost, but he still had to retreat in the end," Shen Pei insisted. "Will Yan be able to supply his army indefinitely...? I think not!"

"...I hope that's true," Shen Rong sighed.

Cao Cao invited his officers to his command tent and said, "We have achieved great things, but we're getting nowhere with Shen Pei. I little expected such a craven, hitherto-incompetent toady to be such an obstacle. Is there some great mind in there that we've been unaware of...?"

"No, Excellency," the defector Su Yòu insisted. "Rather it is that Shen Pei fears for his own life and works tirelessly to preserve it. Yuan Tan wants to destroy him, and he imagines that you wish to do the same, so his usual poor performance is replaced by this formidable defence."

Cao Cao laughed and said, "You are quite right! But there must be some way to defeat him."

"We proceed as we have and wait for another key defection," Xu Yòu suggested.

"I agree with Xu Ziyuan," Guo Jia said. "I imagine that there are many others that tire of this now."

"...But is simply hoping for someone to open the gates enough, gentlemen...?" Cao Cao wondered. "The men to the south of here are getting sick from being so close to Yanpi Marsh, and the rivers on three sides are inhibitive. Supplies will not last forever. What 'key defection' can there be if Su Yòu is already here...?"

"There are others," Guo Jia replied. "If we are patient..."

As the days passed, Shen Pei's disciplinary measures became more and more aggressive and indiscriminate, and soldiers started to complain to their superiors. Wei Prefecture Administrator Gao Fan dismissed the complaints when he was approached, but one officer – Feng Li – refused to accept that his men should suffer the purge of 'potential dissidents' and planned rebellion. Feng Li waited until nightfall and had a group of disaffected men assist him in making a hole in the eastern wall of the city so that the enemy could launch a sudden attack and take the city; the work was quickly spotted by the spies that Shen Pei had despatched throughout the city, and Feng Li's rebels were captured and brought to the command room to face punishment.

"I should have known that you were another wretched traitor, Feng Li!" Shen Pei heckled. "I shall enjoy your execution!"

"Spare me your theatrics, Shen Pei," Feng Li retorted. "You did nothing but slander good men while Lord Yuan Shao lived, and then you conspired to make the wrong son the chieftain; I was blind to your mistake until now. Yuan Shang is somewhere else, sieging his own brother, whose entitlement is greater than his, while the entire northeast falls into the hands of another: no man worthy of such power would make such a mistake. Cao Cao will win, and that's Heaven's will: fortify this place all you want, but you're doomed to follow me soon, you and any other fool that helps you to hold this place for an unworthy lord."

The few officials that were gathered in the command room exchanged worried glances; Shen Pei sneered and said, "I'm glad that you chose those to be your parting words, Feng Li. You hid Su Yòu's treachery, committed your own, and now you urge others to do the same: you are guilty thrice of treason! **GUARDS: DEATH! Death to him and his followers! Death to them all!**"

Shen Rong turned to his uncle as Feng Li and the other rebels were being led away and asked, "Now that you have lost another senior officer, what will you do...?"

"I shall have to take personal command of more of the men and assign more of them to you," Shen Pei replied. "This city will not fall... even if it is eventually the case that I and I alone defend it, this city *will not fall*!"

"And the breach...?" Gao Fan asked.

"We'll let the enemy use it, since they know about it," Shen Pei replied cruelly.

Cao Cao was delighted when a lone soldier approached his camp and informed him of Feng Li's defection and the breach that would allow his soldiers to enter Yè City and surprise Shen Pei: Guo Jia shook his head and said, "Don't send too many good men, Lord Cao. Shen Pei's security is obsessive, and so he's bound to know about the plot and take defensive countermeasures."

"Feng Li is a good man," Xu Yòu retorted. "I know it, Su Yòu knows it, Zhang Hè knows it; Feng's action is genuine, he is cautious, and we should be capitalising on this opportunity, not ignoring it!"

"...I've no choice but to seize the opportunity," Cao Cao said. "I'll send three-hundred men to get inside and open the gates."

But the path that Feng Li had created for Cao Cao's men was now a trap: the 300 men were allowed to rush into the city before Shen Pei ordered rocks and boulders to be dropped on them from above, killing them and ensuring that the path was blocked. The fate of the raiding party affected morale: Shen Pei saw a general increase in confidence in the city, despite the earlier objections to his disciplinary measures, while Cao Cao's forces mourned the losses and wondered if they would ever succeed.

The Qiang warlord Ma Teng heard of Du Ji's arrival in Liang Province and his subsequent meeting with Han Sui; Teng's lack of trust got the better of him, and he hurriedly demanded his own meeting with the Han official that took place on the border with Han Sui's territory.

"...Please state your concerns," Du Ji said to the large collection of Qiang chieftains that he faced.

"Why are you here?" Ma Teng asked. "Why did you meet with Han Sui? What is Cao Cao up to...?"

"I met with Han Sui for the same reason that you now meet with me: he thought that I had come here to make trouble," Du Ji replied. "He thought that I might be another corrupt official or agitator, just as you do, a man looking to divide the Qiang or make some easy money by taxing the people. I'm neither: I'm here to act as a liaison, nothing more."

"...I don't think that we've got anything to worry about with this man," Ma Teng decided.

"Strangely... I agree, Father," Ma Chao said as he glared at the calm, unflinching Du Ji. "This is a man with nothing to hide."

"I'm more than happy to meet with anyone, together or separately," Du Ji insisted. "By all means arrange a meeting with you, General Han, Song Jian and whoever else you want here: if it leads to peaceful relations between Han and Qiang, I will agree to meet whoever I am asked to meet. I'm here to build bridges, General Ma, not burn them."

"...You exude confidence that comes from the honesty of your words," Ma Teng said. "Perhaps we might have that meeting you suggest one day, but for now... I like you, Mister Du Ji, and I think that we will have no serious arguments."

"That warms my heart," Du Ji replied with a smile. "May we soon enjoy a peace that we have all deserved for a long time."

Over the coming days, Cao Cao became increasingly frustrated with his lack of progress against the defenders of Yè: Shen Pei's archers were managing to shoot his mound-based archers, all of the new tunnels had been countered with trenches and the attempts to scale the walls had resulted in piles of fried, boiled and crushed bodies on the ground below and not a single successful climb. Cao Cao assembled his officials within his command tent once again and prepared to make an unsettling declaration that only the wisest of his counsel foresaw; one of the wisest, Guo Jia, was conspicuous by his absence, and everyone knew that it was due to illness.

"The inside perimeter of the city must be a network of trenches with barely a patch of undisturbed ground; my mounds are little more than a distraction!" Cao Cao complained. "There is only one thing for it: I have tried to refrain from repeating this cruel measure, but I have no choice."

"What are you going to do...?" Xiahou Dun asked.

"...The mounds will be demolished," Cao Cao ordered. Then-"

"**Demolished**???" Cao Hong cried. "We only started building them a few weeks ago! Some of them were only just finished!"

"Why would we demolish them?" Xiahou Dun asked.

"We're not retreating *again*, are we Mengde?" Xu Yòu exclaimed. "You promised that we wouldn't! What possesses you???"

"...Please let me finish," Cao Cao replied tonelessly. "First the mounds... then, we will dig a shallow trench around the walls."

"I think I see where you're going with this," Cao Chun said.

"We'd be thwarted if the enemy realised what we were doing," Jia Xu suggested. "The key, as Fengxiao always says, is speed."

"Yes... he would say just that," Cao Cao murmured.

"With the right men assigned to the task, we'd outwit Shen Pei easily, Mengde," Cao Chun said.

"What are we doing...?" Cao Hong asked. "I truly don't understand. A shallow trench will achieve *what*...?"

"I'll explain it to you, Zilian," Cao Pi promised.

"...So you understand, my son," Cao Cao chuckled softly. "I'm glad... for it means that my heir is possessed of the wits he needs to succeed me."

The next day saw Cao Cao order the flattening of the mounds and the digging of the shallow trench: Shen Pei looked over the walls and frowned as he watched the work.

"...This can only be a sign that they're planning to withdraw!" Gao Fan said.

"Perhaps, Administrator... perhaps," Shen Pei replied. "We will know when they show us what they intend to do with this trench."

"...But Uncle, they cannot intend to surround the city with a deep trench to cut us off, or to facilitate more tunnels...?" Shen Rong asked worriedly.

"We'd shoot their workers if we saw such a trench being dug,"

Shen Pei replied. "And no fool would start to dig such a tunnel that close to the walls. No... it is probably for moving obstructive debris – corpses, broken ladders – away from the walls to facilitate the scaling attempts, or just to bury their dead with some dignity before they withdraw."

"As you say, we'll see what it's for soon enough," Gao Fan sighed.

The moat was dug slowly and seemingly unenthusiastically over several days: Shen Pei smiled when he saw that the work on each section of the moat finished when it was no more than two feet deep at the lowest point in any one place, as it seemingly indicated that it was a ruse of some kind.

"They're going!" Shen Pei chuckled. "That must be it! That or his men have lost the will to fight! Look at how feeble the effort is! They can run back and forth across the space! It serves next to no purpose: it looks more like a shallow grave for their festering dead with every passing day!"

"...Are you sure...?" Gao Fan asked.

"I can be sure of nothing that Cao does, not completely, but this... this is an act of desperation," Shen Pei replied. "The mounds have been flattened, but a wide, shallow moat dug in their place: if the extracted earth were for the mounds, I would worry, but with the mounds gone the moat is strategically worthless! It must be a pitiful attempt to deceive us... no doubt there's a rumour that Lord Yuan is soon to return, and that has shattered Cao's resolve!"

"...We should remain vigilant," Gao Fan suggested.

"Is there a man alive that is more vigilant than me...?" Shen Pei retorted. "Their moat will not get any larger, I assure you... if I see any sign of it, we will rain terror down upon them until they withdraw. But I think that moat is for the dead."

Gao Fan smiled and said, "Relief may be given at last..."

Night fell: Shen Pei left a night guard patrol on every wall and retired to plan his strategy for the next day. But within minutes of dawn breaking and the first light bathing the ground around the city, a commotion erupted; within minutes of that, Gao Fan rushed into Shen's sleeping quarters and cried, **"We're *finished*!"**

"...What...?" Shen Pei groaned. "What are you saying...?"

"Come and see for yourself!" Gao Fan replied angrily. **"Come and see what they have done!"**

Gao Fan turned and fled from the room; Shen Pei rubbed his eyes and muttered, "What is that fool on about...?"

Shen Pei dressed in armour and hurried to the eastern wall: his eyes bulged when he saw the ground below, and the only sound that he could manage was a croak. Cao Cao's men had worked under the cover of night to increase the depth of the moat by more than 10 times, and in such numbers that the work encompassed the entire moat. To make matters worse, Cao Cao had taken advantage of the city defenders losing external control of the nearby rivers and done as he had done to the city of Xiapi 6 years before: a complex network of channels had also been dug, and the moat was filled with diverted water from the Huan River. Shen Pei turned and hurried toward the southern wall: the sight was the same, but that water was mostly diverted from the foul waters of the southern marshlands.

"**Don't bother!**" Gao Fan said as Shen Pei prepared to run to toward the west wall. "**It's the same all the way around, Mister Shen... we're completely cut off now.**"

Shen Pei could hear countless men sobbing and cursing; he knew that Cao Cao had, with this seemingly impossible night-time exercise, doomed the inhabitants of Yè to starvation and sickness, and that thoughts would increasingly turn to surrender.

"...We... we must hold!" Shen Pei insisted feebly. "We... we must be strong... they cannot stay forever, they-!"

"**They're not leaving!**" Gao Fan barked. "**We're trapped, and they're outside laughing at us! There's no sign of Lord Yuan Shang returning, and we cannot get a man out to tell him what's happened! We must hope that somehow, some way, he hears of this and returns, or... or all is lost!**"

A sudden scream alerted the men on the wall to a new problem: they all turned and looked at the ground below, where Shen Pei's trenches – dug to thwart tunnelling attempts by Cao Cao's sappers – were now filling with muddy water that was seeping in from the moat outside.

"...**Curse you, Cao Cao!**" Shen Pei shrieked. "**Curse you Su Yòu, and Guo Jia, and Xu Yòu, and Zhang Hè, and Yuan Tan, and...! Curse you ALL!**"

"**What good is that going to do...?**" Gao Fan asked. "**We need answers, Mister Shen, not curses: we cannot suffer the same fate as Lü Bu!**"

Shen Pei covered his face with his sleeve and fled from the wall.

"**Where's he going???**" Gao Fan exclaimed.

"...**Lady Liu must be notified,**" Shen Rong replied. "**And somehow, as you said, we need answers... we need to contact Lord Yuan, *somehow*...**"

Cao Cao looked at Yè City and hummed thoughtfully.

"...This was necessary, I suppose," Liu Yè sighed.

"I do this because of the lives that this will save," Cao Cao insisted. "They cannot hold out now – even the mighty *Lü Bu* could not endure this – so when Yuan Shang does return, it will be to a city under our control. He will have to capitulate then."

Jia Xu hummed thoughtfully.

"...Alright, I know that Shang might be stubborn enough to hold out, even after this, but where would he go...?" Cao Cao asked. "Qing Province and Pingyuan in Bohai are in his older brother's hands, and Bing and Yòu Provinces are too difficult to get to, and besides that, Yuan Xi has enough problems of his own and is obviously trying to remain neutral."

"It all depends on how Shang tries to return now, as previously noted," Jia Xu said.

"...Yes," Cao Cao conceded. "How this ends is in Yuan Shang's hands now."

＊＊＊＊＊＊＊＊＊＊＊＊

47

"...I have decided to go back to Yè."

Yuan Shang's announcement was met by incredulous gasps and sighs of irritated relief; the siege of Pingyuan City in Bohai Prefecture had yielded no positive results, while Cao Cao had rampaged across western Ji Province and seized most of Wei Prefecture and the supply road to Bing Province.

"I am relieved that you have finally made this decision, for I was beginning to despair," Yin Kui admitted.

"We must go at once, Lord Yuan, before Cao Cao does any more damage," Xun Chen pleaded. "We must take the fastest route and surprise them!"

"Let me take the vanguard!" General Zhang Yi said.

"If not General Zhang, then let me, my lord! Let us both!" General Ma Yan implored.

"We will be cautious in our approach," Yuan Shang replied. "Cao controls the area around Li County to the south, and many of the roads to the west of there as well, so we'd be better off re-establishing Handan and Maocheng as part of our supply route and relieving the siege from the north, by way of the roads that straddle the mountain ranges."

"...No," Li Fu said. "We must fight desperately, and-!"

"You're a registrar, not an adviser, Mister Li," Yuan Shang retorted. "You're good with words, but what do you know of warfare...? This is a serious situation! I will have my brother's army biting at my heels and a swathe of conquered regions waiting for me! My men will need constant rest breaks, good food supplies and a tightly-held belief that there will be a victory at the other end of the journey! How can charging blindly at Cao's army with Li County reinforcements and my brother at our rear be anything else but suicide...? We must somehow lose my brother's pursuing army as we travel, and that means moving into territory that he dare not enter! That is obvious, is it not...?"

"...There is more to warfare than what seems obvious, my lord," Li Fu countered.

"I do not need your analysis," Yuan Shang scoffed. "What I need, *Registrar* Li, is your obedience: you will go ahead of us with a team of elite riders and alert the defenders to our approach."

"...You actually want to alert the enemy to our surprise return...?" Li Fu chortled.

"Did I say 'the enemy'...?" Yuan Shang snapped.

"No, but my arrival will mean nothing else but reinforcements to the defenders *and* to Cao Cao!" Li Fu insisted. "We are better off-"

"*Ayah*... Mister Li, you will oppose me no further!" Yuan Shang ordered. "Get ready to depart, please: we need to deliver hope and prepare a coordinated attack to drive Cao back to Li County."

Li Fu clasped his hands together, bowed tersely and said, "As you command, my lord."

Registrar Li Fu gathered the 30 men that had been allocated to him and said, "I will do as I have been ordered, and you will do as I tell you."

"Of course," the captain replied.

"Firstly, Captain Deng, I will not be travelling with this," Li Fu said as he raised his 'staff of authority' – which could, amongst other things, be used to prove his identity at and seize command of friendly outposts – and suddenly snapped it across his knee, which led to anguished gasps.

"Wh-what are you doing???" Captain Deng asked.

"I might as well ask you to cut off my head and deliver it to Cao Cao if I keep this thing on my person," Li Fu replied as he tossed the broken staff to one side. "Right, now for the second thing: there are quite a few of you, but I want to take just three of you, three horsemen, and-"

"We need to report Li Fu to Lord Yuan, Captain," one soldier suggested. "He's mad."

"I am not 'mad'... now please, hear me out," Li Fu retorted. "The south and west are under Cao Cao's control, not Lord Yuan's, so I must travel inconspicuously, paying no heed to nonsense protocols like 'sizes of escorts' and 'needing to carry a staff of authority'. I will not be travelling by day once we get to Wei Prefecture either, nor will I be going by the main roads."

The soldiers exchanged worried glances.

"*Aiee...* I have just explained why!" Li Fu despaired. "*Think*, will you??? All but the three of you that will be accompanying me will do your best to remain out of Lord Yuan Shang's way until I have long departed."

"...Alright," Captain Deng replied. "I admit that I do understand what you're doing."

"Good," Li Fu said. Then you can definitely come with me. Pick two men with more than straw and millet between their ears that can ride a horse well, and we'll get moving as soon as possible."

Yuan Tan stood on the walls of Pingyuan City and watched his brother's army begin its retreat; he then turned to Guo Tu and said, "Now we shall seize Bohai."

"...Perhaps we should now pursue and pincer Yuan Shang, to show unity with Cao Cao," Xin Pi suggested. "After all, his attack has-"

"Cao Cao is not my friend," Yuan Tan retorted. "Yes, we'll pursue, but not for long. And then we seize Bohai while Cao distracts my idiot brother. And then, when we have Bohai... I shall have Shen Pei's head, and then Cao's head."

Xin Pi sighed miserably and said, "As you command, my lord... as you command..."

Registrar Li Fu's small band travelled westward initially, as Yuan Shang intended to do: when they reached the road that led southward to Yè, Li Fu turned to his followers and asked, "Will my orders be heeded...?"

"You've been proven correct at every point so far," Captain Deng replied. "My respect for you is without question, Mister Li. Tell us what we must do."

"We acquired a change of clothes in that last village for a reason," Li Fu said. "We're going to put on a little show... and I shall now explain your roles..."

The northern part of the siege was being overseen by Cao Hong and Xiahou Dun: both men had arrayed their camps effectively and posted sentries throughout to look out for anyone that tried to escape or launch an attack from the north. Li Fu – who was now dressed in expensive robes and carrying a small wooden fan – walked ahead of his two similarly-dressed allies – Captain Deng and a cavalry soldier called Kui – and approached a sentry on the outskirts of the camp; the sentry frowned as the fearless Li Fu looked him up and down and sighed, "Pitiful."

"What?" the sentry exclaimed.

"Don't address me unless I ask something, Private!" Li Fu barked. **"You *never*, *ever* speak to a disciplinary officer unless you are responding to a request!"**

The sentry panicked and bowed humbly.

"And don't bow either, idiot!" Li Fu cried. **"What if I was an imposter, looking to coerce you into taking your eyes off of me so that I could behead you?"**

"S-sorry, sir," the sentry replied.

"...There's no point with you, is there...?" Li Fu chortled. "And you're posted to the perimeter security...? An *army* could march through here."

The sentry's captain approached Li Fu and bowed slightly, saying, "Is there a problem, *Mister*...?"

"Wang Hong," Li Fu replied. "And yes, there is: why is such a scruffy, poorly-trained man placed here...? Is he typical...?"

The captain smiled coldly and said, "General Cao Hong-"

"*Ah*... well, *that's* why," Li Fu scoffed. "And where's he...? In his tent, cavorting with prostitutes, as he is known for...? Perhaps I need to speak to him... or would I be disturbing something...?"

The sentry captain was now convinced that the only man that would dare to criticise or threaten to confront Cao Hong would be a genuine disciplinary officer from Cao Cao's personal staff: he bowed humbly and said, "I will improve the situation personally, Mister Wang. There is no need to disturb General Cao."

"...Fine," Li Fu grunted; he then gestured to his two amused followers and began a slow, meticulous inspection of the entire eastern section of Cao Hong's camp that took him further and further south.

Captain Deng started to worry as they left Cao Hong's camp and entered the eastern portion of Cao Cao's vast encampment, so he asked, "Are we perhaps pushing our luck...?"

"No," Li Fu replied. "Now... I wonder who's in charge here...?"

"I saw a standard reading 'Li Dian'," Kui noted.

"Ah, right," Li Fu said. "He's no idiot... but we can still operate as we were. Cao Cao is known for surprise inspections, after all! Just remain silent as you have done so far and follow me when I gesture, just as you have done up to now."

"That's fine by me: I'm too scared to do anything else," Kui admitted. "Where are we going?"

"Now you've said what you've said, it's probably better that I don't tell you," Li Fu replied. "Just trust me."

The trio approached a wandering sentry, who asked, "Who goes there? Who are you?"

"Disciplinary Officer Wang Hong," Li Fu replied gruffly. "I want to speak to General Li Dian about the state of his security... I had heard good things, but it seems that I heard wrong."

The sentry was dumbstruck.

"Who is your immediate superior?" Li Fu asked.

The sentry's eyes turned toward a captain that was approaching at speed: Li Fu smiled and prepared to repeat his ruse.

After several similar confrontations, Li Fu reached the northeast tip of the southern section of the defences: Cao Cao's command tent was located to the far south of the encampment, but Li Fu was unafraid.

"...Don't we run the risk of running into a real disciplinary officer or one of Cao's advisers here, Mister Li...?" Captain Deng asked.

"Of course, but I don't intend to chat anymore," Li Fu replied. "We need to find the men that are in charge of watching the wall."

"...Ah, I understand," Captain Deng said. "Mister Li, I think I see someone: isn't that fellow there a watch captain...?"

Li Fu followed Deng's gaze and smiled, saying, "Yes."

"...Who are you...? What are you doing here?" the watch captain asked as Li Fu approached him.

"I'd be angry if I could be bothered," Li Fu retorted. "But I've never seen such diabolical disorganisation in a camp in my life... I'm actually worn out from telling men like you off and cannot find the energy."

"I beg your pardon?" the watch captain exclaimed.

"The wall is not exactly what you call 'heavily watched', is it...?" Li Fu heckled. "There's such a thin line of men that whole platoons could drop from the wall and cross the moat without being seen!"

"You're exaggerating, whoever you are!" the watch captain retorted. "I've been allocated the proper number of men by my superior for watching a wall that is surrounded by a moat!"

"...I don't know who your superior is, but you need to file a complaint," Li Fu said. "I'll help you write it."

"...What do you mean...?" the watch captain asked.

"Say a desperate band of men did somehow leap from the wall and into the water, and say they survived," Li Fu replied. "How would you deal with them...?"

The watch captain looked at the wall, looked at the moat, turned to Li Fu and laughed, saying, "Who could leap all that way...!"

"...Alright, but say that they lowered themselves down at great speed, all along the wall, lots of them all at once," Li Fu countered. "What would you do...?"

The watch captain smirked and said, "Well, I'd signal for help, of course, and..."

"...And what...?" Li Fu asked. "What then, while you and this tiny group of men you've been allocated are being attacked by desperate, hungry escapees...?"

"...You're right," the watch captain replied. "I need more men!"

"I have the authority to complain on your behalf," Li Fu said. "Let's go to your tent and draw up something."

"At once!" the watch captain replied: he then led Li Fu's group to his command tent, where he was immediately overpowered and tied up.

"There are at least ten other men like this fool: we'll need to get at least the three at this section of the wall," Li Fu explained. "We'll lure them here one at a time."

Shen Pei had been made aware of an apparent commotion near the southern wall: he hurried to the battlements with Gao Fan and peered over the wall just as Li Fu and his allies were swimming across the moat.

"Who are these fools...?" Shen Pei wondered. "That water is foul..."

"...Whoever it is must be mad or on our side," Gao Fan replied.

Li Fu started to wave his arms and shout as soon as he was stood on the narrow stretch of land below the wall: Shen Pei finally realised who it was and cried, "**Here, quickly! Somebody lower a rope at once!**"

"...And then they hoisted him and his friends up the wall," Jia Xu said to a silently smirking Cao Cao. "They've been beating victory drums ever since."

"Well, well...!" Guo Jia chuckled. "There's someone who might be a threat if his little swim in that marshy water doesn't kill him."

"I don't see why you're laughing!" Xiahou Dun complained. "He made fools of my sentries and captains! 'Wang Hong', indeed..."

Cao Cao started to laugh.

"Stop it!" Xiahou Dun whined. "Mengde, you're laughing at our misfortune, ours and yours!"

"Agreed," Xu Yòu said. "I don't see what you and Guo Jia are finding so amusing, Mengde. This can only mean one thing: reinforcements are on their way!"

"This man, whoever he was, is as cunning and inventive as Taishi Ci was when he delivered the letter from his magistrate!" Cao Cao replied. "Such a man is worth recruiting! We've got so many of the Yuan clan's men with us already, and this one sounds like a future hero! We *must* discover his identity, gentlemen!"

"I just want to know what he looks like so I know who to kill," Xiahou Dun growled.

"Don't be such a sore loser, Yuanrang!" Cao Cao said. "Yes, he made a fool of us all: that only serves as the best of references!"

"We'll recruit this mystery genius *if* we win," Xu Yòu heckled. "For now, though, Mengde, shouldn't we be worried about the reinforcements that he foreshadows...?"

"He must get back out to go back to Yuan Shang in order to relay collaborative strategies from Shen Pei," Guo Jia insisted. "And if he can do *that*, I'll be really surprised and impressed, and I yearn for such a feeling."

"So do I," Cao Cao chuckled. "Let this man entertain us some more! We'll still win in the end, Xu Ziyuan."

"*Hopefully*," Xu Yòu muttered.

Li Fu's exploits emboldened the defenders of Yè City, but as Cao Cao and his allies had observed, it was a meaningless 'victory' if Li could not then carry Shen Pei's advice on relieving the city back to Yuan Shang, who was advancing westward while trying to repel his brother's army. Escaping Yè and somehow passing the defences seemed to be an impossible task: Cao Cao waited to see if 'the impossible' could be achieved yet again.

****

48

Shen Pei and Li Fu waited until nightfall and went to the eastern wall to look at the camps below; the ground directly below Yè's walls was piled high with the dead bodies of enemy soldiers and city inhabitants – civilian and military alike – that had been thrown from the wall in an effort to limit the spread of disease inside the city.

"...So sad," Li Fu sighed. "How many have perished...?"

"Forgive my stance for what it implies, but it cannot be discussed right now as it is not relevant," Shen Pei replied. "How are you going to get out? And why did you stop me from silencing the drummers when they started?"

"My man on the outside is caring for our horses: the drums were to tell him that we reached the city," Li Fu explained. "You'll sound them after I've left as well."

"And how will we know that you escaped the camps safely...?" Shen Pei asked.

"I'll start a fire on the edge of the camp," Li Fu replied. "Your drums will then tell our outside man that we're on our way so that he can have the horses ready."

"...Is this all your idea...?" Shen Pei asked.

"It is," Li Fu replied. "Now, as for how we're – I mean 'we're', since I'll need my two aides for the return journey – are going to escape the city, I have planned for that in advance. You'll note that I brought with me several articles of enemy clothing – soldiers' uniforms – that we took from one of the tents... they will facilitate our escape."

Shen Pei smirked and said, "So you're going to dress as their soldiers and just walk out of here...?"

"It seems ridiculous, but that's where my concern at the number of casualties comes in," Li Fu replied. "Like you, I am a pragmatist: I asked because it is essential to the plan."

Shen Pei frowned and said, "You've perplexed and intrigued me, Mister Li. Please elaborate."

"Cao Cao must accept that these losses are outside for all to see: not just soldiers but women, children and the old, the once-gifted and once-promising, are piled up like sacks around the walls, and more will sadly follow," Li Fu replied. "If he wants to avoid having a lasting reputation for massacring the innocents, he has to agree to allow said innocents to flee the city. We will be among them."

Shen Pei laughed and said, "Yes, but they – *and you* – will be evacuated across a *moat*! Any that do not fall into or are not pushed into that foul water as they panic will be penned together as they cross the relatively narrow bridges that will be provided, and in such circumstances, how will you escape??? You'll be watched the whole time by their soldiers, and-!"

"Yes, in a panic situation, where the enemy will be looking for suspicious *civilians*," Li Fu interrupted. "Do you understand now?"

Shen Pei's eyes wandered.

"You do, but you have doubts," Li Fu continued. "But you must do as I suggest, Mister Shen, or we'll never get a trusted man out to coordinate with Lord Yuan."

"...I have little choice," Shen Pei conceded. "I'll have Gao Fan submit the request at dawn."

Wei Prefecture Administrator Gao Fan's request was hurried to Cao Cao, who frowned and said, "Is that the best that they could come up with...? I'm disappointed."
"But we must agree to it!" Guo Jia chuckled.
"Why?" Xu Yòu heckled. "Let them starve! Let them die! They-!"
"Ziyuan... are you my chief campaign adviser...?" Cao Cao asked.
"...No, Mengde, but I don't see how we can agree to this!" Xu Yòu replied. "They'll sneak a man out! That's why they're doing it!"
"And I must accept, or this will become public knowledge and tarnish my reputation further," Cao Cao said irritably. "I have already given myself a monster's reputation by my actions in Xu Province, and the siege of Xiapi did little to help; I want to make friends of the inhabitants of this province, and of Yè especially, and I won't do that by publicly refusing to allow civilians to flee a combat zone!"
"...I see your point," Xu Yòu conceded.
"Thank you for being so considerate," Cao Cao muttered; he then turned his gaze back to the letter from Gao Fan and added, "Now then... how do we minimise the risk of agents mingling with the innocents and escaping my net...?"
"It depends on how ingenious our opponent is," Guo Jia said. "All that we can do is emphasise that the men show the utmost vigilance; every man must know every other man at any given point, and not one person should be allowed to stray from the defined paths that lead to wherever we're putting these civilians. The facility will need to be guarded and fenced, naturally."
"...We'll need to put them in corrals until we can ascertain their innocence," Cao Cao replied. "Women and young children and the very old can be moved to less intimidating but nevertheless secure accommodation fairly quickly... the men and older boys will, of course, need to be vetted more carefully..."
"...This is unsafe," Xu Yòu complained.

Cao Cao, Liu Yè, Xu Yòu, Guo Jia, Jia Xu and the senior officers personally oversaw the preparations for the civilian evacuation: heavy wooden bridges were laid across the moat, designated paths through the camps were created, corrals were cleared of prisoners, oxen and horses to provide temporary containment spaces, and soldiers were prepared for the distress of managing thousands of starved, panicking people.
When all of the preparations were complete, Cao Cao had a drum beaten to notify the defenders and ordered his men to move away from the walls: Shen Pei lined the walls with archers to ensure that the enemy could not suddenly advance, and then he signalled to his men on the ground so that they could open the gates and release the civilian hordes. As soon as the gates opened, order broke down instantaneously: some of the first few rushed out into the fresher air and started toward the bridges that lay in front of them without caring for the welfare of the rest, while others meandered out and started to weep when they saw the bodies that were stacked up on either side of the gateways. Some of the people at the rear of the throngs started to push and shove, and people were trampled or moved aside by the uncaring.

Screaming replaced weeping and murmuring, and the soldiers that were watching were suddenly afraid.

"**STAY CALM!**" Xiahou Dun ordered as his men started to fidget and aim their weapons aggressively; some of the people were staggering and falling into the water, while others had forgotten about escaping the city and were trying to find loved ones among the rotting bodies, and the sight of it was too much for many of the besiegers.

"…This will harm me anyway," Cao Cao muttered.

"But it is… better than refusing," Guo Jia wheezed.

"The bad air is making you sick," Cao Cao said. "It does little for my head, either… this is as organised as it is ever going to be, so let us retreat and leave this to others."

Guo Jia nodded gratefully and retreated with his lord and the silent Liu Yè.

As soon as the last of the civilians were outside, Shen Pei ordered that the gates be shut behind them: some lost their trust and quickly fled back into the city before the gates were fully closed, and once there was no way back others panicked and turned to start hammering on the wooden gates with their fists. With the gates closed, Cao Cao's men could finally advance and try to control the mass of people: they were quickly overwhelmed as people misunderstood their intentions and either cowered or fled in random directions.

"…**CALM DOWN!**" Li Dian cried. "**WE'RE TRYING TO HELP!**"

The area around the walled city was now a sea of people – alive and dead, civilians and soldiers – and there would be no quick sense made of it. Cao Cao's men - including some senior officers – were forced to wade into the mass of people in order to rescue trampled soldiers and civilians or jump into the moat to rescue flailing women, children and elderly that had somehow fallen into it; Shen Pei watched from atop the wall and smiled, saying, "I am impressed, Mister Li… you assessed it perfectly."

Drums sounded within an hour of the civilians being safely contained and escorted from the walls: Cao Cao looked at Guo Jia, who said, "That was theirs, not ours."

"But… why would they do that…?" Xu Yòu asked. "Is it to inspire a revolt among the corralled civilians…?"

"Unlikely," Guo Jia replied. "It might be as some sort of signalled thanks for our cooperation, or-"

"**Damn them!**" Xiahou Dun cried as he ran into the command tent. "**Next time, Mengde, just accept the mark on your reputation! You'll have time to atone for it later!**"

"…Is there some reason for that outburst, General Xiahou…?" Guo Jia asked.

"**Of *course there is*!**" Xiahou Dun barked. "**Don't ask me how, I'm too stupid to figure out how, but they got somebody out! That's why they're on the walls, mocking us and beating those bloody drums!**"

"…*How*…?" Xu Yòu murmured.

Cao Cao was smiling silently: Xiahou Dun looked at him and asked, "**What's there to be smiling about??? They got someone out, they-!**"

"Never mind that, General," Guo Jia said. "We must ascertain *how* this person escaped in order to learn from it and also ensure that there were no agitators placed among the evacuees. It may confine me to my bed again, but I'll oversee it."

Cao Cao, Liu Yè and Xu Chu followed Guo Jia and Xiahou Dun to the main corral: Cao smiled continuously, which unnerved all but Guo Jia, who was doing his best to stifle the urge to smile as well. The herded civilians were studied carefully, but it quickly became clear that they were all innocents and that they would cause no serious trouble.
"…So do we have any information on the ones that evaded us…?" Guo Jia asked of Jia Xu, who had arrived shortly before the inspections reached their conclusion.
"We do," Jia Xu replied. "It seems that they exploited the inevitable chaos by hiding among the civilians, just as one would expect, and then they fled when attention was diverted, just as one would expect."
"But we specifically ordered the men to be vigilant across the camp," Li Dian said. "How could anyone – even one person – get to the north end of the camp without being spotted…?"
"In the same way that they got in: a combination of disguise and bluff," Jia Xu explained. "It seems that they were in soldier's uniforms – our uniform, of course – and were 'soaked through from rescuing civilians by the north gate'. There were three of them – the same three that got in, no doubt – and one of them was 'particularly convincing', despite nobody recognising him.

"They said they were Lü Xiang's men, recently surrendered, and that was the reason why they were unfamiliar, despite it being obvious, surely, that we would not allocate Lü Xiang's men to that particular mission. But most people react to such confidence with blind trust, unfortunately, and so they walked to the edge of the camp without being questioned more than three times and even started a fire within a camp at the outer perimeter to alert the city. They told a passing sentry that they were cooking a fish that they'd caught in the river, and offered to share it when he passed them again if he kept quiet. The fool only realised that they were lying when they ran off and left the fire unattended, piled high with kindling."
Cao Cao started to laugh.
"It isn't funny!" Xu Yòu cried.
"Ah, but it *is*!" Cao Cao said through laughter. "But it may get funnier still! Mister Jia: was this sentry chastised by our visitor for his incompetence on the way in…?"
Jia Xu groaned and replied, "I believe so."
"I ordered his replacement!" Cao Hong insisted.
"It doesn't matter!" Cao Cao said. "What's done is done, Zilian… and I needed a laugh!"
"So did I!" Guo Jia chuckled hoarsely.
"*Aiee*… I don't understand either of you!" Xiahou Dun said. "This is awful! Aren't the enemy on their way…? And isn't the enemy prepared to make a coordinated relief effort now…?"
"Don't fret," Guo Jia insisted. "A meeting will be held… I won't be there, but… Lord Cao won't need me for this."
"I'll still miss your presence," Cao Cao said. "But yes, this is not something that requires great insight now… only luck."

"That man they sent in and out of here made fools of us all!" Cao Hong cried. **"How can we not need brains if he's alive and making more plans???"**
"Because his role is complete, and he is no longer managing affairs," Jia Xu suggested. "His masters, Shen Pei and Yuan Shang, are now making the biggest decisions, and neither man is that impressive. The outcome depends on what Yuan Shang does now: his next move will ensure that victory will be swift or a long time from now."
"Let us go back to the command tent," Cao Cao said. "I will speak with the officers and reassure them that I am still in control... but I must say that this has been most entertaining! That elusive man will make a fine addition to my ranks."
"...Not if I get to him first," Cao Hong grumbled.

Li Fu's twin deceptions had a demoralising effect on the officers, and none more than those whose subordinates had allowed the enemy agent to move freely; Cao Cao's first intention during his afternoon meeting was to reassure the officers that there would be allowances made and that the damage was minimal.
"But the enemy have an intelligence advantage now," Li Dian said.
"I think you are giving them too much praise, and I think that you are smart enough to know that, General," Cao Cao replied. "What could have been discussed in the few days that their agent was trapped in Yè...? There are only a few ways to coordinate attacks for the relief of a sieged city, no matter how clever the methods used to pass information back and forth."
"The worry is that Yuan Shang retreats from Pingyuan with his brother in pursuit," Li Dian explained. "Cao Chun, Zhang Hè, Yue Jin, Zhang Liao, Yu Jin and I have discussed it, and there is the definite risk that Yuan Shang's men will be fighting desperately as they move southward and are therefore ten times as dangerous as any of our men, since normal survival instincts will be replaced entirely by fear and bloodlust... or, in other words, the 'men fighting on death ground' scenario described by Sun Tzu: in that case, they'll catch us in a pincer and we'd have to retreat in order to avoid serious losses."
"...I know that, and of course I would avoid confrontation if they did travel here by the most direct route," Cao Cao replied. "But their agent retreated northward, not eastward, and I think that might be telling. If they choose to go west and approach Yè from the north rather than the east, we will be facing something entirely different... and all their efforts will have been in vain."

Li Fu hurried to Yuan Shang, who had begun his march to the west: he was given an audience immediately, and he began his report with a request that the army change direction and march southwards, towards the region to the east of Yè.
"I will do no such thing!" Yuan Shang insisted. "You're not the only one to suggest it, and that saddens me! What good is there in putting our men on 'death ground' before a major relief effort...?"
"That's precisely where they need to be," Li Fu protested. "I've just passed through most of Ji Province, seen their camps, and I've been in Yè: my lord, Handan City is lost, and the capital is surrounded by a stagnant moat and mounds of corpses. Hundreds

have died... many will be spared by the ruse that got me back here, but hundreds, thousands more are still trapped in the city, those who refused to flee for fear of being abandoned or those that wanted to stay with their relatives in the army... the enemy have completely surrounded the city, and-"

"None of what you say is a surprise," Yuan Shang retorted. "You think I am detached...? My mother, my wife and consorts and young children, and many of my loyal vassals are trapped in that city! My father's temple has not been honoured, and it might be desecrated if the enemy seize the city! A lot of my family's possessions, including many irreplaceable heirlooms, are in that city! I might, in fact, have more to lose than any of you that dare to question me!"

Li Fu sighed and stared at Xun Chen, who smiled strangely.

"We will attack from the northwest," Yuan Shang continued. "We will have our backs to Gao Gan, then, instead of my hankering, treacherous brother. That, I think, will serve us better than being in a pincer: we can then catch Cao in a pincer and rescue my capital before there are any more losses. Did you discuss what you were sent in there to discuss...?"

"...Yes, my lord," Li Fu replied. "They await our signal."

"Then we advance to Handan!" Yuan Shang said. "Victory is near!"

The Inspector of Liang Province, Wei Kang, heard of Du Ji's success in winning the trust of the Qiang warlords and started to lose his own trust in Cao Cao's appointed Magistrate of Xiping: he asked his assistant Yang Fu and military adviser Zhao Ang to come to his study to discuss it privately.

"Fear not," Zhao Ang insisted. "Du Ji is as loyal as any of us."

"Are we sure...?" Wei Kang fretted. "The last men that got on so well with the Qiang were *Dong Zhuo* and *Liu Yan*!"

"Both men were powerful warlords with armies: Du Ji has a handful of officials that were allocated to him by His Excellency, and the military in Xiping is tiny," Zhao Ang replied. "I've been in correspondence with Du Ji, Inspector, and it's just the case that he's a good judge of character: he's appealing to majority of the Qiang chieftains as the strength-revering simpletons that they are, but when it comes to Ma Teng and Han Sui he plays on their origins as Han officials and reassures them that he is not 'a Cheng Qiu or Geng Bi'."

"...Geng Bi was a greedy fool that caused Ma Teng's defection from the Han," Wei Kang noted. "Cheng Qiu... yes, I remember those two. I hope that Du Ji takes care to note that we're not like them either when he makes these grand statements of his."

"Of course... and he also makes it clear that he isn't another Li Xiangru either, which is for our benefit as well as theirs," Zhao Ang replied. "Of course, Li's surrendering of Longxi was crucial to the success of Han Sui's rebellion..."

"He knows his history of the area," Yang Fu said. "He's certainly the right man in every respect."

"...So he is," Wei Kang decided. "Perhaps peace *is* possible...!"

****

49

Yuan Shang's 10,000-strong army marched toward the western edge of Ji Province, collecting supplies as they travelled. Yuan Tan pursued for some time, but only to ensure that his brother left Pingyuan County far behind: he then instructed his small army to concentrate on seizing control of every major settlement in Bohai Prefecture, starting with the city of Nanpi.

Neither of the Yuan brothers' movements escaped Cao Cao's attention: he was angry that Yuan Tan had chosen to ignore Yuan Shang and build a power base instead, but the delight at learning that Shang was taking a longer, less dangerous route to relieve Yè City offset any anger considerably.

"I told you all, did I not, that I was hoping for our enemy to take the cautious path?" Cao Cao said to his assembled officers. "I have invited you all here to the command tent to tell you that my scouts report that Yuan Shang has gone west, intending no doubt to reclaim Handan before marching south to relieve Yè."

"...And that's good...?" Xiahou Dun prompted.

"What, you didn't know that Ji Province is already mine...?" Cao Cao chuckled. "You'll see it clearly soon enough!"

"...Are you alright, Mengde...?" Cao Hong asked.

"I am just fine," Cao Cao insisted. "I am not afflicted: the signs are there for the enlightened to see, and soon the victory will be there for all to see. We must do our part though, and not leave our enemies' destruction entirely to them! We will advance at once and prepare to engage Yuan Shang and Shen Pei!"

"Shen Pei...?" Cao Hong exclaimed. "What-?"

"You'll see!" Cao Cao promised. "You'll see soon enough!"

Yuan Shang began a military reclamation of the Handan region with the help of General Ju Hu, who had fled the city during its capture and fled to a nearby village: once the smaller settlements were back under Yuan control, Shang gathered his officers and said, "We now go to Yangping."

"We passed that place on the way here!" Ma Yan cried.

"Why would we go back to that little village when we've just exhausted the men marching all the way here...?" Yin Kui asked.

"Cao Cao will never suspect that we're going to attack from Yangping!" Yuan Shang cackled. "This will ensure his downfall, as well as the relief of my capital! And with Handan restored to our control, it will not take long for us to regain Maocheng, re-establish contact with Cousin Gan and bring his men here to drive the old villain into an early grave!"

"...You're leaving Ju Hu here with that kind of task...?" Li Fu asked.

"He's survived being routed and rebuilt his militia," Yuan Shang replied. "I trust him to do this for me. He will have the help of Xun Chen and of Jiang Yiqu's men that fled here when Jiang was surprised at Yè and presumably killed... or maybe he has survived and will reappear to aid us when we liberate Yè."

"There are too many presumptions in your analysis," Li Fu said.

"And what do you know...?" Yuan Shang retorted. "You think that you are a master strategist because you fooled a few sentries and carried a message or two...? I was taught the art of war by my father's tutors, and I carry the very same copy of Sun Tzu's text that my father used throughout his life!"

"...I will say no more," Li Fu sighed.

"Once we reach Yangping, we'll wait until nightfall and light a signal fire as arranged," Yuan Shang continued. "When Shen Pei responds, we'll begin our surprise advance and destroy our enemy! General Zhang Yi, General Ma Yan: prepare your men for the glorious victory that awaits us! Even Sun Tzu would marvel at the way that we will turn this situation around and bring an end to Cao Cao once and for all!"

"As you command," Zhang Yi replied.

"...As you command, Lord Yuan," Ma Yan said tonelessly.

Yuan Shang's army marched to Yangping Village, which sat on the bank of the Fu River that ran toward Yè City. The towering signal fire that Yuan Shang's men lit could be seen from a great distance away: Shen Pei laughed when it was reported to his court.

"Can we be sure that it's our allies, Uncle...?" Shen Rong asked.

Shen Pei waved his hand dismissively and said, "Of course it is! This is our last day of suffering these terrible conditions, gentlemen! Gao Fan: respond with our own fire at once! The rest of you: ready the crossing bridges and prepare to open the northern gates!"

The officials touched their right fists to their chests and responded as one.

An hour passed: the northern gates of Yè City opened, and an army of 3,000 weary, hungry men marched forth under cover of darkness with Shen Pei at the helm; Yuan Shang advanced southward with 7,000 of his men in order to rendezvous with his chief adviser.

But the two armies would never meet: Shen Pei cried out in anguish when his way was blocked by Zhang Liao, who asked, **"Where do you think you're headed...?"**

"Fight, fight for your lives!" Shen Pei ordered, but it was futile: Su Yòu, Li Dian and Cao Hong attacked from other directions and drove Shen Pei back to Yè City.

"And that's where you'll stay!" Cao Hong cackled as Shen Pei disappeared into the open gateway: Hong was forced to retreat after the defenders fired arrows into the darkness at Gao Fan's command, but the desired outcome had been achieved.

Yuan Shang fared little better: Cao Cao, Cao Pi, Cao Chun, Cao Xiu, Yu Jin, Xu Huang and an army of 5,000 men awaited him on the route to Yè, and the river was to his left, preventing free movement. The shock of being attacked during a supposedly secret sortie caused many of Yuan Shang's men to panic: some attacked anyone and everyone, while others tried to flee and fell into the river, where many drowned.

"We're being routed!" Yuan Shang cried.

"Cao Cao is poorly guarded!" Ma Yan noted. **"I will charge at him personally!"**

Ma Yan took ten of his elite men and fought past Cao Cao's infantry, but they had forgotten about Cao Cao's bodyguard, Xu Chu: the giant knocked one rider from his horse with one swipe of his heavy halberd, kicked a second to the ground, turned his horse and took hold of the throat of a third rider, lifting him from his horse.

"Cao Cao has a demon for a guardian!" Ma Yan said as he turned and fled.

"HELP ME!" the captured man shrieked.

"You're beyond help," Cao Cao chuckled.

Xu Chu twirled his halberd and stuck it into the ground so that he could drive his chubby fingers into the eye sockets of his captive.

"Don't *play with him*, you fat fool! Just kill him! NOW!" Xu Yòu screeched.

"Yes... kill him, Zhongkang," Cao Cao ordered.

Xu Chu snapped the howling captive's neck and let his body fall to the ground before retrieving his halberd.

"Have we won...?" Xu Yòu wondered.

"...We have won," Cao Cao said.

Yuan Shang's army was in full retreat; Cao Cao gave no orders, which started to unnerve and irritate Xu Yòu.

"...So we're pursuing...?" Xu Yòu asked at last.

"We are," Cao Cao replied. **"At once."**

Yuan Shang returned to Yangping, but the village was now under the control of Lü Kuang and Lü Xiang, who had scattered the 2,000 men that had been left there.

"Traitors!" Yuan Shang screamed. **"Traitors to your true lord! Heaven will punish you for your ways!"**

But Cao Cao's army had pursued relentlessly: Yuan Shang was caught in a pincer, which led to more loss of life as men fell into the river or suffered an attack by Cao Chun's cavalry.

"We shall go west!" Yuan Shang cried. **"West to Quzhang, where we can regroup!"**

The Yuan army began another humiliating retreat.

Cao Cao did not pursue Yuan Shang immediately: he allowed his men to rest and spent some time wandering around and reassuring the inhabitants of Yangping. Scouts reported Yuan Shang's movements in the early evening, after Cao Cao himself had taken a much-needed rest; he gathered his officers in the command tent of his temporary camp and had the scouts relay what they had learned.

"So he's gone to Quzhang," Cao Cao said.

Xu Yòu looked at the battle map and said, "I don't know where he'd go from there."

"It's another river position," Cao Cao replied. "He's not given up on the idea of defeating me, it seems... even after this. He's as stubborn as his father was."

"But Quzhang's main settlement is a small city, and hence a better defensive position that Yangping," Xu Yòu noted. "He's maybe preparing for a siege...?"

"I don't want to juggle two sieges at once," Cao Cao replied.

"Should we ask Yuan Tan to contribute...?" Cao Chun asked.

"He's 'conducting his own business'," Cao Cao said. "We'll have to do this ourselves: how many men is Shang likely to have now...?"

"Far from the ten-thousand he had to begin with... perhaps half, or even less," Xu Yòu replied. "I'm guessing that he has not done much to earn their loyalty: Ma Yan and Zhang Yi are still with him,

unfortunately, but if that changes..."
"...Then we will advance to Quzhang, surround him, and crush his army utterly, leaving nothing for his brothers to salvage," Cao Cao decided. "We shall end Yuan rule in Ji Province *now*."

While Cao Cao began his advance to Quzhang, Jia Xu oversaw the surrounding of Yè City to prevent further excursions by Shen Pei; Shen visited Lady Liu to inform her of the failure to rendezvous with her son Yuan Shang. Yuan Xi's wife, Lady Zhen, quietly watched the discussion from the doorway, as she was eager to know whether Xi would be invited to aid the relief of Yè.
"...And judging by the lack of pressure that the enemy faced, it is safe to assume that they routed Lord Yuan as well," Shen Pei concluded. "We've had no signs at all... so he was routed or has been forced to abandon us."
"...My son will return," Lady Liu insisted. "When he sees that I am in danger, and that his father's great legacy is at risk, he will certainly return..."
"...But why does he not seek aid from my husband...?" Lady Zhen proposed. "He-"
"I did not ask for your contribution," Lady Liu heckled. "In fact, I did not allow you to be present! **Get out!**"
"I seek to help!" Lady Zhen protested. "And I am the lord's sister-in-law!"
"**And I am the lord's *mother*!**" Lady Liu snapped. "**Were he the sovereign, I would be *Dowager*: would you dare to challenge me then...? I think not! But as the mother of a lord that rules a quarter of the Empire, I am suddenly *unimportant*, am I...?**"
"...I will withdraw," Lady Zhen murmured.
"Silly girl," Lady Liu scoffed as Lady Zhen retreated. "She was spoiled by having her own money: her father should have ensured that she married before he died so she didn't get any ideas above her place."
"...I should go as well," Shen Pei said. "I have to watch the walls."
"Yes, go," Lady Liu ordered. "And do not lose faith in my son: he will return..."

****

50

Yuan Shang became increasingly desperate as Cao Cao tightened his grip on northern Ji Province. The Yuan chieftain's army only numbered around 6,000, and it was then reported that Handan County had fallen for a second time; the victors made it clear that Ju Hu and Xun Chen had not survived, and although some strongly doubted the fact, most accepted it with regret. Cao Cao's army was now gathering around Quzhang, and it became clear that difficult decisions needed to be made.

"...So Shen Pei is trapped in Yè, while I am trapped here," Yuan Shang said soberly. "What should I do...?"

"You have a few options," Yin Kui replied. "You can submit to Yuan Tan in exchange for his help, though he might just kill you and take your army for himself; you can submit to Cao Cao, who, *if* he accepts your submission, will no doubt strip you of your wealth and power but let you live in order to humiliate you and make you an example to others that defy him; you can ask the Wuhuan for aid, and hope that your current weakness doesn't drive them toward Cao Cao or Yuan Tan; or, lastly, you could ask Yuan Xi for aid and hope that he does not refuse for fear of angering Tan."

"...I must surrender to Cao Cao, then," Yuan Shang decided.

"As easily as that...?" Ma Yan exclaimed. "Your father-!"

"Leave Father out of this!" Yuan Shang barked. **"Was Father ever hemmed in by a river, with nothing but a tiny, inconsequential city for defence and six-thousand men??? If I must submit to survive, then so be it!"**

Ma Yan muttered irritably.

"...I must do so now, while Quzhang is not yet compromised," Yuan Shang continued; he then turned to Chief Secretary Chen Lin and said, "You are a master of words, Mister Chen."

"He is indeed," Li Fu said dryly. "His denunciation of Cao Cao is quite famous."

"Shut up!" Yuan Shang barked. **"Regardless of its content, it was a well-written document that presented its arguments succinctly and professionally!"**

"And it is a document that is certain to shorten my life if Cao wins," Chen Lin sighed.

"I... I know that you have reservations, but I don't think that Cao Cao will harm you," Yuan Shang said. "Turn your marvellous talent to penning the letter to him: make him understand that I submit sincerely in order to prevent further bloodshed!"

"I... shall set to work at once," Chen Lin replied.

"Good, good," Yuan Shang said. "And then you and Mister Yin can deliver the submission to Cao Cao and-"

"*What*...?" Zhang Yi exclaimed. "So you're going to kneel to Cao Cao, throwing away over a hundred years of Yuan clan achievements... and you're going to send both Yin Kui and *Chen Lin* to do it???"

"Why send Chen's whole body, Lord Yuan, when all Cao wants is his head...?" Ma Yan scoffed. "I'm sure Yin Kui wouldn't mind carrying it."

"Stop questioning me, all of you!" Yuan Shang bellowed. **"I am your *lord*! No, I am not happy with this, but it is my only**

proper option! And as my vassals, you should be pledging to share my fate, not heckling me!"
The larger number of officials murmured uneasily.
"...And you can stop that muttering as well, all of you," Yuan Shang ordered. "I... I *must* do this. As you were, Chen Lin... and when your words are prepared, I will provide the seal, and then you and Mister Yin can go, and then we can be done with this unfortunate matter."
"...At once, Lord Yuan," Chen Lin replied as he looked at Li Fu, who was visibly sympathetic but utterly powerless to intervene.

Cao Cao laughed when he learned of the negotiators' arrival at his camp: he had Yin Kui and Chen Lin brought to the command tent and said, "Well, well... it's been quite a while, hasn't it, Mister Chen Kongzhang."
"...It has," Chen Lin replied meekly.
"Kill him!" Xiahou Dun cried. **"Kill that wretched-!"**
"No, Yuanrang... no," Cao Cao replied gently. "Now then, gentlemen: once again, I am surprised and disappointed by what I learn of your lord Yuan Shang. I'm sure that I am not alone in saying that this plea to submit is a pitiful end to the great Yuan clan, and that your lord is a selfish, hankering coward that conspired with Shen Pei and Pang Ji to steal his brother's claim to the chieftainship, repeating and going beyond Yuan Shu's earliest crime, but lacks the strength to keep what he steals; I also doubt that I am alone in saying that when this desperate moment – a moment born of stupidity and failure to recognise obvious danger – came about, your lord's first instinct was to save himself, tacitly offering Chen Lin as a sacrifice to satiate me and reduce the likelihood that I will hurt him for dragging me here for a second time to rein him in."
Yin Kui was silent; Chen Lin laughed nervously and said, "Lord Yuan has received some criticism for submitting, Excellency."
"...And how do you feel, gentlemen, now that you are here...?" Cao Cao asked. "I am angry at your lord; I am angry at his subordinates; I am especially angry at Chen Lin, whose words portrayed me as the worst of villains, a creature more despicable than Dong Zhuo... is that what you suppose...?"
"It... is an obvious inference," Yin Kui replied.
"...There will be no easy end," Cao Cao declared. "Your lord, Yuan Shang, has brought shame upon the clan and–"
"He's offering to submit!" Xu Yòu interrupted. "*Accept*, Mengde, and then–!"
"Silence!" Cao Cao barked. **"We are not alone in a room drinking tea right now, Xu Yòu, so act as you find!"**
Xu Yòu hung his head and muttered angrily.
"...I do not mean to shout, Ziyuan, but please do not interrupt me, for I have a reason for my aggressive stance," Cao Cao said as he returned his gaze to the terrified envoys. "I was Yuan Benchu's friend... you, of all men, know that well, Chen Kongzhang. Yes, he was muddle-headed, and yes, he could be pompous... but never, ever was he a coward. If he had been faced with this situation, he would fight to the last man, as he once fought the 'Ten' in the palace despite being under threat of arrest for high treason, and those men that he commanded would follow him gladly; he would

keep talents close, and do his best to save them, as he once saved the 'partisans' that those same eunuchs tormented for so many years. I have had many a conversation with Chen Qun, whose father and grandfather suffered exile and Yuan Benchu's protection, and he sometimes admitted that fighting Benchu saddened him... as it saddened me."

Xu Yòu snorted irritably.

"And so I would not be doing Benchu a service by allowing his runt of a third son to throw away generations of earned fame, fortune and power to save his own lousy life, would I...?" Cao Cao continued. "And yes, I had hate in my heart when I read your denunciation, Kongzhang... but I am a stronger man than most."

"...I am lost," Yin Kui admitted.

"You're not the only one," Xu Yòu muttered.

"Here I am, surrounded by Benchu's former allies!" Cao Cao chuckled. "How strange life is...!"

"...It is," Chen Lin replied timidly.

Cao Cao smiled and said, "Now, Mister Yin Kui, I will clarify things for you. There will, as I said, be no easy peace: Yuan Shang will fight and die a warrior's death as his father wanted, and earn something resembling a reputation so that I can face Benchu's temple and tell him that his son was a worthy opponent. You will deliver that answer of mine to your lord... and Chen Kongzhang will remain here."

Yin Kui looked at Chen Lin and smiled sympathetically.

"But Kongzhang will remain here to ensure his preservation, not his death, as his lord no doubt intended," Cao Cao continued. "Kongzhang is a fine scholar... Yuan Shang does not know how to use men properly. I do."

"...Reconsider!" Yin Kui pleaded.

"I'm afraid not," Cao Cao replied. "You may go now, Mister Yin."

Chen Lin and Yin Kui exchanged terrified glances as Yin was escorted from the tent by two of Xiahou Dun's soldiers.

"Now the other one's gone, you can kill that little bastard!" Xiahou Dun cackled. "He should die a thousand times for what he-!"

"I am a man of my word, Cousin," Cao Cao insisted. "Kongzhang will be spared."

Xiahou Dun scowled and said, "Oh, Mengde, you really-!"

"I spared Jia Xu for a lot more," Cao Cao replied. "Kongzhang can now write for the Han as he once did, years ago, before all of this madness engulfed us."

"I will do anything for the Han, Excellency," Chen Lin promised.

"...Tell me, Kongzhang: who was it that carried the message into Yè, and then escaped with such cunning...?" Cao Cao asked.

"That would be Li Fu, The Registrar of Ji Province," Chen Lin replied. "I beseech you, Excellency, to spare him if you are offered the chance, as you did me."

"I will *employ him* if I can!" Cao Cao chuckled. "I should direct you toward Yang Xiu – who is a fine scholar that is now in my employ – and whose mother is Benchu's sister..."

"I recognise him," Chen Lin said as he looked at the slim, frail trainee registrar and smiled warmly; Yang Xiu smiled and bowed slightly in return.

"So you can trust me when I say that I will employ any able man if I can," Cao Cao continued. "I am not petty, Kongzhang."

"...I wish that I could say the same for Lord Yuan Shao or his sons," Chen Lin said with absolute honesty. "I served Lord Yuan Shao because he was a great man, and I still say that he was, right to the last, despite losing his way; Yuan Shang has squandered opportunities, misused men, intrigued when it was not necessary and lost a massive army by himself. His mother has more influence in Yè than the advisers do, and although I do not consider Yuan Tan to be as great as his father, he can surely not be worse than Yuan Shang, who has already done irreparable damage to the Yuan name."

"...Perhaps I should have you write another denunciation!" Cao Cao chuckled.

"I speak as I find," Chen Lin replied. "Or, where I am not close enough to find, I speak as I see or hear... though that might not always be right."

"You do not need to apologise," Cao Cao insisted. "You did as you were asked, and I left myself open to criticism. My complaint is not with you, but the man that commissioned the document, for he was no less flawed, and should have known better than to resort to what he once decried his brother for."

"...Indeed," Chen Lin replied.

"You should go with Yang Xiu, who will provide you with accommodation and arrange for you to travel to Li County," Cao Cao continued. "I may have need of you as a negotiator later on."

"If I can bring about peace, then instruct me and I shall obey, Your Excellency," Chen Lin replied.

Cao Cao nodded, and Yang Xiu escorted Chen Lin from the tent after a brief exchange of polite bows.

"...So we spared him after all," Xiahou Dun grumbled. "And what about Yuan Shang...?"

"There will be no mercy for him," Cao Cao replied. "We will intensify the pressure on Quzhang and either drive him from Ji Province or kill him outright."

"That, at least, is *something*," Xu Yòu said angrily.

Yuan Shang was ashen-faced and silent after Yin Kui delivered Cao Cao's response.

"So what was achieved in the end???" Ma Yan cried. "We've lost Chen Lin: that's all that came of it!"

"...We will just have to fight as valiantly as we can," Yin Kui said.

"We've lost another hundred men since you left, Mister Yin, and mainly to desertion!" Zhang Yi heckled. "Quzhang is no place to expect a victory!"

"But nonetheless, we must hold!" Yin Kui protested. "Perhaps we can write to Yuan Xi and request assistance!"

"...Yuan Xi will dither, because he has local problems," Li Fu said.

"He cannot **afford** to dither!" Yuan Shang bellowed. "**Our clan is on the verge of losing all that our ancestors fought so hard to gain! Write at once, Li Fu: he *must* aid me, or he is as guilty as Tan and I are of failing in our duty!**"

"...This is resolve that should have been shown already, or perhaps 'never lost'," Zhang Yi complained. "I have had a lot of trouble preventing men from rebelling and defecting because they see you as weak, Lord Yuan! There are, or were, a quarter of a million men that serve the Yuan cause across the four provinces:

show strength, earn their respect again and turn this around!"
"If it is at all possible, then I shall!" Yuan Shang promised.

A northbound messenger barely escaped Quzhang before Cao Cao's enormous army surrounded the city and laid siege to it: the civilians and regular defenders were ill-prepared for the horrors that now faced them, and there were repeated attempts to throw the gates open to the enemy. Yuan Shang assembled his tiny group of officials after several days of resistance and said, "There's not enough food in the city depot for a long siege, and nothing to throw at them from the walls except pebbles and planks: what can I do now...?"
"You can either hold here and wait to see if Yuan Xi sends help," Yin Kui replied, "or you can escape when it's dark and go somewhere else that is easier to defend."
"I suggest Lankou, in the Qi Hills, if we do flee," Li Fu said. "If the waters are running down from that place it will impede attacks, and it is high ground regardless."
"...I will leave," Yuan Shang decided. "My request to submit did a lot of damage to the morale of the locals, and the river is more of an impediment than a benefit... especially if Cao decides to use it to flood this place as he did to Yè. How soon can we get out of here without abandoning too many supplies...?"
"We can leave tonight," Yin Kui replied.
"...So our supply situation is that bad," Yuan Shang sighed.
"We'll need to confiscate the city's supplies," Yin Kui said. "We'll do that and then flee before Cao Cao can get in or be let in."
"...Yes," Yuan Shang agreed. "Tonight it is."

Cao Cao ordered his men to abandon the city walls as night fell: Yuan Shang's small army retreated within hours, but Cao refused to pursue immediately.
"I know we need to worry about 'cornered tigers', Mengde, but that's a pretty feeble and mangy tiger that just fled," Xu Yòu said.
"He's running out of places to run to," Cao Cao replied. "Fengxiao's written to suggest that he might run to Lankou, in the Qi Hills, since that provides natural-"
"REPORT...!"
Cao Cao turned to the newly-arrived messenger, who added, **"Yuan Tan has seized Bohai and Hejian Prefectures and is advancing to take Anping!"**
"He's taking Ji for himself!" Xu Yòu exclaimed. **"Mengde, you cannot let him-!"**
"Hush," Cao Cao whispered as he smiled at the messenger and gestured that he should leave the command tent; once the messenger was gone, Cao Cao turned to Xu Yòu and said, "You must learn to control your temper, Ziyuan."
"That was a trusted man reporting just now!" Xu Yòu protested.
"Yes, but I would prefer that we didn't let the lower ranks see us panicking," Cao Cao replied calmly. "I am as anxious to be rid of the Yuan brothers as you are, but we must be careful. Until Yuan Shang is defeated or destroyed, I cannot fight Tan."
"...So we're going to let him take over Ji...?" Xu Yòu asked. "Doesn't his increased might risk his impressing the Wuhuan...?"
"He's seizing the cities and forcibly recruiting men, and yes, if he

becomes too powerful, the Wuhuan will, as you say, transfer allegiance to him," Cao Cao replied. "The Wuhuan tribes have stayed out of this so far, perhaps sensing that Shang is not the great leader that Benchu was, and yes, Tan is potentially more impressive, I know... but I have found a man to deal with that later, when it is safe to confront him. For now, Yuan Tan cannot risk confronting me either, not until his brother is vanquished... and once Shang's army is pushed out of Ji, I intend to force Tan to be the one to end Shang's life if he still lives."
"How...?" Xu Yòu asked.
"Let's see where Shang runs to next," Cao Cao replied. "If he goes to the hills, we will defeat him there; if he goes to Yòu Province, we'll turn around and very noisily return to Yè to finish the siege."
"...But doesn't pushing Shang into Xi's territory and then forcing Tan to confront one or both of them risk the three meeting, reconciling and turning their swords against you...?" Xu Yòu asked.
"Maybe," Cao Cao said, "but in the end, we've won."

****

51

Yuan Shang's militia assembled in the Lankou area of the western Qi Hills and awaited Cao Cao's next move: few expected a direct attack on an elevated position, so Yuan Shang relaxed and took the opportunity to draft letters to his allies around the northeast.

"I will write to Xi again, reminding him of the urgency of the situation," Yuan Shang said to Registrar Li Fu. "In addition to that, I'll speed a man to Yè to let them know that we live, so they don't yield the city... and I'll contact Louban and Tadun as well."

"Be careful in your dealings with the Wuhuan," Li Fu warned. "They're showing no signs of lending us support instinctively, and we've received a report that suggests that Yuan Tan is in the process of taking Bohai Prefecture: he might have done so in the time since that report, and perhaps moved on to other places."

"...Maybe I should write to him as well, and remind him that we are bound by blood, and that his support for Cao Cao is ultimately self-destructive," Yuan Shang replied. "Perhaps... perhaps I should consider relinquishing the chieftainship to him in exchange for that support. Tan will wrest the chieftainship from me with Cao's help if I don't cede it, but as Cao is certain to betray Tan afterward, such an act might preserve the Yuan clan in the long-term."

"...And *you*, my lord, in the short-term," Li Fu noted.

"I care not for my own well-being!" Yuan Shang snapped. "I tried to submit to spare the people, Li Fu! I only consider tendering the chieftainship to Tan in order to protect my father's legacy! Father wanted me to inherit his power, but if the current situation renders that impossible, then-!"

"REPORT!"

"...Speak," Yuan Shang said as he turned to his messenger.

"C-Cao Cao has begun a-an attack on Lankou!" the soldier continued. **"Zhang Yi and Ma Yan recommend that we-!"**

"I will fight!" Yuan Shang said as he leapt to his feet. **"Come, Li Fu! Let us fight valiantly, as Yin Kui has suggested!"**

Yuan Shang joined his generals in battle, but his cause was already lost: Cao Chun's cavalry was leading an uphill charge with Zhang Liao, Xu Huang, Li Dian, Cao Hong and Cao Xiu providing infantry support and additional horsemen, and the defenders had procured little more than some medium-sized rocks and a few logs to roll down the hill. The overconfidence that many of Yuan Shang's lower-ranked officers had shown since reaching the high ground was now their downfall, as the incline could only provide protection when the defenders made the proper use of it; the attackers were even able to ride past the defenders and attack from an even higher position, and that was enough to break the defenders' resolve and scatter them.

"Enough!" Zhang Yi bellowed as he found himself confronted by Xu Huang and Li Dian. **"I have had enough..."**

Ma Yan saw that his colleague had surrendered and quickly did the same, along with most of his subordinates; Li Fu was separated from Yuan Shang and surrounded by Cao Hong's men, but he managed to break free of the entrapment and rendezvoused with Yuan Shang and Yin Kui, who had started a retreat to the north.

"We have him, Mengde!" Xu Yòu cried as a scout finished

making a report to the commanders at the foot of the hills. **"If we
pursue Yuan Shang now, it is over!"**

"...**Pursue...? ...Into Yòu Province...? ...No, Ziyuan... now
he's his older brothers' problem, Xi and Tan both,"** Cao Cao
replied. **"Yuan Shang's fangs and claws are blunted, but he
hides in the den of a second tiger with fangs and claws that
are very much intact, and I have no friends in Yòu
Province. We must turn our attentions back to Shen Pei,
using the spoils of this campaign as propaganda to force
his submission before Yuan Tan completes his acquisition
of Anping and Ganling and moves to take the city himself:
and don't dismiss for a moment the notion that others
beside Shen Pei would rather yield to a Yuan than to me,
and that Shen Pei might not be 'overruled', shall we say.
The man that controls Yè City controls Ji Province... and it
is not reserved for the most powerful Yuan. I would like it
to be _me_... for the Han."**

"...I don't like it, but... you're right," Xu Yòu conceded.

Yuan Tan had spies monitoring Cao Cao's progress against his
younger brother; he was still preoccupied with taking control of
northern Ji Province, which typically involved taking the cities by
way of a siege and forcing the magistrates and administrators to
submit. Yuan Tan was in the process of sieging a small city in
Anping Prefecture when Yuan Shang's defeat at Quzhang was
finally reported; Tan turned his attention away from the walls and
said, "This is excellent! Shang is worm food and without me
moving a muscle! My enemy does my work for me! If Shang can
just hold on for a few weeks more...! ...And then I can finish taking
the north and go and take Yè while he distracts Cao for me!"

"Don't underestimate Cao's cunning," the adviser Xin Ping warned.

"...Indeed," Xin Pi said reluctantly. "He might leave Yuan Shang's
ultimate fate for you to decide."

"...Why would he do that?" Yuan Tan scoffed.

"Would he dare divide his forces further and invade Yòu when he
can barely maintain the siege of Yè and fight an exhausted Shang
simultaneously...?" the adviser Guo Tu asked pointedly.

"...A fair point," Yuan Tan admitted. "But then I don't want to
invade Yòu Province either, really, do I, Mister-"

A sudden chorus of cheering interrupted the discussion: Yuan
Tan's soldiers had reached the battlements of the sieged city and
were in the process of overwhelming the tiny defence force so that
they could open the gates.

"...A 'textbook siege victory', methinks," Guo Tu chuckled. "Our
fourth, and with less than fifty casualties between them...! If only
every siege was this easy... except for the ones that our enemies
undertake, of course."

"Of course," Xin Pi said coldly.

"...We'll monitor Cao and see what he does," Yuan Tan declared.
"If he does leave Shang alive, I'll have to drop everything and go
and destroy him before he goes whining to Xi and gets
reinforcements. I've got a lot more men now, so I can defeat him
easily enough if he's got less than five thousand now, right...?"

"Yes... but as I said, be careful," Xin Ping replied. "Don't forget
that every place that we 'liberate' adds another displaced militia to

the potential list of sources that Yuan Shang could look to for reinforcements. And while we're spying on Cao, Cao will be spying on us... don't forget that either."
Xin Pi smiled and said, "My brother is right, Lord Yuan."
"Let him spy," Yuan Tan chuckled. "In fact, I will send you to update Cao Cao on my exploits, Xin Pi! You can go at once!"
"...As you command," Xin Pi said cautiously.
"You can stay with him then, and keep me informed of things!" Yuan Tan continued. "All that their spies will see is victory after victory: the true lord of the Yuan clan reclaiming that which is his by right! And soon enough, I'll have Yè for my capital and the heads of my enemies for sacrifices to Father's temple! It is Heaven's will!"

The battle at Lankou was definitive: Yuan Shang had been forced to abandon anything that was not essential to survival when he began his retreat toward the border with Yòu Province, and that included state seals, standards and valuables. Cao Cao had his army march back to Yè City so that he could parade the captured articles at the foot of Ye's eastern wall and show the defenders that resistance was pointless; Shen Pei fought tears of rage as he retreated to the governor's mansion and prepared to address his demoralised followers.
"It isn't over, no matter what that collection of *supposed* spoils of a *supposed* victory over our lord conveys!" Shen Pei said defiantly. "They've surrounded us with water, starved us, beaten us back when we've tried to charge and mocked us relentlessly, but we have not yielded: why should we now give up...?"
"...Because we're holding this city for our lord," Wei Prefecture Administrator Gao Fan retorted. "If our lord is gone, then we're holding the city for some other reason."
"Are you accusing me of maintaining a defence to save myself at the expense of others, Mister Gao...?" Shen Pei asked angrily.
"Are you...?" Gao Fan countered.
"We serve the Yuan clan, Mister Gao, and the Yuan clan is resilient!" Shen Pei said. "Yes, Lord Yuan Shang has been routed, and he has lost his standard, but where is his head, or the rest of his body for that matter...? If Cao Cao had that to parade, he would do it, but he does not!"
Yuan Shang's mother, Lady Liu, sobbed audibly as she cowered in her hiding place behind a curtain on the left side of the hall.
"...Lord Yuan Shang is very much alive, safe, and out of Cao's reach, no doubt in Yòu Province, where he will be seeking support from his allies, which is why Cao Cao ran back here and started waving that captured standard!" Shen Pei continued. "Cao Cao is desperate to trick us into surrendering before Lord Yuan Shang returns with an army of Wuhuan cavalrymen from Yòu Province and overwhelms Cao's gaggle of defectors, stolen armies and bandits in soldier's clothing! *Hold*, gentlemen, and we will look back on this day as one of our finest!"
The officials murmured agreeably; Gao Fan sighed and said, "You pose a valid point, Mister Shen... so I will stand at your side and continue to hold. Let's hope that the relief arrives quickly."
"Look at how they dance and laugh, Mister Gao, and wonder why they put on such a show with such a small amount of actual proof

of victory," Shen Pei retorted. "I believe that it is not only a sign that aid is on its way, but that it is imminent! *Hold*, Mister Gao, and we can expect a victory in a month or much, much less!"
The officials cheered weakly and pledged that they would continue to hold the city with what energy they had left; Shen Rong turned to Shen Pei and asked, "Are you really so certain that help is on its way so soon, Uncle...?"
"We *hold*, Nephew," Shen Pei replied tersely. "We *hold*."
Shen Rong realised that Gao Fan might have been right about Shen Pei's real reason for maintaining the siege: he frowned, thought of his own young family, and made a difficult decision.

Yuan Tan's gradual takeover of northern Ji Province was still proceeding according to his plans when he received word that Cao Cao had retreated to Yè City without ensuring that Yuan Shang was captured or killed.
"That treacherous villain!" Yuan Tan cried. **"Now Shang is on his way to Yòu Province, where...!"**
"You were warned, Lord Yuan," Xin Ping said.
"...I must pursue and attack Shang before he can regroup or get assistance from my brother," Yuan Tan decided.
"My own attempts to contact Yuan Xi have gone unanswered, as though he is not even in his capital," Guo Tu said bemusedly. "Regardless of the situation thus far, he has responded to letters... this is very strange."
"He is probably ignoring me because I have been disinherited," Yuan Tan replied. "But he shall regret that decision... were we not born from the same father *and* mother...? Why, then, would he side with Lady Liu's dog...?"
"...His wife, Lady Zhen, is Lady Liu's hostage in Yè, so perhaps he has been warned off of speaking to you cordially," Xin Ping suggested. "If we rout Yuan Shang, he might join us in order to save his wife."
"Where *specifically* is Shang now...?" Yuan Tan asked.
"How can we know that...?" Guo Tu replied. "The information is always days old, no matter how quickly it gets here! But I suspect that he'll be somewhere in Zhongshan Prefecture, on the border, not in Yòu itself, not until he knows that his brother will help him and not kill him."
"...I have ten-thousand men now," Yuan Tan noted. "If half of them stay here in Ji and... ... ...yes! Let's leave at once! Send scouts ahead to track Shang down! We'll finish what Cao Cao started... and then, with Xi's help, we'll finish Cao Cao!"
"As you command," Xin Ping sighed.

Yuan Shang heard of Yuan Tan's swift approach within the next two days and expected the worst.
"There is still no word from Yuan Xi," Registrar Li Fu said. "It is as though he is not in his capital... but perhaps he ignores you because you-"
"I know," Yuan Shang interrupted. "I cannot be sure that he wouldn't side with Tan, what with their being full brothers and my only hold over Xi to this point being my mother having his wife as a hostage in all but name. No, Xi is more likely to take me captive and demand his wife's return... and Tan wants me dead for 'what I

have done'. No, I must defend... and I must win!"

"Without several decent field generals, that's unlikely," Yin Kui replied. "Yuan Tan is a ferocious man in battle."

"Whereas I am not," Yuan Shang sighed. "I know that too... but I must *try*!"

When Yuan Tan arrived at northern Zhongshan, he was in no mood for negotiating or giving his younger half-brother any chances: his army tore into Yuan Shang's ill-prepared forces and scattered them.

"**Regroup! REGROUP!**" Yuan Shang ordered desperately.

"**No, Lord Yuan: we are outmatched, and we must flee!**" Yin Kui replied. "**Flee first, Lord Yuan, and I will cover you!**"

Yuan Shang reluctantly took Yin Kui's advice and retreated before his brother could reach him.

Li Fu was separated from his lord once again, but he would not be able to evade capture for a second time: Xin Ping intercepted him with a group of riders and said, "**Registrar Li! You're quite a good catch for our net!**"

"**...I would rather die!**" Li Fu barked.

"**But we want you alive!**" Xin Ping retorted. "**Restrain Li Fu!**"

Li Fu was quickly overpowered and his bodyguards killed; the Registrar of Ji Province was then brought to Yuan Tan, who smirked silently.

"**...Kill me and be done with it!**" Li Fu shouted defiantly.

"**You'll remember your place as the servant of the true chieftain of the Yuan clan, Mister Li... and that true chieftain is me,**" Yuan Tan replied. "**You can think about it in prison... take him away!**"

"**We cannot find Yuan Shang, my lord,**" Xin Ping reported as three men took Li Fu toward a prison cart. "**Two lesser officers have also been captured, a Major Gan Li and-**"

"**Kill them,**" Yuan Tan ordered. "**They will set an example. And as for my wicked brother... we must pursue before he reaches Yòu Province! Onward!**"

Xin Ping advanced with the intent of capturing Yin Kui and adding to his reputation further: the armies of the two former colleagues met on a road edged with foliage and fought desperately, since both sides knew that reinforcements for the other could be on their way. Xin Ping appeared to have secured a victory after several minutes of intense battle, but Yin Kui was strangely calm as his enemy finished dispatching his rear guard and confronted him.

"**Surrender, Yin, or die a dog's death!**" Xin Ping shouted.

"**I'm not the one that's going to die a dog's death, Xin Ping!**" Yin Kui retorted; he then raised his arm, and, seconds later, a volley of arrows from the nearby foliage struck Xin Ping and his men. Yin Kui urged his horse forward a little so that he could look over Xin Ping's corpse; he then turned, raised his arm for a second time and cried, "**ONWARD!**" before leading his men northward once again.

"...*Aiee*...! What a waste...!" Guo Tu cried as his own forces reached the road where Xin Ping had fallen. "He... he is...!"

"**Men die!**" Yuan Tan barked. "**He slowed them down, which means he died a meaningful death! If you want to do**

something, Guo Tu, then avenge him!"

"…Of course," Guo Tu replied. "Someone… gather them for burial."

"**And the rest will continue!**" Yuan Tan urged. "**Death to my brother and his followers: death to them all!**"

Guo Tu stared at Xin Ping's body as he passed it; Xin's death had elevated Guo to the position of Yuan Tan's only senior adviser, but it also robbed him of an ally at a critical moment. Guo Tu grunted ambiguously and continued on his way.

Yuan Shang's remaining followers were repeatedly defeated as they moved northward: they were eventually forced to flee into Yòu Province, regardless of what reception they might get from the hitherto-silent Yuan Xi. Yuan Tan did not dare to cross into Xi's territory, even though he still feared Shang's revival: he returned to Anping instead to complete the takeover of the prefecture and grow his army.

****

52

In addition to tormenting Yè City's defenders with the spoils of his victories at Quzhang and Lankou, Cao Cao ordered the reconstruction of the mounds so that his men could fire upon the walls more easily: he personally supervised the work on a daily basis, despite repeated protestations by his officials.
"Excellent…!" Cao Cao chuckled as he watched his men pile earth onto a mound near the east wall: it was late in the afternoon, and the sky was clouding over as if it were about to rain.
"It's a mound of earth," Cao Hong sighed.
"It's more than that, Zilian," Cao Cao replied. "It's a show of strength… for they cannot topple them, no matter how much they want to. They're trapped, and soon, they will yield!"
The sector captain ran to Cao's horse and bowed humbly, saying, "Do not linger, Excellency! The enemy occasionally fire at us to slow our work!"
"I'm not afraid of their arrows, Captain," Cao Cao insisted.
"At least lower your standard, Mengde," Cao Hong pleaded. "What sense is there in advertising your presence…?"
"It depresses them further," Cao Cao retorted.
"…There's a lot of activity on the wall," Liu Yè noted.
"They always scurry around like that," Cao Cao replied dismissively. "Don't worry: we'll get some warning if they plan to start shooting at us."

Shen Pei was alerted to Cao Cao's presence near the east wall and travelled to the battlements to see for himself; the adviser cackled maniacally when he saw the Excellency of Works' standard and said, "We can end this campaign in a single moment! Administrator Gao: who is your best crossbowman…?"
"I have three expert shots on the south wall, and two on this wall," Gao Fan replied.
"Assemble them and have them begin firing!" Shen Pei ordered.
"But the light is poor!" Gao Fan protested. "Crossbow ammunition is precious and should be reserved for-!"
"What better target is there than the 'Crafty Villain' himself…?" Shen Pei retorted. **"Have them fire, damn you! Assemble them at once!**"

Within minutes, Cao Cao's horse was startled by a crossbow shot that barely missed Cao's right leg: a second shot struck the ground in front of the horse, and a third shot whistled past Cao's plumed helmet.
"Back!" Cao Hong cried. **"Your life is in danger, Mengde!"**
Cao Cao laughed and turned his horse to flee; a fourth shot missed him by a fraction, which led him to shout, **"Heaven itself deflects your shots, Shen Pei: can you not see it is over???"**
"You're impossible!" Cao Hong complained as he took Cao Cao's reins and led him away; more shots rained down, but none of them found their mark. The Han soldiers started to taunt the crossbowmen by repeating Cao Cao's defiant words: that only demoralised the defenders further.

"...I don't understand," Shen Pei said as he watched Cao Cao being led away from the wall. "Not one shot... not one... they hit *nothing*... not even his *horse*...!"

"I said that the light was bad," Gao Fan protested. "And the men are tired, Mister Shen, and the lack of good food has weakened them, affected their eyesight-"

"Your men are useless!" Shen Pei retorted. **"It takes no strength to fire a crossbow: I'd have had more luck if I'd shot at him myself: next time I *will*!"**

Gao Fan was going to say something else, but Shen Pei shoved him aside and retreated from the wall; the crossbowmen glared at Shen as he walked away. Gao Fan turned to Shen Rong and said, "Talk to your uncle, please, and explain that telling these men that they're useless is not a good way to retain their support."

"...I am not sure that I have the words to explain it to him," Shen Rong replied.

"Just *explain*!" Gao Fan said as Shen Rong walked away in a daze.

Cao Cao laughed about the 'crossbow incident' for the rest of the evening; Xu Yòu, Jia Xu and Cao Hong were not amused, and Xin Pi – who had just arrived – did not know what to think, but Guo Jia – who was feeling better – smiled and said, "Your luck has probably done more for our victory than the mounds will."

"That's exactly what I was thinking!" Cao Cao replied.

"Hopefully, Excellency, the end will come soon," Xin Pi said. "Yuan Tan is gathering men as easily as a farmer harvests grain after a good crop, and reports suggest that Ganling is likely to be his now in addition to the rest."

"I'm ready to deal with him," Cao Cao promised. "The exact timings of it all are now up to Shen Pei... and I doubt that he'll keep us waiting long."

"Yes," Guo Jia said. "Wenruo often refers to Shen as being 'strong-willed but tactless': he'll make more enemies than friends now, and hand himself over."

"He cannot do it soon enough," Xu Yòu sighed.

****

53

Three days passed: the mounds were rebuilt, and the walls of Yè City were once again exposed to elevated arrow fire. Shen Pei personally oversaw the defence of the walls, but the atmosphere was obviously tainted by Shen's increasing levels of abuse, physical and verbal, of the soldiers that he commanded. Some soldiers and civilians were secretly hoping that someone might betray the city and bring an end to their suffering: and when night fell, one man decided to do just that.

"Shen! Shen! We've been betrayed!"
Shen Pei sat up and turned his weary gaze toward Gao Fan, who had entered Shen's sleeping quarters in full armour.
"Did you hear me?" Gao Fan continued. **"The enemy are in the city! We must fight for our lives!"**
"…You *cannot be right*!" Shen Pei screeched. **"My *nephew*-!"**
"He's the one that let them in!" Gao Fan retorted. **"Now come on, man, before we lose any more ground! We have to repel them and close the east gate!"**
Shen Pei followed Gao Fan as far as the street, but the fighting was already close by and any chance of victory was long gone.
"What do we do???" Gao Fan asked.
"…They will not outlive me!" Shen Pei cried as he turned and ran toward a guarded house to the west.
"Who???" Gao Fan asked. **"Who do you…? Where are you going??? SHEN PEI! You are *needed*, Shen Pei! SHEN PEI!"**
Shen Pei ignored Gao Fan as he continued on his very personal journey to the house where a number of families – including those of Xin Pi, Xin Ping, Guo Tu and other 'traitors' – were being kept: he intended to slay them all before the night was over, since that was the only small victory that he could now salvage.

Wei Prefecture Administrator Gao Fan returned to the front line of the battle, but he did not last long: Cao Chun's cavalry were leading the charge as always, and their efficiency had already decimated the men that had rushed to the eastern gates to counter the breach. Some of Cao Chun's horsemen rode through the city to capture and then open the other gates before more of the defenders could be roused for battle while the infantry started to make its presence felt: the end was sudden and swift, and it was not long before a search was being conducted for Shen Pei and the other leaders that had survived.

Shen Pei was found on a western road, bound with rope and brought to an improvised execution ground in the centre of the city: Cao Cao looked the adviser up and down and asked, "Have you anything to say…?"
Shen Pei turned to his nephew, Shen Rong, and spat at him.
"You brought this on yourself!" Shen Rong shouted angrily.
"Shen killed my family!" Xin Pi cried. **"He deserves-!"**
"*I* shall decide what Shen Pei deserves," Cao Cao said. "Now I ask again: have you anything to say, Shen Pei…?"
Shen Pei turned his steely gaze to look at all of the men that Cao Cao had brought with him: Xu Yòu, Xin Pi, Lü Kuang, Lü Xiang, Su

Yòu and Zhang Hè were all glaring at him hatefully, as he had been at least partly responsible for their own decisions to leave the Yuan cause.

"...So many traitors," Shen Pei heckled. "I, Pei, choose to die as a Yuan loyalist, just as I lived. Those men are dogs."

"Kill him, Excellency!" Su Yòu implored. **"Even just for the kin of your followers that he's killed, you must-!"**

"I stand beside Jia Xu," Cao Cao interrupted. "Know that I strive to be an extraordinary man... a man that looks beyond the personal for the sake of the state. Shen Pei, I admit that you intrigue me: your loyalty and outspokenness at this late hour makes a mockery of your reputation as a self-serving, craven toady. Someone told me that you were trying to hide in a well, but I now find that hard to believe!"

"At this 'late hour', as you put it, I am surrounded by traitors, having just been betrayed by my own nephew, and I am looking at being remembered as the man that let Yè fall to the infamous 'Crafty Villain'," Shen Pei retorted. "The least I can do for my lord is reaffirm my pledge to him in my last moments."

"Your slanderous rhetoric turned us away from the Yuans and made us their enemies, just as it turned the Yuans away from the light and made them enemies of the Empire," Zhang Hè said. "You're evil, Shen Pei, and should not be left alive."

"It is a pity that I had no kin of yours to execute, Zhang Hè," Shen Pei retorted. "Yours was one of the worst betrayals of all, for it handed a complete victory to Cao Cao by relieving Guandu... after that wretch Xu Yòu had done the most damage by betraying the importance of Wuchao."

"I regret nothing but leaving family here for you to hurt," Xu Yòu said bitterly.

"I could spare you, Shen Pei," Cao Cao declared. "What have you to say to that...?"

Shen Pei harrumphed and said, "My only regret is that a mischievous demon deflected the bolts that my crossbowmen fired at you the other day! Heaven did not save you, Cao Cao: it was the netherworld lords that you serve!"

"Bastard!" Xiahou Dun cried.

Cao Cao laughed and said, "You are truly magnificent in such a situation, Shen Pei. Could you not turn your talents to serving the Han as you once did...?"

"*Ayah*! Do not offer this man work, my lord!" Xin Pi implored. **"He killed the kin that my brother and I left here in good faith! I cannot show the strength you show, Excellency, and work with such a man!"**

Cao Cao hummed thoughtfully.

"He's got a history of turning his lord's vassals against each other and conspiring to interfere with his lord's choice of successor," Jia Xu noted. "Such a man cannot be expected to serve well if he even betrays a lord that he claims to serve loyally."

"Kill him, Mengde!" Xu Yòu cried. **"This man slandered my wife and brought ruin to my family: remember the debt you owe me and kill him!"**

Many of the other officials added their voices to a growing chorus that demanded Shen Pei's execution: Cao Cao gestured that they should be silent and smiled at Shen Pei, saying, "It is out of my hands, I think."

"I was going to refuse your request anyway," Shen Pei replied. "I just have one request that even my enemies should not mind."

"**Grant him *nothing*!**" Xu Yòu heckled.

"...What do you 'request', Shen Pei...?" Cao Cao asked.

"I would like to be facing north at the moment of my death," Shen Pei replied. "That is where my lord is."

"...Your wish shall be granted," Cao Cao said. "Guards...!"

Shen Pei smiled as he was led to the spot where he would be beheaded; Cao Cao then turned his attentions to a group of former prisoners that had just arrived.

"Mister *Cui Yan*...!" Cao Cao chuckled. "Have you been in a cell all this time...?"

"I refused to choose which brother I served," Cui Yan replied. "My most recent accommodation was better, after Yin Kui and Chen Lin argued for me to be punished less severely. I understand that the Yuan brothers are still fighting."

"They are," Cao Cao said. "Will you now aid me, Jigui, in bringing an end to the chaos that they have brought down upon the people of Ji Province...?"

"I cannot," Cui Yan replied. "I owe the Yuans a debt of service, and so I must politely remain outside of your employ, at least for the time being."

"But I am the Excellency of Works," Cao Cao pleaded. "You would be serving the *Han*, Jigui! Chen Kongzhang is with me now, Cui Jigui, and you could be too!"

"I... I must still refuse for now," Cui Yan insisted. "Ask me again when certain things have changed."

"...Alright," Cao Cao said. "I shall proceed without your sagely advice... for now."

"My thanks," Cui Yan replied.

At that moment, Jia Xu approached Cao Cao with a nervous look on his face: Cao frowned and asked, "What's the matter...?"

"A... an awkward situation has arisen," Jia Xu replied. "Your son travelled to the Yuan residence as ordered, but... he has developed a fixation with a certain Lady Zhen and apparently refuses to part with her."

"...I shall pretend that I do not understand and see for myself," Cao Cao said angrily. "Pi had better have a good explanation for this... **Guo Jia, Jia Xu, Cao Hong: follow me, please!**"

When Cao Cao arrived at the Yuan family mansion and entered the grand audience hall, he was greeted by an unusual sight: Yuan Shao's widow, Lady Liu, was sat on the ground near the host seat, surrounded by her handmaidens and under the watchful eye of Cao Xiu, while Cao Pi – who had been instructed to gather everyone together – was nowhere to be seen.

"...Where is my son...?" Cao Cao asked tensely.

"He... he is in the bedchamber of Lady Zhen," Cao Xiu replied.

"He...! **Wait here, Xu Chu!**" Cao Cao exclaimed: he then tore his battle helmet from his head, threw the helmet to the floor and marched into the inner halls of the vast house to locate his son.

"...Lord Cao is *very angry*," Xu Chu sighed.

"*Aiee*... what has Pi done...?" Cao Hong asked as he picked up Cao Cao's helmet.

"*Nothing*!" Cao Xiu insisted. "He just... wants to be able to sit and talk to Lady Zhen, and... look at her."

"But she is *Yuan Xi's wife*," Jia Xu said. "This is not appropriate."

"...I know," Cao Xiu replied.

"Your reputations are deserved!" Lady Liu heckled.

"Shut up!" Cao Hong replied. **"You'll be lucky if Mengde doesn't order you to be dragged into the courtyard and strangled for all the damage you've caused!"**

Lady Liu lowered her head and groaned miserably.

Cao Cao finally found Lady Zhen's bedchamber and speechlessly pointed an accusing finger at his teenaged son, who was stood on the opposite side of the room to the lady and her bemused servants.

"I have not done anything!" Cao Pi insisted.

"...He has not touched me, Your Excellency," Lady Zhen said. "He just... wished to protect me from Lady Liu."

"Lady Liu is *insane*, Father!" Cao Pi cried. "She mutilated Yuan Shao's consorts and took Lady Zhen as a hostage to ensure her son's ascension as chieftain!"

Cao Cao looked at Lady Zhen and hummed with admiration for her incredible beauty.

"Is she not magnificent...?" Cao Pi said. "Such beauty and wit...!"

"...Is my husband alive...?" Lady Zhen asked.

"...I cannot say, my lady," Cao Cao replied. "He is, however, a fugitive and an enemy of the Han that has defied royal decrees to submit, and-"

"It is not so, Excellency!" Lady Zhen protested. "My husband is good, and kind, and he has not gotten involved in his brothers' feuding! Spare him, Excellency, and allow me to return to him!"

"...I cannot do that," Cao Cao replied. "You will remain in my protective custody... and if Yuan Xi is found alive, then you will be given the opportunity to divorce him or share his fate."

"...If that is how it must be," Lady Zhen said.

Cao Cao glared at his son, grunted tersely and turned to leave.

"Father, *wait*!" Cao Pi cried. "I have something to ask!"

"...Do not *dare*!" Cao Cao growled as he started toward the audience hall with the anxious Cao Pi in pursuit.

"Please... is there no way that I can have her...?" Cao Pi asked.

"She is *married*!" Cao Cao barked. "She is married to an enemy lord that has a right to the Yuan clan chieftainship if his brothers are destroyed! Yuan Xi is the most agreeable of the three, a man that has done nothing to anger the Han, and if there is any way to preserve that noble family, it is through Yuan Xi!"

"But Father, she is all that I crave in a wife!" Cao Pi implored. "And I thought that you wanted to destroy the Yuans and bring an end to their grip on Ji Province and on the Han! What sons will Yuan Xi produce with Lady Zhen, and what will they be like...? Will *they* be 'agreeable'...?"

Cao Cao halted.

"If... if there were some way that I could have Lady Zhen, she would be a fine wife for the heir to your legacy," Cao Pi continued. "She is loyal, brave, honest, intelligent, peerlessly beautiful-"

"I suspect that it is solely the last of those things that is driving this conversation," Cao Cao chortled.

"Your own gaze was hardly free of guilt," Cao Pi countered. "Is it that you fear accusations of impropriety, or is it that she appealed to you and my interest has-?"

"*Enough*," Cao Cao ordered. "I... will consider the options. If I am honest, I would rather see the Yuans' legacy absorbed into other clans and this region brought under my control: I can hardly take Wei Prefecture as my new capital if a worthy Yuan lives to stake a stronger claim that others at court might use to undermine me."

"...So you intend to kill him...?" Cao Pi asked.

"... ... ...I do," Cao Cao admitted. "But that might – *will* – take months or even years, and she would be in custody until then, and that won't do. Perhaps I can use some sort of technicality to divorce her from Yuan Xi so that she can be wedded to you as soon as possible."

"I... would be eternally grateful, Father," Cao Pi said.

"Is that so...?" Cao Cao chortled.

"...As I am grateful to you for all that you have done for me, esteemed father," Cao Pi added.

"Return to her for now," Cao Cao said. "Don't touch her until she is no longer wedded to Yuan Xi, though: do you understand...?"

"I do," Cao Pi promised.

Cao Pi returned to Lady Zhen's chambers, and Cao Cao returned to the main hall, where Lady Liu was sat sobbing pitifully; Xu Yòu had arrived, and he immediately said, "You owe me for this victory, Mengde!"

"You betrayed my husband and caused this terrible day!" Lady Liu shrieked. **"Damn you, Xu Yòu! *Damn you*!"**

"Curse me all you want, you despicable woman," Xu Yòu retorted. "Your death will be a thousand times worse than mine. Isn't that so, Mengde...?"

"...Lady Liu, I should like to apologise to you for the death of your husband, who was, not so long ago, my *friend*," Cao Cao declared.

Cao Xiu, Cao Hong and Xu Yòu exclaimed simultaneously.

"Silence, please," Cao Cao ordered. "I must say my piece: Lady Liu, you were with Benchu in his last moments, and it saddens me to think that I was his enemy and played a part in his early end. I should like to pay my respects to his tomb... and I should like to ensure that you are properly cared for as his widow."

"I... I am grateful," Lady Liu replied.

"I wish that I could care for his sons, but they still oppose the will of the Han," Cao Cao continued. "If there were some way to restore order and bring the Yuan brothers back here humbly, as the servants of the Han, and spare them further harm... I assure you, my lady, that I will do all that I can to negotiate with them."

"I... hope that my son is not stubborn, Excellency," Lady Liu replied. "I... should like for him to survive."

Cao Cao smiled sadly and said, "I should like the same."

"Are you being serious...?" Xu Yòu chortled. "Mengde, this woman slashed the faces of Yuan Shao's consorts to deface them in the afterlife! She conspired with Pang Ji and Shen Pei to compromise natural law and elevate her son to chieftain of the Yuan clan! Her meddling deserves punishment!"

"She has suffered enough," Cao Cao retorted. "She may lose the son she fought so hard to elevate... so perhaps she has yet to suffer the worst."

Lady Liu lowered her head and whimpered.

"Let us go to the tomb of my friend and pay our respects," Cao Cao said.

"I'll do no such thing!" Xu Yòu heckled. "I was slandered and sentenced to imprisonment and maybe death by that muddle-headed drunk! I saved you from him, Mengde, and now you want me to kowtow to him...? He locked up my wife! He slandered you! He'd have *killed you* if it weren't for me!"

"This is *not the time*, Ziyuan," Cao Cao growled.

"It's just the right time!" Xu Yòu retorted. "How can you expect me to show respect for him? Why would you-?"

"**Do it because it is the proper thing!**" Cao Cao barked. "**Show that you are a worthy statesman, Ziyuan!**"

"I at least deserve an Excellency role for saving you, Mengde," Xu Yòu chuckled. "So who do I have to impress...? But alright: I'll show respect to the old fool... if only to stop your complaining."

Xu Yòu turned and left the mansion; Xu Chu looked at Cao Cao, who nodded tersely and grunted ambiguously in response.

****

54

Cao Cao escorted Lady Liu and Yuan Shang's young family to the tomb of his former friend Yuan Shao, which was to the west of the city; Cao Pi escorted Lady Zhen, who was starting to become suspicious of Pi's motives as his language and behaviour became increasingly intimate and persuasive. The gathering – which included Cao Cao, Xu Yòu, Liu Yè, Yang Xiu, Man Chong, Cao Pi, Cao Xiu, Cao Chun, Cao Hong, Xiahou Dun, Jia Xu, Guo Jia, Xu Chu, Xin Pi, Cui Yan, Su Yòu, Lü Kuang, Lü Xiang, Lady Liu, Lady Zhen, Zhang Hè and the newly-arrived Chen Lin – bowed before the stone structure and muttered respectful words.

"…**I am sorry, Benchu!**" Cao Cao declared. "**I am sorry that this is how it had to end! We were friends, such good friends… like brothers, we were, in those heady days in Luoyang that are now long gone!**"

Guo Jia smirked at the words.

"**How long we fought the injustices together!**" Cao Cao continued. "**You and I, we opposed the 'Ten' and their cruelties, sheltering the innocent scholars that they branded as criminals! You sheltered the most… and then, when the 'Ten' threatened Commander-in-Chief Hè Jin and his nephew the Son of Heaven, you and you alone stood at that great man's side and avenged him in the anxious moments after his death! But then we were faced with Dong Zhuo, the worst of evils, who raped and pillaged and, at the suggestion of Li Ru, slaughtered your kin in the capital and melted your ancestors' statues to make worthless coins that brought down our economy!**"

Jia Xu covered his face with his sleeve and groaned as he pondered his own part in Dong Zhuo's atrocities.

"**Only** *you*, **Benchu, could lead the magistrates and administrators and governors against that evil tyrant!**" Cao Cao continued. "**Only you, Benchu, could form the Eastern Pass Coalition and force the villain to abandon the capital! But oh, then your cruel and greedy brother made his fraudulent claim to the clan chieftainship, splitting the wealth and influence of that great clan and dragging us into seven years of futile civil war that harmed all of the land and forced the Son of Heaven to suffer imprisonment in Chang'an!**"

Lady Liu sobbed as she pondered the similarities between Yuan Shu's actions and the chaos that she had brought about by supplanting Yuan Tan.

"**But Heaven spoke, and Yuan Shu – who dared to do what you never would, and claimed that he was divine – was destroyed by his own hand!**" Cao Cao continued. "**But by then, Benchu, look at where we were! I had become a great warlord and the guardian of the Son of Heaven… but you, in your boundless grief, were swayed by wicked liars that had already poisoned you against loyal officers and officials – men like Dong Zhao and Qu Yi – and came to believe that I was a villain! How I tried to make you understand, Benchu, that despite some past mistakes, we were still the** same friends! But hankering toadies had done their damage... and what's done cannot be undone. They ruined our friendship, drove us apart... and caused us to do battle at Guandu."**

Lady Zhen was forced to lower her head in order to ignore Cao Pi's attempts to smile at her.

"Oh, how I regret what took place, perhaps more than anything!" Cao Cao cried. **"Benchu, we were tricked into fighting in that place! We should have been united against the remaining enemies of the Han, but instead we were working alongside those wretches to harm each other! Men like Liu Bei and Liu Biao strove to divide us further and realise their own baseless claims to greatness, and I swear that they will be punished!"**

Xiahou Dun grunted as he thought of his hatred for Liu Bei's general Guan Yu, who had briefly aided Cao Cao before returning to Liu Bei's side.

"Fate robbed you of Wen Chou and Yan Liang, and selfish advisers caused you to find fault in more of your loyal followers, like Xu Yòu and Zhang Hè and Gao Lan, which may have benefitted my cause, Benchu, but it harmed my soul!" Cao Cao continued. **"To think that men that once pledged to die for you were then compelled to seek a new lord in order to escape slander... but they are here today, Benchu, to say that they still respect you for who you were, and to mourn your passing."**

Xu Yòu scoffed.

"Sadly, the rout at Guandu was not the end of it, and our armies clashed one last time," Cao Cao said sombrely. **"Yet again, your forces were driven back, and you died in despair as all that you had fought to build in the northeast was seemingly imperilled... but I vow to you, Benchu, that I will personally oversee the reconstruction of what has been destroyed and that I will finish what you and I started all those years ago! I will restore the Han, and one day, your name will be remembered as a martyr to that great ambition! Let all remember the name 'Yuan Shao'... the name of a hero."**

Most of the gathering joined Cao in paying further respects to Yuan Shao; only Xu Yòu refused to show the proper courtesy, which was noticed by everyone and angered Cao Cao greatly.

Once the ceremony ended, the majority of the mourners dispersed and returned to their homes or their tents; only Cao Cao, Xu Yòu, Guo Jia, Jia Xu, Chen Lin, Liu Yè, Yang Xiu, Man Chong, Cao Xiu, Xin Pi and the hulking Xu Chu remained at the tomb.

"...Your uncle was a great man, Yang Xiu," Cao Cao insisted.

"I know that he *was*," Yang Xiu replied. "He *was*... at one time, long ago."

"Perhaps... a *very* long time ago," Xu Yòu scoffed. "After Dong Zhuo killed everyone in Luoyang, Yuan Shao became progressively worse, more and more arrogant and stupid, until-"

"Silence, Ziyuan!" Cao Cao barked. **"You only embarrass yourself with your disrespectful words!"**

"Spare me the pantomime show of respect, Mengde," Xu Yòu

chuckled. "You and Yuan Shao were irreconcilable, and mostly because of Shen Pei – who you actually wanted to *recruit* – and Guo Tu, and Xun Chen, and Pang Ji... oh, and Chen Lin there and that thing that he wrote denouncing you."
Chen Lin sighed miserably.
"You stand here doing all that sobbing for him, but would he have done the same if he'd beaten you at Guandu and not the other way around...?" Xu Yòu heckled. "If I had not saved you – and it was my information alone that saved you – it would be *your* tomb that men would be visiting, Mengde, and 'Benchu' would not be one of them!"
"I... *urge you*... to be *silent*," Cao Cao growled.
"You *owe me*," Xu Yòu retorted. "I will keep saying it, Mengde, because it is true: that drunken idiot was going to *kill you* if-!"
Cao Cao's bodyguard, Xu Chu, suddenly raised his halberd and, using the blunt side of his halberd blade, struck the top of Xu Yòu's head with enough force to shatter Xu's skull; Xu jerked violently, squealed and fell to the ground. The act was a complete surprise to most: Guo Jia seemed to have expected it, and Cao Cao seemed to be momentarily unfazed before he became animated and ran to the fallen body of his friend.
"*Aiee*...! Xu Chu, you reacted to his free and open ways too harshly!" Cao Cao said as he touched Xu Yòu's shoulder and shuddered dramatically. "He was the last of them... the last of my friends from those old times...!"
Jia Xu bit his hand and stared at Cao Cao silently.
"...Oh, Xu Ziyuan, it is true that you were too outspoken, but did you deserve *this*...?" Cao Cao lamented. "Did you deserve such an undignified end...?"
"Sorry, but... yes," Cao Xiu said. "He drew stares for his behaviour, showed no respect for you or anyone else, and-"
"He was my *friend*...!" Cao Cao sobbed; Xu Chu suddenly became nervous as Cao Cao's grief became increasingly convincing.
"...But he was also untrustworthy," Xin Pi admitted. "There was some truth in some of what was said about him, Excellency... and one wonders what he would have demanded as his arrogance inflated, or what he might have done if his allegiances shifted for a second time. Perhaps... ... ... sorry, Excellency, but perhaps this was for the best."
"...Perhaps," Cao Cao groaned. "But... first poor Wei Zi, and then Lü Boshe, then Yuan Boye, and then Zhang Mengzhuo, and Yuan Benchu... and now, with Ziyuan gone, I am alone. Was Xu Ziyuan so flawed that he did not deserve a chance...?"
"I'm sorry, Lord Cao," Xu Chu pleaded. "I thought that-!"
"You did what you thought to be right," Cao Cao replied. "As Xin Zuozhi has said... perhaps this was for the best. Perhaps, in some way... his death is a sacrifice to Benchu... perhaps it is Heaven's way of setting things right."
Jia Xu shuddered.
"...Now I must try and do what I can to bring peace to this region," Cao Cao said as he got to his feet and stood over the crumpled heap that used to be Xu Yòu. "Sad to say, I must begin by questioning my alliance with Yuan Tan... whose behaviour is an even greater affront to Benchu's memory. Cao Xiu: have your men collect the remains of my friend and ensure that he is buried

262

respectfully... for regardless of our opinions of him, we should set an example. Xu Chu, Liu Yè, Man Chong, Yang Xiu..."

"I'm right behind you, Excellency," Yang Xiu replied as he followed Cao Cao, Man Chong, Liu Yè and the confused Xu Chu.

"...After you, Fengxiao," Chen Lin prompted.

Guo Jia stifled laughter as he followed his lord's retreat from the tomb; Chen Lin stared and Xu Yòu and smiled slightly before he followed Guo Jia.

"I won't miss the man," Cao Xiu scoffed as he crouched over Xu Yòu and nudged his lifeless arm.

Xin Pi looked at Jia Xu and asked, "Are you alright...?"

"Y-yes," Jia Xu replied. "After you..."

"Xu Yòu was a coward and a traitor," Xin Pi said as he walked with Jia Xu. "Although his betrayal at Guandu has been beneficial, he did not do it for the right reasons, and he was too dangerous to be left alive. As we saw with Yuan Shao, all it takes is one depot to be compromised... and for that, all it took was one moment of misplaced self-preservation."

"I do see that," Jia Xu insisted. "It just... surprised me."

"I'd have thought that nothing would surprise you after working for Dong Zhuo, Li Jue, Guo Si and Zhang Xiu," Xin Pi said.

"...Nothing except- ... ...Nothing," Jia Xu replied.

Guo Jia walked alongside Cao Cao and said, "That happened rather abruptly."

"...It is for the best," Cao Cao replied. "He... he went too far."

"And would have gone further," Guo Jia suggested. "Now, he goes nowhere. But you, Lord Cao, have seized Yè, and by doing so, you have taken Ji."

"Almost," Cao Cao replied. "I have almost taken Ji... and taking it completely should be my next objective, I think."

Guo Jia smiled and said, "Quite right."

The siege of Yè City had concluded controversially, but it had concluded nonetheless: Cao Cao immediately ordered the city's reconstruction and began making plans to deal with the 3 divided Yuan brothers, who were still active across the northeast. Yuan Tan reacted to the fall of Yè by half-heartedly congratulating Cao Cao; Yuan Xi remained silent; Yuan Shang was horrified at the loss of his capital and the capture of his family but remained determined that he could somehow save his clan's great name, even if it was at the expense of his esteemed place within it. Many wondered which of the Yuan brothers would be Cao Cao's first target: the answer would be known soon enough.

****

ACT V: THE BATTLE OF NANPI

55

The Han Empire's Excellency of Works, Cao Cao, had promised that he would defeat every one of the warlords that he had declared to be enemies of the state, and it was becoming harder to doubt his word.

None had expected that Cao Cao could vanquish the tens of thousands of Yellow Turban cultists that plagued Runan Prefecture, but they now numbered in the hundreds; the entire nation assumed that Cao would lose when Yuan Shao, lord of the northeast, declared war and threatened to attack the capital, Xuchang, with his 250,000-strong army of Han Chinese infantry and Wuhuan tribal cavalry, but Cao Cao used information passed by his friend and defecting official Xu Yòu to burn Yuan's supplies and humiliate Yuan's army at Guandu; nobody believed that the violent and rebellious Qiang tribes of the northwest could be forced to submit to the Han, but Cao Cao had exploited a internecine feud to achieve just that; the idea that the Mount Tai Bandits of Qing Province could be turned into a loyalist army was laughed at, but their 'king', Zang Ba, was now a field general that obeyed Cao's every command.

The only men that still threatened Cao Cao in any way were Liu Biao, the Governor of Jing Province, Sun Quan, the lord of the Jiangdong region in southern China, and the Yuan brothers, who still commanded a massive army and a quarter of the Han Empire; but the previous Yuan chieftain, Yuan Shao, had died after a series of crippling defeats at Cao Cao's hands, and the subsequent debate over who would succeed him – his eldest son Tan, his quiet middle son Xi, or his studious youngest son Shang – had ended with a shock announcement that Shang would be clan chieftain and that Tan would be adopted to a dead uncle. Tan immediately and violently contested the decision, which led in turn to a civil war in the northeast that divided and weakened the Yuans.

Regardless of all of those surprises, the announcement that Cao Cao would march northward and take Yè City, the seat of the once-infallible Yuan clan, from its young ruler in 2 years or less with an army of 50,000 was still met with ridicule and cynicism: but once again, Cao Cao had exploited the divisions within the region and taken the city after a costly siege while Yuan Tan – who had, as a further surprise, formed an alliance with Cao Cao – fought his brother Yuan Shang for the clan chieftainship and exhausted the family's resources still further.

The fall of Yè City and the subsequent death of the defector Xu Yòu – who had, it was explained, 'shown unacceptable disrespect to the temple of Yuan Shao' – were met with surprise, but it was Cao Pi's announcement that he was to marry Lady Zhen – a woman whose husband, Yuan Xi, was known to be very much alive – that caused the most shock and criticism. Lady Zhen's opinion was never publicly sought during the debacle, since it was not considered to be relevant: her marriage to Yuan Xi was simply annulled with her supposed agreement, and Cao Pi married her during a lavish ceremony in the weeks thereafter. The rumours that then circulated around the capital Xuchang – that Lady Zhen was showing signs of early pregnancy, and that the only way for that to be possible was if she engaged in relations with Cao Pi before their marriage or, more controversially, if Yuan Xi had somehow met with her at some point before the fall of Yè – did harm to Cao Pi's reputation and gave valuable ammunition to the small number of detractors that Cao Cao still had.

And then there was the matter of Lady Zhen's first husband, Yuan Xi: he was still the unsanctioned Governor of Yòu Province, and he now had reasons of his own to defy the Cao-led Han regime. Yuan Shang was now hiding in Yuan Xi's territory after his latest defeat at the hands of Yuan Tan, who now commanded an impressive army and half of Ji Province in addition to his gifted fief of Qing Province and the resources that came with it. And then there was Gao Gan, the Governor of Bing Province and cousin to the feuding Yuan brothers, who had been fighting Cao from a distance until news of the fall of Yè finally reached him: Cao Cao pondered all of this as he sat in the private study of the governor's mansion in Yè City with two of his advisers, Guo Jia and Jia Xu.

"So, gentlemen... do you think that Gao Gan's surrender is genuine...?" Cao Cao asked of his most trusted counsel.

"No," Guo Jia chuckled. "He's surrendered while he tries to figure out what to do next, of course. Yuan Shang's future is uncertain, while Yuan Tan's future looks brighter... for now, of course. Have you decided how you will address Yuan Tan in your next communication, Lord Cao...?"

"I know what I *want* to say," Cao Cao replied.

"Elder Cheng writes from Li County," Jia Xu said. "In addition to complaining that he is 'bored to death' of 'sitting in a safe place' while we 'have all the fun', Elder Cheng asks the same question as Guo Fengxiao."

"Don't you have a suggestion...?" Cao Cao asked.

"...I do, but I'm sure that Fengxiao does as well," Jia Xu replied.

"I... notice that you've been more hesitant since Xu Ziyuan's unfortunate death, Mister Jia," Cao Cao prompted.

"I have, because I had seen the two of you and knew of your lifelong friendship, and I realised upon his death that the world is a very complex place," Jia Xu replied. "He was not liked at all for his ways by many of your vassals and kin."

"But why has that made you hesitant...?" Cao Cao asked.

"You are an extraordinary statesman, as you said you wished to be," Jia Xu replied. "Xu Yòu was a braggart and intended to exploit his single advantage, having learned nothing from exploiting similar things while he served Yuan Shao. He betrayed Yuan Shao to save his own life, and it was obvious that he owed allegiance to nobody but himself, and I wonder how long it would have been before he went to the Yuans with information about you... and others wonder the same, Excellency."

"...So you believe that I had him killed before he became a threat, then...?" Cao Cao asked.

"I believe that your bodyguard reacted to a highly inappropriate and public show of gross contempt toward Yuan Shao's tomb and then toward the Han's Excellency of Works," Jia Xu replied. "Some might say that it was disproportionate, but that would be when taking into account the friendship between Your Excellency and Xu Yòu, which, at such a high level of state and in a public, protocol-driven scenario, is irrelevant. You may have to punish friends and even your kin for state offences at some point, Excellency, and it is precisely because Yuan Shao was incapable of such things – such as when he tried to save his heretic brother rather than condemn him – that he ultimately lost the right to claim to be a true servant of the state."

Cao Cao clapped his hands together and laughed, saying, "That is the truth, Mister Jia Xu! You have cleared away the clouds and brought forth clarity!"

"And as for my suggestion on how to deal with Yuan Tan, I think I am far from alone in saying that his current behaviour points to his being by far the most dangerous of the three brothers," Jia Xu continued. "He is closest; he is the only one with a sizeable army; he has control of most of Qing and half of Ji; he is the oldest, and hence the rightful heir on the basis of primogeniture; he still enjoys counsel from Guo Tu – though Xin Ping has apparently died – while the others have little or no counsel at all now; and above all, he is militarily experienced. None of those things would be a problem, but he has faults. He is arrogant yet without pride; he is untrusting yet untrustworthy; he blindly hates you, Excellency, for your role in his father's downfall, despite knowing all of the facts; he will do whatever he believes to be necessary to facilitate his survival and growth, as shown by his willingness to rescue Yuan Shu after he had declared as an emperor and his willingness to turn to you after what happened at Guandu and Li County; he is violent and ill-tempered, and not very bright; and he is guilty of wilful civil administrative incompetence and corruption, which makes him a poor ally even if he did not have the other faults. That is why so many were willing to go along with Lady Liu, Shen Pei, Pang Ji and Yuan Shang."

Cao Cao looked at Guo Jia, who said, "I agree completely."

"But there are three brothers," Cao Cao retorted. "What of the other two...? And what about Gao Gan...? What do we know that makes them less of a threat...?"

"Mister Jia can elaborate," Guo Jia said. "I am sparing my voice."

"...Yuan Xi is meek, relatively honest, and lacking in ambition," Jia Xu began cautiously. "He was... he was due to be happily married to Lady Zhen, of course, until Lady Liu took the lady hostage and had her allies fool Yuan Shao into sending Yuan Xi away."

Cao Cao smiled sadly and said, "I am aware that my son's behaviour has caused me some criticism... and, perhaps, some harm... but you are free to discuss whatever needs to be discussed for the purpose of defeating the Yuans. Please go on."

"...Very well," Jia Xu replied. "It is obviously the case that Yuan Xi – once he resurfaced after a conspicuously long period of silence – expressed his dissatisfaction at his marriage being annulled and his wife remarrying, and to your heir of all men. It might have pushed Yuan Xi to consider allying with Yuan Shang, or it might not... at present, Yuan Xi seems to be allowing his younger half-brother to reside in Yòu Province as a good vassal should, but he has not committed to a military alliance... not yet, at least. He may or may not be waiting to see what Yuan Tan does, which adds to the importance of routing Yuan Tan."

"...I see your points," Cao Cao said. "Please go on."

"My simple point is that Yuan Xi and Gao Gan will not act alone at present," Jia Xu continued. "They will only act under two circumstances: when they see another – be it the other, or be it Yuan Tan or Yuan Shang – acting in some way, or when they are completely isolated. Yuan Tan has at least one experienced adviser, ten-thousand or more men, control of half of this province and, to his mind, total control of another: if you do not break faith, he reasons, before he can act, he can march southward to attack you here before Zang Ba can mobilise in Qing and harm his supply route, and Gao Gan, at the very least, will lend aid ... if not all of the other three, depending on Tan's choice of words."

"...And Yuan Shang...?" Cao Cao asked.

"Yuan Shang has, at the most, five thousand men, Yin Kui as an adviser-general, and no base of his own, so he will need Yuan Xi's help. Yuan Xi is overwhelmed with rebellions, tribal incursions, administrative corruption, poverty, food shortages, and he has a small standing army that will be quite ineffective on its own, since it was designed to work in concert with Wuhuan tribal support that he does not have: it is up to Tan or Shang to bring that vital Wuhuan support to the battlefield, and right now it is not there and Yuan Tan is the only man with the reputation to obtain it... yet another argument for dealing with him first."

"And Gao Gan...?" Cao Cao asked. "You're sure that he will not attack when my back is turned...?"

"Only if you are under attack or seemingly losing, at present... though that may change," Jia Xu replied. "Gao Gan lost a lot of men when his attack on Hedong failed, Excellency, and the threat of further attacks from that direction still worries him enough to stay his hand. Like Yuan Tan, he is reliant on being able to act before you can issue orders to your local army, and being able to defeat you before you can call upon them for help."

"...Then I must deal with Yuan Tan first," Cao Cao decided. "It was my own thought, but I wanted to be sure that I had not missed anything. How should I approach this...? Should I just attack him, or should I be more cautious...?"

"He promised, as part of a formal military alliance, to aid the siege of Yè, and he did not," Guo Jia replied.

"No... instead, he started to conquer the rest of the province," Cao Cao grumbled.

"And that means that he is guilty of failing to honour the conditions of your alliance, Excellency," Jia Xu said. "Inform him of this, and then attack him when all are aware that your alliance has ended. Attacking him without warning could – and most likely *will* – lead to one thing that we do not desire..."

"...He'll call on the others, and they'll all retaliate together," Cao Cao supposed.

"Yuan Shang was prepared to submit to you, Excellency, when he was so desperate during the siege at Quzhang: he'd ally with Yuan Tan and even relinquish the chieftainship if it would preserve his life," Jia Xu explained. "Yuan Tan would agree to work with Shang – even being prepared to accept his brother's chieftainship – if it would save him from you; Yuan Xi and Gao Gan will support whoever is doing something meaningful, and the fifth concern –

the Wuhuan – will join in if they are impressed by the show of force and the opportunity to enjoy violence."

"...One more thing... the Qiang," Cao Cao said. "I have avoided discussing those troublesome pests on the northwest frontier because I have been so busy trying to stabilise the northeast frontier: the war in Liang Province is being fought with bluff, placating words, vague promises and maintaining a state of 'uniting division' between Ma Teng and Han Sui, but I worry that those two will start to find genuine unity and make trouble at a moment when I cannot properly deal with them."

"We receive regular reports, Excellency, and for now you need not fear," Jia Xu promised. "Zhao Ang's reorganisation of the region's military proceeds nicely, with all of Dong Zhuo's former vassals and their supporters now fully purged or rehabilitated; Inspector Wei Kang's honest, sensible government has won hearts and minds and removed most of the threats of rebellion among the Han populace, which was the real cause of the rise of the Qiang warlords twenty years ago; and Xiping Magistrate Du Ji's work is doing wonders for keeping the Qiang and Han rebel elements locked in meaningful discussions and remaining optimistic for the future. It would take a total disaster to see a breakdown in order right now, and that's highly unlikely."

"So I can forget about the northwest for now...?" Cao Cao asked.

"You can, completely," Guo Jia replied.

"...So I must, in order, break ties with Yuan Tan, prevent Tan allying with the Wuhuan, put pressure on Qing Province to limit Tan's military effectiveness and keep him in Ji Province, and then attack him with full force," Cao Cao prompted.

"And you must kill him," Guo Jia said. "Nothing less than death will do, or this campaign will last another eight to ten years... kill him, and it will be over in three or four at the most, including the final pacification of the Wuhuan tribes."

"...That's ambitious," Jia Xu suggested.

"Why strive for the top of a hill when Heaven is within reach, Mister Jia...?" Guo Jia asked. "At the very least ascend a mountain, or what is the point...?"

Cao Cao hummed thoughtfully and said, "You've convinced me, gentlemen. I knew that I would be here in this region for a while, which is why I wanted to make a base of Yè City... perhaps I will move my family here when the damage done by the siege is repaired. But I do not want to be here fighting for a decade! I want to bring peace to this region, and if I cannot do that without killing Yuan Tan... then kill him I must, and kill him I will. I'll make sure he knows the situation as soon as I can."

"And be ready to march, or at the very least defend," Jia Xu replied. "The battle with Yuan Tan could be a swift one if luck and the heavens are with us."

"It will be a swift end," Guo Jia said. "I'm certain of it."

****

56

Emperor Xian demanded a court session in order to ask about the campaign in Ji Province: Xun Wenruo spoke for his lord Cao Cao.

"His Excellency Cao has secured the region around Yè City, while Yuan Tan has secured the north of Ji Province," Xun Wenruo reported. "The precise outcome is as yet unclear, but an amicable relationship with the rightful heir to the Yuan clan might still be possible, Your Majesty."

"We see that the signs of accord are there," Emperor Xian said. "But at the same time, we wonder if the man that once rode into Xu Province to personally rescue his uncle – an uncle that had dared to lay claim to our throne – is the right man to be parleying with, Mister Xun."

"His Excellency Cao Cao does, I admit, have his own concerns about Yuan Tan, Your Majesty," Xun Wenruo replied. "B-but the situation is complicated."

Emperor Xian smiled dryly and said, "So we understand."

Many officials guessed that their sovereign's response was alluding to Cao Pi's marriage to Lady Zhen or the sudden death of Xu Yòu. Kong Rong smirked and asked for permission to speak, which unnerved his friend Zhi Xi and disappointed his friend Wang Lang: but Xun Wenruo guessed that Kong Rong wanted to heckle Cao Cao in some way, so he ignored the request.

"All that I can add, Your Majesty, is that relief is being given to southern Ji, and that the people are grateful for the end to Yuan rule," Xun Wenruo said. "The recent unrest was the fault of Yuan Shang, and Yuan Tan's offence was committed during his father's rule: I am certain that His Excellency will do what is right."

"...We are reassured for now," Emperor Xian replied.

"...Fool!" Zhi Xi said to Kong Rong as they left the Imperial audience hall.

"I am not a fool," Kong Rong retorted. "Cao Cao makes a mockery of us! Yes, I am glad that he spared Chen Kongzhang and that Cui Jigui is safe, but has there been any word of Wenruo's wayward brother Xun Chen, or Ying Shao...?"

"You're picking faults as usual, Wenju," Wang Lang said. "You're annoyed that His Excellency spared Chen Lin, in truth, because by doing so it rightly invalidates that hideous denunciation that Yuan Shao forced him to write."

"...I am happy that Chen Kongzhang lives, and I dislike the insinuation that I would wish the man dead to prove my distrust of Cao Cao is justified!" Kong Rong replied quietly. "But at the same time, Jingxing, it is likely, is it not, that Cao only 'spared' Kongzhang to clear his own name...? Will we get to ask Kongzhang anything, or will he slip on a large mouse dropping and fall onto an upturned axe blade and decapitate himself before he can come to Xuchang and face his friends...?"

Zhi Xi covered his smiling face with his sleeve.

"...That, I presume, was a childish reference to what happened to Xu Yòu," Wang Lang sighed. "That nasty little man got what he long deserved."

"And he only 'got it' after his usefulness had ended... and Cao is such a shameless villain that he didn't even wait a few months!" Kong Rong retorted. "Xu was killed *immediately after Yè fell*; that is surely a record for 'tying up loose ends'!"

"I think that you are seeking fault because he is on good terms with Yuan Tan, and you must try and put your hate to one side for the state," Wang Lang said.

"But there is that other matter: his heir marrying Lady Zhen," Kong Rong said. "I cannot let that affront to our civilisation go by without commenting!"

"Are you that desperate for an early grave...?" Zhi Xi asked.

"I intend to write to Cao and let him know what I – and others without the courage – think of his son's impropriety," Kong Rong declared. "I must. I would be failing in my capacity as a statesman if I ignored it like everyone else is doing. If he really is a hero and not another Dong Zhuo, he must be made aware of what that looks like."

"I think he knows," Wang Lang scoffed.

"But allowed it anyway...?" Kong Rong chortled. "That's worse!"

"...I cannot talk you out of your folly," Wang Lang conceded.

"No, you can't," Kong Rong said. "I will have my say."

"...And suffer for it," Zhi Xi sighed.

Emperor Xian retired to his chambers and dismissed his servants with a silent wave of his hand; Empress Fu frowned and asked, "What is it, Majesty...?"

"Nothing is different," Emperor Xian replied. "It's as we heard already: Cao has allied with Yuan Tan to depose the younger son and conquer Yè. Cao Cao's lackey Xun Yu was mumbling something about Cao seizing Yè as a first step to pacifying the Wuhuan and stabilising the north between his bouts of kowtowing and simpering squeaks... I can only hope that Cao plans to double-cross that traitor Yuan Tan when his usefulness is ended, just as he does to everyone else."

Empress Fu nodded and said, "But when the Yuans are gone..."

"...Then there will only be Liu Biao and Liu Bei, who did nothing while Cao Cao sieged Yè, so I doubt that they'll do anything now," Emperor Xian replied. "But that's the least of my concerns: I do not like what I am hearing about Cao's heir."

"Why, Majesty...?" Empress Fu asked. "What about that matter bothers you so...?"

"He takes what is not his," Emperor Xian replied. "Taking the widow of an enemy is one thing; taking the wife of a *living opponent* – a provincial governor with a claim to an influential chieftainship – and, some say, making her pregnant with child before he'd even married her, suggests that Cao Pi is as bad as, if not worse than his father... and he will one day be who I must deal with unless something changes. What else might Cao Pi take a liking to... and decide to take...?"

Empress Fu guessed the meaning of Emperor Xian's words and sighed miserably.

✱✱✱✱✱✱✱✱✱✱✱✱

57

Yuan Tan had returned to Pingyuan in the east of Ji Province after his victory over his brother Yuan Shang and the acquisition of Bohai, Hejian, Ganling and Anping Prefectures: he was unsure of what his next move should be, but he knew that he had to act against either Cao Cao or his brother.

There was an expectation that Cao Cao would, at the very worst, demand an explanation for Yuan Tan's seizure of 4 prefectures without seeking Cao's guidance; Tan was shocked when Cao Cao sent a mid-ranking official to Pingyuan in order to deliver a scathing denunciation.

"His Excellency placed the utmost faith in General Yuan Tan and even went as far as to propose an alliance of the Cao and Yuan clans, but General Yuan has, in exchange, shown nothing but contempt and failed to make a worthy contribution to the agreed efforts to stabilise the region," the official relayed. "When His Excellency was sieging Yè, General Yuan took the opportunity to attack and take possession of numerous counties in northern Ji; while His Excellency exhausted the men and resources of the Han Empire in an effort to bring peace to the people, General Yuan brought war to the people, forcing men into his service and stealing resources for reasons as yet undeclared. Such an ally is not an ally at all."

Yuan Tan was as angry as he was afraid: he looked at Guo Tu, who was not sure whether he should heckle the official in a show of support for his lord or maintain a respectful silence.

"It has come to His Excellency's attention that General Yuan took as a captive the Registrar of Ji Province, Li Fu," the official continued. "But instead of sending that vital administrative figure to Yè upon his capture, General Yuan has chosen to retain him for purposes unknown."

"So I was supposed to send him to a flooded-out ruin of a city...?" Yuan Tan asked aggressively. **"To do what???"**

"...My lord, it is proper etiquette to let the esteemed gentleman finish reading the decree," Guo Tu said nervously.

"And I *shall* finish," the official said. "Once again, General Yuan has shown that his interests are purely his own, with no regard to the needs of the state or the will of His Majesty: it is therefore decided that all prior agreements are annulled, including the marriage alliance, and the truce between His Excellency and General Yuan is effectively ended."

The last part of the announcement was met with astonished gasps: Yuan Tan leapt to his feet and pointed at the official, saying, **"Fine! Let there be an end to the false accord! And you shall be the first casualty of our renewed hostility!"**

"Stop!" Guo Tu cried as Yuan Tan drew his sword and prepared to charge at the cowering official. **"Let him go, Lord Yuan! Nothing is to be gained from murdering a Han official when Cao Cao is the enemy!"**

Yuan Tan halted, looked at his sword and muttered, "Yes... you're... quite right."

Guo Tu nodded at the official, who retreated while Yuan Tan was distracted; Guo then turned to Tan and said, "Your next move

should be to consolidate your forces, Lord Yuan. Cao Cao will certainly have sent word to Zang Ba, which will impact on our supply line from Qing Province; we must order Wang Xiu and Guan Tong to send as much as they can now, and we must reinforce this city and relocate to Longcou, where-"
"Why would we abandon Pingyuan for Longcou...?" Yuan Tan asked derisively. "Do I not have a strong army...? Is Cao Cao's army not part exhausted and part derived from my brother's army, which was my father's, and therefore should – and *will* – be mine...? Hasn't Supuyan of the Wuhuan suddenly moved southward and shown signs that he would like to add his swords to ours...?"
"All that you say is true, which is precisely why I said that we should relocate to Longcou – not 'abandon Pingyuan'," Guo Tu replied. "We will reinforce Nanpi as well, creating three strong points of defence that Cao Cao must either divide his forces to manage or risk exposing his army to a pincer by picking a single target. In the meantime, we will send a man to liaise with Supuyan and assure him of our ever-growing strength."
"...I think I see what you are trying to do," Yuan Tan said. "Alright, we'll fortify Pingyuan and Nanpi and build a camp at Longcou. And we'll have Wang Xiu establish an emergency supply chain."
"But wouldn't we be better off going back to Qing Province, where we are established, and fending our enemies off from a position of solid strength...?" an official asked.
"That's a valid point," Yuan Tan said. "Have you an answer, Mister Guo Tu...?"
"By retreating from northern Ji, we abandon the province to become Cao Cao's," Guo Tu retorted. "Surely you cannot believe that to be the proper course...?"
"...I don't know what I believe," Yuan Tan admitted. "I am concerned about Xin Pi, who surely must have been taken hostage if we have now broken ties and he has not returned... that, or... ...
...but I refuse to believe such a thing."
"Xin Pi is not our concern right now," Guo Tu said coldly. "He helped us to forge an alliance that has now collapsed, and he is not and will not be here."
"...You're right," Yuan Tan decided. "The only priority now is the destruction of Cao Cao! Write to Wang Xiu at once!"
"...I shall," Guo Tu replied.

Cao Cao received Kong Rong's letter while he was preparing to march toward Pingyuan: he read the known detractor's correspondence with an expectant frown on his face.

"Humble greetings to Your Excellency.

Firstly, I should like to congratulate you on your swift victory in Ji Province. I am glad that you have managed to tame the animal that is Yuan Tan and put him to good use for the state; perhaps he can atone for his past misdemeanours. Tan's stepmother, Lady Liu, has done incalculable harm to the Yuan clan by appointing her own son, but would appointing Tan as the heir have led to any better a conclusion for the state?

Secondly, I should like to laud you for sparing and employing Chen Lin when other men might have destroyed him for his words. It is a fine thing indeed when a ruler understands that a man cannot be chastised for expressing an opinion or conveying the will of his lord.

Many interesting things are happening right now, and men are being forced to re-evaluate other men and look to the past to see the future. Take the fall of the Yuans and the rise of your own clan: no man could have foreseen it as it has happened! I was the first to say that the Yuans could not be beaten, but time and again you have bested them, proving me to be mistaken! I truly failed to see what the Caos were capable of. And when I see what has just transpired, I am again surprised: truly, it is as it was in the old times, when King Wu of Zhou defeated Zhou and married the beautiful Daji to the Duke of Zhou. Who could have foreseen what happened next!

I look forward to your next exploits.

Regards,

Kong Rong"

"...Mm... I must admit, I am pleasantly surprised," Cao Cao chuckled as he passed Kong Rong's letter to Guo Jia. "Perhaps I am on the way to having one less critic!"
Guo Jia frowned as he read the letter and replied, "Perhaps."
"You have some interpretation that I have missed, Fengxiao...?" Cao Cao asked.
"I don't think so," Guo Jia replied as he handed the letter to Jia Xu and moved his eyes from the letter to his fellow adviser in a pointed manner.
"Praise from Kong Wenju is a fine thing if it is sincere," Cao Cao said. "After all, I have, until just now, been allied to Yuan Tan, whose treatment of the Kong family was most discourteous, and Wenju has long suspected me of being unjust. Even if he still has doubts, I expect that he will like me more when I destroy Yuan Tan! Perhaps he will invite me to one of his banquets!"
"...Indeed," Jia Xu replied as he finished reading the letter and looked at Guo Jia with surprise.
"Remember when he chastised me for the alcohol ban, Fengxiao...?" Cao Cao chuckled. "That was so petty, heckling me for banning wastage of crops during a famine... and when he brought that man Mi Heng to me...? Oh, how angry I was!"
"...But now he is less confrontational," Guo Jia replied carefully.
"I will be glad when we can call each other 'Mengde' and 'Wenju', and we can be true friends," Cao Cao continued. "He's right, too: who could not miss the similarity between the way that Daji brought down the Shang with her vile actions and the way that

the beautiful but vicious Lady Liu has harmed the Yuans! But enough of that: we must press on!"

"...Indeed we must," Jia Xu said.

The leader of the former Mount Tai Bandits, Zang Ba, was forced to calm his allies and subordinates yet again when Cao Cao's latest orders reached them.

"**This is ridiculous!**" Chang Xi screamed. "**I won't go along with it anymore, Zang! 'Fight Yuan Tan!' 'Be friends with Yuan Tan!' 'Kill Yuan Tan!' It's one set of contradictory instructions after another!**"

"**...So you're dropping out of the confederacy, then...?**" Zang Ba asked icily.

"**What 'confederacy'???**" Chang Xi heckled. "**'We're not bandits anymore.' Your words, not mine! What 'confederacy' is there...? All we are now is a set of dogs of different breeds that bark for an ungrateful master!**"

Some of the other bandit leaders murmured agreeably; Zang Ba's long-time ally Sun Guan leant sideways toward Zang and said, "You're losing them."

"**...I like the constantly changing orders no more than you lot do,**" Zang Ba declared as he got to his feet. "**Yeah, I know you've heard me say that far too many times recently, but I have to move with the times! Cao Cao is bringing order! The Yuans are on the way out! Yuan Tan has been bad for Qing Province! We should all be glad that Cao was just using him instead of it being a real alliance! What else is there to say...?**"

Many looked to Chang Xi, who said, "**I still respect you, Zang... _just_. I'll go along with this one more time... but if Cao Cao turns around and tells us to kiss Yuan Tan's arse again, I won't just turn on Cao... I'll turn on _you_!**"

"**Fine, you do that,**" Zang Ba retorted. "**Just know that I won't go easy on you.**"

"**You think it'll just be me...?**" Chang Xi heckled. "**Don't place a bet on it, 'King of Kaiyang'.**"

"**Calm down, Chang!**" Sun Guan said cheerfully. "**There won't be any more silly orders now: Cao told us to lay off attacking Yuan Tan until he'd taken Yè. Now we get to deal with Tan: it's what we all want!**"

"**...Alright,**" Chang Xi huffed. "**But I mean it, Zang Ba... _one more chance_.**"

Zang Ba sat down and groaned wearily: Sun Guan sensed that Zang was in need of a moment to think and issued orders on his behalf that would take the former Mount Tai Bandits back to the north of Qing Province and pit them against Wang Xiu and Guan Tong yet again.

∗∗∗∗∗∗∗∗∗∗∗∗

58

Cao Cao's advance did not solicit the reaction that Yuan Tan had hoped for: many saw the arrival of the Excellency of Works as a further sign of the erosion of Yuan clan influence in Ji Province, and some villages and smaller cities around Pingyuan opened their gates willingly. The rumours that the Wuhuan chieftain Supuyan was advancing southward did little to aid Yuan Tan either, despite his seeing it as a military advantage: even more villages and cities across the north of Ji considered submitting to Cao Cao rather than facing more raids by their tribal neighbours, and some even started to rebel before the Han armies could ever reach them.

"...**What do I do???**" Yuan Tan shrieked. "*Seven reports of...!* **Guo Tu, you stand there like a statue, and the rest of you, you just linger like ghosts! Give me some *advice*, damn you! SAY SOMETHING!**"

"We must abandon Pingyuan, of course," Guo Tu replied. "Longcou may or may not be tenable."

"...**I cannot be beaten so easily!**" Yuan Tan cried. "**I am a tiger of the battlefield!**"

"But Cao Cao has gained the confidence of the people," Guo Tu retorted. "Like it or not, the long-established policy of allowing the Wuhuan to run rampant has finally shown that it has consequences: yet now we must turn to the very people that cause the villages and cities to turn against us, because we need their costly aid."

"Very poetic," Yuan Tan scoffed. "Have you anything more useful to contribute?"

"I can add nothing to what I have already said," Guo Tu replied. "We must recall the men in Pingyuan to Longcou and make preparations for a retreat to Nanpi if we cannot hold Longcou."

"...Where is my family?" Yuan Tan asked.

"In Nanpi," Guo Tu replied miserably; news of Shen Pei's massacre of the families of defectors and Yuan Tan loyalists had reached Pingyuan, and the effect on morale had been devastating.

"...Where is Li Fu?" Yuan Tan asked.

"In Pingyuan," Guo Tu replied.

"**What?!**" Yuan Tan cried. "**I expected you to say 'Nanpi' or 'here', you fool! Pingyuan will be the first place to fall, and Cao will–!**"

"**We wouldn't want Li Fu as the registrar anyway!**" Guo Tu snapped. "**Let Cao have the man, Lord Yuan: Cao can take his anger out on him!**"

"...**Send word to Pingyuan!**" Yuan Tan ordered. "**I don't care what you say, Guo Tu, I want – *need* – Li Fu to submit to me and be the Registrar of Ji! It validates me as the ruler of this province!**"

"I'll do as you say, Lord Yuan, but evacuating soldiers and supplies comes first!" Guo Tu replied.

Pingyuan's capital was in the process of evacuating when Cao Cao's vanguard – led by Cao Chun, Cao Hong, Lü Kuang and Lü Xiang – arrived at the western gates: Yuan Tan's soldiers abandoned their transport carts and fled toward Longcou before they could be routed by Cao Chun's now-infamous Tiger and Leopard Cavalry.

"...It isn't just supplies," Cao Chun reported to Cao Cao.

"Oh...? What else?" Cao Cao asked.

"Prisoners... and of particular interest is one man that Lü Kuang has identified as being Li Fu, the Registrar of Ji Province," Cao Chun replied.

Cao Cao clapped his hands together and said, "We have Li Fu!"

"So it seems!" Guo Jia chuckled.

"Zilian wanted to kill him, but I have placed him under guard," Cao Chun explained. "Mister Li is unwilling to speak."

"He'll speak to *me*," Cao Cao replied. "Bring him to me at once."

Li Fu was brought, unbound, before Cao Cao by Cao Chun and Cao Hong.

"It is Heaven's will that we meet today, Li Zixian!" Cao Cao said.

"You refer to me by my courtesy name, yet I have shown no courtesy to you and do not intend to," Li Fu retorted. "Kill me and be done with it!"

"I'll not let a hair on your head be so much as twisted," Cao Cao said. "I have need of the help of men like you if I am to stabilise the north and undo the terrible damage that has been done by this generation of Yuans... for sad to say, they make a mockery of their father's admittedly fine reputation and act more like their treasonous uncle."

"...I cannot betray the Yuans!" Li Fu pleaded.

"They have betrayed themselves, Zixian," Cao Cao retorted. "They're fighting each other; please try and understand that I only act as I do through lack of choice. If I could preserve the Yuans I would, but... they are their own undoing."

Li Fu turned to look at Chen Lin, who said, "I saved Lord Yuan Shao once, long ago, but I could not save him from his own folly. He did not name his heir, and-"

"That's because... well, you can see why!" Li Fu retorted. "Yuan Tan is a mindless animal that resorts to violence easily! I did not like Pang Ji, but he did not deserve to be splattered across the floor for passing on a refusal of aid! Lord Yuan Shang had every quality necessary for a great ruler: primogeniture is only applicable when the oldest is not an unstable monster that will bring ruin to clan and state!"

Cao Cao hummed thoughtfully.

"I will serve Lord Yuan Shang until my death, and that is that," Li Fu continued. "So you might as well make my death quick: spare me and I will only try to return to my lord and need to be killed, like Ju Shou before me."

"But I cannot kill such a man as you, Zixian," Cao Cao said. "The way that you outwitted my entire army twice at Yè has impressed me too much."

"...You know that I...!" Li Fu exclaimed. "And yet... yet you'd still spare me...?"

"I have a reputation as a 'monster', but I am not," Cao Cao insisted. "I want to reunite the land under the Son of Heaven's benevolent rule, nothing more. The Yuans have strayed from the path, Li Zixian: help me guide Yuan Shang and Yuan Xi back to the light if that is possible."

Li Fu looked at Chen Lin, Su Yòu and Guo Jia in turn before he

said, "I would be fooling myself if I continued to say that the
Yuans have not strayed, given that I look at some of the most
honest, decent men in the land and see them by your side,
Excellency, instead of Yuan Shang's: they were all misused, as I
have been, while the power has flowed to the likes of Shen Pei
and Guo Tu, who elevated themselves using slander and intrigue."
"So you'll help me...?" Cao Cao asked.
Li Fu fell to his knees, kowtowed penitently and said, "I, Fu,
pledge my service to the Han and to the Excellency of Works. I
only hope that I can be of useful service."
"To your feet, man, to your feet!" Cao Cao pleaded. "I will have no
needless shows of obeisance! You retain your post as Registrar of
Ji Province... and your first act can be to help me restore proper
order in Pingyuan!"
Li Fu got to his feet, bowed humbly and said, "As you command,
Your Excellency."
"And you can rest assured that I will send you on no mad missions
to scheme your way past guards and scale the walls of cities!" Cao
Cao continued. "Your place will be the one that you have earned:
the keeper of the peace and the manifestation of order in Ji
Province... nothing more, nothing less."
"I have found my true lord, then," Li Fu said.

Pingyuan City was quickly pacified and reorganised with the
unexpected help of Registrar Li Fu: the road to the camp at
Longcou was clear, and it would be the next obstacle on the path
to defeating Yuan Tan.

＊＊＊＊＊＊＊＊＊＊＊＊

59

Cao Cao's forces attacked Yuan Tan's army on the outskirts of Longcou and scattered many of the men that Tan had recently compelled to join him: Guo Tu immediately sought an audience with his lord and said, "If the outer perimeter fell with such ease, we cannot hope for the rest to do better."

"Are you suggesting that we run again…?" Yuan Tan heckled. "I will not fold so easily! Cao Cao was stuck at Yè for months! You're suggesting that-!"

"Longcou was only ever going to be a strong position if Pingyuan held, and Pingyuan has fallen!" Guo Tu explained desperately. "If we want to survive, we must alert Wang Xiu to the situation and-"

"**But Wang Xiu and Guan Tong are under attack by Zang Ba!**" Yuan Tan cried.

"**Can we care???**" Guo Tu retorted. "If we must choose between keeping northern Ji and keeping northern Qing, which is more use to us…?"

Yuan Tan was silent.

"…We must choose, and the choice is obvious," Guo Tu continued. "Ji is the heart of the Yuan clan's territory: Qing, Bing and Yòu are neither as important as Ji nor likely to remain part of the Yuan clan's territory if Ji is lost!"

Yuan Tan shuddered angrily.

"We'll do no better in Qing," Guo Tu insisted. "The Mount Tai Bandits control the centre and the south: we have Le'an, Ji'nan, Beihai and Donglai Prefectures, and little else besides! The-!"

"*Fine*… fine," Yuan Tan said desperately. "Either I can stay here or I can't; either I can hold Nanpi or I can't. I can stay and fight or run to Qing and lose. I'll stay."

"It is the proper course," Guo Tu huffed. "We will abandon Longcou and consolidate around Nanpi, building a forest of camps like the one around Li County that perplexed and defeated the villain before and seeking the assistance of Supuyan's cavalry. When Cao Cao retreats – and he will when he is faced with a Wuhuan cavalry – we will pursue and gather more help along the way, for the cowards that fled when they mistook Cao's charge for strength will soon come back to avoid your wrath."

"…I'll do as you suggest with regard to using Supuyan, but I will not yield Qing," Yuan Tan said. "Wang Xiu will remain in Qing. Han Xun: break camp."

General Han Xun touched his fist to his chest and said, "As you command, my lord."

News of Yuan Tan's second retreat was met with some surprise in Cao Cao's camp.

"…My brother is definitely dead," Xin Pi sighed. "He'd never have yielded this quickly, not after being made to look weak once; this is Guo Tu's idea."

"I… am sorry, Xin Zuozhi," Cao Cao said. "I did not want you to lose your brother… I had hoped to sway him, to reunite you both as servants of the Han."

"He was stubborn in his ways, and he truly intended to serve Yuan Tan to the end," Xin Pi replied. "I mustn't forget that he was Yuan

Tan's adviser when Tan rode south to save Yuan Shu, which was perhaps beyond justification."

"I was intending to ignore that transgression," Cao Cao said.

"He was aiding Guo Tu's intriguing when I saw him last, which was something that I never thought that I would see, so... so... so like Xu Yòu, his death is perhaps for the best," Xin Pi replied. "Shen Pei killed everyone that he cared about, except, I hope, me, and... and Guo Tu is more manageable when alone."

"...Fine," Cao Cao said soberly. "So, then... what next...?"

The question was met with silence.

"...Are we now suddenly at a loss...?" Cao Cao asked.

"Sorry, my lord, I was instinctively waiting for Xu Yòu to make some sort of comment before I tried to answer," Guo Jia replied. "His absence is proving to be something of a difficult thing to adjust to after what, nearly four years of him...?"

"...Yes," Cao Cao grunted. "I, too, await the heckling on occasion."

"But gone he is, so I shall answer," Guo Jia continued. "Here we are in Longcou, but with nobody to fight: Guo pitted against Guo, somehow related but very, very distantly and far from equal in talent. Guo Tu has schemed all of his colleagues to death, so now he is, at last, where he always wanted to be: he is the lone counsel to the self-proclaimed chieftain of the Yuan clan, but without rivals to plot against and other talents to be actually doing all of the work while he plots, he is at a loss. They have withdrawn to Nanpi, where there can be only one outcome..."

"...A *siege*," Cao Cao grumbled. "*Another siege.*"

"But this siege will be an unrefined, brutal, costly affair, as Guo Tu will be unable to contain Yuan Tan's bloodlust without other strong voices of reason to aid him," Guo Jia continued. "To make it more costly still, the Wuhuan will definitely be involved this time if we do not sabotage communications between them – which will be nigh-on impossible – or send a man that outperforms Yuan Tan's man and impresses the Wuhuan chieftain so much that he chooses to aid us or not to fight at all."

"...Supuyan, correct...?" Cao Cao prompted.

"It is," Xin Pi confirmed. "He... he brings five-thousand cavalry."

"*Aiee*...! With such a sudden bolstering of his forces, Tan might even win the entire campaign, never mind repel my force from Nanpi!" Cao Cao exclaimed. "Five-thousand fresh cavalrymen, and bloodthirsty ones at that, and Tan's own men, led by two like-minded thugs, when my own forces, great in size though they are, are tired, some homesick, some ill, some newly gained from the Yuans and prone to defection at the first sign of a change of fortunes... no, no, that won't do. We must turn Supuyan back."

"But how...?" Xin Pi asked.

"I have a number of men in mind," Cao Cao said. "I could send one of Yuan Shao's famous generals, such as Zhang Hè, but the Wuhuan, fickle though they are, have a hypocritical contempt for 'Han men' that switch sides and Yuan Tan's envoy will know that. The man I send must be intimidating, clever, unreadable, courageous, quick-witted, skilful with sword and polearm, a natural horseman, but at the same time he must be... well..."

"...Expendable," Guo Jia supposed.

"...Yes," Cao Cao admitted. "I must send someone that has yet to be given command of a lot of men, so that his loss – which is a

possibility – does not leave one of my militias without a head. Otherwise I'd send Cao Chun, who is everything that I have just described... but this is a dangerous mission."
"Might I make a suggestion...?" Xin Pi asked.
"By all means," Cao Cao replied.
"Anping has fallen to Yuan Tan but now suffers a resurgence of unrest," Xin Pi explained. "Amongst the defenders of Anping is one Qian Zhao, styled 'Zijing', a native of Guanjin County that quickly proved to be a fine military leader and was promoted quickly. He's had dealing with the Wuhuan in times when they were both enemies and allies of the Yuans, and he will certainly impress them. He's expressed a desire to surrender to the Han now that Yuan Shang has faltered, so, if Your Excellency approves of it..."
"...And he isn't just going to recruit the Wuhuan men for Yuan Shang...?" Cao Cao asked pointedly. "I don't need to take the sword from one of them and pass it to the one I just humbled, Zuozhi, or I'll be fighting the Yuans for the rest of my life!"
"I have met Qian Zhao," Xin Pi said. "He's honest, clever... clever enough, at least, to make the right decision. If he submits, Excellency, he does so sincerely."
"...Alright, well, have him come here to Longcou," Cao Cao ordered. "We shall speak with him and, if he is useable, we will send him to Supuyan."
"At once, Excellency," Xin Pi replied.

Qian Zhao impressed Cao Cao immediately upon his arrival at Longcou: he was tall, athletic, strong-featured and confident, and that was exactly what was needed to repel the Wuhuan.
"You know why you are here, Qian Zijing," Cao Cao prompted.
"...I am to do some service for the Han Empire," Qian Zhao replied. "I care not what it is, Excellency, so long as it allows me to atone for my mistakes."
"And why do you assume that you are invited here to do a service for the Han...?" Guo Jia asked.
"First, I am not bound," Qian Zhao replied. "Second, His Excellency refers to me by my courtesy name, which implies that I can be a friend of the Empire; thirdly, I could not know why I am here if the intent was to kill me, for I have surrendered honestly and done nothing to deserve punishment, so telling me that I know why I am here can only mean that I am here as a submitted vassal, as was my intent."
"...Good," Cao Cao said. "I want you to go to the Wuhuan chieftain Supuyan and turn him back before he joins forces with Yuan Tan: can you do that...?"
"I believe that I can," Qian Zhao replied. "I know the Wuhuan: they hate, fear or begrudgingly respect us 'Han men', and only our level of strength and how we manifest it dictates which it is. But in this case, it is not that I should challenge *their* strength but the strength of the rival that seeks their aid. Yuan Tan will have an envoy placed among them: by humiliating that envoy, I can sway Supuyan and have him turn back."
"You need no briefing!" Cao Cao chuckled. "I have every faith in you: go at once!"
Qian Zhao bowed humbly and said, "As you command."

The Wuhuan chieftain Supuyan had set up an informal camp to the north of Nanpi: the men – in addition to constant training – raided nearby villages for food and whatever else they wanted, and the Wuhuan women ensured that everybody was fed amply. Their activities were watched over by an envoy from Yuan Tan, just as Cao Cao's inner circle had guessed: Yuan Shang's envoys had been chased away at every attempt since the defeat at Zhongshan, and Yuan Xi had never tried to appoint one. Supuyan spent most of his time sat close to a cooking fire with his closest allies and Yuan Tan's envoy, enjoying cooked meat and random displays of strength and skill.

"...We eat, rest, and then we go south to see your master," Supuyan said to the envoy.

"Indeed," the envoy replied: he was a tall, strong and arrogant officer that had been chosen for his rugged appearance and military skills, and he was quickly becoming respected among Supuyan's subordinates.

"...Yuan Tan wants Cao Cao crushed," Supuyan said.

"He does," the envoy replied. "Completely. And then the Yuan clan and the Wuhuan can do as they please."

Supuyan laughed, tore a piece of meat from a pig rib with his teeth and said, "We already do as we please! But we get to do that everywhere...?"

"Everywhere," the envoy replied. "When Cao is dead, the–"

"SOMEONE IS HERE!"

All eyes turned to a Wuhuan sentry, who was accompanied by Qian Zhao.

"Who are you...?" Supuyan growled. **"You are an envoy from Yuan Shang...?"**

The envoy got to his feet and pointed at Qian Zhao, saying, **"I know you!"**

"Teng Du, isn't it...?" Qian Zhao heckled.

"Teng Dao!" the envoy retorted. **"Don't pretend you don't know me, Qian Zhao! We both served Yuan Shao!"**

"And now you serve his idiot son that only knows how to run at swords," Qian Zhao said. **"For the time that I was blind enough to serve the Yuan brothers, I at least picked the clever one."**

"You chose to serve Yuan Shang, who is weak and lost everything!" Teng Dao countered. **"I chose Lord Yuan Tan, who now rules–!"**

"Who now 'rules' Nanpi, and that's only at knifepoint," Qian Zhao interrupted. **"He isn't strong at all: all he's done so far is retreat from His Excellency Cao."**

The Wuhuan men exchanged confused glances.

"...You... serve *Cao Cao* now...?" Teng Dao asked.

"I serve *the Han* now," Qian Zhao replied.

Supuyan's allies laughed at the idea; Supuyan himself smirked and said, **"The Han...? The Han emperors only know how to be prisoners now!"**

"If you'd come here as Yuan Shang's man, that would be bad enough," Teng Dao heckled. **"Go away, Qian Zhao! You are a weak fool serving a weak fool that pretends to be serving a weak emperor!"**

"You're all mouth," Qian Zhao retorted. **"Cao Cao is not weak:**

282

he came here and took Yè from Yuan Shang, who was busy defeating your lord with ease! It is Yuan Tan that is weak, the weakest of all, and you are his subordinate, which makes you even weaker!"

Supuyan smirked and said, "**This man 'Qian Zhao' makes a good point.**"

"**N-not at all!**" Teng Dao protested. "**Yuan Tan took all of northern Ji and defeated Yuan Shang at Zhongshan!**"

"**He 'took all of northern Ji' while Cao Cao took Yè, which Tan could not even get close to,**" Qian Zhao retorted. "**He 'defeated Yuan Shang at Zhongshan' after His Excellency Cao Cao had already defeated him and taken all of his best men from him!**"

The Wuhuan men started to murmur agreeably.

"...**Dog!**" Teng Dao cried. "**You-!**"

"**Tan has lost all of northern Ji except for Nanpi, and he failed to kill Yuan Shang even when he had more men!**" Qian Zhao continued. "**Weak... WEAK!**"

Teng Dao could tell that Qian Zhao's arguments were swaying the Wuhuan; in a last, desperate show of defiance, Teng drew his sword and said, "**I, Dao, will show you that I am not all mouth, Qian Zhao! You will see why Yuan Tan favours me!**"

Qian Zhao drew his own sword, and the two envoys started to duel; it began as cautious circling with the occasional slash or swipe, but it soon devolved into a hand-to-hand brawl that ended when Qian Zhao – who was the stronger of the two – wrestled Teng Dao to the ground and kicked him in the chest. The Wuhuan started to converse in their native tongue: it was clear to both envoys that Qian Zhao had done enough damage to Yuan Tan's reputation, and that the real fight was over.

"E-enough...!" Teng Dao pleaded.

"...'**Enough**'...?" Qian Zhao taunted. "**What kind of man are you...? Get up and fight!**"

Supuyan got to his feet, approached Qian Zhao and slapped his arm, saying, "**You are strong! You are clever! Cao Cao has strong men!**"

"...I am nothing special," Qian Zhao replied. "His Excellency Cao Cao sent me because he can afford to lose me: he has a hundred others like me."

"Really...?" Supuyan exclaimed. "That is interesting. What does Cao Cao want?"

"He wants peace in the land, between everyone, where everyone gets what they need," Qian Zhao replied. "The Yuans are stupid and cannot be trusted. They will use you and then betray you."

"...So will Cao Cao, maybe," Supuyan retorted. "What does Cao Cao want... from *me*, *right now*? He wants us to fight Yuan Tan with him?"

"He wants you to turn back so that he can fight Yuan Tan with just his own army against Yuan Tan's army," Qian Zhao said. "His Excellency Cao Cao needs no help: and if Yuan Tan is strong, then he will win, won't he? He shouldn't need you to save him."

Supuyan smiled dryly and replied, "That is true. I will not waste time on weak men that cannot win without being saved first. I will turn back. If Yuan Tan is stronger than Cao Cao, let him prove it, and then I will join him again."

Qian Zhao bowed slightly and said, "You are a wise chieftain."

"...Cao Cao has many strong men working for him... very interesting," Supuyan continued. "Maybe Cao Cao will win."

"What will happen to Teng Dao now?" Qian Zhao asked.

"He can go away," Supuyan scoffed. "He is weak and stupid. Let Yuan Tan send someone better. Will you feast and drink with us before you leave?"

Qian Zhao laughed and said, "I should like that very much!"

Yuan Tan was infuriated when Teng Dao returned to Nanpi to report his own defeat at Qian Zhao's hands and the subsequent withdrawal of Supuyan's Wuhuan reinforcements.

"**Imbecile!**" Yuan Tan cried. "**Your weakness and incompetence has harmed my cause! Death to you, you worthless bastard! GUARDS!**"

"**Aiee! No, my lord, wait!**" Teng Dao pleaded as he was dragged out of the command tent. "**Give me another chance!**"

"To do what...?" Yuan Tan scoffed.

Guo Tu waited until Teng Dao had been removed from the tent before he turned to Yuan Tan and said, "You have lost your Wuhuan reinforcements, my lord. We are on our own... now is the time to write to Wang Xiu and ask for more men from Qing."

"But I will lose Qing!" Yuan Tan complained.

"It is better than losing your life," Guo Tu retorted. "I shall be honest: if we cannot hold here, you are finished."

Yuan Tan looked at his small retinue of officials: each man hung his head as his eyes met theirs.

"...Write to Wang Xiu," Yuan Tan said. "Tell- ...Tell him to hurry."

"I shall," Guo Tu replied.

"But do not think that I am accepting some sort of defeat as possible!" Yuan Tan continued. "I want Wang Xiu to come here to aid the pursuit of Cao Cao when we rout him! I am the great Yuan Shao's heir! I am not defeated at all! Let Zang Ba and his bandits take Qing Province: I will take it back soon enough!"

"You shall, my lord," Guo Tu replied. "You shall."

Cao Cao clapped his hands together and laughed when Qian Zhao entered his command tent; the assembled officers cheered enthusiastically, which prompted Qian to say, "I have done nothing much, really."

"Nonsense!" Cao Cao replied. "You have averted a crisis! Supuyan was going to turn Yuan Tan into a threatening force that might have reversed my fortunes; now Yuan Tan is little more than an obstacle in my path to inevitable victory!"

"...But a strong, stubborn, potentially effective obstacle," Guo Jia said. "What Qian Zhao has achieved here is most impressive and of great benefit... but we must not become complacent. Now Yuan Tan is the very definition of a 'cornered tiger', Lord Cao, and we must exercise caution, or we will lose a lot of men."

"But in the end, we will still defeat him in a year or less, and for now, that is enough to lift my spirits!" Cao Cao replied. "And that is all due to Qian Zhao: my thanks to you, Qian Zijing, will be more than words. Expect rewards when this is over."

"If I can do more, I eagerly will," Qian Zhao said humbly.

Cao Cao's forces were emboldened by the news that there would be no Wuhuan cavalry coming to strengthen Yuan Tan: the ring of Han military camps around Nanpi isolated Tan completely and ensured that any attempts to call for or receive reinforcements from Qing Province would be thwarted or severely impeded. It was now a matter of engaging in rare but increasingly violent skirmishes, and both Yuan and Cao knew that such a 'war of attrition' had to be resolved quickly. But days became weeks, and an end was nowhere to be seen.

****

60

The esteemed physician Hua Tuo completed a tour of the east of China and returned to his home in Pei County, Xu Province: the Chancellor of Pei, Chen Gui, heard of Hua's arrival and immediately confronted him at his residence. Hua Tuo's leathery skin, foreign features and sunken eyes gave him the appearance of a 100-year-old mountain hermit, and it was almost certain that he had at travelled from the lands to the west or north of Han China in search of expanding his vast array of knowledge; Chen Gui was reluctant to confront Hua but knew that he would be scolded for failing to do so.

"...I have just returned, Mister Chen, and I do not intend to stay long," Hua Tuo grumbled. "I have too much to see and too little time in the world to see it all as it is without becoming the court physician, which is, I can tell, why you're here... *again*."

"You are a wise man and a gifted man, but you are far too aloof and unaware of what you are facing," Chen Gui retorted. "You are refusing to treat the Han's Excellency of Works, Master Hua, for a condition that should pique your curiosity! Why does his ailment mean so little to you...?"

"Severe headaches are a common thing to men that hold high office," Hua Tuo replied. "Many a night spent reading and writing under poor light, the military campaigns, deaths and executions, the pressures of having such responsibility... why is his headache so different to any other man's...?"

"You do not like him," Chen Gui sighed.

"Did we not do this before?" Hua Tuo asked plainly. "His role ensures that he will preside over wars, sieges, executions, massacres, and so on, and I accept that. I have just said that I do not understand what is so different about his headache!"

"I have seen him under the effects of one," Chen Gui replied. "He is crippled by the pain, and can be quite a different man: the pounding of blood that he feels, and the way in which he can become... quite..."

"Violent," Hua Tuo said. "Yes, but I have no reason to believe that his violent turns are anything more than a result of frustration at being in pain. I am trying to find a cure for the plague, Mister Chen; I am trying to discover how the ways of animals and our copying those ways could make us healthier; I am trying to find ways to open men up without killing them to reach internal ailments and cure them; I am trying to find a way to relieve even the most crippling pain."

"And you could test your marvellous pain reliefs on His Excellency!" Chen Gui suggested.

"...And if they fail...?" Hua Tuo asked. "You yourself speak of his fiery temper when he is ill... and I would be punished for failing to help him."

"You're wrong!" Chen Gui protested. "When he returns from Ji Province, I beseech you, Master Hua, to visit him and-!"

"If I have no other case that is more pressing or intriguing, then I will meet with His Excellency," Hua Tuo promised. "Now please... my wife, who is as old as me, has been very poorly, which is why I have returned. Another time, perhaps...?"

Chen Gui sighed, bowed humbly and said, "I shall leave you, Master. I wish your wife well."
Hua Tuo watched Chen Gui walk away and muttered, "I should leave again soon."

Kong Rong was receiving news from Ji Province via Xun Wenruo, who still considered him a friend despite his constant criticism of Cao Cao; Kong waited until one of his popular banquets had ended and most of the guests had left – leaving only his close friends present – before he turned to Zhi Xi and said, "Now Cao fights Yuan Tan... that's good."
"Did you expect anything else...?" Wang Lang asked.
"His Excellency only intended to support Yuan Tan until Yè was taken and Yuan Shang chased away or defeated," Xun Wenruo said. "I expected a man as clever as you to realise that without being told, Wenju."
"It isn't that I didn't expect the deception, it is more a case of being surprised by how far it was taken," Kong Rong replied.
"...And I was surprised by your recent correspondence to His Excellency," Xun Wenruo said tonelessly. "That part about Daji..."
"Indeed, Uncle," Xun Gongda scoffed. "Why do you try to agitate His Excellency, Wenju...?"
Zhi Xi looked at Kong Rong, who smiled and said, "I'm afraid that I don't see the problem, gentlemen. I remarked on the similarity between events."
"Yes, and you're lucky that he misunderstood which event you were finding a similarity with: that was foolish!" Xun Wenruo scolded. "I know that you were annoyed at the alliance with Yuan Tan, but as I just said, you should have known that it was a ruse and wouldn't last!"
"...And it is over, but what comes next...?" Kong Rong asked. "Your lord, the Excellency of Works, has Yè City for a base and Ji Province as a new fief. The-"
"He has *nothing of the sort*!" Xun Wenruo cried.
"But what about the suggestion by some officials that His Excellency should be given the governorship of Ji Province...?" Kong Rong asked.
"...Yes, I know that there are some that suggest that His Excellency should receive the governorship of Ji when it is taken," Xun Wenruo replied cagily. "But that is only to be expected! He will certainly refuse it!"
"But whose will it be if not his, Wenruo...?" Kong Rong asked. "Who will be the lords of those provinces when the Yuans are finally vanquished...?"
"It won't be the lord and his eldest sons, if that is what you imply," Xun Wenruo retorted. "The Yuans have been a lesson in idiocy for us all."
"...Indeed yes," Yuan Huan sighed.
"I meant no offence," Xun Wenruo pleaded.
"And none is taken," Yuan Huan insisted. "I am a Yuan clansman, as is Yang Xiu by blood, but there is no further tie to those traitors, I assure you. I mistakenly served Yuan Shu for a time, becoming something of a cackling villain myself at times, perhaps, as the madness of it all took its toll. But I have seen sense now, and I serve His Majesty gratefully. Yuan Shu... was truly beyond

salvation. At first, some of what he said made sense, but... at the end... he was demented, and rightly died. But Yuan Shao was, at the end, much the same: a rambling drunk, unable to decide if he was trying to save the Han, control the Han or supplant the Han, and more often doing more to control or supplant them, whether that was his intent or not. And now his sons repeat the madness despite, as you say, having the lesson of their father and uncle to look to and avoid such self-destructive folly. They *are* idiots... no other words will do."

"...So why did Cao spare Lady Liu...?" Kong Rong asked. "He doesn't intend to make a concubine of her, does he, as he did with Lady Zou...?"

"Petty, Wenju, petty! Such conduct is beneath a man of your wit!" Xun Wenruo heckled. "*His Excellency* spared her out of respect for his dead friend that he did not want to fight! He certainly wouldn't marry her now, not even to ensure that she was kept! It would be disrespectful and, given her temperament, dangerous."

Kong Rong hummed thoughtfully: he considered bringing up the subject of Lady Zhen's apparently forced marriage to Cao Pi, but he ultimately decided that there was no point.

"What amazes me is the apparent speed of Yuan Tan's decline," Xun Gongda said.

"I agree, Nephew," Xun Wenruo replied. "It took such great effort to defeat Tan and Shang and take Li County; the siege of Yè was expensive to prepare for and tedious to see through; Tan had half of Ji Province, the promised support of a Wuhuan chieftain and tens of thousands of men, but now the reports indicate that he has little more than Nanpi City and some camps around it. Tan was a ferocious tiger that men feared while Shang was seen as feeble by comparison... yet Shang will probably outlive Tan despite his setbacks. Some things are truly hard to fathom."

"...I wonder if Tian Chou will fight for the Yuans or submit," Xun Gongda said.

"He'll submit," Xun Wenruo replied. "He went home to support his home region, not to join the Yuans in a struggle to the death."

"...I should go," Wang Lang said suddenly.

"As should we all, as much as it would be a nice thing to stay longer," Xun Wenruo declared. "Wenju, you are a gracious, generous host... even if you will insist on riling His Excellency at every turn. Please try to view him anew: he is not flawless, I know, but he craves stability and has done more than any other man to achieve it, which even you have to admit."

"I will never shy away from challenging him, but if he is the hero that you say that he is, I will one day speak better of him than any man," Kong Rong replied.

The officials rose and exchanged polite bows: the guests then left their host and returned to their own homes. One of Kong Rong's two young sons approached him as the last of the guests departed and asked, "Why do you challenge Cao Cao, Father...?"

Kong Rong smiled and replied, "Because *somebody* has to."

****

61

The heir to the Yuan clan chieftainship, Yuan Shang, had been hiding in Zhuo Prefecture in the southwest of Yòu Province since his defeat at his own brother Tan's hands at Zhongshan in northwest Ji Province; his half-brother and governor of Yòu Province, Yuan Xi – whose stance since the death of their father had been to remain aloof and neutral as Tan and Shang argued – had initially hesitated in approaching Shang, but he relented and visited Zhuo after repeated requests for him to do so.

"Brother, I wish that we could have met sooner, and under better circumstances," Yuan Shang said as he greeted Xi at the gates of his camp. "I am, as you can see, understaffed: shall we alight to my command tent…?"

"…As you command," Yuan Xi replied tonelessly.

Yuan Shang's adviser and senior general, Yin Kui, noted Yuan Xi's frosty response and hummed thoughtfully.

"Please, Brother, sit!" Yuan Shang said as soon as he was sat at his own host within the command tent.

"…As you wish," Yuan Xi replied as he sat at a distance from his brother; Yin Kui looked at Yuan Shang with a pointed expression.

"I can see that you are confused as to whether you should sit as my brother or as my vassal, but I assure you that I see you as the latter," Yuan Shang said nervously.

"But I am both," Yuan Xi retorted. "And you must excuse my lack of warmth, as I am currently grieving for the 'loss', for no better way of putting it, of my lady wife."

"I… I do not know what to say about that," Yuan Shang admitted.

"I knew that Cao Cao was a villain, and I knew that he had taken Lady Zou at Wan City to his own detriment, but I little expected that the son would be worse than the father. I vow to you, Brother, that when we turn this situation around-"

"Is that possible?" Yuan Xi's aide Jiao Chu asked snidely.

"**You forget your place!**" Yin Kui barked. "**Do not interrupt your lord!**"

"I wonder, Mister Yin, if Yuan Shang is truly worthy or indeed possessed of that role," Jiao Chu retorted. "After all, where is it that Yuan Shang rules now…?"

"Here," Yuan Xi said before any other man could reply. "Lord Yuan Shang is the chieftain of the Yuan clan, by my father's dying decree, and so he is the lord of his brothers and the domains that they hold."

Yuan Shang laughed awkwardly and replied, "That is quite true, Brother, but-"

"In fact," Yuan Xi said as he locked gazes with Yuan Shang, "it is entirely within Lord Yuan Shang's power to demand that I forfeit my governor's seal, my military authority and all of my other responsibilities so that he can rule Yòu absolutely and directly."

"That is so," Yuan Xi's adviser, Mister Fan, agreed.

"…But I will not do that," Yuan Shang insisted. "I am here as… as a guest in your province, Brother, having recently been defeated by our older brother, who has seen fit to ally with the man that killed our father, the villain Cao Cao, who is also the father of the man that stole your wife."

"Which is why I am here as your ally and not Tan's without any internal conflict," Yuan Xi replied. "He and I were born from the same womb in addition to having the same father; I will be completely honest and admit that I have no time for your mother, Lady Liu, after the disgraceful way that she treated my wife or for her deliberately cold treatment of us in her capacity as our stepmother, but... but Tan's betrayal eclipses all that has gone before. He would probably say that I deserved to lose Lady Zhen as punishment for not supporting his claim to the chieftainship, or perhaps others might say I deserved it for my lack of military support during the siege of Yè, but-"

"No, never," Yuan Shang insisted. "You were, in your capacity as a vassal, waiting for my command, which you did not receive until after the city was all but lost. That's entirely my fault, because you were not just a vassal-governor... you were, and are, my brother, and although I could lie and say that I forgot that obvious truth amid the haze of dealing with an unexpected rise to power, I also allowed my advisers, Shen Pei and Pang Ji, to convince me that you were a potential threat. I was wrong, and my folly cost you your wife, who would have been in Fanyang, not Yè, when Cao Pi's father had his victory."

"...Which is the worst part of it is difficult to fathom," Yuan Xi admitted. "I never knew Lady Zhen well enough to truly miss her company, for we were together for such a short time; I must be honest and say that it is the implied part of it that riles me most."

"That you are dead, or as good as, and that Cao Pi married a widow," Yin Kui supposed.

"Very much so, Mister Yin," Yuan Xi replied. "My counsel was of a mind that Cao Cao might have considered negotiating with me, primarily because of my neutral stance during your feud with that heartless older brother of ours... and that perhaps, just perhaps, I could save us all by brokering a peace, and the Yuans would endure for a hundred years more, even if it was as Cao Cao's puppets. But when Cao Pi did that awful thing, he made me a dead man walking and confirmed that Cao Cao intends to exterminate our clan, regardless of what he might say."

"And our fool brother failed to see that obvious thing," Yuan Shang said. "He failed to see a lot of things... including why I was appointed as the heir instead of him. But which of us is the chieftain is now irrelevant, for as you say, our clan's very survival is at stake. I know that I ask a lot of you, Brother, after letting you down so badly, but I have nowhere else to turn at present: Yè has fallen, Gao Gan has surrendered, Tan is now being attacked by Cao – though I could never willingly work with him again – and most of my army has defected to Cao Cao."

"So to return to a previously unanswered point, how do we 'turn this around'?" Jiao Chu asked. "Our reports spoke of Ma Yan, Zhang Yi, Lü Kuang, Lü Xiang and Su Yòu abandoning the Yuans, of Registrar Li Fu being captured, and of hundreds, thousands deserting or defecting; Yòu Province, as you should know, is rife with its own problems. The Wuhuan run rampant as they do everywhere else, but their crimes in this region are frequent and worst in their nature; criminals that claim to support Lord Yuan Xi are little better, but must be tolerated because they are often needed as muscle to repel the Xianbei that all too often stray into the area to pillage the poor people still further; rebellions are commonplace, and completely justifiable. Yes, there are thousands of soldiers and officials in service, but they are former followers of Yuan Shao, Gongsun Zan, Liu Yu and Han Fu... all with their own ideas, all with their own loyalties, all with their own local problems. What kind of army do you hope to make of them, Lord Yuan Shang, and to what end...?"

"Pompous man!" Yin Kui heckled. "How dare you!"

"He is right to ask," Yuan Shang conceded. "I know not what I can achieve now, but it is as my brother has said: if we attempt to yield, as I did at Quzhong, then we will be met with swords, not treaties. Our clan faces certain destruction unless we fight, and so we will fight. We have no choice."

"...I can see that," Jiao Chu replied.

"We must appeal to our remaining followers across the four provinces and urge them to consolidate here for a final battle with Cao Cao," Yuan Shang continued. "We must even be prepared to use Tan if he survives Cao's siege... he can answer for his selfishness later. The survival of our clan must take priority."

"I agree," Yuan Xi said reluctantly. "My resources are at your disposal, my lord, and-"

"For this to work, we must be who we are," Yuan Shang insisted. "You must call me 'Brother', for that is what we are... brothers."

Jiao Chu grimaced.

"...My resources are at your disposal, *lord and brother*, and no demand shall be refused," Yuan Xi continued. "Yòu Province is now our base for the reclamation of our lands and the defence of our clan. Come with me to Fanyang, and I will provide men to reinforce this defensive position should Tan or Cao Cao dare to invade; we can liaise with our cousin Gao Gan, who has surely not deserted us completely, and between us, Cao Cao can be defeated. If Cao could reverse his fortunes at Guandu, why can't we do the same now...?"

"That is exactly what I believe, Brother," Yuan Shang replied. "Lead the way, and I shall follow."

Yuan Shang left his camp in Zhou Prefecture and travelled eastward with Yuan Xi to the provincial capital Fanyang; Jiao Chu followed his lords quietly and unenthusiastically.

****

62

A third skirmish with Cao Cao's forces allowed Yuan Tan to sneak a second messenger out of the Nanpi region; the first had obviously been caught, but the second man was able to make the two dangerous river crossings and reach Qing Province without being intercepted. Yuan Tan's appointed guardian, Wang Xiu, met the messenger at the gates of the capital Linzi and took the letter from his lord.

"…This is serious," Wang Xiu muttered.

"More serious than our own situation?" General Guan Tong asked.

"…We must speak privately," Wang Xiu replied.

Once Wang Xiu and Guan Tong were safely installed in the governor's mansion, Wang said, "Our lord has lost all of his gains in Ji Province: Anping, Bohai, Hejian… all are falling to rebellions, and he is trapped in Nanpi with Cao Cao's men on all sides. He only has Guo Tu for counsel, and his only halfway competent officer in Han Xun, who is no match for the dozens of officers that Cao can call upon, including men that know Han Xun inside out and could predict when he will sneeze."

"*Ayah*… then our lord will be destroyed if he not relieved!" Guan Tong exclaimed.

"And if he is killed or captured – most likely *killed* – then what's left of our armies here will crumble and Qing will fall into Zang Ba's hands… not that any of that matters of our lord is dead," Wang Xiu continued.

"Would we join Yuan Xi in that case…?" Guan Tong asked.

"If Lord Yuan Tan were to die… then we would perhaps consider surrendering to Yuan Xi or even Cao Cao, but not Yuan Shang," Wang Xiu replied. "If he were to be captured, then we must be loyal and do all we can to liberate him, even if it means charging directly at Cao Cao's swords."

"…I agree," Guan Tong said. "Go and relieve Lord Yuan: you can rely on me to hold northern Qing against Zang Ba."

Wang Xiu hummed thoughtfully and replied, "I only hope that I am in time…"

Cao Cao watched as his men were repelled from the extensive network of camps around Nanpi City for a fourth time: the encounters had generated as many casualties as Cao had suffered during the siege of Yè, and it was obvious that there would be many, many more before Yuan Tan was defeated.

"Yuan Tan will die for this!" Cao Cao cried. **"There will be no last-minute reprieve! Yuan Tan will *die*!"**

Yuan Tan had taken to the battlefield in person while Guo Tu held the city and acted as the overall strategist: Tan only had Han Xun for tactical support but that was enough, since his desperate men – who were mostly fighting with every ounce of strength that they had and lacking in any hesitation – were the ones that were deciding the outcome.

"COME ON, ALL OF YOU!" Yuan Tan screamed as he rode around and lunged at soldiers with his decorated spear. **"COME ON, THE TRAITORS AND INVADERS ALIKE: COME HERE AND DIE AT MY HANDS!"**

"**...Order a withdrawal,**" Cao Cao said. "**Fengxiao, we must talk at once.**"
"**As you command,**" Guo Jia replied.

Cao Cao returned to his command tent, sat at his host seat and said, "I am seriously contemplating some sort of temporary cessation of violence."
"I can see why," Guo Jia admitted.
"...Hundreds are being maimed and killed, Fengxiao, and that won't do," Cao Cao continued. "We were dealing with another Gongsun Zan until the Wuhuan were turned back, and now he's another Lü Bu!"
"I did say that he shouldn't be underestimated," Guo Jia replied.
"...You did," Cao Cao sighed. "Now I am paying the price for... I was going to say 'arrogance', but was I being arrogant...? He has less men, is surrounded, and lacks outside support of any merit."
"There are reports of two armies moving west from the Le'an and Ji'nan regions of Qing Province," Guo Jia said. "They are certainly reinforcements for Yuan Tan... reinforcements that might give him added strength or make him complacent and be his undoing. I am not yet sure."
"You're unsure...?" Cao Cao exclaimed.
"I cannot fully assess the desperate or the demented," Guo Jia replied. "He is both. But one thing is clear: while he is isolated like this, his loyal men are going to fight like ten men each, and we'll see losses equal to those we've seen on the last four occasions. You can either persist or make your temporary peace, but you must have an alternate target if you make peace, else the Wuhuan will be back."
"...I must think it over," Cao Cao decided.

"Cao's buckling!" Yuan Tan cackled as he returned to his command tent with Han Xun. "His men are buckling too: we are breaking their spirit with our resolve!"
"Should I attack them while they are demoralised, Lord Yuan...?" Han Xun asked.
"No, no... we'll wait a while," Yuan Tan replied. "Let them suffer. It's like Guo Tu said: they're deep into our territory now, with a stretched supply line, and every action that they take to fix that will make them more unpopular. If they stay, they lose men and look weak; if they flee or seek peace, they look weak, the Wuhuan will return to my side, and I have as good as won. Let them suffer, Han Xun... let them suffer!"

"...So Shang and Xi are allied at last."
Bing Province Governor Gao Gan finished reading a letter from Yòu Province and turned to his adviser Gao Rou, adding, "And we have established cordial relations with Wang Yi of Hedong."
"We have," Gao Rou replied uneasily. "But I must remind you, Lord and kin, of the penalty for submitting and then 'rebelling' again. *Death... painful* death."
"I know it," Gao Gan said. "But Cao Cao allowed me to stay in my post; apart from appointing that annoying man 'Zhang Zhi' as some sort of spy, he has left me be, despite my ties to the Yuans. Wang Yi is angry because Cao has abandoned Hedong after subjecting it to 'protection' by Qiang tribal 'guardians' that

probably showed little respect for the people; he is obviously unhappy with Cao Cao. And now Lord Yuan Shang is safely installed in Yòu Province with Yuan Xi as his ally. I do not know how the battle between Yuan Tan and Cao Cao will end, but it can only end in two ways: Cao Cao can win, at which point he will travel northward and attack Lord Yuan Shang; or Cao Cao can lose, at which point Yuan Tan will call on others to aid his rout. In each case, we will be expected to act: could we aid a fleeing Cao Cao by fighting our own kin...?"
"...A valid question," Gao Rou replied.
"If Cao wins, then our dilemma is similar: can we aid Cao's destruction of the Yuans when we are asked to...?" Gao Gan asked pointedly. "After all, that is his intent: it has to be, else why allow Cao Pi to steal Lady Zhen from Cousin Xi?"
"...Again, a valid point," Gao Rou replied. "I can only recommend seeing what happens and acting accordingly. If, at any point, Cao Cao is vulnerable and our path is clear, then we should act. But remember that the Black Mountain Bandits are now helping Cao Cao, and that help includes preventing free movement into Ji Province through Maocheng."
"They're already losing supporters as 'the lines become blurred'," Gao Gan insisted. "And we didn't have Hedong as an ally before! In fact, ironic as it sounds, we might even have smaller Qiang tribes in Hedong aiding us in addition to the Southern Xiongnu rebels and Wuhuan 'rebels' that traditionally assist us! Perhaps Ma Chao will add his formidable spear to ours!"
"...Perhaps, my lord," Gao Rou replied. "We'll wait, though, and see what happens."
"And in the meantime, I'll continue to cultivate alliances," Gao Gan said. "The Yuans are not defeated yet... there is still hope...!"

Cao Cao was once again forced to do without Guo Jia when the adviser fell sick again; he was sat in his command tent and dreading the onset of another of his migraines when his cousin Cao Chun approached him.
"...You're done in Pingyuan...?" Cao Cao asked.
"I've left the place to others: Yuan Tan won't be regaining that place any time soon," Cao Chun replied. "But I've been asking around, Mengde, and it sounds like you want to parley now."
Cao Cao nodded silently.
"Don't," Cao Chun pleaded. "The-!"
"Challenge me during the meeting I've called," Cao Cao interrupted. "But your challenge should be a good one, Zihe. You've seen the situation...?"
Cao Chun exhaled loudly and said, "Yes, I have."
"Coffins... coffins upon coffins," Cao Cao complained. "Unburied dead... so many dead, and the injured... so many injured. Yuan Tan's become a mighty cornered tiger – nay, a lord of an army of cornered tigers – and now my men are fighting half-heartedly. This is what I feared of Yuan Shang when he advanced from Pingyuan to save Yè: Yuan Tan has rightly adopted the 'death ground' approach and sent his men to fight to the last. Guo Jia is sick; Jia Xu is preoccupied with a pro-Yuan Tan rebellion in western Anping that has also robbed me of Xu Huang and Qian Zhao's presence; Yue Jin is wounded, though it is thankfully

minor; we're short of horses; some of Lü Kuang's men defected; Cheng Yu is also preoccupied with pro-Yuan Tan rebellions in Li County; Yuan Shang's few remaining supporters are also rising up, requiring separate contingents to deal with *them*; and there are at least two armies moving west to relieve Tan, one of which is being delayed by Zang Ba, but for how long can he do that while he has his own problems, and while those armies pass through Ji'nan, where I am less popular than Dong Zhuo...?"

"...I see your dilemma, Cousin Mengde," Cao Chun admitted. "But I have an answer."

"I look forward to it," Cao Cao sighed.

Cao Cao summoned his officials to the command tent an hour later and said, "I want to call a truce with this savage, unbridled tiger that we face before he does us too much harm."

"Don't give up now, Mengde!" Cao Hong pleaded.

"Keep fighting!" Xiahou Dun said. "He isn't made of stone!"

"No, but his resolve is making his army like stone, and my poor men, new and old, like so many eggs being dashed against that stone," Cao Cao retorted. "I see the huddled men, hear the grumbling... we are losing support, and so we must be more cautious in our dealings with Yuan Tan."

"I disagree," Cao Chun said. "Our predicament is obvious: we're deep in enemy territory; our supply line is stretched; our efforts to procure supplies locally are riling the people, who already distrust us."

"That's your long-awaited argument?" Cao Cao scoffed. "That reinforces my desire to call a truce!"

"I am not finished," Cao Chun insisted. "Yes, if we stay, we suffer harm, but if we flee or have the truce you seek, that will be exactly what they want. When they win, they become vain, and we fear worse defeats... they know that. But we must use that growing fear against their growing vanity, becoming 'cornered tigers' ourselves to deflate their arrogance, and that way we are sure to win."

"...An offensive stance," Cao Cao mused.

"I am prepared to stake my own reputation on it," Cao Chun said.

Cao Cao looked to Xin Pi, who said, "I agree with Cao Chun."

"...Cao Chun: you will act in whatever way you see fit," Cao Cao ordered. "Had I been using your cavalry and attitude from the onset, I might have known better results: do as you have suggested, Zihe, and destroy them once and for all."

"I shall not disappoint you," Cao Chun promised.

Cao Chun had the war drums prepared and arrayed the armies of Xiahou Dun, Cao Hong, Li Dian and Zhang Hè in preparation for a follow-up rout; Chun's own elite cavalry then most to the front line, and Yuan Tan advanced to meet them. Cao Cao left his command tent and rode to the rear of the army with Xin Pi at his side: he silently hoped that Cao Chun's gamble worked.

"IF WE LOSE HERE, DEATH IS ALL THAT AWAITS!" Cao Chun declared. **"FIGHT THIS FIGHT AS THOUGH IT IS YOUR LAST, BECAUSE IF YOU LOSE, IT *WILL* BE YOUR LAST!"**

The soldiers were startled and emboldened by the announcement.

"YUAN TAN DIES THIS DAY, OR THE HAN IS LOST!" Cao Chun

continued. "**ALL OF YOU: BE READY!**"

Yuan Tan watched the enemy army's preparation and laughed, saying, "**Look at how they try to intimidate us with their numbers! But our men are each worth ten, no, twenty of theirs! Let's finish this now!**"

Yuan Tan's charge did surprising damage and threw the Han forces into a panic, just as he had intended: Cao Chun took personal control of the main war drum and beat it with all of his strength, and his galvanised cavalry responded with a charge that finally started to match Yuan Tan's front lines and gradually destroy them.

"**IDIOTS!**" Yuan Tan cried. "Han Xun… **HAN XUN!**"

Han Xun had been part of the front line, and he was as dead as his men; Yuan Tan urged his men to fall back and regroup, but the whole of Cao Cao's army was now charging, and it far outnumbered his. The anger and desperation that had driven Yuan Tan's men and made them stronger had now been effectively matched by the enemy, negating that small advantage and restoring organisation and numbers to their place as the main factors of the outcome. Yuan Tan tried to flee to the city, but Yue Jin had led a force to attack the east wall and had seized it while the defenders were distracted by the field battle; in addition, Cao Chun's cavalrymen had hacked their way through Tan's bodyguards and were within striking distance on all sides: Tan turned his horse to flee to the east, but it stumbled and threw him to the ground.

"**Somebody come to my aid!**" Yuan Tan cried as he hurriedly got to his feet; he looked in all directions, but his remaining men were too busy fighting.

"**Where is Yuan Tan???**" Xiahou Dun screamed. "**I want his head taken!**"

Yuan Tan continued his retreat on foot, but he was intercepted by one of Cao Chun's cavalrymen, who closed in and raised his sword to strike. Yuan Tan looked up at the horseman, smiled, harrumphed and said, "**You know who I am! Spare me, soldier, and I will make you a rich ma-**"

The cavalryman brought his sword down with all of his might, nearly severing Yuan Tan's head from his shoulders; Tan's body fell backwards, and the cavalryman jumped down from his horse so that he could finish what he had started. Word travelled quickly, and the resistance around the city of Nanpi disappeared.

"**REPORT! Yuan Tan has been killed, and Yue Jin has taken Nanpi City!**"

Cao Cao frowned when the messenger finished his report.

"**…Are you not going to say something, Your Excellency…?**" Xin Pi asked.

Cao Cao started to laugh; the messenger grinned involuntarily.

"**Very good young man… very good!**" Cao Cao chuckled. "**Go and celebrate with your colleagues… while I prepare to reward Zihe and Yue Wenqian for this incredible feat!**"

The messenger retreated.

"So soon," Xin Pi murmured.

"**I did not hear your words, but I suspect that the suddenness of this has taken you aback, as it has me!**" Cao

Cao said. **"But he is dead, Zuozhi, and now Nanpi is ours! Heaven favours me again!"**

Registrar Li Fu arrived just as Cao Cao was preparing to enter Nanpi: he asked to speak with Cao and said, "Please, Excellency, do all that you can to reassure the people and execute only those that are guilty of the highest service to Yuan Tan."

"The city aided Yuan Tan," Cao Cao countered. "Does that not deserve some punishment…?"

"The people were frightened," Li Fu replied. "The Yuans have been their masters since Han Fu was ousted. Your arrival is unsettling. If you sack the city, they'll turn to Yuan Shang and Yuan Xi. Treat them well and allow the city to return to normal, Excellency, and this province is yours to command."

"Li Zixian is quite right," Xin Pi said. "Nanpi must be an example of how you intend to govern all of Ji… and all of the Empire."

"…It shall be as you say, Li Zixian," Cao Cao declared. "I entrust you with reassuring the people, Li Zixian: I have the business of dealing with Guo Tu and the other wretches to attend to."

"Guo, I have no pity for," Li Fu replied. "His end is long overdue."

Cao Cao commandeered the mansion's audience hall and had Guo Tu and the other Yuan Tan loyalists brought before him. Yuan Tan's severed head was placed on a small table in front of the host seat: Cao Cao smirked and said, "Look, gentlemen, at the man you pledged your lives to. Your end will be much the same."

Many of Yuan Tan's officials started to wail and plead for forgiveness; Guo Tu scowled and replied, "Wicked villain! You won't be satisfied until the Yuans and all of their great achievements are dust!"

"In a way, Guo Tu, I have you to thank for many of my victories," Cao Cao heckled. "You conspired to ruin your lord Han Fu and hand Ji Province to Benchu; you then whittled away all of your 'rivals' – Xu Yòu, Dong Zhao, Qu Yi, Tian Feng, Ju Shou – with slander and traps. More men have come over to me because of you, Shen Pei, Pang Ji and Xun Chen than through any of my own efforts. It is, in part, your treachery that gave me Zhang Hè and Gao Lan as well! I am as much in your debt, in a way, as I was to Xu Yòu for that victory at Guandu, but such debts to such men as you are best left unpaid."

Guo Tu's eyes wandered.

"You were set to reach the greatest heights, but then you were outfoxed by Shen and Pang, who made Yuan Shang the clan chieftain and left you with no choice but to serve Yuan Tan," Cao Cao continued. "But yet again, you were set upon being the lone counsel… I'm sure that Xin Ping's death was probably not much of a disappointment."

Xin Pi scowled at Guo Tu, who hung his head in shame.

"…Your death alone will not suffice," Cao Cao continued. "Your clan will know destruction to the third degree: your children, consorts, siblings, parents, servants… whoever I can get my hands on, they're all dead."

"Spare them, Excellency!" Guo Tu pleaded. "I cannot face them in the afterlife and-!"

"You brought this misfortune upon them and yourself," Cao Cao said. "Your vile, needless toadying and intriguing made enemies of Benchu and me, exacerbated the Yuan feud, caused the Son of Heaven and the court to endure untold horrors and put cruel, seditious thoughts in Benchu's kind heart. We are where we are today because of men like you... and none of you will go unpunished. Death to you all, and death to your families. Your bloodlines must harm the Han no more. **GUARDS!**"

Guo Tu and the other officials pleaded for their lives for one last time, but their cries were ignored as they were dragged from the hall by pitiless soldiers.

"...Was that not all true of *Shen Pei*, Excellency...?" Xin Pi asked.

"A wise lord listens and learns," Cao Cao replied. "I would not spare Shen Pei if he were here again now."

Xin Pi looked at the head of Yuan Tan and asked, "What of their lord's family...?"

"...There can be no future quests for revenge," Cao Cao replied. "A wise lord listens and learns, as I said: I'm hearing about events in Jiangdong, for example, where the Suns are suffering assassinations at the hands of loyalists and kin of their victims. Already, Sun Ce has fallen to Xu Gong's son and Sun Quan's younger brother Yi to former vassals of Sheng Xian. And then there is Yi Governor Liu Zhang's fractured relationship with Zhang Lu of Hanzhong. To prevent such things, all of Yuan Tan's loyalists and kin must share his fate."

"...Wang Xiu is still advancing," Xin Pi noted. "Spare *him* if you can, Excellency. He is a great asset."

"If he yields and does as I ask of him, then I will gladly spare him," Cao Cao said as he turned his own gaze to Yuan Tan's severed head. "...But the other Yuans... must end their days as this one has. It has gone on too long... and must end."

Wang Xiu surrendered as soon as he arrived in Nanpi, at Li Fu and Xin Pi's suggestion: word of Yuan Tan's demise then travelled to Qing Province, where it was met with rebellions and protests against Yuan Tan's last remaining loyalist, Guan Tong. The rebellions and continued attacks by Zang Ba's former Mount Tai Bandits forced Guan Tong out of the capital Linzi and pushed him toward Le'an Prefecture in the northwest corner of Qing Province: the capital, named for the place, had the Ji River to the west and north and the sea to the east as natural barriers, so Guan hoped that he could defend the place for no other reason than to defy Cao Cao. The gesture was meaningless: Yuan Tan's death had placed all of Ji and Qing Provinces under Cao Cao's control and left the only obstacle to conquest – the two surviving Yuan brothers in You Province – geographically isolated; the additional submission in entirety of the Black Mountain Bandits indicated that an end to the great northern campaign was near at last. But there were still a few surprises left for the weary Excellency of Works as he prepared to go northward.

****

63

Emperor Xian and his court were stunned and silenced by the news that the eldest of Yuan Shao's sons had been killed at Nanpi; Kong Rong smiled gratefully, as it gave him the desired conclusion to the acrimony between Tan and the Kong family.

"...So *quickly*...?" Emperor Xian exclaimed.

"It is a genuine surprise to all, Your Majesty," Xun Wenruo said. "There is now an opportunity to pacify Ji and Qing and then advance to Yòu Province and end the Wuhuan threat in addition to the Yuan threat."

"We can truly believe that Mister Cao has it within his ability," Emperor Xian replied. "Ji and Qing Provinces are so quickly and easily returned to our control... we look forward to seeing Bing and Yòu Provinces liberated soon as well."

"As do we all, Majesty," Xun Wenruo said.

"How long does His Excellency Cao intend to remain on campaign without returning to Xuchang...?" Kong Rong asked.

"For now, it is too important that His Excellency remains close to the enemies of the state," Xun Wenruo replied. "His intent, for now at least, is to establish Yè as a main base of operations and coordinate everything from there and a series of other key cities such as Li County City, Nanpi, Pingyuan, Zhongshan and Handan, depending on the exact nature of the problem."

"And what of Qing Province...?" Kong Rong asked. "If Yuan Tan is no longer the governor by his treasonous father's decree, then who *is*...?"

"...That has not been decided," Xun Wenruo replied awkwardly. "For now, the province is still suffering some pockets of resistance, primarily at Le'an."

"But the capital, Linzi, is in the hands of the former Mount Tai Bandits," Kong Rong noted. "Whoever controls the capital of a province controls the province."

The statement was met by some stifled gasps and muffled snickering across the rows of identically-dressed officials; Emperor Xian detected another thinly-veiled attack on Cao Cao and looked at Xun Wenruo with interest.

"...Zang Ba is not the Governor of Qing Province, if that is what you imply," Xun Wenruo retorted. "He is acting as a deputised officer of the Han in order to atone for past crimes, and he is, at best, guarding the place until the proper man is found to be appointed as governor... or inspector; whichever is deemed to be more appropriate."

"But I am guessing that I will not be asked to resume the role," Kong Rong said pointedly.

"That is not the best course," Xun Wenruo replied. "It is better suited to a general in these difficult times."

Kong Rong harrumphed quietly.

"...We are most pleased with Mister Cao's progress," Emperor Xian declared. "He shall be rewarded handsomely when this campaign has ended. Is there any other matter to discuss...?"

"Yes, Your Majesty," Xun Wenruo replied. "Agricultural reports..."

At the conclusion of the meeting, Kong Rong left the court with Zhi Xi and Wang Lang; Wang smiled dryly and asked,

"Are you annoyed that you will not be allowed to return to Qing Province, Wenju...?"

"No more than you crave a return to Kuaiji to fight the Suns," Kong Rong retorted. "I am more concerned that Zang Ba might be appointed as governor... and no matter what Wenruo says, I still suspect that to be Cao's intent."

"'Cao' killed your enemy Yuan Tan, and yet you still despise him," Wang Lang sighed.

"I-! ...I... I am grateful," Kong Rong replied. "I am just... underwhelmed by the news."

"You expected Yuan Tan's death to be some great burden of regret lifted from your shoulders, but you are still miserable," Wang Lang said.

"Tan humiliated my family and me, and he deserved what happened," Kong Rong replied. "But Qing Province, which I still have an attachment to from my days as governor, is still unstable... who knows when that will change...?"

Guan Tong's grip on Le'an Prefecture in northwest Qing Province pushed Cao Cao's patience to its limits; he summoned the newly-submitted Wang Xiu to the command room of his temporary base at Nanpi City and said, "Guan was your colleague in Qing Province. I graciously spared you at the request of others that value you, but I am weary of your friend and see no choice but to send you to destroy him for me."

Wang Xiu fell to his knees and replied, "Do not ask that of me, Your Excellency!"

"Do it, Wang Xiu, or I will reconsider my decision to spare you," Cao Cao growled. "Or perhaps you are the most wrong of men to send... would you join him...?"

"...It is not that I disobey your order out of some buried loyalty for Yuan Tan, who is dead and gone now," Wang Xiu promised. "It is rather that I consider Guan Tong to be a most principled, decent, loyal, courageous man that would be wasted in a coffin, Excellency. He is showing loyalty to his lord, even when the lord is dead, because his grief is clouding his judgement and he has nobody to help him see the truth. I will gladly go to Le'an, but only if I am going there to beg him to submit to the Han as I have. If I cannot do that, then I must sincerely refuse your demand and await your punishment."

Cao Cao looked at Guo Jia, Xin Pi and Li Fu before he said, "I am... moved by your honesty and loyalty to your colleagues, Mister Wang Xiu. If you can win Guan Tong over to me, then by all means do: I should also like to employ you properly, if you would serve me as well as you served Yuan Tan."

"I would gladly serve the Empire," Wang Xiu replied.

"...Then by all means go at once, please," Cao Cao ordered, and Wang Xiu retreated.

"That deals with Wang and Guan," Guo Jia said hoarsely.

"You are still not recovered," Cao Cao sighed.

"My ailment takes a little more of me each time, Lord Cao," Guo Jia replied. "But I am still here, am I not...? Anyhow, we digress: you must now pacify Ji and Qing Provinces properly. You must end the perpetual hatred for you in Ji'nan, and win the hearts of the people so that no other force – and that includes Zang Ba – can ever question your authority with any success."

"...How do I achieve it...?" Cao Cao asked.

"You must be inclusive," Guo Jia explained. "That will include working with undesirables in the interim, of course, but none are worse than the Wuhuan, who must be treated in the opposite way. We must invite the gentry to contribute to the government, even families that are not entirely honest, but we must start to dilute their power and influence once they have exposed their activities to scrutiny."

"...And I must force the crime families to make peace as well," Cao Cao supposed.

"Their feuds are costly, and made it impossible for you to remain in Ji'nan," Guo Jia said. "The Empire's future is at stake: they will make peace or face prison."

"...And it gives me closure on an unpleasant chapter in my life," Cao Cao said; he hummed thoughtfully, and then asked, "Tell me, Fengxiao, what do you think of another plan of mine to force men to pay the proper taxes and spend less on memorials to themselves and their associates, whether they be alive or dead...? Would it help or harm me to tell men that they are not kings and should not – or rather, *will not be able to* – create expensive tombs and suchlike...?"

"It is a good idea," Guo Jia replied. "You will earn the respect of the less fortunate if you do such things."

"That has long been an idea that I shared with my mentor Qiao Xuan," Cao Cao said. "I must remember to take an offering for him this year... I must not forget."

"And will you go back to the capital as well...?" Guo Jia asked.

"...I should prefer not to, not until I am done with the Yuans," Cao Cao replied. "It is not that I fear an attempt on my life – after all, I am less safe in Ji – but rather that I do not want to keep conversing with His Majesty about matters unresolved. I want to go back when the Yuans are purged and the Wuhuan are tamed."

"...And what about Zang Ba...?" Guo Jia asked. "What do you intend for him?"

"I... do not know," Cao Cao admitted. "I have to decide, since I know that his presence in Qing – especially in a military capacity with no supervision – worries some. When Guan Tong yields Le'an – which gives me full control of Qing – I will decide what to do."

Guo Jia coughed uncomfortably and said, "That is best."

Zang Ba's followers had surrounded Guan Tong at Le'an, and the expectation was that the Yuan Tan loyalist would be sieged and killed; several leaders – including the characteristically cynical Chang Xi – were angered by the arrival of a negotiating party led by Wang Xiu and General Yu Jin.

"Don't start with the 'That was my last chance' speech, Chang," Zang Ba said as Chang Xi and his growing band of followers confronted him in his camp command tent. "This isn't a turnabout: Yuan Tan is dead, killed by Cao's men, and this-"

"We should get Qing Province now!" Chang Xi heckled. "We should get Xu as well, but we're at least owed our home to run!"

Chang Xi's followers murmured agreeably.

"...That isn't going to be how it goes," Zang Ba replied. "We're reformed bandits, Chang: we escaped death for our activities, and we got jobs in the administration. That's it: when this is over, we go home and-"

"I reckon we are all of us leaders entitled to be prefectural administrators," Chang Xi said. "You should be Governor, just because you were our 'king', but-"

"That would involve me demanding it from Cao Cao, and I'm not doing that," Zang Ba interrupted. "In fact, I intend to go to Yè with a tribute and to see what Cao Cao hints that he wants from us now."

"A *tribute*...?" Chang Xi scoffed. "**We won this bloody province for him and-!**"

"**Get it through your thick skull!**" Zang Ba shouted angrily. "**We have all that we are going to get, and we should be grateful for it!**"

Chang Xi grunted irritably.

"...If Wang Xiu convinces Guan Tong to submit, I'll go back with him and Yu Jin, and see Cao Cao in Yè," Zang Ba continued. "And whatever he wants us to do next, we do it... alright...?"

The murmurs and grumbles told Zang Ba that the majority were with him, but Chang Xi's supporters increased with every statement that Zang was forced to make.

General Yu Jin approached Chang Xi at the end of Zang Ba's meeting.

"...Yu Wenze!" Chang Xi exclaimed. "You... heard us in there...?"

"I have just arrived," Yu Jin replied tonelessly. "Wang Xiu has already talked Guan Tong into yielding Le'an City and submitting to the Han, so I am here to tell Zang Ba that we're going back."

"You can tell me, friend," Chang Xi said. "Are we getting Qing Province as a reward...?"

"...I have not heard anything of that kind," Yu Jin replied. "His Excellency is not likely to 'give' the province to you. There may be better appointments as rewards, but no, I don't think there will be ab independent Qing run by you and the rest."

"There *should be*," Chang Xi grumbled. "We-!"

"For your own good, say no more," Yu Jin urged. "I will have a drink with you before I leave, but I must speak to Zang at once."

"...Fine," Chang Xi replied; Yu Jin continued on his mission to speak with Zang Ba, leaving Chang Xi to wonder if he should accept his lot or do something drastic.

Cao Cao moved back to Yè City once Nanpi had been stabilised: restoration work was proceeding well, and most of the provincial capital was operating normally once again. Wang Xiu, Guan Tong, Yu Jin and Zang Ba announced their arrival within days, and a banquet was arranged to celebrate the end of the first part of the campaign to destroy the Yuan brothers. When word reached Xuchang, many of the officials wanted to attend and sought leave from their work; Kong Rong was particularly keen to go to Yè, to the horror of his friend Zhi Xi.

"Don't be a fool!" Zhi Xi pleaded. "I know that you-!"

Kong Rong ignored Zhi Xi's protests and told a junior official, "You will look after my office until I return."

The official bowed humbly.

"...You want to challenge him again!" Zhi Xi whined.

"I will behave impeccably," Kong Rong replied. "I am saddened that you will not be joining me... but I have Wang Jingxing to talk to on the way there."

Zhi Xi took Kong Rong to one side and whispered, "Don't trust Wang Lang so much. He's shifty."

"Jingxing is a man that adapts to circumstance, which is altogether different to 'shifty'," Kong Rong insisted. "I know what I am doing."

Zhi Xi lowered his head and sighed miserably.

While Cao Cao was preparing to celebrate the death of Yuan Tan, Tan's siblings – Yuan Shang and Yuan Xi – were unsure of what they should be thinking when the news finally reached them in Yòu Province's capital Fanyang. The two sat quietly in the main audience hall of the governor's mansion while their senior subordinates – Yin Kui, Jiao Chu, Mister Fan and Zhang Nan – looked on wearily.

"...Are we meant to be glad...?" Yuan Shang wondered.

"I am now upset, even after his willingness to be an ally of that wife-stealer," Yuan Xi admitted. "I suppose that I accept that he would have betrayed Cao eventually."

"His death ends the contest of my chieftainship, on the other hand, and acts as a unifying force," Yuan Shang said coldly. "All those that support the Yuan clan no longer have cause to be confused: I am the sole light for them to look to now, and that will surely benefit us over the coming months. We can approach Tadun and Louban, re-establish communications with Gao Gan, appeal to everyone in Ji and Qing that still yearns for our sound governance or, if not that, hates Cao Cao at least and wants him dead as we do... today, the Yuan resurgence begins anew."

Jiao Chu and Zhang Nan exchanged tired glances: the two had just about endured Yuan Xi for some time, but the idea of supporting both of the surviving Yuan brothers had pushed them to the point of seeking alternative lords.

Cao Cao – along with his son Cao Pi and his cousins Cao Chun and Cao Xiu – greeted the banquet guests at the gates of what was now the Cao residence in Yè City; Cao Cao was surprised at Zang Ba's attendance, since its meaning was unclear, but the sight of Kong Rong did not fill him with the usual sense of unease.

"Wenju," Cao Cao chuckled. "It is good to see you again."

Kong Rong smiled and said, "You are a true marvel, Excellency."

"That last letter from you gave me quite a start, but now it makes me smile," Cao Cao continued. "Your comment about Daji was very poignant... although I did not recognise the exact form of the accompanying quote. Might I enquire the source...?"

"Source...?" Kong Rong replied as he briefly turned his eyes toward Cao Pi. "Observation, nothing more: I saw what happened here in the present and thought 'It must have been so'."

Cao Cao's smile faded, and his expression hardened; Kong Rong bowed slightly and passed the welcoming party without another word. The next guest, Wang Lang, approached Cao Cao and bowed humbly, but Cao Cao was lost in a daze and did not acknowledge him.

"...Mengde...?" Cao Chun prompted.

"Uh...? Oh, uh... Wang Jingxing," Cao Cao bumbled. "You, uh... are

most welcome, Jingxing... most welcome."
"Your work here is incredible, Excellency," Wang Lang replied. "Soon the Empire will be united once again."
"I... I hope so," Cao Cao said quietly. "It... is good to see you."
Wang Lang sensed that Cao Cao had been affected by the conversation with Kong Rong and continued on his way after a polite bow.
"...Mengde, what is it...?" Cao Chun asked.
"N-nothing," Cao Cao replied as he finally gained control over his anger. "We have more guests to greet!"

The banquet proceeded well enough, despite Cao Cao having to constantly refrain from glaring hatefully at the smugly smirking Kong Rong, who was as popular with the intelligentsia as ever and was enjoying the discussions greatly. Zang Ba was noticeably uncomfortable in his place among the generals; most of the veterans of Cao's campaign against Lü Bu remembered the effort and costs of apprehending Zang after Bu's death, and – with the apparent exception of Xu Huang, Yu Jin and Zhang Liao – were not quick to forgive him. The entertainment included dancers, music and an eclectic mix of food from around the various provinces, all accompanied by heated wine and tea: as the evening wore on, Cao Cao became more and more curious as to why Zang Ba had asked to attend and said, **"Mister Zang! I should like to thank you for your support during this recent campaign. Your father would be proud."**
Many of the banquet guests stopped talking when they heard Cao Cao speak.
"...I'm just glad t'be of use, Excellency," Zang Ba replied uneasily. "I never wanted t'be a bandit, see... my father always hated criminals. The 'Ten' turned us to it with their rampant corruption."
"I feel the same," Xu Huang said. "Many 'White Waves' were desperate, angry... the criminals in the government made criminals of us. Now we can be who we want to be, Mister Zang."
"I think so," Zang Ba sighed.
"Forgive my directness, Mister Zang, but... why are you here...?" Cao Cao asked.
Zang Ba smiled awkwardly and replied, "I... want to move my family to Yè."
Guo Jia, Xun Wenruo, Xun Gongda, Yuan Huan, Jia Xu and Xin Pi smiled as one.
"...If that is what you want to do, then so be it," Cao Cao said. "Thank you, Mister Zang."
Zang Ba bowed humbly, ending the brief but eventful exchange.

When the banquet ended, Cao Cao retired to his private study with his many advisers and his bodyguard Xu Chu.
"...I understand that Kong Rong said something unhelpful earlier," Guo Jia prompted.
"I'm drunk, and don't want to talk about it," Cao Cao replied.
"You should," Guo Jia insisted.
"... ... ...That little *wretch*!" Cao Cao cried as his face contorted in anger. "He...! He...! His letter, when he spoke of Daji, he... he did not mean Lady Liu at all!"
"I suspected as much," Guo Jia sighed.
"Then why not say something???" Cao Cao retorted. **"Why let**

me decide that he was being cordial???"

"Kong Rong is popular," Xun Wenruo said. "He's also careful in his heckling, and-"

"**You knew for certain as well???**" Cao Cao exclaimed.

"It... was better that we said nothing," Xun Wenruo insisted.

"As you have just hinted, Lord Cao, you knew that there was possible venom in his words all along but chose to disregard the notion," Guo Jia said. "That is, of course, because he is popular, as Wenruo has already noted... and careful."

"...Popular, but not invincible," Cao Cao growled. "I've... I've toppled taller trees than Kong Rong. Careful, yes... but not always. He'll slip up again, like he did when... when he challenged me on the alcohol ban. But next time... he'll lose more than his job, popular or not."

"...Be lenient," Xun Wenruo pleaded. "Wenju is a rare talent."

"He's a mediocrity," Cao Cao retorted. "Everyone's blinded by him being a... a descendant of Confucius, but... his poems are no match for mine or my sons'."

"Let us change the subject," Chen Qun said. "That announcement by Zang Ba was an unexpected gift!"

Cao Cao forced a smile and replied, "Will his friends be as cooperative, though...?"

"They still fear and respect him... mostly," Yuan Huan said. "I understand from General Yu Jin that there is a growing faction that feels that Zang has gotten weak and wants to go back to their old ways. His submission may hasten their descent."

"If they do, they die," Cao Cao replied coldly.

"...We should retire," Xun Wenruo decided.

"I agree, Uncle," Xun Gongda said. "Sleep well, Excellency."

Cao Cao grunted drunkenly; the advisers bowed respectfully and left the room.

"...Did you want me to hit Kong Rong on the head now?" Xu Chu asked innocently.

Cao Cao laughed and said, "No, no, Zhongkang... dealing with 'Wenju' requires *patience*."

Zang Ba left the governor's mansion after the banquet and walked toward the eastern gates of the city; he was suddenly approached by Yu Jin, who said, "Your announcement came as a genuine shock to me."

"Yeah, well... I see the changing times," Zang Ba replied. "I meant what I said: I was pushed into the bandits out of lack of choice, and in the end I became a bigger criminal than most."

Yu Jin laughed and said, "Life is often strange."

"Now I have to go back and face the others," Zang Ba continued. "Wish me luck, General... and hope that this choice of mine doesn't lead to violence."

Yu Jin hummed ambiguously, and Zang Ba reluctantly continued on his way to the eastern gates in order to begin the return journey to Qing Province.

****

64

Cao Cao invited the scholar and former statesman Cui Yan to his court within days of his banquet: Cui entered the busy hall, bowed and said, "Your Excellency has achieved much in a short time, although is much, much more to do."

Cui Yan's strong posture, commanding voice and fearless gaze was enough to make him strangely intimidating; the official Sima Lang nodded soberly as he studied a man that had long been a friend and wondered what he would do.

"I hope that your calling me by my title indicates that you intend to join my staff," Cao Cao replied. "Look, Cui Jigui, at how many of your former colleagues from the days of Yuan Benchu are now here in his former capital as my aides!"

Cui Yan looked to his right: Guo Jia, Xun Wenruo, Xun Gongda, Xin Pi, Wang Xiu, Chen Lin and Registrar Li Fu – who had all, at some point, served Yuan Shao and even one of his sons in some cases – were prominently placed among the officials. Cui Yan nodded thoughtfully and looked to his left: Generals Zhang Hè, Gao Lan, Zhu Ling, Su Yòu, Lü Kuang, Lü Xiang, Guan Tong and Qian Zhao had all been invited to emphasise the striking number of high-level military defections.

"Some might say that I insult Benchu by sitting at his seat within his capital and surrounded by his vassals, but I was his vassal too, once... and before that, I was his friend," Cao Cao added. "This has not ended as either of us wanted it to."

"...I know that, Excellency," Cui Yan replied. "Though it was very, very rare and always dismissed by Guo, Xun, Pang or Shen, Lord Yuan Shao did sometimes express his regret that the two of you had grown so far apart when you were once so very alike in your aims and principles. It was initially difficult to see which of you had strayed from the proper path: in a sense, you both have, but it is the nature of the men that remain that indicates who has found their way back. If there is any way that I can assist you in restoring order, Excellency, I am ready to serve."

Cao Cao clapped his hands together and said, "Marvellous! Mister Cui Yan, you are famed for your honesty and your understanding of men. I should like that you were now to become a consultant on all matters of state."

"If that is your wish, Excellency, then it is so," Cui Yan replied.

"Marvellous, marvellous," Cao Cao said cheerfully. "If you don't mind, Mister Cui Jigui, we can begin now. The wayward Yuan brothers are still at large, and I must put a stop to that by the only workable means. I have been perusing the official records, and there are three-hundred-thousand soldiers under my command now. Ji Province is indeed great in size and value, but I know that I am unable to use these troops for various reasons. How do I make them available to me?"

"I'm disappointed already," Cui Yan replied. "The Han Empire is in turmoil and the nine provinces are divided, while the Yuan brothers still cause trouble, the Wuhuan go unchecked, rebellions are understandably rife, bodies go unburied and disasters go unrelieved. There is your 'various reasons'!"

Cao Cao's expression was unnervingly unreadable.

"The people have no clue as to how you will bring benevolent government, disaster relief and, if I might be so optimistic, peace to them after so many years of war," Cui Yan continued. "But the first thing you do is to check the records for the numbers of troops and military equipment you've obtained: is this what you think the people of this province expect of you, Excellency...? Is that what you think is right...?"

"*Aiee*... he's dead," Sima Lang muttered.

"...Excellency," Xun Wenruo said uneasily, "I-!"

Cao Cao gestured that Xun Wenruo should be silent; he then got to his feet, which caused many of the officials – and even some of the generals – to shrink backwards reflexively. Cao Cao passed his low table, looked at Cui Yan and bowed humbly, saying, "You have corrected a grave error, Mister Cui, and I am grateful. My faith in you has doubled, and my understanding of how much I have yet to learn is better for your words. Tell me what must be done, and it will be done."

"...A true hero," Cui Yan declared. "To bow so humbly before me, to lower yourself in front of your vassals and so readily admit your faults... you are the hero that the Han Empire has need for so long. You shall have my unreserved help, Excellency."

Cao Cao smiled and said, "My thanks again, Mister Cui. As 'Attendant Officer', you will help me build the peaceful Empire that we have all been so long denied."

Cao Cao retired to his private study after the meeting: Xun Wenruo joined him for one last face-to-face meeting before returning to Xuchang.

"...Now I have Cui Yan," Cao Cao said. "Next, I will attack the Yuans in Yòu."

"That is the right course, Your Excellency," Xun Wenruo replied.

"I know from Cao Ren that Runan needs stronger governance: I intend to appoint Man Chong to that role, unless you can suggest another," Cao Cao prompted.

"He is just the right man for that role," Xun Wenruo replied.

"...And Mao Jie could be promoted," Cao Cao said.

"It's overdue," Xun Wenruo replied. "He's a fine fellow."

"...Yang Xiu is showing promise as a registrar, but Liu Yè will need to stay in that role for now," Cao Cao continued. "And Jia Kui will make an excellent Administrator for Hongnong... though I wanted him in my counsel. I must find a promising man to put in Hongnong, but while it is so beset with unrest..."

"You will doubtlessly find someone, Excellency," Xun Wenruo said.

"...This is proving to be most taxing," Cao Cao admitted.

"His Majesty supports you, Excellency," Xun Wenruo replied. "The whole state supports you in this most important of ventures."

"Yes... it might even be the last great obstacle to peace," Cao Cao said thoughtfully. "If I can topple the Yuans and tame the Wuhuan, then who is left...? Zhang Lu of Hanzhong, who is isolated and doomed; the Qiang of the northwest, who are already partly tamed; the Shanyue and Sun Quan in Jiangdong; and, of course, Liu Biao and Liu Bei in Jing Province. None of them are as dangerous as the Yuans, so why shouldn't this be the end of the hardest stage of the journey...?"

"And then, as you say, the Empire will be reunited, Excellency,"

Xun Wenruo replied.

Cao Cao grunted ambiguously and said, "But then there is…"

"…But then there is what, Excellency …?" Xun Wenruo asked after a short silence.

"…Never mind," Cao Cao insisted. "That's another conversation for a man other than yourself to partake in: go back to Xuchang and continue to serve as my bridge between vassal and sovereign."

Xun Wenruo bowed humbly and said, "Heaven speed you in your great mission."

"…And besides… that conversation must wait," Cao Cao murmured as he watched Xun Wenruo leave his study. "It… is not time yet."

With Cui Yan's help, Cao Cao began to distribute aid to stricken areas of western Ji Province and quell the rebellions. Qian Zhao and Zhang Hè provided support in driving back the most daring of the Wuhuan chieftains in eastern Ji Province without provoking a full-scale Wuhuan-Han war that it was not yet time for; that provided relief to that part of the province and increased the popularity of the Excellency of Works. Qing Province stabilised under the guiding hands of men that Cao entrusted with the task, although Zang Ba's submission had left the Mount Tai Bandits bitterly divided and posed a threat to the mid-term stability of the region. The surviving Yuan brothers and their weary subordinates watched as the preparations for an inevitable Yòu Province campaign intensified. There were differing ideas about how to react among the many administrators, magistrates, rebel groups, bandit gangs, tribal leaders, magnates and criminals in Yòu as the Yuan brothers prepared to do what they believed to be right: defend the imperilled Yuan clan – and their own lives – to the very last and by any means necessary.

****

ACT VI: THE CONQUEST OF BING PROVINCE

65

The Han Empire had once been inseparable from the wealthy and influential Yuan clan of Ru County, but times had changed. When the clan's last great chieftain, Yuan Shao, was the loser of the campaign that is known to history as 'The Battle of Guandu', he was left humiliated and his opponent – the Han Empire's Excellency of Works, Cao Cao – was left with close to absolute power. Yuan Shao's subsequent premature death apparently left his estate without a clear heir, and two of his three sons – the eldest, Yuan Tan, and the youngest, Yuan Shang, whose mother and advisers had apparently connived to have him appointed as the heir with a forged will – fought as Shao and his brother Shu had done years before.

The second generation of feuding Yuan brothers had almost solely preoccupied Cao Cao for 3 years: the renegade warlord Liu Bei and his distant relation, the Jing Province Governor Liu Biao, were a more desirable target, but they had to wait. A series of surprise opportunities had allowed Cao Cao to kill Yuan Tan, humble Yuan Shang and seize two of the Yuan clan's four provincial holdings – Ji and Qing – in addition to securing the reluctant submission of the governor of Bing Province, Gao Gan: that left the northernmost Yòu Province, which was in the tenuous grip of the relatively meek second Yuan brother, Xi, and the third brother and clan chieftain, Yuan Shang. Yòu Province was a notoriously troubled place: it was on the frontier and constantly threatened by the Xianbei and Northern Xiongnu peoples that lived beyond the Great Wall, while indigenous Wuhuan tribes were known for raids on settlements that Yuan Shao – in exchange for the use of their formidable cavalry – had allowed. The instability made Yòu Province a place where crime syndicates and bandit militias thrived as much as the tribal raiders, and rebellions by disaffected people were a matter of course: it would be the most unpredictable and dangerous of battlegrounds for Cao Cao as he prepared for what he hoped to be the final campaign against the sons of his former friend, and proper planning was crucial.

"I wonder what will happen next," Cao Cao said as he moved his eyes along the rows of officials and officers that sat on either side of his audience hall in Yè City, the capital of Ji Province. "We now have more information, I understand; what can we expect from the Yuans if we are honest?"
"Yòu Province was already at breaking point, so I understand," Cao Cao's most trusted adviser, the sickly Guo Jia, replied. "Yuan Xi is seen as a bumbling mediocrity, unable or unwilling to deal with the crime families and Wuhuan tribes that harass his worn-down people. Yuan Shang's arrival with what was left of his once-mighty army has done little to help, as his first wish was to make an army from the locals so that he could come back to Ji Province and reverse his losses."
"Will Yuan Xi aid him as he hopes...?" Cao Cao asked.
"Yuan Xi might have refused to aid Shang under other circumstances, but... but it is a widely accepted fact that he resents the taking of his wife, and... and that the matter has made

it somewhat personal for him, Lord Cao," Guo Jia said with uncharacteristic hesitation.

"Yes, well... what's done is done," Cao Cao grumbled as he turned his gaze toward his heir, Cao Pi, who had taken Yuan Xi's wife, Lady Zhen, for himself after the fall of Yè City several months earlier; Cao Pi was torn between hanging his head in shame and discreetly smiling with satisfaction that he had won an argument and obtained a desired possession, so he opted to do both.

"Yuan Xi is a traitor to the Empire, and so he will soon be executed and he knows it: his 'anger' at losing his wife is an obvious attempt to distract everyone from the real issues," Cao Cao continued. "If they will fight together, they will die together, and that is better for me as it reduces the length of this already-too-long campaign. I have been fighting the Yuan brothers for three years, gentlemen – three years! They seem to have a propensity for causing others to suffer drawn out, costly conflicts... but this will be no seven-to-eight-year affair like the feud between their father and uncle. This will go on no longer than *five years*, gentlemen, preferably *less*."

"We can talk about time frames until the sun sets and rises ten more times, but Heaven has its own ideas," the aged, bitter adviser Cheng Yu said. "The question is whether we march the army northward straight away or wait until something happens. Which will it be...?"

"I favour patience in this instance," Guo Jia replied. "The Yuan brothers are united: when Yuan Tan and Yuan Shang united at Li County and Yè, they made a two-week siege into a six-month war of attrition that forced us to withdraw. By withdrawing and focussing on a false Jing Province campaign, we fooled them into destroying themselves."

"Yes Fengxiao, but that only worked because Tan and Shang hated one-another anyway," the adviser Xin Pi noted. "Xi and Shang have no such animosity between them: yes, Lady Zhen was held hostage by Shang, but that is it. Xi did not contest Shang's chieftainship as Tan did, and they now have a common enemy that, in their minds, has stolen three quarters of their holdings from them and more besides."

"It is not a division of the brothers that I await, Xin Zuozhi," Guo Jia replied. "It is the division of lords from vassals."

Xin Pi nodded thoughtfully and said, "You think that the administrators and magistrates will turn against them."

"Unless they are idiots, yes," Guo Jia replied. "Ji and Qing have fallen; Bing has surrendered. Gao Gan is not the only one: the Black Mountain Bandits have completely submitted and all but disbanded, and the gentry in Ji and Qing are now working with us. If there is no force to aid the Yuans without, then a force within is meaningless, for all it can do is keep attackers out without gaining ground, and that is barely possible in a stable region... and 'stable' is not really a word that applies."

"So we are to focus on making Ji and Qing as stable as possible, and leave the Yuans to be 'betrayed' – if that is, indeed, the right word – by their own vassals," Cao Cao said. "That's good, actually... unless, perhaps, we should use the lull to attack Liu Biao again...?"

"No, Excellency," Jia Xu replied. "I am, as per your instruction, still in close contact with General Zhang Xiu in Nan County, and his spies report that Liu Biao and Liu Bei are not doing anything beyond fortifying the borders and desperately recruiting from what is a quite unenthusiastic populace."

"Yes... the intelligentsia in Jing Province is surprisingly resistant to preparations for war, despite their hating me," Cao Cao said sadly. "And... well, I know that this is a war meeting, but has there been any word about Ying Shao...? That fine scholar should be here, in Yè, finishing his work in safety."

"He's proving elusive," Attendant Officer Cui Yan replied. "I, too, would like to see Ying Zhongyuan safely installed in Yè until this crisis is over. I know that his work entirely involves research into common folklore, but now is not the time to be in random villages asking questions."

"...I know that you're doing what you can," Cao Cao sighed.

"So with that digression at an end, can we return to dealing with Ji Province...?" Cheng Yu asked gruffly. "I will return to Li County and continue to aid the restructuring of the local army and-"

"And, perhaps, disbanding the bandit militias that you created to destabilise the region when Yuan Shang was running it," Guo Jia teased. "You really were a little too effective there, Elder Cheng! You might have ensured that they would behave when they were no longer needed!"

"...They'll disband," Cheng Yu retorted. "Have I failed before?"

"As Mister Cui Yan has already pointed out, there are nine provinces under my partial or total control now, and we must not now forget that Yan Province, Yu Province, Xu Province, Liang Province and Central Province require government," Cao Cao said. "Mister Cheng, you are perhaps due to return to Dong Prefecture and ensure that everything is fine there. I have Registrar Li Fu, Mister Xin Pi and host of other local officials to help me stabilise Li County if Jia Xin cannot do it alone."

"As you wish, Excellency," Cheng Yu replied.

"...And I'll need to inform His Majesty that we're not marching straight away, which will no doubt set the hecklers off again," Cao Cao complained.

"There are all of ten hecklers these days," Guo Jia replied. "Kong Rong being the worst of them tells you that we have nothing to worry about."

"The silent ones are the most dangerous, Fengxiao!" Cao Cao retorted. "If the likes of Kong Rong are the only loud voices, and they only resort to cheap snipes disguised as compliments, then the other dissenters – and they will exist – are now afraid to speak and conspire in shadows instead of confronting me openly! If I am to be an effective statesman, then my rivals, enemies and critics must be visible and vocal so that I can counter them and make them see that I am well-meaning, else how can I avoid another 'Girdle Edict' in the years to come...?"

"Perhaps it is just that you have proven the majority of your critics wrong, silenced your petty rivals and expunged your baseless enemies," Jia Xu suggested.

"Agreed," Chen Qun said. "Wenruo can manage the court well enough, Excellency."

"And my brother Ren can handle the threats in Yu Province, Cousin Mengde," Cao Chun insisted. "You have Cousin Miaocai watching over Yingchuan as well, and Dong Zhao has stabilised Xu Province since being made Inspector."

"...I'm hearing of rebellions against us in Qing Province now, though!" Cao Cao cried. "Didn't we just get rid of their useless ruler for them???"

"The situation is complicated, as you well know, Excellency," Cheng Yu said calmly. "Of *course* there are rebellions: the 'provincial governor', Yuan Tan, has been slain, Zang Ba has submitted to the government, and no clear administration exists: Wang Xiu, as a former vassal of Tan and Kong Rong, can provide some continuity, but that isn't enough. Tan ousted Kong Rong, and Kong has supporters; you ousted Tan, and some – mostly crime lords and bandits – actually liked him. Furthermore, you are unpopular in some quarters anyway, due to your own history with Qing, and until you've proved that the mistrust and hatred were and are misplaced, that will continue to be so."

Cao Cao nodded slowly.

"...It will be something for Zang Ba to deal with," Guo Jia suggested. "He can use it to reassert his authority over the other former bandit leaders, primarily by showing that he can still fight."

"...Yes," Cao Cao agreed. "Write to Zang Ba and have him deal with it. Now what about Gao Gan...? Is it safe to leave him in his post as Governor of Bing...?"

"It is less safe to try to remove him while the Yuan brothers live," Guo Jia replied. "He submitted: he may be dishonestly submitting, but that doesn't matter. If you try to remove him, others that submitted will worry that you intend the same for them and we will have more unrest."

"Guo Fengxiao is right," the official Wang Xiu said. "I know you to be sincere and completely understand why you want Gao Gan removed, but others might not be so understanding. It is better to watch him from a distance."

"That is what I shall do, then," Cao Cao replied. "I don't want to remove him: I want him to understand why I am acting as I am toward his cousins, that they have gone the way of their uncle and become rebels and traitors! I respect his adviser Gao Rou very much and would like for us to all be allies!"

"Perhaps we will be," Guo Jia said. "But that, sadly, is up to the Yuans once again."

"Let them fall soon," Cao Cao groaned. "Heaven, be kind and... have them fall."

****

66

Yuan Shang and Yuan Xi were becoming increasingly desperate as news poured in from Ji and Qing Provinces: the brothers had hoped that the death of their elder brother Yuan Tan would turn the people toward Shang and provoke rebellions against Cao Cao's rule, but the reality was different.

"The fact is, Lord Yuan Shang, that Cao Cao is doing such a good job of ending people's suffering and playing at being the perfect statesman that he is winning hearts and minds instead of losing them," Yuan Shang's adviser, Yin Kui, reported to the court in Yòu Province's capital Fanyang. "The story is the same everywhere, I'm afraid: across Ji and Qing, he is-"

"I... I can read for myself," Yuan Shang said as he lowered a written report to his lap. "Tan did such an awful job in Qing that the Yuans have lost the support of the gentry, the peasants and the army, and the Mount Tai Bandits cannot be bought. The only ray of sunshine is that the people of Qing are rebelling, which should cause Cao Cao some grief."

"And – just for my information – the situation in Ji Province is the same is it...?" the Administrator of Zhou Prefecture, Wang Song, asked irreverently.

"...It is," Yuan Xi's aide Jiao Chu confirmed. "Zhongshan is with Cao; Anping, Handan, Hejian... even *Bohai*, Lord Yuan Shao's old seat, is mostly with Cao Cao. Yes, there are the odd places here and there that still support the Yuans, the odd man here and there, but... the rest, they-"

"Damn that Cui Yan!" Yuan Shang cried. **"This is because of that shifty, faithless man, I just know it! Damn Li Fu as well! Curses upon them all for-!"**

"Your laments serve no purpose," Yuan Xi interrupted.

Yuan Shang turned and glared at Yuan Xi.

"Cao Pi stole my wife and made an indecent woman of her, but I've realised that cursing him won't do anything, Brother, any more than cursing Cao Cao for killing our father has," Yuan Xi continued. "We need a plan, and so far, nothing satisfies."

Yuan Shang relaxed his gaze and smiled apologetically, saying, "I momentarily forgot that this crisis harms you in as many if not more ways than it does me. Yes, Brother, we need a plan, but if Ji and Qing are with Cao, then our only hope lies with a letter reaching Cousin Gan in Bing Province."

"If the Black Mountain Bandits have surrendered to Cao Cao, then they are a new army for Cao to use, like the Mount Tai Bandits in Qing," Jiao Chu said. "The likelihood is that they'll prevent messengers getting through and, perhaps, start attacking western Yòu for Cao, just as they once attacked Lord Yuan Shao's armies in western Yòu to aid Gongsun Zan."

"Yes, and it is my prefecture that will bear the brunt of that!" Wang Song snapped. **"And right after that, Administrator Xianyu in Yuyang will-!"**

"Is it that Zhuo and Yuyang are the only places in the world that matter...?" Yuan Shang retorted.

"...I agree with Administrator Wang," the Administrator of Yuyang Prefecture, Xianyu Fu, declared. "Zhongshan has, at varying times, been classed as part of Ji, and, at other times, part of Yòu; regardless of its ownership, my lord, its allegiances have been, in recent times, with the Yuans, not least because of the harm caused by Gongsun Zan. Now they are not, and that is telling."

"Telling of *what*, Administrator...?" Yin Kui asked aggressively.

"...Of changing times," Xianyu Fu replied. "And Zhongshan is very important strategically."

"Yes, because it a gateway to Zhuo, which I will be tasked with defending!" Wang Song said. "And who will side with me, mm...? The people are fed up!"

"They must not lose sight of who we're dealing with!" Yuan Xi pleaded. "This is *Cao Cao* at our gates, gentlemen! Have you all forgotten his long list of crimes?"

"But is there a truly guiltless man among the warlords...?" Wang Song retorted.

"I have harmed nobody willingly," Yuan Xi insisted. "Cao Cao, from birth, has been a source of mischief and chaos and suffering, and his progeny are obviously the same! As a boy, he was famous for destructive antics! As a young official, he was exiled to Ji'nan for harming the uncle of a eunuch, and when he got there he turned the entire place against him with his unjust behaviour! When he 'fled Dong Zhuo' – while his shifty, dishonest father remained safe in Luoyang, I might add – he slaughtered a close friend's family on the way and stole their money! His first military assignment resulted in the needless death of yet another 'close friend' at Xingyang and emboldened Dong Zhuo's armies instead of harming them!"

The magistrate of Wuzhong County, Tian Chou, scowled at Yuan Xi's appraisal.

"My brother is right!" Yuan Shang said excitedly. "Cao's first administrative role as Governor of Yan Province saw him wage an unjustifiable war against Xu Province, where he slaughtered tens of thousands of innocents and piled their bodies in the Si River! He then 'rescued' the Son of Heaven from the White Wave Bandits at Dong Cheng's request, after which he did what, gentlemen...? He made a puppet of His Majesty, just like Dong Zhuo, Li Jue and Guo Si before him, used that Imperial authority to promote himself, and then declared all of his enemies and rivals – including Father – as traitors! Oh, yes, and then he had a *pregnant* Imperial consort strangled for being Dong Cheng's daughter! *In the palace*! In the *palace*, gentlemen, while the Son of Heaven remonstrated to no avail!"

"Dong Cheng falsified an Imperial edict against Excellency Cao, which is treason punishable by extermination to at least the third degree," Tian Chou retorted. "Chen Lin – the man that wrote your father's famous accompanying denunciation – now serves Cao Cao willingly and fearlessly."

"You speak as an idiot would!" Yuan Shang heckled. "You have the wrong version of events!"

"Do I...?" Tian Chou retorted. "I've listened and learned: Gongsun Zan aided your father's takeover of Ji Province from Han Fu, and then Gongsun murdered Governor Liu Yu, who had notably vexed your father when he earlier refused to be a replacement sovereign for the one we have now! And where is Liu Hè...?"

"Father fought Gongsun Zan, and later killed him!" Yuan

Shang barked. "**The-!**"

"The point, as Wang Song said, is that the warlords are all of them far from guiltless," Tian Chou interrupted. "I'm sick of seeing the aftermath of Wuhuan raids – and now *Xianbei* raids as well, now that those monsters have smelled blood too – and having to console people that have suffered such... ... ...and your father gave the Wuhuan implicit *permission*! By not confronting the Wuhuan, so do *you*!"

The other officials murmured agreeably; Jiao Chu looked at his colleague Zhang Nan, who nodded in response.

"...And the Xiongnu, the Qiang, and the various armies of bandits that Cao Cao sees fit to employ are employed without consequences, are they...?" Yuan Shang asked. "The necessity at this point is-"

"'Necessity'! 'Necessity'! To the lowest level of Hell with your 'necessity'!" Tian Chou heckled. "The people are not with you, Yuan Shang, because *you* are not with *them*!"

The majority of the assembled officials stared to chatter agreeably; Yuan Xi turned to Yuan Shang and whispered, "We must not ally with-"

"**We need the Wuhuan,**" Yuan Shang said coldly. "That is that, gentlemen... that is that. We also need the support of the people if we are to repel the 'Crafty Villain' and restore the order that Father brought to the region."

"*Order*...?" Wang Song chortled. "Where...? When...?"

"...This region has always been troublesome!" Yuan Shang insisted. "Governor Liu Yu could not control the agitators without Gongsun Zan, and Gongsun couldn't manage alone! Father made a difference; what will Cao Cao do...? Will he dam rivers with bodies and needlessly feed the flesh of men to his soldiers as he did in Xu and Yan, and siege cities until they bleed corpses, as he has done before in Yè and Xiapi...?"

The officials grumbled disconcertedly; Wang Song's weary eyes turned to Jiao Chu, who nodded purposefully. Wang Song's eyes wandered for a moment: he then looked at Jiao Chu for a second time, whereupon Jiao nodded slowly and gestured toward his colleague Zhang Nan. Wang Song smiled, turned to look at Xianyu Fu and nodded; Xianyu smiled and nodded in response.

"...We must do all we can to repel this menace when he comes," Yuan Shang continued. "We will not have the support of the people of Ji or Qing: fine, we'll survive without them. We will have trouble getting a letter to Gao Gan: fine, but if a worm like Li Fu can pass Cao Cao's best men to deliver a message to Yè City, then we can find another man to pass a few bandits and get to Bing Province. We will not have the full support of Yòu Province's people: fine, we'll force assistance where it is not offered, according to military tradition! But this province will not yield to Cao Cao, gentlemen: it cannot and should not and will not!"

Jiao Chu smiled and said, "It is probably best for everyone to return to their respective domains now in order to prepare."

Wang Song and Xianyu Fu nodded at Jiao Chu and Zhang Nan, who returned the subtle gesture.

"...Yes, yes... dismissed," Yuan Shang huffed.

"We're not at all popular," Yuan Xi noted as he watched the officials retreat.

"I don't care," Yuan Shang replied. "They are my vassals and must obey my commands, Brother, no matter how much they detest the commands or me. They will understand the necessity of my approach when their lives are bettered by Cao Cao's destruction."

"...I am with you to the end, lord and brother," Yuan Xi promised. "The Caos have taken almost everything from us... but they'll lose more than they took."

"...Tian Chou, Wang Song and Xianyu Fu were particularly vocal," Yin Kui said.

"I think that we must be concerned about the extent of the disaffection," Yuan Xi's adviser, Mister Fan, suggested. "Xianyu Fu and Wang Song are holding key areas for us, and they might need to be watched or replaced if-"

"They are clever men that understand the problems of the day," Jiao Chu insisted. "Let them be, Mister Fan, and they will do the right thing at the critical moment."

"I agree," Zhang Nan said. "They are both the right men for the roles that they hold."

"...Cao must not win," Yuan Shang muttered. "We *must* prevail."

Wang Song and Xianyu Fu met at the western gates of Fanyang to have one last conversation: Wang bowed humbly and said, "Thank you for seeing me off, Mister Xianyu. Next time I shall see you off at the eastern gates."

"...Heaven speed you, and Heaven favour us," Xianyu Fu replied.

"Yes... for time is not with us," Wang Song said. "Good luck to you, Mister Xianyu."

The two men then parted company; Wang Song went west to Zhuo Prefecture's capital, and Xianyu Fu went eastward to his own capital in Yuyang Prefecture.

Days passed: Yuan Shang and Yuan Xi became lost in their preparations for war, despite the reports from the south speaking of nothing but continued stabilisation efforts throughout Ji Province. But as soon as Wang Song and Xianyu Fu were sure that the other was safely returned to their prefecture, the two rebelled against the Yuans and pledged their allegiance to Cao Cao: rebellions broke out across the province, and the unrest eventually reached the settlements around Fanyang City, forcing the Yuan brothers to close the gates of the capital.

"**Traitors! *Knaves*!**" Yuan Shang cried as he paced back and forth across the hall of the governor's mansion. "How can they betray us so...?"

"...Easily, I fear," Yuan Xi replied. "We've made ourselves unpopular, as Mister Tian and Mister Wang said."

"But Cao Cao is the most evil of them all!" Yuan Shang retorted.

"Yes, but Cao Cao isn't behind the Wuhuan raids and the crime lords here in Yòu, is he...?" Yuan Xi noted. "People blame and hate the people responsible for their own hardships and don't much care whether the other person is worse."

"...**Fools, ingrates and churls, the entire lot of them!**" Yuan Shang snapped.

"You do sound like Father," Yuan Xi sighed.

"And I truly understand how he felt now!" Yuan Shang replied. "They betray their *lord*! I am their *lord*! They are my vassals! They

are *mine*! How *dare* they-!"
"WE ARE BETRAYED!"
Yuan Shang and Yuan Xi turned at faced the battered, blood-soaked Yin Kui, who added, "Jiao Chu, Zhang Nan, and... ... ...f-flee, lords, at once!"
"Mister Fan???" Yuan Xi cried.
"Gone! *Dead*!" Yin Kui replied. "P-please... **run!**"

The Yuan brothers were now without most of their closest aides and under attack on all sides: their instincts took over, and they – along with what remained of their elite guard units – fought their way to the northern gates of Fanyang while Yin Kui did what he could to delay the majority of their pursuers. The Yuans escaped the city and fled eastward, but the cost of the unforeseen betrayal had been heavy.
"Where now...?" Yuan Xi asked.
"...Where...?" Yuan Shang replied numbly.
"Yes, *Lord Yuan Shang*: 'where'?" Yuan Xi asked irritably.
"Lord of *what*...?" Yuan Shang chuckled.
"We don't have time!" Yuan Xi pleaded. **"Where do we go???"**
"I don't know anything about Yòu Province!" Yuan Shang retorted.
"It's your province! ...It *was* your province... but now it belongs to those... those *wicked, evil*...!"
"...If Wang Song, Xianyu Fu, Jiao Chu and Zhang Nan betrayed us, then Liaoxi and Youbeiping are unlikely to serve as safe havens either," Yuan Xi supposed.
"Yes, that's... probably right," Yuan Shang said. "...Wait: if... if we could get past the wall to Liucheng, to the Wuhuan... we might be able to turn things around."
The soldiers looked at one-another and grimaced.
"...You suggest that we put ourselves completely at the mercy of Tadun and Louban...?" Yuan Xi exclaimed. "Go *beyond the Great Wall*??? That's guaranteed-!"
"Do we have a choice???" Yuan Shang barked. **"Look, Brother, at our mighty army!** ...A handful of tired, rightly disaffected men that fought for us to get out of that den of traitorous wretches, and... and for what, Brother, if we now die...?"
Yuan Xi looked at the soldiers and sighed miserably.
"We must go north, far to the north, to Liucheng," Yuan Shang continued. "We will seek refuge with the Wuhuan peoples, procure men and resources and make a triumphant return at the head of an army the like of which our father only dreamed of! We'll take back Yòu, and then Ji, and Qing... we'll rescue the Son of Heaven, restore peace...!"
"Restore peace... at the head of an army of Wuhuan tribesmen...?" Yuan Xi said desperately.
"It will work!" Yuan Shang insisted. "Thousands of disaffected Han peoples have joined the Wuhuan, and we'll soon procure more! They'll be anxious to see an end to Cao Cao's villainy, and they'll fight, fight for their lives and for the Yuan clan!"
"...Alright, fine, it's the only choice we have," Yuan Xi conceded. "Which way?"
"I... don't know," Yuan Shang admitted. "We'll have to ask the locals as we travel... unless one of our men knows...?"
"...The only safe way to the north that anyone knows is to go east,

around the Great Wall where it ends at the coast, past Liaoxi," one soldier – a Wuzhong resident – suggested. "That's a long journey, Lord Yuan, and-"
"We don't really have a choice," Yuan Shang retorted. "If that's the only known way, then we should start moving now and not stop until we get out of the Empire."
"…Really, lord and brother, I don't know," Yuan Xi said. "This-"
"It will be fine!" Yuan Shang insisted. "We'll dress as peasants- no, as merchants, travelling merchants, and ask directions as we move. We'll be fine, Brother… we'll be *fine*!"
Yuan Xi hummed cynically.

The mutinies in Fanyang City, Zhou Prefecture and Yuyang Prefecture had yielded most of Yòu Province to Cao Cao without the Excellency of Works putting a single boot or hoof in the region. But the fight for Yòu Province was far from over.

❋❋❋❋❋❋❋❋❋❋❋❋

67

Cao Cao laughed when reports of the mass uprisings and submissions in Yòu Province reached Yè City: he summoned his followers to his court and said, "This is Heaven's will! The Yuans are now wandering the wastelands, searching for some sort of sanctuary, but will they find one...?"

"Not in the Empire," Guo Jia replied.

"...They will retreat to the Wuhuan territories beyond the Great Wall," Jia Xu agreed. "The only question at that point, Excellency, is to ask what type of reception they will get from Louban, Tadun and the rest of them."

"The Wuhuan only respect strength," Chen Qun noted. "Won't the Yuan brothers coming to the Wuhuan heartland with next to nothing lead to the Yuan brothers being laughed away...?"

"Not necessarily," Guo Jia replied. "We must remember that the Wuhuan have thrived under the Yuans, who allowed them to do as they pleased; Lord Cao, by contrast, humbles tribes like theirs and forces their obedience, as he has done with the Qiang, and the Wuhuan will know that or be told so by the Yuans."

"And so we can expect the Wuhuan to aid those boys because it will ensure that the entire northeast – if not more – will be their playground again and forever, which is something that I will not allow," Cao Cao said. "Benchu and I agreed on a lot of things in the past, and we might still agree on some things now, were he alive... but to allow those tribes to inflict horror upon the people in exchange for armies... was one of his greater crimes against the Empire, against its people. The Wuhuan chiefs will bend at the knee or part at the neck, gentlemen, for it can go on no longer."

"And you'll have total support, Excellency," Ji Province Registrar Li Fu promised.

"...And the defectors... especially the new 'Inspector of Yòu Province', Jiao Chu... should I grant them the roles that they so casually claim for themselves...?" Cao Cao asked.

"Is there a Liu Hè to give the seal of office to...?" Guo Jia retorted. "Let Jiao be the Inspector: he would be worrying me if he claimed to be the Governor, but he does not go that far. In fact, he's doing the right thing: by appointing himself as such, he's giving continuous leadership rather than waiting like a puppy and throwing the region into even more chaos. Zhang Nan is 'General of the Household', which is fair enough... the other men simply state that they are in the roles that Yuan Shao gave them, and why not...? They are competent and they have submitted."

"I just wanted to be sure," Cao Cao replied. "Send word to them that we accept the submissions... and hasten preparations for a march northward."

"As you command," Jia Xu said.

Yuan Shang and Yuan Xi were forced to go to the east and weave their way around the Great Wall at the point at which it met the sea: they then continued northward to Liucheng, which was a settlement deep in the mountains. Wuhuan scouts spotted the small party as it travelled and brought them to Louban and Tadun, who were surprised and amused at the sight of humbled, weary but courageous guests from the Han Empire.

"Yuan Shang... and Yuan Xi," Tadun said tonelessly. "You look very... tired."

"We have been betrayed," Yuan Shang replied. "There is no sense working up to it: we have been betrayed and chased out of our domain. Cao Cao will soon take control of all of the northeast."

"Cao Cao...?" Tadun exclaimed. "That's not good. Cao Cao will not let us live as we please."

"...No, he will not," Louban said sombrely; Yuan Shang noticed that Louban was not as confident as he had been in previous meetings, and that Tadun now seemed to be wielding more power than the chosen heir.

"...We must help the Yuans," Tadun decided. "Where is your army hiding, Yuan Shang?"

"I wish we knew," Yuan Xi chuckled quietly.

"Mm...? You say something...?" Tadun prompted.

"My brother... is tired and angry," Yuan Shang replied. "Cao Cao's son, Cao Pi, took my brother's wife to insult him, and now we have lost everything because our own men betrayed us out of fear of Cao Cao. Our army is gone: my brother Tan stole some of my army and then he was defeated by Cao Cao and killed."

"We know about Yuan Tan: Supuyan told us," Louban said bitterly.

"Cao Cao has made everyone fear him, so many have gone to him because he seems to be strongest," Yuan Shang explained. "But he is not: he dares not go into Yòu without the men that have submitted. Cao Cao pretends to be strong and they submit. If we take Yòu back from the traitors, Cao Cao can do nothing, and then we can fight him and get everything else back."

Tadun turned to Louban and said something in their shared Wuhuan language: Louban replied tonelessly, and Tadun nodded.

"...What do you think...?" Yuan Xi asked quietly.

"I think you should be quiet and be patient," Yuan Shang replied.

Tadun had started to say something else to Louban: the two conversed for few moments more before Tadun turned to the Yuans and said, "We will help. We will summon all of the chieftains and get them to help us attack your enemies, because they are also our enemies. What is your plan...?"

"We will attack Yuyang Prefecture, where Xianyu Fu, one of the worst of them, is in charge," Yuan Shang explained. "We will raid villages, collect people and food, build an army, and then we will take Fanyang City from the men there. After that, we can take Zhou Prefecture from another man to close the western routes into Yòu Province to block Cao Cao, and then we can take everything else."

"...We will attack Yuyang... good," Tadun said. "We start soon!"

A week passed.

The submissions of Zhou Prefecture and Yuyang Prefecture and the revolt in Fanyang City were not to everyone's liking: two wealthy clan chieftains, Zhao Du and Huo Nu, were left with less political influence as a result of the Yuans being ousted, so they resolved to do what they could to return things to as they were. Zhao Du assembled as many men as he could while Huo Nu tried to establish contact with the exiled Yuan brothers; the two addressed their followers in a hastily-constructed military camp on Zhuo Prefecture's eastern border.

"The Yuans live," Zhao Du confirmed. **"They are liaising with the Wuhuan."**

The announcement was met by anxious murmurs and cheers.

"The Wuhuan can be negotiated with," Zhao Du promised. **"We can find them some new victims... Cao Cao's lot, for one. Anyway, this is the plan: Wang Song's guarding Zhou Prefecture, which gives Cao Cao a straight march northward, which we can't allow, so we'll take Zhou. Xianyu Fu's not so much of a threat, and the Wuhuan can deal with him; that leaves control of Fanyang, and whoever controls that city controls Yòu Province. We must defeat Jiao Chu and Zhang Nan and take Fanyang back before Cao Cao gets here!"**

News from Yòu Province travelled quickly, but not quickly enough to make a difference; Cao Cao's court in Yè was horrified when a messenger arrived and said, **"REPORT! A 'Zhao Du' and a 'Huo Nu' have attacked Zhou Prefecture's capital and the provincial capital Fanyang simultaneously! Inspector Jiao Chu is missing, presumed dead! General Zhang Nan is dead! Administrator Wang Song is dead! Zhuo Prefecture and Fanyang are in the hands of the rebels! Wuhuan tribes are attacking Gongping! Xianyu Fu-!"**

"Give me the report and get some rest," Jia Xu said miserably; the messenger handed a bamboo tube to Jia and retreated silently.

"This is far from ideal," Xin Pi admitted.

Cao Cao exhaled loudly.

"And Guo Jia is sick *again*," Chen Qun complained.

"Yes well if Hua Tuo would stop *evading me*, Mister Chen, he might cure my headaches and Guo Jia's ailments as well!" Cao Cao snapped. **"Beyond noting *that*, why point out the obvious???"**

Chen Qun lowered his head.

"...Sorry, but I have a migraine right now, and this is... unwanted," Cao Cao continued. "Where did these two rebels come from? Why didn't Jiao and Zhang make sure they were not so easily got at after exploiting similar weakness? How could they fail and die so easily after achieving so much?"

"It is merely a case of being taken by surprise," Jia Xu said. "Dong Zhuo was killed just as easily, if you recall, and you'd think that *he'd* have been more careful."

"...True," Cao Cao grumbled. "So what now, gentlemen...? This is a setback, is it not...?"

"Sadly, yes," Chen Qun said as he raised his head and stared at Cao Cao. "With the roads to and through Zhou blocked once again, we will be forced to take difficult routes into the province."

"And we're dealing with two serious problems," Registrar Liu Yè said. "Firstly, these two men 'Zhao Du' and 'Huo Nu', who are obviously popular and act for the Yuans specifically; and secondly the Wuhuan, who ostensibly act for the Yuans but would help anyone who agreed to let them run rampant."

"And worse still, the report suggests that the Wuhuan are not just attacking Xianyu Fu," Jia Xu said. "They're abducting families by the hundreds from Yuyang, Excellency, and making them travel to the lands beyond the Great Wall."

"...The Yuan brothers have gone too far this time!" Cao Cao cried.

"Our first priority is to eliminate Zhao Du and Huo Nu," the adviser Yuan Huan suggested. "They're blocking the artery roads and giving legitimacy to the Yuans."

"How long before we can safely march...?" Cao Cao asked.

"Ji Province is stabilised enough for us to allocate more men to the main army, Excellency," Cui Yan replied. "An army of fifty-to-eighty thousand is feasible, but I do not recommend anything beyond the lower number if I am honest."

"I only need fifty thousand," Cao Cao growled. "I toppled Yuan Shao, liberated Yè and killed Yuan Tan with fifty thousand. Dealing with two scruffy rebels and a handful of Wuhuan raiders hardly needs more."

"But Excellency, Tadun has committed the entire Wuhuan confederacy to this," Jia Xu protested. "Last estimates placed that army at three-hundred thousand."

The court was filled with gasps.

"...Zhao Du and Huo Nu will be dealt with first," Cao Cao said calmly. "When the roads are clear, we can move more supplies and more men if we need to. Yuan Yaoqing is right when he says that Zhao and Huo must be worried about and dealt with before we start fretting about how many Wuhuan there are. All of you get to your duties... waste no more time talking to me."

The court slowly dispersed; only Yuan Huan, Jia Xu, Xin Pi and Chen Qun remained to provide further counsel.

"The secondary problem is the 'ripples from the impact'," Jia Xu said. "We must be prepared for trouble from Gao Gan."

"Zhang Zhi reports regularly," Xin Pi replied. "We'll know if Gao Gan acts."

Cao Cao's trusted aide Xun Wenruo was delighted when a messenger informed him of the imminent arrival of the former Administrator of Yuzhang Prefecture, Hua Xin; he personally greeted the 49-year-old veteran of southern politics at the gates of Xuchang City and brought him to the chancellery, where Wenruo's nephew, Xun Gongda, was waiting enthusiastically.

"What brings you to the capital, Hua Ziyu...?" Xun Wenruo asked once all were seated and tea had been served.

"I am answering the call for men to come to the capital and serve," Hua Xin replied. "There is no sense in my remaining in Yang Province, Wenruo: the Suns don't trust me completely, so I'd be of no use as a spy; and the preparations for war with Liu Biao are too much for me... it is with thanks to Sun Ce that I have sixty-year-old bones in this fifty-year-old body already."

"You're welcome here, although there's little to do but fight here in the north," Xun Wenruo admitted. "And we certainly haven't got a prefecture for you right now."

"Not a problem," Hua Xin insisted. "Any role will do, so long as it involves meaningful service to the Han."

"We'll notify His Excellency of your arrival," Xun Gongda said. "Your knowledge of southern affairs will be crucial in the future."

"I doubt it," Hua Xin sighed. "Did I save Governor Liu Yao...?"

"In what way were you capable of doing so...?" Xun Gongda asked.

"We've talked to Wang Lang, who tried to liaise with you from Kuiaji, and he has already informed us of what you were up against; Jiang Ziya himself would have struggled, as the attempts by Wang's adviser Xu Jing and Liu Yao's adviser, Xu Shao – both of them infamous appraisers – should tell you."

"Xu Shao's death was truly vile," Hua Xin said bitterly. "Such a great man... and he died a meaningless death in the undeveloped south, a victim of Sun Ce's thuggish ambition and the greed of that heretic Ze Rong. And now, there is Sun Quan... who is unfathomable. He allies with wicked pirates and great heroes at the same time, like his brother, but he is less accessible, so I do not much about him beyond his staggering unpopularity in some parts of his vast domain."

"We've heard about it," Xun Wenruo replied. "But enough of the Suns for now; would you help us eliminate the treacherous Yuans and their allies...?"

"Give me Yuan Shang, Yuan Xi or Gao Gan to fight," Hua Xin said. "For the Han, I will gladly face any of them."

"Wonderful!" Xun Wenruo exclaimed. "We'll send you on to aid His Excellency at once... he could use the extra counsel."

"Consider me halfway there," Hua Xin replied.

Bing Province Governor Gao Gan did not receive any word from Yuan Shang, but he did not need to: the news of the double defeat of the pro-Cao faction led by Wang Song, Xianyu Fu, Jiao Chu and Zhang Nan was enough to tell Gao Gan that the time might be right for him to stage his own attack on Cao Cao.

"This is our moment, Cousin!" Gao Gan said to his adviser, Gao Rou. "I will contact Wang Yi in Hedong and we can coordinate something as soon as Cao Cao leaves Yè to try to fight Zhao Du and Huo Nu!"

"...Just be sure and make no mistakes," Gao Rou pleaded.

"There will be no mistakes," Gao Gan insisted. "Cao Cao will be caught in a pincer and destroyed... and the Yuan clan will be rescued. It is Heaven's will!"

****

68

Cao Cao completed hasty preparations for war, appointed his son Cao Pi, Provincial Registrar Li Fu, Attendant Officer Cui Yan and Cao Hong as the guardians of Yè City and began a northward march at the head of an army of 50,000 men: Cao's first targets, Zhao Du and Huo Nu, assembled an army of 35,000 to make a stand in Zhuo Prefecture. The two armies met for the first time at Zhuo's southern border; the rebel army was at a numerical disadvantage and lacked a large number of professional soldiers, but their fear and resolve once again placed the Han forces at odds with an army on 'death ground'. The first, almost immediate skirmish ended with the rebel army border guard retreating northward: Cao Cao then ordered the construction of a temporary camp and assembled his generals in the command tent as soon as it was available.

"There can be no mistakes," Cao Cao said. "Zhao and Huo are popular: no, they are no 'Li Jue and Guo Si' militarily, but they claim to fight for the people and seem to have the support of many of the people. We must once again do what we can to win not only battles but hearts; we must turn not only enemy armies, but confused minds."

"I reckon we went the wrong way," Xiahou Dun grumbled. "What about Liu Bei and Liu Biao?"

"They won't move," Guo Jia said dismissively. "If anyone will move, General Xiahou, it will be Gao Gan of Bing Province."

"Then why leave him in the job?" Xiahou Dun asked snidely. "If he's bound to betray us, Mengde, then *why*…?"

"Continuity and conciliation," Cao Cao replied. "It is Gao Gan that breaks the peace, then, for betraying our trust rather than us for trying to supplant him. We've done that enough times before, Yuanrang, so why does it still confuse you…?"

"Because it *never works*!" Xiahou Dun retorted. "It isn't like when the generals and advisers and politicians join us! The governors and administrators and magistrates *always betray us*, and always when we really don't need the trouble!"

"Ah, yes, but the outcome has always been favourable to us in the end, General, so why complain?" Guo Jia teased. "And besides, 'always' is not strictly true."

"…'Mostly', then… 'almost always'," Xiahou Dun retorted. "Too many times to risk Gao Gan when we-!"

"*Enough*, Cousin Yuanrang," Cao Cao ordered. "Our enemies might be far from up to the standard of opponent that we've faced recently, but that doesn't mean that we have time to bicker and whinge! Zhao and Huo have consolidated their main force around the prefectural capital with the intention of fighting to the last man, and that is as undesirable as it was when we fought Yuan Tan. We must preserve the lives of the amateur soldiers that Zhao and Huo employ and restore stability. Mister Jia Xu, is there any word from the men that followed Wang Song?"

"A few," Jia Xu replied. "Wang Song's followers were scattered and left confused, so we'll have trouble reorganising them. Fortunately, Zhao Du and Huo Nu have both come here, so if we capture or kill them both, their rebellion is likely over."

"Kill, for certain," Cao Cao said. "They killed Wang Song, so I must show that he has been avenged. What word from Zhang Yan...?"

"*Zhang Yan*...?" Xiahou Dun exclaimed. "You mean 'Flying Swallow' Zhang Yan, don't you...? You want to use the *Black Mountain Bandits* on this campaign...?"

"I just want them to provide a blockade," Cao Cao insisted.

"By being an 'unmoving wing' in the west, we prevent Zhao and Huo running in any other direction but east, where we can trap them," Guo Jia explained.

"...The people won't like us using bandits," Xiahou Dun suggested.

"The Black Mountain Bandits *are* the people, worn by years of poor treatment that actually worsened under Benchu's rule," Cao Cao replied. "That is why they submitted to us, Yuanrang, but not to the Yuans: they won't turn the people of Zhuo against us, I assure you. Now then, Mister Jia... what word...?"

"They are moving northward," Jia Xu said. "It leaves Gao Gan freer to act, so we had better hope that Zhao and Huo are eliminated quickly."

"They will be," Cao Cao insisted.

Gao Gan received word that the Black Mountain Bandits were abandoning many of their positions to the south and east of Bing Province and moving northward to aid Cao Cao's campaign; Gao then sent word to Hedong Administrator Wang Yi, who summoned his known loyalists to a private meeting and said, "It is time to act at last."

"Can we be absolutely sure that we should act...?" the official Wei Gu asked. "We do not want to commit our lives to a cause that's doomed to failure."

"The Qiang are not in this region anymore," Wang Yi replied. "Gao Gan reports that Zhang Yan has gone northward with most of his men, making the reclamation of Maocheng Fortress possible; Cao Cao is also in the north fighting the Yuan loyalists, leaving little in the way of a defensive garrison at Yè. If we take Hedong and collaborate with Gao – and, hopefully, Liu Biao – to seize Ji Province and then Yan Province, we can bring Cao Cao's evil reign to an end and save the Son of Heaven!"

"...But we're going to take action regardless of whether Liu Biao and Liu Bei add their swords to the cause...?" the official Fan Xian asked uneasily.

"We are to set an example that others might follow," Wang Yi replied. "When Liu Biao sees that we are doing something, he will surely join us. Now, gentlemen: here is the plan..."

Li Fu and Cui Yan watched over Yè diligently, but Cao Pi and Cao Hong were not so reliable: Li and Cui despaired at the lack of seriousness exhibited by the Cao clan members, and their discontent worsened with the arrival of the Hedong official Wang Ling and the news that he brought with him.

"Gao Gan has somehow coerced Administrator Wang into joining him in rebelling against the Han!" Wang Ling explained. "Wei Gu and Fan Xian – under the pretext that they are 'pacifying areas of concern' – have taken control of several cities in Hedong!"

"And you're sure that Wang Yi is allied to these two men...?" Cui Yan asked.

"He must be," Wang Ling replied. "My superior and I tried to report what happened to Administrator Wang and he was strangely dismissive: when we suggested contacting His Excellency, we were suddenly attacked and chased away. I travelled through Bing to get here, Mister Cui, and Gao's men are gradually seizing control of cities and fortifying them as they move north and east; Administrator Jia Kui is experiencing some problems in western and northern Hongnong as well, which is why I has to go through Bing."

"We must write to His Excellency at once," Li Fu said. "Yòu Province must wait."

"...Hedong... aligned with the Yuans...?" Cui Yan murmured. "*Why*...? ...Or... or am I being wilfully ignorant...? Should I have seen this coming...?"

"Your concern was staying alive wherever Yuan Shang put you, Mister Cui, and mine was protecting Ji Province," Li Fu said as he started to pen a letter to Cao Cao. "Hedong Prefecture's leaders are being very foolish... it will cost them."

Cao Cao grimaced when he received the letter from Li Fu a day later: his armies were gaining ground against Zhao Du and Huo Nu, but the Wuhuan confederacy's attack on Yuyang Prefecture had not, as yet, been challenged, and Administrator Xianyu Fu was becoming increasingly desperate.

"...Did you anticipate Hedong aiding Gao Gan...?" Cao Cao asked as he turned to look at Guo Jia, Xin Pi, Jia Xu and his new consultant, Hua Xin.

"I confess that I considered the possibility of it," Guo Jia replied. "It was a remote, 'worst-case scenario', if you will, but yes. The presence of the Qiang and our subsequent 'abandonment' – Wang Yi's word, not mine – of the region have led to Wang taking this foolish decision to ally with the Yuans when their time is short."

"But what do I do???" Cao Cao asked. "I am entrenched here in Yòu Province with the task less than half done! If I retreat now, I'll surely have three-hundred-thousand Wuhuan tribesmen at my heels and lose the entire region to them!"

"Oh, certainly," Guo Jia replied. "You must stay, at least until Zhao and Huo are dead and the Wuhuan hordes are pushed back to their lairs beyond the Great Wall."

"But I will lose Bing and Hedong, and maybe Hongnong as well!" Cao Cao cried. "Hedong will not stay under the stable control of a man like Wang Yi for long, will it? The proximity to Xiongnu and Qiang settlements will guarantee that Hedong becomes another Xiliang! And Gao Gan might advance into Ji if left unchecked!"

"Assign one good general to the cause of retaking Hedong from Wang Yi and we can 'buy some time'," Hua Xin said. "Maocheng and Handan are being guarded by competent men, so Gao Gan will be halted at the provincial border at the very worst. The first priority is to deal with Zhao Du and Huo Nu here and deal with Wang Yi in Hedong."

"...Whom do I send...?" Cao Cao asked. "Can I spare any of my most ferocious generals when Maocheng, Handan, Yè, Zhuo and Yuyang will need their talents...?"

"I cannot help you there, Excellency," Hua Xin admitted.

"Neither can I," Guo Jia said. "You're right, Lord Cao, to suggest

that a man should not be deployed from Ji or Yòu: perhaps you
need to consult Wenruo...?"
"...I wish I had Chen Lin here," Cao Cao grumbled. "My own words
shall have to do: bring me a pen and paper."

Word of the rebellion in Hedong reached Jing Province's northern
capital Xiangyang within a very short time: the guest-warlord Liu
Bei hurried to Governor Liu Biao's private study and said,
"Jingsheng, this is our moment, a moment that was believed to be
passed and gone but is now upon us!"
"...I should have my advisers here," Liu Biao suggested; his
cynical wife, Lady Cai, was obviously watching the conversation
from the doorway.
"By all means confer with them, but do not be swayed from taking
action!" Liu Bei pleaded. "Cao Cao has miscalculated, Jingsheng!
He is now in the far north, locked in battle with the Yuan brothers,
while Xuchang and the villain's new capital at Yè are left
understaffed! Governor Gao and Administratror Wang have
rebelled, bringing Bing Province and Hedong Prefecture over to
our cause!"
Liu Biao's eyes wandered as he thought about Liu Bei's as yet
unspoken but obvious suggestion.
"...This might be our last opportunity," Liu Bei warned. "If Gao and
Wang are defeated, then Cao Cao will rule uncontested in Bing
and Hedong; if Cao also defeats the Wuhuan tribes and the Yuan
brothers, then Jing will be completely isolated and-"
"*Ah*... so it *was* Liu Bei that I saw," the adviser Kuai Yue said as he
entered the study with his colleagues Wang Can and Fu Xun.
Liu Biao smiled and said, "Xuande was just making one or two
suggestions about-"
"The rebellions in Hedong and Bing," Kuai Yue sighed.
"...You don't think much of them...?" Liu Biao prompted.
"Wang Yi is a mediocrity that was just at war with Gao Gan and
lost pitifully, forcing him to rely on Qiang aid that he then
denounced," Kuai Yue replied. "And Gao Gan may have a province
full of fighting men, but where are they...? Half a million of them
are the Black Mountain Bandits – and therefore his enemies – and
many of the rest are Southern Xiongnu settlers that are divided
between serving Cao and serving the Yuans. Gao has, at most,
thirty-thousand at his disposal, and many of them are committed
to maintaining order across the province, so in reality he has ten-
to-fifteen-thousand that he can send against Cao Cao."
"That is hardly going to achieve anything!" Liu Biao chortled.
"*Ayah*... why do you men seek to turn Jingsheng away from taking
action that will save the province from later harm?" Liu Bei asked.
"The Yuan brothers have been toppled," Wang Can retorted. "Yuan
Tan was the strongest of them, and he is dead; Yuan Shang is a
poor chieftain, and Yuan Xi is feeble as a governor. Both of them
combined pose no threat to Cao Cao, so they have employed a
Wuhuan army that will be their undoing. Gao Gan could not take
Hedong when his opponent was Wang Yi, and he crumbled when
Ma Chao appeared: why, then, could he defeat Cao Cao now...?
And the aforementioned Wang Yi is no match for a feeble Gao
Gan, so how can he last long, especially when a hungry Ma Chao
lurks nearby...?"

Liu Bei turned to Liu Biao and said, "Jingsheng...!"

"...My advisers are right," Liu Biao decided. "Gao and Wang were just enemies: their alliance is unreliable and a feeble one at that. I won't help such useless men. Besides, can I commit to that when Sun Quan is at my door again...?"

Liu Bei sensed that he would not sway Liu Biao now that his advisers had arrived; he bowed humbly to each man in turn and left the room.

"...We arrived just in time," Fu Xun chuckled.

"In time to do *what*...?" Liu Biao asked as he wavered again.

"In time to save you from being another Tao Qian or Che Zhou," Wang Can replied.

"Had he tricked you into helping Gao and Wang, then you would soon have been humiliated, my lord, and that sometimes leads to men gathering in shadows and proposing regime change, which is a tactic that Bei's used before," Kuai Yue said. "Even if we must fight alone, it is better than fighting alongside unreliable allies: the Guandu fiasco taught us that."

"...I hope that you are right, gentlemen," Liu Biao replied. "Because if that really is my last chance to fight Cao with allies, then... then I think that I have just put a knife to my own throat."

The advisers exchanged glances.

"...I should like to be left alone now," Liu Biao said.

The advisers bowed politely and withdrew.

"...Why am I now so unsure...?" Liu Biao croaked. "Who can I really trust out of them all...?"

A messenger was sped to Xuchang with Cao Cao's request for guidance on managing the Hedong rebellion: Xun Wenruo retired to the chancellery study to read the letter, and his nephew Xun Gongda joined him.

"What a dilemma," Xun Gongda sighed.

"It was expected, but... not right now," Xun Wenruo replied. "Now, then... who to send to Hedong to face Wang Yi...? I don't know: I truly- ... ...Du Ji."

"Du Ji...?" Xun Gongda exclaimed.

"I may regret it, I may not, but... I think that this is a task for Du Ji," Xun Wenruo said. "I'll write back with the suggestion... and see what His Excellency says."

Cao Cao received Xun Wenruo's surprise response and invited his advisers to the command tent once again.

"...Du Ji...?" Xin Pi exclaimed.

"The man's in the far west, where I understand that he has quickly gained the respect of the Qiang," Cao Cao replied thoughtfully. "I... I admit that I can see why Wenruo has made this odd suggestion."

"Du Ji would have the Qiang at his back if he were in Hedong, and a man that they respect would keep them away or employ them with relative ease, depending on the necessity of the moment," Guo Jia said. "He's a qualified official that can lead an administration or an army with equal confidence, so he'll adapt to the situation as it changes. We would be right to give such a man a chance while we cannot move ourselves. The worst that he can do is fail, and he'll have still given us some time."

Cao Cao stared at Xun Wenruo's letter for several minutes while he wrestled with the choice that he had to make: when it became clear that no better solution was going to materialise, Cao groaned and said, "Heaven enjoys its games, as always... and if I must endure another loss, so be it. I will send Du Ji."

The official Du Ji was summoned to Yè City from his post in the far west of Liang Province; he travelled quickly, passing through Central Province rather than taking the quicker route through Hedong Prefecture. When word of the Hedong rebellion and Du Ji's movements reached the Qiang, Ma Chao met with his father Ma Teng and said, "You're the chieftain of our clan and our tribe, Father, and yet you fail to smell drawn blood and act on it."
"...You'd have me aid those feeble idiots in Bing and Hedong?" Ma Teng chortled.
"Gao and Wang are weaklings, doomed to lose if they fight Cao whether they work together or not," Ma Chao retorted. "But with *our* help..."
"Nonsense," Ma Teng scoffed. "I won't risk a-"
"'Risk'...?" Ma Chao exclaimed. "You, a Qiang clan chieftain, one of the three powerful 'kings amongst kings' in Liang Province, speak of 'risk'...?"
"Cao is a dangerous man," Ma Teng replied. "*When* Gao and Wang lose, we will be facing a triumphant Cao alone, with Han Sui to the rear. What will happen then...?"
"How can Cao win?" Ma Chao asked. "He fights the Yuans, who have recruited what must be the entire Wuhuan people to fight for them in Yòu Province, along with a large local army; Gao Gan fights in Bing, Wang Yi fights in Hedong, and Liu Biao will surely join in soon."
"You presume too much, my son," Ma Teng replied. "The Wuhuan fight because they fear losing their power in the region, but Cao can turn them back as he has done before: you think I am blind, but I watched Yuan Tan's defeat and know that Supuyan's retreat ensured it. And that 'local army' you speak of is angry villagers and a few wealthy men that have the Yuans to thank for their money; Cao will soon disperse them. That leaves Gao and Wang, and no, I don't think that Liu Biao will join in if he has not already done so. And Cao Cao has moved Du Ji to Hedong to counter this threat: Du Ji is very clever and honest, and most importantly he ensures that there are a lot of lesser Qiang chieftains that would rather aid Cao's man than the rebels, which means that it might already be over."
"So you will just sit and *watch*???" Ma Chao cried.
"I will sit and watch and *learn*," Ma Teng retorted. "Learn to do the same, son, or you will lose in the future."
Ma Chao turned and retreated angrily; Ma Teng shook his head and frowned miserably.

****

69

The official Du Ji was met at the gates of Yè City by Li Fu and Cui Yan, who immediately sped him to the audience hall of the governor's mansion.

"His Excellency is on the northern frontier, as you know," Cui Yan said as he studied Du Ji; the stresses of administrating Xiping had taken their toll, but he was not as haggard, wasted or rugged as some men might have been. Du Ji had managed to retain an air of refined dignity and strength, and none of the local influences had altered his appearance: he looked very much like a man that had been serving the Han court in Xuchang.

"We are looking at a sizeable but dispersed army of rebels in Bing, and Hedong is now under the control of Wang Yi's cronies since they control every key city," Li Fu explained. "You can only be allocated a thousand men at present."

"I shall manage," Du Ji replied. "I am, after all, supposed to provide a temporary distraction while His Excellency completes his northern campaign: if I do not overstretch, I cannot lose."

"That's precisely the right attitude," Li Fu said.

"What parts of Bing do we control...?" Du Ji asked.

"At the moment, very little," Cui Yan replied. "Shanjin Ford is still ours, though, which gives you a crossing point."

"I won't waste any more time," Du Ji said. "I'll hurry to Hedong and confront these men before any of their gains can be made more permanent."

"Heaven's will be with you," Li Fu replied.

Cao Cao's army in Zhou Prefecture had managed to defeat all of Zhao Du and Huo Nu's rebel forces across the south of the region: the prefectural capital would be the final battleground before Cao could finally turn his attentions to fighting the Wuhuan tribes in Yuayang Prefecture. Zhao Du and Huo Nu had realised that the Black Mountain Bandits had blocked any escape routes to the west, so contacting Gao Gan for assistance was pointless; Cao Cao's men had similarly blocked all of the viable roads to Fanyang City, and the early loss of the only tenable fortress – Yijing – was causing the two leaders and their senior subordinates to argue.

"The place was still partly in ruins!" Zhao Du protested. "And besides, who wanted to be trapped in Yijing with the ghosts of Gongsun Zan and his family...?"

The lesser leaders of the Zhou rebels – who were sat facing Zhao Du and Huo Nu in the command tent of the rebel camp – exchanged irritated glances and grumbled incoherently.

"I know that this is far from ideal," Zhao Du continued. "But Yijing would have been worse. I looked the place over, and Yuan Shao obviously left the place as it was as a warning: the tunnels, the burned-out buildings, all still as it was, with more rats in the place than I wanted to count."

"That's not what I was told by my people," Huo Nu said. "I was told that Yijing was part rebuilt and–"

"Part, yes, and a very small part as well," Zhao Du insisted. "We're better off here. And anyway, Cao Cao would still have us pinned, and unlike Gongsun, we don't have the bandits as our friends: they're stopping us from-!"

"**ATTACK!**"

"**An attack???**" Zhao Du exclaimed in response to the sudden alarm. "*Now???*"

"**Will it end if we just sit here?!**" Huo Nu retorted.

The rebel leaders leapt to their feet as one and rushed to the gates of their camp: Cao Cao had ordered a full-scale attack on every part of the rebel defence network at the same time.

"**Bastards!**" Zhao Du cried.

Generals Cao Chun, Xiahou Dun, Cao Xiu, Li Dian, Zhang Liao, Yu Jin, Yue Jin, Zhang Hè and Xu Huang were scattering the rebels with ease; Zhao Du and Huo Nu retreated toward the city with several hundred of their followers, but the city-dwellers – who knew that admitting the rebel leaders would inevitably lead to a siege – had overpowered the small number of guards that had been left within the walls and closed the gates.

"**NO! LET US IN, YOU IDIOTS!**" Huo Nu screamed desperately. "**We**... we'll be *killed*...!"

"**Make a stand!**" Zhao Du ordered. "**Die proudly and take as many of them with us as we can!**"

Zhao and Huo readied their men as Cao Chun and Xu Huang advanced on their position: the rebels met their ends after a short, uneven battle that left the victors with a sense of unease.

"...So how many died in the end...?" Cao Cao asked of his assembled generals; the command tent was silent and sombre.

"...A thousand or so," Xin Pi reported at last. "Zhao and Huo among them, as the head display will tell you."

"I didn't know either of them," Cao Cao sighed.

"I met them both on a routine trip to this region some years back, Excellency," Xin Pi replied. "I can confirm that they are dead."

"...Their popularity was evident," Cao Cao said. "This is the end of the rebellion in Zhuo, though, I understand...?"

"The others have surrendered," Jia Xu replied.

"We should advance quickly, then, and waste no more time here in Zhuo," Guo Jia said. "We must restore Yijing to a credible outpost, leave someone in Zhuo to reassure the populace of our good intentions, and move at once to Yuyang."

"...I shall do as you suggest," Cao Cao replied. "Qian Zhao...?"

The officer Qian Zhao nodded obediently.

"I shall soon have need of your 'diplomacy skills' again," Cao Cao continued. "The Wuhuan must be turned back quickly so that I can deal with Gao Gan."

"I shall do my very best, Excellency," Qian Zhao replied.

"...And our 'friend' Zhang Yan will need to be ordered to go southward to harry Gao Gan's forces now that they are no longer needed here," Cao Cao said.

"I shall write at once," Xin Pi promised.

The surviving Yuan brothers, Shang and Xi, were disturbed by the news that their strongest non-Wuhuan allies had been routed by Cao Cao; the two met in Shang's command tent and studied the map of Yòu Province.

"Older Brother, we are now in dangerous territory," Yuan Shang said quietly.

"Oh, I'm well aware of that," Yuan Xi replied. "Without Zhao and Huo, we'll be taking Yòu Province – and anywhere else – back with the near-sole help of the Wuhuan, so Yuan rule is a thing of the past regardless of who wins."

"But to let Cao Cao win would be to hand our severed heads to him," Yuan Shang retorted. "Will he let you live after giving your wife to his son...?"

"...Of course not," Yuan Xi said angrily. "And I'd never surrender so easily."

"We can still win, even without Zhao and Huo," Yuan Shang suggested. "They are not the only ones that have refused to betray us: Tian Chou, the Magistrate of Wuzhong, has not gone over to Cao Cao, and the Administrators of the eastern prefectures did not join Jiao Chu's rebellion either. We can rely upon them when Cao's weakness is exposed... I am sure of it."

"As you said, Brother and lord, we are unable to submit to Cao Cao," Yuan Xi replied. "He has, by the nature of his actions, stated very clearly that we will die if he were to defeat us. That being the case, we will fight until we kill Cao or die in battle ourselves."

"...Indeed," Yuan Shang sighed. "Indeed."

Du Ji outwitted the forces of Gao Gan's subordinate Zhang Sheng and led his 1,000-strong militia toward Shanjin Ford: Zhang notified Gao, who sent word to Hedong Administrator Wang Yi.

"**Can Gao Gan not deal with this man Du Ji himself???**" Wang Yi cried. "**Haven't I got enough to worry about with all the rebels that still serve Cao Cao???**"

Wang Yi's officials stared at each other blankly.

"...**Someone send word to Fan Xian and Wei Gu at once!**" Wang Yi continued. "**Shanjin Ford must be taken!**"

Fan Xian and Wei Gu both sent men to Shanjin to seize control of the vital crossing point: the main defender, Zhang Zhi, had already been repelled when Du Ji arrived.

"There's no point trying to take it back, General Du," Zhang Zhi sighed. "The enemy are on either side, and a pincer is-"

"Firstly, Mister Zhang, I should point out that I have been appointed as the Administrator of Hedong," Du Ji interrupted. "That may help us to win this battle with greater expediency than swords will."

Zhang Zhi bowed humbly and said, "Forgive me, Administrator, for my-"

"You need not be so meek, Mister Zhang," Du Ji said with a smile. "I get the impression that you will be appointed as Inspector of Bing Province after this is over, so you still outrank me."

Zhang Zhi straightened up, laughed and replied, "You are a remarkably easy fellow to get along with, Mister Du. You do not have the manners of a man that's spent months on the western frontier with nothing but Qiang savages for company."

"What is a savage...?" Du Ji asked pointedly. "Han Sui, Dong Zhuo, Lü Bu, Yuan Shu... they are all the same in the end. Now, then, we should think about how we proceed: one of us will need to write to His Excellency and tell him that the rebels have seized all of the major crossing points and effectively surrounded us. I imagine that the Black Mountain Bandits will be deployed to distract Gao

Gan if they have not been already, but that leaves these idiots Wei and Fan…"

"And Wang Yi," Zhang Zhi suggested.

"No, he's no problem," Du Ji replied casually. "He buckled immediately when Gao Gan sent Guo Yuan to attack him: he hasn't been overthrown by Wei and Fan yet, but he certainly would be eventually. It's them that we must defeat… and defeat them we will."

"I'll write to His Excellency and request reinforcements," Zhang Zhi promised.

The arrival of Zhang Zhi's plea coincided with Cao Cao's arrival in western Yuyang Prefecture, where he intended to do battle with the Wuhuan tribes despite their outnumbering his forces by as much as 6 to 1: Cao groaned as he read the words, which led Guo Jia to ask, "How will you respond…?"

"Do I not respond appropriately already?" Cao Cao whimpered. "I am a hair's breadth away from weeping, which is how any man, no matter how bold, should respond to such a dilemma!"

"But it won't solve anything," Guo Jia retorted.

"You're the adviser, 'Fengxiao'," Xiahou Dun growled. "Advise!"

Guo Jia laughed weakly and said, "I am indeed, 'Yuanrang'. And if I am honest, I would suggest sending *you* with an army of thousands to smash these rebels, for I believe that your anger alone would do half the job."

Xiahou Dun smirked gratefully.

"…It was my idea as well," Cao Cao admitted. "But can I spare Yuanrang and a large portion of my forces when I am about to face overwhelming odds here…?"

"This battle – and, I think, Du Ji's as well – will be won more by words and schemes and posture than by swords," Guo Jia replied. "You can spare General Xiahou and a few thousand men: the rest can be recruited during the march from areas that are stabilised."

"Sounds fine to me," Xiahou Dun said. "Can I go *now*, Mengde, if Fengxiao says that I should go quickly…?"

"He did not, but he no doubt implied it, as he always does," Cao Cao replied. "Yes, Yuanrang, you may depart at once with Chen Qun as your counsel: I'll speed a man ahead to notify Du Ji."

Xiahou Dun cackled, leapt to his feet and left the command tent.

"…*Aiee*… I cannot comment," Cao Cao sighed.

"He'll not lose the other eye," Guo Jia insisted. "Wang Yi and his friends are no match for us: this is about bringing a speedy end to an annoying distraction."

"…I hope so, Fengxiao," Cao Cao said. "Yuanrang, like all of my family, blood ties or not, means a lot to me."

Zhang Zhi received Cao Cao's messenger and listened soberly.

"…You may go," Zhang Zhi said once the weary, battered messenger had spoken.

"We will not see this army for at least a week," Du Ji suggested once the messenger had departed. "That poor lad obviously struggled to get here, which suggests that Zhang Sheng is gathering more and more support for his lord Gao Gan and making the east more and more impassable: General Xiahou must fight his way here once he arrives in Bing Province, and we will be

attacked once that happens."
"So what do we do...?" Zhang Zhi asked. "Have you any ideas...?"
"...I do," Du Ji replied. "But my plan requires your absolute trust."
"If His Excellency appointed you as a general and an administrator, then he has your trust; who am I to doubt his judgement?" Zhang Zhi said. "Tell me my role and I will assist you in any way that I can."
"Firstly, I will need to know where the nearest small ford is: one that is not considered to be a viable military crossing and hence is not heavily guarded," Du Ji explained. "After that, I will need a small group of smart, trustworthy men, some horses, and..."

Wei Gu and Fan Xian had arrayed their men along the western bank of the Yellow River and insisted on daily heckling and chanting to unnerve Du Ji's men on the opposite side: Du, in turn, had ordered his men to ignore the taunts and conduct drills as normal. There was no suggestion of any sort of concession or negotiation by either side, so it alarmed Wei and Fan when a scout suddenly reported the arrival of Du Ji and a small band of officials.
"They are nigh-on unarmed, you say...?" Wei Gu asked of the scout, who nodded excitedly in response.
"...What does this mean...?" Fan Xian wondered.
"We'll only find out by asking," Wei Gu replied. "And something tells me that we might be blessed by Heaven!"
Wei Gu and Fan Xian had Du Ji brought to their command tent and sat awaiting his words.
"...As you two gentlemen might have guessed, I've been sent here to relieve Wang Yi of his position as Administrator of Hedong and stabilise the region," Du Ji said. "But the situation is obviously beyond the understanding of some, and so I have come here to bring an end to this in a more realistic fashion."
Wei Gu and Fan Xian exchanged bemused glances.
"Firstly, I think that Wang Yi does not know talent when he sees it, nor does he recognise his own mediocrity," Du Ji continued.
"You are here, guarding the ford, while he hides in his capital: he sees that you are his sword and shield, but I am sure that he has not properly rewarded you, nor will he ever. I have heard of your exploits, and I marvel at them: you-"
"Stop right there," Wei Gu chuckled.
"You're trying to win us over to Cao Cao, but that is impossible!" Fan Xian heckled.
"I'm trying to do nothing of the sort," Du Ji replied. "I've just been in Xiping on the western frontier, where I am *very popular*, gentlemen; ask around."
Wei Gu and Fan Xian exchanged unfathomable glances.
"I, Ji, bring with me skills that will benefit a joint cause... *our* joint cause," Du Ji continued.
"...You're coming over to us...?" Wei Gu exclaimed.
"But only if I am given the role that Cao has let me take," Du Ji replied. "We can exploit the inferior judgement of Cao and Wang both: I will become the Administrator, which will delay Cao's coming here, and you two will, in turn, gain the highest offices in my administration."
"But we'll betray our alliance with Gao Gan by doing that, won't we?" Fan Xian asked. "And what about the rebellions against us in

Hedong Prefecture...?"

"Gao Gan can be made to understand," Du Ji insisted. "As for the rebellions, that's due to Wang Yi's poor instruction. To win hearts and minds, you must show compassion. Instead of sieging the cities, open them and restore normal activity; rather than oppressing the defiant officials, grant their requests; rather than letting your followers do as they please, discipline them as you would a proper army. Fail to do these things and the rebellions will grow and we will be routed: heed my advice and the populace will turn to us and we will be invincible."

"...Alright, that makes sense," Wei Gu admitted. "I, for one, will be honest and say that we were losing ground in some places before you arrived; we'll do everything that you have suggested, Mister Du. What about Zhang Zhi...?"

"He's a stubborn loyalist, but to the Han, not to Cao Cao," Du Ji insisted. "Keep him surrounded, and when we've stabilised Hedong, he'll see that we're the ones that he should be helping and come over to us."

"...We're blessed by your arrival, Mister Du!" Fan Xian said. "With your assistance, Hedong will be ours!"

News of Du Ji's apparent defection reached Xiahou Dun's army as it approached Bing Province; Xiahou screamed angrily and said, **"Du Ji's the first one to die!"**

"...Something is suspicious about that, my lord," Xiahou Dun's deputy, Han Hao, suggested carefully. "I wonder if we should give Du Ji a chance."

"You think he's pretending to defect, then...?" Xiahou Dun asked.

"His Excellency would not appoint such an easily-swayed man to such a role," Han Hao replied. "He defected almost immediately after requesting the help that we are here to provide: that suggests some plan to placate the enemy."

"...They must be very stupid to fall for such a plan," Xiahou Dun suggested. "...Mind you, I wanted to kill him, so *I* fell for it."

"And thank Heaven that they *did* fall for it," Xiahou Dun's adviser, Chen Qun, said gratefully. "We'll be stuck there for weeks fighting our way past Zhang Sheng if initial reports are anything to go by."

"...So what should we do...?" Xiahou Dun asked.

"We should stop at Handan and Maocheng and prepare carefully," Chen Qun replied. "We're expected, so there's no point trying to surprise them: the best course is to feign a lack of readiness and insufficient men and resources so that they think we have no intention of attacking for a long time... and then, if Du Ji is on our side, he'll surely see what we're doing and tell us what will help his own plan."

"Alright," Xiahou Dun said. "But I detest the waiting: Mengde is so lucky that he gets to have a real fight!"

Cao Cao's forces in Yuyang Prefecture were immediately forced onto the defensive by the ferocity of the Wuhuan attacks: the tribal warriors compensated for lack of organisation and strategy with their fearlessness and unflinching attitude to killing their enemies. Cao Chun, Cao Xiu, Zhang Liao, Li Dian, Yu Jin, Yue Jin, Xu Huang and Qian Zhao confronted the forces of Tadun, Louban, Supuyan and Wuyan repeatedly, and the Han army's losses were becoming impossible to justify; Cao Cao retired to his command tent after one particularly violent encounter and said, "Hundreds, we're losing, gentlemen... hundreds, and with nothing but held ground to show for it."

"Don't lose heart, Mengde," Cao Chun replied. "We're drawing blood too; reports indicate that some tribes have not joined Tadun, and if there are abstainers while they are winning, there will be others that will flee when they are seen to lose."

"...I know that, I do, but I am pained!" Cao Cao said. "Even Qian Zhao could do nothing to turn them back this time: I am lucky that they spared him to return to us!"

Qian Zhao lowered his head and sighed miserably.

"...You turned back Nanlou, for which I am grateful," Cao Cao insisted. "I have not forgotten your achievements, Qian Zijing."

"I sigh for my recent failings, not because I fear that you have forgotten my earlier successes, Your Excellency," Qian Zhao replied. "If I could change the weather and change the course of rivers for the Han, I would, and I am angry at my uselessness when dealing with these chieftains – even Supuyan, whose army I turned back once before!"

"Repelling Nanlou is still a good thing," Jia Xu said.

"...I am at a loss, gentlemen!" Cao Cao admitted. "What will it take to chase them from this region???"

"As we hold our ground, men flock to us," Jia Xu replied. "Zhao Du and Huo Nu's rebellion was popular, yes, but now that it is crushed the greater population – the ones that supported the original 'rebellion' by Jiao Chu, Wang Song and Xianyu Fu – are emerging from their homes once again and offering all types of support, from food to lodgings to soldiers. We now have seventy-thousand men to fight the Wuhuan, and once we have relieved the prefectural capital there will be many, many more and the Wuhuan will return to their lairs beyond the Great Wall."

"...I know that too, but it seems to be a lofty ambition," Cao Cao said. "Of all our allies in this region, only Xianyu Fu remains, and maybe – hopefully – those magistrates that serve him."

Guo Jia – who was very sickly and therefore limited in his ability to contribute to the meeting – smiled knowingly.

"All of you... all of you should go and rest, and thank your men for their efforts on my behalf as well as your own," Cao Cao ordered. "Don't stay here listening to me lament like an old woman."

The majority of the officials and officers withdrew, leaving Cao Cao with Xu Chu, Guo Jia, Jia Xu, Hua Xin and Xin Pi for company.

"...You are saddened by Tian Chou's apparent defiance," Guo Jia said weakly.

"Yes," Cao Cao admitted. "I am here to save this region, but he stays in Wuzhong and proffers nothing, not even a word of thanks or encouragement!"

"Do not... be too harsh," Guo Jia suggested. "Wuzhong is... isolated at the moment, Lord Cao, and... and it-"

"Save your strength, Fengxiao," Cao Cao said warmly. "I am allowing worry and vexation to make a court fool of me in word and deed, but not in thought."

"Very good...!" Guo Jia chuckled feebly. "I'll retire, then."

Cao Cao nodded; Guo Jia got to his feet and staggered out of the command tent.

"...He's fading," Cao Cao bleated. "Time and Heaven are cruel masters indeed!"

"You have a migraine, don't you...?" Xin Pi guessed.

"The onset of one," Cao Cao replied. "I will be of little use, so..."

"You can trust us completely to act in your stead, Excellency," Jia Xu promised.

Cao Cao looked at Jia Xu – who had once served the tyrant Dong Zhuo and Cao's former nemesis Zhang Xiu – and then at Xin Pi – who had, until recently, served the same Yuans that he was now fighting – and laughed quietly before leaving the tent with his fretful bodyguard Xu Chu.

"...It *is* funny, I suppose," Xin Pi said.

Jia Xu hummed thoughtfully and replied, "But also true."

Xin Pi turned to Hua Xin and asked, "Have you anything to contribute that we might have missed...?"

"Such a simple situation lacks complexity to miss," Hua Xin replied. "All I can say is that I believe this situation to be nowhere near as desperate as when Liu Yao faced Sun Ce or when I was confronted by the likes of Zhou Tai with no army to speak of; I confess that I rambled like a fool at times when faced by approaching armies, so I know how His Excellency feels when the burden of failure rests on one's own shoulders. We will, ultimately, succeed, I think, but only being resolute, as Sun Ce was when faced by bandits or Shanyue tribes, or indeed when His Excellency faced overwhelming numbers at Guandu. If the right man is found to stymie the Bing Province rebellion and the right tactic is used against the Wuhuan here, we can bring this thing to an end."

"...Quite right," Xin Pi said.

"And sometimes, gentlemen, we must look to our enemies for inspiration as well as our heroes, especially when those enemies once faced our current foes," Hua Xin continued. "If it brings victory, why not...?"

"...That's quite right as well," Jia Xu said. "You've given me a few ideas, Mister Hua...!"

****

70

Cao Cao's armies finally started to force the Wuhuan to flee from the west and south of Yuyang Prefecture with the assistance of the locals and a steadily growing army; at around the same time, Xiahou Dun's army – with the aid of Zhang Yan's Black Mountain Bandits – finally managed to push through the human wall of resistance that stood on the western side of Maocheng Fortress and cross into Bing Province properly. Gao Gan and his senior subordinates were now busy in the south, however, since Cao Cao's only remaining agent in the province, Zhang Zhi, was proving difficult to uproot from Shanjin Ford now that Cao Cao's appointed Administrator of neighbouring Hedong Prefecture, Du Ji, had successfully coerced Gao Gan's strongest allies in that region, Wei Gu and Fan Xian, to betray their leader, Wang Yi, and focus on 'winning hearts and minds' rather than destroying mutual enemies. Gao Gan had hoped that Wang Yi would somehow sway his former allies back to him, but Du Ji's suggested tactics were actually working and driving Wei Gu and Fan Xian closer to him with every passing day.

"You're a genius," Wei Gu chuckled as he read a report from the east of Hedong. "We've been trying to convince Wenxi to submit for ages and getting nowhere, Du Bohou, and now its defenders are with us!"

"I know Pei Qian well, so it was easy," Du Ji replied. "All it took was to show the lenience and discipline that I suggested."

"And now we're as invincible as you promised!" Fan Xian cackled. "Let that Xiahou Dun fellow come to Hedong now! Lü Bu's man might have been satisfied with one eye, Mister Du, but we'll take his whole head!"

"…What, I wonder, of Wang Yi…?" Du Ji prompted.

"He's holed up in Anyi with a few loyalists, but he'll soon cede the seal of office to you, Bohou," Wei Gu said. "Now I have a similar question: what of Zhang Zhi?"

"Yes, I think that a few weeks is enough," Du Ji replied. "He's had enough time to see that we know what we're doing: I'll go and parley with him."

"Once Zhang Zhi is with us, we can all turn that idiot Xiahou around and start pushing east into Ji Province!" Wei Gu said excitedly. "Who knows what we can achieve after that…?"

"What indeed," Du Ji replied dryly. "We shall certainly meet again soon, gentlemen."

Du Ji took his new elite guard and close to 50 cavalry and infantry for the return crossing: he approached Zhang Zhi's camp to the east of Shanjin Ford and met with the bemused Zhang at the western gates.

"I'm down to twelve-hundred men, including what's left of yours," Zhang Zhi explained. "Whatever you've got in mind, I hope it includes reinforcements!"

"It's all arranged," Du Ji promised. "Our friends Wei and Fan are about to get a very nasty surprise; and as for Gao Gan, well… General Xiahou will have plenty of time to reach us and chase him away now that we have four-thousand men."

"...*Four thousand*...?" Zhang Zhi exclaimed. "From where...?"
Du Ji smirked and said, "We have Wei Gu and Fan Xian to thank for them!"

Wei Gu and Fan Xian were as angry as they were surprised when many cities – including the recently-pacified Wenxi – rose up against them once again as supporters of Du Ji, who had somehow recruited thousands of men from Hedong Prefecture without them realising.
"**Bastard!**" Fan Xian cried. "**That sneaky, vile bastard!**"
"...And all the time, we thought that *we* were 'winning hearts and minds'," Wei Gu grumbled. "Letting the officials move about, move their families to safety, make plans, organise... yes, he fooled us completely. But when we've turned this around again we'll destroy the lot of them!"
"But how will we turn things around?" Fan Xian protested. "We've lost all the cities, even the ones that we'd captured, and so all we have left is Anyi, and Wang doesn't trust us now! We're isolated!"
"**Yes, and Wang is *useless*! He *needs us*!**" Wei Gu insisted. "Stay calm, man, and let's just focus on getting Du Ji and Zhang Zhi and taking Shanjin before Xiahou Dun breaks out of the blockade around Maocheng! With us and Gao Gan pouring all of our efforts into it, how can we lose?"

Cao Cao was delighted when Du Ji reported his efforts in Hedong, which puzzled some of his weary generals.
"He's got some more men and held a small camp near a ford," Li Dian noted. "I know that I should perhaps be more positive, Excellency, but what can he do when he is surrounded by – and outnumbered by – enemies at a strategic river crossing with no allies nearby...?"
"Aha, but his even having lasted this long shows that he is a future asset!" Cao Cao replied cheerfully. "All he has to do is delay the enemy until Yuanrang can reach and relieve him. And it looks like we might soon be able to lend our own swords to the fight for Bing Province, so I am right to be generally pleased!"
"...I am glad that you are more optimistic now, Mengde," Cao Chun said. "Within a few weeks or less, we will have rendezvoused with Xianyu Fu and chased the Wuhuan and their Yuan friends into the wilds."
"Yes, but will that be enough...?" Li Dian asked. "We'd need to leave a large army here to stop them from coming back, which leaves us under-resourced when we attack Bing Province."
"The remaining people of this region will be grateful to be rid of the Wuhuan that have made their lives a misery for so long," Xin Pi suggested.
"But the key word there is 'remaining'," Li Dian retorted. "This region is now under-populated as well."
Cao Cao frowned and said, "Quite right."
"...Yes, General Li Dian makes a valid point, but one that answers itself," Jia Xu replied. "The Wuhuan have abducted tens of thousands from Yuyang: those that remain are angry, frightened, distressed at the loss of loved ones... and of all those things, they're mostly angry, very angry, and will fight as hard as any of us. They've already proved that, I think. We will have no trouble

forming defence militias."

Cao Cao's smile returned, and he said, "Good. We'll continue as we are, then."

The Grand Magistrate of Chang'an, Zhong Yao, was becoming increasingly worried about the unrest that was now spilling out of Hedong Prefecture: he summoned his officials and said, "We're going to be forced to ask the Qiang for help again if this situation gets any worse, gentlemen. Should I lend aid?"

The Inspector of Liang Province, Wei Kang – who was visiting Chang'an on business – shook his head and replied, "Lend aid to whom...? Wang Yi seems to be fighting against us this time, and until we know who our friends are, we might make matters worse. Focus instead on two things: keeping our own people from joining in with this madness, and keeping the Qiang from supporting the rebels as well."

"...You're right," Zhong Yao decided. "Hasn't Ma Chao gone west?"

"He has," Wei Kang replied worriedly. "I don't know if he's exploiting the reduced number of respected Han officials since Du Ji went east, or whether he intends to fight Han Sui or make peace with him, or... ... ...I just try not to think about it."

"*Aiee...* I said it before, and I say it again: the Yuans must lose their grip in the northeast, or there will never be peace!" Zhong Yao declared. "Hurry, Excellency, and rid us of those traitors before any more harm can befall us!"

Du Ji and Zhang Zhi were able to resist the constant attacks by the combined forces of Gao Gan, Zhang Sheng, Wei Gu and Fan Xian with surprising ease, despite being outnumbered: it was partly due to their enemies' lack of proper coordination, but the completely defensive stance also allowed for a calm response to the increasingly angry and desperate attempts to breach the camp. Du and Zhang held on for in excess of a month, after which time Xiahou Dun's army finally arrived in Shanjin and dealt a crippling blow to Gao Gan's supply line and rear guard.

"We'll need to retreat!" Gao Gan's adviser, Gao Rou, insisted as the order in Gan's Shanjin camp broke down altogether. **"We must go back to the capital!"**

Gao Gan frowned and asked, **"But what about Wang Yi, Wei Gu and Fan-?"**

"*Leave them*!" Gao Rou snapped. **"It's Wei and Fan's fault that Du Ji was able to recruit so many men and hold on here for so long! If they die, it serves them right! But we will die too if we try to stay here!"**

"...Alright," Gao Gan conceded. **"Tell Zhang Sheng to prepare to fight our way out of here, then."**

Du Ji led a force out of the eastern gates of his camp as soon as Gao Gan started to retreat and pursued the defeated Governor for close to an hour: once Gao Gan was considered unlikely to return, Du met with Xiahou Dun, who saw his battle standard, laughed and said, **"You had me fooled too, Du Ji! You're a wily one!"**

"Gao Gan may be gone, but the other two are still at Shanjin," Du Jin replied. **"We should not let them escape!"**

Xiahou Dun and Du Ji charged toward Shanjin Ford,

chased Wei Gu and Fan Xian's men back to their camp and sieged the fenced enclosure until the majority of Wei and Fan's demoralised soldiers abandoned them and threw the gates open: Wei and Fan were both captured, bound with rope and brought before Xiahou Dun and Du Ji.

"You'll die a wretched death, Du Ji," Fan Xian growled as he glared at the man that had so easily fooled and betrayed him.

"Most men do," Du Ji retorted. "But I'll live longer than either of you two."

"**GUARDS!**" Xiahou Dun cackled. "**DEATH!**"

"**Heaven curse you, Du Ji!**" Wei Gu cried as he was led away. "**Heaven curse you, you servant of a tyrant...!**"

"**Dogs and rats! Dogs and rats!**" Fan Xian screamed. "**I'm going to a better place, but where are you going??? You'll wish you spared us! Damn you...!**"

Du Ji sniggered dismissively and turned to the official Pei Qian, who said, "You've saved us all from terror, Administrator."

"You're here to be congratulated for your part in keeping Wenxi out of their hands for so long, Mister Pei," Du Ji replied. "Any word on Wang Yi...?"

"He fled, apparently, but where can he go...?" Pei Qian insisted. "The important thing is that Anyi is freed from his control, as is the rest of Hedong."

A group of captured officials was brought before Xiahou Dun while Du Ji spoke: Xiahou turned to Du and asked, "What about these, Mister Du...?"

"Ah, right, yes," Du Ji said as he turned and looked at Wei Gu and Fan Xian's terrified subordinates. "You're all pardoned, gentlemen, and free to resume your work. Guards: release them, please."

"Uh... pardon...?" Xiahou Dun exclaimed. "They...! ...Wait. You're no idiot. I won't argue. You know what you're doing. But... but all the same, could you explain it to me, please...?"

Du Ji waited until the freed officials had finished apologising, expressing their thanks and retreating from the command tent before he said, "Fear and confusion are powerful weapons, as you well know, General. Those men followed Wei and Fan, yes, but while I was working alongside them I realised that they were doing what they believed to be right and had been left frightened and confused by the 'state of things' in recent times. Now that they have been pardoned, I will ensure that they are never swayed from serving the Han again."

"And that's your job from now on, Mister Du," Xiahou Dun replied. "Now I have to find out what Mengde – His Excellency – wants *me* to do next."

"Kill Gao Gan," Du Ji said. "What else...?"

∗∗∗∗∗∗∗∗∗∗∗∗

71

The defeat of the Hedong rebels had left the Yuan clan-appointed Governor of Bing Province, Gao Gan, without a key ally and dangerously exposed: the Black Mountain Bandits immediately started to press all of the northern towns and cities that were still loyal to Gao while Xiahou Dun slowly recaptured strategic points in the southwest of the province. The Han forces would also benefit from a second flow of supplies and reinforcements from Hedong, which was now under the near-total control of its new Administrator, Du Ji: Cao Cao clapped his hands and laughed when the news reached his camp in Yuyang Prefecture.

"Du Ji and my dear Yuanrang have achieved a great victory and given us more than just hope!" Cao Cao said as he stood before his generals in the command tent. "With that hope comes more support: day after day, more leaders and officials turn away from the Yuans or end their stubborn neutrality! Ji Province is ours, Qing Province is ours, and western Yòu Province is ours! Bing Province is slipping from Gao Gan's grip now that his foolish assumption that we were defeated has been proven incorrect! All we need now, gentlemen, is one decisive strike against our Wuhuan enemies that blunts them, causes them to respect us and compels them to retreat!"

"I volunteer to lead a force against them, Excellency," Zhang Liao declared. "I have performed poorly and wish to atone for it: nobody would believe that I was once the lieutenant of the mighty Lü Bu, and I wish to change that."

"This will be a joint effort, not the work of one officer alone," Cao Cao replied. "This is not about glory or restoring reputations."

Zhang Liao bowed and said, "Forgive me, Excellency, for that was not my intent."

"I know," Cao Cao replied. "The 'rebuke', if it must be seen as such, was aimed at one and all, including me: we've all been strained by the sight of gutted, emptied villages and weeping villagers, and, of course, the sight of our dead and injured. We must be controlled and show raw power driven by determination, not passionate anger. They interpret such anger as weakness."

"Thank goodness that Yuanrang and Zilian are elsewhere, then," Cao Chun said. "Such orders are wasted on them."

"Mm… indeed," Cao Cao replied. "Go and prepare, gentlemen: this must be our last battle before we turn southward at last!"

"And let us hope," Jia said as he turned his gaze toward Hua Xin, "that a long-dead enemy of the Han's trick will work twice."

"Indeed, Mister Jia," Hua Xin sighed. "Think of how many lives it would save…"

"When our enemy is as superstitious as Tadun, how will it fail…?" Cao Cao asked. "We can at least *try*! Now let us proceed!"

The Yuan brothers had joined in the Wuhuan confederacy's siege of Yuyang Prefecture's capital city, but they immediately retreated when they heard that Cao Cao's was personally advancing with an army of 70,000; the Wuhuan chieftains then convened a meeting that the Yuans reluctantly attended.

"Cao Cao comes here to die quickly," Tadun declared. "We will bury him here!"

"We've had losses," Yuan Shang said. "Otherwise, how could he-?"

"Men die!" Tadun retorted. "Yes, he killed some of my people to get here, but death is part of life! Cao Cao will learn that now!"

"...Cao Cao boasted that he was strong," Supuyan said. "His man, Qian Zhao, said that he was strong, that he had a lot of strong men, and it is true."

"We are more in number and stronger, coward!" Tadun heckled.

"**I am not a coward!**" Supuyan retorted; he then continued his rant in the Wuhuan language, which immediately alienated the Yuan brothers.

"We might as well not be here," Yuan Xi sighed.

"...**Listen to me!**" Yuan Shang bellowed: the Wuhuan chieftains stopped their arguing and turned to face the young heir to the Yuan clan legacy, who added, "I was wrong to speak words that caused doubt in our ability to fight and win. Of course we can! Louban, Tadun: you are the highest of all the Wuhuan chiefs, and I appreciate your support in getting rid of Cao Cao, who will harm us all if he wins. We must win or we will suffer."

"...Tadun may answer," Louban muttered sarcastically.

"There is nothing more to say about whether we fight," Tadun declared. "Of course we will fight! What I want to know is 'how' and 'where' and 'when'."

"Now, here, and by throwing every man and horse we have at them!" Yuan Shang replied. "If they relieve Yuyang's capital, others will join them and we will have to waste time killing more of the people that we could be using ourselves!"

Yuan Xi shook his head sadly.

"Yes," Tadun said. "We will not move away: we will fight here, by the city. We will charge straight away and scare them like the mice they are."

"And my standard will be beside yours," Yuan Shang promised. "I have regained a small army of around three-thousand men, and there will be more when we win. And my brother also has a militia, do you not, Brother...?"

"I do," Yuan Xi replied numbly.

"Then we attack at once!" Tadun ordered.

Cao Cao's forces arrayed neatly and prepared to engage the disorganised but overwhelming Wuhuan hordes.

"...**There are more barbarian men than there are blades of grass!**" Xin Pi exclaimed.

"**Stay calm,**" Cao Cao ordered.

"**I am calm, Excellency,**" Xin Pi insisted.

"**They are preparing to overwhelm us,**" Jia Xu said tensely.

"**But their intent will not match the outcome,**" Cao Cao replied. "**Mister Jia, Mister Xin: show our friends the skills of array-forming!**"

Drums and flag-bearers moved into position behind Cao Cao's front lines: the soldiers stared at their formidable enemies and prepared for their approach.

"**Cao Cao intends to play music for his men!**" Tadun chuckled.

"...**No! They plan to use Han arrays!**" Louban exclaimed.

"...***Arrays...?***" Tadun said: his face fell, and he turned to face Yuan Shang.

"**I am only mildly versed in arrays,**" Yuan Shang admitted.

"**Which means *what*?**" Louban asked cynically.

"**I... I am unfamiliar with all but the simplest arrays, great chieftain,**" Yuan Shang replied nervously. "**And... and that is not a simple array.**"

"**You Han fool!**" Wuyan cried. "**Always, always, you brag about your stupid book in your pocket that you got from your father!**"

"**That's Sun Tzu's book about the 'art of war'!**" Yuan Shang retorted. "**It does not cover arrays because they are the technical side of war, and-!**"

"**And for all your years, you never read a book about 'technical side of war'?**" Tadun heckled. "**You were going to leave everything to someone else?**"

"**...Yes!**" Yuan Shang admitted. "**But at least I-!**"

"*Aiee...* **that's a big array,**" Yuan Xi groaned.

The front line of the Han forces had divided into a set of distinct 'chains' of men that were either standing perfectly still or continually running in synchronised motion; the soldiers were additionally forming either rings or rectangular 'walls' with deliberate, baiting openings. The Han cavalry – of which Cao Chun's 'Tiger and Leopard Cavalry' were the most ferocious – were dispersed among the different parts of the array and providing internal and external contributions. The large battle drums were being beaten to time, and flags were being used to order sudden shifts in movement: the frenetic activity unnerved the Wuhuan warriors and led to conflict over how best to react.

"**...This is dangerous,**" Yuan Shang decided.

"**Pah! This is why you lost!**" Tadun heckled. "**You are a Han man, but you know nothing of your own strategies, your own arrays! You expect others to do everything, and when there is nobody clever or strong to do your work for you, you lose! But Tadun needs no arrays and strategies! I will break them like dry twigs! CHARGE!**"

Tadun personally advanced, and Louban, Wuyan and Supuyan followed: thousands of Wuhuan infantry and cavalrymen poured across the battlefield like a swarm of locusts and entered the human net that Cao Cao's advisers had prepared for them. As soon as no more Wuhuan men could be absorbed into the array, the openings disappeared; Han soldiers raised their weapons and shields to either repel those that were outside of the trap or cause harm to those that were within while their cavalry colleagues rode around and hacked at the confused tribesmen. Panic spread quickly throughout the ranks of the Wuhuan: one in every three men that entered the array was killed, and the chieftains were cut off from their increasingly anxious followers, which led to more careless and costly charges.

"**...And once they are broken, we will scare them some more!**" Cao Cao chuckled. "**Have Cousin Chun bring in our 'secret weapon'!**"

Jia Xu signalled to the rear of the army, who signalled to some far-off allies in turn: Jia Xu then gave a second signal, and the array opened to let the survivors flee.

"**These Han men are cowards!**" Tadun complained as he fled to his own front line.

"**Their tricks are too much!**" Louban said. "**They-!**"
"**...White horses!**" Wuyan exclaimed. "**Holy demons attacking us on white horses!**"
The entire Wuhuan army was stunned by the line of identically-dressed horsemen – all with white capes, white tunics, grey boots and silver-coloured helms with white plumes – that was now advancing: every horse was white or close to being entirely white, which struck fear into the more superstitious of Tadun and Louban's followers.
"**It's a *trick*!**" Yuan Shang cried. "**Gongsun Zan employed the same trick against-!**"
"**What 'trick', Han fool???**" Wuyan retorted. "**They are the white horses of legend! I will not stay!**"
Tadun was unsure of what he should do, but his mind was made up for him: the panic at the sight of so many white horses was already leading to tens of thousands of men retreating, and there was no point to staying without an army.
"**No, no you...! ...Damn their feeble minds!**" Yuan Shang cried as he watched Tadun and the other leaders turn and flee. "**We'll have to flee as well, Brother, or we're dead!**"
Yuan Xi was bitterly angry at having missed an opportunity to strike at Cao Cao, but he knew that his brother was right and retreated silently. The Wuhuan men that stayed were quickly massacred by the Han soldiers that had suffered so much at their hands; Cao Cao watched with pitiless eyes and smiled coldly.

Once the battle was over, Cao Cao rode to the open gates of Yuyang's capital, where the Administrator of Yuyang, Xianyu Fu, was waiting with his seal of office in his hands.
"That's for you to keep for now, Mister Xianyu," Cao Cao insisted.
"...But I have failed the Han," Xianyu Fu said meekly. "I-!"
"We've all failed the Han at some point," Cao Cao replied. "But you have aided the purging of the Yuans from Yòu Province and avenged those harmed by the Yuans and their ally-turned-rival Gongsun Zan. I only wish that I could stay and finish what I have started here today, but that is something that must sadly wait."
"...You're leaving Yuyang?" Xianyu Fu exclaimed. "B-but Wuzhong and other places are-!"
"I have to destroy Gao Gan and pacify Bing Province before I can continue my work against the Wuhuan in person," Cao Cao insisted. "But you will have a lot of help from now on, Administrator Xianyu: I shall leave Qian Zhao, Wang Xiu, Su Yòu and a host of other men here to continue the fight against the Wuhuan and the Yuans that so selfishly tolerated their cruelties against the people."
Xianyu Fu bowed low and said, "The Empire has a hero at last!"
"...I vow that I shall be back in a year or less," Cao Cao replied. "Until then, you will probably have a little trouble, but they will not hurry back in great numbers. Until then, do as you have done and continue to inspire the people... while I punish Gao Gan for forcing me to leave here and abandon you."
"**Heaven curse him, the wretch!**" Xianyu Fu cried.
"It does," Cao Cao chuckled. "Now, I must go... I have little time."
Xianyu Fu and Cao Cao exchanged bows for one last time before Cao left the relieved city and began an immediate journey

southward to Yè City in Ji Province with the bulk of his army. While costly and far from finished, the campaign had ended with the destruction of all of the Yuan brothers' most powerful non-Wuhuan allies in the region, the purging of the Wuhuan confederacy and the pacification of three quarters of the province: that alone was met with surprise and respect in the Han Imperial capital Xuchang.

"I... I still genuinely fail to believe it," Kong Rong said as he sat with Wang Lang, Yang Biao and Zhi Xi in Kong's living quarters; they had just enjoyed another of Kong's popular banquets, where the news of Cao Cao's conquests had, unsurprisingly, dominated the conversation.
"Believe it, Wenju," Wang Ling replied. "It is quite incredible, but believe it nonetheless for it is what happened. Believe it so we can talk about something else!"
"...The Wuhuan, driven from Yòu Province... Yuan Tan slain, his brothers deposed from power, and now only Gao Gan remains," Kong Rong said soberly.
"Yes, and it will still be so if you say it another thousand times," Wang Lang sighed.
"I must confess that I am also 'bored with discussing it'," Yang Biao said. "My son's welfare and the fate of my wife's clan are driving forces for that 'boredom'."
"Oh... yes, of course," Kong Rong replied. "Yuan Tan is – *was* – your wife's nephew, of course, and Gao Gan-"
"Yes, exactly," Yang Biao said. "Perhaps we can discuss the news from the south."
"Yes... the Sun clan's sudden loss of luck," Wang Lang snickered. "I hope that they all die painful deaths for what they did to me and other loyal men like me."
Yang Biao and Zhi Xi happily discussed the southern situation, but Kong Rong was silently haunted; his hatred of Cao Cao prevented him from thinking about anything other than the situation in Bing Province, which was about to change forever.

****

72

Cao Cao returned to Yè City as a hero that had once again managed to achieve something that had been deemed impossible. Registrar Li Fu, Attendant Officer Cui Yan and the rest of the officials lined the road that led from the gates to the governor's mansion and bowed as Cao Cao's carriage passed them. Cao Pi and Cao Hong met the carriage at the mansion gates: Cao Cao looked at his son Pi and grunted ambiguously.

"...Are you not *happy*, Father...?" Cao Pi asked.

"I am not sure," Cao Cao replied. "That would depend on *timings*."

Cao Hong shuddered as Cao Cao passed him with the hulking bodyguard Xu Chu; Cao Chun frowned and said, "I am obviously ignorant of something."

"...I perhaps should have mentioned it when word arrived," Cao Xiu said as he looked at the expressionless Cao Pi. "Lady Zhen has given birth to a son."

"...Ah, I see," Cao Chun sighed.

"What do you 'see'...?" Cao Pi asked snidely.

"The situation," Cao Chun replied. "I am not judging, Cousin."

"Lady Zhen and I are besotted husband and wife, Zihe," Cao Pi insisted. "Nothing improper has happened."

"...No, I am sure that it hasn't," Cao Chun replied. "Perhaps we should follow Mengde now."

Cao Pi nodded silently and led the procession of family members into the living quarters, where Cao Cao was already seated as the host and clan chieftain.

"I want to rest, but I cannot," Cao Cao said once his kin were seated. "Yuanrang is trying to fight Gao Gan, but he is unfamiliar with Bing Province and needs assistance. "But I must prepare properly before I undertake such a journey myself, and so others must go ahead of me."

"I will gladly go," Cao Chun declared.

"Me as well," Cao Hong said. "If Yuanrang's in trouble, then–"

"No, no...!" Cao Cao chuckled. "Not you, Zilian: one of you two is bad enough... I'd never send both of you. And you need to reorganise your 'Tiger and Leopard Cavalry' after two devastating losses, Zihe, and that cannot be done on campaign. No, I'm going to send Yue Jin and Li Dian. Yue Jin was the one that took Nanpi while Yuan Tan's back was turned; Li Dian is a man that has already saved Yuanrang once and will be listened to. And both men are sensible and are therefore bound to work together well."

"...Not necessarily," Cao Chun replied. "They argued quite a bit during the Yuyang campaign, Mengde."

"That campaign was violent and costly, and what men said to each other during that horror is not indicative of normality," Cao Cao insisted. "They'll be fine."

Cao Pi could not contain himself any longer: he raised his hand and said, "Father, I must–"

""I... really do not want to hear about it right now," Cao Cao admitted. "We will discuss it later, son. For now, I must restrict my time to the Bing Province campaign, or we will never defeat the Yuans before I lose Fengxiao."

"...Is Guo Jia's health even worse, then...?" Cao Hong asked.

"He was more sick than healthy on this occasion," Cao Cao replied. "I fear that if he does not get rest, he will be completely unable to accompany me on my return to Yòu Province. I will need him there... I *must* have him there. So... so I have granted him leave, much to his consternation, from the Bing campaign."

"You've more advisers than you'll ever need, so I wouldn't worry," Cao Hong said. "You have Old Cheng, Xin Pi, Chen Qun, Yuan Huan, Xun Yu, Xun Yòu..."

"...And someone obvious that you deliberately neglected to mention," Cao Cao replied with amusement. "Yes, you're right, Zilian, that I have a lot of other advisers. But... but Fengxiao is a unique talent, perhaps only matched by the man whose name you refuse to utter... and, like you, I still hesitate to fully trust him. If I am to survive past Fengxiao's demise... that has to change."

The fugitive warlord Liu Bei had been watching the situation in the north closely since his failure to convince Jing Governor Liu Biao that a coordinated attack on Cao Cao was in their best interests; Bei and his close associates viewed Cao Cao's recent victories over the Yuans and the northern tribes as a crushing blow to their hopes for a future victory.

"...On the other hand," Jian Yong said, "we'd be stuck doing business with the Wuhuan if Cao had lost."

"Xianhe, you're my friend of many years, and I genuinely appreciate your attempts to be serious, but I cannot agree with your implied conclusion that 'this was for the best'," Liu Bei retorted. "Cao Cao is the worst of all of the villains! The Han is surely doomed while he is Chancellor of State in all but name! Even a temporary alliance with the Wuhuan is tolerable when the ultimate goal is the removal of a man whose predilection for evil eclipses Wang Mang and Dong Zhuo!"

"Even his best attempts to woo me away with kind words, gold and titles could hide what he really is," Guan Yu said as he stroked his long beard thoughtfully.

"But the Wuhuan were harming the people," Jian Yong noted.

"Cao Cao will ultimately harm them more," Mi Zhu said. "My clan has served the Han at a high level for a long time, and so I have heard stories about high and low points in the past... I think that things have not been this bad since Wang Mang generally."

"Yes, and now you don't even have your clan's wealth and influence to be able to do anything about it," Liu Bei whimpered. "You're stuck in Jing with me, the man that frittered it all away on futile actions!"

"That is not at all true," Mi Zhu replied. "My clan's fortune and very existence were endangered from the moment that Cao Cao invaded my home province and started to massacre the people without discretion or restraint: your 'futile actions' saved tens of thousands, perhaps hundreds of thousands of lives, Lord Liu, and you might still save more in the future."

"...But I cannot even get Liu Biao to act when the moment is obviously upon us!" Liu Bei complained. "Now Cao Cao has killed Yuan Tan, humbled the Wuhuan tribes, chased Yuan Shang and Yuan Xi out of Yòu-"

"Yeah, and stole Yuan Xi's wife from him and gave her to his son, who got her pregnant before he married her, which he shouldn't have been able to do either, not while she was still married to someone else that was still alive," Zhang Fei suggested. "The Caos are all the same."

Guan Yu – who was still angry at Cao Cao 'snatching' the supposedly-widowed Lady Du from him and taking her as his own consort – harrumphed and said, "I could not agree more, Yide. Though Qin Yilu's reappearance would have made the 'Lady Du situation' as difficult for me as Cao Pi's current predicament, I at least thought, as everyone else did, that Qin was dead… the Caos *know* that Yuan Xi is alive and intend to harm him when there are better, more appropriate options for ending the Yuan conflict."

"…With all due respect, I do not care if Cao and his sons make consorts of the wives of walking dead men," Mi Zhu admitted. "I care that he and his sons are not themselves among those 'walking dead'. I care that, instead of their being fugitives from justice, they rule the Imperial court and, as Lord Liu was saying, have some sort of luck demon on their side that has enabled them to placate the Qiang, tame the Mount Tai Bandits *and* the Black Mountain Bandits, repel the Wuhuan, disband the Yellow Turbans, topple the most powerful clan in the Empire and make sensible, intelligent men by the hundreds – Han loyalists to the core, like Xun Yu – think that they mean well when they obviously don't. It… makes no sense."

"It does if you have the wrong perspective," Jian Yong suggested. "Men like Xun Yu are seeing the whole story from one side, just like we have in the past. Face it, friends: if you're looking at the state of things through the wrong lens right now, Cao Cao is the 'Hero of Chaos' that Xu Shao predicted, only he's ending the chaos, not perpetuating it. Cao Cao's done all the things that *we* wanted to do – well, except the 'toppling the Yuans' part, anyway – and if it were anyone else but him – *anyone* – then we'd be hailing him for achieving the impossible and stabilising the Empire. Men like Xun Yu are looking at Cao for what he's done, not who he is and what he might do later, and that's never sensible, but there you go."

"…That's the most serious that you've been in a long time," Liu Bei replied. "If only you and Mi Zizhong had the answers as well as the observations, and then I wouldn't need to recruit Zhuge and Pang so urgently."

"When do you intend to approach 'Crouching Dragon' again…?" Jian Yong asked.

"Soon," Liu Bei replied. "For now, I'm watching what Cao does."

"Yes, since we may need to flee if he suddenly sends his new, hundred-thousand-strong army at us without warning instead of attacking Gao Gan as he is expected to," Mister Sun said. "And I've been talking to my 'fellow politicians', like Huan Jie, and it seems that there is a genuine worry that we could see Sun Quan attack Jiangxia within the next two years. That'd be an effort led by the likes of Taishi Ci and doubtlessly costly to Liu Biao."

"…There are rumours that Taishi Ci is sick, or even dead," Guan Yu noted.

"That would be terrible," Liu Bei replied. "I know that the Suns are possible future enemies of the Han, but Taishi is a true hero, not like Cao Cao… he does the right thing in the end, as he did when he borrowed our troops to save Kong Rong from the Yellow

Turbans. I hope the rumours prove false: heroes like him should live for ninety years or more and die content, or at least die a worthy, memorable death."

"That is my own hope," Guan Yu said. "May Heaven be kind and grant it."

"...I wonder how long Gao Gan can survive for," Mister Sun said suddenly. "Should we suggest to Liu Biao that we assist Gao Gan in some way...?"

"A waste of time," Liu Bei admitted. "Jingsheng's wife, brother-in-law and advisers are watching us, and whenever I approach him they circle like carrion birds, heckling me and scaring him away from the proper course. Gao Gan, sad to say, is on his own... and that is that. Heaven help him."

"Which it *won't*," Jian Yong said miserably. "And when he and the Yuans are defeated, it'll just be Jing left... Heaven help *us*."

Liu Bei was not the only one that shuddered at the prospect.

Cao Cao personally saw Yue Jin and Li Dian to the gates of Yè City when their moment of departure for Bing Province arrived.

"Do not fail to keep me informed of your movements, Generals," Cao Cao ordered.

Yue Jin and Li Dian bowed simultaneously.

"Yuanrang has managed to stay alive and well, but he is not the man to face Gao Gan, who is a relative mediocrity but still wily enough to do harm," Cao Cao continued. "His counsel, Gao Rou, is not a fool, and Zhang Sheng seems to be a competent senior officer, so do not be complacent because this enemy is not as formidable as the last."

"We will not err, Excellency," Li Dian promised.

"...No, no, of course not," Cao Cao chuckled. "Heaven be with you all the same."

Once the two generals and their armies had started their departure, Guo Jia coughed weakly and asked, "Should they not have counsel...?"

"You shouldn't even be here," Cao Cao replied. "Did I not order you to rest?"

Guo Jia smiled and said, "You did. I shall retire now that my question is posed."

"...He's right," Cao Chun said once Guo Jia was gone. "Li and Yue are not fools, but they'll have Chen Qun between them and Yuanrang, and that's not ideal."

"I might have a lot of advisers and seemingly enough to spare one here and there, but that is not so," Cao Cao replied. "They must help me train the men to use arrays effectively, scout out new talents, watch for activity in Liang, Jing, Qing, Yòu and the Jiangdong region, and most importantly help me prepare for the future battles with the Wuhuan. Li and Yue will be fine... they *have* to be fine."

****

73

When Li Dian and Yue Jin reached Bing Province they encamped on the field to the west of Maocheng Fortress and asked locals about Gao Gan's movements.

"...He's hiding in his capital, that much we've ascertained, but what do we do next...?" Li Dian wondered. "If the roads are guarded, and even the Black Mountain Bandits are unable to harass him effectively, we're unlikely to do better."

Yue Jin smiled and said, "With all due respect, General, I killed Sui Gu before he could join Yuan Shao and recruited the men of Henei; I routed the armies of Yuan Shao at Yan Ford with the help of Yu Jin; I killed Yan Jing in Li County and ended the siege as a result; and I scaled the walls of Nanpi to rescue Cao Chun's cavalry from Yuan Tan and ensure Tan's demise. I am not one for doubting that I can achieve something: I just achieve it."

"*Aiee*... I am not being pessimistic, Wenqian, but rather *pragmatic*!" Li Dian retorted. "I have contributed to the campaigns against Lü Bu and Yuan Shao, and-!"

"As a *logistics officer*," Yue Jin scoffed. "You manage supplies and suchlike. Your one attempt at leading an army was to defeat Gao Fan's navy 'almost single-handed'; a pity that it was a feeble excuse for a navy. Oh, and before that you had to rescue Xiahou Dun from a trap that he walked into because you and Yu Jin couldn't talk him down. You were appointed Administrator of Lihu after your brother died because 'Inspector of Qing' was deemed too much of a responsibility for you: even now, after all of your 'contributions', His Excellency has been quicker to entrust the place to *Zang Ba* than he has been to entrust it to you."

Li Dian's eyes steeled.

"So before you try to compare our achievements, *don't*," Yue Jin continued. "You're here to manage the supplies while I do battle."

"...You have been needlessly confrontational and unfair," Li Dian replied. "Why, I do not know, and nor do I care: if you wish to act alone, by all means do so."

"I don't need your help or anyone else's, not to deal with a nobody like Gao Gan," Yue Jin said. "I would be surprised that His Excellency thought that I did, but his giving me you as a second shows that he is simply ensuring that I am not without proper logistics – which is your expertise – else he would have assigned Zhang Liao, Xu Huang or some other 'tiger of the battlefield'."

"As I said, I am happy to let you lead the way," Li Dian insisted. "What do you intend to do, General Yue?"

"The roads are, as you say, blocked by Gao's forces, and no doubt most of them since he has lost support and so many are distracted elsewhere, and I intend to exploit that obvious fact," Yue Jin explained. "I will go around him, to the north and west, circling around his defensive positions to hit his capital on what will be its undefended western side."

Li Dian hummed thoughtfully.

"You have something to contribute...?" Yue Jin asked tensely.

Li Dian bowed politely and replied, "Not at all, General Yue."

"...Then we'll set out at once," Yue Jin continued. "There will be no need for His Excellency to come here: Gao Gan will fall to our forces long before another boot or hoof has left Yè!"

Within a day, Xiahou Dun received word from Yue Jin that his forces should remain in the south of Bing Province and continue to supress the remnants of the Hedong rebels.
"Is he trying to annoy me?" Xiahou Dun asked of his campaign adviser Chen Qun.
"General Yue... seems to be succumbing to hubris," Colonel Han Hao suggested.
"Yes, Colonel, and that's a shame," Chen Qun said at last. "He is a great warrior."
"But just like Lü Bu, he's getting a big head about it," Xiahou Dun grumbled. "I am family to Mengde, while he's a vassal! How dare he order me about!"
"While I don't agree with his choice of words, his suggestion is valid," Chen Qun admitted. "Zhang Zhi can't inspire the people alone, and a lot of Wei Gu and Fan Xian's remaining supporters are fleeing here now that Du Ji governs Hedong and the rebellions in other places are failing. Let Yue Jin do what he thinks he can do against Gao Gan: we'll stay here and ensure that Gao gets no more help from Hedong, Hongnong or anywhere else."
"...Alright," Xiahou Dun sighed. "But I don't like his tone."

General Yue Jin travelled at the helm of his army of 10,000 as it circled around the human defensive perimeter that Gao Gan had formed around his capital: General Li Dian alternated his time between the different parts of the convoy in order to minimise time spent with his co-commander. But despite the utmost care being taken, the discovery of the large force was inevitable and Gao Gan learned of it within days.
"...What should I do...?" Gao Gan asked of his assembled officials.
"You have two choices," the adviser Gao Rou replied. "You can stay here in the capital and endure a siege, or you can move to a more strategic location."
The other officials murmured uneasily.
"A siege is not at all ideal," Gao Gan said. "This 'Yue Jin' is known to me as a valiant general, with his boasts including the capture of Nanpi while Yuan Tan was in the field. And he is only a precursor to future horrors, is he not...?"
"Certainly," Gao Rou replied. "Though Yue Jin is obviously sent here to try for a 'swift decapitation', his failure to do so will inevitably be followed by a larger army led by Cao Cao himself. If Yuan Tan could not survive such a siege when pressed by an army half the size of what Cao has post-Yòu Province, then we must expect less for our own efforts... by which I mean that we would lose within a few weeks rather than a few months. And that's if the people don't throw the gates open or someone doesn't somehow get to the top of the wall, which Yue Jin has done against stronger opponents than us."
"...That is a poor choice of words," Zhang Sheng heckled. "You're paid to inspire and provide ideas: if you have no ideas, Gao Rou, then be silent!"
"Calm down," Gao Gan said. "Cousin Rou is being honest about our chances, and he mentioned a 'more strategic location': might I now enquire, Cousin Rou, what you meant by that...?"

"There are some that might say 'Why abandon a city to defend a gate?' but in this case it is the proper course," Gao Rou replied. "If we take one of the mountain passes, we will have the high ground, and passage between two places, depending on our choice. My own suggestion is Hu Pass, Governor, because the fortress is one of the most formidable: we could whittle down their resources in such a place, and all the while we can wait for Lord Yuan Shang to return to Yòu Province with his army and reach out to other nearby allies, such as Liu Biao of Jing."
"Liu Biao...? ...I have little faith in receiving aid from that old coward, but Lord Yuan Shang might indeed return, and besides, we cannot surrender, not when the penalty for rebelling after submitting is certain death," Gao Gan said soberly. "We will therefore feign ignorance of Yue Jin's movements using decoy forces while we move our main army to Hu Pass. Zhang Sheng...?"
"I shall begin preparations at once," Zhang Sheng declared.

Yue Jin cried out in anger when he realised that Gao Gan had abandoned the provincial capital: his forces were now poised to strike at a relatively undefended city with no strategically valuable inhabitants, although any attempts to siege the walls would visibly be met by stubborn resistance.
"...I suppose you think this is *funny*," Yue Jin growled as he turned to an expressionless Li Dian.
"Why would I think it is funny...?" Li Dian asked. "Haven't we all just wasted time going halfway around Bing Province for-?"
"Not 'funny', perhaps, but your retort reeks of 'I told you so'!" Yue Jin shouted.
"...Retort...?" Li Dian chortled. "I-!"
"I've been made to look like a fool, ignoring advice and wasting time and resources!" Yue Jin snapped.
"...I made no suggestions... I gave no advice," Li Dian said calmly.
"Gao Gan has abandoned his capital and yet he has made it as far from worthwhile as he could to take the place," Yue Jin noted. "We will have to pursue him to wherever he had gone to... might he have gone southward...?"
"...My own thought is that he would not have gone southward for fear of encountering General Xiahou," Li Dian replied carefully. "He would be seeking another strong defensive or offensive position... a riverside settlement, maybe, or a mountain fort."
"...Well, we left five-thousand recruits guarding the road to Maocheng, so that's safe," Yue Jin muttered. "We'll ask around: north leads to the Black Mountains, and he wouldn't go there. Either east or west... and west leads to Liang Province, which isn't so ridiculous if the Yuans can team up with the Wuhuan... although the Qiang are with *us*, in a sense..."
Li Dian nodded patiently.
"...We'll ask around," Yue Jin continued. "And... and I suppose we'll have to... to write to His Excellency, and... and let him know what... what has happened. You're more eloquent than me, General Li, so... so you can do it."
"I shall ensure that you are happy with what I have prepared," Li Dian promised.
Yue Jin smiled falsely and said, "My *thanks*, General."

Cao Cao could not hide his disappointment when Li Dian's letter reached him: he summoned his officers, officials and advisers – save for Guo Jia, who was still recuperating – and said, "This is not ideal at all. I admit that I had hoped that Yue Jin and Li Dian would bring a swift end to Gao Gan's feeble rebellion, but now we must face the prospect of that shifty opportunist being behind the walls of some grand fortress! ...**I need to get back to Yòu Province! This idiot is WASTING MY TIME!**"

"...Other intelligence is pointing to Gao Gan possibly being at Hu Pass," Yuan Huan reported.

"*Aiee*... Hu Pass is a good defensive position," Zhang Liao said miserably. "In the days of Inspector Ding Yuan, we always dreaded the idea of having to face an opponent that had taken that place. The only option is to overwhelm it."

Cao Cao clutched his aching head and asked, "What would it take to 'overwhelm' Hu Pass, gentlemen...? Is this something that Yue Jin, Li Dian and Yuanrang can do without further assistance...?"

"...Gao Gan has obviously sent word to various agitators across the region," Jia Xu replied. "We've got everything from river pirates to renegade Southern Xiongnu rising up now, and-"

"So I must go there in person," Cao Cao said irritably. "Gao Gan *might*, just *might*, have enjoyed clemency if he had not done this thing: he *will* die a dog's death – that much is certain – but I swear to you all that if this delay in any way results in the Yuans and their Wuhuan friends returning to fighting strength and returning to the Empire to cost more valuable lives, **I will have Gao Gan's corpse desecrated and his name denounced for the next six hundred years!**"

"...Who will you take on your campaign, Father...?" Cao Pi asked.

"You'll stay here," Cao Cao replied angrily. "You can source your next consort from some other place at a later date."

Many men covered their faces with their sleeves and stared at the floor; Cao Pi fought tears of rage and embarrassment as he bowed and said, "I will guard Yè City with my life, Father."

"Cui Yan will remain in Yè to ensure discipline," Cao Cao continued. "I will take every available man and horse, gentlemen, and 'overwhelm' Gao Gan at Hu Pass."

"We can be ready in a few days," Jia Xu said.

"I... I must wait until this accursed headache passes anyway," Cao Cao replied as he got to his feet and started to make his way out of the hall by a side entrance that led to his study. "If I had not had them all my life, I'd say they were another 'gift' from the last man that sat here as the lord... to thank me for our friendship."

The hall was silent for several minutes before Yuan Huan said, "We should get back to our work."

The officials exchanged respectful bows and retreated via the main entrance; Cao Pi, Cao Hong, Cao Chun and Cao Xiu were left seated along the right side of the hall in stunned silence.

"...Mengde's headaches are indeed cruel," Cao Chun said at last.

"I was *humiliated*," Cao Pi replied tonelessly.

"Forgive my frankness, Zihuan, but Mengde made a vague comment that caused many a man in the court to recall crueller words that are whispered by allies and critics alike in many a shadowy corner of Yè, Xuchang, and Heaven knows where else," Cao Chun retorted. "The entire matter of Lady Zhen and your 'early' son with her is, like it or not, 'controversial', and the comments and rumours reach Mengde, like *that* or not."

"...Lady Zhen and I are *besotted*," Cao Pi insisted. "No impropriety has taken place... and *yes*, I know about the 'rumours', Zihe... rumours that include the nonsense idea that Yuan Xi somehow snuck into Yè during the siege and left Lady Zhen with child before sneaking out again, apparently days or even *hours* before the city fell, if the timings are to work! If Yuan Xi is so *incredible* – if Yuan Xi is another Li Fu that somehow outwitted everyone *twice*, *somehow*, *again* – then why is he now hiding in barbarian territory with *nothing to his name*, the powerless older brother to the illegitimate heir to a once-great clan left with *nothing*?"

"...Did I say that I believed any of it...?" Cao Chun asked.

"No, you didn't, and I didn't accuse you of believing it... I am hurt, I am offended, and I am speaking my mind about it," Cao Pi replied. "I am the heir to the Cao clan, the man that will inherit all of the wealth, power and burdens that my father now bears, and... and I detest the idea that people dare to accuse me of raping my wife before we married or being some fool that is raising Yuan Xi's son and future avenger."

"Put like that, yes I see your anger," Cao Chun sighed. "But-"

"There's no 'but', Zihe," Cao Pi retorted. "I will one day be their lord, and after me, my son... *my* son, Zihe, not Yuan Xi's magic son conceived one foggy night during a violent siege when Lady Zhen was under constant watch by Lady Liu. I deserve the respect of the officials, and so does my son... unless, of course, I am assumed to be 'fallen from favour', and they are all suspecting that I will be passed over, like Yuan Tan..."

"That's nonsense," Cao Hong chuckled. "Mengde would never do that. He's smart: he'd never do what Yuan Shao did, not after he's seen what happened, no matter how pissed off he might be."

Cao Xiu groaned quietly at Cao Hong's choice of words.

"But I am an *embarrassment*, Zilian!" Cao Pi chuckled angrily. "Yuan Tan was an embarrassment, was he not...? And Father has his favourites, Zhi and Chong-"

"Stop it... stop harming yourself," Cao Xiu said sternly. "You're like a brother to me, Zihuan, and Mengde is a friend and father both. I do not believe for a moment that Mengde would ever disinherit or 'pass over' you in favour of another."

Cao Pi got to his feet and said, "I am going to go and see my son. I... I thank you all for listening to me. I shall do all that I can to restore my standing with Father."

Cao Pi left the hall; Cao Hong shook his head and sighed.

"*You're* sighing...?" Cao Xiu heckled. "You said-!"

"Zilian knows what he said," Cao Chun interrupted. "Let us go and attend to our armies... for we're doubtless going to Bing Province with Mengde. Zihuan has his own battles to fight that we cannot assist him with: he's on his own."

Cao Hong and Cao Xiu reluctantly agreed with Cao Chun's words and followed him out of the hall.

****

74

Hu Pass Fortress was an elevated structure that enjoyed additional strength from the mountains on either side: the rocky incline was difficult to traverse, near-impossible to dig through and too dangerous for any but the most cost-ignoring attempts at an uphill charge. If supplies and morale had not been an issue, Gao Gan would have been almost impossible to dislodge, but the need to open some sort of supply route and maintain communications with potential allies forced Gao to send his army out of the fortress to engage General Yue Jin's weary besiegers. Both sides lost men, but Gao Gan's side was suffering most: that did nothing to appease Yue Jin, however, since his reputation was, in his mind, at stake.

"Why will this man not accept defeat and let me rid the world of him before His Excellency marches out of Yè???" Yue Jin cried as he paced back and forth across the command tent; Li Dian sat to the left of the host seat and watched him silently. **"We've met on the field four times now,"** Yue Jin continued, **"and I have humiliated his army every time!"**

"You really don't need to shout, General Yue, it's only me here," Li Dian urged. "And stop pacing: it serves no purpose other than to wear yourself out."

Yue Jin marched to the host seat and sat down abruptly.

"His Excellency is probably already on his way," Li Dian continued. "We just have to accept that Gao Gan outmanoeuvred us, took a very sensible defensive posture in a very formidable fortress, and that we will not uproot him without overwhelming him."

"...Gao Gan has ruined my reputation," Yue Jin complained.

"No he hasn't," Li Dian replied. "Gao Gan's stubborn, and as you said you've-"

"My reputation is one of a man that gets things done, General Li," Yue Jin said irritably. "Gao Gan has outwitted me, outrun me and now he sits in his high fortress laughing at me."

"You've killed hundreds of his men," Li Dian noted.

"And yet his defence of Hu Pass inspires others," Yue Jin retorted. "Every day that I fail to get him out of there, another village or town turns back to him! Every day that I do not end his life, pirates and rebels flock to him! What if the Black Mountain Bandits defect to him, or Huchuquan's Xiongnu tribes, or-!"

"They won't," Li Dian insisted. "A handful of pirates making trouble and a few sympathetic rebellions breaking out is none of it worth crying about, and many of those started before Gao even got to Hu Pass. Compared to Yòu Province, this is-"

"I was feared in Yòu Province!" Yue Jin snapped. **"I was feared in Ji as well! Here I'm that short, useless general that cannot get rid of a runt like Gao Gan!"**

"...Let's go outside," Li Dian sighed. "They're bound to charge again soon."

Yue Jin did not have to wait long for Li Dian's prediction to come true: within an hour, Zhang Sheng led a 1,000-strong militia down the hillside to attack the edge of the Han camp. Yue Jin personally led the counter-attack, but the intention of the latest assault was intimidation and demoralisation, so Zhang retreated before any serious harm could be inflicted on his army.

"COME BACK HERE, COWARD!" Yue Jin screamed as he raised the spear in his right hand above his head. **"GIVE ME YOUR HEAD FOR MY LORD CAO CAO!"**

"Calm down, Wenqian!" Li Dian pleaded as he rode to Yue Jin's side and tried to take hold of Yue's left arm.

"You are not my friend, Li Dian! Don't address me as such!" Yue Jin retorted.

"...Fine," Li Dian sighed. **"I shall return to the command tent, then, General Yue."**

"Do as you please!" Yue Jin barked. **"I shall wait here for that coward to come back!"**

Li Dian grunted irritably and retreated.

Cao Cao's preparations for departure came to an end, and he held one last meeting in his grand audience hall before leaving Yè City.

"...Firstly, I should like to say that I will be leaving the security of this city in the hands of my son and heir, Pi, and Attendant Officer Cui Yan," Cao Cao said with a tone that suggested humility, pragmatism and, some suspected, resignation. "I must bring a swift end to Gao Gan's rebellion, gentlemen, else I will be facing further unrest not just in Bing and Yòu, but everywhere. That means taking a very large force to Hu Pass."

"Is such a small defensive force in Yè enough when Gao Gan holds Hu Pass...?" Cao Chun asked.

"It will have to be," Cao Cao replied. "I will, of course, have an army harassing the other side of the pass if I can, but the rivers make that awkward. Believe me, Zihe, when I say that I am distressed at this: your brother Ren has been stuck in Runan for a long time now, poor Miaocai will soon take root in Yingchuan if he must stay there any longer, and I want more than Li Tong and a few of my less-seasoned officers in Jing Province. But if I do not defeat Gao Gan definitively and set an example to any others that are pondering similar action, this will never end. The Qiang, the Wuhuan, the Suns of Jiangdong, Liu Biao, Liu Bei, and maybe even some of the Mount Tai Bandits."

"I'm keeping an eye on that last situation for you, Excellency," General Yu Jin promised. "The principal agitator, Chang Xi, is a fellow townsman and trusts me, so he tends to be very honest in his communication. If he or anyone else plots against Zang Ba or the Han, we will know about it."

"...Very good," Cao Cao replied as he turned to look at Cao Pi.

"I will not fail you, Father," Cao Pi insisted. "Travel content in the knowledge that Yè is in safe hands."

"...I have faith," Cao Cao replied carefully. "And hopefully, I will not be gone long, for I know the stress of protecting a new family and defending a city from my days in Ji'nan... it is not easy. I have instructed Attendant Officer Cui to be your 'guide' – your mentor, if you will – and further refine your nature so that you are ready for the responsibilities that shall one day be yours. I have faith that you are worthy."

Cao Pi clasped his hands together and bowed humbly as his father returned his steely gaze to the wider audience.

"...We will show no mercy to Gao Gan," Cao Cao declared. "Headache or no headache, he has greatly vexed me and harmed

the state: no mercy... *none*."
The officials silently agreed.

The small number of determined Yuan loyalists that remained in Ji Province were dispersed evenly so that they could discover new information and quickly relay it to their exiled lord Yuan Shang: word of Cao Cao's departure for Bing Province was met with a brief period of excitement and frenzied planning in the Yuan brothers' new base beyond the frontier, but it quickly became clear that any attempt to march into Yòu Province for a second time would be met by fierce, near-total opposition.

"I would have to enslave or destroy most of Yòu Province in order to retake it," Yuan Shang complained. "I have erred in my judgement, Elder Brother."

"It was my province to govern, so I must at the very least share the blame," Yuan Xi insisted.

"...It was Father's policy – policy that I willingly continued – that led to our lack of popularity with the people," Yuan Shang admitted. "But what can we do?"

"We must send agents into the province to try and sway minds back to us," Yuan Xi suggested. "If we can make the people understand that Cao Cao is a villain, another Dong Zhuo... tired though that argument is, and sick though the people might be of hearing it, it is no less true. They thank him for repelling the Wuhuan now, but when he is stealing their daughters for his harem – or those of his sons – and crushing old women under the wheels of his carriage for fun, will they be so grateful...?"

"We can try, Brother," Yuan Shang said. "...Incidentally, do you suspect as I do that Tadun is now the 'chief of chiefs' of the Wuhuan, and not Louban...?"

"Tadun sometimes implies power-sharing to cover his tracks, but it's no diarchy," Yuan Xi replied. "I doubt that it ever was: Tadun feigned deference to the young, inexperienced Louban, gained support through shows of strength and took the power without Louban realising... much like Cao Cao's takeover of the Han court. Now, like the Han court, Tadun wields the power while still feigning deference to Louban, but Louban knows what's going on... you can see it. When disaffected court officials that resigned their posts and fled to Ji spoke of the atmosphere in Xuchang, and spoke of the exchanges between Cao and the Son of Heaven, their descriptions match the tension seen between Louban and Tadun: a powerless monarch sarcastically demonstrating authority next to the real wielder of power."

"...I wonder if we are safe," Yuan Shang admitted.

"So do I, sometimes, but my belief is that Tadun needs us to get back into the Empire, and we're safe until his foothold is regained," Yuan Xi replied. "He still needs Louban as well, so Tadun is not that secure... at the moment."

"...Just like Cao," Yuan Shang chuckled. "And that being the case... a victory is still possible. We'll send agents as you suggested... and wait for the right signs."

Cao Cao's army arrived in Bing Province and spread out across the region, seeking out pockets of resistance and eliminating them; Cao himself took Cao Chun, Cao Xiu, Yu Jin, Zhang Liao and Xu

Huang to Hu Pass, where Yue Jin's forces were still trying to pass the defences and take the fortress. When Cao Cao's vanguard reached the friendly camp at the base of the pass, Yue Jin greeted his lord in person and fell to his knees, saying, **"I have failed you, Excellency!"**

"You are incorrect, Wenqian," Cao Cao replied. **"I cannot find any man that says that taking Hu Pass is anything less than 'severely taxing'. You have done well, in fact."**

Yue Jin got to his feet and allowed Cao Cao's carriage to pass through the gates.

"We *must be quick*," Cao Cao said to Jia Xu, who was sat opposite him in the carriage. "Our enemies will know that we are concentrated here in Bing Province."

"Indeed, Excellency," Jia Xu replied.

Cao Cao smiled and said, "You are quietly pained that I repeat that point so often, aren't you...? But I must tell myself this so often because I am... nervous. Terrified, in fact."

The bodyguard Xu Chu – who was sat to Cao Cao's left – frowned at the statement and asked, "Do you not think that I can protect you, Excellency?"

Cao Cao laughed quietly and said, "I am not afraid of any man that tries to attack me directly, Zhongkang, for I know that you will tear him to shreds. No, am terrified of the unseen enemy, or the horde that one guard cannot repel alone. Bing is between Ji and Yòu Provinces to the east – both being recently pacified and under threat from the Wuhuan – and Liang Province to the west, where Qiang and Du tribes are always a worry to me. So far, they have remained 'tame'... but that will not last if I fail to defeat Gao Gan quickly."

Jia Xu hummed quietly.

"When Wang Yi betrayed me and turned Hedong over to the Yuans, Hongnong was quick to follow and more still after that," Cao Cao continued. "Du Ji seems to be the right man to keep Hedong stable for me, but if he is not... then this is a dangerous place for me to be, because there are two other serious threats: the Xianbei are beyond the Great Wall to the north, and Jing Province is beyond the Yellow River to the south. I am potentially surrounded and far from Xuchang or Yè... and if my enemies united at this point... one bodyguard, no matter how strong, will not make much of a difference."

Jia Xu hummed for a second time.

"...You are pondering the similarity of this to other things, Mister Jia...?" Cao Cao chuckled. "Am I like Dong Zhuo, with my very own Lü Bu sat next to me, surrounded by the angry and hateful many that look to harm me...?"

"Not at all," Jia Xu replied immediately. "Dong Zhuo was rightly hated, whereas you, Excellency, are just misunderstood. The Qiang will do nothing; the Wuhuan will, I think, stay where they are, and so will the Xianbei; Liu Biao will, as always, sit there and do nothing. The now-confirmed death of Taishi Ci will delay Sun Quan a little while he honours his brother's closest ally after Zhou Yu of Lujiang, but there will be no peace between Liu Biao and the Suns, and it is that certain threat from the south that will keep Liu Biao from listening to Liu Bei's attempts to rouse him to act against you now."

"…Taishi Ziyi, I regret that you were unable to see that I should have been your lord," Cao Cao lamented. "Now you are gone: such a shame."
"It is," Jia Xu replied.
"But it is also a fact that cannot be changed," Cao Cao continued. "You are right to say that I am safe for now, Mister Jia. I will be more optimistic about defeating Gao Gan, no matter how long it takes. And once Gao Gan is dead, I can make enquiries about… other matters."
"…'Other matters', Excellency…?" Jia Xu said cautiously.
"Years ago, a faction of the Southern Xiongnu committed a terrible – seemingly insignificant, but terrible – wrong in northern Liang Province," Cao Cao replied. "For some time now, I have wanted to right that wrong since they will not, and now that I am in the territory that they have settled in, I want to begin the process. It… would seem silly to some, but it is something that I absolutely have to do."
"…Cai Yong's eldest daughter, Lady Cai Yan," Jia Xu guessed. "I feel that I am in part responsible for her plight, since Dong Zhuo's forcing her father to attend his mockery of a court – a court that I was instrumental in realising – was the main reason that Director Wang Yun was given cause to execute him and indirectly condemn his family to exile and destruction. It would please me greatly to see at least some of the damage repaired."
"Then we have common ground, Jia Wenhe," Cao Cao replied. "May we find more in the years to come."
Jia Xu bowed slightly and smiled.
"But for now," Cao Cao said, "we must focus on Gao Gan…"

✳✳✳✳✳✳✳✳✳✳✳✳

75

The initial reports from Bing Province calmed the nervous officials that had remained in Ji Province to maintain stability and good governance: the news was particularly well received in Yè City, where confidence in the main defender, Cao Pi, was not high. Cui Yan despaired more than any: he had been entrusted with 'refining the nature' of Cao Pi's character, but Cao Cao's heir was interested in little more than music, poetry and spending time with Lady Zhen and his new son. Cao Pi was not oblivious to the concern, but he was as aware as ever of the rumours and jokes at his expense and did whatever he could to avoid too much communication with the officials, including Cui Yan.

"They all criticise me... they criticise *us*, my lady," Cao Pi said to Lady Zhen, who was sat facing him in their living quarters. "They are all quite cruel. That is why I behave as I do toward them: I should have said so before, but-"

"Forgive my interruption, but I know of it all from my maids," Lady Zhen admitted.

"...All of it...?" Cao Pi asked.

"The accusations, the rumours, the spite... all of it, Husband," Lady Zhen replied.

"I want to protect you, me, and our son from it all, but I cannot," Cao Pi sighed.

"...They do not understand, Husband," Lady Zhen replied. "I was confused at first, but when I see how... how that man that I am loath to speak of... abandoned me to suffer continual venom from Yuan Shao's widow, and then made no effort to... ... ...but I am treated well now, and I am nothing less than content. Let them speak ill of us, for their ignorance will undo them in the end."

"...I am not respected," Cao Pi suggested. "There is more to it than just our marriage and our child: they all of them view me as a mediocrity, like Yuan Tan, that will one day be cast aside so that one of my brothers can inherit everything. Father insists that I am his heir, but then he fawns on Chong and Zhi, and tells me that I need some stubborn little pedant to help me 'improve myself'. How can I then be sure...?"

"You were left in charge of Yè," Lady Zhen noted.

"A false responsibility," Cao Pi scoffed. "Cui Yan has been left in charge of Yè."

"...So what will you do until His Excellency returns...?" Lady Zhen asked as Cao Pi suddenly got to his feet and brushed his robes down needlessly.

"I will do as all noblemen do to keep their wits and skills intact," Cao Pi replied. "I shall assemble my friends and go on a hunt. We shall reconvene later, my lady: until then, stay well."

Lady Zhen nodded silently, and Cao Pi departed.

"*Ayah*... hunting...?"

The young official Yang Xiu nodded in response to Attendant Officer Cui Yan's 'question' about Cao Pi's current whereabouts.

"...*Hunting*," Cui Yan grumbled. "The entire northeast is on a political cliff edge, and he has gone hunting. Is it that we are mad and they sane, or am I just unlucky...?"

"I am not going to answer that, Mister Cui," Yang Xiu said dryly.

"No, no... that's the sensible thing," Cui Yan muttered.

"What will you do...?" Yang Xiu asked.

"His Excellency instructed me to be his son's mentor," Cui Yan replied. "If I now ignore this blatant disregard for responsibility, what kind of mentor would I be...?"

"So what will you say...?" Yang Xiu asked.

"I am tempted to point out that another son of a famous hero went hunting when his enemies were nearby, but it would no doubt be misconstrued," Cui Yan replied as he took up a pen and started to write on a piece of cloth paper. "I know that the Caos can be touchy, and being compared to Sun Ce should flatter the lad, but he'll get angry instead, since Sun Ce is a 'rustic pirate' or some such. I shall keep my words simple and straightforward... and also stern. He might get angry, but I would rather incur the wrath of the son than the wrath of the father."

"I quite understand... though I will not say why," Yang Xiu said.

"...You must be disappointed that His Excellency has not taken you on campaign this time," Cui Yan prompted.

"I am only twenty-one years of age," Yang Xiu replied, "and I have much to learn. And as Registrar Liu Yè has said, I must manage things here while he is away. I have many more years left to achieve great things, Mister Cui."

"...While Cao Pi, who is only two years younger than you, cannot seem to control his urge to act like a child," Cui Yan complained. "This will have to do... I only hope that it results in his improved behaviour and not me losing my life."

A junior official delivered Cui Yan's letter to Cao Pi when the latter returned to his home after a moderately successful hunt; Pi retired to his study and read the letter carefully.

"...Is something wrong, Husband...?" Lady Zhen asked when she entered the study a short time later and caught sight of Cao Pi's pained expression.

"This man... denounces me!" Cao Pi replied tensely. "But... but he does so with such eloquence that... ... ...he frames his arguments so well that... without resorting to a single word of malice, a single barbed comment!"

"Who denounces you for what...?" Lady Zhen asked.

"...Cui Yan," Cao Pi replied numbly. "He is truly a great man. I would learn much from him."

Lady Zhen frowned; she did not know if the reply was intended to be sarcastic or sincere.

"...I mean it," Cao Pi said after a long pause. "I have been foolish. Though this letter is meant to rebuke me for the hunting trip, it goes on to speak of other things that – intended or not – show that I have reacted wrongly to a great many things. I *do* need to 'refine my nature', my lady... and I shall begin by composing a fitting reply."

Cui Yan was briefly afraid when one of Cao Pi's soldiers arrived at his home and knocked abruptly; his servants readied their simple weapons and prepared to defend their master to the end if necessary, but the soldier was only delivering a letter. Cui Yan sighed with relief, thanked the soldier needlessly and retired to his living quarters to read Cao Pi's response to his own rebuke. Two friends – his colleague Sima Lang, and the scholar Song Jie – were visiting at the time, and they awaited Cao Pi's words with interest and dread.

"… … …There is nothing to fear, gentlemen," Cui Yan said at last. "The lad may yet be a hero."

"What did he say…?" Sima Lang asked.

"He has apologised for his 'gross folly' and destroyed his hunting equipment so that he cannot 'err and neglect his duties again'," Cui Yan reported. "He has explained his personal situation with clarity and a perspective that I must confess to be quite plausible and understandable… he has thanked me for my 'lecture' – a strong word, yes, but better than 'rebuke' – and has said that he hopes that I will still agree to help him to 'become a better man'."

"So there will be no angry killing," Song Jie chuckled. "I am happy for you."

"So you should be," Cui Yan said with a smile. "Then you'd have to care for Gongsun Fang's children and my own family, and your salary is already stretched."

"Cao Pi's poor behaviour to this point will hopefully be the last, then," Sima Lang said. "It's just added to my brother Yi's lack of interest in serving the Han."

"Which is a shame, as I have always said, since he's the smartest of the 'Eight Sima' and the one that could go furthest," Cui Yan replied. "Is he still 'ill'…?"

"*Aiee*… you make it sound like a cheap trick!" Sima Lang protested. "If-!"

"If he were to be caught feigning illness to avoid service, that would be bad," Cui Yan said. "I only hope that it is genuine, for such tricks won't fool Cao Cao for long. Zhongda might just have to accept that he is destined to serve in the court."

"Yi's ever so slightly- …Well, I hate to use the word, but… he is 'vindictive'," Sima Lang noted. "He doesn't like being forced to do *anything*, and so forcing him to serve the Han might be… unwise."

"Sima Yi will one day serve the court, for better or worse," Cui Yan replied. "His Excellency will demand it. What happens next is up to Sima Yi."

"…And you'll live to see it," Song Jie joked. "Lucky you!"

"Cao Pi has surprised me, and pleasantly for once," Cui Yan said as he turned to look at the letter once again. "He is no Yuan Tan… no, he is a smarter, more thoughtful man than that thug ever was. He might just make a fine heir."

"So will you be informing His Excellency of the matter…?" Sima Lang asked.

"I am obliged to, Boda, and others seeking to elevate themselves – Wang Lang is one name that springs to mind – might feel the need to mention it if I do not," Cui Yan replied. "I will be fair and speak of Pi in the highest terms… as he deserves."

Cao Cao retired to his command tent to read Cui Yan's letter, after which he hummed thoughtfully; several days had passed since the incident that Cui referred to, and the campaign in Bing Province was going well enough for Cao to be annoyed but not furious at his son's behaviour.

"Is there anything that we need to discuss…?" Xin Pi asked.

"Mm...? ...Uh, no, no, it is a trifling issue that can wait until I return to Yè," Cao Cao replied as he handed the letter to his registrar, Liu Yè; he then turned to Consultant Hua Xin and asked, "How go our scouting exercises...?"

"Zhang Liao's men report a few high mountain paths that can be used to attack the fortress from the sides," Hua Xin replied. "It seems that Gao Gan was not sensible enough to secure them."

"Nor was I 'clever enough' to even be aware of them," General Yue Jin said as he glared at General Zhang Liao. "It seems that you will be the man to end this campaign quickly, Zhang."

"I served in Bing Province under Inspector Ding Yuan for many years, which you know, General Yue," Zhang Liao retorted. "Can I help it if my men and I are more knowledgeable about Hu Pass than yours, and why should I apologise...?"

Yue Jin pointed at Zhang Liao and said, "*You*-!"

"I will put an end to this argument before it goes any further," Cao Cao said sternly. "How many times must I reprimand grown men for such bickering? You're both heroes and should respect each other and my authority enough to argue no more."

Zhang Liao bowed slightly and said, "I have no quarrel with you, General Yue."

"...And I acknowledge General Zhang Liao's achievements," Yue Jin growled.

"*Aiee*... go and inspect your men, both of you," Cao Cao ordered, and the two officers left the command tent; Cao then turned to Xin Pi, Yuan Huan, Jia Xu, Hua Xin and Liu Yè and said, "Sun Tzu would weep at the fact that men's minds have developed so little over the centuries and that I still need to heed basic advice about infantile generals posturing and fighting over their reputations."

"Zhang Liao is not going to fight Yue Jin without some serious provocation," Yuan Huan suggested.

"But Yue Jin is becoming difficult: he also quarrels with Li Dian regularly," Cao Cao replied uneasily. "All of them are formidable, but their bickering is dangerous."

"Indeed," Jia Xu said. "I recall an unfortunate time – unfortunate for Dong Zhuo, I mean, which was, of course, much deserved and fortunate for the rest of the world – when he sent three of his finest generals to fight Sun Jian and they quarrelled and lost."

Cao Cao smiled and replied, "Ah, yes... the Battle of Yangren, was it not...?"

Jia Xu nodded silently.

"While I was bested by one of Dong's officers – Xu Rong – at Xingyang, Sun Jian defeated *three* – Hu Zhen, *Hua Xiong* and the mighty *Lü Bu* – at Yangren," Cao Cao recalled. "Truly that was a case of 'the sum failing to match the parts'; Lü Bu's ego harmed the defenders at Yangren, and it cost Dong Zhuo the service of Hua Xiong. I might need to remind Yue Jin of it at some point: his service is undeniably among some of the finest work, but he'll be of no use to me if he cannot work with others."

"It's a shame," Yuan Huan said. "Yue Jin has been so reliable up to now. What has changed?"

"Too many incredible victories followed by a predictable setback," Cao Cao replied. "He expects incredible victories at every turn now and is disappointed when they do not materialise... I have seen it before in others and must avoid succumbing to such feelings in

the future, should I do what I intend to do and succeed."
"...What will we do about the fortress, Excellency...?" Jia Xu asked
after a short silence.
"I think that we will bring this nonsense to a swift conclusion," Cao
Cao replied. "Gao Gan is nothing special: he has only a few
thousand men and little grain, a lack of projectiles to roll down at
us as we charge, and nowhere to run to or summon help from. We
will hit the fortress on all sides and break the defenders' spirits,
and then Heaven will decide the outcome, which I already know.
We will wait for three days... and then he will die."

****

76

Gao Gan regularly travelled to the walls of Hu Pass Fortress to see what his enemies were doing, and their apparent lack of activity unnerved him.

"Perhaps we should charge again," Gao Gan suggested.

"We lost over two hundred men last time," the adviser Gao Rou retorted. "We should be maintaining a tight defence and looking for allies."

Zhang Sheng harrumphed and said, "Allies...? What, such as Liu Biao, who has watched this unfold from a short distance away and done nothing to save his own neck or ours...?"

"I was hoping that Liu Bao, heir apparent to the Southern Xiongnu title of Chanyu, might be able to help," Gao Rou replied. "He does not like Cao Cao, mainly because he blames Cao for the death of his father Yufuluo. They are not far from here, so-"

"I already sent a man to them, and they rebuked him," Gao Gan said. "Liu Bao might be heir apparent, but his uncle Huchuquan is the current Chanyu, and Huchuquan will not confront Cao Cao. Liu Bao has limited support and would risk war with his uncle if he disobeyed him."

"Ah yes, that's right," Gao Rou said numbly.

"...There must be *someone*!" Gao Gan cried.

"There is Lord Yuan, who is currently 'exiled' in the lands beyond the Great Wall," Zhang Sheng said. "Besides him, I see no one."

"So we're to just sit here and wait for Cao's supplies to run out, then...?" Gao Gan heckled. "Send another messenger to Liu Biao! Reach out to *Zhang Xiu* if you must! We need allies! We will be defeated without allies!"

"I doubt we'll get a messenger past Cao's camps, but I shall see what I can do," Gao Rou promised.

Three days passed: Gao Gan had retired to his bed after an anxious night of pacing the walls in expectation of a night attack that never came. Morale had slowly eroded as Cao Cao's men engaged in sorties that brought them close to the walls while never really doing anything; security was also becoming lax due to fatigue, and that was what Cao Cao had been waiting for. Suddenly, drums started to sound and the shouts of men rang out in all directions: Gao Gan awoke with a start and rushed out of his headquarters in time to see his men rushing toward all of the walls with whatever they could use as projectiles.

"...Attacks from the *sides*...?" Gao Gan exclaimed.

"**Governor! Governor, we are at risk!**" Gao Rou cried as he approached Gao Gan. "**We... we're facing attacks from all sides, Governor... they found mountain paths that took them around us so that they could-**"

"**Drat! How is it that we did not know about these roads???**" Gao Gan snapped.

"...**We knew, but we could not secure them without difficulty,**" Gao Rou replied. "**It was hoped that the enemy would not learn of them; I forgot that they employ a number of Ding Yuan's former followers that know this region well.**"

"We cannot hope to survive this, can we, Cousin...?" Gao Gan asked plainly.

"...Not really," Gao Rou admitted. **"You should flee, Governor, and I will hold the fortress for as long as possible."**

"But where would I go???" Gao Rou asked desperately.

"Jing Province," Gao Rou replied. **"Liu Biao might be a poor ally, but he's given sanctuary to Liu Bei, so why not you...?"** Gao Gan did not have time to think and he knew it: he nodded and said, **"I shall depart at once. Heaven be with you."**

Gao Gan disguised himself as a common soldier and, with a small group of trusted men, fled Hu Pass Fortress by climbing down the wall when Cao Cao's men were reeling from a boiling oil attack and retreated briefly; Gao Rou took charge of the walls and did what he could to inspire the defenders, but it was obviously over. The west wall was taken by Zhang Liao's men, who then fought their way to the gates and opened them to Yue Jin's main force. The subsequent battle was violent and unforgiving: Gao Rou was captured, but most of the defenders – who had decided to die as loyal subordinates of Gao Gan – were slaughtered.

Cao Cao waited until the battle was truly over before he had the very small number of captured defenders brought to his command tent; Gao Rou was brought to him first, bound with rope and dishevelled from days of fighting.

"Gao Wenhui," Cao Cao said as he studied the face of the emotionally broken adviser. "Zhang Sheng is no more, which is regrettable, but you are alive, and I have the power to spare you: will you submit to the Han...?"

"...I have nothing to say," Gao Rou replied. "Kill me and-"

"How I *tire* of that phrase," Cao Cao interrupted. "How I tire, Wenhui, of good men being brought to me and saying 'Kill me and be done with it'. Evil men say it too, of course, but I have no problem with agreeing to their wishes. But you, you're a good man. Why die needlessly...? What good is there in dying for Gao Gan...? I hear that you even tried to pretend that you were he! *Why*, Wenhui...?"

"He is my cousin and my lord," Gao Rou retorted. "As my lord, I owe him my unyielding service."

"...So was it you that advised him to rebel again after submitting?" Xin Pi asked.

"I... no, but it was the right thing to do!" Gao Rou retorted.

"It wasn't, as the outcome shows," Cao Cao said coldly. "And I should inform you that Gao was intercepted as he fled... for as my knowledge of what *you* look like prevented you from dying in his place, so other men's knowledge of what *he* looked like prevented his disguise being of much use."

Gao Rou groaned miserably and lowered his head.

"If Gao Gan is dead, then what lord do you have...?" Cao Cao continued. "I regret it, Wenhui, I truly do: I have known Gao Gan my entire life. But Gao sent Guo Yuan to fight his own uncle, Zhong Yao, and cost Guo his life, which I cannot forgive; he allowed Pang Ji and Shen Pei to upset the proper passing of Benchu's estate, and only to ensure that he gained an impressive fief, which is a grave offence; he turned Administrator Wang Yi away from the light and brought chaos to Hedong and Hongnong,

which was another grave offence; he submitted insincerely and then pulled me away from achieving a swift and much needed victory against the cruel Wuhuan, which is actually two offences, both grave; that's all recent, but we both know that there's more, and that you were there for a lot of it... the worst, perhaps, being the decision to leave His Majesty to rot when he was trying to escape Li Jue and Guo Si. But I am a man that dislikes seeing good men go to waste, no matter how much they have strayed from the proper path."
Gao Rou looked at Jia Xu and said, "So I see."
"So what will it be...?" Cao Cao asked. "Will you join me in bringing peace to the Empire, or will you die a pointless death to honour a dead lord whose crimes are so many and so grave...?"
"...I have long known that the Yuans have been resorting to tactics that cause harm to the innocents, all in the name of 'victory'," Gao Rou admitted. "I have long despised the decision to use the Wuhuan in exchange for letting them do as they like... and Liu Bao's poor behaviour is no better."
"That we agree upon," Cao Cao said.
"Your control of the Qiang makes use of them without tolerating cruelties, and that has not escaped me," Gao Rou continued. "Chanyu Huchuquan is completely pacified... and if you could do the same to the Wuhuan tribes, the north would be at peace. I wonder if Lord Yuan Shao's tactics guaranteed anything at all."
"I don't doubt that he'd have brought them to heel eventually, but he was taking too long to do it, and for the wrong reasons," Cao Cao replied. "Defeating me became more important than being a good man to his subjects."
Gao Rou nodded soberly and said, "That is true. But I can see the truth now. The Yuans lost sight of righteousness a long time ago."
"They did, and I failed to see it either," Xin Pi said. "But now, with His Excellency Cao, I am bringing peace to the north. Join us and do good, Wenhui!"
"The Yuan brothers are my kin, but they are as gone astray as their treasonous uncle Shu that I so foolishly served!" Yuan Huan suggested. "Take this opportunity to bring peace to the Empire, Wenhui: submit and pledge service to the Han!"
Gao Rou fought tears as he fell to his knees and cried, "I, Rou, submit and pledge allegiance to the Han and to you, Your Excellency, with all humility, in the hope that I can atone for my long time in the darkness!"
"...Someone free him," Cao Cao ordered: Cao Xiu helped Gao Rou to his feet and cut his bonds.
"I will not fail the Han again, Excellency," Gao Rou promised.
"I can see that you are sincere, Wenhui," Cao Cao replied. "You are a smart man: you will now serve me as part of my counsel."
"What next, Excellency...?" Yuan Huan asked.
"As previously discussed, Zhang Zhi shall be the Inspector of Bing Province," Cao Cao declared. "I shall consult others on the proper men to take up Administrator and Magistrate titles. I will remain here briefly and oversee the pacification in person: I will also have Cao Hong, Cao Xiu and others go into Hongnong and Henei Prefectures and ensure that those regions are properly stabilised. And then, when I am certain that there will be no more problems here, I will begin preparations for a second, definitive march

against the Wuhuan tribes: there will be no turnabout, no concessions and no mercy shown. The Wuhuan chieftains will either submit and live alongside us or they will be consigned to history: it is their choice. And as for the Yuan brothers... they will be consigned to history. Heaven has spoken."

The Yuan brothers learned of the defeat of Gao Gan within a week; the news shocked and demoralised them, since it meant that they now had no allies apart from the unpredictable Wuhuan tribes. Jing Governor Liu Biao and his tenant Liu Bei were also rattled by the news of the fall of Bing Province: they were now as isolated as the Yuan brothers and the likelihood of any kind of collaborative effort against Cao Cao working at such great distances seemed to be unlikely. And for Cao Cao, an end seemed to be in sight at last, one way or another: if his latest ambitious campaign ended as he intended it to, he would be remembered for the greatest achievement in recent military history, but if he failed, the consequences could be severe. That thought haunted the Excellency of Works as he oversaw a number of changes, small and large, in the fractured Bing Province region.

****

ACT VII: BEYOND THE GREAT WALL

77

The Han Dynasty's Excellency of Works, Cao Cao, was now poised to end the presence or even the existence of two of the Han Empire's most enduring elements: the influential Ru County Yuan clan that had once dominated the palace court for generations and the Wuhuan tribal confederacy that had long existed alongside – and often come into conflict with – the Han Chinese people in the northeast provinces of Yòu and Ji. Cao Cao's many critics were now largely silent, as talk of things being 'impossible' no longer seemed to be appropriate.

After Cao Cao's defeat of former friend and now-deceased Yuan clan chieftain, Yuan Shao, at the Battle of Guandu – which was, in itself, deemed impossible – he went on to do things that here history in the making: Cao 'tamed' and then enlisted the aid of the ferocious Qiang tribes of the northwest, even going so far as to use them to end an invasion of Hedong Prefecture by the army of Gao Gan, the Yuan-appointed Governor of Bing Province; Zhang Xiu – the last of the 'unrepentant' followers of the tyrant Chancellor Dong Zhuo and perceived murderer of Cao's eldest son and heir during 'The Battle of Wan City' – was now an agent of the government that was maintaining pressure on the Governor of Jing Province, Liu Biao, for Cao; the Mount Tai Bandits of Qing Province were now a mercenary army that acted for the Han and had actually been instrumental in Cao's swift defeat of the formidable eldest Yuan brother, Tan; and the victory over the defenders of the Yuan clan's capital, Yè City, led to countless defections and the surrender of the million-strong Black Mountain Bandit confederacy of northern Bing Province. The last of those important submissions allowed Cao Cao to attack and destroy Bing's ruler, Gao Gan, in a few months and leave the Yuans with no more allies in northern China. The exiled Yuan chieftain, Shang, and his older brother Xi had also been expelled from the Empire along with their Wuhuan tribal allies, so all of the provinces that had been ruled by the Yuans – Ji, Qing, Bing and Yòu – were partially or entirely under Han government control for the first time in many years.

For the cynical 26-year-old Emperor Xian, Excellency Cao Cao's victories were a bitter pill: he had been the sovereign since his half-brother was deposed and then murdered by Dong Zhuo 16 years before, and half of those 16 years had been spent as a puppet to the self-appointed Chancellor Dong Zhuo and later his subordinates Li Jue and Guo Si, who had styled themselves as 'Regents' and continued to rule as their assassinated predecessor had done. Emperor Xian had exploited tension between the ambitious regents and escaped them, but his subsequent calls for aid were ignored by almost all of his warlords in the east of the Han Empire: they were all fighting for themselves or in the name of Yuan Shao or his younger half-brother Shu, who had started a feud over who the rightful heir to the Yuan clan should be.

"None of this had been forgotten," Emperor Xian said to his principal partner, Empress Fu: the two were alone so that the sovereign could speak freely and without being restricted to

conversational protocol. "Yuan Shao ignored a direct request to allow me and my court to settle in Ji Province, while Yuan Shu went even further and decided that he was a fitting replacement sovereign, citing the age-old notion of the 'Mandate of Heaven' and declaring that the Han has lost the said mandate to govern. That... was not helpful."
Empress Fu nodded silently.

The 'Way of Peace' – a nationwide cult that had grown strong during an era when the court was beset by corruption and the land by famine and poverty – had spread a mantra that similarly declared the Han's mandate as exhausted, so Yuan Shu's announcement only served to inspire the surviving acolytes: the military arm of the cult – known as the 'Yellow Turbans', and numbering around a million at its heights – had only been defeated by paid militias because of the poor state of the Imperial Army, and they had never been fully eradicated. Yuan Shu had even employed men that he knew to be Yellow Turbans during his attempts to seize the throne, and it emerged that he had been funding the Runan Yellow Turbans – and thus strengthening them – for many of the years that he had been feuding with his brother, purely so that they would serve as local agitators.

"The Yuans, when I ponder it, have been a menace," Emperor Xian continued. "When the younger brother's treason caused his followers to desert him, that should have been the end of it, but the older one never really served me, did he...?"
"...He was a difficult man to assess, Majesty," Empress Fu replied.
"A diplomatic answer," Emperor Xian chuckled. "I assessed him regularly, and I was always unsure of his true motives... just like his friend Cao Cao."

Cao Cao had been the one to rescue the Imperial court and bring them to his capital, which annoyed Yuan Shao and led to accusations that Cao was plotting sedition: the landless warlord Liu Bei, Jing Governor Liu Biao and a number of disaffected courtiers found common ground with Yuan Shao in the form of a 'Girdle Edict' – said to be written by Emperor Xian himself – that called for Cao Cao's arrest and assassination, but in the end it was Yuan Shao alone that challenged Cao at Guandu and suffered a humiliating defeat. Liu Biao had been forced to retreat and defend his southern border from the warlord Sun Quan, who still sought revenge for his father's death at Biao's order; Liu Bei's attempts to seize Xu Province ended with a humiliating rout; the plotters in the capital were executed along with their relatives, which included, in one case, a pregnant consort of Emperor Xian.

"...I must decide which is worse, my lady," Emperor Xian said tonelessly. "A man that stood in this very room, armed, and ordered my soldiers to take Consort Dong away and strangle her... or his friend Yuan Shao, who supposedly saw sense and rallied the warlords against Cao, but saw fit to send a mercenary army of less-than-former Yellow Turbans from Runan to attack this city to 'save me'... a man that once turned kin against kin by proposing that Governor Liu Yu replace me when I was Dong Zhuo's hostage. Cao Cao supposedly disagreed with that, but has no problem with strangling my consorts against my wishes."

"...I cannot be sure either, Majesty," Empress Fu sighed.

"Yuan Shao is dead, so his motivations hardly matter now," Emperor Xian noted. "I must now evaluate his sons... and what a motley bunch they seem to be. The eldest was disinherited by his stepmother's scheming, so we are told... but he continued to defy the court nonetheless. The middle brother is, we are told, an uninspiring ditherer that now has to suffer the humiliation – and obvious ill omen – of Cao Cao's heir marrying his wife while he still lives. And the youngest, Shang, has led the clan to definitive ruin and been forced to hide in the barbarian wastelands beyond the Wall. Am I supposed to be pleased with that...?"

"I... cannot say," Empress Fu replied.

"I ask unfair questions that are, in fact, directed only at me," Emperor Xian continued. "I am watching as Cao becomes more and more influential, powerful, and worst of all, *popular*. If that man intends to supplant my clan with his own, he is doing everything properly: he shows discretion in punishing crimes, bans excessive shows of wealth, relieves those affected by disease, famine and poverty, ensures that the army is happy, well-fed and well-equipped, and he is actually doing something about the bandits and tribes that doesn't involve compromises that harm the people. He is a model statesman... and, some might say, a model sovereign."

Empress Fu exhaled loudly.

"And now, he plans a foreign expedition," Emperor Xian sighed. "That is either the end of his run of luck and the precursor to a Xianbei invasion... or the greatest achievement in living memory and a certain start to calls for him to be given a duchy... or a kingdom. Which should I hope for...?"

"...The Yuans are not likely to return to Yòu Province in the near future, so we must go to them before they feel ready to return," Cao Cao said to his assembled officials: he was still in a military camp near Hu Pass in Bing Province following the defeat of Gao Gan, but planning for a northern campaign was well underway.

"Forgive my hesitation, but... you speak of going north, beyond the Wall," the adviser Chen Qun noted. "Is this one of Guo Jia's insane ideas...?"

"No, it is my insane idea," Cao Cao replied. "I understand the caution, gentlemen: I remember the day that I heard that the Han army had marched north to fight the Xianbei confederacy. I discussed it with Yuan Shao, and we neither of us could believe it... not the campaign so much, for that was inevitable, but the condition of the army... men with no food, no water pouches, or in the worst cases, no weapons, no armour and, in the very worst, no clothes."

Cao Hong and Xiahou Dun started snickering quietly.

"Funny though it might sound, it was no laughing matter," Cao Cao continued. "Sending an army of malnourished, demoralised, half-naked men with no weapons to fight a horde of well-trained, well-fed professional cavalrymen whose entire culture is based around the care of warhorses and weapons was the conceit of an incompetent government, corrupt eunuchs and privateers, and an oblivious, ignorant monarch that was content to blame the outcome on a witch."

"Yes... a 'witch' that we were related to, Cousin Mengde," Cao Chun sighed.

"The temporary loss of status was bearable," Cao Cao replied. "I was genuinely more aggrieved by the fact that the army was decimated, because of what it might lead to and what it *did* lead to: would we have had to fund militias ourselves to fight the Yellow Turbans – or would the Yellow Turbans have ever come into being – if not for the army being left in such a state...? Would the Qiang rule the northwest if the army had been strong and the officials placed there honest...?"

The ensemble murmured agreeably.

"I say 'decimated', but *less, far* less than one in ten men came back from fighting the Xianbei, in fact, and we had to marry a number of women – including princesses – off to their chieftains and ply them with gold and silk to prevent an invasion... equivalent to or greater than the riches that had been embezzled from the military and civil funds by the 'Ten' and their friends to pay for their gilded roofs and banquets, and hence the same riches that – had they been left where they were – would have ensured that a funded army of fed, clothed and armed men went north," Cao Cao continued. "And it is an army of fed, clothed, armed and trained men that I intend to send north, gentlemen: I will show the world how it should be done, and I will make amends for all of the mistakes of the past that I was once forced to watch unfold from a distance with such a sense of powerlessness. Every Wuhuan and Xianbei man that lives beyond the Great Wall will know that the Han is restored, and every man, woman and child that they have abducted will be returned."

The officers cheered enthusiastically.

"...This will be *our* achievement, not mine," Cao Cao insisted. "Let no man speak of it being my victory and therefore my purse that needs filling in the aftermath: every man that commits to this will be rewarded, if only by knowing that the Xianbei and the Wuhuan will never bother us again... and that the Yuans are, at last, a threat to the Han no more."

Many of the officials and officers voiced their approval.

"Go and continue with your fine work, gentlemen," Cao Cao concluded. "There is still much to be done in Bing Province: let us get it done so that we can move forward and end decades of division and chaos... once and for all time."

The majority of the officials retreated from the command tent, leaving Cao Cao with his bodyguard Xu Chu, his registrar Liu Yè, the advisers Yuan Huan, Jia Xu, Hua Xin and Chen Qun and his generals Xiahou Dun and Cao Chun.

"...I did not expect so many of you to remain," Cao Cao admitted.

"Since your main reason for your still being in Bing Province is the seeking of closure, we have been working to give you that closure," Cao Chun replied. "Mister Jia Xu has finally received word of the scholar Ying Shao..."

"...Oh...?" Cao Cao said excitedly. "How is Zhongyuan? Has he forgiven me at last and...? ...Your faces betray that he has died."

"We do not know how," Jia Xu explained. "But... yes, he is dead."

"*Aiee...* I do all this for men like him more than any other!" Cao

Cao cried. "I do all of this to preserve culture and civilisation! Why else do we do all of this? His work was so valuable... and now it falls to others to finish what he has started... but will any work as tirelessly to record the beliefs and cultures of the people...?"

"Don't be sad, Mengde," Xiahou Dun pleaded. "He was old, and he might have just died of old age."

"But I must still entertain the idea that the wars that I have contributed to have robbed the world of Ying Zhongyuan," Cao Cao retorted. "I... can only hope that he did not suffer... and I will be a patron for any new work that has been or is later found. Was that all...?"

"Our recent liberation of Wuhuan-controlled territories in Yòu Province has given us another useful expert in Wuhuan affairs," Yuan Huan reported. "Yan Rou, originally from Guangyang."

Cao Cao hummed thoughtfully and said, "Styled...?"

"He has no style name at present," Yuan Huan explained. "He... was captured by the Wuhuan at quite a young age... I need not say more."

"No... you need not," Cao Cao sighed. "He's rational, though...?"

"Rational enough, Excellency, and eager to help us bring the Wuhuan tribes under control," Yuan Huan replied. "He will rendezvous with us at Yijing."

"Fine... very good," Cao Cao said. "Anything else...?"

"...We have found a Lady Cai," Chen Qun reported.

"...'A' Lady Cai...?" Cao Cao prompted.

"This is... quite unbelievable," Jia Xu admitted. "It seems that the younger Lady Cai, who would have been but a young girl at the time that her sister was abducted, was not, as her mother wished, killed before the Xiongnu could take her. She survived Liu Bao's attacks on Liang Province... and is very much alive."

Cao Cao laughed strangely and said, "I... am speechless. It is definitely her...?"

"She speaks of things that can only be known by a resident in Cai Yong's household, although her memories of twelve years ago and more are understandably hazy," Jia Xu explained. "Additionally, I met Cai Yong's family, and her features are familiar. It is definitely her, Excellency."

"...The world has lost Ying Shao, but regained the younger Lady Cai!" Cao Cao said with delight. "Forgive what will sound like a very selfish question, but... has she demonstrated any of the intelligence of her father and sister...?"

"Her life was cruelly changed twelve years ago, Excellency, and at a time when any talent was yet to manifest," Chen Qun replied. "She was a child... and it seems that she is not possessed of any great intelligence now, even if she was then."

"That's unfortunate, but it is enough that she lives," Cao Cao said insistently. "I am even more driven now in my quest to liberate her sister from the Xiongnu: it will sadly have to wait, since I must first demonstrate strength... is that not true...?"

"Sadly, yes," Yuan Huan replied. "The Xiongnu Chanyu, Huchuquan, has expressed unwillingness to demand that his heir and nephew cede a woman to the Han, regardless of the circumstances of her becoming part of Liu Bao's harem. Only by impressing them with a show of strength will you make them do as you ask."

"Their autonomy is obviously a privilege that must come under review when my northern campaign is over," Cao Cao said irritably. "Was that all...?"

Xiahou Dun sighed and said, "Zilian has-"

"Not now, Yuanrang," Cao Chun pleaded.

"...Is this prostitutes again...?" Cao Cao asked angrily.

"No, no, it's Zilian trying to impress you," Cao Chun replied. "He's learned of the scholar Sima Yi and is trying to get the man to befriend him and help him to 'refine his character'."

Cao Cao covered his face with his right hand and laughed desperately at the notion.

"He knows you're annoyed about all the business with the prostitutes and him picking on Tubby- ...Uh, I mean picking on *Zhen*," Xiahou Dun bumbled. "He thinks that making friends with a clever fellow like this Sima Yi will-"

Cao Cao lowered his right hand and said, "He would impress me *more* if he'd stop paying the women and stop picking on Zhen! What good is there in him forcing some poor academic to be his friend if he still intends to behave in the same way???"

"...*You* still buy prostitutes, Mengde," Xiahou Dun retorted. "And-!"

"*Enough*," Cao Cao ordered; Yuan Huan, Chen Qun, Hua Xin and Jia Xu were covering their faces with their sleeves and Xu Chu was smiling uncontrollably.

"...Sorry," Xiahou Dun sighed.

"Yes, I still employ the services of women *with my own money* here and there," Cao Cao continued, "but I think that Zilian's habit of hiring many, many women for his strange banquets *with his military budget* is something else entirely. If he intends to befriend Sima Yi and genuinely learn from him, that's fine: if it is a cheap attempt to deflect me from seeing and decrying his obvious flaws, then he is wasting his time. Was *that* all...?"

Xiahou Dun mumbled incoherently, bowed slightly and withdrew; Cao Chun smiled dryly and said, "I have nothing to add."

"...I wanted to recruit Sima Yi," Cao Cao sighed.

"He is ill, or so I understand," Jia Xu replied. "Should we enquire?"

"...I already do," Cao Cao admitted. "Sima Yi is as frail as a man three times his age, from what I've been told: he walks with a cane, has failing eyesight and hearing, and must be carried on occasion when his legs fail him."

"How cruel," Hua Xin said.

"That sounds slightly odd," Chen Qun suggested. "He's only in his late twenties, Excellency: it's either the result of excessive vice, like Guo Jia, or some rare and bizarre illness... *if* it is true."

"...And it is when I think about Fengxiao's rapidly failing health that I take Sima Yi's plight most seriously, Mister Chen," Cao Cao retorted. "You always voice your disapproval of him, but has any man done as much for me as Fengxiao...? Perhaps Sima Yi is as similarly bored of life... which is sad but understandable. *If* he is feigning illness, he will not be let off lightly, but he *will serve me*."

Chen Qun hummed ambiguously.

"...If the elder Lady Cai and others cannot be rescued without first scaring the Xiongnu, then there is no point to me remaining here," Cao Cao continued. "I will return to Yè and direct the campaign preparations from there."

"Yè...?" Chen Qun exclaimed. "You're not returning to Xuchang...?"

"What for...?" Cao Cao scoffed. "Wenruo speaks for me at the court; there are no dangerous plots against me; my family are gradually relocating to Yè. What sense is there in going to Xuchang in the middle of a campaign...?"

"...I understand," Chen Qun replied.

"And, hopefully, so will everybody else," Cao Cao said. "There will be no more time-wasting and meaningless adherence to protocol. For now... that is all."

The last of the officials retreated after paying respects: Cao Cao was, apart from his bodyguard, alone. After a moment of thought, Cao Cao sighed and said, "Ying Zhongyuan, you are gone. But through your work, you are immortal. Will *I* be as fortunate...?"

The scholar Ying Shao's *Fengsu Tongyi* – a comprehensive study and encyclopaedia of Eastern Han Dynasty Chinese customs and folklore – would, as Cao Cao hoped, continue to educate, inform and inspire for generations to come; Cao's own legacy would be more famous – and infamous – but no less or more important in shaping China's past and future.

****

78

Cao Cao's returning entourage was greeted at the gates of Yè City by Ji Province Registrar Li Fu and Attendant Officer Cui Yan.

"Where is my son...?" Cao Cao asked.

"His child had a slight cough, Excellency, so he remained with him," Cui Yan replied.

"...A father should care about his son, just as the son should honour the father," Cao Cao declared. "I will not reprimand him, for his excuse is justifiable. All is well...?"

"The Yuans are not reported as having returned to Yòu Province, Excellency, and there are no serious rebellions in any of the provinces," Cui Yan replied.

"...Mister Li, it is good to see you again," Cao Cao said as he turned to face Li Fu. "It seems that we are lucky and there is going to be minimal resistance in the four provinces!"

Li Fu bowed humbly and replied, "Only because you have made so many wise decisions, Excellency. Though I knew Gao Gan and am saddened by his passing, he made it necessary and so he should not complain about it in the next world."

Gao Gan's cousin and adviser, Gao Rou, sighed woefully and said, "What Mister Li Fu says is very true."

"Gao Rou...?" Cui Yan exclaimed. "You have also aligned yourself with the Excellency of Works...?"

"I have, Mister Cui," Gao Rou replied. "My only regret is that I have only just done so."

"...To recruit men like Jia Xu and Gao Rou shows that you are incomparable as a statesman, Excellency!" Cui Yan said. "Shall we go to the meeting hall or will you be resting first?"

"I am tired," Cao Cao admitted. "I must rest, see my family... and also Guo Fengxiao. Has he recovered at all...?"

"We have barely seen him, Excellency," Li Fu replied. "I do not like to say it, but he does look very poorly."

"...*Fool*," Chen Qun muttered.

"I will visit him," Cao Cao sighed. "I *must* know his opinion."

"I wish him well," Cui Yan said sadly.

"...Your cousin Cui Lin has been appointed as Magistrate of Wu County," Cao Cao replied. "I remembered that you spoke well of him, even though others have little to say... he seems unremarkable, but I know that you are right about him."

"I have confidence that he will impress Inspector Zhang and you, Excellency," Cui Yan said gratefully. "He is not as unremarkable as he seems."

"...And I must appoint some others to key roles," Cao Cao continued. "**Wang Ling!**"

Wang Ling – who was stood behind Cui Yan – moved so that he could bow humbly and ask, "What would you have me do for the Empire, Excellency...?"

"I have heard good things about you, Wang Yanyun," Cao Cao continued. "You will be my Administrator of Zhongshan."

Wang Ling kowtowed and said, "I will not fail you, Excellency!"

"Rise, please," Cao Cao ordered. "There's no need for that, Yanyun. Your uncle was Inspector of Yu Province, and after that Minister over the Masses, and after that the Director of the

Imperial Secretariat, and he was worthy of all of the appointments; it was his genius that rid the world of Dong Zhuo, ironically using Lü Bu as the murder weapon and avenging Ding Yuan in two ways at once. Yes, his treatment of Cai Yong was… unfortunate… but no man is perfect… and any nephew of his – taught in the ways of good governance by such as he – is wasted on a small role."

"You are too kind, Excellency!" Wang Ling replied.

"…Forgive me gentlemen, but I am fatigued," Cao Cao said. "We will discuss other matters later…"

Cui Yan, Li Fu, Wang Ling and the rest of the welcoming party stood aside and watched Cao Cao's carriage pass them; Cui Yan smiled and said, "Yè City has a fine lord once again, and the world has a hero that will save it."

"I truly hope that His Excellency does achieve what he intends to achieve," Li Fu replied. "I believe that nothing is impossible, so I know that he *can*… I just hope that he *does*."

Cao Cao went to his home and found his son, Cao Pi, sat by his own young son's bedside with his wife Lady Zhen.

"…Is he seriously ill…?" Cao Cao asked.

"F-Father," Cao Pi stammered.

"Calm down," Cao Cao said as Cao Pi tried to get to his feet and turn to face him; Lady Zhen was also being overly humble.

"It is nothing, Father," Cao Pi insisted. "In fact, I should have greeted you and-"

"I am not angry," Cao Cao said calmly. "In fact, I am impressed by your compassion and hope that you continue to show such care for your family. I am aware of your behaviour while I was away, and I am a little disappointed, but the fact that you responded with an apologetic letter instead of an attack on Cui Yan shows that you are becoming a fine man. That pleases me."

Cao Cao turned and walked away without waiting for a reply; Cao Pi stared vacantly and murmured, "It… pleases him."

"That is good," Lady Zhen said. "That is very good indeed."

Cao Pi smiled and nodded agreeably.

When Cao Cao reached his own study, he was confronted by Cao Pi's mother, Lady Bian, who asked, "How will you reprimand our son for his mistakes…?"

"He's apologised for his mistakes," Cao Cao replied. "I think that no more need be said of them."

Lady Bian smiled gratefully.

"Are my other children well…?" Cao Cao asked. "I did not want the usual formal greeting when I returned, so I have not set eyes on half of them yet."

"Chong continues to amaze us with his ideas," Lady Bian replied. "Zhi still composes his poetry; Zhang is Zhang. The others are much as you left them too."

"…Very good," Cao Cao said. "Now, then: shall we convene for some sort of proper family banquet…?"

"I think that would be a very good idea," Lady Bian replied.

"…I don't know whether to invite Guo Fengxiao," Cao Cao said. "I know that he unnerves some of you with his manner, but he is a good man with an intelligent son that will one day serve me as his father does... and if he... ... ...if Fengxiao were to pass, then I would bring his son into our home and see to his needs, at the very least as thanks for all that Fengxiao has done for me."

"Our home is as big as it needs to be," Lady Bian replied. "Our door is as open as you wish it to be, Husband."

"...Fengxiao is ill, so he cannot attend, and so I will not ask," Cao Cao decided. "But I will still look after his son and widow should the worst occur... *when* the worst occurs. At some point, I shall visit him... yes... and I shall tell him... I shall promise him... so that he is assured that I will not forget him."

Cao Cao held his banquet for his large family; he was still smiling when he attended his court on the following morning.

"You are looking... very optimistic, Lord Cao!" a familiar voice said.

"**Fengxiao???**" Cao Cao exclaimed; Guo Jia was present, although he was obviously frail and tired.

"I thought that... I should attend court," Guo Jia continued. "Once I am comfortable, I... will need to pause less often. I look far more unwell than I am!"

"You're lying, but I appreciate your being here," Cao Cao replied. "I know that I should be quick: I have summoned Dong Zhao from Xu Province to act as supervisor on a large canal-digging project."

Guo Jia nodded agreeably and said, "He is knowledgeable about such things."

"Indeed he is," Li Fu said. "He was once the Administrator of this prefecture, and it has to be said that he could govern any place and succeed."

"His time as Governor of Xu Province has brought peace and eroded all of the surviving support for Tao Qian and Liu Bei," Cao Cao noted. "He's just the man to work on such a project because everyone knows him and everyone trusts him."

"...How strange it will be to see Dong Gongren in Yè again after all these years!" Xin Pi said. "He left here a wrongly-slandered man... I might not have believed that slander, and he knew that, but I owe him an apology for not having helped him."

"There wasn't any way to help him," General Zhang Hè suggested. "At that time, the court was a playground for Guo Tu, Pang Ji, Shen Pei and Xun Chen, and they were always going to be listened to. Dong Gongren, like me, survived their slander, *unlike* Qu Yi and Tian Feng, and that's all that matters."

"...Such history," Cao Cao sighed.

"Your rule has put things right the things that Yuan Shao did wrong, Excellency," Cui Yan said. "Now the slanderers are buried and the good men are restored to the roles that they are meant for. Now you will undo the decades of misrule and deal with the Wuhuan once and for all."

"Indeed I will!" Cao Cao chuckled. "Indeed I will!"

The respected second brother of the 'Eight Da of Sima', Sima Yi, had been successful in avoiding recruitment by feigning illness: he hobbled about on a cane every day and did a good job of convincing people that his sight, hearing and mental faculties were failing. Sima even went so far as to maintain his ruse in front of the household staff, which meant that any time spent behaving normally within his own home had to be very carefully planned with his wife, Lady Zhang.

"...Forgive my asking, Husband, but for how long must we maintain this ruse...?" Lady Zhang asked when she and her husband were alone in Sima Yi's private study.

"There is no imminent end to it, my lady," Sima Yi replied. "I am either discovered and killed or we must remain like this forever, or until I can find some far-off place where Cao Cao and his family have no jurisdiction. I am pondering Jiangdong, or maybe Jiaozhi... even Cao Cao cannot hope to conquer Jiaozhi any time soon... although Sun Quan might. Why must I be born into an age of greedy 'heroes' that force intelligent men to aid them in their pointless conquests...?"

"We can't live like this forever," Lady Zhang complained. "The effort, Husband, is too much! How can we guarantee with certainty that none of our staff, a passing guest or a surprise visit by Cao Cao's armed men won't lead to-?"

"**I know that, woman!**" Sima Yi barked. "For Heaven's sake, did I not just say that I am looking into where we can go...?"

"You're a genius, Husband," Lady Zhang retorted. "I am smart enough to see it, and others see it too. Wherever you go, you'll be asked to join the local warlord as soon as you speak to anybody."

"...Which is why I haven't gone to Jing already," Sima Yi admitted. "Wherever you go, you get Liu Biao, Liu Bei, Sun Quan, Cao Cao... or one of their many, many agents. That 'Cao Hong' that pestered us recently was a joke, though: if that is the class of men that Cao has as his close kin, then he will surely fail."

Lady Zhang smiled.

"I know that I will be pestered wherever I go, but I refuse to submit quietly!" Sima Yi declared. "I do not want to serve the Han! The Han is doomed! And I do not want to serve the warlords either! They're all violent thugs that harm the state! And Cao Cao is one of the worst! I don't care what excuses he has: he has the blood of a hundred-thousand innocents on his hands for Xu Province alone!"

"So we must continue this farcical game of pretending that you are a premature invalid and senile fool," Lady Zhang said. "Very well... so be it. I will do whatever it takes to ensure that I have done my best to protect you, Husband. But do remember that you will be childless if you do not find a way to-"

"Yes, yes, I know," Sima Yi grumbled. "I know, I know! 'How can a senile cripple father children?' they would say; I am looking for a way out of this mess. Trust me."

Lady Zhang smiled cynically and said, "I do."

✳✳✳✳✳✳✳✳✳✳✳✳

79

Cao Cao visited the Yè City home of his increasingly frail chief adviser, Guo Jia, and sat with him in the living quarters.

"I won't join you with regards to the wine, as much as I'd like to: it might be bad for my health," Guo Jia joked. "So! What brings you here, Lord Cao...?"

"...Just this once, Fengxiao, I'd like to insist that you call me 'Mengde'," Cao Cao replied. "And... and as for why I've come here... it's to discuss my transition from man to monster."

"...Go on," Guo Jia prompted.

Cao Cao sighed and said, "I must first share with you my observations, as uncomfortable as they are. I am now in my fifties, and I have seen, sad to say, most of what the world has to offer. Since a boy, I have witnessed the first 'Partisan Crisis' caused by the 'Ten', and the numerous revivals of that cruel persecution of the intelligentsia; I have seen near-naked soldiers marched into the frontier lands to 'fight' the Xianbei and mostly die; I have seen the disaffected people rise up as one with the symbol of yellow on their brow, decrying the Han and declaring its mandate as being at an end; I have watched as warlords that claimed to be trying to save the Han then divided up the Empire amongst themselves, causing more chaos than they had ever quelled; and now, Fengxiao, I am witness to chaos that I am supposedly prophesied to exist for. But am I supposed to end the chaos or perpetuate it...? Am I supposed to save the Han Dynasty or... or am I supposed to supplant it for the good of the people...?"

Guo Jia smiled and hummed ambiguously.

"I... I know that I went from a set of oft-trod observations to an unfair question, but I am inwardly torn," Cao Cao continued. "If only it were simple! But I have just learned of a minor plot – destined to fail – against me by very junior officials that were obviously deluded when it came to their own influence. But I have suffered attacks by Dong Cheng – bad enough – and also Yuan Shao, which hurt me greatly. And I cannot rule out the Son of Heaven's involvement in some or all of those plots... so if my clan is to survive... I wonder what I must do."

"...Of course," Guo Jia said tonelessly.

"And then I think some more, and... and I now see why you tire of the world," Cao Cao continued. "We all gather, secure in our superiority, to denounce the 'barbarians' and mock them, wallowing in our own brilliance, our own culture... while calling them 'uncultured'. But when I look closely, I see more similarities than I do differences. I look at Ma Teng and Han Sui, and how they hurt and kill each other's kin and then casually reunite when mutually beneficial opportunities to kill and conquer others arise... and I think of me and Zhang Xiu; when I think of the tensions between Huchuquan and Yufuluo that divided the Southern Xiongnu, I think of Yuan Shao and Yuan Shu, or of Shao's sons; when I hear courtiers scoffing at the false loyalty shown toward Louban by some Wuhuan leaders, or toward Huchuquan, I then think about the many men that pledge loyalty to His Majesty while looking to steal lands, or even the throne."

"...Nothing that you say is new to me, as you have more or less noted," Guo Jia said.

"But it is to me in a way, but I have chosen to ignore it," Cao Cao replied. "I look at the peoples of this Empire of ours with open, honest eyes and I see a collection of peoples that all have a right to be here in one way or another, but they all want it for themselves: the Han and all the kingdoms before it claim that they bring peace by subjugating the 'uncultured, violent barbarians', but the Yuans, Gongsun Zan, and especially the likes of Dong Zhuo prove that it is in us all... what peace did Dong Zhuo bring to the people...? ...What peace did *I* bring when I massacred the people of western Xu...? We heckle the Di, the Wuhuan, the Shanyue, the Qiang and the Xiongnu for being like animals... for raids, kidnapping girls, massacring villages and cities full of people, forced slavery or servitude, the committing of rapes, torture, murders, cannibalism, pillaging... but when I think of Zhang Fei, Yuan Shao, Yuan Shu, Gongsun Zan, Dong Zhuo, Lü Bu... and worst of all, *me*... I wonder if the only so-called 'civilisation' that separates 'us' from 'them' is a groundless self-importance based in how we write, speak, dress and walk about, and a belief that we have better excuses and justifications for the same bad behaviour."

"...Where is this going...?" Guo Jia asked.

"...Nowhere," Cao Cao admitted. "I can't change something as fundamental as how people think, not when I am as prone to err as the rest of them: I like to think that I am an academic, a scholar, a poet, a musician and a scribe, but I am also a politician, a warlord-governor, and a man with a man's needs and urges. I am no Cai Yong or Ying Shao that puts society's need before personal desires... no, I would throw the likes of them in prison for failing to cooperate, or I would force them to perform for me like puppets in order to make me look cultured... just like Dong Zhuo. I am 'complex', some say – even me, in my own defence – but I am not complex really, I just find complex excuses for the worst of my behaviour. Some say I will undo myself... so do and so will all the warlords. Dong Zhuo, Lü Bu, Sun Ce – to name but three – were their own undoing. I ruined my own cause at Xingyang and then again, worse still, at Wan City, and I am now certain that Wan is not the worst failure that I will be known for. Liu Bei has always been his own worst enemy too: that we have in common, and I'm sure *his* worst humiliations are yet to come. All great heroes are unconquerable by all but themselves... that's the funniest part of it all... of the 'grand game'...!"

"I cannot disagree," Guo Jia said.

"I want to be a man that changes things... truly, I do... but I'll probably just create a 'different version of the same', since I am not as enlightened as I sometimes profess to be," Cao Cao continued. "The people that do try to change the way that men think are always crushed, and usually by the very lords and kings that regularly mourn the fact that nothing ever changes. *Power* will always be the driving force behind 'civilisations', because we do not have the imagination to find another way and wilfully ignore or destroy those that do. We'll always hide behind calligraphy, sculpture, scripture, music, poetry and faith because they are our invented entitlement to what others have, our justification for the *killing*, the *stealing*, the-"

"I ask again, *Mengde*... where is this going...?" Guo Jia said. "And please do not say 'Nowhere' again... you would not rouse me from my sickbed to rant like this when you have others to listen to you, like Wenruo and Old Cheng."

"The first of those men would not like my question, which is already asked of you; the second would answer controversially in order to sound like a man without boundaries, but his reaction to the killing of Consort Dong shows that there are some realities that he cannot find the courage to face," Cao Cao replied. "Only *you*, Fengxiao, are blessed with the vision I need."

"You've just answered your own question by answering my statement," Guo Jia said. "You already know what you need or want to do."

"...But am I *right*???" Cao Cao cried. "For the last decade or more, I have sheltered that untrusting, ungrateful sovereign in Yan Province, at first tolerating a symbolic displacement as 'Marquis of some other place' before sense was seen and I was restored to the position of Yan's governor; I have spent a lot of my clan's hard-earned wealth building a temporary palace and then a bustling capital city around that sovereign, but nothing is ever enough! Nothing will ever be enough!"

"...Go on," Guo Jia prompted once again.

"I *know* that we must show strength, Fengxiao, so that our borders do not suffer incursion by the frontier tribes or by the armies of the foreign kings that buy our silk and other wares only because they daren't risk trying to take it from us!" Cao Cao continued. "But that sovereign just sits there, Fengxiao, expecting others to exhaust their life energies strengthening and rebuilding that which... which past sovereigns – for I concede that the fault does not lie with the incumbent – weakened and destroyed through their greed, foolishness and blindness! The previous sovereign is commemorated as being incompetent, which is an *understatement*! And the one before that, he actually made thinking a crime when he allowed the eunuchs to make 'partisans' of the learned! And it's no wonder, after the diabolical shambles that we call a 'war' with the Xianbei Confederacy, that the likes of Zhang Jue had no difficulty convincing people that the Han's mandate had extinguished! It's no surprise even now... not even to loyalists like me."

Guo Jia sat silently and waited for Cao Cao to continue.

"...The Han's *mandate* may or may not still exist... I will not be goaded into saying any such thing... but the Han's *credibility* is all but gone," Cao Cao said. "When I marched against Luoyang over a decade ago, I did so to rescue the Son of Heaven from the White Wave Bandits, who 'rescued' the court from Li Jue and Guo Si, who inherited it from Dong Zhuo, who dominated it when Hè Jin died after taking control away from the 'Ten', who took the control from Liang Ji... I could go on. The Han Empire has been controlled by others for longer than I have been alive, Fengxiao, so the ability to stand unaided has been lost to the sovereigns... they are reliant on others for strength, but they will not place trust in the right people, and so they alienate themselves from their protectors and invite wolves into the house."

"It is a tale told a thousand tedious times," Guo Jia sighed.

"Others accuse me of intending to overthrow the sovereign, and so I suffer coup attempt after assassination attempt after condemnation by some distant warlord or other... and I know that ultimately, my reward for my great expense will be imprisonment, exile or death if I do not take steps to protect my clan as much as I protect the throne," Cao Cao continued. "Sometimes protecting one will mean harming the other... and I must choose carefully, because an action intended to preserve might unintentionally condemn... but I have no other option but to stay, finish what I started and ensure that my heir follows me, do I...? I am the 'Hero of Chaos'! Like the great warrior or debater that tries to retire but finds his legendary skill constantly challenged by younger, lesser-known men that want to make names for themselves, so will I be chased down if I retire, no matter where I run to! My clan will be hunted down as well, and no doubt exterminated! That is so, is it not...? I cannot just retire when the Yuans are put down and peace restored in the northeast, can I...?"

"No, you can't," Guo Jia replied tonelessly.

"...I must see this to the end," Cao Cao said. "In a way, that depresses me, but... but it also excites me, the idea that I am poised to make my clan as legendary as the Yuans once were... perhaps greater still. But I cannot survive without surrounding the sovereign with *my* people, can I...? He must be married to my daughters, have my sons as his generals and courtiers... so that no other man can try and take from me what is earned, what is rightly mine. But what I describe... sounds almost like... like a play for power, doesn't it...? But what else can I do...?"

"To *that*, the answer is 'Nothing'," Guo Jia replied.

"...But it all bores you, doesn't it...?" Cao Cao chuckled miserably. "A part of you perhaps wondered if you were joining me on an exciting quest to create a new world where new ways of thinking took hold, where everything was about something other than 'the usual things'..."

"I never had such a silly idea," Guo Jia replied. "You said it yourself: you cannot change the way that people think. I never cared one way or the other whether we ended up with something different or something that was exactly the same; I simply wondered whether I could correctly guess every situation and every person that I encountered... and I have done rather well. I've always known who you really are, Mengde, and what you intended and intend to do."

Cao Cao lowered his head and smiled silently.

"Soon you'll be leaving to face the last of the troublemakers in the northeast... and then you'll need to do the things that you know that you need to do," Guo Jia continued. "I may or may not be there when you take those steps... right now, Mengde, I suspect that I will not be. Regardless, you'll do what must be done, and then you'll face the rest of them: Liu Biao and Liu Bei in Jing, and Sun Quan in Jiangdong; Zhang Lu in Hanzhong, and the Qiang and Di in the northwest; and then, at the last, you might need to break some alliances and rein in the likes of Liu Zhang, Zang Ba, or the Xiongnu Chanyu."

"...If I am not assassinated, arrested by my untrusting sovereign, or struck down by illness or my own legendary idiocy first," Cao Cao sighed.

"Illness will not be your downfall," Guo Jia insisted. "And let the sovereign distrust you: you will reunite the northeast with the capital region, something that no other man has been able to do. Uniting the rest... might take time. Some might temporarily form opposing states that seem 'unconquerable', but in the end, those states will implode and the entire empire will be reunited: it might be left to your heir, some other descendent, or to some other ambitious man, but in the end, it *will* reunite... if only so it can divide again and bore some as-yet-unborn adviser to death as it does me."

Cao Cao laughed softly and said, "I will miss you, Fengxiao, when... ... ...but I'd prefer that you delayed the inevitable for a while longer."

"...It is out of my hands now," Guo Jia replied.

Cao Cao was silent for a few moments before he said, "Your family... they will be *my* family, Guo Fengxiao, when... when that day comes."

"My thanks to you, Mengde," Guo Jia replied. "I would have it no other way."

****

80

Cao Cao's efforts had not been missed by his rival warlords, and one of them – the self-proclaimed lord of Jiangdong, Sun Quan – was quick to send tribute.

"...An *elephant*...?" Cao Cao exclaimed.

"An elephant," Cheng Yu grumbled. "Do you think I'd be here if it wasn't something unusual...? Would any of us be here...?"

"...He sent me an elephant...?" Cao Cao chuckled. "Sun Quan sent me an *elephant*...?"

"Yes! Yes, Sun Quan sent you an elephant!" Cheng Yu snapped.

"...What a strange lad he is," Cao Cao said as he looked at the silent, ponderous Hua Xin. "Where is it now, Mister Cheng?"

"*In my sleeve*," Cheng Yu replied irritably.

"It's on its way from Xuchang," Registrar Liu Yè reported. "We didn't think – Wenruo didn't think – that such a grand gift, meant for you, should remain in the city for jealous men to mutter about, Your Excellency."

"...Or, in other words, toadies and plotters that wanted an excuse to accuse me of sedition would tell the Son of Heaven, who would want to know why *he* didn't get an elephant from Sun Quan," Cao Cao suggested. "I hope that Sun did provide some sort of tribute to His Majesty..."

"He's sent a lot of things to His Majesty, including an elephant or two for the royal zoo, but the idea of *you* receiving one is obviously seen as 'controversial', since you are a vassal, not a king," Cheng Yu replied.

"Perhaps that is the intent," Hua Xin said quietly.

Cao Pi, Cao Zhi and Cao Chong had approached Cao Cao as he spoke with his advisers; Zhi could not contain his excitement any longer and asked, "Will we be able to ride the elephant, Father?"

"Elephants are very large, Brother," Cao Chong said seriously. "It would take a lot of effort for–"

"I am not a child any longer," Cao Zhi retorted. "I am fourteen, almost fifteen, and more than capable of riding an elephant if some barbarian fool can do so!"

"And although I am only ten and strangely frail, I don't doubt that I could ride it, but that isn't the point as such," Cao Chong said. "You have to get to its back by way of a ladder and then stay there, and we do not know how tame it is."

"Sun Quan wouldn't be stupid enough to send us a wild or dangerous elephant," Cao Zhi heckled.

"Don't be so sure," Cao Chong retorted. "The Suns are renowned for reckless acts."

"...I'm more worried about the people seeing it than who gets to ride it," Cao Cao admitted. "City folk are used to seeing strange animals from foreign places, but the rural folk are superstitious and easily startled... like the Wuhuan, they balk at the sight of too many white or black horses... and the large foreign steeds cause even more panic: how will they react to an elephant?"

"Like the idiots that they are," Cheng Yu grumbled. "If it were me, gentlemen, I–"

"If it were you, Elder Cheng, you'd trample a few of the 'idiots' because you hate them so much," Liu Yè suggested. "But we are

trying to endear ourselves to the people of Ji Province, and that
wouldn't help."

"...I was going to say that we might use it to scare the Wuhuan,"
Cheng Yu retorted.

"I won't be using a gift as a weapon," Cao Cao insisted. "If it were
hurt or killed, I would need to explain how it happened."

"...Wenruo, Gongda and the rest of them are acting like children,"
Cheng Yu scoffed. "They're *all* coming to Yè with the elephant. If
you need military funds, Excellency, then I suggest charging them
all for rides before they remember that they are grown men with
important jobs and go back again."

Cao Cao laughed and said, "I might ride it myself, you miserable
old man! In fact, I may make *you* ride it! You might actually enjoy
the thrill of it!"

Cheng Yu sneered.

"...We need some light relief after years of war," Cao Cao
continued. "I realise that there has been no real respite for... oh,
goodness, *years*. I have been fighting the Yuans for almost seven
years, and there were few quiet moments before *that*."

"And to think that the 'light relief' comes from Sun Quan, of all
men!" Cheng Yu heckled. "Isn't he next after Liu Biao...?"

"Not necessarily," Cao Cao retorted. "He might negotiate or even
submit. Remember, Mister Cheng, that he will be the only one left
at that point unless he wants to forge alliances with Zhang Lu, the
Nanman and the Qiang; our marriage alliances must also play
some part in his decision-making as well, I think. His cousin Ben's
daughter is my daughter-in-law, and my niece is the widow of his
younger brother."

"And said 'cousin Ben' – with whom you are on good terms – is a
past clan chieftain, acting or not, and a very receptive and
cooperative individual... am I right...?" Cheng Yu asked pointedly.

Cao Cao smiled silently.

"The elephant will arrive in a few days' time," Liu Yè said. "Its
presence will certainly be a talking point, one way or another."

Cao Cao laughed and replied, "Indeed it will."

Sun Quan's gifted elephant was the talk of Wei Prefecture when it
finally reached Yè City's gates: most of Cao Cao's court gathered
to review the colossal animal, which towered over everything and
generated awe and fear.

"...So are you not bored of it yet after travelling here with it...?"
Cheng Yu asked of Xun Wenruo and Xun Gongda.

"How can you be 'bored' of such a marvel, Mister Cheng...?" Xun
Gongda retorted.

"What does it *do*?" Cheng Yu heckled.

"...Not a lot, but it is aesthetically pleasing," Xun Wenruo replied.

"How so...?" Cheng Yu asked. "It is an ugly, fat, hairless, wrinkly
grey thing. It is Dong Zhuo in his nineties! Its size is its only
'marvel', and-"

"Please stop whinging, Zhongde," Yuan Huan sighed.

Cao Zhi turned to Hua Xin and Wang Lang and asked, "Are there
lots of elephants roaming around in Jiangdong?"

"I saw one or two near the border with Jiaozhi, both of them tame
and in use as beasts of burden," Wang Lang replied. "Wild ones
may be abundant somewhere, but nowhere that I was."

"My answer would be much the same, young master," Hua Xin said meekly.

"The peasants are running around scared," Cheng Yu grumbled.

"Indeed yes," Xun Wenruo sighed.

"The journey here was truly an insight," Xun Gongda said. "We had a number of priests come to the roadside on our way here: some to bless us and some to exorcise the 'giant demon'. Children liked it, though."

"Its eyes are kind," Cao Chong suggested. "They radiate intellect."

"If Heaven had blessed it with the power of speech and some hands instead of a long nose, that intellect might have some point," Cheng Yu retorted.

"They are very strong," Wang Lang noted. "They can push over trees or rip them out of the ground as though they were rootless twigs. And for a creature of such power, they are amazingly docile. It takes a lot to truly rile them once tamed, so I'm told."

"That's good to hear," Cao Cao said as he stared upward at the face of the giant beast. "Did you still want to ride it, Zhi'er...?"

"...No, Father," Cao Zhi replied.

"Xiong'er...?" Cao Cao said as he looked at his youngest son by Lady Bian. "Don't you want to ride it...?"

"I won't, Father," Cao Xiong replied. "I always feel a bit dizzy when I climb too high."

"It's so big," Cao Zhang sighed. "What a sight a general would be atop such a monster. It made the ground shake as it walked!"

Cao Cao hummed thoughtfully and said, "That's a point... I wonder how heavy it is."

"How would you assess such a thing...?" Cao Pi wondered.

"There must be some way," Cao Cao said. "I am surrounded by great minds, so somebody must have an idea. Fengxiao...?"

Guo Jia smiled and said, "I am not a mathematician, Lord Cao. I can only measure a man's intelligence and predictability."

"...Elder Cheng...?" Cao Cao said as he turned to Cheng Yu. "You've done nothing but moan about what use it will be, but can you determine its weight...?"

"I am no mathematician either," Cheng Yu replied.

"There's no point asking me either," Yuan Huan said.

"Nor me," Liu Yè chuckled.

"Wang Can is the sort of mind you'd look to, for his mentor Cai Yong might have known such a thing, or the hermit Lou Zibo that lives on Mount Zhongnan," Cui Yan suggested.

"An enemy adviser, a corpse and a vagrant: that's the only capable mathematical minds in the Empire, Cui Yan...?" Cheng Yu asked snidely.

"If it is, that's no fault of ours," Cui Yan replied.

"Zhi...?" Cao Cao prompted.

"I am at a loss, Father," Cao Zhi admitted. "I am a poet, a singer, a writer, but I am not a scientist."

"That sort of thing is something for the likes of Wang Can if anyone," Yang Xiu said.

"That's if he didn't react to the elephant in the same way that he reacts to donkeys," Xun Wenruo chuckled. "And before you ask, Excellency, I know nothing of such things. Dong Gongren's canal-digging team might have someone that knows."

"Like Uncle, I am not that kind of scholar," Xun Gongda said sadly.

"Such problems are too much for me. But Uncle is right, though: what about Dong Zhao's men...?"

"They're working from books that are specifically about canal digging," Cao Cao replied miserably. "Besides, their work must not be disturbed."

"Cai Yong's student Wang Can must once again be mentioned," Liu Yè said.

"I wouldn't count on him lasting if Liu Bei takes over Jing Province," Cheng Yu grumbled. "Bei's a hardened Legalist: they have no time for arts and science."

"I also believe that Legalism has merits, Elder Cheng, but I value art and science," Cui Yan insisted. "Like every other philosophy, it has different schools."

"...I cannot ask Wang Can, gentlemen, so there is no point to repeatedly mentioning him," Cao Cao sighed. "That beast's weight may have to remain a mystery..."

"Why do you even want to *know*, Father...?" Cao Zhang asked.

"Curiosity, mainly," Cao Cao replied. "But it would also be interesting to know whether it could be loaded onto a particular vehicle for transportation. Somebody must have known how big and strong a ship to risk loading it onto in order to send it here from across the Great River. Is it that Sun Quan has better mathematicians in his stable than I do...?"

The gathering was silent in response to the statement.

"Is there *nobody*...?" Cao Cao chortled. "A great state cannot just be about poems, songs and paintings, any more than it can be just about ploughing tools and swords! Chong'er: I have avoided putting pressure on a ten-year-old boy, regardless of his obvious intelligence, but I am *desperate*! Can you think of a way to weigh this marvellous animal...?"

"I can and have," Cao Chong said; the boy's calm reply caused many men to gasp and mumble excitedly or cynically.

"...What is your proposal...?" Cao Cao asked.

"When one places an object in water, the 'level' – the height of the surface of the water – rises accordingly, because the object displaces the water," Cao Chong explained. "If we were to place the elephant in a strong boat – itself placed in a body of water where the level is measured prior – then the beast's weight would cause the water level to rise, at which point we would mark the new level: if we then remove the elephant, get smaller heavy objects whose weights are already known, and place them in the boat until the level reached the same height as the elephant – ensuring that the level before we began that second measurement is the same as before the elephant was weighed, of course – we can get the elephant's weight from the sum of the weight of the smaller objects."

The officials stared at each other silently.

"...That is what we shall do," Cao Cao declared. "My son is a genius! What father would not be boundlessly proud of such a gifted son?"

Cao Pi glared at Cao Chong with seething jealousy and fear for his own place as Cao Cao's heir; Cao Zhi was also irritated at having to share such glowing praise with a child, but he hid his feelings more carefully.

"Come on, gentlemen, and prepare a sturdy boat: we can use the

training lake or one of the smaller pools… yes, one of the pools!"
Cao Cao ordered. "I am eager to learn the beast's weight! If there
are any questions, ask my wondrous son, who might, one day, be
another Cai Yong!"
"I am not the first to realise such things, Father," Cao Chong
insisted. "Please do not compare me to prodigies like Cai Yong."
"I shall do so if I wish!" Cao Cao chuckled. "Come, gentlemen, let
us hurry!"

The weighing of the elephant became as much of a spectacle as
its arrival: Cao Cao was delighted when Cao Chong's suggestion
yielded a weight that closely matched the estimates made by
others, since that meant that the method was sound and could be
used to measure the weight of large, heavy objects in the future.
It was probably not the first time that the idea that is known to
many as *Archimedes' Principle* had been discovered or used in
China, but centuries of indiscriminate wars and casual destruction
had robbed – and would, perhaps, go on to rob – China and the
rest of the world of many works of science, art and philosophy,
and Cao Cao knew it all too well. The Excellency of Works was
moved by the idea that his prodigious son might rediscover some
of that lost knowledge or even make new discoveries, but he knew
that Cao Chong's talent was far from enough if his own legacy was
to be more than a conqueror.

****

81

Cao Cao journeyed to the site of one of his transport canals after three months of digging: the project supervisor, Xu Province Governor Dong Zhao – whose courtesy name was 'Gongren' – hurried to Cao's carriage and bowed low, saying, "Your Excellency, I hope that my efforts are enough."

Cheng Yu – who was sat in Cao Cao's carriage facing the bodyguard Xu Chu – sneered and turned his gaze to the floor; Registrar Liu Yè – who was facing Cao – smiled politely and bowed his head to Dong Gongren as a sign of respect.

"We're on schedule," Cao Cao replied. "How are you doing?"

"I'm… fine, Excellency," Dong Gongren replied.

"Very good!" Cao Cao chuckled.

"…I am glad that you are in good spirits, Excellency," Dong Gongren said.

"We all enjoyed that bit of excitement some few weeks back with the elephant," Cao Cao replied. "Now my son Chong – a true genius in the making – is helping me in the law courts as well! He is, at just eleven years of age, a future statesman without compare! He is my finest son, and were it not for the obsession with primogeniture, he would be my heir without question!"

"…I have heard about the elephant, Excellency, and I have also heard about your son's method of assessing its weight," Dong Gongren said cautiously. "Some are comparing him to Shang Gao, Cai Yong and other great minds of times past."

"Might any of your men have come to the same conclusion…?" Cao Cao asked.

"Not likely," Dong Gongren replied. "We're working from copies of the Nine Chapters to get this job done, of course, but we're not going to be analysing or adding to it, Excellency. It is agreed that your son is a prodigy, and I say that as a sincere point rather than a sycophantic effort."

"I know that you are above such awful toadying, Gongren," Cao Cao insisted. "And I am very impressed at the work that you've already carried out… very impressed."

"We've got so many strong and healthy captured soldiers and tribesmen to use for the digging that it really is possible to finish earlier than planned," Dong Gongren suggested. "But I won't promise any such thing, just in case."

"And I wouldn't expect you to," Cao Cao said. "Now, uh… I have a question for you, Gongren."

"I hope that I can answer it," Dong Gongren prompted.

"…What is your opinion about my plan…?" Cao Cao asked.

"You know my style of governance, Excellency, for it is very similar to your own," Dong Gongren replied. "I would never have given the Wuhuan so much freedom. I'm hearing about what has gone on here, and I am sickened. People are rejoicing that you have chased the Wuhuan away; if the planned expedition only results in their never returning to these provinces, Excellency, that would be enough. But if you achieve what you truly intend – the complete defeat of the Wuhuan – then there will be no greater hero than you in our time. I believe that it is the right thing to do and I also believe that it is possible."

"...My generals are sceptical," Cao Cao admitted. "I thank you for your support... and, of course, for your marvellous work here."
Dong Gongren bowed humbly; Cao Cao ordered his driver to turn the carriage and began a return journey to Yè City.
"...We came all this way to look at a half-dug trench and ask a couple of questions...?" Cheng Yu complained.
"If he had been well enough, I'd have brought Fengxiao," Cao Cao retorted. "I actually value Dong Zhao greatly. I want him to join my main counsel."
"An excellent idea," Liu Yè said.
"And who will be Governor of Xu Province?" Cheng Yu asked.
"There's always someone else," Cao Cao replied. "Men like Dong Gongren are wasted in such roles when the dangers have passed."
"...That's true enough," Cheng Yu admitted. "Anyhow... the trench we looked at will be dug and filled with water in the next couple of months, and I imagine the same can be said for the other one. What then...?"
"I am still unsure about the enormity of this, if I am honest," Cao Cao replied. "I must have a proper debate about it in order to allay not only my fears but those of my generals, whose fight it will actually be... and when we return, we shall."
"And if the outcome is that the risks outweigh the potential benefits...?" Cheng Yu asked pointedly.
"...Then I will reinforce the provinces and parley with our foreign enemies, and turn my attentions elsewhere for now," Cao Cao replied. "Toward Liu Biao, perhaps... or Zhang Lu."
"Do not attack Zhang Lu without first removing the threats posed by Liu Biao and Sun Quan, or they will attack Xuchang and Yè while your back is turned," Cheng Yu warned. "In fact, you must also ensure that the Qiang confederacy is either completely pacified or utterly defeated before you invade Hanzhong. At least force submission from the leaders, or-"
"I will forget about Zhang Lu for now," Cao Cao said miserably. "...'Pacify', 'defeat'... 'force submission'... or in other, more honest words, 'kill them all'. That always seems to be the sole way to achieve the peace that I seek. My name will be remembered for creating a sea of blood instead of an ocean of knowledge!"
"But your name *will* be remembered," Cheng Yu retorted. "I'm sick of saying it, but I'll say it again anyway: three or four people will remember Cai Yong; *everyone* will remember Lü Bu. That is how the people 'think', Excellency... if that is the right word to use."
"*Aiee*... I wish that I had not discussed it with you now, you cantankerous man," Cao Cao groaned.

Cao Cao's exploits were as much a source of conversation as they had always been, even after the unusual distraction of Sun Quan's gifted elephant; the officials eventually found that the Excellency of Works was dominating their time once again whenever they met at one of Kong Rong's banquets in the capital Xuchang. The only attempts at changing the subject usually led to a discussion about Luoyang, the true capital of the Han Empire, which was still undergoing reconstruction following Dong Zhuo's destructive retreat almost 15 years before.
"Here we are, in Xuchang, after *ten years*... will Luoyang's restoration ever be finished...?" Kong Rong complained; Yang Biao

and Zhi Xi were his only remaining guests after a typically pleasant banquet.

"The place was looted and gutted by Dong Zhuo... which I saw first-hand, of course, as one of his hostages," Yang Biao said bitterly. "I still remember the fires, the death... and then all of those 'banquets'..."

"So do a lot of other people that get as upset as you do, and we should stop talking about the worst of it all... for your health," Zhi Xi insisted. "But yes, the city was gutted... and then left in that state for five years while the Yuans fought. It is only because of the late Zhang Yang's hard work – and, it has to be admitted, Cao Cao's determination to see the city reborn – that has ensured that it is no longer a shell."

"But still... *ten years*...?" Kong Rong chortled.

"We're fighting a war with most of the rest of the Empire, Wenju," Zhi Xi retorted. "Wars are not cheap... and nor is restoring a city the size of Luoyang, especially given the damage done to it. It might take *another* ten years, or maybe *more*!"

"Yes, and in the meantime we're being struck down by excessive taxes," Kong Rong grumbled. "No, gentlemen, I'm not blaming Cao for the taxes... but he had better win that war that he's starting with the Wuhuan!"

"*Aiee*... we're back to *that* again," Yang Biao groaned.

"What choice have we got?" Kong Rong asked plainly. "It's got to be the talking point of all sensible men! I have children that I happen to care a lot about! I don't want them to end up like Cai Yong's poor lot!"

"...That, by the way, is remarkable," Yang Biao said. "To have found Master Cai's younger daughter after *twelve years*! It only adds credibility to His Excellency's plan to rescue other girls from the Xiongnu."

"Cai Bojie's son is still dead," Kong Rong retorted. "All of *our* sons will be dead and our daughters their slaves if the Wuhuan defeat Cao and invade the Empire."

"They won't win," Zhi Xi said.

"They have won on every other occasion," Kong Rong retorted. "Cao had better hope that he is as magnificent as his ego leads him to believe."

The 'tolerated' ruler of Nan County, Zhang Xiu, was alarmed when his trusted general Huche'er announced the unexpected arrival of Cao Cao's local military commander Li Tong.

"Does he plan to attack me at last?" Zhang Xiu fretted.

"He would encounter strong opposition if he did, my lord," Huche'er promised.

"But we would still lose in the end," Zhang Xiu said sadly. "Times have changed dramatically since my now-infamous victory over Cao Cao here; now the genius adviser that conceived that victory works for him, not me, and he commands most of Yuan Shao's hordes as well."

"Thankfully, my lord, Li Tong is not here to fight," Huche'er replied. "He is not in full armour and claims to have a message from Cao Cao."

"...Why did it not come to me through Mister Jia...?" Zhang Xiu asked pointlessly.

"We can only assume that it is an official order," Huche'er said. "Shall I allow Li an audience...?"

"...Yes, yes," Zhang Xiu replied nervously.

Within an hour, Li Tong entered Zhang Xiu's courtroom and bowed slightly as a sign of respect; Li Tong had requested that only the most trusted of Zhang's followers attend, so there were only a few soldiers and officials present.

"Your presence is welcome, General," Zhang Xiu said soberly. "I understand that you have a message for me from His Excellency Cao Cao...?"

Li Tong smiled and reached into his right sleeve; Huche'er and the rest of Zhang Xiu's guards tensed and raised their weapons as Li Tong produced a small wooden tube.

"...Why the secrecy...?" Zhang Xiu asked.

"Put simply, General Zhang, you and your best men will not be here," Li Tong replied as he handed the tube to Zhang Xiu's registrar. "It was deemed... 'undesirable'... for Liu Biao to know too much too soon."

Zhang Xiu took the unfurled letter from his registrar and read the document carefully.

"I shall now return to my camp," Li Tong said tonelessly.

"...You must hurry away, General...?" Zhang Xiu asked once he had finished reading.

"I have preparations to make for my own actions, General Zhang," Li Tong replied. "And you can rest assured that there is no plot to seize Nan County in your absence... no more than there was when you aided His Excellency in person before. I am stationing close to the county border in case of Liu Biao hearing of your departure and exploiting it."

"Well then... a safe journey, General Li," Zhang Xiu said.

Once Li Tong had fully retreated, Huche'er turned to his lord and asked, "What are our instructions...?"

"...We shall return to my study," Zhang Xiu replied. "My advisers shall join us."

"...This is a grand expedition," Zhang Xiu said once he was sat in his private study with his officials. "Cao Cao wants to attack and destroy the Wuhuan... in their own territory."

"*Ayah*... when have such brash actions ever led to good things...?" one adviser asked.

"I agree," Huche'er admitted. "The Imperial army has a poor record against fighting foreign 'barbarians': their last campaign against the Xianbei was a bit before my time, my lord, but I know as well as anyone that it ended very badly. Has Cao been consumed by hubris again...?"

"Whether he has or he hasn't isn't the point," Zhang Xiu said. "We're not his opponent this time: we're his trusted ally. He's asked us to bring our own formidable swords to the battle, knowing that we're some of the best that there are. We are not in a position to refuse. We must prepare at once."

"Then we shall," Huche'er replied.

The former Mount Tai Bandit Zang Ba also received orders that were delivered to his Qing Province headquarters by a robe-wearing official.

"We're to support Cao Cao should he need us to," Zang Ba explained to his agitated subordinates. "**Our main role is pacifying Qing Province, as always, but with Dong Zhao being in Yòu Province digging canals, Xu Province has no governor so-**"

"**So we should seize the bloody place instead of waiting for thrown scraps!**" Chang Xi heckled.

"**That's not going to happen,**" Zang Ba said. "**For one, the 'risk of harm' involved is-**"

"What 'risk of harm'?" Chang Xi taunted. "**None of *us* have given our families over to Cao as hostages!**"

Several bandit chieftains chattered agreeably.

"**...I didn't give them over as hostages!**" Zang Ba said angrily. "**I sent them without being asked to in order to show that I'm committed to serving the Han... as we should *all be*. Don't do what you keep hinting at, Chang... you-**"

"**Who's hinting?**" Chang Xi said aggressively. "**Xu Province has no governor, and we're bandits! It weren't so long ago that you'd be leading us to Xiapi!**"

"**Xu Province is stable now,**" Zang Ba retorted. "**The-**"

"**Liu Bei, weakling that he is, took Xu *twice*!**" Chang Xi heckled. "**Xu Province *hates Cao Cao*: what'll we look like if we ignore an opportunity to-**"

"**What 'opportunity', you fool...?**" Zang Ba chortled. "**Cao has half a million men now! The Black Mountain boys have *surrendered*! The White Waves are *gone*! The Qiang have *submitted*! Xu Province hates bandits *more*! Times have changed, and if you don't see that soon, friend, we'll be *burying you*!**"

Chang Xi gestured rudely and left the hall with his growing following; Zang Ba turned his gaze to his long-time friend Sun Guan, who smiled sadly.

"**...Alright,**" Zang Ba sighed. "**I'll carry on where I left off...**"

****

82

Cao Cao's military officers were concerned about the northern campaign's scope and the other risks that it posed: Cao was eventually forced to address those concerns as the canal-digging project neared completion.

"The entire idea is too risky!" Li Dian suggested. "If we just faced the Yuans and the Wuhuan tribes, then I would not object, but we have other enemies that will be behind us when we march!"

"Yeah, and some of them will be right behind us, like *Zhang Xiu*, and *Zang Ba*," Xiahou Dun complained.

"You're wrong to worry about Zhang Xiu, Cousin Yuanrang," Cao Cao insisted. "He'll not trouble us again."

"But what about Liu Biao, Liu Bei and the pirate Guan Cheng...?" Li Dian asked. "What about Zhang Lu and the Qiang tribes...? What about *Sun Quan*...?"

"Sun Quan is posturing but is, at present, unable to attack anybody, not even his hated enemy Liu Biao," Guo Jia said with obvious strain.

"I am inclined to agree, despite seeing Sun Quan's strength first-hand," Hua Xin said.

"And Guan Cheng is an obvious concern that I intend to deal with immediately," Cao Cao announced. "I won't have a grubby pirate ruining my grand ambition."

"And the rest...?" Yu Jin asked. "Forgive the concern, Excellency, but Li Dian and I are not alone."

Many of the mid-ranking officers murmured agreeably.

"...I will despatch Yue Jin, Zhang Hè and Li Dian to deal with Guan Cheng," Cao Cao proclaimed.

"I need no seconds for defeating a pirate!" Yue Jin barked. **"My one setback at Hu Pass should not be held against me, Your Excellency!"**

"...Nothing is being held against you, General," Cao Cao replied tonelessly. "I want this self-styled 'king of the rivers' crushed quickly... and a three-pronged attack will achieve that."

"*Three*-pronged...?" Yue Jin exclaimed. "Then why assign Li Dian?"

"*Aiee*... again, you insult me groundlessly!" Li Dian complained.

"Stop bickering," Cao Cao ordered. "I am sat in Yuan Shao's seat, and I employ a lot of Yuan Shao's former vassals, but I am not Yuan Shao!"

Li Dian and Yue Jin bowed humbly and mumbled apologies.

"...The three of you will go together to destroy Guan Cheng, after which you will join my northern campaign," Cao Cao continued. "Zhang Lu and the Qiang are not problems at the moment and need not be mentioned further."

"But that still leaves Liu Biao and Liu Bei," Major Han Hao suggested. "Excellency, I have been serving you as General Xiahou Dun's subordinate for some years now, and before that I served Wang Kuang. I've seen and heard a lot, and I shall now relay what I see and hear. The consensus is that there is a serious risk of attacks from the south while we turn our attentions toward a blunted sword. Yuan Shang has fled the Empire and has no soldiers; the Wuhuan are a treacherous, inconstant bunch that only aid the Yuans in exchange for impunity in the north that they cannot now promise, so why should the barbarians help the brothers now...?"

"That is quite reasonable," Cao Cao admitted. "Go on."

"On the other hand, Liu Biao and Liu Bei are running out of potential allies and will surely resort to desperate acts of self-preservation," Han Hao continued. "Whether it be to save the Yuans or to save themselves, they will consider attacking Xuchang while the army is entrenched in the lands beyond the wall: while it is agreed that Liu Biao has not got the stomach for such things, there is a risk that Liu Bei might convince him to act, and if that happens we will be too far away to have second thoughts and prevent a catastrophe. And Xuchang *will* be vulnerable: a handful of defenders could not repel even a weakened Liu Biao, doubly so if Huang Zu commits to it also."

Cao Cao hummed thoughtfully.

"...Many of the officials share similar concerns," Cui Yan admitted. "Our plans are there for the world to see: won't the Yuans learn of the canals...?"

"Such matters cannot be ignored," Li Dian said. "A campaign such as this will take months at the very least: if the enemy shows any resolve – which, let us be honest, has been the Yuans' sole strong point – we could be out there for *years*!"

Cao Cao exhaled fiercely and lowered his head.

"Time, of course, is the main concern."

All eyes turned to the frail Guo Jia.

"Naturally, Mister Guo," Li Dian prompted.

"It is my only concern," Guo Jia continued. "Truly, 'Swiftness is the key in war': it is what has won us most of our victories, gentlemen, for as Sun Tzu said, 'While haste is never advocated, delay is never wise'."

"Meaning *what*...?" Cao Hong asked.

"There are ways to make this campaign very short indeed, but I... excuse me... ... ...I shall keep my words to allaying fears about the 'Two Lius of Jing' and the nature... of the enemy," Guo Jia continued. "The Wuhuan are arrogant when they are in our lands: they will be doubly so in their own. They react to surprise with disorder that we can and will exploit. They are deluded, believing that they are safe in their mountain strongholds and that any attack will come with ample warning, but they are wrong. If we were to attack them before any reasonable expectation then they will be destroyed."

"Nonsense!" Li Dian exclaimed. "I'm in charge of supplies, as I am so often chided for, and I know what this will involve: for an army to march such a distance, they'll need to take-"

"Forgive me, but... might I finish...?" Guo Jia said weakly.

"Let Fengxiao finish, Mancheng," Cao Cao ordered.

"...I am a veteran of supply management as well, so I know what is usually involved as well, General, but I have a remedy for that," Guo Jia continued. "I... excuse me."

Guo Jia was forced to pause and wait for a pain in his gut to pass; the adviser Chen Qun scowled and shook his head disdainfully.

"...Even if you have some miracle method for sending men to war on empty stomachs, there is still the matter of Liu Bei and Liu Biao," Li Dian said irritably. "I have the utmost respect for you, Fengxiao, but the idea that we are going to commit to this without destroying that easier target... is nonsense. If we wait, then Sun Quan might attack Jing, and that complicates things further, since we would then need to wade into that feud."

"I... know," Guo Jia replied. "Sun Quan is not ready yet... expect nothing from him for another half-year at the least. And as for Liu Biao... and Liu... Bei... if we attack them first, the Yuans will definitely recover and be harder to defeat... and they'll take back lands that they've lost... be certain of that. We've not pacified the provinces entirely. There are more Zhao Dus and Huo Nus out there... that must not be allowed to bring the Yuans back."

"Indeed yes," Yuan Huan said. "It took four years to chase the brothers out of the Empire: we can't risk them regaining a foothold, not if it means trying to regain Bing, Yòu and northern Ji all over again. Liu Biao, by contrast, weakens even when he is left alone to think."

"Exactly... right," Guo Jia wheezed. "Liu Biao knows only how to sit and talk... and Liu Bei cannot persuade him... to do anything."

"We cannot be certain of that," Han Hao suggested.

"Oh, we can!" Guo Jia chuckled softly. "Liu Bei is still kept low... even after defending Bowang from a superior force. Liu Bei is actually more competent than Liu Biao... and Biao knows it. Bei has always been restricted by the size of his army and the quality of his counsel... and if Biao gave him any way to grow, Jing would become Bei's thereafter. Liu Biao must balance... rewarding Bei with limited power with... avoiding insufficient reward that... causes Bei to grumble."

"Save your strength, Fengxiao," Cao Cao said. "Your words ring true as always, my friend, and you need say no more. Guan Cheng will soon yield or die; Liu Bei will get nowhere with Liu Biao, who will do nothing but look southward and sigh; the Wuhuan will laugh and disregard the threat that we pose until it is too late."

The officials murmured anxiously.

"Yue Jin, Zhang Hè, Li Dian: you will go to Bing Province to challenge Guan Cheng on the Yellow River," Cao Cao ordered. "I will personally oversee the northern campaign, since its success or failure will bless or damn us all. I will advance to Yijing Fortress and establish a base there within the coming weeks."

"...That is... the proper course," Guo Jia said quietly.

Cao Cao's canal-digging activity was impossible to miss: various spies soon reported it to Jing Governor Liu Biao and his warlord tenant Liu Bei.

"There is only one reason that Cao Cao would be ordering such canals to be dug: he intends a full-scale invasion of Yòu Province and, perhaps, the Wuhuan territories beyond the Great Wall... which matches as the rumours," the adviser Kuai Yue said to Liu Biao's packed court in Xiangyang City.

"...**So how is it that I cannot be in the south at this critical moment, when my enemy Sun Quan looks poised to act against Huang Zu?!**" Liu Biao cried.

"Our agents report that Zhang Xiu is mobilising, and that can only mean two things," the adviser Wang Can said. "One possibility is that the canals are dug as a deception and that he actually feigns this 'grand march northward' with the true intent of turning about to attack Jing when we are at ease; the other is that he desires Zhang Xiu's aid in the upcoming battle, which leaves Nan County understaffed, though we daren't risk trying to seize it while Sun Quan's lurking."

"We shouldn't...?" Liu Biao prompted.

"Don't let Liu Bei or his allies talk you into a suicidal attack on Nan County or Xuchang," Kuai Yue chuckled. "If Nan County is 'understaffed', it is only as bait to lure us out!"

"Quite right," Wang Can said. "We're dealing with *Guo Jia* here."

"...I suppose so," Liu Biao sighed.

"Cao Cao has achieved the near-impossible already: he has Yuan Shao's army as his own, and the Wuhuan have been chased out of Yòu and Ji," Kuai Yue said. "I see no instance where he would now leave Nan County or Xuchang 'understaffed' so that he can gain the frontier and lose his home province."

"Cao Cao is rarely based in Xuchang these days," Huan Jie noted. "I hear stories about him having elephants gifted to him by Sun Quan, and family banquets, and luxury enhancements being made to his home... and all of it refers to his base in *Yè*, not Xuchang."

"Yes, and that elephant was sent because *why*...?" Kuai Yue said pointedly. "Cao Cao and Sun Quan are not friends. The only reason that Sun Quan would be sending such a present to Cao Cao is to protect his own position as lord of Jiangdong from his vastly more experienced cousin Sun Ben – whose daughter has Cao Cao for a father-in-law – and to show unity with Cao... unity before some action that is personally or mutually beneficial. Sun Quan is, at the very least, preparing to attack us now because he hates Lord Liu Biao, but regardless of his reasons, it pins us here. We cannot attack Nan County *or* Xuchang, no matter what-"

Liu Biao started to cough painfully.

"Father, you are sick," Liu Qi said empathetically.

"...I... am *fine*," Liu Biao insisted. "Mister Kuai is quite right when he... when he says that we should not be rash. Far from attacking, we should be preparing for a great defence... defence against Sun Quan in the south and Cao Cao's minions to the north and east."

"That is the proper course," Kuai Yue said wearily. "Let none tell you otherwise."

Liu Bei and his new adviser – the 27-year-old 'Crouching Dragon', Zhuge Liang – would later attempt to sway Liu Biao toward action against Cao Cao while his back was turned, but their efforts were in vain, just as Guo Jia had predicted; Nan County would also be safe after Zhang Xiu left the region to aid the Han in Ji Province.

****

83

Han Generals Yue Jin, Zhang Hè and Li Dian arrived in Bing Province with a combined army of 15,000; they were greeted at the border by Inspector Zhang Zhi, who immediately said, "Your aid is most welcome."

"We were only just here, and now this scabby pirate has dragged us back," Yue Jin complained. "Rest assured, Inspector, that Guan Cheng will die a dog's death."

"Only if his death is unavoidable," Zhang Hè suggested. "Guan Cheng commands support from thousands of competent river fighters; they might be useful in future confrontations with the likes of Liu Biao, whose navy is–"

"We won't need pirates," Yue Jin retorted. "Am I not a competent river warrior? And what is there to it anyway? Even Li Dian has won river battles with ease."

Li Dian sighed and said, "For the sake of this discussion, I concede that Gao Fan was no Guan Cheng. And General Zhang is right to suggest that–"

"We won't need pirates!" Yue Jin snapped. "His Excellency has not undertaken his mission to keep giving power to the likes of–!"

A man in Zhang Zhi's welcoming party coughed loudly and deliberately, which ended the conversation and drew all eyes to him; he was 'Flying Swallow' Zhang Yan, leader of the recently-surrendered Black Mountain Bandits.

"Yes...?" Yue Jin prompted.

"The 'likes of Guan Cheng' is no diff'rent to the likes of Zang Ba, or to the likes o' *me*, General Yue," Flying Swallow said plainly. "Weren't your mate Xu Huang one o' the top men in the White Waves not so long ago...?"

"...Yes, he was," Yue Jin conceded. "But this Guan is–!"

"'This Guan', as you put it, is trying his luck," Flying Swallow said. "Yeah, they ain't in it for the same reason that most o' my lot was, but you can't write them all off; if you kill them all, it'll annoy a lot o' people, make them scared... including some o' my boys – and their families – that still don't trust you."

"...Your point is taken, Zhang Yan," Yue Jin replied. "We'll try and get him to submit."

"Wise move," Flying Swallow insisted. "His boys are good river fighters... prob'ly only the Jing Province navy and the Sun clan's lot are better."

"We'll need boats to fight them on the rivers and siege equipment for attacking their fortress," Li Dian said.

"And you'll get them," Zhang Zhi promised. "Shall we move on?"

Cao Cao busied himself with preparations for departure, but concerns over the growing number of rumours about his heir Cao Pi drove him to seek counsel from Guo Jia once again; he was greeted at the door by Jia's son Yi.

"My father is weary, Excellency," Guo Yi said as he led Cao Cao and Xu Chu into the living quarters.

"I know... I will not keep him long," Cao Cao promised.

Guo Yi bowed humbly and left the room.

"...Why is Mister Guo so sick?" Xu Chu asked suddenly.

"He... ... ...he is sick of everybody, I suppose you could say," Cao Cao replied. "We all sicken him... we all bore him... he speeds up the sickness, that's all."
"What did we do to make him sick?" Xu Chu asked.
"Nothing different," Cao Cao replied miserably.
After a few minutes, Guo Yi and a household servant brought Guo Jia into the room and guided him to his seat.
"*Ayah*... every time I see you, you...!" Cao Cao exclaimed.
"Enough about me," Guo Jia replied. "Must we speak privately?"
"Indeed yes," Cao Cao said as he gestured for Xu Chu to back away. "This is a delicate matter about family and state."
Guo Jia turned to his son and servant and smiled; the pair bowed and departed, after which Guo said, "You don't intend to employ my son in the same capacity then...?"
"I, like you, assess each man individually," Cao Cao replied. "If he is capable, I will use him. But regardless, Fengxiao, he will be like a son to me. This is a matter that I would not even discuss with Lady Bian or my sons themselves."
"Ah... so this is about Cao Pi," Guo Jia guessed.
"Two, nearly three years have passed since the end of the siege of Yè," Cao Cao said. "Yet his conduct after that event is still a talking point... and, in some cases, a laughing matter. Lady Zhen's sudden pregnancy and, of course, the very nature of her marriage to my son... make easy sport for my enemies. What must I do?"
"What did you do after Wan?" Guo Jia asked.
Cao Cao laughed and said, "Well met. I have, as you have so deftly put it, made a bigger fool of myself than my son has done, but I faced the criticism and overcame it by becoming a greater man. Pi must do the same."
"So what other course did you have in mind...?" Guo Jia asked.
"...*Disinheritance*... in favour of Chong," Cao Cao admitted.
Guo Jia hummed thoughtfully and said, "I can entirely understand that if I am honest, Mengde. Chong is one of the ablest minds in the land."
"And every bit the deserving heir!" Cao Cao replied excitedly. "He is skilled in the fields of mathematics, law, history, military strategy and literature: even now, as a boy, he makes all but my most brilliant adult officials look utterly incompetent."
"But at the same time, Mengde, he is not even your third son," Guo Jia noted. "Before him come three of Lady Bian's sons: Pi, Zhang and Zhi."
"...Yes," Cao Cao sighed. "And Lady Bian is my principal wife and my favourite."
"She is also very shrewd and sensible, and I think that she would probably understand why you would make such a choice, even if your choice is not one of her children," Guo Jia said. "The problem is 'the sons themselves'... is it not...?"
"Yes," Cao Cao replied. "Pi and Zhang are both very... 'assertive'. They would not stand for seeing their younger half-brother elevated over them... and I should not do so, not after watching the Yuans destroy themselves by making that very same mistake... but..."
"...I wish that I could help... but I am a winner of battles and wars," Guo Jia said. "Family disputes are not my specialty."
"Nor are they of any remote interest to you, except as ways of

defeating muddle-headed opponents: am I right...?" Cao Cao chuckled miserably.

Guo Jia smiled and said, "You are correct to see the error in allowing this to become a public, long-standing issue. I am not the only strategist in the world, and the rest are not going to automatically gravitate toward you. If Liu Biao, Liu Bei, Sun Quan – or, ridiculous as it might sound, the lesser likes of Liu Zhang or Zhang Lu – were ever to recruit men with insight, such a weakness could topple you as it toppled the Yuans. Make a decision and stick to it, Mengde... and let fate do the rest."

Cao Cao hummed thoughtfully.

"...Zhang Xiu will be here soon, I understand," Guo Jia prompted.

"He is on his way here," Cao Cao replied carefully. "But there is no need to discuss Zhang Xiu, Fengxiao: that matter is resolved."

Guo Jia hummed a laugh.

"So I have no need to harass you further," Cao Cao continued. "Rest, my old friend, and please try to recover... or else you will not see the fruits of your labours. You at least want to see your efforts made real...?"

"...I have seen enough," Guo Jia replied. "The rest is obvious."

Cao Cao exhaled loudly and turned to summon Xu Chu; Guo Jia called for his servants, who hurried to his side to help him back to his bed.

"...I will not bother you again until I am ready to depart," Cao Cao said as he prepared to leave. "Until then, I order you to take care of yourself!"

Guo Jia smiled and replied, "Until then, Lord Cao... I shall."

Cao Cao left the Guo residence with a frown on his face; he knew that he would soon lose his strongest guiding light, and the thought of it filled him with fear.

Guan Cheng heard that Cao Cao had finally decided to confront him and summoned most of his followers – who numbered in the thousands – to the Yellow River to block the Han boats as they travelled toward Guan's stronghold. Even Yue Jin was stunned at the sight of so many enemy boats; Yue's deputy shook his head and said, "**We underestimated him, I think.**"

"**Speak for yourself!**" Yue Jin retorted. "**Yes, they are intimidating to the common eye, but my eye is uncommon! Let them send a *hundred thousand* against us! Pirates are pirates, nothing more!**"

Yue Jin's men were emboldened by their commander's words – whether they were heard first-hand or relayed by others – and started to cheer enthusiastically. The pirates had been heckling the Han forces, but the sight of so many men crying out fearlessly caused them to become hesitant and wonder whether they could survive against professional soldiers.

"**We must use this moment to our advantage!**" Yue Jin barked. "**ATTACK!**"

But the battle would not be as straightforward as Yue Jin expected: his men numbered only half of his actual force, since many had become distressed or sick when trying to move freely on the bobbing boats. The soldiers that had managed to overcome the problems associated with simple travelling on boats were now faced with having to fight on such unstable platforms, and that was a specialised form of combat that few had been expected to undertake before; the pirates, by contrast, were each and every one of them proficient in moving and fighting, and that quickly proved to be an unassailable advantage.

"**Damn them!**" Yue Jin cried. "**Damn their clumsy, useless...!**"

The smaller Han naval force was at risk of being decimated: the pirates' losses were at least half in number, and they already outnumbered Yue Jin's men. The close-quarters fighting was, at times, embarrassing to watch: the recruits that lacked training were flailing and staggering as the boats moved under them, which gave the pirates plenty of opportunities to cut them down, while those that did know how to manoeuvre were being overwhelmed by attacks from multiple directions that were as skilful as their own at the least.

"**...I CANNOT RETREAT!**" Yue Jin screamed; he then advanced with his elite unit to fight the enemy in person. Yue Jin had learned the art of naval combat, so he was no match for the older or slower pirates that met him initially; the shock of his arrival also harmed the morale of the more skilful pirates and led to a general shift in the tide of battle. Zhang Hè suddenly added his own forces to the battle at that point: his men were approaching from the opposite direction, which was unexpected and left the pirate fleet with nowhere to go.

"**Fall back, lads! FALL BACK!**" Guan Cheng ordered.

"**Fall back *where*???**" another pirate asked desperately.

The pirates either attempted to fight their way past Zhang Hè or fled to the western bank, where Li Dian's men were waiting for them: local forces and volunteer militias comprised of commoners that had tired of the constant attacks gave the Han army a sudden advantage as the battle shifted mainly to the land, where the pirates were not as adept. Guan Cheng's followers were scattered, leaving the pirate king with two choices: submit or die in battle.

"**Weapons down! WEAPONS DOWN!**" Guan Cheng ordered.

The majority of the pirates surrendered as soon as they knew that Guan Cheng had conceded defeat; Yue Jin commandeered a horse and loomed over Guan with his reins in one hand and a halberd in the other.

"**I hope you didn't take that horse on a boat,**" Guan Cheng heckled. "**Horses don't like boats much... the movin' about makes 'em-**"

"**SILENCE!**" Yue Jin bellowed. "**Do you yield or not, you dog?**"

"**What does it look like???**" Guan Cheng retorted.

Li Dian smiled and said, "**We must be clear. Do you submit, Guan Cheng?**"

"**...Yeah, I do,**" Guan Cheng replied. "**I give up... I submit.**"

"**Then help us talk down the last of the men that are still fighting,**" Li Dian continued. "**They're more use alive than dead, are they not...?**"

Guan Cheng nodded slowly and joined the Han officers' calls for the battle to end: Guan's pirates were then absorbed into the local defence forces or imprisoned, depending on their known crimes.

"...Excellent," Cao Cao chuckled as he read Yue Jin's report in front of his court. "Yet again, gentlemen, my great generals make quick work of our enemies!"

"You are being far too dismissive of the main content," the adviser Cheng Yu suggested. "It clearly says that 'naval training was generally inadequate', Excellency. They were going to be fighting *pirates*... and pirates are, typically, bandits that operate along the waterways, I think, using boats. So why were so many of our men unprepared for it...?"

Cao Cao's face fell.

"Jing Province has the best professional navy in the land... or, at worst, the second-best if Sun Quan's navy has somehow surpassed them," Cheng Yu continued. "If Liu Biao is our next target after the Wuhuan, Excellency, then-"

"Your point is noted, Mister Cheng," Cao Cao said irritably. "We defeated Guan Cheng... which is, for now, all that matters. The Wuhuan fight on land and in the hills, and for that we are well-prepared. We'll worry about the 'river rats of Jing' when it is time to do so!"

"...As you wish, Excellency," Cheng Yu sighed.

"What news of Zhang Xiu?" Cao Cao asked as he turned to Jia Xu.

"My former lord is delayed by sudden illness, Excellency," Jia Xu replied. "It seems to afflicting all of his vitals... it started after his first stop in Henei."

Cao Cao's eyes wandered as he said, "I hope that he is not suffering too much. If he is delayed, so be it, but... what a shame it is that he is poorly."

Jia Xu frowned as he replied, "It *is* a shame, Your Excellency... it *is* a shame."

"I must proceed nonetheless," Cao Cao said. "The end of the long road is very near now..."

****

84

The defiant scholar Sima Yi continued his pretence of being seriously ill, despite his fairly young age of 28 and the potential consequences of being discovered: his wife Lady Zhang - who was 10 years his junior – was saddened by their inability to have a family but remained loyal to her husband's desire to remain disconnected from the Han court that had now employed most of his 7 brothers and his father. The act was becoming harder and harder to sustain, however: Sima was actually being harmed by the need to remain indoors for long periods and keep his dishevelled and sickly appearance through deliberate malnourishment, and the extra added stress of keeping all but one trusted vassal ignorant of the truth meant that Sima was not able to relax his guard at any time.

"...Who is in the house...?" Sima Yi whispered to the miserable Lady Zhang. "I want to go outside: who is in the house...?"

"Both kitchen workers are out buying supplies, and the maid is cleaning the bedrooms," Lady Zhang replied. "Be careful all the same, Husband."

"I got this far," Sima Yi groaned as he got to his feet and flexed his right ankle. "I will do this until I am grey-haired if I must and they won't catch me."

"...Such a shame," Lady Zhang sighed as she watched her husband walk to the garden with three bamboo books tightly clutched in his left hand and his walking cane in his right.

The sky was cloudy, and the breeze was strengthening: Sima Yi breathed the clean air as though it were the most precious of things and smiled gratefully. Sima's wooden chair was carefully positioned so that he would have advance warning of a surprise guest, and the small table that sat next to it was placed so that a sudden dash past it and into the house was possible; Lady Zhang was forced to act as a lookout whenever her husband decided that he needed such a liberated moment, and that meant that she had to clear her mind of distractions and be ready to react instinctively to even the slightest threat of being discovered.

"...Why, oh why, can the Han not die...?" Sima Yi murmured as he read his copy of 'The Spring and Autumn Annals'. "A fine horse such as myself will wither away to nothing if it must be stabled for too much longer..."

"*Husband*! *Husband*!"

Sima Yi immediately turned to face his wife, whose hissed words were obviously some sort of warning: Lady Zhang pointed at her husband's legs and added, "*Your cane...!*"

Sima Yi looked down and saw that his cane had dropped to the ground: he smiled and leant forward to pick it up and rest it against his left leg while his wife returned her gaze to the house. The maid had just finished her cleaning duties and approached Lady Zhang, saying, "I can do the living quarters now, Mistress."

"...Not yet," Lady Zhang replied. "I forgot to tell the others to buy paper for my husband to write... it's his only little pleasure. I asked for ink, but not paper... please go and buy some."

"Very well, Mistress," the maid said obediently.

Once the maid was gone, Lady Zhang smiled and went to her

husband's side.

"She out...?" Sima Yi chuckled.

"It's just us," Lady Zhang replied.

"...I know this is frustrating," Sima Yi said, "but I imagine that we will soon be rewarded by some great upheaval. Cao Cao's challenging the Wuhuan, which will end in him becoming the ruler of the land or bringing an end to the Han once and for all: one way or another that might be the time for me to cast this ridiculous cane aside and do some good."

"You're a brilliant man... you should not be forced to rot here," Lady Zhang said as she stroked Sima Yi's shoulder gently.

"...Yes, well... when did the state ever know how to treat talented men properly...?" Sima Yi asked. "I must be 'of use': if my skills cannot be made to serve some selfish motive then I am discarded, regardless of my ability. Cao Cao might, perhaps, be a man that knows how to treat people... or perhaps not. It is difficult to tell."

Lady Zhang hummed thoughtfully and looked to the ground: it was then that a sudden heavy rain shower began.

"Oh for-! ...I was enjoying the air!" Sima Yi complained.

"Inside, quickly!" Lady Zhang cried as she ran indoors. **"You mustn't get soaked! *Inside*!"**

Sima Yi panicked at the sudden urgency in his wife's voice and dashed into the house with his cane firmly clutched in his right hand; the rain intensified, so he was forced to stand at the door and stare at his garden with a sense that he had been foiled by some greater power.

"That's it... that's what it is," Sima Yi muttered. "Heaven has done this to make fun of me."

Lady Zhang sighed wearily.

"Did this happen to Yue Yi, or Jiang Ziya...?" Sima Yi chuckled. "Perhaps it did, and they didn't bother to include it in the- ... ...

...My *books*!"

"What?" Lady Zhang exclaimed.

"My *books*, you stupid woman!" Sima Yi retorted as he dropped his cane and started toward his garden chair. **"You made me forget them with your idiot screaming! They'll be damaged! They're *irreplaceable*!"**

"No, no, come back!" Lady Zhang pleaded as she grabbed at her husband's arm. **"You'll be soaked through, and-!"**

"Get off me, imbecile!" Sima Yi barked as he shrugged his wife's hand away violently; Lady Zhang could only watch as Sima marched toward the chair and bent over to pick up his bamboo reading material.

"Mistress!"

Lady Zhang froze: the maid – who had returned to escape the rain – ran to her and said, **"Mistress, forgive me, but I didn't want to-!** ...What...?"

Lady Zhang's eyes alternated between the stunned maid – who had now seen her healthy master, Sima Yi, collecting his books in the rain – and Sima Yi himself, who had frozen with fear when he realised that he had been discovered.

"B-but... I don't understand," the maid murmured. "Mistress, I- ...I don't understand. Mistress, it's... it's a miracle, isn't it...? Has Master Sima recovered...?"

Sima Yi stared at his wife with bulging eyes and croaked feebly.

"It's a miracle!" the maid said excitedly. "He was so sick! But look, Mistress, he's fine now! He... he was so *sick*... he *was* sick, wasn't he, Mistress...?"

Lady Zhang turned and walked toward the kitchen's preparation table slowly and silently.

"...Mistress, I... I don't understand," the maid complained as she trotted after Lady Zhang. "What's going on...?"

Lady Zhang sighed miserably and moved her hands across the table, which was littered with bits of chopped vegetable and cutting knives.

"...Was Master Sima not sick...?" the maid asked at last. "He... he could get into trouble if people knew... we *all could...*!"

Lady Zhang exhaled loudly.

"We could all get into trouble!" the maid whined. "We-!"

Lady Zhang turned with frightening speed and grabbed the maid, spinning her around and drawing her close before she could understand what was going on.

"**Mistress???**" the maid cried.

"Quiet, now," Lady Zhang whispered softly: she then slit the maid's throat with a large kitchen knife and held her tightly while she made her last futile movements and slowly sank to the floor.

"...Quiet, now," Lady Zhang whispered.

"*Ayah*... what have you done...?" Sima Yi exclaimed: he had watched the entire murder from the doorway.

"...Did you want to be discovered...?" Lady Zhang asked calmly.

"I...! ...No, I did not," Sima Yi replied.

"You yourself said that you would resort to anything... and I, as your wife, must do the same," Lady Zhang said as she stood up and returned the knife to the table. "She must be dealt with now... so now that you have your books, you must go to our bedroom, change out of those wet clothes and return to bed. I will clean up, prepare dinner and manage the staff."

Sima Yi nodded uneasily.

"You do not need to remain," Lady Zhang insisted. "I will manage everything. There will be no trace of this incident when I am done... and it had to be done. We cannot, after all of our efforts, be compromised by a simple-minded girl that's paying off her family's debts: that would be ridiculous."

"...Yes... I suppose so," Sima Yi murmured.

"I will not allow you to be discovered," Lady Zhang promised. "Whatever it takes, Husband... whatever it takes. Now go and get out of those wet clothes before you *really* get sick."

Sima Yi passed his wife and left the kitchen.

"...What must I do first...?" Lady Zhang wondered as she stared at the twitching corpse of her former maid. "I must... slaughter a pig to explain the blood..."

"...I forgot to say, in the midst of my understandable bewilderment... that I am impressed," Sima Yi said as he suddenly returned to the entrance to the kitchen. "I am truly impressed, my lady: you are the formidable woman that I need at my side."

Lady Zhang smiled gratefully and replied, "Your approval is all that I seek."

Sima Yi smirked, hummed thoughtfully, and resumed his journey to the bedroom.

Lady Zhang was forced to concoct an elaborate story to explain the sudden disappearance of the maid – who, like many household staff, was a serf that worked to pay off a family debt – but the entire matter was resolved with the aid of a large sack, some unscrupulous labourers and a hastily-purchased pig to explain the blood that Lady Zhang could not remove. It would be the most dramatic and memorable of Sima Yi's efforts to avoid service, but it would not be the last: Cao Cao was determined to employ him and every other capable man in the land, and that would ensure no end to the scrutiny of Sima's health in the months to come.

****

85

Cao Cao's continuing preparations for war reached the surviving Yuan brothers, who repeatedly lobbied the Wuhuan leaders, Tadun and Louban, but their concerns were met with ridicule.

"You know nothing about the land near your 'Great Wall', either of you, yet you say you rule it!" Tadun heckled.

"Cao Cao is digging canals and massing weapons and men for a great war with us – with *you* – and yet you are not worried at all...?" Yuan Shang countered.

"When can he attack?" Tadun asked.

"Whenever he wants!" Yuan Shang retorted. "He has a great army, canals, boats, equipment–"

"All useless when the rains come," Tadun scoffed.

"Rains...?" Yuan Xi prompted; his ignorance was met with much laughter amongst the Wuhuan leaders and much chattering about the Yuans' lack of knowledge in their own language.

"You, Yuan Xi, are 'Governor of Yòu Province'!" Louban chortled. "You know nothing of the great rains...?"

"...I confess that I do not," Yuan Xi replied. "But I have only been the governor for a short time, and I have been based in–"

"You Han men always have such excuses for knowing nothing about your people or your land!" Tadun said with glee. "Soon the rains will come in the east, where they need to go to get to us. All the area around what you call 'Liaoxi', right to the sea, will become mud that no man or animal can move through!"

Yuan Shang smirked and said, "Perfect! If there is no other way to go but around the Great Wall and along the coastline, then–"

"Then they cannot attack until the rains stop and the land dries again, which is not for a long, long time," Tadun interrupted. "So let Cao Cao dig his canals and sail his boats. He will not be able to sail his boats or march his men through mud!"

"What about the rivers...?" Yuan Xi asked.

"We are not fools," Louban replied. "You call us 'barbarians', which makes you feel that we are stupid and violent while you are clever and gentle. We know about the rain and you do not; we know about the rivers too and have put men near them to guard them. Cao Cao will not get here easily or, maybe, at all."

"And in the meantime, Brother, we can cultivate loyalty amongst the 'Han people' that have come to this region and grow our army!" Yuan Shang suggested.

"That won't be easy," Yuan Xi retorted. "They were abducted, weren't they?"

Tadun harrumphed and said, "You take and use Wuhuan people, Xiongnu people, Qiang, Du, Shanyue... you take our land too, to become your 'provinces', but that is all called 'pacifying'; we take and use your people and live on what you say is 'your land' – land which was *our land* – and that is called 'abducting' and–"

"Don't lecture us, Tadun," Yuan Shang retorted. "We Yuans let you share the land with us, whoever it truly belongs to, unlike Cao Cao, who will destroy you, take *all of your land* and, as you say, call it 'pacifying'; and unlike my brother I am aware that many of the people here are people that left the Empire voluntarily."

"*Voluntarily*...?" Yuan Xi exclaimed.

"Yes… strange though that may seem," Yuan Shang replied. "The abducted ones will be hard to convince, yes, but there are generations of people that fled the chaos, the famines, the poverty… and live here quite happily."

"*Aiee*… I knew nothing of it," Yuan Xi admitted.

"You know nothing of anything," Tadun heckled. "Was there anything else you wanted to say, or did you two 'Han noblemen' just come here to beg us to do something about Cao Cao again…?"

"We have nothing else to say," Yuan Shang replied. "We shall go now, great chieftains, and let you plan, since you seem to know what you are doing."

Tadun grinned and said, "At least you understand that now."

Yuan Shang and Yuan Xi started the journey back to their accommodation – a pair of animal skin tents – in the Liucheng camp; Yuan Xi was suddenly more aware of his surroundings and was looking at the Wuhuan people more objectively. The smiles of the children were genuine, and while the majority of the culture was alien, there were obvious signs that the people – some of whom were at least part Han Chinese – were at the very least comfortable.

"…You're very quiet," Yuan Shang noted.

"I… I suppose I am just waking up a bit," Yuan Xi replied.

"To what…?" Yuan Shang asked.

"…Let's get back to your tent before we speak of it, Brother and lord," Yuan Xi replied.

"Very well," Yuan Shang said.

A short time later, Yuan Shang and Yuan Xi sat on comfortable animal skin rugs in Shang's tent and prepared to resume their conversation.

"So, then… what have you awoken to…?" Yuan Shang asked dryly.

"We've not seen their whole 'being' while we've been in the Empire," Yuan Xi suggested.

"*You* haven't," Yuan Shang retorted. "I visited Tadun, Louban, Supuyan and the rest on a number of occasions once I became chieftain: I've seen what you're seeing a fair few times."

"The people are not constantly afraid," Yuan Xi noted. "They laugh and joke, they cook and make clothes, the children play… like any village with no serious worries. All I ever hear – *heard* – from my subordinates was that the Wuhuan are monsters – wicked, immoral murderers and rapists – that we should exterminate for our own good. And that's all that I ever saw of them; the villages after they'd pillaged them, the crying people, the-"

"Dong Zhuo left a similar mark, I think," Yuan Shang interrupted. "Cao Cao did it in Xu Province – his own clan's home region – and the pirates and bandits do very similar things. Most of them were or are 'Han people', like us."

"…I really didn't know that some people were here by choice," Yuan Xi sighed.

"The 'Ten' caused a lot of people to flee: it isn't everyone that joined the Black Mountain Bandits or the Yellow Turbans or some other group of dissidents or cultists or criminals," Yuan Shang said. "No, it isn't that we've got it all the wrong way around about the Wuhuan; *some* Wuhuan people do raid villages and abduct people, rape women, murder people, steal food and animals, and

412

so on... just as *some* 'Han people' do the same thing. The vassals – even men like Shen Pei and Pang Ji that suggested it in the first place – whinged about the marriage alliances, but how many marriage alliances do we make with other 'Han people' that are any better...?"

"...Until my wife was taken by Cao Pi I would not have understood your point quite as well," Yuan Xi admitted. "Yes, I had heard of past sovereigns' harems and the likes of Cao Cao taking women against their will, but... it all felt... as though it might be misinformation, as though it might be misunderstood..."

"We are in quite a situation!" Yuan Shang joked. "Here we are, two Han nobles, trapped in the frontier lands as guests of 'barbarians' that actually don't look so peculiar when dealing with them face-to-face... we haven't the benefit of lofty distance to use to look down upon them anymore, so we must be objective. But the signs that we only choose to see now have always been there... for after all... isn't it the case that Ma Teng and Han Sui, the mightiest of the Qiang warlords, are former Han vassals...?"

"...That is true," Yuan Xi realised. "Wasn't Ma Teng a major in the Liang Province military...?"

"And Han Sui was a local official... and not that low-ranked either," Yuan Shang noted. "Yet now they wear the fur hats and tribal robes of Qiang men and father children with Qiang women. And there are a lot of Han people living in Xiliang voluntarily, people that didn't want to join rebellions and fight the corrupt government... people that just wanted to get away and find peace elsewhere. And they found the peace they sought with the Qiang... so they cannot be all bad."

"...We laugh at their fear of white horses, we scoff at their obsession with strength, and we deride their lack of knowledge of our military tactics, but... we didn't even know that Liaoxi had monsoons at this time of year, and we have our own superstitions," Yuan Xi mused.

"...And we Yuans – a high-ranking noble family – bickered over who should be clan chieftain, with our older brother citing not primogeniture as the basis of his birth right, but *strength*," Yuan Shang said. "Dong Zhuo deposed His Majesty Shaodi citing his *weakness* as the reason... and all the warlords, Father included, recruited men based on their 'strength'... for what else is useful when one is a warlord...?"

"...What a shame it is that we cannot just stay here and live," Yuan Xi sighed.

"I... cannot agree," Yuan Shang admitted. "I hunger for what I have lost, wrong though that might be. I miss the power to do something meaningful; I could not live here as a warrior and spend my time practising horseback archery and wrestling. I miss my books, the art, the musicians and the dancing girls... yes, the Wuhuan girls are pretty enough, but their music does not appeal and they lack literature, even in their own language. I miss 'the trappings', Brother... and I want them back. And yes, I am prepared to fight Cao Cao and risk death to reclaim them. Don't you at least want to avenge your humiliation at the hands of the Caos...? Don't you at least want to go back and rescue Lady Zhen, put Cao Pi's head on a spike and-?"

"I partly agree, and then again I partly don't," Yuan Xi said. "Lady

Zhen is his now, which is something that I must accept. She is his wife, so any attempt to 'reclaim her' – as though she were a wine dish or a fine piece of pottery – would leave her further tainted. The humiliation has happened, and so all I can do now is cut the heads off of men that are still laughing at me, which doesn't undo what's been done. I stayed out of the succession crisis for the same reason that the refugees came to be here in the frontier lands: I didn't want to fight. It's as you said about them... I just want to be somewhere that I can find peace. And Lady Zhen was an arranged bride, so... I can never be sure that we were actually happy anyway."

"You're being cowardly," Yuan Shang suggested. "Or, at least, that is how it will be seen: how do you think the people that ran away from the problems are seen by the ones that stayed and tried to fix them, mm...? Will any children that you do eventually have with whoever you end up with – an exiled Han woman, maybe, or a Wuhuan 'princess' – thank you for condemning them to a life as a tent-dwelling nomad beyond the Great Wall when they eventually learn – and they will – that you were once-"

"That I was once a 'Han nobleman'...?" Yuan Xi scoffed.

"Cao Cao is coming here, so you cannot 'stay here and live in peace'," Yuan Shang heckled. "Sooner or later, Brother, you must fight: why later, when the odds will be stacked even more against you than they are now...?"

Yuan Xi exhaled fiercely and averted his gaze.

"...The problems and their solutions are not wherever you now look to, they're right in front of us," Yuan Shang continued. "You stayed out of the 'succession crisis' – which was entirely the fault of our hankering older brother – because you had no proper place within that crisis other than to take the side of one of us against the other. Yes, I am slightly irritated that you did not show your support for *me*, as Father wished it, but-"

"You were contemplating surrendering to Cao Cao recently, saying that you'd cede the chieftainship or the clan's wealth if you had to, just to survive; now you're prattling about your entitlement again!" Yuan Xi exclaimed. "I'm not the only one that '*was once* a Han nobleman'."

"...Assuming that we've lost, Brother, which we *haven't*," Yuan Shang growled.

"I...! ...Alright, alright, I *would* be running away," Yuan Xi conceded. "I detest the idea of invading the Empire with a Wuhuan army, especially when the army is made up of the ones that like to do all that pillaging that we hate so much, but... but Cao's got the Qiang as his vanguard in the west, so he can't criticise, and all that we're facing out here is certain death. I *do* see that. But the odds..."

"The Wuhuan number in the hundreds of thousands and this is their territory, so if Cao Cao attacks them here after those rains clear, they cannot lose," Yuan Shang suggested. "If he is just securing Yòu Province with his canals and troops, then he is scared of our return: we can then recruit from the refugee men – and, with a little explanation of our motives, from the abducted men as well – and be returning to the Empire with an army of Han men that matches or exceeds the army that Cao stole from us! Will Su Yòu, Lü Kuang, Zhang Hè or any of the others that

abandoned our clan to serve Cao Cao be so sure that they were right when half-a-million Han men and three-hundred-thousand Wuhuan warriors pour over the border and descend on them...?"
Yuan Xi nodded silently.
"And, dear Brother – for I know what concerns you and share your concern – what will those Wuhuan warriors demand from us when a hundred-thousand or more men defect back to us and Cao Cao is defeated...?" Yuan Shang continued. "They will be facing an army of equal or greater numbers on hostile foreign land... and we will not acquiesce to their unreasonable demands for a second time. They will not raid *our lands* any more... they will learn to respect us and accept that Ji and Yòu are *not* former Wuhuan lands as they like to suggest... they will accept that they are Han Imperial provinces."
"...I know that I cannot hide anywhere," Yuan Xi said miserably. "I will remain at your side and fight, Brother and lord, until Cao Cao is vanquished and we are back where we belong, in the Empire, as guardians of the person and laws of the Son of Heaven."
"Well put," Yuan Shang replied. "Don't lose heart... for as Cao Cao once thought that Father seemed to be invincible and defeated him regardless, so we shall turn the tide of this struggle for a second time and restore order. It is Heaven's will."

****

86

Cao Cao was visibly moved when a white-robed envoy from Zhang Xiu's travelling party entered his great hall, bowed low and said, "Your Excellency, I... I must report that my Lord Zhang Xiu has passed away...!"
Xiahou Dun, Cao Hong and many of Cao Cao's other close allies and relations were forced to conceal their satisfaction at the news.
"...I am truly saddened!" Cao Cao proclaimed. "I will ensure that his marquisate title – though awarded by the false regents – is, as thanks for his recent work for the Han cause, preserved, and that he is treated with the utmost respect!"
"Why?" Cao Hong asked.
"...Say no more," Cao Cao retorted. "Marquis Zhang will be remembered for his merits, not his faults! You may go now, envoy, and I will forward appropriate condolences to his family."
Zhang Xiu's envoy retreated after casting a cutting glance in Jia Xu's direction.
"...You're not really upset, are you, Mengde...?" Xiahou Dun asked.
"Strange though it might seem... yes, I am," Cao Cao replied. "Zhang Xiu taught me a valuable lesson that I must never forget."
"I wonder if I might be allowed to take the condolence letter to the Zhang family, Your Excellency," Jia Xu said.
"It was my intention," Cao Cao replied. "And... and as mercenary an attitude as it might be, Mister Jia... I would like to know that General Huche'er intends to continue his march and provide the support that his late lord promised me."
"Rest assured that I will discover his intentions," Jia Xu said.
"...So who is the Magistrate of Nan County now that Zhang is gone...?" Cao Xiu asked.
"It can remain under Li Tong's control for now," Cao Cao replied. "That place is a vital base for my future battles with Liu Biao, so I cannot afford to let the county fall into the hands of another, especially Liu Biao."
"That is quite right," Yuan Huan said.

The signs of mourning in Nan County were too obvious for Liu Biao and Liu Bei to miss them; Liu Bei went to Jing's northern capital Xiangyang once again and asked to speak with the governor.
"No 'Crouching Dragon' this time, Xuande...?" Liu Biao sniggered.
"He is busy reorganising my troops and acquainting them with complex arrays at the moment," Liu Bei explained. "But enough of that, Jingsheng! It is quite obvious that something has changed in Nan County! The-!"
"Zhang Xiu is dead," Liu Biao interrupted. "Yes, I'm aware of it."
"...So it is true, then," Liu Bei murmured.
"Yes it is, but I will not be acting upon it," Liu Biao insisted. "So you might as well go back to Xinye or Bowang or wherever it is that you and your militia are currently operating."
"Why are you being so distant, Jingsheng...?" Liu Bei asked. "I am here to suggest that we take back what is yours from an enemy! If needs be, I'll take Nan County back with my own men, with your consent!"
"After which I presume that you'd like to be named the

magistrate...?" Liu Biao asked cuttingly.

"...*Aiee*... you have allowed your advisers and your kin to poison you against me wrongly and groundlessly!" Liu Bei exclaimed. "Have I harmed you...?"

Liu Biao faltered; he cupped his head in his hands and said, "I... do not know who I can trust anymore, Xuande! My advisers only want what's best and have defended me against many an enemy, but when they speak ill of you it confuses me! But I am surrounded by hankerers! I recently suffered the repeated suggestion that I supplant Huang Zu – who is 'becoming feeble and incompetent', so some say – with my eldest son Qi, but can I do that when it loses me the Huangs of Jiangxia and the many, many vassals that serve them and not me...?"

"I do not know what to say," Liu Bei replied. "Some of the officials seem to be discussing your successor, which is most distasteful. Some act as though I intend some sort of coup, which I most certainly do not; others want to see primogeniture dictate the issue and rightly state that Qi is your successor though there is no need for such a discussion at present; others, it seems, are coalescing around your younger son Cong..."

"...Say no more of it, Xuande," Liu Biao pleaded. "I feel like there is some hideous curse affecting all of the great men in the land! Yuan Shao and Yuan Shu dragged us all into that succession row of theirs, and then Shao's sons destroyed themselves after their father's death by arguing over the succession when the answer was clear; the plotters appointed the youngest as heir – which made no sense at all – and, once again, we all pay the price!"

"So true," Liu Bei said, "but-!"

"Cao Cao has, thanks to the late Zhang Xiu's actions at Wan City ten long years ago, been left with a deviant as his heir that steals married women from their living husbands and fathers children with the women out of wedlock!" Liu Biao continued. "Even the throne is beset with strife, what with the incumbent being where he is thanks to the forced abdication of his brother and subsequent regicide by Dong Zhuo!"

"But he is the true Son of Heaven!" Liu Bei protested.

"I don't contest that!" Liu Biao retorted. "I am just pointing out that the great heroes of the land, good or evil, are all being brought down by their heirs, one way or another! Look at Liu Yan! Alright, he turned away from the light when he joined forces with the Qiang and attacked Chang'an, but he was still a hero that stabilised Yi Province and brought the heretic Zhang Lu to heel! Now look at what's happened: all three of his worthy eldest sons died in various ways, leaving his fourth son, the inept Liu Zhang, to inherit and ultimately undo all of his good work!"

"There are other interpretations, Jingsheng, but I see your point," Liu Bei said.

"Now it is my turn!" Liu Biao continued. "Everything is clear... or at least it *was*! I, a scion of the royal house, am governor by royal appointment, and my eldest son, Qi, is to inherit the province: it should be as simple as that! But instead, Xuande, I have Cao Cao calling me a rebel and trying to 'arrest me' and take the province, no doubt for one of his many sons to rule; I have Sun Quan blaming me for his father's death and trying to steal Jing as 'reparation'; and then I have my advisers divided on whether my

sickly eldest son or my unequipped, juvenile younger son should
inherit the province – if it isn't stolen by Cao or Sun first – while I
am far from being dry bones! And when all of the suspicions about
you are added to it... it makes me ill!"

"...I can say nothing to change things," Liu Bei sighed.

"No, you can't... and invading Nan County won't make things any
better," Liu Biao replied. "Cao Cao is in Yè, his lackey Du Ji is in
nearby Hedong, and the man that Cao's left in Nan County, Li
Tong, is apparently quite competent. And that's all without
considering Cao's dozens of famous generals and thousands of
men that he now has since stealing everything from the Yuans.
We must let him go northward as he obviously intends and hope
that it is Heaven's will that he fails and presents the Son of
Heaven with the chance to issue another decree. Fighting Cao Cao
at the height of his powers isn't just folly: it's suicide."

"...I will say no more of attacking Nan County," Liu Bei declared.
"But it is a shame... because Zhang was always a man that might,
just might, be bargained with, and now it is Cao's loyal man in
Nan County."

"I thought you said that you'd 'say no more'," Liu Biao chortled.
"What, then, is 'saying something else'...?"

Liu Bei bowed humbly and left Liu Biao's private study.

"...I am so *tired*," Liu Biao groaned. "Whatever *next*...?"

Weeks passed.

The Han army's preparations for war were suddenly halted by the
news that the planned route had been hit by heavy rains; Cao Cao
hurried to Guo Jia and begged an audience with him via his son Yi.

"...Have... the monsoons come, then...?" Guo Jia chuckled as he
shuffled into his living quarters.

"*Ayah*... you knew about them?" Cao Cao despaired.

"A better question... might be 'Why didn't *you*...?'" Guo Jia retorted
as Guo Yi lowered him to his seat. "I think that the second of... the
'Five Fundmentals' that... that Sun Tzu refers to in his opening
statements in the 'Art of War' covered 'knowing the seasons', Lord
Cao: it isn't... exactly hidden away. Part of 'knowing the seasons'
is knowing weath- ...weather conditions that arise from those
seasons in a... given area."

Cao Cao was silent.

"Every battle is... is affected by the weather, just as they are
affected by the time of day," Guo Jia continued. "They're all
affected, even if it is- ...is just by the absence of it. The Wuhuan
knew... about the rain and winds... and you did not. That handed
them an easy first morale victory, didn't it...?"

"We can't be sure that the Wuhuan knew of the rains," Cao Cao
said irritably.

"They're traditionally *nomadic*, Mengde... they move around to
avoid droughts, famines, and... *monsoons* and such," Guo Jia
wheezed. "It's only us 'civilised' *fools* that... insist on staying
somewhere that changes so dramatically."

"I feel foolish," Cao Cao admitted.

"But will you *remain* foolish...?" Guo Jia retorted. "That's... not up
to me... n-never was and... *won't be*."

"...Your plan for swift movement," Cao Cao said humbly. "It will be met with cynicism, or maybe even *derision*... what do I-?"

"Implement it or don't," Guo Jia replied. "It will work... if it is given a chance."

"...Why must you wither, Fengxiao...?" Cao Cao pleaded. "I need your guidance!"

"There are other clever m-men, Mengde," Guo Jia replied. "Listen to them as you have I-listened to me, and you will still be alright."

"...I have promoted Hua Xin to a senior military adviser as you suggested, but... I will not forget your contribution to my cause," Cao Cao promised.

"You've... said as much before," Guo Jia retorted.

"Yes, but... I am leaving Yè shortly," Cao Cao explained. "I will be going to Yijing, as you know, and... and you will be... remaining here, will you not."

"I can't come with you, that m-much is certain!" Guo Jia joked.

"...Yes... it is," Cao Cao said as he got to his feet. "So this... is 'goodbye', Fengxiao."

Guo Yi fought tears as he watched his father and Cao Cao have what would likely be their final conversation.

"You have the w-words of wisdom, Mengde... mine and others. All you need to do is... read them or hear them and *heed them*... *understand them*," Guo Jia said seriously. "That and always remember... 's-swiftness is...'"

"...'Swiftness is the key in war'," Cao Cao sighed. "I will always remember your words of wisdom."

"N-not... *my* wisdom... a *shared* wisdom, across ages," Guo Jia replied painfully. "The principle is in... the 'Art of War'. Read and... you'll find it."

Cao Cao fell to his knees and clasped Guo Jia's hands tightly, saying, "Fengxiao! The world can do without me, but can it do without you...?"

"It will go on," Guo Jia replied with a smile. "So will you."

Cao Cao released Guo Jia's hands and slowly got to his feet for a second time.

"...Farewell, Mengde," Guo Jia said. "Go and make your name."

Cao Cao fell to his knees for a second time and kowtowed to Guo Jia as if he were the emperor; Guo Jia sighed sadly but lacked the strength to respond as he wanted to. His tribute completed, Cao Cao rose for a third time and left his adviser of 10 years to the care of Guo Yi and the rest of his family.

****

87

Yuan Shang's attempts at recruiting men from the Han Chinese migrants proved to be more difficult and less rewarding than he had anticipated: many were openly bitter and considered the Yuan clan to be part of the problem.

"**Go away!**" one man shrieked. "**You're all the same!**"

Yuan Xi turned and looked at the small number of men that had chosen to join his brother; some were wavering as the disaffected made their feelings known.

"**I did not force you to leave the Empire!**" Yuan Shang protested. "**Was it not the 'Ten Attendants' that were the source of the rampant corruption...?**"

"**You're a Ru County Yuan!**" a second man heckled. "**Your family was always close to the throne and did nothing to change things!**"

"**Yeah, and my family fled your father's war with Gongsun Zan!**" the first man said. "**Don't come here and tell us you're different! What will you do different to your father...?**"

Yuan Xi looked at Yuan Shang, who replied, "**I vow to you that I will go back, fight Cao Cao, liberate the north, and then rescue the Son of Heaven and restore order to the Empire so that we can all-!**"

"**All that is is 'Fight', 'Fight', 'Rescue'!**" the second man said. "**You want us all to be your soldiers so you can fight Cao Cao like your father did!**"

"**But I will restore order to the Empire and bring change!**" Yuan Shang protested.

"**Bugger off!**" a third man shouted.

"*Aiee...* **I give up!**" Yuan Shang cried as the potential recruits started to heckle him; he turned to those that had already agreed to serve him and said, "**Let's go!**"

Yuan Shang and Yuan Xi led the relatively small group of recruits away from the civilian camp.

"...So are we going to try the abducted people now...?" Yuan Xi asked snidely.

"I don't expect such taunts from you, Brother," Yuan Shang retorted. "We're both dead if we cannot get more than a hundred men to join us! Tens of thousands live out here! We have to keep trying! We have to make recruiters of our recruits and send them back to state our case to the rest!"

"But how long will that take, Brother?" Yuan Xi asked. "There aren't many charismatic generals among the men we've recruited... in fact, they're-"

"They're the insightful ones," Yuan Shang insisted. "They must go back to the rest and explain that this supposedly safe life that they have made here will soon be destroyed by a horde of Cao Cao's worst, just as it was in Xu Province fourteen years ago! Some of these people fled the war between Cao Cao and Tao Qian, others from the war between Cao and Lü Bu! We can start with them! No, we'll probably have to give up on the ones that blame Father's war with Gongsun for their misfortune, but that's not the majority! A lot of them wavered when we mentioned the

'Ten'! Father slaughtered the 'Ten', and if it weren't for Dong Zhuo perpetuating and building upon the harm caused by the 'Ten' then they might have felt safe to return!"

"...That's true," Yuan Xi conceded.

"We're not through yet," Yuan Shang insisted. "And for once, time is on our side; we won't be seeing Cao Cao for a while, and when he does appear... he'll die."

****

88

Cao Cao became increasingly nervous as he travelled to Yijing, which was the site of the warlord Gongsun Zan's defeat at the hands of Yuan Shao 8 years earlier; his own chances of victory over Yuan Shao's surviving sons were now being called into question as the rains became heavier and heavier. The arrival at Yijing was, therefore, a sombre affair: Cao retired to his designated command headquarters and watched as Registrar Liu Yè, the trainee registrar Yang Xiu and a small team of servants hurriedly turned the living quarters of the governor's mansion into a 'war room'.

"...Even Fengxiao's plan cannot work now, surely," Cao Cao muttered. "Damn these rains!"

"We have not been enlightened, Your Excellency," Chen Qun replied. "What *is* the plan, exactly...?"

"...Perhaps it is folly to pursue any sort of march right now," Cao Cao sighed. "I have never advocated marching weary men through bitter cold and pounding rain... not even for a campaign as vital as this one."

"It would be folly to leave the Wuhuan with three months to regain their confidence, and it would be even more folly to let the Yuans go unchecked for the same amount of time, not when they are in possession of a hundred-thousand captured men that might be compelled or won over," Chen Qun suggested.

"I agree," Jia Xu said quietly.

Cao Cao looked to his latest acquisition – the former Wuhuan captive Yan Rou – who shook his head and said, "You cannot risk retreat after advancing so far, or they'll see it as weakness: that is an obvious fact that any man that's dealt with them for a moment can tell you, Excellency. And if you do not deal with them now, they'll be back, and next time they'll take *more* people, cause *more* harm..."

"...Too true," Qian Zhao sighed. "I can't advocate turning back now either, Excellency, not now I've seen so many abducted."

"...We must continue onward, gentlemen," Cao Cao decided. "I could sit here, as Gongsun Zan once did, waiting for the enemy to come back, but I prefer to seize full control of Yuyang Prefecture since Xianyu Fu appears to be unable to."

The advisers exchanged nervous glances.

"...Your silence implies that you are worried that I intend to inflict some horror on Tian Chou," Cao Cao chuckled. "If he surrenders, that won't be necessary."

Cao Cao left his campaign base at Yijing and moved east and north, toward the centre of Yuyang Prefecture; the last remnants of Wuhuan and rebel fighters proved to be small obstacles, and the Han army reached the outskirts of Wuzhong County – seat of the official Tian Chou – in swift order.

"...He will know that I am coming," Cao Cao said as he stared eastward. "But what will he do...?"

"He did not come here to serve the Yuans," Yuan Huan noted.

"No... he came here to get away from *me*," Cao Cao retorted.

"Not necessarily, Your Excellency," Jia Xu said. "Mister Tian was a loyal servant of Yòu Province Governor Liu Yu, who, as we know, was murdered by Gongsun Zan and his son, Liu Hè, captured by Yuan Shu. As we also know, Yu's son escaped Shu's custody and joined Yuan Shao's campaign against Gongsun Zan, but he then 'disappeared' after Yuan Shao's conquest of the province; Mister Tian could not come here to search for clues as to his lord's son's whereabouts while the son of Liu Yu's murderer-by-proxy, Yuan Shao, was Governor, but with the collapse of Shao's army at Guandu came an opportunity that his 'reservations about the government structure' gave secondary 'motivation to action' to."

"...I can see how that violent bumpkin Dong Zhuo and those two cretin regents held onto power for as long as they did," Chen Qun heckled. "You could make *anything* justifiable, couldn't you...?"

Jia Xu sighed miserably.

"Tian Chou *walked away*!" Chen Qun continued. "I have tried to be fair to him, but he should have surrendered when his current lord, Prefectural Administrator Xianyu Fu, did so a year ago!"

"...You are both correct, gentlemen, so all that remains is to see what Mister Tian Chou now does," Cao Cao declared. "Let us continue onward."

Word of Cao Cao's approach reached Wuzhong County's capital: Magistrate Tian Chou summoned his officials and said, "I intend to submit to the Excellency of Works."

"*Aiee...* I cannot fathom you, Magistrate!" one official cried. "We might, could and should have done that already if that was always your intention!"

Tian Chou smiled and said, "I believe that there is a proper time for everything, gentlemen, and that the proper time is now. Send a man to inform His Excellency of my decision at once."

Cao Cao was delighted when Tian Chou's submission request reached him; the two were finally reunited at the western gates of Wuzhong City, where Magistrate Tian brought his seal of office on a wooden tray and presented it as a sign of his deference.

"Why have you waited so long for this moment, Tian Zitai...?" Cao Cao asked.

"Wuzhong is where you need to be, Your Excellency," Tian Chou replied. "I have remained neutral as the Yuans did battle and various factions rose and fell, and I know everything that is to be known about the situation here. As an additional selfish point, this is my home, the place where I was born, and so I had to be here and see that it survived that harm that was being done."

"...But you left my service because you doubted me, also," Cao Cao prompted.

"No man should draw his conclusions about a matter by only looking at one aspect, else he is not truly seeking the right answers," Tian Chou replied. "Yes, I had doubts, as all open-minded men should, but by coming back here and seeing the state of the Yuan clan's little personal empire from within, I could judge who was best placed to restore order if that had been my concern... and I wonder if it ever was."

"Such an evasive answer, Zitai!" Cao Cao chuckled.

"I prefer to see it as an answer that reflects the uncertainty of the times," Tian Chou insisted. "But that is not the point... the point,

Lord Cao, is that this place was not at all benefitting from Yuan clan rule, not while they allowed abusive factions of the Wuhuan to act as they pleased. Since your arrival here the Wuhuan have retreated and the people have rejoiced; if Dong Cheng's slanderous, groundless document had been allowed to dictate the scheme of things then Wuzhong County would be a living hell. Those that call you the 'Hero of Chaos' do so out of spite, for any man that truly looks can see that the chaos is driven out whenever you set foot in a place, Your Excellency, and that makes you a hero of order."

"...It pleases me to hear that," Cao Cao admitted. "I-... ... ...Never mind. Let us get through the formalities: I accept your submission, Magistrate Tian, but I refuse to take the seal. You will remain as the magistrate until a more fitting post can be found for you, Mister Tian."

Tian Chou bowed humbly and said, "I thank you for your magnanimity, Excellency."

"...Wuzhong is strategically critical to any attack on the Wuhuan peoples," Cao Cao continued. "I intend to march into their territory beyond the Wall and destroy them."

"Oh, really...?" Tian Chou chuckled.

"...You are cynical," Cao Cao supposed.

"Not at all," Tian Chou replied. "It is a challenge, for sure, but... well, I'm sure that your resourcefulness will win out in the end, Excellency. Will you accompany me to my residence to banquet your officials...? You must all be in need of some light relief after your recent trials."

"Indeed yes," Cao Cao sighed.

Cao Cao's reacquisition of Tian Chou was an important victory for a number of reasons that were immediately obvious to his advisers: it vindicated the Excellency of Works as a statesman, showed that he was a magnanimous lord and proved that he was a capable military tactician. But fate would have it that Tian Chou would provide one further victory that was far less indirect and far more important: he would soon prove to be critical to the outcome of the Wuhuan pacification campaign, which might, under other circumstances, have had a very different conclusion.

****

89

A week passed: Cao Cao's army left Wuzhong and continued to move eastward, but the monsoon rains worsened and reports came in that spoke of the sandy soil terrain that Cao Cao's army had intended to traverse becoming seas of impassable mud.
"We can't march through mud," Yuan Huan said. "And with the reports suggesting that it is knee-deep in some places and waist or even *neck-deep* in others…"
"I am truly at a loss," Cao Cao admitted. "The Wuhuan are, perhaps, completely safe for at least the next three months while we wait for the roads to become passable again. But by then…"
"Your Excellency… we cannot leave them be," Chen Qun suggested. "There must be some way to get to them… there *must be*. Perhaps the reports are exaggerated."
Tian Chou hummed quietly.
"…Guo Fengxiao spoke of the rains as 'monsoons' and spoke of them being a long, miserable affair," Cao Cao recalled. "But I have come this far: sound the advance, General Zhang!"
Zhang Liao sent word that the soaked, miserable army of men should continue along the road to the coastline, and they reluctantly complied.
"The supplies are getting soaked," Jia Xu noted.
"***Everything* is getting soaked!**" Chen Qun cried.
"But as you have said, we must continue," Cao Cao sighed.

The weather reports were proven to be true: the vast majority of the terrain was all but impassable and the heavy rain and winds pounded the soldiers until they were ready to weep.
"…**Will the accursed rains never cease???**" Cao Cao shrieked.
"We are almost at a river that we can use to reduce the burden, Excellency," Chen Qun noted. "The scouts report that the riverbanks have kept their integrity and provide a-"
"**AAAAAAAGH! MY LEG! MY LEG!**"
A group of soldiers had strayed from the main road and become trapped in the swampy mud; several of their colleagues rushed to aid them, but the situation was exacerbated when a poorly-attended supply cart almost tipped over as the ground gave way underneath it.
"…This was madness," Cao Cao sobbed. "I should not have done this! The humiliation will be my ruin!"
"Don't admit defeat just yet, my lord," Tian Chou pleaded. "Let us see what the river offers us in the way of options… and then plan from there."
Cao Cao eyed Tian Chou cautiously and said, "I… shall you as you say, Zitai."

The terrain in the Liaoxi region that led to the sea was, in itself, a muddy sea; one river provided possible salvation to the Han army as the rains defied expectation by being even heavier and even more demoralising. Local fishing vessels and the small number of military boats were quickly confiscated in order to use them to cross the river, but hopes were quickly dashed when a small group of Wuhuan warriors attacked the boats as they reached the northern banks.

"Order them back! ORDER THEM BACK!" Cao Cao shrieked; his voice then cracked and he succumbed to a heavy cough. Cao Xiu, Zhang Liao and Yue Jin joined the rescue efforts and managed to bring some of the men back, but the supplies were lost and the majority of the boats were captured, sunk or left to drift downstream. The Wuhuan hollered triumphantly and heckled the Han soldiers, who were mostly too sickly, wet, cold and demoralised to demand a response.

"RETREAT!" Jia Xu ordered. **"Back to the camp!"**

Cao Cao entered his Liaoxi command tent and sat on his low stool; he winced as he realised that he had sat on his drenched battle cape.

"...We can't get past their defences," Cao Chun suggested. "It's dark, wet, cold, windy and just about every other bad thing; my cavalry won't be of much use."

"The oxen are not as robust as they look," Li Dian noted. "We none of us are up to such conditions."

"I... know all that," Cao Cao said as he removed his cape with Registrar Liu Yè's help. "I cannot go forward at nature's decree... but I cannot go back at my reputation's decree. If I am forced to retreat, gentlemen, then I will be the laughing stock of all the land. The Qiang will rise up, defiant elements in Qing will rise up, Liu Biao and Liu Bei will march on Xuchang-"

"And the sky will rain piglets, and tigers will emerge from the wells to devour the washerwomen, and rats with human heads will come out of the ground to nibble our shoes, and fish the size of horses will laugh at us as we sail by them," Cheng Yu heckled. "What calamities await us if we cannot go on!"

Several men stifled smiles as Cao Cao huffed and replied, "That helps us in no way, Mister Cheng!"

"And neither does your whinging, Excellency!" Cheng Yu retorted. "We will either have to wait for another opportunity when the rains clear or we must find another route if one exists!"

"...Yes... *if* one exists," Cao Cao grumbled. "There certainly isn't another way near here, is there...? Is there another way in some other place...?"

The question was met with silence.

"...Mister Yan Rou, you were... well, we all know that you were their prisoner for a long time, and that they forced you to accompany sorties as a 'beast of burden'," Cao Cao said. "Did they ever speak of other roads in and out of the Empire...? Were you ever led into the Empire by some other route...?"

"If they did know of other roads, Excellency, then they never used them," Yan Rou replied. "They used to go around the Wall via the beach, just as we're trying to do."

"...Where is Mister Tian Chou...?" Cao Cao asked.

"He was sent back to his tent to give instruction to his own men," Jia Xu reported.

"Zitai... knows Wuzhong better than any man here," Cao Cao said. "If any man can get us out of this 'calamity', it is Tian Zitai. Summon him, please."

"I will go, Excellency," Yang Xiu said.

"No... I should go," Registrar Liu Yè insisted.

"Be quick, Mister Liu," Cao Cao murmured. "In the meantime, you gentlemen shall retire and I shall change out of these clothes."
The officials retreated quietly.

Within an hour, Wuzhong Magistrate Tian Chou was sat before Cao Cao, who was now dressed in his state robes; Jia Xu, Cheng Yu, Chen Qun, Yuan Huan, Yan Rou and Liu Yè were the only ones that had returned for the meeting.
"You have come back to me willingly, Zitai, so I hope that my request is not asking too much of you too quickly," Cao Cao began. "I... I very much need your guidance."
Chen Qun harrumphed quietly.
"...Your Excellency desires an alternative route to the lands beyond the Wall so that the campaign may continue," Tian Chou guessed.
"Tadun has matched me," Cao Cao admitted. "Far from being a talentless brute, he has ensured that the mountain passes are watched, the rivers are guarded, and there is doubtlessly a large force awaiting us if we should somehow get around the coastline."
"Indeed, Excellency, it is the case that the conventional route is, by the will of Heaven and the unexpected professionalism of Tadun's defences, beyond our usage," Tian Chou replied. "It is very much the case that every known road will be similarly impassable... but there is one road that they will not guard, a road that, if taken in this desperate hour, will allow us to attack where they do not expect us to and take Tadun's head without fighting a single battle to a drawn-out conclusion."
"Oh...?" Cao Cao exclaimed. "What road is it that you speak of...?"
"I should like to know that myself," Cheng Yu scoffed. "What magical road is this, Tian Zitai...?"
Tian Chou smiled and said, "There is a road to the north of Wuzhong that was once used to advance into the frontier lands."
"**To the *north of Wuzhong*...?**" Chen Qun cried. "**Then why did you allow us to march to the *east* all of this way, you-!**"
"Hear him out," Cao Cao ordered.
"...I did not suggest it because it carries its own hazards that might have exceeded the ones that we have, unfortunately, found here in Liaoxi," Tian Chou insisted. "It should be of no surprise to any that know what is directly north of Wuzhong..."
"...The Xianbei territories," Cheng Yu sighed.
Cao Cao looked at Yan Rou, who shrugged and said, "Elder Cheng would be right: any roads north of Wuzhong would lead to the Xianbei territories, where the Wuhuan would never dare go unless looking for a war."
"*Ayah*... **that's no option!**" Chen Qun cried. "Why would *we* risk a confrontation with them when-!"
"If... if the only way through is by way of that road and past the Xianbei, then so be it," Cao Cao declared. "Budugen will have his opportunity to strike at us if he is indeed capable... though our reconnaissance shows that to be unlikely."
"That's quite right," Tian Chou said. "Since the death of Tanshihuai, the stability of the Xianbei Confederacy has diminished considerably: they have done their best to hide the weakness, but Budugen – who is, admittedly, a better ruler than Tanshihuai's inept son and Budugen's older brother ever were – does not inspire as Tanshihuai did, so we have little to fear so long

as we do not attack them or are mistakenly perceived to be intending to."

"...By being erroneously seen to 'borrow passage to destroy Guo'...?" Yuan Huan suggested.

"Precisely," Tian Chou replied. "We must make it clear that we do not intend to loiter or establish bases on their borders."

"That only adds greater importance to following Guo Fengxiao's plan properly... as I should have done in the first place," Cao Cao said. "We will do as you suggest, Zitai, and march northward from Wuzhong, using this forgotten road to take us into the frontier lands, and from there we will travel eastward, behind their defensive positions, and advance to the sea to resume the march to Liucheng from the coast. Such a route will confound and divide the Wuhuan and convince Budugen that we will not be confronting the Xianbei... this time."

"Let us hope that we never have to," Tian Chou replied. "They have their lands and we have ours; if neither side advances, then peace is achievable."

"...Yuan Huan, Chen Qun, Jia Xu: distribute orders to retreat," Cao Cao said. "We will, of course, insinuate that this is a *full retreat*..."

Tadun laughed when his scouts repeatedly brought word of Cao Cao's difficulties in advancing, but the news of the retreat was met with some initial scepticism.

"I don't believe it," Yuan Shang said.

"Why not?" Tadun asked tersely.

"Cao Cao is stubborn to a fault, as Xingyang proved," Yuan Shang replied. "Every single one of his campaigns, in truth, is begun with impetuous, stubborn advance when all others say that it is foolish to do so. I don't believe that a man that marches against armies that are four to five times the size of his own would retreat because it is raining."

"Go, then, and see how far you can get," Louban heckled. "The mud will swallow you up to your waist, or even your neck! The rivers are swollen!"

"And guarded," Tadun said. "As are the mountain roads."

"All the same," Yuan Shang retorted, "the-"

"He leaves signs for his lost men!" Tadun said angrily. "They say that-! ...What did they say...?"

Yuan Shang scoffed as a Wuhuan scout passed a transcription of the roadside sign to Tadun.

"Why do you laugh...?" Louban asked.

"...He laughs because he is arrogant," Tadun said as he read the transcription. "The sign says 'The summer weather is bad, the... road can- ...cannot be passed, and... and we-"

"It'll be quicker to pass it to me to read for myself, great chieftain," Yuan Shang suggested dryly.

"...It would," Tadun growled as he thrust his letter-bearing hand out for Yuan Shang to take it from him.

"...'Notice to all: the summer weather is obstructive, making the road impassable,'" Yuan Shang relayed. "...'We are now waiting until the summer rains have passed; return the way you came at His Excellency's decree.'."

"Well, Mister Yuan...?" Louban asked as Yuan Shang lowered the letter to his lap.

"...It is written in the proper manner," Yuan Shang replied. "And... and if the weather is as bad as I am led to believe, then perhaps he has genuinely retreated for now. Perhaps... perhaps we are safe as you predicted we would be."

"Cao Cao cannot come here," Tadun insisted. "We – *you* – are 'safe', Yuan Shang."

"So we will have time to build our army," Yuan Xi said.

"Indeed we will, Brother," Yuan Shang replied. "Indeed we will!"

****

90

Cao Cao's demoralised army returned to Wuzhong without common knowledge of the full plan: the generals waited to vent their frustration until the first official meeting was held in a camp on the eastern Wuzhong County border.

"Do you know how many of my men are sick…?" Xiahou Dun asked. "Cousin Mengde, I don't usually like to confront you, but–!"

"It… is understandable," Cao Cao conceded.

"This retreat goes against your every principle, Excellency, and so it makes no sense," Zhang Liao suggested. "Never, since I yielded to you in Xiapi eight years ago, have I known you to so quickly turn your back to an enemy."

"Quite right, General Zhang," Li Dian agreed. "I am hoping that there is some plan that we are now to be informed of."

Cao Cao smirked and said, "There is, indeed, a plan."

The officials exchanged glances and mutterings.

"It has come to my attention that there is a road to the north of Wuzhong County that will take us to where we want to go," Cao Cao continued.

"…Any road to the north of Wuzhong would take us into the Xianbei territories, where they graze their animals and practice their horsemanship," Zhang Liao noted. "We would be unwise to loiter there for long, Excellency."

"And that, in itself, will be impossible to avoid if we adhere to the logic associated with a successful march," Li Dian suggested. "I–"

"Here he goes… the 'expert on supplies'," Yue Jin heckled.

"*Aiee*… I am trying to make a valid point!" Li Dian despaired. "Do you want your men to march, demoralised and tired as they already are, with inadequate rations???"

"It is precisely *my* intent, General Li, even if it is not General Yue's," Cao Cao announced.

"Are you joking?" Cheng Yu asked.

"Not at all," Cao Cao replied. "Guo Fengxiao has recommended to me but one thing throughout his magnificent tenure: *speed*, for 'swiftness is the key in war'. Yes, I know; it says such a thing in Sun Tzu's 'Art of War', and Fengxiao himself remarked to me that he merely 'shares wisdom' with that great master. Were we all to *read the thing* instead of carrying it around like some sort of magical military talisman that will grant us victory by virtue of its very possession, then–"

"I ask again, for your own sake," Cheng Yu interrupted as disaffected murmuring turned to irritated heckling. "Are you joking, Excellency?"

"Absolutely not," Cao Cao replied. "We will achieve the swiftness that victory demands by doing as Guo Fengxiao suggested to me before we left: we will advance at double-time – or triple-time, if at all possible – into the Wuhuan territory, taking days where weeks would be expected and hours where there should be days. We will achieve this great speed by not having the usual baggage train that slows down the–"

"We cannot march an army of thousands – *tens of thousands* – through hostile enemy territory without food, water or additional clothes, weapons and regular rest periods!" Li Dian protested.

"I reluctantly agree with the 'master of supplies'," Yue Jin said. "That isn't doable, not for an army of this size."

"I expected more ambition from you, Yue Jin," Cao Cao retorted.

"'Fengxiao' is obviously suffering a malady of the brain in addition to his rotting body," Chen Qun said angrily. "How dare he suggest such a destructive idea and then be too sick to be here to see it fail! When I next see that fool, I-!"

"That meeting is unlikely to take place," Cao Cao interrupted. "And if any of you know of a better way to continue our campaign and not do the most demoralising and damaging thing of all – retreat and give the Yuan brothers and the Wuhuan time to build a grand army to invade the Empire, to name just that one consequence – then *please*, gentlemen... enlighten me."

The question was met by silence.

"...I thought so," Cao Cao continued. "Gentlemen, we will follow Fengxiao's plan – quite possibly his last plan – through to the end, whatever that end might be. With Tian Chou's help, we have one last chance, a road that is not known to our enemies: a road that we can use to go northward and strike at them unexpectedly. Let us not waste such a chance to end the chaos."

"It is certainly doable, though far from straightforward," Zhang Hè said. "The utmost discipline would need to be enforced, especially when we are passing the Xianbei crop fields."

"My men will know the penalties for even the smallest crime," Yue Jin promised.

"Every man will need to know the penalty for failure: the complete destruction of the Han Empire and with it our entire way of life," Cao Cao said ominously. "We will have the Qiang, the Southern Xiongnu and Liu Biao behind us, the million-strong Xianbei Confederacy to the west and our intended target – three-hundred-thousand or more Wuhuan tribesmen and a quarter-of-a-million confused Han migrants – to the east and north of us. We cannot afford to fail."

The statement was met by sombre silence.

"...You're all dismissed," Cao Cao continued. "You will prepare your men for this, the greatest campaign undertaken in our time; and once again, I stress to you... don't any of you underestimate what we are about to do or allow others to do so. Go."

The officers left the command tent quietly and thoughtfully.

"It makes no *sense*," Cheng Yu grumbled. "How can none but *Tian Chou* know of this road...?"

Tian Chou lowered his head and exhaled miserably.

"...And *no baggage train*...?" Chen Qun murmured.

"*Yes*, Mister Chen Qun, no baggage train!" Cao Cao snapped. **"And *yes*, Mister Cheng Yu, knowledge of the road's existence is lost to all but the most studious! What guided me to my victories over Yuan Shao and him to his ridiculous losses, mm...? How did Dong Zhuo, most ignorant and stupid of men, confound us all...? To be more relevant, which men knew of the northeast region's monsoon rains, then, such that this road's little-known existence is so strange...? To be more relevant still, did we not defeat Gao Gan recently because he knew nothing of roads that were within walking distance of his fortress???"**

"That... is all quite true," Cheng Yu admitted. "Excellency, I... I...!"

"I... as Elder Cheng now struggles to say... I hope that the Heavens truly favour us," Yuan Huan sighed.

"So do I, Yaoqing," Cao Cao replied as he clutched his aching head. "So do I, because we have been pushed to this... which means that the inevitable destruction of our culture, our history and our people that would follow defeat would then be the will of Heaven: *that*, more than *anything*, would make no sense."

Cao Cao's weary army was allowed to rest for a few days before the next phase of the campaign began. Morale had been harmed by the trials of the eastward march, and Cao Cao knew it; he summoned Jia Xu, Hua Xin and Cheng Yu for one last pre-march meeting and said, "I might gain some comfort from discussing the future times."

"The future that springs forth from a victory here in the north will be a brilliant one, Your Excellency," Hua Xin replied. "The rebels in Jing and Jiangdong will either surrender or be crushed by the half-a-million men that you will have under your command after such an endeavour as this one. Men will call for you to be rewarded with a-"

"Stop there," Cao Cao ordered. "I appreciate that you correctly read my need for a positive vision to look toward, Mister Hua, but I do not want that vision to include what some might consider as 'sycophantic' predictions about my career prospects."

Hua Xin bowed humbly and said, "I meant no such offence."

"If you say so," Cheng Yu grumbled. "But I see no point in looking to the future for 'comfort', Excellency. What is ahead of us other than more wars...? Even if Liu Biao, Liu Bei and Sun Quan bend at the knee, there's the Shanyue of the Jiangdong region, the Di and Qiang of Liang Province, the Nanman people that live to the south of Yi Province, numerous pirates, bandit armies and-"

"*Why*, Elder Cheng...?" Cao Cao cried. "*Why, why, why* do you insist on being so miserable, pessimistic and frankly *irritating* at such a moment...?"

Cheng Yu lowered his gaze.

"I am aware that I face many fights in the future," Cao Cao continued. "I am not a fool: I know that one of the worst fights – be it with pen or sword – will be with my own distrusting sovereign, who will certainly try to curb my powers after I have pacified the Empire for fear that I will become another Dong Zhuo or Wang Mang!"

"That... is a genuine problem, Excellency," Hua Xin said. "I have spoken openly with Wang Jingxing since arriving in the north, our having been joined at a distance in our struggle against the Suns of Jiangdong, and we agreed upon one other thing besides the need to eradicate the Suns and restore Han rule in the south: we must secure the nation against future villains, and there is only one way to do that... we must empower *you*, Your Excellency, as much as possible."

Cao Cao grunted ambiguously and turned his gaze toward the unreadable Jia Xu.

"It is true," Cheng Yu sighed.

"Of course it is," Hua Xin continued. "Since I was a child and before that, in fact, the court has been mired in corruption; first Liang Ji, then the 'Ten', then Dong Zhuo, then the 'regents', and then Dong Cheng and the White Wave Bandits... and the Empire crumbled as a result of it. Since your rise to power, Excellency, we have seen *tuntian* feed the armies that bring peace to long-troubled places; we have seen the Mount Tai Bandits and crime families of Qing, the Qiang of Liang Province, the Black Mountain Bandits of Bing Province and even the Yellow Turbans of Runan bend at the knee and submit to the Han; we have seen a court populated by honest men, decent men that want to bring peace to the Empire and normalise relations with the rest of the world under Heaven."

"Quite right," Cheng Yu said. "You know that I refused to serve Liu Dai because, despite his similar placement as the powerful and influential Governor of Yan Province – and, in addition, his standing as a scion of the royal house – he would not and could not have achieved what you have achieved, despite his famous public defence of Lu Kang that made him an enemy of the 'Ten'. Likewise, Yuan Shao was the man that charged into the royal palace – with his brother Shu at his side – to destroy the 'Ten', but look how that ended. Those men made stands, yes, but they lacked the moral fibre and courage to do everything necessary."

"It is just as Elder Cheng says," Hua Xin insisted. "You, Excellency, have tamed the wicked and restored order in the north; Liu Dai and Yuan Shao share the shame of doing some sort of harm. You, Excellency, have used your power wisely and justly to bring order, and every man that hankered for your power has been proven to be another villain: *that* is why I suggested empowering you more, not as a 'sycophantic act' but as a pragmatic, logical act, for it is sometimes necessary to make a benevolent tree a more rigid one by covering it with thorns. Regardless of any mistakes that you might have made, we are about to bring an end to centuries of threats from the Wuhuan: you could have been satisfied with destroying the Yuans and ruling the nation from behind the throne as Liang Ji, Dong Zhuo and others have done or Yuan Shao, Dong Cheng and others would have done, but instead you seek true order. We cannot risk any action – however well-intentioned it might be – taking you away from your great mission."

"...You understand me well, Mister Hua," Cao Cao replied. "But you suggest 'empowering me more', which is not exactly easy, since I am already one of the three ducal ministers and there is no need for a regent to an adult sovereign."

"There is a way," Hua Xin suggested.

"...We should probably discuss this in some detail when our victory is assured," Jia Xu said knowingly. "What we have gained from this discussion, gentlemen, is a need to know what must come next, and... I do agree."

Cao Cao hid a smile.

＊＊＊＊＊＊＊＊＊＊＊＊

91

The march northward began as dawn broke: many of the soldiers were noticeably distressed at the lack of a baggage train and the need to forego heavy armour to increase marching speed, but their supply sacks were filled with enough food and water to last them for several days and that did something to calm them. The road into the Xuwu Hills was fairly solid despite the rains, and the hills themselves were not much more troublesome than at any other time of year; the upward march was, nonetheless, taxing on the men and horses, especially since they were moving at almost twice the usual speed without any scheduled rest periods outside of stopping for the night. No man could keep moving forever, but the hilltop camps that were finally established would only give a few hours of rest before the army started onward once again.

The march continued until the army reached a natural breach in the Great Wall at Lulong Pass, whereupon they finally left the Xuwu Hills – and, more importantly, Han Imperial China – and continued along the treacherous valley paths that sat alongside the Luan River. Many a man almost slipped from the paths and fell into the waters as hunger and fatigue started to take their toll; even the campaign's senior general, Zhang Liao, was starting to wonder if there should be some change of plan, but Cao Cao remained defiant when he finally had an open-air meeting during a necessary stop.

"We are almost at what we call Pinggang," Cao Cao said. "So far, we have seen not one Wuhuan person, man, woman or child... not *one*. This route is as unknown to the enemy as Tian Zitai promised it would be, but we are still at risk of being discovered, and so no unnecessary stop will be undertaken."

"The men are not made of stone," Yu Jin protested.

"They must still, however, be made of something strong if they are to make history," Cao Cao retorted. "My sustenance is little better than theirs: am I feasting everyone here with pork, chicken and wine...? No, I am not: we all eat what we brought with us, little though that is, and we make it last, just as the men do. I therefore think that I can speak as an honest man and say that we are all suffering hardship together, hardship that is worth it for the reward of knowing that we will be safe from the barbarians in future times. I've said it often enough before and I do quite honestly despair when I have to keep on reiterating it to you... the common men, yes, perhaps, but you are their leaders, their supposed betters in terms of understanding!"

"...Is there a baggage train of *any kind*, Mengde...?" Xiahou Dun asked desperately.

"General Li Dian is not here, which would, I think, indicate that there is, but that the main army is not waiting for it to catch up to us," Cao Cao replied wearily. "I do not expect the men to starve, but they must be strong until we have won the crucial first victory against our enemy! The baggage will be here in time to feed the men amply after their supplies are exhausted! Honestly, gentlemen, you surprise me! You all know what 'marching double-time' involves and have done so before, or have at least trained for it!"

"But we have never marched double-time into another country with the intention of fighting an enemy that outnumbers us by at least five-to-one on their own ground, Excellency," Yue Jin suggested. "I am fearless, yes, but I am not blind or stupid. We face great odds anyway, but-"
"You've all of you outlined this before, and my answer is the same," Cao Cao insisted. "We will continue as we are."
"But we're about to go through Xianbei-controlled territory, Excellency," Chen Qun protested. "We-!"
"They will not act if we move quickly and quietly," Cao Cao insisted. "All of you must be strong so that the men can be strong: your weakness will affect them, and I would consider that to be a great disservice to the Han."
Chen Qun was not alone in deducing that such a 'great disservice' might be heavily punished: the gathering remained silent in response to Cao Cao's words.
"The last dangerous obstacle before the confrontation itself is that march through the Xianbei territory, but I am not concerned," Cao Cao continued. "As Guo Fengxiao articulated to me on at least two occasions, Budugen will not – or, rather, *cannot* – act without the agreement of his 'subordinate' chieftains, and although he *should* act – it would bolster him and make him a man of action – he lacks enough respect, ironically enough, to attack us and hence gain the respect he needs. Such is life when your culture is based on strength *and* idiocy."
The majority laughed, albeit uneasily.
"I cannot reassure you, gentlemen, and I would be a fool to expect that I could," Cao Cao concluded. "All that I can do is ask – *plead* – that you trust in our success and do your best to pass your optimism, false or otherwise, on to your men."
"...I, for one, shall do as you ask, Excellency," Zhang Liao promised. "What is our course after we cross the Xianbei lands...?"
"We will go into the mountains and proceed toward the sea," Cao Cao replied. "We will reach the sea – our original destination – but be *behind* their defences... and by the time that they realise... it will be too late."
The officers chattered enthusiastically: their confidence restored, they retreated to their individual militia camps and prepared to march once again.

The Han march through the Xianbei fields alarmed the locals, who immediately reported it to their chieftains: that march was almost complete by the time that the news finally reached the vast, undefended series of animal skin tents and horse enclosures that served as the current headquarters of the Xianbei Confederacy's supreme ruler, Budugen.
"...They are going east, toward Wuhuan land," Budugen noted.
"What will we do about it?" one chieftain asked.
"You ask me but I cannot answer you," Budugen retorted. "Maybe I should attack; who would help me...?"
The small group of assembled Xianbei chieftains exchanged awkward glances.
"You would, all of you, but many are not here and would not come here if I asked them to," Budugen continued. "Yes, the Han men might want to fight, but the last time – over thirty years ago –

they were smashed by the Great Tanshihuai and left most of their
men here as corpses. The Han men have not come here to fight
us, I think: they sneak through our land like rats, hoping that we
will not confront them, and it is just as well, isn't it, since I *can't*
confront them, not without being sure of what the rest will do. Will
our 'brothers' do nothing, or will they raid and pillage our lands
and try to establish a new king of kings while I am busy fighting,
or will they actually help me…? And can I afford to do nothing…?
Would the Han men attack us after attacking the Wuhuan, if it is
at all possible that they might win…?"
"Should we warn the Wuhuan?" another chieftain asked.
"What for…?" Budugen scoffed. "They want our grazing lands.
They would take everything if they could. They are not willing to
join us and be part of our coalition, making their own coalitions
instead. They made deals with Han men, like the Southern
Xiongnu, and they will one day be slaves to the Han men, just like
the Southern Xiongnu. The Wuhuan would not warn us… so why
should we warn them and be dragged into it…? There are tens of
thousands of Wuhuan, so why do they need our help…?"
The chieftains mumbled agreeably.
"There are only about twenty, thirty… at the most fifty-thousand
Han men, and they do not have any supplies with them," Budugen
continued. "They are not stopping and setting up camps… so why
should I worry right now…? If the Wuhuan lose, then we would
need to make temporary peace with the Han men, and if the
Wuhuan win then it is the Wuhuan that we would have to parley
with or fight. Let us see what happens… mainly because that is
our only option."

The Han march through Xianbei territory was, as expected,
unhindered: the army then turned and moved into the mountains
that straddled the frontier border in order to make use of existing
plank roads and valley paths. The rains that had impeded the
previous march were almost as heavy in the mountains, so the
roads were treacherous: Cao Cao was often forced to stop as men
stumbled and slipped over and horses briefly lost their footing. A
wide valley road offered the much-needed opportunity for a rest,
despite there being Wuhuan scouts nearby: Cao Cao reluctantly
ordered the army to halt and huddle in groups along the
windswept, waterlogged path to enjoy one tiny meal and a short
sleep before the final advance to the northern and western banks
of the Daling River.
"On the one hand, I have never been more frightened… and on
the other hand, never have I been so excited," Cao Cao admitted
to his adviser Jia Xu. "Here I am, outside of the Empire, just a day
away from the sea… and one of the most important battles that
will ever be fought in our lifetime, no matter how brief it is and
regardless of its outcome."
"I understand your feelings, Excellency," Jia Xu replied. "As
miserable as our surroundings are, I am warmed, strangely, by
the knowledge that what we are doing is history, that we are
doing something worthwhile that will strengthen the Empire."
"…How strange it is that I see a trustworthy friend in you, Jia
Wenhe… but I do," Cao Cao said. "We are sure to achieve great
things now that we are allies rather than enemies."

"I am glad of it also, Excellency," Jia Xu replied.

"…You suspect that your former lord Zhang Xiu's death was not natural," Cao Cao prompted.

"It wouldn't matter if it wasn't," Jia Xu replied. "Zhang Xiu was the nephew of a man that seized Nan County illegally, regardless of what benevolent motives one might want to apply to it. Zhang Ji was a vassal of Dong Zhuo that enjoyed a lot of power in the regency regime that I, sad to say, part-facilitated. Zhang Xiu should have surrendered the county, but nothing was clear at the time. Everything is very clear to me now, Excellency… and I acknowledge that I was acting as an enemy of the state when I opposed you as Zhang Xiu's adviser at Wan City, just as I was wrong when I acted as the adviser to Dong Zhuo, Li Jue and Guo Si before that. Zhang Xiu was glad of being forgiven and allowed to serve as a Han vassal when others were baying for his head… and all men die eventually."

"…A sound answer, Wenhe," Cao Cao said. "I thank you for it."

Cao Chun approached at that moment and said, "The rains are worsening, Mengde."

"It is noticeable," Cao Cao replied. "We can march again in an hour, I think, and cover some more ground before it is too dark."

"I'd advise it, Excellency," Jia Xu said. "We're very likely to be noticed now."

"…Almost certainly," Cao Cao sighed.

"We must hope that the shock of our sudden arrival has the desired effect," Cao Chun said as he turned to walk away. "Either way, we're almost there."

"…Almost at the end," Cao Cao muttered.

✳✳✳✳✳✳✳✳✳✳✳✳

92

Tadun and Louban were in the middle of holding a banquet to raise morale amongst their men and continue celebrations of the withdrawal of the Han army when a distressed Wuhuan scout entered their grand tent and screamed in his native Wuhuan language, **"The enemy are here!"**

Louban almost choked, but Yuan Shang and Yuan Xi were unwillingly ignorant of the announcement that had rattled the Wuhuan guests; Tadun glared at the scout and asked, "What are you talking about?"

"The Han men are at the river!" the scout replied. **"Thousands of them, on our side of the river, they-!"**

"IMPOSSIBLE!" Tadun screamed. **"You are stupid! You-!"**

"What's going on?" Yuan Shang asked.

Tadun turned to Yuan Shang and said, "Han men have been spotted at the river to the south, on our side of the river. Are they your men?"

"I... I have no men there, no, Great Chieftain," Yuan Shang replied as he tried to ignore his brother Xi's agitated gaze. "Is there some mistake, perhaps...?"

Louban started to interrogate the scout in the Wuhuan language: the exchange lasted for several minutes, after which Tadun got to his feet and shouted in that same language, **"The banquet is over! Recall our men from the river or they will all be killed! Alert Nanlou, Supuyan, Pufulu and all of the other chieftains! Tell them to come to White Wolf Mountain! We must prepare for *war*!"**

Yuan Shang turned to the chieftain Wuyan and asked, "What is going on, please?"

"Cao Cao has come here," Wuyan replied as he got to his feet and turned to leave the tent.

"Cao Cao???" Yuan Xi exclaimed. "B-but...!"

"...That's *impossible*," Yuan Shang murmured. "That's...! Tadun, you told me that a march was impossible... you promised me that it was *impossible*!"

Tadun turned to Louban and said, "We must prepare our own men for war and meet Cao Cao at the foot of White Wolf Mountain."

"I agree," Louban replied powerlessly. "But-"

"You said that it was impossible!" Yuan Shang cried as he moved between Tadun and Louban and tried to stare Tadun down. **"You sat here and told me that there was no way that Cao Cao could get here, and now he's-!"**

"Stop whining!" Tadun barked. **"Will shouting at me make him go away?"**

"We... w-we only have a few thousand men," Yuan Shang fretted. "W-we are nowhere near capable of providing a worthy contribution to this battle with-"

"He invades *our* territory now, not yours!" Tadun interrupted. **"Cao Cao is here to fight Wuhuan men, and he shall get what he wants! We will all of us fight! We will all of us fight to the death!"**

Yuan Shang and Yuan retreated to their own camp in order to

prepare for the sudden arrival of Cao Cao's army: Shang sighed angrily as soon as he was within his command tent and said, "This is impossible! This *must be wrong*!"

"...Tadun and Louban seem to be very sure," Yuan Xi suggested.

"I don't care if they are!" Yuan Shang retorted. "It... it cannot be possible! Cao Cao retreated! He left signs and retreated! The roads were sodden mud pits and the riverbank was guarded by hundreds of Wuhuan warriors! He couldn't get here without being spotted, yet he is here, like some sort of magical demon!"

"...Perhaps Cao Cao has utilised some supernatural power," Yuan Xi suggested.

"I... I am inclined to agree, Brother, until I am offered some other explanation," Yuan Shang admitted. "He bested Father at Guandu with such ease that one wonders if there was witchcraft at work... perhaps the rumours that Empress Song, a distant relation of Cao's, was a witch that caused the Han army's destruction thirty years ago was true... perhaps she did it so that Cao could now have this amazing victory... but... no, that cannot be it. He is not a demon! He lost his son at Wan! He was outfoxed by Liu Bei! There is some other explanation!"

Yuan Xi was studying a map as Shang rambled: he pointed at the region to the north of Wuzhong County and said, "I see only one way that he could have done this, Brother... he must have marched double-time through some pass that we were unaware of, that someone – Xianyu Fu, perhaps, or Tian Chou – failed to notify us of but alerted Cao Cao to it."

"That would have taken him into the Xianbei's territory," Yuan Shang scoffed.

"And...?" Yuan Xi retorted. "When has Budugen ever seemed to be a credible threat...? If they marched quickly enough..."

"...No, no, that's ridiculous," Yuan Shang insisted. "The Wuhuan knew Yuyang Prefecture like the backs of their own hands... if there had been some way to retreat to this region by going directly northward through some pass or other then they'd have known of it."

"...So it is magic, then," Yuan Xi sighed. "Cao has a magician in his employ... so what is the point of fighting...?"

"We... are wasting time talking about it," Yuan Shang replied. "Let's prepare."

Tadun's messengers went to all of the Wuhuan chieftains as quickly as they could: two of the chieftains, Nanlou and Pufulu, ignored the request to hurry to White Wolf Mountain and met to discuss what they should do.

"I think that we should wait and see what happens when they first fight," Nanlou admitted.

"I agree, else I wouldn't be here," Pufulu replied. "Tadun wants to be a great coalition leader like Tanshihuai of the Xianbei, but he is not like Tanshihuai. He cannot defeat the Han men if the Han men are properly equipped: he did not defeat them in their own lands when his Han friends, the Yuan brothers, had men of their own, so why should he win now when he is taken by surprise like this?"

"We will wait, then," Nanlou decided.

Cao Cao's forces intercepted the Wuhuan men that were trying to retreat from the mountains and riverbanks and killed or captured them: the road to Liucheng was now open, despite the continued downpours chilling the men to their bones and the lack of new food supplies starting to take its toll. Cao Cao was forced to hold a brief emergency meeting before the march resumed, and the atmosphere was understandably tense.

"What we've got from the Wuhuan won't last us," Cheng Yu said.

"Oh, no... don't you dare!" Xiahou Dun heckled. "If you are even *thinking* about suggesting cannibalism to solve our supply needs, Old Cheng, then-!"

"**Shut up you imbecile!**" Cheng Yu snapped. "I was not about to say anything of the sort! In fact, I was about to say that we must do all that we can to avoid such a catastrophe!"

"...You'd better have been," Xiahou Dun grumbled.

"We are badly under-resourced, though," Cao Chun noted. "Aren't there any crop fields or game animals nearby, Mengde...?"

"Scouts report that there are small Han immigrant communities along the route to Liucheng, but we shouldn't be raiding them," Cao Cao replied. "In fact, we should be advancing as quickly as we can now that it seems likely that the Wuhuan know that we're on our way."

"We don't know that," Cao Hong suggested.

"Why were the men fleeing northward then...?" Cheng Yu asked.

"*Think*, you fool! They were recalled by Tadun! They're probably fortifying the passes that lead to their mountain strongholds as we speak! Though I never truly advocated this ridiculous campaign, we're forced to act quickly now in order to avoid destruction!"

"Elder Cheng is correct once again," Yan Rou declared. "They would not retreat as they do unless ordered to, because it would be punished with death: mass retreats during a rout are one thing, but abandoning defensive positions before a battle, giving time to an enemy to approach more quickly... those men would be dead and their chieftains beaten senseless at the very least if they were going home uninstructed."

"Then we must be quick," Cao Cao said. "What is our situation supply-wise now, Mister Yuan...?"

"The river route is cleared of defenders, so a Liaoxi supply route can be established as soon as the rains have lessened sufficiently," Yuan Huan replied. "In addition to that, a supply train will reach us in the next week or so if Li Dian's march is not stymied by the Xianbei. The worst part of the campaign is actually at an end, technically."

"*Technically*," Cheng Yu heckled. "Now all that's left is fighting the three-hundred-thousand-strong Wuhuan horde on empty stomachs! I feel better already!"

"...And the men only have light armour until the supplies arrive," Yue Jin noted. "We must be very, very aggressive."

"We have just outflanked the Wuhuan army and terrified them into retreating within their own territory, gentlemen!" Cao Cao chortled desperately. "Can you not be more *constructive*...?"

"...As Mister Cheng said, we're here now," Cao Chun replied. "We'll advance quickly and strike at them before they can organise properly. Perhaps we'll be able to scavenge supplies as we take ground from them."

"Yes, perhaps," Cao Cao said impatiently. "This meeting is at an end: we cannot afford to dawdle any longer!"

The Han army advanced northward toward the mountain range that the Wuhuan leaders used as their main headquarters: they met with little opposition but found little in the way of sustenance either, which lowered morale even further as hunger became unbearable. The Wuhuan had been expected to fortify the hills and mountains, but Tadun had assembled an army of what scouts estimated to be over 100,000 men at the foot of White Wolf Mountain instead; Cao Cao was exasperated by the news and convened yet another emergency meeting before the two armies could meet on the relatively flat ground that lay ahead.
"Excellency, we can't fight an army that's at least twice the size of ours when they're rested and fed and we're tired and hungry!" Chen Qun heckled.
"And they might not be heavily armoured, but neither are we, which only adds to the possible disadvantages," General Zhu Ling said. "My men are scared."
"So should we write to Tadun and say, 'We did not want to trouble you by making you invade the Empire again, so we have come here to deliver our heads to you'?" Cheng Yu retorted. "We haven't a choice now, have we?"
"…No, we don't," Cao Cao sighed.
"Know that I will fight to the last for you and for the Son of Heaven, Excellency," Zhang Liao promised.
"We all will," Yu Jin said.
"This is by no means impossible," Zhang Hè insisted.
"Winning at Guandu was deemed impossible," Xu Huang noted.
"As Guo Fengxiao said, we can win by striking quickly and unexpectedly," Cao Chun suggested.
"I will be the first to attack if I am permitted to!" Yue Jin declared.
"…Very good!" Cao Cao said. "But we cannot just attack blindly: if there is a strong point then we must avoid it if possible, and if there is some weakness to exploit then we must exploit it."
"They have not harassed us as we marched and do not appear to intend to," Yuan Huan noted.
"Yes, and the scouts report little in the way of organisation," Hua Xin said.
"They're scared… unbelievable, perhaps, but they're scared," Jia Xu suggested. "Our sudden appearance must have rattled them and led them to suspect some supernatural force at work."
"And the numbers do not sound right," Yan Rou said. "If they are scared and disorganised then there is a chance that some of the lesser chieftains – perhaps some of the more powerful and influential ones – have neglected to show."
"They are, after all, a coalition of coalitions of small, competitive tribes that put their own survival foremost, and that has always been the weakness of these peoples," Cheng Yu suggested. "The Di, the Qiang, the Shanyue, the Xiongnu, the Xianbei, the Wuhuan, the Nanman, they are all the same in the end: hit the weak point and they scatter to the winds."
"…I need a high place from which to observe their ranks: find it at once," Cao Cao ordered.

Cao Cao and a small retinue of elite guards and advisers sped ahead of the already-swift march of the main army and found a safe viewing point in a steep slope that was situated close to the road to White Wolf Mountain: Cao looked at the vast army of Wuhuan infantry and cavalry and said, "Look at that: if they had seized this slope, littered the road with ambushes and harassed us continually, we would be in no state to fight such a horde by the time that we got here."

"As I am always saying, they're idiots," Cheng Yu replied.

"Do you see what I see, Excellency...?" Yan Rou asked.

"I do indeed, Mister Yan... I do indeed!" Cao Cao cackled: the Wuhuan battle lines were thin, disordered even by Wuhuan standards and visibly troubled by in-fighting.

"There is no way that the entire Wuhuan confederacy is here for this battle," Yan Rou suggested. "Yes, they might have some sort of trap planned, but it is unlikely."

"If they do, Mister Yan, then I have no choice but to walk right into it," Cao Cao retorted. "We cannot turn about now or we'd be smashed like a sparrow's egg against a boulder. But if we hit those weak points and they are true..."

"...Then there is a chance that this could be over with in an hour or less, just as I suggested before, Excellency," Tian Chou said. "Now is the time: let us not delay any longer."

"Indeed, Mister Tian," Cao Cao replied. "Back to the army: we have orders to issue!"

What followed was as brief as it was terrifying: after weeks and months of planning and posturing, the entire campaign was decided in one short, climactic battle. Zhang Liao led his fellow officers – among them Cao Chun, Cao Xiu, Cao Hong, Xiahou Dun, Yue Jin, Xu Huang, Zhang Hè, Yu Jin and Zhu Ling – in an apparently suicidal frontal assault on the Wuhuan front lines that awaited them at the foot of White Wolf Mountain: the Wuhuan cavalry was totally unprepared for such an attack and crumpled under the pressure of Han infantry and cavalry while the Wuhuan infantry started to panic and resort to survivalist behaviour, be that running or fighting in an individualistic manner.

"**We need organisation!**" Yuan Shang pleaded. "**We need to issue orders and strengthen the ranks or we'll be routed!**"

"**I am trying to do that, you fool!**" Tadun retorted.

The Wuhuan cavalry was considered to be one of the best in the known world, but their disorganisation made a mockery of that reputation: Cao Chun's elite Tiger and Leopard Cavalry tore into them from the centre while cavalries led by Generals Zhang Liao, Zhang Hè, Yue Jin and Xu Huang gradually encircled the larger Wuhuan cavalry and humiliated them completely. The Wuhuan confederacy started to show exactly what it was made of – an unstable collection of smaller, uneasy alliances of small tribes – when, one by one, the lowest chieftains attempted to flee the battlefield in order to save their own small following and inspired others to do the same: that gradual fragmentation of alliances started to affect the more powerful coalition chieftains like Wuyan, Supuyan and Tadun himself, who left the line of leaders and tried to inspire some kind of proper fightback from the centre of his disintegrating army.

"**I am not staying here!**" Wuyan said. "**This is certain defeat!**"

"If you go, I will find you and kill you!" Louban threatened.
"Is your sword sharper than Cao Cao's...?" Wuyan retorted.
"His is closer to my neck – and yours!"
The Han infantry had completed their advance and were now doing serious damage to the already-weakened, quickly-shrinking Wuhuan army: Louban sensed that defeat was, as Wuyan had said, inevitable and imminent, so he prepared to flee from the battlefield as some of his subordinates were trying to do.
"We have to try and fight!" Yuan Shang protested.
"Forget it!" Yuan Xi said. **"This is over before it even started!"**
"We go east, Yuan Shang!" Louban declared. **"Quickly, now, we must go!"**
"What about Tadun?" Yuan Xi asked.
"What about him?" Louban retorted.
Louban, Yuan Shang, Yuan Xi, Wuyan, Supuyan and a collection of other, less important chieftains started to retreat eastward while Tadun did what he could to reverse a guaranteed rout: the loss of most of the leaders quickly caused mass dissent amongst the remaining Wuhuan forces, and that left Tadun dangerously exposed as he finally realised that he had to flee as well.
"Tadun is ours!" Cao Chun cried. **"A fine reward for the man that captures him alive for his Excellency!"**
The Tiger and Leopard Cavalry descended on Tadun's position and surrounded him: the Wuhuan chieftain's bodyguards fought bravely but were no match for a cavalry that was as well trained as they were. Tadun was pulled from his horse, tied tightly with rope and brought before Cao Cao alongside a group of lesser Wuhuan chieftains.
"Well, well... so you are Tadun," Cao Cao said as he looked down at the fallen chief of chieftains from the saddle of his warhorse.
"What will you do, Cao Cao...?" Tadun asked defiantly.
"You have the temerity to ask that of me after what has taken place here today...?" Cao Cao retorted. "Look at what you have caused, you worthless man, and wonder whether you have the right to be called a man!"
Tadun turned as best he could and observed the battlefield: thousands of Wuhuan men lay dead and dying while frustrated and hungry Han soldiers scavenged for anything edible or useable.
"I had to march here through biting rains that nearly drowned my men in mud, only to be turned back and forced to find other ways to surprise you," Cao Cao continued. "That I did, because you were no match for me strategically... and thank the Heavens that you were so stupid, else our entire way of life was in danger."
"And what about *our* way of life...?" Tadun asked.
Yan Rou glared at Tadum with near-tangible anger.
"You think that I care...?" Cao Cao chuckled angrily.
"...I am defeated," Tadun growled. "I am defeated, but-"
"*No*, Tadun... your entire *people* are defeated, *all of you*," Cao Cao replied. "I will chase down the rest of them... Louban, Supuyan, Wuyan, Nanlou... and I will humble or destroy them as I will destroy you now."
"...What about my family?" Tadun asked.
"Our culture punishes men to various degrees: your entire clan will be punished severely," Cao Cao explained. "There can be no more Taduns."

"...They would rather join me in the afterlife than live as your slaves," Tadun said.

Yan Rou – who could not shake memories of his time as a Wuhuan slave – finally lost his composure altogether and cried, **"Bastard savage, you DARE-!"**

"*Enough*, Mister Yan," Cao Cao pleaded. "Go and rest, Mister Yan, and I will deal with this: your work is done."

Cao Cao watched as Yan Rou cast one last look at Tadun, snorted contemptuously and retreated; Tadun snorted a laugh and muttered abuse in his own language.

"...You heckle me with talk of slaves when you've abducted so many...?" Cao Cao said as he returned his attention to Tadun. "You wanted to be another Tanshihuai, I hear: you are no great chieftain, Tadun. You're a scruffy rebel, like Yufuluo was, and you'll die a rebel's death. **GUARDS: DEATH!"**

Tadun was dragged away silently by two unsympathetic soldiers.

"...**And the rest... what will you do...?**" Cao Cao asked as he looked at the other chieftains: some pleaded and pledged allegiance while others lowered their heads and quietly awaited death. Cao Cao shook his head and said, **"Those that submit are to be spared: those that do not... can join Tadun."**

The defiant chieftains were dragged away by soldiers while the submissive few were quickly freed and allowed to join their corralled subordinates.

"You said that you would pursue the others," Tian Chou noted. "Will you do that personally, Excellency...?"

"...I want to wait for the supplies, but at the same time I must be sure to break them completely," Cao Cao replied.

"You've done that already," Cheng Yu said. "I've never seen them react as they do: their collective spirit is broken, Excellency, and all in the space of one day."

"...But we cannot be sure of peace until Louban and the Yuan brothers are apprehended or killed," Cao Cao replied. "We know that they have gone eastward: let us see if we can get to them before they seek shelter."

"Shelter...? ...With whom...?" Cheng Yu scoffed. "What fool would shelter them now...?"

"...I have been informed of one possibility," Cao Cao replied.

The fleeing Wuhuan chieftains and their Yuan clan allies had little more than 3,000 men and horses when they left the battlefield at White Wolf Mountain: their escape took them north and eastward toward the Liaodong Peninsula, which was the domain of nominal Han vassal Gongsun Kang. Some – including the fugitives themselves – wondered whether the motley band of Wuhuan men and Han Chinese 'rebels' would really be admitted and given asylum, and to the surprise of many, they apparently were. The next stage of the campaign was now in the hands of a man that nobody had considered to be relevant with the exception, perhaps, of Guo Jia: it would now be a matter of waiting to see what Gongsun Kang would do with his new guests.

****

93

Yuan Shang and Louban immediately despatched a messenger to Liaodong's capital and led their small army toward the nearest settlement to await an answer.

"We'll pitch a camp," Yuan Shang said sombrely.

"**We should go into the village and seize houses!**" Louban retorted. "**I am a prince! You are a prince! We-!**"

"I am not intending our current situation to be a long-standing one," Yuan Shang interrupted. "We are both fallen nobles, Louban, and must endure that for a while, else we might make enemies of these people before we have a solid footing. Cao Cao might not have followed us into Liaodong... *yet*... but he is still close behind."

Louban and Yuan Shang continued their argument while the rest of the Wuhuan chieftains huddled to discuss their plight in their own language.

"I am the Chanyu of what the Han men call 'Yòubeiping', but I have only a few hundred followers now and no home," Wuyan complained. "This is humiliating!"

"I am a Chanyu as well, and I once had Cao Cao sending men to impress me and turn my army back from Nanpi," Supuyan recalled. "Now I have less men than some of the clan chieftains that I used to have kneeling before me. Tadun has harmed us."

"Tadun is probably dead now," Wuyan said. "But what about Louban...? Should we still follow him...?"

"Louban was not Chanyu of Chanyus before, not while Tadun was alive," Supuyan replied. "We let Tadun become powerful when Louban should have been; Louban wanted to do things differently, and maybe we'd still be powerful if he'd been ruling us. Let's see what Louban does now and decide later."

"...Alright," Wuyan said miserably.

In the meantime, the argument between Yuan Shang and Louban was reaching a conclusion.

"...Alright, I will agree to camp outside the village," Louban conceded. "But I will not kneel before this 'Gongsun Kang'! You can if you want to, but-!"

"I intend no such thing," Yuan Shang insisted. "I am heir to a chieftainship that entitles me to expect *him* to bend at the knee to *me*! I will observe his countenance and plan from there... but rest assured, Chanyu of Chanyus, we are here to rebuild our respective armies and return to the battlefield as winners, not rot in exile."

"I need no 'assurance'," Louban replied. "I am rebuilding whether you do or not. I want to go back soon and-"

"That is not an option right now," Yuan Shang insisted.

"Cao Cao cannot stay in the frontier lands forever, lord and brother," Yuan Xi suggested.

"No, Brother, he can't, but he will stay for a month at the least and try to repatriate the displaced Han peoples and subjugate the Wuhuan chieftains that remain," Yuan Shang explained. "He had supplies... they were left behind so that he could attack us swiftly from wherever he came from. He'll have at least a month's worth, enough to do some more damage before morale and other threats – such as our ally Liu Biao, the Qiang warlords and the self-styled 'lord of Jiangdong', Sun Quan, compel him to withdraw."

"We should contact your allies," Louban suggested.

"I intend to once we're settled properly," Yuan Shang promised. "I will contact Liu Biao and Liu Bei in Jing, Sun Quan in Jiangdong, Ma Teng, Han Sui and Song Jian in Liang Province and the bandit leaders of Qing and Bing, who will certainly have doubts about their choice of allegiance by that time: if even half of them respond favourably, then that will be enough! And if we cite the 'Girdle Edict' as our motivation, especially after Cao Cao has finished rewarding himself with grand titles..."

"...Then we will certainly stand a chance of winning, lord and brother," Yuan Xi supposed.

"We are certain to win," Yuan Shang said. "Cao Cao will be his own undoing!"

Liaodong Administrator Gongsun Kang received Yuan Shang's messenger in his audience hall and hummed thoughtfully as he listened to a brief account of recent events and the subsequent plea for shelter.

"...And so you see, Administrator, that there is little time," the robed messenger concluded. "Forgive my lord's impatience, but he needs a swift response."

"...You will be given enough food and water for the return journey," Gongsun Kang declared. "You will take word that I will receive your lord and his 'friends' here as soon as it is possible."

The messenger-official kowtowed and said, "Thank you, Administrator Gongsun!"

Gongsun Kang smiled politely and watched as Yuan Shang's messenger withdrew from the hall with two of Kang's junior staff; the administrator then turned to his frowning brother Gongsun Gong and asked, "What do you think...?"

"...Can we talk privately...?" Gongsun Gong said cautiously.

"...Alright," Gongsun Kang replied.

The Liaodong Administrator and his most trusted advisers retired to a private meeting room to discuss the latest situation.

"I ask again," Gongsun Kang said. "What do you think...?"

"This is unwise," Gongsun Gong replied. "The Yuans are close to extinction, lord and brother, and any who aid them will meet a similar fate."

"...The Yuans once ruled Ru County – the whole of Yu Province, in fact – and the entire northeast of the Empire proper," Gongsun Kang retorted. "Is that not a strong ally to have...?"

"Not at all," Gongsun Gong replied. "Yuan Shu forfeited their clan's ancestral power base in Yu Province to Cao Cao when he declared as a false emperor ten years ago; and Cao Cao has taken every last part of the northeast from them over the last four years with surprising, painful ease."

"But Cao Cao is considered to be a villain," Gongsun Kang noted.

"Cao Cao's a very successful villain; Yuan Shang is, at best, an unsuccessful one," Gongsun Gong retorted. "Look at who the fool brings with him: his humiliated and powerless older half-brother, three Wuhuan Chanyus and their tribal subordinates. It would be a surprise if any of the three-thousand-or-so 'soldiers' that they have with them are Han people: the Yuan brothers have betrayed their Han heritage and all but become Wuhuan warlords, just as Han Sui, Song Jian and Ma Teng have become Qiang kings in

Liang Province."

"…That's a slight exaggeration," one adviser suggested.

"Not at all," Gongsun Gong insisted. "Yuan Shao is known to have married women to the Wuhuan chieftains and allowed the barbarians to act as they pleased in Yòu and Ji Provinces: Yuan Shang continued the tradition when he inherited the chieftainship, which is, in itself, contested."

"Ah, yes, that's right: Yuan Shang is the youngest brother," Gongsun Kang recalled.

"And the least qualified," Gongsun Gong suggested. "He's proved that: he inherited a quarter-of-a-million men – mostly Han men – and a quarter of the Empire for a fief when Yuan Shao died. Now he is a penniless refugee with Wuhuan princes for bodyguards. Yuan Tan's incompetence reached our ears here in Liaodong because we overlook northeast Qing, so yes, we know he was an idiot… but could he have lost so much with such ease in such a short time…?"

The advisers murmured agreeably.

"Yuan Shang and his father betrayed their people by forging alliances with the Wuhuan that benefitted the barbarians more than their own people," Gongsun Gong continued. "Shang betrayed his father's will by betraying his brothers and seizing power when primogeniture dictated that Tan was heir and politics dictated that Xi was a preferable second choice; why wouldn't he now live up to his reputation as a hankering snob and try to seize control of Liaodong so that it can serve as a base for yet another failed attempt by the Yuans to conquer the Empire…?"

"…I have already invited him here," Gongsun Kang noted.

"And by all means welcome him warmly, but only so that you can separate the man's head from his shoulders and send the head to Cao Cao, along with his brother's," Gongsun Gong replied. "He's no friend, lord and brother: kill him *and* his brother and spare us a coup and-or a war with Cao Cao!"

"…I'll have him here and monitor him closely," Gongsun Kang decided. "I won't shed his blood without good cause."

"He will give you good cause," Gongsun Gong said. "That I'm certain of."

Cao Cao had halted his army when scouts reported that the fugitives had crossed the Liaodong border: Cao's instructions alarmed his advisers, who wondered why their lord would react in such a way when dealing with a Han vassal like Gongsun Kang.

"It is better that I do not act against the rebels now," Cao Cao said to his assembled officials. "We'll concentrate on pacifying the remaining Wuhuan in Liucheng and ensuring that the support for Louban and his allies is as blunted as the support for the Yuans is in their old domains."

"Gongsun Kang is a Han official," Cheng Yu noted.

"Yes, but Liaodong is not joined to the Empire by land, so Gongsun enjoys a lot of autonomy that I cannot currently interfere with," Cao Cao retorted.

"So we're going to let Gongsun harbour them after all we've been through?" Cao Hong protested. "We marched all the way here on empty stomachs and-!"

"And we've crushed the Wuhuan utterly as a result," Cao Cao said insistently. "Do not place any importance on their escape, for it is a short-lived achievement."

"Gongsun's given them asylum!" Chen Qun cried.

"Has he...?" Cao Cao retorted. "He's let them into Liaodong and invited them to his capital, yes, but that is not the same as giving them asylum. He will hear them out, provided that they are worth hearing out... but by taking no military action, I am arranging it so that Gongsun Kang will not give them shelter. In fact, gentlemen, I predict that he will, in fact, deliver the heads of the Yuan brothers to me shortly."

"Gongsun Kang is deserving of a thrashing!" Xiahou Dun said. "How dare he even speak to them when he has the Excellency of Works at his door demanding their heads!"

"And as I have just said, Yuanrang, he will deliver them without my having to ask," Cao Cao replied. "Be patient."

"I beg of you, Excellency, don't let them escape and regain the strength to come back and hurt more people and take more people away from everything they know – *please*!" Yan Rou rambled. "We wasted our time coming here if-!"

"*Patience*, Mister Yan," Cao Cao insisted. "Patience... patience. I know what I'm doing."

The gathering protested audibly, but Cao Cao was unmoved: there would be no invasion of Liaodong Peninsula.

"...We are lucky," Yuan Xi said: his only company – his younger half-brother, Yuan Shang – smirked and stared at the ground. The two were sat in a guest room within one of Liaodong Administrator Gongsun Kang's large western residences, and their Wuhuan allies were quartered in adjacent rooms; the brothers were soon to advance to the capital and meet Gongsun Kang's court in the grand audience hall.

"...Why did you smile like that...?" Yuan Xi asked.

"I smiled because you are right," Yuan Shang said as he raised his eyes and stared at his older brother. "We are indeed fortunate to have such a warm and trusting host."

"...What do you mean...?" Yuan Xi whispered.

"Why are you whispering?" Yuan Shang chortled. "We're guests of a man that sees our noble breeding and knows that we are his superiors: he is not at all like the Gongsun that Father dealt with."

"...Are they closely related...?" Yuan Xi asked.

"What, Gongsun Zan and Gongsun Kang...?" Yuan Shang said. "At some point, in some way and for some reason, yes, of course, if they share the same name. The Gongsuns of Liaoxi – from which our father's enemy descended – will doubtless be not far removed from the Liaodong Gongsuns. The similarities abound, since these Gongsuns – starting with Kang's father, Gongsun Du, in fact – invaded Goguryeo for the Han – or rather, on the orders of Dong Zhuo – and took control of what we call Xuantu and Lelang, just as Gongsun Zan seized land for others and then himself."

"I'm vaguely familiar with Gongsun Du's 'acquisitions'," Yuan Xi admitted. "But can we really hope for asylum...?"

"I have grander hopes than mere asylum, Brother," Yuan Shang replied. "But yes, if we must settle for that, then yes: Gongsun Du famously gave asylum to Taishi Ci after that whole 'petition' fiasco, if you recall, so why not the Ru County Yuan clan chieftain and his brother...?"

"...But Gongsun Du wanted to kill a famous academic that Taishi Ci then had to rescue and smuggle out of Liaodong," Yuan Xi noted.

"Self-inflicted," Yuan Shang insisted. "Taishi Ci was too quick to play the hero, even when it made a villain of him. We're Han nobles that require a base to rebuild our army, and this region will do nicely."

"...I doubt that Gongsun Kang would let us do that," Yuan Xi said.

"I don't intend to ask nicely," Yuan Shang retorted. "He will give us control or I will take it from him."

"We don't have the men to seize control of Liaodong and we shouldn't be trying to!" Yuan Xi protested.

"We have thousands of Wuhuan men with us that need a temporary base as much as we do," Yuan Shang retorted. "Louban is a wet fish that let Tadun steal his crown, so why can't *I* make use of him...? And Wuyan and Supuyan will not oppose us in a place that's ruled by 'Han men' when most of their followers are gone. Cao Cao has overstretched and dares not invade an isolated Han territory: we will be able to rally an army and destroy the villain with an attack that is as underhanded and unexpected as his was! Victory is still within our grasp!"

"...I want no part of it," Yuan Xi muttered.

"You have no choice," Yuan Shang retorted. "You are my vassal, Brother... and you have as much to lose as I do."

"...Alright," Yuan Xi said. "I... ... ...alright."

"Soon, Brother, we will be in the Liaodong capital," Yuan Shang chuckled. "And then the moment will be upon us...!"

****

94

Cao Cao was almost alone in his optimism regarding Gongsun Kang: as the days passed, scouts reported the movements of the fugitive Yuans and their Wuhuan allies to the Han encampment on the Liaodong border and created more tension among Cao's weary and frustrated subordinates.

"You don't seriously intend to just *sit here*???" Xiahou Dun asked.

"...We'll need to return to the Empire soon," Cao Cao replied.

"*Empty-handed*...?" Cao Hong asked snidely.

"*Aiee*... in what way are we going back empty-handed, you thick-skulled ignoramus...?" Cao Cao retorted. "Perhaps you *do* need to be friends with Sima Yi after all!"

"...Alright, alright, I know we've done a lot," Cao Hong sighed.

"...'A lot'...?" Cao Cao chortled.

"We've just pacified the second-largest military threat to the Han Empire, Zilian," Cao Chun said with disdain. "The Xianbei have not harassed our supply train, which means that it will be here tomorrow, on schedule, to finally end our hunger, and that the Xianbei have seen our might and chosen to remain at a distance!"

"...That's a fair point," Xiahou Dun said. "We're under-resourced, tired, hungry and badly equipped, so if the Xianbei attacked now they'd get this land, kill most of the Han army's leadership and have a clear run at-"

"I'm aware of that," Cao Cao interrupted. "I'm hoping that Budugen remains hesitant until we're well on our way back to Yòu Province... via the coast, not through their grazing fields again. The rains are subsiding now, which means that the roads will be traversable again."

"But the winter is setting in early, Excellency, which isn't ideal," Tian Chou noted.

"...This was an enormous risk," Cao Cao groaned. "The cost of failure would have been catastrophic: what was I *thinking*...?"

"As is the oft-cited mantra these days, Excellency: 'We are here now'," Cheng Yu grumbled.

"And we achieved what we set out to do," Cao Chun said hoarsely.

"Your voice is strained, Zihe," Cao Cao noted.

"I've been subjected to intense rain for weeks and gone without proper sustenance, as everyone else has," Cao Chun replied. "I am a little poorly, that's all. It will pass once I've had a couple of hot meals and some rest."

"...A lot of men are sick," Cao Cao murmured.

"Perhaps 'Fengxiao' wants to make everyone ill like he is," Chen Qun suggested bitterly.

"...Fengxiao... Guo Fengxiao... I wonder whether his health has improved," Cao Cao said. "I have not been able to receive word of him whilst on this campaign... and I will need him for the next."

"Where are we going *now*...?" Cao Hong whined.

"Never fear: that will be an internal campaign," Cao Cao replied. "We've no need to leave the Empire again, Zilian: the Xianbei *and* the Qiang will behave now."

"...Liu Biao and Liu Bei," Cao Chun supposed.

"Naturally," Cao Cao replied. "And after them, Sun Quan... and after them, Zhang Lu... and after them, I will force the Qiang 'kings' to surrender all of their ill-gotten gains and the Southern Xiongnu to appoint a leader that we approve of... and after that... the Empire will be reunited at last."

"We get a rest first though, right...?" Cao Hong asked.

"Of course," Cao Cao replied. "We cannot march toward Jing – and, hopefully, take it without a fight – without doing some administrative reorganisation in Xuchang. I must have absolute authority in order to act so finally against the sanctioned governor of Jing Province, and an attack on the south requires two things: a large navy – which I will acquire from Sun Quan's enemy, Jing Province – and the knowledge that I will not be stabbed in my back when I am facing southward."

"Always planning ahead," Cao Chun chuckled.

"But this entire plan relies on our destroying the Yuans once and for all, and that relies on Gongsun Kang attacking and killing them, which he is not doing!" Cheng Yu heckled. "Send a few troops and an ultimatum his way to force his hand!"

"I expected better of you, Elder Cheng," Cao Cao teased. "You are reading the situation wrongly! By sitting here and saying nothing I guarantee the desired outcome... just wait and see."

"This is not the same as when we 'turned and looked the other way' in order to goad the Yuan brothers into fighting!" Cheng Yu suggested. "Gongsun Kang's father was acting on Dong Zhuo's orders when he attacked Goguryeo and annexed that land! He probably fears reprisals for aiding Dong Zhuo and-!"

"*Wait and see*," Cao Cao said forcefully. "I know what I'm doing."

The Han army's supply train arrived at the main camp near White Wolf Mountain on the following morning, where it was greeted by Generals Yu Jin and Zhu Ling: the supply convoy commander, General Li Dian, bowed humbly and said, "I am too late to see good service. Where is His Excellency...?"

"The main army is now at the Liaodong border," Yu Jin explained.

"*Liaodong*...?" Li Dian exclaimed. "Why? We're not invading Liaodong now, are we...?"

"The survivors of the rout fled to Liaodong," Zhu Ling explained. "His Excellency's placed the bulk of the army there as an 'intimidating measure'."

"...I'd better take some supplies to them, then," Li Dian sighed.

"Please do," Yu Jin replied. "I'm showing a lot of self-control right now by not shoving you aside and eating that food you've brought, bags and all, and I'm far from the only one."

"Oh, right, yes, we should start distributing at once," Li Dian said. "I'll take some to His Excellency in person."

"Any word from home...?" Zhu Ling asked.

"None, but we were moving along a secret route so I don't expect any," Li Dian replied. "But I heard that the coastal route's open now, so..."

"...I must be hungry to be asking such a stupid question," Zhu Ling sighed.

"I'll advance straight away," Li Dian said. "I'll leave local distribution to you, gentlemen."

Liaodong Administrator Gongsun Kang was alerted to the arrival of Yuan Shang, Yuan Xi and the Wuhuan chieftains and relocated to his audience hall to greet them.

"How will you manage the 'guests', lord and brother...?" Gongsun Gong asked.

"Cao Cao has not moved... and I am a little more aware of the Yuans' intentions now," Gongsun Kang replied. "I will greet them as allies when they arrive... and move forward constructively."

"...'Move forward constructively'...?" Gongsun Gong exclaimed.

"Trust me," Gongsun Kang replied. "I will act properly at the critical moment."

Days passed: Li Dian brought supplies to Cao Cao's Liaodong border camp and gave the soldiers a badly-needed energy boost and better equipment. Nothing in the way of news was emerging from Liaodong, however, so expectation was as low as it had been. And then, on one cold, frosty afternoon, two Liaodong soldiers crossed the border with two large wooden boxes and asked for an audience with Cao Cao that was quickly and enthusiastically granted.

"...It can't be," Tian Chou murmured as the two visitors entered the command tent with their boxes clutched to their chests.

"...It is, Mister Tian!" Cao Cao replied as the two soldiers fell to their knees before their large audience and proffered the boxes to the host seat.

"What do you bring us...?" Jia Xu asked.

One soldier raised his head and replied, "**The heads of Yuan Shang and Yuan Xi!**"

"**Yes!**" Xiahou Dun cried. "**We've-!**"

"**Silence, please!**" Cao Cao ordered. "Now: place the boxes on my table so that I might inspect them, please."

Four of Cao Cao's soldiers took the boxes from their holders and removed the lids so that their master could view the lifeless contents: the officials gasped when Cao Cao – who was smiling broadly – had the heads shown to them.

"You were right, Excellency!" Registrar Liu Yè said with disbelief.

"The idea was proven right, yes," Cao Cao said as he gestured for the lids to be replaced and the boxes to be put to one side. "The two men that brought us these most welcome gifts shall be rewarded with rest and food before they leave: they shall take a letter of thanks with them."

One Liaodong soldier took a wooden tube from his belt and offered it to Jia Xu, saying, "**This is from Administrator Gongsun!**"

"Thank you," Jia Xu replied.

Cheng Yu waited until the two visitors had been escorted from the tent before he asked, "How did you know that Gongsun Kang would react in this way...?"

"How else...?" Chen Qun said with a sneer. "The peerless wisdom of 'Fengxiao'."

"Indeed it was," Cao Cao replied. "Guo Fengxiao anticipated that the survivors of the battle – were it as swift as he hoped – might flee in one of three directions: north, which was not ideal and might have saved them, but the way was too difficult; west, to the Xianbei, which was a better choice but likely to end in the Wuhuan being forced to cede their territories and no real support; and lastly east, to Liaodong. Gongsun Kang is the son of a man that invaded foreign kingdoms for Dong Zhuo but kept the spoils when that father died, so he is fierce, and he has ruled autonomously for years, so he is confident and likely to bargain at the least."

"I can see that," Cheng Yu admitted.

"There were two fears that Fengxiao highlighted: the first was that Gongsun would agree to an alliance with the Yuans and help them to grow a new army," Cao Cao continued. "The second was that Yuan Shang would try to kill Gongsun and seize Liaodong for himself. Both scenarios relied upon Gongsun trusting Yuan Shang as an ally or at the least seeing 'a fellow rebel'. If I had advanced, I'd have ensured that Gongsun – who knows what we have achieved – would have assumed that we were doing so to take Liaodong from him, and he would definitely have sought a friendship with the Yuans. By remaining on the border I gave Gongsun the chance to reflect and try to analyse not only us but his guests, who were so stupid and greedy that they probably discussed seizing Liaodong openly enough to be overheard."

"Another correct guess from Fengxiao, then," Cheng Yu sighed. "What does the letter from Gongsun Kang say, Mister Jia...?"

"It says that he extends his full respect and knows only humble obedience to the Son of Heaven and those that act for the throne," Jia Xu replied. "He 'punished these rebels on our behalf' and 'congratulates us on an amazing victory over barbarians and rebels in the north'. The Wuhuan men have all been executed as well but he 'did not think their worthless heads were of interest', although he will 'send them on if requested'."

"...That will do," Cao Cao said. "The campaign is at an end: we will now go home."

"I will stay in this region for now," Yan Rou insisted.

"*Stay*???" Cheng Yu exclaimed.

"...But why in Heaven's name would you want to do that, Mister Yan...?" Tian Chou asked.

"The people that think that they want to stay... are probably very confused," Yan Rou replied. "If they barely remember anything different – like me – then they might think that they want to stay here when deep down, they don't... and besides, I don't trust the Wuhuan, and I want to see for myself that they are definitely a broken people... as broken as I am."

"What you say... is something that I must bear in mind when I begin my quest to retrieve someone that has endured as much – and more – and who, sadly, may be as 'confused' as you suggest of others, and might actually resist being rescued," Cao Cao said. "What you say... I will remember."

Yan Rou bowed slightly.

"...And you can stay if that is what you want, Mister Yan," Cao Cao continued. "Qian Zhao will maintain contact with you and ensure that you are alright."

"Thank you for understanding, Excellency," Yan Rou replied.

"...We can go *home*... which is *great*!" Cao Hong sighed.

"Too bad, 'Master of Supplies'," Yue Jin heckled as he glared at Li Dian. "You came all this way as 'Head of Catering' but haven't achieved anything!"

"...I refuse to rise to it," Li Dian retorted.

"General Li Dian brought the supplies through hostile enemy territory without incident despite having an inadequate defensive militia, for which he – along with everyone that contributed to this campaign – will be rewarded," Cao Cao declared. "Now, as I have said, let us go *home*... I think that we have all endured enough."

The Han army began a triumphant but subdued march southward: biting winter winds and the gradual depletion of water supplies and food made the journey difficult, but the destination was home so spirits were higher than they had been during the previous weeks. A large number of Wuhuan prisoners and Han Chinese migrants – close to 200,000 in all – travelled with the army, but many embittered settlers that had fled Han China voluntarily chose to stay and were not forced to do otherwise.

The army halted when it reached Liaoxi in northeast Yòu Province: supplies that had travelled down Dong Gongren's canals were waiting for them, so many – soldier, civilian and prisoner alike – enjoyed better meals and a proper rest after a long and arduous journey. Cao Cao was glad to be home and was, initially, nearly always smiling: that changed when a messenger announced that a youth in white robes had arrived in Yijing.

"...It is not... *Guo Yi*...?" Cao Cao asked pleadingly.

"...It is," Jia Xu replied.

The court anxiously awaited Cao Cao's response, but they were forced to wait for several minutes while Cao – whose head fell forward upon hearing Jia Xu's words – absorbed the news that Guo Jia had finally passed away.

"Mengde, I'm sorry," Cao Chun said quietly.

"Fool...!" Chen Qun sobbed. "That... that *fool*...!"

"Mengde, please... *say something*," Xiahou Dun whimpered.

"... ... ...**D'AAAAAAAAGH...! I-!** I...! ...I have dreaded this day more than the day of my own death!" Cao Cao lamented. "He is my brains, my wits, my... my *friend*...! Does *any man* understand me as Fengxiao did...?"

"...Mengde...?" Cao Hong said weakly.

"Nobody understands me as he did," Cao Cao continued. "He... he knew when to sway me, when to allow me to advance or falter... he could make certain defeats into victories... he was without compare. My enemies laugh at my misfortune... they sigh with relief that Guo Jia is no more, and they will **die a thousand deaths for it!**"

"I... I am sorry that I called him a fool, Excellency," Chen Qun pleaded. "I... I...!"

"He... he *was* a fool, but only to himself," Cao Cao replied. "You need not fear me, Chen Changwen; your remonstrations were born of concern for his welfare that was rightly offered and wrongly ignored."

Chen Qun lowered his head and exhaled miserably.

"We will all wear white to mourn his passing, Excellency," Liu Yè said. "I will ensure that there are enough garments for-"

"You... need say no more, Ziyang," Cao Cao interrupted. "I brought something white to wear because of the unwavering awareness that... that *someone*... would deem it necessary. That it is Fengxiao comes as no surprise, but why it must always be the case that the 'flame that burns the brightest wanes the fastest' is, to me, a cruel matter that so often robs the world of its finest talents in their youth and leaves it cursed with a multitude of old, stale mediocrities."

The 66-year-old Cheng Yu harrumphed irritably.

"I... I am aware that my last comment was poorly thought out, gentlemen," Cao Cao continued. "I am just so very, very upset that my plan to celebrate this great victory has been marred by such a loss to my counsel."

"...Fengxiao's genius served us to the last," Cao Chun said warmly. "Our victory over the Wuhuan was partly his doing."

"Partly... but mostly it was luck and the tenacity of those that were there," Cao Cao replied. "I said that I would reward everyone that contributed – and your cavalry, Cousin Zihe, earns you praise once again for its acquisition of Tadun – but I will doubly reward those that tried to talk me out of embarking on the campaign at all, because... because despite the fact that I have won, this... this was a ridiculous idea that only worked because we were fortunate at the critical moments."

The gathering was stunned by Cao Cao's frank admission.

"None of you need pretend that you suddenly believe the venture to be some great and magnificent adventure or that you always did... not for my sake nor anyone else's," Cao Cao continued. "The wisdom of the doubters was only 'wrong' because Heaven favoured us and Guo Fengxiao correctly estimated the enemy's stupidity... and for no other credible reason."

Chen Qun bowed humbly and said, "You are a most wise and magnanimous lord, Your Excellency: the Empire is blessed to have you as its guiding light."

The majority of the officials echoed Chen Qun's words.

The mood in Cao Cao's camp was subdued because of the mixture of disbelief at what had apparently been achieved beyond all expectation – the total subjugation of the Wuhuan people – coupled with the relief that the main objectives – killing the last of the troublesome Yuan brothers and escaping the frontier lands alive – had been met along with the physical and emotional impact of such an exhaustive campaign and the saddening news that the genius Guo Jia had died – regardless of how much it was expected – in his mid-thirties, leaving the Excellency of Works without his most reliable and trusted counsel. It would take some time before the enormity of it all would truly set in: history had genuinely been made.

The Wuhuan that had lived so freely and so confidently for centuries were a broken people, and the Yuan clan of Ru County that had been at the centre of Han Imperial politics for as long as anyone could remember had been hollowed by the deaths of all of the heirs to the chieftainship; there were still known heirs to the Yuan legacy, but none of them – Minister Yang Biao's son, Yang Xiu, and Cao Cao's adviser Yuan Huan, to name but two – would be seeking what little was left of the wealth, land and power that had caused their relations to destroy each other and themselves. Yet another new political era had begun, and for once there was no clear sense of what might or should happen next.

∗∗∗∗∗∗∗∗∗∗∗∗

ACT VIII: AN OPPORTUNITY FOR HEALING

95

The whole of Han Dynasty China was surprised and in some cases distressed by the news that gradually emerged from the northeast of the empire. The Han's Excellency of Works, Cao Cao, had famously pledged that he would confront and defeat the three heirs to the powerful Ru County Yuan clan, and many guessed that he would probably win since his victory over their father, Yuan Shao, at Guandu was deemed impossible and happened nonetheless: the eldest of the brothers, Yuan Tan, met his end after trying – and failing – to use Cao Cao to regain the Yuan clan chieftainship from his younger half-brother Shang, whose mother and subordinates had found a way to circumvent the usual rules regarding succession and elevated their lord at Tan's expense and who then defeated Tan repeatedly in battle. Cao Cao had not only twisted Yuan Tan's plan to suit himself and seized the capital of the Yuans' domains while the brothers fought; Cao then served as Tan's executioner after the latter had been tricked into chasing Shang out of Ji Province. The next phase of Cao's plan – to defeat Yuan Shang and the middle brother, Yuan Xi, in the frontier region known as Yòu Province – resulted in more quick victories that forced the brothers and their Wuhuan tribal allies to flee the empire altogether, but Cao was briefly prevented from finishing his work by the need to put down the last of the Yuans' allies in neighbouring Bing Province: that done, he began very public preparations for a march that would take the Han army out of China for the first time in 32 years.

The idea of a march into foreign territory to fight a foreign enemy on their own ground had been met with near-universal scorn and protestation: the last campaign of that nature had ended with the near-total destruction of the army and was considered as one of the reasons why the Yellow Turban Rebellion that followed 9 years later was so successful in its early stages. But Cao Cao had refused to be swayed: his strategist – the brilliant but sickly Guo Jia – had formulated a plan that, if luck was on the army's side, would deliver victory before any of Cao Cao's enemies in the empire could mobilise and exploit his absence. The most proactive of those enemies – the itinerant warlord Liu Bei – repeatedly asked his current host, Jing Governor Liu Biao, to 'march to the capital Xuchang and free the Son of Heaven from the villain Cao Cao' when it became clear that Cao was planning to leave the heart of the empire exposed, but Biao – who feared his powerful neighbour and enemy Sun Quan and the consequences of failure – failed to act. But Cao Cao was still considered by most to be playing with fire and unlikely to succeed.

Against all odds, Cao Cao had done everything that he had set out to do: he had defeated not only the Yuan brothers but the formidable Wuhuan tribes that had previously enjoyed unchecked movement between Han China and the harsh frontier lands and acted with impunity. Even the Yuans, while claiming total control of the northeast after seizing it via a series of deals and conquests, had been forced to parley with the Wuhuan chieftains and yield to the majority of their demands in exchange for the use of their brilliant cavalrymen, but Cao Cao – after taking the Yuans' lands from them with surprising swiftness – had ended decades of raids and mass abductions by driving the Wuhuan out of China and then taking the fight to their homelands beyond the Great Wall. The seemingly-impossible had, once again, been achieved: the Wuhuan had been defeated in one short, impulsive battle and their allies the Yuan brothers, after being put to flight, had been betrayed and executed by the semi-autonomous warlord Gongsun Kang.

Once Cao Cao had returned to his campaign headquarters in Yijing Fortress and regained his composure after mourning the untimely loss of his irreplaceable strategist Guo Jia to illness, he had a man travel to the current imperial capital, Xuchang, to confirm what had transpired.
"...And... that's it," Cao Cao's ally Xun Wenruo said as he finished reading the report that his lord had submitted to the dumbstruck imperial court. "His Excellency conveys his utmost respect, of course, to the Son of Heaven and longs for the right moment to come here and bask in Your Majesty's divine presence."
"We... are truly impressed," Emperor Xian admitted. "We have never known a time when the Wuhuan people were not a menace to the people of the north, and now... that time appears to be at an end."
The official Kong Rong asked to be heard and said, "And the Yuan brothers, they... are all of them destroyed...?"
"That is what I relayed, Mister Kong," Xun Wenruo replied. "The Yuans' heads were delivered to His Excellency by Liaodong Administrator Gongsun Kang after they tried – and failed – to seize control of Liaodong Peninsula with the remnants of their Wuhuan allies."
"It is scarcely believable," the official Wang Lang said. "The Wuhuan are truly crushed...? What of the Xianbei Confederacy that occupies the neighbouring territory...? Will they now pose any threat to us...?"
"The Xianbei's ruler, Budugen, is not the great warlord king that his ancestor Tanshihuai – the man that humiliated our army over thirty years ago – was," Xun Wenruo replied. "Budugen took no action against our army while it marched, took no action when he saw that the Wuhuan were in danger and took no action as the army withdrew to the Empire."
"But what about the people that reside in the Wuhuan lands...?" Minister Yang Biao asked. "Will the Xianbei now move eastward and seize those lands...?"
"We'll reoccupy those lands at a later date, but for now they are civilian residential territories that are, yes, occupied by a mixture of Wuhuan families and migrant families from the Empire," Xun Wenruo replied. "As I have relayed already, about two-hundred-thousand travelled with the army and the rest – anywhere between another two-hundred-thousand and a million depending on whose estimate you want to believe – have either opted to follow later or remain where they are... mostly the latter."
The officials fought the urge to discuss the announcement.
"...Our people would rather remain in such hostile lands when the option to return is open to them...?" Emperor Xian exclaimed. "We are genuinely surprised and saddened by that fact."

"As is His Excellency Cao, Your Majesty," Xun Wenruo replied. "It dampened his spirits... as did the news that Mister Guo Jia has finally succumbed to his long-standing illness."
Emperor Xian noted the large number of officials that were wearing white articles and said, "We are saddened by the loss of such a valuable asset to our administration. We trust that Mister Cao has arranged for Mister Guo's family to be given proper treatment as reward for his service...?"
"They will be his family and live in his home," Xun Wenruo replied.
"...Which home...?" Emperor Xian asked with sudden iciness.
"Th-the Excellency of W-Works' home in Yè, f-for now, Your Majesty," Xun Wenruo stammered. "B-but the-"
"Perhaps we are being unfair," Emperor Xian said with a smirk. "We are sure that Mister Cao has earned a second home in Yè City as a reward for his efforts. Perhaps he would like to be made 'Governor of Ji Province' as has been suggested before...?"
"His Excellency Cao prefers to remain as 'Governor of Yan Province' so that he can be sure of maintaining stability here in the capital," Xun Wenruo replied immediately. "His being appointed as the governor of two provinces would be inappropriate, so he cannot assume that role."
Emperor Xian's smile disappeared as he said, "Yes... Mister Cao wishes to 'maintain stability here', of course... and that is *critical*, is it not...?"
"It is," Xun Wenruo replied innocently. "His Excellency Cao wishes to avoid more 'unfortunate incidents'. His Excellency seeks only the preservation of the Han... which is why he risked everything to end the enduring scourge of the Wuhuan in the northeast. And while I return to that matter, I should add that we can probably expect the Qiang warlords and others – even the heretic Zhang Lu – to capitulate now that the once-invincible Wuhuan tribes are humbled. We may well see the end of the unrest in Liang Province or the return of Hanzhong to Han rule next, Your Majesty: they are certainly long-term goals."
Emperor Xian forced a smile and said, "We are most pleased with Mister Cao's long list of achievements, and... and he will certainly be rewarded for them."
Xun Wenruo bowed humbly and replied, "Knowing that he has served the Han so well is reward enough, Majesty."
Kong Rong and several others were unable to supress contemptuous sneers.

Kong Rong returned to his home when the court session ended: he was then visited within an hour by his friend Zhi Xi, two like-minded officials named Geng Ji and Wei Huang and finally Wang Lang in quick succession.
"Why are you here...?" Kong Rong asked as he opened the door to Wang Lang.
"You're answering the door yourself now...?" Wang Lang teased.
"I... was already entertaining guests," Kong Rong replied. "Zhi Xi, Geng Ji and-"
"I'm not surprised," Wang Lang sighed. "I'm here to say one thing, Wenju: please do not start heckling Excellency Cao when he comes to the court. I have it on good authority that he is still most displeased with your last stunt."

"…'Stunt'…?" Kong Rong scoffed. "I take it that you are referring to my letter."

"And the barbed comment that followed," Wang Lang replied. "Don't push your luck, Wenju: I say that as your friend. You heard what Wenruo said at the meeting: there can be no more 'unfortunate incidents'."

"I am a critic, not a rebel," Kong Rong retorted. "Since when has it been illegal to criticise a statesman…? Didn't Cao Cao shelter men like me during the 'Partisan Crisis' and openly decry such an attitude when it was manifested by-?"

"Don't try to be too smart," Wang Lang interrupted. "Casual criticism is one thing; career chastising is another. Your comments incite others to cast excessive doubt on His Excellency's motives. Look at what he has just done and wonder whether his faults are acceptable when his merits are so many and so valuable."

"…I'll heed your words," Kong Rong replied.

"And I will not stay: I have things to do," Wang Lang said. "Enjoy your banquet."

Wang Lang turned and departed before Kong Rong could say anything else; Kong then returned to his three guests and said, "That was Wang Jingxing."

"Come to 'warn you', I presume…?" Wei Huang asked.

"…Yes," Kong Rong replied uneasily. "Perhaps he had a point: I don't want to be mistaken for a rebel. I am trying to curb Cao Cao's power and point out his many obvious faults, not facilitate a coup attempt."

"Sometimes there is no way to avoid challenging an ambitious man more directly than that," Geng Ji suggested. "Your words accord with my own long-held thoughts, Wenju: Cao is a tyrant, a 'Chancellor in all but name', as some have called him in the past."

"Yes… perhaps… but I must still avoid being seen as being too critical when praise is deserved," Kong Rong replied. "And what he's achieved… deserves praise."

"You're quite right," Wei Huang said. "But-!"

"No, Mister Wei… it deserves praise, not sniping that will be construed as petty," Kong Rong pleaded. "Cao will doubtless give us excuses to criticise in the future, but for now we must give credit where it is due."

"That's right," Zhi Xi said. "We must not be seen as agitators!"

"…But isn't this our one last chance to 'curb his power'…?" Geng Ji suggested. "It is precisely because the court will 'give credit where it is due' that I worry so much: Cao will certainly be promoted for his 'great achievements', and there is every chance that he will revert to the old ducal system to give himself more power!"

"Cao Cao, Chancellor of State…? …I'll never give assent to that," Wei Huang muttered.

"No, Mister Wei, and neither will I, and neither will a lot of others, including Xun Wenruo," Kong Rong insisted. "For Cao Cao to emulate Dong Zhuo now – for that is what he would be doing by adopting that title – that would be his *undoing*, surely. There are plenty of his followers that are still Han loyalists above all else… he wouldn't *dare*…"

Emperor Xian had returned to his private quarters and sat opposite Empress Fu without dismissing his servants: the empress knew from his expression that the sovereign needed to talk but lacked the composure to act.

"...Leave us, please," Empress Fu said at last: the servants looked to Emperor Xian, who nodded agreeably, whereupon they left the sovereigns alone.

"...He has defeated the Wuhuan," Emperor Xian said after a long, thoughtful silence. "If... if anyone else... *anyone else...* had achieved such a thing, I might have rewarded them with whatever they desired without so much as a thought."

"When you say 'defeated', Majesty... what do you mean...?" Empress Fu asked.

"Defeated, subjugated, humbled, humiliated, crushed... any word you care to use," Emperor Xian replied. "He took the army into the frontier lands and defeated the entire Wuhuan Confederacy in a single battle: they and the Yuans no longer have any power... like so many others that Cao has crossed paths with."

"...Is he supernatural...?" Empress Fu asked.

"I am inclined to wonder that myself, my lady," Emperor Xian chuckled miserably.

"...And the Yuans are dead...?" Empress Fu prompted.

"Their severed heads delivered to Cao by Gongsun Kang, my 'loyal Administrator of Liaodong Peninsula and the annexed territories'," Emperor Xian replied. "I had completely forgotten about the Gongsuns of Liaodong, to be honest... and now they suddenly remind me of their existence by killing the men that I had secretly hoped to be my saviours. But at the same time, I am relieved, and rightly so... for after all, what kind of saviour would they have been...? Cao Cao has prevented the Yuans from marching a horde of three-quarters-of-a-million men – one and all of them disaffected Han emigrants and Wuhuan barbarians – into the Empire in a year or two to do who-knows-what."

"...I suppose so," Empress Fu sighed.

"Never have I been more confused," Emperor Xian admitted. "That is why I could not find the strength to dismiss the servants and start a conversation: what can I say...? Is Cao Cao the Heaven-sent hero that the nation needs, or is he a wicked hegemon that will one day steal the throne...? Every time he does something to prove one theory, he then does something to prove the opposite! This is the single greatest service that anyone has done for the Empire in years! If those cretins that my father despatched to fight Tanshihuai thirty years ago had done half as well as this, then there would never have been any crises! What 'Yellow Turban Rebellion'...? What 'Liang Province Rebellion'...? What 'White Wave Bandits'...? What 'Dong Zhuo', or 'Li Jue' or 'Guo Si'...? What '*Cao Cao*', for that matter...?"

Empress Fu nodded silently.

"But Cao Cao there is, and I *must* acknowledge his achievements!" Emperor Xian continued. "He has pacified the northeast and brought it under our control again! He has terrified the Xianbei Confederacy into extending courtesies and will no doubt coax submissions from the Qiang, Liu Biao, Sun Quan, Zhang Lu...! ...How can I not reward the man, even though I *hate him*...? But how do you reward such achievements when the recipient has so much already, mm...? What will I be asked – or *told* – to give him...?"

"...I understand," Empress Fu replied.
"But as usual, I am powerless," Emperor Xian continued. "What I want to do matters as much as it ever done... not at all. His cronies will push for whatever it is that he wants on his behalf, and I will have to grant it... just as it has always been. And now that the Yuans are gone, I must hope that this man really is as benevolent as his lackey Xun Yu constantly protests, because the only other strong men left now are Liu Biao, Liu Bei and Sun Quan, and I cannot be sure of any of them, not even Liu Bei."
"And as usual, Majesty, I cannot help," Empress Fu sighed.
"You... you understand, and that is a comfort," Emperor Xian replied. "This would be worse if I were truly alone. And I must be positive: Dong Zhuo – who was a burden that I had to deal with alone – seemed to be invincible, and yet he was flesh and blood and met his end one day. 'Heaven's will' might not be clear, but every other villain has fallen eventually and... and Cao Cao will surely be no different."
Empress Fu smiled encouragingly and said, "Quite right."
"...I shall have the servants return," Emperor Xian decided. "We can discuss the events more trivially and have it known that we're pleased with the end to the suffering in the north. Worrying about the possibilities solves nothing; let us be glad of this end to a threat not just to the throne but to our very way of life. The Wuhuan were eroding the lives of the people... and now they are no longer able to cause harm. That... is *good*."

****

96

Cao Cao remained in Yijing in order to oversee the last of the administrative reorganisation in Yòu Province and manage any situations that might arise from his conquest of Tadun's Wuhuan Confederacy: his crippling migraines continued to render him unable to hold court for several days at a time, and with the campaign at an end The Excellency of Works' thoughts turned to his own health once again.

"...Are you well again, Excellency...?" Registrar Liu Yè asked as Cao Cao took his place as the host and reviewed the audience hall.

"The pain lingers," Cao Cao replied. "I'll not tolerate this any longer: I want Hua Tuo found and escorted to Yè or Xuchang, whichever is closer to where he is found."

"Perhaps he... can help me with this cold... while he's around," Cao Chun wheezed.

"I will have Hua Tuo located for you, Excellency," Liu Yè promised.

"...And this time, I want no excuses," Cao Cao insisted. "The man finds the time to sit around imitating monkeys: he can *make* the time to help me with these blasted headaches!"

"...We will locate him," Liu Yè replied.

"...Now I shall move from Hua *Tuo* to Hua *Xin*," Cao Cao said as he turned to face his nervous adviser. "What news from the frontier border, Mister Hua...?"

"The reports are correct," Hua Xin replied. "Nanlou and Pufulu did not participate in the battle at White Wolf Mountain and now desire a meeting so that they can formally surrender to the Han, Your Excellency."

"...They are sensible," Cao Cao said. "I will meet them. What of Khan Budugen...?"

"He sends what can best be described as 'adequate tribute'," Cheng Yu reported.

"A show of strength and conciliation... which is, again, sensible," Cao Cao said. "It looks like I will be able to go southward in the coming weeks, then."

"The north can manage now," Xin Pi insisted. "Administrator Wang Ling has already managed to bring greater stability to Zhongshan; Administrator Xianyu Fu has dealt with the last of the rebels in Yuyang; the death of Tadun has left the officials in his 'seat of power', Liaoxi, able to restore order; Li Fu has informed us that Ji and Qing Provinces are settling down now; and Bing Province Inspector Zhang Zhi, Hedong Administrator Du Ji and Hongnong Administrator Jia Kui all report that the Qiang and Southern Xiongnu are making no trouble and the rebels are contained."

"...*Yes*... the Qiang and the Xiongnu," Cao Cao sighed.

"They are making no trouble," Cheng Yu said. "Why put that tone in your voice...?"

"Ma Teng and Han Sui are aggressive and ambitious whether they operate alone or in concert," Cao Cao replied. "I do not feel comfortable leaving them as they are."

"But Huchuquan is another matter, so why mention the Xiongnu, Excellency...?" Chen Qun asked.

"Liu Bao – Huchuquan's heir and the son of the rebel chieftain Yufuluo – is my concern, not Huchuquan," Cao Cao explained. "I want to send a warning to that young prince, but I also have a request that I can finally make now that I have proved that I am not to be trifled with."

"...Lady Cai," Jia Xu said.

"But if he refuses to hand over Lady Cai, doesn't that mean a war with the Southern Xiongnu...?" Cao Hong asked.

"He won't refuse: the most he'll do is set a high ransom that I am prepared to pay, no matter how high it may be," Cao Cao replied. "I will not allow the daughter of the Empire's finest mind to remain as the property of a barbarian prince any longer."

"Just be careful, Excellency," Chen Qun warned. "Our victory over the Wuhuan tribes should not lead us to become overconfident and careless."

"It *won't*," Cao Cao growled. "Am I a fool...?"

"N-no, Excellency," Chen Qun bleated.

"...My... *apologies*, Changwen," Cao Cao sighed. "My temper got the better of me."

"It... is understandable, Excellency," Chen Qun replied.

"...I think that my affliction is lingering with too much malice for me to continue," Cao Cao said as he got to his feet and started to leave the hall. "You may continue without me, gentlemen..."

Cao Chun watched Cao Cao depart by way of a side door and groaned miserably.

"Really, Mister Liu Yè, you must hurry and find Hua Tuo," Cao Hong said. "Mengde is being driven mad by those headaches, and it's a waste of a great man's time to be bedridden so often."

"Rest assured that I will do all that I can," Liu Yè replied.

"And I will prepare the response to the Wuhuan chieftains, sir," Yang Xiu suggested.

Cao Cao's eldest living son, Cao Pi, was quietly pleased when he learned that his wife Lady Zhen's previous husband, Yuan Xi, had been killed, but he knew that his feelings might not be shared; after many days of avoiding the subject he finally requested a solitary audience with Lady Zhen and asked, "How do you feel...?"

"...Numb," Lady Zhen replied.

"...'Numb'...?" Cao Pi exclaimed.

"Yes, dear husband, 'numb'... I don't feel anything," Lady Zhen replied. "Nothing has changed since the marriage was annulled. As I have said before, Yuan Xi and I were married and then separated from one-another almost immediately by his stepmother, something which he never truly contested; I spent the entire marriage as a prisoner of Lady Liu, so I did not really ever know him. You and I are husband and wife now and parents as well: Yuan Xi is someone that no longer matters."

Cao Pi smiled and said, "It pleases me to hear you say that."

"I am surprised that you expected to hear me say anything else," Lady Zhen replied. "I would not be a dutiful wife or an intelligent woman if I mourned his death."

"...I know from his surrendered courtiers that he was determined to reclaim you," Cao Pi said. "I also know that the two of you were matched because of your similar characters, your philanthropy..."

"Or, perhaps, because I was a wealthy orphan," Lady Zhen replied. "Young, unmarried women still pay five times the standard rate of tax, Husband, as an 'incentive' to find a match,

and I had 'concerned relatives' that 'did not want to see me pay such excessive fines for celibacy' and pushed me toward the Yuans; that and Yuan Shao was probably looking to replace lost monies and thought my inheritance to be an ideal source. I was given the impression that Yuan Xi was good-natured, but he went to the frontier after the wedding and did nothing to rescue me and be a proper husband, so how can I know?"
Cao Pi laughed at his wife's frankness.
"...I have been too outspoken," Lady Zhen supposed.
"It is refreshing," Cao Pi chuckled. "Never feel that you cannot tell me your thoughts!"
"I am content now," Lady Zhen insisted. "The Caos are doing great things here and everywhere else; your father has brought peace to the northeast and given the people respite that all of my money could not buy. I should still like to do something to aid the disadvantaged wherever possible, but His Excellency's achievements humble me. When I think of how ridding the provinces of the threat of raids by bandits and barbarians will change people's lives... it is heart-warming."
"I will try to be as much of a hero as Father if only to please you, my lady," Cao Pi said.
"We are a happy family," Lady Zhen replied. "That is enough."

The officials and intelligentsia in the former Yuan clan capital, Yè City, were collectively stunned by the news that all of the Yuan brothers were now gone: Ji Province Registrar Li Fu met with a fellow former Yuan vassal, Attendant Officer Cui Yan, and asked, "Was this the right outcome, Jigui...?"
"I hate to say it, Zixian, but yes," Cui Yan replied. "My main concern about the 'new masters of the house', so to speak, was the true nature of Cao Pi, and he has proven to be more agreeable than Yuan Tan – who was violent and stupid – or Yuan Shang, who was arrogant, selfish, stubborn and fatally prone to indulging in needless intrigue. Yuan Xi's an unnecessary casualty, perhaps, but it complicated Cao Pi's situation to have Xi alive and pledging revenge over a change in circumstances that Lady Zhen is, by the look of things, perfectly content with. Xi's timidity, inconstancy and willingness to be a vassal to whichever of his brothers held the power made him a poor choice for heir, anyway, and it is precisely because he was not his own man that he condemned his wife to house imprisonment and died such an ignominious death."
"...All that you say is true," Li Fu sighed. "And it brings the entire Yuan clan chieftainship crisis to an end, I suppose... unless there is some distant relation that will appear to claim it...?"
"Yang Xiu, Yuan Huan and Gao Rou – all of whom now serve as some of the closest heirs, and Yang Xiu, being Yuan Shao's nephew, is most obvious – also serve His Excellency in some capacity and wouldn't risk their places in the Han court by raising such an ugly matter," Cui Yan suggested. "Yuan Shu's son and daughter are both alive and living in Jiangdong as 'guests' of the Sun clan, so I understand, but their father's fate and their current circumstances make them unlikely claimants. His Excellency might decide to honour his former friend and appoint an heir from the surviving relatives, but then what is there to claim...? Is there anything left but an empty, meaningless title...?"

"...Not really," Li Fu realised. "The money's gone."

"And His Excellency is now the lord of Yè," Cui Yan said. "Ru County is, like the rest of Runan, the responsibility of Administrator Man Chong now, and most of the Yuans' influence bled away from that place years ago. The Yuans are part of history now."

"...Which is a strange notion after such a long time," Li Fu replied.

"But a notion that we must adapt our thinking to," Cui Yan said. "The Caos are now the guiding force in the land, Zixian, and what an improvement that is already! If, just a few weeks ago, you'd asked me what would really make a difference here in the northeast of the Empire, I'd have answered by saying, 'Pacifying the Wuhuan', and the idea would have been met, most likely, by unanimous laughter at the ridiculousness of it. Now it is so, by Cao Cao's hand, and I can only thank Heaven for the so-called 'Hero of Chaos'; the man that gave that strange title to Mengde, the wise Xu Shao, certainly meant that as a compliment and a premonition of greatness to come, no matter what some commentators thought."

"...There were moments when 'some commentators' seemed to be right," Li Fu suggested.

"Oh, yes, I know," Cui Yan replied. "The early mischief, the debacle when he was District Captain in Luoyang, the whole 'Xu Province incident', the 'Wan City incident' and, most controversial of all, his solution to the problem of Dong Cheng's pregnant daughter... but I am a Legalist at heart because I understand that the unpolished nature of man means that no hero has clean hands and not every situation can be remedied without resorting to unpleasant tactics. What matters in the end is the outcome: a better, more stable, less corrupt, happier state has resulted from Mengde's actions, and I cannot say the same for the state that Yuan Shao was building. He courted the Wuhuan, and we let him, which is my shame when I now see how easy it was to humble them instead."

"...So what next, do you think...?" Li Fu asked.

"I don't know," Cui Yan replied. "I'd imagine that His Excellency wants to see the Qiang submit properly, but Zang Ba's horde of reformed brigands are starting to fragment as they tire of being honest men... so I wonder if pacifying at least some of them before they drag Qing Province back into the sea of chaos might be what comes next... and after that, Liu Biao."

Li Fu hummed thoughtfully, gasped suddenly and said, "Oh yes, I forgot to ask, Jigui... how is Gongsun Fang?"

"...Not at all good," Cui Yan replied miserably. "He might be meeting our teacher again soon."

"I'm sorry," Li Fu sighed.

"Such is life," Cui Yan replied. "He, Song Jie and I were but three of Zheng Xuan's students, and how lucky we were to know that wise old man; we've remained friends ever since, even when we were separated by the famines, the wars... and if he passes, then I will do for his family what His Excellency is doing for Guo Jia's. We must all do what we can when we can... and we must accept that good and talented men, like all men, die when their time comes, no matter when that might be. Ying Shao, Cai Yong, Zheng Xuan... they were all losses to art and science, math and literature, philosophy... but as I said, such is life. They live on through their work, though."

"And their families," Li Fu said. "Is it true that His Excellency still plans to confront the Southern Xiongnu and demand the return of the elder Lady Cai...?"

"Yes, and it is another magnificent action," Cui Yan replied. "That poor girl has suffered enough. So if Zang Ba and his friends, Ma Teng and Han Sui, Liu Biao and all of the other rebels in the land can just give His Excellency some breathing space... then perhaps a small but significant wrong can be righted."

The last of the 'great Chanyus of the Wuhuan', Nanlou and Pufulu, declared that they would bring their subordinate chieftains and a small army of their warriors to the Yi River in Yòu Province with the intention of formally submitting to the Han Emperor's Excellency of Works, Cao Cao. The Han representation arrived before the Wuhuan and ensured that there would be no ambushes or unexpected challenges; Cao Cao was glad to be spared the horrors of a migraine for the meeting, which would be tense enough without extreme pain and confusion.

"...What a cold day," Cao Cao said tonelessly.

"And yet we have much to feel warmed about," Jia Xu replied. "This is an important moment, Excellency: but what will we do with them afterward...?"

"I do not want them living beyond the frontier in large numbers, waiting for another Tadun or Louban to excite them to rebellion," Cao Cao said. "They will all of them live here, in the Empire, as subjects of His Majesty and integrate fully; I will agree with my late friend Benchu that their knowledge of horses and horsemanship will prove invaluable, and – unless I am compelled by strong advice to do otherwise – I will mould them into a reliable army as our ancestors did with the Southern Xiongnu of Bing Province. Is there some other course...?"

"No, Excellency, that's the proper course," Jia Xu replied.

"I agree," Hua Xin said. "The Wuhuan are best watched and if possible assimilated."

"...When this meeting is concluded, I will begin the withdrawal to Yè," Cao Cao declared. "I have been too long away from my dear Lady Bian, my other consorts and my children and grandchildren, and I am best placed to negotiate with Huchuquan and Liu Bao from there."

"You are still determined to demand the return of Lady Cai, then...?" Cheng Yu grumbled.

"I am," Cao Cao replied. "The- ...Ah, I see that our 'friends' are arriving at last."

The man charged with negotiating with the Wuhuan leaders, Qian Zhao, hummed thoughtfully and said, "They are."

The attentions of the 5,000-strong Han delegation turned northward: the Wuhuan leaders and their 300 followers approached at speed on well-groomed horses and halted in a disorderly and somehow unnerving fashion that caused many of the Han infantrymen to take one step backward. Generals Zhang Liao, Yue Jin, Zhang Hè and Zhu Ling ordered their cavalries to be ready for a sudden attack, but the concern passed when Chanyu Nanlou dismounted and ordered his followers to part, revealing that the rear of their party was made up of rider-less horses laden with gifts.

"Ah, good," Qian Zhao said with a smile. "Very good indeed...!"

"We are impressed by Cao Cao, the Han's great general!" Chanyu Pufulu bellowed. **"We bring you many fine horses, food, cloth and other things!"**

"...The best part is the 'many fine horses'," Tian Chou noted. "It means that they're serious, as Yan Rou suggested in his letter."

"I'm aware of it, Zitai," Cao Cao replied. "Let us get this necessary show of false courtesy over with quickly."

The leaders of the two cultures met at close quarters and exchanged pleasantries that marked the end of hostilities. The Wuhuan chieftains departed at the end of a cordial open-air banquet and, with well-hidden sadness and frustration, went back to the frontier lands to begin the process of mass migration and inevitable cultural extinction; Cao Cao's entourage returned to Yijing and began formally winding down the northern campaign altogether. The Xiongnu and other tribal peoples would absorb and assimilate those Wuhuan families that did not make the southward journey and opted to stay or go east, west or north: within two generations, the name 'Wuhuan' would be all but lost to the ages.

****

97

The latest of Cao Cao's temporary envoys to the Southern Xiongnu travelled to their settlement in Ping County, Bing Province and asked for an audience with the appointed ruler, Huchuquan: the request was granted, and the envoy met with the Xiongnu leadership in a vast enclosure in the centre of their camp.

"...Cao Cao has won a great victory," Huchuquan said. "He is a great warrior, brave and decisive."

"He is, great chieftain," the envoy replied.

"Why are you here?" Huchuquan's heir and nephew, Liu Bao, asked aggressively. "You want tribute, you want-!"

"Quiet, please, Nephew," Huchuquan ordered. "Let this man talk."

"...His Excellency does indeed hope that his achievement will be recognised and that tribute will be sent to the Son of Heaven as reaffirmation of your pledge to serve and respect the Han throne and its peoples in exchange for your right to settle here," the envoy explained. "But there is another, more delicate matter that His Excellency wishes to negotiate with you shortly, great chieftain... the matter of a woman taken during a raid in Liang Province around twelve years ago that he would like returned."

Huchuquan briefly turned to glare at Liu Bao before he said, "The Southern Xiongnu are grateful for the land that the Han emperor has given us; we do not repay kindness by doing as you suggest. If the raid happened in Liang Province and it happened when you say it happened – twelve years ago – then why are Southern Xiongnu blamed and not the Qiang...?"

"Survivors of the raids confirm that it was Southern Xiongnu *rebels*," the envoy replied. "They went north and east after the raids, not south or west, and wore the clothes and had the ways of the Xiongnu."

"If they went 'north and east' and 'had the ways', why are they Southern Xiongnu and not our former brothers that came from our homeland beyond the Wall...?" Huchuquan countered.

"...This has been carefully researched," the envoy insisted. "I would not have been sent here to make unfounded accusations."

"These... 'rebels'... that you speak of... are known...?" Huchuquan asked warily.

The envoy was about to reply when Liu Bao lost his composure and shouted, "**No more games! I will not-!**"

Huchuquan turned to Liu Bao and said in their native language, "Do not embarrass yourself in front of this man, Nephew! Things have changed now! The Wuhuan's fate will be ours if we try to keep certain things that we can do without!"

"...I am your nephew *and* your heir," Liu Bao retorted. "Your cooperation with them will harm me!"

"That goes without saying," Huchuquan insisted. "But by copying your father's behaviour and doing what you did, you harmed yourself. Nonetheless... I will do what I can."

Liu Bao nodded tersely and grunted.

"...What should I take to His Excellency from this meeting, great chieftain...?" the envoy asked politely.

Huchuquan smiled and said in the Han Chinese language, "I am prepared to discuss this matter further... with the right people."

"His Excellency knows this," the envoy replied. "I shall leave now."
The envoy then bowed; Huchuquan nodded slowly and gestured to
his guards, who escorted the envoy from the enclosure.
"They should not be able to come here and speak like that!" Liu
Bao complained.
"...Did you take all of the women from this raid for yourself...?"
Huchuquan asked.
"I... do not know which raid they refer to," Liu Bao admitted.
"...This is... this is very *bad*, Nephew," Huchuquan sighed.
"Make them reward us well or tell them 'no'," Liu Bao insisted.
"Remember, Uncle, that I am the next Chanyu and that this
woman either belongs to me or one of my trusted followers."
"I will not give her away cheaply," Huchuquan replied. "Of course
I know that we must be careful, yes, but not too humble, or we'll
lose more than this woman of yours. But I warn you, Nephew:
make no more mistakes or you might doom us all."
Liu Bao scoffed and left the enclosure.

Cao Cao's return to Yè City was a muted affair: the majority wore
white articles to show their grief at the loss of Guo Jia. Cao
himself was dressed from head to foot in white and colourless
clothing as he rode through the gates with Guo Jia's son Yi at his
side: Cao then had Yi return to his family's allocated rooms within
his vast mansion while he went to his audience hall to chair a
meeting of his senior officials.
"The Wuhuan are dealt with: now I must properly mourn the
genius that made this victory possible," Cao Cao declared; Cheng
Yu shook his head disappointedly.
"...You want to have a grand memorial service for Guo Jia," Ji
Province Registrar Li Fu said.
"Guo Fengxiao is in a coffin but is yet to be entombed," Cao Cao
replied. "I asked this of his son and heir because I cannot bear the
thought of his memorial being left to any man but me, the man
that he turned from a lizard to a dragon."
Cheng Yu snorted irritably but quietly; some guessed the reason
behind his gesture and silently agreed.
"...I wonder if there will ever be another man that can do as he
did," Cao Cao continued. "In ten years, gentlemen, he reversed
my fortunes, bringing me back from the brink and enabling me to
defeat Yuan Shu, Yuan Shao and Tadun in quick succession: he
could turn me away from the path of folly with a glance, a smirk
or a cogent quip. We would not be sat here as the guardians of
Wei Prefecture, the Yuan brothers crushed, the tribes humbled if
not for Fengxiao... I will scream to the Heavens for his return a
thousand times!"
"...As will we all, Your Excellency," Registrar Liu Yè said as he
stared at Cheng Yu, who was visibly struggling with the urge to
speak out.
"I pray that I haven't a headache on that day," Cao Cao sighed.
"It would... harm my ability to give my all to mourning my friend."
"We're close to securing Hua Tuo's service," Liu Yè insisted. "Your
physical suffering might then be at an end."
"...Yes," Cao Cao murmured. "That would be *something*."

Cao Cao finished his work for the day and went to his living quarters: his principal wife, Lady Bian, poured tea for him and asked, "Does all go well, Husband...?"

"As well as one can expect," Cao Cao replied. "But I don't want to talk about business; I have devoted enough of my life to the Han recently that one evening's relaxation cannot be seen as a vice."

"I shall say no more of your work, Husband," Lady Bian promised.

"Why would you want to?" Cao Cao asked. "You embraced me upon my return and spoke of how I had been missed; it is that work that took me away, so be glad that I am as sick of it as you should be."

"...Are you pleased that our eldest son's first child is doing well...?" Lady Bian asked nervously.

"I'm done being angry with Pi," Cao Cao insisted. "Yuan Xi is dead now, so the controversy is at an end. The child is his: those ridiculous rumours are just that. Yuan Xi was a pathetic individual that lacked the backbone to stand up to his brothers, the Wuhuan, his own subordinates or his stepmother: we are expected to believe that he heroically smuggled his person into this city while it was under siege by most of my army for a night of passion with his imprisoned wife and then had her swear to secrecy...?"

Lady Bian smiled at the idea.

"*Li Fu* got in, yes, but he is smart and courageous," Cao Cao continued. "Yuan Xi...? ...That gutless fool wouldn't have got past the mad woman that awaited him at the door of his wife's bedchamber, never mind the high walls and street patrols that his own brother placed as defences to keep Xi out as much as anyone and the tens of thousands of men that I had around the city to catch whichever of the Yuans came my way. Let my detractors continue to fantasise that a 'Yuan in the fold' will one day inherit my legacy... for all the good it would do them. It's *nonsense*."

"...And how do you feel about your other children, Husband...?" Lady Bian asked.

"Yellow-beard still disappoints me with his lack of interest in using his brain, but so be it," Cao Cao replied. "Zhi is so very talented... every bit the future scholar or statesman. My daughters are beautiful and wise and will make good matches for the heroes that I will introduce them to. Chong... continues to amaze and frighten me with his intellect and precociousness; to think that he can preside over legal cases at the age of eleven with the wits of a man six times his age... incredible. Forgive me, my lady, but even though I love my eldest sons very dearly and will not move away from the logical choice of making Pi my heir... Chong is the son that I would most like to leave my legacy to. He may be too frail for the saddle or the sword, and he may be too gentle and good-natured for the tastes of some, but he is a prodigy that would make the Empire the envy of the world."

"I know it," Lady Bian admitted. "And I can see your reasoning for harbouring such ideas, Husband. Chong never ceases to amaze, as you say, and he is so kind, so thoughtful, so honest and so intelligent that it is difficult not to like him."

"But I will obey the proper law of succession," Cao Cao insisted. "Pi has shown that he can be a great statesman, and I gladly speak of him as my son and heir."

"...The Guo family are settling in well," Lady Bian said.

"I'm glad," Cao Cao replied. "Fengxiao was... *is*... irreplaceable as a confidante and friend. I wish that I could do more to honour him."

"...What will you do next...?" Lady Bian asked. "I hear you speaking of Lady Cai Yan; you intend to rescue her from the Xiongnu. I know what it is to be trapped from my time as a courtesan, paying off family debts with my entire being... so when I think of that girl being the creature of some barbarian prince for *twelve years...*"

"...Truly, she was abandoned by the gods," Cao Cao replied wistfully. "I now know that she was married before her abduction, but that her husband died at some point soon after they were wed. The chaos of the time – and the destruction of records – makes it difficult for me to know if the poor fellow was ill, or if the Xiongnu or Qiang killed him, or if he was a victim of a purge that Li Jue and Guo Si – or Wang Yun – carried out."

"Can you not ask Jia Xu...?" Lady Bian said.

"He pleads ignorance and I choose to believe him," Cao Cao replied. "I suppose it doesn't matter in the end; the man died. And then, after the pain of losing her father and her husband, she was abducted by the followers of Liu Bao, heir apparent of the Southern Xiongnu; twelve years, as you rightly said, of being his creature, granting him two children in the process that I will not be allowed to take when I free her..."

"How terrible," Lady Bian sighed.

"But I *must* rescue her, and she must accept the loss of contact with her offspring by that 'barbarian prince'," Cao Cao said. "That wrong must be righted."

"...Will you marry her...?" Lady Bian asked.

"No," Cao Cao replied immediately. "I have found a match for her sister and will do the same for her; I must not be seen to be ransoming her from Liu Bao and then marrying her... such a move might provoke a certain type of criticism. It will be another man's job to protect her and restore her faith in Heaven and men."

"Choose well, Husband," Lady Bian pleaded. "The poor thing has suffered enough."

Cao Cao nodded silently.

"...When will you do this...?" Lady Bian asked.

"As soon as possible," Cao Cao replied. "But I must first go to the capital to hopefully – *hopefully* – receive reward in the form of higher rank that should make that task and others even easier to accomplish. I *must* capitalise on the shock and disarray that were generated by my victory before they ebb away... or my task will be a thousand times more challenging. If only my head would not hurt so often..."

"Heaven is surely with you, Husband," Lady Bian said. "Heaven is surely with you."

Two days passed: Cao Cao's envoy to the Southern Xiongnu left Ping County and immediately travelled to Yè City to meet with Cao Cao privately.

"They'll discuss it, will they...?" Cao Cao chuckled.

"They will," the envoy replied pointlessly.

"My thanks," Cao Cao said. "You may go back to Yangqu now, and give my regards to Inspector Zhang."

The envoy bowed low, turned and retreated from Cao Cao's private study; Cao then turned to Jia Xu, Yuan Huan and Hua Xin and said, "I will go and negotiate this in person after I have been to Xuchang. I want to go before that, but I won't."

"That's wise," Hua Xin replied. "The Son of Heaven-"

"Will not be kept waiting long," Cao Cao said. "Now then: I understand that Hua Tuo has been found...?"

"He has been *sighted*... on a road leading to Pei County," Yuan Huan said. "Chen Gui will not allow him to leave the region."

"...I hoped to get everything done before I was beset by another headache, but I can feel another brewing within my skull already," Cao Cao continued. "I do not want to be at anything other than my best... I *have* to be at my best."

"He will soon be on his way here," Registrar Liu Yè promised.

"...May he be the marvellous saviour that I have heard about," Cao Cao muttered.

"Dong Zhao has asked whether he should return to Xu Province now," Yuan Huan said suddenly.

"Oh, right, yes... I'd almost forgotten about him, what with everything else that I've had to deal with," Cao Cao replied. "For now, yes... but tell him to be cautious. I've posted Yu Jin to the Ji-Qing border in expectation of trouble from the former Mount Tai Bandits... something else that poor Fengxiao warned me of before... ... ...well, anyway, I expect some trouble there, and Xu Province has been guarded by Zang Ba's friend Sun Guan since Gongren moved north to oversee the canals, and Sun might not want to go home without an argument."

"Sun Guan is, like Zang Ba, a more agreeable type that won't push his luck," Yuan Huan suggested. "The general belief is that it is Wu Dun or Chang Xi that will 'return to their old ways', not Zang or Sun or Yin Li."

"Thank you for being so informed," Cao Cao replied. "I want to reassign poor Miaocai away from Yingchuan: he's been there for years now and Man Po'ning has stabilised Runan Prefecture sufficiently enough for there to be no need for such a fearsome gate guard at Yingchuan anymore. I want to prepare for the next campaigns straight away and embark upon the first of them within the next two-to-four months."

"That's too soon," Yuan Huan suggested. "We've only just-"

"The troops that fought in the north will mostly remain here," Cao Cao said. "The generals are coming with me to Jing, of course, but Li Tong, Lu Zhao and Feng Kai have their own men that I can use for this and I expect Jing to yield without a fight anyway."

"...There's no way that Liu Biao would yield Jing to you, Excellency," Hua Xin suggested. "I've been on the Jiangxia border long enough to know that."

"Ah, but you know something else, don't you, Mister Hua...?" Cao Cao chuckled.

"...Sun Quan is preparing to attack Jiangxia again," Hua Xin said.

"And this time, Hua Ziyu, there will be no retreat," Cao Cao suggested. "Sun Quan has been pacifying the Shanyue and amassing forces for this for a couple of years. He lost his finest naval officer in the last battle, so I hear, and Taishi Ci passed away last year as well; he's looking to do as I have just done and end the feud with Huang Zu once and for all. Sun Quan might not find the going smooth, but he will ultimately win as I did, and Huang Zu will die: that will weaken Liu Biao's grip and harm his already failing health, and that ensures that I will either be dealing with a sickly, senile Liu Biao or one of his sons... neither of which impresses me."

"But doesn't Biao's illness leave an opening for Liu Bei to seize power in Jing?" Hua Xin asked.

"Liu Biao's wife, Lady Cai, and her brother Cai Mao are, from what I understand from my time in Nan County, much like Empress Dowager Hè and Hè Jin, or Empress Dowager Liang and Liang Ji before them," Jia Xu replied. "Lady Cai has a lot of influence in Liu Biao's inner court, mainly because her brother is the Chief Admiral of the navy and Acting Commander-in-Chief of the army in northern Jing; Lady Cai is also the childhood guardian of Liu Cong, Biao's younger son, and is said to have a preference for him over the elder son Qi despite neither being of her blood. In fact, my last intelligence reports pointed toward her having arranged a marriage between Cong and one of her nieces, which would tie the Liu and Cai clans for a successive generation, just as the Liangs did before they were destroyed."

"Your point being...?" Hua Xin asked as politely as he could.

"Liu Bei is hated, quite frankly, by everyone in Liu Biao's inner circle," Jia Xu continued. "Liu Biao is said to trust him and argue for him, but the consensus is that Liu Bei will, as you suggest, want to try to seize power at any given opportunity, which means that Bei is always kept at a distance. At the moment, Bei is in Xinye, which is far enough away from the northern capital Xiangyang for him to be the last one to know when some change of regime is needed."

"...Xinye is across the Han River, quite some distance north and east of Fan City," Hua Xin noted. "He really is being kept at a distance, isn't he...?"

"And he must ask permission to speak with Liu Biao, usually going through Kuai Yue or Wang Can, who both detest him," Jia Xu said. "If Biao were to fall ill, the advisers will coalesce around Cai Mao and Lady Cai, and the successor will be of their choosing, either Liu Qi – who is afflicted by vice – or Liu Cong, who is at worst another Yuan Shang but more likely another Liu Zhang."

"If he is as much of a cowardly sycophant as Liu Zhang of Yi Province, Cong would either pay tribute and beg to remain as Governor or submit and tender the seal outright," Yuan Huan suggested. "And if he is, 'at worst', another Yuan Shang, then he will be as dead as my rebel cousin by the end of next year."

"...I am more optimistic already!" Cao Cao chuckled. "But no more about Jing for now: let us focus on other matters now."

Cao Cao got his wish and led a memorial service for Guo Jia four days later: every official without urgent duties was instructed to attend. The front yard of the Cao mansion was a sea of white robes and turbans, and white flags hung from countless poles across the city: Cao Cao knelt before the coffin and cried, **"Fengxiao! Fengxiao! Why have you left me, Fengxiao, and gone back to the Heavens when so much is left to do...? Who else is there, Fengxiao...? FENGXIAO!"** Xun Wenruo noticed that Cheng Yu was grimacing angrily and frowned disapprovingly in the hope that the older man would see him and show more sorrow.

"**Ten years ago, Fengxiao, I was a wandering fool!**" Cao Cao continued. "**I had great power, but was unable to make proper use of it! I had a great army, but lacked the skill to properly deploy it! I had wise heads at all sides, but none could sway me! Only** *you*, **Fengxiao, truly knew how my mind worked, and only** *you*, **Fengxiao, could have guided me to the many victories that are so bitter-sweet when pondering your early passing! But now you are gone, Fengxiao, and... and that cannot be so! You are my friend, Fengxiao! Return, Fengxiao! FENGXIAO!**"

The gathering wailed and gesticulated in a unified show of grief; Cheng Yu, Kong Rong and some of the other, more cynical guests were more reserved but participated to a certain degree.

"**...Fengxiao...!**" Cao Cao sobbed. "**Fengxiao, I... I have not the words! This should be a moment for fine poetry that commemorates your life and mourns your passing, but I am at a loss! What words could truly do justice to your short time on this world under Heaven...? How could I, A'Man, possibly craft a suitable eulogy to a man whose only peers are men like Jiang Ziya, Zhang Liang and Sun Tzu...?**"

The mass mourning continued; Cheng Yu bit his hand and started to weep for an entirely different reason.

"**...You repaired my army after the loss at Wan, humbled the heretic Yuan Shu, routed the villain Liu Bei and smashed Yuan Shao's mighty hordes at Guandu!**" Cao Cao continued. "**Time and again, it was your foresight that predicted the weakness of men, preparing the way for others to do their part! When other men acted, they acted in accordance with your brilliant assessment of their character! Truly, Fengxiao, you knew men better than they knew themselves! You knew that Yuan Shu would be his own undoing! You knew that Xu Yòu would come to me with the key to victory at Guandu! You knew that Yuan Shang and Yuan Tan would bicker when we turned our backs, that Tadun's three-hundred-thousand would crumble if attacked unexpectedly, and that Gongsun Kang would deliver the heads of the brothers to me if I waited patiently! Who else could see...? Who else...? ...FENGXIAO!**"

The mourning reached a crescendo.

"**FENGXIAO!**" Cao Cao screamed. "**Fengxiao, you are an irreplaceable loss to me! You are my friend, my confidante, my conscience, my eyes and ears, my sense of reason, and now you are gone! Why did you not leave a clue for me, a clue to the man that can take your place and guide me as you did...? Who will help me save the Han now, Fengxiao...? FENGXIAO...! Come back, Fengxiao...!**"

The mourners began to chant pleas for Guo Jia's return between their anguished wailing; even Cheng Yu, in the end, started to cry out for Guo Jia out of desperation.

"...Fengxiao...!" Cao Cao sighed as he placed his hands on the coffin and rested his forehead against it. "You... must come back to me...!"

Cheng Yu retired to his office after the exhausting ritual; Xun Wenruo followed him and asked, "Why did you act that way, Elder

Cheng…? …And don't pretend that you do not know what I mean."

"…The problem here, Xun Yu, is that you *don't* need to pretend that *you* do not know what *I* meant, else you'd not ask such a stupid question," Cheng Yu retorted.

"You're right, I don't understand," Xun Wenruo said. "We were mourning a colleague, a friend, a man that did amazing things! Even Chen Changwen, who constantly decried his self-destructive ways and heckled his ideas, was out there crying his head off, but you were unmoved! Why are you so heartless…? Is it that-?"

"Don't *dare* accuse me of jealousy, Wenruo," Cheng Yu snapped. "You know that isn't it."

"…It's customary to speak in grandiose terms when mourning the dead and calling them back!" Xun Wenruo protested. "What were we to do, cry out, 'We were a team, and you did your part, and we are just upset at losing one of many, many talented men that surround the Excellency of Works because it means more work for us in the future'…?"

"Are you really so dense…?" Cheng Yu scoffed. "Or maybe I'm being unfair; you are, after all, missing a lot of the little snipes that the rest of us have to hear because you are in Xuchang. But he's going to join you in the capital in the coming weeks… we'll see if you can be so wilfully ignorant then."

Xun Wenruo huffed irritably and said, "I will never understand you, you…! …You miserable, bitter old man!"

Cheng Yu snorted a laugh; Xun Wenruo retreated without responding further.

The Chancellor of Pei County, Chen Gui, heard that Hua Tuo had returned to his home in the region, so he visited the property and demanded an audience.

"…You are more forceful in your tone than you were before," Hua Tuo said. "Is this because your lord is now more powerful…?"

"You're aware enough to know that His Excellency has defeated the Wuhuan and the Yuans and brought peace to the northeast, then," Chen Gui retorted. "You should then be aware of the time taken to achieve all of these wondrous things."

"The term 'wondrous' is subjective, Mister Chen," Hua Tuo replied. "A lot of people died so that 'peace was brought': Ying Shao was a man that, as a fellow scholar, I respected immensely, especially since we shared an interest in rescuing finite knowledge from the abyss of wilful ignorance."

"The battle for the soul of the northeast was a necessary one," Chen Gui insisted. "You cannot blame His Excellency alone for-"

"I did not say that I blamed any one man for it," Hua Tuo said. "But you have once again turned the conversation to Cao Cao, so I assume that you are here about his headaches yet again…?"

"You are strangely lacking in compassion!" Chen Gui suggested. "His Excellency has, as I tried to say before, achieved a lot in a short time, and he would be able to do even more in even less time – perhaps with the consequence of a lower loss of life – if he were only spared the pain of his headaches!"

"The pressures of his high office or a trauma on the brain caused by injury during one of his many battles to 'bring peace' are the two most likely causes," Hua Tuo retorted. "Will he relinquish power or let me – or any man – take an axe near his skull to look

476

inside it...?"

"There are other possibilities and you know it," Chen Gui scoffed. "Stop trying to avoid assisting Excellency Cao: you harm the Empire in the process."

"...I will visit His Excellency in Yè and review him during an attack of his affliction," Hua Tuo conceded. "If I can help then I will help: if I cannot I will probably be killed, but won't that happen if I continue to refuse...?"

"You... should not say such things," Chen Gui retorted.

Hua Tuo smiled and said, "May I fetch my medical bag...?"

"You will need it," Chen Gui replied. "A travel bag is also advised: you will be gone for some time."

Hua Tuo sighed irritably and retreated to his study.

"...Finally," Chen Gui murmured.

****

98

Cao Cao was struck down with another migraine before he was due to depart for Xuchang: Hua Tuo – who had just arrived in Yè – was rushed to Cao's bedside.

"I will need to know *everything* regarding the patient, Registrar Liu," Hua Tuo said.

"...'Everything'...?" Liu Yè exclaimed.

"**Why???**" Cao Cao screamed. "**What more do you need to know but what is wrong with me?! I have a pain in my head! Is that not obvious???**"

"...An affliction is not always what is seems to be," Hua Tuo explained. "I apply a holistic approach to medicine: pain in the head can actually be caused by a malady of the stomach, or-"

"**What are you talking about???**" Cao Cao snapped. "**The pain is in my head! My HEAD! If it was my stomach then my stomach would hurt! Are you mocking me, Hua Tuo???**"

"I am answering your question," Hua Tuo insisted. "The body is a complex thing, Your Excellency: think of it as being much the same as food entering and exiting the body by different paths and as different substances, or how the brain manifests creative ideas through the hands and mouth."

"...Can you help me or not?" Cao Cao whimpered.

"Please say that the answer is 'yes'," Liu Yè whispered.

"...I might be able to help," Hua Tuo replied. "The answer might be medicine – though I would need to know what causes the pain – or acupuncture, which requires my knowing the right acupuncture point or points, which again requires my knowing the root cause of the pain."

"If you... help me, Master Hua, then you can... name your reward," Cao Cao pleaded. "Name your... your price, and it is yours, for when you... restore my health you... you guarantee the security of the Empire."

"I only ask that I be allowed to continue my work, Your Excellency" Hua Tuo replied.

"**A great man!**" Cao Cao cried. "A great... man... that seeks so little for doing... so much!"

"Let us avoid praise until I have done something," Hua Tuo said. "I must now repeat my request to know everything about the patient's medical history... what Chancellor Cao eats, how much sleep he gets, how much exercise he has, the balance of his humours, the condition of his hair and skin, past physical and emotional traumas... everything that is relevant."

"What you need to know, you will know it," Cao Cao insisted. "Ziyang, give him the answers that he requires."

"...As you wish, Excellency," Liu Yè replied.

"If I can help as well, please say so," Lady Bian said anxiously.

"...I shall first catalogue His Excellency's diet," Liu Yè suggested.

"That is a good place to start," Hua Tuo replied.

Cao Cao writhed and groaned as his migraine persisted: Hua Tuo finished his assessment and said, "I diagnose acupuncture to be the solution and will apply the technique with Your Excellency's permission."

"*Anything*," Cao Cao replied. "Just get rid of this pain!"

"...Very good," Hua Tuo said. "I will need hot water for sterilisation of my instruments: might someone fetch me a kettle...?"

"Yes, yes," Liu Yè said: Lady Bian retreated to personally fetch a kettle of hot water before Liu Yè had the chance to ask.

"Lack of cleanliness of the medical instruments is a surprisingly common issue that harms the patient more than some obviously realise," Hua Tuo said as he reached into his bag and produced a small roll of cloth that contained a collection of long, extremely thin needles.

"What are you going to do with those...?" Liu Yè asked.

"This is the remedy that I will apply," Hua Tuo explained. "The pain in the head is caused by something that is best described as 'travelling through the body from another place'. What the exact cause is, I cannot say for certain yet, but if I apply the needle to the point that I call 'bubbling fountain', His Excellency should see an almost immediate improvement in his condition."

"...You... you want to stick a *needle* into His Excellency's body...?" Liu Yè exclaimed.

"That is the essence of acupuncture," Hua Tuo replied. "Do I have permission or not, Excellency...?"

Cao Cao stared at the needle with bulging eyes but said nothing.

"...I must ask again, Your Excellency, if I have permission," Hua Tuo prompted.

"...**Xu Chu,**" Cao Cao barked; the giant bodyguard took a step forward and stared at Hua Tuo as Cao Cao added, "I am aware of the 'acupuncture' treatment and its unavoidable use of needles, but this man may be a friend of one of my many enemies. Xu Chu: you and Liu Yè will watch this man carefully, and if he does anything suspicious you will stop him – and kill him if necessary – before he can harm me seriously."

Hua Tuo sighed miserably and shook his head.

"...I give you permission to treat me, Hua Tuo," Cao Cao continued. "But be warned: if you are an assassin you will not live to take another job."

"If I were an assassin, Excellency, then the task would already be done," Hua Tuo retorted. "A needle in the wrong place can paralyse or kill a man; and simply touching some plants for a moment or breathing the spores of some fungi in all innocence can condemn a man to death in days."

Liu Yè shuddered.

"Now may I please have a kettle of boiling water...?" Hua Tuo asked again.

"Lady Bian has gone to request a kettle," Liu Yè replied. "There should be one available any- Ah, here we are."

A servant entered the room with a kettle of water and placed it on a small table near Cao Cao's bedside; Lady Bian returned to her place near the door and watched intently.

"...And this treatment... will reduce the pain...?" Cao Cao asked.

"With any luck, Excellency, it will get rid of the pain altogether," Hua Tuo replied as he studied one of his long acupuncture needles in order to ensure that it was free of defects. "I will now sterilise the needle."

The audience watched as Hua Tuo dipped the needle into the boiling water and subsequently dried it with a piece of cloth; the physician examined the needle for a second time as he said, "You

will need to lift your shirt, Excellency: the 'bubbling fountain' point
is in the diaphragm area, above the stomach."
"*Again* you are talking about treating my head by treating my
stomach!" Cao Cao heckled. "What do you hope to achieve by
sticking needles into-!"
"*Aiee*... do you want my help or not, Your Excellency...?" Hua Tuo
asked wearily.
Cao Cao winced as he sat up slightly and tugged at his shirt to
expose his chest and stomach.
"Lay as flat as you can please, Your Excellency," Hua Tuo ordered,
and Cao Cao complied.
"...Will it hurt...?" Liu Yè asked as Hua Tuo prepared to insert the
needle into his patient's body.
"It cannot hurt more that this headache, Ziyang!" Cao Cao
snapped. "Get it over with, please, Mister Hua, and-!"
"You *must stay still*, Excellency," Hua Tuo ordered.
Cao Cao fought the urge to writhe in agony and tensed his body;
Hua Tuo leant forward and – with steady hands and uncanny
accuracy – slowly and carefully inserted the needle into the flesh
that concealed Cao Cao's thoracic diaphragm.
"How do you feel, Excellency...?" Hua Tuo asked.
Cao Cao's eyes widened as he realised that something had
changed almost immediately; he smiled broadly and said, "It... it
has cleared!"
Lady Bian gasped and bit her hand; Liu Yè laughed disbelievingly.
"It has cleared!" Cao Cao reiterated. "It has cleared, gone,
disappeared! How did you-!"
"Please do not be so animated, Excellency," Hua Tuo said. "You
must be careful how you move while the needle is in place."
"How...?" Cao Cao asked. "How is this possible...?"
"As I have already said, Excellency, the exact reasoning is
unknown to me as yet," Hua Tuo replied. "The muscle at that
point seems to have some great significance and affects the most
unusual things."
"I imagine that you have a better answer that only your own
profession understands," Cao Cao said. "How the scholar of arts or
literature can be considered to be above the medical physician
when a man can be cured of such horrible pain in an instant is
truly beyond me!"
"All the same, I am a scholar first and a physician second," Hua
Tuo replied.
"...How exact is the art of 'acupuncture', Master...?" Liu Yè asked.
"If any fool is unleashed upon the body with these needles, bad
things are certain to follow," Hua Tuo replied. "I've heard of
incompetent students of skilled practitioners that have inflicted
cruel and sometimes permanent damage; the user requires a
steady hand, a sharp mind, the ability to sense the exact point of
application and the understanding of exactly how far to insert the
needle. Any small deviation from that essential accuracy is
potentially serious... very serious."
"But what a thing it is when done properly!" Cao Cao said with
barely-contained excitement. "Master Hua, I have endured these
headaches with ever-increasing ferocity since I was a youth! If I
had only encountered this remedy ten years ago, I might still have
my eldest son and all of the work might already have been done!"

"I am glad that I could help," Hua Tuo replied. "I shall remove the needle after a set time; the pain will not recur when I do so, because the affliction will have passed."

"Leave it there for as long as it must be there!" Cao Cao said. "Can it be there longer than the horrible pain, the confusion and the exhaustion...?"

"Bless you, Master Hua Tuo!" Lady Bian cried.

"...There must, of course, be a longer-term solution," Hua Tuo suggested. "There are other men that either possess the same level of proficiency in acupuncture or have the latent talent for it: there is one man, Fan A of Peng, that-"

"I will not risk anyone – even a man that you recommend – taking your place, Master Hua," Cao Cao said. "It must be you. You are henceforth appointed as my personal physician."

"I must travel in order to learn more, Excellency," Hua Tuo insisted. "There are many others that have or can learn the skills needed to perform acupuncture, but there are a million afflictions, including yours, that might have cures that have yet to be found. If they are to be found, then-"

"I am in good spirits; please do not ruin the moment," Cao Cao said. "I am the Excellency of Works, Master Hua, and I have a lot of important work to do: the next most important job in the land after filling my head with knowledge is keeping it from hurting, and that job is now yours."

Hua Tuo exhaled loudly and nodded in resignation.

"If I am spared the pain and the weariness that comes afterward, then I can travel to Xuchang in the morning," Cao Cao decided. "And rest assured that I shall!"

Liu Yè and Xu Chu grinned and laughed as they shared in Cao Cao's relief; Lady Bian was crying and repeatedly thanking Hua Tuo under her breath. Hua Tuo was the only person present that was unhappy; he hated the idea of being permanently attached to Cao Cao's entourage and was already constructing escape plans in his mind.

****

99

The former Mount Tai Bandits of Qing Province were as surprised by the outcome of Cao Cao's northern campaign as everyone else, but the mood was still defiant in some quarters.

"Could Cao have marched north and done any of what he's done without us watching his back...?" the senior ex-bandit Chang Xi asked of a large, divided audience. **"Could he have marched at all if we hadn't taken Qing for him...? Wouldn't he still be in Xuchang biting his nails and waiting for opportunities without our help, and wouldn't the Yuans still be alive and have all the northeast provinces...?"**

A number of men voiced their agreement.

"I already know your point, but I'm going to waste time asking anyway, just for *clarity*... and to give you an out," the overall coalition leader, Zang Ba, retorted angrily. **"Where are you leading...?"**

"We should be rewarded!" Chang Xi replied. **"We're doing all the work here in Qing! We put down the rebellions, keep the crime families in check and we even collect the bloody taxes so Cao Cao's little men in robes can pay themselves as a pat on the back for our hard work! We deserve *power*, and if we're not given it then we should *take it*!"**

The declaration provoked some enthusiastic chanting.

"We'll get whatever we're offered!" Zang Ba heckled. **"Who are you now, eh...? You reckon you're stronger than Yuan Shang or Tadun...?"**

"You're a bloody coward!" Chang Xi countered. **"You went down on one knee and gave your family over as hostages without even being asked to! At least Yuan Shang and Tadun put up a fight!"**

Zang Ba instinctively turned to his left to seek the support of his friend Sun Guan, but Sun was in Xu Province as acting guardian; Zang then turned to look at Yin Li, who said, **"I agree with you, Xuangao, but Chang's winning more hearts by the day and I can't do much about it. A lot of our blokes are pissed off with it all."**

"That's right!" Chang Xi cried. **"We've most of us had enough! We've been the Han's dogs for years now, and nothing ever gets any better! Where will we be sent next, ay...? Will we be expected to fight Gongsun Kang in Liaodong, or the Qiang in Liang, or the Shanyue in Jiangdong...? Where will we be sent to be the front line next, to die in the place of Cao's soldiers while they get all the rewards...?"**

"How should I know???" Zang Ba replied desperately. **"I-!"**

"We're even putting down our own now!" Chang Xi complained. **"Twice now, me and Wu Dun have had to kill our old mates because they were accused of 'going back to their old ways'!"**

"But they *had*!" Zang Ba protested. **"They raided villages, and we can't-!"**

"*No*, Zang, *no*!" Chang Xi interrupted. **"*Enough* is *enough*! We don't get the *supplies* we need, the *money* we need, the symbols of *authority* that we need, just the dirty work and**

being ordered to run at swords with bugger all in the way of rewards! This is going *nowhere*!"

The majority voiced their agreement with Chang Xi.

"**You *can't* go back to being bandits, you fools!**" Zang Ba protested. "**It was a reckless enough idea before, but after what's just happened, it's *certain death*! He'll come after you, and-!**"

"**And so will *you*, won't you, you two-faced bastard!**" Chang Xi heckled. "**Just like you went after Ren and Liao!**"

"**...Yeah, I will!**" Zang Ba retorted. "**I'll *have to*, because-!**"

"**Because Cao Cao *owns you now*!**" Chang Xi snapped; most of the other hecklers fell silent at that moment since they were still inwardly loyal to Zang Ba and were not prepared to go as far as Chang Xi.

"**...See...?**" Zang Ba chuckled.

"**See *what*...?**" Chang Xi growled.

Zang Ba exhaled loudly and said, "**Being angry is one thing; being stupid is another! We can't bargain from the outside, Chang: didn't all those years of trying to and failing teach you that at all...?**"

"**...Fine! Fine! You stay and carry on being Cao Cao's shields and cart-horses!**" Chang Xi retorted. "**I'm done with this now! You hear me...? I'm DONE!**"

The hall fell silent as Chang Xi and his large group of followers retreated; Zang Ba's following still outnumbered the dissenters but they had obviously diminished in number significantly.

"...What will you do, Xuangao...?" Yin Li asked quietly.

"...Report it to Cao Cao and hope that Chang Xi's content with sulking," Zang Ba replied. "Chang's an old mate: I don't want to fight him, Yin, but if he forces my hand, then I have no choice."

Cao Cao's other 'mercenary force' – the Qiang tribal confederacy led by Ma Teng – was also suffering from divided reactions to the defeat of the Wuhuan and the submissive stances adopted by the Xianbei Confederacy and the Southern Xiongnu.

"Cao will demand *our* submission next," Ma Teng's eldest son, Ma Chao, said before an audience comprised of his father, brothers and some subordinate chieftains. "But we are not the Wuhuan! We are stronger than the Wuhuan and-!"

"Son... please say no more," Ma Teng interrupted. "Yes, he will probably demand tributes and a hostage in order to ensure our continued cooperation, and I'm surprised that he has not done so already, but he will demand similar things from Han Sui and Song Jian and-"

"None of us should agree to it!" Ma Chao snapped. "Do we want to be theirs forever...?"

"...We must be patient," Ma Teng insisted. "I intend to have some sort of discussion with Han Sui in the future, and I believe that we'll be more likely to cooperate without fighting if we're both hurting from having family taken from us by the Han emperor. We can unite, take some place and demand the return of their hostages in exchange for ours, and then we can start to build a proper coalition that will shame Tadun and, maybe, inspire Budugen and coerce the Xianbei into fighting."

"...And who would the Han want as a hostage...?" Ma Chao asked

snidely. "They like to take the eldest son of the leader in most cases; you really think that I'll let them take me as a hostage...?"
"I imagine that Cao will demand someone else... since he knows what a handful you would be," Ma Teng replied dryly.
"This is not a laughing matter," Ma Chao growled. "Who would you let him take?"
"Whoever he asks for," Ma Teng sighed. "Like I said, we can bargain later when we've re-established peace with Han Sui."
"The Han lackeys here will *laugh at us*," Ma Chao muttered.

Liang Province's Army Adviser, Zhao Ang, was monitoring the movements of the Qiang rulers with the utmost caution from his home in Ji City; his wife, Lady Wang, became concerned about his health and said, "You ask your agents to visit this house with information at all hours: why can you not entrust more people with this task, Husband...?"
"Put simply, I am too frightened of the complacency that others seem to show at the worst moments," Zhao Ang replied. "I took on this awful role because I felt that it might prevent another... another 'avoidable dilemma'... and the chances of such a thing might have increased now, rather than what might be expected."
"...You can speak more openly," Lady Wang said. "Liang Shuang's ability to have a hold over our family haunts you as it does me."
"And he was a mere criminal, a rebel," Zhao Ang replied. "Yet all the same, he outwitted me, killed our sons and almost..."
Zhao Ang stopped talking, lowered his head and shuddered violently as he thought of his fallen sons and the horrors that followed Liang Shuang's successful rebellion in their hometown.
"...'Almost'," Lady Wang said with a sad smile. "But our daughter is alive and I am not violated or, self-pitying fool that I was for a while afterward, dead; our sons died as heroes, defending our hometown from a villain, and would not want us to be left unguarded by their passing."
"...Quite so," Zhao Ang said soberly. "And do not chastise yourself: you were brave when it mattered, and any woman would have been confused after-"
"The details are known to us both," Lady Wang interrupted. "Explain your sudden need to increase your workload and exhaust yourself, please."
"Ma Teng and Han Sui are great dragons to Liang Shuang's tiny lizard, my lady, and their appetites are equally larger," Zhao Ang replied. "The two of them tore Liang Province apart twenty years ago and again a few years later when they attacked Chang'an with that hankerer Liu Yan; I am excited by the news that the Wuhuan tribes have been defeated and hope that it provokes a lot of submissions across the Empire, Liang Shuangs and Ma Tengs alike, but... but news such as this sometimes solicits the opposite reaction to the desired."
Lady Wang nodded and said, "You fear their fear."
"Precisely," Zhao Ang replied. "If they react to this news by trying to secure Liang Province before Excellency Cao can finish stabilising the northeast and mobilise another army, then we might have to endure something terrible... and I want to be prepared for it if at all possible, especially given that Inspector Wei is one of many men that are considering travelling to Xuchang

to congratulate Excellency Cao on his victory and back various petitions, which leaves the region understaffed and even more vulnerable than it usually is."

"...If there is any way that I can help, I will," Lady Wang insisted. "If I can help you to avert or predict a crisis then by all means show me how; if the worst happens and I must take up a weapon and fight at your side, then I will."

"Thank you, my lady," Zhao Ang said. "I only hope that Inspector Wei is as strong and defiant as you when the moment comes; he seems to start considering 'peaceful options' at the most inappropriate moments."

Zhao Ang and Lady Wang would experience the crisis that they feared, but they would wait for three years for a confrontation that would be a direct consequence of yet another unexpected moment in military history.

The ageing Governor of Jing Province, Liu Biao, sat alone at the desk in his private study and drummed his fingers erratically; he was haunted by the news that all of his potential allies in the northeast had been annihilated by Cao Cao, and the thought of what might follow had already impacted on his health. Biao's wife, Lady Cai, watched him intently from a distance: she and her brother, Admiral Cai Mao, would be left with the responsibility of leading the administration forward if Biao perished, and the twin threats of Cao Cao to the north and a vengeful Sun Quan to the south made that a less than desirable prospect.

"...Either say something or go somewhere, woman," Liu Biao said at last. "Stop loitering like a ghost."

"If Sun Quan attacks us now, what will you do?" Lady Cai asked.

"I will have Huang Zu repel him as usual," Liu Biao replied.

"...And if Cao Cao attacks us now, Husband, what will you do?" Lady Cai asked.

"I will have your brother and Liu Bei repel him as they did before," Liu Biao replied. "Have you any more pointless questions...?"

"...If Cao Cao and Sun Quan coordinated and attacked simultaneously, what would you do...?" Lady Cai asked.

"That... would not happen," Liu Biao insisted.

"Their clans are united by marriage," Lady Cai noted.

"**That *would not happen*!**" Liu Biao snapped. "Cao Cao is not going to attack us with the aid of a state rebel! His marriage alliances are a divisive measure aimed at provoking Sun Ben to challenge his cousin Quan for control of the Sun clan! His chosen Inspector of Yang, Liu Fu, is at odds with the Suns! His agents have been killing the Suns one by one!"

"All the suppositions of your counsel," Lady Cai scoffed.

"They have been shown to be right so far!" Liu Biao retorted. "Or at least, I hope so: the only way that they might have been wrong – fatally wrong – is with regard to something that you actually agree with them about, namely the suggestions offered by my relative and guest Liu Xuande!"

"That insincere little man is a hankerer," Lady Cai said. "His advice is barbed, designed to make you take terrible risks so that he can seize the province! In what way would you have benefitted by marching against Xuchang as he suggested...?"

"I...! ...Alright, yes, I would have been wrong to march on this occasion, yes, because Cao won so quickly," Liu Biao conceded, "but if I had acted before, then-!"

"At what moment?" Lady Cai heckled. "When Cao was at Wan? When Cao was in Xu Province fighting Lü Bu? When Cao was in Guandu? When Cao was trying to take Yè? When Cao was in-"

"At some point like... like, well, any one of those that you mention, some of which *predate* Liu Xuande's time here!" Liu Biao replied. "I have been indecisive and it has cost me dearly! I should have done *more*! *Perhaps* I should have gone southward and aided Huang Zu in destroying Sun Ce or Sun Quan at some point! *Perhaps* I should have taken Nan County back from Zhang Xiu before he died and inadvertently bequeathed it to Cao Cao! *Perhaps* I should have completed my march on Xuchang when Cao was in Guandu! I know that I should have done *something* that I did not do, else... I...!"

Liu Biao was halted by a violent coughing fit.

"...The Suns were threatening your southern borders at every moment that Cao was busy, and they still do," Lady Cai suggested. "I hear your arguments with Liu Bei and your advisers, and my own thought is that Cao Cao would be a better ally than an enemy."

"He... demands... my governor's seal... if not my *head*!" Liu Biao protested through his persistent coughing. "He... *invaded* Jing once... *already*! He *won't*... be an ally...!"

"Then you might have to consider surrendering – to the Son of Heaven, of course – before you are forced to fight," Lady Cai replied. "You have two sons, neither of them warriors, that cannot govern a province under siege, and-"

"How *dare you*...!" Liu Biao said as he pointed an accusing finger at his wife. "You... dare suggest that... I yield my province to...!"

"You're ill," Lady Cai replied. "Huang Zu is senile and robbed of his courage. If you do not replace him you will lose Jiangxia."

"With my eldest son, I suppose...?" Liu Biao heckled. "I know that you want him out of the way so-!"

"I don't care who you send, and it is not my place to choose the most suitable person anyway; my only suggestion is 'not Liu Bei', and I'm sure your advisers will say the same," Lady Cai interrupted. "All I want is a safe place to live for our family, including your sons: your sons are neither of them mine, Husband, but I care what happens to them both."

"...I *know you do*," Liu Biao chuckled sarcastically.

"By which you mean what...?" Lady Cai asked gruffly.

Liu Biao waited for his cough to fully pass before he replied, "Your brother openly criticised Qi at a meeting recently, and I know that much of what you're saying is part of a planned, sustained campaign to make my younger son – who is now your niece's husband inasmuch as he is my son – my heir over Qi, over whom you have next to no control."

"That is an unfair accusation!" Lady Cai snapped.

"Is it...?" Liu Biao retorted. "You think that I am a senile old fool, the pair of you, and that I don't know that you're trying to turn all of the conversations toward making Cong my heir over Qi so that you will rule Jing Province from the shadows like Empress Dowager Liang or Yuan Shao's widow, Lady Liu, when I am gone. Did the outcome of the recent Yuan clan chieftainship crisis teach you *nothing*, woman...?"

"...Qi is unfit to rule Jing Province," Lady Cai replied icily. "You have pushed me to saying it, and it is true: his obvious lack of strength of will and self-inflicted poor health aside, he is easily manipulated and seeks audiences with Liu Bei and his would-be kingmaker Zhuge Liang."

"...You're accusing my *son* of colluding with Liu Bei now...?" Liu Biao exclaimed.

"He is publicly seeking advice from improper persons," Lady Cai replied. "That is all that I am saying because that is all that I know to be fact. I don't raise the matter lightly: I am related by marriage to Zhuge Liang, so I speak with great reluctance when I say that-"

"Enough of your constant intriguing," Liu Biao ordered. "So my son is talking to Liu Bei and Zhuge Liang: *I* have talked to Liu Bei and Zhuge Liang! Do I plot against myself...?"

"That isn't an argument and you know it," Lady Cai retorted. "You know that Qi is sickly and weak-willed, and that's why you don't trust him with too much responsibility even though you're ill, because you know that he might lose the province if you did so; my only suggestion is that you give Cong, who is also your son, a chance to-"

"*Yes*, I'm ill, but I am *not dying*!" Liu Biao retorted. "I'm sick of you and your arrogant brother constantly willing me dead with every word you utter about succession! You're lucky I don't count it as treason!"

Lady Cai did not react to her husband's words in any way.

"Qi is my heir by right of primogeniture and because he is a *worthy son*, regardless of his faults, and *that is that*!" Liu Biao continued. "I will not let Cao Cao *or* Sun Quan take this province from me! I'll fight them both *at the same time* if I have to! And if Liu Bei really does want to steal my province then I'll fight *him* as well! I'll fight *anyone* that is trying to steal the province from me, and if that includes you and your ungrateful brother then so be it: either have the courage to challenge me here and now or **leave me in *peace*!**"

Lady Cai retreated silently.

"...Yes, I am isolated," Liu Biao muttered. "But I *will not yield*! Not to *anyone*!"

****

100

Emperor Xian was disturbed by the news that Cao Cao was coming to the capital to address the court: he was still nervous when the day arrived and the officials gathered to hear the Excellency of Works' account of the northern campaign.

"...Your Majesty, and my respected colleagues, it is a pleasure to be addressing the court as a victorious servant of the Han," Cao Cao began. "Forgive my not returning immediately, Your Majesty, but we had to receive tribute and formal submission from the last of the Wuhuan princes and bring their people into our lands to-"

"Is that wise, Excellency...?" the military official Geng Ji asked. "Shouldn't the Wuhuan have been left where they were, beyond the Great Wall...?"

"...We wonder the same, Mister Cao," Emperor Xian said.

Cao Cao smiled before he replied, "It is the right course, Majesty. If we left the Wuhuan in their own lands they might find a new king and grow in strength again or they might be absorbed into the Xianbei Confederacy and become a vengeful 'left arm' for Budugen. The Wuhuan are momentarily shaken by the humiliation that they have suffered, but the distress and fear will, over time, turn to frustration and then anger and regret that they did not fight harder: by bringing them into the Empire and showing them leniency and tolerance in exchange for their obedience and willingness to adapt to our way of life, we will tame them long before they can break free of the fragile leash that holds them."

"That is quite right," Wang Lang suggested. "The Shanyue of the south are best dealt with in the same way."

"And it has to be said that we could achieve the same when dealing with the Qiang in the northwest," Hua Xin said. "The Southern Xiongnu tribes prove that there is a chance that we can tame even the wildest beasts and make use of them."

"...To a point," Cao Cao replied. "The Southern Xiongnu also prove that even a refugee nation that owes its host for what culture and security they retain can, unfortunately, become ungrateful under the right circumstances, such as the selection of an overambitious chieftain, and I agree with Geng Ji's caution to some extent because of that. I have not forgotten Yufuluo, and the occasional affront still occurs; we will certainly see the same from the Wuhuan and indeed the rest."

"But we see that an enemy is best kept close and *watched*, Mister Cao," Emperor Xian said with a dry smile. "We understand your choice of action."

Cao Cao sensed the sovereign's dual meaning but bowed and replied, "I strive to do everything that will ultimately stabilise the Empire, Majesty."

"...In addition to the destruction of the Wuhuan Confederacy, Excellency Cao also exterminated the Yuans of Ru County," the official Wei Huang said. "What will become of their holdings?"

"I think that 'exterminated' is a strong word," Yuan Huan suggested. "Partly because it implies excessive force, Mister Wei, but mainly because Yang Xiu and I, amongst others, would therefore be dead as we sit here now."

Many officials stifled smiles.

"…The immediate heirs are purged," Kong Rong noted. "What will the governments of Qing, Ji, Yòu and Bing Provinces now look like, Your Excellency…?"

"Zhang Zhi is Inspector of Bing Province," Cao Cao replied. "Finding the right man to be Inspector of Yòu Province is my greatest challenge, since that man inherits political, economic and social instability that might actually outweigh any seen anywhere save for the north of Liang Province. Qing Province is equally troublesome but for different reasons, though rest assured that I am pondering the matter daily. I know that there have been calls for me to become Inspector or Governor of Ji Province but I will not take on two governorships at once and cannot yield Yan Province – home to the current capital – to anyone without being worried that I invite disaster upon the Empire."

"And in the meantime, Excellency, you will continue to build a second home in Wei Prefecture," Kong Rong prompted.

"…In *Yè City* in Wei Prefecture," Cao Cao replied tersely. "I have but one house in that city, Mister Kong."

"And a pet elephant," Kong Rong chuckled. "I forget how much it weighed now."

"…I hardly think that you are pursuing a proper direction of conversation, Mister Kong," Wang Lang scolded. "We are gathered here to hear of His Excellency's pacification of four provinces and the stabilisation of a quarter of the Empire after decades of unrest! Are one house and an elephant more important…?"

Kong Rong scowled at his old friend but said nothing.

"…Thank you, Mister Wang," Cao Cao said. "I shall return to the original point – the *elimination* of the seditious Yuan brothers. We know how it started: those young men followed their father, Yuan Shao, as he slowly took control of the northeast with the aid of his Wuhuan allies, whose callous treatment of the people earned righteous scorn. There was no low that Yuan Shao would not stoop to as his vicious advisers corrupted his spirit and turned him away from the path that he had once trodden so insistently: the first signs were found as early as his founding of the Eastern Pass Coalition, when he tried to supplant the Son of Heaven."

Emperor Xian sighed at the words.

"Liu Yu refused to agree to Yuan Shao's request that he take the throne, and the rebel Gongsun Zan later killed poor Liu Yu and seized Yòu Province," Cao Cao continued. "Prior to that murder, Gongsun Zan had secretly entered into a pact with Yuan Shao to harass the appointed Governor of Ji Province, Han Fu, and trick him into yielding Ji to Yuan, which he famously did and then died suddenly while in the care of Chenliu Administrator Zhang Miao… another friend of mine that proved to be too easily swayed by the lure of greater power. I doubted Zhang Miao's involvement in the suicide or assassination of Han Fu, but time and later happenings – Zhang's involvement in the villain Lü Bu's attempted seizure of Yan Province – make a man wiser."

Kong Rong frowned at the versions of events that Cao Cao was relaying to the court.

"The older Yuan Shao was not a man that kept promises, sad to say, though how much of that was down to the likes of Guo Tu and Pang Ji we will never know," Cao Cao continued. "It saddens me to think that he was once the hero that stormed the palace –

risking execution for treason – and rescued Your Majesty from the wicked 'Ten'."

"Indeed, Mister Cao," Emperor Xian replied dryly. "We find his transformation from the saviour of the Han to its worst enemy as baffling as you do."

Cao Cao paused for a moment and stifled his anger; he then smiled and said, "It is, nonetheless, the truth: Yuan Shao quickly went from saving Your Majesty's divine life to seeking to supplant the throne and seizing provinces from himself... which brings me back to Gongsun Zan's fate. When what I shall call the 'older Yuan brothers' – Shao and Shu – infamously became estranged at the expense of Your Majesty's rescue from Dong Zhuo and dragged the entire east of the Empire into a meaningless and selfish war over that long-coveted prize – the Ru County Yuan chieftainship – Shao's first mission was the acquisition of Qing, Yan, Yu, Bing, Yòu and Central Provinces while his brother initially sought Yang, Yu, Xu and Jing."

Emperor Xian nodded silently.

"No man, Your Majesty, was able to escape that selfish war: neither combatant was a benign hero, which only made it worse," Cao Cao continued. "Both Yuans claimed that they were 'good' and the other 'evil', and that they were trying to stabilise the Empire while the other coveted it... each brother said that they were protecting places by occupying them, in order to defend them from invasion by the other... but in truth, they were the same. It wasn't obvious at first, but as their ability to disguise their motives deteriorated with the increase in corruption, degeneration of sanity, hubris and the more frequent use of immoral tactics, so their façades slipped. Yuan Shu eventually committed a crime that I scarcely utter in Your Majesty's presence, as we all know so painfully..."

Emperor Xian recalled Yuan Shu's proclamation that he was the 'First Emperor of the Zhong Dynasty' and hummed angrily at the thought of it.

"...And Yuan Shao, though more subtle, coveted the same, as he showed when he was then willing to rescue his heretic brother – after all that they had put the Empire through! – in exchange for the Imperial Seal that Shu professed to have," Cao Cao continued. "It is then that what I shall call the 'younger Yuan brothers' – Yuan Tan, Yuan Xi and Yuan Shang – begin to appear and show that they are no better. It was Yuan Tan – who had already wrested Qing Province from its rightful governor, Mister Kong Rong – that was entrusted with rescuing Yuan Shu from government forces, and it is only luck and the swift actions of General Zhu Ling – and another fellow that we shall come to later – that spared us more of the villain's antics."

"We shall not dispute that Yuan Shu was a wretch and that Yuan Shao and his son were wrong to protect them if that was, indeed, their intent," Emperor Xian retorted.

"They claimed to the last that it was not, but time and events, once again, make a man wiser," Cao Cao insisted. "If the Yuans had then pledged loyalty to the throne and acted as loyal subjects should then there would be no doubt: they then attacked Gongsun Zan while the state needed his help in apprehending Lü Bu and pacifying the Mount Tai Bandits in Xu Province, which prolonged

the suffering of the people of Xu, and that was because Gongsun –
a friend of that deceitful fellow *Liu Bei* that I promised to come
back to – could testify against Yuan Shao if anyone ever asked
how either man ended up as lords of provinces that were not at all
meant to be theirs."
"You simplify matters, *Your Exellency*," Wei Huang suggested.
"Furthermore, you-!"
"Do I...?" Cao Cao asked. "There are enough former members of
Yuan Shao's court that are now in the Han court's employ that can
and will corroborate my statements, Mister Wei."
Wei Huang lowered his gaze.
Cao Cao smiled and said, "While I was trying to save Xu Province
from Lü Bu-"
"Xu Province was obviously grateful for your presence,
Excellency," Kong Rong snapped.
Cao Cao's smile disappeared as he said, "Yes, I know that I am
charged with weakening Xu Province in the first place when I
attacked Tao Qian, but we also have several men from Tao's
government in the court's employ that will substantiate my
version of events, so might I continue...?"
"Please do," Emperor Xian chuckled.
"When I was fighting Lü Bu, Yuan Shao killed Gongsun Zan to take
Yòu Province, had his cousin Gao Gan take Bing Province by
subterfuge and then he sat there, like a spoiled prince, demanding
excessive taxes from the downtrodden inhabitants of his four ill-
gotten provinces and complaining that he had not been given
enough titles and rewards for his 'considerable efforts': what were
they...?" Cao Cao asked. "He then gave credibility to that
treasonous document that Dong Cheng forged and aided Liu Bei's
illegal seizure of Xu Province, bringing more hardship on those
poor people than I ever did by forcing me to send yet another
army to get it back for a third time."
"Yuan Shao had no shame," Hua Xin suggested.
"No, he did not, Mister Hua, and neither did *Liu Bei*, who repaid
His Majesty's kind recognition of his royal lineage after years of
disinheritance by becoming a rebel and capturing provinces," Cao
Cao replied. "Yuan then sheltered Liu Bei and formed an alliance
with Liu Biao, the Wuhuan tribes, rebellious Southern Xiongnu and
other disparate elements so that he could use that 'Girlde Edict',
as he called it, to do... well, we know not what, but he had
another, more willing 'Liu Yu' in Liu Bei, so perhaps he planned to
supplant the throne again...?"
"It... is possible," Emperor Xian admitted.
"Again, the facts shape the scenario for us," Cao Cao continued.
"Liu Bei travelled in secret to Runan and – with an army of bandits
and *Yellow Turbans* – attacked the capital from the west while I
engaged Yuan Shao's forces at the region to the north of Guandu.
Thankfully, Your Majesty, both Liu Bei and Yuan Shao were
thwarted, and Bei sought shelter with Liu Biao – who will soon be
dealt with – while Yuan held onto Cangting and prepared to attack
again. I repelled him for a second time and he rightly died a
broken man, leaving what was left of his pretender's empire to his
three sons... who immediately began the cycle of chaos again.
Where, I ask, is the loyal scion of the Han when we examine Liu
Bei's actions and where, I ask, is the descendant of loyal subjects

when we look at Yuan Shao...?"

"...Please continue, Mister Cao," Emperor Xian ordered after a short silence.

"Thank you Majesty, Cao Cao said. "There are some that say that I should have intervened differently, awarding the chieftainship to the eldest son, Yuan Tan, sparing Yuan Xi and punishing Yuan Shang, but to them I ask a question: was I to punish Shang – a usurper that, with the aid of his mother and those same treacherous advisers that corrupted his father, vowed to take up his father's sword and wage war on the Han court – whilst at the same time elevating 'loyal' Yuan Tan – who seized Qing with violence and tried to save Yuan Shu from divine punishment – and sparing 'harmless' Yuan Xi, who did nothing to curb the Wuhuan's atrocities in the province that he held...?"

"The Excellency of Works is correct," the former Magistrate of Wuzhong, Tian Chou, insisted.

"But I did try to liaise with Tan, as everyone knows!" Cao Cao continued. "I forgave past offences and really, truly tried to restore order with his cooperation, which proved to be false. When Yè finally yielded and Yuan Shang fled, I dealt with the treacherous Yuan Tan, who had pretended to see the proper path and used me to try to take control of his clan. Shang and Xi – who had willingly joined forces in Yòu Province – then went on to use the Wuhuan hordes as their army when their own forces defected to the Han cause, allowing them to abduct thousands – tens, perhaps hundreds of thousands – from their villages and force them to emigrate to the frontier lands beyond the Wall... and let us not forget that they also used local criminal gangs to attack and kill Han officials in-between all that."

"...You defeated the Yuans in Yòu Province and their cousin Gao Gan in Bing Province, liberating all four of those illegally governed provinces that Yuan Shao had seized in past times," Xun Wenruo said. "What then, Excellency, for the benefit of the records...?"

"I was then faced with a dilemma," Cao Cao replied. "When the Yuans fled beyond the Great Wall, I knew that they would return with a Wuhuan army at some point in the future, so I resolved that I would defy military convention and attack them in their own territory with a smaller army that lacked proper provisions... though not as lacking as that debacle thirty years ago, of course."

"And with this campaign you have righted that wrong, Excellency," Minister Yang Biao suggested. "Thirty years ago, Your Majesty, the Empire was on its knees: foreign visitors thought that we were to be exploited and foreign empires lusted after our resources. The eunuch faction that we call the 'Ten Attendants' had gone from being saviours to being the cause of the erosion: they embezzled military funds and allowed our army to march into the frontier lands to fight Tanshihuai – the greatest Xianbei king that ever lived – without even the most basic equipment, and we suffered a loss that was only prevented from being the beginning of the end of the Han Empire by Heaven's will that foreign nations had their own problems and the Xianbei lacked the foresight to follow on from their victory, contenting themselves with bribes from that same corrupt 'Ten' that gave them their victory. That loss was the catalyst for the other calamities: the Yellow Turban Rebellion, the Liang Province Rebellion, the rise of Dong Zhuo, Li Jue and Guo

Si's 'regency', the birth of the numerous 'bandit armies' and the abuses inflicted by the Wuhuan, and they, in turn, closed our doors to the outside world, which has only been less serious than it should be because, again, the other great nations are beset with their own problems.

"Now, Majesty, the situation is reversed: despite being outnumbered by as much as seven-to-one, His Excellency Cao Cao took an army into foreign territory and 'broke the back of the beast', ending decades of torment and scaring the once-invincible Xianbei Confederacy into sending us tribute instead of the other way around. The roads out of the Empire can, over time, once again open fully, allowing us to demonstrate that we are a great and powerful nation that cannot be taken for granted; the immediate effects are obvious as one bandit army, rebel, pirate and tribal confederacy after another submits or breaks under the feet of our rejuvenated army and crops are once again sufficient to feed the people. One cannot underestimate or undervalue the great debt of gratitude that we owe His Excellency Cao Cao for what he has done... nor should we reward him insufficiently. His Excellency has begun the true process of restoring the Han, and only by ensuring that he has the appropriate authority can he finish what he has started."

Emperor Xian shuddered uncontrollably as his worst fears were seemingly about to be realised at that very moment.

"I motion that – if only for the duration of the crisis that is still, undeniably, upon us – the old ducal system should be restored and that His Excellency Cao Cao should be titled 'Chancellor of State'," Yang Biao continued.

"*What...?*" Xun Wenruo exclaimed.

"**Ridiculous!**" Kong Rong cried.

"**This is not the proper course!**" Zhi Xi protested.

"**A hero does not demand a villain's title!**" Geng Ji said.

"**I cannot support such a motion!**" Wei Huang insisted. "**Have you gone mad, Yang Biao...?**"

"I don't support this decision lightly," Yang Biao insisted. "There are many gentlemen in this room, including me, that suffered the worst of Dong Zhuo's tenure as Chancellor of State: but if one were to avoid empowering any man because of the mistake made by empowering but one, then we'd have no court to speak of."

"**We don't need a Chancellor of State!**" Kong Rong heckled.

"**Cao Cao has managed perfectly well against his rivals as the Excellency of Works! Give Cao Cao the seal of 'Commander-in-Chief' if that's what he needs to swing his club more fiercely, but-!**"

"**His Excellency cannot hold two ducal roles at once!**" Hua Xin retorted.

"**Then find another Excellency of Works!**" Geng Ji said. "**The old system is broken, unbalanced, and open to corruption!**"

"...'Chancellor of State'...?" Xun Wenruo murmured as he looked at Cao Cao, who was obviously unsettled by the amount of resistance to the proposal. "This would not have been suggested without... ... ... *why...?*"

Xun Gongda noted his uncle Wenruo's disbelief at what was unfolding and quietly agreed with him.

"**I... am honoured that you wish to bestow this upon me,**

gentlemen, but I must politely refuse," Cao Cao declared. "It is not a popular move."

"There! That should be an end to it!" Wei Huang said.

"This must be done!" Hua Xin protested.

"Necessary moves are not always popular!" Wang Lang insisted. "Only a Chancellor of State, with all of the powers that the role entitles one to, can intimidate Liu Biao, Liu Bei, Sun Quan, Zhang Lu and the bandits, heretics and tribal hordes of the north, south, east and west that still defy the will of the Son of Heaven!"

"Wang Lang???" Kong Rong exclaimed. "*You support this*, Wang Lang???"

Wang Lang avoided meeting Kong Rong's gaze or responding to his rebuke.

"There is still a national crisis!" Hedong Administrator Du Ji bellowed. "We have finally found an honest man that can undo the damage and has already done so much! Why do so many of you now wish to clip his wings while he is in full flight and prolong the people's suffering???"

"Du Bohou is right!" Hongnong Administrator Jia Kui said. "We barely contain the unrest in our regions, but there would be no stability at all if not for the Excellency of Works!"

"Inspector Wei Kang and I came all the way here to support this because it *must be done*!" Chang'an's Grand Magistrate, Zhong Yao, shouted over the debate. "Like it or not, we *have no choice*! The Empire needs a hero with genuine power!"

"*Ayah*! Zhong Yao as well???" Kong Rong exclaimed.

"Do not obstruct the road to peace!" Wang Lang proclaimed. "Support the end to thirty years of chaos! Support the total restoration of the Han!"

"I *cannot believe this*...!" Kong Rong sobbed.

Emperor Xian sat back and fought the urge to scream as the naysayers gradually lost the argument against Cao Cao being elevated to the highest ministerial rank of the older 'Ducal Minister' system; it would make Cao Cao close to invincible, and that was something that the young sovereign could not bear to think about as it edged closer to becoming a reality.

****

101

Cao Cao retired from the first day of Imperial court discussions about the future of the Han administration in an optimistic mood; he went to his chancellery office to have a private meeting with his own core counsel, which he expected to be unanimously behind him being promoted to Chancellor of State.

"I think that the small handful of doubters will come around to our way of thinking, Excellency," Hua Xin said as Cao Cao looked at Xun Wenruo.

"...Speak your mind, old friend," Cao Cao prompted.

"I... am just surprised, that's all," Xun Wenruo replied uneasily. "I am a devout Han loyalist, Excellency, so I'm a little surprised at the suggestion that there should be a return to a ducal system that is so commonly associated with... well..."

"...Usurpers...?" Cao Cao prompted.

"B-but that's only in a few extreme cases," Xun Wenruo insisted. "I am well aware that the new system was created because of a few wicked hegemons, men like Wang Mang and Dong Zhuo that exploited the lack of scrutiny. You, Excellency, are the type of man that the system was invented for."

"Then why the doubt...?" Xiahou Dun asked menacingly.

"Don't be like that, Yuanrang," Cao Cao scolded.

"He's acting like you're another Dong Zhuo, Mengde," Cao Hong said. "Why shouldn't we be angry about that...?"

"I assure you that I am not hesitant because I doubt His Excellency's virtue," Xun Wenruo replied as he tried to ignore his nephew Gongda's probing gaze. "I worry because it might give our political opponents cause to sow distrust."

"And how many of *them* are there...?" Cao Hong scoffed. "Practically the whole court's made up of family members and men that came with Mengde from the old days, like you, so-"

"**Shut up, you cretin!**" Cao Cao bellowed.

"...But it's true!" Cao Hong protested.

"It most certainly is not," Cao Cao retorted. "My old mentor and long-time supporter Sima Fang is not 'one of my men from the days', and nor are Yang Biao and Zhong Yao, who have always held higher posts than me in the past; Du Ji is not my long-time subordinate, and Wang Lang used to serve *Tao Qian*."

"You don't need to convince *us*, Excellency," Xun Wenruo insisted.

"*Who*, then...?" Xiahou Dun asked.

"The usual people," Cheng Yu grumbled. "Kong Rong, Wei Huang, Geng Ji, Fu Wan-"

"*Fu Wan*???" Hua Xin chortled.

"He's the Empress's father," Cheng Yu said.

"I know who he is, but I don't see where you get the idea of adding that simpering shadow of a man to that very, very short list of dissenters!" Hua Xin retorted.

"They're not dissenters, Mister Hua," Cao Cao insisted. "They're *outspoken critics*."

"They're the same thing in the end," Hua Xin scoffed.

"...That's exactly the stance that was taken by the 'Ten Attendants' toward the likes of me during the worst days of the 'Partisan Crisis'," Cao Cao warned.

"And be honest, Excellency... they were right," Cheng Yu suggested. "You were labelled as a dissenter for a few outspoken comments because they knew that you were probably doing more than that in secret, and you *were*. Who knows how many promising minds have now been twisted and corrupted by Kong Rong's 'innocent critical comments' and will later prove to be-"
"I refuse to put rebels, seditionists and critics in the same condemnatory category," Cao Cao insisted. "Yes, I supported the 'Partisans' while I openly defied the 'Ten' in the court, but I did not support or even know about the attempts to kill them. I don't believe that Kong Rong is planning anything, and nor are Geng Ji, Wei Huang or the timid and unimpressive Fu Wan, who didn't even *frown* at that meeting."
"Harsh words can lead to other things," Hua Xin said.
"...If they're met with swords, then yes," Cao Cao retorted. "I will not harm Kong Wenju or anyone else for a few brave, unguarded comments. I must thrive on criticism and better myself as a counter to it."
"So what next...?" Xiahou Dun asked. "They're going to promote you for certain, Mengde, and then we'll be able to fight whoever we want to fight."
"...'They' do not promote me, Yuanrang," Cao Cao retorted. "The Son of Heaven is the only authority."
"But it'll be decided by the court," Cao Chun suggested. "And the court is almost entirely convinced that your promotion is the right way forward, so the Son of Heaven will certainly accept their educated judgement."
"...Most likely," Cao Cao replied tonelessly.
"I... still have doubts about it, as Uncle does," Xun Gongda admitted. "Three career hecklers that would probably oppose a voluntary *demotion* if it went against His Excellency's will are one thing: there are dozens of officials that do not like the idea of another Chancellor of State, no matter who it is. If... well, to be completely honest, if something were to happen to His Excellency Cao, we must accept that his successor would -rightly or wrongly - automatically be the Chancellor of State with all of the same power but potentially without the same moral strength."
"I won't risk my own position of strength because I might die and leave power to one who was less worthy: there would be no kings and emperors in the world if everyone worried about that inevitability," Cao Cao replied. "The reason that the 'Mandate of Heaven' – which existed before Wang Mang's infamous use of it to topple the Han two hundred years ago – was conceived in the first place was to have a safeguard against a deviant, simpleton or maniac becoming the Son of Heaven and undoing everything that their ancestors had worked so hard for. There are safeguards at *all levels*: one need only show strength of heart and *use them*! If my successor – or, indeed, if I myself – be found to be truly unfit for the role of Chancellor, just as with *any other role*, including the one that I currently occupy and *yes*, including the *throne*, then unseat the unworthy!"
"...But the worry is that an all-powerful Chancellor of State would be exempt from such measures," Xun Wenruo suggested.
"No more than an unfit Son of Heaven," Cao Cao retorted. "The Mandate of Heaven can be used to unseat a man made divine:

why, then, can a humble Chancellor not be removed from office...? The answer, gentlemen, is a combination of complicity and cowardice, just as it has always been: Dong Zhuo, by himself, was a stupid thug that bled when cut and fell when pushed, just like any other man, once his muscle and his brains – forgive me for making this point at your expense, Wenhe – were no longer acting as his sword and shield."

Jia Xu bowed humbly and said, "You are right to use that very relevant example, Excellency. If Lü Bu and I had not served him as we did – along with a dozen other generals and officials and an army of thousands that obeyed his every word – then Dong Zhuo was just another man from the hills of Mei County."

"Yes, and any man that ever gains power – including me – does so as a leader of a collective effort: I did not defeat the Wuhuan alone, and nor did anyone else, just as Tadun did not raid villages and terrify the Yuans by himself," Cao Cao continued. "Tadun isn't the only warrior king that will be born to the Wuhuan, so we took the steps that we took to bring them into the Empire so that we can watch for new agitators and manage them as they emerge, avoiding more sights of impressionable men following charismatic lunatics on paths of violence for no good reason; you similarly need to watch the court carefully and prevent the rise of tyrants."

"The Wuhuan followed Tadun because they feared him and fled because he was proven to be ordinary and not frightening at all," Xiahou Dun suggested. "The men that followed Dong Zhuo were the same: what can anyone do about that...?"

"The Wuhuan chieftains that intimidated their own followers into serving them – and, by proxy, Tadun - didn't *have* to follow Tadun: they *chose to*, even if their subordinates didn't, just as they chose to abandon him later, because they always knew that he was just a man and abandoned him when he no longer promised greatness, not because some great veil of deception regarding some supernatural power had suddenly been lifted," Cao Cao retorted. "Which brings me back to my point: give me the power of Chancellor of State because you want to and *only* because you want to, gentlemen, because I am not a god that can strike you down if you refuse. By that same truth, demote me if I prove unworthy, because I am but one man and you are many: what powers do I have that will stop you doing so...?"

"The power of the 'complicit' that you mentioned," Cheng Yu replied. "The men that served Dong Zhuo, Tadun and, incidentally, the 'Ten Attendants' as well, who were frail, emasculated weaklings that epitomised 'unthreatening', mostly served the villains because, as you said, doing so promised greatness, and they intimidate and kill the good men on the villain's behalf."

"But why would the complicit – the weak of will that, at worst, occupy the lower roles in the court – succeed if there are enough brave men among *you* – who are the heart and soul and fist of the court – that are willing to do the right thing...?" Cao Cao countered. "Wouldn't the only reason for me or any other man being able to rule as a tyrant be because none of you did anything to stop it...? I selected all of you for your roles because of your courage, loyalty and above all *honesty*, and so I expect you to honour me by doing the right thing."

"...I won't contest the decision," Xun Wenruo said, "because I believe that you are going to use the power to do more good. But I beseech you, Your Excellency… always use the power wisely. Do not succumb to hubris or demand more again when your later campaigns bring victories."

"What else is there to demand…?" Cao Chun asked.

"It doesn't matter, because I will demand nothing," Cao Cao said before Xun Wenruo could respond. "I will use my power wisely, Wenruo, you can be sure of that. I will bring the peace that I have brought to the northeast to the other three quarters of the Empire… and then my work will be done. Perhaps I will become 'Grand Tutor'!"

Xun Wenruo smiled and said, "A fine ambition, Excellency."

"You may all retire now, gentlemen," Cao Cao continued. "There is nothing else to say now until the decision is made… and that decision will be made in the Imperial court, as it should be… not here or any other place."

"Quite right, Excellency!" Xun Wenruo said excitedly.

The officials paid their respects to their lord and left the hall one by one: Cao Cao waited until Cao Pi, Cao Chun, Cao Hong, Xiahou Dun and his bodyguard Xu Chu were his only company before he said, "I did not expect the Xuns to be so resistant to the idea."

"*Ingrates*," Xiahou Dun muttered.

"I think that they genuinely worry about the future," Cao Chun replied. "I'm not completely convinced either, even when it is Mengde that we elevate, but that's just because of what that title has meant in the past. They'll calm down soon enough."

Cao Cao hummed thoughtfully and said, "I hope so."

Wang Lang visited Kong Rong's home after he finished his work, but Kong was unwilling to admit him.

"Don't be petty, Wenju," Wang Lang sighed.

"*Petty*…?" Kong Rong chortled.

"Yes, Wenju," Wang Lang replied. "If it were any other man but Cao Cao, you'd-"

"I'd have reacted the same way!" Kong Rong insisted. "Chancellor of State…? Have you and the rest gone mad…? Have Yang Biao and Zhong Yao got some strange urge to relive the long walk from Chang'an…? Does Du Ji want to go back into hiding…?"

"You're being needlessly dramatic," Wang Lang replied. "And *please*, Wenju, let me in so that we can talk indoors: it's cold."

"Yes, Mister Wang, it *is* cold, mainly because I feel a sudden loss of warmth," Kong Rong said bitterly. "Why would I want to let you in here to defend the indefensible…? Try your deceitful rhetoric on some of your staff or some other man of lower intellect."

"*Deceitful*…?" Wang Lang exclaimed.

"You had the nerve to accuse me of worry too much before," Kong Rong replied. "'Cao Cao is no hegemon', you said. 'Cao Cao is an honest statesman', you said. 'With men like you and I to protect the Han, what can happen?' you said! And then, after all that, after convincing me that you were as loyal to the Han as me, and that you would defend the Han to the last, you go and do *this*!"

"Do *what*…?" Wang Lang chortled. "His Excellency is-!"

Kong Rong harrumphed and flicked his sleeve.

"Don't do that!" Wang Lang protested.

Kong Rong flicked his sleeve and harrumphed for a second and then a third time before closing his door.

"...You disappoint me, Wenju," Wang Lang sighed as he turned and walked away.

"Was that Wang Lang...?" Zhi Xi asked as Kong Rong returned to his living quarters.

"Who else...?" Kong Rong replied miserably.

"...You rebuked him," Zhi Xi supposed.

"Of *course I did*!" Kong Rong replied. "That wicked toady stood up in the court and argued for the empowerment of a tyrant! That self-serving wretch promised me that he'd never do anything to harm the Son of Heaven!"

"...Wang Lang has gained favour with Cao Cao," Zhi Xi noted.

"I think that I noticed that," Kong Rong muttered as he sat in his host seat, picked up the nearby tea kettle and poured some into his dish. After a few moments, Kong Rong laughed disdainfully and recited a poem:

"To think that a man such as he,
Who once claimed such staunch loyalty
Who promised to protect the throne
As well as if it were his own
Who once had such principles great
That I gave him the right to berate
Would now stoop so brazenly low,
And promote such a hegemon so!

Truly, my heart is aggrieved
For I feel so cruelly deceived
By a man that professed to be kind
That had just his career on his mind
Driven solely by rewards for his deeds
He cares only for personal needs
And with not one single thought for what's right
Gives a villain a Chancellor's might."

Kong Rong was silent for moment before he added, "Curse him... curse that lying fool and all the rest as well!"

"He might report you to Cao Cao," Zhi Xi suggested.

"Let him," Kong Rong replied. "Even when Cao has awarded himself the Nine Dignitaries and asked his lackeys to start lobbying for a duchy, I will still be there arguing for what's right."

"...Hopefully," Zhi Xi sighed.

Emperor Xian had retreated to his personal quarters, dismissed his staff and sat quietly since the court session had ended; Empress Fu waited patiently for close to three hours before she asked, "Should I call the staff back, Majesty...?"

"It's started," Emperor Xian replied. "*Chancellor of State*, he will be by the end of tomorrow's session... *Chancellor of State*!"

Empress Fu stifled a gasp.

"None of the loyal ones... none of them can do *anything*," Emperor Xian continued. "Not that there are many... I look around that hall and I see nothing but unfriendly faces these days... damn near all of them *his* people... I don't think that there were more than twenty voices of dissent in a room with hundreds of men in it... no, the majority were cawing and fawning on that old villain and calling for him to be made *Chancellor of State*, and there is *nothing* that I can do about it!"

Empress Fu sighed sadly and said, "What will become of-?"

"I *cannot*," Emperor Xian snapped as his composure failed him. "It is all that we ever do these days, and... *no*! I *cannot* have that same *pointless* conversation again so soon, not when it changes *nothing* and... and... **SERVANTS!**"

"But you *need* to talk!" Empress Fu protested. "Even if it *is* 'pointless', you-!"

"*No*, my lady... I want to, but... no," Emperor Xian said as the servants started to return to the room; the young sovereign briefly contemplated sending them away again but quickly relented and said, "There is no point... none at all."

Empress Fu covered her face with her sleeve.

"...*Chancellor of State*...!" Emperor Xian muttered. "The-! ...The *fools*... the... *fools*."

The following day saw a short but fiery debate that ended with the officials deciding overwhelmingly that they would support Cao Cao being promoted to the position of Chancellor of State: Emperor Xian accepted their verdict quietly and miserably, and the plan was actioned immediately.

Some efforts were made to follow some sort of administrative procedure and make the fateful transition from the newer three-role 'Ducal Minister' system – which comprised of the 'Excellency of Works', the 'Excellency over the Masses' and 'Commander-in-Chief' – to the older, more controversial three-role model – which comprised 'Chancellor of State', 'Imperial Counsellor' and 'Grand Commandant' – seem to be a matter-of-fact event that should not be a cause for alarm: it did little to placate the likes of Kong Rong and Geng Ji, who watched with angry tears in their eyes as a man that they did not trust adopted a title that had last been used by the worst tyrant that the empire had seen in an age.

Cao Cao was not blind to the bitter and frightened expressions on the faces of his critics and even some of the men that traditionally looked to him as a force for good: he was especially saddened by Xun Wenruo and Xun Gongda, whose discomfort was obvious to all. But regardless of the lingering doubts, the court had promoted Cao Cao to Chancellor of State and the discussions were at an end: Cao retired from the court and began plans for sending another envoy to the Southern Xiongnu settlement in Bing Province while the staff of the Imperial Secretariat penned the letters that would announce the change to the rest of Han Dynasty China.

****

102

"...*Chancellor of State*???"

Jing Governor Liu Biao could barely contain his anger and distress: his assembled advisers were mostly unsympathetic, as most of them were already preparing for life after their ailing lord's rule.

"**That wretched, villainous bastard!**" Liu Biao cried. "Is it not enough that he was 'Excellency of Works' and 'Acting Commander-in-Chief' and that his appointed 'Excellency over the Masses' is one of his cronies??? Does he seek to outdo Dong Zhuo now...? ...Why do I even *ask*...? Dong Cheng was *right*: he plots the fall of the Han! And that wickedness will continue with *my* destruction and then beyond it!"

"What do we do, Father...?" Liu Qi asked.

"...This has all been done with the consent of the Son of Heaven," the politician Huan Jie said calmly.

"That's right, my lord," the adviser Wang Can said. "Chancellor Cao is trying to unify the Empire, and it must be conceded – even by you – that the end to the Wuhuan aggression in the northeast is a popular move that only added to his list of supporters."

"We must accept that Chancellor Cao is now considered to be a force for good and that we are at risk of being seen universally as rebels," the politician Hè Qia suggested. "If there is a chance that we can submit then we should do so immediately."

"...Is there a single one of you that actually continues to serve me, or have you all decided to shift your allegiances to Cao Cao...?" Liu Biao heckled. "You there, the Pangs, and Kuai Yue... Huan Jie, Fu Xun, Han Song... are you all determined to convince me that I should yield to 'Chancellor Cao'...? Will you again slander my eldest, who has done nothing to harm you...?"

Kuai Yue, Huan Jie and the Pang brothers lowered their eyes and said nothing.

"...We're being pragmatic," the politician Fu Xun replied.

"Ah, yes... the 'pragmatism' argument," Liu Biao chuckled. "How I love that most overused of politicians' arguments."

"Our role is to ensure that the province is stable and properly governed," Han Song said. "We are not always going to find the answers to the pressing questions in the places that you would prefer that we-"

"**I employ you to do what is *right*!**" Liu Biao screamed. "**How is...** is...!"

Liu Biao was interrupted by yet another coughing fit.

"...And what is 'right', Lord Liu, is that we ensure that the province and its people are protected from harm where possible," Wang Can said.

"...How... *far* you've come, Wang Can, from the... the donkey-obsessed *child* that I gave such fine opportunities to," Liu Biao wheezed. "How far you've come, young man, that... you now openly speak of me as though I am... this province's *ruin*."

"You are being unfair to us," Huan Jie said.

"**How dare you!**" Liu Biao snapped. "Go... back to your... old masters in Jiangdong, two-faced-!"

"Don't overexert yourself, Father!" Liu Qi pleaded.

"I am your loyal vassal, Lord Liu!" Huan Jie said. "I hate the Suns of Jiangdong as much as you do! But they are not the same as the Chancellor of the Han!"

"All of you, traitors one and all," Liu Biao muttered as he got to his feet and started to leave his audience hall. "*Traitors.*"

"Lord and esteemed brother-in-law, your misunderstand," Admiral Cai Mao insisted. "We are just trying to assess all options."

"Aha! I wondered when you would start talking, 'esteemed brother-in-law'," Liu Biao said as he stopped and turned to face Cai Mao. "So tell me then: in what order will these 'options' be explored…? Does loyalty to me come before your fear of Cao Cao…? Does your loyalty to my son and heir come before you and your sister's desire to see my younger son, with whom you have greater ties, sat in my seat when I'm gone…? When Cao's men come here again – and remember that this would be a second invasion – will you rush to submit or first defend the people from the horrors that he will inflict upon them…?"

"If he attacked the people, my lord, we would not then consider diplomacy," Fu Xun promised. "But we only have the word of others, like the eternal liar and hankerer Liu Bei, that-"

"Xuande warned me that I should have done something sooner, but I listened to all of you, and did nothing, and now I am completely isolated, unless I want to do as the Yuan brothers did and seek allies like the Qiang," Liu Biao heckled. "If I had helped those lads when they asked for it, they might have avoided suicidal pacts with Tadun and scored early victories, making this day an amusing topic at banquets, a fictional nightmare scenario instead of a horrible reality. Cao Cao *did* lay waste to western Xu Province and murder a hundred-thousand of its people, and he *did* make an unwilling whore of Lady Zou, and he *did* let his loyal son and heir die in his place at Wan so that *he* could live another day, and he *did* murder a pregnant consort, and now he tightens his grip on power, all in readiness for the day when he seizes the throne for himself, and the world must look on helpless… or grovel and seek a place in his court, as you all do. *Pathetic.*"

Liu Biao left the audience hall.

"…We will not submit if Chancellor Cao is seen to be a villain," Wang Can said.

"Of course not," Han Song replied. "I'll go to the front line myself."

"But if he is a proper statesman and simply demands our surrender in an exchange for an end to hostilities, then we *must* consider it," Hè Qia said.

"Of course," Fu Xun replied.

"…**Father is right!**" Liu Qi cried as he got to his feet and left the hall at speed.

"…But what about Sun Quan?" Han Song asked.

"That's altogether different," Huan Jie insisted. "The Suns will destroy Jing Province and kill every one of us if they get past Huang Zu. We must resist them if they attack Jiangxia and provide whatever support is needed."

"But would Sun Quan dare to attack Jiangxia now that Cao Cao is the Chancellor of State and intends an invasion of his own…?" Fu Xun asked.

"…Whether they are allies or not, Cao Cao and Sun Quan will both attack this province over the coming months," Kuai Yue said. "Sun Quan will probably attack first; we may *lose* Jiangxia… that is actually a strong possibility."

"Huang Zu would fight to the end," Huan Jie replied.

"...Yes, he would," Kuai Yue said. "I don't doubt that."

"...And without Huang Zu, we are all the poorer," Fu Xun sighed.

"What a shame it is that our nearest friendly neighbour is such a coward," Han Song said. "If Liu Zhang were even half the man his father was, would we need to speak as we do...?"

It took considerably longer for the Han government's messengers to reach the westernmost part of the Empire: the Governor of Yi Province – the frail, scrawny Liu Zhang – summoned his followers to his Chengdu court to hear the news from the Imperial capital and immediately began discussions about the tributes that would need to be sent.

"A grand tribute will be sent to Chancellor Cao, of course!" Liu Zhang chuckled.

"*How* grand, lord and brother-in-law...?" General Wu Yi asked. "We must remember that he is a chancellor, not a prince."

"Surely we must show Chancellor Cao the utmost respect!" Liu Zhang replied.

"Utmost respect, yes: downright toadying, no," the adviser Zhang Song said. "Don't be too overeager, my lord."

"You are being too familiar, Mister Zhang," Liu Zhang suggested.

"Rudeness is not familiarity," the politician Huang Quan said. "Zhang Song is as crude on the inside as he is on the outside."

"I may be 'crude in appearance and in speech', Huang Quan, but I'm trustworthy," Zhang Song retorted. "I always speak my mind and for the good of Lord Liu and the province. I'm saying that Cao Cao is a man with a mixed reputation and that we should not be seen to grovel to him too much. Send him what we'd have sent him if he was being made Excellency of Works, because he still is, or rather he should be. 'Chancellor of State'...? After everything that's happened...?"

"...I admit that I agree," Wu Yi said. "Limit your gifts *and* your praise, Lord Liu."

"And risk being accused of trying to remain neutral when Chancellor Cao is looking for war with Liu Biao and, perhaps, Sun Quan as well...?" Liu Zhang asked pointedly. "And shouldn't I want him to be generous toward us if we need his help in our struggle against our eternal enemy, Zhang Lu of Han'ning...? What say you, Elder Yang Jixiu...?"

The middle-aged politician Yang Hong smiled and said, "Offer tribute to Chancellor Cao by all means, Governor Liu, but be careful not to include any gifts that might imply that you see Cao Cao as a future duke or prince; we do not want the Son of Heaven to think that we are pledging support to Cao Cao if he later reveals himself as an ambitious villain, do we...?"

Many of the more cynical officials smiled as Liu Zhang mumbled nervously and replied, "Wise thinking, wise thinking... we might be wise to send a more modest tribute than I had in mind... while also sending grander tribute to His Majesty to reaffirm our loyalty to the Han. That's what Zhang Song meant as well, isn't it...? ...Yes, and I will take it to heart."

Yang Hong bowed and said, "That is the right course."

"Indeed it is," Zhang Song grumbled. "Don't forget that the

esteemed Xu Jing, brother of the man that once labelled Cao Cao as a 'Crafty Villain', is a refugee from violence in this very province, Lord Liu, and he would balk at the idea of us sending a prince's gifts to a-"

"I understand," Liu Zhang insisted. "I will be reserved."

"One possible benefit is the fear that this will strike into all of our enemies," Huang Quan suggested. "Chancellor Cao cannot fight the Yuans and the Wuhuan and the Yellow Turbans and then ignore the Qiang and the Nanman and Zhang Lu."

"*That* is something that we agree upon," Zhang Song said. "Zhang Lu's days are surely numbered as the other enemies of the Son of Heaven disappear; maybe we'll see Cao Cao attacking 'Han'ning' in the next two years."

"That would be wonderful," Liu Zhang sighed. "Peace at last...!"

Liu Zhang's northern neighbour, Zhang Lu, was understandably concerned about the future of his unconventional independent state, which some described as the "Theocratic State of Han'ning". The Han government was reluctant to send a messenger into what was, in effect, a rogue nation within the Empire, but they also wanted to send a warning to Zhang Lu in the hope that he might submit before an invasion was necessary.

"They send me this messenger to tell me that 'Cao Cao' is 'Chancellor of State'," Zhang Lu said to his assembled courtiers. "They make thinly-veiled threats and hope that I will crumble, but I am **not Yuan Shao! I am not Dong Zhuo! I am not Tadun, or Budugen, or Zhang Jue!**"

The assembly bowed as one and said, "**We hear you, Great Master Zhang!**"

"...Increase the border patrols," Zhang Lu ordered. "See if we can trade for better weapons with someone, anyone, and watch Liu Zhang even more closely: Cao Cao likes to use others to do his work for him."

"**It will be done, Master Zhang!**" a general responded.

"...I shall now retire to my study," Zhang Lu said. "Mister Yan, Mister Yang, Younger Brother... you will come with me, please."

The advisers Yan Pu and Yang Bo and Zhang Lu's younger brother, Zhang Wei, followed Zhang Lu's exit through a side entrance while the rest left by way of the main entrance to the hall.

"It has been twenty years," Zhang Lu said as he sat facing his three subordinates. "Twenty long, difficult years... and there must be twenty more!"

"And there will be, Heaven willing," Yan Pu replied.

"When the first 'Governor of Yi Province', Liu Yan, 'sent me here' all those years ago, he did so with the idea that I would seize Hanzhong for him and him alone, but instead I took it for Heaven and all of the people of the world," Zhang Lu continued. "Since then, I have first endured Liu Yan and then his son holding my mother and others as hostages, forcing me to let them treat us as a buffer between them and the Han administration in Liang Province, and then endured the pain of learning that Liu Zhang – a wretched, cowardly fool of a son that was a curse upon Liu Yan as punishment for his greed and violence – slayed my kin as though he thought it would further entrench me as his slave, when it not only set me free but left me with a need to see him die."

"Yes," Zhang Wei said. "*I* will kill Liu Zhang if *you* can't, brother and master."

"...But we must worry that he will now have Cao Cao's help if we attack him and that he would aid Cao Cao should there be a decision to invade," Zhang Lu replied. "A pincer would be dangerous... and I worry."

"...As do I," Yang Bo admitted.

Zhang Lu sighed and said, "I have founded a peaceful state: I have abolished money to eliminate greed and vice and ensured that everyone – be they healthy or lame, weak or strong, young or old, male or female – has what they need to live a full life as Heaven desires. The Heaven-defying Han cannot say the same, which is why they are constantly forced to wage war against their own hungry, poor, undervalued people; here there is barely a murmur of discontent, save for the moneylenders and businessmen that pass through and find that their poison cannot be spread."

"Heaven and the people praise your name for it, brother and master," Zhang Wei insisted.

"But by building a place of peace, I am then too weak for war, and when you are surrounded by hankerers that would destroy what I have built to reclaim this little place 'for the Han' so that the people can go back to that unrewarding existence... being unready for war is not an option," Zhang Lu said. "We must do even more than I have dared to say so far: we must grow the army and look for allies."

"*Allies*...?" Yan Pu exclaimed. "Master Zhang, we-!"

"I am blessed with Heaven's will but not the complete knowledge of how that will should be done, which is why I employ your talents," Zhang Lu said. "We must find allies: *you* must find a way to find them."

"...There are only the tribes of Liang Province to the north and the Nanman to the far south," Yang Bo suggested. "The rest – Liu Biao, Du Ji, Sun Quan – see us as heretics."

"When it is *they* who are the heretics," Zhang Lu replied. "They kowtow before a man – a plain, ordinary man – bedecked in gold and silk that idles in his one of his many palaces within one of his many kingdoms and demands the world as his personal possession whilst gives nothing in return save for more demands that lead to more violence and more taking from others: Heaven is angry, and every sign points to the collapse of that foul regime, and yet men like Cao Cao and Liu Biao continue to deny the will of Heaven because it brings an end to their vast material wealth and meaningless power over others and would make the world the possession of Heaven and Heaven's gift to all men once again. They can ignore the changes, the patterns of the stars and the whispers on the winds but it is as my wayward rival Zhang Jue once said in his famous mantra that inspired a million men to don a yellow scarf: they can bruise the flesh, shed the blood and dash the brains of as many of their detractors as they like, but the Han's time is over."

"Yes... a *million men*... if only we could have such an army and not need the help of others that do not share our enlightenment and have their own vices that rival the Han," Zhang Wei complained.

"The Qiang are a rough sort but know that Heaven resides in all of us and above us, not in the form of that pampered boy in Xuchang," Zhang Lu declared. "If the Qiang tribes can be parleyed with, Mister Yan, then do so: the Nanman people, on the other hand, are a waste of time, for they lay claim to our lands and pray to false gods."

Yan Pu bowed slightly and said, "I will do as you ask, Master."

"I will never yield Han'ning to such wicked men as Cao Cao!" Zhang Lu vowed. "Cao Cao, Liu Zhang, Liu Biao, Sun Quan, Liu Bei and all the rest shall smash their armies against us like eggs, for we are the rock of Heaven! *None* shall devour us!"

The bandit Chang Xi gathered his trusted allies and travelled to a village to the west of the Mount Tai Prefectural capital to gather more support.

"**Enough is enough!**" Chang Xi proclaimed. "**Cao Cao's taking the piss! The Han government lied to me and to all of you about what they wanted to do, and I say that we teach 'em a lesson!**"

"**By doing what...?**" one villager asked.

"**They talked us all out of being bandits 'cause they said we'd be pardoned, given good jobs, given respect!**" Chang Xi replied. "**They lied! They've had us going here and there, beating up old mates and picking fights with crime families that never showed us no disrespect, and fighting the Yuans, and what do we get in return...? Have any o' you known any peace since the Han's been running Qing...?**"

"I dunno, boss," one of Chang Xi's allies said. "It weren't that peaceful under-"

"**Shut up!**" Chang Xi snapped.

"**You never answered my question,**" the villager prompted.

"**...Look, what I'm saying is obvious!**" Chang Xi replied. "**I know a lot o' you, and I know that you all gave up being bandits after the Han cracked down on Zang and the rest of us, mainly 'cause you were promised – like we were – that things would be better if we 'behaved'. But look, mates, at what it's like nowadays! I'm telling you that I haven't had a single flippin' day where I haven't been sent this way, sent that way, messed about all the time, told that I'm fighting Yuan Tan on one day and then being friends with him two days later, after he's killed two o' my friends! I don't know how I never got fed up and walked away from it all before!**"

"**...Oh, no, Chang, no way!**" a second man heckled. "**I thought you'd seen sense and given up on all that!**"

"**Oh, well, at least you get what I'm saying,**" Chang Xi despaired. "**Look, mates, I didn't come to this decision lightly! It means fighting Zang Ba, who's given his family over to Cao Cao and all but crawled up the man's arse, but he's still a friend and I really don't want to fight him, but I might have to!**"

"**Stop babbling and tell us what you want!**" one woman shouted angrily.

"**Isn't it obvious?**" another woman said. "**Well he can go away! My husband got hurt following his friend Wu Dun, and so I'm damned if I'm letting him talk my son into going off and robbing other villages and making himself a target for**

Cao Cao's soldiers!"

"**I'm doing this for everyone!**" Chang Xi protested. "**Cao Cao is a liar! The Han officials are all of 'em liars! They pretended to let us all off, and said there'd be no more corruption, but they're going to go back on it, I tell you! We have to go back to our old ways and send them a message!**"

"**So you're saying that they might come after men what joined the bandits before, even if they gave up...?**" one older man asked.

"**They're two-faced!**" Chang Xi replied. "**The corruption, the lies, it's all coming back again! We need to get back to making noise again now, send them a message and make them change their minds again! If we don't, then I'm telling you that when there's no one else left for Cao Cao to beat up he'll come back here and finish what he started!**"

"**...I'm with you!**" one young man cried.

"**Me as well!**" a second youth said. "**My uncle got hurt fightin' Yuan Tan's men in Beihai and never got *nothing*! To Hell with the Han!**"

Chang Xi smiled: one by one, more and more men added their voices to an enthusiastic group of volunteer bandits.

"**Let's all of us march on the prefectural capital and string up the toadies that Cao Cao put in to run it!**" one middle-aged man suggested.

"**While we're at it, let's string up the bastards that run this village!**" a farmer said. "**That'll teach 'em to tax me after the year that I've had!**"

"...This is brilliant," Chang Xi sniggered. "This is better than I'd hoped for...!"

"I dunno," one bandit said. "They're pretty fired up now."

"That's the whole *point*, Red Crest!" Chang Xi replied irritably.

Another of Chang Xi's allies frowned and said, "Uh, boss... this is 'cause you're pissed at not getting a decent job from Cao Cao. How are you going to calm everyone down again if you get what you want...?"

"We'll worry about that when we get to it, Long-toes," Chang Xi replied. "Stop worrying, lads: it'll be fine."

Chang Xi would visit more villages and towns as he moved across Qing Province: he rejoiced when he found majority support and looted those that showed no interest in joining his uprising. But as he continued his campaign of spreading discontent, other forces tapped into the raw anger, frustration and despair that was commonly felt – even if the reasons for them varied dramatically – and tried to use them for their own ends; one group in particular would prove to be a serious short-term threat to Cao Cao's plan to restore order, and their success was as far from being on Chang Xi's list of intended consequences as was possible.

****

103

A second envoy travelled to Ping County and asked for an audience with Southern Xiongnu Chanyu Huchuquan.

"...So Cao Cao is now 'Chancellor'," Huchuquan said as he studied the new envoy.

"He is," the envoy replied.

"I said that I would discuss this 'matter' with him, so why does he send *you*...?" Huchuquan asked.

"I am here to discover a convenient time for Chancellor Cao to come here and discuss the 'particularly delicate matter' with you," the envoy replied.

"...The Han Chancellor cares when I would like to talk...?" Huchuquan scoffed. "I am a guest in this place: we all are. When will he arrive...?"

"He would prefer to speak with you as soon as possible," the envoy explained.

"...Go and tell him that I am always ready," Huchuquan replied.

The envoy bowed and departed; Huchuquan then turned to his nephew and heir Liu Bao and said, "You will *cooperate*."

Liu Bao grunted angrily.

"...You've just been made Chancellor, and now your first commands are 'bring me Hua Tuo' and 'prepare to go to Ping County' when they are obviously far from compatible with each other," Cheng Yu complained as Cao Cao clutched his head and rocked back and forth in his host seat in the Xuchang chancellery audience hall.

"I don't value your flippancy right now," Cao Cao retorted. "My head feels like it is about to *explode*! **I want Hua Tuo brought here at once!**"

Cheng Yu winced and said, "Fine, fine, *shout*: as you've already said, *Chancellor*, you are but a mortal man with no special powers to speak of, so shouting at us will not make a man that cannot be found appear!"

"I can... still make people *suffer*, Old Cheng, and by the gods I will tear that bastard's entrails out myself if I find that he is doing something trivial!" Cao Cao growled. "**Find him! I don't care what it takes: FIND HIM!**"

"But he could be anywhere!" Cao Hong said.

"**Who let him leave in the first place???**" Cao Cao shrieked.

"He said that he needed to fetch something from his home that he needed to diagnose a cure for you and that seemed reasonable enough," Xun Wenruo said.

"**D'AAAAAAGH! He should have been chained to the floor!**" Cao Cao retorted. "**And you fools should all be reassessed if you're stupid enough to make such a mistake! I need that man here! The EMPIRE NEEDS THAT MAN TO BE HERE! FIND HIM! FIND HIM *NOW*!**"

"...We're doing everything possible, Mengde," Cao Chun pleaded.

"I... know," Cao Cao replied meekly. "And... I... am *sorry*, Elder Cheng. I know that you, Liu Yè, Jia Xu, Wenruo, Gongda and a host of other men are doing all that they can... but I want to *behead myself*, the pain is so unbearable, and I have *so much to do...* and so little time *anyway...!*"

"Yes, and Chen Gui will stop him leaving Pei County when he inevitably returns to see his ailing wife," Cheng Yu said. "But is there nobody else that can perform acupuncture...?"

"Even Master Hua says that there are others, but Chancellor Cao is adamant that Master Hua and only Master Hua act as his physician," Liu Yè explained.

"If Hua Tuo is so cruel, then we *must* find another doctor," Cao Chun said. "Is he really better than the physicians that tend to the Son of Heaven...?"

"I've... tried... the court ph-physicians... even the likes of... Ji Pi couldn't... help me, so he... is... last *chance*, m-maybe," Cao Cao panted. "O Heaven, you... you make it *worse still*...! Is this because I... made myself *Chancellor*...?"

"...He'll be found, Mengde," Cao Chun insisted. "And I'll tie a rope around him and drag him here myself if I must, and we won't let him go again."

"So *sorry*, Lady Cai...!" Cao Cao whimpered. "You... whom Heaven has so cruelly tortured... must suffer longer while Heaven... has its fun with *me*...!"

"...*Aiee*... what a thing," Cheng Yu grumbled as he turned and left the hall. "We have an intelligent, decisive leader that's periodically crippled by *his own brain*... what *nonsense*."

Cao Cao did not have long to wait before Hua Tuo was forced to return to his home in Pei County; the Chancellor of Pei, Chen Gui, immediately led a force of men to the house and insisted on yet another audience with the famed physician.

"You pester me again, Chen Gui," Hua Tuo heckled. "And you bring soldiers this time as well: are you here to arrest me...?"

"Times have changed, Master Hua," Chen Gui replied. "Cao Cao was the Excellency of Works before, and his work was already of the utmost importance; now he is the Chancellor of State, and-"

"*Ayah*... so Caoi Cao is beginning the walk down *that* road now," Hua Tuo exclaimed.

"...I shall pretend that I did not hear that implicit accusation and fail to report it: you're in enough trouble as it is for being so defiant," Chen Gui said. "I implore you, Master Hua: do not make me bind you with ropes!"

"...There are a hundred other men that can perform acupuncture treatment!" Hua Tuo protested. "You're a skilled man: I could probably show *you* how to do it and then *you* could be the Chancellor's physician!"

"You're a clever man: don't say such nonsense," Chen Gui scoffed.

"My wife is sick," Hua Tuo retorted. "I-"

"Tend to her as you always do and then prepare to leave as you always do... but this time, Master Hua, you will be going to Xuchang," Chen Gui said.

"...I can see that I am without options," Hua Tuo conceded. "Alright, I will go to the capital and tend to the Chancellor's headaches again... but I will not become a court physician. I will treat the ailment again and then I will leave again."

Chen Gui laughed disbelievingly and said, "You really do not understand what you are about to face, do you...? ...But then I suppose that blissful ignorance of danger is the privilege of eccentric scholars."

"It claimed Cai Yong," Hua Tuo retorted. "Why not me...?"

"...You do understand, and yet you refuse to be cooperative," Chen Gui realised. "The world needs you, Master, so don't throw your life away by being needlessly difficult. Chancellor Cao has no sense of humour when he is afflicted."

"...I've seen that for myself," Hua Tuo said. "I will need my bag: may I fetch it...?"

"It is as it was before: fetch whatever you need for this long journey that will take you away from your home until you are no longer needed," Chen Gui replied. "But please hurry: word of your presence will reach Chancellor Cao's close allies, and they would not be so patient with you."

Hua Tuo grumbled angrily and retreated from his front door to fetch his famous medicine bag yet again.

"...Stubborn man," Chen Gui sighed. "You'll be your own undoing, just like all the others..."

Cao Cao was still incapacitated by his latest migraine when Hua Tuo reached the capital under armed escort: Xun Wenruo rushed the physician to Cao's bedside, where Court Physician Ji Pi was already in attendance.

"Master Hua Tuo!" Ji Pi exclaimed.

"I am here now, Chancellor," Hua Tuo said.

"**Why did you leave???**" Cao Cao screamed. "**Did you not understand a shred of what I have told you???**"

"...I treated you for several attacks and made it perfectly clear to your staff that I needed to leave to conduct research," Hua Tuo explained as he began the usual preparations for treatment. "How will I cure you if I do not-"

"**If a cure is not known then it must wait!**" Cao Cao snapped. "**The Empire needs me, you difficult man! Keep me healthy and sane until I have united the provinces and tamed the wicked, and then you can research all you want!**"

"...I am probably not even the best acupuncturist in the Empire, Chancellor," Hua Tuo insisted as he checked his needles. "I am a scholar first: I don't just study acupuncture, I study animal forms, medicine development, meditative processes-"

"**The needle *works*!**" Cao Cao cried. "**Just do what *works*!**"

"Please cooperate, Master Hua," Ji Pi whispered. "Don't risk His Excellency's anger."

Cao Cao bared his chest and glared at Hua Tuo, saying, "**Hurry and *help me*!**"

"...I might be able to help in other ways, but we will, as you say, do what works for now, Chancellor," Hua Tuo replied as he leant forward and moved the needle over Cao Cao's chest. "The final answer might be surgery, medicine – though I would need to know what causes the pain – or some other acupuncture point."

"So there are many different types of headaches that require completely different solutions...?" Ji Pi exclaimed.

"Oh yes," Hua Tuo replied once he had inserted the acupuncture needle. "And if I apply the wrong solution by being hasty, I risk doing further damage or even beginning the onset of new headaches in addition to the current. Patience and careful diagnosis is the vital first step."

Cao Cao exhaled contentedly as the pain passed.

"...Amazing," Ji Pi murmured. "Truly amazing."

"I am done," Hua Tuo said.

"...Thank you , Master Hua," Xun Wenruo replied. "Mister Ji, you will no longer be needed, but thank you for trying your best."

Ji Pi turned to Hua Tuo and said, "It is a pleasure to have viewed your work here today, Master Hua."

"I extend my own respects to you, Mister Ji," Hua Tuo replied; the two physicians then bowed to each other politely before Ji Pi left the room.

"You are quite incredible, Master Hua," Xun Wenruo said.

"...I shall leave now," Hua Tuo replied.

"You must *stay now*, Master Hua," Cao Cao said. "You *must* stay... you *will* stay."

Hua Tuo grunted irritably and looked at the floor.

News of Hua Tuo's 'apprehension' travelled quickly; Kong Rong hosted a banquet that he had hoped that Hua Tuo would be able to attend, but Cao Cao's entourage refused to let Hua leave Cao's family mansion.

"What a cheek," Kong Rong said to his guests. "That fine mind is unparalleled, but he is forced to come to court and be the 'guest' of a demanding Chancellor of State: is this the beginnings of a repeat of that other incident...?"

"And what incident is that...?" Wang Lang asked coldly.

Kong Rong harrumphed and refused to answer.

"...This is the first time that I have been allowed to attend one of your banquets since the recent promotion of Chancellor Cao, and I am glad that I am here," Wang Lang prompted. "I do, of course, know that you refer to Cai Yong. Forgive me."

"I have barely had the time for more than three banquets since then, and I have not 'allowed' you, Wang Lang," Kong Rong retorted. "You are here because I have been too many times scolded for being petty and because I am well aware that most of this room voted as you did and would banquet next to nobody if I clung to my rarely-held beliefs."

"We 'voted' for a 'Chancellor Cao' over an 'Excellency Cao' because we need a man with that kind of authority at this moment in time," Yang Biao said insistently. "That will change, hopefully, and then we can review whether the new ducal model should be restored. I doubt that Chancellor Cao will protest: he will be sixty or more and anxious to retire to a more passive role, I imagine!"

"You'd better hope so," Kong Rong muttered.

"...I admit that I do worry about the way in which Master Hua is being treated," Zhi Xi said. "I was surprised enough when Chen Gui – a man that was the 'quiet hero' of that terrible 'Lü Bu' crisis ten years ago – jostled Master Hua into the city as he did, but I thought that would be the end of it."

"At least he wasn't bound with rope," Geng Ji suggested. "I might have taken action if he had been."

"Chancellor Cao suffers great pain when those headaches affect him," Wang Lang said. "I knew from others that his agony is tangible when the worst attacks occur: I have now been present for a bad one myself and it is terrifying to think that such pain can be invisible to the eye and yet as bad as the worst plague or prolonged amputation. Acupuncture relieves the pain immediately, and in addition to that Master Hua has been tasked with making a more thorough prognosis and finding a permanent cure."

"...I concede that Master Hua's movements might be restricted so that he misses nothing, and that he may, perhaps, be 'voluntarily restricted'," Kong Rong replied. "But if Chancellor Cao is cured and Master Hua is still detained, then what should be done...?"

"Don't you think that we should wait for such an event before we start plotting an armed rescue, Wenju...?" Yang Biao asked; his comment was met with laughter.

"...I hope that Master Hua can help," Sima Lang said. "Father and I have seen Chancellor Cao at his best, and he is a true hero."

"He *is* a hero, my son... when he is not compelled by the need to be mischievous," Sima Fang joked.

"Ah, yes... 'District Captain Cao Cao'," Yang Biao chuckled.

Sima Fang smiled thoughtfully and added, "But then I have not seen that 'wily prankster' part of Mengde's character for some years; he has matured into a hero that has brought peace to a quarter of the land."

"Will your most famous son be joining us soon, Jiangong...?" Yang Biao asked.

"Zhongda...? No, no... he's very ill," Sima Fang replied. "It makes me cry inside to know that such a promising youth has been afflicted so... just like Chancellor Cao, I suppose."

Yang Biao frowned and asked, "What is it that ails him, exactly...?"

"He's prematurely lame and senile," Sima Lang replied. "It sounds incredible, I know, but my brother hobbles around on a cane and talks gibberish."

"...Terrible," Zhi Xi sighed.

"Maybe Master Hua can find some cure for his affliction as well," Kong Rong suggested.

"...That is a thought," Sima Fang said. "I shall broach the subject if I can."

"What a pity it is that he cannot cure the Empire," Geng Ji muttered bitterly. "That is the weakest patient of them all..."

Cao Cao was kept under observation for several days: Hua Tuo studied him intently whilst providing Cao with the treatment that guaranteed relief from the pain.

"...Well...?" Cao Cao asked. "Can you see any pattern, any signs of something that points to a cure...? Is a cure even necessary if the symptoms can be instantly eliminated...?"

"The acupuncture will clear the pain, but we do not know that the affliction does not do some greater harm," Hua Tuo replied. "A long-term solution is needed in order to extend your life span."

"...I see," Cao Cao said. "Well then... I shall hope for a cure."

"I must come and go in order to research such a cure," Hua Tuo replied. "You must trust that I will return eventually... and you must please trust me when I say that there are others that can perform the acupuncture. My wider skillset is being ignored and other medical breakthroughs left undiscovered if I am restricted."

"...A proper search will be conducted for the right man in good time, but for now you must remain and serve as my personal physician," Cao Cao insisted. "You will go where I go and provide immediate care: the headaches affect me with increasing frequency and severity as my workload and worries mount, and that cannot be so."

Hua Tuo sighed and said, "Alright... alright."

"To see such relief administered in such a short time that works so well... leaves me speechless!" Xun Wenruo said. "I am left fighting tears of joy, Chancellor: and Master Hua, I am – along with the entire nation - forever in your debt."

Hua Tuo hummed ambiguously.

"Now I can get back to business more quickly, without the usual exhaustion that I suffer after an attack," Cao Cao said. "I will now attend my meeting with Chanyu Huchuquan... and he had better be prepared!"

Chang Xi's growing army of bandits started to divide into militias in order to attack multiple targets: some of Chang's allies were growing increasingly concerned at the rhetoric that their leader was resorting to in his search for support and suggested that he change his tactics as they concluded a violent raid on a farming village in Yangdu County.

"Look, I'm not just doing this for myself anymore," Chang Xi insisted. "I'm doing it for all of us, and for the people, alright...?"

The bandits looked at the looted village and silently pondered their leader's words.

"We all took part in what just happened," Chang Xi protested, "so don't bother doing the 'What you did was wrong' bit on me. We looted villages before: these people are conspirators! They're put here by Cao Cao to farm the land and pay taxes that fund his army! They grow food for his army for his, you know, that 'tuntian' thing he's got going. They're part-time soldiers."

"...Yeah, but we're still talking like rebels when we go looking for new blood, and that's dangerous," 'Long-toes' suggested.

"Look, mate, if people responded to 'We have to fight because we won't get what we want if we just sit here', then I'd stick to saying that, but they don't react to it!" Chang Xi retorted. "The fact is that Cao Cao is just another villain: he's made himself 'Chancellor of State' now, which means he's another Dong Zhuo!"

"...Yeah, Chang, you have kind of said that a few times already," 'Red Crest' said. "But you sound like you're calling for a rebellion against the Han now, when I thought that we were just-"

"Of course we're rebelling against the Han!" Chang Xi despaired. "Cao Cao is the Han! Cao Cao has had us fighting endlessly for no reward, and it's all in the name of the Han, isn't it...?"

Chang Xi's allies were silent.

"...Look, if you've decided I'm wrong, then go," Chang Xi continued. "Go back to Zang, or go home, or whatever you want, alright...? I already lost two o' you for attacking their home villages, and I still have thousands on my side because I'm right: the Han have lied to us and we've got to hit back. I don't want to be an attack dog for the rest o' my life: neither should any of you. Zang's sold out and joined Cao: good for him. But the reason that half o' Ji'nan and Juping is with me is 'cause they know how we've been treated by the Han government in the past and they know that Cao is a two-faced, lying bastard that'll have us fighting and whittling ourselves down in the name of the emperor and then he'll lock up whoever didn't fall on a sword."

The bandits murmured agreeably.

"So is the little mutiny over now, mm…?" Chang Xi heckled. "Can we get back to showing the Han that we've had enough of being trod on now…?"

"…I'm done," one man said. "I get what you're saying, Chang, but the way you're putting it, it's getting people worked up, and I reckon we're gonna have people turning on us when you get what you want, or maybe turning to someone else when we're alright and they're not. Good luck and all that, but I'm going home."

"…Fine," Chang Xi replied. "Like I said, Frog-eyes, I don't care: I still got loads o' blokes that understand what I'm doing."

The rest of the bandits watched as their ally 'Frog-eyes' turned and walked away slowly; some expected Chang Xi to attack him, but the lone dissenter was left to depart without incident.

"…Anyone else…? …Good," Chang Xi grumbled. "I'm right… I'm right, I tell you! The only way that we'll get what we want is to turn this province upside-down and tip all the corrupt bastards out of it and send them back to Xuchang!"

"…He was right, though," 'Long-toes' said. "People'll ask where theirs is when we get ours and stop all this."

"And I'll answer that as I already did before: stop worrying!" Chang Xi replied. "Everyone'll get what they deserve… including Zang Ba."

The bandits exchanged nervous glances.

"We're going to Kaiyang next… and we're going to make Zang wish that he'd told us the truth and not sold us out," Chang Xi continued. "We'll deal with him, and then we'll take Beihai properly, and once we've got Linzi, we'll run the whole province! No more crawling for scraps, lads: we'll take what we should have been given!"

****

104

On the eve of his intended departure from Xuchang, Cao Cao summoned Jia Xu, Hua Xin, Yuan Huan and Cao Chun to his private study within the chancellery and said, "I am blessed by the Heavens at present, gentlemen, and I intend to make the most of that. I am fully recovered following my recent illness and am now ready to go and deal with Liu Bao of the Xiongnu. I should also like to look at potential new recruits and make some other administrative changes."

"That's all very sensible, Chancellor," Hua Xin replied. "But... is leaving now entirely wise...? The court is still reeling from your promotion, and there are signs that something serious is about to happen in the south."

"I am aware of Sun Quan's movements," Cao Cao promised. "As for the feelings of the court, I only ask that they be good-natured regarding my next mission."

"Some might say that you should remain here," Yuan Huan suggested. "Only you can properly argue for your cause right now, Your Excellency."

"Xun Wenruo is a fine ambassador for my cause and argues it well enough," Cao Cao retorted. "And as I have already said, I hope that my wanting to negotiate the return of the gifted daughter of one of the Empire's greatest prodigies will be seen as a forgivable diversion, even by my harshest critics."

"...Who will accompany you, Mengde?" Cao Chun asked.

"Hua Tuo, of course, to deal with my affliction... and I must take a sizeable force in order to intimidate the young 'prince' that I will be bartering with," Cao Cao replied. "The Qiang might not like it, but I must hope that they will not react aggressively... I am not yet ready to make my demands of them."

"So you *do* intend to demand hostages from them," Hua Xin said.

"I do," Cao Cao replied with a smile. "And they will be surprised at my choices, I think!"

Cao Cao left Xuchang with his army on the following morning: Emperor Xian was notified of the exact reason for the expedition by Xun Wenruo, who held the meeting in a smaller hall with less than 20 officials – all of them Cao Cao's loyalists – in attendance.

"...We are taken aback," Emperor Xian admitted. "Mister Cao intends to retrieve Lady Cai with funds from his own treasury...?"

"Cai Yong's family was destroyed and their modest wealth lost due to years in exile," Xun Wenruo explained. "And although the lady's sister's father-in-law is a prefectural administrator, he is not a wealthy man; Chancellor Cao, however, still has some considerable wealth despite the loss of much of what his father carried with him on that Xu Provincial road on that fateful day fifteen years ago, and-"

Xun Wenruo hesitated and lowered his eyes tellingly.

"...And what he has expended while turning this city into a capital fit for the Son of Heaven," Emperor Xian guessed. "And, no doubt, what he has also spent on the reconstruction of Luoyang."

"I, Yu, am unworthy!" Xun Wenruo cried. "I did not mean to offend Your Majesty by implying that-!"

"Say no more of it, Mister Xun," Emperor Xian said gently. "You do in fact remind us of exactly how much Mister Cao has done for the Empire over the last decade. Perhaps we should remember the financial sacrifices with more vigour, for they are often forgotten amidst the haze of wars and meetings."

"...Chancellor Cao is aware that the timing is not perhaps convenient, Your Majesty," Xun Wenruo prompted.

"There will never be a good time to do anything while the realm is beset by such chaos," Emperor Xian replied. "One must act when one can. We are more than happy with the explanation given: you gentlemen may return to your duties now."

Xun Wenruo and the rest of the officials kowtowed and retreated from the hall.

"...I will never understand him," Emperor Xian sighed quietly.

Huchuquan and his heir Liu Bao personally greeted Cao Cao at the edge of the Southern Xiongnu settlement in Ping County; in addition to travelling in a carriage that one might have mistakenly assumed to be housing someone grander still, the Chancellor of State had brought Generals Cao Hong, Zhang Hè and Xu Huang and a force of 2,000 men as a sign that Cao was prepared to fight if needs be, but the Xiongnu had no appetite for confrontations of that kind.

"Your strength is great," Liu Bao said as he glared at Cao Cao.

"It is, and I am not afraid to use it," Cao Cao retorted. "I hope that my request will be granted."

Liu Bao grinned and said, "Tell us, Han Chancellor!"

"I will be straightforward," Cao Cao replied. "I am here to... as distasteful as it sounds... buy back a-"

"We will discuss this privately," Huchuquan ordered.

Huchuquan led the Han delegation to his grand enclosure and had them sit as guests: Cao Chun, Jia Xu, Yuan Huan, Hua Xin, Xin Pi, the hulking bodyguard Xu Chu and Registrar Liu Yè joined their lord while the generals watched for dangers.

"...Your bodyguard is like a great warrior god," Liu Bao said as he looked at Xu Chu. "I would like to test his strength."

"No more distractions," Cao Cao replied. "I am here on behalf of the late father of Cai Yan to pay a ransom for her return to what is left of her family: I already know that she is part of your harem, Prince Bao: I now want to know your price."

"And I want to know why I should give up this woman," Liu Bao retorted. "She is *mine*! Nobody has ever dared come and demanded her before!"

"Believe me, Prince Bao, when I say that if I could have come here and taken her from you at any point after I dealt with your father, then I would have," Cao Cao replied coldly.

Liu Bao scowled bitterly.

"We should be less aggressive," Huchuquan pleaded. "**More food! More drink!**"

Several maids brought jars of wine and long dishes of food and laid them down for the guests.

"...My father's death was *your fault*, Cao Cao," Liu Bao heckled. "Why should I now want peace? Why should I now want to give you one of my women?"

"You will do it because I have the strength to fight you if I must and the will to do so," Cao Cao replied. "In the past, your people have enjoyed the freedom to live here in Bing Province as you please; in exchange, you provide men and horses to serve in the army. I now have the humbled remnants of the Wuhuan paying homage and a pledge from the Qiang peoples as well, and both can and will provide the same service without complaint or dissent; how much can you bargain...?"

Liu Bao's eyes wandered.

"I have not interfered in your chieftainship selection process as previous Han courts have done," Cao Cao continued. "I *could*, though: do you think that there are no complaints...? Do you think that there are no voices saying, 'How can you let the brother of the troublemaker Yufuluo be the king of the Xiongnu?' Do you think that there are no men asking, 'Why is Liu Bao, a man who claims links to the Han throne by way of the royal princess ancestors that he has, a man that is the *son* of the troublemaker Yufuluo, allowed to be the next king?' I face questions like that all of the time, but I let you keep your freedom to choose, even after what Yufuluo did."

"Yes, and we are grateful," Huchuquan said.

"...The woman is *mine!*" Liu Bao protested.

"'The woman', *Lady Cai Yan*, is the daughter of the famous genius Cai Yong, and she belongs in the Han court, continuing what her father started," Cao Cao replied.

"She belongs to *me!*" Liu Bao retorted. "The woman belongs *here*, with *me!*"

"She was taken by you, yes... as any man can take something and then say, 'It is mine'," Cao Cao replied calmly. "I could take something from you and say 'It is mine'... one of your women, perhaps, or your right to be the next Chanyu of the Southern Xiongnu... couldn't I...?"

Liu Bao grunted angrily.

"I'm choosing to reimburse you for the loss, even though you abducted her and murdered most of her family in the process, which is actually a crime that I could punish," Cao Cao said with a smile. "I think that's very reasonable."

Liu Bao looked at Xu Chu; Huchuquan looked at Liu Bao and wondered whether he should intervene.

"...I want money – *a lot of money* – and gold, silk, horses and wine, and you cannot have any children she produced," Liu Bao announced after a long pause for thought. "You will pay what a prince would be paid for taking a wife from another chieftain: you know how much that is."

"The children are Xiongnu children and future heirs to your chieftainship," Cao Cao replied. "They should and will remain here with your people."

"And you will give me what I ask...?" Liu Bao prompted.

"I *shouldn't*," Cao Cao said, "but I *will*... since I see no sense in more bloodshed if it can be avoided. Money and possessions are worthless to the dead."

"You are a wise man, Cao Cao," Huchuquan declared. "Nephew, you should-"

"The woman will be delivered when I get what I have asked for," Liu Bao said angrily. "*Not before.*"

"I want to see her and know that I am getting the woman that I am paying the ransom for, and not some other, less favoured consort of yours chosen at random," Cao Cao insisted.

"Fine," Liu Bao said; he then shouted orders at one of his subordinates, who left the enclosure. "We will go outside and you can see her before you go," Liu Bao added with evident bitterness. "Then you will go and get my price and bring it here."

"...Thank you," Cao Cao said uneasily.

The Han delegation was rattled and distressed at the sight of Lady Cai Yan when she was finally brought before them: she was totally devoid of any signs of thought or emotion. The 30-year-old Cai Yan was dressed in traditional Xiongnu clothing but her features were undeniably those of a person of Han Chinese descent; Liu Bao had summoned the entirety of his harem as an apparent act of spite, however, and many others were Han Chinese girls that he had probably acquired in exactly the same way.

"Which one is it, then...?" Liu Bao asked.

Cao Cao turned to Jia Xu, who sighed miserably and pointed at Cai Yan without speaking.

"...You are the daughter of 'Cai Yong'?" Liu Bao asked as he glared at the emotionless consort.

"...Yes," Cai Yan replied. "I was."

"*Aiee*... part of me wants to *kill* these scum," Xin Pi muttered.

Liu Bao barked orders at a Xiongnu warrior that then led the harem away; two of the girls looked back as they were being forcibly moved, but Cai Yan was moving as though she were without a will of her own and did not do the same.

"She will be yours when you pay, Chancellor Cao Cao," Liu Bao heckled. "You can go now."

"Remember that I have the power to take all of this from you," Cao Cao said as he turned to Huchuquan. "No *tricks*."

"You will get the woman when the price is paid: I promise," Huchuquan replied.

Cao Cao cast one last look at the group of girls as they retreated and said, "We're going now, gentlemen."

Cao Cao was sombre when he returned to the command tent of his temporary camp at the outskirts of Ping County.

"Can't we just do what we did to the Wuhuan?" Cao Hong asked.

"...Huchuquan might not seem to be very agreeable, but he is," Cao Cao replied. "He has to work with Liu Bao, just as Louban had to work with Tadun; the relationship is the same in many ways, and Huchuquan might even thank me for intervening in the Chanyu selection process and denying his obnoxious nephew the chance to doom his people."

"They were *our* girls!" Cao Hong protested. "Any one of the others could be a Yuan, a Cao, a-!"

"I have no intention of letting the Xiongnu retain their autonomy, not after what I've just seen," Cao Cao promised. "Liu Bao has the eyes of a future problem that we can well do without. We won't be able to do anything straight away – not with the Qiang watching – but in times to come, we'll break the Xiongnu's will and retrieve the others. But the Qiang must be dealt with first."

"Will they have working minds by then...?" Yuan Huan asked.

"Lady Cai was as empty-eyed as a wooden puppet! Not a trace of a soul on her face! Does she even possess a mind anymore after *thirteen years* of…!"

"…I am fighting the urge to weep as well, Yaoqing, but I must try to remember that Liu Bao is a monster that serves as a poor example of his people," Cao Cao replied. "Others – many others – have the same morals as we do… and a number of our most loyal cavalrymen are at least part Xiongnu."

"Mengde is right," Cao Chun said. "I have quite a few Xiongnu in my own cavalry, and they are good people."

"…Other nations might say the same as us were they to judge us by citing Dong Zhuo as the model… and let us not forget that Zhang Fei took Miaocai's daughter, though there will be no ransom given to *that* old criminal," Cao Cao continued. "But enough of that: let us get this over with."

Liu Bao smiled as Cao Cao's soldiers brought the vast wealth that he had demanded into the Xiongnu camp; a large number of tribesmen gathered to watch what seemed to be some sort of victory for their people.

"**Do not mistake this for power!**" Cao Cao warned. "**This is no *tribute*: this is my attempt at honouring the spirit of the man on whose behalf I pay this ransom.**"

"…**You are not misunderstood,**" Huchuquan promised.

"**Now the lady will be handed over,**" Cao Cao urged once the treasures had been delivered in full; Liu Bao smirked and clapped his hands theatrically.

"…I really want to do something else entirely," Cao Chun muttered as Cai Yan was brought forth and told to walk toward her liberators; she said nothing as she walked forward, showing neither sadness at abandoning her children nor joy at returning to her people.

"She is still an empty ghost," Liu Yè noted.

"I have an idea that may help," Cao Cao replied as Jia Xu took Cai Yan's hand and led her toward the chancellor's carriage.

"**Our business is done,**" Liu Bao declared.

"**For now,**" Cao Cao retorted. "**But I can assure you, Prince Bao, that there will be more 'business' in the future.**"

Huchuquan shuddered; Cao Cao turned and boarded his carriage, and the Han delegation departed.

"If he wants to buy more of my Han women for as much money as this, he is welcome to!" Liu Bao joked. "I will be rich enough to-!"

"You should be glad if he does not now do to us what he has done to the Wuhuan!" Huchuquan scolded. "I warn you: do not celebrate your little 'victory', Nephew… not *yet*."

The journey back to the Han camp was a sombre one: Cai Yan did not answer any of Cao Cao or Hua Tuo's enquiries about her health or state of mind. Cao Cao summoned his senior officials to his command tent immediately upon returning to the camp and said, "Master Hua Tuo says that the lady's ailment is entirely of the spirit and cannot be cured by medicine or needles as mine can. I have asked Yang Chai to escort his wife to Yè so that the sisters can be reunited: it will, with any luck, reawaken Lady Cai Yan's broken spirit."

"That might work," Jia Xu said. "But... I don't know, Excellency... I fear that the damage to her mind might be too great to-"

"I refuse to think like that," Cao Cao interrupted. "She is my last hope, Wenhe: if she does not recall any of the great works that her father created, then those treasures of the mind – worth more than any of the baubles that I have just given that soulless barbarian prince – will be lost forever."

"...Is that the only reason why you've done all this...?" Cao Hong asked without thinking.

Cao Chun shoved Cao Hong and shouted, **"Shut up you-!"**

"I... am aware that some will label me as a selfish villain for saying this, but... that is almost entirely correct," Cao Cao admitted. "There were, as Zilian has already pointed out, a lot of Han girls in that harem brought before us, and the other chieftains will have similar 'spoils'."

The gathering was silent.

"...Apart from the fact that I lacked the funds to buy back every last one of them at the prices that the man was demanding and the fact that I did not desire a fight to win them back, I must acknowledge the fact that I would then have to do the same a thousand times over with the Di, the Qiang, the Shanyue, the Wuhuan... and then, some would say, some of our own people," Cao Cao continued. "But can I do that? Women are a spoil of war: the wives and daughters of our defeated enemies become *our* consorts after we have slain the men... and that is how it has always been."

"That's during *war*, Mengde," Cao Hong protested. "Liu Bao is a savage that did that to villages when-"

"The discussion is over," Cao Cao ordered.

"So when will Yang Chai get here...?" Cao Chun asked.

"...Soon," Cao Cao replied. "I can do no better than that."

The young official Yang Chai brought his wife – the younger daughter of Cai Yong, known affectionately as 'Xiaocai' – from his current home in Mount Tai Prefecture, where his father was now the Administrator, to the city of Yè; the sisters were reunited in the main audience hall of Cao Cao's residence, although care was taken to keep any but the most necessary officials from being in attendance. Cai Yan had been given Han robes and had her hair altered to match the Han style, but there had been no change in her lifeless countenance and still none when her sister entered the hall with her husband.

"Pray this works, gentlemen," Cao Cao murmured.

"...*Older Sister*...?" Xiaocai exclaimed. "...Older sister! Older sister! It *is* you!"

The first signs of emotion appeared on Cai Yan's face as she studied the younger woman that was approaching her and realised that it was the sister that she had thought to be dead.

"...You...are... *Xiaocai*...?" Cai Yan exclaimed. "But... I saw...!"

"The chaos of the moment blinded you to the truth, sister-in-law," Yang Chai said. "Here she is, alive and well."

Cai Yan shook her head slightly and whispered, "Younger sister...?"

"Older sister!" Xiaocai pleaded. "Older sister...!"

Cai Yan tried to move forward, but years of often-violent 'training' had removed much of her free will: it was left to Xiaocai to act first and throw her arms around Yan. That gesture worked: Cai Yan was suddenly overcome by grief, trauma and joy that broke the mental hold that her Xiongnu husband still had and allowed her to sob and reciprocate the embrace.

"A promising start," Hua Tuo suggested. "However..."

"...It's a start," Cao Cao said. "Let us hope it is the start of something better."

Cai Yan gradually ceased to be an automaton and became the person that she had once been as the days wore on: the process was strangely exhausting to all that witnessed it. Cao Cao wanted to enjoy his semi-altruistic act for as long as he could, but he knew that there could be no more time spent on the matter than was absolutely necessary: he planned his return to the capital and left Cai Yan in the temporary care of her sister and Yang Chai.

****

105

Cao Cao immediately set about looking at the credentials of potential recruits and promotable officials upon his return to Xuchang; he summoned Xun Gongda after two days of deliberations and said, "Call Bao Xun to the chancellery."

"…Bao Xun…?" Xun Gongda prompted.

"Yes, Gongda, Bao Xun," Cao Cao said irritably. "Bao Xun, styled 'Shuye', son of Bao Xin of Mount Tai Prefecture that served Liu Dai in this very province."

"…I will have a messenger go at once, Your Excellency," Xun Gongda replied. "He is where…?"

"*Here*, in Xuchang, in a junior role," Cao Cao scolded. "You used to be more alert: you've forgotten who Bao Xun is…?"

"Excellency, I am just about keeping up with the names of my staff," Xun Gongda replied. "Bao Xin's son is, to be honest, a little obscure. Why him…?"

"Bao Xin was an ally during my early days in this province, which you should know," Cao Cao retorted. "He and I fought the Yellow Turbans that I turned into my Qing Province Corps, but not before they claimed his life."

"…And so you want to give his son a job," Xun Gongda prompted.

"His son is properly educated," Cao Cao promised. "This is not some favour that will see some mediocrity given a high rank: Shuye is, I understand, outspoken and honest, and unafraid to confront even the highest of men with their faults."

"…Well then he is ideal," Xun Gongda said.

"Which is why I want him promoted!" Cao Cao chuckled.

Xun Wenruo entered the office and said, "You are in good spirits today, Chancellor Cao."

"Just call me 'Excellency' as you have always done," Cao Cao replied. "I am, after all, still a 'Ducal Excellence'."

"…As you wish," Xun Wenruo said.

"And yes, I am in good spirits!" Cao Cao continued. "Knowing that I will never again be impeded by those blasted headaches for days on end is enough to make me want to *sing*… though I will not."

Xun Wenruo looked at Cao Cao's registrar, Liu Yè, who returned a resigned expression.

"Ah! Since you're here, Wenruo, you can tell me whether there is any word on Sima Yi's condition," Cao Cao continued. "Is he really as sick as I am told, and can he not be cured by the marvellous Hua Tuo…?"

"…His father, Elder Sima Fang, wonders the same," Xun Wenruo replied. "I'll admit that I am starting to wonder what we're dealing with… but I am perhaps being ridiculous. Who would risk imprisonment for feigning illness so that he could avoid a well-paid role at the top of the Han Imperial administration…?"

"That's my main – if not my only – reason for believing that Sima Yi is ill," Cao Cao admitted. "Though I contradict my desire to employ him by saying this, I shall anyway: for his own sake, he had better be ill."

"…Yes, Your Excellency," Xun Wenruo said. "Is there any word from Yang Chai…?"

"It is too soon for correspondence, Wenruo," Cao Cao replied. "I have only just got back to Xuchang! But Lady Cai was showing strong signs of recovery when I left Yè, so I am optimistic. Oh, yes: has Hua Tuo said anything else about isolating and eliminating my headaches completely...?"

"No... he just complains that he needs to be able to travel, as usual, and asks whether there is any correspondence from his household in Pei," Xun Wenruo said.

"It might be wise to find another man – or preferably men – that can help," Hua Xin suggested. "We can ill afford to have him gaining some great hold over you, Excellency, by his being the only man that can help you and one day realising the benefits of such a position."

"Hmm... that's true," Cao Cao realised. "You are quick-thinking, Hua Ziyu! That's just the thing that I need from all of you, gentlemen, now that Fengxiao is gone: quick thinking!"

"...Are you alright, Excellency...?" Xun Gongda asked carefully.

"Fine, Gongda: quite fine!" Cao Cao chuckled. "I feel like I used to feel oh-so-many years ago, when I was not so dragged down by my affliction, all the while dreading its return, writhing when it strikes and feeling exhausted in its wake! Heaven bless Hua Tuo! He might need to be controlled or replaced, as you say, but Heaven bless him anyway!"

"...That is good, Excellency," Xun Gongda said.

"Now then, gentlemen," Cao Cao continued. "Any other matters that need to be brought to my attention...?"

"We... we don't have confirmation yet, Excellency, but... there is strong evidence to suggest that Chang Xi – one of the more prominent chieftains of the former Mount Tai Bandits – has... has attacked a village near their old Kaiyang stronghold and tried to seize control of it," Xun Wenruo explained. "General Yu Jin is monitoring the situation and has asked Zang Ba to look into the matter as well."

"There's no end to it, is there...?" Cao Cao said calmly. "Ah, well... 'A man whose thoughts lead oft to crime succumbs and gravely errs in time'. I'm surprised that it is just one of them that I am dealing with. But Yu Jin will manage well enough!"

"...I'm glad that you are responding to the news as you do, Excellency," Xun Wenruo replied.

"Just keep me informed," Cao Cao said. "I have so much to do, and so little time! When can I lament about a lapsed criminal...? Carry on as you are, and I shall do the same! Can I keep Ma Teng waiting any longer...?"

"...Whatever it is you're doing, be careful," Xun Wenruo warned.

"I'm not scared of the Qiang!" Cao Cao chuckled. "And there will be even less to be scared of soon enough!"

The leader of the former Mount Tai Bandits, Zang Ba, was angered by the news that his former ally Chang Xi was apparently moving toward their old Kaiyang stronghold with his small army; Zang assembled his remaining allies in his base in Mount Tai City and said, "What does this idiot think he's doing???"

"He's got plans," Sun Guan sighed.

"He's a dead man that's got a year to live at best, that's what he's got!" Zang Ba replied. "I *warned him*!"

"We're not really gonna go after Chang, are we, boss...?" Wu Dun asked miserably.

"He's brought this on himself," Zang Ba replied. "If I can take him alive I will, but... Yu Jin's involved now."

"*Aiee*... that Han toady will want the kill for his own reputation," Yin Li said.

"And worse yet, Chang still thinks that Yu Jin's his mate 'cause they're both from Juping," Sun Guan replied. "We need to get to Chang first."

"We'll cooperate with Yu Jin, not compete with him," Zang Ba insisted. "If we're caught trying to save Chang we'll be punished."

"That's true," Wu Dun said. "Oh well... it's like you said then, Xuangao: it's him or us and he'll have to go."

"I *didn't say that*... but... yeah," Zang Ba replied. "It *is* him or us."

While the former Mount Tai Bandits prepared to do battle with Chang Xi, the Qiang tribes of the northwest – which had already become divided and had been fighting each other for some time – were about to be tested by Cao Cao's latest demand to be made of the senior chieftain Ma Teng. A Han envoy marched into the leader's enclosure within Ma Teng's current headquarters – a bivouac camp near Mei County – and said, "**The Chancellor of State, Cao Cao, calls for General Ma Teng, self-styled 'king of chieftains' among the Qiang tribes of Xiliang, to offer tribute and a formal submission to the Son of Heaven!**"

Ma Teng shuddered.

"**An invitation to Yè City in Ji Province is extended to General Ma Teng: close family should also be in attendance,**" the envoy continued.

"**Treachery!**" Colonel Pang De cried. "**You used us as your army to save Hedong and now you try to abduct our lord! If the lord's eldest son were here, you-!**"

"**Calm down, Colonel!**" Ma Teng urged. "I'm glad that Chao is not here... because this man does not come alone."

"**Let them come here, Father!**" Ma Tie shouted over the angry cries of his fellow Qiang chieftains. "**The-!**"

"**No!**" Ma Teng bellowed. "**Be quiet, all of you!**"

Pang De nodded to two lesser chieftains that quietly left the enclosure; the rest gradually fell silent.

"**You will be awarded an Imperial military rank upon your arrival in Yè,**" the envoy continued. "**The Chancellor of State will ensure that you are properly respected, General Ma.**"

"...I am grateful to the Chancellor," Ma Teng replied.

"**...I will now depart,**" the envoy said. "**The Chancellor of State demands a swift reply to his request.**"

"**And he will get it,**" Ma Teng promised. "**Tell the chancellor that I will prepare for my journey to Yè immediately.**"

The envoy nodded tersely, turned and retreated.

"...You do not really intend to go, do you Father...?" Ma Tie asked.

"I have no choice," Ma Teng replied. "Cao Cao has outmanoeuvred me, but-"

"Take me with you, Father!" Ma Xiu pleaded.

"...You will both be going with me, and so will all of my consorts, servants, and younger children," Ma Teng replied. "Only your elder brother will remain."

"Cao Cao will not like that," Ma Tie suggested.

"Chao will not be forced to go," Ma Teng replied. "That is
something that Cao Cao will have to accept if he is going to resort
to taking me hostage."
"But what if Chao responds to this with violence...?" Ma Tie asked.
"He would be condemning most of his clan to extermination," Ma
Teng replied. "No pious son that respects his father and mother
would then risk their lives. Cao Cao knows that, which is why he
takes this action."
"Will he do the same to Han Sui?" Ma Xiu asked.
"I honestly don't know," Ma Teng said. "I didn't expect *this*, so
how can I know?"
"If you want to fight, I will fight," Pang De declared. "We all will!"
"No, Colonel... no," Ma Teng ordered. "I saw that you sent two
men away to fetch Chao, but I will not allow armed confrontation
over this. I want you and the others to honour me by remaining
here in Liang Province and living peacefully with Han Sui and Song
Jian and with the Han people. Let Cao Cao and his agents be the
ones that destroy the peace, not my son or Han Sui or anyone
else, because Cao Cao will use whatever action we take as an
excuse to annihilate us."
"I understand," Pang De replied. "I cannot promise that I can calm
Mengqi, but I will do my very best."
"...Well then... I should prepare to leave," Ma Teng sighed.

Ma Chao screamed angrily when he learned of his father's
dilemma and subsequent decision: he left his base by the Wei
River and hurried to Mei County, but his father and family were
gone by the time that he arrived.
"Calm down," Pang De pleaded.
"... ... ...I... *swear*... that I will find a way, Pang Lingming," Ma Chao
growled. "I will find a way to get to Cao Cao... I will find a way to
destroy him...!"
"Do not fight!" Pang De said. "He will kill your entire clan!"
"I will not let this go," Ma Chao retorted. "I will find a way... there
has to be a way..."
"The answer is *unity*, Cousin," Ma Dai suggested quietly.
"...It is," Ma Chao replied. "Only by uniting will we smash Cao
Cao... and so I must go and speak to Han Sui and Song Jian."
"Don't waste time talking to Song Jian," Ma Dai said. "He just
stays in his little 'kingdom' and refuses to do anything."
"Just Han Sui, then," Ma Chao replied. "We will go now."

Ma Teng was welcomed at the gates of Yè City by Cao Cao's heir
Cao Pi, Ji Province Registrar Li Fu and Attendant Officer Cui Yan.
"Father – the Chancellor of State – is currently in Xuchang," Cao
Pi explained. "He will invite you to his court to show you the
proper respect when he returns. In the meantime, General Ma, we
have prepared your new accommodation, and you will find that it
is more than sufficient for you and your clan."
"...I thank you," Ma Teng replied quietly.
"I do not see any sign of your famous eldest son, Ma Chao," Cui
Yan said. "Is he not accompanying you...?"
"No, and you should be glad that he has not!" Ma Tie snapped.
"...Is that so...?" Cao Pi replied. "I shall bear that in mind."
"Pay no attention to my son's outburst," Ma Teng said. "Chao is

famous for his short temper, as you no doubt know, but he is no threat. He remains in Liang to tend to business and protect my lands from my rival, General Han Sui."

"That old life is no longer yours to worry about," Li Fu declared. "Your place now is here in Yè City or, perhaps, the Imperial capital in the future, General Ma: you will receive appropriate rank for that new life."

Ma Teng smiled sadly and said, "I am unlikely to see Liang Province again, then…?"

"You know that to be the case," Li Fu replied. "You and Han Sui are like the two fierce tigers of the proverb: Chancellor Cao acts to preserve your lives and make the best use of you both."

Ma Teng laughed and said, "How generous."

"Let us go and settle your family in your new home," Li Fu replied.

"…Lead the way," Ma Teng sighed.

Han Sui was puzzled when Ma Chao's arrival was announced: he readied his best men, hid the best ten of those men behind screens with swords at the ready and invited his rival's son into his enclosure.

"Remember… watch him closely," Han Sui whispered to his adviser, Chenggong Ying, who nodded silently in response.

"Greetings, General Han," Ma Chao said as he entered the tent at speed and fell to one knee; Pang De and Ma Dai followed shortly afterward and bowed humbly.

"…Up, please, Ma Mengqi," Han Sui replied cautiously. "I won't have my friend's son – which makes you my friend also – showing such deference."

Ma Chao straightened up and said, "I thank you, Han Wenyue."

"To what do I owe this visit…?" Han Sui asked.

Ma Chao sighed theatrically and said, "Are you aware that my father and most of the rest of my clan – including my eldest brothers, Tie and Xiu – have been taken hostage by Cao Cao…?"

Han Sui's court reacted with genuine surprise.

"…So you do not," Ma Chao realised.

"Cao Cao, that-! …No… *dare he treat us like this*???" Han Sui exclaimed. "Chenggong Ying: how should I react? Am I next…?"

"…To answer your last question, I think that the answer is 'no', else they would have been here before Ma Chao," Chenggong Ying replied. "To answer your first question – regardless of who you aimed it at – I think that the answer is, 'He has already done so'; to answer the remaining question, my lord – 'How to react' – the answer is 'With unity'."

"Which is why I am here," Ma Chao declared. "For the last few years, we've done the Han's dirty work for them without realising it, and we have to stop. They want us to fight when they do not need us, and they divide us; and when they need us, they keep us divided so that they can use our lack of trust in each other to control our every move. We must stop killing each other and become a strong confederacy again."

"…Why…?" Han Sui asked. "You can't fight Cao Cao without losing your clan."

"I will find a way to harm Cao Cao," Ma Chao promised. "But until then, Han Wenyue, we must be fearsome and prevent them from taking anything else from us. And if the worst must happen, then... then I cannot allow my clan to become the cause of the destruction of our people."

"...I see," Han Sui said as he briefly turned his eyes toward Chenggong Ying, who nodded discreetly. "From this day, Ma Mengqi, we will fight no more; we are now like blood brothers, you and I, against the Han."

Ma Chao stood up and extended a hand of friendship: Han Sui got to his feet and clasped Ma Chao's hand tightly.

"No more weakness," Ma Chao said. "We meet every challenge with a challenge."

"Yes," Han Sui replied. "The Han will not disrespect us again!"

Cao Cao received word of Ma Teng's arrival in Yè and smiled, saying, "'General Ma' has capitulated... that's good. I do not appear to have caught Ma Chao in my net, but I have enough of his clan to control him, which will do."

"You seem a little less animated, Excellency," Xun Wenruo noted.

"Alas, I am about to suffer another bout of my affliction: I can feel the signs of it," Cao Cao replied. "I am still saddened by that inevitability... but I am less distressed than I would have been now that I know that my friend Hua Tuo has provided a way to ease my suffering."

"...And you're sure that you do not mind his departure...?" Xun Wenruo asked.

"He is only going for a while, and he is waiting until this latest headache has passed," Cao Cao replied. "The letter from Pei said that his wife's condition has deteriorated; what sort of lord would I be if I let a man's wife die needlessly...?"

Xun Wenruo nodded silently.

"If, as he says, his wife is too sick to be moved, then I must be generous, especially since Master Hua has done so much for me," Cao Cao continued.

Xun Wenruo nodded agreeably.

"He will return, Wenruo," Cao Cao said with a strange smile. "He will return; only a fool would not."

Xun Wenruo nodded uneasily.

Two days passed: once Cao Cao's migraine was successfully treated, Hua Tuo hurried to the eastern gates of Xuchang and departed the city in a simple carriage. The scholar-doctor clutched his medicine bag to his chest and silently hoped not only that Cao Cao would not change his mind and call him back before he could get out of the county, but that he would never see the Chancellor of State again; unbeknownst to Cao, Hua had lied when he said that he would return once he had seen to his wife, who was not as sick as he had suggested.

"I *must* be free," Hua Tuo murmured. "I *must be*, or what else will I learn before I die, old as I am...?"

The carriage left the capital county without incident, but it would not, as the physician hoped, be the last time that Hua Tuo would see the city or encounter the persistent Chancellor of State.

****

Zang Ba, Sun Guan, Wu Dun and Yin Li led their followers to different parts of eastern Qing Province in order to quell the uprisings that Chang Xi was inspiring with his latest actions: Zang insisted that he would be the one that actually confront Chang Xi, which he eventually did at a village to the west of Kaiyang.

"**SURRENDER, CHANG!**" Zang Ba ordered. "**DON'T MAKE ME KILL YOU!**"

"**YOU BETRAYED US!**" Chang Xi replied. "**YOU JOINED CAO CAO AND SENT HIM YOUR FAMILY!**"

"**WE'VE BEEN THROUGH THAT YOU–!** ...Oh, why am I bothering...?" Zang Ba said. "He's determined to do this..."

"**WHAT'S THE MATTER?**" Chang Xi heckled. "**YOUR VOICE GONE NOW? TRY YÈ, WHERE YOU SENT YOUR COURAGE AND YOUR FAMILY!**"

"I'm done with this," Zang Ba said. "**GET READY, LADS!**"

"**GET READY TO DIE!**" Chang Xi screamed. "**CHARGE, EVERYONE! CHARGE!**"

The two armies of bandits – one reformed, one returned to their old ways – charged at each other and clashed for several minutes; Chang Xi's followers suffered a slight numerical advantage, but their resolve made them more effective in comparison to Zang Ba's disillusioned, confused and demoralised men, so the battle started to go in favour of Chang. But just as Zang Ba was about to contemplate retreating, a second army appeared that carried banners reading 'Yu Jin, General that Punishes Bandits'; Chang Xi's men were unable to fend off two armies from two different directions, so they started to scatter.

"**PUSH THE ADVANTAGE!**" Zang Ba ordered. "**GET CHANG XI!**"

Chang Xi fled the battlefield with little more than than 1,000 of his original following.

"...That was nearly very dangerous," Zang Ba sighed to himself as he observed the battlefield and tried to estimate the body count. "*Damn* that idiot... *damn him...!*"

General Yu Jin approached Zang Ba and said, "**Was Chang Xi apprehended, Mister Zang?**"

"No," Zang Ba replied. "**But I did try to get, him, honestly.**"

"**I believe you,**" Yu Jin promised. "**Why would you lie?**"

"...Yeah," Zang Ba sighed. "Why would I...?"

"**We should pursue at once,**" Yu Jin suggested.

"**And kill him in battle,**" Zang Ba said.

"**Not necessarily,**" Yu Jin replied. "**If he can be captured in battle, then that would suffice.**"

"...I'll secure this area, then," Zang Ba said.

"**Yes, and I shall pursue Chang Xi,**" Yu Jin replied. "**Every effort will be taken to take him alive so that justice can be properly served.**"

Zang Ba nodded respectfully, and Yu Jin rode away; Zang pondered Yu Jin's words and smiled, saying, "What a shifty man."

Cao Cao was starting to suffer the initial effects of a migraine when Bao Xun finally reported to his office and said, "You asked to see me, Chancellor...?"

"I am not at my best," Cao Cao replied. "I am glad to see you, Shuye... even if it took you longer to report to me than I had hoped for."
Xun Wenruo and Liu Yè frowned nervously.
"...I was first delayed by an illness in my family," Bao Xun explained. "And when I later asked about the right time to speak with you, I was informed that you were very busy with important state affairs: if that was not the case then I should not have been told so."
Cao Cao laughed and said, "As direct as I had been told. You know that I knew your father well...?"
"I know that you knew him, Chancellor," Bao Xun replied. "As to how well, I am ignorant. Father died some fifteen, sixteen years ago now, while in the service of the Han, and against the Yellow Turbans that were attacking this province."
"And I greatly regret that I was unable to provide support to him, but I was trapped in Yingchuan and Chenliu, fighting Li Jue and Guo Si's raiding parties," Cao Cao explained. "Although there wasn't much that I could do, I still regret it."
"Do not," Bao Xun said. "Why wish that you could have added your corpse to that bungled assault...? Your survival led to the taming of the Yellow Turbans and a lot of other incredible achievements after that; that's a better outcome."
"I thank you for saying that," Cao Cao replied. "Now I will tell you of your new role, which should make better use of you."
"Do not reward me for soothing your conscience or being the son of a better man than I can profess to be," Bao Xun said. "That would be wrong."
Cao Cao smiled and replied, "I appreciate your directness, Shuye. You will henceforth be an Officer within the chancellery, and you can expect other promotions to follow if you continue to be honest, forthright and competent."
"I hope that I shall prove worthy," Bao Xun said. "To whom should I report...?"
"You'll report to me," Xun Wenruo explained. "I'll get you started."
"You do that," Cao Cao said as he got to his feet. "I... think that I had better retire to my study, where the light is less intense. Carry on as you are."
Xun Wenruo, Registrar Liu Yè and Bao Xun bowed to their lord before he retreated.
"...So the headaches really are as disruptive as I had heard," Bao Xun said.
"Worse, perhaps," Liu Yè suggested. "We have been lucky enough to enjoy the immediate relief provided by Hua Tuo's acupuncture for some time now, but... things will be different – or rather, as they used to be – this time, I'm afraid, since Hua Tuo is... temporarily absent."
"I see... where is Hua Tuo, then...?" Bao Xun asked.
"He is *temporarily absent*," Xun Wenruo replied tersely.
"...Ah, I see," Bao Xun said. "I shall say no more."
"But he'll return to us," Xun Wenruo insisted. "He *must*."

Liang Province Inspector Wei Kang was understandably surprised when the news of Ma Teng's removal from the province and Ma Chao's subsequent meeting with rival warlord Han Sui were reported within days of each other; Wei summoned Military Consultant Zhao Ang and Assistant Officer Yang Fu to speak with him privately and said, "Should we be worried...?"

"Of course we should," Zhao Ang replied. "We should be extremely concerned."

"I agree in one sense, but I refuse to panic," Yang Fu said. "For now, the two troublemakers are in western Tianshui and will hopefully stay there to avoid Chancellor Cao abducting anyone else from their midst."

"So what concerns you both, exactly...?" Wei Kang asked.

"*Ayah*... you invited us here, Inspector, but seem to be the least concerned," Zhao Ang despaired. "We were notified that Chancellor Cao intended to take hostages, but not close to two-hundred members of the Ma clan without taking Ma Chao!"

"...But that makes Ma Chao less of a threat, surely, gentlemen," Wei Kang said.

"Only if he has a shred of decency and upholds the values that most men have regarding honouring one's parents," Zhao Ang replied. "I actually doubt that when I hear about him: he has that same impulsive, feral way about him that *Lü Bu* had."

"In battle, he is a fair comparison," Wei Kang agreed.

"And in other ways, I'll wager," Zhao Ang retorted. "Heaven knows what happened to Bu's real father, but we know what happened to his adoptive ones, don't we...? He killed them both when they were least aware of the threat, and an adoptive father is as precious as any other: other men will exist that are just as violent, capricious and immoral as Bu, and Ma Chao is similar in enough ways to be such a man."

"...That's true," Yang Fu admitted. "But we must assume that he is a loyal son and hope that Chancellor Cao's actions have done us a great favour. If Ma Chao and Han Sui are putting a greater distance between their homes and the seat of power then it is to avoid confrontation as well as recruitment, and that is surely a good thing."

"So we should be optimistic...?" Wei Kang prompted.

"Never," Zhao Ang replied. "I will continue to worry because that's my role. I admit that the greatest threats now come from Zhang Lu attempting to form an alliance and Chancellor Cao accidentally provoking the Qiang with some rash action, and both of those are hopefully unlikely."

Wei Kang smiled and said, "At least we have ways to bargain with them! We might even see an improvement in relations in the coming years! Perhaps the Qiang will be able to live alongside us again, as they did before the rebellion twenty years ago. After the Chancellor's pacification of the Wuhuan, I am prepared to believe that anything is possible."

"...The tribes that live in different parts of the Empire are not identical," Zhao Ang replied. "Some might be reasoned with, while others must be crushed; some might submit, while others might prefer to fight to the death. We'll be sensible and watch the Qiang carefully... I won't let my guard down again."

Chang Xi's multi-targeted rebellion was met with counterattacks across eastern Qing Province that blunted every army and restored order to every settlement that they affected. Han General

Yu Jin pursued Chang Xi to the Qing-Xu provincial border and trapped him in an abandoned fortress; the bandit leant over the battlements and shouted, **"WHY ARE YOU HOUNDING ME, YU JIN? WHY HAVE YOU FORGOTTEN THE PAST...?"**
Yu Jin smiled and replied, **"IT'S BECAUSE I REMEMBER THOSE DAYS IN JUPING THAT YOU ARE STILL ALIVE, CHANG XI!"**
Chang Xi hummed thoughtfully.
"YOU KNOW THE PENALTY FOR REBELLING AFTER SUBMISSION," Yu Jin said. **"WHY HAVE YOU DONE THIS?"**
"WE'VE BEEN MISTREATED!" Chang Xi protested. **"WE KEPT QING SAFE WHILE JI AND YÒU AND BING WERE TAKEN: OTHERS GET RANK, SO WHY HAVEN'T WE? ALL YOUR LORD DID WAS TAKE ZANG'S FAMILY HOSTAGE!"**
"YOU WERE TOO IMPATIENT!" Yu Jin retorted. **"IF YOU HAD ONLY *WAITED*, CHANG XI!"**
Chang Xi's eyes wandered erratically.
"IT IS NOT TOO LATE!" Yu Jin said. **"I HAVE NOT FORGOTTEN JUPING! I WILL ENSURE THAT JUSTICE IS DONE!"**
"...You will?" Chang Xi asked.
"SUBMIT, CHANG XI, AND END THIS FOOLISH REBELLION BEFORE OTHERS ARE SENT HERE THAT DO NOT UNDERSTAND YOU!" Yu Jin pleaded. **"DO THE RIGHT THING!"**
"...I'LL SURRENDER!" Chang Xi decided. **"WAIT THERE!"**
Yu Jin smiled silently.

"You can't surrender, you fool!" Chang Xi's wife pleaded. "He'll kill you!"
"He remembers our time as children in Juping," Chang Xi insisted. "He'll do everything to ensure justice is done, he said. We can't win if they start sending more troops, anyway."
"We're better off holding!" 'Long-toes' suggested. "Lü Bu didn't-!"
"That was when we held Ju City, not this shabby place," Chang Xi interrupted. "And a lot o' blokes died holding off Lü Bu... more than I can afford to lose."
"But we never got nothin' for what we fought for!" another bandit said. "We still ain't got nothin' for risin' up! If we held, we-!"
"Maybe it's like Zang Ba said, about us negotiating with 'em when we can instead of fighting," Chang Xi suggested. "Yu Wenze is a Juping man, an' I'm a Juping man, so we can do a deal! Maybe I'll end up as Inspector of Xu Province!"
"...Not likely," Chang Xi's wife sighed.
"I'll go out and surrender now," Chang Xi declared. "Wish us luck."

Yu Jin waited until Chang Xi was less than a metre from him before he said, "I have to arrest you formally, Chang Xi."
"What...?" Chang Xi exclaimed.
"Everything must be done properly," Yu Jin said as a group of soldiers descended on Chang Xi and bound him with rope. "Colonel: apprehend the rest of them."
A subordinate colonel led some men toward the fortress.
"...Don't disappoint me, Wenze!" Chang Xi pleaded. "We're Juping men! You said that! We're friends from Juping!"
"That we are," Yu Jin replied. "And I meant every word of what I said, don't you worry. We'll go and meet up with your old friends now and discuss what comes next."
"R-right, y-yeah, I-I get it," Chang Xi stammered. "The future..."

Zang Ba, Sun Guan and Wu Dun received word from Yu Jin that Chang Xi had been caught and met with the Han general at a makeshift camp to the north of Kaiyang.

"…Moron," Zang Ba said as he stared at Chang Xi, who was still bound with rope.

"D-do I have to still be bound with rope now?" Chang Xi asked nervously. "Isn't now a good time to, y'know, untie me so's we can talk properly…?"

"No," Yu Jin replied coldly. "Guards: take Chang Xi to the prisoner corral, please."

Two soldiers escorted Chang Xi away from the command tent.

"So what happens to him now?" Sun Guan asked. "My guess is that he needs to be sent to Chancellor Cao for final-"

"And you would be mistaken," Yu Jin interrupted. "Chang Xi has committed a serious crime – rebelling after submitting – that is terrible enough, but-"

"What?" Wu Dun exclaimed.

"I said that I would ensure that justice is done, and it will be," Yu Jin retorted. "You all submitted after being troublemakers and received military rank; that was a reward enough for pardoned rebels. But Chang Xi broke his word, forfeited his rank and returned to banditry: that must be punished with death."

"*Death???*" Wu Dun cried.

"Of course," Yu Jin retorted.

"So what happened to his death 'not being necessary', then…?" Zang Ba teased.

"I said that his death in battle would not be necessary, and I vowed that justice would be done," Yu Jin replied. "Justice demands death from a rebel that first broke a pact with the-"

"Wait, wait," Sun Guan said. "Chang has to be properly heard."

"That's right," Zang Ba said. "General Yu, the right procedure is-"

"I need no instruction regarding proper procedure," Yu Jin insisted. "Were his only crime the rebellion itself, then I might agree to wasting Chancellor Cao's valuable time – or, more precisely, that of his staff – by sending Chang Xi to Yè or the capital; but do none of you know that there can be no pardon for those that submit while being besieged…?"

"Since when?" Wu Dun heckled.

"Who would ever survive a siege if that was the case…?" Zang Ba asked pointedly. "You're saying that the new rule is that the only options are 'Hold on to the last and die' or 'Submit early on and die'. Like Wu Dun said: since *when*…?"

"In this case – where the besieged is guilty of a serious offence that the siege relates to – that is the rule," Yu Jin replied.

"Sounds like *bollocks* to me," Wu Dun growled.

"That, regardless of your feelings, is the rule," Yu Jin insisted. "I shall do him the honour of telling him the decision in person."

"Yeah, I'm sure that he'll be grateful for that," Zang Ba said as he watched Yu Jin leave the command tent.

"We're not gonna stop this…?" Wu Dun asked.

"…No," Zang Ba replied. "Chang brought this on himself."

     "*Death???*" Chang Xi cried as Yu Jin concluded his grim and condemnatory announcement.

"I… I do not do this lightly, old friend!" Yu Jin said through tears. "The rules are the rules! I cannot pardon a man that submits during a siege when he already has a serious charge hanging over him! The submission is then taken as an admission of guilt, and... it is the *law*, Chang Xi, and I *cannot* disobey the law!"

"Long-toes, R-Red Crest, a-an' the others," Chang Xi stammered. "I promised 'em that I'd get us all pardons! I-!"

"They are already dealt with," Yu Jin replied. "Sorry, but it is as I said... this is the only way that the law allows me to deal with what you have done."

"...But... but I only submitted because... you *told me to*, Wenze!" Chang Xi whimpered.

"I... I know that, my friend, and... I must bear that burden for the rest of my days," Yu Jin replied. "I can say no more... and I can delay no more."

"**Don't I even get to see my *family*???**" Chang Xi screamed.

"It... is only too lucky for you that they are spared the same fate, Chang Xi," Yu Jin replied with apparent sadness. "You must die content in the knowledge that they will go on living."

Chang Xi closed his eyes and sobbed bitterly.

"...I will always remember those days in Juping," Yu Jin said as he placed his hands on Chang Xi's shoulders and briefly embraced him. "Your friendship will always mean something to me... and my memories of times when duty and the law were not the cause of our division. Goodbye, Chang Xi... goodbye."

"...I... s-submitted... b-because...!" Chang Xi bleated. "W-Wenze... Wenze, *please*...!"

Yu Jin exhaled loudly and shouted, "**GUARDS! DEATH!**"

Chang Xi screamed maniacally as he was led to his place of execution; Yu Jin snorted loudly, hummed thoughtfully and returned to the command tent, where Zang Ba had remained.

"...Your allies have gone...?" Yu Jin prompted.

"Yeah, they have," Zang Ba said. "I imagine that you'll get a nice promotion for single-handedly ending the rebellion so quickly and personally capturing the leader; his swift execution – in line with the law, of course – will ensure that the whole grubby matter of you two being from the same village won't be a problem."

"I intend to notify Chancellor Cao of my connection to Chang Xi if he does not know already," Yu Jin replied. "My loyalty to the Han exceeds any personal matter in terms of its importance, and this sorry incident makes that clear, I think."

Zang Ba smirked and said, "I think so, yeah. I, uh... I think I'll be going myself now, General. Well played."

General Yu Jin nodded respectfully; Zang Ba reciprocated the gesture and retreated.

Cao Cao was forced, for the first time in quite a while, to endure his first full migraine without the aid of Hua Tuo's pain-reducing treatment; when it cleared, he asked to read Yu Jin's report and smiled, saying, "If I was completely free of pain and not so damned tired, I'd laugh out loud. Wenze has shown yet again that he is one of, if not my finest general."

"How so, Excellency...?" Registrar Liu Yè asked.

"I treated him with suspicion and heckled him at every opportunity when he first joined me, because he had come to me from Wang Lang when Wang still served my enemy Tao Qian, and yet he served without reservation, saving me from disaster when I was retreating from Wan City," Cao Cao explained. "He dealt with dissent and kept the army together when the ranks collapsed and morale plummeted, and all whilst enduring slanders that might have led to his arrest: that was his first great achievement. Now he has apprehended a man that he knew as a childhood friend and rightly put him to death for treason and rebellion. I have had to do the same, and so I know how difficult that can be; even if you think that you can do it, the moment when you are actually faced with the decision is... most painful."

"I... imagine so, Excellency," Liu Yè replied.

"I... have had to do that terrible thing so many times now," Cao Cao continued. "Oh, how I regret that Mengzhuo- ...that *Zhang Miao* had to be destroyed... but he forced my hand with his vile treachery; and Yuan Shao... Benchu... oh, how I regret that... I even had to slay his *sons... all of them...*"

Liu Yè nodded nervously.

"...Enough of that," Cao Cao decided. "I digress too easily when I am afflicted."

"It's understandable, Excellency," Liu Yè replied.

"Yu Wenze has done the right thing, resisting all urges to save his friend... and that proves, along with that prior achievement, that he is consistently marvellous," Cao Cao said. "I shall ensure that he is promoted to... to 'General with a Tiger's Might' – that is appropriate, I think – and I shall make him my vanguard general."

Liu Yè nodded silently.

"...Hua Tuo should be back soon," Cao Cao continued. "The acupuncture alone is worth looking forward to, but... I hope that he has discovered something else during his short absence. I hope that he is able to cure me properly... I... I so hope that he can."

"Anything is possible," Liu Yè replied.

"I *must* be cured," Cao Cao said quietly. "I... *need* to be cured..."

"The Han is diseased! The Han has infected us all with that disease, and only the teachings of our slain master, Zhang Jue, can restore the health of the people and the nation!"

A village in Ji'nan region of Qing Province was host to a party of Yellow Turbans: these were mostly brawny, athletic men that were wearing an assortment of armour in addition to their signature headwear.

"We've been silenced time and again, but the time has come to find our voice and shout again, and to shout louder than ever before, and I, Hou Shu, shall be the one to rouse you here today!" the Yellow Turban leader continued. **"The so-called bandit, Chang Xi, saw the light and turned away from the corruption that swallowed the souls of his brothers! Now his light is extinguished, but our lights still burn strong! The only way out of the darkness is on a path thick with blood, but that blood will be theirs instead of ours if we take the fight to them! Let us not allow Chang Xi's defiant stand be a lone and meaningless gesture!"**

One villager turned to the man standing next to him and whispered, "Didn't Zang's lot fight these lot before...?"

The other man shrugged indifferently.

"The only way to bring an end to the violence and death that the Han rulers inflict upon us the people is to fight!"

Hou Shu continued. **"The only way to defeat the sickness is to cut away the rotting flesh, the flesh of the Han emperor and his villainous 'Chancellor of State', *Cao Cao*!"**

The region still had a shared dislike of Cao Cao that mostly stemmed from his time as the local administrator decades before: some in the crowd became increasingly receptive to the idea of rising up once again, if only to spite Cao.

"Some say that the answer to our woes lies with the Han Chancellor and his local puppet Zang Ba, but how can that be, when Zang was a thief that robbed your villages to fill his treasury and his belly...?" Hou Shu asked of the crowd.

"No! No, he is not the answer! The answer to Cao Cao and his 'Way of War' is Master Zhang Jue's 'Way of Peace'! To those that said that a Han victory would restore prosperity, I ask this: where is that prosperity...?"

"With the few!" one man replied instinctively.

"Yes, with the few, as it always has been!" Hou Shu replied. **"Master Zhang Jue's dream was ridiculed: a world where there would be no 'Son of Heaven' in a palace of gold, surrounded by minions that oppress the many with taxes and brutality! What's wrong with that...? What's wrong with prosperity and happiness for all, and not just a self-appointed 'privileged few'...?"**

"Yellow Sky! Yellow Sky!" some chanted. **"The azure sky must fall!"**

"That's right!" Hou Shu said. **"The Han Dynasty's mandate – if it ever existed – certainly doesn't exist now! Men rise up in anger time and again, and they will rise up again, and again, and again and again and again until that wicked Son of Hell – its *lowest level* – is unseated and the people are made their own masters in a world of peace, a world of peace that can only be taken from the wicked few by taking their war to them!"**

The crowd were then encouraged to recite the mantra that had inspired every previous Yellow Turban army to fight:

**"Han's mandate has passed!
Yellow Sky, soon here!
In this renewing year,
Prosperous all, at last!"**

"...We're ready," Hou Shu said to a subordinate. "Distribute the scarves... and choose the best men for immediate training. The enemy must have no chance to smother us before we have taken root: we start at once."

****

107

Two weeks passed: Cao Cao's migraines continued to plague him, but the physician Hua Tuo had not returned to provide any relief.

"...*Hua Tuo*... is starting to unnerve me," Cao Cao admitted.

The Xuchang chancellery court was awkwardly silent.

"He... may have been forced to travel to the frontier in either the northeast or northwest," Xun Wenruo suggested. "The-"

"I... have my future campaigns to plan, gentlemen," Cao Cao said with growing anger. "I do *not*... have *time*... for a carefree scholar that comes and goes as he pleases when **my well-being is essential to the survival of the *entire* Empire!**"

"Another man has been sent to Pei," Xun Gongda revealed.

"...'Another'...?" Cao Cao chortled. "How many have been sent to Pei County, exactly...?"

"...A few," Xun Gongda replied. "Mister Hua was only present on one of the occasions, and he politely explained that he was procuring herbs and keeping watch on his wife's condition, since her health is still-"

"Alright," Cao Cao interrupted. "If... if his wife is still in Pei, that means that he is busy with some matter that I will assume to be the procurement of ingredients for some sort of medicine to cure me. I am doing my best to restore normal border trade, and if some of those ingredients are from foreign lands then I must play my part in making them easier to obtain. I am going back to Yè now; Wenruo, you will continue your duties here; Gongda will accompany me to Yè. Hua Xin: you are now promoted to Imperial Secretary and will remain here. Wang Lang: you are promoted to an adviser and will accompany me to Yè."

"Wait, wait, what...?" Xiahou Dun exclaimed. "You're moving everyone around like a madman, Mengde!"

"Be thankful that I am," Cao Cao replied. "Miaocai is moving from Yingchuan; he will eventually be with us permanently, in Yè, but for now he must go to Qing Province to oversee the development of proper government and the implementation of *tuntian* on a massive scale now that Zang Ba has overcome the latest rebellion with General Yu Wenze's help."

"...But my lord, that rebellion has caused a rapid rise in the number of active Yellow Turbans," Xun Wenruo said nervously. "The situation is-"

Cao Cao laughed strangely and said, "*Yellow Turbans*...?"

"...Yes, Excellency," Xun Gongda replied. "Thousands of them."

"I thought that they were pacified now," Bao Xun said.

"Yellow Turbans...?" Cao Cao chuckled. "*Yellow Turbans*...!"

"...Please don't laugh like that, Mengde," Cao Chun pleaded.

"What am I supposed to do...?" Cao Cao retorted through more strange laughter. "I have been hard at work for years and years and years now... it all started with Yellow Turbans and the unrest in Qing Province, and now, after all that I have endured all that I have done, it is still the *same nonsense*...! I had really hoped that my headaches would be cured, and that the rebels would be quelled, and that there would be no more barbarian hordes, no more cultist armies, no more pirates and bandits, and the Empire would be at peace! But it is obviously a waste of time, isn't it...?

What else can it be when we're seeing the resurgence of the *Yellow Turbans* in Qing Province! It has all gone around in a bloody circle and come back to where it started! ***AGAIN!* Nothing I have done has changed a thing!"**

"…You're being unduly pessimistic, Excellency," Xun Wenruo insisted. "The Wuhuan are permanently broken; the Qiang are tamed; Liu Biao is isolated; Hedong is pacified; the Yuans-"

"I would not now be surprised if the Yuan brothers clawed their way out of the earth, found their displaced heads, reattached them and led an army of my slaughtered enemies toward Yè!" Cao Cao retorted. **"How many more times must I fight the peddlers of that blasted mantra???"**

"Why is it bothering you so much now when we've put up with it for so long…?" Cao Hong asked. "Why should we care more now that they're just in Qing Province? You weren't half as upset as this when they were everywhere."

"*Because*, Zilian, their mantra foretells *my* defeat now, *my* failure!" Cao Cao replied furiously. **"Every time that they chant that vile curse, I am being threatened with the complete reversal of all of my efforts! I am the *Chancellor of State*! The survival of the Han Empire is now *my* burden, *my* responsibility! If the Empire collapses whilst *I* am its guardian, history will blame *me*!** …I would wander the netherworld forever after such a failure… how could my spirit ever know rest…?"

Xun Wenruo sighed and said, "You truly are the most loyal of us all, Excellency."

"…I cannot allow even one Yellow Turban to be reciting that mantra," Cao Cao insisted. "Miaocai will still travel to Qing, but it will be to aid Zang Ba's destruction of the Yellow Turbans, once and for all this time."

"Can we trust Zang with that task?" Xiahou Dun asked. "Didn't most of the bandit armies grow out of the Yellow Turbans in the first place? Isn't that why that Chang Xi fellow's rebellion caused them to reappear…?"

"You're right that the bandit armies did, a lot of them, grow out of the Yellow Turban remnants in the wake of their first rebellion being crushed, but as you *should* remember – I swear that we had this conversation already – Zang Ba's bandit army was the exception," Cao Cao replied. "His bandits actually joined the government's efforts to destroy the Yellow Turbans, which is one of the reasons why we have always been so lenient toward them… do you remember now…?"

"Yeah, yeah, I do," Xiahou Dun sighed. "Sorry, Mengde."

"…I must hurry to Yè," Cao Cao continued. "I want to check on Lady Cai Yan's recovery, properly welcome my 'guest' Ma Teng, ensure that my heir is behaving, and see Chong and find out what brilliant thoughts he has had recently. I will be better placed to assist Miaocai as well, and I can plan the invasion of Jing, and… … …there is still so much to do."

Cao Cao lowered his head and covered his face with his hands.

"There is still… so, so much that I must do… without the return of old problems and these blasted headaches wasting so much of my time!" Cao Cao whimpered. "*Please*, Master Hua… hurry back… hurry back…!"

The officials exchanged nervous glances.

Zang Ba and Sun Guan had moved their former bandit armies –
which they now referred to as the 'Qing Province Militias' – to the
outskirts of Beihai Prefecture so that they could defend the
provincial capital Linzi from one particularly aggressive army of
Yellow Turbans: the two leaders were wandering their main camp
and conducting inspections when Zang Ba suddenly laughed and
said, "It's like the old days, isn't it, Zhongtai...?"
"And that's *funny*...?" Sun Guan exclaimed.
"No... no, not really," Zang Ba replied. "I'm not laughing because
it's funny, Zhongtai... I think I may be losing my mind."
"This has been a really, really awful year, and it's barely started,"
Sun Guan complained. "I never liked Chang Xi, but I still can't
believe that he's dead."
"I admit that I regret what happened," Zang Ba replied. "I
wouldn't say that in front of Wu Dun... or Yin Li, if I'm honest. But
yeah, I regret it. Chang was pissed off and couldn't pretend that
he was happy anymore... if he ever did. And maybe he was the
honest one. But he was still wrong to rebel like that."
"Will Yu Jin be coming back here to help us...?" Sun Guan asked.
"No," Zang Ba replied. "He's Cao Cao's favourite soldier now; he'll
be part of their next big invasion of wherever-it-is-that-Cao's-
wanting-to-take-next... which'll be Jing, probably. No, we're
getting Xiahou Yuan this time."
"...Cao Cao's cousin...?" Sun Guan exclaimed.
"Supposedly he is, yeah," Zang Ba chuckled.
"...What's he like...?" Sun Guan asked.
"He's supposed to be a really cheerful, easy-to-get-along-with sort
of bloke," Zang Ba replied. "There's a tavern tale about Xiahou
taking the blame for some crime that Cao committed in his youth,
and that Cao really values him for it."
"...I'm not surprised," Sun Guan said.
"Yeah, and he's honest too, really honest," Zang Ba continued.
"He's Administrator of Yingchuan *and* Chenliu, but supposedly as
poor as the next man: again, this is 'tavern talk' from when I was
in Yè, but the rumours are that Xiahou's so honest that his entire
family chops firewood, make shoes and so on to cover costs
'cause he gives all his wages to the running of the state. Yeah, he
can't tax his people too hard 'cause he has to keep them happy
and stop them becoming rebels an' all that, but he supposedly
don't take *any money at all* from the treasuries... not a coin."
"...That *is* honest," Sun Guan sighed. "And he's *cheerful*...?"
Zang Ba shrugged and said, "If he's still 'cheerful' after what I
heard about one of Liu Bei's generals abducting his daughter and
marrying her, then he must be a *really* nice bloke... that or he's a
bloody good actor."
"Honest, patient, no bad temper... is that really the sort of man
that should be sent to deal with this lot...?" Sun Guan wondered.
"Cao seems to think so," Zang Ba replied. "Let's hope he's right."

Cao Cao decided that he would have a family banquet upon his
return to to Yè City: he reviewed his vast audience of residents
from his host seat and said, "I might need to consider an even
bigger mansion!"

"If we are occupying essential space, Excellency, then please say so," Guo Yi replied. "My father would not want us to be a burden."

"No, Boyi: you and your family are no burden, and you never need say such things again," Cao Cao said warmly. "Your father, Guo Fengxiao, is the man that made my living in this city possible; how can you be a burden...?"

Guo Yi bowed slightly and replied, "You are a good and kind lord, Your Excellency."

"...Has there been any word from Qin Lang...?" Cao Cao asked.

"Not as yet," Cao Pi replied.

"Where is he, then...?" Cao Hong asked.

"...You weren't listening at all, were you...?" Cao Cao sighed.

"I know he's gone, Mengde," Cao Hong retorted. "I know he's 'seeing the world' or whatever it was he said it was, but I just wondered if we knew where he was."

"And I just said that we've heard nothing from him," Cao Pi said derisively. "If we've heard nothing, then we don't know where he is, do we, Zilian...?"

"...No, Zihuan, we don't," Cao Hong replied miserably. "I'm being stupid again."

"What a surprise," Cao Zhen muttered.

"...What role will Qin Lang take when he returns...?" Guo Yi asked.

"*Is* there a suitable role...?" Cao Zhi chortled.

Cao Cao looked at his haughty third son and said, "That's an unkind comment, Zhi. He cannot help being relatively ordinary. In any other household, he would be magnificent. I am very proud of my foster son."

"That's evident from the undue praise he enjoyed and the preferential treatment that you showed him for no good reason, Father," Cao Zhang suggested. "And now you let him wander the land because he's a mediocrity that-"

"*Enough*, Zhang," Cao Cao growled.

Cao Zhang bowed slightly, saying, "Forgive my outburst."

"...You must learn better manners, Yellow-beard," Cao Cao continued. "Qin Lang is my foster son, which means that he is your brother: respect your brother."

"I am wrong, Father," Cao Zhang conceded. "I will be more thoughtful in future."

"I hope so," Cao Cao replied. "I am weary enough of Zilian and Yuanrang without thinking that I must add my second son to a growing list of tactless braggarts."

"That's harsh," Xiahou Dun complained.

"And I didn't say anything, Mengde!" Cao Hong protested.

"You called me fat again!" Cao Zhen said. "How many more times do I have to say that I am not at fault for my condition?"

"Perhaps the famous Hua Tuo can help you with your involuntary weight gain, Zidan," Cao Chong suggested.

"I already asked," Cao Zhen grumbled. "He at least acknowledged that my weight is not my fault, but-"

"He said that it 'might not be your fault'," Cao Hong heckled. "So in the end, he'll only know for sure if he sees how many buns and cakes you secretly stuff down your neck when nobody's looking!"

"**Zilian!**" Cao Cao snapped.

"Ah, I don't care anymore, Cousin Mengde," Cao Zhen said. "Let him mock me: I'm fat, yes, but that's not as inhibitive as being

stupid. I'm old enough to take a role in the government or the military now, and I'll soon surpass that brainless idiot."
Cao Hong glared at Cao Zhen and mumbled quietly.
"...I would appreciate it if we could not mention Hua Tuo anymore, since the man has vexed me greatly," Cao Cao admitted. "I know that you meant well, Chong'er, so please do not consider that to be a rebuke."
The 11-year-old Cao Chong nodded seriously and said, "I'll say no more, Father, after one last question: is there no other acupuncturist of his calibre...? And if not, then is it not an art that I might perfect, maybe, so that you can know that the needle-bearer is completely trustworthy...?"
"*Aiee*... he's a court judge, a mathematician, an artist, a musician, a poet, a writer, and now he wants to be a bloody doctor as well!" Cao Hong cried. "*Why*, Cangshu? Doctors are what, the same class as merchants, if not *lower*...?"
"And that's wrong," Cao Chong retorted. "Physicians are healing the sick, solving the oldest mysteries that our world has known: before there were numbers, pictures, armies, songs and words, there were illnesses and injuries as men fought to become something greater in this harsh existence."
"...I didn't understand a word of that," Xiahou Dun sighed.
"You should try to," Cao Chong insisted. "Physicians suffer a low place in the scheme of things precisely because people do not understand what they do, and they ridicule what they do not understand. Obsessive acolytes of Taoism do little to help: they say that the body cannot and should not be cut open to remove ailments deep within because that is the worst of wrongs, akin to the punishments inflicted on criminals, but if it restores a man to good health it should be lauded, not villainised! If we ignored the unduly cynical priests and scoffing officials and elevated the medical practitioner to the same level as the poet, we may see marvels that far surpass anything seen in history!"
"...Can Hua Tuo – or any other doctor – make my eye grow back...?" Xiahou Dun asked as he pointed at his disfigured face.
"Not now, perhaps, but who knows what might be achieved if only we opened our minds?" Cao Chong replied. "If we are asked to blindly believe in the gods and the heavens, then why are we figuratively blind to the concept of growing a new eye and literally restoring sight...? If, as some say, Hua Tuo has found potions that make the body numb so that he can open a man up to clean the entrails and remove harmful tumours, and it is true that he can then seal up the wounds and apply ointments that protect that wound from disease, then-"
"That sounds like nonsense," Cao Zhang suggested.
"...Maybe it is, but if it is not, Elder Brother, then such pioneering work should be revered, not ridiculed or persecuted!" Cao Chong retorted. "And yet I hear that most of the work to further the profession is carried out in secret, mostly by women; and the court further muddies the waters by having physicians to tend for the lucky few while decrying the need for them in the speeches to the many. Illness is a villain that claims as many lives as war... more, perhaps... and it is more indiscriminate than the worst tyrant when it comes to choosing its victims."
"I understand your passion, Chong'er, but your single question

has evolved into a scathing attack on faith and a demand for a change to the standing of certain professions, neither of which would be popular at court," Cao Cao scolded. "I'll answer your question by saying that you have better things to do with your time than sticking needles in your father to get rid of his headaches; the other points are best shared privately with family and trusted officials, because a heated debate with the wrong people about elevating physicians could lead to serious harm."

"Even when they maintain the health of the Son of Heaven and his Chancellor of State...?" Cao Chong asked.

"...Hua Tuo has fled from me," Cao Cao replied. "He is not 'maintaining the health' of *anyone*... he is wandering the land carefree, exchanging unproven remedies and incantations with local purveyors of superstition, when he should be *here*, in Yè, attending to me with something that has been proven to work!"

Cao Chong sighed and said, "But-!"

"There is no 'but'!" Cao Cao continued. "He's already harangued me with talk of being deprived of the opportunity to do research, but research is something that is carried out when the answers are not evident! He has a way to treat me, so what does he need to research...? A cure, maybe, yes, but what good is the search for a cure when I, in the meantime, am left to suffer and underperform in my role as this Empire's most important servant at a time of great crisis...? He is being *irresponsible!*"

"...I see your point, Father," Cao Chong admitted.

Cao Cao leant forward and said, "I've heard word now of Administrator Li Teng of Guangling, who died and had to be replaced by... by... that would probably be that naïve cretin Zhao Yu, but it doesn't matter. The point is that Li had eaten raw fish that left him with stomach parasites."

"Nice," Cao Hong chuckled.

"He learned of Hua Tuo and employed him to find a solution," Cao Cao continued. "Hua is supposed to have given Li 'some marvellous potion' that caused him to expel the parasites, curing him *temporarily*. Hua then left vague instructions to 'find a good doctor' and said that Li would die three years' hence of a recurrence of the same condition if he was not treated. And, just as Hua promised, three years later, as I have already revealed... die he did."

"...Hua Tuo did not return to help him...?" Cao Zhi exclaimed.

"*No*, my son, he did *not*," Cao Cao replied ominously. "And *now* I understand that one of Hua Tuo's disciples, Wu Pu, hails from Guangling, and that a second student – another foreign man called 'Fan A' that was, if I recall, one of Hua's suggestions for replacement acupuncturist – was in nearby Peng. They, too, either did not or could not help Li Teng. Hua himself was 'not in the area'... so I ask, one and all, what the point is of such a man. He did not return to help Li Teng; so, I ask, will he ever help *me*...?"

"Hua Tuo sounds like a prodigious misfit," Cao Xiu said. "Was he perhaps hoping for some great 'ransom' in exchange for his help, Cousin Mengde, and let Li Teng die when he did not receive it...?"

"I cannot say," Cao Cao replied. "But I will say this: I will not place any more blind faith in his ability to help me indefinitely. He may have fled because he knows that his 'miracle cure' will no longer work and fears my reaction when I am not helped for the first time... or he may just find my affliction 'boring' and be seeking other challenges. Perhaps he follows the Buddhist faith that is so prevalent in Xu Province; most of the migrant people from the lands to the west of the Empire seem to be of that faith, and Hua Tuo is not of Han origin. If that were the case, he might have hoped to convert me and others to his faith as part of the conditions for treatment. He risks offending me, whatever his motivations... and I am running out of patience. Now I want to say no more of him and enjoy the remainder of the banquet; I ask that I be heeded."

"As you wish, Father," Cao Chong said.

"...Perhaps some poetry composition or music is in order," Cao Cao suggested. "I think... that music is best. **MUSIC!**"

Cao Cao's musicians started to play a cheerful melody.

"...How is Lady Cai Yan now...?" Cao Chong asked. "I hope that she is continuing to regain her spirit after those long years of unimaginable suffering."

"You are such a thoughtful boy," Cao Cao chuckled. "She is recovering... slowly."

"I hope that she does recall her father's work," Cao Chong said. "I should like to read the lost teachings and hear the poems and lyrics that were produced by that marvellous scholar."

"...As would I, my son," Cao Cao sighed. "As would I."

Cao Pi observed the closeness and familiarity that his half-brother Chong enjoyed with their father and quietly seethed; Pi knew that the young, good-natured genius was still the favourite and that his father was quietly determined to find a way to make Chong his heir. Unpleasant thoughts filled Cao Pi's mind: he fought the urge to wish Chong dead and muttered angrily.

"Are you alright, Cousin Zihuan...?" Cao Xiu asked.

Cao Pi smiled falsely and replied, "Fine, Wenlie... I'm just *fine*."

****

108

Xiahou Yuan arrived in Qing Province and met with Zang Ba and Sun Guan in their Beihai camp.

"I understand that these Yellow Turbans are a bit more organised than was usual in past times," Xiahou Yuan said.

"There're two types, I think," Zang Ba replied. "The first lot that we've been having on-off problems with for a couple o' years are really well organised but weren't that popular 'til recently. The other lot are new recruits that are more like what we fought twenty years ago."

"*Right*," Xiahou Yuan sighed as he rubbed his bearded chin. "Mengde was right..."

"...Pardon?" Zang Ba prompted.

"Mengde – Chancellor Cao – supposed that the main Yellow Turban faction is made up of men that were Yellow Turbans here fifteen years ago, that took part in the siege of Dongping County," Xianhou Yuan explained. "They killed Yan Governor Liu Dai and his aide Bao Xin before they were finally supressed and told that they needed to join what became known as-"

"The Qing Province Corps," Sun Guan interrupted. "We know that history of the Yellow Turbans in Qing, General Xiahou; what you're saying is that the new lot are actually Qing Corps men that have gone back to their old ways...?"

"Yes," Xiahou Yuan replied. "When Chancellor Cao – I shall have to get used to calling him that – was ambushed by Zhang Xiu at Wan City, he lost more than his son and his bodyguard: the Qing Corps mutinied in the thousands, and we were forced to pacify them. I chased quite a few bands of them out of Yingchuan, and they had to go somewhere... the late Guo Jia, Chancellor Cao and others have speculated that they made the journey back to Qing, and that's likely to be right, it seems, given that they're organised enough to suggest mass military training."

"But they're still stealing what they could be growing and acting like- ...well, criminals," Zang Ba said sheepishly.

Sun Guan laughed at Zang Ba's unintended hypocrisy.

"...I'm used to dealing with the Qing Corps rebels and the usual type of cultist, so I can be of use," Xiahou Yuan continued. "But that wasn't why I was posted here, of course..."

"So why were you posted here, then...?" Zang Ba asked.

"I'm supposed to make proper use of Qing and Xu Provinces as farming land and recruitment regions," Xiahou Yuan explained. "I'll need your help with that, of course, gentlemen."

"'Gentlemen'...!" Sun Guan snickered. "Me, a 'gentleman'...!"

"We've been called that before," Zang Ba said. "Anyway, enough of that; we're here to cooperate with the Han government in any way that we can, General Xiahou, so you point us in the direction you want us to go, alright...?"

"This will be a collaborative effort, Mister Zang," Xiahou Yuan insisted. "You have your armies that follow you, not me, and you know the area better than I do."

"I reckoned that we should call our armies something proper, so we're not always being called 'former bandits'," Zang Ba suggested. "We're the 'Qing Militias' now if that doesn't sound too much like what the enemy's called."

"That's perfectly fine, Mister Zang," Xiahou Yuan replied. "Now then: where shall we turn to next...?"

Xiahou Yuan and Zang Ba's Qing Militias reported to Yè regularly; Cao Cao might have been pleased at their swift progress at any other time, but he was now suffering another migraine and he was once again forced to endure the pain. Hua Tuo had been expected to return to provide acupuncture treatment and, Cao still hoped, a more permanent solution, but the physician had stayed away and reverted to his usual pattern of travelling the country and visiting his home in Pei County.

"That wicked little man!" Cao Cao cried as he sat at his host seat and rocked back and forth with his head in his hands. **"He knows the importance that is attached to my well-being: he endangers the Empire with his carefree meandering, and he shall pay the price for it!"**

"B-but his servants have promised that he will return soon!" Xun Gongda protested. "His wife is too ill for him to stay away from home for too long, they say, and-"

"I will be patient this *one... last... time*," Cao Cao growled. "I need... to return to Xuchang on business: that will be a better journey for him. Tell Chen Gui that... that I want a physician to visit Hua Tuo's home with some soldiers and officials as aides to prevent mischief by the staff: if Hua Tuo's wife is sick, I will *personally* forward gifts of lentils by the bushel and allow him to remain with his wife until her condition changes, even if... even if it means that I must continue to suffer."

"You are a magnanimous lord, Excellency," Xun Gongda said.

"But if he is found to be lying to me, Gongda, then he will suffer the same pain as I suffer, all over his body," Cao Cao continued. "He will be apprehended, taken to Xuchang and interrogated until he confesses for the record."

"Until he 'confesses', Mengde...?" Cao Chun said. "To what...?"

"To refusing to obey an order to attend court from the Chancellor of State, which is defiance of the law of the land, and for disobeying military law by remaining away from one's state duty beyond the allotted leave period," Cao Cao explained. "I am within my rights to demand any punishment at such a dangerous hour... including a death sentence."

"You can't kill Hua Tuo!" Cheng Yu protested. "The-!"

"If Hua Tuo is a rebel, Elder Cheng, then he must be made an example of," Cao Cao retorted. "My word is final: Mister Liu Yè, prepare the order."

"...Yes, Excellency," Registrar Liu Yè said tonelessly.

The tall, imposing Cheng Yu was left as unnerved as he had been when Cao Cao ordered the death of Emperor Xian's pregnant consort 8 years before; the elder adviser quietly and seriously pondered whether it would be safe to criticise or oppose Chancellor Cao in the years to come.

Hua Tuo travelled to the Peng region and visited his colleague and student – a man known as Fan A – before he returned to Pei County. The two men – who both had unusual features and names that suggested foreign origins – sat together in Fan's living quarters and shared a pot of tea.

"Mister Wu sends his regards," Fan A said.

"Very good," Hua Tuo replied. "Please reciprocate on my behalf."

"...Is Cao Cao still trying to get you to go back?" Fan A asked.

Hua Tuo exhaled miserably.

"So he is, then," Fan A said.

"He's impossible to reason with," Hua Tuo replied. "I try to recommend other men to do the acupuncture – including you – but he just dismisses the idea and insists that 'It must be me'. I know that I will be arrested eventually, but I would rather risk that than be trapped, like a bird in a cage, working for an unpleasant man like that until I die of old age."

"...So his temperament is not the direct result of his ailment...?" Fan A prompted.

"As far as I can see, not at all," Hua Tuo replied. "He is mischievous, impatient and ambitious... and it is *my* assessment that he always has been; the appraiser Xu Shao famously called him a man that would be 'a crafty villain in times of chaos', and I entirely agree with *his* assessment. Cao Cao is not a good man at all: the headaches are one of his many excuses for hegemonic, brutish and tyrannical behaviour."

"That's a shame," Fan A said. "He professes to be a guardian of the intelligentsia, and yet he threatens your freedom for his own selfish ends."

"I could be fair and say it is born of mistrust," Hua Tuo replied. "His medical history understandably included emotional traumas: he lost a friend unexpectedly during the war with Dong Zhuo and suffered an increase in severity of his affliction thereafter. The death of his father and the subsequent massacres that he carried out here in Xu Province weigh on his mind continually and added further severity and frequency; Zhang Miao and Yuan Shao, who were two of his best friends, became his bitter enemies and 'harmed his mind', and he executed another friend, Xu Yòu, for 'unpardonable contempt' after memorialising Yuan Shao."

"...That's important to note," Fan A suggested. "Would he want a Peng resident that survived his massacres, such as me, to be his personal physician...?"

"He's dismissing anyone and everyone that I suggest," Hua Tuo replied. "But where is such a man popular...? He is even despised by some that live in Pei, his ancestral home."

"...On the subject of Pei, I have to ask: why do you keep returning to your home...?" Fan A asked. "Why do you not flee to some remote place...?"

"There is no such thing as a 'remote place' if a man pursues his calling and makes himself conspicuous," Hua Tuo replied. "Cai Yong hid in a small, insignificant village in Jiangdong, but Dong Zhuo still found him and forced him to return to the court because the poor man could not sit idle and taught classes for the locals; Ying Shao retreated to a 'remote place' to complete his work, but Cao's wars still claimed him indirectly because he could not hide and do his work as well; and there are no kind or far-sighted men to hide 'partisans' anymore, unless you count Liu Biao of Jing, the next man that Cao Cao – who was, once, such a man until he was corrupted by power – intends to destroy. There is nowhere that I can go... I must therefore accept Heaven's will."

"Can you not at least *try* and run...?" Fan A pleaded.

"I risk abandoning someone – my wife, perhaps, or a loyal servant – to some terrible fate, and I will not do that," Hua Tuo replied. "I will go back when I leave here."

"But if he harms you, Master Hua, your work will be lost!" Fan A said worriedly.

"I was going to leave my life's work with you now, but... perhaps that is not the right thing to do," Hua Tuo replied. "If Cao Cao intends to harm me, then I will use my last hours to write down everything that I know and then entrust it to another because, yes, it will otherwise be lost... but if I act too soon I will be endangering others needlessly. But... if he *does* harm me... you should not give up, whether my work is saved or lost; what we do is more important than either of us."

"You have my word," Fan A said. "I will always carry on."

Hua Tuo made the short journey to Pei County, where he was immediately confronted by Chen Gui and a small militia.

"...This is becoming an unfortunate recurrence," Hua Tuo quipped.

"You really are as stupid as you are clever," Chen Gui retorted. "You hide in plain sight, abandon proven arts to chase myths and show groundless contempt for men with no patience by peddling lies with not a shred of false proof to shroud them. And now it will cost you."

"I am to return to Xuchang," Hua Tuo supposed.

"...This time, Hua Tuo, you go as a prisoner, and believe me, I do this very, very reluctantly," Chen Gui replied.

Hua Tuo eyed the prison cart that he had previously failed to see and asked, "On what charges...?"

"Your wife is not as sick as you said she was: you lied to the Chancellor to obtain leave from state service, which is your first offence," Chen Gui explained. "You then prevaricated and further exaggerated your wife's poor health, taking you beyond the leave of absence that you had falsely obtained in the first place; you have therefore refused a summons by the Chancellor, which is your second offence. Your leave was granted to you so that you could return home to tend to your sick wife, not so that you could wander the land at your leisure; you therefore ignored the conditions of that leave which you obtained falsely and lengthened illegally, which your-"

"Three will do," Hua Tuo interrupted. "I'm sure there are thousands of offences, Chancellor Chen, but you'll never get me back to Cao's bedside tonight if you list them all."

"You're not going to his home," Chen Gui replied. "You're going to prison, where you'll be questioned formally and-"

"*Prison*...?" Hua Tuo chortled. "...'Questioned'...? You mean 'interrogated', which means *torture*, which will leave me a broken shadow with shattered nerves and unsteady hands if I have hands at all: what use will I be to the man then...?"

"You should have thought of that," Chen Gui replied miserably. "I'm sorry, Master Hua, but... that is your fate. **GUARDS!**"

"I-! M-my *work*, Chen Gui!" Hua Tuo cried. "My work is too important for him to treat me like this! And I am *innocent*, Chen Gui! I was pursuing *knowledge*! **What or *who* is more important than *knowledge*???**"

"Tell it to your judges, Master Hua," Chen Gui replied. "You waste your words on a local official like me."

A small crowd was gathering to watch as Hua Tuo was taken by his arms and dragged toward the prison cart by two unsympathetic soldiers; the physician continued to plead his innocence and protest the importance of his work, but his words were ignored.

"...Importance is subjective, Master Hua," Chen Gui sighed. "You *knew that.*"

Hua Tuo's imprisonment was done secretly, but it did not take long for word of his public arrest to reach Xuchang and the grumblings of disapproving officials to be deliberately shared with the wider population in the capital.

"This is worse than I had feared!" Geng Ji said to a gathering that included his like-minded colleague Wei Huang, Wang Lang and the outspoken Kong Rong.

"What if Cao's thugs do harm to Hua's steady hands and calm mind...?" Wei Huang asked. "Won't he then be of no use at all...?"

"Most of Hua Tuo's skills and the severity of his treatment are speculation," Wang Lang suggested. "They say he can cut men open and handle their exposed entrails without them screaming in pain: what nonsense! They also say that he can then put the butchered man back together again and that he will be as he was or even cured of internal ailments; again, gentlemen, I ask you how that is even possible!"

"He was curing the Chancellor with acupuncture," Kong Rong heckled. "Is that now 'nonsense', Wang Lang...?"

"It's so often the case these days that we are on opposing sides, Kong Rong," Wang Lang lamented. "But you will insist on decrying the proven and lauding the shifty! This is yet again an example of Chancellor Cao's actions being mistaken for villainy! Hua Tuo used secretive, unshared methods of pain control and then absconded without curing the condition: in fact, he left the Chancellor in even greater pain! Hua Tuo has allies in places where Chancellor Cao is still unpopular, so it may be fair to assume that Hua teased a solution as an act of spite, as some strange revenge for the people of Xu Province and other places!"

"...I admit that I have my own doubts about Hua Tuo's professed exploits," Yang Biao said. "He's a marvellous herbalist, there's no doubt about that, but... a potion that makes the entire body numb and halts breathing without killing the patient...? Cutting a man open and sealing him up again...? That's more ridiculous than some peasant myths I've read about in Ying Shao's book on folklore. And furthermore, it's sacrilegious."

"He was treating the Chancellor with acupuncture," Kong Rong reiterated. "Or so we were told: are we all to believe that was a lie, now...?"

"...I cannot say what tricks Hua Tuo used," Wang Lang replied. "That's not the point now: he left the service of the state without proper cause and defied orders to return, and once he confesses his guilt he will be punished for it."

"Since when has Cao Cao cared about evidence of guilt...?" Kong Rong heckled.

"Watch your words, Kong Wenju," Yang Biao warned. "You accuse the Chancellor of State of killing men without reason. What's *your* proof of *that*…?"

"…Your point is made," Kong Rong conceded.

"But *my* point is not made strongly enough," Geng Ji said. "Hua Tuo is respected among the physician class and even above that. Tales of his wonderful remedies are, despite the dismissive words of Yang Biao and Wang Lang, commonly known and properly verified in some cases: yes, the full-body surgery is disputable, but he's done localised surgery on people where incense, acupuncture and medicine didn't work… and the success of those treatments is even more widely lauded."

"…Yes, I know what you speak of," Yang Biao admitted. "And yes, it's all spoken of if not absolutely proven."

"And we'd let such a man be callously beaten, starved and shouted at until he confesses to being a criminal, at which point Cao Cao can kill him…?" Geng Ji asked pointedly. "We should be protesting against that!"

"…Hua Tuo will be managed appropriately," Wang Lang insisted.

Two days passed.

Cao Cao rocked back and forth and bit his hand as Xun Wenruo relayed the latest news from Qing Province to his chancellery court; Cao was not listening to the report at all, partly because of the pain that he was enduring but mainly because he could not stop thinking about the man that had once managed that pain.

"…And so the 'siege of Xiami' – if it can even be termed as such – is now over," Xun Wenruo concluded. "It sounds like we might have eliminated some of the senior leaders as well!"

"That's good news, isn't it, Excellency…?" Xun Gongda prompted.

"Mm…? Oh, uh… yes, Gongda, yes, it's excellent news, yes," Cao Cao replied indifferently.

"*Aiee*… you are badly afflicted today, Mengde," Cao Chun sighed.

"There's nothing I can do about it," Cao Cao replied. "Nothing… not now that I do not have that man as my physician… nothing at all… but he will wish that he had not tried to barter my health for high status… he will *confess*… and *then*…!"

"…We really should try and find another acupuncturist," Yuan Huan said.

"And have another rat that tries to use his position as leverage…?" Cao Cao retorted. "That, perhaps, is why those wretched physicians are as low as they are… because they abuse their importance to gain undeserved favour! But they will enjoy no favour from me! I was born to bring an end to the corruption and to bring an end to the corrupt, regardless of their value!"

The court was morbidly silent.

"Now, gentlemen… I understand that I have a visitor from Yi Province," Cao Cao prompted.

"A strange, scruffy little man called Zhang Song, bringing tribute from Governor Liu Zhang," Xun Wenruo replied disdainfully. "It has to be said, I'm surprised at Liu Zhang, actually: I thought that he was at worst a sycophant, but in some way loyal and deferential, and yet he's sent this ugly, uncouth, rude-"

"A 'Mi Heng' that Liu Zhang wants me to dispose of for him," Cao Cao chuckled. "Well, too bad: I have no intention if that's the case... but I'll see him."

Cao Cao invited the Yi Province envoy Zhang Song to a packed chancellery audience hall and said, "So, then, Mister Zhang Song... you bring me tribute from your master."
Zhang Song smirked and replied, "I do indeed: tribute befitting a high-ranking Han minister. Is that *sufficient* tribute, Chancellor...?"
"Impertinent man!" Chen Qun cried. **"You-!"**
"*Enough*, Mister Chen," Cao Cao said. "You... are *brave*, Zhang Song... and I would be a hypocrite if I heckled you for it while demanding the same from my own vassals. So your lord Liu Zhang hopes for cordial relations...?"
"He desires nothing else, Chancellor," Zhang Song replied. "He has long served as the guardian of the remote region known as Yi Province, threatened by the wicked heretic Zhang Lu to the north and the greedy Nanman tribes to the south; he hopes that he can work with the Han court to preserve order in the future."
"...If it is my decision that Liu Zhang is the right man to be guarding such a place, then I will leave him where he is and aid him in his mission," Cao Cao said. "If, on the other hand, I consider him to be a mediocrity, then I will be forced to remove him from his post as I will soon unseat his unworthy, rebellious neighbour Liu Biao."
Xun Wenruo balked and whispered, "Excellency, you-"
"It is no secret that I intend to invade Jing Province, Wenruo," Cao Cao insisted. "This defiant fellow will, as far away as he is, be aware of it already if he is an 'envoy' and 'adviser' to his lord, else he does his lord no service. And it is better that Liu Zhang understands that truth now: I do not bargain with *anyone*. If I do not approve of Liu Zhang, then I will unseat him as I will soon unseat Liu Biao: why should he not know that...?"
Zhang Song sighed disappointedly.
"Something that I say displeases you...?" Cao Cao heckled.
"I admit that I am surprised," Zhang Song replied. "My lord has done no wrong, and yet your response to his humble yet sizeable tribute is a threat to unseat him."
"His father obtained Yi through treachery!" Cao Cao retorted. **"He took it with lies, held it with violence and kept Zhang Lu, that worst enemy of the Han, as a guard dog in Hanzhong! Liu Yan tried to seize the throne with the help of the Qiang, which, now I have thought about it, angers me greatly! Perhaps I will take the place back from Liu Zhang when I'm done with Liu Biao and that rebel rat *Liu Bei* that he is sheltering as well!"**
Zhang Song was ponderously silent.
"...I can see that you've nothing more of value to say, which does not suggest to me that you are a particularly remarkable envoy," Cao Cao scoffed. "I am busy, Zhang Song, so you'll excuse me if I now move on to other affairs: you'll be invited to any banquets that are held before you leave, of course."
Zhang Song bowed ever-so-slightly and said, "I thank you, Excellency, for your boundless hospitality."
Cao Cao harrumphed; Zhang Song turned and left the hall with a confident stride.
"...He was *terrible*," Xun Wenruo said. "Is that ugly, irreverent

man the best that-?"
"Perhaps he struggled to find good words," Jia Xu suggested. "I know that *I* would."
"And given the men that you've defended in the past, Wenhe, that's quite a rebuke," Xun Wenruo said dryly. "Perhaps that *is* it, though... but was warning him wise...?"
"I don't care," Cao Cao admitted. "Liu Zhang is laughable, and moreover he can wait: his 'envoy' can tell him whatever he likes. What will he do...?"

Zhang Song left the chancellery building and hummed thoughtfully: he had realised that he could not defend Liu Zhang any more than he could tolerate Cao Cao. A new plan had formed in his mind: when he did finally leave Xuchang, he would first travel to Jing Province and seek an audience with the fugitive warlord Liu Bei, whose name seemed to pass Cao Cao's lips like a curse word. That meeting would be the beginning of Liu Bei's journey to Yi Province: that was a journey that would lead to the birth of the smallest of the legendary 'Three Kingdoms', Shu Han.

****

109

The new Yellow Turban uprising in Qing Province was proving easy to contain but difficult to eradicate; the cultists could gain no new ground without quickly losing it, but they were too well trained to be affected by dwindling resources and support. Zang Ba's Qing Militias were divided between Zang himself, Sun Guan, Wu Dun, Yin Li and visiting Han general Xiahou Yuan, while armies led by former Yuan loyalists such as Lü Kuang and Su Yòu kept the cultist army from spilling into neighbouring Ji Province; administration in Qing was supported by Wang Xiu and Guan Tong, who were brought in because they knew the region well from their time as Yuan Tan's subordinates.

There were no great generals among the ranks of the Yellow Turbans, but their resolve was undeniable: they once again found solace and strength in the mantra that had been taught to them by the 'Way of Peace' founder, Zhang Jue, 25 years before.

**"Han's mandate has passed!
Yellow Sky, soon here!
In this renewing year,
Prosperous all, at last!"**

"Oh, how I missed those words," Zang Ba sighed sarcastically.
The Yellow Turbans had decided to attack the provincial capital Linzi for a second time after failing to gain new support or take cities in the Mount Tai, Donglai and Ji'nan regions; Zang Ba, Sun Guan and Xiahou Yuan were engaging the cultists from a camp located some distance away from the city while Guan Tong and Wang Xiu oversaw the siege defences from within. The Yellow Turbans were now taunting the external camp by reciting their mantra outside the gates in large numbers; the leaders barely managed to control the tempers of their former bandit soldiers, who just wanted a swift, decisive fight.
"This is once time when 'less is more' makes for bad reading," Xiahou Yuan said as he read a report from Le'an Prefecture in the northwest of the province. "Yin Li says he's struggling against a force that's half the size of his."
"I'll go," Sun Guan suggested.
"I'll join you when this lot are chased off," Zang Ba replied.
Sun Guan left the command tent and led a force of around 3,000 men away from the camp to aid Yin Li; Xiahou Yuan shook his head and said, "We should really try something before too many more of these wretched heretics arrive."
"...What about a second lot of us feigning leaving here to lend support to Yin Li and then doubling back to pincer them...?" Zang Ba suggested.
"It's worth a try, General Zang," Xiahou Yuan replied. "It wouldn't work on a Han general with a half-decent adviser, but it might just work on these men."
"I'll lead them myself," Zang Ba said. "I don't really have a great set of thinkers to send in my place."

Zang Ba led another force of 3,000 out of the western gates of the camp; the Yellow Turbans guessed that they were on their way to Le'an and did not obstruct them. Zang Ba travelled far enough away from Linzi to make the ruse convincing before he prepared to go back; he was alerted to the approach of a second army from the east that turned out to be Sun Guan's militia turning about. Zang Ba was puzzled at the development, so he hurried to meet with his friend and get an explanation.

"...So you had the same idea," Sun Guan chuckled.

"You... feigned leaving the camp to launch a pincer attack...?" Zang Ba exclaimed. "What about Yin Li...?"

"Yin'll either hold for another week or be dead by the time I got there," Sun Guan replied. "It's more important to get these bastards away from the capital, I reckoned: saving Le'an and losing Linzi is a stupid trade."

"...You're right," Zang Ba realised. "Let's give 'em a surprise, then: I'll circle around and attack from the east."

Xiahou Yuan travelled to the northern gates of his camp and stared at the Yellow Turban agitators; he was now tasked with pacifying his mostly borrowed army, which was collectively losing its patience. All the while, the familiar words were being chanted by hundreds of men:

**"Han's mandate has passed!
Yellow Sky, soon here!
In this renewing year,
Prosperous all, at last!"**

"We should be smashing them, not sitting here!" a Qing Militia captain shouted. **"If this bloke Cao Cao sent here won't order us to charge, then-!"**

A sudden din outside the gates caused the cultists to end their barrage of taunts and look to the east and west; Zang Ba and Sun Guan were charging at speed from both directions.

"Why weren't we warned???" a Yellow Turban commander asked angrily. **"How did they-"**

"CHARGE!"

Xiahou Yuan's cry urged a third army of 4,000 out of the camp to complete the pincer; those Yellow Turbans that were not former Qing Corps either scattered or buckled under the pressure of being attacked by a superior army, while the better-trained men staged an effective fighting retreat toward the city, where reinforcements awaited them.

"Let them go!" Xiahou Yuan ordered. **"We'll regroup and make a plan!"**

Sun Guan looked at Zang Ba, who shrugged and said, **"He's right, I reckon."**

"DON'T PURSUE!" Sun Guan ordered. **"BACK TO THE CAMP!"**

The order quickly spread throughout the Qing Militia ranks, and the victorious defenders returned to their camp.

"The next fight," Xiahou Yuan said, **"will be outside the city, when it will be relieved once and for all."**

"I'll drink to that... rules permitting!" Zang Ba joked.

Cao Cao's incarceration of Hua Tuo was starting to make him

noticeably unpopular with the physicians and some of the more open-minded officials as the weeks wore on; Xun Wenruo took the opportunity to discuss it with Cao Cao privately after one tense court session.

"I... I know that you really are angry with the man, and I see why, for I was angry myself at first," Xun Wenruo began. "But Your Excellency, we must learn from what we have learned. Since his incarceration, Master Hua has protested his innocence and enquired after his elderly wife, who, he stresses, was doing better on the day that she was visited but suffers from a condition that, like yours, changes in severity from day to day."

Cao Cao grunted unsympathetically.

"His achievements are known far and wide, and I confess to becoming somewhat of a supporter of his ideas and intentions rather than a detractor," Xun Wenruo continued. "I know that some – Wang Lang, Hua Xin and, until recently, Cheng Yu, to name but three – have argued that he's been deliberately stalling his treatment to provoke offers of great rewards, or that he used some sort of 'binding magic' and that the needles were part of some occult ritual, or that he is an outright fraud... I don't agree. If he wanted rewards, he'd have replied to your early insistence that he be rewarded handsomely."

"Not necessarily," Cao Cao replied. "If a man wants the best rewards, he feigns altruism and extols virtue so as to build a reputation that he cannot be bought, which forces the desperate lord to offer more than he would otherwise consider."

"That may be true of some, Excellency... but not Hua Tuo," Xun Wenruo said. "And even if that were the case, he is a man whose skills are unique and beneficial to so many: have we the right to deprive the world of such a man...?"

"You cannot know any of that for certain, Wenruo," Cao Cao scoffed. "Can you be sure that he is not another Ze Rong, peddling false cures to me in order to persuade the court to adopt his faith...?"

"Like you, Excellency, I assume that Master Hua is a Buddhist, but Ze Rong was a Buddhist *cultist*, as Zhang Jue and Zhang Lu are *Taoist cultists*," Xun Wenruo retorted. "The practitioners of that faith that remain in Xu Province are not at all like Ze Rong, just as Shi Xie, ruler of Jiaozhi in the far south, is not a monster, nor are his people cultists. Please don't turn this into a religious matter if it can be avoided: Hua Tuo has never shown any evidence of cultist behaviour in the past."

"Has he ever had the Chancellor of State as a patient before...?" Cao Cao snapped.

"...I say again, Excellency... be kind to Hua Tuo," Xun Wenruo pleaded. "He is a marvellous man that has brought relief from suffering to rich and poor alike: I say again, have we the right to deprive the world of such a man...?"

Cao Cao smiled coldly as he announced, "Ah... but Hua Tuo has finally *confessed*."

"Confessed...?" Xun Wenruo exclaimed. "To *what*, Excellency...?"

"To all that he was being held for," Cao Cao replied. "Must I repeat the charges?"

"...No, Excellency, I remember them well enough," Xun Wenruo said miserably. "But I implore you, Excellency, to be lenient."

"Oh, I shall be," Cao Cao chuckled. "...*Death*."

"*Ayah*! *No*, Excellency, *no*: you must show *clemency*!" Xun Wenruo protested. "Master Hua Tuo is loved and respected by so many, from the lowly peasant to the wealthy landowner! Hua Tuo has cured diseases, perfected complex surgery, developed amazing potions and brought relief with exercises derived from the animals that even some Taoist priests hail as being Heaven's gift! You cannot harm such a unique, special man!"

"Bah! Are there really no other rats that can do what he does?" Cao Cao retorted. "My word is final, Wenruo, and if I learn that he has been secreted away or that some pedant has gone crying to the Son of Heaven with appeals for 'clemency', then I will put those that tried to save him to the sword as well!"

Xun Wenruo shuddered uncontrollably.

"...*Death to him*, Wenruo," Cao Cao muttered. "*Death to him...*"

It took several days for the news that Hua Tuo had been executed to reach the wider city: many officials donned white garments in a show of solidarity with the famous physician.

"...Cao Cao has outdone even Dong Zhuo with his latest evil," Geng Ji said to his associate Wei Huang. "Cai Yong was a crime enough: what Cao has done has deprived the world of its finest medical mind."

Court Physician Ji Pi, Kong Rong and Zhi Xi were also present at the meeting in Geng Ji's home: Zhi Xi looked about him nervously and said, "We should be careful now, you know. If Cao can kill Hua Tuo and an Imperial consort, then-"

"We cannot become too frightened to meet or speak or act," Geng Ji replied. "That's when we cease to be a solution and become part of the problem."

"I'll continue to speak out, don't you worry," Kong Rong promised. "Cao Cao has gone too far: his careless warmongering cost us Ying Shao, but we could not say too much because his was a shared responsibility; he cleverly sent my friend Mi Heng to Huang Zu so that his murder was another man's fault; he slandered Consort Dong's father as a traitor to the throne and so we held our tongues; this latest murder is inexcusable and beyond explaining, even by a wily schemer like Cao Cao."

"The very worst part is the loss of the wonderful work that he did," Ji Pi whimpered.

"...First Geng Ji, and now you," Zhi Xi said. "Explain why everyone feels that his work has been lost: he has students, doesn't he...?"

"They'll go into hiding now, else they'll be rounded up for whatever reason," Geng Ji replied.

"But he had a bag of some kind," Kong Rong said. "What happened to it...?"

"That's the most nonsensical part of it all," Geng Ji replied. "This, gentlemen, is the story that we are expected to believe: in his last hours, the genius Hua Tuo wrote down what had not already been written and passed those notes – together with his 'green bag book' – to his prison warder, saying 'Take this and become a successful physician'."

Kong Rong frowned cynically.

"This warder – whose identity is not currently known to me, and just as well if he's real – supposedly took Hua's imparted knowledge home after the execution and showed it all to his lady wife," Geng Ji continued. "Then, apparently, she – in a fit of demented fearfulness – convinced him that only a fool would want to be a famous doctor and talked him into *burning everything*."

"*Ayah*...! It's too ridiculous to be true and yet insane enough and cruel enough to be true!" Zhi Xi cried.

"That is utter *drivel*," Kong Rong muttered. "Why would Hua Tuo offer his bag to an uneducated prison guard and expect it to transform him into another genius...?"

"This warder, as the last man to speak to Hua before he was beheaded, was then asked about the bag upon his return to work the next morning, at which point he broke down and confessed his guilt," Geng Ji said with disdain. "That, gentlemen, is the story of the end of the 'green bag book' and everything that Hua Tuo struggled to compile."

"...True or not, it is still a confirmation that, one way or another, the knowledge is gone," Kong Rong scoffed. "Chancellor Cao Cao – who paid a king's ransom to a Southern Xiongnu chieftain in order to retrieve a mentally-disturbed woman so that she could recite and rescue her father Cai Yong's *poetry* for all the world to enjoy – has just destroyed most of the medical research in the known world and the only man that properly understood it."

"He's a menace," Wei Huang suggested. "We-!"

"Say no more," Geng Ji warned. "Smarter men than us have tried and failed. We must hope that the last of his enemies – Liu Biao and Sun Quan – have the sense to bury their differences and defeat Cao Cao on the battlefield, which is the only way that such a man can be felled."

"...At least it's being said that Xun Yu lobbied vigorously for clemency," Ji Pi said. "If even he – who is, perhaps, Cao Cao's most loyal minion – now has doubts, then perhaps Cao will be reined in by his own disaffected followers."

Kong Rong shook his head and replied, "One can only hope so."

Cao Cao retreated to his chancellery study after every meeting and spent the evening rocking back and forth while biting his hand; he knew the ramifications of what he had done and there was no way to undo it. Xun Wenruo had waited for several days before choosing to confront Cao Cao privately once again and saying, "I can offer nothing to justify, condemn, reassure or scare you, Excellency, for you are doing a good enough job of being your own judge: I can see it in your face."

"I don't want to talk about it, Wenruo," Cao Cao insisted. "What word from Qing?"

"General Xiahou reports that the siege of Linzi is lifted," Xun Wenruo replied. "The main fronts are now to be found in villages and cities around Langya and Le'an."

"...But the Qing capital is again relieved," Cao Cao noted. "That's good. What word is there from my 'intelligence-gathering team' in *Wen County*...?"

Xun Wenruo was silent.

"...Aha...! So there is *another* liar to be dealt with!" Cao Cao said.

"His father is your greatest patron, Excellency," Xun Wenuo pleaded. "Do not follow one bad mistake with another!"

"You at least have the courage to admit that you feel that my

killing Hua Tuo was a 'bad mistake', which is something," Cao Cao heckled. "You failed to convince me at the critical moment, though, so why complain...? Only Fengxiao knew me well enough to convince me to do the impossible... and now he is *gone*."
"...Don't kill Sima Yi, Your Excellency," Xun Wenruo whimpered. "His father would-!"
"I do not intend to kill Sima Yi," Cao Cao revealed. "I will scare him, yes, but he will live to lend his devious mind to my cause... and, maybe, help me to continue what I started with Fengxiao at my side. None of the rest of you seems to be able to convince me of anything: perhaps Sima Yi will do better."
Xun Wenruo lowered his head and said, "Yes, Excellency..."

Hua Tuo's demise brought the advance of pioneering medical research in Han Imperial China to an abrupt halt: the loss of his journals meant that the extent of his knowledge – which supposedly included acupuncture, local and general anaesthesia, complex surgery and a range of remedies for everything from intestinal parasites to infectious diseases – will never be known. Wherever he hailed from – and the possibilities are as vast as his purported range of skills – Hua Tuo lived his last years in Han Dynasty China and died a criminal's death while the bulk of his life's work simultaneously ceased to exist or, at best, fell into public disuse by others out of fear of suffering a similar fate. Cao Cao would be verbally cursed for the rest of his days and beyond that, which he was well aware of: to Cao, that was insignificant compared to the loss of the first man to offer relief to his affliction and, soon enough, the only man that might have spared him from what would be, perhaps, the greatest personal tragedy that he would ever have to endure.

****

110

Zang Ba and Sun Guan led their Qing Militia armies to Le'an Prefecture after lifting the siege of Linzi, while Xiahou Yuan went eastward to aid Wu Dun in Langya Prefecture; the Yellow Turbans were finally starting to show signs of weakness as the local crime lords, volunteer peasant militias and a small reinforcement army from Ji Province led by Lü Kuang left them with nowhere to turn.

Zang Ba and Sun Guan's arrival caused the Yellow Turban army around the Le'an capital to panic: Yin Li led an army out of the main gates that was almost annihilated and would have been if not for Zang Ba's quick thinking. The Yellow Turbans were caught in yet another pincer and routed completely; Yin Li was then welcomed into Zang Ba's main camp and given a dish of wine to calm his nerves while Sun Guan secured the region against further attacks.

"Won't be long now," Zang Ba chuckled.

"...Did I say 'thanks' for rescuing me, Xuangao...?" Yin Li wheezed.

"Once or twice," Zang Ba joked.

"This is... bloody Chang Xi's fault, all this is," Yin Li complained. "*He* started this with his rebellion!"

"Yeah, well, he paid a high price for it in advance, didn't he," Zang Ba replied.

"Your tone says a lot," Yin Li prompted.

"...It was done wrong," Zang Ba replied. "He needed dealing with, but you know, we might have got a lot more blokes back on side if Yu Jin hadn't talked Chang down with lies. A lot of why this has been difficult is 'cause a lot o' blokes didn't pick up a weapon and fight until we were half done. That's as much Yu Jin's fault as Chang's, I reckon. It's taken a long time to get the trust back."

"...Yeah, you're right," Yin Li said. "You were always right... ... ...You know that Wu Dun nearly joined Chang."

"O' course I do," Zang Ba replied. "I think we all considered it at least once, Yin. Even me. Maybe that's why I gave my family over to Cao Cao."

"I wondered that," Yin Li admitted.

"...But I'm glad I didn't go back to banditry now," Zang Ba insisted. "Yeah, we probably won't get much of a reward for all this – Xiahou Yuan will though – but it's better than being chased and having to steal from other needy people all the time. Dad'd cry a waterfall from the Heavens if I went back to that now."

Yin Li smiled.

"...O' course, there's the risk that Wu Dun might rebel if we're not rewarded again," Zang Ba suggested.

"And if he does rebel, we'll deal with him," Yin Li replied. "And after that, it's you, me and Sun, and we're none of us stupid enough to rebel, so that'll be that."

Zang Ba sipped some wine from his dish and said, "I'm glad to hear that."

"So you were worried about me as well, then!" Yin Li chuckled.

"Look, Zang, you saved us – me – a lot of times, and I'd be an ingrate if I turned on you. Man's gotta have principles."

Zang Ba laughed and said, "Yeah... even bandits!"

Weeks went by, and the Yellow Turban problem in Qing Province gradually disappeared: the news was generally well received, but Cao Cao had other concerns: his favourite son, Cao Chong, was suddenly struck down by illness that confined him to his bed and forced Cao to rush back to Yè City to be with him.

"Hua Tuo cursed my dear Chong from beyond the grave... that or some wicked doctor in this region found a way to poison him," Cao Cao said to his gathered officials that included his son Cao Pi, Attendant Officer Cui Yan and Ji Province Registrar Li Fu. "I want a man found at once!"

"You think that we haven't been trying...?" Cui Yan retorted.

"A lot of physicians are reluctant to treat the Caos after Hua Tuo's execution," Li Fu admitted. "But every man that we've found says the same thing... that..."

Cao Cao's eyes filled with tears as he said, "That 'it is hopeless'... am I right...?"

"...There may be someone," Li Fu replied. "Believe me, Chancellor, when I say that we are doing everything possible."

"I know," Cao Cao said. "Anyhow, gentlemen... I must dispel the myth that my clan's needs come before the state, mustn't I...? I am pleased with Zang Ba and Sun Guan and intend to reward them properly this time... though the titles that I shall bestow will be signs of superficial power and nothing more."

"What titles, Excellency...?" the adviser Hua Xin asked.

"I intend to make those two loveable misfits, Zang and Sun, the Inspectors of Xu and Qing Provinces respectively," Cao Cao replied. "Dong Zhao is wasted on that role he has, so I'll bring him into government permanently; Miaocai – my cousin Xiahou Yuan – will be stationed in the region and be the one to possess the actual authority in both provinces, which is something that I shall make clear with *his* new title."

"But you said that Miaocai would be able to join us here in Yè!" Xiahou Dun protested.

"I must go back on that promise, Yuanrang," Cao Cao replied. "The needs of the state come first. Now, uh... I must apologise, gentlemen, and retire: I see that I am being asked to go."

The audience turned to look at the side entrance to the hall: an anxious servant was stood at the door with Cao Cao's principal wife Lady Bian.

"...As you were," Cao Cao said as he got to his feet and left the hall; Li Fu shook his head sadly and gestured that the meeting should continue.

"What is the matter...?" Cao Cao said as he followed Lady Bian and the servant to Cao Chong's quarters.

"He asked for you," Lady Bian replied.

"I... I cannot just drop everything when the boy wants to hold my hand!" Cao Cao said emotionally. "Is his mother not by his side?"

"Lady Huan is losing composure," Lady Bian explained. "She has fled the room and gone to seek an audience with..."

"...With Lady Ding," Cao Cao supposed.

"...Yes, Husband," Lady Bian replied. "With Lady Ding."

Cao Cao groaned miserably. Lady Ding was Cao Cao's second wife and the woman that raised his deceased eldest sons, Ang and Shuo, after their biological mother, Lady Liu, died young; she and Cao had not spoken since the death in battle of Cao Ang at Wan

City – which she considered to be entirely Cao's fault – and the subsequent death due to sickness of Cao Shuo, which she considered to be hastened by Cao's prolonged absence. Cao Cao surmised that Lady Huan would only visit Lady Ding's isolated cottage on the mansion complex for one reason: she feared that her son Chong would soon be dead and wanted advice on how to deal with it.

"...I wonder... does she somehow blame me as Lady Ding does...?" Cao Cao murmured.

"She should not," Lady Bian replied.

"...I am not so sure," Cao Cao said. "Is this Heaven's punishment... for Hua Tuo...?"

"If it is, then I wish that Heaven would stop punishing the innocent and be more direct," Lady Bian replied. "What good is there to be had in robbing the world of such a wonderful child...?"

Cao Cao sobbed bitterly as he succumbed to the belief that he was somehow responsible; he was still crying when he reached the entrance to his son's room.

"Father...!" Cao Chong cried; the boy's voice was more childlike and pleading than Cao was used to, and that harmed him further.

"I... I am at a loss for words!" Cao Cao admitted as he fell to his knees and grasped his son's hand. "You... you are my little genius that... that I... I want to bequeath it all to... *everything*...!"

"I *ache*, Father," Cao Chong replied. "I am... so *tired*..."

Cao Cao kissed his son's hand and said, "Don't... *don't sleep*. It must all be *yours*."

Lady Bian sighed, turned and walked away.

The 29-year-old Sima Yi had enjoyed years of avoiding service in the Han government, but it was now about to come to an end: he was sat in his garden with a book in his hand when a small army of soldiers forced their way past his servants and took control of his home.

"*Soldiers*, Husband!" Lady Zhang hissed as she ran into the garden and snatched Sima Yi's book from him. "*Soldiers*... they-!"

"Calm down," Sima Yi ordered. "I can-"

"**Sima Yi.**"

Sima Yi and Lady Zhang turned to face a stern military captain, who said, "I am here with a simple message from Chancellor of State Cao Cao: serve the Han or be prepared to prove that you are ill... if you *can*."

"...I understand, Captain," Sima Yi replied with strength in his tone. "Tell Chancellor Cao that I will respond appropriately in the next two days."

The captain smirked and ordered his men to withdraw.

"...You dropped your pretence, just like that," Lady Zhang complained once the soldiers were gone. "I killed a servant to keep our secret, I-!"

"Until recently, I might have considered doing otherwise," Sima Yi said. "But if Cao Cao can destroy Hua Tuo for feigning his wife's illness, what will he do to me... and to you...?"

Lady Zhang nodded agreeably.

"...It has been fun while it has lasted, but we were not going to be able to pretend forever," Sima Yi continued. "My father's patience would have worn thin soon enough, and, eventually, another Hua

Tuo would have appeared that would have been asked to assess me, and I cannot feign such illnesses to an expert."

"So... so what will we do now...?" Lady Zhang asked.

"If Cao Cao wanted to punish me, then he'd have told his men to seize me today, but he was content with a warning," Sima Yi noted. "That means that he wants my service badly enough to overlook my deceitful behaviour. I will get a good job now... and I will be able to build a fortune... and we will finally be able to start a family."

Lady Zhang smiled gratefully.

"And I will finally be able to get some sun and eat properly!" Sima Yi joked as he poked at his wiry body. "This needn't be seen as a bad day... it might well be the beginnings of something good, even if I do now work for a sickly, psychotic tyrant and a feeble, doomed emperor with no authority and a crumbling empire enjoying brief respite."

"We can start a family at last," Lady Zhang said. "That is good enough for me."

"And I will be treated well... or, at least, I should be, if they want my help and not some other response," Sima Yi replied ominously. "I did not want to work for them, and I have harmed myself and you, my lady wife, in my efforts to avoid working for them, but they have, at long last, forced my hand; they will regret it if they are not now very, very careful."

Zang Ba and Sun Guan retreated to their old fortress base at Kaiyang after the final defeat of the Yellow Turbans: they received imperial messengers within days that brought them news of their hollow titles.

"...Governor of Qing Province," Sun Guan murmured.

"...Governor of Xu Province," Zang Ba sighed.

"...And Xiahou Yuan made 'Chief Logistics Officer for Xu and Qing Provinces', which basically makes him the military commander in both provinces," Sun Guan said dolefully. "The administrative power's mostly devolved to the prefectural administrators, so... bugger-all to do all day."

"It's better than nothing," Zang Ba replied. "We've still got our armies, even if we have to go to Xiahou with a begging bowl whenever we want to do something... I mean, what are we gonna do that don't involve an order from Cao Cao anyway...?"

"...Yeah," Sun Guan sighed. "We're going our separate ways, then; you'll be surrounded by them 'Buddhists', and as for me, I'll..."

"Buddhists are alright all-in-all, and there'll be plenty of excuses for meeting up and sharing a dish o' wine, Zhongtai: like you said, we won't have much to do," Zang Ba insisted. "But yeah, this says I have to go and accept the seal of office from Dong Zhao at once. And that marquis title Cao promised me a year ago is coming an' all, even I never wanted it... glad I didn't get it before or we'd have been fighting Wu Dun as well."

"...I suppose we'd better get going," Sun Guan groaned. "I have to go to Linzi if I'm Inspector- sorry, *Governor* of Qing Province."

"...Time for one dish of wine, I reckon," Zang Ba suggested.

Sun Guan laughed and said, "Why not, Marquis Zang: why not?"

Cao Cao was left a shadow of his usual self when Cao Chong – his favourite son and preferred heir to his legacy – died at the age of 12 after a short, aggressive illness. There was a need to maintain stability and continuity, so Cao Cao resisted the urge to leave his responsibilities to others and conductied state affairs as usual; the only difference was the sudden sight of every man and woman in Yè wearing at least one white garment, although some were actually being worn to mourn Hua Tuo.

Cai Yong's eldest daughter, Lady Cai Yan – who now bore the style name 'Wenji' – started to appear in Cao Cao's court at around the same time. Cai Wenji was now married, whether she liked it or not, to the official Dong Si, and she was beginning the long and sometimes emotionally painful process of reciting her father's extensive library of works from memory; she was also composing her own, almost always melancholy musical and poetic works that she would perform at banquets by request. Cai Wenji's compositions spoke of her many misfortunes and personal losses, and they were known for driving the guests to tears: for Cao Cao, they were strangely cathartic, although he rarely cried openly.

"...I worry," Cao Pi whispered to his cousin, Cao Xiu, as they sat and enjoyed a more cheerful piece of music alongside a large number of banquet guests.

"...Worry about what...?" Cao Xiu asked.

"I tried to tell him that I was sorry... about Chong," Cao Pi explained as he stared at his cold-eyed, oblivious father. "And... and he said, 'Chong's passing is my great misfortune, but for you and your brothers, it is a great advantage'. And then he wouldn't say any more... he waved his hand to dismiss me."

"*Aiee*... I see why you worry," Cao Xiu replied.

The court musicians concluded their tune, and the guests showed their appreciation.

"**Now,**" Cao Cao said, "**Cai Wenji will perform once more.**"

"Oh no... not again," Xiahou Dun complained.

The guests then enjoyed – or, perhaps, endured – a pessimistic and melancholy work of Cai Wenji's invention titled 'Poem of Sorrow and Anger' – performed by Wenji herself – while Cao Cao looked on with emotionally broken eyes. One of his guests – the Qiang hostage-official Ma Teng – struggled with the misery that Wenji's semi-autobiographical lyrics awoke within him; another guest – the newly-appointed official Sima Yi – fought the urge to smile at the depressing atmosphere that Cao was inflicting on his guests for no good reason.

It had been an eventful opening to a new year: in the wake of his surprise victory over the Yuans and the Wuhuan tribes, Cao Cao had completely restructured the government, rescued Cai Yong's daughter and intellectual legacy from the Southern Xiongnu, subjugated the Qiang and Wuhuan races, won the hatred of the medical profession by extinguishing their brightest star and recruited one of the most important men in the history of the period against his will. But the most incredible – and most famous – of the year's events were yet to come.

****

ACT IX: THE INVASION OF JING PROVINCE

111

Han Dynasty China had seen a lot of change in a very short time. The most important official in the empire, Cao Cao, was now titled 'Chancellor of State' as a reward for his victories over the Wuhuan tribes of the northeast and the destruction or subjugation of the numerous bandits, pirates, cultist armies and rogue warlords that had brought the nation to its knees; but Chancellor Cao was, as he had always been, far from universally popular. There were some that saw Cao Cao's latest promotion as the necessary empowerment of a man that had brought stability, but there were others that worried that Cao might go on to emulate the last man to hold the Chancellor's title: the infamous tyrant, Dong Zhuo.

There were many reasons for Cao Cao to be compared to a man that had tortured and killed hundreds of officials and their families, committed regicide, appointed a new sovereign against popular wishes and razed the capital, Luoyang, after looting the tombs of past emperors. Cao Cao had recruited Jia Xu, Dong Zhuo's chief adviser, to his own counsel; he had forced a famous doctor, Hua Tuo, to attend court and then killed him for refusing to cooperate; he had purged the court of dozens of officials that were part of alleged plots and killed many of their family members including, in one notorious instance, a pregnant imperial consort; and then there was the title 'Chancellor of State', which required an older, less accountable ministerial appointment system to be reinstated, an act that was seen by some as unnecessary. Others went further, citing Emperor Xian's futile attempts to plead clemency for his consort as a sign that Cao Cao had reduced the sovereign to a puppet, just as Dong Zhuo had done: but the majority – including victims of Dong Zhuo's regime and, to the surprise of some, men that had actively participated in plots to remove Dong Zhuo – saw Cao Cao as quite the opposite of a tyrant and were prepared to defend him at all times.

The problem was that, unlike Dong Zhuo, Cao Cao was many things to many people: Cao had been the only warlord-governor to rush to Emperor Xian's aid when the court was fleeing Dong Zhuo's successors, the 'co-regents' Li Jue and Guo Si, and he had worked tirelessly to restore Luoyang to its former glory while turning one of his own counties into the temporary capital, Xuchang, at great personal expense. The powerful Yuan clan chieftain Yuan Shao – whom many expected to be the saviour of the homeless, famine-stricken court after rescuing the young monarch from treasonous palace eunuchs and subsequently leading the coalition against Dong Zhuo in past years – was busy feuding with his own brother for control of their clan and quietly amassing wealth and land, and was even said to have referred to sheltering the court as 'a burden'. So when Yuan Shao later challenged Cao Cao for 'custody of the Son of Heaven' – citing an imperial edict of dubious origin, dubbed the 'Girdle Edict', as one of his justifications – the majority of the courtiers continued to place their faith in Cao and reacted positively to the series of defeats that Yuan suffered at the hands of Cao Cao's smaller army. Yuan Shao's premature death from despair and illness led to a second succession crisis that caused the Yuan clan to implode: Cao followed his victories over the Yuans by pacifying their unpopular Wuhuan allies and bringing relative stability and peace to the northeast, which led in turn to his promotion to Chancellor. Since then, Cao Cao had, in addition to his unpopular actions, forced the Qiang tribes to submit after years of confrontation, rescued the famed scholar Cai Yong's daughter, Cai Wenji, from her life as a Xiongnu consort and implemented measures that reduced corruption, ensured fairer taxation and promised famine relief through better crop production and storage. Now a campaign to defeat the last of the 'rebel warlords' – Liu Biao of Jing Province, Zhang Lu of Hanzhong and, if he did not submit, Sun Quan of Yang Province – was being planned: that was, for Cao Cao, as controversial and divisive as everything else.

"Quiet please, gentlemen," the adviser Xun Gongda asked of his fellow officials. "The Chancellor is about to arrive."
The Yè audience hall fell silent; moments later, Cao Cao entered the hall with his bodyguard Xu Chu and sat in his host seat.
"The northeast is as quiet as it will ever be," Cao Cao began. "The efforts of General Xiahou Yuan, Governor Zang Ba and Governor Sun Guan have brought stability to Qing Province, ending the need for large numbers of troops to be in that region. The production of food has been increased, and training for naval warfare has begun, although I understand it to be… I believe the term used was 'inadequate'."
"It is," the official Bao Xun replied. "Woefully inadequate, in fact, Excellency: Jing Province has a number of artery rivers running through it, in the north *and* in the south, and none more obvious than the Han River that divides the north and the Xiang River and Great River that divide north from south and east from west."
"So what am I to do about it…?" Cao Cao asked.
"…Pray or hope, Chancellor, depending on your level of faith," the adviser Sima Yi suggested dryly.
"You've been here a few weeks and already you're asking for a blade across your neck!" Xiahou Dun shouted. "Why is this lying, treacherous man even here, Mengde?"
"He was lying about being sick to get out of working for us!" Cao Hong heckled. "Why spare him but not-!"
"*Don't*, Zilian," Cao Cao warned. "The next words that you were about to utter… are not to be uttered again."
Cao Hong scowled and lowered his head.
"…This is entirely my fault for appearing to be flippant, Chancellor," Sima Yi suggested. "I apologise if that was construed, for it was not my intent."
"What *was* your intent, then…?" Cao Xiu asked.
Sima Yi smiled and replied, "To provoke the answer, 'For what?' to which the answer is, 'Liu Biao dying', which solves everything."
"I agree," the adviser Jia Xu said. "What we absolutely do not want is an armed confrontation with Jing's navy: that was the only force that ever got the better of the 'Tiger of Jiangdong', Sun Jian, and we must not underestimate its power even now."
"They just about repelled us five years ago," General Li Dian suggested. "We faltered at Bowang, but where else did they get the better of us…? Generals Li Tong, Feng Kai and Lu Zhao were not given many troops for that campaign but still suffered no

defeats worth mentioning."

"That's because neither side was really trying," Sima Yi retorted.

"**Bastard!**" Xiahou Dun cried. "I nearly died at Bowang, you-!"

"Silence, Yuanrang," Cao Cao ordered. "You brought that disaster upon yourself, if you recall. And Zhongda is quite right to-"

"Mm...?" Cheng Yu said suddenly. "Have I missed something...?"

"...I said 'Zhong*da*', not 'Zhong*de*'," Cao Cao chuckled. "When have I called you by your style name at meetings, Elder Cheng...?"

"Oh... I was distracted," Cheng Yu replied.

"You're old and senile," Cao Hong teased. "Why are you even here...? Do we need your old bones anymore?"

"Watch your tongue, you witless oaf!" Cheng Yu retorted. "Even if I *was* senile, I'd still have ten times the brains that you have!"

"...A sad fact," Cao Cao chuckled. "May I go on now...?"

Cao Hong grumbled quietly and lowered his head again.

"As I was saying, Sima Zhongda was quite right to point out that our last campaign was a ploy to deceive the Yuans," Cao Cao continued. "Even from afar and while feigning illness, Zhongda could see it, while the likes of Guo Tu, Pang Ji and Xun Chen saw nothing... *that*, Yuanrang and Zilian, is why I hired him."

Xiahou Dun sneered; Cao Hong did not respond at all.

"If either side had truly committed everything to the campaign, then the battles would have moved from the land to the water, and that is where our problems would have started," Cao Cao continued. "We have only ever used rivers as means to transport goods from one place to another... and while doing so, the men suffer. Is that not so, Gongren...?"

"Indeed, yes, Excellency," the former Governor of Xu Province, Dong Gongren, said sadly. "Throughout my time working on those canals for the Wuhuan campaign, I watched as men fell sick from spending too much time on the unstable decks of the boats... and those canals were nowhere near as wide and turbulent as the rivers they would have to fight on. It's too common a problem for men that are not used to it."

"And I don't want to be reliant on surrendered pirates," Cao Cao complained. "But it's just a sad fact: northern men that are used to fighting and living on the land are mostly left nauseous at the very least when on a boat. My training lake looks more like an infirmary. And speaking of infirmaries, we haven't even begun to discuss resistance to water-borne diseases yet... *aiee*."

"Can't we recruit fishermen...?" Cao Hong asked.

"...Shut up," Cheng Yu heckled. "You think Cai Mao's navy is made up of ten men with fishing rods...?"

"It was just a suggestion!" Cao Hong protested.

"Don't bother next time," Cao Cao retorted.

"The signs are that Sun Quan intends to attack Jiangxia at some point in the next year or two," the adviser Hua Xin said. "If that happens, Excellency, surely the navy will be forced to move southward, which will leave the north exposed."

"Yes, and me exposed to accusations that I collude with Sun Quan to divide Jing between us if I were to exploit that diversion," Cao Cao retorted. "I will not be the Yuan Shao to his Gongsun Zan."

"Can we ignore such an opportunity if it arose...?" the adviser Yuan Huan asked.

"But Sun Quan might be spoken of as a Han ally," Hua Xin

realised. "That won't do... the Suns are the worst enemy of the state after Zhang Lu!"

"I think that the vast majority of us agree upon that," Wang Lang replied: Hua Xin, Yuan Huan and Liu Yè – who, like Wang, had all been forced to flee the Sun clan after a defeat of some kind – murmured agreeably.

"Four of you does not make a 'vast majority'," Cheng Yu said. "The Suns of Jiangdong are like any other band of rebels that we've encountered and must be considered as allies if possible: we cannot base all of our decisions on the need to soothe the damaged egos of a handful of men. If that were not the case, could we have worked with Zhang Xiu...?"

Wang Lang and Hua Xin were visibly irritated while Yuan Huan and Liu Yè quietly conceded that Cheng Yu was correct.

"...Far from being senile, Elder Cheng, you are as sharp as always if not sharper," Cao Cao replied. "We must not rule out a working relationship with Sun Quan... but he must not be allowed to think that he can bargain. Any part of Jing that submits to or is conquered by the Suns must then return to government control."

"And that, Excellency, is where Sun Quan will disappoint," Hua Xin insisted. "He wants all of Jing, and Jiangxia most of all: he will kill Huang Zu – which should be enough to satiate his desire for revenge – and then he will take the land as 'reparation for his loss'. I will be proved right."

"...And then there is the risk that the Qiang or Zhang Lu might decide to do something – separately or together – while I am distracted, or the other sizeable risk that Liu Bei seizes Jing during the confusion and puts up a more solid defence," Cao Cao suggested. "And, of course, there is the plain, simple possibility that Liu Biao will surprise us by being a stalwart ruler."

"First, I will quell your last worry," Cheng Yu replied. "Kuai Liang sends ignored ideas from his sickbed like a second-rate Guo Jia to a first-rate Yuan Shao, and that's if he's still alive; his brother, Kuai Yue, has abandoned the enfeebled Huang Zu to provide ineffective advice to Liu Biao instead and to be close to him when his end arrives; the Pangs do little more than look to Kuai Yue or stare at the floor; Wang Can veers between prodigy and simpleton as he acts between the brays of the donkeys; Hè Qia, Huan Jie, Fu Xun and Han Song are politicians first and will therefore do whatever benefits them while claiming that they do it 'for the state'; Cai Mao and his sister are gradually becoming the real power in Jing, but they lack the courage to fight; Biao's heir, Liu Qi, is a sickly whiner that has lost the faith of the entire court but not his father, who is almost certainly senile."

Cao Cao smirked and asked, "And my other worries...?"

"A case of treading well-trod ground," Cheng Yu replied. "If Zhang Lu could act, he would have, but even the pathetic Liu Zhang can keep him trapped in Hanzhong: his silly state can't buy weapons because the rest of us don't consider rice to be a viable currency. And it's been said often enough that the Qiang won't do anything unless we go near them, especially after our acquisition of most of the Ma clan as hostages. And Liu Bei...? ...*Aiee*. We really shouldn't be worried about him anymore, not after his many famous defeats and humiliations, but we're right to worry... we should in most cases, but not this one. The-"

"Stop talking in riddles, old man!" Xiahou Dun heckled. "Should we worry or not?!"

"...*Not in this case*, as I *just said*," Cheng Yu retorted. "Liu Bei is, like Liu Qi, hated by the Jing court; they all despise and suspect him, and although he is popular with the common people – who are stupid beyond belief, as they are everywhere else – he cannot shake his reputation for stealing provinces and then losing them. I think that Cai Mao would be prepared to fight Liu Bei if it came to it, and that wouldn't be much of a fight."

"Your cantankerous speeches are almost enough to make me forget how sad I am, Elder Cheng," Cao Cao said: he had started to think of his recently-deceased son Chong and lose focus.

"...Should we adjourn, Excellency...?" Jia Xu asked.

"No, no... I have an Empire to oversee," Cao Cao replied. "Is there any other business...?"

The court session ended after another hour of discussion: Cao Cao then retired to his study with his registrar, Liu Yè, and the advisers Xun Gongda, Jia Xu, Hua Xin, Yuan Huan and Sima Yi.

"...Forgive me, gentlemen, for my sudden bout of melancholy," Cao Cao said. "It... it just occurs to me that... well, no, it is a recurring thought."

"What thought, Excellency...?" Xun Gongda asked.

"...Your uncle, Wenruo, pleaded clemency for Hua Tuo, but I ignored the pleas and put the man to death," Cao Cao replied. "I have had time to think, and I genuinely believe now that Hua was able to cure me but withheld that permanent treatment as part of a cynical attempt to gain favour and rank through a combination of essential pain relief and feigned reticence... no, he would never have cured me. But... had I spared him... he might have saved my son. That I must live with."

The officials were silent.

"...But that is my problem, gentlemen, not yours or the Empire's," Cao Cao continued. "Liu Biao, Zhang Lu, Han Sui and Ma Chao, Sun Quan... they are the remaining tumours that must be purged for the patient to recover, and it is only sharp cutting implements that can do the job, for no medicine exists and poking at them with the needles of diplomacy has only offered temporary peace. I am, however, prepared to try that diplomacy one last time... with the first and last of those that I mentioned. If Liu Biao will relinquish the rebel Liu Bei and submit his seal of office to me, then I will be lenient; if Sun Quan will accept Inspector Liu Fu's authority, yield control of his personal army and allow the government to select the administrators in Yang, then I will allow him to be Administrator of Kuaiji or Wu – his choice – and forget his past errors. I can be no fairer than that."

"And if we receive no helpful responses...?" Hua Xin asked.

"...Then I will wage war upon them, and any that perish must only blame themselves," Cao Cao replied. "I have been patient enough: there will be no more rebels at the end of this year. The chaos ends *now*."

****

112

Weeks passed in which careful preparations for a campaign against Jing Province continued; Liu Biao rejected the call to submit, which led many to expect that a costly armed confrontation was imminent. But then, one day, a surprising piece of news reached Cao Cao's home in Yè City.

"**Chancellor!**" the adviser Hua Xin cried as he ran into Cao Cao's audience hall and halted sharply.

"...Is there some great problem...?" Cao Cao asked flippantly.

"Sun Quan... has attacked Jiangxia!" Hua Xin explained through exhausted panting. "He... his forces... they apparently exceed... *forty-thousand*!"

"*Ayah*... that's surely impossible!" Yuan Huan exclaimed.

"...Sneaky," Cao Cao said with a frown. "I knew he'd been preparing something, but I did not expect him to be ready so *quickly*. He must have his own Guo Jia."

"Some say... he has *two*," Hua Xin replied.

"And who are these men...?" Cao Cao asked.

"Zhou Yu, styled 'Gongjin', son of former Luoyang Magistrate Zhou Yi and Lü Fan, styled 'Ziheng'," Hua Xin replied.

"Hmm... the same men that aided Sun Ce," Cao Cao recalled. "Such continuity goes against my hope that Sun Quan's support was diminished, as does the news that he can muster an army of forty thousand and deploy it so secretly. That second point also makes me question the loyalty of my 'contacts' in Jiangdong..."

"What do we do?" Yuan Huan asked. "Should we intervene?"

"...No time, not if the armies are that large," Cao Cao replied. "No, that's an *invasion force* that Sun Quan has assembled: Huang Zu is surely doomed... and then Jiangxia will be annexed into Jiangdong, which is not to my liking at all."

"We'll monitor things," Xun Gongda promised.

"Yuan Huan, Liu Yè, Hua Xin and Wang Lang are best placed to do that," Cao Cao suggested. "They are all of them veterans of the 'Jiangdong political situation', after all. Oh, and we'll also need to see how this – and the outcome – affect our dear friend Liu Biao, will we not! I imagine the loss of Huang Zu will be damaging to the old relic... fatal, even... which is just what we wanted."

"It is imperative that we monitor this," Sima Yi insisted. "If Liu Biao does die, then the subsequent succession crisis will weaken the north of Jing and make it prone to invasion as well by Sun Quan or by others."

"...And by 'others', I presume you mean Liu Zhang and Zhang Lu," Cao Cao prompted.

"Either man might want to extend their eastern border," Sima Yi replied. "We must be prepared to accept that it is within their ability and ambition."

"And we should not forget the four so-called 'semi-autonomous prefectures' to the south of Jiangling and the west of Jiangxia," Jia Xu said. "Their loyalty to Liu Biao is based on fear of Huang Zu and a need for unity against the various ethnic tribes, Sun Quan and the Nanman: if Liu Biao and Huang Zu both die, they will also become prone to invasion and will be on Sun Quan's list as a priority. Since the westernmost of them, Wuling and Lingling, are bordering Yi to an extent, that'll start Liu Zhang whining or, as Zhongda said, plotting to seize the prefectures for himself."

"...My, this is going to be a mess, isn't it...?" Cao Cao replied. "I'm guessing that you're all trying to tell me that I have to attack Northern Jing before Sun Quan can advance too far or 'others' can get silly ideas."

"Even if he retreats, Excellency, you must attack Northern Jing and attack it quickly: *now*, if at all possible," Jia Xu said. "The ox has been fatally wounded: it will struggle to keep going, but it is surrounded by wolves and carrion birds that will poke it to death and then divide it between them. Do it a service and ensure that it becomes a meal for His Majesty and not some lesser creature."

"...Fine, then: Sun Quan has forced my hand," Cao Cao declared. "I will travel to Xuchang and denounce that boy's envoy in court while the rest of you prepare to advance on Xiangyang. Oh, and make sure that Liu Zhang and Zhang Lu don't get any ideas as well: polite warnings will do. Chen Lin...?"

The scribe Chen Lin bowed and said, "I shall begin writing at once, Chancellor Cao."

Huang Zu's defence of Jiangxia was faltering and recovering, which led to some confusing reports making their way to Jing Province Governor Liu Biao's northern capital, Xiangyang: word of Cao Cao's preparations for war were coming in from the east as well, which only made Biao feel worse.

"I... am truly isolated now," Liu Biao said to his generally unsympathetic court. "Huang Zu... is my southern sword and shield... and now it looks like Sun Quan might soon hold Jiangxia's seal in one hand and Huang's head in the other!"

Liu Biao's younger son, Liu Cong, had been told to attend court by his stepmother, Lady Cai, and her brother Cai Mao: he smiled encouragingly and said, "Calm down Father; Huang Zu may still defeat that villain Sun Quan."

"That's... highly unlikely," Liu Biao replied. "His hidden ships will supposedly surprise Sun Quan, so this last report says, but Sun's army is... ... ...we'd need to send everything we have to Jiangxia to repel him, and thanks to Cao Cao we cannot do that! I must face the truth... and accept... that Jiangxia will... fall."

"This is the moment when we must submit to the Han court," the adviser Wang Can suggested.

"*Never*," Liu Biao retorted. "Submit to the 'Crafty Villain'...? Tell it to the donkeys, Wang Can."

"What choice will we have...?" the politician Fu Xun asked.

"We can *fight*!" Liu Biao replied. "We can resist these villains!"

"Sun Quan is, without doubt, a villain, but Chancellor Cao is a hero of the age," the politician Hè Qia said. "He has subjugated the tribes, pacified the-"

"I have heard it all before, gentlemen," Liu Biao scoffed.

"Then please, Governor, heed it," Huan Jie said. "We still have a chance to get amnesty, seek peaceful-"

"Do we...?" Liu Biao asked. "Or... do *you*...?"

Huan Jie exhaled irritably.

"All of you... yes, you'll be rewarded for talking me into surrendering, but what will become of Xuande and me...?" Liu Biao asked angrily.

"*Aiee*... why should you care what happens to Liu Bei?" Kuai Yue replied. "He's mainly why we are in this mess, to be quite frank! If we had not sheltered him after he was defeated in Runan – him and his *Yellow Turban allies* – Chancellor Cao might have forgiven our earlier-"

"'Forgiven'???" Liu Biao exclaimed. "You-! ...You...!"

Liu Biao was overcome by a coughing fit: his brother-in-law, Admiral Cai Mao, moved toward him and said, "You should rest."

"You... should be... elsewhere...!" Liu Biao spluttered. "Who guards... the rivers...?"

"Zhang Yun and Wen Ping are guarding against threats from the north and east," Cai Mao promised. "I am here to decide whether we should be sending a relief force to Jiangxia... which is possible. Huang Zu might yet be saved. But *you* must *rest*, my lord... leave this to *us*."

"...Fine," Liu Biao wheezed. "You... yes... fine."

"Guards: escort our lord to his bed," Cai Mao ordered.

"I will accompany you, Father," Liu Cong said.

"You're... a good lad," Liu Biao replied. "You-"

Liu Biao suddenly stumbled; many of the courtiers gasped and called out, but Liu Biao slowly regained his footing, gestured weakly but dismissively and continued his slow, shuffling retreat.

"...He's done," Fu Xun murmured.

"...I think so," Wang Can replied.

Once Liu Biao and Liu Cong were gone, Huan Jie sighed angrily and said, "Cao Cao is coming here with an army of ridiculous size: we know that!"

"...Yes," Cai Mao replied calmly.

"So how can you be planning to take an army to relieve Jiangxia?" Huan Jie asked.

"...I'm not," Cai Mao said with a smile.

"We must be ready to defend Xiangyang and Jiangling against the Sun clan," Kuai Yue explained. "We must also try to negotiate with Cao Cao... and keep Liu Bei out of it all at the same time."

"Where is Liu Qi?" Fu Xun asked.

"Stationed in Fan City at the moment, but supposedly on his way to Jiangxia, as he supposedly has been for weeks and is still here procrastinating," Wang Can replied. "Someone has to be seen to respond to the occupation of Jiangxia, should it happen, or assist in holding it otherwise... and we must be seen to be sure of who we want in charge."

"The lord's not likely to be returning to this court," Kuai Yue suggested. "We must be decisive on his behalf, gentlemen."

"...Yes, we should," Cai Mao replied. "And after this meeting... we must talk."

Cai Mao, Kuai Yue, Wang Can, Huan Jie and Fu Xun met in Cai's private office once the main meeting was adjourned.

"Why did you wish to speak with us, Admiral...?" Kuai Yue asked.

"...We must be decisive on our lord's behalf in all matters," Cai Mao said. "His vitals are fading... and he will not last much longer if he gets any more bad news. Yes, we may see some recovery if Huang Zu survives, but that simply isn't going to happen in my opinion. In fact, I suspect that the next communication that we receive will be to tell us that Sun Quan has taken Jiangxia."

"...I agree," Kuai Yue admitted.

"And at that point, Governor Liu will be killed by shock," Cai Mao suggested. "We then face the prospect of Governor *Liu Qi*, a sad, sickly fellow that is all too easily manipulated by the likes of Liu Bei and Zhuge Liang. In other words, we'll have Governor Liu *Bei* in next to no time, or Bei controlling Qi from the shadows."

"...That won't do," Wang Can said. "I'd sooner surrender to Cao Cao than endure the province being taken over by Liu Bei. We must make sure that Liu Qi is not selected as the heir."

"We must take a calculated risk," Cai Mao suggested. "This, gentlemen, is my proposal: my sister has been ensuring that Liu Cong – who, as you saw, is agreeable and free from the afflictions that devour his elder brother – has his father's approval. She has spoken well of him and had him attend court, impressing Lord Liu with his superior countenance and understanding of court etiquette. Governor Liu was resistant at first, but as his resolve has weakened, so has his heart softened to the idea of ignoring the often-incorrect principle of primogeniture and supporting the worthy son over a sickly, stupid son that he now openly admits to be a disappointment and embarrassment to him."

"...You want to announce that Lord Liu has appointed Liu Cong as his heir," Kuai Yue supposed.

"Exactly that," Cai Mao confirmed. "Liu Qi will come here demanding an audience with his father, but we must be resolute and insist that he instead travel to Jiangxia. We need a decree with a seal stamp on it that he cannot refuse or ignore."

"...Leave that to me," Wang Can said. "I will draft the required document personally, and the stamp can be requisitioned by Mister Kuai."

"Lord Liu pretty much leaves me with the thing nowadays, so there's nothing to procure," Kuai Yue revealed. "We can have the order to leave and the succession announcement ready tonight."

Liu Qi would hear that his brother Liu Cong had been appointed as his father's heir to the governorship at the same time that he was given a formal decree commanding him to lead an army to the Jiangxia border: when his protests ended without success, he consulted with Liu Bei and Zhuge Liang, who suggested that he go southward and await opportunities to reverse his situation. Liu Qi retreated, and the Cais took control of the court while the oblivious Liu Biao neared his end.

****

113

The official Kong Rong continued to stage his popular banquets after the death of Hua Tuo and revelled in making as many critical comments of Chancellor Cao Cao as he could; the majority of his guests found his fearless verbal assaults discomforting but did little to stop him. Kong Rong held one last banquet before Cao Cao was due to return to Xuchang and announce his plans to attack Liu Biao: the attendance was as high as ever but nerves were strained.

"I am glad to see the Empress's father, Fu Wan, has chosen to attend," Kong Rong said. "I am only sorry that we cannot discuss the great peace of mind and faith in the future that we enjoy: we might as well discuss the imps that live in water wells."

"Please do not go on as much as you usually do, Wenju, it isn't good to do so," Zhi Xi whined.

"Why should I be silent?" Kong Rong retorted. "That madman has hired Sima Yi now!"

"Who is my *son*, Wenju, so please be mindful," Sima Fang warned. "Also note that I respect the Chancellor of State greatly and always have done."

"Sima Yi lied to everyone, including you, about his health so that he could avoid service," Kong Rong retorted. "And while I do not blame him for it and think that his desire to avoid serving Cao Cao is a credit to him, I am baffled once again by the inconsistency displayed by Cao! Hua Tuo was killed because he feigned the severity of his wife's illness, so we're told... why, then, is such dishonest behaviour acceptable from Sima Yi, who – and I mean no offence when I say this – would not be as much of a loss to the world as Hua Tuo now is."

"That's my brother you speak of," Sima Lang said.

"...But his argument is valid," Yang Biao admitted. "While I still question Hua Tuo's purported brilliance, he was still very clever and committed no worse a crime than Sima Yi."

"And now, gentlemen, Cao comes here to tell us that the last bastion of intellectual freedom, Northern Jing Province, will soon be as Xu Province was fifteen years ago," Kong Rong suggested. "Liu Biao is the new Tao Qian, and–!"

"You're being entirely unfair now!" Xun Wenruo snapped. "I have remained silent and listened, Wenju, but you go too far! How many tens of thousands of innocent villagers were killed when Chancellor Cao liberated Ji, Bing, Qing and Yòu...? He didn't even massacre the Wuhuan, and the wretches deserved it!"

"Cao Cao needed the people of those four provinces to believe that he was their saviour, Wenruo, else he could not have his new headquarters at Yè," Kong Rong retorted. "That duchy in all but name that he now has in Wei Prefecture is far removed from Xuchang so he can do as he pleases, living the life that he stole from his old friend Yuan Shao, right down to the chairs and cushions that he sits on!"

Some of the guests mumbled anxiously.

"...You misunderstand!" Xun Wenruo protested.

"Do I...?" Kong Rong chuckled.

"Cao Cao has appointed two leaders of the Mount Tai Bandits as the governors of Xu and Qing," the official Geng Ji said. "I don't care what Zang Ba and Sun Guan have supposedly done for the state: you don't give power like that to criminals! Even Cao's sons being given the provinces would have been better than that!"

"And repeat the casual nepotism employed by Yuan Shao...?" Xun Wenruo retorted. "You all decried him at the time as a man with too much ambition!"

"And Chancellor Cao employs *tuntian* – an idea that I proposed to many, but only Chancellor Cao would listen – to feed the nation and its army; he's also making worthy statesmen and soldiers out of bandits and heretics," the official Zao Zhi noted. "Zang Ba and Sun Guan are rehabilitated, like the former White Wave Bandit Xu Huang, Lü Bu's former lieutenant Zhang Liao and the former rebel fortress defender Xu Chu."

"That's right," the official Xue Ti said. "Yes, Xu Province was 'problematic', but here in Yan, things are considerably better since the days of Liu Dai. And as a veteran of Lü Bu's invasion of this province, I can tell you that Chancellor Cao is a more remarkable man than some give credit. You're especially quick to point out the bad, Wenju, and too slow to note the good."

"Half of what Cao does makes perfect sense, and the other half makes no sense at all," Kong Rong suggested. "That is either a symptom of madness or a symptom of trying to offset each bad act with a good one: and if it is the latter, then does he really think he can fool the all-seeing Heavens with such antics...?"

"I shall excuse myself now," Fu Wan said suddenly. "Good evening, gentlemen."

"Yes, and I must go as well," the official Mao Jie said. "A good evening to all."

"...Good evening," Kong Rong replied courteously.

Fu Wan, Mao Jie and a number of the other guests exchanged bows and left the banquet; Xun Wenruo then turned to Kong Rong and said, "You are saying dangerous things, Wenju, and Mister Fu Wan is frightened."

"Fu Wan is the father of the Empress," Kong Rong retorted. "Why should he be frightened...?"

Xun Wenruo's eyes wandered; more guests – including Zao Zhi and Xue Ti – suddenly decided to leave and did so as quickly as they could.

"I don't know when you'll understand... when it's too late, probably," Kong Rong continued. "Your master assured us that his new power would be used wisely: we all hoped that he meant 'all of the time', but perhaps we should have secured that additional assurance beforehand."

"...His Excellency Cao Cao is a wise and benevolent lord," Xun Wenruo protested. "His actions have reason behind them that is sometimes hard to see, but-!"

"Nothing can justify Hua Tuo's fate," Kong Rong insisted. "I haven't forgotten about Mi Heng either, Wenruo: you don't send an outspoken and honest man like that to a thug like Huang Zu."

"...It was Liu Biao that sent Mi Heng to Huang Zu, not the Chancellor," Xun Wenruo replied. "And as for your criticism of the Chancellor's attack on Jing, it is because Huang Zu is currently being attacked by Sun Quan and Jing's stability is threatened! His Excellency is seizing Jing to protect it from the Suns, who will surely do something terrible to Jing, like-!"

"Like Cao Cao did to Xu Province, perhaps," Kong Rong heckled. "So His Excellency Cao Cao sees a like mind in Sun Quan and acts first... how *thoughtful*."

Xun Wenruo's eyes wandered yet again.

"I'm going now, Wenju," Yang Biao declared. "I might have left with the Simas, but I wanted to hear your reasoning, and I must say that I'm disappointed. If Southern Jing fell to Sun Quan and the north became destabilised, then Sun – or worse yet, that heretic *Zhang Lu* – might seize the region and reignite the flames of chaos. What else can Chancellor Cao do but take Jing before others can...?"

"...Agreed," Xun Wenruo decided. "I must remember that some things are unfortunately *necessary*, Wenju... and so should you."

"Not that," Kong Rong insisted. "Not harming Jing. There *has* to be another way."

"If there is another way, Wenju, then find the wisdom of your ancestor, Confucius, and provide the way," Yang Biao said. "If you cannot – much as none of Chancellor Cao's many brilliant advisers have not – then please accept what we must all accept and stop your troublemaking before it leads to you being harmed."

"...I will still challenge him!" Kong Rong insisted as Yang Biao exchanged respectful bows with the few remaining guests and left the house. "No man can be without critics! And powerful men must have them more than any!"

"He understands that," Xun Wenruo said. "But there is a difference between criticism and slander... and between challenging and opposing. You too often cross the lines, Wenju, and that... that will harm you."

"If needs be, Wenruo," Kong Rong retorted. "But no matter how many lashes and cuts and amputations that a tyrant inflicts on a man that is right, the man is still right... they just make the tyrant more wrong."

"...I'll listen no more," Xun Wenruo said. "Good evening, all."

Xun Wenruo was accompanied by more guests as he departed: that left Zhi Xi, Geng Ji, Wei Huang and three members of Geng Ji's staff.

"...You're right about everything, Wenju," Wei Huang said. "But please do not challenge Cao Cao publicly: he's better challenged in other ways."

"I disagree," Kong Rong replied. "He's a wicked old schemer that relies on being able to operate in the shadows: he used Huang Zu to kill Mi Heng, a legal technicality to kill Hua Tuo, the privacy of royal corridors to kill Consort Dong and division to kill the Yuans and the Wuhuan kings. He can't resort to 'Hongmen' in front of the Son of Heaven: the court is where I am safest."

"...But be measured if you absolutely must challenge him," Zhi Xi pleaded. "Your life is as precious as all the others that he's taken!"

Kong Rong turned and looked at his two children, who had decided to come and see why the noise of the banquet had subsided: he dismissed them with a wave of his hand and said, "I *have* to speak out... *somebody has to*."

The bedridden Governor of Jing Province, Liu Biao, glared at the reports from Jiangxia and wheezed uncomfortably. Sun Quan was last reported as having taken the entirety of southern Jiangxia with no difficulty: the security was compromised with the aid of a pirate-turned-mercenary called Gan Ning that Huang Zu had wrongly disrespected. Huang Zu had retreated toward Jiangxia's capital, which was now under threat as well: Liu Biao knew that the consequences of losing both the city and its guardian would be far-reaching and catastrophic.

"...This... is... a *disaster*!" Liu Biao said miserably.

"Remember that Huang Zu has a new fleet of warships that the Suns' intelligence source is almost certainly unaware of," the adviser Wang Can suggested. "This can end in more than one way... in can end with a great victory for us."

"...It better had," Liu Biao croaked. "I... I *cannot lose Huang Zu*...!"

"Try and remain optimistic, Governor," Wang Can pleaded. "You can then recover and reassume control."

"...My son... does well...?" Liu Biao asked.

"Your son... is doing fine," Wang Can replied.

"That's... good," Liu Biao said. "That... at least... is good."

Wang Can looked at Liu Biao's physician, whose expression betrayed a belief that Biao was probably unlikely to recover whether Huang Zu survived or not: Wang was quietly glad, since that eliminated a number of complicated scenarios and paved the way for a peaceful transition of power in the weeks to come.

****

114

Emperor Xian presided over a meeting of his court that was obviously intended as the platform for a grand announcement; Chancellor of State Cao Cao waited until the audience was slightly apprehensive before he finally broke the silence.

"As most of you will or should know, the self-appointed 'Lord of Jiangdong', Sun Quan, has launched an attack on the Jiangxia region of southern Jing Province," Cao Cao began. "As quite a few will already know, I intended to stage a campaign against 'Governor' Liu Biao anyway, but this latest development has advanced my schedule somewhat."

"Do you have the right to be planning a campaign without first seeking approval from the Son of Heaven in this court...?" Kong Rong asked. "It is, after all, His Majesty's army... not yours."

Cao Cao smiled coldly and replied, "I can plan things without seeking approval for their action, Mister Kong; surely I must plan campaigns well enough to know if they are worth embarking upon before I waste the court's time by proposing them...?"

Kong Rong harrumphed quietly.

"Now, as I was saying... my plan was always to seek a peaceful submission from Liu Biao and resort to violence only if it was absolutely necessary," Cao Cao insisted. "Sun Quan's unexpected... 'manoeuvrings', shall we say... have made peaceful solutions far less likely now, sad to say."

"...You seem to be accusing my lord Sun Quan of taking illegal action against Liu Biao, who is, a-as you yourself have said, Chancellor Cao, a rebel and enemy of the state, while my lord Sun Quan is the son of a great hero and a friend of the Empire with... with family ties to your own clan," the Jiangdong envoy said nervously. "The feud between the Sun family and Liu Biao's criminal band is well documented, and the matter has not been-"

"You should not be trying to justify what your lord has done," Cao Cao interrupted. "Yes, I have ties to the Sun clan by marriage: my son is wed to a cousin of your lord, and my niece, now a widow, was married to a brother of your lord. But I cannot be seen to allow anyone – even relations by birth or marriage – to flout the law of the land and attack neighbouring provinces without proper cause or authorisation."

"Our lord acts in self-defence!" the envoy protested.

"...*Self-defence*...?" Wang Lang chortled. "Will the Suns never tire of blaming others for their violence...?"

"You are being unfair, sir," the envoy retorted.

"No I'm not," Wang Lang said. "I think that you know who I am: I was the appointed Administrator of Kuaiji Prefecture, but I was chased away by your lord's brother so that he could start building his little empire in the south."

"The Jiangdong envoy briefly studied Emperor Xian's face before he replied, "It is not an empire! You dare accuse my lord of being a hegemon???"

"When was he appointed as Governor of Yang Province...?" Hua Xin asked. "Do you know who Liu Fu is...?"

"...I know who *you* are, sir," the envoy scoffed. "You can spare me your self-serving view of-"

"No, I'll say my piece," Hua Xin insisted. "I was the appointed Administrator of Yuzhang Prefecture; I was forced to retire from the role because your lord disapproved of my dislike of his obvious intent to seize all of the south!"

"My lord is being misrepresented!" the envoy protested. "I beseech Your Majesty to seek some other opinions and better understand the matters that govern-!"

"You dare to suggest that the court is somehow unfairly biased...?" Cao Cao asked.

"...This matter is more complicated than the version being presented," the envoy replied. "I worry that some unfair judgement will be passed."

"If you came to this court to find fair judgement, you were mistaken in your thinking," Kong Rong suggested. "Chancellor Cao Cao – after appointing himself as such in the wake of his lucky victory over the Wuhuan – has a reputation for-"

"**HOLD YOUR TONGUE!**" Hua Xin bellowed.

"**I will *not*!**" Kong Rong retorted. "**I will speak, as is my right!** ...Or is the Chancellor now completely unaccountable to this court and His Majesty...?"

Cao Cao's eyes steeled; Xun Wenruo contemplated interrupting Kong Rong but something prevented him from doing so.

"...The Chancellor of State has a long-standing reputation for distorting facts, invading lands for dubious reasons and inflicting disproportionate punishment upon men for unproven offences, and that has never been truer than it is here and now," Kong Rong continued. "That being the case, why should Sun Quan expect any different?"

The court was painfully silent; even Zhi Xi started to shrink away from Kong Rong, who was glaring at Cao Cao fearlessly and awaiting a response.

"...I have tolerated you, Kong Rong, because you are a descendant of the great philosopher Confucius and highly respected in your own right, though Heaven-only-knows why," Cao Cao said calmly. "But when you come to this court and have the temerity to slander and heckle the Chancellor of State – His Majesty's most senior appointed minister and, therefore, an extension of His Majesty's authority – in front of the envoy of a foreign state, you force my hand."

"A *foreign state*...?" Kong Rong chuckled. "*Jiangdong*...?"

"A *rogue* or a *rival* state, then," Cao Cao retorted. "The crime that you've committed is the same."

"No, Excellency," Xun Wenruo whispered.

"Alas, Majesty and esteemed colleagues, I am unable to act in any other way," Cao Cao continued. "**GUARDS!**"

"Are you mad...?" Kong Rong chortled disbelievingly. "You... y-you cannot do this! **Will no one speak out???**"

Xun Wenruo, Wang Lang, Geng Ji and Zhi Xi hung their heads or averted their eyes with everyone else and did nothing to defend Kong Rong, who was now being led from the court by two of the eunuch palace guards.

"**Speak out, gentlemen, for the state's sake if not mine!**" Kong Rong protested.

"...*Forgive me*, Wenju," Zhi Xi bleated.

Cao Cao waited until Kong Rong had been removed before he

turned to the unsettled Jiangdong envoy and said, "Your lord has gone too far, and it is sadly too late to prevent the inevitable now. Either Jiangxia or Jiangdong will fall – most likely Jiangxia – and that will be that. If Huang Zu prevails, then your lord's clan will be faced with an invasion by the Jing army that I will put a stop to because – and only because – that will be against the rule of law. If Sun Quan prevails, then he has a choice: he can enjoy smiting his father's murderer, relinquish Jiangxia and everything else to His Majesty and await a more fitting appointment, or he can defy this court... and believe me, that would not be wise."

The envoy's eyes wandered.

"This attack alone has made your lord a foreign power, a rival and a rebel and an enemy, which saddens me," Cao Cao continued. "I suggest that you and your delegation return to Jiangdong at once and convey the court's dissatisfaction: normal relations will resume when your lord sees sense."

The envoy retreated from the hall with his aides.

"...I am genuinely sorry that it has come to this, Your Majesty," Cao Cao said as he turned to the mortified sovereign. "But Liu Biao and Sun Quan cannot do better than the mighty Yuans and the Wuhuan Confederacy, so peace is still within reach."

Emperor Xian nodded slowly and said, "It... can be."

"Excellency... what will you do with Kong Rong...?" Xun Wenruo asked meekly.

"What else can I do...?" Cao Cao replied. "It is a grave offence to abuse state ministers in front of enemy envoys, because it gives an impression of weakness or disunity that could affect the outcome of negotiations. Kong Rong's words might have been the difference between peace and war... and now he – and his clan – must answer for it as the law dictates."

Wang Lang sighed quietly; Zhi Xi and Xun Gongda closed their eyes tightly and covered their faces; Xun Wenruo fought tears.

"...*Death*, to the third degree," Cao Cao declared. "And that is an end to it."

The majority of Kong Rong's friends – and he still had many – stifled sobs at the announcement; Wang Lang shook his head but was otherwise visibly unmoved.

"I should like to continue my announcement now," Cao Cao said. "Hopefully, there will be no more interruptions..."

There were not.

"...*Excellency*...! *Clemency, please*, Excellency...!" Xun Wenruo said as he followed Cao Cao's retreat from the imperial audience hall.

"That annoying little man has made his last mistake," Cao Cao replied. "And none can say that I trapped him, framed him, slandered or provoked him: he interrupted a discussion about a genuine national emergency to take sides with a rebel against me and condemned himself by doing so."

"You have never liked him, and he is partly to blame for that if not wholly, but please, Excellency, he is one of the last links to the great philosopher!" Xun Wenruo retorted. "Is he not worth preserving for that reason?"

"...I agree," Attendant Officer Cui Yan said. "Each case must be assessed individually. Kong Rong is known for being outspoken and tactless, but it is Your Excellency's desire to be challenged, and that was what he was doing."

"The 'tactless' part is the problem," Cao Cao retorted. "He knew the penalty for doing what he did: how dare he think that he was above the law while simultaneously accusing me of assuming the same of myself...?"

"...At least spare his family, Excellency!" Xun Wenruo pleaded. "Wang Jingxing, he is your friend as he is mine: why do you not say something in his defence...?"

"I cannot defend his actions, Wenruo," Wang Lang replied. "Yes, I am his friend, but I would be no friend if I allowed him to live dishonourably as a prisoner, which is the best that he could expect for his crime. As for his family... yes, I do agree that exterminating his clan is unfortunate, but it is the appropriate sentence and should not be commuted because he is in some way special. The law should apply properly to all of the people."

"*Ayah*... what a mess!" Xun Wenruo cried. "I am truly pained! I want to intervene, Heaven forgive me, but I cannot!"

"Destroying former friends or being a helpless witness to their death both hurt the soul, Wenruo, and I should know, for I have endured those situations many times," Cao Cao replied. "But the law must always take precedence... which is, I believe, what Kong Rong himself was trying to say. How fitting, then, that he should make himself such a fitting example."

Kong Rong's household were given no warning of what awaited them: soldiers stormed the house within an hour of Kong's arrest, killing his wife and any servants that resisted or tried to protect Kong's children, who were playing a game of *weiqi* – a form of chess – on a low table in the garden.

"**You must flee!**" a blood-spattered servant said. "**They will kill us all!**"

The elder of the two children – an 8-year-old boy – smiled and asked, "When the nest falls, won't the eggs be broken...?"

The stunned servant did not get the chance to answer the unexpected retort; he was cut down moments later by a soldier that then turned his blade on the children.

Kong Rong pleaded for his family until his final moments, although they had already been slaughtered; the officials had been too scared to warn the household or make further pleas for clemency. The 55-year-old descendant of Confucius – who would be posthumously named as a member of the so-called 'Seven Scholars of Jian'an' by Cao Pi – was beheaded unceremoniously in the prison and then left on public display in Xuchang's main square; a small notice informed the residents of his crime – a form of high treason – and implicitly warned of severe penalties for any who collected the body or showed remorse.

"This is not right," Wei Huang said as he and Geng Ji observed Kong Rong's corpse from a distance. "He deserved better than this... a great statesman, magnificent poet and skilled orator... rotting in the street like a common criminal. Isn't this humiliating spectacle the same fate that Wang Yun inflicted on Dong Zhuo, and isn't that as wrong as it can be...?"

"...Yes... Kong Rong is being treated just as Dong Zhuo was," Geng Ji replied miserably. "...And here comes his Cai Yong."

Zhi Xi could no longer contain his grief and shame: he slowly shuffled toward his friend's body until he was close enough to touch it and shuddered uncontrollably.

"*Ayah*... what is he doing???" Wei Huang exclaimed.

"We can do nothing," Geng Ji said. "We didn't help Kong Rong, and he was the greater loss; will we now forfeit later opportunities to do something meaningful by trying to save Zhi Xi...? Will we add our own names to the list of failed 'conspirators' of times past, like Dou Wu and Chen Fan, and Hè Jin and Yuan Shao, and Dong Cheng, Zhong Ji and Wang Fu, by acting without proper preparation to save one emotional fool...?"

"...No," Wei Huang decided. "Heaven forgive me, but... no."

Zhi Xi fell over Kong Rong's body and wailed uncontrollably, saying, "**Wenju! Wenju, my friend! Now you are gone from this world, who can I talk to that understands me...?**"

Wang Lang was watching Zhi Xi's lament from his own distant viewing point; he shook his head, turned and walked away as two soldiers finally dragged Zhi Xi toward the prison.

Cao Cao learned of Zhi Xi's defiant mourning and said, "We'll let him go."

"What about 'adherence to the law of the land', Excellency...?" Xun Wenruo asked pointedly.

"...I almost detect some bitterness in your tone, Wenruo," Cao Cao replied. "It's understandable, but I hope that it does not evolve into the same meaningless heckling that cost 'Wenju' his life."

"I am not that foolish," Xun Wenruo said. "I... I do understand why Kong Rong had to be punished as he was."

"Zhi Xi is alone in his actions and therefore an irrelevance," Cao Cao continued. "Nobody went to the prison to plead for Zhi's life: despair will probably claim him in the coming days. Any that follow his example will treated differently, of course."

"...Of course," Xun Wenruo murmured.

"Now we must return to genuinely important matters," Cao Cao said. "Liu Biao must be ousted and a stable, Han-appointed government established in Northern Jing that can deal with Liu Bei within and Sun Quan without. There will be no more dallying: the announcement is made, so the army must be ready to march in no more than six days. Miaocai is coming here to take part in this campaign personally now that the 'Qing Militias' and their leaders are installed in Qing and Xu; perhaps we will procure him a wife from Bei's men as revenge..."

"...Yes, Your Excellency," Xun Wenruo replied.

"That, Wenruo, is one thing that I can guarantee," Cao Cao growled. "Liu Bei... will be *harmed*."

∗∗∗∗∗∗∗∗∗∗∗∗

115

Days passed: once the Han army was finally ready to depart from Xuchang, Cao Cao had the officers gather in a training ground so that he could address them. This was one of the largest collections of senior officers that Cao Cao had been able to assemble for a single campaign: Cao Pi, Cao Chun, Cao Xiu, Cao Hong, Cao Ren, Cao Zhen, Xiahou Yuan, Xiahou Dun, Yu Jin, Xu Huang, Yue Jin, Zhang Liao, Li Dian, Zhu Ling and Zhang Hè would be the leading generals while many veterans of earlier campaigns would serve as colonels, majors and the like.

"This will be the penultimate phase of our grand mission!" Cao Cao said. **"Liu Biao has long been a thorn in the side of the Empire; like Liu Yan of Yi in times past, Liu Biao hankers for the throne and has often attempted to seize it while our backs were turned. Now he will finally answer for his wickedness!"**

The officers responded enthusiastically.

"And when we smite Liu Biao, we have the good fortune of eliminating another long-time enemy of the Empire; *Liu Bei,* **a hankerer among hankerers!"** Cao Cao continued. **"Long has he been a menace to stability, stealing the seals of magistrates, administrators and governors alike in his quest to wear the robes of a sovereign: that mat weaver from the frontier will soon know a blade across his neck, and then the Son of Heaven can sleep more soundly, knowing that a vile, rotten scion that once brought an army of heretics to the gates of this very city exists no longer!"**

"I want to be the man that kills Liu Bei!" Xiahou Dun barked.

"No, let me!" Cao Hong cried. **"I'll kill Liu Biao as well!"**

"Let every man have his chance to destroy those two villains!" Cao Cao replied. **"The rewards for victory will be many, for this will leave us with mongrels and rats for enemies! With the fall of Jing, there will be none that can stand in the way of our mission to restore peace!"**

"Glory to the Han!" Yue Jin bellowed.

The officers echoed Yue Jin's enthusiastic cry.

"...You've prepared the Son of Heaven's chariot carriage, Your Excellency," Jia Xu noted.

Xun Wenruo, Xun Gongda, Sima Yi, Registrar Liu Yè and others turned to look at the regal carriage – which was topped with a yellow parasol – as Cao Cao replied, "I have. I had hoped that the Son of Heaven might want to accompany the army on this less-dangerous campaign within the boundaries of the Empire and frighten our enemies into submitting –thereby ending the chaos even more quickly – but I'm afraid that there will be no such occurrence... so I will travel in it myself."

"*Ayah...* you can't do that!" Xun Wenruo protested. "The-!"

"It is a *carriage*, Wenruo, not a throne or a jade seal," Cao Cao scoffed. "And I act as His Majesty's appointed Chancellor of State in the field: wherever I am, His Majesty is there in spirit."

Xun Wenruo exhaled loudly.

"I do wish you'd stop seeing the worst in my actions," Cao Cao scolded. "Either challenge me, Wenruo, and demand that I cede this power that I have been given or allow me to use it to restore order in the Empire: stop whining and then doing and saying nothing of any substance!"

"I... have not lost faith in you, Excellency," Xun Wenruo replied.

"...Good," Cao Cao said. "Cheng Yu, Xun Yòu, Jia Xu: you will be my principal advisers on this campaign. Liu Yè: you are, as always, my trusted registrar and another source of wisdom and will be at my side at all times; Yang Xiu will shadow you. Attendant Officer Cui Yan: you are my liaison with Yè and yet another wise mind that I shall need when I am reorganising the administration in Jing. Bao Xun, Gao Rou: you will assist Cui Yan."

Cheng Yu, Xun Gongda, Jia Xu, Liu Yè, Yang Xiu, Cui Yan, Bao Xun and Gao Rou bowed humbly.

"Hua Xin, Yuan Huan, Wang Lang: you are entrusted with watching Sun Quan's movements and reporting to me via your fellow 'Jiangdong veteran', Liu Yè," Cao Cao continued. "Don't rule out the idea that he might see that I am advancing on Jing Province and try to reclaim Lujiang and Jiujiang, or even make an attempt to race to Xuchang. Assume nothing, expect anything."

Hua Xin, Yuan Huan and Wang Lang bowed humbly.

"Dong Zhao, Xue Ti, Sima Yi: watch Zhang Lu and the Qiang, keeping in touch with Chang'an Magistrate Zhong Yao, Inspectors Wei Kang and Zhang Zhi and Administrators Du Ji and Jia Kui at all times so that there are no surprises coming from Liang Province or the adjacent regions," Cao Cao ordered.

Dong Gongren, Xue Ti and Sima Yi bowed humbly.

"Xun Yu, Zao Zhi, Bao Xun, Mao Jie: you will guard the capital against what few threats remain able to harm it," Cao Cao concluded. "I need Cao Ren, but you can rely on those men that he has hand-picked to serve in his place. Liaise at all times with Li Fu and Xin Pi in Yè."

Xun Wenruo, Zao Zhi, Bao Xun and Mao Jie bowed humbly; Wenruo was noticeably rattled.

"...All is ready," Cao Cao said. "**LET US MARCH!**"

The Qiang warlord Ma Chao was avoiding travelling to the region around Chang'an until he knew that his actions would not be used as an excuse for Cao Cao to harm his family; his colleague Pang De approached him one day and asked, "Have you heard about the events in the south, my lord?"

"I have," Ma Chao replied. "The son of the 'Tiger of Jiangdong' has decided to be more like his father and brother instead of a cowardly mouse. He is a man that I could work with. And Cao Cao plans to attack Liu Biao... which will mean that he is bringing a large army westward that we must watch carefully. Jing Province is a 'central point' in their empire: Cao Cao can attack in any direction from Jing, and he will want to attack Hanzhong, Yi, Jiangdong or us next."

"You... don't intend to fight the Han army while this is going on, do you...?" Pang De asked.

"I want to, but no," Ma Chao replied. "I would be accused of condemning my father and other close family to early graves; I will watch. I will be vigilant and react to what happens as it happens... that's what Father would want."

Sun Quan's attack on Jiangxia Prefecture led to a decisive victory, seizing the region and claiming the life of Liu Biao's strongest ally, Administrator Huang Zu, a man that some suggested to be the real power in the province as a whole. The rulers of the four prefectures to the west of Jiangxia – Changsha Administrator Han Xuan, Wuling Administrator Jin Xuan, Lingling Administrator Liu Du and Guiyang Administrator Zhao Fan – reacted immediately by strengthening their defences and writing impassioned letters to their lord in his northern capital Xiangyang. The southern capital of Jing, Jiangling, was overwhelmed by refugees seeking escape from Jiangxia and Changsha: and, as expected, the news of Huang Zu's death caused an immediate decline in Liu Biao's already-failing health.

"...He's fading," Kuai Yue said to a selected group of trusted officials. "Lord Liu will probably be dead within days if not hours."

"It is a good thing, then, that we finalised the succession process," Wang Can replied. "Liu Cong can replace his father immediately. But we must consider how we will handle *Liu Bei*, gentlemen..."

"...He must not be allowed to get near the governor or Lord Liu Cong," Cai Mao said. "None of that bunch of troublemakers must be allowed to get near the inner capital: not Bei, not his adviser Zhuge Liang, not his lobbyists like Mi Zhu or Sun Qian, and definitely not his generals. If Zhang Fei, Guan Yu or Zhao Yun were to be ordered to fight, it would cost lives: that's why I have remained here and quietly prepared a defence force."

"...So what are we going to do?" the politician Fu Xun asked. "The wolves are everywhere: Cao Cao is on his way, Sun Quan is at the back door, Zhang Lu loiters at our west gate and Liu Bei is already in the house! And Lou Gui, annoying little man that he is, has left the capital and gone who-knows-where!"

Kuai Yue sighed miserably and said, "We needed him too."

"In such a situation, the only answer is to submit," Wang Can insisted. "Cao Cao is a benevolent man in the end; every suspicious or bad action can be met with a number of sound decisions and heroic actions. Governor Liu Biao regrets being called a rebel, and if not for Yuan Shao and Liu Bei's schemes dragging him into an abyss of intrigue he would be healthy and govern with the full trust of His Majesty."

"Indeed yes," the politician Hè Qia said. "Liu Bei and the Yuans are to blame for this: we must encourage Lord Liu Cong to change course and do the right thing."

Cai Mao looked at Huan Jie and asked, "What do you think...?"

"What do I think...? What do you think that I think?" Huan Jie retorted. "I was a vassal of the Suns: I have lived among them and seen what sort of men they are. They view me as the worst of traitors when their beloved patriarch would have been thrown in a ditch if not for me: I 'defected' to Governor Liu because I saw that the next generation of Suns were irrational, violent, ambitious and untrustworthy, and they have done nothing since that tells me otherwise. If we try to negotiate with the Suns, they'll demand land, blood and more land; a deal with Zhang Lu is out of the question, and we cannot rule out his attempting to seize Fangling; Liu Zhang, far from being an ally, is a spineless opportunist that may try to seize Yiling County or extend offers of collaboration to the Administrator of Wuling; the Qiang barbarians are, once again, out of the question. That leaves Chancellor Cao Cao, who is in no mood to bargain, so there can be no alliance, only submission."

"I concur," Kuai Yue said. "Our course is clear, gentlemen: we hope that Liu Qi and what's left of Huang Zu's forces can keep Sun Quan away from Jiangling long enough for us to convince Lord Liu Cong that surrendering the province to Chancellor Cao Cao is the only way forward, preferably without having to deal with Liu Bei, who will then be Cao Cao's problem."

"Leave Liu Bei to me," Cai Mao replied. "Talking my nephew into relinquishing his seal is going to require a more convincing man that I will ever be: whichever of you feels that they are up to the job, I leave it to them."

"Mister Wang Can," Han Song suggested.

"There is no one else," Fu Xun agreed.

"Only Wang Can could sway Lord Liu Cong," Hè Qia said.

"...You all say that, gentlemen, but did I sway Yuan Shang in any way...?" Wang Can replied. "This is a very similar situation in many ways: I am to ask a young man that is grieving the loss of his father to discard brotherly affection – just as Yuan Shang did – and become our lord. But at that point, my words will be intended to steer Lord Liu Cong toward yielding his estate, not defending it as we wanted with Yuan Shang: if I was unable to make a man do everything to protect what he has been bequeathed, how will I be any more successful when I ask Lord Liu to make his first act as holder of the seal of the Governor of Jing Province the tendering of that self-same governor's seal – and all of the military power, wealth, political influence and respect that goes with it – to Chancellor Cao...?"

"You have to be successful, Zhongxuan, because, like the Yuans, the actual power, wealth, influence and respect that he inherits are depleted and close to total exhaustion, and refusing to take this course will lead to another 'Siege of Yè' that Cao Cao will easily win," Kuai Yue said. "Resisting will be a pointless exercise in shedding blood: we must calm the populace, reassure them that there will be a peaceful transition of power and then make good on our promises. Lord Liu Cong must repel Sun Quan, rebuke Liu Bei and welcome Cao Cao: there is no other course, and there is no other man that can find the words as you do."

"You're doing well enough," Wang Can retorted.

"You are better at making such situations easier to live with," Kuai Yue insisted. "Don't refuse anymore, Zhongxuan: you are our chief negotiator with our own lord and with Chancellor Cao."

"...Alright," Wang Can conceded. "I will talk to Lord Liu Cong when the moment is right."

When Cao Cao reached Yingchuan's capital, he summoned the man that Xiahou Yuan had left in charge – an official named Zhao Yan – and said, "My men will rest briefly in a camp close to this city. How go things?"

"Production is up, Chancellor, and the local troops are in good spirits," Zhao Yan replied. "Zang Ba and Sun Guan maintain contact: the first supplies from Qing and Xu will start arriving shortly. Furthermore, I've kept in contact with Administrator Man Chong and together we've begun a pacification and training program for the captured bandits and former Yellow Turbans.

We're using them for construction, farming and low-level military roles – when deemed of good character, of course, to avoid the errors made when forming the Qing Corps. So far we're seeing recruits by the hundreds, and the damage done by Liu Bei, Gong Du, Liu Pi and the like is almost a thing of the past."

"...I'm impressed," Cao Cao said. "Miaocai was right to leave you in charge, but I could use an organised man like you on the campaign, since we're intending to rehabilitate and make use of a lot of Jing's army and navy, and maybe draft in some surrendered pirates. **Gao Rou!**"

The adviser Gao Rou stepped forward.

"Gao Rou: you are now Administrator of Yingchuan and a vital part of the artery that transports the lifeblood of my army – most of all grain – from Yan, Ji, Bing, Qing, Xu, Yu and Central Province," Cao Cao declared. "I have every faith in you."

Gao Rou bowed and said, "I will not disappoint you, Excellency."

"Zhao Yan, you will accompany me to Jing Province, and from there, to Jiangdong," Cao Cao ordered. "We'll make proper use of men and resources and leave everything a thousand times more efficient than we found it!"

Zhao Yan bowed humbly and said, "I hope that I am as capable as you are presuming, Chancellor: I will work tirelessly to meet the standards that are demanded of loyal servants of His Majesty."

"Very good," Cao Cao replied. "...I remember when I began my work in Yingchuan and neighbouring Chenliu. Dong Zhuo had just enjoyed an unbelievable 'victory' by being able to retreat from the burnt-out husk of Luoyang with all of its people, wealth and resources; Li Jue and Guo Si were attacking Central Province and the regions that we were defending, and the heroes of old, like Zhu Jun, were humiliated and their gifted lands sacked. Yellow Turbans had risen up again in Qing, and Governor Liu Dai and Bao Xin had gone to deal with it. It was... me, Yuanrang, Miaocai, Wenruo, and Meng- ...Zhang Miao."

"I was there too, Mengde," Cao Xiu said.

"...I know, cousin," Cao Cao chuckled. "You were a lad then."

"We were so frustrated," Xiahou Yuan recalled. "And then Liu Dai was killed, and we had to go and deal with the Yellow Turbans as well... and then Yuan Shao made you Governor of Yan."

"Yes... that was where it all started, in a way," Cao Cao said. "The rise to power... the start of the road that led to where I am now."

"Yeah, and now you're Chancellor, or 'Prime Minister', or whatever," Xiahou Dun replied. "All that suffering was worth it in the end, eh...?"

Cao Cao smiled and said, "Yes... for now I am able to do all of the things that I wanted to do then, and more... and already, I have done much... but there is much, much more to do. I will be remembered... forever."

Xun Gongda frowned at Cao Cao's choice of words and tone.

"...Enough of that!" Cao Cao chuckled. "Let's rest... and then on to Nan County!"

＊＊＊＊＊＊＊＊＊＊＊＊

116

Jing Province Governor Liu Biao's death was sudden but not surprising: he stopped breathing and ended his days at the age of 65. Biao's eldest son Liu Qi was on his way to the southern capital Jiangling at the time, so the role of leading the mourning – which would be restricted because of the current military situation – was given to Biao's young heir Liu Cong.

"I do not see why I cannot instruct the people to begin mourning!" Liu Cong complained as he chaired his first court session. "I am your governor now, at your own suggestion and per your preference: why do you all try to defy me?"

"We don't 'defy you', Governor," Wang Can insisted. "Liu Bei is nearby, demanding to see you and to pay respects."

"Then let him!" Liu Cong retorted. "What harm can he do?"

"Untold harm," Kuai Yue replied. "Has no one told you about his past behaviour...?"

"...I know of it, of course, because I have heard it from all of you," Liu Cong said. "But he stayed away as my father's health deteriorated so... so...!"

Liu Cong's composure failed momentarily.

"This is not fair, I know, but you must be strong, Lord Liu," Fu Xun said. "Cao Cao will soon attack, and Sun Quan could decide to hack his way past your brother and attack Jiangling at any moment. Liu Bei is no friend, so he must not be allowed to come into the courtroom and talk you into the same sort of mad nonsense that sent your father to the netherworld twenty years too early."

"...But... it is the *Suns* that drove Father to his death!" Liu Cong retorted. "O Heaven, why have you denied me the strength to avenge my father as Sun Quan does his...?"

"...Do you want to retire for now...?" Wang Can asked.

"I do, Mister Wang," Liu Cong replied. "I need to go to my father's study – which is now mine – and reflect. I... am concerned about making the wrong choices."

The officials turned and looked at Wang Can, who said, "I have some ideas if you will hear them, Governor."

"Follow me, then, Mister Wang, and we'll discuss your ideas privately," Liu Cong ordered.

"...Hopefully, he'll convince him immediately," Fu Xun said as he watched Liu Cong and Wang Can retreat from the hall.

"If anyone can, Zhongxuan can," Huan Jie replied.

Liu Cong waited until he and Wang Can were seated in his study before he asked, "What ideas do you have?"

"There can only be one choice made, and once made it is final," Wang Can replied. "You have three problems: the first – Sun Quan – is obvious enough."

"He is," Liu Cong sighed.

"There can be no reasoning with him," Wang Can continued. "He is less uncouth and violent than Sun Ce, but he is still lord of the pirates and a hankerer that wants Jing for his southern empire. We can and must oppose him, but our ability to do so is hampered by our second problem... Chancellor of State Cao Cao."

"Why does Chancellor Cao intend such harm...?" Liu Cong asked.

"You already know that, my lord," Wang Can replied. "Since the 'Dong Zhuo Crisis', your late father has been accused of inaction: he was then the closest to the Son of Heaven when the court fled Li Jue and Guo Si, and he was seen as not only doing nothing – again – but allowing Dong Zhuo's general Zhang Ji to shelter in Nan County, even though everybody knew that Zhang had seized the place with violence and the Suns' constant attacks made retrieving the place impossible until Zhang's nephew was too entrenched to remove. And then, of course, your late father not only sided with Yuan Shao when Dong Cheng's dubious 'Girdle Edict' appeared: he formed a coalition with Yuan and with the man that serves as your third problem... Liu Bei."

"...But Father was determined to believe that Liu Bei was a good man," Liu Cong protested. "Father called Bei 'Xuande' and argued for him constantly with my stepmother and uncle."

"Your late father was too kind for his own good," Wang Can insisted. "Liu Bei fought alongside Gong Du – a bandit king – and the Yellow Turbans when he was operating in Runan. Far from being 'a good man', my lord, he is a devious villain."

Liu Cong's eyes wandered.

"Liu Bei came here under false pretences, claiming to be a friend when he does, in fact, want to seize Jing as he twice seized Xu," Wang Can continued. "Again and again he urged your late father to advance on Xuchang, which would have left the province vulnerable to the Suns and a coup by Liu Bei, not to mention further widening the chasm between your father and the Son of Heaven. Liu Bei must not be welcomed: he must be thrown to Chancellor Cao's dogs as a token of goodwill."

"...So I should betray Liu Bei to Cao Cao...?" Liu Cong prompted.

"I wouldn't use the word 'betray', for after all, how can you betray a treacherous villain that planned to steal Jing from your father...?" Wang Can replied.

"...And you feel that handing Liu Bei over would placate the Chancellor...?" Liu Cong asked optimistically.

"I... do not feel that doing so would serve much more of a purpose than opening a dialogue," Wang Can admitted. "You must go further, Governor."

"... ... ...No, no, no... no!" Liu Cong chortled. "*Never!*"

"My lord, I must be honest and say that there are no options left," Wang Can continued. "The-"

"You're going to tell me that I should submit and tender my seal of office!" Liu Cong guessed. "You have just convinced me to chase Liu Bei away to save the province, only to follow it up by telling me to yield the province anyway!"

"The situation is *dire*, Lord Liu, and you must understand that properly and swiftly or risk terrible loss," Wang Can implored. "If you do not submit to Chancellor Cao, you will then face three – or maybe four, or even *five* – warlords at once, all competing for Jing like dogs over a single piece of meat.

"Sun Quan will continue his advance, Liu Bei will sense danger and try to storm Xiangyang with his formidable generals, and Chancellor Cao will continue *his* advance; Zhang Lu and Liu Zhang may also try to take pieces of the province, and I almost forgot about your own brother, who may launch an attack of his own if Sun Quan doesn't destroy him on the way here. Cai Mao can only do so much: the remnants of our army and navy will be divided along two-to-five fronts, torn apart and scattered, and you *will* be toppled by *someone*... most likely Chancellor Cao since he has the largest army."

"...I see what you're saying," Liu Cong sighed.

Wang Can smirked and said, "Yes, *Bei* could take the province – with or without your brother's assistance – because he has the advantage of being in Jing Province already, and all that means is your certain death – because Bei *will* kill you, citing your 'treacherous betrayal of your brother'. He'll use and discard your brother to get at you, kill you, take Jing and then lose Jing to Chancellor Cao anyway because Liu Bei *always* loses what he steals because he's incompetent."

Liu Cong lowered his eyes and stared at the floor.

"Yes, Sun Quan might get here before Chancellor Cao and once again, that's your death and nothing achieved," Wang Can continued. "Sun will flee when his in-law Chancellor Cao threatens him, so the Chancellor gets the province in the end."

"I'm sensing a pattern," Liu Cong sighed.

"...Submit to Chancellor Cao, and Sun Quan will retreat as soon as he knows about it," Wang Can continued. "Liu Bei might attempt to storm Xiangyang anyway, but at least he'll do so with Cao Cao – as our ally – behind him and there will no Sun Quan behind *us* to impede our efforts to contain the situation; but it's more likely that Bei's advisers will tell him to flee, and with less than three-thousand followers – ignoring the inevitable desertions – he will not get far, for he can only flee southward, where he has no friends. Zhang Lu and Liu Zhang wouldn't dare try to attack once the Han army is here to relieve rather than rout us; and while you are unlikely to be allowed to keep Jing Province, your connection to the royal house entitles you to a high office *somewhere*."

Liu Cong looked to the doorway: his stepmother Lady Cai nodded slowly as a sign that she agreed with everything that Wang Can had proposed.

"...I am unlikely to receive alternative advice from anyone but Liu Bei, who is a self-serving hegemon, so... I will submit," Liu Cong decided. "May my father forgive me for my weakness... he did everything in his power to hold onto this province..."

"But in the end, I would be having the exact same conversation with him had he not passed away, and he would be forced to make the exact same choice," Wang Can insisted. "You are a prisoner of fate, Lord Liu... sad to say."

"...Fine," Liu Cong sighed stoically. "What has to be done...?"

Liu Bei was horrified when he discovered that he had been kept away from Liu Cong so that the courtiers could persuade the young governor to submit to the approaching Han army and consequentially abandon Bei to Cao Cao's wrath; he hurriedly made plans for a retreat southward before Cao could reach Xinye.

Cao Cao halted at Wan City and asked to speak with Li Tong, who was managing the garrisons in Nan County.

"All is well, Chancellor," Li Tong said.

"What sort of resistance are facing?" Cao Cao asked.

"A 'Wen Ping' and a 'Zhang Yun' lead the troops, and a 'Lou Gui' seems to offer advice intermittently," Li Tong replied. "Generals Feng Kai and Lu Zhao are engaging the enemy officers at present since they knew you were coming."

"Ah, good," Cao Cao said. "I hope that we can employ some of these men rather than kill them, though: the navy is especially useful for the times ahead."

"We are aware of it, Chancellor, and do our best to avoid killing men unnecessarily," Li Tong replied.

"Very good," Cao Cao said. "Ah, but this place... brings back unpleasant memories once again, of avoidable mistakes and excessively punished faults. I will commemorate my fallen son, nephew and protector... and Dian Wei most of all, for his sacrifice – one born of duty – was most touching of all."

"...I am finally able to come here and mourn, Father," Cao Pi said.

"Ah, yes, you haven't accompanied me to Wan before, have you," Cao Cao realised. "You wish to mourn your older brother... another loss that harmed some whilst working to the advantage of others."

Cao Pi scowled at Cao Cao's barbed comment and said, "Father, I have to insist that-!"

"*Enough*," Cao Cao ordered. "Men say things... and I have said something. That is that. Your response will have to wait until a more private arena for discussion is found."

Cao Pi nodded angrily.

"General Li Tong, I am extremely impressed with your work here," Cao Cao said.

"Huche'er provided a lot of the stability: I inherit a job well done and do my best to do the same," Li Tong insisted. "Will you be staying in the city for your short visit, Chancellor...?"

"No, I will rest in the camp outside the city," Cao Cao replied. "I still... cannot face this place completely... especially not the governor's mansion, which is where I- ...Well, anyway... perhaps I will commemorate Zhang Xiu as well. After all, our fight was as two tigers, and we were both wounded deservedly... I digress. General Li Tong, we will advance over the next day or so and crush the enemy army's vanguard if they refuse to submit. Be ready for a decisive battle."

"I will do as you ask," Li Tong promised.

Cao Cao retreated to the command tent of his temporary Nan County camp with his bodyguard Xu Chu: Cao Pi followed him so that he could continue their argument.

"Save for Xu Chu, we are alone, Pi'er," Cao Cao noted. "Now that we are seated... speak your mind."

"You have twice implied that I am a poor brother – first to Chong, and then to Ang – and that's on top of your occasional criticism of my worthiness as a son... and an heir," Cao Pi said. "Why must I be so excessively judged...?"

"...What do you seek...?" Cao Cao asked wearily.

"*Fairness* is all I seek," Cao Pi replied. "I will mourn Dian Wei, Anmin and Ang most of all, because despite your assumptions he was my beloved older brother and *his* death – while giving his life for yours, not as a *son* but as a *vassal*, and therefore out of a sense of *duty* – is the most touching. Perhaps I might have to do the same one day."

"...Well met," Cao Cao said awkwardly. "I desire the loss of no

more of my sons, especially as a result of my own folly. And... I was wrong to speak of Dian Wei as the greatest loss and then imply – unintentionally – that you were not sincere. That would suggest that I care more for my own well-being... which is already being said after I allowed Ang to... to...!"
Cao Cao covered his face with his hands to hide his tears.
"...Father, please do not weep so," Cao Pi sighed.
"I let him give me his horse!" Cao Cao sobbed as he hunched forward and started to rock back and forth slightly. "I... I took my son's horse so that I could escape, and left him to die!"
Xu Chu – who had been present at the time of Cao Ang's noble sacrifice – frowned as he pondered his lord's actions with as much intelligence as he could muster.
"A son... must honour his father," Cao Pi said tonelessly.
"Not like that!" Cao Cao retorted. "Not... not by yielding his only means of escape to me! Not by running into battle to delay their pursuit at the cost of his own life! It's all wrong... all of it! He... was such a good lad...!"
Cao Pi exhaled irritably.
"Shuo too... Chong too!" Cao Cao continued. "They were my boys, more precious than gemstones and jade, and...! ...Lady Ding is right to despise me!"
"I... cannot find words to answer you, Father," Cao Pi said. "I shall leave you and wait until you are ready to hold a ceremony."
"...It will be soon," Cao Cao promised.
Cao Pi bowed slightly and retreated.
"...I am a terrible man, really," Cao Cao murmured. "I stole my son's horse to flee a disaster of my own creation... slaughtered Boshe's household without first obtaining proper proof of guilt... and murdered tens of thousands of people for the crimes of two men. But yet it is Heaven's will that I am the only man that can bring order... how *laughable*."

The self-appointed ruler of Han'ning, Zhang Lu, was distressed at the close proximity of such a large Han army and determined to react properly to it; he summoned his most trusted followers to a private meeting and demanded their views.
"We cannot fight such a large force, Master," the adviser Yan Pu said. "We lack the numbers and resources at present."
"...So what should I do?" Zhang Lu asked. "Should I be advancing to Fangling and securing that region...?"
"I wouldn't set a single man on the path toward that army, Master," Yan Pu replied.
"...I must hope that Cao Cao does not intend to attack this region when he is done with Jing," Zhang Lu supposed.
"I'm afraid so, Master," Yan Pu replied. "And I do not think that he can attack Han'ning next, in fact: Sun Quan will be the villain's next target."
"...Then we must hope that Heaven grants Sun Quan the power to defeat Cao Cao, or that Cao succumbs to his famous ego and defeats himself as he has done in the past," Zhang Lu said. "It's decided then: we will continue our preparations for resisting an invasion, but we will not try to expand our borders. We will place our fate in Heaven's trust."

"...So Cao Cao is finally attacking Jing..."
Yi Province Governor Liu Zhang looked at the recent reports from his eastern border and shuddered.
"Stay away from this argument between Jing and the Son of Heaven," the politician Yang Hong protested. "Ignore those that say that we should seize Yiling or Wuling!"
The senior general Zhang Ren harrumphed angrily and muttered, "What *cowardice*."
"I agree with Yang Jixiu," Zhang Song said. "We must not rile that unstable villain."
"I don't agree with your assessment of the chancellor at all, Zhang Song," the minister Wang Lei said. "Might it not be that you were rude to him, Zhang Song, just as you are rude to your colleagues here in this court...?"
"It would be no surprise," the politician and general Huang Quan suggested. "We should not have sent Zhang on such a mission."
"*Ayah*... why say that now...?" Liu Zhang despaired.
"They're trying to blame me for Cao Cao's attitude, but you can ask for witnesses to the conversation and they'll tell you that I speak the truth, Lord Liu," Zhang Song insisted. "Cao Cao threatened invasion, citing-"
"**Yes yes I know!**" Liu Zhang snapped. "I... I know. The most that I can do is ensure that every pass and river is guarded well and make petitions to the Son of Heaven pleading my case. I cannot be held responsible for any wrongs committed by my father and his cronies."
The general Wu Yi sighed and said, "I am your brother-in-law and the son of one of those 'cronies' that you refer to, Lord Liu. If it's true that Cao Cao made threats, then I can only say that my own belief is that Cao has been misinformed... willingly or otherwise. Don't create villains out of your father and his loyal followers when you petition or-"
"**Alright, alright!**" Liu Zhang cried. "I understand your point, Wu Ziyuan! I will not mention anything of the sort! I will keep my arguments to the present day."
"And we are likely to see refugees from Jing, more than we have already seen," the adviser Zhang Junsi said. "We will benefit from more talents coming here."
"Provided, of course, that we make proper use of them," the adviser Fa Zheng sighed quietly.
"...We will welcome any man that wants to come here," Liu Zhang decided. "Sad though Sun Ce's conquest of Yang was, it brought us wise Xu Jing; perhaps there will be some strange consolation to be had from Cao Cao's violence. Perhaps, gentlemen, Yi Province will grow as a result..."
Zhang Song bowed and said, "That's always possible, my lord. There are some in Jing that might make Yi a much, much stronger and better place were they to come here... Heaven willing."
Fa Zheng – who would, along with Zhang Song, be instrumental to Liu Bei's future conquest of Yi – smiled at Song's intentional foreshadowing of things to come.

****

117

The Jing Province general Wen Ping was startled by the speed, skill and overall professionalism of Cao Cao's army as it engaged his forces over the next day at the Nan County border; Wen's surprise was sensed by the hermit-turned-adviser Lou Gui, who said, "You shouldn't worry: Cao Cao wants to recruit the men of Jing for his fight with Sun Quan. That's why he's trying to impress us and not capitalising on opportunities."

"...I sensed as much, but I refuse to surrender unless we are told to by Governor Liu Biao," Wen Ping replied.

"I... don't know if I broach this properly, but... Governor Liu Biao... is dead," Lou Gui said apprehensively. "Xiangyang is currently sealed to all but the most trusted visitors."

"...*Aiee*... our lord... is *dead*...?" Wen Ping exclaimed. "I knew he was ill... but...!"

"I would like to think that our new lord, Governor Liu Cong, is probably deciding whether he should try and negotiate with Cao Cao," Lou Gui continued. "But I am not a fool: he's being persuaded to submit by a group led by Wang Can, Kuai Yue and Admiral Cai Mao, and he won't argue forever."

"...So it is over, then," Wen Ping said.

"I should not answer that with 'Yes', but... yes," Lou Gui replied. "My suggestion to you, General, is that you withstand the attacks as you are and await an urgent messenger that will be heading toward Cao Cao, not us."

"...I want to fight to the last," Wen Ping said.

"I commend your spirit, General, but... do not waste your life," Lou Gui replied.

"...If the Chancellor is too formidable and there is no means of defending the province, I know that I would be a fool to die a worthless death," Wen Ping said. "If, at that point, an opportunity to submit is provided, then I will do so."

"I will go home," Lou Gui admitted. "There will be few men that will not surrender or go home when the order comes... because the lustre of past times is gone, and has been for some time. There is nothing left to defend."

"...Oh, but then there is Liu Bei," Wen Ping exclaimed.

"He's not worth your time, General Wen," Lou Gui insisted. "He'll falter irrecoverably one day, be that in a day, month, year or twenty years. The future of the nation rests in the hands of Chancellor Cao. Perhaps I will serve Cao Cao myself one day, if I consider him to truly be as great as his achievements suggest."

"...If that is true, then I will gladly submit," Wen Ping replied. "But I too must first be suitably convinced."

A group of messengers was despatched from Xiangyang within hours and hurried toward each of the defending armies and the Chancellor of State: Cao Cao had his visitor address his travelling court in the command tent of his Nan County border camp.

"Governor Liu Cong sends greetings to the Chancellor of State," the messenger – an official in robes – said penitently. "I have been sent here by horse to bring a desire to see a peaceful solution to Governor Liu Cong's inherited conflict with the state."

"Oh...? So he wishes to submit, then...?" Cao Cao exclaimed.

The messenger was taken aback by Cao Cao's bluntness and paused momentarily before replying, "That is correct, Chancellor. Governor Liu Cong is looking forward to tendering the seal of office formally, and he can either bring it to you or greet you at the gates of Xiangyang, Fan or Xinye, whichever is preferable for the swift transition of power."

"Well, that is good news!" Cao Cao chuckled.

"...How shall we receive the seal from Liu Cong, Chancellor...?" Cheng Yu prompted.

"Oh, yes, yes, right... I should like the seal to be brought to Xinye," Cao Cao replied. "Xinye is, of course, the city that Liu Biao's guest, the wanted fugitive *Liu Bei*, uses as his base, and so I would be collecting that valuable prize at the same time. You may return to your lord and tell him that I will advance to Xinye at once: time is against us so you will have to convey my answer without a formal letter."

"Uh, Excellency... might we enquire the 'military stance' that we can expect from Governor Liu Cong's subordinates...?" Xun Gongda asked.

"Oh! Yes, yes, of course," Cao Cao said. "Have Liu Cong's men been told to submit?"

"They... have been ordered to do so, Chancellor, and they *should* do so," the messenger replied awkwardly.

"...But there are one or two stubborn fools that might want to keep fighting," Cao Cao sighed. "Alright, fine... you may go."

The messenger bowed low and retreated.

"We'll have no trouble from Zhang Yun," Cheng Yu suggested. "He's Cai Mao's relation, and the Cais will be behind this decision to surrender."

"...So the only potential problem is Wen Ping," Cao Cao said. "Alright, well... I'll have troops advance down both sides of the Yu River and try to pincer the man: I will offer him the chance to submit to me, which he should consider an honour if he is as clever as he is stubborn."

Jing Governor Liu Cong prepared to leave Xiangyang and begin the journey to Xinye; he was suddenly afraid, and Wang Can could guess the reasons.

"Liu Bei will not try to assassinate you, Lord Liu," Wang Can insisted. "And Cao Cao cannot be seen to do you harm, not after-"

"Not after he killed Hua Tuo, the finest physician in the world, and now there are rumours that he killed Kong Rong, one of Confucius' last descendants, before he left Xuchang!" Liu Cong snapped. "Where is this man's reason...?"

"...I respected Kong Rong greatly," Wang Can admitted. "He and I were future rivals in the realm of poetry and verse, and he was considered to be a fine philosopher – not as marvellous as his famous ancestor, but certainly very gifted. But he supposedly spoke ill of Chancellor Cao in front of an envoy from Sun Quan, and that's not at all correct."

"...No... if I were slandered in front of an envoy from that villain Sun Quan, I would not care which man it was," Liu Cong replied. "Even you, or Mister Kuai, for all your long years of service... I could not let such a disrespectful man go unpunished."

"And Hua Tuo's case is not known in its entirety," Wang Can suggested. "We must look at what Chancellor Cao has done that is fully known, Lord Liu: he has placated the tribes, brought peace to Ji, Bing, Qing, Yòu, Xu, Yu, Yan and Central Provinces, and he has rescued my late master Cai Yong's daughters from Southern Xiongnu captivity."

"...Cao Cao is no villain," Liu Cong murmured.

"No, in fact he is a hero," Wang Can insisted. "The famous province thieves, Liu Bei and Sun Quan, are the villains, even if Bei is hopeless at conquest; and then there are Liu Zhang and Zhang Lu, whose holdings are illegal as well. Your father would frown at your decision initially, of course, but he would understand in the end."

"...And you're sure that Liu Bei won't attack us...?" Liu Cong said.

"Since our surrender, Admiral Cai and the rest of our army and navy have turned their attentions toward saving this province from other threats: most of all, Lord Liu, the threat of Liu Bei," Wang Can promised. "Liu Zhang and Zhang Lu are also being watched carefully; your journey will be quiet and uneventful."

"That's good," Liu Cong sighed. "Where is Bei now?"

"On his way to Xinye to rescue his tiny army and flee before Chancellor Cao arrives," Wang Can replied. "With Wen Ping to the north of him and Zhang Yun to the east, he must go south, but as I have said before, Lord Liu, he cannot get far."

"...He has some clever men around him," Liu Cong noted. "He's got some of my courtiers and officers around him, I hear."

"Xiang Lang, Pan Jun, Yi Ji, Wei Yan... men we can survive without," Wang Can insisted. "Most contributed little until now, so forget them."

"It doesn't matter, does it...?" Liu Cong said dryly. "They are not my vassals anymore once I hand the seal over anyway! How many will follow me to wherever I am sent...? Will *you*...?"

"...If I am permitted to," Wang Can replied carefully. "I am famous for my connection to Cai Yong, and Chancellor Cao values Cai Yong, so... I will very likely be asked to join his inner circle, and I cannot refuse."

"You... are quite right," Liu Cong said. "I... must stay focussed on Liu Bei and the other threats to my safety while I am transporting this seal."

"And as I have said, Liu Bei is no threat," Wang Can insisted. "He has a few of our junior ministers and a few low-ranking military officers; most of the men that chose to leave began the journey westward to Yi Province. And as for Bei's existing loyalists, well... Mi Zhu, Mi Fang, Sun Qian and Zhuge Liang for senior officials and Guan Yu, Zhang Fei, Zhao Yun and Chen Dao for senior officers; Bei could not take a *county* with eight half-decent men and a tiny militia, let alone a *province*. Bei *cannot* risk trying to take the seal from you in an effort to seize the province: he must run before Cao Cao can catch him."

"...I am distressed!" Liu Cong admitted. "This is the end of my clan's rule in Jing, and I will be held responsible! My brother will despise me, my ancestors will-!"

"You have done the right thing," Wang Can insisted. "The Liu clan are the royal line: you are a distant prince! Jing is too dangerous for you to hold at the moment, but there are now eight pacified

594

provinces that do not all of them have governors, so be positive, my lord, look to your future responsibilities and forget Jing."

"...I must, therefore I shall," Liu Cong replied. "Let's speak no more: I can't keep the chancellor waiting."

Wen Ping looked on with despair as armies led by Generals Feng Kai, Li Tong, Xu Huang and Yue Jin advanced on his twin camps along the bank of the Yu River; Lou Gui had departed to advise Zhang Yun, so Wen would have to act alone.

"What shall we do...?" a captain asked.

"...I will not yield this position," Wen Ping decided. "I will prove my loyalty to Governor Liu Biao, unlike his unworthy son!"

Wen Ping's defiant stance impressed Cao Cao's generals, who found that the defenders were blunting attempts to seize the camps and liaising with Wen's small naval force to carry out flash raids against the attacking armies' flanks; Yue Jin went to Cao Cao's command tent and said, "You have to see if this man will yield, Governor. He's smarter than we gave him credit, commands unbelievable loyalty from his men and uses all manner of tricks to hold those camps."

"...Pull everybody back and give this man a chance to think," Cao Cao replied. "If he still hesitates, a man will be sent to Wen Ping to negotiate an end to this: we'll let him know that Zhang Yun has surrendered and- ...No, wait: I'll have Zhang add his voice to my chorus once the messenger has been seen."

"Shall I pen something...?" Liu Yè asked.

"Not yet, Ziyang," Cao Cao replied. "Let's see what he does."

Cao Cao's officers ended their attacks on Wen Ping's camps and withdrew to their own camp on the Nan County border; Wen Ping realised that he was being given a chance to surrender and pondered it carefully.

"...This is a man who has recruited heroes for his vanguard," Wen Ping mused. "We will not need further persuasion... Chancellor Cao has proven that he recruits able men and uses them properly. We will surrender at once."

Wen Ping's senior colonel bowed slightly and said, "As you command, General."

Cao Cao, Jia Xu, Cheng Yu, Liu Yè and the surrendered general Zhang Yun met with Wen Ping at the entrance to Wen's western camp.

"You're late," Cao Cao teased. "Why did you make me wait for your surrender, Wen Zhongye...?"

Wen Ping bowed humbly and said, "I was ordered to defend the northern border by Governor Liu Biao, Prime Minister, and felt obligated to obey my lord's dying wish at any cost. I never wanted to submit and am still reluctant to do so: if I am honest, I wanted to resist until the last man had fallen, but here I am anyway."

Cao Cao laughed and replied, "You are the sort of man that the Han should give great responsibility to, Wen Zhongye! You successfully defended an outpost with inadequate forces and refused to submit when others had long kowtowed in deference! If a grand army and a high commission were bestowed upon you, then, why, you would be immovable!"

"You flatter me without proper cause, Prime Minister," Wen Ping replied. "I am ordinary in comparison to your generals."

"You underestimate your talent," Cao Cao insisted. "My generals are very impressed with you... and so am I. You will remain at the rank of general and retain some – not all – of your men. The rest I shall need for my next campaign, but they shall be returned to you if all goes well."

"My troops are at the Han's disposal, Prime Minister, as am I," Wen Ping replied. "Command and I will obey."

"...Magnificent," Cao Cao said. "And I'll have the legendary Lou Gui as well...!"

Zhang Yun smiled sadly and replied, "He... went home."

"He went home...?" Cheng Yu exclaimed. "To the mountains...?"

"He asked why you would you need 'a rascal like him' when you have the likes of Jia Xu and Cheng Yu at your command, Excellency," Zhang Yun explained.

"But Lou Zibo is very highly spoken of," Cao Cao said. "I'd like his sagely advice."

"He's... very *outspoken*, very 'honest', Chancellor," Cheng Yu suggested. "He... might be better used on a campaign where tempers will not be put to the test quite so much."

"I'll take your warning for what it is," Cao Cao replied. "Forget Lou Gui for now, then, and we'll concentrate on getting to Xinye City to receive Liu Cong's seal and Liu Bei's head."

"Liu Bei is a troublemaker that was planning to steal the province from my lord," Wen Ping said angrily. "He is greedy and crafty, Prime Minister, and should not be allowed to escape and try his tricks in some other place."

"I think that you and I are going to get along just fine, Wen Zhongye!" Cao Cao chuckled.

"I'll advance with my cavalry," Cao Chun suggested.

"...You will advance with General Wen Ping," Cao Cao ordered.

"You shouldn't be trusting a mission to a man that's just surrendered, Mengde," Xiahou Dun said. "What if he betrays us?"

"My hatred of Liu Bei is sincere," Wen Ping promised. "And if he knows about Governor Liu Biao's death and Governor Liu Cong's surrender then he'll be up to something in Xinye, and I should like to hurry there before he can set any traps."

"Go, then, at once," Cao Cao said. "I will not be far behind."

Wen Ping and Cao Chun led a force of 5,000 men to Xinye to intercept Liu Bei and prepare the way for their lord.

"...We have a new champion in Wen Ping," Cao Cao declared. "Liu Biao will regret not making better use of him."

Generals Wen Ping and Cao Chun led a brutal assault on Liu Bei's retreating army – and, unavoidably, his civilian entourage – as they fled toward Southern Jing. That confrontation – known as the 'Battle of Steep-slope' – would be an emotional milestone that defined the rest of the conflict between Liu Bei and Cao Cao.

****

118

Cao Cao was taken aback by the lack of citizens when he reached Xinye City: he turned to his registrar Liu Yè and asked, "Was this city evacuated by Liu Biao...?"

"Neither Zhang Yun nor any of the others that we've encountered have made any mention of such a move, Your Excellency," Liu Yè replied uncomfortably.

"...Then did my forces scare the people away...?" Cao Cao asked. "Did Xinye's prefect order an evacuation when they got word of our approach...?"

"Evacuating as many people as are obviously missing... could not be done in such a short time," Jia Xu suggested. "This must have been done a day or so ago at the very least, Excellency."

"...Liu Cong should not have done this," Cao Cao said. "But then he could not have done this... else we'd know from Zhang Yun... unless it is a trap of some kind."

"If it were a trap, it would have been sprung already, Your Excellency," Cheng Yu suggested.

"...No trap... too long ago for... this makes no sense," Cao Cao murmured. "Not... not unless...!"

"...Unless what...?" Cheng Yu prompted.

Cao Cao's eyes steeled.

"...It is most likely that the inhabitants took it upon themselves to evacuate to some nearby place when they heard that something was going to happen here, especially if Liu Bei came back here in a hurry," Jia Xu suggested. "I'll look into it, Excellency."

"Yes... yes, it is most likely that they fled in anticipation of a siege," Cao Cao decided. "I... have initiated enough of them in recent times, have I not...?"

Cao Cao's strange smile compelled Xun Gongda, Cheng Yu and Liu Yè to nod frantically and mumble agreeable responses; Jia Xu hummed thoughtfully and replied, "They will surely be nearby in temporary camps."

"...Enough of that for now," Cao Cao said with obvious sadness. "We have... we have a seal of office to collect from an unfit governor that is only slightly more wise than he is cowardly."

"You feel that Liu Cong should have fought you, Excellency...?" Cheng Yu exclaimed.

"...I suppose that I should not be saying such things," Cao Cao replied. "Think no more of my ill-chosen words, gentlemen. Where is Liu Cong now...?"

"He is nearly here," Xun Gongda said.

"...Yes... he is nearly here," Cao Cao muttered. "But will all obey the order to submit...? And where is *Liu Bei*...?"

The mood in the four semi-autonomous regions to the south of Jiangling was cautiously defiant: the Administrator of Wuling Prefecture, Jin Xuan, called his officials to his main audience hall and said, "We cannot submit to Cao Cao."

"...You're suggesting secession," a minister guessed.

"I have been a loyal Han vassal for my entire life, at one point serving a notable role in Luoyang," Jin Xuan replied. "I am not convinced that Cao Cao is the great hero that some claim him to be; not yet, at least. I will wait until I see how he deals with Sun Quan: in the meantime, we maintain neutrality, telling Cao Cao that we were loyal to Liu Biao, that our people were loyal to Liu Biao and that will need time to placate the people properly or until Liu Qi makes his position clear. Cao will either confront Sun Quan militarily or receive Sun's submission over the coming year, so we'll have clarity soon enough."

"...And what if Chancellor Cao decides to attack us, Father...?" the official Jin Yi asked.

"I do not expect him to," Jin Xuan replied. "I'm more worried about Liu Bei, to be honest; then again, our late lord's *presumed* heir, Liu Qi, is rumoured to be in alliance with Bei, making matters difficult to fathom. Until we can be sure that Cao Cao, in alliance with Cai Mao, has not seized power from Liu Qi in a coup, and that the official account – that 'sickly, unfit' Liu Qi was sidestepped in favour of Liu Cong at Governor Liu Biao's insistence – is correct, then we *must* remain neutral."

"But we have Sun Quan to the east, tribal chiefs at all sides and Liu Zhang to the west!" an official said. "Can we really afford to isolate ourselves...?"

"We must wait," Jin Xuan insisted. "We cannot yield to a tyrant: we must wait, gentlemen, and see who Cao Cao really is and how he deals with his enemies."

The desire to maintain a temporary state of neutrality was echoed to the east of Wuling in Changsha Prefecture, where the hatred of the Sun clan that some felt was matched by the memory of Sun Jian's time as the region's Administrator some 20 years previous.

"Sun Quan might not be as villainous as some would have us believe," a minister proposed. "His father, the famous hero Sun Jian, defeated Ou Xing and brought stability to Changsha, Administrator Han."

"It's known to me," Administrator Han Xuan replied. "It's also known to me that there are many that would like to see Changsha join forces with Liu Qi or Sun Quan against Cao Cao, but that cannot happen. I have discussed it at length with the others, and neutrality is the only option at present!"

"...I feel so worthless," the veteran general Huang Zhong said. "I'm old and useless: I could have been in the north, resisting the advance of the villain with men like Wang Wei and Wen Ping, but instead I am semi-retired, rotting away here and watching the world change around me!"

"There are a lot of things that are going to change, old general," Huan Xuan replied. "The death of Governor Liu Biao will inevitably lead to the boundaries being altered; some say that Jiangxia is unlikely to remain part of Jing, and yet Sun Quan is, for all those that hail him, a rebel that annexes territory illegally. We could see Sun absorb us into a rival empire that endures for twenty years before being trampled, but he would have to defeat Cao Cao and Liu Qi's loyalists first; on the other hand, Liu Qi could produce some proof that he was overthrown by a group of plotters and rally enough support to fight Cao Cao for Jing, but wouldn't Sun Quan attack Liu Qi while his back was turned in the hope of gaining more land...? As I have already said, the choice is joining Liu Qi *or* Sun Quan: there is no option for joining them both, for they are mortal enemies!"

"...So we must somehow remain neutral while Liu Qi, Sun Quan, the Chancellor of State and Liu Bei fight between themselves...?" an official asked.

"We are not vassals of any of those men: we are vassals of the Son of Heaven," Han Xuan replied. "Our role is to maintain stability in Changsha, and any who do otherwise are our enemies. We will have an unofficial pact with our three neighbours and stay out of the theatre of violence; we owe the people that much."

The mood was similar in Guiyang Prefecture, which was to the south of Changsha; but the Administrator of Guiyang, Zhao Fan, was more disturbed by the news of the fighting in Jiangxia and what it might mean.

"The Suns are moving closer and closer to us," Zhao Fan said. "I can only worry that they intend to seize Guiyang soon unless Cao Cao defeats them."

"You must maintain neutrality as agreed," the visiting Administrator of neighbouring Cangwu, Wu Ju, replied insistently. "We have no idea what Cao Cao intends to do after he's finished 'pacifying' your province."

"You hate Cao Cao," Zhao Fan suggested.

"No, I don't 'hate Cao Cao', but I don't like him especially either," Wu Ju retorted. "He is persecuting a friend of mine, which doesn't help his case, admittedly, but I also refer you to his past as an indiscriminate murderer of civilians – by the *tens of thousands* – in Xu Province. Pledge allegiance to him now and you may find yourself allied to a man that put most of Jing's inhabitants in a trench and covered them over."

Zhao Fan's officials quietly agreed.

"...And Sun Quan...?" Zhao Fan asked. "Am I to ignore his continued slithering toward my northeast border...?"

"Like it or not, you must not involve yourself or the inhabitants of this region in a fight between Cao Cao, Sun Quan and the remnants of Liu Biao's collapsed regime," Wu Ju said. "I enjoy semi-autonomy from my province's main government, just as you did from yours, and I should like that to remain the case for me at the very least. Cangwu is south of Lingling as well as Guiyang, so what you do next affects us, which is why I am here. Let the tigers fight: they need no help from you."

"...I'll certainly ponder what you've said," Zhao Fan replied. "It is a common feeling amongst my officials, but... I can only have doubts when faced with orders to submit from the Governor and the Chancellor of-!"

"Chancellor Cao... I need say no more, for his self-appointed title says everything that need be said," Wu Ju countered. "Governor – *former* Governor – Liu Cong sent orders to submit, yes, before yielding his governor's seal and invalidating his claim to authority over you. So you are submitting to 'Chancellor Cao', who is self-styled as having absolute power, like Dong Zhuo before him."

"That's quite right," an adviser said. "I have already made that point myself, Adminis-"

"Yes, yes, I know," Zhao Fan grumbled. "I'll wait."

"...I only hope that the other three keep their word."

Lingling Administrator Liu Du opted for a private meeting with three of his most trusted advisers; he worried that Wuling to the north, Changsha to the northeast and Guiyang to the east – which acted as buffers between his region and neighbouring provinces – were all vulnerable to attack or prone to submission.

"There is no advantage to surrender for any of them," one adviser replied. "And there is no advantage to alliances with anyone but each other and us, my lord."

"...Well... at least Governor Shi Xie is a pious, trustworthy neighbour," Liu Du said. "I should really pity the others while I fear their weakness; Wuling has Cao Cao to the north and Liu Zhang to the west, Changsha has Cao to the north and Sun Quan to the east, while Guiyang has Sun Quan at their door in two directions at once. The others must come under attack first for Lingling to be in any serious danger, and at that point, we can unite against the threat."

"...And we *should*, *must* unite in such a situation, my lord," a second adviser warned. "There is no surviving alone."

"And I would in all but the most extreme circumstances," Liu Du insisted. "But... if the others were to yield or fall in short order... what then...? Would we submit to save lives...?"

"That would depend on whose banner they fell to," the third adviser replied. "We might submit to Liu Qi if he were the true heir to Lord Liu Biao, but we cannot be sure at present; we might submit to Chancellor Cao if he can prove that he obtained the governor's seal without bloodshed or intrigue; we cannot submit to Sun Quan or, ridiculous as the notion sounds, Liu Bei."

"*Liu Bei*...?" the first adviser scoffed. "He can't attack us!"

"But he might try to," the third adviser retorted. "We must not disregard the idea, nor should we dismiss the idea that he might convince our late lord's son, Liu Qi, to do so as a rebel. In that case or in the case of Sun Quan, we would then be submitting to rebels and become rebels ourselves: we are obligated to resist, no matter the cost to the region."

"...Then I would," Liu Du declared. "If Liu Bei comes here, or Sun Quan... then we will fight to the last man before we give such rebels a scrap of Lingling."

Liu Cong finally reached Xinye and ceremonially proffered the seal to Cao Cao at the gates; Cong had hoped that Cao would refuse and return the seal immediately, as often happened, but he was quickly disappointed.

"You have been wise," Cao Cao said coldly. "Your submission has saved the lives of a lot of soldiers, Liu Cong."

"I... I am sorry that it has taken so long for this errant scion to 'come home', Chancellor Cao," Liu Cong replied. "Father... 'lost his way', somewhat."

"Indeed he did," Cao Cao said. "Sheltering rebels... striking at the capital while my back was turned... but Liu Biao was Liu Biao, and you are Liu Cong. The matter is closed with the tendering of Jing's seal. I will now send a messenger to Sun Quan informing him that the submission was sincere and is completed: he will retreat or he will face my fed and eager army, which is now bolstered by the acquisition of yours. Where is the head of the navy...?"

Cai Mao bowed humbly.

"...Admiral Cai Mao, you will keep your position," Cao Cao continued. "I want preparations made for a full-scale attack on Jiangdong: be as public about it as you like once Sun Quan has retreated, but not before."

Cai Mao grinned and replied, "I will relish it, Excellency!"

"Wang Can, Kuai Yue: welcome home," Cao Cao said as he turned to face the two advisers. "Mister Kuai: I had no time to speak with you when you were in Commander-in-Chief Hè Jin's employ, but now you are in mine, and I assure you that we will speak often as I value you greatly. I once said that I could pacify the Empire with you at my side, and I believe that Heaven has finally answered!"

Kuai Yue bowed humbly.

"...And you, Wang Can, are doubly prized!" Cao Cao continued. "Oh, how I have regretted that you have been on the opposite side of a river of enmity for so long. I am trying to rescue the many works that Cai Yong was responsible for: will you help me with that great task in addition to lending me your own wits...?"

"I was entrusted with some of Master Cai's writings when he was preparing for his end at Wang Yun's hands, Chancellor Cao," Wang Can replied. "I can also recall some of them from memory and have written some down in my own hand."

"Wonderful, wonderful!" Cao Cao said. "But... I should note that I now employ Wang Yun's nephew Wang Ling as Administrator of Zhongshan Prefecture..."

"I know of it," Wang Can replied. "Wang Yun is Wang Yun, and he is Wang Ling. The matter is closed."

Cao Cao laughed and said, "I shall look forward to working with you, Zhongxuan!"

Wang Can bowed low and replied, "The pleasure is mine, Chancellor. To serve the Han... is every good man's wish."

"Indeed," Cao Cao said as he turned to the senior politicians. "Fu Xun, Hè Qia, Han Song, Huan Jie: you are all of you most welcome in the Han court."

"I will serve the Han tirelessly, Chancellor!" Han Song vowed.

"As will I, Chancellor!" Hè Qia promised.

"I only hope that I can serve as well I want to, Chancellor!" Fu Xun said.

"It is a great honour, Chancellor!" Huan Jie proclaimed.

"...Huan Jie... you are now about to serve a third lord, if I recall," Cao Cao said with feigned uncertainty of his facts.

"I... dishonoured myself by lending my talents to the Sun clan, Chancellor," Huan Jie replied. "It was too late that I realised that Sun Jian was no longer a hero, and I found myself serving as his senior politician and envoy on the illegal Jing campaign. I switched my allegiance to Governor Liu Biao as soon as an opportunity arose in order to escape serving the rebel and heretic Yuan Shu for a moment longer than was necessary."

Liu Yè hummed thoughtfully and said, "You're one of Liu Biao's senior politicians: I commend you for seeing the error of serving Yuan Shu before I did, Huan Jie, but why did you persist in serving Liu Biao after he had joined a coalition led by Yuan *Shao* that tried to abduct the Son of Heaven...?"

"We were fooled by the 'Girdle Edict'!" Huan Jie protested. "We were confused by the stories that we were hearing! You know that the intelligentsia in Jing is biased against Chancellor Cao: many refugees came to this region from Yan and Xu fifteen years ago peddling stories of-!"

"I... am aware of the stories," Cao Cao interrupted. "We should let this matter drop as well, I think: I choose to forget the mistakes made by good men here in Jing, just as I chose to forget the mistakes made by men that served the Yuan brothers and realised their folly. Our goals now must be shared and achieved in short order: Liu Bei must be apprehended or killed – either suits me – before he can escape to some safer place, and then Sun Quan, Liu Zhang, Zhang Lu and the tribes must be brought to heel, one by one and in that order."

"You will find no man in Jing that will refuse to join a campaign against the Suns of Jiangdong," Huan Jie promised. "They are rightly hated throughout the province, so destroying them would-"

"If they can be subjugated peacefully, so be it," Cao Cao insisted. "If they must die, then yes, so be it, but I want to reunite the Empire as bloodlessly as is possible, gentlemen; if I did otherwise, I would be no hero, would I...?"

"...I suppose not, Chancellor," Huan Jie sighed.

"Now, then... we have more talents for the court, so the next thing to do is advance and destroy the rebel Liu Bei!" Cao Cao declared with false cheer.

"...A question, Zhongxuan," Jia Xu said as he looked at Wang Can. "This city is sparsely populated to say the least; where might the inhabitants have-?"

"I... think that we should worry about the inhabitants of Xinye later," Cao Cao said with a growing sense of unease. "We must focus on Liu Bei: his death will remove many of the anxieties that burden me!"

"...Yes, Excellency," Jia Xu replied.

Word of the swift progress of the Jing Province campaign reached Yè, where it was generally welcomed.

"We can expect Jing to be completely returned to government control within the next three months: it is only the relief of Jiangxia that is expected to be problematic, since the wayward Liu Qi and his villainous ally Liu Bei might seize the region upon Sun Quan abandoning it," Ji Province Registrar Li Fu reported. "After the full liberation of Jing, we can expect Chancellor Cao to take action against another of the Empire's enemies: he could southward and rein in the ambitious Sun Quan, or he move westward to finally reclaim Hanzhong from Zhang Lu."

"...*Wonderful*," Ma Teng muttered; his sons, Ma Tie and Ma Xiu, closed their eyes and silently lamented their situation.

"What will happen to Liu Cong...?" Xin Pi asked.

"Former Jing Province Governor Liu Cong will be brought here to Yè, where he will remain until a suitable post becomes available," Li Fu explained.

"Liu Cong will have a long wait," Liu Xun scoffed. "I have been here and in Xuchang for years now: close to nine, in fact, and where is my 'suitable post'...? He made my adviser into his personal assistant, but nothing for me! I was the Administrator of Lujiang! Where is-!"

"There are a lot of issues that need to be resolved," Xin Pi replied.

"A nonsense answer!" Liu Xun heckled. "Time and again, it is hinted that I am being 'assessed' because I was a close ally of Yuan Shu: Mengde's trusted adviser Yuan Huan was once Yuan Shu's adviser and is related to the man as well! Mengde's registrar Liu Yè was my adviser in Lujiang, so is more to blame for the bad decisions than I am! Generals Qin and Qi are still being used by Mengde, and they were Yuan Shu's generals! Liu Fu, Inspector of Yang is a former Yuan Shu vassal that-!"

"You've made your point, Liu Xun!" Li Fu snapped. "The-!"

"Liu Fu is Inspector of Yang and has in his service Lei Bo and Chen Lan, both of them Yuan Shu's generals!" Liu Xun continued defiantly. "Mengde is being inconsistent! I submitted and pledged my service to the Han, just like the rest, but all I do is go back and forth between Yè and Xuchang being given roles that ill befit a man of my breeding, stature and experience! **Why am I not made proper use of???**"

Ma Teng smirked and lowered his head.

"...Chancellor Cao is going to undertake a restructuring of the administration when he returns from campaign," Xin Pi said. "You will be included in the list of men that require proper appointments, Mister Liu Xun."

"I'll believe it when it happens," Liu Xun scoffed.

"If we might move on... what about the rumours that the prefectures to the south of Jiangling are breaking away from Jing...?" Sima Fang asked.

"Wuling, Lingling, Changsha and Guiyang," Xin Pi noted.

"There is some confusion about the intent of the four administrators of those prefectures," Li Fu admitted. "They should not shelter Liu Qi or Liu Bei, and they should not yield to or join forces with either Sun Quan or Liu Zhang... but there is always the possibility that one or more of them might... 'disappoint us'. But they will pay a heavy price if they do."

Cao Cao's principal spouse, Lady Bian, was delighted by the news that her husband and eldest son Pi were well and that Jing had fallen without serious incident; she visited Pi's wife Lady Zhen and said, "They will be home sooner than expected!"

"I miss him," Lady Zhen replied.

Lady Bian looked at her 4-year-old grandson Rui and said, "My... how lively he is!"

"He babbles and totters about, full of life," Lady Zhen sighed.

"...Why did you say that with such a forlorn tone, daughter-in-law...?" Lady Bian asked.

"Because... because I know that there are still some cruel men that huddle in corners and whisper about his lineage," Lady Zhen replied. "Mother-in-law, I am distressed at the thought that he will be chastised and laughed at, and that I will be-!"

"Hush," Lady Bian ordered. "You speak to a woman that knows how cruel others can be."

"I... must plead ignorance," Lady Zhen said.

"If that is true, then my son saves you what he feels to be shame, else you are being characteristically kind," Lady Bian replied. "I was a courtesan in a brothel when my future husband first encountered me during a trip to Kaiyang."

"...Were you indebted...?" Lady Zhen asked.

Lady Bian smiled and said, "Exactly that. My family was penniless, and my beauty became a way to reimburse those that knew no pity. My future husband viewed me not as a wretched creature but as a strong, brave person deserving of respect, not pity, for facing difficult times and stoically doing what had to be done in a world where a woman's choices are few. Yes, I might have been an astrologer or physician or midwife if I were of the right class to be poor, but that was not the case: I lacked an education for such things to be choices. My future husband settled all of my family's debts, brought me into his home and made a respectable woman of me; and so I see a side of him that many others do not see."

"...I have met so many that suffered the same fate," Lady Zhen replied. "I wanted to help them all, but there was only so much that I could do, and the taxes were so oppressive, and I faced poverty myself if I made too many mistakes..."

"The fact that you sought to bring relief to the burdened is... well, it makes me view you as a friend, Lady Zhen," Lady Bian said. "My son spoke of being mesmerised by your beauty, but you were not the first beauty that he had ever seen, so I think that it was the beauty of your soul that captivated him above all else. You are a truly good person, Lady Zhen, and so you must ignore the gossips and focus on raising your son... my grandson... as another great man."

Lady Zhen looked as Cao Rui as she replied, "All the same, I... I worry. Will they ever let him be...?"

"My husband's relatives – and his principal wife at the time, Lady Ding – all of them looked down on me, viewed me with disdain, but I proved my worth when I was the only one that still believed him to be alive after Dong Zhuo carried out his first purge," Lady Bian said. "Now I cannot remember the last time that anyone mentioned my past; it will be the same for you. Yuan Xi is gone, and that boy there bears no resemblance to him, so all the 'controversies' are, as my husband would say, 'turned to dust'. Your husband – my son – will one day be Chancellor of State at the very least, and, after him, your son will inherit that responsibility. Who will whisper in dark corners then...?"

"...You are kind and strong, Lady Bian," Lady Zhen replied. "I hope that I can be as strong as you one day."

"That means a lot to me," Lady Bian said. "My son... is very lucky indeed to have you at his side. May he always understand that."

****

119

Cao Cao was elated when he learned that Liu Bei's tiny army had been intercepted and humiliated at Steep-slope; Cao ordered a swift advance toward the region, all the while ignoring the anger that he felt at learning that Liu Bei had somehow convinced around 100,000 of the inhabitants of Xinye, Fan and Xiangyang to gather their worldly belongings and follow his flight. Liu Bei had, to Cao Cao's frustration, managed to escape yet again by the time that Cao reached Steep-slope, and his beloved cousin Cao Chun had suffered injury during the chase.

"...My lord, don't be disheartened," Liu Yè pleaded as he followed Cao Cao into a hastily-assembled command tent. "There's still a chance that Generals Xiahou Yuan, Xiahou Dun, Xu Huang and Li Dian will apprehend Bei at the river."

"We despatched them less than ten minutes ago, Liu Ziyang," Cheng Yu heckled. "So I'm sure that His Excellency remembers who was sent."

"I was reminding us all that four good men have been sent," Liu Yè retorted. "And Bei might be dallying, especially given the captives we've taken."

"Yes... and *almost took*," Jia Xu sighed.

"...That bastard near robbed me of Cousin Zihe!" Cao Cao complained. "Bei's lured the civilians into a trap to serve as bait that was set to catch *me*, and then he's...!"

"Zihe's alive," Cao Hong said.

"...But hurt," Cao Zhen murmured.

"...Is his brother Ren at his side...?" Cao Cao asked.

"He is," Jia Xu replied.

"...I'll visit Zihe shortly," Cao Cao decided. "I must first decide how we handle this mess that Bei has created to slander us."

"Keep the civilians out of the report as much as possible," Cheng Yu suggested. "If the Son of Heaven learns of it, bad enough; if our critics, few though they may now be, learn of it, they'll-"

"You think I don't know that???" Cao Cao bellowed.

"...I was thinking aloud, Your Excellency," Cheng Yu pleaded with uncharacteristic weakness.

"...Yes, of course you were," Cao Cao sighed. "Sorry."

"We... have quite a few prisoners," Jia Xu noted.

"Anyone important...?" Cao Hong asked.

"...Liu Bei's daughters," Jia Xu replied. "Both of them."

"Aha! That's perfect!" Cao Hong cackled. "Miaocai can-!"

"Miaocai has already told me that he does not want to take women from Bei's camp as revenge for his daughter," Cao Cao said. "And... well, I have bitter taste in my mouth about such things after recovering Lady Cai Wenji."

"Liu Bei's not the same as Cai Yong," Cao Hong suggested. "And if Miaocai doesn't want one, then-"

"*Shut up*, please, Zilian," Cao Cao sighed.

"...Well what will you do with them...?" Cao Zhen asked.

"Zihe's cavalrymen were the ones that captured them; I will gift them to Zihe, both of them, and he can be their judge or their master," Cao Cao replied.

"He's *injured*," Cao Hong whined. "He-!"

"*Don't*... you *dare*," Cao Cao ordered. "My word is final... and Zihe will be quite alright. Was there anyone else worth mentioning...?"
"A 'Xu Shu', styled 'Yuanzhi', originally from Yingchuan," Jia Xu replied. "He is an amateur cartographer, geographer and junior adviser to Liu Bei."
"He *was* the man's adviser," Cao Cao growled. "Now he will serve the Han or–!"
"I'd... try to recruit him," Xun Gongda suggested. "He's part of the 'great Jing intelligentsia', spoken of kindly by the eccentric 'Master Still Water', Sima Hui of Yingchuan, and also friends with the likes of the two misguided young geniuses that Wang Can was telling us about."
"...Pang Tong and Zhuge Liang," Cao Cao recalled.
"Yes... or 'Young Phoenix' and 'Crouching Dragon', as they prefer to be known," Cheng Yu said with contempt. "Men cannot and should not take such grandiose names without proving themselves first... such hubris invites disaster."
"Liu Bei only has the latter of the two in his service, I understand," Xun Gongda explained. "The other – Pang Tong, styled 'Shiyuan' – declined to serve Liu Bei and took work as a character appraiser in Jiangling."
"Oho, so young Pang Tong fancies himself to be another Xu Shao, does he...?" Cheng Yu sniggered.
"Evidently yes," Xun Gongda replied. The important thing is that he chose not to serve Bei... and neither did Xu Shu's other well-known acquaintances, Shi Tao, Cui Zhouping and Meng Jian, who have all come over to us voluntarily and speak very highly of Xu Shu, so I understand."
"...Cheng Yu, Xun Yòu: speak with this 'Xu Shu' while I see Zihe in the infirmary," Cao Cao decided. "Reason with him if you can... imprison him if you cannot, and we will review his fate later, when tempers are calmed."
"...Yes, Excellency," Xun Gongda replied.
Cao Cao left the tent with Xu Chu, Liu Yè, Cao Hong and Cao Zhen; Xun Gongda then turned to Cheng Yu and said, "*I* will talk with this man, Elder Cheng: this has no need for two important men's time."
"Fine by me," Cheng Yu scoffed. "I'll take my worthless, mediocre old bones somewhere else while you carry on recruiting all of these wonderful young talents in Jing!"
"...Are you insecure...?" Xun Gongda exclaimed. "Is that why you've dyed your hair black again and–?"
"I am... concerned that I cannot reach His Excellency as well as Fengxiao, because our success might well depend upon it," Cheng Yu admitted. "I am concerned whether *any of us* can truly convince him as Fengxiao did so often: he snaps at us when we question him, when he would laugh and concede when challenged by Fengxiao with far less tact than even I would resort to."
Jia Xu hummed thoughtfully.
"*Yes*... you've seen it before, no doubt... with Li Jue and Dong Zhuo," Cheng Yu snickered. "Such power can unwittingly cause hubris in even the most rational man; add some unbelievable victories and you have the perfect storm. But we're about to fight the wily Liu Bei – who's outwitted us before from weaker positions than he currently endures – and Sun Quan, whose advisers turned

a family of rustic bumpkins into pirate kings and the lords of a quarter of the Empire: *we* must be eternally cautious, and our lord must be eternally mindful. We can promise the first of those things, but the second... is out of our hands."

"His Excellency won't make any more mistakes like those made at Xingyang and Wan," Xun Gongda insisted. "As long as we make our opinions known and protest or debate as appropriate, then-"

"Did your uncle's protestations save Kong Rong or Hua Tuo...?" Cheng Yu asked. "Even I am shocked at their fates... and I wonder if there is a 'line drawn upon the ground' that we daren't cross for fear of ending up like them."

Xun Gongda's eyes wandered.

"...I, 'cantankerous' and 'outspoken' as I am, gentlemen, now... now fear – yes, *fear* – that I must watch my words and be more diplomatic in future," Cheng Yu continued. "I will occasionally test the ground, but as his counsel grows, and as I age, and as his unhealthy obsession with Fengxiao's 'unparalleled genius' grows, so I will be more careful, for my past achievements have obviously been forgotten, shrouded – by accident or with intent – by the all-smothering cloud that is Guo Fengxiao's contribution to the cause."

"Your accusation is unfair," Xun Gongda said.

"Is it...?" Cheng Yu retorted. "Fengxiao joined our lord around the time that we invited the Son of Heaven to Xuchang: that invitation was, primarily, your uncle's suggestion, and it was heeded. Now your uncle cannot suggest anything, not even the logical step of pardoning a gifted poet descended from Confucius, or at least commuting the sentence to just the death of the man himself! Kong Wenju was your uncle's friend, and your uncle was with our lord even before I was, building his administration and preparing him for his role as Governor of Yan!"

"...That's true," Xun Gongda conceded.

"To this very moment and no doubt beyond, Wenruo speaks for us in the Han court, deflecting the heckling and managing a sovereign that, to be blunt, doesn't trust us at all and resents the execution of Consort Dong," Cheng Yu continued. "But these days he is taken for granted: one wonders if our lord's memoirs will not just say, 'One day I met Fengxiao, who travelled back in time and did everything that happened before he arrived'."

Xun Gongda sighed miserably.

"I miss Fengxiao, truly I do, but he is being overstated, and I do not say that out of jealousy but out of *concern*!" Cheng Yu continued. "Every now and then, we must hear it: 'If only Fengxiao were here'... 'Fengxiao would know what to do'... 'Fengxiao could convince me'... 'When will I find a man like Fengxiao?' ...That sort of talk is defeatist and can only lead to ignored advice and disaster. But Heaven help me, gentlemen, my age has caught up with me and robbed me of my nerve, and I won't risk finding out how far my outspokenness will be tolerated when our lord's mood is poor. I can only pray that some other man has the courage to say what I dare not."

Cheng Yu's words were met by a short silence; the adviser exhaled shamefully and retreated, leaving Jia Xu and Xun Gongda to ponder his words.

"...Did you want me to stay for your talk with Xu Shu...?" Jia Xu asked hesitantly.

"...No... no, Wenhe, you... you go and prepare for the march on Jiangling," Xun Gongda replied. "I'll deal with this."

Jia Xu bowed humbly and retreated.

"...*Aiee*... I...! ...I am speechless," Xun Gongda said miserably.

Cao Cao and his ever-present bodyguard Xu Chu travelled to the open-air infirmary and located Cao Chun, who was laid out on a stretcher in a section reserved for important people; Chun's brother, Cao Ren, bowed humbly and said, "It is good to see you here, Mengde."

"...M-Mengde...!" Cao Chun whispered.

"Don't speak if it tires you," Cao Cao ordered. "I... don't wish to lose you, Zihe. Your cavalry was instrumental to my victories at Yè, Nanpi, Zhongshan, Yuyang, Hu Pass, White Wolf Mountain... and... you are a friend, Cousin."

"...Liu... B-Bei's son... was...!" Cao Chun rasped.

"I know all about the child," Cao Cao replied. "Forget about it, Zihe; your life is worth more than any one victory. And... and I have a present for you."

"P-present...?" Cao Chun spluttered.

"...Miaocai declined, but I must insist when it comes to you," Cao Cao said. "Liu Bei's daughters were captured by your men, were they not...?"

"...They were," Cao Chun replied.

"They are now yours... both of them, Zihe," Cao Cao declared. "Treat them in any way you see fit: Knowing you as I do, I'm sure that you'll probably treat them very well, but I will not judge you if you do not."

"...Take... the cavalry," Cao Chun said. "I'm... retired, I think."

Cao Cao frowned and asked, "Why do you say such things...?"

"P-*pragmatism*, Mengde," Cao Chun replied dryly. "People... forget... th-that I'm actually r-rather smart."

"...Are you that badly injured...?" Cao Cao whimpered.

"Enough... that... I'm not... going any further," Cao Chun replied. "Take the cavalry, Mengde, don't... don't leave them behind."

"I... I won't leave them behind, Zihe... I *can't*, I need them," Cao Cao admitted. "But... if you are hurt, then... then you cannot be expected to continue: I will divide them between Cousin Zhen, Cousin Xiu and Xu Chu."

"Me...?" Xu Chu exclaimed. "But-!"

"No 'buts', Zhongkang," Cao Cao insisted. "No one man has the right to lead that cavalry... it will be divided between three trusted men until... until Zihe is deemed to be well enough to resume command of them."

Cao Chun smiled knowingly and said, "If that's how you... want to proceed, Mengde, then... who am I... to argue...?"

"I... still have things to do," Cao Cao sighed. "But-"

"Then go... and do them, Mengde," Cao Chun insisted. "We'll... talk later, sometime."

Cao Cao bowed respectfully and gestured that Cao Ren should follow his slight retreat from Cao Chun's bedside.

"You wanted to say something, Mengde...?" Cao Ren asked as soon as he and Cao Cao had moved away from Cao Chun.

"I'm... heartbroken," Cao Cao admitted. "But... if he is injured, then so be it."

"...What now, Mengde...?" Cao Ren asked.

"Zihe must go home to convalesce," Cao Cao replied. "He will go home to Pei, where it's peaceful, as soon as he can be moved; he can take his new consorts with him, and they can tend to him as good consorts should."

"I don't know... entrusting a sick man to the women that he abducted from their father...?" Cao Ren whispered. "Is that really wise, Mengde...?"

"If they wish to live, then they will accept their fates," Cao Cao replied. "Their father will soon be dead, so what else is there for them...? They will be grateful to be spared, and they will be in Pei County, surrounded by our clansmen; they will travel a day behind him for safety."

"...He won't die, will he, Mengde...?" Cao Ren asked miserably. "My brother is... my friend as well. He *won't* die... he *can't*...!"

"*Strength*, Cousin Zixiao," Cao Cao ordered. "We both of us have more work to do... and we'll avenge Zihe's injuries as we smite those that inflicted them."

Cao Ren nodded agreeably and said, "I'll let him know, Mengde, and then I'll get back to marching on Jiangling."

"Please do, Zixiao," Cao Cao replied. "In the meantime, Liu Bei... must *die*."

The young adviser Xu Shu was brought before Xun Gongda, who asked, "Why did you not submit to the Chancellor at the same time as your friends...?"

"...I do not know of whom you speak," Xu Shu replied. "I heard that my mother had been captured by your soldiers, so I obeyed the rules set down to us and returned to her side as a filial son."

"I speak of Shi Tao, Meng Jian and Cui Zhouping, who have all spoken well of you," Xun Gongda said. "They are all happy to serve the Han: why did you run...?"

"...*Ayah*... I did not think that those men would yield to your master," Xu Shu replied.

"**Show respect!**" Xun Gongda snapped.

"**Your master massacred the innocents!**" Xu Shu cried.

Xun Gongda fought the urge to strike Xu Shu and said, "You... are shackled to a myth, Mister Xu. Chancellor Cao is no villain. We are now aware that 'Xu Province' was the precedent cited by Liu Bei to trigger this hysterical mass migration, but-"

"And what happened here *just now* doesn't evoke Xu Province...?" Xu Shu sobbed angrily. "Innocent people are dead, cut down by *your master's men*!"

"...Innocents that were led to their destruction by that shameless rebel Liu Bei, who tricked them into serving as a human shield to block the route that he was taking during his cowardly escape!" Xun Gongda retorted.

"His senior generals and staff doubled back to defend the civilians!" Xu Shu countered. "What 'cowardly escape'...?"

"...The men that harmed civilians deliberately will be punished for it," Xun Gongda promised.

"And Lord Liu Bei's daughters...?" Xu Shu asked. "Will they be your master's whores now, like Lady Zou when he took Wan from-!"

"Do not push your luck, Mister Xu," Xun Gongda warned. "You're lucky that I chose to see you and ask for your submission personally; I could have delegated this to a junior official that might have been a lot less patient."

Xu Shu snorted disdainfully.

"...Chancellor Cao is not a villain," Xun Gongda insisted. "You are here in Jing Province seeing only what others tell you that they've seen, hearing only what others claim to have heard... but in the capital and the places that have been relieved by the Chancellor's efforts, things are different. Are you saying that noble, decent men like Yang Biao, Sima Fang, Wei Kang, Zao Zhi and Zhong Yao are villains too...?"

"You came here at the head of an army, you and your master, to seize Jing's seal by force if necessary," Xu Shu heckled. "If Governor Liu Biao had not died of despair, then your master would have killed him! It is only because of Cai Mao's treachery and Liu Cong's cowardice that this poor province fell into Cao's hands with such ease!"

"...We came here on a just mission to retrieve Jing Province from the hands of one sick, dying rebel before it was taken – by force, whether necessary or not – by another rebel, namely Sun Quan of Fuchun," Xun Gongda retorted. "This is a Han Imperial army, sanctioned by the throne."

"And led by a Chancellor of State that has learned only from past tyrants and is remorseful about nothing," Xu Shu said. "Otherwise, then, why would he have Dong Zhuo's brain trust *Jia Xu* on one side of him and *Cheng Yu* – an evil old man that fed the flesh of murdered civilians to his soldiers during the Xu Province campaign – on the other...? Did the throne sanction the murder of Consort Dong or the executions of Hua Tuo and Kong Rong...?"

"...I won't imprison you, though I should," Xun Gongda replied. "You can return to your mother as a 'filial son' for now, and we'll speak again some other time... when you've had time to reflect and put aside the lies and distortions that you willingly allow to cloud your judgement. **Guards...!**"

The soldiers that had brought Xu Shu to Xun Gongda's tent then led Xu away again.

"...You make it very hard for me to defend you, Excellency," Xun Gongda said involuntarily; he immediately realised what he had uttered and thanked the Heavens that he had not been heard.

✳✳✳✳✳✳✳✳✳✳✳✳

120

Cao Cao was in a strange yet optimistic mood as he stood with his son Pi, his cousin Ren and his campaign advisers and observed his army's military drills from atop the walls of Jiangling City: Liu Bei had escaped with the aid of Liu Qi and a naval relief force led by Guan Yu, but the cost of Bei's retreat had been great and the fugitive warlord was now trapped in occupied Jiangxia and completely dependent on others militarily.
"Do you have thoughts that you wanted to share, Chancellor…?" Jia Xu asked.
"…Oddly enough, no," Cao Cao replied. "I… am actually overwhelmed by the enormity of what now awaits us."
"Sun Quan and Liu Bei – and in the latter case, only because he can make use of Liu Qi's army – are the last of the dangerous rebels," Cheng Yu suggested.
"…That they are," Cao Cao replied. "I don't fear the Qiang, or the 'Way of Five Pecks', though perhaps I *should*… I certainly don't fear Liu Zhang."
Cao Pi smiled and said,

"A man from Pei County most bold,
A brave hero that Xu Shao foretold,
Who had foes most fearsome to face,
But most are put in their place,
Now just these two rebels to go,
Divided by feuds from so long ago,
Their fight is a fight against fate,
A war on their sovereign most great,
That dooms them to pain much deserved,
When justice, by us, is finally served,
And then the last of the fools,
Those men that live by evil rules,
Who pour such scorn upon the throne,
Whose power is owed to distraction alone,
Will finally know our long tempered wrath,
Their people put back on Heaven's path,
The land will no longer be blighted,
And the Han then at last reunited,
The hero from Pei, his dream disbelieved,
Can rest at last, his task achieved,
And in times far removed from now,
All men will know the name 'Cao',
Who did what no other could do:
He brought peace to all men anew."

"…You managed to maintain a pattern of seven words to each line," Cao Cao exclaimed. "Did you compose that now, or…?"
"I did, Father, but I am no match for you or Zhi," Cao Pi replied.
"…Interesting," Cao Cao said. "Did you mean those words…?"
"I did," Cao Pi replied. "You are the envy of every aspiring man, Father. How could I – or any sensible person – not understand the magnitude of your achievements and respect you for them…?"
"…I was going to compose a poem, but I must bow to my son's

talent and say that he has done my job for me!" Cao Cao chuckled. "My spirits are lifted: I can truly believe that we are almost at the end of the journey!"

Cheng Yu hummed cynically.

"Liu Qi and Sun Quan are irreconcilable," Cao Cao continued. "Liu Bei must choose to betray his 'nephew' for an army of fifty-thousand pirates or cling to tenuous family ties and make do with, at the most, thirty-thousand disaffected Liu Qi loyalists that will soon return to the light when they have faced a few defeats. Either way, gentlemen, Liu Bei will soon be dead and the Empire will be on the way to full restoration! A year from now, we will only know peace!"

"…Yes, Excellency," Liu Yè said tonelessly.

"Liu Qi, Liu Bei, Sun Quan… send word to them all, demanding their surrender… and send more letters to Sun Ben and Sun Fu as well, prompting them to action," Cao Cao ordered. "Be subtle, but be clear: if Sun Ben can overthrow his cousin Quan…"

"We should and shall be very, very subtle, Excellency," Jia Xu replied. "Sun Ben is not exactly loved, and after the victory at Jiangxia, the-"

"Sun Quan is not much loved either, and the victory at Jiangxia was entirely down to Quan's advisers and generals, not Quan himself," Cao Cao insisted. "Yes, they are happy that they have slain Huang Zu and taken a shaky foothold in Jiangxia, but they now face the might of the Han army, an army that we will tell them is made up of eight-hundred-thousand – no, wait, a *million* – men, yes, a million, and that their fifty-thousand is eggs against boulders. Will Sun Quan be popular when he hides in his capital and orders his brave vassals to commit loyal suicide by running at a million swords…?"

"…We shall see, Excellency," Cheng Yu suggested.

"*Pah*… we shall only see capitulation or destruction!" Cao Cao retorted. "Victory is certain… Heaven demands it!"

The Han Imperial court was informed of the tense standoff in the south by Cao Cao's ever-loyal spokesman Xun Wenruo; Emperor Xian listened intently with a strange mixture of fear and hope in his heart.

"So this, to summarise, is the situation," Xun Wenruo said. "Northern Jing Province has completely submitted now, which is everything north of and including the southern capital Jiangling. The four large prefectures to the south of Jiangling – though some call them counties due to their sparse population – are refusing to submit properly but have not declared war either, opting for neutrality that we must begrudgingly accept at present. Liu Qi has taken control of western Jiangxia and is refusing to accept that his father's seal of office was passed to his younger brother Liu Cong at his father's decree… in short, he has rebelled. Sun Quan has withdrawn his army to eastern and southern Jiangxia, and we are currently awaiting a response to a demand that he surrender. Liu Bei has escaped and is currently based in northern Xiakou, where, so some rumours suggest, he is desperately trying to form an alliance between Liu Qi and Sun Quan against the government."

"…We understand the situation, if not the finer points of it," Emperor Xian declared.

"It is badly muddied water, Majesty," Xun Wenruo sighed.

"So after fifteen years of feuding – which far eclipses even the internecine struggle that consumed the elder Yuan brothers – there might actually be a truce between *Liu Qi* and *Sun Quan* against the Han government…?" Minister Yang Biao exclaimed. "Is that really possible, Wenruo…?"

"…It is not for me to say," Xun Wenruo replied. "I don't know what wily-tongued politicians work for either man, or for that 'third arm' in this equation, Liu Bei, who has the most to lose. Stranger things have happened: with Liu Qi and Sun Quan set to lose all of their lands as punishment for their behaviour and Liu Bei set to lose his wretched life for the crime of high treason, a common cause – survival born of desperation – might do what years of failed negotiations could not."

"And if this ridiculous alliance of rebels came to pass, Mister Xun, what sort of army might they have between them…?" the official Geng Ji asked.

"…Sun Quan professes to have fifty-to-a hundred-thousand men, but half of them will be needed to guard his many stolen prefectures and contested borders," Xun Wenruo replied. "Liu Qi… is surprisingly popular, sad to say: he has reassembled what's left of Huang Zu's army under his own banner and enjoys the support of quite a bit of his father's army, meaning anywhere up to… I don't know… thirty-thousand…?"

"And the Chancellor has – he claims – up to a *million men* at his disposal," Geng Ji noted. "What percentage of that is useable…?"

"…Or *real*," Wei Huang scoffed quietly.

"His Excellency the Chancellor of State took an army of two-hundred-thousand men to Jing," Xun Wenruo revealed to astonished gasps that quickly increased in number and volume. **"Jing's army and navy – both crucial to any invasion of the south – add another hundred-thousand to the total when the threat of attacks removes their need to be dispersed throughout the province. A second Han army is now advancing westward that will take the total to four-hundred thousand."**

"*Four-hundred-thousand*???" Yang Biao exclaimed. "The Chancellor is a miracle-worker! Before he took office the Imperial army was a joke that could barely tame our own rebels, let alone protect our borders! Now it is magnificent enough to conquer any place under Heaven!"

"But we will show *restraint*," Xun Wenruo suggested. "At the end of this campaign – and, of course, the subsequent campaigns against Zhang Lu and whoever then refuses to submit – the Han Empire will be the strongest force in the world under Heaven; the Nanman, the Xianbei, An Xi, even the far-flung Da Qin… none of the peoples beyond our borders will threaten us again. We will be secure, safe and at peace… thanks to Chancellor Cao."

Emperor Xian waited for the excited chattering to die down before he said, "We… are grateful to Chancellor Cao for all of his achievements. We shall, of course, await the outcome – no matter how inevitable it might seem – of his latest campaign against the rebel Sun Quan and those two disgraced scions of our clan. When that is over… let us see."

Xun Wenruo sensed the emperor's discomfort at the idea of Cao

Cao's impending victory and replied, "Only good can come of this, Your Majesty."

Emperor Xian smiled icily and said, "We should certainly hope so, Mister Xun Yu."

Xun Wenruo shuddered involuntarily.

Chen Qun – who was now posted to the office of the Imperial Secretariat – followed Xun Wenruo to his office and said, "You were like a ghost as you shuffled here, Wenruo. What is it that's bothering you...?"

"...The Son of Heaven is quietly hostile, and... ... ...nothing," Xun Wenruo replied.

"I think that 'hostile' is a slight exaggeration," Chen Qun suggested. "His Majesty has a strange sense of humour that is quite understandable after years of being mistreated by the likes of Dong Zhuo and Li Jue."

"...You are quite right, Changwen," Xun Wenruo replied with false cheer. "I am just overwhelmed by the enormity of His Excellency's achievements and worry too much about possible setbacks."

"His Excellency has been 'close to victory' before, and then you've been forced to stand and watch the opportunity slip away, so that's quite understandable," Chen Qun said. "But this will not be another Wan City."

"I know that," Xun Wenruo promised.

"...It's almost over," Chen Qun insisted. "And then what happened to me and my father can never happen to anyone else: there will be no more villains, no more tyrants, no more 'partisans', no more rebels, no more cultists... it will be over."

"...Yes," Xun Wenruo sighed. "...It will be over..."

Emperor Xian retired to his private chambers, dismissed his servants, sat opposite Empress Fu and said, "It shall soon be over, so they say."

"What will, Majesty...?" Empress Fu asked.

"The- ...well, *everything*," Emperor Xian replied. "He's about to destroy the 'last three', as some call them... Liu Bei, Liu Qi, and Sun Quan."

"...And then there will be no strong warlords left to oppose his will," Empress Fu said.

"That... is what is being said," Emperor Xian replied. "They don't seem to be worried about Zhang Lu, the Qiang or the Southern Xiongnu; they claim that the 'last three' will signal an end to the strife at last... that after they are gone, there will be peace... but there will still be 'Chancellor Cao'. He will demand great rewards... a duchy... a kingdom... I should be overjoyed that there are no more rebels, but when I hear that Liu Bei claims that he fights to restore the Han to 'its proper lustre', and when I hear that I am called a 'puppet of Cao Cao' by some... I... I want those 'rebels' to win. I want another Guandu, where it is Cao that suffers the surprise defeat... and subsequent destruction. It is the only way that I – *we* – can survive."

Empress Fu nodded silently.

"I don't care what they say in that court... I trust my instincts, and my instincts say that Cao is a hankerer that is eliminating everyone that might be a rival or obstacle to his staking his own claim to my throne," Emperor Xian continued. "I don't see a loyal man when I look into his eyes... I see another Dong Zhuo, another Li Jue. I am not naïve like my father, who was told of Wang Mang but had no examples to draw from; I've seen evil, I've lived in its shadow, and so I recognise it no matter how keen and convincing the disguise. If Cao Cao is not stopped, then he will devour me... and the throne will be his."

"...But there really is nothing that we can do, Majesty," Empress Fu whispered.

"No, there isn't... except to pray, maybe, to appeal to the Heavens," Emperor Xian replied. "I am the Son of Heaven: is my will ignored by that same Heaven...? How is it that I can be sat here helpless while yet another hegemon slowly tightens his grip on *my* Empire, *my* mandated rule...? I am appealing to Heaven... *pleading*, if I must... for someone to be granted the strength to topple this mad tyrant Cao Cao. If it must be Liu Qi, Liu Bei or Sun Quan, then so be it... but *please*... after *four-hundred years*... it cannot end like *this*."

For Emperor Xian, the waiting would, perhaps, be most difficult of all: Cao Cao's army and navy were poised to score yet another victory over yet another of the Han Empire's defiant rebels, and there were next to none in the land that believed that anything other than victory for Cao Cao was possible. But the same had been said of Yuan Shao and Cao Cao's encounter at Guandu, and that famous upset of 8 years previous was about to be upstaged by the outcome of another, more famous battle at a place called 'Red Cliffs'.

There would be one last reprieve for the Han Dynasty: it would endure for another 12 years as Chancellor Cao Cao did what he could to reverse his fortunes, counter the growing strength of Liu Bei and Sun Quan and quietly build a power base of his own in Wei Prefecture to prevent his clan meeting the same fate as the Yuans of Ru County. Some continued to see hope for the Han, but in the end, fate sided with the feuding warlords instead of their sovereign, and the Han would give way to Cao Pi's Cao Wei Dynasty, Liu Bei's Shu Han Dynasty and Sun Quan's Sun Wu Dynasty, which co-existed in a state of perpetual, three-way conflict where constantly shifting alliances and rivalries would be the norm: that was the 60-year-long era that would come to be known as 'Three Kingdoms'.

∗∗∗∗∗∗∗∗∗∗∗∗

EPILOGUE: THE SCENE NOW SET

"...Unbelievable...!"

"Cao Cao did so much...?"

"That was a lot to keep up with!"

"There were still Yellow Turbans...?"

"So Red Cliffs happened next, then...?"

"He said that already!"

"I was just checking!"

"I still can't get over that..."

"Over what...?"

"The Yuans... teamed up with *barbarians*???"

The old storyteller sat and smiled as he listened to his audience and their varied reactions to the tale that he had told.

"That... was probably the longest version of that part of the story that I ever heard, elder," the young farmer said.

"Yes, well, as I said, I don't often get asked to go into detail about it," the old man replied. "Most people prefer the short version because they just want to hear about Cao's fleet being burnt."

"So what were the Sun family doing during all that stuff that you just talked about, then...?" one woman asked.

"Oh, don't ask me to elaborate on *that*," the storyteller pleaded. "That's something else that has a popular short version that I prefer to stick to: Sun Ce died before Red Cliffs, Sun Quan replaced him and grew his army for revenge on Huang Zu and Liu Biao, which, as you just heard, he got... in part, anyway."

"Oh, right," the woman said. "But there's more to it, though...?"

"I've heard long versions from Sun clan loving travellers from the south, yes," the old man replied. "But all that you'll get from me is Red Cliffs and beyond... some other time."

The crowd gradually and noisily dispersed.

"...I shall continue tomorrow," the old man promised.

"Thanks," the young farmer said. "That was... different."

Once the crowd was gone, the old man sighed and said, "In some ways, yes..."

The years after Cao Cao seized Jing Province were busy and famous ones: no event was perhaps more famous than Red Cliffs, which would be forever spoken of as the defining moment in the time period. More rebellions, uprisings, betrayals, coups, pretenders and disasters would follow Red Cliffs, and – as in any era – talking about some of them in a particular way was dangerous. History could be a source of entertainment, but it could also include lessons, warnings and ideas: some were more welcome than others.

"But weren't those different men guilty of the same repeated follies and unheeded consequences as the men that went before and those that followed them...?"

But despite his feelings about the plethora of stories that he felt compelled to share, that old storyteller – and many others like him – would continue to tell the story of the Han Dynasty's fall and the formation of the Three Kingdoms for generations to come, and there would always be an audience willing to listen: such was the power of that story and the characters within.

****

CHARACTER PROFILES AND NAME PRONUNCIATION GUIDE

It may or may not come as a surprise that the author of a novel about China cannot actually read, write or converse in Chinese (yes, that is still the case, five books in...): that could be seen as an indication of how interesting this era can be regardless of knowing the language or culture well, but it severely reduces what you can find in the way of further reading or information. The Three Kingdoms era is very popular in Far East Asia, so there are a lot of works based on the period, although there are only a few that have been translated to English and other European languages. But even when you find the work in your language, there is the pronunciation hurdle to jump; this is a (admittedly simplistic) guide for the completely uninitiated to at least get started, although I should note that I am not a professional historian, language teacher or linguist of any kind and that my guide is not meant to be a professional start of a Chinese language course. That said, here we go.

Pronunciation of Chinese names can be awkward, since renderings generated by the Hanyu-Pinyin system are sometimes misleading (Cao Cao, for example, is often mistaken for 'Cow Cow'). The first attempt at translating *Three Kingdoms* by C. H. Brewitt-Taylor used a different redering method, known as the Wade-Giles system, wherein Cao Cao was spelt T'sao T'sao: the modern approach assumes awareness of 'C' never being used as a 'K' (as in, say, *continue*), but always as an 'Ts' (similar to its usage in *central*). The pronunciation guide below does not use either Wade-Giles or Pinyin, and might itself be open to interpretation: hopefully, it will serve as a rough guide for English speakers. The characters are ordered alphabetically rather than by order of appearance or affiliation. Place names are completely or partially translated depending on what I felt was best.

In every case, the family name is first, the given name second: nobles often take on a 'style name' in addition, which is often used to differentiate the friend, focus of respect, or ally from a stranger or enemy in conversation, hence I say 'in familiar terms' after the style name. Some of the details have been rewritten or corrected where mistakes were found post-publishing (I'm still only human... and I'm really trying to avoid the errors I made while editing East of the River's appendices this time).

Some of the information provided along with the character name – intended as a refresher, as an explanation as to what happened to them after they disappeared from the narrative, or to elaborate where the person was only mentioned in some context – can sometimes spoil surprises for a first-time reader. **You have been warned.**

NB: 'ow' on its own or after an apostrophe in a compound should be pronounced as it is in 'cow', 'ay' as in 'pay' and 'eye' as is. 'X' is a tough one, as is 'J': I vary my approach to the latter quite a bit, since it is a soft 'ch' that's almost a 'j' (just as 'B' is a soft 'P' and 'G' is a soft 'k'), but 'X' can be seen as 'Sh' or 'Hs' (I use 'Sh' because it best reflected it so far as my research went).

Name [Pronunciation] – *brief refresher on who the person was.*
*Any other name they were known by, typically their style name.

PEOPLE

Bao Xin [P'ah-oh Shin] – *official in Yan Province that died during a Yellow Turban assault on the north of the province*

Bao Xun [P'ah-oh Shun] – *son of Bao Xin that Cao Cao employed as an official*
*Known by the courtesy name Shuye [S'oo-yer]

Bing Yuan [P'ing Yoo-arn] – *a scholar and official that resided in Liaodong Peninsula until he offended the administrator and had to be rescued by Taishi Ci (recounted in 'East of the River')*
*Known by the courtesy name Genju [K'ern-ch'oo]

Bo Ju [P'oh Ch'oo] – *Yellow Turban rebel general in Runan* ('FICTIONAL' CHARACTER CREATED FOR NARRATIVE COHESION)

Budugen [Boo-t'oo-k'ern] – *the khan of the Xianbei tribal confederacy during the events of this work*

Cai Mao [Ts'eye Mah-oh] – *high-ranking military officer and official in Jing Province whose sister married Governor Liu Biao*
*Known by the courtesy name Degui [T'er-k'oo-ee]

Cai Yan [Ts'eye Yan] – *highly intelligent eldest daughter of Cai Yong that was kidnapped by Southern Xiongnu prince Liu Bao and became his unwilling consort; she is later brought back to the court by Cao Cao to act as the last link to her father's works, which she had committed to memory.*
*Known in adult life by the courtesy name Wenji [Wern-jee]
*Her actual courtesy name might have actually been 'Zhaoji' [Ch'ah-oh-ch'ee], changed to Wenji in records to avoid the 'naming taboo' (a conflict with Jin Dynasty founder Sima Zhao)

Cai Yong [Ts'eye Yong] – *famous polymath and Han official that was responsible for saving the unaltered works of many classical literati by petitioning the court for the creation of the Xiping Stones; he later earned the ire of the 'Ten Attendants' and suffered a long period of exile in the north and east of the country. During his stay in the east, he educated Gu Yong, one of the men that helped the Sun family to found the state of Eastern Wu. He is responsible for launching the careers of many other men, including the calligrapher Zhong Yao (whose son, Zhong Hui, was famous in his own right later on) and scholar-prodigy Wang Can, author of the Cao Wei Empire's official histories.*
*Known by the courtesy name Bojie [P'oh-jee-er]

Cao Ang [Ts'ao Arng] – *Cao Cao's eldest son and heir; he gave his life to defend his father's retreat toward the end of the Battle of Wan City, which led to Cao Pi becoming Cao Cao's heir*
*Known by the courtesy name Zixiu [Tz'ee-shee-oo]

Cao Anmin [Ts'ao Arn-min] - *Cao Cao's nephew*

Cao Bao [Ts'ao P'ah-oh] – *the Chancellor of Xiapi; he was openly critical of Liu Bei during the latter's tenure as Governor of Xu Province and was murdered by an enraged Zhang Fei, which led in turn to Liu Bei losing the province to Lü Bu*

Cao Cao [Ts'ao Ts'ao] – *one of the main characters and a significant figure of the era*
*Known by the courtesy name Mengde [Mung-der].
*Also known as A'Man [Ah-Marn] as a child and for varying reasons in adulthood, from affectionate to derisive.
*Once labelled a *jianxiong* [jee-arn-shee-ong] (which the author translates at various points as 'Crafty Villain' and 'Hero of Chaos', as either might apply) by the appraiser Xu Shao.

Cao Chong [Ts'ao T'ong] – *son of Cao Cao by Lady Huan that was said to be an extraordinary polymath from an early age*
*Known by the courtesy name Cangshu [Ts'arng-s'oo]

Cao Hong [Ts'ao Hong] – *cousin of Cao Cao that served as a senior officer on many of Cao Cao's campaigns*
*Known by the courtesy name Zilian [Zee-lee-arn]

Cao Pi [Ts'ao Pee] – *eldest of Cao Cao's sons by Lady Bian; he becomes the founder of the Cao Wei Dynasty after his father's death, ending centuries of Han rule*
*Known by the courtesy name Zihuan [Tz'ee-hoo-arn]

Cao Ren [Ts'ao Rern] – *cousin of Cao Cao that joined his army as a senior-ranking subordinate*
*Known by the courtesy name Zixiao [Tz'ee-shee-ow]

Cao Shuo [Ts'ao Shoo-oh] – *Cao Cao's second son; he died of illness not long after the death of his elder brother Ang, enabling Cao Pi's rise to heir to the Cao clan*

Cao Song [Ts'ao Song] – *hereditary marquis, Cao Cao's father, adopted son of the influential eunuch attendant Cao Teng. He held a range of posts including Director of Retainers, Minister Herald and Commander-in-Chief, but he retired to his ancestral home in Pei County with his wealth when Dong Zhuo became Chancellor of State and was later robbed and murdered as he travelled through Xu Province, triggering a violent war between his son and Xu Governor Tao Qian. He was idolised by Cao Cao.*

Cao Teng [Ts'ao Tung] – *a favourite eunuch of at least one Han Emperor (prior to Emperor Ling) that adopted Cao Cao's father, Cao Song, beginning the rise fo the Cao clan*

Cao Xing [Ts'ao Shing] – *Cao Cao officer that once served the famous warlord Lü Bu*

Cao Xiong [Ts'ao See-ong] – *son of Cao Cao by Lady Bian*

Cao Xiu [Ts'ao Shee-oo] – *cousin of Cao Cao that served as a senior officer; he was a close friend of his cousin Cao Pi*
*Known by the courtesy name Wenlie [Wern-lee-er]

Cao Zhang [Ts'ao Ch'arng] – *second son of Cao Cao by Lady Bian*
*Known by the courtesy name Ziwen [Tz'ee-wern]
*Known by the nickname 'Yellow-beard'

Cao Zhi [Ts'ao Ch'ee] – *third son of Cao Cao by Lady Bian*
*Known by the courtesy name Zijian [Tz'ee-jee-arn]

Captain Deng – *officer that accompanies Li Fu during the latter's infiltration of the besieged Yè City*
('FICTIONAL' CHARACTER CREATED FOR NARRATIVE COHESION)

Chang Xi [T'arng Shee] – *ally of Mount Tai Bandit leader Zang Ba and bandit chieftain in his own right*

Che Zhou [T'er Ch'oh] – *Han official that Cao appointed as Governor of Xu Province after the Battle of Xiapi; he was subsequently murdered by Liu Bei when the latter tried to retake the province during the 'Girdle Edict Crisis' that preceded the Battle of Guandu*

Chen Dao [Ch'en T'ow] – *possibly a former Danyang Brigade member; regardless of his origins, he became Liu Bei's trusted bodyguard. His fictional role is usually either minimal or non-existent, with Zhao Yun adopting many of his duties.*
*Known by the courtesy name Shuzhi [S'oo-ch'ee]

Chen Deng [Ch'en T'erng] – *eldest son and heir of Chen Gui, the chieftain of the wealthy and influential Chen clan of Xiapi in Xu Province and a pivotal figure; he was a main conspirator during the plots to rid Xu Province of first Liu Bei and then Lü Bu, after which he was appointed as Administrator of Guangling by Cao Cao*
*Known by the courtesy name Yuanlong [Yoo-arn-long]

Chen Fan [Ch'en Farn] – *Commander-in-Chief at the end of the reign of Emperor Huan and Grand Tutor for the first few months of the reign of Emperor Ling; he lost the first role when he defended Partisans like Li Ying and gained the second when his ally Dou Wu took over the court through his daughter the Empress Dowager. He then joined Dou Wu's failed plot to oust the 'Ten Attendants'. He is cited in this work as an example of an overanxious plotter.*
*Known by the courtesy name Zhongju [Ch'ong-joo]

Chen Gong [Ch'en K'ong] – *adviser that initially served Cao Cao; he rebelled against Cao after the latter indiscriminately attacked Xu Province and its people, yielding Yan Province to Lü Bu. Cao Cao successfully reclaimed Yan, and Chen Gong went on to serve as an adviser to Lü Bu; they exploited a rift between then-governor of Xu Liu Bei and the local officials, ruling Xu until the two were killed following Cao Cao's siege of the capital Xiapi.*
*Known by the courtesy name Gongtai [K'ong-t'eye]

Chen Gui [Ch'en K'oo-ee] – *the chieftain of the wealthy and influential Chen clan of Xiapi in Xu Province and father to Chen Deng; he was instrumental to the many regime changes that occured in Xu Province and briefly advised Lü Bu until he betrayed him for the good of the region. Chen Gui was then appointed as the Chancellor of Pei County: this work portrays a number of encounters between Chen and the doctor Hua Tuo, whose home was in Pei County.*
*Known by the courtesy name Hanyu [Harn-yoo]

Chen Ji [Ch'en Jee] – *the father of Cao Cao's adviser Chen Qun. He studied diligently whilst in exile in his youth, and when the 'Partisan Crisis' ended he became an official in the Han Court. He briefly served Dong Zhuo in the capital before fleeing to Qing Province with his family and serving Liu Bei. He then followed Liu Bei to Xu Province, but when Liu Bei was seen to be an unfit successor to Governor Tao Qian he joined a plot to remove Bei and replace him with Lu Bu and Chen Gong: this was then proven to be a terrible mistake, so Chen Ji joined a second plot to remove Lü Bu. He is only referred to in this work.*
*Known by the courtesy name Yuanfang [Yoo-arn-farng]

Chen Lan [Ch'en Larn] – *an officer serving Yuan Shu that later rebelled and became a 'Qian Hills Bandit'; he then submitted to Yang Province Inspector Liu Fu and aided the latter's efforts to stabilise the region in the wake of Yuan Shu's death*

Chen Lin [Ch'en Lin] – *Han official and later secretary to Hè Jin and then Yuan Shao. He is famous for a document that he authored prior to the Battle of Guandu.*
*Known by the courtesy name Kongzhang [Kong-ch'arng]

Chen Qun [Ch'en Choon] – *the eldest son of the respected author, scholar and statesman Chen Ji (Yuanfang). He served Liu Bei in Pingyuan alongside his father; he aided the successive plots to remove Liu Bei and Lu Bu from power in Xu Province and joined Cao Cao's counsel, which is where he is in this work*
*Known by the courtesy name Changwen [T'arng-wern]

Cheng Qiu [T'erng Ch'ee-oo] – *a corrupt official in Liang Province that made himself unpopular and contributed to the great rebellion that elevated Ma Teng, Han Sui and Song Jian to Qiang warlords and made Han rule close to impossible for years; Du Ji refers to him while he is negotiating with the Qiang*

Cheng Yu [Ch'erng Yoo] – *an adviser to Cao Cao. He was quite old, relatively speaking, when he joined Cao Cao (around 50), and he was known in earlier years of service for being cantankerous, frank and devoid of conscience when matters required it; the author gradually 'softens' his character in the wake of Cao Cao's reaction to Dong Cheng's plot being uncovered, since Cheng Yu is notably quieter, more humble and less influential by the time that he is chief adviser to Cao Cao during the infamous Red Cliffs campaign against Liu Bei and Sun Quan. That 'softening' continues in this work, where he is shown to be increasingly apprehensive as*

Cao Cao become more powerful and more brazen in his actions.
*Known by the courtesy name Zhongde [Ch'ong-der]

Chenggong Ying [Ch'erng-k'ong Ying] – *adviser to Han Sui*

Chunyu Qiong [T'oon-yoo Chee-ong] – *Han official and colonel of the short-lived 'Army of the Western Garden'; he later joined Yuan Shao as a general and adviser. He was famously trusted to guard the Wuchao storage depot during the Battle of Guandu: he failed in his duty and was executed (these events are portrayed in '"Yellow Sky"' and '"Turmoil"'. In fiction he was an absent-minded alcoholic that was drunk at the time of the attack on Wuchao.*
*Known by the courtesy name Zhongjian [Ch'ong-jee-arn]

Consort Dong [T'ong] – *one of Emperor Xian's consorts and daughter of the official Dong Cheng; she was infamously strangled at Cao Cao's instruction in the wake of the failed 'Girdle Edict' plot, and most controversially, she was pregnant.*

Cui Lin [Ts'oo-ee Lin] – *a relation of Cui Yan that Cao Cao employs*
*Known by the courtesy name Deru [T'eh-roo]

Cui Yan [Ts'oo-ee Yarn] – *a scholar and student of the elder statesman Zheng Xuan that wandered the country after the Yellow Turban Rebellion; he later served Yuan Shao and the Han court.*
*Known by the courtesy name Jigui [Ch'ee-k'oo-ee]

Cui Zhouping [Ts'oo-ee Ch'oh-ping] – *a scholar in Jing that was an acquaintance of Zhuge Liang, Pang Tong and Xu Shu*

Dian Wei [Dee-arn Way] – *famous bodyguard to Cao Cao; he died protecting Cao Cao during the Battle of Wan City.*

Ding Yuan [T'ing Yoo-arn] – *a Han official and Inspector of Bing Province at the time of the Liang Province Rebellion and the Black Mountain Bandit attacks in the north; he later discovered and took the warrior Lü Bu to be his foster son. He became a known force of benevolence: his other notable subordinate was Zhang Yang, the Administrator of Henei that provided support to Emperor Xian after the collapse of Li Jue and Guo Si's 'Regency' regime. Lü Bu murdered him as a sign of loyalty to his next master, Dong Zhuo.*
*Known by the courtesy name Jianyang [Jee-arn-yarng]

Dong Cheng [T'ong Cherng] – *began his career as a subordinate of Dong Zhuo and then the 'co-regents' Li Jue and Guo Si (how and why is not known at the time of writing) but eventually had a change of heart and rescued Emperor Xian with Cao Cao's help (amongst others), for which he was rewarded with a general's rank. He may have been a relative of Dong Zhuo or the late Grand Empress Dowager Dong, or another Dong clan altogether. He was the senior architect of the 'Girdle Edict' plot that ended in failure (and his execution as a traitor) but gave many of Cao Cao's enemies – most notably Yuan Shao – the justification that they needed to fight Cao (events portrayed in '"Turmoil"').*

Dong Si [T'ong See] – *an official that is wedded to Lady Cai Wenji after her rescue*

Dong Zhao [T'ong Ch'ow] – *known as Dong Gongren throughout to avoid confusion, with the exception of certain dialogue (his name is so similar at a glance to that of the more famous Dong Zhuo that the author felt it wise); he was a prodigious, promising subordinate of Yuan Shao that later joined Administrator Zhang Yang in Henei after a series of 'misunderstandings' and went on to serve the Han court and become Governor of Xu Province.*
*Known by the courtesy name Gongren [K'ong-rern]

Dong Zhuo [T'ong Ch'oo-oh] – *the infamous Liang Province warlord-general that seized control of the capital after the deaths of Emperor Ling, Commander Hè Jin and the 'Ten Attendants' and ruled with cruelty, protected by his foster son Lü Bu and a host of formidable allies. His actions – which included pillaging, treason, torture and regicide – inspired Yuan Shao to form the Eastern Pass Coalition and challenge him militarily (his exploits are covered extensively in '"Yellow Sky"').*
*Known by the courtesy name Zhongying [Ch'ong-ying]

Dou Wu [T'oh Woo] – *a respected scholar and father to Emperor Huan's last empress, Lady Dou. He tried to purge the 'Ten Attendants', but his plan, though thwarted, had serious and far-reaching consequences.*
*Known by the courtesy name Youping [Yoh-ping]

Du Ji [T'oo Ch'ee] – *a Han official that went into hiding during the 'Dong Zhuo Crisis' but resurfaced to become a senior statesman and ancestor to Jin Dynasty emperors*
*Known by the courtesy name Bohou [P'oh-hoo]

Duan Wei [T'oo-arn Way] – *officer that served Dong Zhuo and then the regent Li Jue: he later killed his lord*

Emperor Huan of the Han [Hoo-arn] – *predecessor to Emperor Ling (but not his father: Huan died without issue).*

Emperor Ling of the Han [Ling] – *the successor to Emperor Huan and father to Emperors Shao and Xian; some blame Ling for the demise of the Han (he was emperor during the 'Yellow Turban Rebellion' and 'Liang Province Rebellion', both of which were blamed on government mismanagement). His death was followed by the rise of Dong Zhuo and the fission that resulted from that.*
*Also known as (Han) Lingdi [(Harn) Ling-t'ee] (lit. Han Emperor Ling) when Lingdi is a better option for conciseness.
*Known as Liu Hong [Lee-oo Hong], Marquis of Jieduting [Jee-er-doo-ting]) before being created Emperor.

Emperor Shao of Han [S'ah-oh] – *Emperor Ling's eldest son, born to Empress Hè. He became Emperor shortly after the death of his father (after a short but unpleasant conflict between his grandmother's clan and his mother's clan that resulted in the purge of his grandmother's clan from the court), but when Dong*

Zhuo seized power in the capital Shao was deposed, created the Prince of Hongnong and replaced by his younger brother Liu Xie, who became Emperor Xian, the last Emperor of the Han Dynasty. He and his mother were then murdered by Dong Zhuo's allies.
*Known alternatively within the text as (Han) Shaodi [(Harn) S'ah-oh-t'ee] (lit. Han Emperor Shao) when Shaodi is a better option for conciseness.
*Known as Liu Bian [Lee-oo P'ee-arn], Prince of Hongnong [Hong-nong] after being deposed by Dong Zhuo.

Emperor Xian of Han [Shee-an] – *Emperor Ling's second son, Liu Xie was born to Consort Wang rather than Empress Hè: the jealous empress then poisoned his mother. There were a lot of inauspicious prognostications being made at that point in time, so Lingdi had his sons 'adopted' to others prior to their coming of age; Liu Xie was entrusted to his grandmother, Empress Dowager Dong. He was first created the Prince of Bohai and then the Prince of Chenliu after the 'adoption' period ended, but despite being a second son by a consort, he would later become Emperor Xian after Dong Zhuo seized power and deposed his brother, hence he was never truly accepted by some. It is no secret or 'plot spoiler' that the Han Dynasty was finally eradicated in the early 3rd Century; Xiandi had the 'privilege' of being the last Han Emperor. He is said to have lived for over a decade after abdicating as the Duke of Shanyang; his given date of death is unusually close to – as in not long after – the death of Zhuge Liang, Chancellor/Prime Minister of the independent state of Shu Han, whose self-appointed duty it was to restore the Han in some form.*
*Also known as (Han) Xiandi [(Harn) Shee-an-t'ee] (lit. Han Emperor Xian) when Xiandi is a better option for conciseness.
*Known as Liu Xie [Lee-oo Shee-er], Prince of Chenliu [Ch'en-lee-oo] prior to his ascension.

(Grand) Empress Dowager Dong [T'ong] – *the mother of Emperor Ling; Ling installed his mother as Dowager when the opportunity arose, wherein she started to meddle in the affairs of state. She raised Liu Xie, her younger grandson, when court superstition dictated that her son's heirs should not be raised as princes. When her son died Lady Dong became Grand Dowager, but she and her Hejian Dong clan were then forced to contest the rival Hè family's plans for the succession: the Dongs of Hejian lost, and Lady Dong died a miserable, broken woman.*

Empress Dowager Hè [Her] – *the second empress taken by Emperor Ling; her brother, Hè Jin, would go on to become Commander-in-Chief. She was the mother of Liu Bian, later Emperor Shao and Prince of Hongnong; she shared his fate – death – when Dong Zhuo seized power.*

Empress Fu [Foo] – *daughter of Han official Fu Wan and (one of, if not the) first consort to Emperor Xian; she was then made Empress when Li Jue and Guo Si founded their 'co-regency' government. Empress Fu was said to be a confidante to Emperor Xian; the author takes the liberty of portraying the relationship between the young monarchs as frank, affectionate and relatively informal in order to give the audience an idea of what they might think about events at any given point.*

Empress Dowager Liang [Lee-arng] – *sister of the influential Liang Ji and stepmother to Emperor Huan; she was purged along with her brother by the 'Ten Attendants' and Emperor Huan.*

Empress Song [Song] – *Emperor Ling's less than favoured first empress; when the under-resourced Han army was annihilated by the Xianbei Confederacy, the 'Ten Attendants' needed a scapegoat for the disaster and, along with some jealous consorts, had Empress Song branded as a witch that had caused the loss as an act of spite. Her connection to the Cao clan meant that they – including the famous Cao Cao – suffered a temporary loss of favour, which only intensified Cao's hatred for the eunuchs (events portrayed in '"Yellow Sky"').*

Fa Zheng [Fah Ch'erng] – *a low-ranking member of Liu Zhang's court in Yi Province that later aided Liu Bei's takeover of Yi.*
*Known by the courtesy name Xiaozhi [Sh'ee-ow-ch'-ee]

Fan A [Farn Ah] – *a scholar and student of Hua Tuo*

Fan Xian [Farn Shee-arn] – *an official in Hedong Prefecture that becomes an agitator at the Administrator's request*

Feng Kai [Fung K'eye] – *Cao Cao officer that is depicted as serving in Jing Province. He is named as one of the main generals during the ill-fated Red Cliffs campaign, but he is included in this work in a nominal role since the author could not locate any useful information about him: it is assumed that he is one of the many casualties that resulted.*

Feng Li [Fung Lee] – *Yuan clan officer*

'Flying Swallow' Zhang Yan [Ch'arng Yarn] – *known as 'Flying Swallow' for his great speed and dexterity, Chu Yan (as he was first known) was a bandit leader that formed an uneasy alliance with 'Oxhorn Zhang' to raid a village; Oxhorn was mortally wounded by the defending forces, but to the surprise of all, Chu Yan helped his temporary ally to safety. Oxhorn saw in Chu Yan a man that could do something amazing, and he bequeathed his bandit army to Chu Yan as he lay dying. Chu Yan then changed his named to Zhang Yan in honour of Oxhorn, and went on to become the charismatic leader of a million-strong coalition known as the Black Mountain Bandits.*
*Formerly known as Chu Yan [T'oo Yarn]

'Frog-eyes' – *a former Mount Tai Bandit affiliated to Chang Xi*
('FICTIONAL' CHARACTER CREATED FOR NARRATIVE COHESION)

Fu Wan [Foo Wahn] – *a Han official and descendant of the scholar Fu Sheng and the Han loyalist official Fu Dan; he is father-in-law to Emperor Xian (his daughter is Empress Fu)*

Fu Xie [Foo Shee-er] – *a senior official in the Han court at the time of the great Qiang uprising in Liang Province. He was eventually posted to Liang Province to serve the current Governor and died fighting the rebels Ma Teng and Han Sui, who went on to become prominent Qiang warlords (portrayed in '"Yellow Sky"').*

Fu Xun [Foo Shoon] – *a politician serving Jing Governor Liu Biao.*
*Known by the courtesy name Gongti [K'ong-tee]

Gan Li [K'arn Lee] – *Yuan clan officer*

Gao Fan [K'ao Farn] – *Yuan clan official that was promoted to Administrator of Wei Prefecture in Ji Province*

Gao Gan [K'ao K'arn] – *nephew/vassal of Yuan Shao that served as Shao's Governor of Bing Province*

Gao Lan [K'ao Larn] – *Cao Cao officer that once served Yuan Shao and worked with future legend Zhang Hè*

Gao Rou [K'ao Roh] – *Yuan clan official that served as his cousin Gao Gan's adviser and later joined the Han court*
*Known by the courtesy name Wenhui [Wern-h'oo-ee]

Gao Shun [K'ao S'oon] – *a subordinate of Lü Bu that remained with Bu until his death; the two men had a difficult working relationship. He was a very competent field commander; he (or one of his subordinates) was likely responsible for the infamous arrow that robbed Xiahou Dun of one of his eyes.*

Geng Bi [K'erng P'ee] – *Inspector of Liang Province whose corrupt and incompetent rule was one of the main catalysts of the Liang Province Rebellion (events portrayed in '"Yellow Sky"')*

Geng Ji [K'erng Ch'ee] – *a Han official in Xuchang: he is a critic of (and later plotter against) Cao Cao.*
*Known by the courtesy name Jixing [Ch'ee-shing]

Gong Du [K'ong T'oo] – *bandit in Yu Province that collaborated with Yuan Shao's forces during the Guandu campaign.*

Gongsun Du [K'ong-soon T'oo] – *the semi-autonomous administrator of Liaodong Peninsula until the time of the Siege of Yè City: he seized parts of Korea (known regionally as Goguryeo) at Dong Zhuo's instruction and gave asylum to Taishi Ci*
*Known by the courtesy name Shengji [S'erng-ch'ee]

Gongsun Fang [K'ong-soon Fung] – *scholar and friend of Cui Yan*

Gongsun Gong [K'ong-soon K'ong] – *younger son of Gongsun Du that serves his older brother Kang as an adviser*

Gongsun Kang [K'ong-soon Karng] – *Administrator of Liaodong Peninsula after his father, Gongsun Du, passed away*

Gongsun Zan [K'ong-soon Tz'arn] – *a military officer and warlord in the last two decades of the 2nd Century; he was a friend of the warlord Liu Bei, and was known for his tumultuous relationship with the Ru County Yuan clan. He collaborated with Yuan Shu from time to time and briefly worked with Yuan Shao to seize and divide Ji Province between them, but when his beloved nephew – who was 'on loan' to Yuan Shu's general Sun Jian – was killed in battle with Yuan Shao's army Zan and Shao became irreconcilable enemies. Gongsun then fought Yuan Shao for control of Ji, Qing and Yòu provinces; he killed Yòu's governor, Liu Yu, became self-appointed ruler of Yòu and waged a proxy war with Shao using the Black Mountain Bandits when the Imperial Regency court ordered the two to stop fighting. The feud resumed when Emperor Xian was rescued and installed in Xuchang by Cao Cao, effectively annulling the regency decree: Yuan Shao then exploited his friend-turned-rival Cao's attention being forcibly turned to fighting Lü Bu in Xu Province and destroyed Gongsun Zan, finally adding Yòu Province to his list of territories.*
*Known by the courtesy name Bogui [P'oh-goo-ee]

Guan Cheng [K'oo-arn T'erng] – *a river pirate king in Bing Province: he once fought Zhang Hè, Yue Jin and Li Dian (the precise timing was difficult to determine at the time of writing, so the author places this battle before Cao Cao's Invasion of Jing)*

Guan Tong [K'oo-arn Tong] – *Yuan Tan official in Qing Province*

Guan Yu [K'oo-arn Yoo] – *an early ally of Liu Bei who would gain a magnitude of fame and worship after his death that exceeded that enjoyed by his master; he is known for his long beard, his green robes, his learnedness, his lofty demeanour, his 'Green Dragon' weapon (which the author has retained despite its being a possible fiction), his fictional inheritance of the equally-fictional 'Red Hare' warhorse from Lü Bu, and his similarly fictional unmatched skill in battle, although his historical skill is still quite impressive. He is revered by the lawful and the lawless alike, since he is seen as a man that applied morals when and where appropriate to achieve an ultimate end. His contribution to this work amounts to a few 'cameo appearances', since Liu Bei's faction is not shown often: his early career is covered in "Yellow Sky" and '"Turmoil"', while his later career – which overlaps with this work on the timeline - is depicted in 'Crouching Dragon'.*
*Known by the courtesy name Yunchang [Yoon-charng]

Guo Jia [K'oo-oh Jee-ah] – *senior adviser to Cao Cao that briefly served Yuan Shao; he is one of the most important advisers that Cao Cao ever had, and his absence from the first major campaign after his untimely death – the acquisition of Jing Province and subsequent 'Battle of Red Cliffs' – is largely blamed – and by none more than Cao Cao himself – for the disastrous outcome. It might be said that he is, for the first six acts, a central character of this work and a driving force behind its overall structure, since it is his advice that drives Cao Cao until his victory over the Wuhuan.*
*Known by the courtesy name Fengxiao [Fung-shee-ow]

Guo Si [K'oo-oh See] – *a general serving Dong Zhuo; he cooperated with fellow Liang Province general Li Jue and became 'co-regent' after Dong Zhuo's death. Guo and Li's joint rise to power is depicted in the last acts of '"Yellow Sky"' and their fall from power – and deaths – are depicted in '"Turmoil"'.*

Guo Tu [K'oo-oh Too] – *an adviser to Yuan Shao that once served – and then betrayed – Ji Province governor Han Fu, allowing Yuan to seize Ji and begin building his strength. He later joined Yuan Tan during the second Yuan succession crisis.*
*Known by the courtesy name Gongze [K'ong-tz'er]

Guo Yi [K'oo-oh Yee] – *son of the famous genius Guo Jia that later becomes an official in Cao Cao's government.*
*Known by the courtesy name Boyi [P'oh-yee]

Guo Yuan [K'oo-oh Yoo-arn] – *Gao Gan officer that was related by marriage to the Han official Zhong Yao.*

Han Fan [Harn Farn] – *Yuan clan official that serves as the Magistrate of Yiyang County*

Han Fu [Harn Foo] – *the Governor of Ji Province until the onset of the 'Dong Zhuo Crisis'; Han Fu later lent his forces to the campaign against Dong Zhuo. He had many vassals that were notable in their own right, such as Qu Yi and Zhang Hè: the former was a hero of the Yellow Turban suppression campaign, while the latter would go on to serve Yuan Shao and Cao Cao in succession and become one of the most famous generals of the 'Three Kingdoms' era. After trying to escape his obligations to the Eastern Pass Coalition, Han was attacked by Gongsun Zan (who was acting at Yuan Shao's behest), betrayed by a large number of his vassals and forced to cede his post to Yuan Shao and go into exile in Yan Province; he committed suicide whilst living under the protection of Cao Cao's friend Zhang Miao, Administrator of Chenliu (presumably because he suspected that he and his family would be killed by Yuan Shao's agents otherwise).*
*Known by the courtesy name Wenjie [Wern-jee-er]

Han Hao [Harn Ha-oh] – *Cao Cao officer under Xiahou Dun; he was a subordinate of Wang Kuang at the time of the 'Dong Zhuo crisis' and joined Cao Cao after Wang Kuang retired.*
*Known by the courtesy name Yuansi [Yoo-arn-see]

Han Juzi [Harn Ch'oo-tz'ee] – *Yuan Shao officer: he was killed during Cao Cao's infamous attack on the Wuchao supply depot (the success of which led to Cao's victory at Guandu).*

Han Song [Harn Mung] – *politician serving Jing Governor Liu Biao*
*Known by the courtesy name Degao [T'er-k'ow]

Han Sui [Harn Soo-ee] – *a former Han official that was captured during the great Liang Province Rebellion and 'turned' by events; he quickly became a powerful Qiang warlord along with sometimes-ally, sometimes-rival Ma Teng, who was also a former*

Han official. His role in this work is minor: his (many) early exploits are depicted in '"Yellow Sky"' and '"Turmoil"'.
*Known by the courtesy name Wenyue [Wern-yoo-er]

Han Xian [Harn Shee-an] - *the leader of the White Wave Bandits; he was a good friend of the Han officer Yang Feng, who later joined the bandits. Han and his allies briefly 'protected' Emperor Xian from the co-regents, but when they demanded too much the official Dong Cheng enlisted Cao Cao's aid in repelling the bandits. Han Xian's reduced following was then recruited by Yuan Shu, who sent them to Xu Province to fight Lü Bu: Han and his friend Yang Feng were later captured and executed by Liu Bei.*

Han Xuan [Harn Shoo-arn] – *Liu Biao's appointed administrator of Changsha; he surrendered to Liu Bei after Red Cliffs*

Han Xun [Harn Shoon] – *Yuan Tan officer*
('FICTIONAL' CHARACTER CREATED FOR NARRATIVE COHESION)

Hè Jin [Her Jin] – *the brother of Empress Hè; Jin rose to Commander-in-Chief of the Imperial army once his sister was elevated as Lingdi's second empress. He was lauded for his victories over the Yellow Turbans, but he also became an enemy of the 'Ten Attendants', who convinced Emperor Ling to form a second force, the 'Army of the Western Garden', to counter Jin's growing influence. When Lingdi died, Jin thwarted Grand Empress Dowager Dong's attempts to alter the succession line and secured his nephew as Emperor Shao. Jin then tried to purge the 'Ten Attendants', but he was pitted against his own sister, Empress Dowager Hè (who was being blackmailed by the 'Ten' for her part in Consort Wang's death) and forced to invite General Dong Zhuo to the capital to aid his cause. Jin was killed by the 'Ten' before Dong Zhuo reached the capital, which allowed Dong – who was now the highest-ranking officer – to seize power. All of these events are depicted in '"Yellow Sky"'.*
*Known by the courtesy name Suigao [Soo-ee-gah-oh]

Hè Qia [Her Chee-ah] – *politician serving Jing Governor Liu Biao*
*Known by the courtesy name Yangshi [Yarng-s'ee]

Hè Xian [Her Shee-an] – *son of Hè Jin; Xian died young, and Cao Cao took Xian's widow Lady Yin into his own home as a consort.*

Hè Yan [Her Yarn] – *son of Hè Xian by Lady Yin (and grandson of Hè Jin); he was adopted by Cao Cao when Cao took his mother as a consort*
*Known by the courtesy name Pingshu [Ping-s'oo]

Hou Shu [Hoh S'oo] – *Yellow Turban leader in Qing Province*
('FICTIONAL' CHARACTER CREATED FOR NARRATIVE COHESION)

Hu Zhen [Hoo Ch'ern] – *an influential Liang Province general serving Dong Zhuo; he had a minor rivalry with Lü Bu that was not always friendly (it is this rivalry that is referred to in this work when Cao Cao is discussing Yue Jin with his advisers). Hu put his*

feud with Bu to one side to aid Wang Yun's plot to kill Dong Zhuo, but when future regents Li Jue and Guo Si gained the upper hand Hu switched sides and aided Li and Guo's victory over Lü Bu and Wang Yun. He was rewarded with rank but died suddenly; Regent Li Jue was suspected to be behind his conspicuous end.
*Known by the courtesy name Wencai [Wern-ts'eye]

Hua Tuo [Hoo-ah Too-oh] – *a famous scholar and doctor that lived and worked through the time of the last three Han Emperors; he is already very old at the time that he is introduced – as a major character – in this work. He was said to have created beneficial exercises based on the physical postures and movements of several animals and practised a range of medicinal treatments including anaesthesia, surgery and the more traditional acupuncture. The fates of Hua and his 'Book of the Green Bag' are dealt with in detail in this work.*
*Known by the courtesy name Yuanhua [Yoo-arn-hoo-ah]

Hua Xin [Hoo-ah Shin] – *a Han official that served as Administrator of Yuzhang Prefecture in Yang Province before deciding to leave the south and seek employment with the central government in the north; he has a grudge against the Sun clan (some of the circumstances leading to that grudge are depicted in 'East of the River').*
*Known by the courtesy name Ziyu [Tz'ee-yoo]

Hua Xiong [Hoo-ah Shee-ong] – *Dong Zhuo general that is most famous for his death in fiction: in 'Sanguo Yanyi' (Romance of the Three Kingdoms), Hua Xiong was shown to be second only to Lü Bu (whose strength is also greatly exaggerated); Hua bests every general sent to challenge him, including the formidable Sun Jian (who had the most to do with his historical defeat), but he is finally killed with ease during a duel with Guan Yu. Historically, Hua Xiong is far less exciting, and it is this Hua Xiong that the author chose for the sake of producing more factual works, namely his appearances in '"Yellow Sky"' and 'East of the River'. Hua is briefly mentioned during a discussion about Yue Jin.*

Huan Jie [Hoo-arn Jee-er] – *a politician that served Sun Jian until the latter's death in Jing Province; Huan successfully lobbied Liu Biao to have Sun's body returned to his family and then joined Liu Biao. Huan Jie later joined the Han government and the Cao Wei Empire that succeeded it.*
*Known by the courtesy name Boxu [P'oh-shoo]

Huang Quan [Hoo-arng Choo-arn] – *an official serving Yi Governor Liu Zhang; he later served Liu Bei and the Cao Wei Empire.*
*Known by the courtesy name Gongheng [K'ong-Herng]

Huang Shè [Hoo-arng S'er] – *the son of the Jiangxia (southeast Jing Province) warlord Huang Zu*

Huang Zhong [Hoo-arng Ch'ong] – *a veteran Han general that served Liu Biao (mentioned but never shown) and then the Changsha Administrator Han Xuan (where he only makes a*

'cameo appearance') before being recruited by Liu Bei (which is depicted in 'Crouching Dragon'). Huang's main contribution to history – besides being an impressive example of a man that is still fighting on the front line in his seventies – is defeating and killing Cao Cao's senior general Xiahou Yuan during the Hanzhong campaign in the late 210s.
*Known by the courtesy name Hansheng [Harn-s'erng]

Huang Zu [Hoo-arng Tz'oo] – ostensibly a vassal of Jing Province Governor Liu Biao, but Huang Zu was autonomous in the southeast Jiangxia region and had immense influence.

Huangfu Song [Hoo-arng-foo Song] – a prominent Han Dynasty general; he scored many victories against the Yellow Turbans, and he was renowned for his morals and generosity. He challenged the 'Ten Attendants' and suffered a temporary downturn in his career; he had one last significant victory against the Qiang rebels but was forced (due to the death of Lingdi) to retreat to the capital before he could finish his work. He retired in poor health and died during the brief 'co-regency' period.
*Known by the courtesy name Yizhen [Yee-ch'ern]

Huche'er [Hoo-cher Er] – a man of non-Chinese origin that served as an officer to the Liang Province warlord Zhang Ji and then his nephew Zhang Xiu; he is said to have been strong and resourceful, and he was pivotal to the victory over Cao Cao's forces during the 'Battle of Wan City'. He disappears from history after that encounter, but the author retains him for the few scenes in this work that require Zhang Xiu to have followers.

Huchuquan [Hoo-t'oo-chooarn] – elected Chanyu (supreme chieftain) of the Southern Xiongnu tribes that reside in Bing Province and brother of the famous Southern Xiongnu renegade chieftain Yufuluo (and, by proxy, uncle of future Chanyu Liu Bao)

Huo Nu [Hoo-oh Noo] – a minor magnate in Yòu Province that supports the rule of the Yuan clan

Ji Pi [Jee Pee] – a Han court physician that is briefly depicted in this work as a foreshadowing of his later role as plotter against Cao Cao: the author hints that Hua Tuo's death might have been a motivational factor. He is usually known as Ji Ben, but the author understands that his actual name was changed due to 'naming taboo' (as Cao Pi was an emperor)

Jia Kui [Jee-ah Koo-ee] – a Han official that served as Administrator of Hongnong (the author places him in this role during this work) and then as Cao Cao's registrar (beyond the timeline of this work). Jia Kui is most famous for preventing the 'Battle of Shiting/Stone Town' – fought between Cao Wei and Sun Quan's forces in the Three Kingdoms era – becoming a total rout by seeing through an enemy ruse and rescuing Cao Xiu. He is only introduced in this work and does nothing significant.
*Known by the courtesy name Liangdao [Lee-arng-t'ow]

Jia Xin [Jee-ah Shin] – *a Han official that is appointed as guardian of Li County by Cao Cao*

Jia Xu [Jee-ah Shoo] – *an adviser and politician; Jia Xu first served the tyrant Dong Zhuo and then advised Dong's generals Li Jue and Guo Si when they governed as co-regents. When the regents faltered, Jia Xu joined their former vassal Zhang Xiu in Wan City: it is there that he inflicted one of the most famous and costly defeats of Cao Cao's career upon him. Jia later served Cao Cao and the Cao Wei Empire. He is probably one of the most divisive and decisive figures of the period, and is, it might be argued, one of the greatest strategists of the time, an equal or perhaps superior to more famous figures such as Zhuge Liang, Pang Tong, Zhou Yu, Lü Meng, Lu Xun, Sima Yi and Guo Jia.*
*Known by the courtesy name Wenhe [Wern-her]

Jian Shuo [Jee-arn S'oo-oh] – *a senior member of the 'Ten Attendants'; he conceived and commanded the militia-based 'Army of the Western Garden'. He met his end when his fellow 'Ten Attendants' abandoned him after a failed attempt to assassinate Hè Jin: he is briefly mentioned in this work, used as a form of insult. His uncle was arrested and flogged by the then-District Captain of Luoyang, Cao Cao, for flouting a curfew law, which led to Cao being 'exiled' to Ji'nan by the 'Ten Attendants' (this is mentioned in a separate conversation).*

Jian Yong [Jee-arn Yong] – *official of and friend to Liu Bei; he was said to be vulgar and direct, so the author tends to use him as a means for lightening the mood (and he is, once again, depicted as a constant companion to Liu Bei).*
*Known by the courtesy name Xianhe [Shee-an-her]

Jiang Yiqu [Jee-arng Yee-choo] – *Yuan clan officer*

Jiao Chu [Jee-ow T'oo] – *Yuan clan official in Yòu Province*

Jin Xuan [Ch'in Shoo-arn] – *Administrator of Wuling until Liu Bei seized the region after the Battle of Red Cliffs*
*Known by the courtesy name Yuanji [Yoo-arn-jee]

Jin Yi [Ch'in Yee] – *Han official and son of Jin Xuan that fled to Xuchang when Liu Bei seized Wuling; he later joined a plot to assassinate Cao Cao that failed terribly.*
*Known by the courtesy name Dewei [T'er-way]

Ju Hu [Joo Hoo] – *Yuan clan officer and son of Ju Shou*

Ju Shou [Joo S'oh] – *an official and adviser to Yuan Shao; he was formerly a subordinate official of Ji Province governor Han Fu, and was one of the men that convinced Han that he should cede the province quietly. He was one of Yuan Shao's most important advisers, although his advice was frequently ignored; he decided that he would die a loyal death at Guandu instead of joining Cao Cao as others did.*

Kong Rong [Kong Rong] – *a descendant of the famous philosopher Confucius and a popular poet and philosopher in his own right. His last years are portrayed in this work.*
*Known by the courtesy name Wenju [Wern-joo]

Kong Rong's children [Kong] – *whether they were two boys or a boy and girl (or maybe there were more than two?) is not clear at the time of writing: they met a grisly end after their father erred and gave Cao Cao an opportunity to destroy him and his clan. The (apocryphal?) famous last words of one son are recounted in this work as they are too well known to ignore.*

Kuai Liang [Koo-eye Lee-arng] – *adviser to Jing Governor Liu Biao: he is depicted as sick (and then dead) in this work, due to his true fate being difficult to determine*
*Known by the courtesy name Zirou [Tz'ee-roh]

Kuai Yue [Koo-eye Yoo-er] – *adviser to Huang Zu and Liu Biao and brother of Kuai Liang; also a former subordinate of Hè Jin*
*Known by the courtesy name Yidu [Yee-t'oo]

Lady Bian [P'ee-arn] – *Cao Cao's principal wife*

Lady Cai (1) [Ts'eye] – *sister of Jing Admiral Cai Mao and second wife of Governor Liu Biao*

Lady Cai (2) [Ts'eye] – *younger sister of Cai Yan (Wenji). The author concedes that she is all but explicitly depicted as having died in '"Yellow Sky"', but that was unintended: she not only survived but served as mother to at least one future person of note (late Cao Wei official Yang Hu). The author uses the Da/Xiao prefix – used when referring to the Qiao sisters of Jiangdong – as a way to differentiate between this Lady Cai and Liu Biao's wife.*
*Referred to almost exclusively as Xiaocai [Shee-ow-ts-eye]

Lady Cao [Ts'ao] – *eldest daughter of Cao Cao by Lady Liu*

Lady Ding [T'ing] – *Cao Cao's second wife and carer to his first 3 children after the early death of Lady Liu; she all but divorced Cao Cao after the loss of Cao Ang (in battle) and Cao Shuo (to illness) and lived in a separate building on Cao Cao's estate. She is only mentioned in this work.*

Lady Du [T'oo] – *consort to Cao Cao and formerly the wife of Lü Bu's general Qin Yilu; she was briefly pursued by Guan Yu, who still holds a grudge against Cao for 'stealing her'.*

Lady Huan [Hoo-arn] – *one of Cao Cao's consorts and mother to his favourite son, the short-lived prodigy Cao Chong*

Lady Liu (1) [Lee-oo] – *Yuan Shao's last principal wife and mother to his favourite third son Yuan Shang*

Lady Liu (2) [Lee-oo] – *Cao Cao's deceased first wife*

Lady Sun [Soon] – *a different Lady Sun to the more famous 'Shangxiang' depicted in 'Crouching Dragon' and 'East of the River': she is Sun Ben's daughter, married to Cao Zhang*

Lady Wang [Warng] – *the famous historical figure Wang Yi, who took up arms during Ma Chao's siege of Ji City (this occurs 'off-stage' in 'Crouching Dragon' and is outside of this work's timeline: she is introduced here because her husband is a prominent defender of Liang Province and her backstory is interesting)*

Lady Xiahou [Shee-ah-hoh] – *a daughter of Xiahou Yuan that, controversially, was abducted and forcibly married to Liu Bei's famous general Zhang Fei. The author deliberately avoided this element of the story when writing 'Crouching Dragon', but here it is: it does make some of Xiahou Yuan's dialogue in that other work seem improper, but the casual attitude to women's rights – or, rather, the lack of them – actually makes his stance plausible. In Zhang Fei's defence – if that is even the right term – he did treat Lady Xiahou well: that allowed for a few high-profile defections, one of which – Xiahou Lan – is depicted in this work.*

Lady Yin [Yin] – *consort to Cao Cao, widow of Hè Jin's son Xian and mother Hè Yan*

Lady Yuan [Yoo-arn] – *Yuan Shao's sister, wife of Yang Biao and mother of Yang Xiu; she is only mentioned.*

Lady Zhang [Ch'arng] – *the principal wife of Sima Yi and mother of future regents Sima Shi and Sima Zhao*

Lady Zhen [Ch'ern] – *wife to Yuan Xi and then Cao Pi, and mother to the future Cao Wei emperor Cao Rui; she is a fairly important character in this work.*

Lady Zou [Tz'oh] – *beautiful wife of Zhang Ji that became an unwilling catalyst for the Battle of Wan City*

Lei Bo [Lay P'oh] – *rebel/bandit leader that once served Yuan Shu alongside Chen Lan (who is now a fellow rebel/bandit)*

Li Cheng [Lee T'erng] – *Yuan Shao's appointed Administrator of Wei Prefecture in Ji Province that was killed by Black Mountain Bandits; his successor, Gao Fan, is reminded of this*

Li Dian [Lee T'ee-an] – *Cao Cao officer specialising in supplies*
*Known by the courtesy name Mancheng [Man-t'eng]

Li Fu [Lee Foo] – *Ji Province Registrar under the Yuan clan*
*Known by the courtesy name Zixian [Tz'ee-shee-arn]

Li Jue [Lee Joo-er] – *one of Dong Zhuo's subordinate officers; he later took charge of Chang'an with fellow officer Guo Si after Dong Zhuo's death and became a co-regent (his rise to power is depicted in '"Yellow Sky"'). He claimed to be descended from two famous historical figures: one was Lao Tzu, founder of Taoism,*

and the other was Li Guang, a Han commander known as the 'Flying General'. He was later betrayed by some of his followers – who allowed Emperor Xian to flee to Luoyang – and murdered.
*Known by the courtesy name Zhiran [Ch'ee-rarn]

Li Kan [Lee Karn] – *Qiang officer serving Ma Teng*

Li Ru [Lee Roo] – *an adviser to Dong Zhuo that assisted his takeover of the Imperial court; he usually worked alongside the more famous Jia Xu. He 'retired' after being publicly castigated by Emperor Xian and all but threatened for his role in the regicide of Emperor Shao (depicted in '"Yellow Sky"').*
*Known by the courtesy name Wenyou [Wern-yoh]

Li Shu [Lee S'oo] – *Sun clan officer that was directly involved in the assassination of Cao Cao's first appointed Inspector of Yang Province, Yan Xiang: he rebelled and tried to seize Lujiang Prefecture when Sun Quan was named as successor to Sun Ce. He is never mentioned by name in this work.*

Li Teng [Lee Terng] – *a former Administrator of Guangling that was said to have been temporarily cured and then 'allowed to die' by the physician Hua Tuo*

Li Tong [Lee Tong] – *Cao Cao officer*
*Known by the courtesy name Wenda [Wern-dah]

Li Xiangru [Lee Shee-arng-roo] – *Administrator of Longxi that defected to the rebels during the Liang Province Crisis of 185; Du Ji mentions him when liaising with the Qiang warlords.*

Li Zheng [Lee Ch'erng] – *the eldest son of Han official Li Qian, the elder brother of Han general Li Dian and former Inspector of Qing Province; he is mentioned when Yue Jin is heckling Li Dian.*

Liang Ji [Lee-arng Jee] – *controlled the court of Emperor Huan until he was outwitted by Huan and his eunuchs and executed for sedition. A highly divisive figure, praised for reforms by some but vilified for moral corruption by others*

Liang Shuang [Lee-arng S'oo-arng] – *a rebel in Liang Province that briefly had Zhao Ang's wife Lady Wang and their daughter as hostages after causing the deaths of their sons: he is depicted as the cause of emotional trauma and Zhao Ang's heightened caution when dealing with the Qiang.*

Liu Bao [Lee-oo P'ao] – *eldest son of exiled Southern Xiongnu chieftain Yufuluo and heir to the Southern Xiongnu chieftainship: his abduction (and taking as a consort) of Lady Cai Yan is a major plot point in this work. His descendants go on to conquer part of China, citing Han lineage as their justification for creating their own empire.*

Liu Bei [Lee-oo P'ay] – *an ancestrally-disinherited scion of the ruling Liu family; Bei was forced into a life of weaving straw shoes*

and mats with his mother as a result. He was later supported by a wealthy relative, and was schooled alongside Gongsun Zan, a future friend that he aided during the Yellow Turban Rebellion. He famously aided the southern warlord Sun Quan during the conflict known as the Battle of Red Cliffs, and then he had an uneasy alliance with the Suns for over a decade. He eventually became First Emperor of the western state of Shu Han, which was one of the famous 'Three Kingdoms', but died shortly thereafter, leaving the task of reunifying the country to his trusted aide Zhuge Liang. Liu Bei's early career is depicted in '"Yellow Sky"' and '"Turmoil"'; his later career is depicted in this work until the timeline runs parallel to 'Crouching Dragon', after which he is only referred to.
*Known by the courtesy name Xuande [Shoo-arn-der]

Liu Biao [Lee-oo P'ee-ow] – *the Governor of Jing Province; he had a famous feud with the Sun clan of Jiangdongthat is still raging at the start of this work. His final years are depicted in this work.*
*Known by the courtesy name Jingsheng [Jing-s'ung]

Liu Cong [Lee-oo Ts'ong] – *the second son of Jing Provincial Governor Liu Biao; he was favoured by Biao's second wife, Lady Cai and her brother General Cai Mao when contemplating succession (and was married to their niece). His most famous contribution to history is portrayed in this work.*

Liu Dai [Lee-oo T'eye] – *royal Liu clan member and the Governor of Yan Province after the Yellow Turban Rebellion; he died fighting an army of Yellow Turban rebels, whereupon Cao Cao successfully petitioned Yuan Shao for the role of governor.*
*Known by the courtesy name Gongshan [K'ong-s'arn]

Liu Du [Lee-oo T'oo] – *Administrator of Lingling Prefecture under Jing Governor Liu Biao*

Liu Feng [Lee-oo Fung] – *the adopted son of Liu Bei (previously known as Kou Feng [Koh Fung]); he was actually connected to the royal house by marriage, so it was a partly political adoption that Liu Bei made while in Jing Province. Liu Feng should have been Bei's heir, since Bei had no sons when Feng was adopted, but Bei's biological son Shan was born shortly afterward, leaving doubt that eventually led to Feng abandoning Guan Yu to die at Fan and being subsequently disowned and ordered to commit suicide by a furious Liu Bei (portrayed in 'Crouching Dragon')*

Liu Fu [Lee-oo Foo] – *Cao Cao's appointed Inspector of Yang Province at the start of this work: he left Lujiang (and Yuan Shu's rule) to join the Han government some time before (depicted in 'East of the River' and '"Turmoil"'). Fu pacified the local bandits and oversaw the initial construction of the famous Hefei Fortress that would test the Sun clan's army to its limits for some years after the Battle of Red Cliffs*
*Known by the courtesy name Yuanying [Yoo-arn-ying]

Liu Hè [Lee-oo Her] – *the eldest son of Yòu Governor Liu Yu, who was suggested as an alternative emperor by Yuan Shao during the*

'Dong Zhuo Crisis'; he was held hostage by Yuan Shu (detail is provided in '"Yellow Sky"') for many years. He was released during the chaos surrounding Yuan Shu's declaration as an emperor and joined Yuan Shao's campaign against Gongsun Zan, who had murdered his father Yu. His final fate after Gongsun's defeat at Yijing (shown in '"Turmoil"') is unknown by the author at the time of writing: his status is given as 'whereabouts unknown'.

Liu Pi [Lee-oo Pee] – a Yellow Turban leader in Runan that took part in most of the uprisings and worked as a mercenary for several warlords, the last being Yuan Shu (taking his first presumed death date) or Yuan Shao (taking his second, more likely death date that the author assumes as correct). He is shown aiding Liu Bei's attack on Xuchang in '"Turmoil"' and being killed in battle shortly afterward; Bei then has to deal with the remnants of his followers in the opening act of this work.

Liu Qi [Lee-oo Chee] – the eldest son of Jing Provincial Governor Liu Biao; he is depicted here and in the author's other works as being in poor health due to vice, which may or may not be correct (he died shortly after the Battle of Red Cliffs, inadvertently bequeathing his army to Liu Bei in the process).

Liu Shan [Lee-oo S'arn] – Liu Bei's infant son that is obliquely referred to during this work; he was rescued by Zhao Yun at the Battle of Steep-slope, which occurs 'off-stage' in Act IX. He will go on to be the Second Emperor of Shu Han.

Liu Xun [Lee-oo Shoon] – Yuan Shu's appointed Administrator of Lujiang Prefecture until Shu died, at which point he declared autonomy and seized Shu's family; he was defeated by Sun Ce prior to the Battle of Guandu and joined the court in Xuchang.
*Known by the courtesy name Zitai [Tz'ee-t'eye]

Liu Yan [Lee-oo Yarn] – a royal Liu clan member who served as a court official in the imperial capital; he seized an opportunity to suggest upgrading certain inspectors to regional governors to reduce pressure on the Han administration, and he was then made Governor of Yi Province. He forged an alliance with Zhang Lu, leader of the 'Way of Five Pecks' cult in Yi. His fourth son Liu Zhang inherited his position when he died shortly after a failed attempt to defeat the co-regents and seize Chang'an with the aid of the Qiang warlords (depicted in '"Yellow Sky"').
*Known by the courtesy name Junlang [Joon-larng]

Liu Yao [Lee-oo Yah-oh] – a member of the royal Liu clan and brother of Yan Province Governor Liu Dai; he was later made Governor of Yang Province when the court wanted to curb the ambitions of Yuan Shu and his allies, but he was routed by Sun Ce (events depicted in 'East of the River'). His main adviser was Xu Shao, the man that famously appraised Cao Cao.
*Known by the courtesy name Zhengli [Ch'erng-lee]

Liu Yè [Lee-oo Yer] – Cao Cao official and later his registrar and adviser; he once served as an adviser to Yuan Shu's Administrator

of Liujiang Prefecture, Liu Xun
*Known by the courtesy name Ziyang [Tz'ee-yarng]

Liu Yu [Lee-oo Yoo] – *a member of the imperial Liu clan; he was made Governor of Yòu Province and given the responsibility of pacifying the tribes and rebels in that frontier region, which he did with the vital support of his vassal Gongsun Zan. Liu Yu was considered as an alternative emperor after the demise of Emperor Shao, but he refused the appointment. His relationship with Gongsun Zan eroded as Gongsun's power grew, and when he challenged Gongsun's 'business activities', Gongsun killed him and seized the province as an independent territory.*
*Known by the courtesy name Bo'an [P'oh An]

Liu Zhang [Lee-oo Ch'arng] – *fourth son of the Governor of Yi Province, Liu Yan; he inherited his father's role, since his elder brothers had all died. Liu Zhang is only shown briefly in this work: his governorship (and loss) of Yi and his strained relationship with his distant relative Liu Bei are depicted in 'Crouching Dragon'.*
*Known by the courtesy name Jiyu [Jee-yoo]

'Long-toes' – *a former Mount Tai Bandit affiliated to Chang Xi*
('FICTIONAL CHARACTER CREATED FOR NARRATIVE COHESION)

Lou Gui [Loh K'oo-ee] – *a hermit that lives in Jing Province: he leant sporadic advice to Liu Biao until the fall of Jing and later served Cao Cao at the Battle of Tong Pass*
*Known by the courtesy name Zibo [Tz'ee-boh]

Louban [Loh-barn] – *the appointed Chanyu (king) of the Wuhuan people of northeast China; his relative Tadun (who served as his 'regent' until he came of age) actually holds all of the power*

Lu Kang [Loo Karng] – *Han official, respected pacifier of troublemakers and an Administrator of Lujiang; he was one of the first men to suffer at the hands of Sun Ce, who sieged him to death. He was, ironically enough, the uncle of the famous Sun clan strategist Lu Xun that routed Liu Bei at Xiaoting. His later life and death are depicted in '"Yellow Sky"' and 'East of the River').*
*Known by the courtesy name Jining [Jee-ning]

Lu Zhao [Loo Ch'ah-oh] – *Cao Cao officer that is shown serving in Jing Province. He is named as one of the main generals during the famous Red Cliffs campaign, but he is only included in this work in a nominal role since the author could not locate any useful information about him: it is assumed that he is one of the many casualties of the rout.*

Lu Zhi [Loo Ch'ee] – *a scholar of the Han court; he tutored the future warlords Liu Bei and Gongsun Zan and was lauded for his military efforts against the Yellow Turbans.*
*Known by the courtesy name Zigan [Tz'ee-garn]

Lü Boshe [L' P'oh-sher] – *a friend of Cao Cao whose family was butchered by an untrusting Cao as he fled the capital to escape*

Dong Zhuo; an adapation of his famous story, be it apocryphal or not, is depicted in '"Yellow Sky"' and referenced occasionally.

Lü Bu [L'Boo] – one of the most famous men of the era; he is known particularly for his disloyalty, inconstancy, and inevitable downfall. In fiction, he is portrayed as a near-invincible warrior that rides a similarly unparalleled horse, 'Red Hare'; famous scenes include him successfully keeping Liu Bei, Guan Yu and Zhang Fei at Bei simultaneously and with ease, retreating only when the three attacked at exactly the same time (the author chose to homage the scene in '"Turmoil"', during the Battle of Xiapi). Historically and in fiction, Lü Bu is a poor tactician, but in history that serves as a greater handicap since he is not an invincible warrior. He began his career as the adopted son to Bing Province Inspector Ding Yuan, but he killed Ding Yuan and became the bodyguard and foster son of the tyrant Dong Zhuo. The loyalist courtier Wang Yun persuaded Bu to betray Dong Zhuo less than three years later, but Lü Bu was then chased from the capital by former allies Li Jue and Guo Si. Bu then drifted from place to place, gaining greater notoriety as he went; he gained temporary control of Yan Province with the aid of Chen Gong but was defeated by Cao Cao and chased into Xu Province, where he sheltered under and then usurped power from Liu Bei. Bu lost the confidence of Xu's officials, who betrayed him to Cao Cao and – after a long campaign that saw Bu veer between serving the Han and allying with the pretender Yuan Shu – finally tricked the warlord into isolating himself. Bu died an ignominious death – strangulation – after being captured by his own men during a siege on Xu's capital Xiapi by Cao Cao and Liu Bei, who were enjoying a rare – and short-lived – alliance.
*Known by the courtesy name Fengxian [Fung-shee-arn]

Lü Fan [L'Farn] – Sun clan adviser that helped Sun Ce and Sun Quan to build their impressive independent state
*Known by the courtesy name Ziheng [Tz'ee-herng]

Lü Kuang [L'Koo-arng] – Yuan clan officer

Lü Xiang [L'Shee-arng] – Yuan clan officer

Ma Chao [Mah T'ao] – son and heir of Qiang warlord Ma Teng; he later becomes the leader of a consequential rebellion in Liang Province. He later joined the warlord Liu Bei and assisted his takeover of Yi Province before dying uneventfully
*Known by the courtesy name Mengqi [Mung-chee]

Ma Dai [Mah T'eye] – Qiang officer and cousin of Ma Chao that later joined Shu Han and became a loyal general that famously aided the quelling of Wei Yan's rebellion after Zhuge Liang's death.

Ma Teng [Mah Tung] – a major in the Han army that defected to the Liang Province rebels and became a Qiang warlord; he is the father of the famous Qiang warlord Ma Chao.
*Known by the courtesy name Shoucheng [S'oh-t'ung]

Ma Tie [Mah Tee-er] – *younger son of the warlord Ma Teng*

Ma Xiu [Mah Shee-oo] – *younger son of the warlord Ma Teng*

Ma Yan [Mah Yarn] – *Yuan clan officer*

Man Chong [Marn T'ong] – *an official serving Cao Cao that becomes an important adviser in later years; his courtesy name is changed to "P'oning" in the text*
*Known by the courtesy name Boning [P'oh-ning]

Mao Jie [Mah-oh Chee-er] – *official serving Cao Cao*
*Known by the courtesy name Xiaoxian [Shee-ow-shee-arn]

Mei Qian [May Chee-arn] – *a leader of the Qian Hill Bandits in Yang Province: he agreed to work with Liu Fu and is passive during the timeframe of this work*

Meng Jian [Merng Ch'ee-arn] – *an acquaintance of Pang Tong, Zhuge Liang and Xu Shu that joined Cao Cao*
*Known by the courtesy name Gongwei [K'ong-way]

Mi Fang [Mee Farng] - *the younger brother of Mi Zhu; he became an early supporter of Liu Bei. Some of his complicated later career – including his role in Guan Yu's famous loss of Jing Province – is covered in 'Crouching Dragon'.*
*Known by the courtesy name Zifang [Tz'ee-farng]

Mi Heng [Mee Herng] – *prodigious but irreverent young scholar that was recommended to Cao Cao by Kong Rong in a letter that survives; his fate is depicted in '"Turmoil"'*
*Known by the courtesy name Zhengping [Ch'erng-ping]

Mi Zhu [Mee Ch'oo] – *an influential clan chieftain in Xu Province that became an early supporter of Liu Bei; his early career is covered in '"Yellow Sky"' and '"Turmoil"' and his later career and death are depicted in 'Crouching Dragon'.*
*Known by the courtesy name Zizhong [Tz'ee-ch'ong]

Mister Fan [Farn] – *Yuan Xi's adviser*
('FICTIONAL' CHARACTER CREATED FOR NARRATIVE COHESION)

Nanlou [Narn-loh] – *a Wuhuan tribal leader in Yòu Province*

Niu Fu [Nee-oo Foo] – *Dong Zhuo's son-in-law*

Ou Xing [Oh Shing] – *a rebel/bandit in Changsha that Sun Jian defeated in his early career prior to the 'Dong Zhuo Crisis'*

Pan Jun [Parn Ch'oon] – *Liu Biao official that went on to serve Liu Bei and Sun Quan in later years*
*Known by the courtesy name Chengming [T'ung-ming]

Pang brothers [Parng] – *Liu Biao advisers (most likely Pang Degong [Parng T'er-k'ong] and Pang Shanmin [Parng S'arn-min])*

*that the author does not make much use of; they are related to
the famous strategist Pang Tong*

Pang De [Parng Der] – *Qiang officer that served Ma Teng and then
Ma Chao before joining Cao Cao; his role in Guan Yu's famous
siege of Fan City is covered in 'Crouching Dragon'.*
*Known by the courtesy name Lingming [Ling-ming]

Pang Ji [Parng Jee] – *an adviser to Yuan Shao*
*Known by the courtesy name Yuantu [Yoo-arn-too]

Pang Rou [Parng Roh] – *Pang De's brother; he went on to serve
Shu Han while Pang De served Cao Cao*

Pang Tong [Parng Tong] - *the famous strategist and friend/rival of
Zhuge Liang; he is only referred to in this work (his short career
serving is Liu Bei covered in 'Crouching Dragon').*
*Known by the courtesy name Shiyuan [S'ee-yoo-arn]
*Known by the Taoist name 'Young Phoenix'

Pufulu [Poo-foo-loo] – *a Wuhuan tribal leader in Yòu Province*

Qi Ji [Chee Jee] – *Cao Cao officer that once served Yuan Shu*

Qian Zhao [Chee-arn Ch'ah-oh] – *Yuan clan officer that joins Cao
Cao and becomes a Wuhuan liaison*
*Known by the courtesy name Zijing [Tz'ee-jing]

Qiao Xuan [Chee-ow Shoo-arn] – *an scholar and senior official
during the later years of the Han Dynasty; he was said to have
been so certain of the importance of law over all that when his
closest family were held for ransom, he approved an armed
assault on the kidnappers and gave no thought to payment. His
wife and children died at the hands of their doomed captors, but
Qiao Xuan was unapologetic, saying that future kidnappers could
expect no money or mercy; the number of kidnappings – which
had been increasing to that point – was reduced to next to
nothing thereafter. He held almost every important court rank that
there was at one time or another, and was one of the men that
launched the career of the prodigy Cai Yong. He also endorsed
Cao Cao, calling him 'A hero of future times', and the two
remained friends until Qiao Xuan's death.*
*Known by the courtesy name Gongzu [K'ong-tz'oo]

Qin Bonan [Chin P'oh-narn] – *an old acquaintance of Cao Cao's
that gives his life for Cao during Cao's campaign against Yufuluo
(depicted in '"Turmoil"'): this story may, like that of Lü Boshe, be
an invention, but the author chose to include the story and refer
to it. Some accounts suggest that Qin was the natural father of
Cao Zhen (who later served as Commander-in-Chief to the Cao
Wei Emperor and fought against Shu Han Prime Minister Zhuge
Liang on a number of occasions), and that Cao adopted Zhen as a
way of honouring Qin's sacrifice; alternative accounts have Cao
Zhen as an actual relation, however.*

Qin Lang [Chin Larng] – *son of the general Qin Yilu; he was adopted by Cao Cao when Cao took his mother as a consort. He was said to be a mediocrity but enjoyed favour nonetheless*
*Known by the courtesy name Yuanming [Yoo-arn-ming]

Qin Yi [Chin Yee] – *military officer serving Yuan Shu; he later defected to Cao Cao*

Qin Yilu [Chin Yee-loo] – *officer and official serving Lü Bu; he later abandoned his wife, Lady Du, and became an envoy to Yuan Shu's court in Shouchun. Cao Cao took Lady Du as a consort and adopted his son after defeating Lü Bu; Qin Yilu was eventually killed by Liu Bei's forces (depicted in '"Turmoil"')*

Qiuliju [Chee-oo-lee-joo] – *father of Louban and the previous Wuhuan Chanyu (king)*

Qu Yi [Choo Yee] – *a talented military officer during the time of the Yellow Turban Rebellion that worked for Ji Governor Han Fu and his successor Yuan Shao. Qu Yi crushed Gongsun Zan's army at the Battle of Jie Bridge, but he was slandered and fled/died.*

'Red Crest' – *a former Mount Tai Bandit affiliated to Chang Xi*
('FICTIONAL' CHARACTER CREATED FOR NARRATIVE COHESION)

Shen Pei [S'ern Pay] – *Yuan clan adviser*
*Known by the courtesy name Zhengnan [Ch'erng-narn]

Shen Rong [S'ern Rong] – *the nephew of the adviser Shen Pei*

Sheng Xian [S'erng Shee-arn] – *appointed Administrator of Wu Prefecture that was overthrown by Xu Gong and forced into exile; he is only referred to in this work, but is a secondary character in 'East of the River'. He was killed by Sun Quan's agents, which led his followers to kill Quan's brother Yi in retaliation*
*Known by the courtesy name Xiaozhang [Shee-ow-ch'arng]

Shi Huan [S'ee Hoo-arn] – *an officer serving Cao Cao*
*Known by the courtesy name Gongliu [K'ong-lee-oo]

Shi Tao [S'ee Tah-oh] – *an acquaintance of Pang Tong, Zhuge Liang and Xu Shuthat chose to serve Cao Cao*
*Known by the courtesy name Guangyuan [K'oo-arng-yoo-arn]

Shi Xie [S'ee Shee-er] – *Governor of Jiaozhi 'Province' (actually part of modern Vietnam) that ran the region as a benevolent, semi-autonomous Buddhist state*
*Known by the courtesy name Weiyan [Way-yan]
*Known in Vietnamese Buddhist worship as King Si [See]

Shisun Rui [S'ee-soon Roo-ee] – *politician and staunch Han loyalist that became involved in many plots to remove Dong Zhuo and the co-regents; he died before the court was rescued.*
*Known by the courtesy name Junrong [Ch'oon-rong]

Sima Fang [Ss-mah Farng] – *Han official and father of Sima Yi*
*Known by the courtesy name Jiangong [Jee-arn-k'ong]

Sima Fu [Ss-mah Farng] – *younger brother of Sima Yi*
*Known by the courtesy name Shuda [Shoo-t'ah]

Sima Hui [Ss-mah Hoo-ee] – *eccentric scholar from Yingchuan that mostly resided in Jing Province; he recommended Zhuge Liang and Pang Tong to Liu Bei*
*Known by the courtesy name Decao [T'er-tsao]
*Known by the Taoist name 'Master Still Water'
*Known as 'Mister Yes' (pejorative)

Sima Jin [Ss-mah Ch'in] – *younger brother of Sima Yi*
*Known by the courtesy name Huida [Hoo-ee-t'ah]

Sima Kui [Ss-mah Koo-ee] – *younger brother of Sima Yi*
*Known by the courtesy name Jida [Ch'ee-t'ah]

Sima Lang [Ss-mah Larng] – *elder brother of Sima Yi*
*Known by the courtesy name Boda [P'oh-t'ah]

Sima Min [Ss-mah Min] – *younger brother of Sima Yi*
*Known by the courtesy name Youda [Yoh-t'ah]

Sima Tong [Ss-mah Tong] – *younger brother of Sima Yi*
*Known by the courtesy name Yada [Yah-t'ah]

Sima Xun [Ss-mah Shoon] – *younger brother of Sima Yi*
*Known by the courtesy name Xianda [Shee-arn-t'ah]

Sima Yi [Ss-mah Yee] – *a famous official that served Cao Cao and several successive members of the Cao clan; he is also the father of Sima Shi and Sima Zhao and the grandfather of Sima Yan, who were all historically significant in their own right as the founders of the Jin Dynasty. He is just starting his career in this work: his famous rivalry with Zhuge Liang is depicted in 'Crouching Dragon'.*
*Known by the courtesy name Zhongda [Ch'ong-t'ah]

Song Jian [Song Jee-arn] – *a former Han official that rebelled and became one of three Qiang kings that ruled Liang Province when the Han court finally gave up trying to reclaim it (the other two were the more ambitious Han Sui and Ma Teng): his autonomous state lasted for decades.*

Song Jie [Song Ch'ee-er] – *a scholar and friend of Cui Yan*

Song Nie [Song Nee-er] – *a Han official that was appointed as Inspector of Liang Province during the early stages of the rebellion but proved to be naïve, idealistic and too 'soft' to manage the Qiang tribes; Cao Cao refers to him disdainfully.*

Su Yòu [Soo Yoh] – *Yuan clan officer*

Sui Gu [Soo-ee K'oo] – *an officer serving Zhang Yang; he tried to*

join Yuan Shao after Zhang's death but Yue Jin intercepted Sui, killed him and requisitioned his men for Cao Cao.
*Known by the courtesy name Baitu [P'eye-too]

Sun Ben [Soon P'ern] – *cousin of Sun Ce and briefly the head of the Fuchun Sun clan; he is a major character in 'East of the River'*
*Known by the courtesy name Boyang [P'oh-yarng]

Sun Ce [Soon Ts'er] – *the eldest son of the warrior-prodigy Sun Jian and the true founder of the state of Eastern Wu; he was assassinated by the son of the agitator Xu Gong in revenge for Gong's murder, which paved the way for Sun Quan to rule. The Sun clan's early exploits are covered in 'East of the River'.*
*Known by the courtesy name Bofu [P'oh-foo]

Sun Guan [Soon Ts'er] – *a former Mount Tai Bandit chieftain and good friend of Mount Tai Bandit founder Zang Ba*
*Known by the courtesy name Zhongtai [Ch'ong-Tigh]

Sun Jian [Soon Jee-arn] – *a southern man whose military career began during the Yellow Turban Rebellion and continued with a sizeable role in the campaigns against the Liang Province rebels and Dong Zhuo; his progeny founded the state of Eastern Wu.*
*Known by the courtesy name Wentai [Wern-Tigh]

Sun Kuang [Soon Koo-arng] – *a younger son of Sun Jian that was married to Cao Cao's niece but died young (the circumstances of his death were unknown at the time of writing, so the author cites illness). He is only mentioned in this work.*
*Known by the courtesy name Jizuo [Ch'ee-Tz'oo-oh]

Sun Qian [Soon Chee-arn] – *known throughout as 'Mister Sun' (in-keeping with a practice started in 'Crouching Dragon' to differentiate him from members of the southern Sun clan); he and the influential Mi clan of Xu Province turned their allegiances from Tao Qian to Liu Bei and remained with him thereafter. His early career is covered in '"Yellow Sky"' and '"Turmoil"', and the end of his career is covered in 'Crouching Dragon'.*
*Known by the courtesy name Gongyou [K'ong-yoh]

Sun Quan [Soon Choo-arn] – *the second son of Sun Jian and future ruler of Eastern Wu; he is recently installed as ruler of Jiangdong at the start of this work.*
*Known by the courtesy name Zhongmou [Ch'ong-moh]

Sun Yi [Soon Yee] – *younger son of Sun Jian that was considered, by some, to be a better choice for a successor to his elder brother Sun Ce's legacy; Yi happily served under Quan until his untimely death at the hands of assassins that were avenging Sheng Xian.*
*Known by the courtesy name Shubi [S'oo-p'ee]

Supuyan [Soo-poo-yarn] – *a Wuhuan tribal leader in Yòu Province*

Tadun [Tah-doon] – *senior Wuhuan chieftain that acted as regent for young Chanyu (king) Louban but retained the power when*

Louban came of age; he is allied to the Yuan clan against Cao Cao

Taishi Ci [T'eye-sher Ts'er] – *a 'lone wolf' that has become legendary for acts of great heroism, including rescuing Kong Rong from a horde of Yellow Turbans using a combination of ruses and a militia borrowed from Liu Bei. He travelled to Yang Province to aid fellow townsman (and provincial governor) Liu Yao in his battle against Yuan Shu; that initially pitted him against Sun Ce, but the two later became allies (events depicted in 'East of the River').*
*Known by the courtesy name Ziyi [Tz'ee-yee]

Tanshihuai [Tarn-shee-hoo-eye] – *the famous khan of the Xianbei Confederacy that routed the Han army in the year 175*

Tao Qian [Tah-oh Chee-an] – *the Governor of Xu Province during the reign of Emperor Ling; Tao is revered in some fiction as a morally upstanding man, but historical accounts suggest a more multifaceted man that hankered for talented subordinates and reacted badly to any that rejected his work offers. He was held responsible for the death of Cao Cao's father, Cao Song, which led to Cao's famous devastation of Xu. Xu Province passed to Liu Bei after his death (depicted in '"Yellow Sky"' and ' "Turmoil"').*
*Known by the courtesy name Gongzu [K'ong-tz'oo]

Teng Dao [Terng T'ow] – *Yuan Shang's envoy to Supuyan*
('FICTIONAL' CHARACTER CREATED FOR NARRATIVE COHESION)

Tian Chou [Tee-an T'oh] – *official that once served Yòu Province Governor Liu Yu and then joined Cao Cao; he returns to Yòu at the start of this work after being seen to serve Cao in '"Turmoil"', which was 'artistic license' (Tian Chou probably never left Yòu)*
*Known by the courtesy name Zitai [Tz'ee-t'eye]

Tian Feng [Tee-an Fung] – *an adviser to Yuan Shao that was imprisoned by Shao before the Battle of Guandu (for questioning the campaign) and slandered afterward by his peers, which led to Shao ordering his execution (depicted in '"Turmoil"')*
*Known by the courtesy name Yuanhao [Yoo-arn-ha-oh]

Tian Kai [Tee-an K'eye] – *officer and trusted offical serving Gongsun Zan; he died during Yuan Shao's siege of Yijing.*

Wang Can [Warng Ts'arn] – *a Han Dynasty official that served Liu Biao and then Cao Cao; his family were prestigious enough for his grandfather and great-grandfather to be Excellences alongside the Yuan clan. He was said to possess an eidetic memory and have a fascination with donkeys, among other things, and the famed polymath Cai Yong was a vocal sponsor. Wang Can wrote a historical work, 'Record of Heroes', that serves as an alternative biographical compendium to the more famous 'Record of the Three Kingdoms', though it might be seen as biased toward Cao Cao's faction. It includes alternate fates (or even dates of death) for some notable figures, such as Sun Jian.*
*Known by the courtesy name Zhongxuan [Ch'ong-shoo-arn]

Wang Fu [Warng Foo] – *Han official that was part of Dong Cheng's failed 'Girdle Edict' plot to oust Cao Cao*

Wang Kuang [Warng Koo-arng] – *a subordinate of Hè Jin at the end of Emperor Ling's reign; he later became the Administrator of Henei and joined the Eastern Pass Coalition. He retired after a defeat, and his subordinate Han Hao went on to serve Cao Cao.*
*Known by the courtesy name Gongjie [K'ong-Jee-er]

Wang Lang [Warng Larng] – *official that served Han and Cao Wei, great-grandfather of first Jin Emperor Sima Yan. He was a friend of Kong Rong, although this work depicts this friendship being put to the test. His time in Yang Province – where he opposed Sun Ce as Administrator of Kuaiji – is depicted in 'East of the River'.*
*Known by the courtesy name Jingxing [Jing-shing]

Wang Lei [Warng Lay] – *Liu Zhang official*

Wang Ling [Warng Ling] – *nephew of Wang Yun that became a trusted Han official; he also served Cao Wei loyally, but he rebelled against the Sima clan prior to the founding of the Sima-led Jin Dynasty.*
*Known by the courtesy name Yanyun [Yarn-yoon]

Wang Song [Warng Song] – *Administrator of Zhou in Yòu Province*

Wang Wei [Warng Way] – *Liu Biao officer*

Wang Xiu [Warng Shee-oo] – *Yuan Tan official*
*Known by the courtesy name Shuzhi [S'oo-Ch'ee]

Wang Yi [Warng Yee] – *Administrator of Hedong Prefecture*

Wang Yun [Warng Yoon] – *a Han official; he was appointed Director of the Imperial Secretariat when Dong Zhuo relocated the capital to Chang'an. Wang Yun plotted to oust Dong Zhuo: in fiction, he used a beautiful palace maiden (and in some versions, adopted daughter) known as Diaochan to sow discord between Dong Zhuo and Lü Bu: historically, some accounts speak of Dong Zhuo and Lü Bu having fallen out over their interest in the same serving maid, and the author adapted this version of events in "Yellow Sky". Regardless of the exact circumstances, Wang Yun managed to convince Lü Bu to betray Dong Zhuo, and once Dong was dead, Wang Yun took charge in Chang'an, although his success was short-lived and he was killed by the faction of Dong Zhuo's vassals that he had refused to offer amnesty to; he famously executed the polymath Cai Yong for serving and then mourning Dong Zhuo.*
*Known by the courtesy name Zishi [Tz'ee-shee]

Wei Gu [Way K'oo] – *a Hedong official serving Wang Yi*

Wei Huang [Way Hoo-arng] – *a Han official that plotted against Cao Cao with Geng Ji and Jin Yi prior to Cao's death*

Wei Kang [Way Karng] – *a Han official that was appointed as Inspector of Liang Province prior to the Battle of Guandu.*
*Known by the courtesy name Yuanjiang [Yoo-arn-ch'ee-arng]

Wei Xu [Way Shoo] – *Han officer and relative of Lü Bu*

Wei Zi [Way Tz'ee] – *a friend of Cao Cao that joined Cao's assault on Dong Zhuo's retreating army at Xingyang; he was killed during that battle, a fact that haunts Cao periodically.*

Wen Chou [Wern T'oh] – *Yuan Shao officer that died prior to the final stages of the Battle of Guandu; he is famous for his death in fiction, as he is said to be yet another victim of Guan Yu's near-peerless talent as a general. Historically, information about his fate is vague; the author chose to be similarly vague.*

Wen Ping [Wern Ping] – *Liu Biao officer that went on to become a lauded general under Cao Cao*
*Known by the courtesy name Zhongye [Ch'ong-yer]

'White Circles' – *a Black Mountain Bandit chieftain*

Wu Dun [Woo T'oon] – *a Mount Tai Bandit chieftain*

Wu Ju [Woo Joo] – *Administrator of Cangwu and friend of Liu Bei*

Wu Pu [Woo Poo] – *a scholar and student of Hua Tuo*

Wu Xi [Woo Shee] – *a subordinate of Dong Zhuo that served as an officer; he then served the regent Guo Si and later killed him.*

Wu Yi [Woo Yee] – *the brother-in-law of Yi Governor Liu Zhang; his father was a friend of Zhang's father.*
*Known by the courtesy name Ziyuan [Tz'ee-yoo-arn]

Wuyan [Woo-yarn] – *a Wuhuan tribal leader in Yòu Province*

Xi Zhicai [Shee Ch'ee-ts'eye] – *deceased Cao Cao adviser*

Xiahou Dun [Shee-ah-hoh T'oon] – *a close ally (and possible relative) of Cao Cao that serves Cao as an officer; he famously lost an eye during a campaign against Lü Bu in Xu Province (depicted in '"Turmoil'"). In fiction, he is said to have removed the arrow from his eye socket – with the eye attached to it – and consumed the eye before continuing to fight.*
*Known by the courtesy name Yuanrang [Yoo-arn-ranrng]

Xiahou Lan [Shee-ah-hoh Larn] – *a member of the Xiahou clan that surrendered to Liu Bei after the Battle of Bowang and joined his faction sincerely (recounted in this work).*

Xiahou Yuan [Shee-ah-hoh Yoo-arn] – *a close associate (and possible relative) of Cao Cao. He supposedly took the blame for one of Cao Cao's misdemeanours at an early age. He was highly trusted and was often given heavy responsibilities during his*

career. One of his later roles – the protector of the Hanzhong region – brought him into conflict with Liu Bei, and the resultant Battle of Mt. Dingjun – a famous event that has many interesting fictional variations – is covered in 'Crouching Dragon'.
*Known by the courtesy name Miaocai [Mee-ow-ts'eye]

Xiang Lang [Shee-arng Larng] – *an official in Jing Province that joined Liu Bei when the province fell to Cao Cao's forces; he was a friend of Ma Su, Zhuge Liang's protégé, in later years.*
*Known by the courtesy name Juda [Ch'oo-t'ah]

Xianyu Fu [Shee-arn-yoo Foo] – *Han official and Administrator of Yuyang Prefecture*

Xin Pi [Shin Pee] – *Yuan clan official that previously served Ji Governor Han Fu; brother of Xin Ping*
*Known by the courtesy name Zuozhi [Tz'oo-oh-ch'ee]

Xin Ping [Shin Ping] – *Yuan Tan adviser that previously served Ji Province Governor Han Fu; brother of Xin Pi*
*Known by the courtesy name Zhongzhi [Ch'ong-ch'ee]

Xu Chu [Shoo T'oo] – *a purportedly simple-minded man that served voluntarily as the guardian of his village and supposedly repelled an army of 10,000 Yellow Turbans with a combination of prowess and bluff. He later surrendered to Cao Cao, becoming a member of Cao's elite Tiger Guard: when the role of Cao Cao's bodyguard was vacated by the death of Dian Wei, Xu Chu took the role. His quiet, affable, dopey nature outside of combat contrasted heavily with the violent powerhouse that he would become when faced with those that were designated as his enemies.*
*Known by the courtesy name Zhongkang [Ch'ong-karng]
*Known by the moniker Hu Chi [Hoo T'ee] (lit. 'Tiger Fool') by some; the author uses 'Crazy Tiger' instead

Xu Gong [Shoo K'ong] – *a difficult-to-fathom figure that some accounts depict as a rebel that overthrew Sheng Xian, the Administrator of Wu Prefecture in Yang Province, and then received recognition by the Han due to his competence; this is the Xu Gong that the author used for his appearance in 'East of the River'. Xu Gong opposed and then reluctantly collaborated with Sun Ce in his last years; he began to correspond with Cao Cao and unintentionally gave Sun Ce his famous epithet 'Little Conqueror' whilst describing the threat that Ce supposedly posed. Sun Ce learned of the exchanges and had Xu Gong assassinated, but Gong's followers avenged him, killing Sun Ce months later.*

Xu Huang [Shoo Hoo-arng] – *famous Cao Cao officer and former White Wave Bandit; he had a friendly rivalry with Guan Yu.*
*Known by the courtesy name Gongming [K'ong-ming]

Xu Jing [Shoo Jing] – *an official in the Han court; he was the brother of the famous appraiser Xu Shao. He fled Dong Zhuo's court purges and ended up serving Wang Lang in Kuaiji. He fled Kuaiji after Wang Lang's defeat and ended up in Yi Province,*

where he served Liu Zhang. When Liu Zhang ceded Yi to Liu Bei, Xu Jing was highly regarded, even demanding deference from the likes of the Shu Han Prime Minister Zhuge Liang (a fact that is mentioned in 'Crouching Dragon').
*Known by the courtesy name Wenxiu [Wern-shee-oo]

Xu Rong [Shoo Rong] – *talented Dong Zhuo general. Xu decided to aid Wang Yun and Lü Bu's plot to oust Dong Zhuo and his loyalist faction led by Li Jue and Guo Si; he then died fighting against those loyalists.*

Xu Shao [Shoo S'ao] – *a famous appraiser who was known for fearless frankness; it was said that men feared his judgement and would try to curry favour with him in the hope that it would result in a career-boosting response. He is famous for having supposedly judged Cao Cao to be 'An able statesman in times of peace, and a "jianxiong" (meaning a "crafty villain", more or less) in chaotic times'. He later travelled to Xu Province, where he supposedly rated its governor Tao Qian poorly; he then went to Yang Province and served the court-appointed governor Liu Yao until his untimely death (his time in Yang is depicted in 'East of the River').*
*Known by the courtesy name Zijiang [Tz'ee-jee-arng]

Xu Shu [Shoo S'oo] – *a close friend of Zhuge Liang and Pang Tong; he was forced to surrender to Cao Cao during the Battle of Steep-slope (as depicted in this work). He is featured more prominently in the opening acts of 'Crouching Dragon'*
*Known by the courtesy name Yuanzhi [Yoo-arn-ch'ee]

Xu Yòu [Shoo Yoh] – *a lifelong friend of Yuan Shao and Cao Cao, and an adviser to Shao until he was slandered by colleagues; he then betrayed information to Cao Cao that decided the outcome of the Guandu campaign. His last years are depicted in this work.*
*Known by the courtesy name Ziyuan [Tz'ee-yoo-arn]

Xue Ti [Shoo-er Tee] – *Han official serving Cao Cao*

Xun Chen [Shoon T'ern] – *Yuan clan official that once served Ji Governor Han Fu; he is the brother of Cao Cao's trusted adviser Xun Yu (Wenruo)*
*Known by the courtesy name Youruo [Yoh-roo-oh]

Xun Yòu [Shoon Yoh] – *known through the text as 'Xun Gongda'; he is an adviser to Cao Cao and nephew of Xun Yu (Wenruo)*
*Known by the courtesy name Gongda [K'ong-t'ah]

Xun Yu [Shoon Yoo] – *known as 'Xun Wenruo' throughout the text; he was an official in the Han court before joining Yuan Shao as an emissary and adviser. He later 'defected' to Cao Cao and started to find more officials to serve his new lord, including Xi Zhicai, his own nephew Xun Gongda and Guo Jia.*
*Known by the courtesy name Wenruo [Wern-roo-oh]

Yan Jing [Yarn Ch'ing] – *Yuan Tan officer*

Yan Liang [Yarn Lee-arng] – *Yuan Shao officer; he is famous for his fictional prowess and death at the hands of Guan Yu, much like Hua Xiong before him and Wen Chou after him. The one difference is that Yan Liang was actually said to have been killed by Guan Yu (Hua Xiong was killed by Sun Jian's forces, while Wen Chou's death is attributed to Cao Cao's forces in general); his ignominious historical death could – as the author noted when depicting it in '"Turmoil"' – be attributed to Yan's thinking that Guan had come to support him (since Liu Bei – Guan Yu's liege lord – was serving Yan's lord Yuan Shao at the time).*

Yan Pu [Yarn Poo] – *adviser to Han'ning ruler Zhang Lu*

Yan Rou [Yarn Roh] – *former captive of the Wuhuan that aids Cao Cao's Wuhuan pacification campaign*

Yan Xiang [Yarn Shee-arng] – *former adviser to Yuan Shu that seems – unless it was another Yan Xiang – to have been recruited by Cao Cao to serve as the Inspector of Yang Province (the author has chosen to take the two as one and the same). Inspector Yan, whoever he was, was assassinated by Sun Ce's followers, paving the way for Liu Fu's historically important time in the role.*

Yang Biao [Yarng P'ee-ow] – *a senior Han Dynasty politician; he was said to have come up with the scheme that divided Li Jue and Guo Si and effectively ended their co-regency. He was the father of the more famous Yang Xiu that worked for Cao Cao.*
*Known by the courtesy name Wenxian [Wern-shee-arn]

Yang Bo [Yarng P'oh] – *an adviser to Han'ning ruler Zhang Lu*

Yang Chai [Yarng T'eye] – *Han official, husband to Lady Cai (2)*

Yang Feng [Yarng Fung] – *Dong Zhuo officer and friend of the White Wave Bandit leader Han Xian; he aided Emperor Xian's escape from the co-regents but demanded too many rewards, so he and Han Xian chased away by Dong Cheng and Cao Cao. He and Han Xian then served Yuan Shu's campaign against Lü Bu in Xu Province but were captured and killed by Liu Bei's forces.*

Yang Fu [Yarng Foo] – *an insightful man that was invited to serve Liang Province Inspector Wei Kang as an official*
*Known by the courtesy name Yishan [Yee-s'arn]

Yang Hong [Yarng Hong] – *Liu Zhang politician that later served Liu Bei; he aided Zhuge Liang during the Hanzhong Campaign*
*Known by the courtesy name Jixiu [Ch'ee-shee-oo]

Yang Qiu [Yarng Chee-oo] – *Qiang chieftain serving Ma Teng*

Yang Xiu [Yarng Shee-oo] – *gifted son of Minister Yang Biao and Yuan Shao's sister, and future registrar to Cao Cao; he was a victim of the Cao clan succession crisis of later years*
*Known by the courtesy name Dezu [T'er-tz'oo]

Yi Ji [Yee Ch'ee] – *Liu Biao vassal that joined Liu Bei alongside his acquaintance Zhuge Liang*
*Known by the courtesy name Boji [P'oh-ch'ee]

Yin Kai [Yin Kigh] – *Yuan clan's guardian of Maocheng Fortress*

Yin Kui [Yin Koo-ee] – *Yuan clan official*

Yin Li [Yin Lee] – *a former Mount Tai Bandit chieftain*

Ying Shao [Ying S'ow] – *a retired official that was trying to preserve common folklore in a written work that survives to this day – Fengsu Tongyi (lit. "Enduring/Penetrating Customs")*
*Known by the courtesy name Zhongyuan [Ch'ong-yoo-arn]

Yu Jin [Yoo Ch'in] – *Cao Cao officer that was 'given' to Cao by Wang Lang. He was initially mistrusted (as shown in '"Yellow Sky"' and '"Turmoil"'), but he went on to become one of the most renowned generals in Cao Cao's army. His connection to fellow townsman and former bandit Chang Xi is depicted in this work. Yu Jin's later years are covered in 'Crouching Dragon'.*
*Known by the courtesy name Wenze [Wern-tz'er]

Yuan Cheng [Yoo-arn T'erng] – *Yuan Shao's uncle that is asked to advise on the clan succession issue*

Yuan Huan [Yoo-arn Hoo-arn] – *trusted Cao Cao adviser that once served Yuan Shu*
*Known by the courtesy name Yaoqing [Yah-oh-ching]

Yuan Ji [Yoo-arn Ch'ee] – *Yuan Shao's deceased elder brother; Yuan Tan is posthumously adopted to him in order to technically disinherit Tan and make it easier to appoint Shang as clan heir*

Yuan Mai [Yoo-arn Migh] – *Yuan Shao's deceased fourth son*

Yuan Shang [Yoo-arn S'arng] – *Yuan Shao's third son and, arguably, the most pivotal character of the work; he is made chieftain of the Yuan clan by way of what appears to be intriguing by his mother and some of Yuan Shao's advisers, and it is the resultant feud between Shang and his eldest half-brother Tan that dictates what happens everywhere else.*
*Known by the courtesy name Xianfu [Shee-arn-foo]

Yuan Shao [Yoo-arn S'ao] – *head of the influential Yuan clan of Ru County in Yu Province and famous 'Super Warlord' of the period leading up the 'Three Kingdoms' era; he was a friend of Cao Cao, Zhang Miao and other noted up-and-coming figures in the later 2nd Century. He became a colonel in the ill-fated 'Army of the Western Garden', befriended Commander-in-Chief Hè Jin, and personally led the purge of the 'Ten Attendants' in Luoyang. He later led the Eastern Pass Coalition against Dong Zhuo. When that coalition ended, Shao was pitched against his own brother in a power-struggle that lasted for years. He conquered 4 provinces in the north but lost to Cao Cao at the Battle of Guandu: this work*

begins in the months after that famous battle.
*Known by the courtesy name Benchu [P'ern-t'oo]

Yuan Shu [Yoo-arn S'oo] – *brother of Ru County Yuan clan chieftain Yuan Shao: he always felt that his inheritance was snatched from him when his father allowed Shao to be adopted by his heirless older brother – and clan leader – thus placing Shao as the new heir to the clan fortune. As Yuan Shao was technically illegitimate, Yuan Shu felt that he should have been the next in line, and that he was before Shao's adoption took place: Yuan Shu never forgot that 'outrage' and finally waged a violent, costly war with Yuan Shao. Yuan Shu's hubris – and, perhaps, insanity – peaked and he declared as an alternative emperor, losing most of his support – including, most notably, the indentured Sun clan of Jiangdong – and leading ultimately to his death as a humiliated fugitive. Yuan Shu is often under-represented, but his actions are, perhaps, the most important catalysts for defining events in the period, directly or indirectly.*
*Known by the courtesy name Gonglu [K'ong-loo]

Yuan Tan [Yoo-arn Tarn] – *the eldest of Yuan Shao's sons; he served his father as a general.*
*Known by the courtesy name Xiansi [Shee-an-see]

Yuan Xi [Yoo-arn Shee] – *Yuan Shao's second son and first husband to Lady Zhen, who went on to become wife of Cao Wei Emperor Cao Pi and mother to Cao Wei Emperor Cao Rui*
*Known by the courtesy name Xianyi [Shee-arn-yee]
*Known by the courtesy name Xianyong [Shee-arn-yong]

Yuan Yao [Yoo-arn Yah-oh] – *the eldest of Yuan Shu's sons; he is, at the time of this work, a guest or hostage of the Sun clan in Jiangdong (unbelievably, it is more likely the former)*

Yuan Yi [Yoo-arn Yee] – *a cousin of Yuan Shao and Yuan Shu that later served as Administrator of Shanyang Prefecture, Yan Province; he was a founder member of Yuan Shao's Eastern Pass Coalition against Dong Zhuo, serving under his provincial governor Liu Dai. Cao Cao was said to respect him greatly. He was killed in action not long after the Eastern Pass Coalition collapsed.*
*Known by the courtesy name Boye [P'oh-yer]

Yuan Yin [Yoo-arn Yin] – *an adviser to Yuan Shu*

Yue Jin [Yoo-er Ch'in] – *famous Cao Cao officer*
*Known by the courtesy name Wenqian [Wern-chee-an]

Yufuluo [Yoo-foo-loo-oh] – *the chieftain of a breakaway faction of Southern Xiongnu; he had been selected as the Chanyu (king) of his people by a meddling Han court, but instead of accepting Yufuluo the Southern Xiongnu exiled him and his followers (although his brother Huchuquan stayed and was actually elected as the next Chanyu by the Xiongnu themselves). Yufuluo then became a wandering warlord of sorts, but he joined Yuan Shao's Eastern Pass Coalition very briefly; he tired of the inactivity and* rebelled, forging alliances with the Black Mountain Bandits and groups of Yellow Turbans at varying points in time. He was eventually hounded to his death by Cao Cao's forces: his son, Liu Bao, became the next Chanyu and his descendants would enjoy great power in northern China.

Zang Ba [Tz'arng P'ah] – *prison warder's son-turned-founder of the Mount Tai Bandits that took over an entire region of Xu and ruled it as an independent 'crime haven'. His confederacy surrendered to the Han after Lü Bu's defeat, at which point they became a powerful army of enforcers for Cao Cao.*
*Known by the courtesy name Xuangao [Shoo-arng-k'ao]

Zang Jie [Tz'arng Ch'ee-er] – *Zang Ba's father; he was an honest prison warder in Mount Tai Prefecture that was falsely imprisoned for questioning corrupt officials. Zang Ba was forced to go to the criminal underworld for help, which ironically led to Ba becoming one of the most powerful crime lords in northeast China.*
*Known by the courtesy name Yaoqing [Yah-oh-ching]

Zao Zhi [Ch'ao Ch'ee] – *Han official serving Cao Cao; proposed the 'tuntian' military-agricultural system*

Ze Rong [Tz'er Rong] – *a Buddhist cult leader in Xu Province: he was the trusted Administrator of Xiapi – which later became the capital region – and turned the main city into a stronghold and sanctuary for his followers, who eventually numbered in the tens of thousands. He was accused of funding his 'Buddhist Utopia' with misappropriated public monies. He later travelled to Yang Province to join the state-appointed governor Liu Yao's struggle against Yuan Shu, but he looted prefectures and counties along the way and in Yang itself. He was eventually defeated by the remnants of Liu Yao's forces and died at the hands of local tribesmen. He is a major antagonist to Sun Ce in one act of 'East of the River'.*

Zhang Fei [Ch'arng Fay] – *an early ally and sponsor of Liu Bei who is frequently paired with Guan Yu. Fiction typically portrays him as a brash, slow-witted, violent drunk, but in reality he was smart enough to run his pig-butchery business, rally troops and inspire troops, so while the author has retained his usual outspokenness and comic relief aspects from fiction, Zhang Fei is also shown to be more intelligent and not an alcoholic. His contribution to this work is minimal: his early career is covered in "Yellow Sky" and "'Turmoil'", and his later career is depicted in 'Crouching Dragon'.*
*Known by the courtesy name Yide [Yee-der]

Zhang Hè [Ch'arng Her] – *Cao Cao officer that has only recently defected from Yuan Shao at the start of this work (after submitting at the end of the Battle of Guandu); he also served Ji Governor Han Fu. His later career pitted him against Liu Bei's faction many times (as depicted in 'Crouching Dragon').*
*Known by the courtesy name Junyi [Ch'oon-yee]

Zhang Hong [Ch'arng Hong] – *an adviser and envoy that served the Fuchun Sun clan; he appears in Cao Cao's court in this work,*

since he was an ambassador. He may, historically, have been in Xuchang until Cao Cao invaded Jing: the author returns him to Jiangdong and places an unnamed successor in the Han court.
*Known by the courtesy name Zigang [Tz'ee-k'arng]

Zhang Ji [Ch'arng Jee] – *a general serving Dong Zhuo; he was envied for his beautiful wife, Lady Zou. He later left the service of the regents Li Jue and Guo Ji and died seizing Nan County, which was then governed (illegitimately) by his nephew Zhang Xiu.*

Zhang Jue [Ch'arng J'oo-er] – *founder of the Taoist sect 'The Way of Peace' (his name is sometimes Romanised to Zhang Jiao [Ch'arng J'ee-ao], but the author has chosen the older, more traditional version); he travelled the land performing benevolent 'miracles' and spreading word of a new era of peace and enlightenment that required the destruction of the Han empire. As general discontent grew, Zhang Jue and his allies started to plan a nationwide revolution. When their allies within the capital were exposed, Zhang Jue ordered his followers to adopt a common symbol of a yellow turban and form armies to fight the emperor. That uprising – which was known as the Yellow Turban Rebellion – began the careers of many future 'heroes' such as Cao Cao, Liu Bei and Sun Jian, who would then become important to the 'Three Kingdoms' era that followed over 30 years later. Zhang Jue did not even live to see the end of the initial, failed uprising; however, new factions and evolutions of the Yellow Turbans would continue to plague the Han government for many years to come.*

Zhang Liao [Ch'arng Lee-ow] – *famous Cao Cao officer that once served as Lü Bu's trusted second; he earned great fame when he nearly routed Sun Quan while acting as a defender of Hefei.*
*Known by the courtesy name Wenyuan [Wern-yoo-arn]

Zhang Lu [Ch'arng Loo] – *the leader of the 'Way of Five Pecks', a Taoist cult that was most influential in Yi Province and Hanzhong. The newly-appointed governor of Yi Province, Liu Yan, sought his aid when quietly annexing neighbouring Hanzhong: he did as he was asked until Hanzhong was seized, at which point he killed his campaign ally and seized Hanzhong, turning it into the theocratic state of Han'ning and declaring independence from Han rule. Liu Zhang had some control over him by way of keeping his family as hostages: Yan's son and successor Liu Zhang was less cordial and killed the hostages, plunging the two into direct conflict. Liu Zhang fatefully invited Liu Bei to Yi Province to guard against Zhang Lu, but Bei eventually seized the province. Zhang Lu later surrendered to Cao Cao (the later events are depicted in 'Crouching Dragon').*
*Known by the courtesy name Gongqi [K'ong-chee]

Zhang Miao [Ch'arng Mee-ow] – *a lifelong friend of Cao Cao and Yuan Shao; he was said to be very generous and kind, but naively outspoken. His criticism of Yuan Shao's leadership irked Yuan such that the two never spoke again, and he did not support Cao Cao's indiscriminate Xu Province campaign: he eventually allied himself with Chen Gong and seized Yan Province from Cao, which led in turn to Cao ending his Xu campaign, returning to Yan and retaking*

the province, killing Zhang and his entire family in the process.
*Known by the courtesy name Mengzhuo [Mung-ch'oo-oh]

Zhang Nan [Ch'arng Narn] – *Han official in Yòu Province that serves in Yuan Xi's administration*

Zhang Ren [Ch'arng Rern] – *Liu Zhang officer; he later defended Yi from Liu Bei, and his actions led to the death of Liu Bei's famous strategist Pang Tong (depicted in 'Crouching Dragon')*

Zhang Sheng [Ch'arng S'erng] – *Gao Gan officer*

Zhang Song [Ch'arng Song] – *honest, unpolished Liu Zhang official that acts as an envoy for his lord; he later served as a lead conspirator when some of Liu Zhang's officials wanted to replace their lord with Liu Bei, but he was betrayed by his own brother and executed (depicted in 'Crouching Dragon')*
*Known by the courtesy name Ziqiao [Tz'ee-chee-ow]

Zhang Xiu [Ch'arng Shee-oo] – *nephew of Dong Zhuo's ally Zhang Ji; he later received Jia Xu's service after inheriting the conquered Nan County from his uncle. He submitted to Cao Cao to avoid conflict, but when Cao Cao took his widowed aunt, Lady Zou, as a consort, showed general contempt and pondered assassinating Zhang for being angry, Zhang and Jia Xu ambushed Cao's forces and routed them, causing the deaths of Cao's bodyguard Dian Wei, Cao's heir Cao Ang and his cousin Cao Anmin. Cao has apparently forgiven Zhang and is using him as an enforcer by the time that this work begins.*

Zhang Yang [Ch'arng Yarng] – *Ding Yuan general during the time of the Liang Province Rebellion alongside Lü Bu and Zhang Liao; Lü Bu famously murdered Ding Yuan and defected to Dong Zhuo, but Zhang never lost faith in Bu and defended him many times, despite also lending his army to the Eastern Pass Coalition, which was dedicated to the destruction of Dong Zhuo. His contribution to the coalition ended when he was captured by the Xiongnu rebel Yufuluo; Yuan Shao then had to rescue Zhang Yang, after which he was made Administrator of Henei by Dong Zhuo's court in Chang'an. He later gave safe haven to the fugitive Dong Zhao (Gongren) and Lü Bu, which made him an enemy of his former saviour Yuan Shao, who hated both men. He was the first to offer sanctuary to Emperor Xian and later oversaw the restoration of the palace in Luoyang, for which he was promoted; he then undid everything by deciding to aid Lü Bu when Bu was attacked by Cao Cao, and he was killed by one of his own subordinates.*
*Known by the courtesy name Zhishu [Ch'ee-s'oo]

Zhang Yi (1) [Ch'arng Yee] – *Yuan clan officer*

Zhang Yi (2) [Ch'arng Yee] – *Liu Zhang official that later joined Liu Bei; he continued to serve the Shu Han Empire that Liu Bei founded and became a trusted envoy and statesman*
*Known by the courtesy name Junsi [Ch'oon-see]

Zhang Yun [Ch'arng Yoon] – *Liu Biao naval officer and nephew of Admiral Cai Mao*

Zhang Zhi [Ch'arng Ch'ee] – *Han official that Cao Cao appointed as Inspector of Bing Province after Gao Gan was defeated*

Zhao Ang [Ch'ao Arng] – *Han official that was appointed as a senior army consultant by Liang Province Inspector Wei Kang; he is the husband of the well-known figure Lady Wang Yi.*
*Known by the courtesy name Weizhang [Way-ch'arng]

Zhao Du [Ch'ao T'oo] – *a minor magnate in Yòu Province that supports the rule of the Yuan clan*

Zhao Fan [Ch'ao Farn] – *Administrator of Guiyang; he is only notable for an argument with Zhao Yun after submitting to Liu Bei (portrayed in 'Crouching Dragon')*

Zhao Qi [Ch'ao Chee] – *famous scholar and Han official*

Zhao Yan [Ch'ao Yarn] – *Han official that is listed as being a senior contributor to the Red Cliffs campaign, despite there being little information about him at the time of writing: he survived the rout and served for many years thereafter, though the author does little with him due to said lack of information.*
*Known by the courtesy name Boran [P'oh-rarn]

Zhao Yu [Ch'ao Yoo] – *the Administrator of Guangling when Cao Cao began his Xu Province Campaign; he was apparently murdered – and his prefecture looted – by the cultist Ze Rong, whom he mistook for a Buddhist saint as many did.*

Zhao Yun [Ch'ao Yoon] – *Liu Bei officer who once served Gongsun Zan; he has little more than a 'cameo' in this work (most of his impressive career and life are depicted in 'Crouching Dragon').*
*Known by the courtesy name Zilong [Tz'il-ong]

Zheng Xuan [Ch'erng Shoo-arn] – *famous commentator and Confucian philosopher that was a mentor to Cui Yan; he shared a mentor with Lu Zhi, who was Liu Bei and Gongsun Zan's mentor.*

Zhi Xi [Ch'ee Shee] – *Han official that was said to be a good friend of Kong Rong: the author wanted to include him in '"Turmoil"' to avoid a rushed introduction but lacked the space. He was the only man that risked publicly mourning Kong Rong at the last.*

Zhong Ji [Ch'ong Jee] – *Han official and ally of Dong Cheng that took part in the failed 'Girdle Edict' plot and was executed*

Zhong Yao [Ch'ong Yao] – *Han official, student of Cai Yong, calligrapher and father of famous Cao Wei general Zhong Hui; he was also related to Gao Gan's general Guo Yuan by marriage.*
*Known by the courtesy name Yuanchang [Yoo-arn-ch'arng]

Zhou Yi [Ch'oh Yee] – *Magistrate of Luoyang at the time of*

Emperor Ling's death; he was the father of the famous Sun clan strategist and general Zhou Yu (Gongjin), and the flight from Luoyang ensured that Zhou Yu would meet his future lord and friend Sun Ce when the latter travelled from the south with his father, who was on his way to confront Dong Zhuo.

Zhou Yu [Ch'oh Yoo] – *younger son of Luoyang Magistrate Zhou Yi; he joined Sun Ce, the son of the famous prodigy Sun Jian, and the two sowed the seeds of an independent state in the south that endured for decades. Their earlier exploits are depicted in 'East of the River'; Zhou Yu's greatest achievement – destroying Cao Cao's navy at Red Cliffs – is partially depicted in 'Crouching Dragon' and is the next major event to occur after the end of this work.*
*Known by the courtesy name Gongjin [K'ong-jin]

Zhu Jun [Ch'oo J'oon] – *a prominent Han official; he was a 'sponsor' of Sun Jian, and recommended him to good effect whenever he could. He is only mentioned in this work; he has already retired, seen his lands pillaged by Li Jue and Guo Si and dies of illness during the time of the co-regents' civil war.*
*Known by the courtesy name Gongwei [K'ong-way]

Zhu Ling [Ch'oo Ling] – *Cao Cao officer that initially served Yuan Shao; he was sent to aid Cao and decided to remain with him.*
*Known by the courtesy name Wenbo [Wern-p'oh]

Zhuge Liang [Ch'oo-ker Lee-arng] – *a famous polymath that served the warlord Liu Bei and was pivotal to elevating him from minor player to ruler of his own kingdom; he is the protagonist of 'Crouching Dragon' – which is named for one of his Taoist soubriquets – and one of the most famous figures of the era. He is mentioned but never seen in this work.*
* Known by the courtesy name Kongming [Kong-ming]
* Known by the Taoist name 'Crouching Dragon'
* Known by the Taoist name 'Sleeping Dragon'

UNNAMED SUN CLAN ENVOY – *represent Sun Quan in Xuchang* ('FICTIONAL' CHARACTER CREATED FOR NARRATIVE COHESION)

UNNAMED STORYTELLER – *appears in the prologue and epilogue*

HISTORICAL CHINESE FIGURES

Confucius (Romanisation of Kong Fusha, known as Kong Fu-tzu/Kong Fuzi [Kong Foo-tz'er], lit. Master Kong) – *a famous scholar and philosopher whose beliefs and teachings became a philosophy in their own right, with many noted figures throughout Chinese history adopting 'Confucianism' as a way of life. Confucius' 'analects' were seen as the model for a morally correct way of living: their teachings usually sat alongside any other moral or spiritual beliefs that the practitioner had. Kong Rong – a minor protagonist in this work – is his descendant.*

Daji [T'ah-ch'ee] – *a consort of King Zhou of Shang, mentioned by*

Kong Rong in his letter to Cao Cao; see the entry for Jiang Ziya

Fu Sheng [Foo S'erng] – *famed Confucian scholar ancestor of Empress Fu and Fu Wan*

Duke of Zhou [Ch'oh] – *ruler of the ancient Shang [S'arng] kingdom, mentioned by Kong Rong in his letter to Cao Cao; see the entry for Jiang Ziya*

Jiang Ziya [Jee-arng Tz'ee-yah] (a.k.a. Taigong Wang [T'eye-k'ong Warng]) – *a famous genius in ancient China that served as a strategist and adviser to King Wen [Wern] and King Wu [Woo] of Zhou [Ch'oh] in succession, preventing them from prematurely challenging the immoral King Zhou [Ch'oh], whose rule was supposedly tainted further by the sadistic whims of his concubine Daji [T'ah-jee]. King Zhou's Shang [S'arng] Dynasty collapsed and was replaced by the King Wu's Zhou [Ch'oh] Dynasty; Jiang Ziya then served as Prime Minister. A fantastical version of the fall of the Shang Dynasty/rise of the Zhou Dynasty was written during the Ming Dynasty: it is called 'Fengshen Yanyi' (a.k.a. Fengshen Bang, known sometimes as 'Creation/Investiture/ of the Gods' or 'Apotheosis of Heroes' in english).*

King Wu [Woo] – *ruler of the ancient Zhou [Ch'oh] kingdom, mentioned by Kong Rong in his letter to Cao Cao; see the entry for Jiang Ziya*

Lao Tzu [Lao Tz'oo] (sometimes Romanised to Laozi [Lao-tz-er], but the author has opted for the older form) – *famous philosopher and founder of Taoism (again, this can be Romanised to Daoism, but the author has opted for one over the other). Li Jue apparently claimed to be his descendant.*

Liu Bang [Lee-oo P'arng] – *the founder of the Han Dynasty; his region of influence, Hanzhong, gave his dynasty its name. One of his descendants was eventually overthrown by the chancellor Wang Mang; Wang was defeated in turn by a popular uprising led by Liu clan members, and the Han Dynasty was restored. The second of the new line of Han Emperors, Liu Xiu/Emperor Guangwu, moved the capital to the eastern city of Luoyang to create distance between his government and the foreign tribes that threatened to devour the western provinces. As such, some historians tend refer to a Western Han (pre-Wang Mang) and an Eastern Han (post-Wang Mang).*

Shang Gao [S'arng K'ow] – *a mathematician and astronomer that Dong Zhao (Gongren) mentions when discussing Cao Chong with his father Cao Cao: Shang worked for the Duke of Zhou and compiled the Zhoubi Suanjing, a set of arithmetic problems.*

Sun Tzu [Soon Tz'oo] (sometimes Romanised to Sunzi [Soon-tz'er], but the author has opted for the older form) – *a legendary scholar, famed for his work 'The Art of War'; while new technologies outdated some strategies and forced later scholars such as Zhuge Liang to annotate the work, his understanding of* the psychological aspects of warfare were used to great effect, and unlike technology, those references remained relevant since people, unlike their inventions, did not and do not change. The 2nd Century warlord Sun Jian and his progeny claimed descent from Sun Tzu, though this was never completely proven or disputed.

Wang Mang [Warng Marng] – *the regent and Chancellor to the last Chang'an-based Han Emperor and founder of his own short-lived Xin Dynasty. He used the idea of the Mandate of Heaven to delegitimise the entire Han Dynasty rather than a single sovereign. He was eventually overthrown by members of Liu clan, who revived the Han Dynasty. Wang Mang is treated as a villain by Han loyalists and subsequent imperial regimes, while some historians argue that his government was not entirely malevolent. His name was typically used in Han times as a slander to imply that a person was a scheming hegemon.*

Yuan An [Yoo-arn Arn] – *an ancestor of Yuan Shao that provided much support to the Han Dynasty; he was rewarded with grand titles that his descendants inherited, and there were many statues erected to honour him.*

Yue Yi [Yoo-er Yee] – *a famous strategist that was an able statesman in addition, forming alliances with other small nations to defeat the state of Qi during the 'Warring States' era; likening a man to him implies an intention to unite lesser lords against corrupt officials or an evil ruler.*

Zhang Liang – *a famous adviser and strategist that aided the future Han founder Liu Bang; likening men to him was a great compliment that also implied that they would make their lord a future hero at the very least.*
*Known by the courtesy name Zifang [Tz'ee-farng]

PLACES

In this book, land locations are sorted by their provincial-level location and other landmarks – rivers and such – trail the list. In '"Yellow Sky"' and '"Turmoil"', every part of the nation is covered in some way; this work therefore follows the pattern.

Xuchang [Shoo-t'arng] – *the current (temporary) imperial capital, built for Emperor Xian in Yan Province by Cao Cao; it is not as grand as it could be, but it is only meant to serve as the capital until Luoyang is restored (sometimes known as Xu [Shoo] but the author was concerned that it be confused with Xu Province).*

Luoyang [Loo-oh-yarng] – *the eastern and 'actual' capital, used by Han Emperor Guangwu (Liu Xiu) onwards during the second phase of the Han Dynasty; at the start of this work, it has already been looted and left a gutted shell by Dong Zhuo and his allies (prior to their move to the former capital Chang'an). Luoyang does not enjoy a revival until the early 3rd Century, when it becomes the seat of a new dynasty, Cao Wei.*

Chang'an [T'arng Arn] – *the western and former capital, designated so by the Han Dynasty founder Liu Bang and used until the usurper Wang Mang temporarily ended the Han Dynasty and founded his own Xin [Shin] Dynasty. It was still considered to be the capital for a very short time after the restoration of the Han, but for a number of reasons (primarily that the Qiang and other tribes in the west were a constant threat, and Emperor Guangwu had an established power base in the east), a new capital – Luoyang – was created. The court was moved here by Dong Zhuo (shown in '"Yellow Sky"') but was relocated to Xuchang in Yan Province by Cao Cao (shown in '"Turmoil"').*

Yan [Yarn] Province – *located in central China, to the east of Central and Jing Provinces, west of Xu Province and south of Ji Province; Cao Cao is the governor. The Guandu [K'oo-arn-t'oo] Campaign, which is better known as The Battle of Guandu – which is one of the most important battles of the Later Han period and takes place in the last act of '"Turmoil"' – was centred around the place it is named for and several surrounding points in Yan Province. Guandu City is close to a number of rivers and a 'road' that an army can take to attack Cao Cao's temporary imperial capital, Xuchang [Shoo-t'arng] City; Cao Cao chose it to be his last line of defence and sent other forces at Boma [P'oh-mah] City, Meng [Mung] Ford, Yan [Yarn] Ford and Dushi [T'oo-s'ee] Ford to either guard against Yuan Shao's army or harry established military camps. Anmin [Arn-min] is used as part of a ruse during the Cangting campaign.*

Dong [T'ong] Prefecture – located in northeast Yan Province; it is the provincial capital. Cangting [Ts'arng-ting] Ford is located in Dong Prefecture: Cheng Yu fortified this region before Chen Gong could during the former's failed coup, and Yuan Shao tries to hold it after losing at Guandu but fails.

Chenliu [T'ern-lee-oo] Prefecture/Principality – located in southwest Yan Province, on the border with Central Province; Cao Cao's friend Zhang Miao became the administrator prior to the campaign against Dong Zhuo

Yingchuan [Ying-t'oo-arn] – located in southwest Yan Province and northeast Yu Province; it straddles the border between the provinces. Xiahou Yuan was posted here as it is strategically important; he spends the entire text defending the region against Yellow Turbans, Yuan Shu's mercenaries, Yuan Shao's mercenaries, bandits and Liu Bei.

Central Province – *known at the time as 'Sili' [See-lee], but the author chose to refer to the province by its political purpose and geographical location. Luoyang is to the east of the region, and Chang'an is to the west, bordering (and also inhabiting, technically) Liang Province.*

Other places that are mentioned during the narrative include (or may include, due to boundary changes): Xingyang [Shing-yarng] (where Cao Cao fought Xu Rong after Dong Zhuo fled the capital); Anyi [Arn-yee] (located in western Central Province) which became a strategic base for Dong Zhuo's son-in-law Niu Fu after the end of the Dong Zhuo Campaign; Yangren [Yarng-rern], where Sun Jian defeated three of Dong Zhuo's best generals (Cao Cao mentions it to highlight the cost of disunity).

Hedong [Her-t'ong] Prefecture – located to the west; it is the site of an invasion by Gao Gan and then an insurrection led by the Administrator. Shanjin Ford (on the Yellow River) is a crossing point to/from Bing Province and is the site of several battles. The Sima clan's ancestral home, Wen [Wern] County, is here, and Wenxi [Wern-shee] is mentioned as a resisting local rebels.

Hongnong [Hong-nong] Prefecture – located in western-central Central Province, to the west of Luoyang; some rebellions take place here 'off-stage'.

Henei [Her-nay] Prefecture – the capital prefecture of Central Province; Luoyang, the Han capital, is in Henei.

Ji [Jee] Province – *located in the northeast of China, south of Yòu Province, east of Bing Province and west of Qing Province; this is Yuan Shao's power base. Its first capital was Xindu [Shin-t'oo] in the centre of the province, but Yuan Shao relocated the centre of power to the southern city of Yè [Yer] after becoming Governor. Yuan Shang made his last attempts to hold onto the region at Quzhang [Choo-ch'ang] City (in the northwest of the province) and Lankou [Larn-koh] in the Qi Hills (to the northwest of Quzhang).*

Wei [Way] Prefecture – in southern Ji Province; it is the location of Yuan Shao's capital city, and later becomes Cao Cao's capital, duchy and finally kingdom before serving as Cao Pi's fairly obvious choice when naming his imperial dynasty. The Qing [Ching] and Huan [Hoo-arn] rivers run close of Yè, and Yanpi Marsh is to the south: they are all used to flood the city during Cao Cao's siege. Li [Lee] County, to the east, is an early flashpoint after the Guandu campaign; Yiyang [Yee-yarng] and Yin'an [Yin Arn] are seized by Cao Cao during that same early period in the Ji Province campaign.

Bohai Prefecture/Principality – located in the central-east of Ji Province; Yuan Shao was made Administrator of Bohai by Dong Zhuo (as a conciliatory gesture) when he first arrived in Ji. Nanpi City is the site of Yuan Tan's last stand against Cao Cao, depicted in Act V of this work; Pingyuan [Ping-yoo-arn] (which has been classed as part of Qing or Yòu Province in the past) is to the west of Nanpi, and Longcou (where Yuan Tan made one failed attempt to repel Cao) is to the south of the city.

Hejian [Her-jee-an] Prefecture – located in northern Ji Province; it is the ancestral home of the Dong clan that Empress Dowager Dong (mother of Emperor Ling) belonged to. The Qing [Ching] River runs north of Yè, and it is close to a prominent crossing here Jie [Jee-er] Bridge – that Gongsun Zan and Yuan Shao fought of their most important early battles.

Anping [Arn-ping] Prefecture – the region where Xindu, the old provincial capital, was located; Qian Zhao, who repelled Yuan Tan's Wuhuan reinforcements during the Nanpi campaign, hailed from here

Ganling [Garn-ling] Prefecture – located in central Ji Province; Yuan Tan seized it while he was supposed to be aiding Cao Cao's siege of the provincial capital

Zhao [Ch'ao] Prefecture – located in the west of Ji Province, west of Julu and adjacent to the mountains; its location made it a frequent target for the Black Mountain Bandits. Maocheng [Mah-oh-t'eng] Fortress and Handan [Harn-t'arn] County – both important strategic points – are located in this region (Maocheng serves as a gateway to Bing Province).

Yòu [Yoh] Province – *located in the northeast of China, on the frontier; it is therefore prone to frequent attacks by Northern Xiongnu, Wuhuan and other tribes. Liu Yu was made Governor; the famous warlord Gongsun Zan killed Yu and usurped control. Its capital is Fanyang [Farn-yarng]. The Xuwu [Shoo-woo] Hills and Lulong [Loo-long] Pass are part of the route that leads past the Great Wall, out of Han China and into what was then non-Han territory ruled by foreign tribes such as the Xianbei and Wuhuan. The Yi [Yee] River was the site of the final submission by the Wuhuan tribes after their famous defeat.*

Notable places include: Yijing [Yee-ch'ing] City in the northwest, which was Gongsun Zan's last stronghold when Yuan Shao finally attacked him and Cao Cao's chosen headquarters during his Wuhuan campaign; Magistrate of Anxi [Arn-shee] County was future 'super-warlord' Liu Bei's first official post, awarded to him after the original Yellow Turban rebellion; Yòubeiping [Yoh-p'ay-ping]/Right Beiping [P'ay-ping] is a strategic point in the northeast of the province.

Zhuo [Ch'oo-oh] County – located in the northwest of Yòu Province; Gongsun Zan was appointed as the Magistrate after the Yellow Turban Rebellion. A number of uprisings against Cao Cao and the Yuans take place there.

Zhongshan [Ch'ong-s'arn] Prefecture – located in the west-southwest of Yòu Province (and is sometimes classed as being part of Ji Province; Yuan Shang retreats here after several losses to Cao Cao, and Wang Ling is made Administrator when the Yuans are defeated.

Yuyang [Yoo-yarng] Prefecture – located in the centre-north of Yòu Province; Wuzhong County's Magistrate is Tian Chou, the man that provides Cao Cao with a way to surprise the Wuhuan tribes and bring swift end to his pacification campaign.

Liaoxi [Lee-ow-shee] Prefecture – located in northeast Yòu Province; it is Tadun's power base in China and the region that provides the Wuhuan with what is preumed to be the only safe gateway in and out of the empire (via the coast, where the Great Wall cannot fully serve as a barrier).

Bing [P'ing] Province – *located in the centre-north of China, north of Central Province; the capital is Yangqu [Yarng-choo] in Jinyang [Ch'in-yarng]. Lü Bu's mentor and first foster father Ding Yuan was Inspector of the province at one time. The Southern Xiongnu migrants live in the region (most concentrated Ping [Ping] County), and the Black Mountain Bandits are very active here at varying times. Shanjin Ford is on the border with Hedong. The Yuan clan's appointed governor, Gao Gan, makes his last stand at Hu [Hoo] Pass Fortress in the southeast (near the border with Ji Province).*

Qing [Ching] Province – *located in the northeast of China, east of Ji Province and south of Yòu Province; there is a large* *'information hole' when it comes to Qing Province, and the region seems to suffer from high levels of crime and corruption. Linzi [Lin-tz'er] – located in the centre-north of Qing Province – serves as the provincial capital. A place called Xiami [Shee-ar-mee] (to the east of Linzi) is mentioned as being sieged (and relieved) at one point.*

Beihai [P'ay-high] – located in the centre-north of Qing Province. Kong Rong was made Chancellor of Beihai around the time of the death of Emperor Ling and famously required rescuing when an army of Yellow Turbans sieged the city; the hero Taishi Ci borrowed an army from Liu Bei and saved him.

Mount Tai [Tigh] Prefecture – located in the northwest of Qing Province, near the actual Mount Tai; this was the home region of former bandit king Zang Ba and most of his followers. Former bandit Chang Xi and Cao Cao's famous general Yue Jin share Juping [Joo-ping] as a childhood home, which becomes a pivotal plot point in Act VIII.

Ji'nan [Jee Narn] Prefecture – located in the west of Qing Province, near the Ji River; Cao Cao was sent here by the court, but he could not cope with the pressure and retired. He is still unpopular here and in the surrounding regions, which becomes important at varying points.

Langya [Larng-yah] Prefecture – located in the centre of Qing Province, southeast of Beihai; Yangdu [Yarng-t'oo], located in the southwest of Langya Prefecture, was the famous Zhuge clan's ancestral home and is shown as falling victim to a raid by Chang Xi in Act VIII. Cao Cao's principal wife Lady Bian (mother of future emperor Cao Pi) also hails from this prefecture.

Le'an [Ping-yoo-arn] Prefecture – located in the far northwest of Qing Province, near the border with Yòu Province; this is the site of Yuan Tan vassal Guan Tong's last defiant attempts to honour his lord

Donglai [T'ong-ligh] Prefecture – located in northeast Qing Province; it is the home of brothers Liu Dai and Liu Yao and the 'lone wolf' Taishi Ci. It is directly south of Liaodong Peninsula.

Liang [Lee-arng] Province – *located in the far northwest of China; Ji [Jee] County was the capital of the province, and later suffered a siege by the warlord Ma Chao. The region is home to the Qiang and Yuezhi peoples, who rose up against the Han government in semi-organised revolt; many of the local Han Chinese people in the region were as dissatisfied with the government as the Qiang, so they joined the uprising, turning it into a full-blown rebellion that would take many decades for the Han government to fully quell. The northernmost region, Xiliang [Shee-lee-arng], is the region most associated with the Qiang rebels and their famous prodigy Ma Chao; Xiping [Shee-ping] is an important early posting for the official Du Ji.*

Notable places include: Mei [May] County – located in the southeast of Liang Province; it was once Dong Zhuo's power base, but Ma Teng operates out of here at varying points

Longxi [Long-shee] Prefecture – located in western Liang Province; Han Sui and Ma Teng contend for the region

Yu [Yoo] Province – *located south and east of Central Province;*

the famous warlord Sun Jian was once made Inspector of the province by his lord Yuan Shu, and Wang Yun held the role at some point. Cao Cao's forces are stationed at Xiping [Shee-ping] in the far west at one point when facing Liu Biao's forces. Yingchuan [Ying-t'oo-arn] in the northeast is a supply centre and strategic region guarded by Xiahou Yuan for Cao Cao.

Runan [Roo-narn] Prefecture – the capital prefecture of Yu Province, located in its centre; the Yuan clan's ancestral home, Ru [Roo] County, is located here; the warlord Liu Bei, Liu Pi and the bandit Gong Du were all active in this region at varying points. Cao Cao's future bodyguard Xu Chu defended his townspeople's fortress in the region at one point.

Yang [Yarng] Province *– located in the southeast of China, east of southern Jing and south of everything else; it is quite a large province, and can be divided into two as the Yangtze/Great River bisects the province. The southern part is also considered to be east of the Great River, and is sometimes known as Jiangdong [Jee-arng-t'ong] (lit. river-east, or 'east of the river'). Lujiang and Jiujiang Prefectures comprise the majority of the northern part, although Guangling and Danyang could be partially included (and were often considered as annexed into Xu Province as well).*

Jiujiang [Jee-oo-jee-arng] Prefecture – located in the northeast of Yang Province, 'above' the Great River; there are land borders with Yan and Xu Provinces to the north.

Lujiang [Loo-jiang] Prefecture – located in the northwest of Yang Province, 'above' the Great River; there are land borders with Jing, Yu and Yan Provinces. The famous strategist Zhou Yu (Gongjin) hailed from Lujiang. Hefei [Her-fay] is located in the south of Lujiang Prefecture; this strategically useful area was under constant threat of attack by forces in the so-called 'Jiangdong region' (southern Yang Province), and it was eventually fortified by Cao Cao's vassal Liu Fu. The resultant fortress was a major obstacle to the Sun clan's plans to reclaim northern Yang.

Wu [Woo] Prefecture – located in the east of Yang Province, south of Guangling and west of Wu Prefecture, 'below' the Yangtze/Great River; the Sun clan hailed from this region, and the scholar Cai Yong hid here for 12 years. The rebel-turned-official Xu Gong – who was one of the warlord Sun Ce's most vocal critics until he was assassinated – resided here.

Danyang [T'arn-yarng] Prefecture – located in the centre of Yang Province, south of Jiujiang and 'below' the Yangtze/Great River; the region was famous for producing good cavalrymen.

Guangling [K'oo-arng-ling] Prefecture – located in the east of Yang Province, on the coast, north of Wu Prefecture and south of Xiapi in eastern Xu Province; only southern Guangling is part of the Sun clan's domains; the north is Han-controlled.

Kuaiji [Koo-eye-jee] Prefecture – located in the southeast of Yang Province, on the coast, south of Wu Prefecture; Wang Lang administrated Kuaiji until he was driven away by Sun Ce.

Yuzhang [Yoo-ch'arng] Prefecture – located in the southwest of Yang Province, east of southern Jing Province; Hua Xin was Administrator for a time but left after yielding to Sun Ce.

Xu [Shoo] Province *– located in the centre-east of China, south* of Qing Province and east of Yan Province; it was one of the most important places in '"Turmoil"', but is relatively unimportant during the timeline of this work. The capital prior to Cao Cao's campaigns was Peng [Perng] City; then-governor Tao Qian later abandoned this city and moved the capital to Xiapi [Shee-ah-pee] City, which was located in the east of Xu Province, to the east of the Si [See] River (that Cao Cao famously 'dammed with bodies' during that campaign). Haixi [High-shee] – where Liu Bei suffered a year-long siege that permanently affected him – is located to the north of Xiapi. Kaiyang [Kigh-yarng] County (located somewhere in the far north-northeast of Xu Province) was occupied by Zang Ba and made into an independent state when he was the leader of the Mount Tai Bandits.

Pei [Pay] County – located in the west of Xu Province; it was Cao Cao's clan's ancestral home. Chen Gui was made Chancellor of Pei after aiding Cao's defeat of Lü Bu, and Hua Tuo has a home here.

Guangling [K'oo-arng-ling] Prefecture – located in the east of Xu Province, on the coast; only northern Guangling is part of the Han-controlled domains; the rest is ruled by Sun Quan

Yi [Yee] Province – a province located in the centre-west of Han China, south of Hanzhong and west of Jing; it is a relatively harsh and unforgiving place at this point (now it is Szechuan), but Liu Yan craved the governorship precisely because it was isolated enough for him to have complete autonomy. The current capital is Chengdu [T'erng-doo], in the south; the province is governed by Liu Zhang throughout this text.

Hanzhong [Harn-ch'ong] Province – interchangeably known throughout this text as (The Taoist/Theocratic State of) Han'ning [Harn Ning]; this region was the fief of sorts of Liu Bang, founder of the Han Dynasty, and he named his dynasty for this region. When Zhang Lu occupied Hanzhong, he renamed it: if Hanzhong is read as meaning 'Amidst/In Han', Han'ning could, when taking individual characters, mean 'Tranqil Han' or, possibly, 'Rather than Han/Preferable to Han', which fits perfectly with Zhang Lu's beliefs. The capital is Nanzheng [Narn-ch'erng] The province barely features in this text but is very important to past and future events in the later Han and Three Kingdoms periods.

Jing [Jing] Province – a province located in the centre of Han China; it has borders with Yi, Hanzhong, Yu, Yan and Central provinces, which makes it strategically desirable to a would-be conqueror. Jing does not play a large part in the early acts, but the final act depicts the fall of Jing Province that preceded the Battle of Red Cliffs. Xiangyang [Shee-arng-yarng] is located in the lower north of Jing Province; it straddles the south bank of the River Han. The city of Xiangyang is the northern capital of Jing; Jiangling [Jee-arng-ling] is the southern capital. Steep-slope is to the north of Jiangling and is the site of a famous battle. Xinye [Shin-yer] was Liu Bei's base when in Jing; he fought a famous battle with Cao Cao's forces at Bowang [P'oh-warng] Valley during a strategic lull in Cao Cao's northern campaign.

Nan [Narn] County – a county located in the far north of

Jing Province; it borders Yan Province, Yu Province and Central Province, making it strategically invaluable for conquering the north of China. Zhang Xiu is the magistrate of this autonomous county at the start of the work, having negotiated peace with his nemesis Cao Cao, who requires his aid (or, at least, neutrality) while he deals with other threats, such as Liu Biao and the Qiang.

Jiangxia [Jee-arng-shee-ah] Prefecture – located in southeast Jing Province; this is Huang Zu's power base, and is the site of many battles between Huang Zu and the Sun clan.

The four 'semi-autonomous prefectures' – located in the south of Jing: they are, clockwise from northwest, Wuling [Wooling], Changsha [T'arng-shah], Guiyang [K'oo-ee-yarng] and Lingling [Ling-ling]. They are only featured briefly in this work (when they declare full autonomy after Liu Biao dies); they formed part of Liu Bei's early holdings after the Battle of Red Cliffs (his conquests are depicted in 'Crouching Dragon').

Jiaozhi [Jee-ow-ch'ee] Province *– a province located in the far south of Han China that is actually part fo modern Vietnam; it has borders with Yang and Jing provinces, and is too remote to be governed effectively by the Han administration in the imperial capital, so it is an autonomous Buddhist state when Han China proper was Taoist and still highly resistant to the spread of other faiths. Cangwu – the seat of Liu Bei's acquaintance Wu Ju – is arguably part of Yang or Jiaozhi, although the fact that Sun Quan's agent Bu Zhi – or any other man – is sent to 'pacify' the region until the Suns control Jiaozhi suggests the latter. Xu Jing fled here after Wang Lang's defeat in Kuaiji; it is ruled by the clan of Shi Xie (who, as his article notes, is now revered in Vietnam Buddhism as King Si).*

Great Wall [a.k.a. 'The Endless Wall'] – commissioned by various rulers throughout history to repel the Xiongnu and other tribal invaders; it spans the entire northern border. Some Han Chinese lived north of the wall by the end of the Han Dynasty: conversely, the 'Southern Xiongnu' settled south of the wall and contributed to Han society. The early iterations of the wall were mostly earthworks, signal towers and garrisons, and provided limited and ultimately futile defence against the Mongols (successors to the Xianbei that were first led by the infamous Genghis Khan), who went on to conquer China and found the Yuan [Yoo-arn] Dynasty. The Wall has direct plot relevance, as its role as a barrier affects both the tribes and the Han army when Cao Cao is undertaking his seismic Wuhuan pacification campaign.

After the Mongol Yuans were replaced by the Chinese Ming Dynasty, the wall was rebuilt in stone to try and prevent further incursions; this is the more famous wall of modern times. The wall was not completely breached again until the end of the Ming Dynasty, during a popular peasant uprising (that bore great similarity to the Yellow Turban Rebellion in terms of magnitude, cause and purpose). That rebellion had led to the suicide of the last Ming emperor and left the loyalist military generals stationed at the wall with two choices: allow an invasion by the Mongol-Manchu alliance or submit to the will of their own frustrated people. The generals ultimately chose to open the gates to the

Manchus, who overran and conquered China (and were, incidentally, the last imperial rulers of China – the 'Last Emperor', Puyi, was Manchurian, not Han Chinese).

Yangtze [Yarng-tz'ee] River – *spoken of in the text as the Great River, it runs from the west of China to the east, separating the land naturally into north and south.*

Yellow River – *located in the centre-north of China; this vibrant river – which literally runs yellow with sand – runs south and west from the northeast coast to the lands east of Luoyang, whereupon it turns west and runs north of Luoyang as far as the lands east of Chang'an, whereupon it splits and runs north and west.*

The 'lands beyond the Great Wall' – *these demand their own section because Cao Cao spends part of Act VII outside of Han China; White Wolf Mountain is the site of a famous – but brief – battle between Han forces and the Wuhuan tribes that ened with the complete pacification of the latter. The Wuhuan were based in what the Han called Liucheng [Lee-oo-t'erng]; a large settled region known as Pinggang [Ping-k'arng] was on the route that Cao Cao took during that campaign.*

MISCELLANEOUS

Di [Dee] – *a northern, non-Han Chinese race, broken down further into tribes; they were indigenous to the mountains of Hanzhong.*

Hongmen [Hong-mern] – *a commonly-recalled event in Chinese literature, specifically referring to a sword dance or fencing exhibition performed by one or more assassins during a banquet. The host is typically the author of the plot, and they will use a signal – usually dropping or dashing their wine cup – to tell the assassin(s) to strike at the intended victim, who is usually a guest that is blissfully enjoying the proceedings. Any time that a person enters a gathering and notes the host holding a wine cup with caution, they fear a variation of a Hongmen-style assassination, the main variant being hidden assassins (usually behind the hall curtains, or posing as guards). There are several examples in fictional versions of Three Kingdoms: Liu Bei's strategist Pang Tong tries to kill Liu Zhang using this ruse, and Wu General Ling Tong tries to kill fellow general and former enemy Gan Ning during a victory banquet. In this work, it is merely referred to.*

Nan(man) [Narn(-marn)] – *a southern, non-Chinese race, indigenous to Nanzhong, which once included Yi Province until the Han Chinese annexed their territory.*

Qiang [Chee-arng] – *non-Chinese ethnic tribes that lived in the northwest on either side of the Great Wall. The various tribes were typically enemies of the Han Dynasty. Ma Teng and Han Sui famously joined the tribes, and the eldest son of the former, Ma Chao, became a notorious historical warrior king.*

Shanyue [S'arn-yoo-er] – *non-Chinese tribes that lived in and around Yang Province in large numbers; they resented Han rule, but their allegiances shifted dramatically through the eras.*

The 'Ten Attendants' – *a clique of court eunuchs; they began life as loyalists that helped Emperor Huan to regain list power, but by the year 166 they were almost untouchable, and anyone that crossed them was dealt with in the harshest fashion: hundreds of non-complient intelligentsia were labelled as traitors and persecuted, an event known as the 'Partisan Crisis'. They were finally purged after thwarted political action by Commander-in-Chief Hè Jin and decisive military action by his ally Yuan Shao.*

'The Way of Five Pecks' – *a religious cult that was led by Zhang Lu, the ruler of Han'ning; their doctrine was based around a non-monetary system where rice was the currency and community was paramount, although many decried the way that potentially troublesome elements were kept loyal by providing them with whatever they needed at the expense of others.*

'The Way of Peace' – *the religious group that started the Yellow Turban Rebellion; although it can probably be said that many of those that fought were not followers of this Taoist cult, their 16-character mantra was a simple, inspirational way to gather followers and rally other forms of support.*

Wuhuan [Woo-hoo-arn] – *non-Chinese tribes that lived in northeast China and the non-Han territory north of Yòu Province, to the north of the Great Wall; their ultimate fate is a major plot element throughout this work*

Xiongnu [Shee-ong-noo] – *non-Chinese ethnic tribes that lived in the north on either side of the Great Wall; the various tribes were enemies, economic trading partners or allies of the Han Dynasty. The Southern Xiongnu provided troops to the Han army.*

Xianbei [Shee-an-p'ay] – *a confederacy of mostly Xiongnu tribes that became a powerful force in the lands north of the Great Wall.*

Yellow Turbans – *a rebel army that earned their name from the yellow scarves that they used to cover their hair. They were mostly made up of peasants that were tired of poor treatment by the state. The founder was a Taoist cultist, Zhang Jue. The rebellion was eventually crushed by government forces and local militias, but they reappeared many times over the next decade before they were finally suppressed by the Han government.*

✶✶✶✶✶✶✶✶✶✶✶✶